I0831569

THE NOVELS OF F. SCOTT FITZGERALD:

This Side of Paradise,
The Beautiful and Damned,
The Great Gatsby,
Tender is the Night

by
Francis Scott Fitzgerald

BENEDICTION CLASSICS

ISBN: 978-1-78943-336-4.

CONTENTS

THIS SIDE OF PARADISE

BOOK ONE

The Romantic Egotist

I. Amory, Son of Beatrice

Amory Blaine inherited from his mother every trait, except the stray inexpressible few, that made him worth while. His father, an ineffectual, inarticulate man with a taste for Byron and a habit of drowsing over the Encyclopedia Britannica, grew wealthy at thirty through the death of two elder brothers, successful Chicago brokers, and in the first flush of feeling that the world was his, went to Bar Harbor and met Beatrice O'Hara. In consequence, Stephen Blaine handed down to posterity his height of just under six feet and his tendency to waver at crucial moments, these two abstractions appearing in his son Amory. For many years he hovered in the background of his family's life, an unassertive figure with a face half-obliterated by lifeless, silky hair, continually occupied in "taking care" of his wife, continually harassed by the idea that he didn't and couldn't understand her.

But Beatrice Blaine! There was a woman! Early pictures taken on her father's estate at Lake Geneva, Wisconsin, or in Rome at the Sacred Heart Convent—an educational extravagance that in her youth was only for the daughters of the exceptionally wealthy—showed the exquisite delicacy of her features, the consummate art and simplicity of her clothes. A brilliant education she had—her youth passed in renaissance glory, she was versed in the latest gossip of the Older Roman Families; known by name as a fabulously wealthy American girl to Cardinal Vitori and Queen Margherita and more subtle celebrities that one must have had some culture even to have heard of. She learned in England to prefer whiskey and soda to wine, and her small talk was broadened in two senses during a winter in Vienna. All in all Beatrice O'Hara absorbed the sort of education that will be quite impossible ever again; a tutelage measured by the number of things and people one could be contemptuous of and charming about; a culture rich in all arts and traditions, barren of all ideas, in the last of those days when the great gardener clipped the inferior roses to produce one perfect bud.

In her less important moments she returned to America, met Stephen Blaine and married him—this almost entirely because she was a little bit weary, a little bit sad. Her only child was carried through a tiresome season and brought into the world on a spring day in ninety-six.

When Amory was five he was already a delightful companion for her. He was an auburn-haired boy, with great, handsome eyes which he would grow up to in time, a facile imaginative mind and a taste for fancy dress. From his fourth to his tenth year he did the country with his mother in her father's private car, from Coronado, where his mother became so bored that she had a nervous breakdown in a fashionable hotel, down to Mexico City, where she took a mild, almost epidemic consumption. This trouble pleased her, and later she made use of it as an intrinsic part of her atmosphere—especially after several astounding bracers.

So, while more or less fortunate little rich boys were defying governesses on the beach at Newport, or being spanked or tutored or read to from "Do and Dare," or "Frank on the Mississippi," Amory was biting acquiescent bell-boys in the Waldorf, outgrowing a natural repugnance to chamber music and symphonies, and deriving a highly specialized education from his mother.

"Amory."

"Yes, Beatrice." (Such a quaint name for his mother; she encouraged it.)

"Dear, don't *think* of getting out of bed yet. I've always suspected that early rising in early life makes one nervous. Clothilde is having your breakfast brought up."

"All right."

"I am feeling very old to-day, Amory," she would sigh, her face a rare cameo of pathos, her voice exquisitely modulated, her hands as facile as Bernhardt's. "My nerves are on edge—on edge. We must leave this terrifying place to-morrow and go searching for sunshine."

Amory's penetrating green eyes would look out through tangled hair at his mother. Even at this age he had no illusions about her.

"Amory."

"Oh, *yes*."

"I want you to take a red-hot bath as hot as you can bear it, and just relax your nerves. You can read in the tub if you wish."

She fed him sections of the "Fetes Galantes" before he was ten; at eleven he could talk glibly, if rather reminiscently, of Brahms and Mozart and Beethoven. One afternoon, when left alone in the hotel at Hot Springs, he sampled his mother's apricot cordial, and as the taste pleased him, he became quite tipsy. This was fun for a while, but he essayed a cigarette in his exaltation, and succumbed to a vulgar, plebeian reaction. Though this incident horrified Beatrice, it also secretly amused her and became part of what in a later generation would have been termed her "line."

"This son of mine," he heard her tell a room full of awestruck, admiring women one day, "is entirely sophisticated and quite charming—but delicate—we're all delicate; *here*, you know." Her hand was radiantly outlined against her beautiful bosom; then sinking her voice to a whisper, she told them of the apricot cordial. They rejoiced, for she was a brave raconteuse, but many were the keys turned in sideboard locks that night against the possible defection of little Bobby or Barbara....

These domestic pilgrimages were invariably in state; two maids, the private car, or Mr. Blaine when available, and very often a physician. When Amory had the whooping-cough four disgusted specialists glared at each other hunched around his bed; when he took scarlet fever the number of attendants, including physicians and nurses, totalled fourteen. However, blood being thicker than broth, he was pulled through.

The Blaines were attached to no city. They were the Blaines of Lake Geneva; they had quite enough relatives to serve in place of friends, and an enviable standing from Pasadena to Cape Cod. But Beatrice grew more and more prone to like only new acquaintances, as there were certain stories, such as the history of her constitution and its many amendments, memories of her years abroad, that it was necessary for her to repeat at regular intervals. Like Freudian dreams, they must be thrown off, else they would sweep in and lay siege to her nerves. But Beatrice was critical about American women, especially the floating population of ex-Westerners.

"They have accents, my dear," she told Amory, "not Southern accents or Boston accents, not an accent attached to any locality, just an accent"—she became dreamy. "They pick up old, moth-eaten London accents that are down on their luck and have to be used by some one. They talk as an English butler might after several years in a Chicago grand-opera company." She became almost incoherent—"Suppose—time in every Western woman's life—she feels her husband is prosperous enough for her to have—accent—they try to impress *me*, my dear—"

Though she thought of her body as a mass of frailties, she considered her soul quite as ill, and therefore important in her life. She had once been a Catholic, but discovering that priests were infinitely more attentive when she was in process of losing or regaining faith in Mother Church, she maintained an enchantingly wavering attitude. Often she deplored the bourgeois quality of the American Catholic clergy, and was quite sure that had she lived in the shadow of the great Continental cathedrals her soul would still be a thin flame on the mighty altar of Rome. Still, next to doctors, priests were her favorite sport.

"Ah, Bishop Wiston," she would declare, "I do not want to talk of myself. I can imagine the stream of hysterical women fluttering at your doors, beseeching you to be simpatico"—then after an interlude filled by the clergyman—"but my mood—is—oddly dissimilar."

Only to bishops and above did she divulge her clerical romance. When she had first returned to her country there had been a pagan, Swinburnian young man in Asheville, for whose passionate kisses and unsentimental conversations she had taken a decided penchant—they had discussed the matter pro and con with an intellectual romancing quite devoid of sappiness. Eventually she had decided to marry for background, and the young pagan from Asheville had gone through a spiritual crisis, joined the Catholic Church, and was now—Monsignor Darcy.

"Indeed, Mrs. Blaine, he is still delightful company—quite the cardinal's right-hand man."

"Amory will go to him one day, I know," breathed the beautiful lady, "and Monsignor Darcy will understand him as he understood me."

Amory became thirteen, rather tall and slender, and more than ever on to his Celtic mother. He had tutored occasionally—the idea being that he was to "keep up," at each place "taking up the work where he left off," yet as no tutor ever found the place he left off, his mind was still in very good shape. What a few more years of this life would have made of him is problematical. However, four hours out from land, Italy bound, with Beatrice, his appendix burst, probably from too many meals in bed, and after a series of frantic telegrams to Europe and America, to the amazement of the passengers the great ship slowly wheeled around and returned to New York to deposit Amory at the pier. You will admit that if it was not life it was magnificent.

After the operation Beatrice had a nervous breakdown that bore a suspicious resemblance to delirium tremens, and Amory was left in Minneapolis, destined to spend the ensuing two years with his aunt and uncle. There the crude, vulgar air of Western civilization first catches him—in his underwear, so to speak.

A KISS FOR AMORY

His lip curled when he read it.

> *"I am going to have a bobbing party," it said, "on Thursday, December the seventeenth, at five o'clock, and I would like it very much if you could come.*
>
> *Yours truly,*
>
> *R.S.V.P.* *Myra St. Claire.*

He had been two months in Minneapolis, and his chief struggle had been the concealing from "the other guys at school" how particularly superior he felt himself to be, yet this conviction was built upon shifting sands. He had shown off one day in French class (he was in senior French class) to the utter confusion of Mr. Reardon, whose accent Amory damned contemptuously, and to the delight of the class. Mr. Reardon, who had spent several weeks in Paris ten years before, took his revenge on the verbs, whenever he had his book open. But another time Amory showed off in history class, with quite disastrous results, for the boys there were his own age, and they shrilled innuendoes at each other all the following week:

"Aw—I b'lieve, doncherknow, the Umuricun revolution was *lawgely* an affair of the middul *clawses*," or

"Washington came of very good blood—aw, quite good—I b'lieve."

Amory ingeniously tried to retrieve himself by blundering on purpose. Two years before he had commenced a history of the United States which, though it only got as far as the Colonial Wars, had been pronounced by his mother completely enchanting.

His chief disadvantage lay in athletics, but as soon as he discovered that it was the touchstone of power and popularity at school, he began to make furious, persistent efforts to excel in the winter sports, and with his ankles aching and bending in spite of his efforts, he skated valiantly around the Lorelie rink every afternoon, wondering how soon he would be able to carry a hockey-stick without getting it inexplicably tangled in his skates.

The invitation to Miss Myra St. Claire's bobbing party spent the morning in his coat pocket, where it had an intense physical affair with a dusty piece of peanut brittle. During the afternoon he brought it to light with a sigh, and after some consideration and a preliminary draft in the back of Collar and Daniel's "First-Year Latin," composed an answer:

> *My dear Miss St. Claire:*
> *Your truly charming envitation for the evening of next Thursday evening was truly delightful to receive this morning. I will be charm and inchanted indeed to present my compliments on next Thursday evening.*
> *Faithfully,*
>
> *Amory Blaine.*

On Thursday, therefore, he walked pensively along the slippery, shovel-scraped sidewalks, and came in sight of Myra's house, on the half-hour after five, a lateness which he fancied his mother would have favored. He waited on the door-step with his eyes nonchalantly half-closed, and planned his entrance with precision. He would cross the floor, not too hastily, to Mrs. St. Claire, and say with exactly the correct modulation:

"My *dear* Mrs. St. Claire, I'm *frightfully* sorry to be late, but my maid"—he paused there and realized he would be quoting—"but my uncle and I had to see a fella—Yes, I've met your enchanting daughter at dancing-school."

Then he would shake hands, using that slight, half-foreign bow, with all the starchy little females, and nod to the fellas who would be standing 'round, paralyzed into rigid groups for mutual protection.

A butler (one of the three in Minneapolis) swung open the door. Amory stepped inside and divested himself of cap and coat. He was mildly surprised not to hear the shrill squawk of conversation from the next room, and he decided it must be quite formal. He approved of that—as he approved of the butler.

"Miss Myra," he said.

To his surprise the butler grinned horribly.

"Oh, yeah," he declared, "she's here." He was unaware that his failure to be cockney was ruining his standing. Amory considered him coldly.

"But," continued the butler, his voice rising unnecessarily, "she's the only one what *is* here. The party's gone."

Amory gasped in sudden horror.

"What?"

"She's been waitin' for Amory Blaine. That's you, ain't it? Her mother says that if you showed up by five-thirty you two was to go after 'em in the Packard."

Amory's despair was crystallized by the appearance of Myra herself, bundled to the ears in a polo coat, her face plainly sulky, her voice pleasant only with difficulty.

"'Lo, Amory."

"'Lo, Myra." He had described the state of his vitality.

"Well—you *got* here, *any*ways."

"Well—I'll tell you. I guess you don't know about the auto accident," he romanced.

Myra's eyes opened wide.

"Who was it to?"

"Well," he continued desperately, "uncle 'n aunt 'n I."

"Was any one *killed?*"

Amory paused and then nodded.

"Your uncle?"—alarm.

"Oh, no just a horse—a sorta gray horse."

At this point the Erse butler snickered.

"Probably killed the engine," he suggested. Amory would have put him on the rack without a scruple.

"We'll go now," said Myra coolly. "You see, Amory, the bobs were ordered for five and everybody was here, so we couldn't wait—"

"Well, I couldn't help it, could I?"

"So mama said for me to wait till ha'past five. We'll catch the bobs before it gets to the Minnehaha Club, Amory."

Amory's shredded poise dropped from him. He pictured the happy party jingling along snowy streets, the appearance of the limousine, the horrible public descent of him and Myra before sixty reproachful eyes, his apology—a real one this time. He sighed aloud.

"What?" inquired Myra.

"Nothing. I was just yawning. Are we going to *surely* catch up with 'em before they get there?" He was encouraging a faint hope that they might slip into the Minnehaha Club and meet the others there, be found in blasé seclusion before the fire and quite regain his lost attitude.

"Oh, sure Mike, we'll catch 'em all right—let's hurry."

He became conscious of his stomach. As they stepped into the machine he hurriedly slapped the paint of diplomacy over a rather box-like plan he had conceived. It was based upon some "trade-lasts" gleaned at dancing-school, to the effect that he was "awful good-looking and *English*, sort of."

"Myra," he said, lowering his voice and choosing his words carefully, "I beg a thousand pardons. Can you ever forgive me?" She regarded him gravely, his intent green eyes, his mouth, that to her thirteen-year-old, arrow-collar taste was the quintessence of romance. Yes, Myra could forgive him very easily.

"Why—yes—sure."

He looked at her again, and then dropped his eyes. He had lashes.

"I'm awful," he said sadly. "I'm diff'runt. I don't know why I make faux pas. 'Cause I don't care, I s'pose." Then, recklessly: "I been smoking too much. I've got t'bacca heart."

Myra pictured an all-night tobacco debauch, with Amory pale and reeling from the effect of nicotined lungs. She gave a little gasp.

"Oh, *Amory*, don't smoke. You'll stunt your *growth!*"

"I don't care," he persisted gloomily. "I gotta. I got the habit. I've done a lot of things that if my fambly knew"—he hesitated, giving her imagination time to picture dark horrors—"I went to the burlesque show last week."

Myra was quite overcome. He turned the green eyes on her again. "You're the only girl in town I like much," he exclaimed in a rush of sentiment. "You're simpatico."

Myra was not sure that she was, but it sounded stylish though vaguely improper.

Thick dusk had descended outside, and as the limousine made a sudden turn she was jolted against him; their hands touched.

"You shouldn't smoke, Amory," she whispered. "Don't you know that?"

He shook his head.

"Nobody cares."

Myra hesitated.

"*I* care."

Something stirred within Amory.

"Oh, yes, you do! You got a crush on Froggy Parker. I guess everybody knows that."

"No, I haven't," very slowly.

A silence, while Amory thrilled. There was something fascinating about Myra, shut away here cosily from the dim, chill air. Myra, a little bundle of clothes, with strands of yellow hair curling out from under her skating cap.

"Because I've got a crush, too—" He paused, for he heard in the distance the sound of young laughter, and, peering through the frosted glass along the lamp-lit street, he made out the dark outline of the bobbing party. He must act quickly. He reached over with a violent, jerky effort, and clutched Myra's hand—her thumb, to be exact.

"Tell him to go to the Minnehaha straight," he whispered. "I wanta talk to you—I *got* to talk to you."

Myra made out the party ahead, had an instant vision of her mother, and then—alas for convention—glanced into the eyes beside. "Turn down this side street, Richard, and drive straight to the Minnehaha Club!" she cried through the speaking tube. Amory sank back against the cushions with a sigh of relief.

"I can kiss her," he thought. "I'll bet I can. I'll *bet* I can!"

Overhead the sky was half crystalline, half misty, and the night around was chill and vibrant with rich tension. From the Country Club steps the roads stretched away, dark creases on the white blanket; huge heaps of snow lining the sides like the tracks of giant moles. They lingered for a moment on the steps, and watched the white holiday moon.

"Pale moons like that one"—Amory made a vague gesture—"make people mysterieuse. You look like a young witch with her cap off and her hair sorta mussed"—her hands clutched at her hair—"Oh, leave it, it looks *good*."

They drifted up the stairs and Myra led the way into the little den of his dreams, where a cosy fire was burning before a big sink-down couch. A few years later this was to be a great stage for Amory, a cradle for many an emotional crisis. Now they talked for a moment about bobbing parties.

"There's always a bunch of shy fellas," he commented, "sitting at the tail of the bob, sorta lurkin' an' whisperin' an' pushin' each other off. Then there's always some crazy cross-eyed girl"—he gave a terrifying imitation—"she's always talkin' *hard*, sorta, to the chaperon."

"You're such a funny boy," puzzled Myra.

"How d'y' mean?" Amory gave immediate attention, on his own ground at last.

"Oh—always talking about crazy things. Why don't you come ski-ing with Marylyn and I to-morrow?"

"I don't like girls in the daytime," he said shortly, and then, thinking this a bit abrupt, he added: "But I like you." He cleared his throat. "I like you first and second and third."

Myra's eyes became dreamy. What a story this would make to tell Marylyn! Here on the couch with this *wonderful*-looking boy—the little fire—the sense that they were alone in the great building—

Myra capitulated. The atmosphere was too appropriate.

"I like you the first twenty-five," she confessed, her voice trembling, "and Froggy Parker twenty-sixth."

Froggy had fallen twenty-five places in one hour. As yet he had not even noticed it.

But Amory, being on the spot, leaned over quickly and kissed Myra's cheek. He had never kissed a girl before, and he tasted his lips curiously, as if he had munched some new fruit. Then their lips brushed like young wild flowers in the wind.

"We're awful," rejoiced Myra gently. She slipped her hand into his, her head drooped against his shoulder. Sudden revulsion seized Amory, disgust, loathing for the whole incident. He desired frantically to be away, never to see Myra again, never to kiss any one; he became conscious of his face and hers, of their clinging hands, and he wanted to creep out of his body and hide somewhere safe out of sight, up in the corner of his mind.

"Kiss me again." Her voice came out of a great void.

"I don't want to," he heard himself saying. There was another pause.

"I don't want to!" he repeated passionately.

Myra sprang up, her cheeks pink with bruised vanity, the great bow on the back of her head trembling sympathetically.

"I hate you!" she cried. "Don't you ever dare to speak to me again!"

"What?" stammered Amory.

"I'll tell mama you kissed me! I will too! I will too! I'll tell mama, and she won't let me play with you!"

Amory rose and stared at her helplessly, as though she were a new animal of whose presence on the earth he had not heretofore been aware.

The door opened suddenly, and Myra's mother appeared on the threshold, fumbling with her lorgnette.

"Well," she began, adjusting it benignantly, "the man at the desk told me you two children were up here—How do you do, Amory."

Amory watched Myra and waited for the crash—but none came. The pout faded, the high pink subsided, and Myra's voice was placid as a summer lake when she answered her mother.

"Oh, we started so late, mama, that I thought we might as well—"

He heard from below the shrieks of laughter, and smelled the vapid odor of hot chocolate and tea-cakes as he silently followed mother and daughter downstairs. The sound of the graphophone mingled with the voices of many girls humming the air, and a faint glow was born and spread over him:

"Casey-Jones—mounted to the cab-un
Casey-Jones—'th his orders in his hand.
Casey-Jones—mounted to the cab-un
Took his farewell journey to the prom-ised land."

SNAPSHOTS OF THE YOUNG EGOTIST

Amory spent nearly two years in Minneapolis. The first winter he wore moccasins that were born yellow, but after many applications of oil and dirt assumed their mature color, a dirty, greenish brown; he wore a gray plaid mackinaw coat, and a red toboggan cap. His dog, Count Del Monte, ate the red cap, so his uncle gave him a gray one that pulled down over his face. The trouble with this one was that you breathed into it and your breath froze; one day the darn thing froze his cheek. He rubbed snow on his cheek, but it turned bluish-black just the same.

The Count Del Monte ate a box of bluing once, but it didn't hurt him. Later, however, he lost his mind and ran madly up the street, bumping into fences, rolling in gutters, and pursuing his eccentric course out of Amory's life. Amory cried on his bed.

"Poor little Count," he cried. "Oh, *poor* little *Count!*"

After several months he suspected Count of a fine piece of emotional acting.

Amory and Frog Parker considered that the greatest line in literature occurred in Act III of "Arsene Lupin."

They sat in the first row at the Wednesday and Saturday matinees. The line was:

"If one can't be a great artist or a great soldier, the next best thing is to be a great criminal."

Amory fell in love again, and wrote a poem. This was it:

"Marylyn and Sallee,
Those are the girls for me.
Marylyn stands above
Sallee in that sweet, deep love."

He was interested in whether McGovern of Minnesota would make the first or second All-American, how to do the card-pass, how to do the coin-pass, chameleon ties, how babies were born, and whether Three-fingered Brown was really a better pitcher than Christie Mathewson.

Among other things he read: "For the Honor of the School," "Little Women" (twice), "The Common Law," "Sapho," "Dangerous Dan McGrew," "The Broad Highway" (three times), "The Fall of the House of Usher," "Three Weeks," "Mary Ware, the Little Colonel's Chum," "Gunga Din," The Police Gazette, and Jim-Jam Jems.

He had all the Henty biasses in history, and was particularly fond of the cheerful murder stories of Mary Roberts Rinehart.

School ruined his French and gave him a distaste for standard authors. His masters considered him idle, unreliable and superficially clever.

He collected locks of hair from many girls. He wore the rings of several. Finally he could borrow no more rings, owing to his nervous habit of chewing them out of shape. This, it seemed, usually aroused the jealous suspicions of the next borrower.

All through the summer months Amory and Frog Parker went each week to the Stock Company. Afterward they would stroll home in the balmy air of August night, dreaming along Hennepin and Nicollet Avenues, through the gay crowd. Amory wondered how people could fail to notice that he was a boy marked for glory, and when faces of the throng turned toward him and ambiguous eyes stared into his, he assumed the most romantic of expressions and walked on the air cushions that lie on the asphalts of fourteen.

Always, after he was in bed, there were voices—indefinite, fading, enchanting—just outside his window, and before he fell asleep he would dream one of his favorite waking dreams, the one about becoming a great half-back, or the one about the Japanese invasion, when he was rewarded by being made the youngest general in the world. It was always the becoming he dreamed of, never the being. This, too, was quite characteristic of Amory.

CODE OF THE YOUNG EGOTIST

Before he was summoned back to Lake Geneva, he had appeared, shy but inwardly glowing, in his first long trousers, set off by a purple accordion tie and a "Belmont" collar with the edges unassailably meeting, purple socks, and handkerchief with a purple border peeping from his breast pocket. But more than that, he had formulated his first philosophy, a code to live by, which, as near as it can be named, was a sort of aristocratic egotism.

He had realized that his best interests were bound up with those of a certain variant, changing person, whose label, in order that his past might always be identified with him, was Amory Blaine. Amory marked himself a fortunate youth, capable of infinite expansion for good or evil. He did not consider himself a "strong char'c'ter," but relied on his facility (learn things sorta quick) and his superior mentality (read a lotta deep books). He was proud of the fact that he could never become a mechanical or scientific genius. From no other heights was he debarred.

Physically.—Amory thought that he was exceedingly handsome. He was. He fancied himself an athlete of possibilities and a supple dancer.

Socially.—Here his condition was, perhaps, most dangerous. He granted himself personality, charm, magnetism, poise, the power of dominating all contemporary males, the gift of fascinating all women.

Mentally.—Complete, unquestioned superiority.

Now a confession will have to be made. Amory had rather a Puritan conscience. Not that he yielded to it—later in life he almost completely slew it—but at fifteen it made him consider himself a great deal worse than other boys... unscrupulousness... the desire to influence people in almost every way, even for evil... a certain coldness and lack of affection, amounting sometimes to cruelty... a shifting sense of honor... an unholy selfishness... a puzzled, furtive interest in everything concerning sex.

There was, also, a curious strain of weakness running crosswise through his make-up... a harsh phrase from the lips of an older boy (older boys usually detested him) was liable to sweep him off his poise into surly sensitiveness, or timid stupidity... he was a slave to his own moods and he felt that though he was capable of recklessness and audacity, he possessed neither courage, perseverance, nor self-respect.

Vanity, tempered with self-suspicion if not self-knowledge, a sense of people as automatons to his will, a desire to "pass" as many boys as possible and get to a vague top of the world... with this background did Amory drift into adolescence.

PREPARATORY TO THE GREAT ADVENTURE

The train slowed up with midsummer languor at Lake Geneva, and Amory caught sight of his mother waiting in her electric on the gravelled station drive. It was an ancient electric, one of the early types, and painted gray. The sight of her sitting there, slenderly erect, and of her face, where beauty and dignity combined, melting to a dreamy recollected smile, filled him with a sudden great pride of her. As they kissed coolly and he stepped into the electric, he felt a quick fear lest he had lost the requisite charm to measure up to her.

"Dear boy—you're *so* tall... look behind and see if there's anything coming..."

She looked left and right, she slipped cautiously into a speed of two miles an hour, beseeching Amory to act as sentinel; and at one busy crossing she made him get out and run ahead to signal her forward like a traffic policeman. Beatrice was what might be termed a careful driver.

"You *are* tall—but you're still very handsome—you've skipped the awkward age, or is that sixteen; perhaps it's fourteen or fifteen; I can never remember; but you've skipped it."

"Don't embarrass me," murmured Amory.

"But, my dear boy, what odd clothes! They look as if they were a *set*—don't they? Is your underwear purple, too?"

Amory grunted impolitely.

"You must go to Brooks' and get some really nice suits. Oh, we'll have a talk to-night or perhaps to-morrow night. I want to tell you about your heart—you've probably been neglecting your heart—and you don't *know*."

Amory thought how superficial was the recent overlay of his own generation. Aside from a minute shyness, he felt that the old cynical kinship with his mother had not been one bit broken. Yet for the first few days he wandered about the gardens and along the shore in a state of superloneliness, finding a lethargic content in smoking "Bull" at the garage with one of the chauffeurs.

The sixty acres of the estate were dotted with old and new summer houses and many fountains and white benches that came suddenly into sight from foliage-hung hiding-places; there was a great and constantly increasing family of white cats that prowled the many flower-beds and were silhouetted suddenly at night against the darkening trees. It was on one of the shadowy paths that Beatrice at last captured Amory, after Mr. Blaine had, as usual, retired for the evening to his private library. After reproving him for avoiding her, she took him for a long tete-a-tete in the moonlight. He could not reconcile himself to her beauty, that was mother to his own, the exquisite neck and shoulders, the grace of a fortunate woman of thirty.

"Amory, dear," she crooned softly, "I had such a strange, weird time after I left you."

"Did you, Beatrice?"

"When I had my last breakdown"—she spoke of it as a sturdy, gallant feat.

"The doctors told me"—her voice sang on a confidential note—"that if any man alive had done the consistent drinking that I have, he would have been physically *shattered*, my dear, and in his *grave*—long in his grave."

Amory winced, and wondered how this would have sounded to Froggy Parker.

"Yes," continued Beatrice tragically, "I had dreams—wonderful visions." She pressed the palms of her hands into her eyes. "I saw bronze rivers lapping marble shores, and great birds that soared through the air, parti-colored birds with iridescent plumage. I heard strange music and the flare of barbaric trumpets—what?"

Amory had snickered.

"What, Amory?"

"I said go on, Beatrice."

"That was all—it merely recurred and recurred—gardens that flaunted coloring against which this would be quite dull, moons that whirled and swayed, paler than winter moons, more golden than harvest moons—"

"Are you quite well now, Beatrice?"

"Quite well—as well as I will ever be. I am not understood, Amory. I know that can't express it to you, Amory, but—I am not understood."

Amory was quite moved. He put his arm around his mother, rubbing his head gently against her shoulder.

"Poor Beatrice—poor Beatrice."

"Tell me about *you*, Amory. Did you have two *horrible* years?"

Amory considered lying, and then decided against it.

"No, Beatrice. I enjoyed them. I adapted myself to the bourgeoisie. I became conventional." He surprised himself by saying that, and he pictured how Froggy would have gaped.

"Beatrice," he said suddenly, "I want to go away to school. Everybody in Minneapolis is going to go away to school."

Beatrice showed some alarm.

"But you're only fifteen."

"Yes, but everybody goes away to school at fifteen, and I *want* to, Beatrice."

On Beatrice's suggestion the subject was dropped for the rest of the walk, but a week later she delighted him by saying:

"Amory, I have decided to let you have your way. If you still want to, you can go to school."

"Yes?"

"To St. Regis's in Connecticut."

Amory felt a quick excitement.

"It's being arranged," continued Beatrice. "It's better that you should go away. I'd have preferred you to have gone to Eton, and then to Christ Church, Oxford, but it seems impracticable now—and for the present we'll let the university question take care of itself."

"What are you going to do, Beatrice?"

"Heaven knows. It seems my fate to fret away my years in this country. Not for a second do I regret being American—indeed, I think that a regret typical of very vulgar people, and I feel sure we are the great coming nation—yet"—and she sighed—"I feel my life should have drowsed away close to an older, mellower civilization, a land of greens and autumnal browns—"

Amory did not answer, so his mother continued:

"My regret is that you haven't been abroad, but still, as you are a man, it's better that you should grow up here under the snarling eagle—is that the right term?"

Amory agreed that it was. She would not have appreciated the Japanese invasion.

"When do I go to school?"

"Next month. You'll have to start East a little early to take your examinations. After that you'll have a free week, so I want you to go up the Hudson and pay a visit."

"To who?"

"To Monsignor Darcy, Amory. He wants to see you. He went to Harrow and then to Yale—became a Catholic. I want him to talk to you—I feel he can be such a help—" She stroked his auburn hair gently. "Dear Amory, dear Amory—"

"Dear Beatrice—"

So early in September Amory, provided with "six suits summer underwear, six suits winter underwear, one sweater or T shirt, one jersey, one overcoat, winter, etc.," set out for New England, the land of schools.

There were Andover and Exeter with their memories of New England dead—large, college-like democracies; St. Mark's, Groton, St. Regis'—recruited from Boston and the Knickerbocker families of New York; St. Paul's, with its great rinks; Pomfret and St. George's, prosperous and well-dressed; Taft and Hotchkiss, which prepared the wealth of the Middle West for social success at Yale; Pawling, Westminster, Choate, Kent, and a hundred others; all milling out their well-set-up, conventional, impressive type, year after year; their mental stimulus the college entrance exams; their vague purpose set forth in a hundred circulars as "To impart a Thorough Mental, Moral, and Physical Training as a Christian Gentleman, to fit the boy for meeting the problems of his day and generation, and to give a solid foundation in the Arts and Sciences."

At St. Regis' Amory stayed three days and took his exams with a scoffing confidence, then doubling back to New York to pay his tutelary visit. The metropolis, barely glimpsed, made little impression on him, except for the sense of cleanliness he drew from the tall white buildings seen from a Hudson River steamboat in the early morning. Indeed, his mind was so crowded with dreams of athletic prowess at school that he considered this visit only as a rather tiresome prelude to the great adventure. This, however, it did not prove to be.

Monsignor Darcy's house was an ancient, rambling structure set on a hill overlooking the river, and there lived its owner, between his trips to all parts of the Roman-Catholic world, rather like an exiled Stuart king waiting to be called to the rule of his land. Monsignor was forty-four then, and bustling—a trifle too stout for symmetry, with hair the color of spun gold, and a brilliant, enveloping personality. When he came into a room clad in his full purple regalia from thatch to toe, he resembled a Turner sunset, and attracted both admiration and attention. He had written two novels: one of them violently anti-Catholic, just before his conversion, and five years later another, in which he had attempted to turn all his clever jibes against Catholics into even cleverer innuendoes against Episcopalians. He was intensely ritualistic, startlingly dramatic, loved the idea of God enough to be a celibate, and rather liked his neighbor.

Children adored him because he was like a child; youth revelled in his company because he was still a youth, and couldn't be shocked. In the proper land and century he might have been a Richelieu—at present he was a very moral, very religious (if not particularly pious) clergyman, making a great mystery about pulling rusty wires, and appreciating life to the fullest, if not entirely enjoying it.

He and Amory took to each other at first sight—the jovial, impressive prelate who could dazzle an embassy ball, and the green-eyed, intent youth, in his first long trousers, accepted in their own minds a relation of father and son within a half-hour's conversation.

"My dear boy, I've been waiting to see you for years. Take a big chair and we'll have a chat."

"I've just come from school—St. Regis's, you know."

"So your mother says—a remarkable woman; have a cigarette—I'm sure you smoke. Well, if you're like me, you loathe all science and mathematics—"

Amory nodded vehemently.

"Hate 'em all. Like English and history."

"Of course. You'll hate school for a while, too, but I'm glad you're going to St. Regis's."

"Why?"

"Because it's a gentleman's school, and democracy won't hit you so early. You'll find plenty of that in college."

"I want to go to Princeton," said Amory. "I don't know why, but I think of all Harvard men as sissies, like I used to be, and all Yale men as wearing big blue sweaters and smoking pipes."

Monsignor chuckled.

"I'm one, you know."

"Oh, you're different—I think of Princeton as being lazy and good-looking and aristocratic—you know, like a spring day. Harvard seems sort of indoors—"

"And Yale is November, crisp and energetic," finished Monsignor.

"That's it."

They slipped briskly into an intimacy from which they never recovered.

"I was for Bonnie Prince Charlie," announced Amory.

"Of course you were—and for Hannibal—"

"Yes, and for the Southern Confederacy." He was rather sceptical about being an Irish patriot—he suspected that being Irish was being somewhat common—but Monsignor assured him that Ireland was a romantic lost cause and Irish people quite charming, and that it should, by all means, be one of his principal biasses.

After a crowded hour which included several more cigarettes, and during which Monsignor learned, to his surprise but not to his horror, that Amory had not been brought up a Catholic, he announced that he had another guest. This turned out to be the Honorable Thornton Hancock, of Boston, ex-minister to The Hague, author of an erudite history of the Middle Ages and the last of a distinguished, patriotic, and brilliant family.

"He comes here for a rest," said Monsignor confidentially, treating Amory as a contemporary. "I act as an escape from the weariness of agnosticism, and I think I'm the only man who knows how his staid old mind is really at sea and longs for a sturdy spar like the Church to cling to."

Their first luncheon was one of the memorable events of Amory's early life. He was quite radiant and gave off a peculiar brightness and charm. Monsignor called out the best that he had thought by question and suggestion, and Amory talked with an ingenious brilliance of a thousand impulses and desires and repulsions and faiths and fears. He and Monsignor held the floor, and the older man, with his less receptive, less accepting, yet certainly not colder mentality, seemed content to listen and bask in the mellow sunshine that played between these two. Monsignor gave the effect of sunlight to many people; Amory gave it in his youth and, to some extent, when he was very much older, but never again was it quite so mutually spontaneous.

"He's a radiant boy," thought Thornton Hancock, who had seen the splendor of two continents and talked with Parnell and Gladstone and Bismarck—and afterward he added to Monsignor: "But his education ought not to be intrusted to a school or college."

But for the next four years the best of Amory's intellect was concentrated on matters of popularity, the intricacies of a university social system and American Society as represented by Biltmore Teas and Hot Springs golf-links.

... In all, a wonderful week, that saw Amory's mind turned inside out, a hundred of his theories confirmed, and his joy of life crystallized to a thousand ambitions. Not that the conversation was scholastic—heaven forbid! Amory had only the vaguest idea as to what Bernard Shaw was—but Monsignor made quite as much out of "The Beloved Vagabond" and "Sir Nigel," taking good care that Amory never once felt out of his depth.

But the trumpets were sounding for Amory's preliminary skirmish with his own generation.

"You're not sorry to go, of course. With people like us our home is where we are not," said Monsignor.

"I *am* sorry—"

"No, you're not. No one person in the world is necessary to you or to me."

"Well—"

"Good-by."

THE EGOTIST DOWN

Amory's two years at St. Regis', though in turn painful and triumphant, had as little real significance in his own life as the American "prep" school, crushed as it is under the heel of the universities, has to American life in general. We have no Eton to create the self-consciousness of a governing class; we have, instead, clean, flaccid and innocuous preparatory schools.

He went all wrong at the start, was generally considered both conceited and arrogant, and universally detested. He played football intensely, alternating a reckless brilliancy with a tendency to keep himself as safe from hazard as decency would permit. In a wild panic he backed out of a fight with a boy his own size, to a chorus of scorn, and a week later, in desperation, picked a battle with another boy very much bigger, from which he emerged badly beaten, but rather proud of himself.

He was resentful against all those in authority over him, and this, combined with a lazy indifference toward his work, exasperated every master in school. He grew discouraged and imagined himself a pariah; took to sulking in corners and reading after lights. With a dread of being alone he attached a few friends, but since they were not among the elite of the school, he used them simply as mirrors of himself, audiences before which he might do that posing absolutely essential to him. He was unbearably lonely, desperately unhappy.

There were some few grains of comfort. Whenever Amory was submerged, his vanity was the last part to go below the surface, so he could still enjoy a comfortable glow when "Wookey-wookey," the deaf old housekeeper, told him that he was the best-looking boy she had ever seen. It had pleased him to be the lightest and youngest man on the first football squad; it pleased him when Doctor Dougall told him at the end of a heated conference that he could, if he wished, get the best marks in school. But Doctor Dougall was wrong. It was temperamentally impossible for Amory to get the best marks in school.

Miserable, confined to bounds, unpopular with both faculty and students—that was Amory's first term. But at Christmas he had returned to Minneapolis, tight-lipped and strangely jubilant.

"Oh, I was sort of fresh at first," he told Frog Parker patronizingly, "but I got along fine—lightest man on the squad. You ought to go away to school, Froggy. It's great stuff."

INCIDENT OF THE WELL-MEANING PROFESSOR

On the last night of his first term, Mr. Margotson, the senior master, sent word to study hall that Amory was to come to his room at nine. Amory suspected that advice was forthcoming, but he determined to be courteous, because this Mr. Margotson had been kindly disposed toward him.

His summoner received him gravely, and motioned him to a chair. He hemmed several times and looked consciously kind, as a man will when he knows he's on delicate ground.

"Amory," he began. "I've sent for you on a personal matter."

"Yes, sir."

"I've noticed you this year and I—I like you. I think you have in you the makings of a—a very good man."

"Yes, sir," Amory managed to articulate. He hated having people talk as if he were an admitted failure.

"But I've noticed," continued the older man blindly, "that you're not very popular with the boys."

"No, sir." Amory licked his lips.

"Ah—I thought you might not understand exactly what it was they—ah—objected to. I'm going to tell you, because I believe—ah—that when a boy knows his difficulties he's better able to cope with them—to conform to what others expect of him." He a-hemmed again with delicate reticence, and continued: "They seem to think that you're—ah—rather too fresh—"

Amory could stand no more. He rose from his chair, scarcely controlling his voice when he spoke.

"I know—oh, *don't* you s'pose I know." His voice rose. "I know what they think; do you s'pose you have to *tell* me!" He paused. "I'm—I've got to go back now—hope I'm not rude—"

He left the room hurriedly. In the cool air outside, as he walked to his house, he exulted in his refusal to be helped.

"That *damn* old fool!" he cried wildly. "As if I didn't *know!*"

He decided, however, that this was a good excuse not to go back to study hall that night, so, comfortably couched up in his room, he munched Nabiscos and finished "The White Company."

INCIDENT OF THE WONDERFUL GIRL

There was a bright star in February. New York burst upon him on Washington's Birthday with the brilliance of a long-anticipated event. His glimpse of it as a vivid whiteness against a deep-blue sky had left a picture of splendor that rivalled the dream cities in the Arabian Nights; but this time he saw it by electric light, and romance gleamed from the chariot-race sign on Broadway and from the women's eyes at the Astor, where he and young Paskert from St. Regis' had dinner. When they walked down the aisle of the theatre, greeted by the nervous twanging and discord of untuned violins and the sensuous, heavy fragrance of paint and powder, he moved in a sphere of epicurean delight. Everything enchanted him. The play was "The Little Millionaire," with George M. Cohan, and there was one stunning young brunette who made him sit with brimming eyes in the ecstasy of watching her dance.

"*Oh—you—wonderful girl,*
What a wonderful girl you are—"

sang the tenor, and Amory agreed silently, but passionately.

"*All—your—wonderful words*
Thrill me through—"

The violins swelled and quavered on the last notes, the girl sank to a crumpled butterfly on the stage, a great burst of clapping filled the house. Oh, to fall in love like that, to the languorous magic melody of such a tune!

The last scene was laid on a roof-garden, and the cellos sighed to the musical moon, while light adventure and facile froth-like comedy flitted back and forth in the calcium. Amory was on fire to be an habitui of roof-gardens, to meet a girl who should look like that—better, that very girl; whose hair would be drenched with golden moonlight, while at his elbow sparkling wine was poured by an unintelligible waiter. When the curtain fell for the last time he gave such a long sigh that the people in front of him twisted around and stared and said loud enough for him to hear:

"What a *remarkable*-looking boy!"

This took his mind off the play, and he wondered if he really did seem handsome to the population of New York.

Paskert and he walked in silence toward their hotel. The former was the first to speak. His uncertain fifteen-year-old voice broke in in a melancholy strain on Amory's musings:

"I'd marry that girl to-night."

There was no need to ask what girl he referred to.

"I'd be proud to take her home and introduce her to my people," continued Paskert.

Amory was distinctly impressed. He wished he had said it instead of Paskert. It sounded so mature.

"I wonder about actresses; are they all pretty bad?"

"No, *sir*, not by a darn sight," said the worldly youth with emphasis, "and I know that girl's as good as gold. I can tell."

They wandered on, mixing in the Broadway crowd, dreaming on the music that eddied out of the cafes. New faces flashed on and off like myriad lights, pale or rouged faces, tired, yet sustained by a weary excitement. Amory watched them in fascination. He was planning his life. He was going to live in New York, and be known at every restaurant and cafe, wearing a dress-suit from early evening to early morning, sleeping away the dull hours of the forenoon.

"Yes, *sir*, I'd marry that girl to-night!"

HEROIC IN GENERAL TONE

October of his second and last year at St. Regis' was a high point in Amory's memory. The game with Groton was played from three of a snappy, exhilarating afternoon far into the crisp autumnal twilight, and Amory at quarter-back, exhorting in wild despair, making impossible tackles, calling signals in a voice that had diminished to a hoarse, furious whisper, yet found time to revel in the blood-stained bandage around his head, and the straining, glorious heroism of plunging, crashing bodies and aching limbs. For those minutes courage flowed like wine out of the November dusk, and he was the eternal hero, one with the sea-rover on the prow of a Norse galley, one with Roland and Horatius, Sir Nigel and Ted Coy, scraped and stripped into trim and then flung by his own will into the breach, beating back the tide, hearing from afar the thunder of cheers... finally bruised and weary, but still elusive, circling an end, twisting, changing pace, straight-arming... falling behind the Groton goal with two men on his legs, in the only touchdown of the game.

THE PHILOSOPHY OF THE SLICKER

From the scoffing superiority of sixth-form year and success Amory looked back with cynical wonder on his status of the year before. He was changed as completely as Amory Blaine could ever be changed. Amory plus Beatrice plus two years in Minneapolis—these had been his ingredients when he entered St. Regis'. But the Minneapolis years were not a thick enough overlay to conceal the "Amory plus Beatrice" from the ferreting eyes of a boarding-school, so St. Regis' had very painfully drilled Beatrice out of him, and begun to lay down new and more conventional planking on the fundamental Amory. But both St. Regis' and Amory were unconscious of the fact that this fundamental Amory had not in himself changed. Those qualities for which he had suffered, his moodiness, his tendency to pose, his laziness, and his love of playing the fool, were now taken as a matter of course, recognized eccentricities in a star quarter-back, a clever actor, and the editor of the St. Regis Tattler: it puzzled him to see impressionable small boys imitating the very vanities that had not long ago been contemptible weaknesses.

After the football season he slumped into dreamy content. The night of the pre-holiday dance he slipped away and went early to bed for the pleasure of hearing the violin music cross the grass and come surging in at his window. Many nights he lay there dreaming awake of secret cafes in Mont Martre, where ivory women delved in romantic mysteries with diplomats and soldiers of fortune, while orchestras played Hungarian waltzes and the air was thick and exotic with intrigue and moonlight and adventure. In the spring he read "L'Allegro," by request, and was inspired to lyrical outpourings on the subject of Arcady and the pipes of Pan. He moved his bed so that the sun would wake him at dawn that he might dress and go out to the archaic swing that hung from an apple-tree near the sixth-form house. Seating himself in this he would pump higher and higher until he got the effect of swinging into the wide air, into a fairyland of piping satyrs and nymphs with the faces of fair-haired girls he passed in the streets of Eastchester. As the swing reached its highest point, Arcady really lay just over the brow of a certain hill, where the brown road dwindled out of sight in a golden dot.

He read voluminously all spring, the beginning of his eighteenth year: "The Gentleman from Indiana," "The New Arabian Nights," "The Morals of Marcus Ordeyne," "The Man Who Was Thursday," which he liked without understanding; "Stover at Yale," that became somewhat of a text-book; "Dombey and Son," because he thought he really should read better stuff; Robert Chambers, David Graham Phillips, and E. Phillips Oppenheim complete, and a scattering of Tennyson and Kipling. Of all his class work only "L'Allegro" and some quality of rigid clarity in solid geometry stirred his languid interest.

As June drew near, he felt the need of conversation to formulate his own ideas, and, to his surprise, found a co-philosopher in Rahill, the president of the sixth form. In many a talk, on the highroad or lying belly-down along the edge of the baseball diamond, or late at night with their cigarettes glowing in the dark, they threshed out the questions of school, and there was developed the term "slicker."

"Got tobacco?" whispered Rahill one night, putting his head inside the door five minutes after lights.

"Sure."

"I'm coming in."

"Take a couple of pillows and lie in the window-seat, why don't you."

Amory sat up in bed and lit a cigarette while Rahill settled for a conversation. Rahill's favorite subject was the respective futures of the sixth form, and Amory never tired of outlining them for his benefit.

"Ted Converse? 'At's easy. He'll fail his exams, tutor all summer at Harstrum's, get into Sheff with about four conditions, and flunk out in the middle of the freshman year. Then he'll go back West and raise hell for a year or so; finally his father will make him go into the paint business. He'll marry and have four sons, all bone heads. He'll always think St. Regis's spoiled him, so he'll send his sons to day school in Portland. He'll die of locomotor ataxia when he's forty-one, and his wife will give a baptizing stand or whatever you call it to the Presbyterian Church, with his name on it—"

"Hold up, Amory. That's too darned gloomy. How about yourself?"

"I'm in a superior class. You are, too. We're philosophers."

"I'm not."

"Sure you are. You've got a darn good head on you." But Amory knew that nothing in the abstract, no theory or generality, ever moved Rahill until he stubbed his toe upon the concrete minutiae of it.

"Haven't," insisted Rahill. "I let people impose on me here and don't get anything out of it. I'm the prey of my friends, damn it—do their lessons, get 'em out of trouble, pay 'em stupid summer visits, and always entertain their kid sisters; keep my temper when they get selfish and then they think they pay me back by voting for me and telling me I'm the 'big man' of St. Regis's. I want to get where everybody does their own work and I can tell people where to go. I'm tired of being nice to every poor fish in school."

"You're not a slicker," said Amory suddenly.

"A what?"

"A slicker."

"What the devil's that?"

"Well, it's something that—that—there's a lot of them. You're not one, and neither am I, though I am more than you are."

"Who is one? What makes you one?"

Amory considered.

"Why—why, I suppose that the *sign* of it is when a fellow slicks his hair back with water."

"Like Carstairs?"

"Yes—sure. He's a slicker."

They spent two evenings getting an exact definition. The slicker was good-looking or clean-looking; he had brains, social brains, that is, and he used all means on the broad path of honesty to get ahead, be popular, admired, and never in trouble. He dressed well, was particularly neat in appearance, and derived his name from the fact that his hair was inevitably worn short, soaked in water or tonic, parted in the middle, and slicked back as the current of fashion dictated.

The slickers of that year had adopted tortoise-shell spectacles as badges of their slickerhood, and this made them so easy to recognize that Amory and Rahill never missed one. The slicker seemed distributed through school, always a little wiser and shrewder than his contemporaries, managing some team or other, and keeping his cleverness carefully concealed.

Amory found the slicker a most valuable classification until his junior year in college, when the outline became so blurred and indeterminate that it had to be subdivided many times, and became only a quality. Amory's secret ideal had all the slicker qualifications, but, in addition, courage and tremendous brains and talents—also Amory conceded him a bizarre streak that was quite irreconcilable to the slicker proper.

This was a first real break from the hypocrisy of school tradition. The slicker was a definite element of success, differing intrinsically from the prep school "big man."

"THE SLICKER"

1. Clever sense of social values.

2. Dresses well.Pretends that dress is superficial—but knows that it isn't.

3. Goes into such activities as he can shine in.

4. Gets to college and is, in a worldly way, successful.

5. Hair slicked.
"THE BIG MAN"

1. Inclined to stupidity and unconscious of social values.

2. Thinks dress is superficial, and is inclined to be careless about it.

3. Goes out for everything from a sense of duty.

4. Gets to college and has a problematical future.Feels lost without his circle, and always says that school days were happiest, after all.Goes back to school and makes speeches about what St. Regis's boys are doing.

5. Hair not slicked.

Amory had decided definitely on Princeton, even though he would be the only boy entering that year from St. Regis'. Yale had a romance and glamour from the tales of Minneapolis, and St. Regis' men who had been "tapped for Skull and Bones," but Princeton drew him most, with its atmosphere of bright colors and its alluring reputation as the pleasantest country club in America. Dwarfed by the menacing college exams, Amory's school days drifted into the past. Years afterward, when he went back to St. Regis', he seemed to have forgotten the successes of sixth-form year, and to be able to picture himself only as the unadjustable boy who had hurried down corridors, jeered at by his rabid contemporaries mad with common sense.

II. Spires and Gargoyles

At first Amory noticed only the wealth of sunshine creeping across the long, green swards, dancing on the leaded window-panes, and swimming around the tops of spires and towers and battlemented walls. Gradually he realized that he was really walking up University Place, self-conscious about his suitcase, developing a new tendency to glare straight ahead when he passed any one. Several times he could have sworn that men turned to look at him critically. He wondered vaguely if there was something the matter with his clothes, and wished he had shaved that morning on the train. He felt unnecessarily stiff and awkward among these white-flannelled, bareheaded youths, who must be juniors and seniors, judging from the savoir faire with which they strolled.

He found that 12 University Place was a large, dilapidated mansion, at present apparently uninhabited, though he knew it housed usually a dozen freshmen. After a hurried skirmish with his landlady he sallied out on a tour of exploration, but he had gone scarcely a block when he became horribly conscious that he must be the only man in town who was wearing a hat. He returned hurriedly to 12 University, left his derby, and, emerging bareheaded, loitered down Nassau Street, stopping to investigate a display of athletic photographs in a store window, including a large one of Allenby, the football captain, and next attracted by the sign "Jigger Shop" over a confectionary window. This sounded familiar, so he sauntered in and took a seat on a high stool.

"Chocolate sundae," he told a colored person.

"Double chocolate jiggah? Anything else?"

"Why—yes."

"Bacon bun?"

"Why—yes."

He munched four of these, finding them of pleasing savor, and then consumed another double-chocolate jigger before ease descended upon him. After a cursory inspection of the pillow-cases, leather pennants, and Gibson Girls that lined the walls, he left, and continued along Nassau Street with his hands in his pockets. Gradually he was learning to distinguish between upper classmen and entering men, even though the freshman cap would not appear until the following Monday. Those who were too obviously, too nervously at home were freshmen, for as each train brought a new contingent it was immediately absorbed into the hatless, white-shod, book-laden throng, whose function seemed to be to drift endlessly up and down the street, emitting great clouds of smoke from brand-new pipes. By afternoon Amory realized that now the newest arrivals were taking him for an upper classman, and he tried conscientiously to look both pleasantly blasé and casually critical, which was as near as he could analyze the prevalent facial expression.

At five o'clock he felt the need of hearing his own voice, so he retreated to his house to see if any one else had arrived. Having climbed the rickety stairs he scrutinized his room resignedly, concluding that it was hopeless to attempt any more inspired decoration than class banners and tiger pictures. There was a tap at the door.

"Come in!"

A slim face with gray eyes and a humorous smile appeared in the doorway.

"Got a hammer?"

"No—sorry. Maybe Mrs. Twelve, or whatever she goes by, has one."

The stranger advanced into the room.

"You an inmate of this asylum?"

Amory nodded.

"Awful barn for the rent we pay."

Amory had to agree that it was.

"I thought of the campus," he said, "but they say there's so few freshmen that they're lost. Have to sit around and study for something to do."

The gray-eyed man decided to introduce himself.

"My name's Holiday."

"Blaine's my name."

They shook hands with the fashionable low swoop. Amory grinned.

"Where'd you prep?"

"Andover—where did you?"

"St. Regis's."

"Oh, did you? I had a cousin there."

They discussed the cousin thoroughly, and then Holiday announced that he was to meet his brother for dinner at six.

"Come along and have a bite with us."

"All right."

At the Kenilworth Amory met Burne Holiday—he of the gray eyes was Kerry—and during a limpid meal of thin soup and anaemic vegetables they stared at the other freshmen, who sat either in small groups looking very ill at ease, or in large groups seeming very much at home.

"I hear Commons is pretty bad," said Amory.

"That's the rumor. But you've got to eat there—or pay anyways."

"Crime!"

"Imposition!"

"Oh, at Princeton you've got to swallow everything the first year. It's like a damned prep school."

Amory agreed.

"Lot of pep, though," he insisted. "I wouldn't have gone to Yale for a million."

"Me either."

"You going out for anything?" inquired Amory of the elder brother.

"Not me—Burne here is going out for the Prince—the Daily Princetonian, you know."

"Yes, I know."

"You going out for anything?"

"Why—yes. I'm going to take a whack at freshman football."

"Play at St. Regis's?"

"Some," admitted Amory depreciatingly, "but I'm getting so damned thin."

"You're not thin."

"Well, I used to be stocky last fall."

"Oh!"

After supper they attended the movies, where Amory was fascinated by the glib comments of a man in front of him, as well as by the wild yelling and shouting.

"Yoho!"

"Oh, honey-baby—you're so big and strong, but oh, so gentle!"

"Clinch!"

"Oh, Clinch!"

"Kiss her, kiss 'at lady, quick!"

"Oh-h-h—!"

A group began whistling "By the Sea," and the audience took it up noisily. This was followed by an indistinguishable song that included much stamping and then by an endless, incoherent dirge.

"Oh-h-h-h-h
She works in a Jam Factoree
And—that-may-be-all-right
But you can't-fool-me
For I know—DAMN—WELL
That she DON'T-make-jam-all-night!
Oh-h-h-h!"

As they pushed out, giving and receiving curious impersonal glances, Amory decided that he liked the movies, wanted to enjoy them as the row of upper classmen in front had enjoyed them, with their arms along the backs of the seats, their comments Gaelic and caustic, their attitude a mixture of critical wit and tolerant amusement.

"Want a sundae—I mean a jigger?" asked Kerry.

"Sure."

They suppered heavily and then, still sauntering, eased back to 12.

"Wonderful night."

"It's a whiz."

"You men going to unpack?"

"Guess so. Come on, Burne."

Amory decided to sit for a while on the front steps, so he bade them good night.

The great tapestries of trees had darkened to ghosts back at the last edge of twilight. The early moon had drenched the arches with pale blue, and, weaving over the night, in and out of the gossamer rifts of moon, swept a song, a song with more than a hint of sadness, infinitely transient, infinitely regretful.

He remembered that an alumnus of the nineties had told him of one of Booth Tarkington's amusements: standing in mid-campus in the small hours and singing tenor songs to the stars, arousing mingled emotions in the couched undergraduates according to the sentiment of their moods.

Now, far down the shadowy line of University Place a white-clad phalanx broke the gloom, and marching figures, white-shirted, white-trousered, swung rhythmically up the street, with linked arms and heads thrown back:

"Going back—going back,
Going—back—to—Nas-sau—Hall,
Going back—going back—
To the—Best—Old—Place—of—All.
Going back—going back,
From all—this—earth-ly—ball,
We'll—clear—the—track—as—we—go—back—
Going—back—to—Nas-sau—Hall!"

Amory closed his eyes as the ghostly procession drew near. The song soared so high that all dropped out except the tenors, who bore the melody triumphantly past the danger-point and relinquished it to the fantastic chorus. Then Amory opened his eyes, half afraid that sight would spoil the rich illusion of harmony.

He sighed eagerly. There at the head of the white platoon marched Allenby, the football captain, slim and defiant, as if aware that this year the hopes of the college rested on him, that his hundred-and-sixty pounds were expected to dodge to victory through the heavy blue and crimson lines.

Fascinated, Amory watched each rank of linked arms as it came abreast, the faces indistinct above the polo shirts, the voices blent in a paean of triumph—and then the procession passed through shadowy Campbell Arch, and the voices grew fainter as it wound eastward over the campus.

The minutes passed and Amory sat there very quietly. He regretted the rule that would forbid freshmen to be outdoors after curfew, for he wanted to ramble through the shadowy scented lanes, where Witherspoon brooded like a dark mother over Whig and Clio, her Attic children, where the black Gothic snake of Little curled down to Cuyler and Patton, these in turn flinging the mystery out over the placid slope rolling to the lake.

Princeton of the daytime filtered slowly into his consciousness—West and Reunion, redolent of the sixties, Seventy-nine Hall, brick-red and arrogant, Upper and Lower Pyne, aristocratic Elizabethan ladies not quite content to live among shopkeepers, and, topping all, climbing with clear blue aspiration, the great dreaming spires of Holder and Cleveland towers.

From the first he loved Princeton—its lazy beauty, its half-grasped significance, the wild moonlight revel of the rushes, the handsome, prosperous big-game crowds, and under it all the air of struggle that pervaded his class. From the day when, wild-eyed and exhausted, the jerseyed freshmen sat in the gymnasium and elected some one from Hill School class president, a Lawrenceville celebrity vice-president, a hockey star from St. Paul's secretary, up until the end of sophomore year it never ceased, that breathless social system, that worship, seldom named, never really admitted, of the bogey "Big Man."

First it was schools, and Amory, alone from St. Regis', watched the crowds form and widen and form again; St. Paul's, Hill, Pomfret, eating at certain tacitly reserved tables in Commons, dressing in their own corners of the gymnasium, and drawing unconsciously about them a barrier of the slightly less important but socially ambitious to protect them from the friendly, rather puzzled high-school element. From the moment he realized this Amory resented social barriers as artificial distinctions made by the strong to bolster up their weak retainers and keep out the almost strong.

Having decided to be one of the gods of the class, he reported for freshman football practice, but in the second week, playing quarter-back, already paragraphed in corners of the Princetonian, he wrenched his knee seriously enough to put him out for the rest of the season. This forced him to retire and consider the situation.

"12 Univee" housed a dozen miscellaneous question-marks. There were three or four inconspicuous and quite startled boys from Lawrenceville, two amateur wild men from a New York private school (Kerry Holiday christened them the "plebeian drunks"), a Jewish youth, also from New York, and, as compensation for Amory, the two Holidays, to whom he took an instant fancy.

The Holidays were rumored twins, but really the dark-haired one, Kerry, was a year older than his blond brother, Burne. Kerry was tall, with humorous gray eyes, and a sudden, attractive smile; he became at once the mentor of the house, reaper of ears that grew too high, censor of conceit, vendor of rare, satirical humor. Amory spread the table of their future friendship with all his ideas of what college should and did mean. Kerry, not inclined as yet to take things seriously, chided him gently for being curious at this inopportune time about the intricacies of the social system, but liked him and was both interested and amused.

Burne, fair-haired, silent, and intent, appeared in the house only as a busy apparition, gliding in quietly at night and off again in the early morning to get up his work in the library—he was out for the Princetonian, competing furiously against forty others for the coveted first place. In December he came down with diphtheria, and some one else won the competition, but, returning to college in February, he dauntlessly went after the prize again. Necessarily, Amory's acquaintance with him was in the way of three-minute chats, walking to and from lectures, so he failed to penetrate Burne's one absorbing interest and find what lay beneath it.

Amory was far from contented. He missed the place he had won at St. Regis', the being known and admired, yet Princeton stimulated him, and there were many things ahead calculated to arouse the Machiavelli latent in him, could he but insert a wedge. The upper-class clubs, concerning which he had pumped a reluctant graduate during the previous summer, excited his curiosity: Ivy, detached and breathlessly aristocratic; Cottage, an impressive mélange of brilliant adventurers and well-dressed philanderers; Tiger Inn, broad-shouldered and athletic, vitalized by an honest elaboration of prep-school standards; Cap and Gown, anti-alcoholic, faintly religious and politically powerful; flamboyant Colonial; literary Quadrangle; and the dozen others, varying in age and position.

Anything which brought an under classman into too glaring a light was labelled with the damning brand of "running it out." The movies thrived on caustic comments, but the men who made them were generally running it out; talking of clubs was running it out; standing for anything very strongly, as, for instance, drinking parties or teetotalling, was running it out; in short, being personally conspicuous was not tolerated, and the influential man was the non-committal man, until at club elections in sophomore year every one should be sewed up in some bag for the rest of his college career.

Amory found that writing for the Nassau Literary Magazine would get him nothing, but that being on the board of the Daily Princetonian would get any one a good deal. His vague desire to do immortal acting with the English Dramatic Association faded out when he found that the most ingenious brains and talents were concentrated upon the Triangle Club, a musical comedy organization that every year took a great Christmas trip. In the meanwhile, feeling strangely alone and restless in Commons, with new desires and ambitions stirring in his mind, he let the first term go by between an envy of the embryo successes and a puzzled fretting with Kerry as to why they were not accepted immediately among the elite of the class.

Many afternoons they lounged in the windows of 12 Univee and watched the class pass to and from Commons, noting satellites already attaching themselves to the more prominent, watching the lonely grind with his hurried step and downcast eye, envying the happy security of the big school groups.

"We're the damned middle class, that's what!" he complained to Kerry one day as he lay stretched out on the sofa, consuming a family of Fatimas with contemplative precision.

"Well, why not? We came to Princeton so we could feel that way toward the small colleges—have it on 'em, more self-confidence, dress better, cut a swathe—"

"Oh, it isn't that I mind the glittering caste system," admitted Amory. "I like having a bunch of hot cats on top, but gosh, Kerry, I've got to be one of them."

"But just now, Amory, you're only a sweaty bourgeois."

Amory lay for a moment without speaking.

"I won't be—long," he said finally. "But I hate to get anywhere by working for it. I'll show the marks, don't you know."

"Honorable scars." Kerry craned his neck suddenly at the street. "There's Langueduc, if you want to see what he looks like—and Humbird just behind."

Amory rose dynamically and sought the windows.

"Oh," he said, scrutinizing these worthies, "Humbird looks like a knock-out, but this Langueduc—he's the rugged type, isn't he? I distrust that sort. All diamonds look big in the rough."

"Well," said Kerry, as the excitement subsided, "you're a literary genius. It's up to you."

"I wonder"—Amory paused—"if I could be. I honestly think so sometimes. That sounds like the devil, and I wouldn't say it to anybody except you."

"Well—go ahead. Let your hair grow and write poems like this guy D'Invilliers in the Lit."

Amory reached lazily at a pile of magazines on the table.

"Read his latest effort?"

"Never miss 'em. They're rare."

Amory glanced through the issue.

"Hello!" he said in surprise, "he's a freshman, isn't he?"

"Yeah."

"Listen to this! My God!

"'A serving lady speaks:

> *Black velvet trails its folds over the day,*
> *White tapers, prisoned in their silver frames,*
> *Wave their thin flames like shadows in the wind,*
> *Pia, Pompia, come—come away—'*

"Now, what the devil does that mean?"

"It's a pantry scene."

> *"'Her toes are stiffened like a stork's in flight;*
> *She's laid upon her bed, on the white sheets,*
> *Her hands pressed on her smooth bust like a saint,*
> *Bella Cunizza, come into the light!'*

"My gosh, Kerry, what in hell is it all about? I swear I don't get him at all, and I'm a literary bird myself."

"It's pretty tricky," said Kerry, "only you've got to think of hearses and stale milk when you read it. That isn't as pash as some of them."

Amory tossed the magazine on the table.

"Well," he sighed, "I sure am up in the air. I know I'm not a regular fellow, yet I loathe anybody else that isn't. I can't decide whether to cultivate my mind and be a great dramatist, or to thumb my nose at the Golden Treasury and be a Princeton slicker."

"Why decide?" suggested Kerry. "Better drift, like me. I'm going to sail into prominence on Burne's coat-tails."

"I can't drift—I want to be interested. I want to pull strings, even for somebody else, or be Princetonian chairman or Triangle president. I want to be admired, Kerry."

"You're thinking too much about yourself."

Amory sat up at this.

"No. I'm thinking about you, too. We've got to get out and mix around the class right now, when it's fun to be a snob. I'd like to bring a sardine to the prom in June, for instance, but I wouldn't do it unless I could be damn debonaire about it—introduce her to all the prize parlor-snakes, and the football captain, and all that simple stuff."

"Amory," said Kerry impatiently, "you're just going around in a circle. If you want to be prominent, get out and try for something; if you don't, just take it easy." He yawned. "Come on, let's let the smoke drift off. We'll go down and watch football practice."

Amory gradually accepted this point of view, decided that next fall would inaugurate his career, and relinquished himself to watching Kerry extract joy from 12 Univee.

They filled the Jewish youth's bed with lemon pie; they put out the gas all over the house every night by blowing into the jet in Amory's room, to the bewilderment of Mrs. Twelve and the local plumber; they set up the effects of the plebeian drunks—pictures, books, and furniture—in the bathroom, to the confusion of the pair, who hazily discovered the transposition on their return from a Trenton spree; they were disappointed beyond measure when the plebeian drunks decided to take it as a joke; they played red-dog and twenty-one and jackpot from dinner to dawn, and on the occasion of one man's birthday persuaded him to buy sufficient champagne for a hilarious celebration. The donor of the party having remained sober, Kerry and Amory accidentally dropped him down two flights of stairs and called, shame-faced and penitent, at the infirmary all the following week.

"Say, who are all these women?" demanded Kerry one day, protesting at the size of Amory's mail. "I've been looking at the postmarks lately—Farmington and Dobbs and Westover and Dana Hall—what's the idea?"

Amory grinned.

"All from the Twin Cities." He named them off. "There's Marylyn De Witt—she's pretty, got a car of her own and that's damn convenient; there's Sally Weatherby—she's getting too fat; there's Myra St. Claire, she's an old flame, easy to kiss if you like it—"

"What line do you throw 'em?" demanded Kerry. "I've tried everything, and the mad wags aren't even afraid of me."

"You're the 'nice boy' type," suggested Amory.

"That's just it. Mother always feels the girl is safe if she's with me. Honestly, it's annoying. If I start to hold somebody's hand, they laugh at me, and let me, just as if it wasn't part of them. As soon as I get hold of a hand they sort of disconnect it from the rest of them."

"Sulk," suggested Amory. "Tell 'em you're wild and have 'em reform you—go home furious—come back in half an hour—startle 'em."

Kerry shook his head.

"No chance. I wrote a St. Timothy girl a really loving letter last year. In one place I got rattled and said: 'My God, how I love you!' She took a nail scissors, clipped out the 'My God' and showed the rest of the letter all over school. Doesn't work at all. I'm just 'good old Kerry' and all that rot."

Amory smiled and tried to picture himself as "good old Amory." He failed completely.

February dripped snow and rain, the cyclonic freshman mid-years passed, and life in 12 Univee continued interesting if not purposeful. Once a day Amory indulged in a club sandwich, cornflakes, and Julienne potatoes at "Joe's," accompanied usually by Kerry or Alec Connage. The latter was a quiet, rather aloof slicker from Hotchkiss, who lived next door and shared the same enforced singleness as Amory, due to the fact that his entire class had gone to Yale. "Joe's" was unaesthetic and faintly unsanitary, but a limitless charge account could be opened there, a convenience that Amory appreciated. His father had been experimenting with mining stocks and, in consequence, his allowance, while liberal, was not at all what he had expected.

"Joe's" had the additional advantage of seclusion from curious upper-class eyes, so at four each afternoon Amory, accompanied by friend or book, went up to experiment with his digestion. One day in March, finding that all the tables were occupied, he slipped into a chair opposite a freshman who bent intently over a book at the last table. They nodded briefly. For twenty minutes Amory sat consuming bacon buns and reading "Mrs. Warren's Profession" (he had discovered Shaw quite by accident while browsing in the library during mid-years); the other freshman, also intent on his volume, meanwhile did away with a trio of chocolate malted milks.

By and by Amory's eyes wandered curiously to his fellow-luncher's book. He spelled out the name and title upside down—"Marpessa," by Stephen Phillips. This meant nothing to him, his metrical education having been confined to such Sunday classics as "Come into the Garden, Maude," and what morsels of Shakespeare and Milton had been recently forced upon him.

Moved to address his vis-a-vis, he simulated interest in his book for a moment, and then exclaimed aloud as if involuntarily:

"Ha! Great stuff!"

The other freshman looked up and Amory registered artificial embarrassment.

"Are you referring to your bacon buns?" His cracked, kindly voice went well with the large spectacles and the impression of a voluminous keenness that he gave.

"No," Amory answered. "I was referring to Bernard Shaw." He turned the book around in explanation.

"I've never read any Shaw. I've always meant to." The boy paused and then continued: "Did you ever read Stephen Phillips, or do you like poetry?"

"Yes, indeed," Amory affirmed eagerly. "I've never read much of Phillips, though." (He had never heard of any Phillips except the late David Graham.)

"It's pretty fair, I think. Of course he's a Victorian." They sallied into a discussion of poetry, in the course of which they introduced themselves, and Amory's companion proved to be none other than "that awful highbrow, Thomas Parke D'Invilliers," who signed the passionate love-poems in the Lit. He was, perhaps, nineteen, with stooped shoulders, pale blue eyes, and, as Amory could tell from his general appearance, without much conception of social competition and such phenomena of absorbing interest. Still, he liked books, and it seemed forever since Amory had met any one who did; if only that St. Paul's crowd at the next table would not mistake *him* for a bird, too, he would enjoy the encounter tremendously. They didn't seem to be noticing, so he let himself go, discussed books by the dozens—books he had read, read about, books he had never heard of, rattling off lists of titles with the facility of a

Brentano's clerk. D'Invilliers was partially taken in and wholly delighted. In a good-natured way he had almost decided that Princeton was one part deadly Philistines and one part deadly grinds, and to find a person who could mention Keats without stammering, yet evidently washed his hands, was rather a treat.

"Ever read any Oscar Wilde?" he asked.

"No. Who wrote it?"

"It's a man—don't you know?"

"Oh, surely." A faint chord was struck in Amory's memory. "Wasn't the comic opera, 'Patience,' written about him?"

"Yes, that's the fella. I've just finished a book of his, 'The Picture of Dorian Gray,' and I certainly wish you'd read it. You'd like it. You can borrow it if you want to."

"Why, I'd like it a lot—thanks."

"Don't you want to come up to the room? I've got a few other books."

Amory hesitated, glanced at the St. Paul's group—one of them was the magnificent, exquisite Humbird—and he considered how determinate the addition of this friend would be. He never got to the stage of making them and getting rid of them—he was not hard enough for that—so he measured Thomas Parke D'Invilliers' undoubted attractions and value against the menace of cold eyes behind tortoise-rimmed spectacles that he fancied glared from the next table.

"Yes, I'll go."

So he found "Dorian Gray" and the "Mystic and Somber Dolores" and the "Belle Dame sans Merci"; for a month was keen on naught else. The world became pale and interesting, and he tried hard to look at Princeton through the satiated eyes of Oscar Wilde and Swinburne—or "Fingal O'Flaherty" and "Algernon Charles," as he called them in precieuse jest. He read enormously every night—Shaw, Chesterton, Barrie, Pinero, Yeats, Synge, Ernest Dowson, Arthur Symons, Keats, Sudermann, Robert Hugh Benson, the Savoy Operas—just a heterogeneous mixture, for he suddenly discovered that he had read nothing for years.

Tom D'Invilliers became at first an occasion rather than a friend. Amory saw him about once a week, and together they gilded the ceiling of Tom's room and decorated the walls with imitation tapestry, bought at an auction, tall candlesticks and figured curtains. Amory liked him for being clever and literary without effeminacy or affectation. In fact, Amory did most of the strutting and tried painfully to make every remark an epigram, than which, if one is content with ostensible epigrams, there are many feats harder. 12 Univee was amused. Kerry read "Dorian Gray" and simulated Lord Henry, following Amory about, addressing him as "Dorian" and pretending to encourage in him wicked fancies and attenuated tendencies to ennui. When he carried it into Commons, to the amazement of the others at table, Amory became furiously embarrassed, and after that made epigrams only before D'Invilliers or a convenient mirror.

One day Tom and Amory tried reciting their own and Lord Dunsany's poems to the music of Kerry's graphophone.

"Chant!" cried Tom. "Don't recite! Chant!"

Amory, who was performing, looked annoyed, and claimed that he needed a record with less piano in it. Kerry thereupon rolled on the floor in stifled laughter.

"Put on 'Hearts and Flowers'!" he howled. "Oh, my Lord, I'm going to cast a kitten."

"Shut off the damn graphophone," Amory cried, rather red in the face. "I'm not giving an exhibition."

In the meanwhile Amory delicately kept trying to awaken a sense of the social system in D'Invilliers, for he knew that this poet was really more conventional than he, and needed merely watered hair, a smaller range of conversation, and a darker brown hat to become quite regular. But the liturgy of Livingstone collars and dark ties fell on heedless ears; in fact D'Invilliers faintly resented his efforts; so Amory confined himself to calls once a week, and brought him occasionally to 12 Univee. This caused mild titters among the other freshmen, who called them "Doctor Johnson and Boswell."

Alec Connage, another frequent visitor, liked him in a vague way, but was afraid of him as a highbrow. Kerry, who saw through his poetic patter to the solid, almost respectable depths within, was immensely amused and would have him recite poetry by the hour, while he lay with closed eyes on Amory's sofa and listened:

"Asleep or waking is it? for her neck
Kissed over close, wears yet a purple speck
Wherein the pained blood falters and goes out;
Soft and stung softly—fairer for a fleck..."

"That's good," Kerry would say softly. "It pleases the elder Holiday. That's a great poet, I guess." Tom, delighted at an audience, would ramble through the "Poems and Ballades" until Kerry and Amory knew them almost as well as he.

Amory took to writing poetry on spring afternoons, in the gardens of the big estates near Princeton, while swans made effective atmosphere in the artificial pools, and slow clouds sailed harmoniously above the willows. May came too soon, and suddenly unable to bear walls, he wandered the campus at all hours through starlight and rain.

A DAMP SYMBOLIC INTERLUDE

The night mist fell. From the moon it rolled, clustered about the spires and towers, and then settled below them, so that the dreaming peaks were still in lofty aspiration toward the sky. Figures that dotted the day like ants now brushed along as shadowy ghosts, in and out of the foreground. The Gothic halls and cloisters were infinitely more mysterious as they loomed suddenly out of the darkness, outlined each by myriad faint squares of yellow light. Indefinitely from somewhere a bell boomed the quarter-hour, and Amory, pausing by the sun-dial, stretched himself out full length on the damp grass. The cool bathed his eyes and slowed the flight of time—time that had crept so insidiously through the lazy April afternoons, seemed so intangible in the long spring twilights. Evening after evening the senior singing had drifted over the campus in melancholy beauty, and through the shell of his undergraduate consciousness had broken a deep and reverent devotion to the gray walls and Gothic peaks and all they symbolized as warehouses of dead ages.

The tower that in view of his window sprang upward, grew into a spire, yearning higher until its uppermost tip was half invisible against the morning skies, gave him the first sense of the transiency and unimportance of the campus figures except as holders of the apostolic succession. He liked knowing that Gothic architecture, with its upward trend, was peculiarly appropriate to universities, and the idea became personal to him. The silent stretches of green, the quiet halls with an occasional late-burning scholastic light held his imagination in a strong grasp, and the chastity of the spire became a symbol of this perception.

"Damn it all," he whispered aloud, wetting his hands in the damp and running them through his hair. "Next year I work!" Yet he knew that where now the spirit of spires and towers made him dreamily acquiescent, it would then overawe him. Where now he realized only his own inconsequence, effort would make him aware of his own impotency and insufficiency.

The college dreamed on—awake. He felt a nervous excitement that might have been the very throb of its slow heart. It was a stream where he was to throw a stone whose faint ripple would be vanishing almost as it left his hand. As yet he had given nothing, he had taken nothing.

A belated freshman, his oilskin slicker rasping loudly, slushed along the soft path. A voice from somewhere called the inevitable formula, "Stick out your head!" below an unseen window. A hundred little sounds of the current drifting on under the fog pressed in finally on his consciousness.

"Oh, God!" he cried suddenly, and started at the sound of his voice in the stillness. The rain dripped on. A minute longer he lay without moving, his hands clinched. Then he sprang to his feet and gave his clothes a tentative pat.

"I'm very damn wet!" he said aloud to the sun-dial.

HISTORICAL

The war began in the summer following his freshman year. Beyond a sporting interest in the German dash for Paris the whole affair failed either to thrill or interest him. With the attitude he might have held toward an amusing melodrama he hoped it would be long and bloody. If it had not continued he would have felt like an irate ticket-holder at a prize-fight where the principals refused to mix it up.

That was his total reaction.

"HA-HA HORTENSE!"

"All right, ponies!"

"Shake it up!"

"Hey, ponies—how about easing up on that crap game and shaking a mean hip?"

"Hey, *ponies!*"

The coach fumed helplessly, the Triangle Club president, glowering with anxiety, varied between furious bursts of authority and fits of temperamental lassitude, when he sat spiritless and wondered how the devil the show was ever going on tour by Christmas.

"All right. We'll take the pirate song."

The ponies took last drags at their cigarettes and slumped into place; the leading lady rushed into the foreground, setting his hands and feet in an atmospheric mince; and as the coach clapped and stamped and tumped and da-da'd, they hashed out a dance.

A great, seething ant-hill was the Triangle Club. It gave a musical comedy every year, travelling with cast, chorus, orchestra, and scenery all through Christmas vacation. The play and music were the work of undergraduates, and the club itself was the most influential of institutions, over three hundred men competing for it every year.

Amory, after an easy victory in the first sophomore Princetonian competition, stepped into a vacancy of the cast as Boiling Oil, a Pirate Lieutenant. Every night for the last week they had rehearsed "Ha-Ha Hortense!" in the Casino, from two in the afternoon until eight in the morning, sustained by dark and powerful coffee, and sleeping in lectures through the interim. A rare scene, the Casino. A big, barnlike auditorium, dotted with boys as girls, boys as pirates, boys as babies; the scenery in course of being violently set up; the spotlight man rehearsing by throwing weird shafts into angry eyes; over all the constant tuning of the orchestra or the cheerful tumpty-tump of a Triangle tune. The boy who writes the lyrics stands in the corner, biting a pencil, with twenty minutes to think of an encore; the business manager argues with the secretary as to how much money can be spent on "those damn milkmaid costumes"; the old graduate, president in ninety-eight, perches on a box and thinks how much simpler it was in his day.

How a Triangle show ever got off was a mystery, but it was a riotous mystery, anyway, whether or not one did enough service to wear a little gold Triangle on his watch-chain. "Ha-Ha Hortense!" was written over six times and had the names of nine collaborators on the programme. All Triangle shows started by being "something different—not just a regular musical comedy," but when the several authors, the president, the coach and the faculty committee finished with it, there remained just the old reliable Triangle show with the old reliable jokes and the star comedian who got expelled or sick or something just before the trip, and the dark-whiskered man in the pony-ballet, who "absolutely won't shave twice a day, doggone it!"

There was one brilliant place in "Ha-Ha Hortense!" It is a Princeton tradition that whenever a Yale man who is a member of the widely advertised "Skull and Bones" hears the sacred name mentioned, he must leave the room. It is also a tradition that the members are invariably successful in later life, amassing fortunes or votes or coupons or whatever they choose to amass. Therefore, at each performance of "Ha-Ha Hortense!" half-a-dozen seats were kept from sale and occupied by six of the worst-looking vagabonds that could be hired from the streets, further touched up by the Triangle make-up man. At the moment in the show where Firebrand, the Pirate Chief, pointed at his black flag and said, "I am a Yale graduate—note my Skull and Bones!"—at this very moment the six vagabonds were instructed to rise *conspicuously* and leave the theatre with looks of deep melancholy and an injured dignity. It was claimed though never proved that on one occasion the hired Elis were swelled by one of the real thing.

They played through vacation to the fashionable of eight cities. Amory liked Louisville and Memphis best: these knew how to meet strangers, furnished extraordinary punch, and flaunted an astonishing array of feminine beauty. Chicago he approved for a certain verve that transcended its loud accent—however, it was a Yale town, and as the Yale Glee Club was expected in a week the Triangle received only divided homage. In Baltimore, Princeton was at home, and every one fell in love. There was a proper consumption of strong waters all along the line; one man invariably went on the stage highly stimulated, claiming that his particular interpretation of the part required it. There were three private cars; however, no one slept except in the third car, which was called the "animal car," and where were herded the spectacled wind-jammers of the orchestra. Everything was so hurried that there was no time to be bored, but when they arrived in Philadelphia, with vacation nearly over, there was rest in getting out of the heavy atmosphere of flowers and grease-paint, and the ponies took off their corsets with abdominal pains and sighs of relief.

When the disbanding came, Amory set out post haste for Minneapolis, for Sally Weatherby's cousin, Isabelle Borge, was coming to spend the winter in Minneapolis while her parents went abroad. He remembered Isabelle only as a little girl with whom he had played sometimes when he first went to Minneapolis. She had gone to Baltimore to live—but since then she had developed a past.

Amory was in full stride, confident, nervous, and jubilant. Scurrying back to Minneapolis to see a girl he had known as a child seemed the interesting and romantic thing to do, so without compunction he wired his mother not to expect him... sat in the train, and thought about himself for thirty-six hours.

"PETTING"

On the Triangle trip Amory had come into constant contact with that great current American phenomenon, the "petting party."

None of the Victorian mothers—and most of the mothers were Victorian—had any idea how casually their daughters were accustomed to be kissed. "Servant-girls are that way," says Mrs. Huston-Carmelite to her popular daughter. "They are kissed first and proposed to afterward."

But the Popular Daughter becomes engaged every six months between sixteen and twenty-two, when she arranges a match with young Hambell, of Cambell & Hambell, who fatuously considers himself her first love, and between engagements the P. D. (she is selected by the cut-in system at dances, which favors the survival of the fittest) has other sentimental last kisses in the moonlight, or the firelight, or the outer darkness.

Amory saw girls doing things that even in his memory would have been impossible: eating three-o'clock, after-dance suppers in impossible cafes, talking of every side of life with an air half of earnestness, half of mockery, yet with a furtive excitement that Amory considered stood for a real moral let-down. But he never realized how wide-spread it was until he saw the cities between New York and Chicago as one vast juvenile intrigue.

Afternoon at the Plaza, with winter twilight hovering outside and faint drums down-stairs... they strut and fret in the lobby, taking another cocktail, scrupulously attired and waiting. Then the swinging doors revolve and three bundles of fur mince in. The theatre comes afterward; then a table at the Midnight Frolic—of course, mother will be along there, but she will serve only to make things more secretive and brilliant as she sits in solitary state at the deserted table and thinks such entertainments as this are not half so bad as they are painted, only rather wearying. But the P. D. is in love again... it was odd, wasn't it?—that though there was so much room left in the taxi the P. D. and the boy from Williams were somehow crowded out and had to go in a separate car. Odd!

Didn't you notice how flushed the P. D. was when she arrived just seven minutes late? But the P. D. "gets away with it."

The "belle" had become the "flirt," the "flirt" had become the "baby vamp." The "belle" had five or six callers every afternoon. If the P. D., by some strange accident, has two, it is made pretty uncomfortable for the one who hasn't a date with her. The "belle" was surrounded by a dozen men in the intermissions between dances. Try to find the P. D. between dances, just *try* to find her.

The same girl... deep in an atmosphere of jungle music and the questioning of moral codes. Amory found it rather fascinating to feel that any popular girl he met before eight he might quite possibly kiss before twelve.

"Why on earth are we here?" he asked the girl with the green combs one night as they sat in some one's limousine, outside the Country Club in Louisville.

"I don't know. I'm just full of the devil."

"Let's be frank—we'll never see each other again. I wanted to come out here with you because I thought you were the best-looking girl in sight. You really don't care whether you ever see me again, do you?"

"No—but is this your line for every girl? What have I done to deserve it?"

"And you didn't feel tired dancing or want a cigarette or any of the things you said? You just wanted to be—"

"Oh, let's go in," she interrupted, "if you want to *analyze*. Let's not *talk* about it."

When the hand-knit, sleeveless jerseys were stylish, Amory, in a burst of inspiration, named them "petting shirts." The name travelled from coast to coast on the lips of parlor-snakes and P. D.'s.

DESCRIPTIVE

Amory was now eighteen years old, just under six feet tall and exceptionally, but not conventionally, handsome. He had rather a young face, the ingenuousness of which was marred by the penetrating green eyes, fringed with long dark eyelashes. He lacked somehow that intense animal magnetism that so often accompanies beauty in men or women; his personality seemed rather a mental thing, and it was not in his power to turn it on and off like a water-faucet. But people never forgot his face.

ISABELLE

She paused at the top of the staircase. The sensations attributed to divers on spring-boards, leading ladies on opening nights, and lumpy, husky young men on the day of the Big Game, crowded through her. She should have descended to a burst of drums or a discordant blend of themes from "Thais" and "Carmen." She had never been so curious about her appearance, she had never been so satisfied with it. She had been sixteen years old for six months.

"Isabelle!" called her cousin Sally from the doorway of the dressing-room.

"I'm ready." She caught a slight lump of nervousness in her throat.

"I had to send back to the house for another pair of slippers. It'll be just a minute."

Isabelle started toward the dressing-room for a last peek in the mirror, but something decided her to stand there and gaze down the broad stairs of the Minnehaha Club. They curved tantalizingly, and she could catch just a glimpse of two pairs of masculine feet in the hall below. Pump-shod in uniform black, they gave no hint of identity, but she wondered eagerly if one pair were attached to Amory Blaine. This young man, not as yet encountered, had nevertheless taken up a considerable part of her day—the first day of her arrival. Coming up in the machine from the station, Sally had volunteered, amid a rain of question, comment, revelation, and exaggeration:

"You remember Amory Blaine, of *course*. Well, he's simply mad to see you again. He's stayed over a day from college, and he's coming to-night. He's heard so much about you—says he remembers your eyes."

This had pleased Isabelle. It put them on equal terms, although she was quite capable of staging her own romances, with or without advance advertising. But following her happy tremble of anticipation, came a sinking sensation that made her ask:

"How do you mean he's heard about me? What sort of things?"

Sally smiled. She felt rather in the capacity of a showman with her more exotic cousin.

"He knows you're—you're considered beautiful and all that"—she paused—"and I guess he knows you've been kissed."

At this Isabelle's little fist had clinched suddenly under the fur robe. She was accustomed to be thus followed by her desperate past, and it never failed to rouse in her the same feeling of resentment; yet—in a strange town it was an advantageous reputation. She was a "Speed," was she? Well—let them find out.

Out of the window Isabelle watched the snow glide by in the frosty morning. It was ever so much colder here than in Baltimore; she had not remembered; the glass of the side door was iced, the windows were shirred with snow in the corners. Her mind played still with one subject. Did *he* dress like that boy there, who walked calmly down a bustling business street, in moccasins and winter-carnival costume? How very *Western!* Of course he wasn't that way: he went to Princeton, was a sophomore or something. Really she had no distinct idea of him. An ancient snap-shot she had preserved in an old kodak book had impressed her by the big eyes (which he had probably grown up to by now). However, in the last month, when her winter visit to Sally had been decided on, he had assumed the proportions of a worthy adversary. Children, most astute of match-makers, plot their campaigns quickly, and Sally had played a clever correspondence sonata to Isabelle's excitable temperament. Isabelle had been for some time capable of very strong, if very transient emotions....

They drew up at a spreading, white-stone building, set back from the snowy street. Mrs. Weatherby greeted her warmly and her various younger cousins were produced from the corners where they skulked politely. Isabelle met them tactfully. At her best she allied all with whom she came in contact—except older girls and some women. All the impressions she made were conscious. The half-dozen girls she renewed acquaintance with that morning were all rather impressed and as much by her direct personality as by her reputation. Amory Blaine was an open subject. Evidently a bit light of love, neither popular nor unpopular—every girl there seemed to have had an affair with him at some time or other, but no one volunteered any really useful information. He was going to fall for her.... Sally had published that information to her young set and they were retailing it back to Sally as fast as they set eyes on Isabelle. Isabelle resolved secretly that she would, if necessary, *force* herself to like him—she owed it to Sally. Suppose she were terribly disappointed. Sally had painted him in such glowing colors—he was good-looking, "sort of distinguished, when he wants to be," had a line, and was properly inconstant. In fact, he summed up all the romance that her age and environment led her to desire. She wondered if those were his dancing-shoes that fox-trotted tentatively around the soft rug below.

All impressions and, in fact, all ideas were extremely kaleidoscopic to Isabelle. She had that curious mixture of the social and the artistic temperaments found often in two classes, society women and actresses. Her education or, rather, her sophistication, had been absorbed from the boys who had dangled on her favor; her tact was instinctive, and her capacity for love-affairs was limited only by the number of the susceptible within telephone distance. Flirt smiled from her large black-brown eyes and shone through her intense physical magnetism.

So she waited at the head of the stairs that evening while slippers were fetched. Just as she was growing impatient, Sally came out of the dressing-room, beaming with her accustomed good nature and high spirits, and together they descended to the floor below, while the shifting search-light of Isabelle's mind flashed on two ideas: she was glad she had high color to-night, and she wondered if he danced well.

Down-stairs, in the club's great room, she was surrounded for a moment by the girls she had met in the afternoon, then she heard Sally's voice repeating a cycle of names, and found herself bowing to a sextet of black and white, terribly stiff, vaguely familiar figures. The name Blaine figured somewhere, but at first she could not place him. A very confused, very juvenile moment of awkward backings and bumpings followed, and every one found himself talking to the person he least desired to. Isabelle manoeuvred herself and Froggy Parker, freshman at Harvard, with whom she had once played hop-scotch, to a seat on the stairs. A humorous reference to the past was all she needed. The things Isabelle could do socially with one idea were remarkable. First, she repeated it rapturously in an enthusiastic contralto with a soupcon of Southern accent; then she held it off at a distance and smiled at it—her wonderful smile; then she delivered it in variations and played a sort of mental catch with it, all this in the nominal form of dialogue. Froggy was fascinated and quite unconscious that this was being done, not for him, but for the green eyes that glistened under the shining carefully watered hair, a little to her left, for Isabelle had discovered Amory. As an actress even in the fullest flush of her own conscious magnetism gets a deep impression of most of the people in the front row, so Isabelle sized up her antagonist. First, he had auburn hair, and from her feeling of disappointment she knew that she had expected him to be dark and of garter-advertisement slenderness.... For the rest, a faint flush and a straight, romantic profile; the effect set off by a close-fitting dress suit and a silk ruffled shirt of the kind that women still delight to see men wear, but men were just beginning to get tired of.

During this inspection Amory was quietly watching.

"Don't *you* think so?" she said suddenly, turning to him, innocent-eyed.

There was a stir, and Sally led the way over to their table. Amory struggled to Isabelle's side, and whispered:

"You're my dinner partner, you know. We're all coached for each other."

Isabelle gasped—this was rather right in line. But really she felt as if a good speech had been taken from the star and given to a minor character.... She mustn't lose the leadership a bit. The dinner-table glittered with laughter at the confusion of getting places and then curious eyes were turned on her, sitting near the head. She was enjoying this immensely, and Froggy Parker was so engrossed with the added sparkle of her rising color that he forgot to pull out Sally's chair, and fell into a dim confusion. Amory was on the other side, full of confidence and vanity, gazing at her in open admiration. He began directly, and so did Froggy:

"I've heard a lot about you since you wore braids—"

"Wasn't it funny this afternoon—"

Both stopped. Isabelle turned to Amory shyly. Her face was always enough answer for any one, but she decided to speak.

"How—from whom?"

"From everybody—for all the years since you've been away." She blushed appropriately. On her right Froggy was *hors de combat* already, although he hadn't quite realized it.

"I'll tell you what I remembered about you all these years," Amory continued. She leaned slightly toward him and looked modestly at the celery before her. Froggy sighed—he knew Amory, and the situations that Amory seemed born to handle. He turned to Sally and asked her if she was going away to school next year. Amory opened with grape-shot.

"I've got an adjective that just fits you." This was one of his favorite starts—he seldom had a word in mind, but it was a curiosity provoker, and he could always produce something complimentary if he got in a tight corner.

"Oh—what?" Isabelle's face was a study in enraptured curiosity.

Amory shook his head.

"I don't know you very well yet."

"Will you tell me—afterward?" she half whispered.

He nodded.

"We'll sit out."

Isabelle nodded.

"Did any one ever tell you, you have keen eyes?" she said.

Amory attempted to make them look even keener. He fancied, but he was not sure, that her foot had just touched his under the table. But it might possibly have been only the table leg. It was so hard to tell. Still it thrilled him. He wondered quickly if there would be any difficulty in securing the little den up-stairs.

BABES IN THE WOODS

Isabelle and Amory were distinctly not innocent, nor were they particularly brazen. Moreover, amateur standing had very little value in the game they were playing, a game that would presumably be her principal study for years to come. She had begun as he had, with good looks and an excitable temperament, and the rest was the result of accessible popular novels and dressing-room conversation culled from a slightly older set. Isabelle had walked with an artificial gait at nine and a half, and when her eyes, wide and starry, proclaimed the ingenue most. Amory was proportionately less deceived. He waited for the mask to drop off, but at the same time he did not question her right to wear it. She, on her part, was not impressed by his studied air of blasé sophistication. She had lived in a larger city and had slightly an advantage in range. But she accepted his pose—it was one of the dozen little conventions of this kind of affair. He was aware that he was getting this particular favor now because she had been coached; he knew that he stood for merely the best game in sight, and that he would have to improve his opportunity before he lost his advantage. So they proceeded with an infinite guile that would have horrified her parents.

After the dinner the dance began... smoothly. Smoothly?—boys cut in on Isabelle every few feet and then squabbled in the corners with: "You might let me get more than an inch!" and "She didn't like it either—she told me so next time I cut in." It was true—she told every one so, and gave every hand a parting pressure that said: "You know that your dances are *making* my evening."

But time passed, two hours of it, and the less subtle beaux had better learned to focus their pseudo-passionate glances elsewhere, for eleven o'clock found

Isabelle and Amory sitting on the couch in the little den off the reading-room up-stairs. She was conscious that they were a handsome pair, and seemed to belong distinctively in this seclusion, while lesser lights fluttered and chattered down-stairs.

Boys who passed the door looked in enviously—girls who passed only laughed and frowned and grew wise within themselves.

They had now reached a very definite stage. They had traded accounts of their progress since they had met last, and she had listened to much she had heard before. He was a sophomore, was on the Princetonian board, hoped to be chairman in senior year. He learned that some of the boys she went with in Baltimore were "terrible speeds" and came to dances in states of artificial stimulation; most of them were twenty or so, and drove alluring red Stutzes. A good half seemed to have already flunked out of various schools and colleges, but some of them bore athletic names that made him look at her admiringly. As a matter of fact, Isabelle's closer acquaintance with the universities was just commencing. She had bowing acquaintance with a lot of young men who thought she was a "pretty kid—worth keeping an eye on." But Isabelle strung the names into a fabrication of gayety that would have dazzled a Viennese nobleman. Such is the power of young contralto voices on sink-down sofas.

He asked her if she thought he was conceited. She said there was a difference between conceit and self-confidence. She adored self-confidence in men.

"Is Froggy a good friend of yours?" she asked.

"Rather—why?"

"He's a bum dancer."

Amory laughed.

"He dances as if the girl were on his back instead of in his arms."

She appreciated this.

"You're awfully good at sizing people up."

Amory denied this painfully. However, he sized up several people for her. Then they talked about hands.

"You've got awfully nice hands," she said. "They look as if you played the piano. Do you?"

I have said they had reached a very definite stage—nay, more, a very critical stage. Amory had stayed over a day to see her, and his train left at twelve-eighteen that night. His trunk and suitcase awaited him at the station; his watch was beginning to hang heavy in his pocket.

"Isabelle," he said suddenly, "I want to tell you something." They had been talking lightly about "that funny look in her eyes," and Isabelle knew from the change in his manner what was coming—indeed, she had been wondering how soon it would come. Amory reached above their heads and turned out the electric light, so that they were in the dark, except for the red glow that fell through the door from the reading-room lamps. Then he began:

"I don't know whether or not you know what you—what I'm going to say. Lordy, Isabelle—this *sounds* like a line, but it isn't."

"I know," said Isabelle softly.

"Maybe we'll never meet again like this—I have darned hard luck sometimes." He was leaning away from her on the other arm of the lounge, but she could see his eyes plainly in the dark.

"You'll meet me again—silly." There was just the slightest emphasis on the last word—so that it became almost a term of endearment. He continued a bit huskily:

"I've fallen for a lot of people—girls—and I guess you have, too—boys, I mean, but, honestly, you—" he broke off suddenly and leaned forward, chin on his hands: "Oh, what's the use—you'll go your way and I suppose I'll go mine."

Silence for a moment. Isabelle was quite stirred; she wound her handkerchief into a tight ball, and by the faint light that streamed over her, dropped it deliberately on the floor. Their hands touched for an instant, but neither spoke. Silences were becoming more frequent and more delicious. Outside another stray couple had come up and were experimenting on the piano in the next room. After the usual preliminary of "chopsticks," one of them started "Babes in the Woods" and a light tenor carried the words into the den:

"Give me your hand
I'll understand
We're off to slumberland."

Isabelle hummed it softly and trembled as she felt Amory's hand close over hers.

"Isabelle," he whispered. "You know I'm mad about you. You *do* give a darn about me."

"Yes."

"How much do you care—do you like any one better?"

"No." He could scarcely hear her, although he bent so near that he felt her breath against his cheek.

"Isabelle, I'm going back to college for six long months, and why shouldn't we—if I could only just have one thing to remember you by—"

"Close the door...." Her voice had just stirred so that he half wondered whether she had spoken at all. As he swung the door softly shut, the music seemed quivering just outside.

'Moonlight is bright,
Kiss me good night."

What a wonderful song, she thought—everything was wonderful to-night, most of all this romantic scene in the den, with their hands clinging and the inevitable looming charmingly close. The future vista of her life seemed an unending succession of scenes like this: under moonlight and pale starlight, and in the backs of warm limousines and in low, cosy roadsters stopped under sheltering trees—only the boy might change, and this one was so nice. He took her hand softly. With a sudden movement he turned it and, holding it to his lips, kissed the palm.

"Isabelle!" His whisper blended in the music, and they seemed to float nearer together. Her breath came faster. "Can't I kiss you, Isabelle—Isabelle?" Lips half parted, she turned her head to him in the dark. Suddenly the ring of voices, the sound of running footsteps surged toward them. Quick as a flash Amory reached up and turned on the light, and when the door opened and three boys, the wrathy and dance-craving Froggy among them, rushed in, he was turning over the magazines on the table, while she sat without moving, serene and unembarrassed, and even greeted them with a welcoming smile. But her heart was beating wildly, and she felt somehow as if she had been deprived.

It was evidently over. There was a clamor for a dance, there was a glance that passed between them—on his side despair, on hers regret, and then the evening went on, with the reassured beaux and the eternal cutting in.

At quarter to twelve Amory shook hands with her gravely, in the midst of a small crowd assembled to wish him good-speed. For an instant he lost his poise, and she felt a bit rattled when a satirical voice from a concealed wit cried:

"Take her outside, Amory!" As he took her hand he pressed it a little, and she returned the pressure as she had done to twenty hands that evening—that was all.

At two o'clock back at the Weatherbys' Sally asked her if she and Amory had had a "time" in the den. Isabelle turned to her quietly. In her eyes was the light of the idealist, the inviolate dreamer of Joan-like dreams.

"No," she answered. "I don't do that sort of thing any more; he asked me to, but I said no."

As she crept in bed she wondered what he'd say in his special delivery tomorrow. He had such a good-looking mouth—would she ever—?

"Fourteen angels were watching o'er them," sang Sally sleepily from the next room.

"Damn!" muttered Isabelle, punching the pillow into a luxurious lump and exploring the cold sheets cautiously. "Damn!"

CARNIVAL

Amory, by way of the Princetonian, had arrived. The minor snobs, finely balanced thermometers of success, warmed to him as the club elections grew nigh, and he and Tom were visited by groups of upper classmen who arrived awkwardly, balanced on the edge of the furniture and talked of all subjects except the one of absorbing interest. Amory was amused at the intent eyes upon him, and, in case the visitors represented some club in which he was not interested, took great pleasure in shocking them with unorthodox remarks.

"Oh, let me see—" he said one night to a flabbergasted delegation, "what club do you represent?"

With visitors from Ivy and Cottage and Tiger Inn he played the "nice, unspoilt, ingenuous boy" very much at ease and quite unaware of the object of the call.

When the fatal morning arrived, early in March, and the campus became a document in hysteria, he slid smoothly into Cottage with Alec Connage and watched his suddenly neurotic class with much wonder.

There were fickle groups that jumped from club to club; there were friends of two or three days who announced tearfully and wildly that they must join the same club, nothing should separate them; there were snarling disclosures of long-hidden grudges as the Suddenly Prominent remembered snubs of freshman year. Unknown men were elevated into importance when they received certain coveted bids; others who were considered "all set" found that they had made unexpected enemies, felt themselves stranded and deserted, talked wildly of leaving college.

In his own crowd Amory saw men kept out for wearing green hats, for being "a damn tailor's dummy," for having "too much pull in heaven," for getting drunk one night "not like a gentleman, by God," or for unfathomable secret reasons known to no one but the wielders of the black balls.

This orgy of sociability culminated in a gigantic party at the Nassau Inn, where punch was dispensed from immense bowls, and the whole down-stairs became a delirious, circulating, shouting pattern of faces and voices.

"Hi, Dibby—'gratulations!"

"Goo' boy, Tom, you got a good bunch in Cap."

"Say, Kerry—"

"Oh, Kerry—I hear you went Tiger with all the weight-lifters!" "Well, I didn't go Cottage—the parlor-snakes' delight."

"They say Overton fainted when he got his Ivy bid—Did he sign up the first day?—oh, *no*. Tore over to Murray-Dodge on a bicycle—afraid it was a mistake."

"How'd you get into Cap—you old roue?"

"'Gratulations!"

"'Gratulations yourself. Hear you got a good crowd."

When the bar closed, the party broke up into groups and streamed, singing, over the snow-clad campus, in a weird delusion that snobbishness and strain were over at last, and that they could do what they pleased for the next two years.

Long afterward Amory thought of sophomore spring as the happiest time of his life. His ideas were in tune with life as he found it; he wanted no more than to drift and dream and enjoy a dozen new-found friendships through the April afternoons.

Alec Connage came into his room one morning and woke him up into the sunshine and peculiar glory of Campbell Hall shining in the window.

"Wake up, Original Sin, and scrape yourself together. Be in front of Renwick's in half an hour. Somebody's got a car." He took the bureau cover and carefully deposited it, with its load of small articles, upon the bed.

"Where'd you get the car?" demanded Amory cynically.

"Sacred trust, but don't be a critical goopher or you can't go!"

"I think I'll sleep," Amory said calmly, resettling himself and reaching beside the bed for a cigarette.

"Sleep!"

"Why not? I've got a class at eleven-thirty."

"You damned gloom! Of course, if you don't want to go to the coast—"

With a bound Amory was out of bed, scattering the bureau cover's burden on the floor. The coast... he hadn't seen it for years, since he and his mother were on their pilgrimage.

"Who's going?" he demanded as he wriggled into his B. V. D.'s.

"Oh, Dick Humbird and Kerry Holiday and Jesse Ferrenby and—oh about five or six. Speed it up, kid!"

In ten minutes Amory was devouring cornflakes in Renwick's, and at nine-thirty they bowled happily out of town, headed for the sands of Deal Beach.

"You see," said Kerry, "the car belongs down there. In fact, it was stolen from Asbury Park by persons unknown, who deserted it in Princeton and left for the West. Heartless Humbird here got permission from the city council to deliver it."

"Anybody got any money?" suggested Ferrenby, turning around from the front seat.

There was an emphatic negative chorus.

"That makes it interesting."

"Money—what's money? We can sell the car."

"Charge him salvage or something."

"How're we going to get food?" asked Amory.

"Honestly," answered Kerry, eying him reprovingly, "do you doubt Kerry's ability for three short days? Some people have lived on nothing for years at a time. Read the Boy Scout Monthly."

"Three days," Amory mused, "and I've got classes."

"One of the days is the Sabbath."

"Just the same, I can only cut six more classes, with over a month and a half to go."

"Throw him out!"

"It's a long walk back."

"Amory, you're running it out, if I may coin a new phrase."

"Hadn't you better get some dope on yourself, Amory?"

Amory subsided resignedly and drooped into a contemplation of the scenery. Swinburne seemed to fit in somehow.

"Oh, winter's rains and ruins are over,
And all the seasons of snows and sins;
The days dividing lover and lover,
The light that loses, the night that wins;
And time remembered is grief forgotten,
And frosts are slain and flowers begotten,
And in green underwood and cover,
Blossom by blossom the spring begins.

"The full streams feed on flower of—"

"What's the matter, Amory? Amory's thinking about poetry, about the pretty birds and flowers. I can see it in his eye."

"No, I'm not," he lied. "I'm thinking about the Princetonian. I ought to make up to-night; but I can telephone back, I suppose."

"Oh," said Kerry respectfully, "these important men—"

Amory flushed and it seemed to him that Ferrenby, a defeated competitor, winced a little. Of course, Kerry was only kidding, but he really mustn't mention the Princetonian.

It was a halcyon day, and as they neared the shore and the salt breezes scurried by, he began to picture the ocean and long, level stretches of sand and red roofs over blue sea. Then they hurried through the little town and it all flashed upon his consciousness to a mighty paean of emotion....

"Oh, good Lord! *Look* at it!" he cried.

"What?"

"Let me out, quick—I haven't seen it for eight years! Oh, gentlefolk, stop the car!"

"What an odd child!" remarked Alec.

"I do believe he's a bit eccentric."

The car was obligingly drawn up at a curb, and Amory ran for the boardwalk. First, he realized that the sea was blue and that there was an enormous quantity of it, and that it roared and roared—really all the banalities about the ocean that one could realize, but if any one had told him then that these things were banalities, he would have gaped in wonder.

"Now we'll get lunch," ordered Kerry, wandering up with the crowd. "Come on, Amory, tear yourself away and get practical."

"We'll try the best hotel first," he went on, "and thence and so forth."

They strolled along the boardwalk to the most imposing hostelry in sight, and, entering the dining-room, scattered about a table.

"Eight Bronxes," commanded Alec, "and a club sandwich and Juliennes. The food for one. Hand the rest around."

Amory ate little, having seized a chair where he could watch the sea and feel the rock of it. When luncheon was over they sat and smoked quietly.

"What's the bill?"

Some one scanned it.

"Eight twenty-five."

"Rotten overcharge. We'll give them two dollars and one for the waiter. Kerry, collect the small change."

The waiter approached, and Kerry gravely handed him a dollar, tossed two dollars on the check, and turned away. They sauntered leisurely toward the door, pursued in a moment by the suspicious Ganymede.

"Some mistake, sir."

Kerry took the bill and examined it critically.

"No mistake!" he said, shaking his head gravely, and, tearing it into four pieces, he handed the scraps to the waiter, who was so dumfounded that he stood motionless and expressionless while they walked out.

"Won't he send after us?"

"No," said Kerry; "for a minute he'll think we're the proprietor's sons or something; then he'll look at the check again and call the manager, and in the meantime—"

They left the car at Asbury and street-car'd to Allenhurst, where they investigated the crowded pavilions for beauty. At four there were refreshments in a lunch-room, and this time they paid an even smaller per cent on the total cost; something about the appearance and savoir-faire of the crowd made the thing go, and they were not pursued.

"You see, Amory, we're Marxian Socialists," explained Kerry. "We don't believe in property and we're putting it to the great test."

"Night will descend," Amory suggested.

"Watch, and put your trust in Holiday."

They became jovial about five-thirty and, linking arms, strolled up and down the boardwalk in a row, chanting a monotonous ditty about the sad sea waves. Then Kerry saw a face in the crowd that attracted him and, rushing off, reappeared in a moment with one of the homeliest girls Amory had ever set eyes on. Her pale mouth extended from ear to ear, her teeth projected in a solid wedge, and she had little, squinty eyes that peeped ingratiatingly over the side sweep of her nose. Kerry presented them formally.

"Name of Kaluka, Hawaiian queen! Let me present Messrs. Connage, Sloane, Humbird, Ferrenby, and Blaine."

The girl bobbed courtesies all around. Poor creature; Amory supposed she had never before been noticed in her life—possibly she was half-witted. While she accompanied them (Kerry had invited her to supper) she said nothing which could discountenance such a belief.

"She prefers her native dishes," said Alec gravely to the waiter, "but any coarse food will do."

All through supper he addressed her in the most respectful language, while Kerry made idiotic love to her on the other side, and she giggled and grinned. Amory was content to sit and watch the by-play, thinking what a light touch Kerry had, and how he could transform the barest incident into a thing of curve and contour. They all seemed to have the spirit of it more or less, and it was a relaxation to be with them. Amory usually liked men individually, yet feared them in crowds unless the crowd was around him. He wondered how much each one contributed to the party, for there was somewhat of a spiritual tax levied. Alec and Kerry were the life of it, but not quite the centre. Somehow the quiet Humbird, and Sloane, with his impatient superciliousness, were the centre.

Dick Humbird had, ever since freshman year, seemed to Amory a perfect type of aristocrat. He was slender but well-built—black curly hair, straight features, and rather a dark skin. Everything he said sounded intangibly appropriate. He possessed infinite courage, an averagely good mind, and a sense of honor with a clear charm and *noblesse oblige* that varied it from righteousness. He could dissipate without going to pieces, and even his most bohemian adventures never seemed "running it out." People dressed like him, tried to talk as he did.... Amory decided that he probably held the world back, but he wouldn't have changed him. ...

He differed from the healthy type that was essentially middle class—he never seemed to perspire. Some people couldn't be familiar with a chauffeur without having it returned; Humbird could have lunched at Sherry's with a colored man, yet people would have somehow known that it was all right. He was not a snob, though he knew only half his class. His friends ranged from the highest to the lowest, but it was impossible to "cultivate" him. Servants worshipped him, and treated him like a god. He seemed the eternal example of what the upper class tries to be.

"He's like those pictures in the Illustrated London News of the English officers who have been killed," Amory had said to Alec. "Well," Alec had answered, "if you want to know the shocking truth, his father was a grocery clerk who made a fortune in Tacoma real estate and came to New York ten years ago."

Amory had felt a curious sinking sensation.

This present type of party was made possible by the surging together of the class after club elections—as if to make a last desperate attempt to know itself, to keep together, to fight off the tightening spirit of the clubs. It was a let-down from the conventional heights they had all walked so rigidly.

After supper they saw Kaluka to the boardwalk, and then strolled back along the beach to Asbury. The evening sea was a new sensation, for all its color and mellow age was gone, and it seemed the bleak waste that made the Norse sagas sad; Amory thought of Kipling's

"Beaches of Lukanon before the sealers came."

It was still a music, though, infinitely sorrowful.

Ten o'clock found them penniless. They had suppered greatly on their last eleven cents and, singing, strolled up through the casinos and lighted arches on the boardwalk, stopping to listen approvingly to all band concerts. In one place Kerry took up a collection for the French War Orphans which netted a dollar and twenty cents, and with this they bought some brandy in case they caught cold in the night. They finished the day in a moving-picture show and went into solemn systematic roars of laughter at an ancient comedy, to the startled annoyance of the rest of the audience. Their entrance was distinctly strategic, for each man as he entered pointed reproachfully at the one just behind him. Sloane, bringing up the rear, disclaimed all knowledge and responsibility as soon as the others were scattered inside; then as the irate ticket-taker rushed in he followed nonchalantly.

They reassembled later by the Casino and made arrangements for the night. Kerry wormed permission from the watchman to sleep on the platform and, having collected a huge pile of rugs from the booths to serve as mattresses and blankets, they talked until midnight, and then fell into a dreamless sleep, though Amory tried hard to stay awake and watch that marvellous moon settle on the sea.

So they progressed for two happy days, up and down the shore by street-car or machine, or by shoe-leather on the crowded boardwalk; sometimes eating with the wealthy, more frequently dining frugally at the expense of an unsuspecting restaurateur. They had their photos taken, eight poses, in a quick-development store. Kerry insisted on grouping them as a "varsity" football team, and then as a tough gang from the East Side, with their coats inside out, and himself sitting in the middle on a cardboard moon. The photographer probably has them yet—at least, they never called for them. The weather was perfect, and again they slept outside, and again Amory fell unwillingly asleep.

Sunday broke stolid and respectable, and even the sea seemed to mumble and complain, so they returned to Princeton via the Fords of transient farmers, and broke up with colds in their heads, but otherwise none the worse for wandering.

Even more than in the year before, Amory neglected his work, not deliberately but lazily and through a multitude of other interests. Co-ordinate geometry and the melancholy hexameters of Corneille and Racine held forth small allurements, and even psychology, which he had eagerly awaited, proved to be a dull subject full of muscular reactions and biological phrases rather than the study of personality and influence. That was a noon class, and it always sent him dozing. Having found that "subjective and objective, sir," answered most of the questions, he used the phrase on all occasions, and it became the class joke when, on a query being levelled at him, he was nudged awake by Ferrenby or Sloane to gasp it out.

Mostly there were parties—to Orange or the Shore, more rarely to New York and Philadelphia, though one night they marshalled fourteen waitresses out of Childs' and took them to ride down Fifth Avenue on top of an auto bus. They all cut more classes than were allowed, which meant an additional course the following year, but spring was too rare to let anything interfere with their colorful ramblings. In May Amory was elected to the Sophomore Prom Committee, and when after a long evening's discussion with Alec they made out a tentative list of class probabilities for the senior council, they placed themselves among the surest. The senior council was composed presumably of the eighteen most representative seniors, and in view of Alec's football managership and Amory's chance of nosing out Burne Holiday as Princetonian chairman, they seemed fairly justified in this presumption. Oddly enough, they both placed D'Invilliers as among the possibilities, a guess that a year before the class would have gaped at.

All through the spring Amory had kept up an intermittent correspondence with Isabelle Borge, punctuated by violent squabbles and chiefly enlivened by his attempts to find new words for love. He discovered Isabelle to be discreetly and aggravatingly unsentimental in letters, but he hoped against hope that she would prove not too exotic a bloom to fit the large spaces of spring as she had fitted the den in the Minnehaha Club. During May he wrote thirty-page documents almost nightly, and sent them to her in bulky envelopes exteriorly labelled "Part I" and "Part II."

"Oh, Alec, I believe I'm tired of college," he said sadly, as they walked the dusk together.

"I think I am, too, in a way."

"All I'd like would be a little home in the country, some warm country, and a wife, and just enough to do to keep from rotting."

"Me, too."

"I'd like to quit."

"What does your girl say?"

"Oh!" Amory gasped in horror. "She wouldn't *think* of marrying... that is, not now. I mean the future, you know."

"My girl would. I'm engaged."

"Are you really?"

"Yes. Don't say a word to anybody, please, but I am. I may not come back next year."

"But you're only twenty! Give up college?"

"Why, Amory, you were saying a minute ago—"

"Yes," Amory interrupted, "but I was just wishing. I wouldn't think of leaving college. It's just that I feel so sad these wonderful nights. I sort of feel they're never coming again, and I'm not really getting all I could out of them. I wish my girl lived here. But marry—not a chance. Especially as father says the money isn't forthcoming as it used to be."

"What a waste these nights are!" agreed Alec.

But Amory sighed and made use of the nights. He had a snap-shot of Isabelle, enshrined in an old watch, and at eight almost every night he would turn off all the lights except the desk lamp and, sitting by the open windows with the picture before him, write her rapturous letters.

> *... Oh it's so hard to write you what I really feel when I think about you so much; you've gotten to mean to me a dream that I can't put on paper any more.Your last letter came and it was wonderful!I read it over about six times, especially the last part, but I do wish, sometimes, you'd be more frank and tell me what you really do think of me, yet your last letter was too good to be true, and I can hardly wait until June!*Be sure *and be able to come to the prom.It'll be fine, I think, and I want to bring you just at the end of a wonderful year.I often think over what you said on that night and wonder how much you meant.If it were anyone but you—but you see I thought you were fickle the first time I saw you and you are so popular and everthing that I can't imagine you really liking me best.*
>
> *Oh, Isabelle, dear—it's a wonderful night.Somebody is playing "Love Moon" on a mandolin far across the campus, and the music seems to bring you into the window.Now he's playing "Good-by, Boys, I'm Through," and how well it suits me.For I am through with everything.I have decided never to take a cocktail again, and I know I'll never again fall in love—I couldn't—you've been too much a part of my days and nights to ever let me think of another girl.I meet them all the time and they don't interest me. I'm not pretending to be blasé, because it's not that.It's just that I'm in love.Oh, dearest Isabelle (somehow I can't call you just Isabelle, and I'm afraid I'll come out with the "dearest" before your family this June), you've got to come to the prom, and then I'll come up to your house for a day and everything'll be perfect....*

And so on in an eternal monotone that seemed to both of them infinitely charming, infinitely new.

June came and the days grew so hot and lazy that they could not worry even about exams, but spent dreamy evenings on the court of Cottage, talking of long subjects until the sweep of country toward Stony Brook became a blue haze and the lilacs were white around tennis-courts, and words gave way to silent cigarettes.... Then down deserted Prospect and along McCosh with song everywhere around them, up to the hot joviality of Nassau Street.

Tom D'Invilliers and Amory walked late in those days. A gambling fever swept through the sophomore class and they bent over the bones till three o'clock many a sultry night. After one session they came out of Sloane's room to find the dew fallen and the stars old in the sky.

"Let's borrow bicycles and take a ride," Amory suggested.

"All right. I'm not a bit tired and this is almost the last night of the year, really, because the prom stuff starts Monday."

They found two unlocked bicycles in Holder Court and rode out about half-past three along the Lawrenceville Road.

"What are you going to do this summer, Amory?"

"Don't ask me—same old things, I suppose. A month or two in Lake Geneva—I'm counting on you to be there in July, you know—then there'll be Minneapolis, and that means hundreds of summer hops, parlor-snaking, getting bored—But oh, Tom," he added suddenly, "hasn't this year been slick!"

"No," declared Tom emphatically, a new Tom, clothed by Brooks, shod by Franks, "I've won this game, but I feel as if I never want to play another. You're all right—you're a rubber ball, and somehow it suits you, but I'm sick of adapting myself to the local snobbishness of this corner of the world. I want to go where people aren't barred because of the color of their neckties and the roll of their coats."

"You can't, Tom," argued Amory, as they rolled along through the scattering night; "wherever you go now you'll always unconsciously apply these standards of 'having it' or 'lacking it.' For better or worse we've stamped you; you're a Princeton type!"

"Well, then," complained Tom, his cracked voice rising plaintively, "why do I have to come back at all? I've learned all that Princeton has to offer. Two years more of mere pedantry and lying around a club aren't going to help. They're just going to disorganize me, conventionalize me completely. Even now I'm so spineless that I wonder how I get away with it."

"Oh, but you're missing the real point, Tom," Amory interrupted. "You've just had your eyes opened to the snobbishness of the world in a rather abrupt manner. Princeton invariably gives the thoughtful man a social sense."

"You consider you taught me that, don't you?" he asked quizzically, eying Amory in the half dark.

Amory laughed quietly.

"Didn't I?"

"Sometimes," he said slowly, "I think you're my bad angel. I might have been a pretty fair poet."

"Come on, that's rather hard. You chose to come to an Eastern college. Either your eyes were opened to the mean scrambling quality of people, or you'd have gone through blind, and you'd hate to have done that—been like Marty Kaye."

"Yes," he agreed, "you're right. I wouldn't have liked it. Still, it's hard to be made a cynic at twenty."

"I was born one," Amory murmured. "I'm a cynical idealist." He paused and wondered if that meant anything.

They reached the sleeping school of Lawrenceville, and turned to ride back.

"It's good, this ride, isn't it?" Tom said presently.

"Yes; it's a good finish, it's knock-out; everything's good to-night. Oh, for a hot, languorous summer and Isabelle!"

"Oh, you and your Isabelle! I'll bet she's a simple one... let's say some poetry."

So Amory declaimed "The Ode to a Nightingale" to the bushes they passed.

"I'll never be a poet," said Amory as he finished. "I'm not enough of a sensualist really; there are only a few obvious things that I notice as primarily beautiful: women, spring evenings, music at night, the sea; I don't catch the subtle things like 'silver-snarling trumpets.' I may turn out an intellectual, but I'll never write anything but mediocre poetry."

They rode into Princeton as the sun was making colored maps of the sky behind the graduate school, and hurried to the refreshment of a shower that would have to serve in place of sleep. By noon the bright-costumed alumni crowded the streets with their bands and choruses, and in the tents there was great reunion under the orange-and-black banners that curled and strained in the wind. Amory looked long at one house which bore the legend "Sixty-nine." There a few gray-haired men sat and talked quietly while the classes swept by in panorama of life.

UNDER THE ARC-LIGHT

Then tragedy's emerald eyes glared suddenly at Amory over the edge of June. On the night after his ride to Lawrenceville a crowd sallied to New York in quest of adventure, and started back to Princeton about twelve o'clock in two machines. It had been a gay party and different stages of sobriety were represented. Amory was in the car behind; they had taken the wrong road and lost the way, and so were hurrying to catch up.

It was a clear night and the exhilaration of the road went to Amory's head. He had the ghost of two stanzas of a poem forming in his mind. ...

> *So the gray car crept nightward in the dark and there was no life stirred as it went by....As the still ocean paths before the shark in starred and glittering waterways, beauty-high, the moon-swathed trees divided, pair on pair, while flapping nightbirds cried across the air....*

> *A moment by an inn of lamps and shades, a yellow inn under a yellow moon—then silence, where crescendo laughter fades... the car swung out again to the winds of June, mellowed the shadows where the distance grew, then crushed the yellow shadows into blue....*

They jolted to a stop, and Amory peered up, startled. A woman was standing beside the road, talking to Alec at the wheel. Afterward he remembered the harpy effect that her old kimono gave her, and the cracked hollowness of her voice as she spoke:

"You Princeton boys?"

"Yes."

"Well, there's one of you killed here, and two others about dead."

"My God!"

"Look!" She pointed and they gazed in horror. Under the full light of a roadside arc-light lay a form, face downward in a widening circle of blood.

They sprang from the car. Amory thought of the back of that head—that hair—that hair... and then they turned the form over.

"It's Dick—Dick Humbird!"

"Oh, Christ!"

"Feel his heart!"

Then the insistent voice of the old crone in a sort of croaking triumph:

"He's quite dead, all right. The car turned over. Two of the men that weren't hurt just carried the others in, but this one's no use."

Amory rushed into the house and the rest followed with a limp mass that they laid on the sofa in the shoddy little front parlor. Sloane, with his shoulder punctured, was on another lounge. He was half delirious, and kept calling something about a chemistry lecture at 8:10.

"I don't know what happened," said Ferrenby in a strained voice. "Dick was driving and he wouldn't give up the wheel; we told him he'd been drinking too much—then there was this damn curve—oh, my *God!...*" He threw himself face downward on the floor and broke into dry sobs.

The doctor had arrived, and Amory went over to the couch, where some one handed him a sheet to put over the body. With a sudden hardness, he raised one of the hands and let it fall back inertly. The brow was cold but the face not expressionless. He looked at the shoe-laces—Dick had tied them that morning. *He* had tied them—and now he was this heavy white mass. All that remained of the charm and personality of the Dick Humbird he had known—oh, it was all so horrible and unaristocratic and close to the earth. All tragedy has that strain of the grotesque and squalid—so useless, futile... the way animals die.... Amory was reminded of a cat that had lain horribly mangled in some alley of his childhood.

"Some one go to Princeton with Ferrenby."

Amory stepped outside the door and shivered slightly at the late night wind—a wind that stirred a broken fender on the mass of bent metal to a plaintive, tinny sound.

CRESCENDO!

Next day, by a merciful chance, passed in a whirl. When Amory was by himself his thoughts zigzagged inevitably to the picture of that red mouth yawning incongruously in the white face, but with a determined effort he piled present excitement upon the memory of it and shut it coldly away from his mind.

Isabelle and her mother drove into town at four, and they rode up smiling Prospect Avenue, through the gay crowd, to have tea at Cottage. The clubs had their annual dinners that night, so at seven he loaned her to a freshman and arranged to meet her in the gymnasium at eleven, when the upper classmen were admitted to the freshman dance. She was all he had expected, and he was happy and eager to make that night the centre of every dream. At nine the upper classes stood in front of the clubs as the freshman torchlight parade rioted past, and Amory wondered if the dress-suited groups against the dark, stately backgrounds and under the flare of the torches made the night as brilliant to the staring, cheering freshmen as it had been to him the year before.

The next day was another whirl. They lunched in a gay party of six in a private dining-room at the club, while Isabelle and Amory looked at each other tenderly over the fried chicken and knew that their love was to be eternal. They danced away the prom until five, and the stags cut in on Isabelle with joyous abandon, which grew more and more enthusiastic as the hour grew late, and their wines, stored in overcoat pockets in the coat room, made old weariness wait until another day. The stag line is a most homogeneous mass of men. It fairly sways with a single soul. A dark-haired beauty dances by and there is a half-gasping sound as the ripple surges forward and some one sleeker than the rest darts out and cuts in. Then when the six-foot girl (brought by Kaye in your class, and to whom he has been trying to introduce you all evening) gallops by, the line surges back and the groups face about and become intent on far corners of the hall, for Kaye, anxious and perspiring, appears elbowing through the crowd in search of familiar faces.

"I say, old man, I've got an awfully nice—"

"Sorry, Kaye, but I'm set for this one. I've got to cut in on a fella."

"Well, the next one?"

"What—ah—er—I swear I've got to go cut in—look me up when she's got a dance free."

It delighted Amory when Isabelle suggested that they leave for a while and drive around in her car. For a delicious hour that passed too soon they glided the silent roads about Princeton and talked from the surface of their hearts in shy excitement. Amory felt strangely ingenuous and made no attempt to kiss her.

Next day they rode up through the Jersey country, had luncheon in New York, and in the afternoon went to see a problem play at which Isabelle wept all through the second act, rather to Amory's embarrassment—though it filled him with tenderness to watch her. He was tempted to lean over and kiss away her tears, and she slipped her hand into his under cover of darkness to be pressed softly.

Then at six they arrived at the Borges' summer place on Long Island, and Amory rushed up-stairs to change into a dinner coat. As he put in his studs he realized that he was enjoying life as he would probably never enjoy it again. Everything was hallowed by the haze of his own youth. He had arrived, abreast of the best in his generation at Princeton. He was in love and his love was returned. Turning on all the lights, he looked at himself in the mirror, trying to find in his own face the qualities that made him see clearer than the great crowd of people, that made him decide firmly, and able to influence and follow his own will. There was little in his life now that he would have changed. ... Oxford might have been a bigger field.

Silently he admired himself. How conveniently well he looked, and how well a dinner coat became him. He stepped into the hall and then waited at the top of the stairs, for he heard footsteps coming. It was Isabelle, and from the top of her shining hair to her little golden slippers she had never seemed so beautiful.

"Isabelle!" he cried, half involuntarily, and held out his arms. As in the storybooks, she ran into them, and on that half-minute, as their lips first touched, rested the high point of vanity, the crest of his young egotism.

III. The Egotist Considers

"Ouch! Let me go!"

He dropped his arms to his sides.

"What's the matter?"

"Your shirt stud—it hurt me—look!" She was looking down at her neck, where a little blue spot about the size of a pea marred its pallor.

"Oh, Isabelle," he reproached himself, "I'm a goopher. Really, I'm sorry—I shouldn't have held you so close."

She looked up impatiently.

"Oh, Amory, of course you couldn't help it, and it didn't hurt much; but what *are* we going to do about it?"

"*Do* about it?" he asked. "Oh—that spot; it'll disappear in a second."

"It isn't," she said, after a moment of concentrated gazing, "it's still there—and it looks like Old Nick—oh, Amory, what'll we do! It's *just* the height of your shoulder."

"Massage it," he suggested, repressing the faintest inclination to laugh.

She rubbed it delicately with the tips of her fingers, and then a tear gathered in the corner of her eye, and slid down her cheek.

"Oh, Amory," she said despairingly, lifting up a most pathetic face, "I'll just make my whole neck *flame* if I rub it. What'll I do?"

A quotation sailed into his head and he couldn't resist repeating it aloud.

"All the perfumes of Arabia will not whiten this little hand."

She looked up and the sparkle of the tear in her eye was like ice.

"You're not very sympathetic."

Amory mistook her meaning.

"Isabelle, darling, I think it'll—"

"Don't touch me!" she cried. "Haven't I enough on my mind and you stand there and *laugh!*"

Then he slipped again.

"Well, it *is* funny, Isabelle, and we were talking the other day about a sense of humor being—"

She was looking at him with something that was not a smile, rather the faint, mirthless echo of a smile, in the corners of her mouth.

"Oh, shut up!" she cried suddenly, and fled down the hallway toward her room. Amory stood there, covered with remorseful confusion.

"Damn!"

When Isabelle reappeared she had thrown a light wrap about her shoulders, and they descended the stairs in a silence that endured through dinner.

"Isabelle," he began rather testily, as they arranged themselves in the car, bound for a dance at the Greenwich Country Club, "you're angry, and I'll be, too, in a minute. Let's kiss and make up."

Isabelle considered glumly.

"I hate to be laughed at," she said finally.

"I won't laugh any more. I'm not laughing now, am I?"

"You did."

"Oh, don't be so darned feminine."

Her lips curled slightly.

"I'll be anything I want."

Amory kept his temper with difficulty. He became aware that he had not an ounce of real affection for Isabelle, but her coldness piqued him. He wanted to kiss her, kiss her a lot, because then he knew he could leave in the morning and not care. On the contrary, if he didn't kiss her, it would worry him.... It would interfere vaguely with his idea of himself as a conqueror. It wasn't dignified to come off second best, *pleading*, with a doughty warrior like Isabelle.

Perhaps she suspected this. At any rate, Amory watched the night that should have been the consummation of romance glide by with great moths overhead and the heavy fragrance of roadside gardens, but without those broken words, those little sighs....

Afterward they suppered on ginger ale and devil's food in the pantry, and Amory announced a decision.

"I'm leaving early in the morning."

"Why?"

"Why not?" he countered.

"There's no need."

"However, I'm going."

"Well, if you insist on being ridiculous—"

"Oh, don't put it that way," he objected.

"—just because I won't let you kiss me. Do you think—"

"Now, Isabelle," he interrupted, "you know it's not that—even suppose it is. We've reached the stage where we either ought to kiss—or—or—nothing. It isn't as if you were refusing on moral grounds."

She hesitated.

"I really don't know what to think about you," she began, in a feeble, perverse attempt at conciliation. "You're so funny."

"How?"

"Well, I thought you had a lot of self-confidence and all that; remember you told me the other day that you could do anything you wanted, or get anything you wanted?"

Amory flushed. He *had* told her a lot of things.

"Yes."

"Well, you didn't seem to feel so self-confident to-night. Maybe you're just plain conceited."

"No, I'm not," he hesitated. "At Princeton—"

"Oh, you and Princeton! You'd think that was the world, the way you talk! Perhaps you *can* write better than anybody else on your old Princetonian; maybe the freshmen *do* think you're important—"

"You don't understand—"

"Yes, I do," she interrupted. "I *do*, because you're always talking about yourself and I used to like it; now I don't."

"Have I to-night?"

"That's just the point," insisted Isabelle. "You got all upset to-night. You just sat and watched my eyes. Besides, I have to think all the time I'm talking to you—you're so critical."

"I make you think, do I?" Amory repeated with a touch of vanity.

"You're a nervous strain"—this emphatically—"and when you analyze every little emotion and instinct I just don't have 'em."

"I know." Amory admitted her point and shook his head helplessly.

"Let's go." She stood up.

He rose abstractedly and they walked to the foot of the stairs.

"What train can I get?"

"There's one about 9:11 if you really must go."

"Yes, I've got to go, really. Good night."

"Good night."

They were at the head of the stairs, and as Amory turned into his room he thought he caught just the faintest cloud of discontent in her face. He lay awake in the darkness and wondered how much he cared—how much of his sudden unhappiness was hurt vanity—whether he was, after all, temperamentally unfitted for romance.

When he awoke, it was with a glad flood of consciousness. The early wind stirred the chintz curtains at the windows and he was idly puzzled not to be in his room at Princeton with his school football picture over the bureau and the Triangle Club on the wall opposite. Then the grandfather's clock in the hall outside struck eight, and the memory of the night before came to him. He was out of bed, dressing, like the wind; he must get out of the house before he saw Isabelle. What had seemed a melancholy happening, now seemed a tiresome anticlimax. He was dressed at half past, so he sat down by the window; felt that the sinews of his heart were twisted somewhat more than he had thought. What an ironic mockery the morning seemed!—bright and sunny, and full of the smell of the garden; hearing Mrs. Borge's voice in the sun-parlor below, he wondered where was Isabelle.

There was a knock at the door.

"The car will be around at ten minutes of nine, sir."

He returned to his contemplation of the outdoors, and began repeating over and over, mechanically, a verse from Browning, which he had once quoted to Isabelle in a letter:

"Each life unfulfilled, you see,
It hangs still, patchy and scrappy;
We have not sighed deep, laughed free,
Starved, feasted, despaired—been happy."

But his life would not be unfulfilled. He took a sombre satisfaction in thinking that perhaps all along she had been nothing except what he had read into her; that this was her high point, that no one else would ever make her think. Yet that was what she had objected to in him; and Amory was suddenly tired of thinking, thinking!

"Damn her!" he said bitterly, "she's spoiled my year!"

THE SUPERMAN GROWS CARELESS

On a dusty day in September Amory arrived in Princeton and joined the sweltering crowd of conditioned men who thronged the streets. It seemed a stupid way to commence his upper-class years, to spend four hours a morning in the stuffy room of a tutoring school, imbibing the infinite boredom of conic sections. Mr. Rooney, pander to the dull, conducted the class and smoked innumerable Pall Malls as he drew diagrams and worked equations from six in the morning until midnight.

"Now, Langueduc, if I used that formula, where would my A point be?"

Langueduc lazily shifts his six-foot-three of football material and tries to concentrate.

"Oh—ah—I'm damned if I know, Mr. Rooney."

"Oh, why of course, of course you can't *use* that formula. *That's* what I wanted you to say."

"Why, sure, of course."

"Do you see why?"

"You bet—I suppose so."

"If you don't see, tell me. I'm here to show you."

"Well, Mr. Rooney, if you don't mind, I wish you'd go over that again."

"Gladly. Now here's 'A'..."

The room was a study in stupidity—two huge stands for paper, Mr. Rooney in his shirt-sleeves in front of them, and slouched around on chairs, a dozen men: Fred Sloane, the pitcher, who absolutely *had* to get eligible; "Slim" Langueduc, who would beat Yale this fall, if only he could master a poor fifty per cent; McDowell, gay young sophomore, who thought it was quite a sporting thing to be tutoring here with all these prominent athletes.

"Those poor birds who haven't a cent to tutor, and have to study during the term are the ones I pity," he announced to Amory one day, with a flaccid camaraderie in the droop of the cigarette from his pale lips. "I should think it would be such a bore, there's so much else to do in New York during the term. I suppose they don't know what they miss, anyhow." There was such an air of "you and I" about Mr. McDowell that Amory very nearly pushed him out of the open window when he said this. ... Next February his mother would wonder why he didn't make a club and increase his allowance... simple little nut....

Through the smoke and the air of solemn, dense earnestness that filled the room would come the inevitable helpless cry:

"I don't get it! Repeat that, Mr. Rooney!" Most of them were so stupid or careless that they wouldn't admit when they didn't understand, and Amory was of the latter. He found it impossible to study conic sections; something in their calm and tantalizing respectability breathing defiantly through Mr. Rooney's fetid parlors distorted their equations into insoluble anagrams. He made a last night's effort with the proverbial wet towel, and then blissfully took the exam, wondering unhappily why all the color and ambition of the spring before had faded out. Somehow, with the defection of Isabelle the idea of undergraduate success had loosed its grasp on his imagination, and he contemplated a possible failure to pass off his condition with equanimity, even though it would arbitrarily mean his removal from the Princetonian board and the slaughter of his chances for the Senior Council.

There was always his luck.

He yawned, scribbled his honor pledge on the cover, and sauntered from the room.

"If you don't pass it," said the newly arrived Alec as they sat on the window-seat of Amory's room and mused upon a scheme of wall decoration, "you're the world's worst goopher. Your stock will go down like an elevator at the club and on the campus."

"Oh, hell, I know it. Why rub it in?"

"'Cause you deserve it. Anybody that'd risk what you were in line for *ought* to be ineligible for Princetonian chairman."

"Oh, drop the subject," Amory protested. "Watch and wait and shut up. I don't want every one at the club asking me about it, as if I were a prize potato being fattened for a vegetable show." One evening a week later Amory stopped below his own window on the way to Renwick's, and, seeing a light, called up:

"Oh, Tom, any mail?"

Alec's head appeared against the yellow square of light.

"Yes, your result's here."

His heart clamored violently.

"What is it, blue or pink?"

"Don't know. Better come up."

He walked into the room and straight over to the table, and then suddenly noticed that there were other people in the room.

"'Lo, Kerry." He was most polite. "Ah, men of Princeton." They seemed to be mostly friends, so he picked up the envelope marked "Registrar's Office," and weighed it nervously.

"We have here quite a slip of paper."

"Open it, Amory."

"Just to be dramatic, I'll let you know that if it's blue, my name is withdrawn from the editorial board of the Prince, and my short career is over."

He paused, and then saw for the first time Ferrenby's eyes, wearing a hungry look and watching him eagerly. Amory returned the gaze pointedly.

"Watch my face, gentlemen, for the primitive emotions."

He tore it open and held the slip up to the light.

"Well?"

"Pink or blue?"

"Say what it is."

"We're all ears, Amory."

"Smile or swear—or something."

There was a pause... a small crowd of seconds swept by... then he looked again and another crowd went on into time.

"Blue as the sky, gentlemen...."

AFTERMATH

What Amory did that year from early September to late in the spring was so purposeless and inconsecutive that it seems scarcely worth recording. He was, of course, immediately sorry for what he had lost. His philosophy of success had tumbled down upon him, and he looked for the reasons.

"Your own laziness," said Alec later.

"No—something deeper than that. I've begun to feel that I was meant to lose this chance."

"They're rather off you at the club, you know; every man that doesn't come through makes our crowd just so much weaker."

"I hate that point of view."

"Of course, with a little effort you could still stage a comeback."

"No—I'm through—as far as ever being a power in college is concerned."

"But, Amory, honestly, what makes me the angriest isn't the fact that you won't be chairman of the Prince and on the Senior Council, but just that you didn't get down and pass that exam."

"Not me," said Amory slowly; "I'm mad at the concrete thing. My own idleness was quite in accord with my system, but the luck broke."

"Your system broke, you mean."

"Maybe."

"Well, what are you going to do? Get a better one quick, or just bum around for two more years as a has-been?"

"I don't know yet..."

"Oh, Amory, buck up!"

"Maybe."

Amory's point of view, though dangerous, was not far from the true one. If his reactions to his environment could be tabulated, the chart would have appeared like this, beginning with his earliest years:

1. *The fundamental Amory.*

2. *Amory plus Beatrice.*

3. *Amory plus Beatrice plus Minneapolis.*

Then St. Regis' had pulled him to pieces and started him over again:

4. *Amory plus St. Regis'.*

5. *Amory plus St. Regis' plus Princeton.*

That had been his nearest approach to success through conformity. The fundamental Amory, idle, imaginative, rebellious, had been nearly snowed under. He had conformed, he had succeeded, but as his imagination was neither satisfied nor grasped by his own success, he had listlessly, half-accidentally chucked the whole thing and become again:

6. *The fundamental Amory.*

FINANCIAL

His father died quietly and inconspicuously at Thanksgiving. The incongruity of death with either the beauties of Lake Geneva or with his mother's dignified, reticent attitude diverted him, and he looked at the funeral with an amused tolerance. He decided that burial was after all preferable to cremation, and he smiled at his old boyhood choice, slow oxidation in the top of a tree. The day after the ceremony he was amusing himself in the great library by sinking back on a couch in graceful mortuary attitudes, trying to determine whether he would, when his day came, be found with his arms crossed piously over his chest (Monsignor Darcy had once advocated this posture as being the most distinguished), or with his hands clasped behind his head, a more pagan and Byronic attitude.

What interested him much more than the final departure of his father from things mundane was a tri-cornered conversation between Beatrice, Mr. Barton, of Barton and Krogman, their lawyers, and himself, that took place several days after the funeral. For the first time he came into actual cognizance of the family finances, and realized what a tidy fortune had once been under his father's management. He took a ledger labelled "1906" and ran through it rather carefully. The total expenditure that year had come to something over one hundred and ten thousand dollars. Forty thousand of this had been Beatrice's own income, and there had been no attempt to account for it: it was all under the heading, "Drafts, checks, and letters of credit forwarded to Beatrice Blaine." The dispersal of the rest was rather minutely itemized: the taxes and improvements on the Lake Geneva estate had come to almost nine thousand dollars; the general upkeep, including Beatrice's electric and a French car, bought that year, was over thirty-five thousand dollars. The rest was fully taken care of, and there were invariably items which failed to balance on the right side of the ledger.

In the volume for 1912 Amory was shocked to discover the decrease in the number of bond holdings and the great drop in the income. In the case of Beatrice's money this was not so pronounced, but it was obvious that his father had devoted the previous year to several unfortunate gambles in oil. Very little of the oil had been burned, but Stephen Blaine had been rather badly singed. The next year and the next and the next showed similar decreases, and Beatrice had for the first time begun using her own money for keeping up the house. Yet her doctor's bill for 1913 had been over nine thousand dollars.

About the exact state of things Mr. Barton was quite vague and confused. There had been recent investments, the outcome of which was for the present problematical, and he had an idea there were further speculations and exchanges concerning which he had not been consulted.

It was not for several months that Beatrice wrote Amory the full situation. The entire residue of the Blaine and O'Hara fortunes consisted of the place at Lake Geneva and approximately a half million dollars, invested now in fairly conservative six-per-cent holdings. In fact, Beatrice wrote that she was putting the money into railroad and street-car bonds as fast as she could conveniently transfer it.

> *"I am quite sure," she wrote to Amory, "that if there is one thing we can be positive of, it is that people will not stay in one place. This Ford person has certainly made the most of that idea. So I am instructing Mr.*

Barton to specialize on such things as Northern Pacific and these Rapid Transit Companies, as they call the street-cars.I shall never forgive myself for not buying
Bethlehem Steel.I've heard the most fascinating stories.You must go into finance, Amory.I'm sure you would revel in it.You start as a messenger or a teller, I believe, and from that you go up—almost indefinitely.I'm sure if I were a man I'd love the handling of money; it has become quite a senile passion with me. Before I get any farther I want to discuss something.A Mrs. Bispam, an overcordial little lady whom I met at a tea the other day, told me that her son, he is at Yale, wrote her that all the boys there wore their summer underwear all during the winter, and also went about with their heads wet and in low shoes on the coldest days.Now, Amory, I don't know whether that is a fad at Princeton too, but I don't want you to be so foolish.It not only inclines a young man to pneumonia and infantile paralysis, but to all forms of lung trouble, to which you are particularly inclined.You cannot experiment with your health.I have found that out.I will not make myself ridiculous as some mothers no doubt do, by insisting that you wear overshoes, though I remember one Christmas you wore them around constantly without a single buckle latched, making such a curious swishing sound, and you refused to buckle them because it was not the thing to do.The very next Christmas you would not wear even rubbers, though I begged you.You are nearly twenty years old now, dear, and I can't be with you constantly to find whether you are doing the sensible thing.

"This has been a very practical letter.I warned you in my last that the lack of money to do the things one wants to makes one quite prosy and domestic, but there is still plenty for everything if we are not too extravagant.Take care of yourself, my dear boy, and do try to write at least once a week, because I imagine all sorts of horrible things if I don't hear from you.

Affectionately, MOTHER."

FIRST APPEARANCE OF THE TERM "PERSONAGE"

Monsignor Darcy invited Amory up to the Stuart palace on the Hudson for a week at Christmas, and they had enormous conversations around the open fire. Monsignor was growing a trifle stouter and his personality had expanded even with that, and Amory felt both rest and security in sinking into a squat, cushioned chair and joining him in the middle-aged sanity of a cigar.

"I've felt like leaving college, Monsignor."

"Why?"

"All my career's gone up in smoke; you think it's petty and all that, but—"

"Not at all petty. I think it's most important. I want to hear the whole thing. Everything you've been doing since I saw you last."

Amory talked; he went thoroughly into the destruction of his egotistic highways, and in a half-hour the listless quality had left his voice.

"What would you do if you left college?" asked Monsignor.

"Don't know. I'd like to travel, but of course this tiresome war prevents that. Anyways, mother would hate not having me graduate. I'm just at sea. Kerry Holiday wants me to go over with him and join the Lafayette Esquadrille."

"You know you wouldn't like to go."

"Sometimes I would—to-night I'd go in a second."

"Well, you'd have to be very much more tired of life than I think you are. I know you."

"I'm afraid you do," agreed Amory reluctantly. "It just seemed an easy way out of everything—when I think of another useless, draggy year."

"Yes, I know; but to tell you the truth, I'm not worried about you; you seem to me to be progressing perfectly naturally."

"No," Amory objected. "I've lost half my personality in a year."

"Not a bit of it!" scoffed Monsignor. "You've lost a great amount of vanity and that's all."

"Lordy! I feel, anyway, as if I'd gone through another fifth form at St. Regis's."

"No." Monsignor shook his head. "That was a misfortune; this has been a good thing. Whatever worth while comes to you, won't be through the channels you were searching last year."

"What could be more unprofitable than my present lack of pep?"

"Perhaps in itself... but you're developing. This has given you time to think and you're casting off a lot of your old luggage about success and the superman and all. People like us can't adopt whole theories, as you did. If we can do the next thing, and have an hour a day to think in, we can accomplish marvels, but as far as any high-handed scheme of blind dominance is concerned—we'd just make asses of ourselves."

"But, Monsignor, I can't do the next thing."

"Amory, between you and me, I have only just learned to do it myself. I can do the one hundred things beyond the next thing, but I stub my toe on that, just as you stubbed your toe on mathematics this fall."

"Why do we have to do the next thing? It never seems the sort of thing I should do."

"We have to do it because we're not personalities, but personages."

"That's a good line—what do you mean?"

"A personality is what you thought you were, what this Kerry and Sloane you tell me of evidently are. Personality is a physical matter almost entirely; it lowers the people it acts on—I've seen it vanish in a long sickness. But while a personality is active, it overrides 'the next thing.' Now a personage, on the other hand, gathers. He is never thought of apart from what he's done. He's a bar on which a thousand things have been hung—glittering things sometimes, as ours are; but he uses those things with a cold mentality back of them."

"And several of my most glittering possessions had fallen off when I needed them." Amory continued the simile eagerly.

"Yes, that's it; when you feel that your garnered prestige and talents and all that are hung out, you need never bother about anybody; you can cope with them without difficulty."

"But, on the other hand, if I haven't my possessions, I'm helpless!"

"Absolutely."

"That's certainly an idea."

"Now you've a clean start—a start Kerry or Sloane can constitutionally never have. You brushed three or four ornaments down, and, in a fit of pique, knocked off the rest of them. The thing now is to collect some new ones, and the farther you look ahead in the collecting the better. But remember, do the next thing!"

"How clear you can make things!"

So they talked, often about themselves, sometimes of philosophy and religion, and life as respectively a game or a mystery. The priest seemed to guess Amory's thoughts before they were clear in his own head, so closely related were their minds in form and groove.

"Why do I make lists?" Amory asked him one night. "Lists of all sorts of things?"

"Because you're a mediaevalist," Monsignor answered. "We both are. It's the passion for classifying and finding a type."

"It's a desire to get something definite."

"It's the nucleus of scholastic philosophy."

"I was beginning to think I was growing eccentric till I came up here. It was a pose, I guess."

"Don't worry about that; for you not posing may be the biggest pose of all. Pose—"

"Yes?"

"But do the next thing."

After Amory returned to college he received several letters from Monsignor which gave him more egotistic food for consumption.

> *I am afraid that I gave you too much assurance of your inevitable safety, and you must remember that I did that through faith in your springs of effort; not in the silly conviction that you will arrive without struggle.Some nuances of character you will have to take for granted in*

yourself, though you must be careful in confessing them to others. You are unsentimental, almost incapable of affection, astute without being cunning and vain without being proud.

Don't let yourself feel worthless; often through life you will really be at your worst when you seem to think best of yourself; and don't worry about losing your "personality," as you persist in calling it; at fifteen you had the radiance of early morning, at twenty you will begin to have the melancholy brilliance of the moon, and when you are my age you will give out, as I do, the genial golden warmth of 4 P.M.

If you write me letters, please let them be natural ones. Your last, that dissertation on architecture, was perfectly awful— so "highbrow" that I picture you living in an intellectual and emotional vacuum; and beware of trying to classify people too definitely into types; you will find that all through their youth they will persist annoyingly in jumping from class to class, and by pasting a supercilious label on every one you meet you are merely packing a Jack-in-the-box that will spring up and leer at you when you begin to come into really antagonistic contact with the world. An idealization of some such a man as Leonardo da Vinci would be a more valuable beacon to you at present.

You are bound to go up and down, just as I did in my youth, but do keep your clarity of mind, and if fools or sages dare to criticise don't blame yourself too much.

You say that convention is all that really keeps you straight in this "woman proposition"; but it's more than that, Amory; it's the fear that what you begin you can't stop; you would run amuck, and I know whereof I speak; it's that half-miraculous sixth sense by which you detect evil, it's the half-realized fear of God in your heart.

Whatever your metier proves to be—religion, architecture, literature—I'm sure you would be much safer anchored to the Church, but I won't risk my influence by arguing with you even though I am secretly sure that the "black chasm of Romanism" yawns beneath you. Do write me soon.

With affectionate regards, THAYER DARCY.

Even Amory's reading paled during this period; he delved further into the misty side streets of literature: Huysmans, Walter Pater, Theophile Gautier, and the racier sections of Rabelais, Boccaccio, Petronius, and Suetonius. One week, through general curiosity, he inspected the private libraries of his classmates and found Sloane's as typical as any: sets of Kipling, O. Henry, John Fox, Jr., and Richard Harding Davis; "What Every Middle-Aged Woman Ought to Know," "The Spell of the Yukon"; a "gift" copy of James Whitcomb Riley, an assortment of battered, annotated schoolbooks, and, finally, to his surprise, one of his own late discoveries, the collected poems of Rupert Brooke.

Together with Tom D'Invilliers, he sought among the lights of Princeton for some one who might found the Great American Poetic Tradition.

The undergraduate body itself was rather more interesting that year than had been the entirely Philistine Princeton of two years before. Things had livened surprisingly, though at the sacrifice of much of the spontaneous charm of freshman year. In the old Princeton they would never have discovered Tanaduke Wylie. Tanaduke was a sophomore, with tremendous ears and a way of saying, "The earth swirls down through the ominous moons of preconsidered generations!" that made them vaguely wonder why it did not sound quite clear, but never question that it was the utterance of a supersoul. At least so Tom and Amory took him. They told him in all earnestness that he had a mind like Shelley's, and featured his ultrafree free verse and prose poetry in the Nassau Literary Magazine. But Tanaduke's genius absorbed the many colors of the age, and he took to the Bohemian life, to their great disappointment. He talked of Greenwich Village now instead of "noon-swirled moons," and met winter muses, unacademic, and cloistered by Forty-second Street and Broadway, instead of the Shelleyan dream-children with whom he had regaled their expectant appreciation. So they surrendered Tanaduke to the futurists, deciding that he and his flaming ties would do better there. Tom gave him the final advice that he should stop writing for two years and read the complete works of Alexander Pope four times, but on Amory's suggestion that Pope for Tanaduke was like foot-ease for stomach trouble, they withdrew in laughter, and called it a coin's toss whether this genius was too big or too petty for them.

Amory rather scornfully avoided the popular professors who dispensed easy epigrams and thimblefuls of Chartreuse to groups of admirers every night. He was disappointed, too, at the air of general uncertainty on every subject that seemed linked with the pedantic temperament; his opinions took shape in a miniature satire called "In a Lecture-Room," which he persuaded Tom to print in the Nassau Lit.

"Good-morning, Fool...
Three times a week
You hold us helpless while you speak,
Teasing our thirsty souls with the
Sleek 'yeas' of your philosophy...
Well, here we are, your hundred sheep,
Tune up, play on, pour forth... we sleep...
You are a student, so they say;

You hammered out the other day
A syllabus, from what we know
Of some forgotten folio;
You'd sniffled through an era's must,
Filling your nostrils up with dust,
And then, arising from your knees,
Published, in one gigantic sneeze...
But here's a neighbor on my right,
An Eager Ass, considered bright;
Asker of questions....How he'll stand,
With earnest air and fidgy hand,
After this hour, telling you
He sat all night and burrowed through
Your book....Oh, you'll be coy and he
Will simulate precosity,
And pedants both, you'll smile and smirk,
And leer, and hasten back to work....

'Twas this day week, sir, you returned
A theme of mine, from which I learned
(Through various comment on the side
Which you had scrawled) that I defied
The highest rules of criticism
For cheap and careless witticism....
'Are you quite sure that this could be?'
And
'Shaw is no authority!'
But Eager Ass, with what he's sent,
Plays havoc with your best per cent.

Still—still I meet you here and there...
When Shakespeare's played you hold a chair,
And some defunct, moth-eaten star
Enchants the mental prig you are...
A radical comes down and shocks
The atheistic orthodox?
You're representing Common Sense,
Mouth open, in the audience.
And, sometimes, even chapel lures
That conscious tolerance of yours,
That broad and beaming view of truth
(Including Kant and General Booth...)
And so from shock to shock you live,

A hollow, pale affirmative...

The hour's up... and roused from rest
One hundred children of the blest
Cheat you a word or two with feet
That down the noisy aisle-ways beat...
Forget on narrow-minded earth
The Mighty Yawn that gave you birth."

In April, Kerry Holiday left college and sailed for France to enroll in the Lafayette Esquadrille. Amory's envy and admiration of this step was drowned in an experience of his own to which he never succeeded in giving an appropriate value, but which, nevertheless, haunted him for three years afterward.

THE DEVIL

Healy's they left at twelve and taxied to Bistolary's. There were Axia Marlowe and Phoebe Column, from the Summer Garden show, Fred Sloane and Amory. The evening was so very young that they felt ridiculous with surplus energy, and burst into the cafe like Dionysian revellers.

"Table for four in the middle of the floor," yelled Phoebe. "Hurry, old dear, tell 'em we're here!"

"Tell 'em to play 'Admiration'!" shouted Sloane. "You two order; Phoebe and I are going to shake a wicked calf," and they sailed off in the muddled crowd. Axia and Amory, acquaintances of an hour, jostled behind a waiter to a table at a point of vantage; there they took seats and watched.

"There's Findle Margotson, from New Haven!" she cried above the uproar. "'Lo, Findle! Whoo-ee!"

"Oh, Axia!" he shouted in salutation. "C'mon over to our table." "No!" Amory whispered.

"Can't do it, Findle; I'm with somebody else! Call me up to-morrow about one o'clock!"

Findle, a nondescript man-about-Bisty's, answered incoherently and turned back to the brilliant blonde whom he was endeavoring to steer around the room.

"There's a natural damn fool," commented Amory.

"Oh, he's all right. Here's the old jitney waiter. If you ask me, I want a double Daiquiri."

"Make it four."

The crowd whirled and changed and shifted. They were mostly from the colleges, with a scattering of the male refuse of Broadway, and women of two types, the higher of which was the chorus girl. On the whole it was a typical crowd, and their party as typical as any. About three-fourths of the whole business was for effect and therefore harmless, ended at the door of the cafe, soon enough for the five-o'clock train back to Yale or Princeton; about one-fourth continued on into the dimmer hours and gathered strange dust from strange places. Their party was scheduled to be one of the harmless kind. Fred Sloane and Phoebe Column were old friends; Axia and Amory new ones. But strange things are prepared even in the dead of night, and the unusual, which lurks least in the cafe, home of the prosaic and inevitable, was preparing to spoil for him the waning romance of Broadway. The way it took was so inexpressibly terrible, so unbelievable, that afterward he never thought of it as experience; but it was a scene from a misty tragedy, played far behind the veil, and that it meant something definite he knew.

About one o'clock they moved to Maxim's, and two found them in Deviniere's. Sloane had been drinking consecutively and was in a state of unsteady exhilaration, but Amory was quite tiresomely sober; they had run across none of those ancient, corrupt buyers of champagne who usually assisted their New York parties. They were just through dancing and were making their way back to their chairs when Amory became aware that some one at a near-by table was looking at him. He turned and glanced casually... a middle-aged man dressed in a brown sack suit, it was, sitting a little apart at a table by himself and watching their party intently. At Amory's glance he smiled faintly. Amory turned to Fred, who was just sitting down.

"Who's that pale fool watching us?" he complained indignantly.

"Where?" cried Sloane. "We'll have him thrown out!" He rose to his feet and swayed back and forth, clinging to his chair. "Where is he?"

Axia and Phoebe suddenly leaned and whispered to each other across the table, and before Amory realized it they found themselves on their way to the door.

"Where now?"

"Up to the flat," suggested Phoebe. "We've got brandy and fizz—and everything's slow down here to-night."

Amory considered quickly. He hadn't been drinking, and decided that if he took no more, it would be reasonably discreet for him to trot along in the party. In fact, it would be, perhaps, the thing to do in order to keep an eye on Sloane, who was not in a state to do his own thinking. So he took Axia's arm and, piling intimately into a taxicab, they drove out over the hundreds and drew up at a tall, white-stone apartment-house. ... Never would he forget that street.... It was a broad street, lined on both sides with just such tall, white-stone buildings, dotted with dark windows; they stretched along as far as the eye could see, flooded with a bright moonlight that gave them a calcium pallor. He imagined each one to have an elevator and a colored hall-boy and a key-rack; each one to be eight stories high and full of three and four room suites. He was rather glad to walk into the cheeriness of Phoebe's living-room and sink onto a sofa, while the girls went rummaging for food.

"Phoebe's great stuff," confided Sloane, sotto voce.

"I'm only going to stay half an hour," Amory said sternly. He wondered if it sounded priggish.

"Hell y' say," protested Sloane. "We're here now—don't le's rush."

"I don't like this place," Amory said sulkily, "and I don't want any food."

Phoebe reappeared with sandwiches, brandy bottle, siphon, and four glasses.

"Amory, pour 'em out," she said, "and we'll drink to Fred Sloane, who has a rare, distinguished edge."

"Yes," said Axia, coming in, "and Amory. I like Amory." She sat down beside him and laid her yellow head on his shoulder.

"I'll pour," said Sloane; "you use siphon, Phoebe."

They filled the tray with glasses.

"Ready, here she goes!"

Amory hesitated, glass in hand.

There was a minute while temptation crept over him like a warm wind, and his imagination turned to fire, and he took the glass from Phoebe's hand. That was all; for at the second that his decision came, he looked up and saw, ten yards from him, the man who had been in the cafe, and with his jump of astonishment the glass fell from his uplifted hand. There the man half sat, half leaned against a pile of pillows on the corner divan. His face was cast in the same yellow wax as in the cafe, neither the dull, pasty color of a dead man—rather a sort of virile pallor—nor unhealthy, you'd have called it; but like a strong man who'd worked in a mine or done night shifts in a damp climate. Amory looked him over carefully and later he could have drawn him after a fashion, down to the merest details. His mouth was the kind that is called frank, and he had steady gray eyes that moved slowly from one to the other of their group, with just the shade of a questioning expression. Amory noticed his hands; they weren't fine at all, but they had versatility and a tenuous strength... they were nervous hands that sat lightly along the cushions and moved constantly with little jerky openings and closings. Then, suddenly, Amory perceived the feet, and with a rush of blood to the head he realized he was afraid. The feet were all wrong ... with a sort of wrongness that he felt rather than knew.... It was like weakness in a good woman, or blood on satin; one of those terrible incongruities that shake little things in the back of the brain. He wore no shoes, but, instead, a sort of half moccasin, pointed, though, like the shoes they wore in the fourteenth century, and with the little ends curling up. They were a darkish brown and his toes seemed to fill them to the end.... They were unutterably terrible....

He must have said something, or looked something, for Axia's voice came out of the void with a strange goodness.

"Well, look at Amory! Poor old Amory's sick—old head going 'round?"

"Look at that man!" cried Amory, pointing toward the corner divan.

"You mean that purple zebra!" shrieked Axia facetiously. "Ooo-ee! Amory's got a purple zebra watching him!"

Sloane laughed vacantly.

"Ole zebra gotcha, Amory?"

There was a silence.... The man regarded Amory quizzically.... Then the human voices fell faintly on his ear:

"Thought you weren't drinking," remarked Axia sardonically, but her voice was good to hear; the whole divan that held the man was alive; alive like heat waves over asphalt, like wriggling worms....

"Come back! Come back!" Axia's arm fell on his. "Amory, dear, you aren't going, Amory!" He was half-way to the door.

"Come on, Amory, stick 'th us!"

"Sick, are you?"

"Sit down a second!"

"Take some water."

"Take a little brandy...."

The elevator was close, and the colored boy was half asleep, paled to a livid bronze... Axia's beseeching voice floated down the shaft. Those feet... those feet...

As they settled to the lower floor the feet came into view in the sickly electric light of the paved hall.

IN THE ALLEY

Down the long street came the moon, and Amory turned his back on it and walked. Ten, fifteen steps away sounded the footsteps. They were like a slow dripping, with just the slightest insistence in their fall. Amory's shadow lay, perhaps, ten feet ahead of him, and soft shoes was presumably that far behind. With the instinct of a child Amory edged in under the blue darkness of the white buildings, cleaving the moonlight for haggard seconds, once bursting into a slow run with clumsy stumblings. After that he stopped suddenly; he must keep hold, he thought. His lips were dry and he licked them.

If he met any one good—were there any good people left in the world or did they all live in white apartment-houses now? Was every one followed in the moonlight? But if he met some one good who'd know what he meant and hear this damned scuffle... then the scuffling grew suddenly nearer, and a black cloud settled over the moon. When again the pale sheen skimmed the cornices, it was almost beside him, and Amory thought he heard a quiet breathing. Suddenly he realized that the footsteps were not behind, had never been behind, they were ahead and he was not eluding but following... following. He began to run, blindly, his heart knocking heavily, his hands clinched. Far ahead a black dot showed itself, resolved slowly into a human shape. But Amory was beyond that now; he turned off the street and darted into an alley, narrow and dark and smelling of old rottenness. He twisted down a long, sinuous blackness, where the moonlight was shut away except for tiny glints and patches... then suddenly sank panting into a corner by a fence, exhausted. The steps ahead stopped, and he could hear them shift slightly with a continuous motion, like waves around a dock.

He put his face in his hands and covered eyes and ears as well as he could. During all this time it never occurred to him that he was delirious or drunk. He had a sense of reality such as material things could never give him. His intellectual content seemed to submit passively to it, and it fitted like a glove everything that had ever preceded it in his life. It did not muddle him. It was like a problem whose answer he knew on paper, yet whose solution he was unable to grasp. He was far beyond horror. He had sunk through the thin surface of that, now moved in a region where the feet and the fear of white walls were real, living things, things he must accept. Only far inside his soul a little fire leaped and cried that something was pulling him down, trying to get him inside a door and slam it behind him. After that door was slammed there would be only footfalls and white buildings in the moonlight, and perhaps he would be one of the footfalls.

During the five or ten minutes he waited in the shadow of the fence, there was somehow this fire... that was as near as he could name it afterward. He remembered calling aloud:

"I want some one stupid. Oh, send some one stupid!" This to the black fence opposite him, in whose shadows the footsteps shuffled ... shuffled. He supposed "stupid" and "good" had become somehow intermingled through previous association. When he called thus it was not an act of will at all—will had turned him away from the moving figure in the street; it was almost instinct that called, just the pile on pile of inherent tradition or some wild prayer from way over the night. Then something clanged like a low gong struck at a distance, and before his eyes a face flashed over the two feet, a face pale and distorted with a sort of infinite evil that twisted it like flame in the wind; *but he knew, for the half instant that the gong tanged and hummed, that it was the face of Dick Humbird.*

Minutes later he sprang to his feet, realizing dimly that there was no more sound, and that he was alone in the graying alley. It was cold, and he started on a steady run for the light that showed the street at the other end.

AT THE WINDOW

It was late morning when he woke and found the telephone beside his bed in the hotel tolling frantically, and remembered that he had left word to be called at eleven. Sloane was snoring heavily, his clothes in a pile by his bed. They dressed and ate breakfast in silence, and then sauntered out to get some air. Amory's mind was working slowly, trying to assimilate what had happened and separate from the chaotic imagery that stacked his memory the bare shreds of truth. If the morning had been cold and gray he could have grasped the reins of the past in an instant, but it was one of those days that New York gets sometimes in May, when the air on Fifth Avenue is a soft, light wine. How much or how little Sloane remembered Amory did not care to know; he apparently had none of the nervous tension that was gripping Amory and forcing his mind back and forth like a shrieking saw.

Then Broadway broke upon them, and with the babel of noise and the painted faces a sudden sickness rushed over Amory.

"For God's sake, let's go back! Let's get off of this—this place!"

Sloane looked at him in amazement.

"What do you mean?"

"This street, it's ghastly! Come on! let's get back to the Avenue!"

"Do you mean to say," said Sloane stolidly, "that 'cause you had some sort of indigestion that made you act like a maniac last night, you're never coming on Broadway again?"

Simultaneously Amory classed him with the crowd, and he seemed no longer Sloane of the debonair humor and the happy personality, but only one of the evil faces that whirled along the turbid stream.

"Man!" he shouted so loud that the people on the corner turned and followed them with their eyes, "it's filthy, and if you can't see it, you're filthy, too!"

"I can't help it," said Sloane doggedly. "What's the matter with you? Old remorse getting you? You'd be in a fine state if you'd gone through with our little party."

"I'm going, Fred," said Amory slowly. His knees were shaking under him, and he knew that if he stayed another minute on this street he would keel over where he stood. "I'll be at the Vanderbilt for lunch." And he strode rapidly off and turned over to Fifth Avenue. Back at the hotel he felt better, but as he walked into the barber-shop, intending to get a head massage, the smell of the powders and tonics brought back Axia's sidelong, suggestive smile, and he left hurriedly. In the doorway of his room a sudden blackness flowed around him like a divided river.

When he came to himself he knew that several hours had passed. He pitched onto the bed and rolled over on his face with a deadly fear that he was going mad. He wanted people, people, some one sane and stupid and good. He lay for he knew not how long without moving. He could feel the little hot veins on his forehead standing out, and his terror had hardened on him like plaster. He felt he was passing up again through the thin crust of horror, and now only could he distinguish the shadowy twilight he was leaving. He must have fallen asleep again, for when he next recollected himself he had paid the hotel bill and was stepping into a taxi at the door. It was raining torrents.

On the train for Princeton he saw no one he knew, only a crowd of fagged-looking Philadelphians. The presence of a painted woman across the aisle filled him with a fresh burst of sickness and he changed to another car, tried to concentrate on an article in a popular magazine. He found himself reading the same paragraphs over and over, so he abandoned this attempt and leaning over wearily pressed his hot forehead against the damp window-pane. The car, a smoker, was hot and stuffy with most of the smells of the state's alien population; he opened a window and shivered against the cloud of fog that drifted in over him. The two hours' ride were like days, and he nearly cried aloud with joy when the towers of Princeton loomed up beside him and the yellow squares of light filtered through the blue rain.

Tom was standing in the centre of the room, pensively relighting a cigar-stub. Amory fancied he looked rather relieved on seeing him.

"Had a hell of a dream about you last night," came in the cracked voice through the cigar smoke. "I had an idea you were in some trouble."

"Don't tell me about it!" Amory almost shrieked. "Don't say a word; I'm tired and pepped out."

Tom looked at him queerly and then sank into a chair and opened his Italian note-book. Amory threw his coat and hat on the floor, loosened his collar, and took a Wells novel at random from the shelf. "Wells is sane," he thought, "and if he won't do I'll read Rupert Brooke."

Half an hour passed. Outside the wind came up, and Amory started as the wet branches moved and clawed with their finger-nails at the window-pane. Tom was deep in his work, and inside the room only the occasional scratch of a match or the rustle of leather as they shifted in their chairs broke the stillness. Then like a zigzag of lightning came the change. Amory sat bolt upright, frozen cold in his chair. Tom was looking at him with his mouth drooping, eyes fixed.

"God help us!" Amory cried.

"Oh, my heavens!" shouted Tom, "look behind!" Quick as a flash Amory whirled around. He saw nothing but the dark window-pane. "It's gone now," came Tom's voice after a second in a still terror. "Something was looking at you."

Trembling violently, Amory dropped into his chair again.

"I've got to tell you," he said. "I've had one hell of an experience. I think I've—I've seen the devil or—something like him. What face did you just see?—or no," he added quickly, "don't tell me!"

And he gave Tom the story. It was midnight when he finished, and after that, with all lights burning, two sleepy, shivering boys read to each other from "The New Machiavelli," until dawn came up out of Witherspoon Hall, and the Princetonian fell against the door, and the May birds hailed the sun on last night's rain.

IV. Narcissus Off Duty

During Princeton's transition period, that is, during Amory's last two years there, while he saw it change and broaden and live up to its Gothic beauty by better means than night parades, certain individuals arrived who stirred it to its plethoric depths. Some of them had been freshmen, and wild freshmen, with Amory; some were in the class below; and it was in the beginning of his last year and around small tables at the Nassau Inn that they began questioning aloud the institutions that Amory and countless others before him had questioned so long in secret. First, and partly by accident, they struck on certain books, a definite type of biographical novel that Amory christened "quest" books. In the "quest" book the hero set off in life armed with the best weapons and avowedly intending to use them as such weapons are usually used, to push their possessors ahead as selfishly and blindly as possible, but the heroes of the "quest" books discovered that there might be a more magnificent use for them. "None Other Gods," "Sinister Street," and "The Research Magnificent" were examples of such books; it was the latter of these three that gripped Burne Holiday and made him wonder in the beginning of senior year how much it was worth while being a diplomatic autocrat around his club on Prospect Avenue and basking in the high lights of class office. It was distinctly through the channels of aristocracy that Burne found his way. Amory, through Kerry, had had a vague drifting acquaintance with him, but not until January of senior year did their friendship commence.

"Heard the latest?" said Tom, coming in late one drizzly evening with that triumphant air he always wore after a successful conversational bout.

"No. Somebody flunked out? Or another ship sunk?"

"Worse than that. About one-third of the junior class are going to resign from their clubs."

"What!"

"Actual fact!"

"Why!"

"Spirit of reform and all that. Burne Holiday is behind it. The club presidents are holding a meeting to-night to see if they can find a joint means of combating it."

"Well, what's the idea of the thing?"

"Oh, clubs injurious to Princeton democracy; cost a lot; draw social lines, take time; the regular line you get sometimes from disappointed sophomores. Woodrow thought they should be abolished and all that."

"But this is the real thing?"

"Absolutely. I think it'll go through."

"For Pete's sake, tell me more about it."

"Well," began Tom, "it seems that the idea developed simultaneously in several heads. I was talking to Burne awhile ago, and he claims that it's a logical result if an intelligent person thinks long enough about the social system. They had a 'discussion crowd' and the point of abolishing the clubs was brought up by some one—everybody there leaped at it—it had been in each one's mind, more or less, and it just needed a spark to bring it out."

"Fine! I swear I think it'll be most entertaining. How do they feel up at Cap and Gown?"

"Wild, of course. Every one's been sitting and arguing and swearing and getting mad and getting sentimental and getting brutal. It's the same at all the clubs; I've been the rounds. They get one of the radicals in the corner and fire questions at him."

"How do the radicals stand up?"

"Oh, moderately well. Burne's a damn good talker, and so obviously sincere that you can't get anywhere with him. It's so evident that resigning from his club means so much more to him than preventing it does to us that I felt futile when I argued; finally took a position that was brilliantly neutral. In fact, I believe Burne thought for a while that he'd converted me."

"And you say almost a third of the junior class are going to resign?"

"Call it a fourth and be safe."

"Lord—who'd have thought it possible!"

There was a brisk knock at the door, and Burne himself came in. "Hello, Amory—hello, Tom."

Amory rose.

"'Evening, Burne. Don't mind if I seem to rush; I'm going to Renwick's."

Burne turned to him quickly.

"You probably know what I want to talk to Tom about, and it isn't a bit private. I wish you'd stay."

"I'd be glad to." Amory sat down again, and as Burne perched on a table and launched into argument with Tom, he looked at this revolutionary more carefully than he ever had before. Broad-browed and strong-chinned, with a fineness in the honest gray eyes that were like Kerry's, Burne was a man who gave an immediate impression of bigness and security—stubborn, that was evident, but his stubbornness wore no stolidity, and when he had talked for five minutes Amory knew that this keen enthusiasm had in it no quality of dilettantism.

The intense power Amory felt later in Burne Holiday differed from the admiration he had had for Humbird. This time it began as purely a mental interest. With other men of whom he had thought as primarily first-class, he had been attracted first by their personalities, and in Burne he missed that immediate magnetism to which he usually swore allegiance. But that night Amory was struck by Burne's intense earnestness, a quality he was accustomed to associate only with the dread stupidity, and by the great enthusiasm that struck dead chords in his heart. Burne stood vaguely for a land Amory hoped he was drifting toward—and it was almost time that land was in sight. Tom and Amory and Alec had reached an impasse; never did they seem to have new experiences in common, for Tom and Alec had been as blindly busy with their committees and boards as Amory had been blindly idling, and the things they had for dissection—college, contemporary personality and the like—they had hashed and rehashed for many a frugal conversational meal.

That night they discussed the clubs until twelve, and, in the main, they agreed with Burne. To the roommates it did not seem such a vital subject as it had in the two years before, but the logic of Burne's objections to the social system dovetailed so completely with everything they had thought, that they questioned rather than argued, and envied the sanity that enabled this man to stand out so against all traditions.

Then Amory branched off and found that Burne was deep in other things as well. Economics had interested him and he was turning socialist. Pacifism played in the back of his mind, and he read The Masses and Lyoff Tolstoi faithfully.

"How about religion?" Amory asked him.

"Don't know. I'm in a muddle about a lot of things—I've just discovered that I've a mind, and I'm starting to read."

"Read what?"

"Everything. I have to pick and choose, of course, but mostly things to make me think. I'm reading the four gospels now, and the 'Varieties of Religious Experience.'"

"What chiefly started you?"

"Wells, I guess, and Tolstoi, and a man named Edward Carpenter. I've been reading for over a year now—on a few lines, on what I consider the essential lines."

"Poetry?"

"Well, frankly, not what you call poetry, or for your reasons—you two write, of course, and look at things differently. Whitman is the man that attracts me."

"Whitman?"

"Yes; he's a definite ethical force."

"Well, I'm ashamed to say that I'm a blank on the subject of Whitman. How about you, Tom?"

Tom nodded sheepishly.

"Well," continued Burne, "you may strike a few poems that are tiresome, but I mean the mass of his work. He's tremendous—like Tolstoi. They both look things in the face, and, somehow, different as they are, stand for somewhat the same things."

"You have me stumped, Burne," Amory admitted. "I've read 'Anna Karenina' and the 'Kreutzer Sonata' of course, but Tolstoi is mostly in the original Russian as far as I'm concerned."

"He's the greatest man in hundreds of years," cried Burne enthusiastically. "Did you ever see a picture of that shaggy old head of his?"

They talked until three, from biology to organized religion, and when Amory crept shivering into bed it was with his mind aglow with ideas and a sense of shock that some one else had discovered the path he might have followed. Burne Holiday was so evidently developing—and Amory had considered that he was doing the same. He had fallen into a deep cynicism over what had crossed his path, plotted the imperfectability of man and read Shaw and Chesterton enough to keep his mind from the edges of decadence—now suddenly all his mental processes of the last year and a half seemed stale and futile—a petty consummation of himself... and like a sombre background lay that incident of the spring before, that filled half his nights with a dreary terror and made him unable to pray. He was not even a Catholic, yet that was the only ghost of a code that he had, the gaudy, ritualistic, paradoxical Catholicism whose prophet was Chesterton, whose claqueurs were such reformed rakes of literature as Huysmans and Bourget, whose American sponsor was Ralph Adams Cram, with his adulation of thirteenth-century cathedrals—a Catholicism which Amory found convenient and ready-made, without priest or sacraments or sacrifice.

He could not sleep, so he turned on his reading-lamp and, taking down the "Kreutzer Sonata," searched it carefully for the germs of Burne's enthusiasm. Being Burne was suddenly so much realler than being clever. Yet he sighed... here were other possible clay feet.

He thought back through two years, of Burne as a hurried, nervous freshman, quite submerged in his brother's personality. Then he remembered an incident of sophomore year, in which Burne had been suspected of the leading role.

Dean Hollister had been heard by a large group arguing with a taxi-driver, who had driven him from the junction. In the course of the altercation the dean remarked that he "might as well buy the taxicab." He paid and walked off, but next morning he entered his private office to find the taxicab itself in the space usually occupied by his desk, bearing a sign which read "Property of Dean Hollister. Bought and Paid for."... It took two expert mechanics half a day to dissemble it into its minutest parts and remove it, which only goes to prove the rare energy of sophomore humor under efficient leadership.

Then again, that very fall, Burne had caused a sensation. A certain Phyllis Styles, an intercollegiate prom-trotter, had failed to get her yearly invitation to the Harvard-Princeton game.

Jesse Ferrenby had brought her to a smaller game a few weeks before, and had pressed Burne into service—to the ruination of the latter's misogyny.

"Are you coming to the Harvard game?" Burne had asked indiscreetly, merely to make conversation.

"If you ask me," cried Phyllis quickly.

"Of course I do," said Burne feebly. He was unversed in the arts of Phyllis, and was sure that this was merely a vapid form of kidding. Before an hour had passed he knew that he was indeed involved. Phyllis had pinned him down and served him up, informed him the train she was arriving by, and depressed him thoroughly. Aside from loathing Phyllis, he had particularly wanted to stag that game and entertain some Harvard friends.

"She'll see," he informed a delegation who arrived in his room to josh him. "This will be the last game she ever persuades any young innocent to take her to!"

"But, Burne—why did you *invite* her if you didn't want her?"

"Burne, you *know* you're secretly mad about her—that's the *real* trouble."

"What can *you* do, Burne? What can *you* do against Phyllis?"

But Burne only shook his head and muttered threats which consisted largely of the phrase: "She'll see, she'll see!"

The blithesome Phyllis bore her twenty-five summers gayly from the train, but on the platform a ghastly sight met her eyes. There were Burne and Fred Sloane arrayed to the last dot like the lurid figures on college posters. They had bought flaring suits with huge peg-top trousers and gigantic padded shoulders. On their heads were rakish college hats, pinned up in front and sporting bright orange-and-black bands, while from their celluloid collars blossomed flaming orange ties. They wore black arm-bands with orange "P's," and carried canes flying Princeton pennants, the effect completed by socks and peeping handkerchiefs in the same color motifs. On a clanking chain they led a large, angry tom-cat, painted to represent a tiger.

A good half of the station crowd was already staring at them, torn between horrified pity and riotous mirth, and as Phyllis, with her svelte jaw dropping, approached, the pair bent over and emitted a college cheer in loud, far-carrying voices, thoughtfully adding the name "Phyllis" to the end. She was vociferously greeted and escorted enthusiastically across the campus, followed by half a hundred village urchins—to the stifled laughter of hundreds of alumni and visitors, half of whom had no idea that this was a practical joke, but thought that Burne and Fred were two varsity sports showing their girl a collegiate time.

Phyllis's feelings as she was paraded by the Harvard and Princeton stands, where sat dozens of her former devotees, can be imagined. She tried to walk a little ahead, she tried to walk a little behind—but they stayed close, that there should be no doubt whom she was with, talking in loud voices of their friends on the football team, until she could almost hear her acquaintances whispering:

"Phyllis Styles must be *awfully hard up* to have to come with *those two.*"

That had been Burne, dynamically humorous, fundamentally serious. From that root had blossomed the energy that he was now trying to orient with progress....

So the weeks passed and March came and the clay feet that Amory looked for failed to appear. About a hundred juniors and seniors resigned from their clubs in a final fury of righteousness, and the clubs in helplessness turned upon Burne their finest weapon: ridicule. Every one who knew him liked him—but what he stood for (and he began to stand for more all the time) came under the lash of many tongues, until a frailer man than he would have been snowed under.

"Don't you mind losing prestige?" asked Amory one night. They had taken to exchanging calls several times a week.

"Of course I don't. What's prestige, at best?"

"Some people say that you're just a rather original politician."

He roared with laughter.

"That's what Fred Sloane told me to-day. I suppose I have it coming."

One afternoon they dipped into a subject that had interested Amory for a long time—the matter of the bearing of physical attributes on a man's make-up. Burne had gone into the biology of this, and then:

"Of course health counts—a healthy man has twice the chance of being good," he said.

"I don't agree with you—I don't believe in 'muscular Christianity.'"

"I do—I believe Christ had great physical vigor."

"Oh, no," Amory protested. "He worked too hard for that. I imagine that when he died he was a broken-down man—and the great saints haven't been strong."

"Half of them have."

"Well, even granting that, I don't think health has anything to do with goodness; of course, it's valuable to a great saint to be able to stand enormous strains, but this fad of popular preachers rising on their toes in simulated virility, bellowing that calisthenics will save the world—no, Burne, I can't go that."

"Well, let's waive it—we won't get anywhere, and besides I haven't quite made up my mind about it myself. Now, here's something I *do* know—personal appearance has a lot to do with it."

"Coloring?" Amory asked eagerly.

"Yes."

"That's what Tom and I figured," Amory agreed. "We took the year-books for the last ten years and looked at the pictures of the senior council. I know you don't think much of that august body, but it does represent success here in a general way. Well, I suppose only about thirty-five per cent of every class here are blonds, are really light—yet *two-thirds* of every senior council are light. We looked at pictures of ten years of them, mind you; that means that out of every *fifteen* light-haired men in the senior class *one* is on the senior council, and of the dark-haired men it's only one in *fifty*."

"It's true," Burne agreed. "The light-haired man *is* a higher type, generally speaking. I worked the thing out with the Presidents of the United States once, and found that way over half of them were light-haired—yet think of the preponderant number of brunettes in the race."

"People unconsciously admit it," said Amory. "You'll notice a blond person is *expected* to talk. If a blond girl doesn't talk we call her a 'doll'; if a light-haired man is silent he's considered stupid. Yet the world is full of 'dark silent men' and 'languorous brunettes' who haven't a brain in their heads, but somehow are never accused of the dearth."

"And the large mouth and broad chin and rather big nose undoubtedly make the superior face."

"I'm not so sure." Amory was all for classical features.

"Oh, yes—I'll show you," and Burne pulled out of his desk a photographic collection of heavily bearded, shaggy celebrities—Tolstoi, Whitman, Carpenter, and others.

"Aren't they wonderful?"

Amory tried politely to appreciate them, and gave up laughingly.

"Burne, I think they're the ugliest-looking crowd I ever came across. They look like an old man's home."

"Oh, Amory, look at that forehead on Emerson; look at Tolstoi's eyes." His tone was reproachful.

Amory shook his head.

"No! Call them remarkable-looking or anything you want—but ugly they certainly are."

Unabashed, Burne ran his hand lovingly across the spacious foreheads, and piling up the pictures put them back in his desk.

Walking at night was one of his favorite pursuits, and one night he persuaded Amory to accompany him.

"I hate the dark," Amory objected. "I didn't use to—except when I was particularly imaginative, but now, I really do—I'm a regular fool about it."

"That's useless, you know."

"Quite possibly."

"We'll go east," Burne suggested, "and down that string of roads through the woods."

"Doesn't sound very appealing to me," admitted Amory reluctantly, "but let's go."

They set off at a good gait, and for an hour swung along in a brisk argument until the lights of Princeton were luminous white blots behind them.

"Any person with any imagination is bound to be afraid," said Burne earnestly. "And this very walking at night is one of the things I was afraid about. I'm going to tell you why I can walk anywhere now and not be afraid."

"Go on," Amory urged eagerly. They were striding toward the woods, Burne's nervous, enthusiastic voice warming to his subject.

"I used to come out here alone at night, oh, three months ago, and I always stopped at that cross-road we just passed. There were the woods looming up ahead, just as they do now, there were dogs howling and the shadows and no human sound. Of course, I peopled the woods with everything ghastly, just like you do; don't you?"

"I do," Amory admitted.

"Well, I began analyzing it—my imagination persisted in sticking horrors into the dark—so I stuck my imagination into the dark instead, and let it look out at me—I let it play stray dog or escaped convict or ghost, and then saw myself coming along the road. That made it all right—as it always makes everything all right to project yourself completely into another's place. I knew that if I were the dog or the convict or the ghost I wouldn't be a menace to Burne Holiday any more than he was a menace to me. Then I thought of my watch. I'd better go back and leave it and then essay the woods. No; I decided, it's better on the whole that I should lose a watch than that I should turn back—and I did go into them—not only followed the road through them, but walked into them until I wasn't frightened any more—did it until one night I sat down and dozed off in there; then I knew I was through being afraid of the dark."

"Lordy," Amory breathed. "I couldn't have done that. I'd have come out half-way, and the first time an automobile passed and made the dark thicker when its lamps disappeared, I'd have come in."

"Well," Burne said suddenly, after a few moments' silence, "we're half-way through, let's turn back."

On the return he launched into a discussion of will.

"It's the whole thing," he asserted. "It's the one dividing line between good and evil. I've never met a man who led a rotten life and didn't have a weak will."

"How about great criminals?"

"They're usually insane. If not, they're weak. There is no such thing as a strong, sane criminal."

"Burne, I disagree with you altogether; how about the superman?"

"Well?"

"He's evil, I think, yet he's strong and sane."

"I've never met him. I'll bet, though, that he's stupid or insane."

"I've met him over and over and he's neither. That's why I think you're wrong."

"I'm sure I'm not—and so I don't believe in imprisonment except for the insane."

On this point Amory could not agree. It seemed to him that life and history were rife with the strong criminal, keen, but often self-deluding; in politics and business one found him and among the old statesmen and kings and generals; but Burne never agreed and their courses began to split on that point.

Burne was drawing farther and farther away from the world about him. He resigned the vice-presidency of the senior class and took to reading and walking as almost his only pursuits. He voluntarily attended graduate lectures in philosophy and biology, and sat in all of them with a rather pathetically intent look in his eyes, as if waiting for something the lecturer would never quite come to. Sometimes Amory would see him squirm in his seat; and his face would light up; he was on fire to debate a point.

He grew more abstracted on the street and was even accused of becoming a snob, but Amory knew it was nothing of the sort, and once when Burne passed him four feet off, absolutely unseeingly, his mind a thousand miles away, Amory almost choked with the romantic joy of watching him. Burne seemed to be climbing heights where others would be forever unable to get a foothold.

"I tell you," Amory declared to Tom, "he's the first contemporary I've ever met whom I'll admit is my superior in mental capacity."

"It's a bad time to admit it—people are beginning to think he's odd."

"He's way over their heads—you know you think so yourself when you talk to him—Good Lord, Tom, you *used* to stand out against 'people.' Success has completely conventionalized you."

Tom grew rather annoyed.

"What's he trying to do—be excessively holy?"

"No! not like anybody you've ever seen. Never enters the Philadelphian Society. He has no faith in that rot. He doesn't believe that public swimming-pools and a kind word in time will right the wrongs of the world; moreover, he takes a drink whenever he feels like it."

"He certainly is getting in wrong."

"Have you talked to him lately?"

"No."

"Then you haven't any conception of him."

The argument ended nowhere, but Amory noticed more than ever how the sentiment toward Burne had changed on the campus.

"It's odd," Amory said to Tom one night when they had grown more amicable on the subject, "that the people who violently disapprove of Burne's radicalism are distinctly the Pharisee class—I mean they're the best-educated men in college—the editors of the papers, like yourself and Ferrenby, the younger professors.... The illiterate athletes like Langueduc think he's getting eccentric, but they just say, 'Good old Burne has got some queer ideas in his head,' and pass on—the Pharisee class—Gee! they ridicule him unmercifully."

The next morning he met Burne hurrying along McCosh walk after a recitation.

"Whither bound, Tsar?"

"Over to the Prince office to see Ferrenby," he waved a copy of the morning's Princetonian at Amory. "He wrote this editorial."

"Going to flay him alive?"

"No—but he's got me all balled up. Either I've misjudged him or he's suddenly become the world's worst radical."

Burne hurried on, and it was several days before Amory heard an account of the ensuing conversation. Burne had come into the editor's sanctum displaying the paper cheerfully.

"Hello, Jesse."

"Hello there, Savonarola."

"I just read your editorial."

"Good boy—didn't know you stooped that low."

"Jesse, you startled me."

"How so?"

"Aren't you afraid the faculty'll get after you if you pull this irreligious stuff?"

"What?"

"Like this morning."

"What the devil—that editorial was on the coaching system."

"Yes, but that quotation—"

Jesse sat up.

"What quotation?"

"You know: 'He who is not with me is against me.'"

"Well—what about it?"

Jesse was puzzled but not alarmed.

"Well, you say here—let me see." Burne opened the paper and read: "'*He who is not with me is against me*, as that gentleman said who was notoriously capable of only coarse distinctions and puerile generalities.'"

"What of it?" Ferrenby began to look alarmed. "Oliver Cromwell said it, didn't he? or was it Washington, or one of the saints? Good Lord, I've forgotten."

Burne roared with laughter.

"Oh, Jesse, oh, good, kind Jesse."

"Who said it, for Pete's sake?"

"Well," said Burne, recovering his voice, "St. Matthew attributes it to Christ."

"My God!" cried Jesse, and collapsed backward into the waste-basket.

AMORY WRITES A POEM

The weeks tore by. Amory wandered occasionally to New York on the chance of finding a new shining green auto-bus, that its stick-of-candy glamour might penetrate his disposition. One day he ventured into a stock-company revival of a play whose name was faintly familiar. The curtain rose—he watched casually as a girl entered. A few phrases rang in his ear and touched a faint chord of memory. Where—? When—?

Then he seemed to hear a voice whispering beside him, a very soft, vibrant voice: "Oh, I'm such a poor little fool; *do* tell me when I do wrong."

The solution came in a flash and he had a quick, glad memory of Isabelle. He found a blank space on his programme, and began to scribble rapidly:

"Here in the figured dark I watch once more,
There, with the curtain, roll the years away;
Two years of years—there was an idle day
Of ours, when happy endings didn't bore
Our unfermented souls; I could adore
Your eager face beside me, wide-eyed, gay,
Smiling a repertoire while the poor play
Reached me as a faint ripple reaches shore.

"Yawning and wondering an evening through,
I watch alone... and chatterings, of course,
Spoil the one scene which, somehow, did have charms;
You wept a bit, and I grew sad for you
Right here!Where Mr. X defends divorce
And What's-Her-Name falls fainting in his arms."

STILL CALM

"Ghosts are such dumb things," said Alec, "they're slow-witted. I can always outguess a ghost."

"How?" asked Tom.

"Well, it depends where. Take a bedroom, for example. If you use *any* discretion a ghost can never get you in a bedroom."

"Go on, s'pose you think there's maybe a ghost in your bedroom—what measures do you take on getting home at night?" demanded Amory, interested.

"Take a stick" answered Alec, with ponderous reverence, "one about the length of a broom-handle. Now, the first thing to do is to get the room *cleared*—to do this you rush with your eyes closed into your study and turn on the lights—next, approaching the closet, carefully run the stick in the door three or four times. Then, if nothing happens, you can look in. *Always, always* run the stick in viciously first—*never* look first!"

"Of course, that's the ancient Celtic school," said Tom gravely.

"Yes—but they usually pray first. Anyway, you use this method to clear the closets and also for behind all doors—"

"And the bed," Amory suggested.

"Oh, Amory, no!" cried Alec in horror. "That isn't the way—the bed requires different tactics—let the bed alone, as you value your reason—if there is a ghost in the room and that's only about a third of the time, it is *almost always* under the bed."

"Well" Amory began.

Alec waved him into silence.

"Of *course* you never look. You stand in the middle of the floor and before he knows what you're going to do make a sudden leap for the bed—never walk near the bed; to a ghost your ankle is your most vulnerable part—once in bed, you're safe; he may lie around under the bed all night, but you're safe as daylight. If you still have doubts pull the blanket over your head."

"All that's very interesting, Tom."

"Isn't it?" Alec beamed proudly. "All my own, too—the Sir Oliver Lodge of the new world."

Amory was enjoying college immensely again. The sense of going forward in a direct, determined line had come back; youth was stirring and shaking out a few new feathers. He had even stored enough surplus energy to sally into a new pose.

"What's the idea of all this 'distracted' stuff, Amory?" asked Alec one day, and then as Amory pretended to be cramped over his book in a daze: "Oh, don't try to act Burne, the mystic, to me."

Amory looked up innocently.

"What?"

"What?" mimicked Alec. "Are you trying to read yourself into a rhapsody with—let's see the book."

He snatched it; regarded it derisively.

"Well?" said Amory a little stiffly.

"'The Life of St. Teresa,'" read Alec aloud. "Oh, my gosh!"

"Say, Alec."

"What?"

"Does it bother you?"

"Does what bother me?"

"My acting dazed and all that?"

"Why, no—of course it doesn't *bother* me."

"Well, then, don't spoil it. If I enjoy going around telling people guilelessly that I think I'm a genius, let me do it."

"You're getting a reputation for being eccentric," said Alec, laughing, "if that's what you mean."

Amory finally prevailed, and Alec agreed to accept his face value in the presence of others if he was allowed rest periods when they were alone; so Amory "ran it out" at a great rate, bringing the most eccentric characters to dinner, wild-eyed grad students, preceptors with strange theories of God and government, to the cynical amazement of the supercilious Cottage Club.

As February became slashed by sun and moved cheerfully into March, Amory went several times to spend week-ends with Monsignor; once he took

Burne, with great success, for he took equal pride and delight in displaying them to each other. Monsignor took him several times to see Thornton Hancock, and once or twice to the house of a Mrs. Lawrence, a type of Rome-haunting American whom Amory liked immediately.

Then one day came a letter from Monsignor, which appended an interesting P. S.:

> *"Do you know," it ran, "that your third cousin, Clara Page, widowed six months and very poor, is living in Philadelphia? I don't think you've ever met her, but I wish, as a favor to me, you'd go to see her. To my mind, she's rather a remarkable woman, and just about your age."*

Amory sighed and decided to go, as a favor....

CLARA

She was immemorial.... Amory wasn't good enough for Clara, Clara of ripply golden hair, but then no man was. Her goodness was above the prosy morals of the husband-seeker, apart from the dull literature of female virtue.

Sorrow lay lightly around her, and when Amory found her in Philadelphia he thought her steely blue eyes held only happiness; a latent strength, a realism, was brought to its fullest development by the facts that she was compelled to face. She was alone in the world, with two small children, little money, and, worst of all, a host of friends. He saw her that winter in Philadelphia entertaining a houseful of men for an evening, when he knew she had not a servant in the house except the little colored girl guarding the babies overhead. He saw one of the greatest libertines in that city, a man who was habitually drunk and notorious at home and abroad, sitting opposite her for an evening, discussing *girls' boarding-schools* with a sort of innocent excitement. What a twist Clara had to her mind! She could make fascinating and almost brilliant conversation out of the thinnest air that ever floated through a drawing-room.

The idea that the girl was poverty-stricken had appealed to Amory's sense of situation. He arrived in Philadelphia expecting to be told that 921 Ark Street was in a miserable lane of hovels. He was even disappointed when it proved to be nothing of the sort. It was an old house that had been in her husband's family for years. An elderly aunt, who objected to having it sold, had put ten years' taxes with a lawyer and pranced off to Honolulu, leaving Clara to struggle with the heating-problem as best she could. So no wild-haired woman with a hungry baby at her breast and a sad Amelia-like look greeted him. Instead, Amory would have thought from his reception that she had not a care in the world.

A calm virility and a dreamy humor, marked contrasts to her level-headedness—into these moods she slipped sometimes as a refuge. She could do the most prosy things (though she was wise enough never to stultify herself with such "household arts" as *knitting* and *embroidery*), yet immediately afterward pick up a book and let her imagination rove as a formless cloud with the wind. Deepest of all in her personality was the golden radiance that she diffused around her. As an open fire in a dark room throws romance and pathos into the quiet faces at its edge, so she cast her lights and shadows around the rooms that held her, until she made of her prosy old uncle a man of quaint and meditative charm, metamorphosed the stray telegraph boy into a Puck-like creature of delightful originality. At first this quality of hers somehow irritated Amory. He considered his own uniqueness sufficient, and it rather embarrassed him when she tried to read new interests into him for the benefit of what other adorers were present. He felt as if a polite but insistent stage-manager were attempting to make him give a new interpretation of a part he had conned for years.

But Clara talking, Clara telling a slender tale of a hatpin and an inebriated man and herself.... People tried afterward to repeat her anecdotes but for the life of them they could make them sound like nothing whatever. They gave her a sort of innocent attention and the best smiles many of them had smiled for long; there were few tears in Clara, but people smiled misty-eyed at her.

Very occasionally Amory stayed for little half-hours after the rest of the court had gone, and they would have bread and jam and tea late in the afternoon or "maple-sugar lunches," as she called them, at night.

"You *are* remarkable, aren't you!" Amory was becoming trite from where he perched in the centre of the dining-room table one six o'clock.

"Not a bit," she answered. She was searching out napkins in the sideboard. "I'm really most humdrum and commonplace. One of those people who have no interest in anything but their children."

"Tell that to somebody else," scoffed Amory. "You know you're perfectly effulgent." He asked her the one thing that he knew might embarrass her. It was the remark that the first bore made to Adam.

"Tell me about yourself." And she gave the answer that Adam must have given.

"There's nothing to tell."

But eventually Adam probably told the bore all the things he thought about at night when the locusts sang in the sandy grass, and he must have remarked patronizingly how *different* he was from Eve, forgetting how different she was from him... at any rate, Clara told Amory much about herself that evening. She had had a harried life from sixteen on, and her education had stopped sharply with her leisure. Browsing in her library, Amory found a tattered gray book out of which fell a yellow sheet that he impudently opened. It was a poem that she had written at school about a gray convent wall on a gray day, and a girl with her cloak blown by the wind sitting atop of it and thinking about the many-colored world. As a rule such sentiment bored him, but this was done with so much simplicity and atmosphere, that it brought a picture of Clara to his mind, of Clara on such a cool, gray day with her keen blue eyes staring out, trying to see her tragedies come marching over the gardens outside. He envied that poem. How he would have loved to have come along and seen her on the wall and talked nonsense or romance to her, perched above him in the air. He began to be frightfully jealous of everything about Clara: of her past, of her babies, of the men and women who flocked to drink deep of her cool kindness and rest their tired minds as at an absorbing play.

"*Nobody* seems to bore you," he objected.

"About half the world do," she admitted, "but I think that's a pretty good average, don't you?" and she turned to find something in Browning that bore on the subject. She was the only person he ever met who could look up passages and quotations to show him in the middle of the conversation, and yet not be irritating to distraction. She did it constantly, with such a serious enthusiasm that he grew fond of watching her golden hair bent over a book, brow wrinkled ever so little at hunting her sentence.

Through early March he took to going to Philadelphia for week-ends. Almost always there was some one else there and she seemed not anxious to see him alone, for many occasions presented themselves when a word from her would have given him another delicious half-hour of adoration. But he fell gradually in love and began to speculate wildly on marriage. Though this design flowed through his brain even to his lips, still he knew afterward that the desire had not been deeply rooted. Once he dreamt that it had come true and woke up in a cold panic, for in his dream she had been a silly, flaxen Clara, with the gold gone out of her hair and platitudes falling insipidly from her changeling tongue. But she was the first fine woman he ever knew and one of the few good people who ever interested him. She made her goodness such an asset. Amory had decided that most good people either dragged theirs after them as a liability, or else distorted it to artificial geniality, and of course there were the ever-present prig and Pharisee—(but Amory never included *them* as being among the saved).

ST. CECILIA

"Over her gray and velvet dress,
Under her molten, beaten hair,
Color of rose in mock distress
Flushes and fades and makes her fair;
Fills the air from her to him
With light and languor and little sighs,
Just so subtly he scarcely knows...

Laughing lightning, color of rose."

"Do you like me?"

"Of course I do," said Clara seriously.

"Why?"

"Well, we have some qualities in common. Things that are spontaneous in each of us—or were originally."

"You're implying that I haven't used myself very well?"

Clara hesitated.

"Well, I can't judge. A man, of course, has to go through a lot more, and I've been sheltered."

"Oh, don't stall, please, Clara," Amory interrupted; "but do talk about me a little, won't you?"

"Surely, I'd adore to." She didn't smile.

"That's sweet of you. First answer some questions. Am I painfully conceited?"

"Well—no, you have tremendous vanity, but it'll amuse the people who notice its preponderance."

"I see."

"You're really humble at heart. You sink to the third hell of depression when you think you've been slighted. In fact, you haven't much self-respect."

"Centre of target twice, Clara. How do you do it? You never let me say a word."

"Of course not—I can never judge a man while he's talking. But I'm not through; the reason you have so little real self-confidence, even though you gravely announce to the occasional philistine that you think you're a genius, is that you've attributed all sorts of atrocious faults to yourself and are trying to live up to them. For instance, you're always saying that you are a slave to highballs."

"But I am, potentially."

"And you say you're a weak character, that you've no will."

"Not a bit of will—I'm a slave to my emotions, to my likes, to my hatred of boredom, to most of my desires—"

"You are not!" She brought one little fist down onto the other. "You're a slave, a bound helpless slave to one thing in the world, your imagination."

"You certainly interest me. If this isn't boring you, go on."

"I notice that when you want to stay over an extra day from college you go about it in a sure way. You never decide at first while the merits of going or staying are fairly clear in your mind. You let your imagination shinny on the side of your desires for a few hours, and then you decide. Naturally your imagination, after a little freedom, thinks up a million reasons why you should stay, so your decision when it comes isn't true. It's biassed."

"Yes," objected Amory, "but isn't it lack of will-power to let my imagination shinny on the wrong side?"

"My dear boy, there's your big mistake. This has nothing to do with will-power; that's a crazy, useless word, anyway; you lack judgment—the judgment to decide at once when you know your imagination will play you false, given half a chance."

"Well, I'll be darned!" exclaimed Amory in surprise, "that's the last thing I expected."

Clara didn't gloat. She changed the subject immediately. But she had started him thinking and he believed she was partly right. He felt like a factory-owner who after accusing a clerk of dishonesty finds that his own son, in the office, is changing the books once a week. His poor, mistreated will that he had been holding up to the scorn of himself and his friends, stood before him innocent, and his judgment walked off to prison with the unconfinable imp, imagination, dancing in mocking glee beside him. Clara's was the only advice he ever asked without dictating the answer himself—except, perhaps, in his talks with Monsignor Darcy.

How he loved to do any sort of thing with Clara! Shopping with her was a rare, epicurean dream. In every store where she had ever traded she was whispered about as the beautiful Mrs. Page.

"I'll bet she won't stay single long."

"Well, don't scream it out. She ain't lookin' for no advice."

"*Ain't* she beautiful!"

(Enter a floor-walker—silence till he moves forward, smirking.)

"Society person, ain't she?"

"Yeah, but poor now, I guess; so they say."

"Gee! girls, *ain't* she some kid!"

And Clara beamed on all alike. Amory believed that tradespeople gave her discounts, sometimes to her knowledge and sometimes without it. He knew she dressed very well, had always the best of everything in the house, and was inevitably waited upon by the head floor-walker at the very least.

Sometimes they would go to church together on Sunday and he would walk beside her and revel in her cheeks moist from the soft water in the new air. She was very devout, always had been, and God knows what heights she attained and what strength she drew down to herself when she knelt and bent her golden hair into the stained-glass light.

"St. Cecelia," he cried aloud one day, quite involuntarily, and the people turned and peered, and the priest paused in his sermon and Clara and Amory turned to fiery red.

That was the last Sunday they had, for he spoiled it all that night. He couldn't help it.

They were walking through the March twilight where it was as warm as June, and the joy of youth filled his soul so that he felt he must speak.

"I think," he said and his voice trembled, "that if I lost faith in you I'd lose faith in God."

She looked at him with such a startled face that he asked her the matter.

"Nothing," she said slowly, "only this: five men have said that to me before, and it frightens me."

"Oh, Clara, is that your fate!"

She did not answer.

"I suppose love to you is—" he began.

She turned like a flash.

"I have never been in love."

They walked along, and he realized slowly how much she had told him... never in love.... She seemed suddenly a daughter of light alone. His entity dropped out of her plane and he longed only to touch her dress with almost the realization that Joseph must have had of Mary's eternal significance. But quite mechanically he heard himself saying:

"And I love you—any latent greatness that I've got is... oh, I can't talk, but Clara, if I come back in two years in a position to marry you—"

She shook her head.

"No," she said; "I'd never marry again. I've got my two children and I want myself for them. I like you—I like all clever men, you more than any—but you know me well enough to know that I'd never marry a clever man—" She broke off suddenly.

"Amory."

"What?"

"You're not in love with me. You never wanted to marry me, did you?"

"It was the twilight," he said wonderingly. "I didn't feel as though I were speaking aloud. But I love you—or adore you—or worship you—"

"There you go—running through your catalogue of emotions in five seconds."

He smiled unwillingly.

"Don't make me out such a light-weight, Clara; you *are* depressing sometimes."

"You're not a light-weight, of all things," she said intently, taking his arm and opening wide her eyes—he could see their kindliness in the fading dusk. "A light-weight is an eternal nay."

"There's so much spring in the air—there's so much lazy sweetness in your heart."

She dropped his arm.

"You're all fine now, and I feel glorious. Give me a cigarette. You've never seen me smoke, have you? Well, I do, about once a month."

And then that wonderful girl and Amory raced to the corner like two mad children gone wild with pale-blue twilight.

"I'm going to the country for to-morrow," she announced, as she stood panting, safe beyond the flare of the corner lamp-post. "These days are too magnificent to miss, though perhaps I feel them more in the city."

"Oh, Clara!" Amory said; "what a devil you could have been if the Lord had just bent your soul a little the other way!"

"Maybe," she answered; "but I think not. I'm never really wild and never have been. That little outburst was pure spring."

"And you are, too," said he.

They were walking along now.

"No—you're wrong again, how can a person of your own self-reputed brains be so constantly wrong about me? I'm the opposite of everything spring ever stood for. It's unfortunate, if I happen to look like what pleased some soppy old Greek sculptor, but I assure you that if it weren't for my face I'd be a quiet nun in the convent without"—then she broke into a run and her raised voice floated back to him as he followed—"my precious babies, which I must go back and see."

She was the only girl he ever knew with whom he could understand how another man might be preferred. Often Amory met wives whom he had known as debutantes, and looking intently at them imagined that he found something in their faces which said:

"Oh, if I could only have gotten *you!*" Oh, the enormous conceit of the man!

But that night seemed a night of stars and singing and Clara's bright soul still gleamed on the ways they had trod.

"Golden, golden is the air—" he chanted to the little pools of water. ... "Golden is the air, golden notes from golden mandolins, golden frets of golden violins, fair, oh, wearily fair.... Skeins from braided basket, mortals may not hold; oh, what young extravagant God, who would know or ask it?... who could give such gold..."

AMORY IS RESENTFUL

Slowly and inevitably, yet with a sudden surge at the last, while Amory talked and dreamed, war rolled swiftly up the beach and washed the sands where Princeton played. Every night the gymnasium echoed as platoon after platoon swept over the floor and shuffled out the basket-ball markings. When Amory went to Washington the next week-end he caught some of the spirit of crisis which changed to repulsion in the Pullman car coming back, for the berths across from him were occupied by stinking aliens—Greeks, he guessed, or Russians. He thought how much easier patriotism had been to a homogeneous race, how much easier it would have been to fight as the Colonies fought, or as the Confederacy fought. And he did no sleeping that night, but listened to the aliens guffaw and snore while they filled the car with the heavy scent of latest America.

In Princeton every one bantered in public and told themselves privately that their deaths at least would be heroic. The literary students read Rupert Brooke passionately; the lounge-lizards worried over whether the government would permit the English-cut uniform for officers; a few of the hopelessly lazy wrote to the obscure branches of the War Department, seeking an easy commission and a soft berth.

Then, after a week, Amory saw Burne and knew at once that argument would be futile—Burne had come out as a pacifist. The socialist magazines, a great smattering of Tolstoi, and his own intense longing for a cause that would bring out whatever strength lay in him, had finally decided him to preach peace as a subjective ideal.

"When the German army entered Belgium," he began, "if the inhabitants had gone peaceably about their business, the German army would have been disorganized in—"

"I know," Amory interrupted, "I've heard it all. But I'm not going to talk propaganda with you. There's a chance that you're right—but even so we're hundreds of years before the time when non-resistance can touch us as a reality."

"But, Amory, listen—"

"Burne, we'd just argue—"

"Very well."

"Just one thing—I don't ask you to think of your family or friends, because I know they don't count a picayune with you beside your sense of duty—but, Burne, how do you know that the magazines you read and the societies you join and these idealists you meet aren't just plain *German?*"

"Some of them are, of course."

"How do you know they aren't *all* pro-German—just a lot of weak ones—with German-Jewish names."

"That's the chance, of course," he said slowly. "How much or how little I'm taking this stand because of propaganda I've heard, I don't know; naturally I think that it's my most innermost conviction—it seems a path spread before me just now."

Amory's heart sank.

"But think of the cheapness of it—no one's really going to martyr you for being a pacifist—it's just going to throw you in with the worst—"

"I doubt it," he interrupted.

"Well, it all smells of Bohemian New York to me."

"I know what you mean, and that's why I'm not sure I'll agitate."

"You're one man, Burne—going to talk to people who won't listen—with all God's given you."

"That's what Stephen must have thought many years ago. But he preached his sermon and they killed him. He probably thought as he was dying what a waste it all was. But you see, I've always felt that Stephen's death was the thing that occurred to Paul on the road to Damascus, and sent him to preach the word of Christ all over the world."

"Go on."

"That's all—this is my particular duty. Even if right now I'm just a pawn—just sacrificed. God! Amory—you don't think I like the Germans!"

"Well, I can't say anything else—I get to the end of all the logic about non-resistance, and there, like an excluded middle, stands the huge spectre of man as he is and always will be. And this spectre stands right beside the one logical necessity of Tolstoi's, and the other logical necessity of Nietzsche's—" Amory broke off suddenly. "When are you going?"

"I'm going next week."

"I'll see you, of course."

As he walked away it seemed to Amory that the look in his face bore a great resemblance to that in Kerry's when he had said good-by under Blair Arch two years before. Amory wondered unhappily why he could never go into anything with the primal honesty of those two.

"Burne's a fanatic," he said to Tom, "and he's dead wrong and, I'm inclined to think, just an unconscious pawn in the hands of anarchistic publishers and German-paid rag wavers—but he haunts me—just leaving everything worth while—"

Burne left in a quietly dramatic manner a week later. He sold all his possessions and came down to the room to say good-by, with a battered old bicycle, on which he intended to ride to his home in Pennsylvania.

"Peter the Hermit bidding farewell to Cardinal Richelieu," suggested Alec, who was lounging in the window-seat as Burne and Amory shook hands.

But Amory was not in a mood for that, and as he saw Burne's long legs propel his ridiculous bicycle out of sight beyond Alexander Hall, he knew he was going to have a bad week. Not that he doubted the war—Germany stood for everything repugnant to him; for materialism and the direction of tremendous licentious force; it was just that Burne's face stayed in his memory and he was sick of the hysteria he was beginning to hear.

"What on earth is the use of suddenly running down Goethe," he declared to Alec and Tom. "Why write books to prove he started the war—or that that stupid, overestimated Schiller is a demon in disguise?"

"Have you ever read anything of theirs?" asked Tom shrewdly.

"No," Amory admitted.

"Neither have I," he said laughing.

"People will shout," said Alec quietly, "but Goethe's on his same old shelf in the library—to bore any one that wants to read him!"

Amory subsided, and the subject dropped.

"What are you going to do, Amory?"

"Infantry or aviation, I can't make up my mind—I hate mechanics, but then of course aviation's the thing for me—"

"I feel as Amory does," said Tom. "Infantry or aviation—aviation sounds like the romantic side of the war, of course—like cavalry used to be, you know; but like Amory I don't know a horse-power from a piston-rod."

Somehow Amory's dissatisfaction with his lack of enthusiasm culminated in an attempt to put the blame for the whole war on the ancestors of his generation... all the people who cheered for Germany in 1870.... All the materialists rampant, all the idolizers of German science and efficiency. So he sat one day in an English lecture and heard "Locksley Hall" quoted and fell into a brown study with contempt for Tennyson and all he stood for—for he took him as a representative of the Victorians.

Victorians, Victorians, who never learned to weep
Who sowed the bitter harvest that your children go to reap—

scribbled Amory in his note-book. The lecturer was saying something about Tennyson's solidity and fifty heads were bent to take notes. Amory turned over to a fresh page and began scrawling again.

"They shuddered when they found what Mr. Darwin was about,
They shuddered when the waltz came in and Newman hurried out—"

But the waltz came in much earlier; he crossed that out.

"And entitled A Song in the Time of Order," came the professor's voice, droning far away. "Time of Order"—Good Lord! Everything crammed in the box and the Victorians sitting on the lid smiling serenely.... With Browning in his Italian villa crying bravely: "All's for the best." Amory scribbled again.

"You knelt up in the temple and he bent to hear you pray,
You thanked him for your 'glorious gains'—reproached him for 'Cathay.'"

Why could he never get more than a couplet at a time? Now he needed something to rhyme with:

"You would keep Him straight with science, tho He had gone wrong before..."

Well, anyway....

"You met your children in your home—'I've fixed it up!' you cried,
Took your fifty years of Europe, and then virtuously—died."

"That was to a great extent Tennyson's idea," came the lecturer's voice. "Swinburne's Song in the Time of Order might well have been Tennyson's title. He idealized order against chaos, against waste."

At last Amory had it. He turned over another page and scrawled vigorously for the twenty minutes that was left of the hour. Then he walked up to the desk and deposited a page torn out of his note-book.

"Here's a poem to the Victorians, sir," he said coldly.

The professor picked it up curiously while Amory backed rapidly through the door.

Here is what he had written:

"Songs in the time of order
You left for us to sing,
Proofs with excluded middles,
Answers to life in rhyme,
Keys of the prison warder
And ancient bells to ring,
Time was the end of riddles,
We were the end of time...

Here were domestic oceans
And a sky that we might reach,
Guns and a guarded border,
Gantlets—but not to fling,
Thousands of old emotions
And a platitude for each,
Songs in the time of order—
And tongues, that we might sing."

THE END OF MANY THINGS

Early April slipped by in a haze—a haze of long evenings on the club veranda with the graphophone playing "Poor Butterfly" inside... for "Poor Butterfly" had been the song of that last year. The war seemed scarcely to touch them and it might have been one of the senior springs of the past, except for the drilling every other afternoon, yet Amory realized poignantly that this was the last spring under the old regime.

"This is the great protest against the superman," said Amory.

"I suppose so," Alec agreed.

"He's absolutely irreconcilable with any Utopia. As long as he occurs, there's trouble and all the latent evil that makes a crowd list and sway when he talks."

"And of course all that he is is a gifted man without a moral sense."

"That's all. I think the worst thing to contemplate is this—it's all happened before, how soon will it happen again? Fifty years after Waterloo Napoleon was as much a hero to English school children as Wellington. How do we know our grandchildren won't idolize Von Hindenburg the same way?"

"What brings it about?"

"Time, damn it, and the historian. If we could only learn to look on evil as evil, whether it's clothed in filth or monotony or magnificence."

"God! Haven't we raked the universe over the coals for four years?"

Then the night came that was to be the last. Tom and Amory, bound in the morning for different training-camps, paced the shadowy walks as usual and seemed still to see around them the faces of the men they knew.

"The grass is full of ghosts to-night."

"The whole campus is alive with them."

They paused by Little and watched the moon rise, to make silver of the slate roof of Dodd and blue the rustling trees.

"You know," whispered Tom, "what we feel now is the sense of all the gorgeous youth that has rioted through here in two hundred years."

A last burst of singing flooded up from Blair Arch—broken voices for some long parting.

"And what we leave here is more than this class; it's the whole heritage of youth. We're just one generation—we're breaking all the links that seemed to bind us here to top-booted and high-stocked generations. We've walked arm and arm with Burr and Light-Horse Harry Lee through half these deep-blue nights."

"That's what they are," Tom tangented off, "deep blue—a bit of color would spoil them, make them exotic. Spires, against a sky that's a promise of dawn, and blue light on the slate roofs—it hurts... rather—"

"Good-by, Aaron Burr," Amory called toward deserted Nassau Hall, "you and I knew strange corners of life."

His voice echoed in the stillness.

"The torches are out," whispered Tom. "Ah, Messalina, the long shadows are building minarets on the stadium—"

For an instant the voices of freshman year surged around them and then they looked at each other with faint tears in their eyes.

"Damn!"

"Damn!"

The last light fades and drifts across the land—the low, long land, the sunny land of spires; the ghosts of evening tune again their lyres and wander singing in a plaintive band down the long corridors of trees; pale fires echo the night from tower top to tower: Oh, sleep that dreams, and dream that never tires, press from the petals of the lotus flower something of this to keep, the essence of an hour.

No more to wait the twilight of the moon in this sequestered vale of star and spire, for one eternal morning of desire passes to time and earthy afternoon. Here, Heraclitus, did you find in fire and shifting things the prophecy you hurled down the dead years; this midnight my desire will see, shadowed among the embers, furled in flame, the splendor and the sadness of the world.

INTERLUDE

May, 1917-February, 1919

A letter dated January, 1918, written by Monsignor Darcy to Amory, who is a second lieutenant in the 171st Infantry, Port of Embarkation, Camp Mills, Long Island.

MY DEAR BOY:

All you need tell me of yourself is that you still are; for the rest I merely search back in a restive memory, a thermometer that records only fevers, and match you with what I was at your age. But men will chatter and you and I will still shout our futilities to each other across the stage until the last silly curtain falls *plump!* upon our bobbing heads. But you are starting the spluttering magic-lantern show of life with much the same array of slides as I had, so I need to write you if only to shriek the colossal stupidity of people....

This is the end of one thing: for better or worse you will never again be quite the Amory Blaine that I knew, never again will we meet as we have met, because your generation is growing hard, much harder than mine ever grew, nourished as they were on the stuff of the nineties.

Amory, lately I reread Aeschylus and there in the divine irony of the "Agamemnon" I find the only answer to this bitter age—all the world tumbled about our ears, and the closest parallel ages back in that hopeless resignation. There are times when I think of the men out there as Roman legionaries, miles from their corrupt city, stemming back the hordes... hordes a little more menacing, after all, than the corrupt city... another blind blow at the race, furies that we passed with ovations years ago, over whose corpses we bleated triumphantly all through the Victorian era....

And afterward an out-and-out materialistic world—and the Catholic Church. I wonder where you'll fit in. Of one thing I'm sure—Celtic you'll live and Celtic you'll die; so if you don't use heaven as a continual referendum for your ideas you'll find earth a continual recall to your ambitions.

Amory, I've discovered suddenly that I'm an old man. Like all old men, I've had dreams sometimes and I'm going to tell you of them. I've enjoyed imagining that you were my son, that perhaps when I was young I went into a state of coma and begat you, and when I came to, had no recollection of it... it's the paternal instinct, Amory—celibacy goes deeper than the flesh....

Sometimes I think that the explanation of our deep resemblance is some common ancestor, and I find that the only blood that the Darcys and the O'Haras have in common is that of the O'Donahues... Stephen was his name, I think....

When the lightning strikes one of us it strikes both: you had hardly arrived at the port of embarkation when I got my papers to start for Rome, and I am waiting every moment to be told where to take ship. Even before you get this letter I shall be on the ocean; then will come your turn. You went to war as a gentleman should, just as you went to school and college, because it was the thing to do. It's better to leave the blustering and tremulo-heroism to the middle classes; they do it so much better.

Do you remember that week-end last March when you brought Burne Holiday from Princeton to see me? What a magnificent boy he is! It gave me a frightful shock afterward when you wrote that he thought me splendid; how could he be so deceived? Splendid is the one thing that neither you nor I are. We are many other things—we're extraordinary, we're clever, we could be said, I suppose, to be brilliant. We can attract people, we can make atmosphere, we can almost lose our Celtic souls in Celtic subtleties, we can almost always have our own way; but splendid—rather not!

I am going to Rome with a wonderful dossier and letters of introduction that cover every capital in Europe, and there will be "no small stir" when I get there. How I wish you were with me! This sounds like a rather cynical paragraph, not at all the sort of thing that a middle-aged clergyman should write to a youth about to depart for the war; the only excuse is that the middle-aged clergyman is talking to himself. There are deep things in us and you know what they are as well as I do. We have great faith, though yours at present is uncrystallized; we have a terrible honesty that all our sophistry cannot destroy and, above all, a childlike simplicity that keeps us from ever being really malicious.

I have written a keen for you which follows. I am sorry your cheeks are not up to the description I have written of them, but you *will* smoke and read all night—

At any rate here it is:

A Lament for a Foster Son, and He going to the War Against the King of Foreign.

"Ochone
He is gone from me the son of my mind
And he in his golden youth like Angus Oge
Angus of the bright birds
And his mind strong and subtle like the mind of Cuchulin on Muirtheme.

Awirra sthrue
His brow is as white as the milk of the cows of Maeve
And his cheeks like the cherries of the tree
And it bending down to Mary and she feeding the Son of God.

Aveelia Vrone
His hair is like the golden collar of the Kings at Tara
And his eyes like the four gray seas of Erin.
And they swept with the mists of rain.

Mavrone go Gudyo
He to be in the joyful and red battle
Amongst the chieftains and they doing great deeds of valor
His life to go from him
It is the chords of my own soul would be loosed.

A Vich Deelish
My heart is in the heart of my son
And my life is in his life surely
A man can be twice young
In the life of his sons only.

Jia du Vaha Alanav
May the Son of God be above him and beneath him, before him and behind him
May the King of the elements cast a mist over the eyes of the King of Foreign,
May the Queen of the Graces lead him by the hand the way he can go through the midst of his enemies and they not seeing him

May Patrick of the Gael and Collumb of the Churches and the five thousand Saints of Erin be better than a shield to him
And he got into the fight.
Och Ochone."

Amory—Amory—I feel, somehow, that this is all; one or both of us is not going to last out this war.... I've been trying to tell you how much this reincarnation of myself in you has meant in the last few years... curiously alike we are... curiously unlike. Good-by, dear boy, and God be with you. THAYER DARCY.

EMBARKING AT NIGHT

Amory moved forward on the deck until he found a stool under an electric light. He searched in his pocket for note-book and pencil and then began to write, slowly, laboriously:

'We leave to-night...
Silent, we filled the still, deserted street,
A column of dim gray,
And ghosts rose startled at the muffled beat
Along the moonless way;
The shadowy shipyards echoed to the feet
That turned from night and day.

And so we linger on the windless decks,
See on the spectre shore
Shades of a thousand days, poor gray-ribbed wrecks...
Oh, shall we then deplore
Those futile years!
See how the sea is white!
The clouds have broken and the heavens burn
To hollow highways, paved with gravelled light
The churning of the waves about the stern
Rises to one voluminous nocturne,
... We leave to-night."

A letter from Amory, headed "Brest, March 11th, 1919," to Lieutenant T. P. D'Invilliers, Camp Gordon, Ga.

DEAR BAUDELAIRE:—

We meet in Manhattan on the 30th of this very mo.; we then proceed to take a very sporty apartment, you and I and Alec, who is at me elbow as I write. I don't know what I'm going to do but I have a vague dream of going into politics. Why is it that the pick of the young Englishmen from Oxford and Cambridge go into politics and in the U. S. A. we leave it to the muckers?—raised in the ward, educated in the assembly and sent to Congress, fat-paunched bundles of corruption, devoid of "both ideas and ideals" as the debaters used to say. Even forty years ago we had good men in politics, but we, we are brought up to pile up a million and "show what we are made of." Sometimes I wish I'd been an Englishman; American life is so damned dumb and stupid and healthy.

Since poor Beatrice died I'll probably have a little money, but very darn little. I can forgive mother almost everything except the fact that in a sudden burst of religiosity toward the end, she left half of what remained to be spent in stained-glass windows and seminary endowments. Mr. Barton, my lawyer, writes me that my thousands are mostly in street railways and that the said Street R.R. s are losing money because of the five-cent fares. Imagine a salary list that gives $350 a month to a man that can't read and write!—yet I believe in it, even though I've seen what was once a sizable fortune melt away between speculation, extravagance, the democratic administration, and the income tax—modern, that's me all over, Mabel.

At any rate we'll have really knock-out rooms—you can get a job on some fashion magazine, and Alec can go into the Zinc Company or whatever it is that his people own—he's looking over my shoulder and he says it's a brass company, but I don't think it matters much, do you? There's probably as much corruption in zinc-made money as brass-made money. As for the well-known Amory, he would write immortal literature if he were sure enough about anything to risk telling any one else about it. There is no more dangerous gift to posterity than a few cleverly turned platitudes.

Tom, why don't you become a Catholic? Of course to be a good one you'd have to give up those violent intrigues you used to tell me about, but you'd write better poetry if you were linked up to tall golden candlesticks and long, even chants, and even if the American priests are rather burgeois, as Beatrice used to say, still you need only go to the sporty churches, and I'll introduce you to Monsignor Darcy who really is a wonder.

Kerry's death was a blow, so was Jesse's to a certain extent. And I have a great curiosity to know what queer corner of the world has swallowed Burne. Do you suppose he's in prison under some false name? I confess that the war instead of making me orthodox, which is the correct reaction, has made me a passionate agnostic. The Catholic Church has had its wings clipped so often lately that its part was timidly negligible, and they haven't any good writers any more. I'm sick of Chesterton.

I've only discovered one soldier who passed through the much-advertised spiritual crisis, like this fellow, Donald Hankey, and the one I knew was already studying for the ministry, so he was ripe for it. I honestly think that's all pretty much rot, though it seemed to give sentimental comfort to those at home; and may make fathers and mothers appreciate their children. This crisis-inspired religion is rather valueless and fleeting at best. I think four men have discovered Paris to one that discovered God.

But us—you and me and Alec—oh, we'll get a Jap butler and dress for dinner and have wine on the table and lead a contemplative, emotionless life until we decide to use machine-guns with the property owners—or throw bombs with the Bolshevik God! Tom, I hope something happens. I'm restless as the devil and have a horror of getting fat or falling in love and growing domestic.

The place at Lake Geneva is now for rent but when I land I'm going West to see Mr. Barton and get some details. Write me care of the Blackstone, Chicago.

S'ever, dear Boswell,

SAMUEL JOHNSON.

BOOK TWO

The Education of a Personage

I. The Debutante

The time is February. The place is a large, dainty bedroom in the Connage house on Sixty-eighth Street, New York. A girl's room: pink walls and curtains and a pink bedspread on a cream-colored bed. Pink and cream are the motifs of the room, but the only article of furniture in full view is a luxurious dressing-table with a glass top and a three-sided mirror. On the walls there is an expensive print of "Cherry Ripe," a few polite dogs by Landseer, and the "King of the Black Isles," by Maxfield Parrish.

Great disorder consisting of the following items: (1) seven or eight empty cardboard boxes, with tissue-paper tongues hanging panting from their mouths; (2) an assortment of street dresses mingled with their sisters of the evening, all upon the table, all evidently new; (3) a roll of tulle, which has lost its dignity and wound itself tortuously around everything in sight, and (4) upon the two small chairs, a collection of lingerie that beggars description. One would enjoy seeing the bill called forth by the finery displayed and one is possessed by a desire to see the princess for whose benefit—Look! There's some one! Disappointment! This is only a maid hunting for something—she lifts a heap from a chair—Not there; another heap, the dressing-table, the chiffonier drawers. She brings to light several beautiful chemises and an amazing pajama but this does not satisfy her—she goes out.

An indistinguishable mumble from the next room.

Now, we are getting warm. This is Alec's mother, Mrs. Connage, ample, dignified, rouged to the dowager point and quite worn out. Her lips move significantly as she looks for IT. Her search is less thorough than the maid's but there is a touch of fury in it, that quite makes up for its sketchiness. She stumbles on the tulle and her "damn" is quite audible. She retires, empty-handed.

More chatter outside and a girl's voice, a very spoiled voice, says: "Of all the stupid people—"

After a pause a third seeker enters, not she of the spoiled voice, but a younger edition. This is Cecelia Connage, sixteen, pretty, shrewd, and constitutionally good-humored. She is dressed for the evening in a gown the obvious simplicity of which probably bores her. She goes to the nearest pile, selects a small pink garment and holds it up appraisingly.

CECELIA: Pink?

ROSALIND: (Outside) Yes!

CECELIA: *Very* snappy?

ROSALIND: Yes!

CECELIA: I've got it!

(She sees herself in the mirror of the dressing-table and commences to shimmy enthusiastically.)

ROSALIND: (Outside) What are you doing—trying it on?

(CECELIA ceases and goes out carrying the garment at the right shoulder.

From the other door, enters ALEC CONNAGE. He looks around quickly and in a huge voice shouts: Mama! There is a chorus of protest from next door and encouraged he starts toward it, but is repelled by another chorus.)

ALEC: So *that's* where you all are! Amory Blaine is here.

CECELIA: (Quickly) Take him down-stairs.

ALEC: Oh, he *is* down-stairs.

MRS. CONNAGE: Well, you can show him where his room is. Tell him I'm sorry that I can't meet him now.

ALEC: He's heard a lot about you all. I wish you'd hurry. Father's telling him all about the war and he's restless. He's sort of temperamental.

(This last suffices to draw CECELIA into the room.)

CECELIA: (Seating herself high upon lingerie) How do you mean—temperamental? You used to say that about him in letters.

ALEC: Oh, he writes stuff.

CECELIA: Does he play the piano?

ALEC: Don't think so.

CECELIA: (Speculatively) Drink?

ALEC: Yes—nothing queer about him.

CECELIA: Money?

ALEC: Good Lord—ask him, he used to have a lot, and he's got some income now.

(MRS. CONNAGE appears.)

MRS. CONNAGE: Alec, of course we're glad to have any friend of yours—

ALEC: You certainly ought to meet Amory.

MRS. CONNAGE: Of course, I want to. But I think it's so childish of you to leave a perfectly good home to go and live with two other boys in some impossible apartment. I hope it isn't in order that you can all drink as much as you want. (She pauses.) He'll be a little neglected to-night. This is Rosalind's week, you see. When a girl comes out, she needs *all* the attention.

ROSALIND: (Outside) Well, then, prove it by coming here and hooking me.

(MRS. CONNAGE goes.)

ALEC: Rosalind hasn't changed a bit.

CECELIA: (In a lower tone) She's awfully spoiled.

ALEC: She'll meet her match to-night.

CECELIA: Who—Mr. Amory Blaine?

(ALEC nods.)

CECELIA: Well, Rosalind has still to meet the man she can't outdistance. Honestly, Alec, she treats men terribly. She abuses them and cuts them and breaks dates with them and yawns in their faces—and they come back for more.

ALEC: They love it.

CECELIA: They hate it. She's a—she's a sort of vampire, I think—and she can make girls do what she wants usually—only she hates girls.

ALEC: Personality runs in our family.

CECELIA: (Resignedly) I guess it ran out before it got to me.

ALEC: Does Rosalind behave herself?

CECELIA: Not particularly well. Oh, she's average—smokes sometimes, drinks punch, frequently kissed—Oh, yes—common knowledge—one of the effects of the war, you know.

(Emerges MRS. CONNAGE.)

MRS. CONNAGE: Rosalind's almost finished so I can go down and meet your friend.

(ALEC and his mother go out.)

ROSALIND: (Outside) Oh, mother—

CECELIA: Mother's gone down.

(And now ROSALIND enters. ROSALIND is—utterly ROSALIND. She is one of those girls who need never make the slightest effort to have men fall in love with them. Two types of men seldom do: dull men are usually afraid of her cleverness and intellectual men are usually afraid of her beauty. All others are hers by natural prerogative.

If ROSALIND could be spoiled the process would have been complete by this time, and as a matter of fact, her disposition is not all it should be; she wants what she wants when she wants it and she is prone to make every one around her pretty miserable when she doesn't get it—but in the true sense she is not spoiled. Her fresh enthusiasm, her will to grow and learn, her endless faith in the inexhaustibility of romance, her courage and fundamental honesty—these things are not spoiled.

There are long periods when she cordially loathes her whole family. She is quite unprincipled; her philosophy is carpe diem for herself and laissez faire for others. She loves shocking stories: she has that coarse streak that usually goes with natures that are both fine and big. She wants people to like her, but if they do not it never worries her or changes her. She is by no means a model character.

The education of all beautiful women is the knowledge of men. ROSALIND had been disappointed in man after man as individuals, but she had great faith in man as a sex. Women she detested. They represented qualities that she felt and despised in herself—incipient meanness, conceit, cowardice, and petty dishonesty. She once told a roomful of her mother's friends that the only excuse for women was the necessity for a disturbing element among men. She danced exceptionally well, drew cleverly but hastily, and had a startling facility with words, which she used only in love-letters.

But all criticism of ROSALIND ends in her beauty. There was that shade of glorious yellow hair, the desire to imitate which supports the dye industry. There was the eternal kissable mouth, small, slightly sensual, and utterly disturbing. There were gray eyes and an unimpeachable skin with two spots of vanishing color. She was slender and athletic, without underdevelopment, and it was a delight to watch her move about a room, walk along a street, swing a golf club, or turn a "cartwheel."

A last qualification—her vivid, instant personality escaped that conscious, theatrical quality that AMORY had found in ISABELLE. MONSIGNOR DARCY would have been quite up a tree whether to call her a personality or a personage. She was perhaps the delicious, inexpressible, once-in-a-century blend.

On the night of her debut she is, for all her strange, stray wisdom, quite like a happy little girl. Her mother's maid has just done her hair, but she has decided impatiently that she can do a better job herself. She is too nervous just now to stay in one place. To that we owe her presence in this littered room. She is going to speak. ISABELLE'S alto tones had been like a violin, but if you could hear ROSALIND, you would say her voice was musical as a waterfall.)

ROSALIND: Honestly, there are only two costumes in the world that I really enjoy being in—(Combing her hair at the dressing-table.) One's a hoop skirt with pantaloons; the other's a one-piece bathing-suit. I'm quite charming in both of them.

CECELIA: Glad you're coming out?

ROSALIND: Yes; aren't you?

CECELIA: (Cynically) You're glad so you can get married and live on Long Island with the *fast younger married set.* You want life to be a chain of flirtation with a man for every link.

ROSALIND: *Want* it to be one! You mean I've *found* it one.

CECELIA: Ha!

ROSALIND: Cecelia, darling, you don't know what a trial it is to be—like me. I've got to keep my face like steel in the street to keep men from winking at me. If I laugh hard from a front row in the theatre, the comedian plays to me for the rest of the evening. If I drop my voice, my eyes, my handkerchief at a dance, my partner calls me up on the 'phone every day for a week.

CECELIA: It must be an awful strain.

ROSALIND: The unfortunate part is that the only men who interest me at all are the totally ineligible ones. Now—if I were poor I'd go on the stage.

CECELIA: Yes, you might as well get paid for the amount of acting you do.

ROSALIND: Sometimes when I've felt particularly radiant I've thought, why should this be wasted on one man?

CECELIA: Often when you're particularly sulky, I've wondered why it should all be wasted on just one family. (Getting up.) I think I'll go down and meet Mr. Amory Blaine. I like temperamental men.

ROSALIND: There aren't any. Men don't know how to be really angry or really happy—and the ones that do, go to pieces.

CECELIA: Well, I'm glad I don't have all your worries. I'm engaged.

ROSALIND: (With a scornful smile) Engaged? Why, you little lunatic! If mother heard you talking like that she'd send you off to boarding-school, where you belong.

CECELIA: You won't tell her, though, because I know things I could tell—and you're too selfish!

ROSALIND: (A little annoyed) Run along, little girl! Who are you engaged to, the iceman? the man that keeps the candy-store?

CECELIA: Cheap wit—good-by, darling, I'll see you later.

ROSALIND: Oh, be *sure* and do that—you're such a help.

(Exit CECELIA. ROSALIND finished her hair and rises, humming. She goes up to the mirror and starts to dance in front of it on the soft carpet. She watches not her feet, but her eyes—never casually but always intently, even when she smiles. The door suddenly opens and then slams behind AMORY, very cool and handsome as usual. He melts into instant confusion.)

HE: Oh, I'm sorry. I thought—

SHE: (Smiling radiantly) Oh, you're Amory Blaine, aren't you?

HE: (Regarding her closely) And you're Rosalind?

SHE: I'm going to call you Amory—oh, come in—it's all right—mother'll be right in—(under her breath) unfortunately.

HE: (Gazing around) This is sort of a new wrinkle for me.

SHE: This is No Man's Land.

HE: This is where you—you—(pause)

SHE: Yes—all those things. (She crosses to the bureau.) See, here's my rouge—eye pencils.

HE: I didn't know you were that way.

SHE: What did you expect?

HE: I thought you'd be sort of—sort of—sexless, you know, swim and play golf.

SHE: Oh, I do—but not in business hours.

HE: Business?

SHE: Six to two—strictly.

HE: I'd like to have some stock in the corporation.

SHE: Oh, it's not a corporation—it's just "Rosalind, Unlimited." Fifty-one shares, name, good-will, and everything goes at $25,000 a year.

HE: (Disapprovingly) Sort of a chilly proposition.

SHE: Well, Amory, you don't mind—do you? When I meet a man that doesn't bore me to death after two weeks, perhaps it'll be different.

HE: Odd, you have the same point of view on men that I have on women.

SHE: I'm not really feminine, you know—in my mind.

HE: (Interested) Go on.

SHE: No, you—you go on—you've made me talk about myself. That's against the rules.

HE: Rules?

SHE: My own rules—but you—Oh, Amory, I hear you're brilliant. The family expects *so* much of you.

HE: How encouraging!

SHE: Alec said you'd taught him to think. Did you? I didn't believe any one could.

HE: No. I'm really quite dull.

(He evidently doesn't intend this to be taken seriously.)

SHE: Liar.

HE: I'm—I'm religious—I'm literary. I've—I've even written poems.

SHE: Vers libre—splendid! (She declaims.)

> *"The trees are green,*
> *The birds are singing in the trees,*
> *The girl sips her poison*
> *The bird flies away the girl dies."*

HE: (Laughing) No, not that kind.

SHE: (Suddenly) I like you.

HE: Don't.

SHE: Modest too—

HE: I'm afraid of you. I'm always afraid of a girl—until I've kissed her.

SHE: (Emphatically) My dear boy, the war is over.

HE: So I'll always be afraid of you.

SHE: (Rather sadly) I suppose you will.

(A slight hesitation on both their parts.)

HE: (After due consideration) Listen. This is a frightful thing to ask.

SHE: (Knowing what's coming) After five minutes.

HE: But will you—kiss me? Or are you afraid?

SHE: I'm never afraid—but your reasons are so poor.

HE: Rosalind, I really *want* to kiss you.

SHE: So do I.

(They kiss—definitely and thoroughly.)

HE: (After a breathless second) Well, is your curiosity satisfied?

SHE: Is yours?

HE: No, it's only aroused.

(He looks it.)

SHE: (Dreamily) I've kissed dozens of men. I suppose I'll kiss dozens more.

HE: (Abstractedly) Yes, I suppose you could—like that.

SHE: Most people like the way I kiss.

HE: (Remembering himself) Good Lord, yes. Kiss me once more, Rosalind.

SHE: No—my curiosity is generally satisfied at one.

HE: (Discouraged) Is that a rule?

SHE: I make rules to fit the cases.

HE: You and I are somewhat alike—except that I'm years older in experience.

SHE: How old are you?

HE: Almost twenty-three. You?

SHE: Nineteen—just.

HE: I suppose you're the product of a fashionable school.

SHE: No—I'm fairly raw material. I was expelled from Spence—I've forgotten why.

HE: What's your general trend?

SHE: Oh, I'm bright, quite selfish, emotional when aroused, fond of admiration—

HE: (Suddenly) I don't want to fall in love with you—

SHE: (Raising her eyebrows) Nobody asked you to.

HE: (Continuing coldly) But I probably will. I love your mouth.

SHE: Hush! Please don't fall in love with my mouth—hair, eyes, shoulders, slippers—but *not* my mouth. Everybody falls in love with my mouth.

HE: It's quite beautiful.

SHE: It's too small.

HE: No it isn't—let's see.

(He kisses her again with the same thoroughness.)

SHE: (Rather moved) Say something sweet.

HE: (Frightened) Lord help me.

SHE: (Drawing away) Well, don't—if it's so hard.

HE: Shall we pretend? So soon?

SHE: We haven't the same standards of time as other people.

HE: Already it's—other people.

SHE: Let's pretend.

HE: No—I can't—it's sentiment.

SHE: You're not sentimental?

HE: No, I'm romantic—a sentimental person thinks things will last—a romantic person hopes against hope that they won't. Sentiment is emotional.

SHE: And you're not? (With her eyes half-closed.) You probably flatter yourself that that's a superior attitude.

HE: Well—Rosalind, Rosalind, don't argue—kiss me again.

SHE: (Quite chilly now) No—I have no desire to kiss you.

HE: (Openly taken aback) You wanted to kiss me a minute ago.

SHE: This is now.

HE: I'd better go.

SHE: I suppose so.

(He goes toward the door.)

SHE: Oh!

(He turns.)

SHE: (Laughing) Score—Home Team: One hundred—Opponents: Zero.

(He starts back.)

SHE: (Quickly) Rain—no game.

(He goes out.)

(She goes quietly to the chiffonier, takes out a cigarette-case and hides it in the side drawer of a desk. Her mother enters, note-book in hand.)

MRS. CONNAGE: Good—I've been wanting to speak to you alone before we go down-stairs.

ROSALIND: Heavens! you frighten me!

MRS. CONNAGE: Rosalind, you've been a very expensive proposition.

ROSALIND: (Resignedly) Yes.

MRS. CONNAGE: And you know your father hasn't what he once had.

ROSALIND: (Making a wry face) Oh, please don't talk about money.

MRS. CONNAGE: You can't do anything without it. This is our last year in this house—and unless things change Cecelia won't have the advantages you've had.

ROSALIND: (Impatiently) Well—what is it?

MRS. CONNAGE: So I ask you to please mind me in several things I've put down in my note-book. The first one is: don't disappear with young men. There may be a time when it's valuable, but at present I want you on the dance-floor where I can find you. There are certain men I want to have you meet and I don't like finding you in some corner of the conservatory exchanging silliness with any one—or listening to it.

ROSALIND: (Sarcastically) Yes, listening to it *is* better.

MRS. CONNAGE: And don't waste a lot of time with the college set—little boys nineteen and twenty years old. I don't mind a prom or a football game, but staying away from advantageous parties to eat in little cafes down-town with Tom, Dick, and Harry—

ROSALIND: (Offering her code, which is, in its way, quite as high as her mother's) Mother, it's done—you can't run everything now the way you did in the early nineties.

MRS. CONNAGE: (Paying no attention) There are several bachelor friends of your father's that I want you to meet to-night—youngish men.

ROSALIND: (Nodding wisely) About forty-five?

MRS. CONNAGE: (Sharply) Why not?

ROSALIND: Oh, *quite* all right—they know life and are so adorably tired looking (shakes her head)—but they *will* dance.

MRS. CONNAGE: I haven't met Mr. Blaine—but I don't think you'll care for him. He doesn't sound like a money-maker.

ROSALIND: Mother, I never *think* about money.

MRS. CONNAGE: You never keep it long enough to think about it.

ROSALIND: (Sighs) Yes, I suppose some day I'll marry a ton of it—out of sheer boredom.

MRS. CONNAGE: (Referring to note-book) I had a wire from Hartford. Dawson Ryder is coming up. Now there's a young man I like, and he's floating in money. It seems to me that since you seem tired of Howard Gillespie you might give Mr. Ryder some encouragement. This is the third time he's been up in a month.

ROSALIND: How did you know I was tired of Howard Gillespie?

MRS. CONNAGE: The poor boy looks so miserable every time he comes.

ROSALIND: That was one of those romantic, pre-battle affairs. They're all wrong.

MRS. CONNAGE: (Her say said) At any rate, make us proud of you to-night.

ROSALIND: Don't you think I'm beautiful?

MRS. CONNAGE: You know you are.

(From down-stairs is heard the moan of a violin being tuned, the roll of a drum. MRS. CONNAGE turns quickly to her daughter.)

MRS. CONNAGE: Come!

ROSALIND: One minute!

(Her mother leaves. ROSALIND goes to the glass where she gazes at herself with great satisfaction. She kisses her hand and touches her mirrored mouth with it. Then she turns out the lights and leaves the room. Silence for a moment. A few chords from the piano, the discreet patter of faint drums, the rustle of new silk, all blend on the staircase outside and drift in through the partly opened door. Bundled figures pass in the lighted hall. The laughter heard below becomes doubled and multiplied. Then some one comes in, closes the door, and switches on the lights. It is CECELIA. She goes to the chiffonier, looks in the drawers, hesitates—then to the desk whence she takes the cigarette-case and extracts one. She lights it and then, puffing and blowing, walks toward the mirror.)

CECELIA: (In tremendously sophisticated accents) Oh, yes, coming out is *such* a farce nowadays, you know. One really plays around so much before one is seventeen, that it's positively anticlimax. (Shaking hands with a visionary middle-aged nobleman.) Yes, your grace—I b'lieve I've heard my sister speak of you. Have a puff—they're very good. They're—they're Coronas. You don't smoke? What a pity! The king doesn't allow it, I suppose. Yes, I'll dance.

(So she dances around the room to a tune from down-stairs, her arms outstretched to an imaginary partner, the cigarette waving in her hand.)

SEVERAL HOURS LATER

The corner of a den down-stairs, filled by a very comfortable leather lounge. A small light is on each side above, and in the middle, over the couch hangs a painting of a very old, very dignified gentleman, period 1860. Outside the music is heard in a fox-trot.

ROSALIND is seated on the lounge and on her left is HOWARD GILLESPIE, a vapid youth of about twenty-four. He is obviously very unhappy, and she is quite bored.

GILLESPIE: (Feebly) What do you mean I've changed. I feel the same toward you.

ROSALIND: But you don't look the same to me.

GILLESPIE: Three weeks ago you used to say that you liked me because I was so blasé, so indifferent—I still am.

ROSALIND: But not about me. I used to like you because you had brown eyes and thin legs.

GILLESPIE: (Helplessly) They're still thin and brown. You're a vampire, that's all.

ROSALIND: The only thing I know about vamping is what's on the piano score. What confuses men is that I'm perfectly natural. I used to think you were never jealous. Now you follow me with your eyes wherever I go.

GILLESPIE: I love you.

ROSALIND: (Coldly) I know it.

GILLESPIE: And you haven't kissed me for two weeks. I had an idea that after a girl was kissed she was—was—won.

ROSALIND: Those days are over. I have to be won all over again every time you see me.

GILLESPIE: Are you serious?

ROSALIND: About as usual. There used to be two kinds of kisses: First when girls were kissed and deserted; second, when they were engaged. Now there's a third kind, where the man is kissed and deserted. If Mr. Jones of the nineties bragged he'd kissed a girl, every one knew he was through with her. If Mr. Jones of 1919 brags the same every one knows it's because he can't kiss her any more. Given a decent start any girl can beat a man nowadays.

GILLESPIE: Then why do you play with men?

ROSALIND: (Leaning forward confidentially) For that first moment, when he's interested. There is a moment—Oh, just before the first kiss, a whispered word—something that makes it worth while.

GILLESPIE: And then?

ROSALIND: Then after that you make him talk about himself. Pretty soon he thinks of nothing but being alone with you—he sulks, he won't fight, he doesn't want to play—Victory!

(Enter DAWSON RYDER, twenty-six, handsome, wealthy, faithful to his own, a bore perhaps, but steady and sure of success.)

RYDER: I believe this is my dance, Rosalind.

ROSALIND: Well, Dawson, so you recognize me. Now I know I haven't got too much paint on. Mr. Ryder, this is Mr. Gillespie.

(They shake hands and GILLESPIE leaves, tremendously downcast.)

RYDER: Your party is certainly a success.

ROSALIND: Is it—I haven't seen it lately. I'm weary—Do you mind sitting out a minute?

RYDER: Mind—I'm delighted. You know I loathe this "rushing" idea. See a girl yesterday, to-day, to-morrow.

ROSALIND: Dawson!

RYDER: What?

ROSALIND: I wonder if you know you love me.

RYDER: (Startled) What—Oh—you know you're remarkable!

ROSALIND: Because you know I'm an awful proposition. Any one who marries me will have his hands full. I'm mean—mighty mean.

RYDER: Oh, I wouldn't say that.

ROSALIND: Oh, yes, I am—especially to the people nearest to me. (She rises.) Come, let's go. I've changed my mind and I want to dance. Mother is probably having a fit.

(Exeunt. Enter ALEC and CECELIA.)

CECELIA: Just my luck to get my own brother for an intermission.

ALEC: (Gloomily) I'll go if you want me to.

CECELIA: Good heavens, no—with whom would I begin the next dance? (Sighs.) There's no color in a dance since the French officers went back.

ALEC: (Thoughtfully) I don't want Amory to fall in love with Rosalind.

CECELIA: Why, I had an idea that that was just what you did want.

ALEC: I did, but since seeing these girls—I don't know. I'm awfully attached to Amory. He's sensitive and I don't want him to break his heart over somebody who doesn't care about him.

CECELIA: He's very good looking.

ALEC: (Still thoughtfully) She won't marry him, but a girl doesn't have to marry a man to break his heart.

CECELIA: What does it? I wish I knew the secret.

ALEC: Why, you cold-blooded little kitty. It's lucky for some that the Lord gave you a pug nose.

(Enter MRS. CONNAGE.)

MRS. CONNAGE: Where on earth is Rosalind?

ALEC: (Brilliantly) Of course you've come to the best people to find out. She'd naturally be with us.

MRS. CONNAGE: Her father has marshalled eight bachelor millionaires to meet her.

ALEC: You might form a squad and march through the halls.

MRS. CONNAGE: I'm perfectly serious—for all I know she may be at the Cocoanut Grove with some football player on the night of her debut. You look left and I'll—

ALEC: (Flippantly) Hadn't you better send the butler through the cellar?

MRS. CONNAGE: (Perfectly serious) Oh, you don't think she'd be there?

CECELIA: He's only joking, mother.

ALEC: Mother had a picture of her tapping a keg of beer with some high hurdler.

MRS. CONNAGE: Let's look right away.

(They go out. ROSALIND comes in with GILLESPIE.)

GILLESPIE: Rosalind—Once more I ask you. Don't you care a blessed thing about me?

(AMORY walks in briskly.)

AMORY: My dance.

ROSALIND: Mr. Gillespie, this is Mr. Blaine.

GILLESPIE: I've met Mr. Blaine. From Lake Geneva, aren't you?

AMORY: Yes.

GILLESPIE: (Desperately) I've been there. It's in the—the Middle West, isn't it?

AMORY: (Spicily) Approximately. But I always felt that I'd rather be provincial hot-tamale than soup without seasoning.

GILLESPIE: What!

AMORY: Oh, no offense.

(GILLESPIE bows and leaves.)

ROSALIND: He's too much *people.*

AMORY: I was in love with a *people* once.

ROSALIND: So?

AMORY: Oh, yes—her name was Isabelle—nothing at all to her except what I read into her.

ROSALIND: What happened?

AMORY: Finally I convinced her that she was smarter than I was—then she threw me over. Said I was critical and impractical, you know.

ROSALIND: What do you mean impractical?

AMORY: Oh—drive a car, but can't change a tire.

ROSALIND: What are you going to do?

AMORY: Can't say—run for President, write—

ROSALIND: Greenwich Village?

AMORY: Good heavens, no—I said write—not drink.

ROSALIND: I like business men. Clever men are usually so homely.

AMORY: I feel as if I'd known you for ages.

ROSALIND: Oh, are you going to commence the "pyramid" story?

AMORY: No—I was going to make it French. I was Louis XIV and you were one of my—my—(Changing his tone.) Suppose—we fell in love.

ROSALIND: I've suggested pretending.

AMORY: If we did it would be very big.

ROSALIND: Why?

AMORY: Because selfish people are in a way terribly capable of great loves.

ROSALIND: (Turning her lips up) Pretend.

(Very deliberately they kiss.)

AMORY: I can't say sweet things. But you *are* beautiful.

ROSALIND: Not that.

AMORY: What then?

ROSALIND: (Sadly) Oh, nothing—only I want sentiment, real sentiment—and I never find it.

AMORY: I never find anything else in the world—and I loathe it.

ROSALIND: It's so hard to find a male to gratify one's artistic taste.

(Some one has opened a door and the music of a waltz surges into the room. ROSALIND rises.)

ROSALIND: Listen! they're playing "Kiss Me Again."

(He looks at her.)

AMORY: Well?

ROSALIND: Well?

AMORY: (Softly—the battle lost) I love you.

ROSALIND: I love you—now.

(They kiss.)

AMORY: Oh, God, what have I done?

ROSALIND: Nothing. Oh, don't talk. Kiss me again.

AMORY: I don't know why or how, but I love you—from the moment I saw you.

ROSALIND: Me too—I—I—oh, to-night's to-night.

(Her brother strolls in, starts and then in a loud voice says: "Oh, excuse me," and goes.)

ROSALIND: (Her lips scarcely stirring) Don't let me go—I don't care who knows what I do.

AMORY: Say it!

ROSALIND: I love you—now. (They part.) Oh—I am very youthful, thank God—and rather beautiful, thank God—and happy, thank God, thank God—(She pauses and then, in an odd burst of prophecy, adds) Poor Amory!

(He kisses her again.)

KISMET

Within two weeks Amory and Rosalind were deeply and passionately in love. The critical qualities which had spoiled for each of them a dozen romances were dulled by the great wave of emotion that washed over them.

"It may be an insane love-affair," she told her anxious mother, "but it's not inane."

The wave swept Amory into an advertising agency early in March, where he alternated between astonishing bursts of rather exceptional work and wild dreams of becoming suddenly rich and touring Italy with Rosalind.

They were together constantly, for lunch, for dinner, and nearly every evening—always in a sort of breathless hush, as if they feared that any minute the spell would break and drop them out of this paradise of rose and flame. But the spell became a trance, seemed to increase from day to day; they began to talk of marrying in July—in June. All life was transmitted into terms of their love, all experience, all desires, all ambitions, were nullified—their senses of humor crawled into corners to sleep; their former love-affairs seemed faintly laughable and scarcely regretted juvenalia.

For the second time in his life Amory had had a complete bouleversement and was hurrying into line with his generation.

A LITTLE INTERLUDE

Amory wandered slowly up the avenue and thought of the night as inevitably his—the pageantry and carnival of rich dusk and dim streets ... it seemed that he had closed the book of fading harmonies at last and stepped into the sensuous vibrant walks of life. Everywhere these countless lights, this promise of a night of streets and singing—he moved in a half-dream through the crowd as if expecting to meet Rosalind hurrying toward him with eager feet from every corner.... How the unforgettable faces of dusk would blend to her, the myriad footsteps, a thousand overtures, would blend to her footsteps; and there would be more drunkenness than wine in the softness of her eyes on his. Even his dreams now were faint violins drifting like summer sounds upon the summer air.

The room was in darkness except for the faint glow of Tom's cigarette where he lounged by the open window. As the door shut behind him, Amory stood a moment with his back against it.

"Hello, Benvenuto Blaine. How went the advertising business to-day?"

Amory sprawled on a couch.

"I loathed it as usual!" The momentary vision of the bustling agency was displaced quickly by another picture.

"My God! She's wonderful!"

Tom sighed.

"I can't tell you," repeated Amory, "just how wonderful she is. I don't want you to know. I don't want any one to know."

Another sigh came from the window—quite a resigned sigh.

"She's life and hope and happiness, my whole world now."

He felt the quiver of a tear on his eyelid.

"Oh, *Golly*, Tom!"

BITTER SWEET

"Sit like we do," she whispered.

He sat in the big chair and held out his arms so that she could nestle inside them.

"I knew you'd come to-night," she said softly, "like summer, just when I needed you most... darling... darling..."

His lips moved lazily over her face.

"You *taste* so good," he sighed.

"How do you mean, lover?"

"Oh, just sweet, just sweet..." he held her closer.

"Amory," she whispered, "when you're ready for me I'll marry you."

"We won't have much at first."

"Don't!" she cried. "It hurts when you reproach yourself for what you can't give me. I've got your precious self—and that's enough for me."

"Tell me..."

"You know, don't you? Oh, you know."

"Yes, but I want to hear you say it."

"I love you, Amory, with all my heart."

"Always, will you?"

"All my life—Oh, Amory—"

"What?"

"I want to belong to you. I want your people to be my people. I want to have your babies."

"But I haven't any people."

"Don't laugh at me, Amory. Just kiss me."

"I'll do what you want," he said.

"No, I'll do what *you* want. We're *you*—not me. Oh, you're so much a part, so much all of me..."

He closed his eyes.

"I'm so happy that I'm frightened. Wouldn't it be awful if this was—was the high point?..."

She looked at him dreamily.

"Beauty and love pass, I know.... Oh, there's sadness, too. I suppose all great happiness is a little sad. Beauty means the scent of roses and then the death of roses—"

"Beauty means the agony of sacrifice and the end of agony...."

"And, Amory, we're beautiful, I know. I'm sure God loves us—"

"He loves you. You're his most precious possession."

"I'm not his, I'm yours. Amory, I belong to you. For the first time I regret all the other kisses; now I know how much a kiss can mean."

Then they would smoke and he would tell her about his day at the office—and where they might live. Sometimes, when he was particularly loquacious, she went to sleep in his arms, but he loved that Rosalind—all Rosalinds—as he had never in the world loved any one else. Intangibly fleeting, unrememberable hours.

AQUATIC INCIDENT

One day Amory and Howard Gillespie meeting by accident down-town took lunch together, and Amory heard a story that delighted him. Gillespie after several cocktails was in a talkative mood; he began by telling Amory that he was sure Rosalind was slightly eccentric.

He had gone with her on a swimming party up in Westchester County, and some one mentioned that Annette Kellerman had been there one day on a visit and had dived from the top of a rickety, thirty-foot summer-house. Immediately Rosalind insisted that Howard should climb up with her to see what it looked like.

A minute later, as he sat and dangled his feet on the edge, a form shot by him; Rosalind, her arms spread in a beautiful swan dive, had sailed through the air into the clear water.

"Of course *I* had to go, after that—and I nearly killed myself. I thought I was pretty good to even try it. Nobody else in the party tried it. Well, afterward Rosalind had the nerve to ask me why I stooped over when I dove. 'It didn't make it any easier,' she said, 'it just took all the courage out of it.' I ask you, what can a man do with a girl like that? Unnecessary, I call it."

Gillespie failed to understand why Amory was smiling delightedly all through lunch. He thought perhaps he was one of these hollow optimists.

FIVE WEEKS LATER

Again the library of the Connage house. ROSALIND is alone, sitting on the lounge staring very moodily and unhappily at nothing. She has changed perceptibly—she is a trifle thinner for one thing; the light in her eyes is not so bright; she looks easily a year older.

Her mother comes in, muffled in an opera-cloak. She takes in ROSALIND with a nervous glance.

MRS. CONNAGE: Who is coming to-night?

(ROSALIND fails to hear her, at least takes no notice.)

MRS. CONNAGE: Alec is coming up to take me to this Barrie play, "Et tu, Brutus." (She perceives that she is talking to herself.) Rosalind! I asked you who is coming to-night?

ROSALIND: (Starting) Oh—what—oh—Amory—

MRS. CONNAGE: (Sarcastically) You have so *many* admirers lately that I couldn't imagine *which* one. (ROSALIND doesn't answer.) Dawson Ryder is more patient than I thought he'd be. You haven't given him an evening this week.

ROSALIND: (With a very weary expression that is quite new to her face.) Mother—please—

MRS. CONNAGE: Oh, *I* won't interfere. You've already wasted over two months on a theoretical genius who hasn't a penny to his name, but *go* ahead, waste your life on him. *I* won't interfere.

ROSALIND: (As if repeating a tiresome lesson) You know he has a little income—and you know he's earning thirty-five dollars a week in advertising—

MRS. CONNAGE: And it wouldn't buy your clothes. (She pauses but ROSALIND makes no reply.) I have your best interests at heart when I tell you not to take a step you'll spend your days regretting. It's not as if your father could help you. Things have been hard for him lately and he's an old man. You'd be dependent absolutely on a dreamer, a nice, well-born boy, but a dreamer—merely *clever*. (She implies that this quality in itself is rather vicious.)

ROSALIND: For heaven's sake, mother—

(A maid appears, announces Mr. Blaine who follows immediately. AMORY'S friends have been telling him for ten days that he "looks like the wrath of God," and he does. As a matter of fact he has not been able to eat a mouthful in the last thirty-six hours.)

AMORY: Good evening, Mrs. Connage.

MRS. CONNAGE: (Not unkindly) Good evening, Amory.

(AMORY and ROSALIND exchange glances—and ALEC comes in. ALEC'S attitude throughout has been neutral. He believes in his heart that the marriage would make AMORY mediocre and ROSALIND miserable, but he feels a great sympathy for both of them.)

ALEC: Hi, Amory!

AMORY: Hi, Alec! Tom said he'd meet you at the theatre.

ALEC: Yeah, just saw him. How's the advertising to-day? Write some brilliant copy?

AMORY: Oh, it's about the same. I got a raise—(Every one looks at him rather eagerly)—of two dollars a week. (General collapse.)

MRS. CONNAGE: Come, Alec, I hear the car.

(A good night, rather chilly in sections. After MRS. CONNAGE and ALEC go out there is a pause. ROSALIND still stares moodily at the fireplace. AMORY goes to her and puts his arm around her.)

AMORY: Darling girl.

(They kiss. Another pause and then she seizes his hand, covers it with kisses and holds it to her breast.)

ROSALIND: (Sadly) I love your hands, more than anything. I see them often when you're away from me—so tired; I know every line of them. Dear hands!

(Their eyes meet for a second and then she begins to cry—a tearless sobbing.)

AMORY: Rosalind!

ROSALIND: Oh, we're so darned pitiful!

AMORY: Rosalind!

ROSALIND: Oh, I want to die!

AMORY: Rosalind, another night of this and I'll go to pieces. You've been this way four days now. You've got to be more encouraging or I can't work or eat or sleep. (He looks around helplessly as if searching for new words to clothe an old, shopworn phrase.) We'll have to make a start. I like having to make a start together. (His forced hopefulness fades as he sees her unresponsive.) What's the matter? (He gets up suddenly and starts to pace the floor.) It's Dawson Ryder, that's what it is. He's been working on your nerves. You've been with him every afternoon for a week. People come and tell me they've seen you together, and I have to smile and nod and pretend it hasn't the slightest significance for me. And you won't tell me anything as it develops.

ROSALIND: Amory, if you don't sit down I'll scream.

AMORY: (Sitting down suddenly beside her) Oh, Lord.

ROSALIND: (Taking his hand gently) You know I love you, don't you?

AMORY: Yes.

ROSALIND: You know I'll always love you—

AMORY: Don't talk that way; you frighten me. It sounds as if we weren't going to have each other. (She cries a little and rising from the couch goes to the armchair.) I've felt all afternoon that things were worse. I nearly went wild down at the office—couldn't write a line. Tell me everything.

ROSALIND: There's nothing to tell, I say. I'm just nervous.

AMORY: Rosalind, you're playing with the idea of marrying Dawson Ryder.

ROSALIND: (After a pause) He's been asking me to all day.

AMORY: Well, he's got his nerve!

ROSALIND: (After another pause) I like him.

AMORY: Don't say that. It hurts me.

ROSALIND: Don't be a silly idiot. You know you're the only man I've ever loved, ever will love.

AMORY: (Quickly) Rosalind, let's get married—next week.

ROSALIND: We can't.

AMORY: Why not?

ROSALIND: Oh, we can't. I'd be your squaw—in some horrible place.

AMORY: We'll have two hundred and seventy-five dollars a month all told.

ROSALIND: Darling, I don't even do my own hair, usually.

AMORY: I'll do it for you.

ROSALIND: (Between a laugh and a sob) Thanks.

AMORY: Rosalind, you *can't* be thinking of marrying some one else. Tell me! You leave me in the dark. I can help you fight it out if you'll only tell me.

ROSALIND: It's just—us. We're pitiful, that's all. The very qualities I love you for are the ones that will always make you a failure.

AMORY: (Grimly) Go on.

ROSALIND: Oh—it *is* Dawson Ryder. He's so reliable, I almost feel that he'd be a—a background.

AMORY: You don't love him.

ROSALIND: I know, but I respect him, and he's a good man and a strong one.

AMORY: (Grudgingly) Yes—he's that.

ROSALIND: Well—here's one little thing. There was a little poor boy we met in Rye Tuesday afternoon—and, oh, Dawson took him on his lap and talked to him and promised him an Indian suit—and next day he remembered and bought it—and, oh, it was so sweet and I couldn't help thinking he'd be so nice to—to our children—take care of them—and I wouldn't have to worry.

AMORY: (In despair) Rosalind! Rosalind!

ROSALIND: (With a faint roguishness) Don't look so consciously suffering.

AMORY: What power we have of hurting each other!

ROSALIND: (Commencing to sob again) It's been so perfect—you and I. So like a dream that I'd longed for and never thought I'd find. The first real unselfishness I've ever felt in my life. And I can't see it fade out in a colorless atmosphere!

AMORY: It won't—it won't!

ROSALIND: I'd rather keep it as a beautiful memory—tucked away in my heart.

AMORY: Yes, women can do that—but not men. I'd remember always, not the beauty of it while it lasted, but just the bitterness, the long bitterness.

ROSALIND: Don't!

AMORY: All the years never to see you, never to kiss you, just a gate shut and barred—you don't dare be my wife.

ROSALIND: No—no—I'm taking the hardest course, the strongest course. Marrying you would be a failure and I never fail—if you don't stop walking up and down I'll scream!

(Again he sinks despairingly onto the lounge.)

AMORY: Come over here and kiss me.

ROSALIND: No.

AMORY: Don't you *want* to kiss me?

ROSALIND: To-night I want you to love me calmly and coolly.

AMORY: The beginning of the end.

ROSALIND: (With a burst of insight) Amory, you're young. I'm young. People excuse us now for our poses and vanities, for treating people like Sancho and yet getting away with it. They excuse us now. But you've got a lot of knocks coming to you—

AMORY: And you're afraid to take them with me.

ROSALIND: No, not that. There was a poem I read somewhere—you'll say Ella Wheeler Wilcox and laugh—but listen:

"For this is wisdom—to love and live,
To take what fate or the gods may give,
To ask no question, to make no prayer,
To kiss the lips and caress the hair,
Speed passion's ebb as we greet its flow,
To have and to hold, and, in time—let go."

AMORY: But we haven't had.

ROSALIND: Amory, I'm yours—you know it. There have been times in the last month I'd have been completely yours if you'd said so. But I can't marry you and ruin both our lives.

AMORY: We've got to take our chance for happiness.

ROSALIND: Dawson says I'd learn to love him.

(AMORY with his head sunk in his hands does not move. The life seems suddenly gone out of him.)

ROSALIND: Lover! Lover! I can't do with you, and I can't imagine life without you.

AMORY: Rosalind, we're on each other's nerves. It's just that we're both high-strung, and this week—

(His voice is curiously old. She crosses to him and taking his face in her hands, kisses him.)

ROSALIND: I can't, Amory. I can't be shut away from the trees and flowers, cooped up in a little flat, waiting for you. You'd hate me in a narrow atmosphere. I'd make you hate me.

(Again she is blinded by sudden uncontrolled tears.)

AMORY: Rosalind—

ROSALIND: Oh, darling, go—Don't make it harder! I can't stand it—

AMORY: (His face drawn, his voice strained) Do you know what you're saying? Do you mean forever?

(There is a difference somehow in the quality of their suffering.)

ROSALIND: Can't you see—

AMORY: I'm afraid I can't if you love me. You're afraid of taking two years' knocks with me.

ROSALIND: I wouldn't be the Rosalind you love.

AMORY: (A little hysterically) I can't give you up! I can't, that's all! I've got to have you!

ROSALIND: (A hard note in her voice) You're being a baby now.

AMORY: (Wildly) I don't care! You're spoiling our lives!

ROSALIND: I'm doing the wise thing, the only thing.

AMORY: Are you going to marry Dawson Ryder?

ROSALIND: Oh, don't ask me. You know I'm old in some ways—in others—well, I'm just a little girl. I like sunshine and pretty things and cheerfulness—and I dread responsibility. I don't want to think about pots and kitchens and brooms. I want to worry whether my legs will get slick and brown when I swim in the summer.

AMORY: And you love me.

ROSALIND: That's just why it has to end. Drifting hurts too much. We can't have any more scenes like this.

(She draws his ring from her finger and hands it to him. Their eyes blind again with tears.)

AMORY: (His lips against her wet cheek) Don't! Keep it, please—oh, don't break my heart!

(She presses the ring softly into his hand.)

ROSALIND: (Brokenly) You'd better go.

AMORY: Good-by—

(She looks at him once more, with infinite longing, infinite sadness.)

ROSALIND: Don't ever forget me, Amory—

AMORY: Good-by—

(He goes to the door, fumbles for the knob, finds it—she sees him throw back his head—and he is gone. Gone—she half starts from the lounge and then sinks forward on her face into the pillows.)

ROSALIND: Oh, God, I want to die! (After a moment she rises and with her eyes closed feels her way to the door. Then she turns and looks once more at the room. Here they had sat and dreamed: that tray she had so often filled with matches for him; that shade that they had discreetly lowered one long Sunday afternoon. Misty-eyed she stands and remembers; she speaks aloud.) Oh, Amory, what have I done to you?

(And deep under the aching sadness that will pass in time, Rosalind feels that she has lost something, she knows not what, she knows not why.)

II. Experiments in Convalescence

The Knickerbocker Bar, beamed upon by Maxfield Parrish's jovial, colorful "Old King Cole," was well crowded. Amory stopped in the entrance and looked at his wrist-watch; he wanted particularly to know the time, for something in his mind that catalogued and classified liked to chip things off cleanly. Later it would satisfy him in a vague way to be able to think "that thing ended at exactly twenty minutes after eight on Thursday, June 10, 1919." This was allowing for the walk from her house—a walk concerning which he had afterward not the faintest recollection.

He was in rather grotesque condition: two days of worry and nervousness, of sleepless nights, of untouched meals, culminating in the emotional crisis and Rosalind's abrupt decision—the strain of it had drugged the foreground of his mind into a merciful coma. As he fumbled clumsily with the olives at the free-lunch table, a man approached and spoke to him, and the olives dropped from his nervous hands.

"Well, Amory..."

It was some one he had known at Princeton; he had no idea of the name.

"Hello, old boy—" he heard himself saying.

"Name's Jim Wilson—you've forgotten."

"Sure, you bet, Jim. I remember."

"Going to reunion?"

"You know!" Simultaneously he realized that he was not going to reunion.

"Get overseas?"

Amory nodded, his eyes staring oddly. Stepping back to let some one pass, he knocked the dish of olives to a crash on the floor.

"Too bad," he muttered. "Have a drink?"

Wilson, ponderously diplomatic, reached over and slapped him on the back.

"You've had plenty, old boy."

Amory eyed him dumbly until Wilson grew embarrassed under the scrutiny.

"Plenty, hell!" said Amory finally. "I haven't had a drink to-day."

Wilson looked incredulous.

"Have a drink or not?" cried Amory rudely.

Together they sought the bar.

"Rye high."

"I'll just take a Bronx."

Wilson had another; Amory had several more. They decided to sit down. At ten o'clock Wilson was displaced by Carling, class of '15. Amory, his head spinning gorgeously, layer upon layer of soft satisfaction setting over the bruised spots of his spirit, was discoursing volubly on the war.

"'S a mental was'e," he insisted with owl-like wisdom. "Two years my life spent inalleshual vacuity. Los' idealism, got be physcal anmal," he shook his fist expressively at Old King Cole, "got be Prussian 'bout ev'thing, women 'specially. Use' be straight 'bout women college. Now don'givadam." He expressed his lack of principle by sweeping a seltzer bottle with a broad gesture to noisy extinction on the floor, but this did not interrupt his speech. "Seek pleasure where find it for to-morrow die. 'At's philos'phy for me now on."

Carling yawned, but Amory, waxing brilliant, continued:

"Use' wonder 'bout things—people satisfied compromise, fif'y-fif'y att'tude on life. Now don' wonder, don' wonder—" He became so emphatic in impressing on Carling the fact that he didn't wonder that he lost the thread of his discourse and concluded by announcing to the bar at large that he was a "physcal anmal."

"What are you celebrating, Amory?"

Amory leaned forward confidentially.

"Cel'brating blowmylife. Great moment blow my life. Can't tell you 'bout it—"

He heard Carling addressing a remark to the bartender:

"Give him a bromo-seltzer."

Amory shook his head indignantly.

"None that stuff!"

"But listen, Amory, you're making yourself sick. You're white as a ghost."

Amory considered the question. He tried to look at himself in the mirror but even by squinting up one eye could only see as far as the row of bottles behind the bar.

"Like som'n solid. We go get some—some salad."

He settled his coat with an attempt at nonchalance, but letting go of the bar was too much for him, and he slumped against a chair.

"We'll go over to Shanley's," suggested Carling, offering an elbow.

With this assistance Amory managed to get his legs in motion enough to propel him across Forty-second Street.

Shanley's was very dim. He was conscious that he was talking in a loud voice, very succinctly and convincingly, he thought, about a desire to crush people under his heel. He consumed three club sandwiches, devouring each as though it were no larger than a chocolate-drop. Then Rosalind began popping into his mind again, and he found his lips forming her name over and over. Next he was sleepy, and he had a hazy, listless sense of people in dress suits, probably waiters, gathering around the table....

... He was in a room and Carling was saying something about a knot in his shoe-lace.

"Nemmine," he managed to articulate drowsily. "Sleep in 'em...."

STILL ALCOHOLIC

He awoke laughing and his eyes lazily roamed his surroundings, evidently a bedroom and bath in a good hotel. His head was whirring and picture after picture was forming and blurring and melting before his eyes, but beyond the desire to laugh he had no entirely conscious reaction. He reached for the 'phone beside his bed.

"Hello—what hotel is this—?

"Knickerbocker? All right, send up two rye high-balls—"

He lay for a moment and wondered idly whether they'd send up a bottle or just two of those little glass containers. Then, with an effort, he struggled out of bed and ambled into the bathroom.

When he emerged, rubbing himself lazily with a towel, he found the bar boy with the drinks and had a sudden desire to kid him. On reflection he decided that this would be undignified, so he waved him away.

As the new alcohol tumbled into his stomach and warmed him, the isolated pictures began slowly to form a cinema reel of the day before. Again he saw Rosalind curled weeping among the pillows, again he felt her tears against his cheek. Her words began ringing in his ears: "Don't ever forget me, Amory—don't ever forget me—"

"Hell!" he faltered aloud, and then he choked and collapsed on the bed in a shaken spasm of grief. After a minute he opened his eyes and regarded the ceiling.

"Damned fool!" he exclaimed in disgust, and with a voluminous sigh rose and approached the bottle. After another glass he gave way loosely to the luxury of tears. Purposely he called up into his mind little incidents of the vanished spring, phrased to himself emotions that would make him react even more strongly to sorrow.

"We were so happy," he intoned dramatically, "so very happy." Then he gave way again and knelt beside the bed, his head half-buried in the pillow.

"My own girl—my own—Oh—"

He clinched his teeth so that the tears streamed in a flood from his eyes.

"Oh... my baby girl, all I had, all I wanted!... Oh, my girl, come back, come back! I need you... need you... we're so pitiful ... just misery we brought each other.... She'll be shut away from me.... I can't see her; I can't be her friend. It's got to be that way—it's got to be—"

And then again:

"We've been so happy, so very happy...."

He rose to his feet and threw himself on the bed in an ecstasy of sentiment, and then lay exhausted while he realized slowly that he had been very drunk the night before, and that his head was spinning again wildly. He laughed, rose, and crossed again to Lethe....

At noon he ran into a crowd in the Biltmore bar, and the riot began again. He had a vague recollection afterward of discussing French poetry with a British officer who was introduced to him as "Captain Corn, of his Majesty's Foot," and he remembered attempting to recite "Clair de Lune" at luncheon; then he slept in a big, soft chair until almost five o'clock when another crowd found and woke him; there followed an alcoholic dressing of several temperaments for the ordeal of dinner. They selected theatre tickets at Tyson's for a play that had a four-drink programme—a play with two monotonous voices, with turbid, gloomy scenes, and lighting effects that were hard to follow when his eyes behaved so amazingly. He imagined afterward that it must have been "The Jest."...

... Then the Cocoanut Grove, where Amory slept again on a little balcony outside. Out in Shanley's, Yonkers, he became almost logical, and by a careful control of the number of high-balls he drank, grew quite lucid and garrulous. He found that the party consisted of five men, two of whom he knew slightly; he became righteous about paying his share of the expense and insisted in a loud voice on arranging everything then and there to the amusement of the tables around him....

Some one mentioned that a famous cabaret star was at the next table, so Amory rose and, approaching gallantly, introduced himself... this involved him in an argument, first with her escort and then with the headwaiter—Amory's attitude being a lofty and exaggerated courtesy... he consented, after being confronted with irrefutable logic, to being led back to his own table.

"Decided to commit suicide," he announced suddenly.

"When? Next year?"

"Now. To-morrow morning. Going to take a room at the Commodore, get into a hot bath and open a vein."

"He's getting morbid!"

"You need another rye, old boy!"

"We'll all talk it over to-morrow."

But Amory was not to be dissuaded, from argument at least.

"Did you ever get that way?" he demanded confidentially fortaccio.

"Sure!"

"Often?"

"My chronic state."

This provoked discussion. One man said that he got so depressed sometimes that he seriously considered it. Another agreed that there was nothing to live for. "Captain Corn," who had somehow rejoined the party, said that in his opinion it was when one's health was bad that one felt that way most. Amory's suggestion was that they should each order a Bronx, mix broken glass in it, and drink it off. To his relief no one applauded the idea, so having finished his high-ball, he balanced his chin in his hand and his elbow on the table—a most delicate, scarcely noticeable sleeping position, he assured himself—and went into a deep stupor....

He was awakened by a woman clinging to him, a pretty woman, with brown, disarranged hair and dark blue eyes.

"Take me home!" she cried.

"Hello!" said Amory, blinking.

"I like you," she announced tenderly.

"I like you too."

He noticed that there was a noisy man in the background and that one of his party was arguing with him.

"Fella I was with's a damn fool," confided the blue-eyed woman. "I hate him. I want to go home with you."

"You drunk?" queried Amory with intense wisdom.

She nodded coyly.

"Go home with him," he advised gravely. "He brought you."

At this point the noisy man in the background broke away from his detainers and approached.

"Say!" he said fiercely. "I brought this girl out here and you're butting in!"

Amory regarded him coldly, while the girl clung to him closer.

"You let go that girl!" cried the noisy man.

Amory tried to make his eyes threatening.

"You go to hell!" he directed finally, and turned his attention to the girl.

"Love first sight," he suggested.

"I love you," she breathed and nestled close to him. She *did* have beautiful eyes.

Some one leaned over and spoke in Amory's ear.

"That's just Margaret Diamond. She's drunk and this fellow here brought her. Better let her go."

"Let him take care of her, then!" shouted Amory furiously. "I'm no W. Y. C. A. worker, am I?—am I?"

"Let her go!"

"It's *her* hanging on, damn it! Let her hang!"

The crowd around the table thickened. For an instant a brawl threatened, but a sleek waiter bent back Margaret Diamond's fingers until she released her hold on Amory, whereupon she slapped the waiter furiously in the face and flung her arms about her raging original escort.

"Oh, Lord!" cried Amory.

"Let's go!"

"Come on, the taxis are getting scarce!"

"Check, waiter."

"C'mon, Amory. Your romance is over."

Amory laughed.

"You don't know how true you spoke. No idea. 'At's the whole trouble."

AMORY ON THE LABOR QUESTION

Two mornings later he knocked at the president's door at Bascome and Barlow's advertising agency.

"Come in!"

Amory entered unsteadily.

"'Morning, Mr. Barlow."

Mr. Barlow brought his glasses to the inspection and set his mouth slightly ajar that he might better listen.

"Well, Mr. Blaine. We haven't seen you for several days."

"No," said Amory. "I'm quitting."

"Well—well—this is—"

"I don't like it here."

"I'm sorry. I thought our relations had been quite—ah—pleasant. You seemed to be a hard worker—a little inclined perhaps to write fancy copy—"

"I just got tired of it," interrupted Amory rudely. "It didn't matter a damn to me whether Harebell's flour was any better than any one else's. In fact, I never ate any of it. So I got tired of telling people about it—oh, I know I've been drinking—"

Mr. Barlow's face steeled by several ingots of expression.

"You asked for a position—"

Amory waved him to silence.

"And I think I was rottenly underpaid. Thirty-five dollars a week—less than a good carpenter."

"You had just started. You'd never worked before," said Mr. Barlow coolly.

"But it took about ten thousand dollars to educate me where I could write your darned stuff for you. Anyway, as far as length of service goes, you've got stenographers here you've paid fifteen a week for five years."

"I'm not going to argue with you, sir," said Mr. Barlow rising.

"Neither am I. I just wanted to tell you I'm quitting."

They stood for a moment looking at each other impassively and then Amory turned and left the office.

A LITTLE LULL

Four days after that he returned at last to the apartment. Tom was engaged on a book review for The New Democracy on the staff of which he was employed. They regarded each other for a moment in silence.

"Well?"

"Well?"

"Good Lord, Amory, where'd you get the black eye—and the jaw?"

Amory laughed.

"That's a mere nothing."

He peeled off his coat and bared his shoulders.

"Look here!"

Tom emitted a low whistle.

"What hit you?"

Amory laughed again.

"Oh, a lot of people. I got beaten up. Fact." He slowly replaced his shirt. "It was bound to come sooner or later and I wouldn't have missed it for anything."

"Who was it?"

"Well, there were some waiters and a couple of sailors and a few stray pedestrians, I guess. It's the strangest feeling. You ought to get beaten up just for the experience of it. You fall down after a while and everybody sort of slashes in at you before you hit the ground—then they kick you."

Tom lighted a cigarette.

"I spent a day chasing you all over town, Amory. But you always kept a little ahead of me. I'd say you've been on some party."

Amory tumbled into a chair and asked for a cigarette.

"You sober now?" asked Tom quizzically.

"Pretty sober. Why?"

"Well, Alec has left. His family had been after him to go home and live, so he—"

A spasm of pain shook Amory.

"Too bad."

"Yes, it is too bad. We'll have to get some one else if we're going to stay here. The rent's going up."

"Sure. Get anybody. I'll leave it to you, Tom."

Amory walked into his bedroom. The first thing that met his glance was a photograph of Rosalind that he had intended to have framed, propped up against a mirror on his dresser. He looked at it unmoved. After the vivid mental pictures of her that were his portion at present, the portrait was curiously unreal. He went back into the study.

"Got a cardboard box?"

"No," answered Tom, puzzled. "Why should I have? Oh, yes—there may be one in Alec's room."

Eventually Amory found what he was looking for and, returning to his dresser, opened a drawer full of letters, notes, part of a chain, two little handkerchiefs, and some snap-shots. As he transferred them carefully to the box his mind wandered to some place in a book where the hero, after preserving for a year a cake of his lost love's soap, finally washed his hands with it. He laughed and began to hum "After you've gone" ... ceased abruptly...

The string broke twice, and then he managed to secure it, dropped the package into the bottom of his trunk, and having slammed the lid returned to the study.

"Going out?" Tom's voice held an undertone of anxiety.

"Uh-huh."

"Where?"

"Couldn't say, old keed."

"Let's have dinner together."

"Sorry. I told Sukey Brett I'd eat with him."

"Oh."

"By-by."

Amory crossed the street and had a high-ball; then he walked to Washington Square and found a top seat on a bus. He disembarked at Forty-third Street and strolled to the Biltmore bar.

"Hi, Amory!"

"What'll you have?"

"Yo-ho! Waiter!"

TEMPERATURE NORMAL

The advent of prohibition with the "thirsty-first" put a sudden stop to the submerging of Amory's sorrows, and when he awoke one morning to find that the old bar-to-bar days were over, he had neither remorse for the past three weeks nor regret that their repetition was impossible. He had taken the most violent, if the weakest, method to shield himself from the stabs of memory, and while it was not a course he would have prescribed for others, he found in the end that it had done its business: he was over the first flush of pain.

Don't misunderstand! Amory had loved Rosalind as he would never love another living person. She had taken the first flush of his youth and brought from his unplumbed depths tenderness that had surprised him, gentleness and unselfishness that he had never given to another creature. He had later love-affairs, but of a different sort: in those he went back to that, perhaps, more typical frame of mind, in which the girl became the mirror of a mood in him. Rosalind had drawn out what was more than passionate admiration; he had a deep, undying affection for Rosalind.

But there had been, near the end, so much dramatic tragedy, culminating in the arabesque nightmare of his three weeks' spree, that he was emotionally worn out. The people and surroundings that he remembered as being cool or delicately artificial, seemed to promise him a refuge. He wrote a cynical story which featured his father's funeral and despatched it to a magazine, receiving in return a check for sixty dollars and a request for more of the same tone. This tickled his vanity, but inspired him to no further effort.

He read enormously. He was puzzled and depressed by "A Portrait of the Artist as a Young Man"; intensely interested by "Joan and Peter" and "The Undying Fire," and rather surprised by his discovery through a critic named Mencken of several excellent American novels: "Vandover and the Brute," "The Damnation of Theron Ware," and "Jennie Gerhardt." Mackenzie, Chesterton, Galsworthy, Bennett, had sunk in his appreciation from sagacious, life-saturated geniuses to merely diverting contemporaries. Shaw's aloof clarity and brilliant consistency and the gloriously intoxicated efforts of H. G. Wells to fit the key of romantic symmetry into the elusive lock of truth, alone won his rapt attention.

He wanted to see Monsignor Darcy, to whom he had written when he landed, but he had not heard from him; besides he knew that a visit to Monsignor would entail the story of Rosalind, and the thought of repeating it turned him cold with horror.

In his search for cool people he remembered Mrs. Lawrence, a very intelligent, very dignified lady, a convert to the church, and a great devotee of Monsignor's.

He called her on the 'phone one day. Yes, she remembered him perfectly; no, Monsignor wasn't in town, was in Boston she thought; he'd promised to come to dinner when he returned. Couldn't Amory take luncheon with her?

"I thought I'd better catch up, Mrs. Lawrence," he said rather ambiguously when he arrived.

"Monsignor was here just last week," said Mrs. Lawrence regretfully. "He was very anxious to see you, but he'd left your address at home."

"Did he think I'd plunged into Bolshevism?" asked Amory, interested.

"Oh, he's having a frightful time."

"Why?"

"About the Irish Republic. He thinks it lacks dignity."

"So?"

"He went to Boston when the Irish President arrived and he was greatly distressed because the receiving committee, when they rode in an automobile, *would* put their arms around the President."

"I don't blame him."

"Well, what impressed you more than anything while you were in the army? You look a great deal older."

"That's from another, more disastrous battle," he answered, smiling in spite of himself. "But the army—let me see—well, I discovered that physical courage depends to a great extent on the physical shape a man is in. I found that I was as brave as the next man—it used to worry me before."

"What else?"

"Well, the idea that men can stand anything if they get used to it, and the fact that I got a high mark in the psychological examination."

Mrs. Lawrence laughed. Amory was finding it a great relief to be in this cool house on Riverside Drive, away from more condensed New York and the sense of people expelling great quantities of breath into a little space. Mrs. Lawrence reminded him vaguely of Beatrice, not in temperament, but in her perfect grace and dignity. The house, its furnishings, the manner in which dinner was served, were in immense contrast to what he had met in the great places on Long Island, where the servants were so obtrusive that they had positively to be bumped out of the way, or even in the houses of more conservative "Union Club" families. He wondered if this air of symmetrical restraint, this grace, which he felt was continental, was distilled through Mrs. Lawrence's New England ancestry or acquired in long residence in Italy and Spain.

Two glasses of sauterne at luncheon loosened his tongue, and he talked, with what he felt was something of his old charm, of religion and literature and the menacing phenomena of the social order. Mrs. Lawrence was ostensibly pleased with him, and her interest was especially in his mind; he wanted people to like his mind again—after a while it might be such a nice place in which to live.

"Monsignor Darcy still thinks that you're his reincarnation, that your faith will eventually clarify."

"Perhaps," he assented. "I'm rather pagan at present. It's just that religion doesn't seem to have the slightest bearing on life at my age."

When he left her house he walked down Riverside Drive with a feeling of satisfaction. It was amusing to discuss again such subjects as this young poet, Stephen Vincent Benet, or the Irish Republic. Between the rancid accusations of Edward Carson and Justice Cohalan he had completely tired of the Irish question; yet there had been a time when his own Celtic traits were pillars of his personal philosophy.

There seemed suddenly to be much left in life, if only this revival of old interests did not mean that he was backing away from it again—backing away from life itself.

RESTLESSNESS

"I'm tres old and tres bored, Tom," said Amory one day, stretching himself at ease in the comfortable window-seat. He always felt most natural in a recumbent position.

"You used to be entertaining before you started to write," he continued. "Now you save any idea that you think would do to print."

Existence had settled back to an ambitionless normality. They had decided that with economy they could still afford the apartment, which Tom, with the domesticity of an elderly cat, had grown fond of. The old English hunting prints on the wall were Tom's, and the large tapestry by courtesy, a relic of decadent days in college, and the great profusion of orphaned candlesticks and the carved Louis XV chair in which no one could sit more than a minute without acute spinal disorders—Tom claimed that this was because one was sitting in the lap of Montespan's wraith—at any rate, it was Tom's furniture that decided them to stay.

They went out very little: to an occasional play, or to dinner at the Ritz or the Princeton Club. With prohibition the great rendezvous had received their death wounds; no longer could one wander to the Biltmore bar at twelve or five and find congenial spirits, and both Tom and Amory had outgrown the passion for dancing with mid-Western or New Jersey debbies at the Club-de-Vingt (surnamed the "Club de Gink") or the Plaza Rose Room—besides even that required several cocktails "to come down to the intellectual level of the women present," as Amory had once put it to a horrified matron.

Amory had lately received several alarming letters from Mr. Barton—the Lake Geneva house was too large to be easily rented; the best rent obtainable at present would serve this year to little more than pay for the taxes and necessary improvements; in fact, the lawyer suggested that the whole property was simply a white elephant on Amory's hands. Nevertheless, even though it might not yield a cent for the next three years, Amory decided with a vague sentimentality that for the present, at any rate, he would not sell the house.

This particular day on which he announced his ennui to Tom had been quite typical. He had risen at noon, lunched with Mrs. Lawrence, and then ridden abstractedly homeward atop one of his beloved buses.

"Why shouldn't you be bored," yawned Tom. "Isn't that the conventional frame of mind for the young man of your age and condition?"

"Yes," said Amory speculatively, "but I'm more than bored; I am restless."

"Love and war did for you."

"Well," Amory considered, "I'm not sure that the war itself had any great effect on either you or me—but it certainly ruined the old backgrounds, sort of killed individualism out of our generation."

Tom looked up in surprise.

"Yes it did," insisted Amory. "I'm not sure it didn't kill it out of the whole world. Oh, Lord, what a pleasure it used to be to dream I might be a really great dictator or writer or religious or political leader—and now even a Leonardo da Vinci or Lorenzo de Medici couldn't be a real old-fashioned bolt in the world. Life is too huge and complex. The world is so overgrown that it can't lift its own fingers, and I was planning to be such an important finger—"

"I don't agree with you," Tom interrupted. "There never were men placed in such egotistic positions since—oh, since the French Revolution."

Amory disagreed violently.

"You're mistaking this period when every nut is an individualist for a period of individualism. Wilson has only been powerful when he has represented; he's had to compromise over and over again. Just as soon as Trotsky and Lenin take a definite, consistent stand they'll become merely two-minute figures like Kerensky. Even Foch hasn't half the significance of Stonewall Jackson. War used to be the most individualistic pursuit of man, and yet the popular heroes of the war had neither authority nor responsibility: Guynemer and Sergeant York. How could a schoolboy make a hero of Pershing? A big man has no time really to do anything but just sit and be big."

"Then you don't think there will be any more permanent world heroes?"

"Yes—in history—not in life. Carlyle would have difficulty getting material for a new chapter on 'The Hero as a Big Man.'"

"Go on. I'm a good listener to-day."

"People try so hard to believe in leaders now, pitifully hard. But we no sooner get a popular reformer or politician or soldier or writer or philosopher—a Roosevelt, a Tolstoi, a Wood, a Shaw, a Nietzsche, than the cross-currents of criticism wash him away. My Lord, no man can stand prominence these days. It's the surest path to obscurity. People get sick of hearing the same name over and over."

"Then you blame it on the press?"

"Absolutely. Look at you; you're on The New Democracy, considered the most brilliant weekly in the country, read by the men who do things and all that. What's your business? Why, to be as clever, as interesting, and as brilliantly cynical as possible about every man, doctrine, book, or policy that is assigned you to deal with. The more strong lights, the more spiritual scandal you can throw on the matter, the more money they pay you, the more the people buy the issue. You, Tom d'Invilliers, a blighted Shelley, changing, shifting, clever, unscrupulous, represent the critical consciousness of the race—Oh, don't protest, I know the stuff. I used to write book reviews in college; I considered it rare sport to refer to the latest honest, conscientious effort to propound a theory or a remedy as a 'welcome addition to our light summer reading.' Come on now, admit it."

Tom laughed, and Amory continued triumphantly.

"We *want* to believe. Young students try to believe in older authors, constituents try to believe in their Congressmen, countries try to believe in their statesmen, but they *can't*. Too many voices, too much scattered, illogical, ill-considered criticism. It's worse in the case of newspapers. Any rich, unprogressive old party with that particularly grasping, acquisitive form of mentality known as financial genius can own a paper that is the intellectual meat and drink of thousands of tired, hurried men, men too involved in the business of modern living to swallow anything but predigested food. For two cents the voter buys his politics, prejudices, and philosophy. A year later there is a new political ring or a change in the paper's ownership, consequence: more confusion, more contradiction, a sudden inrush of new ideas, their tempering, their distillation, the reaction against them—"

He paused only to get his breath.

"And that is why I have sworn not to put pen to paper until my ideas either clarify or depart entirely; I have quite enough sins on my soul without putting dangerous, shallow epigrams into people's heads; I might cause a poor, inoffensive capitalist to have a vulgar liaison with a bomb, or get some innocent little Bolshevik tangled up with a machine-gun bullet—"

Tom was growing restless under this lampooning of his connection with The New Democracy.

"What's all this got to do with your being bored?"

Amory considered that it had much to do with it.

"How'll I fit in?" he demanded. "What am I for? To propagate the race? According to the American novels we are led to believe that the 'healthy American boy' from nineteen to twenty-five is an entirely sexless animal. As a matter of fact, the healthier he is the less that's true. The only alternative to letting it get you is some violent interest. Well, the war is over; I believe too much in the responsibilities of authorship to write just now; and business, well, business speaks for itself. It has no connection with anything in the world that I've ever been interested in, except a slim, utilitarian connection with economics. What I'd see of it, lost in a clerkship, for the next and best ten years of my life would have the intellectual content of an industrial movie."

"Try fiction," suggested Tom.

"Trouble is I get distracted when I start to write stories—get afraid I'm doing it instead of living—get thinking maybe life is waiting for me in the Japanese gardens at the Ritz or at Atlantic City or on the lower East Side.

"Anyway," he continued, "I haven't the vital urge. I wanted to be a regular human being but the girl couldn't see it that way."

"You'll find another."

"God! Banish the thought. Why don't you tell me that 'if the girl had been worth having she'd have waited for you'? No, sir, the girl really worth having won't wait for anybody. If I thought there'd be another I'd lose my remaining faith in human nature. Maybe I'll play—but Rosalind was the only girl in the wide world that could have held me."

"Well," yawned Tom, "I've played confidant a good hour by the clock. Still, I'm glad to see you're beginning to have violent views again on something."

"I am," agreed Amory reluctantly. "Yet when I see a happy family it makes me sick at my stomach—"

"Happy families try to make people feel that way," said Tom cynically.

TOM THE CENSOR

There were days when Amory listened. These were when Tom, wreathed in smoke, indulged in the slaughter of American literature. Words failed him.

"Fifty thousand dollars a year," he would cry. "My God! Look at them, look at them—Edna Ferber, Gouverneur Morris, Fanny Hurst, Mary Roberts Rinehart—not producing among 'em one story or novel that will last ten years. This man Cobb—I don't tink he's either clever or amusing—and what's more, I don't think very many people do, except the editors. He's just groggy with advertising. And—oh Harold Bell Wright oh Zane Grey—"

"They try."

"No, they don't even try. Some of them *can* write, but they won't sit down and do one honest novel. Most of them *can't* write, I'll admit. I believe Rupert Hughes tries to give a real, comprehensive picture of American life, but his style and perspective are barbarous. Ernest Poole and Dorothy Canfield try but they're hindered by their absolute lack of any sense of humor; but at least they crowd their work instead of spreading it thin. Every author ought to write every book as if he were going to be beheaded the day he finished it."

"Is that double entente?"

"Don't slow me up! Now there's a few of 'em that seem to have some cultural background, some intelligence and a good deal of literary felicity but they just simply won't write honestly; they'd all claim there was no public for good stuff. Then why the devil is it that Wells, Conrad, Galsworthy, Shaw, Bennett, and the rest depend on America for over half their sales?"

"How does little Tommy like the poets?"

Tom was overcome. He dropped his arms until they swung loosely beside the chair and emitted faint grunts.

"I'm writing a satire on 'em now, calling it 'Boston Bards and Hearst Reviewers.'"

"Let's hear it," said Amory eagerly.

"I've only got the last few lines done."

"That's very modern. Let's hear 'em, if they're funny."

Tom produced a folded paper from his pocket and read aloud, pausing at intervals so that Amory could see that it was free verse:

> *"So*
> *Walter Arensberg,*
> *Alfred Kreymborg,*
> *Carl Sandburg,*
> *Louis Untermeyer,*
> *Eunice Tietjens,*
> *Clara Shanafelt,*
> *James Oppenheim,*
> *Maxwell Bodenheim,*

Richard Glaenzer,
Scharmel Iris,
Conrad Aiken,
I place your names here
So that you may live
If only as names,
Sinuous, mauve-colored names,
In the Juvenalia
Of my collected editions."

Amory roared.

"You win the iron pansy. I'll buy you a meal on the arrogance of the last two lines."

Amory did not entirely agree with Tom's sweeping damnation of American novelists and poets. He enjoyed both Vachel Lindsay and Booth Tarkington, and admired the conscientious, if slender, artistry of Edgar Lee Masters.

"What I hate is this idiotic drivel about 'I am God—I am man—I ride the winds—I look through the smoke—I am the life sense.'"

"It's ghastly!"

"And I wish American novelists would give up trying to make business romantically interesting. Nobody wants to read about it, unless it's crooked business. If it was an entertaining subject they'd buy the life of James J. Hill and not one of these long office tragedies that harp along on the significance of smoke—"

"And gloom," said Tom. "That's another favorite, though I'll admit the Russians have the monopoly. Our specialty is stories about little girls who break their spines and get adopted by grouchy old men because they smile so much. You'd think we were a race of cheerful cripples and that the common end of the Russian peasant was suicide—"

"Six o'clock," said Amory, glancing at his wrist-watch. "I'll buy you a grea' big dinner on the strength of the Juvenalia of your collected editions."

LOOKING BACKWARD

July sweltered out with a last hot week, and Amory in another surge of unrest realized that it was just five months since he and Rosalind had met. Yet it was already hard for him to visualize the heart-whole boy who had stepped off the transport, passionately desiring the adventure of life. One night while the heat, overpowering and enervating, poured into the windows of his room he struggled for several hours in a vague effort to immortalize the poignancy of that time.

The February streets, wind-washed by night, blow full of strange half-intermittent damps, bearing on wasted walks in shining sight wet snow plashed into gleams under the lamps, like golden oil from some divine machine, in an hour of thaw and stars.

Strange damps—full of the eyes of many men, crowded with life borne in upon a lull....Oh, I was young, for I could turn again to you, most finite and most beautiful, and taste the stuff
of half-remembered dreams, sweet and new on your mouth.

... There was a tanging in the midnight air—silence was dead and sound not yet awoken—Life cracked like ice!—one brilliant note and there, radiant and pale, you stood... and spring had broken. (The icicles were short upon the roofs and the changeling city swooned.)

Our thoughts were frosty mist along the eaves; our two ghosts kissed, high on the long, mazed wires—eerie half-laughter echoes here and leaves only a fatuous sigh for young desires; regret has followed after things she loved, leaving the great husk.

ANOTHER ENDING

In mid-August came a letter from Monsignor Darcy, who had evidently just stumbled on his address:

MY DEAR BOY:—

Your last letter was quite enough to make me worry about you. It was not a bit like yourself. Reading between the lines I should imagine that your engagement to this girl is making you rather unhappy, and I see you have lost all the feeling of romance that you had before the war. You make a great mistake if you think you can be romantic without religion. Sometimes I think that with both of us the secret of success, when we find it, is the mystical element in us: something flows into us that enlarges our personalities, and when it ebbs out our personalities shrink; I should call your last two letters rather shrivelled. Beware of losing yourself in the personality of another being, man or woman.

His Eminence Cardinal O'Neill and the Bishop of Boston are staying with me at present, so it is hard for me to get a moment to write, but I wish you would come up here later if only for a week-end. I go to Washington this week.

What I shall do in the future is hanging in the balance. Absolutely between ourselves I should not be surprised to see the red hat of a cardinal descend upon my unworthy head within the next eight months. In any event, I should like to have a house in New York or Washington where you could drop in for week-ends.

Amory, I'm very glad we're both alive; this war could easily have been the end of a brilliant family. But in regard to matrimony, you are now at the most dangerous period of your life. You might marry in haste and repent at leisure, but I think you won't. From what you write me about the present calamitous state of your finances, what you want is naturally impossible. However, if I judge you by the means I usually choose, I should say that there will be something of an emotional crisis within the next year.

Do write me. I feel annoyingly out of date on you.

With greatest affection,

THAYER DARCY.

Within a week after the receipt of this letter their little household fell precipitously to pieces. The immediate cause was the serious and probably chronic illness of Tom's mother. So they stored the furniture, gave instructions to sublet and shook hands gloomily in the Pennsylvania Station. Amory and Tom seemed always to be saying good-by.

Feeling very much alone, Amory yielded to an impulse and set off southward, intending to join Monsignor in Washington. They missed connections by two hours, and, deciding to spend a few days with an ancient, remembered uncle, Amory journeyed up through the luxuriant fields of Maryland into Ramilly County. But instead of two days his stay lasted from mid-August nearly through September, for in Maryland he met Eleanor.

III. Young Irony

For years afterward when Amory thought of Eleanor he seemed still to hear the wind sobbing around him and sending little chills into the places beside his heart. The night when they rode up the slope and watched the cold moon float through the clouds, he lost a further part of him that nothing could restore; and when he lost it he lost also the power of regretting it. Eleanor was, say, the last time that evil crept close to Amory under the mask of beauty, the last weird mystery that held him with wild fascination and pounded his soul to flakes.

With her his imagination ran riot and that is why they rode to the highest hill and watched an evil moon ride high, for they knew then that they could see the devil in each other. But Eleanor—did Amory dream her? Afterward their ghosts played, yet both of them hoped from their souls never to meet. Was it the infinite sadness of her eyes that drew him or the mirror of himself that he found in the gorgeous clarity of her mind? She will have no other adventure like Amory, and if she reads this she will say:

"And Amory will have no other adventure like me."

Nor will she sigh, any more than he would sigh.

Eleanor tried to put it on paper once:

"The fading things we only know
We'll have forgotten...
Put away...
Desires that melted with the snow,
And dreams begotten
This to-day:
The sudden dawns we laughed to greet,
That all could see, that none could share,
Will be but dawns... and if we meet
We shall not care.

Dear... not one tear will rise for this...
A little while hence

No regret
Will stir for a remembered kiss—
Not even silence,
When we've met,
Will give old ghosts a waste to roam,
Or stir the surface of the sea...
If gray shapes drift beneath the foam
We shall not see."

They quarrelled dangerously because Amory maintained that *sea* and *see* couldn't possibly be used as a rhyme. And then Eleanor had part of another verse that she couldn't find a beginning for:

"... But wisdom passes... still the years
Will feed us wisdom....Age will go
Back to the old—
For all our tears
We shall not know."

Eleanor hated Maryland passionately. She belonged to the oldest of the old families of Ramilly County and lived in a big, gloomy house with her grandfather. She had been born and brought up in France.... I see I am starting wrong. Let me begin again.

Amory was bored, as he usually was in the country. He used to go for far walks by himself—and wander along reciting "Ulalume" to the corn-fields, and congratulating Poe for drinking himself to death in that atmosphere of smiling complacency. One afternoon he had strolled for several miles along a road that was new to him, and then through a wood on bad advice from a colored woman... losing himself entirely. A passing storm decided to break out, and to his great impatience the sky grew black as pitch and the rain began to splatter down through the trees, become suddenly furtive and ghostly. Thunder rolled with menacing crashes up the valley and scattered through the woods in intermittent batteries. He stumbled blindly on, hunting for a way out, and finally, through webs of twisted branches, caught sight of a rift in the trees where the unbroken lightning showed open country. He rushed to the edge of the woods and then hesitated whether or not to cross the fields and try to reach the shelter of the little house marked by a light far down the valley. It was only half past five, but he could see scarcely ten steps before him, except when the lightning made everything vivid and grotesque for great sweeps around.

Suddenly a strange sound fell on his ears. It was a song, in a low, husky voice, a girl's voice, and whoever was singing was very close to him. A year before he might have laughed, or trembled; but in his restless mood he only stood and listened while the words sank into his consciousness:

"Les sanglots longs
Des violons
De l'automne
Blessent mon coeur
D'une langueur
Monotone."

The lightning split the sky, but the song went on without a quaver. The girl was evidently in the field and the voice seemed to come vaguely from a haystack about twenty feet in front of him.

Then it ceased: ceased and began again in a weird chant that soared and hung and fell and blended with the rain:

"Tout suffocant
Et bleme quand
Sonne l'heure
Je me souviens
Des jours anciens
Et je pleure...."

"Who the devil is there in Ramilly County," muttered Amory aloud, "who would deliver Verlaine in an extemporaneous tune to a soaking haystack?"

"Somebody's there!" cried the voice unalarmed. "Who are you?—Manfred, St. Christopher, or Queen Victoria?"

"I'm Don Juan!" Amory shouted on impulse, raising his voice above the noise of the rain and the wind.

A delighted shriek came from the haystack.

"I know who you are—you're the blond boy that likes 'Ulalume'—I recognize your voice."

"How do I get up?" he cried from the foot of the haystack, whither he had arrived, dripping wet. A head appeared over the edge—it was so dark that Amory could just make out a patch of damp hair and two eyes that gleamed like a cat's.

"Run back!" came the voice, "and jump and I'll catch your hand—no, not there—on the other side."

He followed directions and as he sprawled up the side, knee-deep in hay, a small, white hand reached out, gripped his, and helped him onto the top.

"Here you are, Juan," cried she of the damp hair. "Do you mind if I drop the Don?"

"You've got a thumb like mine!" he exclaimed.

"And you're holding my hand, which is dangerous without seeing my face." He dropped it quickly.

As if in answer to his prayers came a flash of lightning and he looked eagerly at her who stood beside him on the soggy haystack, ten feet above the ground.

But she had covered her face and he saw nothing but a slender figure, dark, damp, bobbed hair, and the small white hands with the thumbs that bent back like his.

"Sit down," she suggested politely, as the dark closed in on them. "If you'll sit opposite me in this hollow you can have half of the raincoat, which I was using as a water-proof tent until you so rudely interrupted me."

"I was asked," Amory said joyfully; "you asked me—you know you did."

"Don Juan always manages that," she said, laughing, "but I shan't call you that any more, because you've got reddish hair. Instead you can recite 'Ulalume' and I'll be Psyche, your soul."

Amory flushed, happily invisible under the curtain of wind and rain. They were sitting opposite each other in a slight hollow in the hay with the raincoat spread over most of them, and the rain doing for the rest. Amory was trying desperately to see Psyche, but the lightning refused to flash again, and he waited impatiently. Good Lord! supposing she wasn't beautiful—supposing she was forty and pedantic—heavens! Suppose, only suppose, she was mad. But he knew the last was unworthy. Here had Providence sent a girl to amuse him just as it sent Benvenuto Cellini men to murder, and he was wondering if she was mad, just because she exactly filled his mood.

"I'm not," she said.

"Not what?"

"Not mad. I didn't think you were mad when I first saw you, so it isn't fair that you should think so of me."

"How on earth—"

As long as they knew each other Eleanor and Amory could be "on a subject" and stop talking with the definite thought of it in their heads, yet ten minutes later speak aloud and find that their minds had followed the same channels and led them each to a parallel idea, an idea that others would have found absolutely unconnected with the first.

"Tell me," he demanded, leaning forward eagerly, "how do you know about 'Ulalume'—how did you know the color of my hair? What's your name? What were you doing here? Tell me all at once!"

Suddenly the lightning flashed in with a leap of overreaching light and he saw Eleanor, and looked for the first time into those eyes of hers. Oh, she was magnificent—pale skin, the color of marble in starlight, slender brows, and eyes that glittered green as emeralds in the blinding glare. She was a witch, of perhaps nineteen, he judged, alert and dreamy and with the tell-tale white line over her upper lip that was a weakness and a delight. He sank back with a gasp against the wall of hay.

"Now you've seen me," she said calmly, "and I suppose you're about to say that my green eyes are burning into your brain."

"What color is your hair?" he asked intently. "It's bobbed, isn't it?"

"Yes, it's bobbed. I don't know what color it is," she answered, musing, "so many men have asked me. It's medium, I suppose—No one ever looks long at my hair. I've got beautiful eyes, though, haven't I. I don't care what you say, I have beautiful eyes."

"Answer my question, Madeline."

"Don't remember them all—besides my name isn't Madeline, it's Eleanor."

"I might have guessed it. You *look* like Eleanor—you have that Eleanor look. You know what I mean."

There was a silence as they listened to the rain.

"It's going down my neck, fellow lunatic," she offered finally.

"Answer my questions."

"Well—name of Savage, Eleanor; live in big old house mile down road; nearest living relation to be notified, grandfather—Ramilly Savage; height, five feet four inches; number on watch-case, 3077 W; nose, delicate aquiline; temperament, uncanny—"

"And me," Amory interrupted, "where did you see me?"

"Oh, you're one of *those* men," she answered haughtily, "must lug old self into conversation. Well, my boy, I was behind a hedge sunning myself one day last week, and along comes a man saying in a pleasant, conceited way of talking:

> *"'And now when the night was senescent'*
> *(says he)*
> *'And the star dials pointed to morn*
> *At the end of the path a liquescent'*
> *(says he)*
> *'And nebulous lustre was born.'*

"So I poked my eyes up over the hedge, but you had started to run, for some unknown reason, and so I saw but the back of your beautiful head. 'Oh!' says I, 'there's a man for whom many of us might sigh,' and I continued in my best Irish—"

"All right," Amory interrupted. "Now go back to yourself."

"Well, I will. I'm one of those people who go through the world giving other people thrills, but getting few myself except those I read into men on such nights as these. I have the social courage to go on the stage, but not the energy; I haven't the patience to write books; and I never met a man I'd marry. However, I'm only eighteen."

The storm was dying down softly and only the wind kept up its ghostly surge and made the stack lean and gravely settle from side to side. Amory was in a trance. He felt that every moment was precious. He had never met a girl like this before—she would never seem quite the same again. He didn't at all feel like a character in a play, the appropriate feeling in an unconventional situation—instead, he had a sense of coming home.

"I have just made a great decision," said Eleanor after another pause, "and that is why I'm here, to answer another of your questions. I have just decided that I don't believe in immortality."

"Really! how banal!"

"Frightfully so," she answered, "but depressing with a stale, sickly depression, nevertheless. I came out here to get wet—like a wet hen; wet hens always have great clarity of mind," she concluded.

"Go on," Amory said politely.

"Well—I'm not afraid of the dark, so I put on my slicker and rubber boots and came out. You see I was always afraid, before, to say I didn't believe in God—because the lightning might strike me—but here I am and it hasn't, of course, but the main point is that this time I wasn't any more afraid of it than I had been when I was a Christian Scientist, like I was last year. So now I know I'm a materialist and I was fraternizing with the hay when you came out and stood by the woods, scared to death."

"Why, you little wretch—" cried Amory indignantly. "Scared of what?"

"*Yourself!*" she shouted, and he jumped. She clapped her hands and laughed. "See—see! Conscience—kill it like me! Eleanor Savage, materiologist—no jumping, no starting, come early—"

"But I *have* to have a soul," he objected. "I can't be rational—and I won't be molecular."

She leaned toward him, her burning eyes never leaving his own and whispered with a sort of romantic finality:

"I thought so, Juan, I feared so—you're sentimental. You're not like me. I'm a romantic little materialist."

"I'm not sentimental—I'm as romantic as you are. The idea, you know, is that the sentimental person thinks things will last—the romantic person has a desperate confidence that they won't." (This was an ancient distinction of Amory's.)

"Epigrams. I'm going home," she said sadly. "Let's get off the haystack and walk to the cross-roads."

They slowly descended from their perch. She would not let him help her down and motioning him away arrived in a graceful lump in the soft mud where she sat for an instant, laughing at herself. Then she jumped to her feet and slipped her hand into his, and they tiptoed across the fields, jumping and swinging from dry spot to dry spot. A transcendent delight seemed to sparkle in every pool of water, for the moon had risen and the storm had scurried away into western Maryland. When Eleanor's arm touched his he felt his hands grow cold with deadly fear lest he should lose the shadow brush with which his imagination was painting wonders of her. He watched her from the corners of his eyes as ever he did when he walked with her—she was a feast and a folly and he wished it had been his destiny to sit forever on a haystack and see life through her green eyes. His paganism soared that night and when she faded out like a gray ghost down the road, a deep singing came out of the fields and filled his way homeward. All night the summer moths flitted in and out of Amory's window; all night large looming sounds swayed in mystic revery through the silver grain—and he lay awake in the clear darkness.

SEPTEMBER

Amory selected a blade of grass and nibbled at it scientifically.

"I never fall in love in August or September," he proffered.

"When then?"

"Christmas or Easter. I'm a liturgist."

"Easter!" She turned up her nose. "Huh! Spring in corsets!"

"Easter *would* bore spring, wouldn't she? Easter has her hair braided, wears a tailored suit."

> *"Bind on thy sandals, oh, thou most fleet.*
> *Over the splendor and speed of thy feet—"*

quoted Eleanor softly, and then added: "I suppose Hallowe'en is a better day for autumn than Thanksgiving."

"Much better—and Christmas eve does very well for winter, but summer..."

"Summer has no day," she said. "We can't possibly have a summer love. So many people have tried that the name's become proverbial. Summer is only the unfulfilled promise of spring, a charlatan in place of the warm balmy nights I dream of in April. It's a sad season of life without growth.... It has no day."

"Fourth of July," Amory suggested facetiously.

"Don't be funny!" she said, raking him with her eyes.

"Well, what could fulfil the promise of spring?"

She thought a moment.

"Oh, I suppose heaven would, if there was one," she said finally, "a sort of pagan heaven—you ought to be a materialist," she continued irrelevantly.

"Why?"

"Because you look a good deal like the pictures of Rupert Brooke."

To some extent Amory tried to play Rupert Brooke as long as he knew Eleanor. What he said, his attitude toward life, toward her, toward himself, were all reflexes of the dead Englishman's literary moods. Often she sat in the grass, a lazy wind playing with her short hair, her voice husky as she ran up and down the scale from Grantchester to Waikiki. There was something most passionate in Eleanor's reading aloud. They seemed nearer, not only mentally, but physically, when they read, than when she was in his arms, and this was often, for they fell half into love almost from the first. Yet was Amory capable of love now? He could, as always, run through the emotions in a half hour, but even while they revelled in their imaginations, he knew that neither of them could care as he had cared once before—I suppose that was why they turned to Brooke, and Swinburne, and Shelley. Their chance was to make everything fine and finished and rich and imaginative; they must bend tiny golden tentacles from his imagination to hers, that would take the place of the great, deep love that was never so near, yet never so much of a dream.

One poem they read over and over; Swinburne's "Triumph of Time," and four lines of it rang in his memory afterward on warm nights when he saw the fireflies among dusky tree trunks and heard the low drone of many frogs. Then Eleanor seemed to come out of the night and stand by him, and he heard her throaty voice, with its tone of a fleecy-headed drum, repeating:

> *"Is it worth a tear, is it worth an hour,*
> *To think of things that are well outworn;*
> *Of fruitless husk and fugitive flower,*
> *The dream foregone and the deed foreborne?"*

They were formally introduced two days later, and his aunt told him her history. The Ramillys were two: old Mr. Ramilly and his granddaughter, Eleanor. She had lived in France with a restless mother whom Amory imagined to have been very like his own, on whose death she had come to America, to live in Maryland. She had gone to Baltimore first to stay with a bachelor uncle, and there she insisted on being a debutante at the age of seventeen. She had a wild winter and arrived in the country in March, having quarrelled frantically with all her Baltimore relatives, and shocked them into fiery protest. A rather fast crowd had come out, who drank cocktails in limousines and were promiscuously condescending and patronizing toward older people, and Eleanor with an esprit that hinted strongly of the boulevards, led many innocents still redolent of St. Timothy's and Farmington, into paths of Bohemian naughtiness. When the story came to her uncle, a forgetful cavalier of a more hypocritical era, there was a scene, from which Eleanor emerged, subdued but rebellious and indignant, to seek haven with her grandfather who hovered in the country on the near side of senility. That's as far as her story went; she told him the rest herself, but that was later.

Often they swam and as Amory floated lazily in the water he shut his mind to all thoughts except those of hazy soap-bubble lands where the sun splattered through wind-drunk trees. How could any one possibly think or worry, or do anything except splash and dive and loll there on the edge of time while the flower months failed. Let the days move over—sadness and memory and pain recurred outside, and here, once more, before he went on to meet them he wanted to drift and be young.

There were days when Amory resented that life had changed from an even progress along a road stretching ever in sight, with the scenery merging and blending, into a succession of quick, unrelated scenes—two years of sweat and blood, that sudden absurd instinct for paternity that Rosalind had stirred; the half-sensual, half-neurotic quality of this autumn with Eleanor. He felt that it would take all time, more than he could ever spare, to glue these strange cumbersome pictures into the scrap-book of his life. It was all like a banquet where he sat for this half-hour of his youth and tried to enjoy brilliant epicurean courses.

Dimly he promised himself a time where all should be welded together. For months it seemed that he had alternated between being borne along a stream of love or fascination, or left in an eddy, and in the eddies he had not desired to think, rather to be picked up on a wave's top and swept along again.

"The despairing, dying autumn and our love—how well they harmonize!" said Eleanor sadly one day as they lay dripping by the water.

"The Indian summer of our hearts—" he ceased.

"Tell me," she said finally, "was she light or dark?"

"Light."

"Was she more beautiful than I am?"

"I don't know," said Amory shortly.

One night they walked while the moon rose and poured a great burden of glory over the garden until it seemed fairyland with Amory and Eleanor, dim phantasmal shapes, expressing eternal beauty in curious elfin love moods. Then they turned out of the moonlight into the trellised darkness of a vine-hung pagoda, where there were scents so plaintive as to be nearly musical.

"Light a match," she whispered. "I want to see you."

Scratch! Flare!

The night and the scarred trees were like scenery in a play, and to be there with Eleanor, shadowy and unreal, seemed somehow oddly familiar. Amory thought how it was only the past that ever seemed strange and unbelievable. The match went out.

"It's black as pitch."

"We're just voices now," murmured Eleanor, "little lonesome voices. Light another."

"That was my last match."

Suddenly he caught her in his arms.

"You *are* mine—you know you're mine!" he cried wildly... the moonlight twisted in through the vines and listened... the fireflies hung upon their whispers as if to win his glance from the glory of their eyes.

THE END OF SUMMER

"No wind is stirring in the grass; not one wind stirs... the water in the hidden pools, as glass, fronts the full moon and so inters the golden token in its icy mass," chanted Eleanor to the trees that skeletoned the body of the night. "Isn't it ghostly here? If you can hold your horse's feet up, let's cut through the woods and find the hidden pools."

"It's after one, and you'll get the devil," he objected, "and I don't know enough about horses to put one away in the pitch dark."

"Shut up, you old fool," she whispered irrelevantly, and, leaning over, she patted him lazily with her riding-crop. "You can leave your old plug in our stable and I'll send him over to-morrow."

"But my uncle has got to drive me to the station with this old plug at seven o'clock."

"Don't be a spoil-sport—remember, you have a tendency toward wavering that prevents you from being the entire light of my life."

Amory drew his horse up close beside, and, leaning toward her, grasped her hand.

"Say I am—*quick*, or I'll pull you over and make you ride behind me."

She looked up and smiled and shook her head excitedly.

"Oh, do!—or rather, don't! Why are all the exciting things so uncomfortable, like fighting and exploring and ski-ing in Canada? By the way, we're going to ride up Harper's Hill. I think that comes in our programme about five o'clock."

"You little devil," Amory growled. "You're going to make me stay up all night and sleep in the train like an immigrant all day to-morrow, going back to New York."

"Hush! some one's coming along the road—let's go! Whoo-ee-oop!" And with a shout that probably gave the belated traveller a series of shivers, she turned her horse into the woods and Amory followed slowly, as he had followed her all day for three weeks.

The summer was over, but he had spent the days in watching Eleanor, a graceful, facile Manfred, build herself intellectual and imaginative pyramids while she revelled in the artificialities of the temperamental teens and they wrote poetry at the dinner-table.

When Vanity kissed Vanity, a hundred happy Junes ago, he pondered o'er her breathlessly, and, that all men might ever know, he rhymed her eyes with life and death:

"Thru Time I'll save my love!" he said... yet Beauty vanished with his breath, and, with her lovers, she was dead...

—Ever his wit and not her eyes, ever his art and not her hair:

> *'Who'd learn a trick in rhyme, be wise and pause before his sonnet there"...So all my words, however true, might sing you to a thousandth June, and no one ever know that you were Beauty for an afternoon.*

So he wrote one day, when he pondered how coldly we thought of the "Dark Lady of the Sonnets," and how little we remembered her as the great man wanted her remembered. For what Shakespeare *must* have desired, to have been able to write with such divine despair, was that the lady should live... and now we have no real interest in her.... The irony of it is that if he had cared *more* for the poem than for the lady the sonnet would be only obvious, imitative rhetoric and no one would ever have read it after twenty years....

This was the last night Amory ever saw Eleanor. He was leaving in the morning and they had agreed to take a long farewell trot by the cold moonlight. She wanted to talk, she said—perhaps the last time in her life that she could be rational (she meant pose with comfort). So they had turned into the woods and rode for half an hour with scarcely a word, except when she whispered "Damn!" at a bothersome branch—whispered it as no other girl was ever able to whisper it. Then they started up Harper's Hill, walking their tired horses.

"Good Lord! It's quiet here!" whispered Eleanor; "much more lonesome than the woods."

"I hate woods," Amory said, shuddering. "Any kind of foliage or underbrush at night. Out here it's so broad and easy on the spirit."

"The long slope of a long hill."

"And the cold moon rolling moonlight down it."

"And thee and me, last and most important."

It was quiet that night—the straight road they followed up to the edge of the cliff knew few footsteps at any time. Only an occasional negro cabin, silver-gray in the rock-ribbed moonlight, broke the long line of bare ground; behind lay the black edge of the woods like a dark frosting on white cake, and ahead the sharp, high horizon. It was much colder—so cold that it settled on them and drove all the warm nights from their minds.

"The end of summer," said Eleanor softly. "Listen to the beat of our horses' hoofs—'tump-tump-tump-a-tump.' Have you ever been feverish and had all noises divide into 'tump-tump-tump' until you could swear eternity was divisible into so many tumps? That's the way I feel—old horses go tump-tump.... I guess that's the only thing that separates horses and clocks from us. Human beings can't go 'tump-tump-tump' without going crazy."

The breeze freshened and Eleanor pulled her cape around her and shivered.

"Are you very cold?" asked Amory.

"No, I'm thinking about myself—my black old inside self, the real one, with the fundamental honesty that keeps me from being absolutely wicked by making me realize my own sins."

They were riding up close by the cliff and Amory gazed over. Where the fall met the ground a hundred feet below, a black stream made a sharp line, broken by tiny glints in the swift water.

"Rotten, rotten old world," broke out Eleanor suddenly, "and the wretchedest thing of all is me—oh, *why* am I a girl? Why am I not a stupid—? Look at you; you're stupider than I am, not much, but some, and you can lope about and get bored and then lope somewhere else, and you can play around with girls without being involved in meshes of sentiment, and you can do anything and be justified—and here am I with the brains to do everything, yet tied to the sinking ship of future matrimony. If I were born a hundred years from now, well and good, but now what's in store for me—I have to marry, that goes without saying. Who? I'm too bright for most men, and yet I have to descend to their level and let them patronize my intellect in order to get their attention. Every year that I don't marry I've got less chance for a first-class man. At the best I can have my choice from one or two cities and, of course, I have to marry into a dinner-coat.

"Listen," she leaned close again, "I like clever men and good-looking men, and, of course, no one cares more for personality than I do. Oh, just one person in fifty has any glimmer of what sex is. I'm hipped on Freud and all that, but it's rotten that every bit of *real* love in the world is ninety-nine per cent passion and one little soupcon of jealousy." She finished as suddenly as she began.

"Of course, you're right," Amory agreed. "It's a rather unpleasant overpowering force that's part of the machinery under everything. It's like an actor that lets you see his mechanics! Wait a minute till I think this out...."

He paused and tried to get a metaphor. They had turned the cliff and were riding along the road about fifty feet to the left.

"You see every one's got to have some cloak to throw around it. The mediocre intellects, Plato's second class, use the remnants of romantic chivalry diluted with Victorian sentiment—and we who consider ourselves the intellectuals cover it up by pretending that it's another side of us, has nothing to do with our shining brains; we pretend that the fact that we realize it is really absolving us from being a prey to it. But the truth is that sex is right in the middle of our purest abstractions, so close that it obscures vision.... I can kiss you now and will. ..." He leaned toward her in his saddle, but she drew away.

"I can't—I can't kiss you now—I'm more sensitive."

"You're more stupid then," he declared rather impatiently. "Intellect is no protection from sex any more than convention is..."

"What is?" she fired up. "The Catholic Church or the maxims of Confucius?"

Amory looked up, rather taken aback.

"That's your panacea, isn't it?" she cried. "Oh, you're just an old hypocrite, too. Thousands of scowling priests keeping the degenerate Italians and illiterate Irish repentant with gabble-gabble about the sixth and ninth commandments. It's just all cloaks, sentiment and spiritual rouge and panaceas. I'll tell you there is no God, not even a definite abstract goodness; so it's all got to be worked out for the individual by the individual here in high white foreheads like mine, and you're too much the prig to admit it." She let go her reins and shook her little fists at the stars.

"If there's a God let him strike me—strike me!"

"Talking about God again after the manner of atheists," Amory said sharply. His materialism, always a thin cloak, was torn to shreds by Eleanor's blasphemy.... She knew it and it angered him that she knew it.

"And like most intellectuals who don't find faith convenient," he continued coldly, "like Napoleon and Oscar Wilde and the rest of your type, you'll yell loudly for a priest on your death-bed."

Eleanor drew her horse up sharply and he reined in beside her.

"Will I?" she said in a queer voice that scared him. "Will I? Watch! *I'm going over the cliff!*" And before he could interfere she had turned and was riding breakneck for the end of the plateau.

He wheeled and started after her, his body like ice, his nerves in a vast clangor. There was no chance of stopping her. The moon was under a cloud and her horse would step blindly over. Then some ten feet from the edge of the cliff she gave a sudden shriek and flung herself sideways—plunged from her horse and, rolling over twice, landed in a pile of brush five feet from the edge. The horse went over with a frantic whinny. In a minute he was by Eleanor's side and saw that her eyes were open.

"Eleanor!" he cried.

She did not answer, but her lips moved and her eyes filled with sudden tears.

"Eleanor, are you hurt?"

"No; I don't think so," she said faintly, and then began weeping.

"My horse dead?"

"Good God—Yes!"

"Oh!" she wailed. "I thought I was going over. I didn't know—"

He helped her gently to her feet and boosted her onto his saddle. So they started homeward; Amory walking and she bent forward on the pommel, sobbing bitterly.

"I've got a crazy streak," she faltered, "twice before I've done things like that. When I was eleven mother went—went mad—stark raving crazy. We were in Vienna—"

All the way back she talked haltingly about herself, and Amory's love waned slowly with the moon. At her door they started from habit to kiss good night, but she could not run into his arms, nor were they stretched to meet her as in the week before. For a minute they stood there, hating each other with a bitter sadness. But as Amory had loved himself in Eleanor, so now what he hated was only a mirror. Their poses were strewn about the pale dawn like broken glass. The stars were long gone and there were left only the little sighing gusts of wind and the silences between... but naked souls are poor things ever, and soon he turned homeward and let new lights come in with the sun.

A POEM THAT ELEANOR SENT AMORY SEVERAL YEARS LATER

"Here, Earth-born, over the lilt of the water,
Lisping its music and bearing a burden of light,
Bosoming day as a laughing and radiant daughter...
Here we may whisper unheard, unafraid of the night.
Walking alone... was it splendor, or what, we were bound with,
Deep in the time when summer lets down her hair?
Shadows we loved and the patterns they covered the ground with
Tapestries, mystical, faint in the breathless air.

That was the day... and the night for another story,
Pale as a dream and shadowed with pencilled trees—
Ghosts of the stars came by who had sought for glory,
Whispered to us of peace in the plaintive breeze,
Whispered of old dead faiths that the day had shattered,
Youth the penny that bought delight of the moon;
That was the urge that we knew and the language that mattered
That was the debt that we paid to the usurer June.

Here, deepest of dreams, by the waters that bring not
Anything back of the past that we need not know,
What if the light is but sun and the little streams sing not,
We are together, it seems... I have loved you so...
What did the last night hold, with the summer over,
Drawing us back to the home in the changing glade?
What leered out of the dark in the ghostly clover?
God!... till you stirred in your sleep... and were wild afraid...

Well... we have passed... we are chronicle now to the eerie.
Curious metal from meteors that failed in the sky;
Earth-born the tireless is stretched by the water, quite weary,
Close to this ununderstandable changeling that's I...
Fear is an echo we traced to Security's daughter;
Now we are faces and voices... and less, too soon,
Whispering half-love over the lilt of the water...
Youth the penny that bought delight of the moon."

A POEM AMORY SENT TO ELEANOR AND WHICH HE CALLED "SUMMER STORM"

'Faint winds, and a song fading and leaves falling,
Faint winds, and far away a fading laughter...
And the rain and over the fields a voice calling...

Our gray blown cloud scurries and lifts above,
Slides on the sun and flutters there to waft her
Sisters on.The shadow of a dove
Falls on the cote, the trees are filled with wings;
And down the valley through the crying trees
The body of the darker storm flies; brings
With its new air the breath of sunken seas
And slender tenuous thunder...
But I wait...
Wait for the mists and for the blacker rain—
Heavier winds that stir the veil of fate,
Happier winds that pile her hair;
Again
They tear me, teach me, strew the heavy air
Upon me, winds that I know, and storm.

There was a summer every rain was rare;
There was a season every wind was warm....
And now you pass me in the mist... your hair
Rain-blown about you, damp lips curved once more
In that wild irony, that gay despair
That made you old when we have met before;
Wraith-like you drift on out before the rain,
Across the fields, blown with the stemless flowers,
With your old hopes, dead leaves and loves again—
Dim as a dream and wan with all old hours
(Whispers will creep into the growing dark...
Tumult will die over the trees)
Now night
Tears from her wetted breast the splattered blouse
Of day, glides down the dreaming hills, tear-bright,
To cover with her hair the eerie green...

Love for the dusk... Love for the glistening after;
Quiet the trees to their last tops... serene...

Faint winds, and far away a fading laughter..."

IV. The Supercilious Sacrifice

Atlantic City. Amory paced the board walk at day's end, lulled by the everlasting surge of changing waves, smelling the half-mournful odor of the salt breeze. The sea, he thought, had treasured its memories deeper than the faithless land. It seemed still to whisper of Norse galleys ploughing the water world under raven-figured flags, of the British dreadnoughts, gray bulwarks of civilization steaming up through the fog of one dark July into the North Sea.

"Well—Amory Blaine!"

Amory looked down into the street below. A low racing car had drawn to a stop and a familiar cheerful face protruded from the driver's seat.

"Come on down, goopher!" cried Alec.

Amory called a greeting and descending a flight of wooden steps approached the car. He and Alec had been meeting intermittently, but the barrier of Rosalind lay always between them. He was sorry for this; he hated to lose Alec.

"Mr. Blaine, this is Miss Waterson, Miss Wayne, and Mr. Tully."

"How d'y do?"

"Amory," said Alec exuberantly, "if you'll jump in we'll take you to some secluded nook and give you a wee jolt of Bourbon."

Amory considered.

"That's an idea."

"Step in—move over, Jill, and Amory will smile very handsomely at you."

Amory squeezed into the back seat beside a gaudy, vermilion-lipped blonde.

"Hello, Doug Fairbanks," she said flippantly. "Walking for exercise or hunting for company?"

"I was counting the waves," replied Amory gravely. "I'm going in for statistics."

"Don't kid me, Doug."

When they reached an unfrequented side street Alec stopped the car among deep shadows.

"What you doing down here these cold days, Amory?" he demanded, as he produced a quart of Bourbon from under the fur rug.

Amory avoided the question. Indeed, he had had no definite reason for coming to the coast.

"Do you remember that party of ours, sophomore year?" he asked instead.

"Do I? When we slept in the pavilions up in Asbury Park—"

"Lord, Alec! It's hard to think that Jesse and Dick and Kerry are all three dead."

Alec shivered.

"Don't talk about it. These dreary fall days depress me enough."

Jill seemed to agree.

"Doug here is sorta gloomy anyways," she commented. "Tell him to drink deep—it's good and scarce these days."

"What I really want to ask you, Amory, is where you are—"

"Why, New York, I suppose—"

"I mean to-night, because if you haven't got a room yet you'd better help me out."

"Glad to."

"You see, Tully and I have two rooms with bath between at the Ranier, and he's got to go back to New York. I don't want to have to move. Question is, will you occupy one of the rooms?"

Amory was willing, if he could get in right away.

"You'll find the key in the office; the rooms are in my name."

Declining further locomotion or further stimulation, Amory left the car and sauntered back along the board walk to the hotel.

He was in an eddy again, a deep, lethargic gulf, without desire to work or write, love or dissipate. For the first time in his life he rather longed for death to roll over his generation, obliterating their petty fevers and struggles and exultations. His youth seemed never so vanished as now in the contrast between the utter loneliness of this visit and that riotous, joyful party of four years before. Things that had been the merest commonplaces of his life then, deep sleep, the sense of beauty around him, all desire, had flown away and the gaps they left were filled only with the great listlessness of his disillusion.

"To hold a man a woman has to appeal to the worst in him." This sentence was the thesis of most of his bad nights, of which he felt this was to be one. His mind had already started to play variations on the subject. Tireless passion, fierce jealousy, longing to possess and crush—these alone were left of all his love for Rosalind; these remained to him as payment for the loss of his youth—bitter calomel under the thin sugar of love's exaltation.

In his room he undressed and wrapping himself in blankets to keep out the chill October air drowsed in an armchair by the open window.

He remembered a poem he had read months before:

"Oh staunch old heart who toiled so long for me,
I waste my years sailing along the sea—"

Yet he had no sense of waste, no sense of the present hope that waste implied. He felt that life had rejected him.

"Rosalind! Rosalind!" He poured the words softly into the half-darkness until she seemed to permeate the room; the wet salt breeze filled his hair with moisture, the rim of a moon seared the sky and made the curtains dim and ghostly. He fell asleep.

When he awoke it was very late and quiet. The blanket had slipped partly off his shoulders and he touched his skin to find it damp and cold.

Then he became aware of a tense whispering not ten feet away.

He became rigid.

"Don't make a sound!" It was Alec's voice. "Jill—do you hear me?"

"Yes—" breathed very low, very frightened. They were in the bathroom.

Then his ears caught a louder sound from somewhere along the corridor outside. It was a mumbling of men's voices and a repeated muffled rapping. Amory threw off the blankets and moved close to the bathroom door.

"My God!" came the girl's voice again. "You'll have to let them in."

"Sh!"

Suddenly a steady, insistent knocking began at Amory's hall door and simultaneously out of the bathroom came Alec, followed by the vermilion-lipped girl. They were both clad in pajamas.

"Amory!" an anxious whisper.

"What's the trouble?"

"It's house detectives. My God, Amory—they're just looking for a test-case—"

"Well, better let them in."

"You don't understand. They can get me under the Mann Act."

The girl followed him slowly, a rather miserable, pathetic figure in the darkness.

Amory tried to plan quickly.

"You make a racket and let them in your room," he suggested anxiously, "and I'll get her out by this door."

"They're here too, though. They'll watch this door."

"Can't you give a wrong name?"

"No chance. I registered under my own name; besides, they'd trail the auto license number."

"Say you're married."

"Jill says one of the house detectives knows her."

The girl had stolen to the bed and tumbled upon it; lay there listening wretchedly to the knocking which had grown gradually to a pounding. Then came a man's voice, angry and imperative:

"Open up or we'll break the door in!"

In the silence when this voice ceased Amory realized that there were other things in the room besides people... over and around the figure crouched on the bed there hung an aura, gossamer as a moonbeam, tainted as stale, weak wine, yet a horror, diffusively brooding already over the three of them... and over by the window among the stirring curtains stood something else, featureless and indistinguishable, yet strangely familiar.... Simultaneously two great cases presented themselves side by side to Amory; all that took place in his mind, then, occupied in actual time less than ten seconds.

The first fact that flashed radiantly on his comprehension was the great impersonality of sacrifice—he perceived that what we call love and hate, reward and punishment, had no more to do with it than the date of the month. He quickly recapitulated the story of a sacrifice he had heard of in college: a man had cheated in an examination; his roommate in a gust of sentiment had taken the entire blame—due to the shame of it the innocent one's entire future seemed shrouded in regret and failure, capped by the ingratitude of the real culprit. He had finally taken his own life—years afterward the facts had come out. At the time the story had both puzzled and worried Amory. Now he realized the truth; that sacrifice was no purchase of freedom. It was like a great elective office, it was like an inheritance of power—to certain people at certain times an essential luxury, carrying with it not a guarantee but a responsibility, not a security but an infinite risk. Its very momentum might drag him down to ruin—the passing of the emotional wave that made it possible might leave the one who made it high and dry forever on an island of despair.

... Amory knew that afterward Alec would secretly hate him for having done so much for him....

... All this was flung before Amory like an opened scroll, while ulterior to him and speculating upon him were those two breathless, listening forces: the gossamer aura that hung over and about the girl and that familiar thing by the window.

Sacrifice by its very nature was arrogant and impersonal; sacrifice should be eternally supercilious.

Weep not for me but for thy children.

That—thought Amory—would be somehow the way God would talk to me.

Amory felt a sudden surge of joy and then like a face in a motion-picture the aura over the bed faded out; the dynamic shadow by the window, that was as near as he could name it, remained for the fraction of a moment and then the breeze seemed to lift it swiftly out of the room. He clinched his hands in quick ecstatic excitement... the ten seconds were up....

"Do what I say, Alec—do what I say. Do you understand?"

Alec looked at him dumbly—his face a tableau of anguish.

"You have a family," continued Amory slowly. "You have a family and it's important that you should get out of this. Do you hear me?" He repeated clearly what he had said. "Do you hear me?"

"I hear you." The voice was curiously strained, the eyes never for a second left Amory's.

"Alec, you're going to lie down here. If any one comes in you act drunk. You do what I say—if you don't I'll probably kill you."

There was another moment while they stared at each other. Then Amory went briskly to the bureau and, taking his pocket-book, beckoned peremptorily to the girl. He heard one word from Alec that sounded like "penitentiary," then he and Jill were in the bathroom with the door bolted behind them.

"You're here with me," he said sternly. "You've been with me all evening."

She nodded, gave a little half cry.

In a second he had the door of the other room open and three men entered. There was an immediate flood of electric light and he stood there blinking.

"You've been playing a little too dangerous a game, young man!"

Amory laughed.

"Well?"

The leader of the trio nodded authoritatively at a burly man in a check suit.

"All right, Olson."

"I got you, Mr. O'May," said Olson, nodding. The other two took a curious glance at their quarry and then withdrew, closing the door angrily behind them.

The burly man regarded Amory contemptuously.

"Didn't you ever hear of the Mann Act? Coming down here with her," he indicated the girl with his thumb, "with a New York license on your car—to a hotel like *this*." He shook his head implying that he had struggled over Amory but now gave him up.

"Well," said Amory rather impatiently, "what do you want us to do?"

"Get dressed, quick—and tell your friend not to make such a racket." Jill was sobbing noisily on the bed, but at these words she subsided sulkily and, gathering up her clothes, retired to the bathroom. As Amory slipped into Alec's B. V. D.'s he found that his attitude toward the situation was agreeably humorous. The aggrieved virtue of the burly man made him want to laugh.

"Anybody else here?" demanded Olson, trying to look keen and ferret-like.

"Fellow who had the rooms," said Amory carelessly. "He's drunk as an owl, though. Been in there asleep since six o'clock."

"I'll take a look at him presently."

"How did you find out?" asked Amory curiously.

"Night clerk saw you go up-stairs with this woman."

Amory nodded; Jill reappeared from the bathroom, completely if rather untidily arrayed.

"Now then," began Olson, producing a note-book, "I want your real names—no damn John Smith or Mary Brown."

"Wait a minute," said Amory quietly. "Just drop that big-bully stuff. We merely got caught, that's all."

Olson glared at him.

"Name?" he snapped.

Amory gave his name and New York address.

"And the lady?"

"Miss Jill—"

"Say," cried Olson indignantly, "just ease up on the nursery rhymes. What's your name? Sarah Murphy? Minnie Jackson?"

"Oh, my God!" cried the girl cupping her tear-stained face in her hands. "I don't want my mother to know. I don't want my mother to know."

"Come on now!"

"Shut up!" cried Amory at Olson.

An instant's pause.

"Stella Robbins," she faltered finally. "General Delivery, Rugway, New Hampshire."

Olson snapped his note-book shut and looked at them very ponderously.

"By rights the hotel could turn the evidence over to the police and you'd go to penitentiary, you would, for bringin' a girl from one State to 'nother f'r immoral purp'ses—" He paused to let the majesty of his words sink in. "But—the hotel is going to let you off."

"It doesn't want to get in the papers," cried Jill fiercely. "Let us off! Huh!"

A great lightness surrounded Amory. He realized that he was safe and only then did he appreciate the full enormity of what he might have incurred.

"However," continued Olson, "there's a protective association among the hotels. There's been too much of this stuff, and we got a 'rangement with the newspapers so that you get a little free publicity. Not the name of the hotel, but just a line sayin' that you had a little trouble in 'lantic City. See?"

"I see."

"You're gettin' off light—damn light—but—"

"Come on," said Amory briskly. "Let's get out of here. We don't need a valedictory."

Olson walked through the bathroom and took a cursory glance at Alec's still form. Then he extinguished the lights and motioned them to follow him. As they walked into the elevator Amory considered a piece of bravado—yielded finally. He reached out and tapped Olson on the arm.

"Would you mind taking off your hat? There's a lady in the elevator."

Olson's hat came off slowly. There was a rather embarrassing two minutes under the lights of the lobby while the night clerk and a few belated guests stared at them curiously; the loudly dressed girl with bent head, the handsome young man with his chin several points aloft; the inference was quite obvious. Then the chill outdoors—where the salt air was fresher and keener still with the first hints of morning.

"You can get one of those taxis and beat it," said Olson, pointing to the blurred outline of two machines whose drivers were presumably asleep inside.

"Good-by," said Olson. He reached in his pocket suggestively, but Amory snorted, and, taking the girl's arm, turned away.

"Where did you tell the driver to go?" she asked as they whirled along the dim street.

"The station."

"If that guy writes my mother—"

"He won't. Nobody'll ever know about this—except our friends and enemies."

Dawn was breaking over the sea.

"It's getting blue," she said.

"It does very well," agreed Amory critically, and then as an after-thought: "It's almost breakfast-time—do you want something to eat?"

"Food—" she said with a cheerful laugh. "Food is what queered the party. We ordered a big supper to be sent up to the room about two o'clock. Alec didn't give the waiter a tip, so I guess the little bastard snitched."

Jill's low spirits seemed to have gone faster than the scattering night. "Let me tell you," she said emphatically, "when you want to stage that sorta party stay away from liquor, and when you want to get tight stay away from bedrooms."

"I'll remember."

He tapped suddenly at the glass and they drew up at the door of an all-night restaurant.

"Is Alec a great friend of yours?" asked Jill as they perched themselves on high stools inside, and set their elbows on the dingy counter.

"He used to be. He probably won't want to be any more—and never understand why."

"It was sorta crazy you takin' all that blame. Is he pretty important? Kinda more important than you are?"

Amory laughed.

"That remains to be seen," he answered. "That's the question."

THE COLLAPSE OF SEVERAL PILLARS

Two days later back in New York Amory found in a newspaper what he had been searching for—a dozen lines which announced to whom it might concern that Mr. Amory Blaine, who "gave his address" as, etc., had been requested to leave his hotel in Atlantic City because of entertaining in his room a lady *not* his wife.

Then he started, and his fingers trembled, for directly above was a longer paragraph of which the first words were:

"Mr. and Mrs. Leland R. Connage are announcing the engagement of their daughter, Rosalind, to Mr. J. Dawson Ryder, of Hartford, Connecticut—"

He dropped the paper and lay down on his bed with a frightened, sinking sensation in the pit of his stomach. She was gone, definitely, finally gone. Until now he had half unconsciously cherished the hope deep in his heart that some day she would need him and send for him, cry that it had been a mistake, that her heart ached only for the pain she had caused him. Never again could he find even the sombre luxury of wanting her—not this Rosalind, harder, older—nor any beaten, broken woman that his imagination brought to the door of his forties—Amory had wanted her youth, the fresh radiance of her mind and body, the stuff that she was selling now once and for all. So far as he was concerned, young Rosalind was dead.

A day later came a crisp, terse letter from Mr. Barton in Chicago, which informed him that as three more street-car companies had gone into the hands of receivers he could expect for the present no further remittances. Last of all, on a dazed Sunday night, a telegram told him of Monsignor Darcy's sudden death in Philadelphia five days before.

He knew then what it was that he had perceived among the curtains of the room in Atlantic City.

V. The Egotist Becomes a Personage

"A fathom deep in sleep I lie
With old desires, restrained before,
To clamor lifeward with a cry,
As dark flies out the greying door;
And so in quest of creeds to share
I seek assertive day again...
But old monotony is there:
Endless avenues of rain.

Oh, might I rise again!Might I
Throw off the heat of that old wine,
See the new morning mass the sky
With fairy towers, line on line;
Find each mirage in the high air
A symbol, not a dream again...
But old monotony is there:
Endless avenues of rain."

Under the glass portcullis of a theatre Amory stood, watching the first great drops of rain splatter down and flatten to dark stains on the sidewalk. The air became gray and opalescent; a solitary light suddenly outlined a window over the way; then another light; then a hundred more danced and glimmered into vision. Under his feet a thick, iron-studded skylight turned yellow; in the street the lamps of the taxi-cabs sent out glistening sheens along the already black pavement. The unwelcome November rain had perversely stolen the day's last hour and pawned it with that ancient fence, the night.

The silence of the theatre behind him ended with a curious snapping sound, followed by the heavy roaring of a rising crowd and the interlaced clatter of many voices. The matinee was over.

He stood aside, edged a little into the rain to let the throng pass. A small boy rushed out, sniffed in the damp, fresh air and turned up the collar of his coat;

came three or four couples in a great hurry; came a further scattering of people whose eyes as they emerged glanced invariably, first at the wet street, then at the rain-filled air, finally at the dismal sky; last a dense, strolling mass that depressed him with its heavy odor compounded of the tobacco smell of the men and the fetid sensuousness of stale powder on women. After the thick crowd came another scattering; a stray half-dozen; a man on crutches; finally the rattling bang of folding seats inside announced that the ushers were at work.

New York seemed not so much awakening as turning over in its bed. Pallid men rushed by, pinching together their coat-collars; a great swarm of tired, magpie girls from a department-store crowded along with shrieks of strident laughter, three to an umbrella; a squad of marching policemen passed, already miraculously protected by oilskin capes.

The rain gave Amory a feeling of detachment, and the numerous unpleasant aspects of city life without money occurred to him in threatening procession. There was the ghastly, stinking crush of the subway—the car cards thrusting themselves at one, leering out like dull bores who grab your arm with another story; the querulous worry as to whether some one isn't leaning on you; a man deciding not to give his seat to a woman, hating her for it; the woman hating him for not doing it; at worst a squalid phantasmagoria of breath, and old cloth on human bodies and the smells of the food men ate—at best just people—too hot or too cold, tired, worried.

He pictured the rooms where these people lived—where the patterns of the blistered wall-papers were heavy reiterated sunflowers on green and yellow backgrounds, where there were tin bathtubs and gloomy hallways and verdureless, unnamable spaces in back of the buildings; where even love dressed as seduction—a sordid murder around the corner, illicit motherhood in the flat above. And always there was the economical stuffiness of indoor winter, and the long summers, nightmares of perspiration between sticky enveloping walls... dirty restaurants where careless, tired people helped themselves to sugar with their own used coffee-spoons, leaving hard brown deposits in the bowl.

It was not so bad where there were only men or else only women; it was when they were vilely herded that it all seemed so rotten. It was some shame that women gave off at having men see them tired and poor—it was some disgust that men had for women who were tired and poor. It was dirtier than any battle-field he had seen, harder to contemplate than any actual hardship moulded of mire and sweat and danger, it was an atmosphere wherein birth and marriage and death were loathsome, secret things.

He remembered one day in the subway when a delivery boy had brought in a great funeral wreath of fresh flowers, how the smell of it had suddenly cleared the air and given every one in the car a momentary glow.

"I detest poor people," thought Amory suddenly. "I hate them for being poor. Poverty may have been beautiful once, but it's rotten now. It's the ugliest thing in the world. It's essentially cleaner to be corrupt and rich than it is to be innocent and poor." He seemed to see again a figure whose significance had once impressed him—a well-dressed young man gazing from a club window on Fifth Avenue and saying something to his companion with a look of utter disgust. Probably, thought Amory, what he said was: "My God! Aren't people horrible!"

Never before in his life had Amory considered poor people. He thought cynically how completely he was lacking in all human sympathy. O. Henry had found in these people romance, pathos, love, hate—Amory saw only coarseness, physical filth, and stupidity. He made no self-accusations: never any more did he reproach himself for feelings that were natural and sincere. He accepted all his reactions as a part of him, unchangeable, unmoral. This problem of poverty transformed, magnified, attached to some grander, more dignified attitude might some day even be his problem; at present it roused only his profound distaste.

He walked over to Fifth Avenue, dodging the blind, black menace of umbrellas, and standing in front of Delmonico's hailed an auto-bus. Buttoning his coat closely around him he climbed to the roof, where he rode in solitary state through the thin, persistent rain, stung into alertness by the cool moisture perpetually reborn on his cheek. Somewhere in his mind a conversation began, rather resumed its place in his attention. It was composed not of two voices, but of one, which acted alike as questioner and answerer:

Question.—Well—what's the situation?

Answer.—That I have about twenty-four dollars to my name.

Q.—You have the Lake Geneva estate.

A.—But I intend to keep it.

Q.—Can you live?

A.—I can't imagine not being able to. People make money in books and I've found that I can always do the things that people do in books. Really they are the only things I can do.

Q.—Be definite.

A.—I don't know what I'll do—nor have I much curiosity. To-morrow I'm going to leave New York for good. It's a bad town unless you're on top of it.

Q.—Do you want a lot of money?

A.—No. I am merely afraid of being poor.

Q.—Very afraid?

A.—Just passively afraid.

Q.—Where are you drifting?

A.—Don't ask *me!*

Q.—Don't you care?

A.—Rather. I don't want to commit moral suicide.

Q.—Have you no interests left?

A.—None. I've no more virtue to lose. Just as a cooling pot gives off heat, so all through youth and adolescence we give off calories of virtue. That's what's called ingenuousness.

Q.—An interesting idea.

A.—That's why a "good man going wrong" attracts people. They stand around and literally *warm themselves* at the calories of virtue he gives off. Sarah makes an unsophisticated remark and the faces simper in delight—"How *innocent* the poor child is!" They're warming themselves at her virtue. But Sarah sees the simper and never makes that remark again. Only she feels a little colder after that.

Q.—All your calories gone?

A.—All of them. I'm beginning to warm myself at other people's virtue.

Q.—Are you corrupt?

A.—I think so. I'm not sure. I'm not sure about good and evil at all any more.

Q.—Is that a bad sign in itself?

A.—Not necessarily.

Q.—What would be the test of corruption?

A.—Becoming really insincere—calling myself "not such a bad fellow," thinking I regretted my lost youth when I only envy the delights of losing it. Youth is like having a big plate of candy. Sentimentalists think they want to be in the pure, simple state they were in before they ate the candy. They don't. They just want the fun of eating it all over again. The matron doesn't want to repeat her girlhood—she wants to repeat her honeymoon. I don't want to repeat my innocence. I want the pleasure of losing it again.

Q.—Where are you drifting?

This dialogue merged grotesquely into his mind's most familiar state—a grotesque blending of desires, worries, exterior impressions and physical reactions.

One Hundred and Twenty-seventh Street—or One Hundred and Thirty-seventh Street.... Two and three look alike—no, not much. Seat damp... are clothes absorbing wetness from seat, or seat absorbing dryness from clothes?... Sitting on wet substance gave appendicitis, so Froggy Parker's mother said. Well, he'd had it—I'll sue the steamboat company, Beatrice said, and my uncle has a quarter interest—did Beatrice go to heaven?... probably not—He represented Beatrice's immortality, also love-affairs of numerous dead men who surely had never thought of him... if it wasn't appendicitis, influenza maybe. What? One Hundred and Twentieth Street? That must have been One Hundred and Twelfth back there. One O Two instead of One Two Seven. Rosalind not like Beatrice, Eleanor like Beatrice, only wilder and brainier. Apartments along here expensive—probably hundred and fifty a month—maybe two hundred. Uncle had only paid hundred a month for whole great big house in Minneapolis. Question—were the stairs on the left or right as you came in? Anyway, in 12 Univee they were straight back and to the left. What a dirty river—want to go down there and see if it's dirty—French rivers all brown or black, so were Southern rivers. Twenty-four dollars meant four hundred and eighty doughnuts. He could live on it three months and sleep in the park. Wonder where Jill was—Jill Bayne, Fayne, Sayne—what the devil—neck hurts, darned uncomfortable seat. No desire to sleep with Jill, what could Alec see in her? Alec had a coarse taste in women. Own taste the best; Isabelle, Clara, Rosalind, Eleanor, were all-American. Eleanor would pitch, probably southpaw. Rosalind was outfield, wonderful hitter, Clara first base, maybe. Wonder what Humbird's body looked like now. If he himself hadn't been bayonet instructor he'd have gone up to line three months sooner, probably been killed. Where's the darned bell—

The street numbers of Riverside Drive were obscured by the mist and dripping trees from anything but the swiftest scrutiny, but Amory had finally caught sight of one—One Hundred and Twenty-seventh Street. He got off and with no distinct destination followed a winding, descending sidewalk and came out facing the river, in particular a long pier and a partitioned litter of shipyards for miniature craft: small launches, canoes, rowboats, and catboats. He turned northward and followed the shore, jumped a small wire fence and found himself in a great disorderly yard adjoining a dock. The hulls of many boats in various stages of repair were around him; he smelled sawdust and paint and the scarcely distinguishable fiat odor of the Hudson. A man approached through the heavy gloom.

"Hello," said Amory.

"Got a pass?"

"No. Is this private?"

"This is the Hudson River Sporting and Yacht Club."

"Oh! I didn't know. I'm just resting."

"Well—" began the man dubiously.

"I'll go if you want me to."

The man made non-committal noises in his throat and passed on. Amory seated himself on an overturned boat and leaned forward thoughtfully until his chin rested in his hand.

"Misfortune is liable to make me a damn bad man," he said slowly.

IN THE DROOPING HOURS

While the rain drizzled on Amory looked futilely back at the stream of his life, all its glitterings and dirty shallows. To begin with, he was still afraid—not physically afraid any more, but afraid of people and prejudice and misery and monotony. Yet, deep in his bitter heart, he wondered if he was after all worse than this man or the next. He knew that he could sophisticate himself finally into saying that his own weakness was just the result of circumstances and environment; that often when he raged at himself as an egotist something would whisper ingratiatingly: "No. Genius!" That was one manifestation of fear, that voice which whispered that he could not be both great and good, that genius was the exact combination of those inexplicable grooves and twists in his mind, that any discipline would curb it to mediocrity. Probably more than any concrete vice or failing Amory despised his own personality—he loathed knowing that to-morrow and the thousand days after he would swell pompously at a compliment and sulk at an ill word like a third-rate musician or a first-class actor. He was ashamed of the fact that very simple and honest people usually distrusted him; that he had been cruel, often, to those who had sunk their personalities in him—several girls, and a man here and there through college, that he had been an evil influence on; people who had followed him here and there into mental adventures from which he alone rebounded unscathed.

Usually, on nights like this, for there had been many lately, he could escape from this consuming introspection by thinking of children and the infinite possibilities of children—he leaned and listened and he heard a startled baby awake in a house across the street and lend a tiny whimper to the still night. Quick as a flash he turned away, wondering with a touch of panic whether something in the brooding despair of his mood had made a darkness in its tiny soul. He shivered. What if some day the balance was overturned, and he became a thing that frightened children and crept into rooms in the dark, approached dim communion with those phantoms who whispered shadowy secrets to the mad of that dark continent upon the moon....

Amory smiled a bit.

"You're too much wrapped up in yourself," he heard some one say. And again—

"Get out and do some real work—"

"Stop worrying—"

He fancied a possible future comment of his own.

"Yes—I was perhaps an egotist in youth, but I soon found it made me morbid to think too much about myself."

Suddenly he felt an overwhelming desire to let himself go to the devil—not to go violently as a gentleman should, but to sink safely and sensuously out of sight. He pictured himself in an adobe house in Mexico, half-reclining on a rug-covered couch, his slender, artistic fingers closed on a cigarette while he listened to guitars strumming melancholy undertones to an age-old dirge of Castile and an olive-skinned, carmine-lipped girl caressed his hair. Here he might live a strange litany, delivered from right and wrong and from the hound of heaven and from every God (except the exotic Mexican one who was pretty slack himself and rather addicted to Oriental scents)—delivered from success and hope and poverty into that long chute of indulgence which led, after all, only to the artificial lake of death.

There were so many places where one might deteriorate pleasantly: Port Said, Shanghai, parts of Turkestan, Constantinople, the South Seas—all lands of sad, haunting music and many odors, where lust could be a mode and expression of life, where the shades of night skies and sunsets would seem to reflect only moods of passion: the colors of lips and poppies.

STILL WEEDING

Once he had been miraculously able to scent evil as a horse detects a broken bridge at night, but the man with the queer feet in Phoebe's room had diminished to the aura over Jill. His instinct perceived the fetidness of poverty, but no longer ferreted out the deeper evils in pride and sensuality.

There were no more wise men; there were no more heroes; Burne Holiday was sunk from sight as though he had never lived; Monsignor was dead. Amory had grown up to a thousand books, a thousand lies; he had listened eagerly to people who pretended to know, who knew nothing. The mystical reveries of saints that had once filled him with awe in the still hours of night, now vaguely repelled him. The Byrons and Brookes who had defied life from mountain tops were in the end but flaneurs and poseurs, at best mistaking the shadow of courage for the substance of wisdom. The pageantry of his disillusion took shape in a world-old procession of Prophets, Athenians, Martyrs, Saints, Scientists, Don Juans, Jesuits, Puritans, Fausts, Poets, Pacifists; like costumed alumni at a college reunion they streamed before him as their dreams, personalities, and creeds had in turn thrown colored lights on his soul; each had tried to express the glory of life and the tremendous significance of man; each had boasted of synchronizing what had gone before into his own rickety generalities; each had depended after all on the set stage and the convention of the theatre, which is that man in his hunger for faith will feed his mind with the nearest and most convenient food.

Women—of whom he had expected so much; whose beauty he had hoped to transmute into modes of art; whose unfathomable instincts, marvellously incoherent and inarticulate, he had thought to perpetuate in terms of experience—had become merely consecrations to their own posterity. Isabelle, Clara, Rosalind, Eleanor, were all removed by their very beauty, around which men had swarmed, from the possibility of contributing anything but a sick heart and a page of puzzled words to write.

Amory based his loss of faith in help from others on several sweeping syllogisms. Granted that his generation, however bruised and decimated from this Victorian war, were the heirs of progress. Waving aside petty differences of conclusions which, although they might occasionally cause the deaths of several millions of young men, might be explained away—supposing that after all Bernard Shaw and Bernhardi, Bonar Law and Bethmann-Hollweg were mutual heirs of progress if only in agreeing against the ducking of witches—waiving the antitheses and approaching individually these men who seemed to be the leaders, he was repelled by the discrepancies and contradictions in the men themselves.

There was, for example, Thornton Hancock, respected by half the intellectual world as an authority on life, a man who had verified and believed the code he lived by, an educator of educators, an adviser to Presidents—yet Amory knew that this man had, in his heart, leaned on the priest of another religion.

And Monsignor, upon whom a cardinal rested, had moments of strange and horrible insecurity—inexplicable in a religion that explained even disbelief in terms of its own faith: if you doubted the devil it was the devil that made you doubt him. Amory had seen Monsignor go to the houses of stolid philistines, read popular novels furiously, saturate himself in routine, to escape from that horror.

And this priest, a little wiser, somewhat purer, had been, Amory knew, not essentially older than he.

Amory was alone—he had escaped from a small enclosure into a great labyrinth. He was where Goethe was when he began "Faust"; he was where Conrad was when he wrote "Almayer's Folly."

Amory said to himself that there were essentially two sorts of people who through natural clarity or disillusion left the enclosure and sought the labyrinth. There were men like Wells and Plato, who had, half unconsciously, a strange, hidden orthodoxy, who would accept for themselves only what could be accepted for all men—incurable romanticists who never, for all their efforts, could enter the labyrinth as stark souls; there were on the other hand sword-like pioneering personalities, Samuel Butler, Renan, Voltaire, who progressed much slower, yet eventually much further, not in the direct pessimistic line of speculative philosophy but concerned in the eternal attempt to attach a positive value to life....

Amory stopped. He began for the first time in his life to have a strong distrust of all generalities and epigrams. They were too easy, too dangerous to the public mind. Yet all thought usually reached the public after thirty years in some such form: Benson and Chesterton had popularized Huysmans and Newman; Shaw had sugar-coated Nietzsche and Ibsen and Schopenhauer. The man in the street heard the conclusions of dead genius through some one else's clever paradoxes and didactic epigrams.

Life was a damned muddle... a football game with every one off-side and the referee gotten rid of—every one claiming the referee would have been on his side....

Progress was a labyrinth... people plunging blindly in and then rushing wildly back, shouting that they had found it... the invisible king—the elan vital—the principle of evolution... writing a book, starting a war, founding a school....

Amory, even had he not been a selfish man, would have started all inquiries with himself. He was his own best example—sitting in the rain, a human creature of sex and pride, foiled by chance and his own temperament of the balm of love and children, preserved to help in building up the living consciousness of the race.

In self-reproach and loneliness and disillusion he came to the entrance of the labyrinth.

Another dawn flung itself across the river, a belated taxi hurried along the street, its lamps still shining like burning eyes in a face white from a night's carouse. A melancholy siren sounded far down the river.

MONSIGNOR

Amory kept thinking how Monsignor would have enjoyed his own funeral. It was magnificently Catholic and liturgical. Bishop O'Neill sang solemn high mass and the cardinal gave the final absolutions. Thornton Hancock, Mrs. Lawrence, the British and Italian ambassadors, the papal delegate, and a host of friends and priests were there—yet the inexorable shears had cut through all these threads that Monsignor had gathered into his hands. To Amory it was a haunting grief to see him lying in his coffin, with closed hands upon his purple vestments. His face had not changed, and, as he never knew he was dying, it showed no pain or fear. It was Amory's dear old friend, his and the others'—for the church was full of people with daft, staring faces, the most exalted seeming the most stricken.

The cardinal, like an archangel in cope and mitre, sprinkled the holy water; the organ broke into sound; the choir began to sing the Requiem Eternam.

All these people grieved because they had to some extent depended upon Monsignor. Their grief was more than sentiment for the "crack in his voice or a certain break in his walk," as Wells put it. These people had leaned on Monsignor's faith, his way of finding cheer, of making religion a thing of lights and shadows, making all light and shadow merely aspects of God. People felt safe when he was near.

Of Amory's attempted sacrifice had been born merely the full realization of his disillusion, but of Monsignor's funeral was born the romantic elf who was to enter the labyrinth with him. He found something that he wanted, had always wanted and always would want—not to be admired, as he had feared; not to be loved, as he had made himself believe; but to be necessary to people, to be indispensable; he remembered the sense of security he had found in Burne.

Life opened up in one of its amazing bursts of radiance and Amory suddenly and permanently rejected an old epigram that had been playing listlessly in his mind: "Very few things matter and nothing matters very much."

On the contrary, Amory felt an immense desire to give people a sense of security.

THE BIG MAN WITH GOGGLES

On the day that Amory started on his walk to Princeton the sky was a colorless vault, cool, high and barren of the threat of rain. It was a gray day, that least fleshly of all weathers; a day of dreams and far hopes and clear visions. It was a day easily associated with those abstract truths and purities that dissolve in the sunshine or fade out in mocking laughter by the light of the moon. The trees and clouds were carved in classical severity; the sounds of the countryside had harmonized to a monotone, metallic as a trumpet, breathless as the Grecian urn.

The day had put Amory in such a contemplative mood that he caused much annoyance to several motorists who were forced to slow up considerably or else run him down. So engrossed in his thoughts was he that he was scarcely surprised at that strange phenomenon—cordiality manifested within fifty miles of Manhattan—when a passing car slowed down beside him and a voice hailed him. He looked up and saw a magnificent Locomobile in which sat two middle-aged men, one of them small and anxious looking, apparently an artificial growth on the other who was large and begoggled and imposing.

"Do you want a lift?" asked the apparently artificial growth, glancing from the corner of his eye at the imposing man as if for some habitual, silent corroboration.

"You bet I do. Thanks."

The chauffeur swung open the door, and, climbing in, Amory settled himself in the middle of the back seat. He took in his companions curiously. The chief characteristic of the big man seemed to be a great confidence in himself set off against a tremendous boredom with everything around him. That part of his face which protruded under the goggles was what is generally termed "strong"; rolls of not undignified fat had collected near his chin; somewhere above was a wide thin mouth and the rough model for a Roman nose, and, below, his shoulders collapsed without a struggle into the powerful bulk of his chest and belly. He was excellently and quietly dressed. Amory noticed that he was inclined to stare straight at the back of the chauffeur's head as if speculating steadily but hopelessly some baffling hirsute problem.

The smaller man was remarkable only for his complete submersion in the personality of the other. He was of that lower secretarial type who at forty have engraved upon their business cards: "Assistant to the President," and without a sigh consecrate the rest of their lives to second-hand mannerisms.

"Going far?" asked the smaller man in a pleasant disinterested way.

"Quite a stretch."

"Hiking for exercise?"

"No," responded Amory succinctly, "I'm walking because I can't afford to ride."

"Oh."

Then again:

"Are you looking for work? Because there's lots of work," he continued rather testily. "All this talk of lack of work. The West is especially short of labor." He expressed the West with a sweeping, lateral gesture. Amory nodded politely.

"Have you a trade?"

No—Amory had no trade.

"Clerk, eh?"

No—Amory was not a clerk.

"Whatever your line is," said the little man, seeming to agree wisely with something Amory had said, "now is the time of opportunity and business openings." He glanced again toward the big man, as a lawyer grilling a witness glances involuntarily at the jury.

Amory decided that he must say something and for the life of him could think of only one thing to say.

"Of course I want a great lot of money—"

The little man laughed mirthlessly but conscientiously.

"That's what every one wants nowadays, but they don't want to work for it."

"A very natural, healthy desire. Almost all normal people want to be rich without great effort—except the financiers in problem plays, who want to 'crash their way through.' Don't you want easy money?"

"Of course not," said the secretary indignantly.

"But," continued Amory disregarding him, "being very poor at present I am contemplating socialism as possibly my forte."

Both men glanced at him curiously.

"These bomb throwers—" The little man ceased as words lurched ponderously from the big man's chest.

"If I thought you were a bomb thrower I'd run you over to the Newark jail. That's what I think of Socialists."

Amory laughed.

"What are you," asked the big man, "one of these parlor Bolsheviks, one of these idealists? I must say I fail to see the difference. The idealists loaf around and write the stuff that stirs up the poor immigrants."

"Well," said Amory, "if being an idealist is both safe and lucrative, I might try it."

"What's your difficulty? Lost your job?"

"Not exactly, but—well, call it that."

"What was it?"

"Writing copy for an advertising agency."

"Lots of money in advertising."

Amory smiled discreetly.

"Oh, I'll admit there's money in it eventually. Talent doesn't starve any more. Even art gets enough to eat these days. Artists draw your magazine covers, write your advertisements, hash out rag-time for your theatres. By the great commercializing of printing you've found a harmless, polite occupation for every genius who might have carved his own niche. But beware the artist who's an intellectual also. The artist who doesn't fit—the Rousseau, the Tolstoi, the Samuel Butler, the Amory Blaine—"

"Who's he?" demanded the little man suspiciously.

"Well," said Amory, "he's a—he's an intellectual personage not very well known at present."

The little man laughed his conscientious laugh, and stopped rather suddenly as Amory's burning eyes turned on him.

"What are you laughing at?"

"These *intellectual* people—"

"Do you know what it means?"

The little man's eyes twitched nervously.

"Why, it *usually* means—"

"It *always* means brainy and well-educated," interrupted Amory. "It means having an active knowledge of the race's experience." Amory decided to be very rude. He turned to the big man. "The young man," he indicated the secretary with his thumb, and said young man as one says bell-boy, with no implication of youth, "has the usual muddled connotation of all popular words."

"You object to the fact that capital controls printing?" said the big man, fixing him with his goggles.

"Yes—and I object to doing their mental work for them. It seemed to me that the root of all the business I saw around me consisted in overworking and underpaying a bunch of dubs who submitted to it."

"Here now," said the big man, "you'll have to admit that the laboring man is certainly highly paid—five and six hour days—it's ridiculous. You can't buy an honest day's work from a man in the trades-unions."

"You've brought it on yourselves," insisted Amory. "You people never make concessions until they're wrung out of you."

"What people?"

"Your class; the class I belonged to until recently; those who by inheritance or industry or brains or dishonesty have become the moneyed class."

"Do you imagine that if that road-mender over there had the money he'd be any more willing to give it up?"

"No, but what's that got to do with it?"

The older man considered.

"No, I'll admit it hasn't. It rather sounds as if it had though."

"In fact," continued Amory, "he'd be worse. The lower classes are narrower, less pleasant and personally more selfish—certainly more stupid. But all that has nothing to do with the question."

"Just exactly what is the question?"

Here Amory had to pause to consider exactly what the question was.

AMORY COINS A PHRASE

"When life gets hold of a brainy man of fair education," began Amory slowly, "that is, when he marries he becomes, nine times out of ten, a conservative as far as existing social conditions are concerned. He may be unselfish, kind-hearted, even just in his own way, but his first job is to provide and to hold fast. His wife shoos him on, from ten thousand a year to twenty thousand a year, on and on, in an enclosed treadmill that hasn't any windows. He's done! Life's got him! He's no help! He's a spiritually married man."

Amory paused and decided that it wasn't such a bad phrase.

"Some men," he continued, "escape the grip. Maybe their wives have no social ambitions; maybe they've hit a sentence or two in a 'dangerous book' that pleased them; maybe they started on the treadmill as I did and were knocked off. Anyway, they're the congressmen you can't bribe, the Presidents who aren't politicians, the writers, speakers, scientists, statesmen who aren't just popular grab-bags for a half-dozen women and children."

"He's the natural radical?"

"Yes," said Amory. "He may vary from the disillusioned critic like old Thornton Hancock, all the way to Trotsky. Now this spiritually unmarried man hasn't direct power, for unfortunately the spiritually married man, as a by-product of his money chase, has garnered in the great newspaper, the popular magazine, the influential weekly—so that Mrs. Newspaper, Mrs. Magazine, Mrs. Weekly can have a better limousine than those oil people across the street or those cement people 'round the corner."

"Why not?"

"It makes wealthy men the keepers of the world's intellectual conscience and, of course, a man who has money under one set of social institutions quite naturally can't risk his family's happiness by letting the clamor for another appear in his newspaper."

"But it appears," said the big man.

"Where?—in the discredited mediums. Rotten cheap-papered weeklies."

"All right—go on."

"Well, my first point is that through a mixture of conditions of which the family is the first, there are these two sorts of brains. One sort takes human nature as it finds it, uses its timidity, its weakness, and its strength for its own ends. Opposed is the man who, being spiritually unmarried, continually seeks for new systems that will control or counteract human nature. His problem is harder. It is not life that's complicated, it's the struggle to guide and control life. That is his struggle. He is a part of progress—the spiritually married man is not."

The big man produced three big cigars, and proffered them on his huge palm. The little man took one, Amory shook his head and reached for a cigarette.

"Go on talking," said the big man. "I've been wanting to hear one of you fellows."

GOING FASTER

"Modern life," began Amory again, "changes no longer century by century, but year by year, ten times faster than it ever has before—populations doubling, civilizations unified more closely with other civilizations, economic interdependence, racial questions, and—we're *dawdling* along. My idea is that we've got to go very much faster." He slightly emphasized the last words and the chauffeur unconsciously increased the speed of the car. Amory and the big man laughed; the little man laughed, too, after a pause.

"Every child," said Amory, "should have an equal start. If his father can endow him with a good physique and his mother with some common sense in his early education, that should be his heritage. If the father can't give him a good physique, if the mother has spent in chasing men the years in which she should have been preparing herself to educate her children, so much the worse for the child. He shouldn't be artificially bolstered up with money, sent to these horrible tutoring schools, dragged through college... Every boy ought to have an equal start."

"All right," said the big man, his goggles indicating neither approval nor objection.

"Next I'd have a fair trial of government ownership of all industries."

"That's been proven a failure."

"No—it merely failed. If we had government ownership we'd have the best analytical business minds in the government working for something besides themselves. We'd have Mackays instead of Burlesons; we'd have Morgans in the Treasury Department; we'd have Hills running interstate commerce. We'd have the best lawyers in the Senate."

"They wouldn't give their best efforts for nothing. McAdoo—"

"No," said Amory, shaking his head. "Money isn't the only stimulus that brings out the best that's in a man, even in America."

"You said a while ago that it was."

"It is, right now. But if it were made illegal to have more than a certain amount the best men would all flock for the one other reward which attracts humanity—honor."

The big man made a sound that was very like *boo.*

"That's the silliest thing you've said yet."

"No, it isn't silly. It's quite plausible. If you'd gone to college you'd have been struck by the fact that the men there would work twice as hard for any one of a hundred petty honors as those other men did who were earning their way through."

"Kids—child's play!" scoffed his antagonist.

"Not by a darned sight—unless we're all children. Did you ever see a grown man when he's trying for a secret society—or a rising family whose name is up at some club? They'll jump when they hear the sound of the word. The idea that to make a man work you've got to hold gold in front of his eyes is a growth, not an axiom. We've done that for so long that we've forgotten there's any other way. We've made a world where that's necessary. Let me tell you"—Amory became emphatic—"if there were ten men insured against either wealth or starvation, and offered a green ribbon for five hours' work a day and a blue ribbon for ten hours' work a day, nine out of ten of them would be trying for the blue ribbon. That competitive instinct only wants a badge. If the size of their house is the badge they'll sweat their heads off for that. If it's only a blue ribbon, I damn near believe they'll work just as hard. They have in other ages."

"I don't agree with you."

"I know it," said Amory nodding sadly. "It doesn't matter any more though. I think these people are going to come and take what they want pretty soon."

A fierce hiss came from the little man.

"Machine-guns!"

"Ah, but you've taught them their use."

The big man shook his head.

"In this country there are enough property owners not to permit that sort of thing."

Amory wished he knew the statistics of property owners and non-property owners; he decided to change the subject.

But the big man was aroused.

"When you talk of 'taking things away,' you're on dangerous ground."

"How can they get it without taking it? For years people have been stalled off with promises. Socialism may not be progress, but the threat of the red flag is certainly the inspiring force of all reform. You've got to be sensational to get attention."

"Russia is your example of a beneficent violence, I suppose?"

"Quite possibly," admitted Amory. "Of course, it's overflowing just as the French Revolution did, but I've no doubt that it's really a great experiment and well worth while."

"Don't you believe in moderation?"

"You won't listen to the moderates, and it's almost too late. The truth is that the public has done one of those startling and amazing things that they do about once in a hundred years. They've seized an idea."

"What is it?"

"That however the brains and abilities of men may differ, their stomachs are essentially the same."

THE LITTLE MAN GETS HIS

"If you took all the money in the world," said the little man with much profundity, "and divided it up in equ—"

"Oh, shut up!" said Amory briskly and, paying no attention to the little man's enraged stare, he went on with his argument.

"The human stomach—" he began; but the big man interrupted rather impatiently.

"I'm letting you talk, you know," he said, "but please avoid stomachs. I've been feeling mine all day. Anyway, I don't agree with one-half you've said. Government ownership is the basis of your whole argument, and it's invariably a beehive of corruption. Men won't work for blue ribbons, that's all rot."

When he ceased the little man spoke up with a determined nod, as if resolved this time to have his say out.

"There are certain things which are human nature," he asserted with an owl-like look, "which always have been and always will be, which can't be changed."

Amory looked from the small man to the big man helplessly.

"Listen to that! *That's* what makes me discouraged with progress. *Listen* to that! I can name offhand over one hundred natural phenomena that have been changed by the will of man—a hundred instincts in man that have been wiped out or are now held in check by civilization. What this man here just said has been for thousands of years the last refuge of the associated mutton-heads of the world. It negates the efforts of every scientist, statesman, moralist, reformer, doctor, and philosopher that ever gave his life to humanity's service. It's a flat impeachment of all that's worth while in human nature. Every person over twenty-five years old who makes that statement in cold blood ought to be deprived of the franchise."

The little man leaned back against the seat, his face purple with rage. Amory continued, addressing his remarks to the big man.

"These quarter-educated, stale-minded men such as your friend here, who *think* they think, every question that comes up, you'll find his type in the usual ghastly muddle. One minute it's 'the brutality and inhumanity of these Prussians'—the next it's 'we ought to exterminate the whole German people.' They always believe that 'things are in a bad way now,' but they 'haven't any faith in these idealists.' One minute they call Wilson 'just a dreamer, not practical'—a year later they rail at him for making his dreams realities. They haven't clear logical ideas on one single subject except a sturdy, stolid opposition to all change. They don't think uneducated people should be highly paid, but they won't see that if they don't pay the uneducated people their children are going to be uneducated too, and we're going round and round in a circle. That—is the great middle class!"

The big man with a broad grin on his face leaned over and smiled at the little man.

"You're catching it pretty heavy, Garvin; how do you feel?"

The little man made an attempt to smile and act as if the whole matter were so ridiculous as to be beneath notice. But Amory was not through.

"The theory that people are fit to govern themselves rests on this man. If he can be educated to think clearly, concisely, and logically, freed of his habit of taking refuge in platitudes and prejudices and sentimentalisms, then I'm a militant Socialist. If he can't, then I don't think it matters much what happens to man or his systems, now or hereafter."

"I am both interested and amused," said the big man. "You are very young."

"Which may only mean that I have neither been corrupted nor made timid by contemporary experience. I possess the most valuable experience, the experience of the race, for in spite of going to college I've managed to pick up a good education."

"You talk glibly."

"It's not all rubbish," cried Amory passionately. "This is the first time in my life I've argued Socialism. It's the only panacea I know. I'm restless. My whole generation is restless. I'm sick of a system where the richest man gets the most beautiful girl if he wants her, where the artist without an income has to sell his talents to a button manufacturer. Even if I had no talents I'd not be content to work ten years, condemned either to celibacy or a furtive indulgence, to give some man's son an automobile."

"But, if you're not sure—"

"That doesn't matter," exclaimed Amory. "My position couldn't be worse. A social revolution might land me on top. Of course I'm selfish. It seems to me I've been a fish out of water in too many outworn systems. I was probably one of the two dozen men in my class at college who got a decent education; still they'd let any well-tutored flathead play football and *I* was ineligible, because some silly old men thought we should *all* profit by conic sections. I loathed the army. I loathed business. I'm in love with change and I've killed my conscience—"

"So you'll go along crying that we must go faster."

"That, at least, is true," Amory insisted. "Reform won't catch up to the needs of civilization unless it's made to. A laissez-faire policy is like spoiling a child by saying he'll turn out all right in the end. He will—if he's made to."

"But you don't believe all this Socialist patter you talk."

"I don't know. Until I talked to you I hadn't thought seriously about it. I wasn't sure of half of what I said."

"You puzzle me," said the big man, "but you're all alike. They say Bernard Shaw, in spite of his doctrines, is the most exacting of all dramatists about his royalties. To the last farthing."

"Well," said Amory, "I simply state that I'm a product of a versatile mind in a restless generation—with every reason to throw my mind and pen in with the radicals. Even if, deep in my heart, I thought we were all blind atoms in a world as limited as a stroke of a pendulum, I and my sort would struggle against tradition; try, at least, to displace old cants with new ones. I've thought I was right about life at various times, but faith is difficult. One thing I know. If living isn't a seeking for the grail it may be a damned amusing game."

For a minute neither spoke and then the big man asked:

"What was your university?"

"Princeton."

The big man became suddenly interested; the expression of his goggles altered slightly.

"I sent my son to Princeton."

"Did you?"

"Perhaps you knew him. His name was Jesse Ferrenby. He was killed last year in France."

"I knew him very well. In fact, he was one of my particular friends."

"He was—a—quite a fine boy. We were very close."

Amory began to perceive a resemblance between the father and the dead son and he told himself that there had been all along a sense of familiarity. Jesse Ferrenby, the man who in college had borne off the crown that he had aspired to. It was all so far away. What little boys they had been, working for blue ribbons—

The car slowed up at the entrance to a great estate, ringed around by a huge hedge and a tall iron fence.

"Won't you come in for lunch?"

Amory shook his head.

"Thank you, Mr. Ferrenby, but I've got to get on."

The big man held out his hand. Amory saw that the fact that he had known Jesse more than outweighed any disfavor he had created by his opinions. What ghosts were people with which to work! Even the little man insisted on shaking hands.

"Good-by!" shouted Mr. Ferrenby, as the car turned the corner and started up the drive. "Good luck to you and bad luck to your theories."

"Same to you, sir," cried Amory, smiling and waving his hand.

"OUT OF THE FIRE, OUT OF THE LITTLE ROOM"

Eight hours from Princeton Amory sat down by the Jersey roadside and looked at the frost-bitten country. Nature as a rather coarse phenomenon composed largely of flowers that, when closely inspected, appeared moth-eaten, and of ants that endlessly traversed blades of grass, was always disillusioning; nature represented by skies and waters and far horizons was more likable. Frost and the promise of winter thrilled him now, made him think of a wild battle between St. Regis and Groton, ages ago, seven years ago—and of an autumn day in France twelve months before when he had lain in tall grass, his platoon flattened down close around him, waiting to tap the shoulders of a Lewis gunner. He saw the two pictures together with somewhat the same primitive exaltation—two games he had played, differing in quality of acerbity, linked in a way that differed them from Rosalind or the subject of labyrinths which were, after all, the business of life.

"I am selfish," he thought.

"This is not a quality that will change when I 'see human suffering' or 'lose my parents' or 'help others.'

"This selfishness is not only part of me. It is the most living part.

"It is by somehow transcending rather than by avoiding that selfishness that I can bring poise and balance into my life.

"There is no virtue of unselfishness that I cannot use. I can make sacrifices, be charitable, give to a friend, endure for a friend, lay down my life for a friend—all because these things may be the best possible expression of myself; yet I have not one drop of the milk of human kindness."

The problem of evil had solidified for Amory into the problem of sex. He was beginning to identify evil with the strong phallic worship in Brooke and the early Wells. Inseparably linked with evil was beauty—beauty, still a constant rising tumult; soft in Eleanor's voice, in an old song at night, rioting deliriously through life like superimposed waterfalls, half rhythm, half darkness. Amory knew that every time he had reached toward it longingly it had leered out at him with the grotesque face of evil. Beauty of great art, beauty of all joy, most of all the beauty of women.

After all, it had too many associations with license and indulgence. Weak things were often beautiful, weak things were never good. And in this new loneness of his that had been selected for what greatness he might achieve, beauty must be relative or, itself a harmony, it would make only a discord.

In a sense this gradual renunciation of beauty was the second step after his disillusion had been made complete. He felt that he was leaving behind him his chance of being a certain type of artist. It seemed so much more important to be a certain sort of man.

His mind turned a corner suddenly and he found himself thinking of the Catholic Church. The idea was strong in him that there was a certain intrinsic lack in those to whom orthodox religion was necessary, and religion to Amory meant the Church of Rome. Quite conceivably it was an empty ritual but it was seemingly the only assimilative, traditionary bulwark against the decay of morals. Until the great mobs could be educated into a moral sense some one must cry: "Thou shalt not!" Yet any acceptance was, for the present, impossible. He wanted time and the absence of ulterior pressure. He wanted to keep the tree without ornaments, realize fully the direction and momentum of this new start.

The afternoon waned from the purging good of three o'clock to the golden beauty of four. Afterward he walked through the dull ache of a setting sun when even the clouds seemed bleeding and at twilight he came to a graveyard. There was a dusky, dreamy smell of flowers and the ghost of a new moon in the sky and shadows everywhere. On an impulse he considered trying to open the door of a rusty iron vault built into the side of a hill; a vault washed clean and covered with late-blooming, weepy watery-blue flowers that might have grown from dead eyes, sticky to the touch with a sickening odor.

Amory wanted to feel "William Dayfield, 1864."

He wondered that graves ever made people consider life in vain. Somehow he could find nothing hopeless in having lived. All the broken columns and clasped hands and doves and angels meant romances. He fancied that in a hundred years he would like having young people speculate as to whether his eyes were brown or blue, and he hoped quite passionately that his grave would have about it an air of many, many years ago. It seemed strange that out of a row of Union soldiers two or three made him think of dead loves and dead lovers, when they were exactly like the rest, even to the yellowish moss.

Long after midnight the towers and spires of Princeton were visible, with here and there a late-burning light—and suddenly out of the clear darkness the sound of bells. As an endless dream it went on; the spirit of the past brooding over a new generation, the chosen youth from the muddled, unchastened world, still fed romantically on the mistakes and half-forgotten dreams of dead statesmen and poets. Here was a new generation, shouting the old cries, learning the old creeds, through a revery of long days and nights; destined finally to go out into that dirty gray turmoil to follow love and pride; a new generation dedicated more than the last to the fear of poverty and the worship of success; grown up to find all Gods dead, all wars fought, all faiths in man shaken....

Amory, sorry for them, was still not sorry for himself—art, politics, religion, whatever his medium should be, he knew he was safe now, free from all hysteria—he could accept what was acceptable, roam, grow, rebel, sleep deep through many nights....

There was no God in his heart, he knew; his ideas were still in riot; there was ever the pain of memory; the regret for his lost youth—yet the waters of disillusion had left a deposit on his soul, responsibility and a love of life, the faint stirring of old ambitions and unrealized dreams. But—oh, Rosalind! Rosalind!...

"It's all a poor substitute at best," he said sadly.

And he could not tell why the struggle was worth while, why he had determined to use to the utmost himself and his heritage from the personalities he had passed....

He stretched out his arms to the crystalline, radiant sky.

"I know myself," he cried, "but that is all."

THE BEAUTIFUL AND DAMNED

The victor belongs to the spoils.
—ANTHONY PATCH

TO
SHANE LESLIE, GEORGE JEAN NATHAN
AND MAXWELL PERKINS

IN APPRECIATION OF MUCH LITERARY HELP
AND ENCOURAGEMENT

BOOK ONE

I. ANTHONY PATCH

IN 1913, when Anthony Patch was twenty-five, two years were already gone since irony, the Holy Ghost of this later day, had, theoretically at least, descended upon him. Irony was the final polish of the shoe, the ultimate dab of the clothes-brush, a sort of intellectual "There!"—yet at the brink of this story he has as yet gone no further than the conscious stage. As you first see him he wonders frequently whether he is not without honor and slightly mad, a shameful and obscene thinness glistening on the surface of the world like oil on a clean pond, these occasions being varied, of course, with those in which he thinks himself rather an exceptional young man, thoroughly sophisticated, well adjusted to his environment, and somewhat more significant than any one else he knows.

This was his healthy state and it made him cheerful, pleasant, and very attractive to intelligent men and to all women. In this state he considered that he would one day accomplish some quiet subtle thing that the elect would deem worthy and, passing on, would join the dimmer stars in a nebulous, indeterminate heaven half-way between death and immortality. Until the time came for this effort he would be Anthony Patch—not a portrait of a man but a distinct and dynamic personality, opinionated, contemptuous, functioning from within outward—a man who was aware that there could be no honor and yet had honor, who knew the sophistry of courage and yet was brave.

A WORTHY MAN AND HIS GIFTED SON

Anthony drew as much consciousness of social security from being the grandson of Adam J. Patch as he would have had from tracing his line over the sea to the crusaders. This is inevitable; Virginians and Bostonians to the contrary notwithstanding, an aristocracy founded sheerly on money postulates wealth in the particular.

Now Adam J. Patch, more familiarly known as "Cross Patch," left his father's farm in Tarrytown early in sixty-one to join a New York cavalry regiment. He came home from the war a major, charged into Wall Street, and amid much fuss, fume, applause, and ill will he gathered to himself some seventy-five million dollars.

This occupied his energies until he was fifty-seven years old. It was then that he determined, after a severe attack of sclerosis, to consecrate the remainder of his life to the moral regeneration of the world. He became a reformer among reformers. Emulating the magnificent efforts of Anthony Comstock, after whom his grandson was named, he levelled a varied assortment of uppercuts and body-blows at liquor, literature, vice, art, patent medicines, and Sunday theatres. His mind, under the influence of that insidious mildew which eventually forms on all but the few, gave itself up furiously to every indignation of the age. From an armchair in the office of his Tarrytown estate he directed against the enormous hypothetical enemy, unrighteousness, a campaign which went on through fifteen years, during which he displayed himself a rabid monomaniac, an unqualified nuisance, and an intolerable bore. The year in which this story opens found him wearying; his campaign had grown desultory; 1861 was creeping up slowly on 1895; his thoughts ran a great deal on the Civil War, somewhat on his dead wife and son, almost infinitesimally on his grandson Anthony.

Early in his career Adam Patch had married an anemic lady of thirty, Alicia Withers, who brought him one hundred thousand dollars and an impeccable entré into the banking circles of New York. Immediately and rather spunkily she had borne him a son and, as if completely devitalized by the magnificence of this performance, she had thenceforth effaced herself within the shadowy dimensions of the nursery. The boy, Adam Ulysses Patch, became an inveterate joiner of clubs, connoisseur of good form, and driver of tandems—at the astonishing age of twenty-six he began his memoirs under the title "New York Society as I Have Seen It." On the rumor of its conception this work was eagerly bid for among publishers, but as it proved after his death to be immoderately verbose and overpoweringly dull, it never obtained even a private printing.

This Fifth Avenue Chesterfield married at twenty-two. His wife was Henrietta Lebrune, the Boston "Society Contralto," and the single child of the union was, at the request of his grandfather, christened Anthony Comstock Patch. When he went to Harvard, the Comstock dropped out of his name to a nether hell of oblivion and was never heard of thereafter.

Young Anthony had one picture of his father and mother together—so often had it faced his eyes in childhood that it had acquired the impersonality of furniture, but every one who came into his bedroom regarded it with interest. It showed a dandy of the nineties, spare and handsome, standing beside a tall dark lady with a muff and the suggestion of a bustle. Between them was a little boy with long brown curls, dressed in a velvet Lord Fauntleroy suit. This was Anthony at five, the year of his mother's death.

His memories of the Boston Society Contralto were nebulous and musical. She was a lady who sang, sang, sang, in the music room of their house on Washington Square—sometimes with guests scattered all about her, the men with their arms folded, balanced breathlessly on the edges of sofas, the women with their hands in their laps, occasionally making little whispers to the men and always clapping very briskly and uttering cooing cries after each song—and often she sang to Anthony alone, in Italian or French or in a strange and terrible dialect which she imagined to be the speech of the Southern negro.

His recollections of the gallant Ulysses, the first man in America to roll the lapels of his coat, were much more vivid. After Henrietta Lebrune Patch had "joined another choir," as her widower huskily remarked from time to time, father and son lived up at grampa's in Tarrytown, and Ulysses came daily to Anthony's nursery and expelled pleasant, thick-smelling words for sometimes as much as an hour. He was continually promising Anthony hunting trips and fishing trips and excursions to Atlantic City, "oh, some time soon now"; but none of them ever materialized. One trip they did take; when Anthony was eleven they went abroad, to England and Switzerland, and there in the best hotel in Lucerne his father died with much sweating and grunting and crying aloud for air. In a panic of despair and terror Anthony was brought back to America, wedded to a vague melancholy that was to stay beside him through the rest of his life.

PAST AND PERSON OF THE HERO

At eleven he had a horror of death. Within six impressionable years his parents had died and his grandmother had faded off almost imperceptibly, until, for the first time since her marriage, her person held for one day an unquestioned supremacy over her own drawing room. So to Anthony life was a struggle against death, that waited at every corner. It was as a concession to his hypochondriacal imagination that he formed the habit of reading in bed—it soothed him. He read until he was tired and often fell asleep with the lights still on.

His favorite diversion until he was fourteen was his stamp collection; enormous, as nearly exhaustive as a boy's could be—his grandfather considered fatuously that it was teaching him geography. So Anthony kept up a correspondence with a half dozen "Stamp and Coin" companies and it was rare that the mail failed to bring him new stamp-books or packages of glittering approval sheets—there was a mysterious fascination in transferring his acquisitions interminably from one book to another. His stamps were his greatest happiness and he bestowed impatient frowns on any one who interrupted him at play with them; they devoured his allowance every month, and he lay awake at night musing untiringly on their variety and many-colored splendor.

At sixteen he had lived almost entirely within himself, an inarticulate boy, thoroughly un-American, and politely bewildered by his contemporaries. The two preceding years had been spent in Europe with a private tutor, who persuaded him that Harvard was the thing; it would "open doors," it would be a tremendous tonic, it would give him innumerable self-sacrificing and devoted friends. So he went to Harvard—there was no other logical thing to be done with him.

Oblivious to the social system, he lived for a while alone and unsought in a high room in Beck Hall—a slim dark boy of medium height with a shy sensitive mouth. His allowance was more than liberal. He laid the foundations for a library by purchasing from a wandering bibliophile first editions of Swinburne, Meredith, and Hardy, and a yellowed illegible autograph letter of Keats's, finding later that he had been amazingly overcharged. He became an exquisite dandy, amassed a rather pathetic collection of silk pajamas, brocaded dressing-gowns, and neckties too flamboyant to wear; in this secret finery he would parade before a mirror in his room or lie stretched in satin along his window-seat looking down on the yard and realizing dimly this clamor, breathless and immediate, in which it seemed he was never to have a part.

Curiously enough he found in senior year that he had acquired a position in his class. He learned that he was looked upon as a rather romantic figure, a scholar, a recluse, a tower of erudition. This amused him but secretly pleased him—he began going out, at first a little and then a great deal. He made the Pudding. He drank—quietly and in the proper tradition. It was said of him that had he not come to college so young he might have "done extremely well." In 1909, when he graduated, he was only twenty years old.

Then abroad again—to Rome this time, where he dallied with architecture and painting in turn, took up the violin, and wrote some ghastly Italian sonnets, supposedly the ruminations of a thirteenth-century monk on the joys of the contemplative life. It became established among his Harvard intimates that he was in Rome, and those of them who were abroad that year looked him up and discovered with him, on many moonlight excursions, much in the city that was older than the Renaissance or indeed than the republic. Maury Noble, from Philadelphia, for instance, remained two months, and together they realized the peculiar charm of Latin women and had a delightful sense of being very young and free in a civilization that was very old and free. Not a few acquaintances of his grandfather's called on him, and had he so desired he might have been *persona grata* with the diplomatic set—indeed, he found that his inclinations tended more and more toward conviviality, but that long adolescent aloofness and consequent shyness still dictated to his conduct.

He returned to America in 1912 because of one of his grandfather's sudden illnesses, and after an excessively tiresome talk with the perpetually convalescent old man he decided to put off until his grandfather's death the idea of living permanently abroad. After a prolonged search he took an apartment on Fifty-second Street and to all appearances settled down.

In 1913 Anthony Patch's adjustment of himself to the universe was in process of consummation. Physically, he had improved since his undergraduate days—he was still too thin but his shoulders had widened and his brunette face had lost the frightened look of his freshman year. He was secretly orderly and in person spick and span—his friends declared that they had never seen his hair rumpled. His nose was too sharp; his mouth was one of those unfortunate mirrors of mood inclined to droop perceptibly in moments of unhappiness, but his blue eyes were charming, whether alert with intelligence or half closed in an expression of melancholy humor.

One of those men devoid of the symmetry of feature essential to the Aryan ideal, he was yet, here and there, considered handsome—moreover, he was very clean, in appearance and in reality, with that especial cleanness borrowed from beauty.

THE REPROACHLESS APARTMENT

Fifth and Sixth Avenues, it seemed to Anthony, were the uprights of a gigantic ladder stretching from Washington Square to Central Park. Coming up-town on top of a bus toward Fifty-second Street invariably gave him the sensation of hoisting himself hand by hand on a series of treacherous rungs, and when the bus jolted to a stop at his own rung he found something akin to relief as he descended the reckless metal steps to the sidewalk.

After that, he had but to walk down Fifty-second Street half a block, pass a stodgy family of brownstone houses—and then in a jiffy he was under the high ceilings of his great front room. This was entirely satisfactory. Here, after all, life began. Here he slept, breakfasted, read, and entertained.

The house itself was of murky material, built in the late nineties; in response to the steadily growing need of small apartments each floor had been thoroughly remodelled and rented individually. Of the four apartments Anthony's, on the second floor, was the most desirable.

The front room had fine high ceilings and three large windows that loomed down pleasantly upon Fifty-second Street. In its appointments it escaped by a safe margin being of any particular period; it escaped stiffness, stuffiness, bareness, and decadence. It smelt neither of smoke nor of incense—it was tall and faintly blue. There was a deep lounge of the softest brown leather with somnolence drifting about it like a haze. There was a high screen of Chinese lacquer chiefly concerned with geometrical fishermen and huntsmen in black and gold; this made a corner alcove for a voluminous chair guarded by an orange-colored standing lamp. Deep in the fireplace a quartered shield was burned to a murky black.

Passing through the dining-room, which, as Anthony took only breakfast at home, was merely a magnificent potentiality, and down a comparatively long hall, one came to the heart and core of the apartment—Anthony's bedroom and bath.

Both of them were immense. Under the ceilings of the former even the great canopied bed seemed of only average size. On the floor an exotic rug of crimson velvet was soft as fleece on his bare feet. His bathroom, in contrast to the rather portentous character of his bedroom, was gay, bright, extremely habitable and even faintly facetious. Framed around the walls were photographs of four celebrated thespian beauties of the day: Julia Sanderson as "The Sunshine Girl," Ina Claire as "The Quaker Girl," Billie Burke as "The Mind-the-Paint Girl," and Hazel Dawn as "The Pink Lady." Between Billie Burke and Hazel Dawn hung a print representing a great stretch of snow presided over by a cold and formidable sun—this, claimed Anthony, symbolized the cold shower.

The bathtub, equipped with an ingenious bookholder, was low and large. Beside it a wall wardrobe bulged with sufficient linen for three men and with a generation of neckties. There was no skimpy glorified towel of a carpet—instead, a rich rug, like the one in his bedroom a miracle of softness, that seemed almost to massage the wet foot emerging from the tub....

All in all a room to conjure with—it was easy to see that Anthony dressed there, arranged his immaculate hair there, in fact did everything but sleep and eat there. It was his pride, this bathroom. He felt that if he had a love he would have hung her picture just facing the tub so that, lost in the soothing steamings of the hot water, he might lie and look up at her and muse warmly and sensuously on her beauty.

NOR DOES HE SPIN

The apartment was kept clean by an English servant with the singularly, almost theatrically, appropriate name of Bounds, whose technic was marred only by the fact that he wore a soft collar. Had he been entirely Anthony's Bounds this defect would have been summarily remedied, but he was also the Bounds of two other gentlemen in the neighborhood. From eight until eleven in the morning he was entirely Anthony's. He arrived with the mail and cooked breakfast. At nine-thirty he pulled the edge of Anthony's blanket and spoke a few terse words—Anthony never remembered clearly what they were and rather suspected they were deprecative; then he served breakfast on a card-table in the front room, made the bed and, after asking with some hostility if there was anything else, withdrew.

In the mornings, at least once a week, Anthony went to see his broker. His income was slightly under seven thousand a year, the interest on money inherited from his mother. His grandfather, who had never allowed his own son to graduate from a very liberal allowance, judged that this sum was sufficient for young Anthony's needs. Every Christmas he sent him a five-hundred-dollar bond, which Anthony usually sold, if possible, as he was always a little, not very, hard up.

The visits to his broker varied from semi-social chats to discussions of the safety of eight per cent investments, and Anthony always enjoyed them. The big trust company building seemed to link him definitely to the great fortunes whose solidarity he respected and to assure him that he was adequately chaperoned by the hierarchy of finance. From these hurried men he derived the same sense of safety that he had in contemplating his grandfather's money—even more, for the latter appeared, vaguely, a demand loan made by the world to Adam Patch's own moral righteousness, while this money down-town seemed rather to have been grasped and held by sheer indomitable strengths and tremendous feats of will; in addition, it seemed more definitely and explicitly—money.

Closely as Anthony trod on the heels of his income, he considered it to be enough. Some golden day, of course, he would have many millions; meanwhile he possessed a *raison d'etre* in the theoretical creation of essays on the popes of the Renaissance. This flashes back to the conversation with his grandfather immediately upon his return from Rome.

He had hoped to find his grandfather dead, but had learned by telephoning from the pier that Adam Patch was comparatively well again—the next day he had concealed his disappointment and gone out to Tarrytown. Five miles from the station his taxicab entered an elaborately groomed drive that threaded a veritable maze of walls and wire fences guarding the estate—this, said the public, was because it was definitely known that if the Socialists had their way, one of the first men they'd assassinate would be old Cross Patch.

Anthony was late and the venerable philanthropist was awaiting him in a glass-walled sun parlor, where he was glancing through the morning papers for the second time. His secretary, Edward Shuttleworth—who before his regeneration had been gambler, saloon-keeper, and general reprobate—ushered Anthony into the room, exhibiting his redeemer and benefactor as though he were displaying a treasure of immense value.

They shook hands gravely. "I'm awfully glad to hear you're better," Anthony said.

The senior Patch, with an air of having seen his grandson only last week, pulled out his watch.

"Train late?" he asked mildly.

It had irritated him to wait for Anthony. He was under the delusion not only that in his youth he had handled his practical affairs with the utmost scrupulousness, even to keeping every engagement on the dot, but also that this was the direct and primary cause of his success.

"It's been late a good deal this month," he remarked with a shade of meek accusation in his voice—and then after a long sigh, "Sit down."

Anthony surveyed his grandfather with that tacit amazement which always attended the sight. That this feeble, unintelligent old man was possessed of such power that, yellow journals to the contrary, the men in the republic whose souls he could not have bought directly or indirectly would scarcely have populated White Plains, seemed as impossible to believe as that he had once been a pink-and-white baby.

The span of his seventy-five years had acted as a magic bellows—the first quarter-century had blown him full with life, and the last had sucked it all back.

It had sucked in the cheeks and the chest and the girth of arm and leg. It had tyrannously demanded his teeth, one by one, suspended his small eyes in dark-bluish sacks, tweeked out his hairs, changed him from gray to white in some places, from pink to yellow in others—callously transposing his colors like a child trying over a paintbox. Then through his body and his soul it had attacked his brain. It had sent him night-sweats and tears and unfounded dreads. It had split his intense normality into credulity and suspicion. Out of the coarse material of his enthusiasm it had cut dozens of meek but petulant obsessions; his energy was shrunk to the bad temper of a spoiled child, and for his will to power was substituted a fatuous puerile desire for a land of harps and canticles on earth.

The amenities having been gingerly touched upon, Anthony felt that he was expected to outline his intentions—and simultaneously a glimmer in the old man's eye warned him against broaching, for the present, his desire to live abroad. He wished that Shuttleworth would have tact enough to leave the room—he detested Shuttleworth—but the secretary had settled blandly in a rocker and was dividing between the two Patches the glances of his faded eyes.

"Now that you're here you ought to *do* something," said his grandfather softly, "accomplish something."

Anthony waited for him to speak of "leaving something done when you pass on." Then he made a suggestion:

"I thought—it seemed to me that perhaps I'm best qualified to write—"

Adam Patch winced, visualizing a family poet with a long hair and three mistresses.

"—history," finished Anthony.

"History? History of what? The Civil War? The Revolution?"

"Why—no, sir. A history of the Middle Ages." Simultaneously an idea was born for a history of the Renaissance popes, written from some novel angle. Still, he was glad he had said "Middle Ages."

"Middle Ages? Why not your own country? Something you know about?"

"Well, you see I've lived so much abroad—"

"Why you should write about the Middle Ages, I don't know. Dark Ages, we used to call 'em. Nobody knows what happened, and nobody cares, except that they're over now." He continued for some minutes on the uselessness of such information, touching, naturally, on the Spanish Inquisition and the "corruption of the monasteries." Then:

"Do you think you'll be able to do any work in New York—or do you really intend to work at all?" This last with soft, almost imperceptible, cynicism.

"Why, yes, I do, sir."

"When'll you be done?"

"Well, there'll be an outline, you see—and a lot of preliminary reading."

"I should think you'd have done enough of that already."

The conversation worked itself jerkily toward a rather abrupt conclusion, when Anthony rose, looked at his watch, and remarked that he had an engagement with his broker that afternoon. He had intended to stay a few days with his grandfather, but he was tired and irritated from a rough crossing, and quite unwilling to stand a subtle and sanctimonious browbeating. He would come out again in a few days, he said.

Nevertheless, it was due to this encounter that work had come into his life as a permanent idea. During the year that had passed since then, he had made several lists of authorities, he had even experimented with chapter titles and the division of his work into periods, but not one line of actual writing existed at present, or seemed likely ever to exist. He did nothing—and contrary to the most accredited copy-book logic, he managed to divert himself with more than average content.

AFTERNOON

It was October in 1913, midway in a week of pleasant days, with the sunshine loitering in the cross-streets and the atmosphere so languid as to seem weighted with ghostly falling leaves. It was pleasant to sit lazily by the open window finishing a chapter of "Erewhon." It was pleasant to yawn about five, toss the book on a table, and saunter humming along the hall to his bath.

"To ... you ... beaut-if-ul lady,"

he was singing as he turned on the tap.

"I raise ... my ... eyes;
To ... you ... beaut-if-ul la-a-dy
My ... heart ... cries—"

He raised his voice to compete with the flood of water pouring into the tub, and as he looked at the picture of Hazel Dawn upon the wall he put an imaginary violin to his shoulder and softly caressed it with a phantom bow. Through his closed lips he made a humming noise, which he vaguely imagined resembled the sound of a violin. After a moment his hands ceased their gyrations and wandered to his shirt, which he began to unfasten. Stripped, and adopting an athletic posture like the tiger-skin man in the advertisement, he regarded himself with some satisfaction in the mirror, breaking off to dabble a tentative foot in the tub. Readjusting a faucet and indulging in a few preliminary grunts, he slid in.

Once accustomed to the temperature of the water he relaxed into a state of drowsy content. When he finished his bath he would dress leisurely and walk down Fifth Avenue to the Ritz, where he had an appointment for dinner with his two most frequent companions, Dick Caramel and Maury Noble. Afterward he and Maury were going to the theatre—Caramel would probably trot home and work on his book, which ought to be finished pretty soon.

Anthony was glad *he* wasn't going to work on *his* book. The notion of sitting down and conjuring up, not only words in which to clothe thoughts but thoughts worthy of being clothed—the whole thing was absurdly beyond his desires.

Emerging from his bath he polished himself with the meticulous attention of a bootblack. Then he wandered into the bedroom, and whistling the while a weird, uncertain melody, strolled here and there buttoning, adjusting, and enjoying the warmth of the thick carpet on his feet.

He lit a cigarette, tossed the match out the open top of the window, then paused in his tracks with the cigarette two inches from his mouth—which fell faintly ajar. His eyes were focussed upon a spot of brilliant color on the roof of a house farther down the alley.

It was a girl in a red negligé, silk surely, drying her hair by the still hot sun of late afternoon. His whistle died upon the stiff air of the room; he walked cautiously another step nearer the window with a sudden impression that she was beautiful. Sitting on the stone parapet beside her was a cushion the same color as her garment and she was leaning both arms upon it as she looked down into the sunny areaway, where Anthony could hear children playing.

He watched her for several minutes. Something was stirred in him, something not accounted for by the warm smell of the afternoon or the triumphant vividness of red. He felt persistently that the girl was beautiful—then of a sudden he understood: it was her distance, not a rare and precious distance of soul but still distance, if only in terrestrial yards. The autumn air was between them, and the roofs and the blurred voices. Yet for a not altogether explained second, posing perversely in time, his emotion had been nearer to adoration than in the deepest kiss he had ever known.

He finished his dressing, found a black bow tie and adjusted it carefully by the three-sided mirror in the bathroom. Then yielding to an impulse he walked quickly into the bedroom and again looked out the window. The woman was standing up now; she had tossed her hair back and he had a full view of her. She was fat, full thirty-five, utterly undistinguished. Making a clicking noise with his mouth he returned to the bathroom and reparted his hair.

"To ... you ... beaut-if-ul lady,"

he sang lightly,

"I raise ... my ... eyes—"

Then with a last soothing brush that left an iridescent surface of sheer gloss he left his bathroom and his apartment and walked down Fifth Avenue to the Ritz-Carlton.

THREE MEN

At seven Anthony and his friend Maury Noble are sitting at a corner table on the cool roof. Maury Noble is like nothing so much as a large slender and imposing cat. His eyes are narrow and full of incessant, protracted blinks. His hair is smooth and flat, as though it has been licked by a possible—and, if so, Herculean—mother-cat. During Anthony's time at Harvard he had been considered the most unique figure in his class, the most brilliant, the most original—smart, quiet and among the saved.

This is the man whom Anthony considers his best friend. This is the only man of all his acquaintance whom he admires and, to a bigger extent than he likes to admit to himself, envies.

They are glad to see each other now—their eyes are full of kindness as each feels the full effect of novelty after a short separation. They are drawing a relaxation from each other's presence, a new serenity; Maury Noble behind that fine and absurdly catlike face is all but purring. And Anthony, nervous as a will-o'-the-wisp, restless—he is at rest now.

They are engaged in one of those easy short-speech conversations that only men under thirty or men under great stress indulge in.

ANTHONY: Seven o'clock. Where's the Caramel? *(Impatiently.)* I wish he'd finish that interminable novel. I've spent more time hungry——

MAURY: He's got a new name for it. "The Demon Lover "—not bad, eh?

ANTHONY: *(interested)* "The Demon Lover"? Oh "woman wailing"—No—not a bit bad! Not bad at all—d'you think?

MAURY: Rather good. What time did you say?

ANTHONY: Seven.

MAURY: (His eyes narrowing—not unpleasantly, but to express a faint disapproval) Drove me crazy the other day.

ANTHONY: How?

MAURY: That habit of taking notes.

ANTHONY: Me, too. Seems I'd said something night before that he considered material but he'd forgotten it—so he had at me. He'd say "Can't you try to concentrate?" And I'd say "You bore me to tears. How do I remember?"

(MAURY *laughs noiselessly, by a sort of bland and appreciative widening of his features.)*

MAURY: Dick doesn't necessarily see more than any one else. He merely can put down a larger proportion of what he sees.

ANTHONY: That rather impressive talent——

MAURY: Oh, yes. Impressive!

ANTHONY: And energy—ambitious, well-directed energy. He's so entertaining—he's so tremendously stimulating and exciting. Often there's something breathless in being with him.

MAURY: Oh, yes.

(Silence, and then:)

ANTHONY: *(With his thin, somewhat uncertain face at its most convinced)* But not indomitable energy. Some day, bit by bit, it'll blow away, and his rather impressive talent with it, and leave only a wisp of a man, fretful and egotistic and garrulous.

MAURY: *(With laughter)* Here we sit vowing to each other that little Dick sees less deeply into things than we do. And I'll bet he feels a measure of superiority on his side—creative mind over merely critical mind and all that.

ANTHONY: Oh, yes. But he's wrong. He's inclined to fall for a million silly enthusiasms. If it wasn't that he's absorbed in realism and therefore has to adopt the garments of the cynic he'd be—he'd be credulous as a college religious leader. He's an idealist. Oh, yes. He thinks he's not, because he's rejected Christianity. Remember him in college? just swallow every writer whole, one after another, ideas, technic, and characters, Chesterton, Shaw, Wells, each one as easily as the last.

MAURY:(Still considering his own last observation) I remember.

ANTHONY: It's true. Natural born fetich-worshipper. Take art—

MAURY: Let's order. He'll be—

ANTHONY: Sure. Let's order. I told him—

MAURY: Here he comes. Look—he's going to bump that waiter. *(He lifts his finger as a signal—lifts it as though it were a soft and friendly claw.)* Here y'are, Caramel.

A NEW VOICE: *(Fiercely)* Hello, Maury. Hello, Anthony Comstock Patch. How is old Adam's grandson? Débutantes still after you, eh?

In person RICHARD CARAMEL *is short and fair—he is to be bald at thirty-five. He has yellowish eyes—one of them startlingly clear, the other opaque as a muddy pool—and a bulging brow like a funny-paper baby. He bulges in other places—his paunch bulges, prophetically, his words have an air of bulging from his mouth, even his dinner coat pockets bulge, as though from contamination, with a dog-eared collection of time-tables, programmes, and miscellaneous scraps—on these he takes his notes with great screwings up of his unmatched yellow eyes and motions of silence with his disengaged left hand.*

When he reaches the table he shakes hands with ANTHONY and MAURY. He is one of those men who invariably shake hands, even with people whom they have seen an hour before.

ANTHONY: Hello, Caramel. Glad you're here. We needed a comic relief.

MAURY: You're late. Been racing the postman down the block? We've been clawing over your character.

DICK: *(Fixing* ANTHONY *eagerly with the bright eye)* What'd you say? Tell me and I'll write it down. Cut three thousand words out of Part One this afternoon.

MAURY: Noble aesthete. And I poured alcohol into my stomach.

DICK: I don't doubt it. I bet you two have been sitting here for an hour talking about liquor.

ANTHONY: We never pass out, my beardless boy.

MAURY: We never go home with ladies we meet when we're lit.

ANTHONY: All in our parties are characterized by a certain haughty distinction.

DICK: The particularly silly sort who boast about being "tanks"! Trouble is you're both in the eighteenth century. School of the Old English Squire. Drink quietly until you roll under the table. Never have a good time. Oh, no, that isn't done at all.

ANTHONY: This from Chapter Six, I'll bet.

DICK: Going to the theatre?

MAURY: Yes. We intend to spend the evening doing some deep thinking over of life's problems. The thing is tersely called "The Woman." I presume that she will "pay."

ANTHONY: My God! Is that what it is? Let's go to the Follies again.

MAURY: I'm tired of it. I've seen it three times. (*To DICK:*) The first time, we went out after Act One and found a most amazing bar. When we came back we entered the wrong theatre.

ANTHONY: Had a protracted dispute with a scared young couple we thought were in our seats.

DICK: (*As though talking to himself*) I think—that when I've done another novel and a play, and maybe a book of short stories, I'll do a musical comedy.

MAURY: I know—with intellectual lyrics that no one will listen to. And all the critics will groan and grunt about "Dear old Pinafore." And I shall go on shining as a brilliantly meaningless figure in a meaningless world.

DICK: (*Pompously*) Art isn't meaningless.

MAURY: It is in itself. It isn't in that it tries to make life less so.

ANTHONY: In other words, Dick, you're playing before a grand stand peopled with ghosts.

MAURY: Give a good show anyhow.

ANTHONY:(To MAURY) On the contrary, I'd feel that it being a meaningless world, why write? The very attempt to give it purpose is purposeless.

DICK: Well, even admitting all that, be a decent pragmatist and grant a poor man the instinct to live. Would you want every one to accept that sophistic rot?

ANTHONY: Yeah, I suppose so.

MAURY: No, sir! I believe that every one in America but a selected thousand should be compelled to accept a very rigid system of morals—Roman Catholicism, for instance. I don't complain of conventional morality. I complain rather of the mediocre heretics who seize upon the findings of sophistication and adopt the pose of a moral freedom to which they are by no means entitled by their intelligences.

(*Here the soup arrives and what MAURY might have gone on to say is lost for all time.*)

NIGHT

Afterward they visited a ticket speculator and, at a price, obtained seats for a new musical comedy called "High Jinks." In the foyer of the theatre they waited a few moments to see the first-night crowd come in. There were opera cloaks stitched of myriad, many-colored silks and furs; there were jewels dripping from arms and throats and ear-tips of white and rose; there were innumerable broad shimmers down the middles of innumerable silk hats; there were shoes of gold and bronze and red and shining black; there were the high-piled, tight-packed coiffures of many women and the slick, watered hair of well-kept men—most of all there was the ebbing, flowing, chattering, chuckling, foaming, slow-rolling wave effect of this cheerful sea of people as to-night it poured its glittering torrent into the artificial lake of laughter....

After the play they parted—Maury was going to a dance at Sherry's, Anthony homeward and to bed.

He found his way slowly over the jostled evening mass of Times Square, which the chariot race and its thousand satellites made rarely beautiful and bright and intimate with carnival. Faces swirled about him, a kaleidoscope of girls, ugly, ugly as sin—too fat, too lean, yet floating upon this autumn air as upon their own warm and passionate breaths poured out into the night. Here, for all their vulgarity, he thought, they were faintly and subtly mysterious. He inhaled carefully, swallowing into his lungs perfume and the not unpleasant scent of many cigarettes. He caught the glance of a dark young beauty sitting alone in a closed taxicab. Her eyes in the half-light suggested night and violets, and for a moment he stirred again to that half-forgotten remoteness of the afternoon.

Two young Jewish men passed him, talking in loud voices and craning their necks here and there in fatuous supercilious glances. They were dressed in suits of the exaggerated tightness then semi-fashionable; their turned over collars were notched at the Adam's apple; they wore gray spats and carried gray gloves on their cane handles.

Passed a bewildered old lady borne along like a basket of eggs between two men who exclaimed to her of the wonders of Times Square—explained them so quickly that the old lady, trying to be impartially interested, waved her head here and there like a piece of wind-worried old orange-peel. Anthony heard a snatch of their conversation:

"There's the Astor, mama!"

"Look! See the chariot race sign——"

"There's where we were to-day. No, *there!*"

"Good gracious! ..."

"You should worry and grow thin like a dime." He recognized the current witticism of the year as it issued stridently from one of the pairs at his elbow.

"And I says to him, I says——"

The soft rush of taxis by him, and laughter, laughter hoarse as a crow's, incessant and loud, with the rumble of the subways underneath—and over all, the revolutions of light, the growings and recedings of light—light dividing like pearls—forming and reforming in glittering bars and circles and monstrous grotesque figures cut amazingly on the sky.

He turned thankfully down the hush that blew like a dark wind out of a cross-street, passed a bakery-restaurant in whose windows a dozen roast chickens turned over and over on an automatic spit. From the door came a smell that was hot, doughy, and pink. A drug-store next, exhaling medicines, spilt soda water and a pleasant undertone from the cosmetic counter; then a Chinese laundry, still open, steamy and stifling, smelling folded and vaguely yellow. All these depressed him; reaching Sixth Avenue he stopped at a corner cigar store and emerged feeling better—the cigar store was cheerful, humanity in a navy blue mist, buying a luxury ....

Once in his apartment he smoked a last cigarette, sitting in the dark by his open front window. For the first time in over a year he found himself thoroughly enjoying New York. There was a rare pungency in it certainly, a quality almost Southern. A lonesome town, though. He who had grown up alone had lately learned to avoid solitude. During the past several months he had been careful, when he had no engagement for the evening, to hurry to one of his clubs and find some one. Oh, there was a loneliness here——

His cigarette, its smoke bordering the thin folds of curtain with rims of faint white spray, glowed on until the clock in St. Anne's down the street struck one with a querulous fashionable beauty. The elevated, half a quiet block away, sounded a rumble of drums—and should he lean from his window he would see the train, like an angry eagle, breasting the dark curve at the corner. He was reminded of a fantastic romance he had lately read in which cities had been bombed from aerial trains, and for a moment he fancied that Washington Square had declared war on Central Park and that this was a north-bound menace loaded with battle and sudden death. But as it passed the illusion faded; it diminished to the faintest of drums—then to a far-away droning eagle.

There were the bells and the continued low blur of auto horns from Fifth Avenue, but his own street was silent and he was safe in here from all the threat of life, for there was his door and the long hall and his guardian bedroom—safe, safe! The arc-light shining into his window seemed for this hour like the moon, only brighter and more beautiful than the moon.

A FLASH-BACK IN PARADISE

Beauty, who was born anew every hundred years, sat in a sort of outdoor waiting room through which blew gusts of white wind and occasionally a breathless hurried star. The stars winked at her intimately as they went by and the winds made a soft incessant flurry in her hair. She was incomprehensible, for, in her, soul and spirit were one—the beauty of her body was the essence of her soul. She was that unity sought for by philosophers through many centuries. In this outdoor waiting room of winds and stars she had been sitting for a hundred years, at peace in the contemplation of herself.

It became known to her, at length, that she was to be born again. Sighing, she began a long conversation with a voice that was in the white wind, a conversation that took many hours and of which I can give only a fragment here.

BEAUTY: (*Her lips scarcely stirring, her eyes turned, as always, inward upon herself*) Whither shall I journey now?

THE VOICE: To a new country—a land you have never seen before.

BEAUTY: (*Petulantly*) I loathe breaking into these new civilizations. How long a stay this time?

THE VOICE: Fifteen years.

BEAUTY: And what's the name of the place?

THE VOICE: It is the most opulent, most gorgeous land on earth—a land whose wisest are but little wiser than its dullest; a land where the rulers have minds like little children and the law-givers believe in Santa Claus; where ugly women control strong men——

BEAUTY: (*In astonishment*) What?

THE VOICE: (*Very much depressed*) Yes, it is truly a melancholy spectacle. Women with receding chins and shapeless noses go about in broad daylight saying "Do this!" and "Do that!" and all the men, even those of great wealth, obey implicitly their women to whom they refer sonorously either as "Mrs. So-and-so" or as "the wife."

BEAUTY: But this can't be true! I can understand, of course, their obedience to women of charm—but to fat women? to bony women? to women with scrawny cheeks?

THE VOICE: Even so.

BEAUTY: What of me? What chance shall I have?

THE VOICE: It will be "harder going," if I may borrow a phrase.

BEAUTY: (*After a dissatisfied pause*) Why not the old lands, the land of grapes and soft-tongued men or the land of ships and seas?

THE VOICE: It's expected that they'll be very busy shortly.

BEAUTY: Oh!

THE VOICE: Your life on earth will be, as always, the interval between two significant glances in a mundane mirror.

BEAUTY: What will I be? Tell me?

THE VOICE: At first it was thought that you would go this time as an actress in the motion pictures but, after all, it's not advisable. You will be disguised during your fifteen years as what is called a "susciety gurl."

BEAUTY: What's that?

(*There is a new sound in the wind which must for our purposes be interpreted as* THE VOICE *scratching its head.*)

THE VOICE: (*At length*) It's a sort of bogus aristocrat.

BEAUTY: Bogus? What is bogus?

THE VOICE: That, too, you will discover in this land. You will find much that is bogus. Also, you will do much that is bogus.

BEAUTY: (*Placidly*) It all sounds so vulgar.

THE VOICE: Not half as vulgar as it is. You will be known during your fifteen years as a ragtime kid, a flapper, a jazz-baby, and a baby vamp. You will dance new dances neither more nor less gracefully than you danced the old ones.

BEAUTY: (*In a whisper*) Will I be paid?

THE VOICE: Yes, as usual—in love.

BEAUTY: (*With a faint laugh which disturbs only momentarily the immobility of her lips*) And will I like being called a jazz-baby?

THE VOICE: (*Soberly*) You will love it....

(*The dialogue ends here, with* BEAUTY *still sitting quietly, the stars pausing in an ecstasy of appreciation, the wind, white and gusty, blowing through her hair.*

All this took place seven years before ANTHONY *sat by the front windows of his apartment and listened to the chimes of St. Anne's.*)

II. PORTRAIT OF A SIREN

CRISPNESS folded down upon New York a month later, bringing November and the three big football games and a great fluttering of furs along Fifth Avenue. It brought, also, a sense of tension to the city, and suppressed excitement. Every morning now there were invitations in Anthony's mail. Three dozen virtuous females of the first layer were proclaiming their fitness, if not their specific willingness, to bear children unto three dozen millionaires. Five dozen virtuous females of the second layer were proclaiming not only this fitness, but in addition a tremendous undaunted ambition toward the first three dozen young men, who were of course invited to each of the ninety-six parties—as were the young lady's group of family friends, acquaintances, college boys, and eager young outsiders. To continue, there was a third layer from the skirts of the city, from Newark and the Jersey suburbs up to bitter Connecticut and the ineligible sections of Long Island—and doubtless contiguous layers down to the city's shoes: Jewesses were coming out into a society of Jewish men and women, from Riverside to the Bronx, and looking forward to a rising young broker or jeweller and a kosher wedding; Irish girls were casting their eyes, with license at last to do so, upon a society of young Tammany politicians, pious undertakers, and grown-up choirboys.

And, naturally, the city caught the contagious air of entré—the working girls, poor ugly souls, wrapping soap in the factories and showing finery in the big stores, dreamed that perhaps in the spectacular excitement of this winter they might obtain for themselves the coveted male—as in a muddled carnival crowd an inefficient pickpocket may consider his chances increased. And the chimneys commenced to smoke and the subway's foulness was freshened. And the actresses came out in new plays and the publishers came out with new books and the Castles came out with new dances. And the railroads came out with new schedules containing new mistakes instead of the old ones that the commuters had grown used to....

The City was coming out!

Anthony, walking along Forty-second Street one afternoon under a steel-gray sky, ran unexpectedly into Richard Caramel emerging from the Manhattan Hotel barber shop. It was a cold day, the first definitely cold day, and Caramel had on one of those knee-length, sheep-lined coats long worn by the working men of the Middle West, that were just coming into fashionable approval. His soft hat was of a discreet dark brown, and from under it his clear eye flamed like a topaz. He stopped Anthony enthusiastically, slapping him on the arms more from a desire to keep himself warm than from playfulness, and, after his inevitable hand shake, exploded into sound.

"Cold as the devil—Good Lord, I've been working like the deuce all day till my room got so cold I thought I'd get pneumonia. Darn landlady economizing on coal came up when I yelled over the stairs for her for half an hour. Began explaining why and all. God! First she drove me crazy, then I began to think she was sort of a character, and took notes while she talked—so she couldn't see me, you know, just as though I were writing casually—"

He had seized Anthony's arm and walking him briskly up Madison Avenue.

"Where to?"

"Nowhere in particular."

"Well, then what's the use?" demanded Anthony.

They stopped and stared at each other, and Anthony wondered if the cold made his own face as repellent as Dick Caramel's, whose nose was crimson, whose bulging brow was blue, whose yellow unmatched eyes were red and watery at the rims. After a moment they began walking again.

"Done some good work on my novel." Dick was looking and talking emphatically at the sidewalk. "But I have to get out once in a while." He glanced at Anthony apologetically, as though craving encouragement.

"I have to talk. I guess very few people ever really *think*, I mean sit down and ponder and have ideas in sequence. I do my thinking in writing or conversation. You've got to have a start, sort of—something to defend or contradict—don't you think?"

Anthony grunted and withdrew his arm gently.

"I don't mind carrying you, Dick, but with that coat—"

"I mean," continued Richard Caramel gravely, "that on paper your first paragraph contains the idea you're going to damn or enlarge on. In conversation you've got your vis-à-vis's last statement—but when you simply *ponder*, why, your ideas just succeed each other like magic-lantern pictures and each one forces out the last."

They passed Forty-fifth Street and slowed down slightly. Both of them lit cigarettes and blew tremendous clouds of smoke and frosted breath into the air.

"Let's walk up to the Plaza and have an egg-nog," suggested Anthony. "Do you good. Air'll get the rotten nicotine out of your lungs. Come on—I'll let you talk about your book all the way."

"I don't want to if it bores you. I mean you needn't do it as a favor." The words tumbled out in haste, and though he tried to keep his face casual it screwed up uncertainly. Anthony was compelled to protest: "Bore me? I should say not!"

"Got a cousin—" began Dick, but Anthony interrupted by stretching out his arms and breathing forth a low cry of exultation.

"Good weather!" he exclaimed, "isn't it? Makes me feel about ten. I mean it makes me feel as I should have felt when I was ten. Murderous! Oh, God! one minute it's my world, and the next I'm the world's fool. To-day it's my world and everything's easy, easy. Even Nothing is easy!"

"Got a cousin up at the Plaza. Famous girl. We can go up and meet her. She lives there in the winter—has lately anyway—with her mother and father."

"Didn't know you had cousins in New York."

"Her name's Gloria. She's from home—Kansas City. Her mother's a practising Bilphist, and her father's quite dull but a perfect gentleman."

"What are they? Literary material?"

"They try to be. All the old man does is tell me he just met the most wonderful character for a novel. Then he tells me about some idiotic friend of his and then he says: '*There*'s a character for you! Why don't you write him up? Everybody'd be interested in *him*.' Or else he tells me about Japan or Paris, or some other very obvious place, and says: 'Why don't you write a story about that place? That'd be a wonderful setting for a story!'"

"How about the girl?" inquired Anthony casually, "Gloria—Gloria what?"

"Gilbert. Oh, you've heard of her—Gloria Gilbert. Goes to dances at colleges—all that sort of thing."

"I've heard her name."

"Good-looking—in fact damned attractive."

They reached Fiftieth Street and turned over toward the Avenue.

"I don't care for young girls as a rule," said Anthony, frowning.

This was not strictly true. While it seemed to him that the average debutante spent every hour of her day thinking and talking about what the great world had mapped out for her to do during the next hour, any girl who made a living directly on her prettiness interested him enormously.

"Gloria's darn nice—not a brain in her head."

Anthony laughed in a one-syllabled snort.

"By that you mean that she hasn't a line of literary patter."

"No, I don't."

"Dick, you know what passes as brains in a girl for you. Earnest young women who sit with you in a corner and talk earnestly about life. The kind who when they were sixteen argued with grave faces as to whether kissing was right or wrong—and whether it was immoral for freshmen to drink beer."

Richard Caramel was offended. His scowl crinkled like crushed paper.

"No—" he began, but Anthony interrupted ruthlessly.

"Oh, yes; kind who just at present sit in corners and confer on the latest Scandinavian Dante available in English translation."

Dick turned to him, a curious falling in his whole countenance. His question was almost an appeal.

"What's the matter with you and Maury? You talk sometimes as though I were a sort of inferior."

Anthony was confused, but he was also cold and a little uncomfortable, so he took refuge in attack.

"I don't think your brains matter, Dick."

"Of course they matter!" exclaimed Dick angrily. "What do you mean? Why don't they matter?"

"You might know too much for your pen."

"I couldn't possibly."

"I can imagine," insisted Anthony, "a man knowing too much for his talent to express. Like me. Suppose, for instance, I have more wisdom than you, and less talent. It would tend to make me inarticulate. You, on the contrary, have enough water to fill the pail and a big enough pail to hold the water."

"I don't follow you at all," complained Dick in a crestfallen tone. Infinitely dismayed, he seemed to bulge in protest. He was staring intently at Anthony and caroming off a succession of passers-by, who reproached him with fierce, resentful glances.

"I simply mean that a talent like Wells's could carry the intelligence of a Spencer. But an inferior talent can only be graceful when it's carrying inferior ideas. And the more narrowly you can look at a thing the more entertaining you can be about it."

Dick considered, unable to decide the exact degree of criticism intended by Anthony's remarks. But Anthony, with that facility which seemed so frequently to flow from him, continued, his dark eyes gleaming in his thin face, his chin raised, his voice raised, his whole physical being raised:

"Say I am proud and sane and wise—an Athenian among Greeks. Well, I might fail where a lesser man would succeed. He could imitate, he could adorn, he could be enthusiastic, he could be hopefully constructive. But this hypothetical me would be too proud to imitate, too sane to be enthusiastic, too sophisticated to be Utopian, too Grecian to adorn."

"Then you don't think the artist works from his intelligence?"

"No. He goes on improving, if he can, what he imitates in the way of style, and choosing from his own interpretation of the things around him what constitutes material. But after all every writer writes because it's his mode of living. Don't tell me you like this 'Divine Function of the Artist' business?"

"I'm not accustomed even to refer to myself as an artist."

"Dick," said Anthony, changing his tone, "I want to beg your pardon."

"Why?"

"For that outburst. I'm honestly sorry. I was talking for effect."

Somewhat mollified, Dick rejoined:

"I've often said you were a Philistine at heart."

It was a crackling dusk when they turned in under the white façade of the Plaza and tasted slowly the foam and yellow thickness of an egg-nog. Anthony looked at his companion. Richard Caramel's nose and brow were slowly approaching a like pigmentation; the red was leaving the one, the blue deserting the other. Glancing in a mirror, Anthony was glad to find that his own skin had not discolored. On the contrary, a faint glow had kindled in his cheeks—he fancied that he had never looked so well.

"Enough for me," said Dick, his tone that of an athlete in training. "I want to go up and see the Gilberts. Won't you come?"

"Why—yes. If you don't dedicate me to the parents and dash off in the corner with Dora."

"Not Dora—Gloria."

A clerk announced them over the phone, and ascending to the tenth floor they followed a winding corridor and knocked at 1088. The door was answered by a middle-aged lady—Mrs. Gilbert herself.

"How do you do?" She spoke in the conventional American lady-lady language. "Well, I'm *aw*fully glad to see you—"

Hasty interjections by Dick, and then:

"Mr. Pats? Well, do come in, and leave your coat there." She pointed to a chair and changed her inflection to a deprecatory laugh full of minute gasps. "This is really lovely—lovely. Why, Richard, you haven't been here for *so* long—no!—no!" The latter monosyllables served half as responses, half as periods, to some vague starts from Dick. "Well, do sit down and tell me what you've been doing."

One crossed and recrossed; one stood and bowed ever so gently; one smiled again and again with helpless stupidity; one wondered if she would ever sit down at length one slid thankfully into a chair and settled for a pleasant call.

"I suppose it's because you've been busy—as much as anything else," smiled Mrs. Gilbert somewhat ambiguously. The "as much as anything else" she used to balance all her more rickety sentences. She had two other ones: "at least that's the way I look at it" and "pure and simple"—these three, alternated, gave each of her remarks an air of being a general reflection on life, as though she had calculated all causes and, at length, put her finger on the ultimate one.

Richard Caramel's face, Anthony saw, was now quite normal. The brow and cheeks were of a flesh color, the nose politely inconspicuous. He had fixed his aunt with the bright-yellow eye, giving her that acute and exaggerated attention that young males are accustomed to render to all females who are of no further value.

"Are you a writer too, Mr. Pats? ... Well, perhaps we can all bask in Richard's fame."—Gentle laughter led by Mrs. Gilbert.

"Gloria's out," she said, with an air of laying down an axiom from which she would proceed to derive results. "She's dancing somewhere. Gloria goes, goes, goes. I tell her I don't see how she stands it. She dances all afternoon and all night, until I think she's going to wear herself to a shadow. Her father is very worried about her."

She smiled from one to the other. They both smiled.

She was composed, Anthony perceived, of a succession of semicircles and parabolas, like those figures that gifted folk make on the typewriter: head, arms, bust, hips, thighs, and ankles were in a bewildering tier of roundnesses. Well ordered and clean she was, with hair of an artificially rich gray; her large face sheltered weather-beaten blue eyes and was adorned with just the faintest white mustache.

"I always say," she remarked to Anthony, "that Richard is an ancient soul."

In the tense pause that followed, Anthony considered a pun—something about Dick having been much walked upon.

"We all have souls of different ages," continued Mrs. Gilbert radiantly; "at least that's what I say."

"Perhaps so," agreed Anthony with an air of quickening to a hopeful idea. The voice bubbled on:

"Gloria has a very young soul—irresponsible, as much as anything else. She has no sense of responsibility."

"She's sparkling, Aunt Catherine," said Richard pleasantly. "A sense of responsibility would spoil her. She's too pretty."

"Well," confessed Mrs. Gilbert, "all I know is that she goes and goes and goes—"

The number of goings to Gloria's discredit was lost in the rattle of the doorknob as it turned to admit Mr. Gilbert.

He was a short man with a mustache resting like a small white cloud beneath his undistinguished nose. He had reached the stage where his value as a social creature was a black and imponderable negative. His ideas were the popular delusions of twenty years before; his mind steered a wabbly and anaemic course in the wake of the daily newspaper editorials. After graduating from a small but terrifying Western university, he had entered the celluloid business, and as this required only the minute measure of intelligence he brought to it, he did well for several years—in fact until about 1911, when he began exchanging contracts for vague agreements with the moving picture industry. The moving picture industry had decided about 1912 to gobble him up, and at this time he was, so to speak, delicately balanced on its tongue. Meanwhile he was supervising manager of the Associated Mid-western Film Materials Company, spending six months of each year in New York and the remainder in Kansas City and St. Louis. He felt credulously that there was a good thing coming to him—and his wife thought so, and his daughter thought so too.

He disapproved of Gloria: she stayed out late, she never ate her meals, she was always in a mix-up—he had irritated her once and she had used toward him words that he had not thought were part of her vocabulary. His wife was easier. After fifteen years of incessant guerilla warfare he had conquered her—it was a war of muddled optimism against organized dulness, and something in the number of "yes's" with which he could poison a conversation had won him the victory.

"Yes-yes-yes-yes," he would say, "yes-yes-yes-yes. Let me see. That was the summer of—let me see—ninety-one or ninety-two—Yes-yes-yes-yes——"

Fifteen years of yes's had beaten Mrs. Gilbert. Fifteen further years of that incessant unaffirmative affirmative, accompanied by the perpetual flicking of ash-mushrooms from thirty-two thousand cigars, had broken her. To this husband of hers she made the last concession of married life, which is more complete, more irrevocable, than the first—she listened to him. She told herself that the years had brought her tolerance—actually they had slain what measure she had ever possessed of moral courage.

She introduced him to Anthony.

"This is Mr. Pats," she said.

The young man and the old touched flesh; Mr. Gilbert's hand was soft, worn away to the pulpy semblance of a squeezed grapefruit. Then husband and wife exchanged greetings—he told her it had grown colder out; he said he had walked down to a news-stand on Forty-fourth Street for a Kansas City paper. He had intended to ride back in the bus but he had found it too cold, yes, yes, yes, yes, too cold.

Mrs. Gilbert added flavor to his adventure by being impressed with his courage in braving the harsh air.

"Well, you *are* spunky!" she exclaimed admiringly. "You *are* spunky. I wouldn't have gone out for anything."

Mr. Gilbert with true masculine impassivity disregarded the awe he had excited in his wife. He turned to the two young men and triumphantly routed them on the subject of the weather. Richard Caramel was called on to remember the month of November in Kansas. No sooner had the theme been pushed toward him, however, than it was violently fished back to be lingered over, pawed over, elongated, and generally devitalized by its sponsor.

The immemorial thesis that the days somewhere were warm but the nights very pleasant was successfully propounded and they decided the exact distance on an obscure railroad between two points that Dick had inadvertently mentioned. Anthony fixed Mr. Gilbert with a steady stare and went into a trance through which, after a moment, Mrs. Gilbert's smiling voice penetrated:

"It seems as though the cold were damper here—it seems to eat into my bones."

As this remark, adequately yessed, had been on the tip of Mr. Gilbert's tongue, he could not be blamed for rather abruptly changing the subject.

"Where's Gloria?"

"She ought to be here any minute."

"Have you met my daughter, Mr.——?"

"Haven't had the pleasure. I've heard Dick speak of her often."

"She and Richard are cousins."

"Yes?" Anthony smiled with some effort. He was not used to the society of his seniors, and his mouth was stiff from superfluous cheerfulness. It was such a pleasant thought about Gloria and Dick being cousins. He managed within the next minute to throw an agonized glance at his friend.

Richard Caramel was afraid they'd have to toddle off.

Mrs. Gilbert was tremendously sorry.

Mr. Gilbert thought it was too bad.

Mrs. Gilbert had a further idea—something about being glad they'd come, anyhow, even if they'd only seen an old lady 'way too old to flirt with them. Anthony and Dick evidently considered this a sly sally, for they laughed one bar in three-four time.

Would they come again soon?

"Oh, yes."

Gloria would be *aw*fully sorry!

"Good-by——"

"Good-by——"

Smiles!

Smiles!

Bang!

Two disconsolate young men walking down the tenth-floor corridor of the Plaza in the direction of the elevator.

A LADY'S LEGS

Behind Maury Noble's attractive indolence, his irrelevance and his easy mockery, lay a surprising and relentless maturity of purpose. His intention, as he stated it in college, had been to use three years in travel, three years in utter leisure—and then to become immensely rich as quickly as possible.

His three years of travel were over. He had accomplished the globe with an intensity and curiosity that in any one else would have seemed pedantic, without redeeming spontaneity, almost the self-editing of a human Baedeker; but, in this case, it assumed an air of mysterious purpose and significant design—as though Maury Noble were some predestined anti-Christ, urged by a preordination to go everywhere there was to go along the earth and to see all the billions of humans who bred and wept and slew each other here and there upon it.

Back in America, he was sallying into the search for amusement with the same consistent absorption. He who had never taken more than a few cocktails or a pint of wine at a sitting, taught himself to drink as he would have taught himself Greek—like Greek it would be the gateway to a wealth of new sensations, new psychic states, new reactions in joy or misery.

His habits were a matter for esoteric speculation. He had three rooms in a bachelor apartment on Forty-forth street, but he was seldom to be found there. The telephone girl had received the most positive instructions that no one should even have his ear without first giving a name to be passed upon. She had a list of half a dozen people to whom he was never at home, and of the same number to whom he was always at home. Foremost on the latter list were Anthony Patch and Richard Caramel.

Maury's mother lived with her married son in Philadelphia, and there Maury went usually for the week-ends, so one Saturday night when Anthony, prowling the chilly streets in a fit of utter boredom, dropped in at the Molton Arms he was overjoyed to find that Mr. Noble was at home.

His spirits soared faster than the flying elevator. This was so good, so extremely good, to be about to talk to Maury—who would be equally happy at seeing him. They would look at each other with a deep affection just behind their eyes which both would conceal beneath some attenuated raillery. Had it been summer they would have gone out together and indolently sipped two long Tom Collinses, as they wilted their collars and watched the faintly diverting round of some lazy August cabaret. But it was cold outside, with wind around the edges of the tall buildings and December just up the street, so better far an evening together under the soft lamplight and a drink or two of Bushmill's, or a thimbleful of Maury's Grand Marnier, with the books gleaming like ornaments against the walls, and Maury radiating a divine inertia as he rested, large and catlike, in his favorite chair.

There he was! The room closed about Anthony, warmed him. The glow of that strong persuasive mind, that temperament almost Oriental in its outward impassivity, warmed Anthony's restless soul and brought him a peace that could be likened only to the peace a stupid woman gives. One must understand all—else one must take all for granted. Maury filled the room, tigerlike, godlike. The winds outside were stilled; the brass candlesticks on the mantel glowed like tapers before an altar.

"What keeps you here to-day?" Anthony spread himself over a yielding sofa and made an elbow-rest among the pillows.

"Just been here an hour. Tea dance—and I stayed so late I missed my train to Philadelphia."

"Strange to stay so long," commented Anthony curiously.

"Rather. What'd you do?"

"Geraldine. Little usher at Keith's. I told you about her."

"Oh!"

"Paid me a call about three and stayed till five. Peculiar little soul—she gets me. She's so utterly stupid."

Maury was silent.

"Strange as it may seem," continued Anthony, "so far as I'm concerned, and even so far as I know, Geraldine is a paragon of virtue."

He had known her a month, a girl of nondescript and nomadic habits. Someone had casually passed her on to Anthony, who considered her amusing and rather liked the chaste and fairylike kisses she had given him on the third night of their acquaintance, when they had driven in a taxi through the Park. She had a vague family—a shadowy aunt and uncle who shared with her an apartment in the labyrinthine hundreds. She was company, familiar and faintly intimate and restful. Further than that he did not care to experiment—not from any moral compunction, but from a dread of allowing any entanglement to disturb what he felt was the growing serenity of his life.

"She has two stunts," he informed Maury; "one of them is to get her hair over her eyes some way and then blow it out, and the other is to say 'You cra-a-azy!' when some one makes a remark that's over her head. It fascinates me. I sit there hour after hour, completely intrigued by the maniacal symptoms she finds in my imagination."

Maury stirred in his chair and spoke.

"Remarkable that a person can comprehend so little and yet live in such a complex civilization. A woman like that actually takes the whole universe in the most matter-of-fact way. From the influence of Rousseau to the bearing of the tariff rates on her dinner, the whole phenomenon is utterly strange to her. She's just been carried along from an age of spearheads and plunked down here with the equipment of an archer for going into a pistol duel. You could sweep away the entire crust of history and she'd never know the difference."

"I wish our Richard would write about her."

"Anthony, surely you don't think she's worth writing about."

"As much as anybody," he answered, yawning. "You know I was thinking to-day that I have a great confidence in Dick. So long as he sticks to people and not to ideas, and as long as his inspirations come from life and not from art, and always granting a normal growth, I believe he'll be a big man."

"I should think the appearance of the black note-book would prove that he's going to life."

Anthony raised himself on his elbow and answered eagerly:

"He tries to go to life. So does every author except the very worst, but after all most of them live on predigested food. The incident or character may be from life, but the writer usually interprets it in terms of the last book he read. For instance, suppose he meets a sea captain and thinks he's an original character. The truth is that he sees the resemblance between the sea captain and the last sea captain Dana created, or who-ever creates sea captains, and therefore he knows how to set this sea captain on paper. Dick, of course, can set down any consciously picturesque, character-like character, but could he accurately transcribe his own sister?"

Then they were off for half an hour on literature.

"A classic," suggested Anthony, "is a successful book that has survived the reaction of the next period or generation. Then it's safe, like a style in architecture or furniture. It's acquired a picturesque dignity to take the place of its fashion...."

After a time the subject temporarily lost its tang. The interest of the two young men was not particularly technical. They were in love with generalities. Anthony had recently discovered Samuel Butler and the brisk aphorisms in the note-book seemed to him the quintessence of criticism. Maury, his whole mind so thoroughly mellowed by the very hardness of his scheme of life, seemed inevitably the wiser of the two, yet in the actual stuff of their intelligences they were not, it seemed, fundamentally different.

They drifted from letters to the curiosities of each other's day.

"Whose tea was it?"

"People named Abercrombie."

"Why'd you stay late? Meet a luscious débutante?"

"Yes."

"Did you really?" Anthony's voice lifted in surprise.

"Not a débutante exactly. Said she came out two winters ago in Kansas City."

"Sort of left-over?"

"No," answered Maury with some amusement, "I think that's the last thing I'd say about her. She seemed—well, somehow the youngest person there."

"Not too young to make you miss a train."

"Young enough. Beautiful child."

Anthony chuckled in his one-syllable snort.

"Oh, Maury, you're in your second childhood. What do you mean by beautiful?"

Maury gazed helplessly into space.

"Well, I can't describe her exactly—except to say that she was beautiful. She was—tremendously alive. She was eating gum-drops."

"What!"

"It was a sort of attenuated vice. She's a nervous kind—said she always ate gum-drops at teas because she had to stand around so long in one place."

"What'd you talk about—Bergson? Bilphism? Whether the one-step is immoral?"

Maury was unruffled; his fur seemed to run all ways.

"As a matter of fact we did talk on Bilphism. Seems her mother's a Bilphist. Mostly, though, we talked about legs."

Anthony rocked in glee.

"My God! Whose legs?"

"Hers. She talked a lot about hers. As though they were a sort of choice bric-à-brac. She aroused a great desire to see them."

"What is she—a dancer?"

"No, I found she was a cousin of Dick's."

Anthony sat upright so suddenly that the pillow he released stood on end like a live thing and dove to the floor.

"Name's Gloria Gilbert?" he cried.

"Yes. Isn't she remarkable?"

"I'm sure I don't know—but for sheer dulness her father—"

"Well," interrupted Maury with implacable conviction, "her family may be as sad as professional mourners but I'm inclined to think that she's a quite authentic and original character. The outer signs of the cut-and-dried Yale prom girl and all that—but different, very emphatically different."

"Go on, go on!" urged Anthony. "Soon as Dick told me she didn't have a brain in her head I knew she must be pretty good."

"Did he say that?"

"Swore to it," said Anthony with another snorting laugh.

"Well, what he means by brains in a woman is—"

"I know," interrupted Anthony eagerly, "he means a smattering of literary misinformation."

"That's it. The kind who believes that the annual moral let-down of the country is a very good thing or the kind who believes it's a very ominous thing. Either pince-nez or postures. Well, this girl talked about legs. She talked about skin too—her own skin. Always her own. She told me the sort of tan she'd like to get in the summer and how closely she usually approximated it."

"You sat enraptured by her low alto?"

"By her low alto! No, by tan! I began thinking about tan. I began to think what color I turned when I made my last exposure about two years ago. I did use to get a pretty good tan. I used to get a sort of bronze, if I remember rightly."

Anthony retired into the cushions, shaken with laughter.

"She's got you going—oh, Maury! Maury the Connecticut life-saver. The human nutmeg. Extra! Heiress elopes with coast-guard because of his luscious pigmentation! Afterward found to be Tasmanian strain in his family!"

Maury sighed; rising he walked to the window and raised the shade.

"Snowing hard."

Anthony, still laughing quietly to himself, made no answer.

"Another winter." Maury's voice from the window was almost a whisper. "We're growing old, Anthony. I'm twenty-seven, by God! Three years to thirty, and then I'm what an undergraduate calls a middle-aged man."

Anthony was silent for a moment.

"You *are* old, Maury," he agreed at length. "The first signs of a very dissolute and wabbly senescence—you have spent the afternoon talking about tan and a lady's legs."

Maury pulled down the shade with a sudden harsh snap.

"Idiot!" he cried, "that from you! Here I sit, young Anthony, as I'll sit for a generation or more and watch such gay souls as you and Dick and Gloria Gilbert go past me, dancing and singing and loving and hating one another and being moved, being eternally moved. And I am moved only by my lack of emotion. I shall sit and the snow will come—oh, for a Caramel to take notes—and another winter and I shall be thirty and you and Dick and Gloria will go on being eternally moved and dancing by me and singing. But after you've all gone I'll be saying things for new Dicks to write down, and listening to the disillusions and cynicisms and emotions of new Anthonys—yes, and talking to new Glorias about the tans of summers yet to come."

The firelight flurried up on the hearth. Maury left the window, stirred the blaze with a poker, and dropped a log upon the andirons. Then he sat back in his chair and the remnants of his voice faded in the new fire that spit red and yellow along the bark.

"After all, Anthony, it's you who are very romantic and young. It's you who are infinitely more susceptible and afraid of your calm being broken. It's me who tries again and again to be moved—let myself go a thousand times and I'm always me. Nothing—quite—stirs me.

"Yet," he murmured after another long pause, "there was something about that little girl with her absurd tan that was eternally old—like me."

TURBULENCE

Anthony turned over sleepily in his bed, greeting a patch of cold sun on his counterpane, crisscrossed with the shadows of the leaded window. The room was full of morning. The carved chest in the corner, the ancient and inscrutable wardrobe, stood about the room like dark symbols of the obliviousness of matter; only the rug was beckoning and perishable to his perishable feet, and Bounds, horribly inappropriate in his soft collar, was of stuff as fading as the gauze of frozen breath he uttered. He was close to the bed, his hand still lowered where he had been jerking at the upper blanket, his dark-brown eyes fixed imperturbably upon his master.

"Bows!" muttered the drowsy god. "Thachew, Bows?"

"It's I, sir."

Anthony moved his head, forced his eyes wide, and blinked triumphantly.

"Bounds."

"Yes, sir?"

"Can you get off—yeow-ow-oh-oh-oh God!—" Anthony yawned insufferably and the contents of his brain seemed to fall together in a dense hash. He made a fresh start.

"Can you come around about four and serve some tea and sandwiches or something?"

"Yes, sir."

Anthony considered with chilling lack of inspiration. "Some sandwiches," he repeated helplessly, "oh, some cheese sandwiches and jelly ones and chicken and olive, I guess. Never mind breakfast."

The strain of invention was too much. He shut his eyes wearily, let his head roll to rest inertly, and quickly relaxed what he had regained of muscular control. Out of a crevice of his mind crept the vague but inevitable spectre of the night before—but it proved in this case to be nothing but a seemingly interminable conversation with Richard Caramel, who had called on him at midnight; they had drunk four bottles of beer and munched dry crusts of bread while Anthony listened to a reading of the first part of "The Demon Lover."

—Came a voice now after many hours. Anthony disregarded it, as sleep closed over him, folded down upon him, crept up into the byways of his mind.

Suddenly he was awake, saying: "What?"

"For how many, sir?" It was still Bounds, standing patient and motionless at the foot of the bed—Bounds who divided his manner among three gentlemen.

"How many what?"

"I think, sir, I'd better know how many are coming. I'll have to plan for the sandwiches, sir."

"Two," muttered Anthony huskily; "lady and a gentleman."

Bounds said, "Thank you, sir," and moved away, bearing with him his humiliating reproachful soft collar, reproachful to each of the three gentlemen, who only demanded of him a third.

After a long time Anthony arose and drew an opalescent dressing grown of brown and blue over his slim pleasant figure. With a last yawn he went into the bathroom, and turning on the dresser light (the bathroom had no outside exposure) he contemplated himself in the mirror with some interest. A wretched apparition, he thought; he usually thought so in the morning—sleep made his face unnaturally pale. He lit a cigarette and glanced through several letters and the morning Tribune.

An hour later, shaven and dressed, he was sitting at his desk looking at a small piece of paper he had taken out of his wallet. It was scrawled with semi-legible memoranda: "See Mr. Howland at five. Get hair-cut. See about Rivers' bill. Go book-store."

—And under the last: "Cash in bank, $690 (crossed out), $612 (crossed out), $607."

Finally, down at the bottom and in a hurried scrawl: "Dick and Gloria Gilbert for tea."

This last item brought him obvious satisfaction. His day, usually a jelly-like creature, a shapeless, spineless thing, had attained Mesozoic structure. It was marching along surely, even jauntily, toward a climax, as a play should, as a day should. He dreaded the moment when the backbone of the day should be broken, when he should have met the girl at last, talked to her, and then bowed her laughter out the door, returning only to the melancholy dregs in the teacups and the gathering staleness of the uneaten sandwiches.

There was a growing lack of color in Anthony's days. He felt it constantly and sometimes traced it to a talk he had had with Maury Noble a month before. That anything so ingenuous, so priggish, as a sense of waste should oppress him was absurd, but there was no denying the fact that some unwelcome survival of a fetish had drawn him three weeks before down to the public library, where, by the token of Richard Caramel's card, he had drawn out half a dozen books on the Italian Renaissance. That these books were still piled on his desk in the original order of carriage, that they were daily increasing his liabilities by twelve cents, was no mitigation of their testimony. They were cloth and morocco witnesses to the fact of his defection. Anthony had had several hours of acute and startling panic.

In justification of his manner of living there was first, of course, The Meaninglessness of Life. As aides and ministers, pages and squires, butlers and lackeys to this great Khan there were a thousand books glowing on his shelves, there was his apartment and all the money that was to be his when the old man up the river should choke on his last morality. From a world fraught with the menace of débutantes and the stupidity of many Geraldines he was thankfully delivered—rather should he emulate the feline immobility of Maury and wear proudly the culminative wisdom of the numbered generations.

Over and against these things was something which his brain persistently analyzed and dealt with as a tiresome complex but which, though logically disposed of and bravely trampled under foot, had sent him out through the soft slush of late November to a library which had none of the books he most wanted. It is fair to analyze Anthony as far as he could analyze himself; further than that it is, of course, presumption. He found in himself a growing horror and loneliness. The idea of eating alone frightened him; in preference he dined often with men he detested. Travel, which had once charmed him, seemed at length, unendurable, a business of color without substance, a phantom chase after his own dream's shadow.

—If I am essentially weak, he thought, I need work to do, work to do. It worried him to think that he was, after all, a facile mediocrity, with neither the poise of Maury nor the enthusiasm of Dick. It seemed a tragedy to want nothing—and yet he wanted something, something. He knew in flashes what it was—some path of hope to lead him toward what he thought was an imminent and ominous old age.

After cocktails and luncheon at the University Club Anthony felt better. He had run into two men from his class at Harvard, and in contrast to the gray heaviness of their conversation his life assumed color. Both of them were married: one spent his coffee time in sketching an extra-nuptial adventure to the bland and appreciative smiles of the other. Both of them, he thought, were Mr. Gilberts in embryo; the number of their "yes's" would have to be quadrupled, their natures crabbed by twenty years—then they would be no more than obsolete and broken machines, pseudo-wise and valueless, nursed to an utter senility by the women they had broken.

Ah, he was more than that, as he paced the long carpet in the lounge after dinner, pausing at the window to look into the harried street. He was Anthony Patch, brilliant, magnetic, the heir of many years and many men. This was his world now—and that last strong irony he craved lay in the offing.

With a stray boyishness he saw himself a power upon the earth; with his grandfather's money he might build his own pedestal and be a Talleyrand, a Lord Verulam. The clarity of his mind, its sophistication, its versatile intelligence, all at their maturity and dominated by some purpose yet to be born would find him work to do. On this minor his dream faded—work to do: he tried to imagine himself in Congress rooting around in the litter of that incredible pigsty with the narrow and porcine brows he saw pictured sometimes in the rotogravure sections of the Sunday newspapers, those glorified proletarians babbling blandly to the nation the ideas of high school seniors! Little men with copy-book ambitions who by mediocrity had thought to emerge from mediocrity into the lustreless and unromantic heaven of a government by the people—and the best, the dozen shrewd men at the top, egotistic and cynical, were content to lead this choir of white ties and wire collar-buttons in a discordant and amazing hymn, compounded of a vague confusion between wealth as a reward of virtue and wealth as a proof of vice, and continued cheers for God, the Constitution, and the Rocky Mountains!

Lord Verulam! Talleyrand!

Back in his apartment the grayness returned. His cocktails had died, making him sleepy, somewhat befogged and inclined to be surly. Lord Verulam—he? The very thought was bitter. Anthony Patch with no record of achievement, without courage, without strength to be satisfied with truth when it was given him. Oh, he was a pretentious fool, making careers out of cocktails and meanwhile regretting, weakly and secretly, the collapse of an insufficient and wretched idealism. He had garnished his soul in the subtlest taste and now he longed for the old rubbish. He was empty, it seemed, empty as an old bottle—

The buzzer rang at the door. Anthony sprang up and lifted the tube to his ear. It was Richard Caramel's voice, stilted and facetious:

"Announcing Miss Gloria Gilbert."

"How do you do?" he said, smiling and holding the door ajar.

Dick bowed.

"Gloria, this is Anthony."

"Well!" she cried, holding out a little gloved hand. Under her fur coat her dress was Alice-blue, with white lace crinkled stiffly about her throat.

"Let me take your things."

Anthony stretched out his arms and the brown mass of fur tumbled into them.

"Thanks."

"What do you think of her, Anthony?" Richard Caramel demanded barbarously. "Isn't she beautiful?"

"Well!" cried the girl defiantly—withal unmoved.

She was dazzling—alight; it was agony to comprehend her beauty in a glance. Her hair, full of a heavenly glamour, was gay against the winter color of the room.

Anthony moved about, magician-like, turning the mushroom lamp into an orange glory. The stirred fire burnished the copper andirons on the hearth—

"I'm a solid block of ice," murmured Gloria casually, glancing around with eyes whose irises were of the most delicate and transparent bluish white. "What a slick fire! We found a place where you could stand on an iron-bar grating, sort of, and it blew warm air up at you—but Dick wouldn't wait there with me. I told him to go on alone and let me be happy."

Conventional enough this. She seemed talking for her own pleasure, without effort. Anthony, sitting at one end of the sofa, examined her profile against the foreground of the lamp: the exquisite regularity of nose and upper lip, the chin, faintly decided, balanced beautifully on a rather short neck. On a photograph she must have been completely classical, almost cold—but the glow of her hair and cheeks, at once flushed and fragile, made her the most living person he had ever seen.

"... Think you've got the best name I've heard," she was saying, still apparently to herself; her glance rested on him a moment and then flitted past him—to the Italian bracket-lamps clinging like luminous yellow turtles at intervals along the walls, to the books row upon row, then to her cousin on the other side. "Anthony Patch. Only you ought to look sort of like a horse, with a long narrow face—and you ought to be in tatters."

"That's all the Patch part, though. How should Anthony look?"

"You look like Anthony," she assured him seriously—he thought she had scarcely seen him—"rather majestic," she continued, "and solemn."

Anthony indulged in a disconcerted smile.

"Only I like alliterative names," she went on, "all except mine. Mine's too flamboyant. I used to know two girls named Jinks, though, and just think if they'd been named anything except what they were named—Judy Jinks and Jerry Jinks. Cute, what? Don't you think?" Her childish mouth was parted, awaiting a rejoinder.

"Everybody in the next generation," suggested Dick, "will be named Peter or Barbara—because at present all the piquant literary characters are named Peter or Barbara."

Anthony continued the prophecy:

"Of course Gladys and Eleanor, having graced the last generation of heroines and being at present in their social prime, will be passed on to the next generation of shop-girls—"

"Displacing Ella and Stella," interrupted Dick.

"And Pearl and Jewel," Gloria added cordially, "and Earl and Elmer and Minnie."

"And then I'll come along," remarked Dick, "and picking up the obsolete name, Jewel, I'll attach it to some quaint and attractive character and it'll start its career all over again."

Her voice took up the thread of subject and wove along with faintly upturning, half-humorous intonations for sentence ends—as though defying interruption—and intervals of shadowy laughter. Dick had told her that Anthony's man was named Bounds—she thought that was wonderful! Dick had made some sad pun about Bounds doing patchwork, but if there was one thing worse than a pun, she said, it was a person who, as the inevitable come-back to a pun, gave the perpetrator a mock-reproachful look.

"Where are you from?" inquired Anthony. He knew, but beauty had rendered him thoughtless.

"Kansas City, Missouri."

"They put her out the same time they barred cigarettes."

"Did they bar cigarettes? I see the hand of my holy grandfather."

"He's a reformer or something, isn't he?"

"I blush for him."

"So do I," she confessed. "I detest reformers, especially the sort who try to reform me."

"Are there many of those?"

"Dozens. It's 'Oh, Gloria, if you smoke so many cigarettes you'll lose your pretty complexion!' and 'Oh, Gloria, why don't you marry and settle down?'"

Anthony agreed emphatically while he wondered who had had the temerity to speak thus to such a personage.

"And then," she continued, "there are all the subtle reformers who tell you the wild stories they've heard about you and how they've been sticking up for you."

He saw, at length, that her eyes were gray, very level and cool, and when they rested on him he understood what Maury had meant by saying she was very young and very old. She talked always about herself as a very charming child might talk, and her comments on her tastes and distastes were unaffected and spontaneous.

"I must confess," said Anthony gravely, "that even *I*'ve heard one thing about you."

Alert at once, she sat up straight. Those eyes, with the grayness and eternity of a cliff of soft granite, caught his.

"Tell me. I'll believe it. I always believe anything any one tells me about myself—don't you?"

"Invariably!" agreed the two men in unison.

"Well, tell me."

"I'm not sure that I ought to," teased Anthony, smiling unwillingly. She was so obviously interested, in a state of almost laughable self-absorption.

"He means your nickname," said her cousin.

"What name?" inquired Anthony, politely puzzled.

Instantly she was shy—then she laughed, rolled back against the cushions, and turned her eyes up as she spoke:

"Coast-to-Coast Gloria." Her voice was full of laughter, laughter undefined as the varying shadows playing between fire and lamp upon her hair. "O Lord!"

Still Anthony was puzzled.

"What do you mean?"

"*Me*, I mean. That's what some silly boys coined for *me*."

"Don't you see, Anthony," explained Dick, "traveller of a nation-wide notoriety and all that. Isn't that what you've heard? She's been called that for years—since she was seventeen."

Anthony's eyes became sad and humorous.

"Who's this female Methuselah you've brought in here, Caramel?"

She disregarded this, possibly rather resented it, for she switched back to the main topic.

"What *have* you heard of me?"

"Something about your physique."

"Oh," she said, coolly disappointed, "that all?"

"Your tan."

"My tan?" She was puzzled. Her hand rose to her throat, rested there an instant as though the fingers were feeling variants of color.

"Do you remember Maury Noble? Man you met about a month ago. You made a great impression."

She thought a moment.

"I remember—but he didn't call me up."

"He was afraid to, I don't doubt."

It was black dark without now and Anthony wondered that his apartment had ever seemed gray—so warm and friendly were the books and pictures on the walls and the good Bounds offering tea from a respectful shadow and the three nice people giving out waves of interest and laughter back and forth across the happy fire.

DISSATISFACTION

On Thursday afternoon Gloria and Anthony had tea together in the grill room at the Plaza. Her fur-trimmed suit was gray—"because with gray you *have* to wear a lot of paint," she explained—and a small toque sat rakishly on her head, allowing yellow ripples of hair to wave out in jaunty glory. In the higher light it seemed to Anthony that her personality was infinitely softer—she seemed so young, scarcely eighteen; her form under the tight sheath, known then as a hobble-skirt, was amazingly supple and slender, and her hands, neither "artistic" nor stubby, were small as a child's hands should be.

As they entered, the orchestra were sounding the preliminary whimpers to a maxixe, a tune full of castanets and facile faintly languorous violin harmonies, appropriate to the crowded winter grill teeming with an excited college crowd, high-spirited at the approach of the holidays. Carefully, Gloria considered several locations, and rather to Anthony's annoyance paraded him circuitously to a table for two at the far side of the room. Reaching it she again considered. Would she sit on the right or on the left? Her beautiful eyes and lips were very grave as she made her choice, and Anthony thought again how naïve was her every gesture; she took all the things of life for hers to choose from and apportion, as though she were continually picking out presents for herself from an inexhaustible counter.

Abstractedly she watched the dancers for a few moments, commenting murmurously as a couple eddied near.

"There's a pretty girl in blue"—and as Anthony looked obediently—" there! No. behind you—there!"

"Yes," he agreed helplessly.

"You didn't see her."

"I'd rather look at you."

"I know, but she was pretty. Except that she had big ankles."

"Was she?—I mean, did she?" he said indifferently.

A girl's salutation came from a couple dancing close to them.

"Hello, Gloria! O Gloria!"

"Hello there."

"Who's that?" he demanded.

"I don't know. Somebody." She caught sight of another face. "Hello, Muriel!" Then to Anthony: "There's Muriel Kane. Now I think she's attractive, 'cept not very."

Anthony chuckled appreciatively.

"Attractive, 'cept not very," he repeated.

She smiled—was interested immediately.

"Why is that funny?" Her tone was pathetically intent.

"It just was."

"Do you want to dance?"

"Do you?"

"Sort of. But let's sit," she decided.

"And talk about you? You love to talk about you, don't you?"

"Yes." Caught in a vanity, she laughed.

"I imagine your autobiography would be a classic."

"Dick says I haven't got one."

"Dick!" he exclaimed. "What does he know about you?"

"Nothing. But he says the biography of every woman begins with the first kiss that counts, and ends when her last child is laid in her arms."

"He's talking from his book."

"He says unloved women have no biographies—they have histories."

Anthony laughed again.

"Surely you don't claim to be unloved!"

"Well, I suppose not."

"Then why haven't you a biography? Haven't you ever had a kiss that counted?" As the words left his lips he drew in his breath sharply as though to suck them back. This *baby*!

"I don't know what you mean 'counts,'" she objected.

"I wish you'd tell me how old you are."

"Twenty-two," she said, meeting his eyes gravely. "How old did you think?"

"About eighteen."

"I'm going to start being that. I don't like being twenty-two. I hate it more than anything in the world."

"Being twenty-two?"

"No. Getting old and everything. Getting married."

"Don't you ever want to marry?"

"I don't want to have responsibility and a lot of children to take care of."

Evidently she did not doubt that on her lips all things were good. He waited rather breathlessly for her next remark, expecting it to follow up her last. She was smiling, without amusement but pleasantly, and after an interval half a dozen words fell into the space between them:

"I wish I had some gum-drops."

"You shall!" He beckoned to a waiter and sent him to the cigar counter.

"D'you mind? I love gum-drops. Everybody kids me about it because I'm always whacking away at one—whenever my daddy's not around."

"Not at all.—Who are all these children?" he asked suddenly. "Do you know them all?"

"Why—no, but they're from—oh, from everywhere, I suppose. Don't you ever come here?"

"Very seldom. I don't care particularly for 'nice girls.'"

Immediately he had her attention. She turned a definite shoulder to the dancers, relaxed in her chair, and demanded:

"What *do* you do with yourself?"

Thanks to a cocktail Anthony welcomed the question. In a mood to talk, he wanted, moreover, to impress this girl whose interest seemed so tantalizingly elusive—she stopped to browse in unexpected pastures, hurried quickly over the inobviously obvious. He wanted to pose. He wanted to appear suddenly to her in novel and heroic colors. He wanted to stir her from that casualness she showed toward everything except herself.

"I do nothing," he began, realizing simultaneously that his words were to lack the debonair grace he craved for them. "I do nothing, for there's nothing I can do that's worth doing."

"Well?" He had neither surprised her nor even held her, yet she had certainly understood him, if indeed he had said aught worth understanding.

"Don't you approve of lazy men?"

She nodded.

"I suppose so, if they're gracefully lazy. Is that possible for an American?"

"Why not?" he demanded, discomfited.

But her mind had left the subject and wandered up ten floors.

"My daddy's mad at me," she observed dispassionately.

"Why? But I want to know just why it's impossible for an American to be gracefully idle"—his words gathered conviction—"it astonishes me. It—it—I don't understand why people think that every young man ought to go downtown and work ten hours a day for the best twenty years of his life at dull, unimaginative work, certainly not altruistic work."

He broke off. She watched him inscrutably. He waited for her to agree or disagree, but she did neither.

"Don't you ever form judgments on things?" he asked with some exasperation.

She shook her head and her eyes wandered back to the dancers as she answered:

"I don't know. I don't know anything about—what you should do, or what anybody should do."

She confused him and hindered the flow of his ideas. Self-expression had never seemed at once so desirable and so impossible.

"Well," he admitted apologetically, "neither do I, of course, but—"

"I just think of people," she continued, "whether they seem right where they are and fit into the picture. I don't mind if they don't do anything. I don't see why they should; in fact it always astonishes me when anybody does anything."

"You don't want to do anything?"

"I want to sleep."

For a second he was startled, almost as though she had meant this literally.

"Sleep?"

"Sort of. I want to just be lazy and I want some of the people around me to be doing things, because that makes me feel comfortable and safe—and I want some of them to be doing nothing at all, because they can be graceful and companionable for me. But I never want to change people or get excited over them."

"You're a quaint little determinist," laughed Anthony. "It's your world, isn't it?"

"Well—" she said with a quick upward glance, "isn't it? As long as I'm—young."

She had paused slightly before the last word and Anthony suspected that she had started to say "beautiful." It was undeniably what she had intended.

Her eyes brightened and he waited for her to enlarge on the theme. He had drawn her out, at any rate—he bent forward slightly to catch the words.

But "Let's dance!" was all she said.

ADMIRATION

That winter afternoon at the Plaza was the first of a succession of "dates" Anthony made with her in the blurred and stimulating days before Christmas. Invariably she was busy. What particular strata of the city's social life claimed her he was a long time finding out. It seemed to matter very little. She attended the semi-public charity dances at the big hotels; he saw her several times at dinner parties in Sherry's, and once as he waited for her to dress, Mrs. Gilbert, apropos of her daughter's habit of "going," rattled off an amazing holiday programme that included half a dozen dances to which Anthony had received cards.

He made engagements with her several times for lunch and tea—the former were hurried and, to him at least, rather unsatisfactory occasions, for she was sleepy-eyed and casual, incapable of concentrating upon anything or of giving consecutive attention to his remarks. When after two of these sallow meals he accused her of tendering him the skin and bones of the day she laughed and gave him a tea-time three days off. This was infinitely more satisfactory.

One Sunday afternoon just before Christmas he called up and found her in the lull directly after some important but mysterious quarrel: she informed him in a tone of mingled wrath and amusement that she had sent a man out of her apartment—here Anthony speculated violently—and that the man had been giving a little dinner for her that very night and that of course she wasn't going. So Anthony took her to supper.

"Let's go to something!" she proposed as they went down in the elevator. "I want to see a show, don't you?"

Inquiry at the hotel ticket desk disclosed only two Sunday night "concerts."

"They're always the same," she complained unhappily, "same old Yiddish comedians. Oh, let's go somewhere!"

To conceal a guilty suspicion that he should have arranged a performance of some kind for her approval Anthony affected a knowing cheerfulness.

"We'll go to a good cabaret."

"I've seen every one in town."

"Well, we'll find a new one."

She was in wretched humor; that was evident. Her gray eyes were granite now indeed. When she wasn't speaking she stared straight in front of her as if at some distasteful abstraction in the lobby.

"Well, come on, then."

He followed her, a graceful girl even in her enveloping fur, out to a taxicab, and, with an air of having a definite place in mind, instructed the driver to go over to Broadway and then turn south. He made several casual attempts at conversation but as she adopted an impenetrable armor of silence and answered him in sentences as morose as the cold darkness of the taxicab he gave up, and assuming a like mood fell into a dim gloom.

A dozen blocks down Broadway Anthony's eyes were caught by a large and unfamiliar electric sign spelling "Marathon" in glorious yellow script, adorned with electrical leaves and flowers that alternately vanished and beamed upon the wet and glistening street. He leaned and rapped on the taxi-window and in a moment was receiving information from a colored doorman: Yes, this was a cabaret. Fine cabaret. Bes' showina city!

"Shall we try it?"

With a sigh Gloria tossed her cigarette out the open door and prepared to follow it; then they had passed under the screaming sign, under the wide portal, and up by a stuffy elevator into this unsung palace of pleasure.

The gay habitats of the very rich and the very poor, the very dashing and the very criminal, not to mention the lately exploited very Bohemian, are made known to the awed high school girls of Augusta, Georgia, and Redwing, Minnesota, not only through the bepictured and entrancing spreads of the Sunday theatrical supplements but through the shocked and alarmful eyes of Mr. Rupert Hughes and other chroniclers of the mad pace of America. But the excursions of Harlem onto Broadway, the deviltries of the dull and the revelries of the respectable are a matter of esoteric knowledge only to the participants themselves.

A tip circulates—and in the place knowingly mentioned, gather the lower moral-classes on Saturday and Sunday nights—the little troubled men who are pictured in the comics as "the Consumer" or "the Public." They have made sure that the place has three qualifications: it is cheap; it imitates with a sort of shoddy and mechanical wistfulness the glittering antics of the great cafes in the theatre district; and—this, above all, important—it is a place where they can "take a nice girl," which means, of course, that every one has become equally harmless, timid, and uninteresting through lack of money and imagination.

There on Sunday nights gather the credulous, sentimental, underpaid, overworked people with hyphenated occupations: book-keepers, ticket-sellers, office-managers, salesmen, and, most of all, clerks—clerks of the express, of the mail, of the grocery, of the brokerage, of the bank. With them are their giggling, over-gestured, pathetically pretentious women, who grow fat with them, bear them too many babies, and float helpless and uncontent in a colorless sea of drudgery and broken hopes.

They name these brummagem cabarets after Pullman cars. The "Marathon"! Not for them the salacious similes borrowed from the cafés of Paris! This is where their docile patrons bring their "nice women," whose starved fancies are only too willing to believe that the scene is comparatively gay and joyous, and even faintly immoral. This is life! Who cares for the morrow?

Abandoned people!

Anthony and Gloria, seated, looked about them. At the next table a party of four were in process of being joined by a party of three, two men and a girl, who were evidently late—and the manner of the girl was a study in national sociology. She was meeting some new men—and she was pretending desperately. By gesture she was pretending and by words and by the scarcely perceptible motionings of her eyelids that she belonged to a class a little superior to the class with which she now had to do, that a while ago she had been, and presently would again be, in a higher, rarer air. She was almost painfully refined—she wore a last year's hat covered with violets no more yearningly pretentious and palpably artificial than herself.

Fascinated, Anthony and Gloria watched the girl sit down and radiate the impression that she was only condescendingly present. For *me*, her eyes said, this is practically a slumming expedition, to be cloaked with belittling laughter and semi-apologetics.

—And the other women passionately poured out the impression that though they were in the crowd they were not of it. This was not the sort of place to which they were accustomed; they had dropped in because it was near by and convenient—every party in the restaurant poured out that impression ... who knew? They were forever changing class, all of them—the women often marrying above their opportunities, the men striking suddenly a magnificent opulence: a sufficiently preposterous advertising scheme, a celestialized ice cream cone. Meanwhile, they met here to eat, closing their eyes to the economy displayed in infrequent changings of table-cloths, in the casualness of the cabaret performers, most of all in the colloquial carelessness and familiarity of the waiters. One was sure that these waiters were not impressed by their patrons. One expected that presently they would sit at the tables ...

"Do you object to this?" inquired Anthony.

Gloria's face warmed and for the first time that evening she smiled.

"I love it," she said frankly. It was impossible to doubt her. Her gray eyes roved here and there, drowsing, idle or alert, on each group, passing to the next with unconcealed enjoyment, and to Anthony were made plain the different values of her profile, the wonderfully alive expressions of her mouth, and the authentic distinction of face and form and manner that made her like a single flower amidst a collection of cheap bric-à-brac. At her happiness, a gorgeous sentiment welled into his eyes, choked him up, set his nerves a-tingle, and filled his throat with husky and vibrant emotion. There was a hush upon the room. The careless violins and saxophones, the shrill rasping complaint of a child near by, the voice of the violet-hatted girl at the next table, all moved slowly out, receded, and fell away like shadowy reflections on the shining floor—and they two, it seemed to him, were alone and infinitely remote, quiet. Surely the freshness of her cheeks was a gossamer projection from a land of delicate and undiscovered shades; her hand gleaming on the stained table-cloth was a shell from some far and wildly virginal sea....

Then the illusion snapped like a nest of threads; the room grouped itself around him, voices, faces, movement; the garish shimmer of the lights overhead became real, became portentous; breath began, the slow respiration that she and he took in time with this docile hundred, the rise and fall of bosoms, the eternal meaningless play and interplay and tossing and reiterating of word and phrase—all these wrenched his senses open to the suffocating pressure of life—and then her voice came at him, cool as the suspended dream he had left behind.

"I belong here," she murmured, "I'm like these people."

For an instant this seemed a sardonic and unnecessary paradox hurled at him across the impassable distances she created about herself. Her entrancement had increased—her eyes rested upon a Semitic violinist who swayed his shoulders to the rhythm of the year's mellowest fox-trot:

"Something—goes
Ring-a-ting-a-ling-a-ling
Right in-your ear—"

Again she spoke, from the centre of this pervasive illusion of her own. It amazed him. It was like blasphemy from the mouth of a child.

"I'm like they are—like Japanese lanterns and crape paper, and the music of that orchestra."

"You're a young idiot!" he insisted wildly. She shook her blond head.

"No, I'm not. I *am* like them.... You ought to see.... You don't know me." She hesitated and her eyes came back to him, rested abruptly on his, as though surprised at the last to see him there. "I've got a streak of what you'd call cheapness. I don't know where I get it but it's—oh, things like this and bright colors and gaudy vulgarity. I seem to belong here. These people could appreciate me and take me for granted, and these men would fall in love with me and admire me, whereas the clever men I meet would just analyze me and tell me I'm this because of this or that because of that."

—Anthony for the moment wanted fiercely to paint her, to set her down *now*, as she was, as, as with each relentless second she could never be again.

"What were you thinking?" she asked.

"Just that I'm not a realist," he said, and then: "No, only the romanticist preserves the things worth preserving."

Out of the deep sophistication of Anthony an understanding formed, nothing atavistic or obscure, indeed scarcely physical at all, an understanding remembered from the romancings of many generations of minds that as she talked and caught his eyes and turned her lovely head, she moved him as he had never been moved before. The sheath that held her soul had assumed significance—that was all. She was a sun, radiant, growing, gathering light and storing it—then after an eternity pouring it forth in a glance, the fragment of a sentence, to that part of him that cherished all beauty and all illusion.

III. THE CONNOISSEUR OF KISSES

FROM his undergraduate days as editor of The Harvard Crimson Richard Caramel had desired to write. But as a senior he had picked up the glorified illusion that certain men were set aside for "service" and, going into the world, were to accomplish a vague yearnful something which would react either in eternal reward or, at the least, in the personal satisfaction of having striven for the greatest good of the greatest number.

This spirit has long rocked the colleges in America. It begins, as a rule, during the immaturities and facile impressions of freshman year—sometimes back in preparatory school. Prosperous apostles known for their emotional acting go the rounds of the universities and, by frightening the amiable sheep and dulling the quickening of interest and intellectual curiosity which is the purpose of all education, distil a mysterious conviction of sin, harking back to childhood crimes and to the ever-present menace of "women." To these lectures go the wicked youths to cheer and joke and the timid to swallow the tasty pills, which would be harmless if administered to farmers' wives and pious drug-clerks but are rather dangerous medicine for these "future leaders of men."

This octopus was strong enough to wind a sinuous tentacle about Richard Caramel. The year after his graduation it called him into the slums of New York to muck about with bewildered Italians as secretary to an "Alien Young Men's Rescue Association." He labored at it over a year before the monotony began to weary him. The aliens kept coming inexhaustibly—Italians, Poles, Scandinavians, Czechs, Armenians—with the same wrongs, the same exceptionally ugly faces and very much the same smells, though he fancied that these grew more profuse and diverse as the months passed. His eventual conclusions about the expediency of service were vague, but concerning his own relation to it they were abrupt and decisive. Any amiable young man, his head ringing with the latest crusade, could accomplish as much as he could with the débris of Europe—and it was time for him to write.

He had been living in a down-town Y.M.C.A., but when he quit the task of making sow-ear purses out of sows' ears, he moved up-town and went to work immediately as a reporter for The Sun. He kept at this for a year, doing desultory writing on the side, with little success, and then one day an infelicitous incident peremptorily closed his newspaper career. On a February afternoon he was assigned to report a parade of Squadron A. Snow threatening, he went to sleep instead before a hot fire, and when he woke up did a smooth column about the muffled beats of the horses' hoofs in the snow... This he handed in. Next morning a marked copy of the paper was sent down to the City Editor with a scrawled note: "Fire the man who wrote this." It seemed that Squadron A had also seen the snow threatening—had postponed the parade until another day.

A week later he had begun "The Demon Lover."...

In January, the Monday of the months, Richard Caramel's nose was blue constantly, a sardonic blue, vaguely suggestive of the flames licking around a sinner. His book was nearly ready, and as it grew in completeness it seemed to grow also in its demands, sapping him, overpowering him, until he walked haggard and conquered in its shadow. Not only to Anthony and Maury did he pour out his hopes and boasts and indecisions, but to any one who could be prevailed upon to listen. He called on polite but bewildered publishers, he discussed it with his casual vis-à-vis at the Harvard Club; it was even claimed by Anthony that he had been discovered, one Sunday night, debating the transposition of Chapter Two with a literary ticket-collector in the chill and dismal recesses of a Harlem subway station. And latest among his confidantes was Mrs. Gilbert, who sat with him by the hour and alternated between Bilphism and literature in an intense cross-fire.

"Shakespeare was a Bilphist," she assured him through a fixed smile. "Oh, yes! He was a Bilphist. It's been proved."

At this Dick would look a bit blank.

"If you've read 'Hamlet' you can't help but see."

"Well, he—he lived in a more credulous age—a more religious age."

But she demanded the whole loaf:

"Oh, yes, but you see Bilphism isn't a religion. It's the science of all religions." She smiled defiantly at him. This was the *bon mot* of her belief. There was something in the arrangement of words which grasped her mind so definitely that the statement became superior to any obligation to define itself. It is not unlikely that she would have accepted any idea encased in this radiant formula—which was perhaps not a formula; it was the *reductio ad absurdum* of all formulas.

Then eventually, but gorgeously, would come Dick's turn.

"You've heard of the new poetry movement. You haven't? Well, it's a lot of young poets that are breaking away from the old forms and doing a lot of good. Well, what I was going to say was that my book is going to start a new prose movement, a sort of renaissance."

"I'm sure it will," beamed Mrs. Gilbert. "I'm *sure* it will. I went to Jenny Martin last Tuesday, the palmist, you know, that every one's *mad* about. I told her my nephew was engaged upon a work and she said she knew I'd be glad to hear that his success would be *extraordinary*. But she'd never seen you or known anything about you—not even your *name*."

Having made the proper noises to express his amazement at this astounding phenomenon, Dick waved her theme by him as though he were an arbitrary traffic policeman, and, so to speak, beckoned forward his own traffic.

"I'm absorbed, Aunt Catherine," he assured her, "I really am. All my friends are joshing me—oh, I see the humor in it and I don't care. I think a person ought to be able to take joshing. But I've got a sort of conviction," he concluded gloomily.

"You're an ancient soul, I always say."

"Maybe I am." Dick had reached the stage where he no longer fought, but submitted. He *must* be an ancient soul, he fancied grotesquely; so old as to be absolutely rotten. However, the reiteration of the phrase still somewhat embarrassed him and sent uncomfortable shivers up his back. He changed the subject.

"Where is my distinguished cousin Gloria?"

"She's on the go somewhere, with some one."

Dick paused, considered, and then, screwing up his face into what was evidently begun as a smile but ended as a terrifying frown, delivered a comment.

"I think my friend Anthony Patch is in love with her."

Mrs. Gilbert started, beamed half a second too late, and breathed her "Really?" in the tone of a detective play-whisper.

"I *think* so," corrected Dick gravely. "She's the first girl I've ever seen him with, so much."

"Well, of course," said Mrs. Gilbert with meticulous carelessness, "Gloria never makes me her confidante. She's very secretive. Between you and me"—she bent forward cautiously, obviously determined that only Heaven and her nephew should share her confession—"between you and me, I'd like to see her settle down."

Dick arose and paced the floor earnestly, a small, active, already rotund young man, his hands thrust unnaturally into his bulging pockets.

"I'm not claiming I'm right, mind you," he assured the infinitely-of-the-hotel steel-engraving which smirked respectably back at him. "I'm saying nothing that I'd want Gloria to know. But I think Mad Anthony is interested—tremendously so. He talks about her constantly. In any one else that'd be a bad sign."

"Gloria is a very young soul—" began Mrs. Gilbert eagerly, but her nephew interrupted with a hurried sentence:

"Gloria'd be a very young nut not to marry him." He stopped and faced her, his expression a battle map of lines and dimples, squeezed and strained to its ultimate show of intensity—this as if to make up by his sincerity for any indiscretion in his words. "Gloria's a wild one, Aunt Catherine. She's uncontrollable. How she's done it I don't know, but lately she's picked up a lot of the funniest friends. She doesn't seem to care. And the men she used to go with around New York were—" He paused for breath.

"Yes-yes-yes," interjected Mrs. Gilbert, with an anaemic attempt to hide the immense interest with which she listened.

"Well," continued Richard Caramel gravely, "there it is. I mean that the men she went with and the people she went with used to be first rate. Now they aren't."

Mrs. Gilbert blinked very fast—her bosom trembled, inflated, remained so for an instant, and with the exhalation her words flowed out in a torrent.

She knew, she cried in a whisper; oh, yes, mothers see these things. But what could she do? He knew Gloria. He'd seen enough of Gloria to know how hopeless it was to try to deal with her. Gloria had been so spoiled—in a rather complete and unusual way. She had been suckled until she was three, for instance, when she could probably have chewed sticks. Perhaps—one never knew—it was this that had given that health and *hardiness* to her whole personality. And then ever since she was twelve years old she'd had boys about her so thick—oh, so thick one couldn't *move.* At sixteen she began going to dances at preparatory schools, and then came the colleges; and everywhere she went, boys, boys, boys. At first, oh, until she was eighteen there had been so many that it never seemed one any more than the others, but then she began to single them out.

She knew there had been a string of affairs spread over about three years, perhaps a dozen of them altogether. Sometimes the men were undergraduates, sometimes just out of college—they lasted on an average of several months each, with short attractions in between. Once or twice they had endured longer and her mother had hoped she would be engaged, but always a new one came—a new one—

The men? Oh, she made them miserable, literally! There was only one who had kept any sort of dignity, and he had been a mere child, young Carter Kirby, of Kansas City, who was so conceited anyway that he just sailed out on his vanity one afternoon and left for Europe next day with his father. The others had been—wretched. They never seemed to know when she was tired of them, and Gloria had seldom been deliberately unkind. They would keep phoning, writing letters to her, trying to see her, making long trips after her around the country. Some of them had confided in Mrs. Gilbert, told her with tears in their eyes that they would never get over Gloria ... at least two of them had since married, though.... But Gloria, it seemed, struck to kill—to this day Mr. Carstairs called up once a week, and sent her flowers which she no longer bothered to refuse.

Several times, twice, at least, Mrs. Gilbert knew it had gone as far as a private engagement—with Tudor Baird and that Holcome boy at Pasadena. She was sure it had, because—this must go no further—she had come in unexpectedly and found Gloria acting, well, very much engaged indeed. She had not spoken to her daughter, of course. She had had a certain sense of delicacy and, besides, each time she had expected an announcement in a few weeks. But the announcement never came; instead, a new man came.

Scenes! Young men walking up and down the library like caged tigers! Young men glaring at each other in the hall as one came and the other left! Young men calling up on the telephone and being hung up upon in desperation! Young men threatening South America! ... Young men writing the most pathetic letters! (She said nothing to this effect, but Dick fancied that Mrs. Gilbert's eyes had seen some of these letters.)

... And Gloria, between tears and laughter, sorry, glad, out of love and in love, miserable, nervous, cool, amidst a great returning of presents, substitution of pictures in immemorial frames, and taking of hot baths and beginning again—with the next.

That state of things continued, assumed an air of permanency. Nothing harmed Gloria or changed her or moved her. And then out of a clear sky one day she informed her mother that undergraduates wearied her. She was absolutely going to no more college dances.

This had begun the change—not so much in her actual habits, for she danced, and had as many "dates" as ever—but they were dates in a different spirit. Previously it had been a sort of pride, a matter of her own vainglory. She had been, probably, the most celebrated and sought-after young beauty in the country. Gloria Gilbert of Kansas City! She had fed on it ruthlessly—enjoying the crowds around her, the manner in which the most desirable men singled her out; enjoying the fierce jealousy of other girls; enjoying the fabulous, not to say scandalous, and, her mother was glad to say, entirely unfounded rumors about her—for instance, that she had gone in the Yale swimming-pool one night in a chiffon evening dress.

And from loving it with a vanity that was almost masculine—it had been in the nature of a triumphant and dazzling career—she became suddenly anaesthetic to it. She retired. She who had dominated countless parties, who had blown fragrantly through many ballrooms to the tender tribute of many eyes, seemed to care no longer. He who fell in love with her now was dismissed utterly, almost angrily. She went listlessly with the most indifferent men. She continually broke engagements, not as in the past from a cool assurance that she was irreproachable, that the man she insulted would return like a domestic animal—but indifferently, without contempt or pride. She rarely stormed at men any more—she yawned at them. She seemed—and it was so strange—she seemed to her mother to be growing cold.

Richard Caramel listened. At first he had remained standing, but as his aunt's discourse waxed in content—it stands here pruned by half, of all side references to the youth of Gloria's soul and to Mrs. Gilbert's own mental distresses—he drew a chair up and attended rigorously as she floated, between tears and plaintive helplessness, down the long story of Gloria's life. When she came to the tale of this last year, a tale of the ends of cigarettes left all over New York in little trays marked "Midnight Frolic" and "Justine Johnson's Little Club," he began nodding his head slowly, then faster and faster, until, as she finished on a staccato note, it was bobbing briskly up and down, absurdly like a doll's wired head, expressing—almost anything.

In a sense Gloria's past was an old story to him. He had followed it with the eyes of a journalist, for he was going to write a book about her some day. But his interests, just at present, were family interests. He wanted to know, in particular, who was this Joseph Bloeckman that he had seen her with several times; and those two girls she was with constantly, "this" Rachael Jerryl and "this" Miss Kane—surely Miss Kane wasn't exactly the sort one would associate with Gloria!

But the moment had passed. Mrs. Gilbert having climbed the hill of exposition was about to glide swiftly down the ski-jump of collapse. Her eyes were like a blue sky seen through two round, red window-casements. The flesh about her mouth was trembling.

And at the moment the door opened, admitting into the room Gloria and the two young ladies lately mentioned.

TWO YOUNG WOMEN

"Well!"

"How do you do, Mrs. Gilbert!"

Miss Kane and Miss Jerryl are presented to Mr. Richard Caramel. "This is Dick" (laughter).

"I've heard so much about you," says Miss Kane between a giggle and a shout.

"How do you do," says Miss Jerryl shyly.

Richard Caramel tries to move about as if his figure were better. He is torn between his innate cordiality and the fact that he considers these girls rather common—not at all the Farmover type.

Gloria has disappeared into the bedroom.

"Do sit down," beams Mrs. Gilbert, who is by now quite herself. "Take off your things." Dick is afraid she will make some remark about the age of his soul, but he forgets his qualms in completing a conscientious, novelist's examination of the two young women.

Muriel Kane had originated in a rising family of East Orange. She was short rather than small, and hovered audaciously between plumpness and width. Her hair was black and elaborately arranged. This, in conjunction with her handsome, rather bovine eyes, and her over-red lips, combined to make her resemble Theda Bara, the prominent motion picture actress. People told her constantly that she was a "vampire," and she believed them. She suspected hopefully that they were afraid of her, and she did her utmost under all circumstances to give the impression of danger. An imaginative man could see the red flag that she constantly carried, waving it wildly, beseechingly—and, alas, to little spectacular avail. She was also tremendously timely: she knew the latest songs, all the latest songs—when one of them was played on the phonograph she would rise to her feet and rock her shoulders back and forth and snap her fingers, and if there was no music she would accompany herself by humming.

Her conversation was also timely: "I don't care," she would say, "I should worry and lose my figure"—and again: "I can't make my feet behave when I hear that tune. Oh, baby!"

Her finger-nails were too long and ornate, polished to a pink and unnatural fever. Her clothes were too tight, too stylish, too vivid, her eyes too roguish, her smile too coy. She was almost pitifully overemphasized from head to foot.

The other girl was obviously a more subtle personality. She was an exquisitely dressed Jewess with dark hair and a lovely milky pallor. She seemed shy and vague, and these two qualities accentuated a rather delicate charm that floated about her. Her family were "Episcopalians," owned three smart women's shops along Fifth Avenue, and lived in a magnificent apartment on Riverside Drive. It seemed to Dick, after a few moments, that she was attempting to imitate Gloria—he wondered that people invariably chose inimitable people to imitate.

"We had the most *hectic* time!" Muriel was exclaiming enthusiastically. "There was a crazy woman behind us on the bus. She was absitively, posolutely *nutty*! She kept talking to herself about something she'd like to do to somebody or something. I was *pet*rified, but Gloria simply *wouldn't* get off."

Mrs. Gilbert opened her mouth, properly awed.

"Really?"

"Oh, she was crazy. But we should worry, she didn't hurt us. Ugly! Gracious! The man across from us said her face ought to be on a night-nurse in a home for the blind, and we all *howled*, naturally, so the man tried to pick us up."

Presently Gloria emerged from her bedroom and in unison every eye turned on her. The two girls receded into a shadowy background, unperceived, unmissed.

"We've been talking about you," said Dick quickly, "—your mother and I."

"Well," said Gloria.

A pause—Muriel turned to Dick.

"You're a great writer, aren't you?"

"I'm a writer," he confessed sheepishly.

"I always say," said Muriel earnestly, "that if I ever had time to write down all my experiences it'd make a wonderful book."

Rachael giggled sympathetically; Richard Caramel's bow was almost stately. Muriel continued:

"But I don't see how you can sit down and do it. And poetry! Lordy, I can't make two lines rhyme. Well, I should worry!"

Richard Caramel with difficulty restrained a shout of laughter. Gloria was chewing an amazing gum-drop and staring moodily out the window. Mrs. Gilbert cleared her throat and beamed.

"But you see," she said in a sort of universal exposition, "you're not an ancient soul—like Richard."

The Ancient Soul breathed a gasp of relief—it was out at last.

Then as if she had been considering it for five minutes, Gloria made a sudden announcement:

"I'm going to give a party."

"Oh, can I come?" cried Muriel with facetious daring.

"A dinner. Seven people: Muriel and Rachael and I, and you, Dick, and Anthony, and that man named Noble—I liked him—and Bloeckman."

Muriel and Rachael went into soft and purring ecstasies of enthusiasm. Mrs. Gilbert blinked and beamed. With an air of casualness Dick broke in with a question:

"Who is this fellow Bloeckman, Gloria?"

Scenting a faint hostility, Gloria turned to him.

"Joseph Bloeckman? He's the moving picture man. Vice-president of 'Films Par Excellence.' He and father do a lot of business."

"Oh!"

"Well, will you all come?"

They would all come. A date was arranged within the week. Dick rose, adjusted hat, coat, and muffler, and gave out a general smile.

"By-by," said Muriel, waving her hand gaily, "call me up some time."

Richard Caramel blushed for her.

DEPLORABLE END OF THE CHEVALIER O'KEEFE

It was Monday and Anthony took Geraldine Burke to luncheon at the Beaux Arts—afterward they went up to his apartment and he wheeled out the little rolling-table that held his supply of liquor, selecting vermouth, gin, and absinthe for a proper stimulant.

Geraldine Burke, usher at Keith's, had been an amusement of several months. She demanded so little that he liked her, for since a lamentable affair with a débutante the preceding summer, when he had discovered that after half a dozen kisses a proposal was expected, he had been wary of girls of his own class. It was only too easy to turn a critical eye on their imperfections: some physical harshness or a general lack of personal delicacy—but a girl who was usher at Keith's was approached with a different attitude. One could tolerate qualities in an intimate valet that would be unforgivable in a mere acquaintance on one's social level.

Geraldine, curled up at the foot of the lounge, considered him with narrow slanting eyes.

"You drink all the time, don't you?" she said suddenly.

"Why, I suppose so," replied Anthony in some surprise. "Don't you?"

"Nope. I go on parties sometimes—you know, about once a week, but I only take two or three drinks. You and your friends keep on drinking all the time. I should think you'd ruin your health."

Anthony was somewhat touched.

"Why, aren't you sweet to worry about me!"

"Well, I do."

"I don't drink so very much," he declared. "Last month I didn't touch a drop for three weeks. And I only get really tight about once a week."

"But you have something to drink every day and you're only twenty-five. Haven't you any ambition? Think what you'll be at forty?"

"I sincerely trust that I won't live that long."

She clicked her tongue with her teeth.

"You cra-azy!" she said as he mixed another cocktail—and then: "Are you any relation to Adam Patch?"

"Yes, he's my grandfather."

"Really?" She was obviously thrilled.

"Absolutely."

"That's funny. My daddy used to work for him."

"He's a queer old man."

"Is he nice?" she demanded.

"Well, in private life he's seldom unnecessarily disagreeable."

"Tell us about him."

"Why," Anthony considered "—he's all shrunken up and he's got the remains of some gray hair that always looks as though the wind were in it. He's very moral."

"He's done a lot of good," said Geraldine with intense gravity.

"Rot!" scoffed Anthony. "He's a pious ass—a chickenbrain."

Her mind left the subject and flitted on.

"Why don't you live with him?"

"Why don't I board in a Methodist parsonage?"

"You cra-azy!"

Again she made a little clicking sound to express disapproval. Anthony thought how moral was this little waif at heart—how completely moral she would still be after the inevitable wave came that would wash her off the sands of respectability.

"Do you hate him?"

"I wonder. I never liked him. You never like people who do things for you."

"Does he hate you?"

"My dear Geraldine," protested Anthony, frowning humorously, "do have another cocktail. I annoy him. If I smoke a cigarette he comes into the room sniffing. He's a prig, a bore, and something of a hypocrite. I probably wouldn't be telling you this if I hadn't had a few drinks, but I don't suppose it matters."

Geraldine was persistently interested. She held her glass, untasted, between finger and thumb and regarded him with eyes in which there was a touch of awe.

"How do you mean a hypocrite?"

"Well," said Anthony impatiently, "maybe he's not. But he doesn't like the things that I like, and so, as far as I'm concerned, he's uninteresting."

"Hm." Her curiosity seemed, at length, satisfied. She sank back into the sofa and sipped her cocktail.

"You're a funny one," she commented thoughtfully. "Does everybody want to marry you because your grandfather is rich?"

"They don't—but I shouldn't blame them if they did. Still, you see, I never intend to marry."

She scorned this.

"You'll fall in love someday. Oh, you will—I know." She nodded wisely.

"It'd be idiotic to be overconfident. That's what ruined the Chevalier O'Keefe."

"Who was he?"

"A creature of my splendid mind. He's my one creation, the Chevalier."

"Cra-a-azy!" she murmured pleasantly, using the clumsy rope ladder with which she bridged all gaps and climbed after her mental superiors. Subconsciously she felt that it eliminated distances and brought the person whose imagination had eluded her back within range.

"Oh, no!" objected Anthony, "oh, no, Geraldine. You mustn't play the alienist upon the Chevalier. If you feel yourself unable to understand him I won't bring him in. Besides, I should feel a certain uneasiness because of his regrettable reputation."

"I guess I can understand anything that's got any sense to it," answered Geraldine a bit testily.

"In that case there are various episodes in the life of the Chevalier which might prove diverting."

"Well?"

"It was his untimely end that caused me to think of him and made him apropos in the conversation. I hate to introduce him end foremost, but it seems inevitable that the Chevalier must back into your life."

"Well, what about him? Did he die?"

"He did! In this manner. He was an Irishman, Geraldine, a semi-fictional Irishman—the wild sort with a genteel brogue and 'reddish hair.' He was exiled from Erin in the late days of chivalry and, of course, crossed over to France. Now the Chevalier O'Keefe, Geraldine, had, like me, one weakness. He was enormously susceptible to all sorts and conditions of women. Besides being a sentimentalist he was a romantic, a vain fellow, a man of wild passions, a little blind in one eye and almost stone-blind in the other. Now a male roaming the world in this condition is as helpless as a lion without teeth, and in consequence the Chevalier was made utterly miserable for twenty years by a series of women who hated him, used him, bored him, aggravated him, sickened him, spent his money, made a fool of him—in brief, as the world has it, loved him.

"This was bad, Geraldine, and as the Chevalier, save for this one weakness, this exceeding susceptibility, was a man of penetration, he decided that he would rescue himself once and for all from these drains upon him. With this purpose he went to a very famous monastery in Champagne called—well, anachronistically known as St. Voltaire's. It was the rule at St. Voltaire's that no monk could descend to the ground story of the monastery so long as he lived, but should exist engaged in prayer and contemplation in one of the four towers, which were called after the four commandments of the monastery rule: Poverty, Chastity, Obedience, and Silence.

"When the day came that was to witness the Chevalier's farewell to the world he was utterly happy. He gave all his Greek books to his landlady, and his sword he sent in a golden sheath to the King of France, and all his mementos of Ireland he gave to the young Huguenot who sold fish in the street where he lived.

"Then he rode out to St. Voltaire's, slew his horse at the door, and presented the carcass to the monastery cook.

"At five o'clock that night he felt, for the first time, free—forever free from sex. No woman could enter the monastery; no monk could descend below the second story. So as he climbed the winding stair that led to his cell at the very top of the Tower of Chastity he paused for a moment by an open window which looked down fifty feet on to a road below. It was all so beautiful, he thought, this world that he was leaving, the golden shower of sun beating down upon the long fields, the spray of trees in the distance, the vineyards, quiet and green, freshening wide miles before him. He leaned his elbows on the window casement and gazed at the winding road.

"Now, as it happened, Thérèse, a peasant girl of sixteen from a neighboring village, was at that moment passing along this same road that ran in front of the monastery. Five minutes before, the little piece of ribbon which held up the stocking on her pretty left leg had worn through and broken. Being a girl of rare modesty she had thought to wait until she arrived home before repairing it, but it had bothered her to such an extent that she felt she could endure it no longer. So, as she passed the Tower of Chastity, she stopped and with a pretty gesture lifted her skirt—as little as possible, be it said to her credit—to adjust her garter.

"Up in the tower the newest arrival in the ancient monastery of St. Voltaire, as though pulled forward by a gigantic and irresistible hand, leaned from the window. Further he leaned and further until suddenly one of the stones loosened under his weight, broke from its cement with a soft powdery sound—and, first headlong, then head over heels, finally in a vast and impressive revolution tumbled the Chevalier O'Keefe, bound for the hard earth and eternal damnation.

"Thérèse was so much upset by the occurrence that she ran all the way home and for ten years spent an hour a day in secret prayer for the soul of the monk whose neck and vows were simultaneously broken on that unfortunate Sunday afternoon.

"And the Chevalier O'Keefe, being suspected of suicide, was not buried in consecrated ground, but tumbled into a field near by, where he doubtless improved the quality of the soil for many years afterward. Such was the untimely end of a very brave and gallant gentleman. What do you think, Geraldine?"

But Geraldine, lost long before, could only smile roguishly, wave her first finger at him, and repeat her bridge-all, her explain-all:

"Crazy!" she said, "you cra-a-azy!"

His thin face was kindly, she thought, and his eyes quite gentle. She liked him because he was arrogant without being conceited, and because, unlike the men she met about the theatre, he had a horror of being conspicuous. What an odd, pointless story! But she had enjoyed the part about the stocking!

After the fifth cocktail he kissed her, and between laughter and bantering caresses and a half-stifled flare of passion they passed an hour. At four-thirty she claimed an engagement, and going into the bathroom she rearranged her hair. Refusing to let him order her a taxi she stood for a moment in the doorway.

"You *will* get married," she was insisting, "you wait and see."

Anthony was playing with an ancient tennis ball, and he bounced it carefully on the floor several times before he answered with a soupçon of acidity:

"You're a little idiot, Geraldine."

She smiled provokingly.

"Oh, I am, am I? Want to bet?"

"That'd be silly too."

"Oh, it would, would it? Well, I'll just bet you'll marry somebody inside of a year."

Anthony bounced the tennis ball very hard. This was one of his handsome days, she thought; a sort of intensity had displaced the melancholy in his dark eyes.

"Geraldine," he said, at length, "in the first place I have no one I want to marry; in the second place I haven't enough money to support two people; in the third place I am entirely opposed to marriage for people of my type; in the fourth place I have a strong distaste for even the abstract consideration of it."

But Geraldine only narrowed her eyes knowingly, made her clicking sound, and said she must be going. It was late.

"Call me up soon," she reminded him as he kissed her goodbye, "you haven't for three weeks, you know."

"I will," he promised fervently.

He shut the door and coming back into the room stood for a moment lost in thought with the tennis ball still clasped in his hand. There was one of his lonelinesses coming, one of those times when he walked the streets or sat, aimless and depressed, biting a pencil at his desk. It was a self-absorption with no comfort, a demand for expression with no outlet, a sense of time rushing by, ceaselessly and wastefully—assuaged only by that conviction that there was nothing to waste, because all efforts and attainments were equally valueless.

He thought with emotion—aloud, ejaculative, for he was hurt and confused.

"No *idea* of getting married, by *God*!"

Of a sudden he hurled the tennis ball violently across the room, where it barely missed the lamp, and, rebounding here and there for a moment, lay still upon the floor.

SIGNLIGHT AND MOONLIGHT

For her dinner Gloria had taken a table in the Cascades at the Biltmore, and when the men met in the hall outside a little after eight, "that person Bloeckman" was the target of six masculine eyes. He was a stoutening, ruddy Jew of about thirty-five, with an expressive face under smooth sandy hair—and, no doubt, in most business gatherings his personality would have been considered ingratiating. He sauntered up to the three younger men, who stood in a group smoking as they waited for their hostess, and introduced himself with a little too evident assurance—nevertheless it is to be doubted whether he received the intended impression of faint and ironic chill: there was no hint of understanding in his manner.

"You related to Adam J. Patch?" he inquired of Anthony, emitting two slender strings of smoke from nostrils overwide.

Anthony admitted it with the ghost of a smile.

"He's a fine man," pronounced Bloeckman profoundly. "He's a fine example of an American."

"Yes," agreed Anthony, "he certainly is."

—I detest these underdone men, he thought coldly. Boiled looking! Ought to be shoved back in the oven; just one more minute would do it.

Bloeckman squinted at his watch.

"Time these girls were showing up ..."

—Anthony waited breathlessly; it came—

"... but then," with a widening smile, "you know how women are."

The three young men nodded; Bloeckman looked casually about him, his eyes resting critically on the ceiling and then passing lower. His expression combined that of a Middle Western farmer appraising his wheat crop and that of an actor wondering whether he is observed—the public manner of all good Americans. As he finished his survey he turned back quickly to the reticent trio, determined to strike to their very heart and core.

"You college men? ... Harvard, eh. I see the Princeton boys beat you fellows in hockey."

Unfortunate man. He had drawn another blank. They had been three years out and heeded only the big football games. Whether, after the failure of this sally, Mr. Bloeckman would have perceived himself to be in a cynical atmosphere is problematical, for—

Gloria arrived. Muriel arrived. Rachael arrived. After a hurried "Hello, people!" uttered by Gloria and echoed by the other two, the three swept by into the dressing room.

A moment later Muriel appeared in a state of elaborate undress and *crept* toward them. She was in her element: her ebony hair was slicked straight back on her head; her eyes were artificially darkened; she reeked of insistent perfume. She was got up to the best of her ability as a siren, more popularly a "vamp"—a picker up and thrower away of men, an unscrupulous and fundamentally unmoved toyer with affections. Something in the exhaustiveness of her attempt fascinated Maury at first sight—a woman with wide hips affecting a panther-like litheness! As they waited the extra three minutes for Gloria, and, by polite assumption, for Rachael, he was unable to take his eyes from her. She would turn her head away, lowering her eyelashes and biting her nether lip in an amazing exhibition of coyness. She would rest her hands on her hips and sway from side to side in tune to the music, saying:

"Did you ever hear such perfect ragtime? I just can't make my shoulders behave when I hear that."

Mr. Bloeckman clapped his hands gallantly.

"You ought to be on the stage."

"I'd like to be!" cried Muriel; "will you back me?"

"I sure will."

With becoming modesty Muriel ceased her motions and turned to Maury, asking what he had "seen" this year. He interpreted this as referring to the dramatic world, and they had a gay and exhilarating exchange of titles, after this manner:

MURIEL: Have you seen "Peg o' My Heart"?

MAURY: No, I haven't.

MURIEL: (*Eagerly*) It's wonderful! You want to see it.

MAURY: Have you seen "Omar, the Tentmaker"?

MURIEL: No, but I hear it's wonderful. I'm very anxious to see it. Have you seen "Fair and Warmer"?

MAURY: (*Hopefully*) Yes.

MURIEL: I don't think it's very good. It's trashy.

MAURY: (*Faintly*) Yes, that's true.

MURIEL: But I went to "Within the Law" last night and I thought it was fine. Have you seen "The Little Cafe"?...

This continued until they ran out of plays. Dick, meanwhile, turned to Mr. Bloeckman, determined to extract what gold he could from this unpromising load.

"I hear all the new novels are sold to the moving pictures as soon as they come out."

"That's true. Of course the main thing in a moving picture is a strong story."

"Yes, I suppose so."

"So many novels are all full of talk and psychology. Of course those aren't as valuable to us. It's impossible to make much of that interesting on the screen."

"You want plots first," said Richard brilliantly.

"Of course. Plots first—" He paused, shifted his gaze. His pause spread, included the others with all the authority of a warning finger. Gloria followed by Rachael was coming out of the dressing room.

Among other things it developed during dinner that Joseph Bloeckman never danced, but spent the music time watching the others with the bored tolerance of an elder among children. He was a dignified man and a proud one. Born in Munich he had begun his American career as a peanut vender with a travelling circus. At eighteen he was a side show ballyhoo; later, the manager of the side show, and, soon after, the proprietor of a second-class vaudeville house. Just when the moving picture had passed out of the stage of a curiosity and become a promising industry he was an ambitious young man of twenty-six with some money to invest, nagging financial ambitions and a good working knowledge of the popular show business. That had been nine years before. The moving picture industry had borne him up with it where it threw off dozens of men with more financial ability, more imagination, and more practical ideas...and now he sat here and contemplated the immortal Gloria for whom young Stuart Holcome had gone from New York to Pasadena—watched her, and knew that presently she would cease dancing and come back to sit on his left hand.

He hoped she would hurry. The oysters had been standing some minutes.

Meanwhile Anthony, who had been placed on Gloria's left hand, was dancing with her, always in a certain fourth of the floor. This, had there been stags, would have been a delicate tribute to the girl, meaning "Damn you, don't cut in!" It was very consciously intimate.

"Well," he began, looking down at her, "you look mighty sweet to-night."

She met his eyes over the horizontal half foot that separated them.

"Thank you—Anthony."

"In fact you're uncomfortably beautiful," he added. There was no smile this time.

"And you're very charming."

"Isn't this nice?" he laughed. "We actually approve of each other."

"Don't you, usually?" She had caught quickly at his remark, as she always did at any unexplained allusion to herself, however faint.

He lowered his voice, and when he spoke there was in it no more than a wisp of badinage.

"Does a priest approve the Pope?"

"I don't know—but that's probably the vaguest compliment I ever received."

"Perhaps I can muster a few bromides."

"Well, I wouldn't have you strain yourself. Look at Muriel! Right here next to us."

He glanced over his shoulder. Muriel was resting her brilliant cheek against the lapel of Maury Noble's dinner coat and her powdered left arm was apparently twisted around his head. One was impelled to wonder why she failed to seize the nape of his neck with her hand. Her eyes, turned ceiling-ward, rolled largely back and forth; her hips swayed, and as she danced she kept up a constant low singing. This at first seemed to be a translation of the song into some foreign tongue but became eventually apparent as an attempt to fill out the metre of the song with the only words she knew—the words of the title—

"He's a rag-picker,
A rag-picker;
A rag-time picking man,
Rag-picking, picking, pick, pick,
Rag-pick, pick, pick."

—and so on, into phrases still more strange and barbaric. When she caught the amused glances of Anthony and Gloria she acknowledged them only with a faint smile and a half-closing of her eyes, to indicate that the music entering into her soul had put her into an ecstatic and exceedingly seductive trance.

The music ended and they returned to their table, whose solitary but dignified occupant arose and tendered each of them a smile so ingratiating that it was as if he were shaking their hands and congratulating them on a brilliant performance.

"Blockhead never will dance! I think he has a wooden leg," remarked Gloria to the table at large. The three young men started and the gentleman referred to winced perceptibly.

This was the one rough spot in the course of Bloeckman's acquaintance with Gloria. She relentlessly punned on his name. First it had been "Block-house." lately, the more invidious "Blockhead." He had requested with a strong undertone of irony that she use his first name, and this she had done obediently several times—then slipping, helpless, repentant but dissolved in laughter, back into "Blockhead."

It was a very sad and thoughtless thing.

"I'm afraid Mr. Bloeckman thinks we're a frivolous crowd," sighed Muriel, waving a balanced oyster in his direction.

"He has that air," murmured Rachael. Anthony tried to remember whether she had said anything before. He thought not. It was her initial remark.

Mr. Bloeckman suddenly cleared his throat and said in a loud, distinct voice:

"On the contrary. When a man speaks he's merely tradition. He has at best a few thousand years back of him. But woman, why, she is the miraculous mouthpiece of posterity."

In the stunned pause that followed this astounding remark, Anthony choked suddenly on an oyster and hurried his napkin to his face. Rachael and Muriel raised a mild if somewhat surprised laugh, in which Dick and Maury joined, both of them red in the face and restraining uproariousness with the most apparent difficulty.

"—My God!" thought Anthony. "It's a subtitle from one of his movies. The man's memorized it!"

Gloria alone made no sound. She fixed Mr. Bloeckman with a glance of silent reproach.

"Well, for the love of Heaven! Where on earth did you dig that up?"

Bloeckman looked at her uncertainly, not sure of her intention. But in a moment he recovered his poise and assumed the bland and consciously tolerant smile of an intellectual among spoiled and callow youth.

The soup came up from the kitchen—but simultaneously the orchestra leader came up from the bar, where he had absorbed the tone color inherent in a seidel of beer. So the soup was left to cool during the delivery of a ballad entitled "Everything's at Home Except Your Wife."

Then the champagne—and the party assumed more amusing proportions. The men, except Richard Caramel, drank freely; Gloria and Muriel sipped a glass apiece; Rachael Jerryl took none. They sat out the waltzes but danced to everything else—all except Gloria, who seemed to tire after a while and preferred to sit smoking at the table, her eyes now lazy, now eager, according to whether she listened to Bloeckman or watched a pretty woman among the dancers. Several times Anthony wondered what Bloeckman was telling her. He was chewing a cigar back and forth in his mouth, and had expanded after dinner to the extent of violent gestures.

Ten o'clock found Gloria and Anthony beginning a dance. Just as they were out of ear-shot of the table she said in a low voice:

"Dance over by the door. I want to go down to the drug-store."

Obediently Anthony guided her through the crowd in the designated direction; in the hall she left him for a moment, to reappear with a cloak over her arm.

"I want some gum-drops," she said, humorously apologetic; "you can't guess what for this time. It's just that I want to bite my finger-nails, and I will if I don't get some gum-drops." She sighed, and resumed as they stepped into the empty elevator: "I've been biting 'em all day. A bit nervous, you see. Excuse the pun. It was unintentional—the words just arranged themselves. Gloria Gilbert, the female wag."

Reaching the ground floor they naïvely avoided the hotel candy counter, descended the wide front staircase, and walking through several corridors found a drug-store in the Grand Central Station. After an intense examination of the perfume counter she made her purchase. Then on some mutual unmentioned impulse they strolled, arm in arm, not in the direction from which they had come, but out into Forty-third Street.

The night was alive with thaw; it was so nearly warm that a breeze drifting low along the sidewalk brought to Anthony a vision of an unhoped-for hyacinthine spring. Above in the blue oblong of sky, around them in the caress of the drifting air, the illusion of a new season carried relief from the stiff and breathed-over atmosphere they had left, and for a hushed moment the traffic sounds and the murmur of water flowing in the gutters seemed an illusive and rarefied prolongation of that music to which they had lately danced. When Anthony spoke it was with surety that his words came from something breathless and desirous that the night had conceived in their two hearts.

"Let's take a taxi and ride around a bit!" he suggested, without looking at her.

Oh, Gloria, Gloria!

A cab yawned at the curb. As it moved off like a boat on a labyrinthine ocean and lost itself among the inchoate night masses of the great buildings, among the now stilled, now strident, cries and clangings, Anthony put his arm around the girl, drew her over to him and kissed her damp, childish mouth.

She was silent. She turned her face up to him, pale under the wisps and patches of light that trailed in like moonshine through a foliage. Her eyes were gleaming ripples in the white lake of her face; the shadows of her hair bordered the brow with a persuasive unintimate dusk. No love was there, surely; nor the imprint of any love. Her beauty was cool as this damp breeze, as the moist softness of her own lips.

"You're such a swan in this light," he whispered after a moment. There were silences as murmurous as sound. There were pauses that seemed about to shatter and were only to be snatched back to oblivion by the tightening of his arms about her and the sense that she was resting there as a caught, gossamer feather, drifted in out of the dark. Anthony laughed, noiselessly and exultantly, turning his face up and away from her, half in an overpowering rush of triumph, half lest her sight of him should spoil the splendid immobility of her expression. Such a kiss—it was a flower held against the face, never to be described, scarcely to be remembered; as though her beauty were giving off emanations of itself which settled transiently and already dissolving upon his heart.

... The buildings fell away in melted shadows; this was the Park now, and after a long while the great white ghost of the Metropolitan Museum moved majestically past, echoing sonorously to the rush of the cab.

"Why, Gloria! Why, Gloria!"

Her eyes appeared to regard him out of many thousand years: all emotion she might have felt, all words she might have uttered, would have seemed inadequate beside the adequacy of her silence, ineloquent against the eloquence of her beauty—and of her body, close to him, slender and cool.

"Tell him to turn around," she murmured, "and drive pretty fast going back...."

Up in the supper room the air was hot. The table, littered with napkins and ash-trays, was old and stale. It was between dances as they entered, and Muriel Kane looked up with roguishness extraordinary.

"Well, where have *you* been?"

"To call up mother," answered Gloria coolly. "I promised her I would. Did we miss a dance?"

Then followed an incident that though slight in itself Anthony had cause to reflect on many years afterward. Joseph Bloeckman, leaning well back in his chair, fixed him with a peculiar glance, in which several emotions were curiously and inextricably mingled. He did not greet Gloria except by rising, and he immediately resumed a conversation with Richard Caramel about the influence of literature on the moving pictures.

MAGIC

The stark and unexpected miracle of a night fades out with the lingering death of the last stars and the premature birth of the first newsboys. The flame retreats to some remote and platonic fire; the white heat has gone from the iron and the glow from the coal.

Along the shelves of Anthony's library, filling a wall amply, crept a chill and insolent pencil of sunlight touching with frigid disapproval Thérèse of France and Ann the Superwoman, Jenny of the Orient Ballet and Zuleika the Conjurer—and Hoosier Cora—then down a shelf and into the years, resting pityingly on the over-invoked shades of Helen, Thaïs, Salome, and Cleopatra.

Anthony, shaved and bathed, sat in his most deeply cushioned chair and watched it until at the steady rising of the sun it lay glinting for a moment on the silk ends of the rug—and went out.

It was ten o'clock. The Sunday Times, scattered about his feet, proclaimed by rotogravure and editorial, by social revelation and sporting sheet, that the world had been tremendously engrossed during the past week in the business of moving toward some splendid if somewhat indeterminate goal. For his part Anthony had been once to his grandfather's, twice to his broker's, and three times to his tailor's—and in the last hour of the week's last day he had kissed a very beautiful and charming girl.

When he reached home his imagination had been teeming with high pitched, unfamiliar dreams. There was suddenly no question on his mind, no eternal problem for a solution and resolution. He had experienced an emotion that was neither mental nor physical, nor merely a mixture of the two, and the love of life absorbed him for the present to the exclusion of all else. He was content to let the experiment remain isolated and unique. Almost impersonally he was convinced that no woman he had ever met compared in any way with Gloria. She was deeply herself; she was immeasurably sincere—of these things he was certain. Beside her the two dozen schoolgirls and debutantes, young married women and waifs and strays whom he had known were so many females, in the word's most contemptuous sense, breeders and bearers, exuding still that faintly odorous atmosphere of the cave and the nursery.

So far as he could see, she had neither submitted to any will of his nor caressed his vanity—except as her pleasure in his company was a caress. Indeed he had no reason for thinking she had given him aught that she did not give to others. This was as it should be. The idea of an entanglement growing out of the evening was as remote as it would have been repugnant. And she had disclaimed and buried the incident with a decisive untruth. Here were two young people with fancy enough to distinguish a game from its reality—who by the very casualness with which they met and passed on would proclaim themselves unharmed.

Having decided this he went to the phone and called up the Plaza Hotel.

Gloria was out. Her mother knew neither where she had gone nor when she would return.

It was somehow at this point that the first wrongness in the case asserted itself. There was an element of callousness, almost of indecency, in Gloria's absence from home. He suspected that by going out she had intrigued him into a disadvantage. Returning she would find his name, and smile. Most discreetly! He should have waited a few hours in order to drive home the utter inconsequence with which he regarded the incident. What an asinine blunder! She would think he considered himself particularly favored. She would think he was reacting with the most inept intimacy to a quite trivial episode.

He remembered that during the previous month his janitor, to whom he had delivered a rather muddled lecture on the "brother-hoove man," had come up next day and, on the basis of what had happened the night before, seated himself in the window seat for a cordial and chatty half-hour. Anthony wondered in horror if Gloria would regard him as he had regarded that man. Him—Anthony Patch! Horror!

It never occurred to him that he was a passive thing, acted upon by an influence above and beyond Gloria, that he was merely the sensitive plate on which the photograph was made. Some gargantuan photographer had focussed the camera on Gloria and *snap*!—the poor plate could but develop, confined like all things to its nature.

But Anthony, lying upon his couch and staring at the orange lamp, passed his thin fingers incessantly through his dark hair and made new symbols for the hours. She was in a shop now, it seemed, moving lithely among the velvets and the furs, her own dress making, as she walked, a debonair rustle in that world of silken rustles and cool soprano laughter and scents of many slain but living flowers. The Minnies and Pearls and jewels and jennies would gather round her like courtiers, bearing wispy frailties of Georgette crepe, delicate chiffon to echo her cheeks in faint pastel, milky lace to rest in pale disarray against her neck—damask was used but to cover priests and divans in these days, and cloth of Samarand was remembered only by the romantic poets.

She would go elsewhere after a while, tilting her head a hundred ways under a hundred bonnets, seeking in vain for mock cherries to match her lips or plumes that were graceful as her own supple body.

Noon would come—she would hurry along Fifth Avenue, a Nordic Ganymede, her fur coat swinging fashionably with her steps, her cheeks redder by a stroke of the wind's brush, her breath a delightful mist upon the bracing air—and the doors of the Ritz would revolve, the crowd would divide, fifty masculine eyes would start, stare, as she gave back forgotten dreams to the husbands of many obese and comic women.

One o'clock. With her fork she would tantalize the heart of an adoring artichoke, while her escort served himself up in the thick, dripping sentences of an enraptured man.

Four o'clock: her little feet moving to melody, her face distinct in the crowd, her partner happy as a petted puppy and mad as the immemorial hatter.... Then—then night would come drifting down and perhaps another damp. The signs would spill their light into the street. Who knew? No wiser than he, they haply sought to recapture that picture done in cream and shadow they had seen on the hushed Avenue the night before. And they might, ah, they might! A thousand taxis would yawn at a thousand corners, and only to him was that kiss forever lost and done. In a thousand guises Thaïs would hail a cab and turn up her face for loving. And her pallor would be virginal and lovely, and her kiss chaste as the moon....

He sprang excitedly to his feet. How inappropriate that she should be out! He had realized at last what he wanted—to kiss her again, to find rest in her great immobility. She was the end of all restlessness, all malcontent.

Anthony dressed and went out, as he should have done long before, and down to Richard Caramel's room to hear the last revision of the last chapter of "The Demon Lover." He did not call Gloria again until six. He did not find her in until eight and—oh, climax of anticlimaxes!—she could give him no engagement until Tuesday afternoon. A broken piece of gutta-percha clattered to the floor as he banged up the phone.

BLACK MAGIC

Tuesday was freezing cold. He called at a bleak two o'clock and as they shook hands he wondered confusedly whether he had ever kissed her; it was almost unbelievable—he seriously doubted if she remembered it.

"I called you four times on Sunday," he told her.

"Did you?"

There was surprise in her voice and interest in her expression. Silently he cursed himself for having told her. He might have known her pride did not deal in such petty triumphs. Even then he had not guessed at the truth—that never having had to worry about men she had seldom used the wary subterfuges, the playings out and haulings in, that were the stock in trade of her sisterhood. When she liked a man, that was trick enough. Did she think she loved him—there was an ultimate and fatal thrust. Her charm endlessly preserved itself.

"I was anxious to see you," he said simply. "I want to talk to you—I mean really talk, somewhere where we can be alone. May I?"

"What do you mean?"

He swallowed a sudden lump of panic. He felt that she knew what he wanted.

"I mean, not at a tea table," he said.

"Well, all right, but not to-day. I want to get some exercise. Let's walk!"

It was bitter and raw. All the evil hate in the mad heart of February was wrought into the forlorn and icy wind that cut its way cruelly across Central Park and down along Fifth Avenue. It was almost impossible to talk, and discomfort made him distracted, so much so that he turned at Sixty-first Street to find that she was no longer beside him. He looked around. She was forty feet in the rear standing motionless, her face half hidden in her fur coat collar, moved either by anger or laughter—he could not determine which. He started back.

"Don't let me interrupt your walk!" she called.

"I'm mighty sorry," he answered in confusion. "Did I go too fast?"

"I'm cold," she announced. "I want to go home. And you walk too fast."

"I'm very sorry."

Side by side they started for the Plaza. He wished he could see her face.

"Men don't usually get so absorbed in themselves when they're with me."

"I'm sorry."

"That's very interesting."

"It *is* rather too cold to walk," he said, briskly, to hide his annoyance.

She made no answer and he wondered if she would dismiss him at the hotel entrance. She walked in without speaking, however, and to the elevator, throwing him a single remark as she entered it:

"You'd better come up."

He hesitated for the fraction of a moment.

"Perhaps I'd better call some other time."

"Just as you say." Her words were murmured as an aside. The main concern of life was the adjusting of some stray wisps of hair in the elevator mirror. Her cheeks were brilliant, her eyes sparkled—she had never seemed so lovely, so exquisitely to be desired.

Despising himself, he found that he was walking down the tenth-floor corridor a subservient foot behind her; was in the sitting room while she disappeared to shed her furs. Something had gone wrong—in his own eyes he had lost a shred of dignity; in an unpremeditated yet significant encounter he had been completely defeated.

However, by the time she reappeared in the sitting-room he had explained himself to himself with sophistic satisfaction. After all he had done the strongest thing, he thought. He had wanted to come up, he had come. Yet what happened later on that afternoon must be traced to the indignity he had experienced in the elevator; the girl was worrying him intolerably, so much so that when she came out he involuntarily drifted into criticism.

"Who's this Bloeckman, Gloria?"

"A business friend of father's."

"Odd sort of fellow!"

"He doesn't like you either," she said with a sudden smile.

Anthony laughed.

"I'm flattered at his notice. He evidently considers me a—" He broke off with "Is he in love with you?"

"I don't know."

"The deuce you don't," he insisted. "Of course he is. I remember the look he gave me when we got back to the table. He'd probably have had me quietly assaulted by a delegation of movie supes if you hadn't invented that phone call."

"He didn't mind. I told him afterward what really happened."

"You told him!"

"He asked me."

"I don't like that very well," he remonstrated.

She laughed again.

"Oh, you don't?"

"What business is it of his?"

"None. That's why I told him."

Anthony in a turmoil bit savagely at his mouth.

"Why should I lie?" she demanded directly. "I'm not ashamed of anything I do. It happened to interest him to know that I kissed you, and I happened to be in a good humor, so I satisfied his curiosity by a simple and precise 'yes.' Being rather a sensible man, after his fashion, he dropped the subject."

"Except to say that he hated me."

"Oh, it worries you? Well, if you must probe this stupendous matter to its depths he didn't say he hated you. I simply know he does."

"It doesn't wor——"

"Oh, let's drop it!" she cried spiritedly. "It's a most uninteresting matter to me."

With a tremendous effort Anthony made his acquiescence a twist of subject, and they drifted into an ancient question-and-answer game concerned with each other's pasts, gradually warming as they discovered the age-old, immemorial resemblances in tastes and ideas. They said things that were more revealing than they intended—but each pretended to accept the other at face, or rather word, value.

The growth of intimacy is like that. First one gives off his best picture, the bright and finished product mended with bluff and falsehood and humor. Then more details are required and one paints a second portrait, and a third—before long the best lines cancel out—and the secret is exposed at last; the planes of the pictures have intermingled and given us away, and though we paint and paint we can no longer sell a picture. We must be satisfied with hoping that such fatuous accounts of ourselves as we make to our wives and children and business associates are accepted as true.

"It seems to me," Anthony was saying earnestly, "that the position of a man with neither necessity nor ambition is unfortunate. Heaven knows it'd be pathetic of me to be sorry for myself—yet, sometimes I envy Dick."

Her silence was encouragement. It was as near as she ever came to an intentional lure.

"—And there used to be dignified occupations for a gentleman who had leisure, things a little more constructive than filling up the landscape with smoke or juggling some one else's money. There's science, of course: sometimes I wish I'd taken a good foundation, say at Boston Tech. But now, by golly, I'd have to sit down for two years and struggle through the fundamentals of physics and chemistry."

She yawned.

"I've told you I don't know what anybody ought to do," she said ungraciously, and at her indifference his rancor was born again.

"Aren't you interested in anything except yourself?"

"Not much."

He glared; his growing enjoyment in the conversation was ripped to shreds. She had been irritable and vindictive all day, and it seemed to him that for this moment he hated her hard selfishness. He stared morosely at the fire.

Then a strange thing happened. She turned to him and smiled, and as he saw her smile every rag of anger and hurt vanity dropped from him—as though his very moods were but the outer ripples of her own, as though emotion rose no longer in his breast unless she saw fit to pull an omnipotent controlling thread.

He moved closer and taking her hand pulled her ever so gently toward him until she half lay against his shoulder. She smiled up at him as he kissed her.

"Gloria," he whispered very softly. Again she had made a magic, subtle and pervading as a spilt perfume, irresistible and sweet.

Afterward, neither the next day nor after many years, could he remember the important things of that afternoon. Had she been moved? In his arms had she spoken a little—or at all? What measure of enjoyment had she taken in his kisses? And had she at any time lost herself ever so little?

Oh, for him there was no doubt. He had risen and paced the floor in sheer ecstasy. That such a girl should be; should poise curled in a corner of the couch like a swallow newly landed from a clean swift flight, watching him with inscrutable eyes. He would stop his pacing and, half shy each time at first, drop his arm around her and find her kiss.

She was fascinating, he told her. He had never met any one like her before. He besought her jauntily but earnestly to send him away; he didn't want to fall in love. He wasn't coming to see her any more—already she had haunted too many of his ways.

What delicious romance! His true reaction was neither fear nor sorrow—only this deep delight in being with her that colored the banality of his words and made the mawkish seem sad and the posturing seem wise. He *would* come back—eternally. He should have known!

"This is all. It's been very rare to have known you, very strange and wonderful. But this wouldn't do—and wouldn't last." As he spoke there was in his heart that tremulousness that we take for sincerity in ourselves.

Afterward he remembered one reply of hers to something he had asked her. He remembered it in this form—perhaps he had unconsciously arranged and polished it:

"A woman should be able to kiss a man beautifully and romantically without any desire to be either his wife or his mistress."

As always when he was with her she seemed to grow gradually older until at the end ruminations too deep for words would be wintering in her eyes.

An hour passed, and the fire leaped up in little ecstasies as though its fading life was sweet. It was five now, and the clock over the mantel became articulate in sound. Then as if a brutish sensibility in him was reminded by those thin, tinny beats that the petals were falling from the flowered afternoon, Anthony pulled her quickly to her feet and held her helpless, without breath, in a kiss that was neither a game nor a tribute.

Her arms fell to her side. In an instant she was free.

"Don't!" she said quietly. "I don't want that."

She sat down on the far side of the lounge and gazed straight before her. A frown had gathered between her eyes. Anthony sank down beside her and closed his hand over hers. It was lifeless and unresponsive.

"Why, Gloria!" He made a motion as if to put his arm about her but she drew away.

"I don't want that," she repeated.

"I'm very sorry," he said, a little impatiently. "I—I didn't know you made such fine distinctions."

She did not answer.

"Won't you kiss me, Gloria?"

"I don't want to." It seemed to him she had not moved for hours.

"A sudden change, isn't it?" Annoyance was growing in his voice.

"Is it?" She appeared uninterested. It was almost as though she were looking at some one else.

"Perhaps I'd better go."

No reply. He rose and regarded her angrily, uncertainly. Again he sat down.

"Gloria, Gloria, won't you kiss me?"

"No." Her lips, parting for the word, had just faintly stirred.

Again he got to his feet, this time with less decision, less confidence.

"Then I'll go."

Silence.

"All right—I'll go."

He was aware of a certain irremediable lack of originality in his remarks. Indeed he felt that the whole atmosphere had grown oppressive. He wished she would speak, rail at him, cry out upon him, anything but this pervasive and chilling silence. He cursed himself for a weak fool; his clearest desire was to move her, to hurt her, to see her wince. Helplessly, involuntarily, he erred again.

"If you're tired of kissing me I'd better go."

He saw her lips curl slightly and his last dignity left him. She spoke, at length:

"I believe you've made that remark several times before."

He looked about him immediately, saw his hat and coat on a chair—blundered into them, during an intolerable moment. Looking again at the couch he perceived that she had not turned, not even moved. With a shaken, immediately regretted "good-by" he went quickly but without dignity from the room.

For over a moment Gloria made no sound. Her lips were still curled; her glance was straight, proud, remote. Then her eyes blurred a little, and she murmured three words half aloud to the death-bound fire:

"Good-by, you ass!" she said.

PANIC

The man had had the hardest blow of his life. He knew at last what he wanted, but in finding it out it seemed that he had put it forever beyond his grasp. He reached home in misery, dropped into an armchair without even removing his overcoat, and sat there for over an hour, his mind racing the paths of fruitless and wretched self-absorption. She had sent him away! That was the reiterated burden of his despair. Instead of seizing the girl and holding her by sheer strength until she became passive to his desire, instead of beating down her will by the force of his own, he had walked, defeated and powerless, from her door, with the corners of his mouth drooping and what force there might have been in his grief and rage hidden behind the manner of a whipped schoolboy. At one minute she had liked him tremendously—ah, she had nearly loved him. In the next he had become a thing of indifference to her, an insolent and efficiently humiliated man.

He had no great self-reproach—some, of course, but there were other things dominant in him now, far more urgent. He was not so much in love with Gloria as mad for her. Unless he could have her near him again, kiss her, hold her close and acquiescent, he wanted nothing more from life. By her three minutes of utter unwavering indifference the girl had lifted herself from a high but somehow casual position in his mind, to be instead his complete preoccupation. However much his wild thoughts varied between a passionate desire for her kisses and an equally passionate craving to hurt and mar her, the residue of his mind craved in finer fashion to possess the triumphant soul that had shone through those three minutes. She was beautiful—but especially she was without mercy. He must own that strength that could send him away.

At present no such analysis was possible to Anthony. His clarity of mind, all those endless resources which he thought his irony had brought him were swept aside. Not only for that night but for the days and weeks that followed his books were to be but furniture and his friends only people who lived and walked in a nebulous outer world from which he was trying to escape—that world was cold and full of bleak wind, and for a little while he had seen into a warm house where fires shone.

About midnight he began to realize that he was hungry. He went down into Fifty-second Street, where it was so cold that he could scarcely see; the moisture froze on his lashes and in the corners of his lips. Everywhere dreariness had come down from the north, settling upon the thin and cheerless street, where black bundled figures blacker still against the night, moved stumbling along the sidewalk through the shrieking wind, sliding their feet cautiously ahead as though they were on skis. Anthony turned over toward Sixth Avenue, so absorbed in his thoughts as not to notice that several passers-by had stared at him. His overcoat was wide open, and the wind was biting in, hard and full of merciless death.

... After a while a waitress spoke to him, a fat waitress with black-rimmed eye-glasses from which dangled a long black cord.

"Order, please!"

Her voice, he considered, was unnecessarily loud. He looked up resentfully.

"You wanna order or doncha?"

"Of course," he protested.

"Well, I ast you three times. This ain't no rest-room."

He glanced at the big clock and discovered with a start that it was after two. He was down around Thirtieth Street somewhere, and after a moment he found and translated the

CHILD'S

in a white semicircle of letters upon the glass front. The place was inhabited sparsely by three or four bleak and half-frozen night-hawks.

"Give me some bacon and eggs and coffee, please."

The waitress bent upon him a last disgusted glance and, looking ludicrously intellectual in her corded glasses, hurried away.

God! Gloria's kisses had been such flowers. He remembered as though it had been years ago the low freshness of her voice, the beautiful lines of her body shining through her clothes, her face lily-colored under the lamps of the street—under the lamps.

Misery struck at him again, piling a sort of terror upon the ache and yearning. He had lost her. It was true—no denying it, no softening it. But a new idea had seared his sky—what of Bloeckman! What would happen now? There was a wealthy man, middle-aged enough to be tolerant with a beautiful wife, to baby her whims and indulge her unreason, to wear her as she perhaps wished to be worn—a bright flower in his button-hole, safe and secure from the things she feared. He felt that she had been playing with the idea of marrying Bloeckman, and it was well possible that this disappointment in Anthony might throw her on sudden impulse into Bloeckman's arms.

The idea drove him childishly frantic. He wanted to kill Bloeckman and make him suffer for his hideous presumption. He was saying this over and over to himself with his teeth tight shut, and a perfect orgy of hate and fright in his eyes.

But, behind this obscene jealousy, Anthony was in love at last, profoundly and truly in love, as the word goes between man and woman.

His coffee appeared at his elbow and gave off for a certain time a gradually diminishing wisp of steam. The night manager, seated at his desk, glanced at the motionless figure alone at the last table, and then with a sigh moved down upon him just as the hour hand crossed the figure three on the big clock.

WISDOM

After another day the turmoil subsided and Anthony began to exercise a measure of reason. He was in love—he cried it passionately to himself. The things that a week before would have seemed insuperable obstacles, his limited income, his desire to be irresponsible and independent, had in this forty hours become the merest chaff before the wind of his infatuation. If he did not marry her his life would be a feeble parody on his own adolescence. To be able to face people and to endure the constant reminder of Gloria that all existence had become, it was necessary for him to have hope. So he built hope desperately and tenaciously out of the stuff of his dream, a hope flimsy enough, to be sure, a hope that was cracked and dissipated a dozen times a day, a hope mothered by mockery, but, nevertheless, a hope that would be brawn and sinew to his self-respect.

Out of this developed a spark of wisdom, a true perception of his own from out the effortless past.

"Memory is short," he thought.

So very short. At the crucial point the Trust President is on the stand, a potential criminal needing but one push to be a jailbird, scorned by the upright for leagues around. Let him be acquitted—and in a year all is forgotten. "Yes, he did have some trouble once, just a technicality, I believe." Oh, memory is very short!

Anthony had seen Gloria altogether about a dozen times, say two dozen hours. Supposing he left her alone for a month, made no attempt to see her or speak to her, and avoided every place where she might possibly be. Wasn't it possible, the more possible because she had never loved him, that at the end of that time the rush of events would efface his personality from her conscious mind, and with his personality his offense and humiliation? She would forget, for there would be other men. He winced. The implication struck out at him—other men. Two months—God! Better three weeks, two weeks——

He thought this the second evening after the catastrophe when he was undressing, and at this point he threw himself down on the bed and lay there, trembling very slightly and looking at the top of the canopy.

Two weeks—that was worse than no time at all. In two weeks he would approach her much as he would have to now, without personality or confidence—remaining still the man who had gone too far and then for a period that in time was but a moment but in fact an eternity, whined. No, two weeks was too short a time. Whatever poignancy there had been for her in that afternoon must have time to dull. He must give her a period when the incident should fade, and then a new period when she should gradually begin to think of him, no matter how dimly, with a true perspective that would remember his pleasantness as well as his humiliation.

He fixed, finally, on six weeks as approximately the interval best suited to his purpose, and on a desk calendar he marked the days off, finding that it would fall on the ninth of April. Very well, on that day he would phone and ask her if he might call. Until then—silence.

After his decision a gradual improvement was manifest. He had taken at least a step in the direction to which hope pointed, and he realized that the less he brooded upon her the better he would be able to give the desired impression when they met.

In another hour he fell into a deep sleep.

THE INTERVAL

Nevertheless, though, as the days passed, the glory of her hair dimmed perceptibly for him and in a year of separation might have departed completely, the six weeks held many abominable days. He dreaded the sight of Dick and Maury, imagining wildly that they knew all—but when the three met it was Richard Caramel and not Anthony who was the centre of attention; "The Demon Lover" had been accepted for immediate publication. Anthony felt that from now on he moved apart. He no longer craved the warmth and security of Maury's society which had cheered him no further back than November. Only Gloria could give that now and no one else ever again. So Dick's success rejoiced him only casually and worried him not a little. It meant that the world was going ahead—writing and reading and publishing—and living. And he wanted the world to wait motionless and breathless for six weeks—while Gloria forgot.

TWO ENCOUNTERS

His greatest satisfaction was in Geraldine's company. He took her once to dinner and the theatre and entertained her several times in his apartment. When he was with her she absorbed him, not as Gloria had, but quieting those erotic sensibilities in him that worried over Gloria. It didn't matter how he kissed Geraldine. A kiss was a kiss—to be enjoyed to the utmost for its short moment. To Geraldine things belonged in definite pigeonholes: a kiss was one thing, anything further was quite another; a kiss was all right; the other things were "bad."

When half the interval was up two incidents occurred on successive days that upset his increasing calm and caused a temporary relapse.

The first was—he saw Gloria. It was a short meeting. Both bowed. Both spoke, yet neither heard the other. But when it was over Anthony read down a column of The Sun three times in succession without understanding a single sentence.

One would have thought Sixth Avenue a safe street! Having forsworn his barber at the Plaza he went around the corner one morning to be shaved, and while waiting his turn he took off coat and vest, and with his soft collar open at the neck stood near the front of the shop. The day was an oasis in the cold desert of March and the sidewalk was cheerful with a population of strolling sun-worshippers. A stout woman upholstered in velvet, her flabby cheeks too much massaged, swirled by with her poodle straining at its leash—the effect being given of a tug bringing in an ocean liner. Just behind them a man in a striped blue suit, walking slue-footed in white-spatted feet, grinned at the sight and catching Anthony's eye, winked through the glass. Anthony laughed, thrown immediately into that humor in which men and women were graceless and absurd phantasms, grotesquely curved and rounded in a rectangular world of their own building. They inspired the same sensations in him as did those strange and monstrous fish who inhabit the esoteric world of green in the aquarium.

Two more strollers caught his eye casually, a man and a girl—then in a horrified instant the girl resolved herself into Gloria. He stood here powerless; they came nearer and Gloria, glancing in, saw him. Her eyes widened and she smiled politely. Her lips moved. She was less than five feet away.

"How do you do?" he muttered inanely.

Gloria, happy, beautiful, and young—with a man he had never seen before!

It was then that the barber's chair was vacated and he read down the newspaper column three times in succession.

The second incident took place the next day. Going into the Manhattan bar about seven he was confronted with Bloeckman. As it happened, the room was nearly deserted, and before the mutual recognition he had stationed himself within a foot of the older man and ordered his drink, so it was inevitable that they should converse.

"Hello, Mr. Patch," said Bloeckman amiably enough.

Anthony took the proffered hand and exchanged a few aphorisms on the fluctuations of the mercury.

"Do you come in here much?" inquired Bloeckman.

"No, very seldom." He omitted to add that the Plaza bar had, until lately, been his favorite.

"Nice bar. One of the best bars in town."

Anthony nodded. Bloeckman emptied his glass and picked up his cane. He was in evening dress.

"Well, I'll be hurrying on. I'm going to dinner with Miss Gilbert."

Death looked suddenly out at him from two blue eyes. Had he announced himself as his vis-à-vis's prospective murderer he could not have struck a more vital blow at Anthony. The younger man must have reddened visibly, for his every nerve was in instant clamor. With tremendous effort he mustered a rigid—oh, so rigid—smile, and said a conventional good-by. But that night he lay awake until after four, half wild with grief and fear and abominable imaginings.

WEAKNESS

And one day in the fifth week he called her up. He had been sitting in his apartment trying to read "L'Education Sentimental," and something in the book had sent his thoughts racing in the direction that, set free, they always took, like horses racing for a home stable. With suddenly quickened breath he walked to the telephone. When he gave the number it seemed to him that his voice faltered and broke like a schoolboy's. The Central must have heard the pounding of his heart. The sound of the receiver being taken up at the other end was a crack of doom, and Mrs. Gilbert's voice, soft as maple syrup running into a glass container, had for him a quality of horror in its single "Hello-o-ah?"

"Miss Gloria's not feeling well. She's lying down, asleep. Who shall I say called?"

"Nobody!" he shouted.

In a wild panic he slammed down the receiver; collapsed into his armchair in the cold sweat of breathless relief.

SERENADE

The first thing he said to her was: "Why, you've bobbed your hair!" and she answered: "Yes, isn't it gorgeous?"

It was not fashionable then. It was to be fashionable in five or six years. At that time it was considered extremely daring.

"It's all sunshine outdoors," he said gravely. "Don't you want to take a walk?"

She put on a light coat and a quaintly piquant Napoleon hat of Alice Blue, and they walked along the Avenue and into the Zoo, where they properly admired the grandeur of the elephant and the collar-height of the giraffe, but did not visit the monkey house because Gloria said that monkeys smelt so bad.

Then they returned toward the Plaza, talking about nothing, but glad for the spring singing in the air and for the warm balm that lay upon the suddenly golden city. To their right was the Park, while at the left a great bulk of granite and marble muttered dully a millionaire's chaotic message to whosoever would listen: something about "I worked and I saved and I was sharper than all Adam and here I sit, by golly, by golly!"

All the newest and most beautiful designs in automobiles were out on Fifth Avenue, and ahead of them the Plaza loomed up rather unusually white and attractive. The supple, indolent Gloria walked a short shadow's length ahead of him, pouring out lazy casual comments that floated a moment on the dazzling air before they reached his ear.

"Oh!" she cried, "I want to go south to Hot Springs! I want to get out in the air and just roll around on the new grass and forget there's ever been any winter."

"Don't you, though!"

"I want to hear a million robins making a frightful racket. I sort of like birds."

"All women *are* birds," he ventured.

"What kind am I?"—quick and eager.

"A swallow, I think, and sometimes a bird of paradise. Most girls are sparrows, of course—see that row of nurse-maids over there? They're sparrows—or are they magpies? And of course you've met canary girls—and robin girls."

"And swan girls and parrot girls. All grown women are hawks, I think, or owls."

"What am I—a buzzard?"

She laughed and shook her head.

"Oh, no, you're not a bird at all, do you think? You're a Russian wolfhound."

Anthony remembered that they were white and always looked unnaturally hungry. But then they were usually photographed with dukes and princesses, so he was properly flattered.

"Dick's a fox terrier, a trick fox terrier," she continued.

"And Maury's a cat." Simultaneously it occurred to him how like Bloeckman was to a robust and offensive hog. But he preserved a discreet silence.

Later, as they parted, Anthony asked when he might see her again.

"Don't you ever make long engagements?" he pleaded, "even if it's a week ahead, I think it'd be fun to spend a whole day together, morning and afternoon both."

"It would be, wouldn't it?" She thought for a moment. "Let's do it next Sunday."

"All right. I'll map out a programme that'll take up every minute."

He did. He even figured to a nicety what would happen in the two hours when she would come to his apartment for tea: how the good Bounds would have the windows wide to let in the fresh breeze—but a fire going also lest there be chill in the air—and how there would be clusters of flowers about in big cool bowls that he would buy for the occasion. They would sit on the lounge.

And when the day came they did sit upon the lounge. After a while Anthony kissed her because it came about quite naturally; he found sweetness sleeping still upon her lips, and felt that he had never been away. The fire was bright and the breeze sighing in through the curtains brought a mellow damp, promising May and world of summer. His soul thrilled to remote harmonies; he heard the strum of far guitars and waters lapping on a warm Mediterranean shore—for he was young now as he would never be again, and more triumphant than death.

Six o'clock stole down too soon and rang the querulous melody of St. Anne's chimes on the corner. Through the gathering dusk they strolled to the Avenue, where the crowds, like prisoners released, were walking with elastic step at last after the long winter, and the tops of the busses were thronged with congenial kings and the shops full of fine soft things for the summer, the rare summer, the gay promising summer that seemed for love what the winter was for money. Life was singing for his supper on the corner! Life was handing round cocktails in the street! Old women there were in that crowd who felt that they could have run and won a hundred-yard dash!

In bed that night with the lights out and the cool room swimming with moonlight, Anthony lay awake and played with every minute of the day like a child playing in turn with each one of a pile of long-wanted Christmas toys. He had told her gently, almost in the middle of a kiss, that he loved her, and she had smiled and held him closer and murmured, "I'm glad," looking into his eyes. There had been a new quality in her attitude, a new growth of sheer physical attraction toward him and a strange emotional tenseness, that was enough to make him clinch his hands and draw in his breath at the recollection. He had felt nearer to her than ever before. In a rare delight he cried aloud to the room that he loved her.

He phoned next morning—no hesitation now, no uncertainty—instead a delirious excitement that doubled and trebled when he heard her voice:

"Good morning—Gloria."

"Good morning."

"That's all I called you up to say-dear."

"I'm glad you did."

"I wish I could see you."

"You will, to-morrow night."

"That's a long time, isn't it?"

"Yes—" Her voice was reluctant. His hand tightened on the receiver.

"Couldn't I come to-night?" He dared anything in the glory and revelation of that almost whispered "yes."

"I have a date."

"Oh—"

"But I might—I might be able to break it."

"Oh!"—a sheer cry, a rhapsody. "Gloria?"

"What?"

"I love you."

Another pause and then:

"I—I'm glad."

Happiness, remarked Maury Noble one day, is only the first hour after the alleviation of some especially intense misery. But oh, Anthony's face as he walked down the tenth-floor corridor of the Plaza that night! His dark eyes were gleaming—around his mouth were lines it was a kindness to see. He was handsome then if never before, bound for one of those immortal moments which come so radiantly that their remembered light is enough to see by for years.

He knocked and, at a word, entered. Gloria, dressed in simple pink, starched and fresh as a flower, was across the room, standing very still, and looking at him wide-eyed.

As he closed the door behind him she gave a little cry and moved swiftly over the intervening space, her arms rising in a premature caress as she came near. Together they crushed out the stiff folds of her dress in one triumphant and enduring embrace.

BOOK TWO

I. THE RADIANT HOUR

AFTER a fortnight Anthony and Gloria began to indulge in "practical discussions," as they called those sessions when under the guise of severe realism they walked in an eternal moonlight.

"Not as much as I do you," the critic of belles-lettres would insist. "If you really loved me you'd want every one to know it."

"I do," she protested; "I want to stand on the street corner like a sandwich man, informing all the passers-by."

"Then tell me all the reasons why you're going to marry me in June."

"Well, because you're so clean. You're sort of blowy clean, like I am. There's two sorts, you know. One's like Dick: he's clean like polished pans. You and I are clean like streams and winds. I can tell whenever I see a person whether he is clean, and if so, which kind of clean he is."

"We're twins."

Ecstatic thought!

"Mother says"—she hesitated uncertainly—"mother says that two souls are sometimes created together and—and in love before they're born."

Bilphism gained its easiest convert.... After a while he lifted up his head and laughed soundlessly toward the ceiling. When his eyes came back to her he saw that she was angry.

"Why did you laugh?" she cried, "you've done that twice before. There's nothing funny about our relation to each other. I don't mind playing the fool, and I don't mind having you do it, but I can't stand it when we're together."

"I'm sorry."

"Oh, don't say you're sorry! If you can't think of anything better than that, just keep quiet!"

"I love you."

"I don't care."

There was a pause. Anthony was depressed.... At length Gloria murmured:

"I'm sorry I was mean."

"You weren't. I was the one."

Peace was restored—the ensuing moments were so much more sweet and sharp and poignant. They were stars on this stage, each playing to an audience of two: the passion of their pretense created the actuality. Here, finally, was the quintessence of self-expression—yet it was probable that for the most part their love expressed Gloria rather than Anthony. He felt often like a scarcely tolerated guest at a party she was giving.

Telling Mrs. Gilbert had been an embarrassed matter. She sat stuffed into a small chair and listened with an intense and very blinky sort of concentration. She must have known it—for three weeks Gloria had seen no one else—and she must have noticed that this time there was an authentic difference in her daughter's attitude. She had been given special deliveries to post; she had heeded, as all mothers seem to heed, the hither end of telephone conversations, disguised but still rather warm—

—Yet she had delicately professed surprise and declared herself immensely pleased; she doubtless was; so were the geranium plants blossoming in the window-boxes, and so were the cabbies when the lovers sought the romantic privacy of hansom cabs—quaint device—and the staid bill of fares on which they scribbled "you know I do," pushing it over for the other to see.

But between kisses Anthony and this golden girl quarrelled incessantly.

"Now, Gloria," he would cry, "please let me explain!"

"Don't explain. Kiss me."

"I don't think that's right. If I hurt your feelings we ought to discuss it. I don't like this kiss-and-forget."

"But I don't want to argue. I think it's wonderful that we *can* kiss and forget, and when we can't it'll be time to argue."

At one time some gossamer difference attained such bulk that Anthony arose and punched himself into his overcoat—for a moment it appeared that the scene of the preceding February was to be repeated, but knowing how deeply she was moved he retained his dignity with his pride, and in a moment Gloria was sobbing in his arms, her lovely face miserable as a frightened little girl's.

Meanwhile they kept unfolding to each other, unwillingly, by curious reactions and evasions, by distastes and prejudices and unintended hints of the past. The girl was proudly incapable of jealousy and, because he was extremely jealous, this virtue piqued him. He told her recondite incidents of his own life on purpose to arouse some spark of it, but to no avail. She possessed him now—nor did she desire the dead years.

"Oh, Anthony," she would say, "always when I'm mean to you I'm sorry afterward. I'd give my right hand to save you one little moment's pain."

And in that instant her eyes were brimming and she was not aware that she was voicing an illusion. Yet Anthony knew that there were days when they hurt each other purposely—taking almost a delight in the thrust. Incessantly she puzzled him: one hour so intimate and charming, striving desperately toward an unguessed, transcendent union; the next, silent and cold, apparently unmoved by any consideration of their love or anything he could say. Often he would eventually trace these portentous reticences to some physical discomfort—of these she never complained until they were over—or to some carelessness or presumption in him, or to an unsatisfactory dish at dinner, but even then the means by which she created the infinite distances she spread about herself were a mystery, buried somewhere back in those twenty-two years of unwavering pride.

"Why do you like Muriel?" he demanded one day.

"I don't very much."

"Then why do you go with her?"

"Just for some one to go with. They're no exertion, those girls. They sort of believe everything I tell them—but I rather like Rachael. I think she's cute—and so clean and slick, don't you? I used to have other friends—in Kansas City and at school—casual, all of them, girls who just flitted into my range and out of it for no more reason than that boys took us places together. They didn't interest me after environment stopped throwing us together. Now they're mostly married. What does it matter—they were all just people."

"You like men better, don't you?"

"Oh, much better. I've got a man's mind."

"You've got a mind like mine. Not strongly gendered either way."

Later she told him about the beginnings of her friendship with Bloeckman. One day in Delmonico's, Gloria and Rachael had come upon Bloeckman and Mr. Gilbert having luncheon and curiosity had impelled her to make it a party of four. She had liked him—rather. He was a relief from younger men, satisfied as he was with so little. He humored her and he laughed, whether he understood her or not. She met him several times, despite the open disapproval of her parents, and within a month he had asked her to marry him, tendering her everything from a villa in Italy to a brilliant career on the screen. She had laughed in his face—and he had laughed too.

But he had not given up. To the time of Anthony's arrival in the arena he had been making steady progress. She treated him rather well—except that she had called him always by an invidious nickname—perceiving, meanwhile, that he was figuratively following along beside her as she walked the fence, ready to catch her if she should fall.

The night before the engagement was announced she told Bloeckman. It was a heavy blow. She did not enlighten Anthony as to the details, but she implied that he had not hesitated to argue with her. Anthony gathered that the interview had terminated on a stormy note, with Gloria very cool and unmoved lying in her corner of the sofa and Joseph Bloeckman of "Films Par Excellence" pacing the carpet with eyes narrowed and head bowed. Gloria had been sorry for him but she had judged it best not to show it. In a final burst of kindness she had tried to make him hate her, there at the last. But Anthony, understanding that

Gloria's indifference was her strongest appeal, judged how futile this must have been. He wondered, often but quite casually, about Bloeckman—finally he forgot him entirely.

HEYDAY

One afternoon they found front seats on the sunny roof of a bus and rode for hours from the fading Square up along the sullied river, and then, as the stray beams fled the westward streets, sailed down the turgid Avenue, darkening with ominous bees from the department stores. The traffic was clotted and gripped in a patternless jam; the busses were packed four deep like platforms above the crowd as they waited for the moan of the traffic whistle.

"Isn't it good!" cried Gloria. "Look!"

A miller's wagon, stark white with flour, driven by a powdery clown, passed in front of them behind a white horse and his black team-mate.

"What a pity!" she complained; "they'd look so beautiful in the dusk, if only both horses were white. I'm mighty happy just this minute, in this city."

Anthony shook his head in disagreement.

"I think the city's a mountebank. Always struggling to approach the tremendous and impressive urbanity ascribed to it. Trying to be romantically metropolitan."

"I don't. I think it is impressive."

"Momentarily. But it's really a transparent, artificial sort of spectacle. It's got its press-agented stars and its flimsy, unenduring stage settings and, I'll admit, the greatest army of supers ever assembled—" He paused, laughed shortly, and added: "Technically excellent, perhaps, but not convincing."

"I'll bet policemen think people are fools," said Gloria thoughtfully, as she watched a large but cowardly lady being helped across the street. "He always sees them frightened and inefficient and old—they are," she added. And then: "We'd better get off. I told mother I'd have an early supper and go to bed. She says I look tired, damn it."

"I wish we were married," he muttered soberly; "there'll be no good night then and we can do just as we want."

"Won't it be good! I think we ought to travel a lot. I want to go to the Mediterranean and Italy. And I'd like to go on the stage some time—say for about a year."

"You bet. I'll write a play for you."

"Won't that be good! And I'll act in it. And then some time when we have more money"—old Adam's death was always thus tactfully alluded to—"we'll build a magnificent estate, won't we?"

"Oh, yes, with private swimming pools."

"Dozens of them. And private rivers. Oh, I wish it were now."

Odd coincidence—he had just been wishing that very thing. They plunged like divers into the dark eddying crowd and emerging in the cool fifties sauntered indolently homeward, infinitely romantic to each other ... both were walking alone in a dispassionate garden with a ghost found in a dream.

Halcyon days like boats drifting along slow-moving rivers; spring evenings full of a plaintive melancholy that made the past beautiful and bitter, bidding them look back and see that the loves of other summers long gone were dead with the forgotten waltzes of their years. Always the most poignant moments were when some artificial barrier kept them apart: in the theatre their hands would steal together, join, give and return gentle pressures through the long dark; in crowded rooms they would form words with their lips for each other's eyes—not knowing that they were but following in the footsteps of dusty generations but comprehending dimly that if truth is the end of life happiness is a mode of it, to be cherished in its brief and tremulous moment. And then, one fairy night, May became June. Sixteen days now—fifteen—fourteen——

THREE DIGRESSIONS

Just before the engagement was announced Anthony had gone up to Tarrytown to see his grandfather, who, a little more wizened and grizzly as time played its ultimate chuckling tricks, greeted the news with profound cynicism.

"Oh, you're going to get married, are you?" He said this with such a dubious mildness and shook his head up and down so many times that Anthony was not a little depressed. While he was unaware of his grandfather's intentions he presumed that a large part of the money would come to him. A good deal would go in charities, of course; a good deal to carry on the business of reform.

"Are you going to work?"

"Why—" temporized Anthony, somewhat disconcerted. "I *am* working. You know—"

"Ah, I mean work," said Adam Patch dispassionately.

"I'm not quite sure yet what I'll do. I'm not exactly a beggar, grampa," he asserted with some spirit.

The old man considered this with eyes half closed. Then almost apologetically he asked:

"How much do you save a year?"

"Nothing so far—"

"And so after just managing to get along on your money you've decided that by some miracle two of you can get along on it."

"Gloria has some money of her own. Enough to buy clothes."

"How much?"

Without considering this question impertinent, Anthony answered it.

"About a hundred a month."

"That's altogether about seventy-five hundred a year." Then he added softly: "It ought to be plenty. If you have any sense it ought to be plenty. But the question is whether you have any or not."

"I suppose it is." It was shameful to be compelled to endure this pious browbeating from the old man, and his next words were stiffened with vanity. "I can manage very well. You seem convinced that I'm utterly worthless. At any rate I came up here simply to tell you that I'm getting married in June. Good-by, sir." With this he turned away and headed for the door, unaware that in that instant his grandfather, for the first time, rather liked him.

"Wait!" called Adam Patch, "I want to talk to you."

Anthony faced about.

"Well, sir?"

"Sit down. Stay all night."

Somewhat mollified, Anthony resumed his seat.

"I'm sorry, sir, but I'm going to see Gloria to-night."

"What's her name?"

"Gloria Gilbert."

"New York girl? Someone you know?"

"She's from the Middle West."

"What business her father in?"

"In a celluloid corporation or trust or something. They're from Kansas City."

"You going to be married out there?"

"Why, no, sir. We thought we'd be married in New York—rather quietly."

"Like to have the wedding out here?"

Anthony hesitated. The suggestion made no appeal to him, but it was certainly the part of wisdom to give the old man, if possible, a proprietary interest in his married life. In addition Anthony was a little touched.

"That's very kind of you, grampa, but wouldn't it be a lot of trouble?"

"Everything's a lot of trouble. Your father was married here—but in the old house."

"Why—I thought he was married in Boston."

Adam Patch considered.

"That's true. He *was* married in Boston."

Anthony felt a moment's embarrassment at having made the correction, and he covered it up with words.

"Well, I'll speak to Gloria about it. Personally I'd like to, but of course it's up to the Gilberts, you see."

His grandfather drew a long sigh, half closed his eyes, and sank back in his chair.

"In a hurry?" he asked in a different tone.

"Not especially."

"I wonder," began Adam Patch, looking out with a mild, kindly glance at the lilac bushes that rustled against the windows, "I wonder if you ever think about the after-life."

"Why—sometimes."

"I think a great deal about the after-life." His eyes were dim but his voice was confident and clear. "I was sitting here to-day thinking about what's lying in wait for us, and somehow I began to remember an afternoon nearly sixty-five years ago, when I was playing with my little sister Annie, down where that summer-house is now." He pointed out into the long flower-garden, his eyes trembling of tears, his voice shaking.

"I began thinking—and it seemed to me that *you* ought to think a little more about the after-life. You ought to be—steadier"—he paused and seemed to grope about for the right word—"more industrious—why—"

Then his expression altered, his entire personality seemed to snap together like a trap, and when he continued the softness had gone from his voice.

"—Why, when I was just two years older than you," he rasped with a cunning chuckle, "I sent three members of the firm of Wrenn and Hunt to the poor-house."

Anthony started with embarrassment.

"Well, good-by," added his grandfather suddenly, "you'll miss your train."

Anthony left the house unusually elated, and strangely sorry for the old man; not because his wealth could buy him "neither youth nor digestion" but because he had asked Anthony to be married there, and because he had forgotten something about his son's wedding that he should have remembered.

Richard Caramel, who was one of the ushers, caused Anthony and Gloria much distress in the last few weeks by continually stealing the rays of their spot-light. "The Demon Lover" had been published in April, and it interrupted the love affair as it may be said to have interrupted everything its author came in contact with. It was a highly original, rather overwritten piece of sustained description concerned with a Don Juan of the New York slums. As Maury and Anthony had said before, as the more hospitable critics were saying then, there was no writer in America with such power to describe the atavistic and unsubtle reactions of that section of society.

The book hesitated and then suddenly "went." Editions, small at first, then larger, crowded each other week by week. A spokesman of the Salvation Army denounced it as a cynical misrepresentation of all the uplift taking place in the underworld. Clever press-agenting spread the unfounded rumor that "Gypsy" Smith was beginning a libel suit because one of the principal characters was a burlesque of himself. It was barred from the public library of Burlington, Iowa, and a Mid-Western columnist announced by innuendo that Richard Caramel was in a sanitarium with delirium tremens.

The author, indeed, spent his days in a state of pleasant madness. The book was in his conversation three-fourths of the time—he wanted to know if one had heard "the latest"; he would go into a store and in a loud voice order books to be charged to him, in order to catch a chance morsel of recognition from clerk or customer. He knew to a town in what sections of the country it was selling best; he knew exactly what he cleared on each edition, and when he met any one who had not read it, or, as it happened only too often, had not heard of it, he succumbed to moody depression.

So it was natural for Anthony and Gloria to decide, in their jealousy, that he was so swollen with conceit as to be a bore. To Dick's great annoyance Gloria publicly boasted that she had never read "The Demon Lover," and didn't intend to until every one stopped talking about it. As a matter of fact, she had no time to read now, for the presents were pouring in—first a scattering, then an avalanche, varying from the bric-à-brac of forgotten family friends to the photographs of forgotten poor relations.

Maury gave them an elaborate "drinking set," which included silver goblets, cocktail shaker, and bottle-openers. The extortion from Dick was more conventional—a tea set from Tiffany's. From Joseph Bloeckman came a simple and exquisite travelling clock, with his card. There was even a cigarette-holder from Bounds; this touched Anthony and made him want to weep—indeed, any emotion short of hysteria seemed natural in the half-dozen people who were swept up by this tremendous sacrifice to convention. The room set aside in the Plaza bulged with offerings sent by Harvard friends and by associates of his grandfather, with remembrances of Gloria's Farmover days, and with rather pathetic trophies from her former beaux, which last arrived with esoteric, melancholy messages, written on cards tucked carefully inside, beginning "I little thought when—" or "I'm sure I wish you all the happiness—" or even "When you get this I shall be on my way to—"

The most munificent gift was simultaneously the most disappointing. It was a concession of Adam Patch's—a check for five thousand dollars.

To most of the presents Anthony was cold. It seemed to him that they would necessitate keeping a chart of the marital status of all their acquaintances during the next half-century. But Gloria exulted in each one, tearing at the tissue-paper and excelsior with the rapaciousness of a dog digging for a bone, breathlessly seizing a ribbon or an edge of metal and finally bringing to light the whole article and holding it up critically, no emotion except rapt interest in her unsmiling face.

"Look, Anthony!"

"Darn nice, isn't it!"

No answer until an hour later when she would give him a careful account of her precise reaction to the gift, whether it would have been improved by being smaller or larger, whether she was surprised at getting it, and, if so, just how much surprised.

Mrs. Gilbert arranged and rearranged a hypothetical house, distributing the gifts among the different rooms, tabulating articles as "second-best clock" or "silver to use *every* day," and embarrassing Anthony and Gloria by semi-facetious references to a room she called the nursery. She was pleased by old Adam's gift and thereafter had it that he was a very ancient soul, "as much as anything else." As Adam Patch never quite decided whether she referred to the advancing senility of his mind or to some private and psychic schema of her own, it cannot be said to have pleased him. Indeed he always spoke of her to Anthony as "that old woman, the mother," as though she were a character in a comedy he had seen staged many times before. Concerning Gloria he was unable to make up his mind. She attracted him but, as she herself told Anthony, he had decided that she was frivolous and was afraid to approve of her.

Five days!—A dancing platform was being erected on the lawn at Tarrytown. Four days!—A special train was chartered to convey the guests to and from New York. Three days!——

THE DIARY

She was dressed in blue silk pajamas and standing by her bed with her hand on the light to put the room in darkness, when she changed her mind and opening a table drawer brought out a little black book—a "Line-a-day" diary. This she had kept for seven years. Many of the pencil entries were almost illegible and there were notes and references to nights and afternoons long since forgotten, for it was not an intimate diary, even though it began with the immemorial "I am going to keep a diary for my children." Yet as she thumbed over the pages the eyes of many men seemed to look out at her from their half-obliterated names. With one she had gone to New Haven for the first time—in 1908, when she was sixteen and padded shoulders were fashionable at Yale—she had been flattered because "Touch down" Michaud had "rushed" her all evening. She sighed, remembering the grown-up satin dress she had been so proud of and the orchestra playing "Yama-yama, My Yama Man" and "Jungle-Town." So long ago!—the names: Eltynge Reardon, Jim Parsons, "Curly" McGregor, Kenneth Cowan, "Fish-eye" Fry (whom she had liked for being so ugly), Carter Kirby—he had sent her a present; so had Tudor Baird;—Marty Reffer, the first man she had been in love with for more than a day, and Stuart Holcome, who had run away with her in his automobile and tried to make her marry him by force. And Larry Fenwick, whom she had always admired because he had told her one night that if she wouldn't kiss him she could get out of his car and walk home. What a list!

... And, after all, an obsolete list. She was in love now, set for the eternal romance that was to be the synthesis of all romance, yet sad for these men and these moonlights and for the "thrills" she had had—and the kisses. The past—her past, oh, what a joy! She had been exuberantly happy.

Turning over the pages her eyes rested idly on the scattered entries of the past four months. She read the last few carefully.

"*April 1st.*—I know Bill Carstairs hates me because I was so disagreeable, but I hate to be sentimentalized over sometimes. We drove out to the Rockyear Country Club and the most wonderful moon kept shining through the trees. My silver dress is getting tarnished. Funny how one forgets the other nights at Rockyear—with Kenneth Cowan when I loved him so!

"*April 3rd.*—After two hours of Schroeder who, they inform me, has millions, I've decided that this matter of sticking to things wears one out, particularly when the things concerned are men. There's nothing so often overdone and from to-day I swear to be amused. We talked about 'love'—how banal! With how many men have I talked about love?

"*April 11th.*—Patch actually called up to-day! and when he forswore me about a month ago he fairly raged out the door. I'm gradually losing faith in any man being susceptible to fatal injuries.

"*April 20th.*—Spent the day with Anthony. Maybe I'll marry him some time. I kind of like his ideas—he stimulates all the originality in me. Blockhead came around about ten in his new car and took me out Riverside Drive. I liked him to-night: he's so considerate. He knew I didn't want to talk so he was quiet all during the ride.

"*April 21st.*—Woke up thinking of Anthony and sure enough he called and sounded sweet on the phone—so I broke a date for him. To-day I feel I'd break anything for him, including the ten commandments and my neck. He's coming at eight and I shall wear pink and look very fresh and starched——"

She paused here, remembering that after he had gone that night she had undressed with the shivering April air streaming in the windows. Yet it seemed she had not felt the cold, warmed by the profound banalities burning in her heart.

The next entry occurred a few days later:

"*April 24th.*—I want to marry Anthony, because husbands are so often 'husbands' and I must marry a lover.

"There are four general types of husbands.

"(1) The husband who always wants to stay in in the evening, has no vices and works for a salary. Totally undesirable!

"(2) The atavistic master whose mistress one is, to wait on his pleasure. This sort always considers every pretty woman 'shallow,' a sort of peacock with arrested development.

"(3) Next comes the worshipper, the idolater of his wife and all that is his, to the utter oblivion of everything else. This sort demands an emotional actress for a wife. God! it must be an exertion to be thought righteous.

"(4) And Anthony—a temporarily passionate lover with wisdom enough to realize when it has flown and that it must fly. And I want to get married to Anthony.

"What grubworms women are to crawl on their bellies through colorless marriages! Marriage was created not to be a background but to need one. Mine is going to be outstanding. It can't, shan't be the setting—it's going to be the performance, the live, lovely, glamourous performance, and the world shall be the scenery. I refuse to dedicate my life to posterity. Surely one owes as much to the current generation as to one's unwanted children. What a fate—to grow rotund and unseemly, to lose my self-love, to think in terms of milk, oatmeal, nurse, diapers.... Dear dream children, how much more beautiful you are, dazzling little creatures who flutter (all dream children must flutter) on golden, golden wings——

"Such children, however, poor dear babies, have little in common with the wedded state.

"*June 7th.*—Moral question: Was it wrong to make Bloeckman love me? Because I did really make him. He was almost sweetly sad to-night. How opportune it was that my throat is swollen plunk together and tears were easy to muster. But he's just the past—buried already in my plentiful lavender.

"*June 8th.*—And to-day I've promised not to chew my mouth. Well, I won't, I suppose—but if he'd only asked me not to eat!

"Blowing bubbles—that's what we're doing, Anthony and me. And we blew such beautiful ones to-day, and they'll explode and then we'll blow more and more, I guess—bubbles just as big and just as beautiful, until all the soap and water is used up."

On this note the diary ended. Her eyes wandered up the page, over the June 8th's of 1912, 1910, 1907. The earliest entry was scrawled in the plump, bulbous hand of a sixteen-year-old girl—it was the name, Bob Lamar, and a word she could not decipher. Then she knew what it was—and, knowing, she found her eyes misty with tears. There in a graying blur was the record of her first kiss, faded as its intimate afternoon, on a rainy veranda seven years before. She seemed to remember something one of them had said that day and yet she could not remember. Her tears came faster, until she could scarcely see the page. She was crying, she told herself, because she could remember only the rain and the wet flowers in the yard and the smell of the damp grass.

... After a moment she found a pencil and holding it unsteadily drew three parallel lines beneath the last entry. Then she printed FINIS in large capitals, put the book back in the drawer, and crept into bed.

BREATH OF THE CAVE

Back in his apartment after the bridal dinner, Anthony snapped out his lights and, feeling impersonal and fragile as a piece of china waiting on a serving table, got into bed. It was a warm night—a sheet was enough for comfort—and through his wide-open windows came sound, evanescent and summery, alive with remote anticipation. He was thinking that the young years behind him, hollow and colorful, had been lived in facile and vacillating cynicism upon the recorded emotions of men long dust. And there was something beyond that; he knew now. There was the union of his soul with Gloria's, whose radiant fire and freshness was the living material of which the dead beauty of books was made.

From the night into his high-walled room there came, persistently, that evanescent and dissolving sound—something the city was tossing up and calling back again, like a child playing with a ball. In Harlem, the Bronx, Gramercy Park, and along the water-fronts, in little parlors or on pebble-strewn, moon-flooded roofs, a thousand lovers were making this sound, crying little fragments of it into the air. All the city was playing with this sound out there in the blue summer dark, throwing it up and calling it back, promising that, in a little while, life would be beautiful as a story, promising happiness—and by that promise giving it. It gave love hope in its own survival. It could do no more.

It was then that a new note separated itself jarringly from the soft crying of the night. It was a noise from an areaway within a hundred feet from his rear window, the noise of a woman's laughter. It began low, incessant and whining—some servant-maid with her fellow, he thought—and then it grew in volume and became hysterical, until it reminded him of a girl he had seen overcome with nervous laughter at a vaudeville performance. Then it sank, receded, only to rise again and include words—a coarse joke, some bit of obscure horseplay he could not distinguish. It would break off for a moment and he would just catch the low rumble of a man's voice, then begin again—interminably; at first annoying, then strangely terrible. He shivered, and getting up out of bed went to the window. It had reached a high point, tensed and stifled, almost the quality of a scream—then it ceased and left behind it a silence empty and menacing as the greater silence overhead. Anthony stood by the window a moment longer before he returned to his bed. He found himself upset and shaken. Try as he might to strangle his reaction, some animal quality in that unrestrained laughter had grasped at his imagination, and for the first time in four months aroused his old aversion and horror toward all the business of life. The room had grown smothery. He wanted to be out in some cool and bitter breeze, miles above the cities, and to live serene and detached back in the corners of his mind. Life was that sound out there, that ghastly reiterated female sound.

"Oh, my *God*!" he cried, drawing in his breath sharply.

Burying his face in the pillows he tried in vain to concentrate upon the details of the next day.

MORNING

In the gray light he found that it was only five o'clock. He regretted nervously that he had awakened so early—he would appear fagged at the wedding. He envied Gloria who could hide her fatigue with careful pigmentation.

In his bathroom he contemplated himself in the mirror and saw that he was unusually white—half a dozen small imperfections stood out against the morning pallor of his complexion, and overnight he had grown the faint stubble of a beard—the general effect, he fancied, was unprepossessing, haggard, half unwell.

On his dressing table were spread a number of articles which he told over carefully with suddenly fumbling fingers—their tickets to California, the book of traveller's checks, his watch, set to the half minute, the key to his apartment, which he must not forget to give to Maury, and, most important of all, the ring. It was of platinum set around with small emeralds; Gloria had insisted on this; she had always wanted an emerald wedding ring, she said.

It was the third present he had given her; first had come the engagement ring, and then a little gold cigarette-case. He would be giving her many things now—clothes and jewels and friends and excitement. It seemed absurd that from now on he would pay for all her meals. It was going to cost: he wondered if he had not underestimated for this trip, and if he had not better cash a larger check. The question worried him.

Then the breathless impendency of the event swept his mind clear of details. This was the day—unsought, unsuspected six months before, but now breaking in yellow light through his east window, dancing along the carpet as though the sun were smiling at some ancient and reiterated gag of his own.

Anthony laughed in a nervous one-syllable snort.

"By God!" he muttered to himself, "I'm as good as married!"

THE USHERS

Six young men in CROSS PATCH'S library growing more and more cheery under the influence of Mumm's Extra Dry, set surreptitiously in cold pails by the bookcases.

THE FIRST YOUNG MAN: By golly! Believe me, in my next book I'm going to do a wedding scene that'll knock 'em cold!

THE SECOND YOUNG MAN: Met a débutante th'other day said she thought your book was powerful. As a rule young girls cry for this primitive business.

THE THIRD YOUNG MAN: Where's Anthony?

THE FOURTH YOUNG MAN: Walking up and down outside talking to himself.

SECOND YOUNG MAN: Lord! Did you see the minister? Most peculiar looking teeth.

FIFTH YOUNG MAN: Think they're natural. Funny thing people having gold teeth.

SIXTH YOUNG MAN: They say they love 'em. My dentist told me once a woman came to him and insisted on having two of her teeth covered with gold. No reason at all. All right the way they were.

FOURTH YOUNG MAN: Hear you got out a book, Dicky. 'Gratulations!

DICK: (*Stiffly*) Thanks.

FOURTH YOUNG MAN: (*Innocently*) What is it? College stories?

DICK: (*More stiffly*) No. Not college stories.

FOURTH YOUNG MAN: Pity! Hasn't been a good book about Harvard for years.

DICK: (*Touchily*) Why don't you supply the lack?

THIRD YOUNG MAN: I think I saw a squad of guests turn the drive in a Packard just now.

SIXTH YOUNG MAN: Might open a couple more bottles on the strength of that.

THIRD YOUNG MAN: It was the shock of my life when I heard the old man was going to have a wet wedding. Rabid prohibitionist, you know.

FOURTH YOUNG MAN: (*Snapping his fingers excitedly*) By gad! I knew I'd forgotten something. Kept thinking it was my vest.

DICK: What was it?

FOURTH YOUNG MAN: By gad! By gad!

SIXTH YOUNG MAN: Here! Here! Why the tragedy?

SECOND YOUNG MAN: What'd you forget? The way home?

DICK: (*Maliciously*) He forgot the plot for his book of Harvard stories.

FOURTH YOUNG MAN: No, sir, I forgot the present, by George! I forgot to buy old Anthony a present. I kept putting it off and putting it off, and by gad I've forgotten it! What'll they think?

SIXTH YOUNG MAN: (*Facetiously*) That's probably what's been holding up the wedding.

(THE FOURTH YOUNG MAN *looks nervously at his watch. Laughter.*)

FOURTH YOUNG MAN: By gad! What an ass I am!

SECOND YOUNG MAN: What d'you make of the bridesmaid who thinks she's Nora Bayes? Kept telling me she wished this was a ragtime wedding. Name's Haines or Hampton.

DICK: (*Hurriedly spurring his imagination*) Kane, you mean, Muriel Kane. She's a sort of debt of honor, I believe. Once saved Gloria from drowning, or something of the sort.

SECOND YOUNG MAN: I didn't think she could stop that perpetual swaying long enough to swim. Fill up my glass, will you? Old man and I had a long talk about the weather just now.

MAURY: Who? Old Adam?

SECOND YOUNG MAN: No, the bride's father. He must be with a weather bureau.

DICK: He's my uncle, Otis.

OTIS: Well, it's an honorable profession. (*Laughter.*)

SIXTH YOUNG MAN: Bride your cousin, isn't she?

DICK: Yes, Cable, she is.

CABLE: She certainly is a beauty. Not like you, Dicky. Bet she brings old Anthony to terms.

MAURY: Why are all grooms given the title of "old"? I think marriage is an error of youth.

DICK: Maury, the professional cynic.

MAURY: Why, you intellectual faker!

FIFTH YOUNG MAN: Battle of the highbrows here, Otis. Pick up what crumbs you can.

DICK: Faker yourself! What do *you* know?

MAURY: What do *you* know?

LICK: Ask me anything. Any branch of knowledge.

MAURY: All right. What's the fundamental principle of biology?

DICK: You don't know yourself.

MAURY: Don't hedge!

DICK: Well, natural selection?

MAURY: Wrong.

DICK: I give it up.

MAURY: Ontogony recapitulates phyllogony.

FIFTH YOUNG MAN: Take your base!

MAURY: Ask you another. What's the influence of mice on the clover crop? (*Laughter.*)

FOURTH YOUNG MAN: What's the influence of rats on the Decalogue?

MAURY: Shut up, you saphead. There *is* a connection.

DICK: What is it then?

MAURY: (*Pausing a moment in growing disconcertion*) Why, let's see. I seem to have forgotten exactly. Something about the bees eating the clover.

FOURTH YOUNG MAN: And the clover eating the mice! Haw! Haw!

MAURY: (*Frowning*) Let me just think a minute.

DICK: (*Sitting up suddenly*) Listen!

(*A volley of chatter explodes in the adjoining room. The six young men arise, feeling at their neckties.*)

DICK: (*Weightily*) We'd better join the firing squad. They're going to take the picture, I guess. No, that's afterward.

OTIS: Cable, you take the ragtime bridesmaid.

FOURTH YOUNG MAN: I wish to God I'd sent that present.

MAURY: If you'll give me another minute I'll think of that about the mice.

OTIS: I was usher last month for old Charlie McIntyre and——

(They move slowly toward the door as the chatter becomes a babel and the practising preliminary to the overture issues in long pious groans from ADAM PATCH'S *organ.)*

ANTHONY

There were five hundred eyes boring through the back of his cutaway and the sun glinting on the clergyman's inappropriately bourgeois teeth. With difficulty he restrained a laugh. Gloria was saying something in a clear proud voice and he tried to think that the affair was irrevocable, that every second was significant, that his life was being slashed into two periods and that the face of the world was changing before him. He tried to recapture that ecstatic sensation of ten weeks before. All these emotions eluded him, he did not even feel the physical nervousness of that very morning—it was all one gigantic aftermath. And those gold teeth! He wondered if the clergyman were married; he wondered perversely if a clergyman could perform his own marriage service....

But as he took Gloria into his arms he was conscious of a strong reaction. The blood was moving in his veins now. A languorous and pleasant content settled like a weight upon him, bringing responsibility and possession. He was married.

GLORIA

So many, such mingled emotions, that no one of them was separable from the others! She could have wept for her mother, who was crying quietly back there ten feet and for the loveliness of the June sunlight flooding in at the windows. She was beyond all conscious perceptions. Only a sense, colored with delirious wild excitement, that the ultimately important was happening—and a trust, fierce and passionate, burning in her like a prayer, that in a moment she would be forever and securely safe.

Late one night they arrived in Santa Barbara, where the night clerk at the Hotel Lafcadio refused to admit them, on the grounds that they were not married.

The clerk thought that Gloria was beautiful. He did not think that anything so beautiful as Gloria could be moral.

"CON AMORE"

That first half-year—the trip West, the long months' loiter along the California coast, and the gray house near Greenwich where they lived until late autumn made the country dreary—those days, those places, saw the enraptured hours. The breathless idyl of their engagement gave way, first, to the intense romance of the more passionate relationship. The breathless idyl left them, fled on to other lovers; they looked around one day and it was gone, how they scarcely knew. Had either of them lost the other in the days of the idyl, the love lost would have been ever to the loser that dim desire without fulfilment which stands back of all life. But magic must hurry on, and the lovers remain....

The idyl passed, bearing with it its extortion of youth. Came a day when Gloria found that other men no longer bored her; came a day when Anthony discovered that he could sit again late into the evening, talking with Dick of those tremendous abstractions that had once occupied his world. But, knowing they had had the best of love, they clung to what remained. Love lingered—by way of long conversations at night into those stark hours when the mind thins and sharpens and the borrowings from dreams become the stuff of all life, by way of deep and intimate kindnesses they developed toward each other, by way of their laughing at the same absurdities and thinking the same things noble and the same things sad.

It was, first of all, a time of discovery. The things they found in each other were so diverse, so intermixed and, moreover, so sugared with love as to seem at the time not so much discoveries as isolated phenomena—to be allowed for, and to be forgotten. Anthony found that he was living with a girl of tremendous nervous tension and of the most high-handed selfishness. Gloria knew within a month that her husband was an utter coward toward any one of a million phantasms created by his imagination. Her perception was intermittent, for this cowardice sprang out, became almost obscenely evident, then faded and vanished as though it had been only a creation of her own mind. Her reactions to it were not those attributed to her sex—it roused her neither to disgust nor to a premature feeling of motherhood. Herself almost completely without physical fear, she was unable to understand, and so she made the most of what she felt to be his fear's redeeming feature, which was that though he was a coward under a shock and a coward under a strain—when his imagination was given play—he had yet a sort of dashing recklessness that moved her on its brief occasions almost to admiration, and a pride that usually steadied him when he thought he was observed.

The trait first showed itself in a dozen incidents of little more than nervousness—his warning to a taxi-driver against fast driving, in Chicago; his refusal to take her to a certain tough café she had always wished to visit; these of course admitted the conventional interpretation—that it was of her he had been thinking; nevertheless, their culminative weight disturbed her. But something that occurred in a San Francisco hotel, when they had been married a week, gave the matter certainty.

It was after midnight and pitch dark in their room. Gloria was dozing off and Anthony's even breathing beside her made her suppose that he was asleep, when suddenly she saw him raise himself on his elbow and stare at the window.

"What is it, dearest?" she murmured.

"Nothing"—he had relaxed to his pillow and turned toward her—"nothing, my darling wife."

"Don't say 'wife.' I'm your mistress. Wife's such an ugly word. Your 'permanent mistress' is so much more tangible and desirable.... Come into my arms," she added in a rush of tenderness; "I can sleep so well, so well with you in my arms."

Coming into Gloria's arms had a quite definite meaning. It required that he should slide one arm under her shoulder, lock both arms about her, and arrange himself as nearly as possible as a sort of three-sided crib for her luxurious ease. Anthony, who tossed, whose arms went tinglingly to sleep after half an hour of that position, would wait until she was asleep and roll her gently over to her side of the bed—then, left to his own devices, he would curl himself into his usual knots.

Gloria, having attained sentimental comfort, retired into her doze. Five minutes ticked away on Bloeckman's travelling clock; silence lay all about the room, over the unfamiliar, impersonal furniture and the half-oppressive ceiling that melted imperceptibly into invisible walls on both sides. Then there was suddenly a rattling flutter at the window, staccato and loud upon the hushed, pent air.

With a leap Anthony was out of the bed and standing tense beside it.

"Who's there?" he cried in an awful voice.

Gloria lay very still, wide awake now and engrossed not so much in the rattling as in the rigid breathless figure whose voice had reached from the bedside into that ominous dark.

The sound stopped; the room was quiet as before—then Anthony pouring words in at the telephone.

"Some one just tried to get into the room! ...

"There's some one at the window!" His voice was emphatic now, faintly terrified.

"All right! Hurry!" He hung up the receiver; stood motionless.

... There was a rush and commotion at the door, a knocking—Anthony went to open it upon an excited night clerk with three bell-boys grouped staring behind him. Between thumb and finger the night clerk held a wet pen with the threat of a weapon; one of the bell-boys had seized a telephone directory and was looking at it sheepishly. Simultaneously the group was joined by the hastily summoned house-detective, and as one man they surged into the room.

Lights sprang on with a click. Gathering a piece of sheet about her Gloria dove away from sight, shutting her eyes to keep out the horror of this unpremeditated visitation. There was no vestige of an idea in her stricken sensibilities save that her Anthony was at grievous fault.

... The night clerk was speaking from the window, his tone half of the servant, half of the teacher reproving a schoolboy.

"Nobody out there," he declared conclusively; "my golly, nobody *could* be out there. This here's a sheer fall to the street of fifty feet. It was the wind you heard, tugging at the blind."

"Oh."

Then she was sorry for him. She wanted only to comfort him and draw him back tenderly into her arms, to tell them to go away because the thing their presence connotated was odious. Yet she could not raise her head for shame. She heard a broken sentence, apologies, conventions of the employee and one unrestrained snicker from a bell-boy.

"I've been nervous as the devil all evening," Anthony was saying; "somehow that noise just shook me—I was only about half awake."

"Sure, I understand," said the night clerk with comfortable tact; "been that way myself."

The door closed; the lights snapped out; Anthony crossed the floor quietly and crept into bed. Gloria, feigning to be heavy with sleep, gave a quiet little sigh and slipped into his arms.

"What was it, dear?"

"Nothing," he answered, his voice still shaken; "I thought there was somebody at the window, so I looked out, but I couldn't see any one and the noise kept up, so I phoned down-stairs. Sorry if I disturbed you, but I'm awfully darn nervous to-night."

Catching the lie, she gave an interior start—he had not gone to the window, nor near the window. He had stood by the bed and then sent in his call of fear.

"Oh," she said—and then: "I'm so sleepy."

For an hour they lay awake side by side, Gloria with her eyes shut so tight that blue moons formed and revolved against backgrounds of deepest mauve, Anthony staring blindly into the darkness overhead.

After many weeks it came gradually out into the light, to be laughed and joked at. They made a tradition to fit over it—whenever that overpowering terror of the night attacked Anthony, she would put her arms about him and croon, soft as a song:

"I'll protect my Anthony. Oh, nobody's ever going to harm my Anthony!"

He would laugh as though it were a jest they played for their mutual amusement, but to Gloria it was never quite a jest. It was, at first, a keen disappointment; later, it was one of the times when she controlled her temper.

The management of Gloria's temper, whether it was aroused by a lack of hot water for her bath or by a skirmish with her husband, became almost the primary duty of Anthony's day. It must be done just so—by this much silence, by that much pressure, by this much yielding, by that much force. It was in her angers with their attendant cruelties that her inordinate egotism chiefly displayed itself. Because she was brave, because she was "spoiled," because of her outrageous and commendable independence of judgment, and finally because of her arrogant consciousness that she had never seen a girl as beautiful as herself, Gloria had developed into a consistent, practising Nietzschean. This, of course, with overtones of profound sentiment.

There was, for example, her stomach. She was used to certain dishes, and she had a strong conviction that she could not possibly eat anything else. There must be a lemonade and a tomato sandwich late in the morning, then a light lunch with a stuffed tomato. Not only did she require food from a selection of a dozen dishes, but in addition this food must be prepared in just a certain way. One of the most annoying half hours of the first fortnight occurred in Los Angeles, when an unhappy waiter brought her a tomato stuffed with chicken salad instead of celery.

"We always serve it that way, madame," he quavered to the gray eyes that regarded him wrathfully.

Gloria made no answer, but when the waiter had turned discreetly away she banged both fists upon the table until the china and silver rattled.

"Poor Gloria!" laughed Anthony unwittingly, "you can't get what you want ever, can you?"

"I can't eat *stuff*!" she flared up.

"I'll call back the waiter."

"I don't want you to! He doesn't know anything, the darn *fool*!"

"Well, it isn't the hotel's fault. Either send it back, forget it, or be a sport and eat it."

"Shut up!" she said succinctly.

"Why take it out on me?"

"Oh, I'm *not*," she wailed, "but I simply *can't* eat it."

Anthony subsided helplessly.

"We'll go somewhere else," he suggested.

"I don't *want* to go anywhere else. I'm tired of being trotted around to a dozen cafés and not getting *one thing* fit to eat."

"When did we go around to a dozen cafés?"

"You'd *have* to in *this* town," insisted Gloria with ready sophistry.

Anthony, bewildered, tried another tack.

"Why don't you try to eat it? It can't be as bad as you think."

"Just—because—I—don't—like—chicken!"

She picked up her fork and began poking contemptuously at the tomato, and Anthony expected her to begin flinging the stuffings in all directions. He was sure that she was approximately as angry as she had ever been—for an instant he had detected a spark of hate directed as much toward him as toward any one else—and Gloria angry was, for the present, unapproachable.

Then, surprisingly, he saw that she had tentatively raised the fork to her lips and tasted the chicken salad. Her frown had not abated and he stared at her anxiously, making no comment and daring scarcely to breathe. She tasted another forkful—in another moment she was eating. With difficulty Anthony restrained a chuckle; when at length he spoke his words had no possible connection with chicken salad.

This incident, with variations, ran like a lugubrious fugue through the first year of marriage; always it left Anthony baffled, irritated, and depressed. But another rough brushing of temperaments, a question of laundry-bags, he found even more annoying as it ended inevitably in a decisive defeat for him.

One afternoon in Coronado, where they made the longest stay of their trip, more than three weeks, Gloria was arraying herself brilliantly for tea. Anthony, who had been down-stairs listening to the latest rumor bulletins of war in Europe, entered the room, kissed the back of her powdered neck, and went to his dresser. After a great pulling out and pushing in of drawers, evidently unsatisfactory, he turned around to the Unfinished Masterpiece.

"Got any handkerchiefs, Gloria?" he asked. Gloria shook her golden head.

"Not a one. I'm using one of yours."

"The last one, I deduce." He laughed dryly.

"Is it?" She applied an emphatic though very delicate contour to her lips.

"Isn't the laundry back?"

"I don't know."

Anthony hesitated—then, with sudden discernment, opened the closet door. His suspicions were verified. On the hook provided hung the blue bag furnished by the hotel. This was full of his clothes—he had put them there himself. The floor beneath it was littered with an astonishing mass of finery—lingerie, stockings, dresses, nightgowns, and pajamas—most of it scarcely worn but all of it coming indubitably under the general heading of Gloria's laundry.

He stood holding the closet door open.

"Why, Gloria!"

"What?"

The lip line was being erased and corrected according to some mysterious perspective; not a finger trembled as she manipulated the lip-stick, not a glance wavered in his direction. It was a triumph of concentration.

"Haven't you ever sent out the laundry?"

"Is it there?"

"It most certainly is."

"Well, I guess I haven't, then."

"Gloria," began Anthony, sitting down on the bed and trying to catch her mirrored eyes, "you're a nice fellow, you are! I've sent it out every time it's been sent since we left New York, and over a week ago you promised you'd do it for a change. All you'd have to do would be to cram your own junk into that bag and ring for the chambermaid."

"Oh, why fuss about the laundry?" exclaimed Gloria petulantly, "I'll take care of it."

"I haven't fussed about it. I'd just as soon divide the bother with you, but when we run out of handkerchiefs it's darn near time something's done."

Anthony considered that he was being extraordinarily logical. But Gloria, unimpressed, put away her cosmetics and casually offered him her back.

"Hook me up," she suggested; "Anthony, dearest, I forgot all about it. I meant to, honestly, and I will to-day. Don't be cross with your sweetheart."

What could Anthony do then but draw her down upon his knee and kiss a shade of color from her lips.

"But I don't mind," she murmured with a smile, radiant and magnanimous. "You can kiss all the paint off my lips any time you want."

They went down to tea. They bought some handkerchiefs in a notion store near by. All was forgotten.

But two days later Anthony looked in the closet and saw the bag still hung limp upon its hook and that the gay and vivid pile on the floor had increased surprisingly in height.

"Gloria!" he cried.

"Oh—" Her voice was full of real distress. Despairingly Anthony went to the phone and called the chambermaid.

"It seems to me," he said impatiently, "that you expect me to be some sort of French valet to you."

Gloria laughed, so infectiously that Anthony was unwise enough to smile. Unfortunate man! In some intangible manner his smile made her mistress of the situation—with an air of injured righteousness she went emphatically to the closet and began pushing her laundry violently into the bag. Anthony watched her—ashamed of himself.

"There!" she said, implying that her fingers had been worked to the bone by a brutal taskmaster.

He considered, nevertheless, that he had given her an object-lesson and that the matter was closed, but on the contrary it was merely beginning. Laundry pile followed laundry pile—at long intervals; dearth of handkerchief followed dearth of handkerchief—at short ones; not to mention dearth of sock, of shirt, of everything. And Anthony found at length that either he must send it out himself or go through the increasingly unpleasant ordeal of a verbal battle with Gloria.

GLORIA AND GENERAL LEE

On their way East they stopped two days in Washington, strolling about with some hostility in its atmosphere of harsh repellent light, of distance without freedom, of pomp without splendor—it seemed a pasty-pale and self-conscious city. The second day they made an ill-advised trip to General Lee's old home at Arlington.

The bus which bore them was crowded with hot, unprosperous people, and Anthony, intimate to Gloria, felt a storm brewing. It broke at the Zoo, where the party stopped for ten minutes. The Zoo, it seemed, smelt of monkeys. Anthony laughed; Gloria called down the curse of Heaven upon monkeys, including in her malevolence all the passengers of the bus and their perspiring offspring who had hied themselves monkey-ward.

Eventually the bus moved on to Arlington. There it met other busses and immediately a swarm of women and children were leaving a trail of peanut-shells through the halls of General Lee and crowding at length into the room where he was married. On the wall of this room a pleasing sign announced in large red letters "Ladies' Toilet." At this final blow Gloria broke down.

"I think it's perfectly terrible!" she said furiously, "the idea of letting these people come here! And of encouraging them by making these houses show-places."

"Well," objected Anthony, "if they weren't kept up they'd go to pieces."

"What if they did!" she exclaimed as they sought the wide pillared porch. "Do you think they've left a breath of 1860 here? This has become a thing of 1914."

"Don't you want to preserve old things?"

"But you *can't*, Anthony. Beautiful things grow to a certain height and then they fail and fade off, breathing out memories as they decay. And just as any period decays in our minds, the things of that period should decay too, and in that way they're preserved for a while in the few hearts like mine that react to them. That graveyard at Tarrytown, for instance. The asses who give money to preserve things have spoiled that too. Sleepy Hollow's gone; Washington Irving's dead and his books are rotting in our estimation year by year—then let the graveyard rot too, as it should, as all things should. Trying to preserve a century by keeping its relics up to date is like keeping a dying man alive by stimulants."

"So you think that just as a time goes to pieces its houses ought to go too?"

"Of course! Would you value your Keats letter if the signature was traced over to make it last longer? It's just because I love the past that I want this house to look back on its glamourous moment of youth and beauty, and I want its stairs to creak as if to the footsteps of women with hoop skirts and men in boots and spurs. But they've made it into a blondined, rouged-up old woman of sixty. It hasn't any right to look so prosperous. It might care enough for Lee to drop a brick now and then. How many of these—these *animals*"—she waved her hand around—"get anything from this, for all the histories and guide-books and restorations in existence? How many of them who think that, at best, appreciation is talking in undertones and walking on tiptoes would even come here if it was any trouble? I want it to smell of magnolias instead of peanuts and I want my shoes to crunch on the same gravel that Lee's boots crunched on. There's no beauty without poignancy and there's no poignancy without the feeling that it's going, men, names, books, houses—bound for dust—mortal—"

A small boy appeared beside them and, swinging a handful of banana-peels, flung them valiantly in the direction of the Potomac.

SENTIMENT

Simultaneously with the fall of Liège, Anthony and Gloria arrived in New York. In retrospect the six weeks seemed miraculously happy. They had found to a great extent, as most young couples find in some measure, that they possessed in common many fixed ideas and curiosities and odd quirks of mind; they were essentially companionable.

But it had been a struggle to keep many of their conversations on the level of discussions. Arguments were fatal to Gloria's disposition. She had all her life been associated either with her mental inferiors or with men who, under the almost hostile intimidation of her beauty, had not dared to contradict her; naturally, then, it irritated her when Anthony emerged from the state in which her pronouncements were an infallible and ultimate decision.

He failed to realize, at first, that this was the result partly of her "female" education and partly of her beauty, and he was inclined to include her with her entire sex as curiously and definitely limited. It maddened him to find she had no sense of justice. But he discovered that, when a subject did interest her, her brain tired less quickly than his. What he chiefly missed in her mind was the pedantic teleology—the sense of order and accuracy, the sense of life as a mysteriously correlated piece of patchwork, but he understood after a while that such a quality in her would have been incongruous.

Of the things they possessed in common, greatest of all was their almost uncanny pull at each other's hearts. The day they left the hotel in Coronado she sat down on one of the beds while they were packing, and began to weep bitterly.

"Dearest—" His arms were around her; he pulled her head down upon his shoulder. "What is it, my own Gloria? Tell me."

"We're going away," she sobbed. "Oh, Anthony, it's sort of the first place we've lived together. Our two little beds here—side by side—they'll be always waiting for us, and we're never coming back to 'em any more."

She was tearing at his heart as she always could. Sentiment came over him, rushed into his eyes.

"Gloria, why, we're going on to another room. And two other little beds. We're going to be together all our lives."

Words flooded from her in a low husky voice.

"But it won't be—like our two beds—ever again. Everywhere we go and move on and change, something's lost—something's left behind. You can't ever quite repeat anything, and I've been so yours, here—"

He held her passionately near, discerning far beyond any criticism of her sentiment, a wise grasping of the minute, if only an indulgence of her desire to cry—Gloria the idler, caresser of her own dreams, extracting poignancy from the memorable things of life and youth.

Later in the afternoon when he returned from the station with the tickets he found her asleep on one of the beds, her arm curled about a black object which he could not at first identify. Coming closer he found it was one of his shoes, not a particularly new one, nor clean one, but her face, tear-stained, was pressed against it, and he understood her ancient and most honorable message. There was almost ecstasy in waking her and seeing her smile at him, shy but well aware of her own nicety of imagination.

With no appraisal of the worth or dross of these two things, it seemed to Anthony that they lay somewhere near the heart of love.

THE GRAY HOUSE

It is in the twenties that the actual momentum of life begins to slacken, and it is a simple soul indeed to whom as many things are significant and meaningful at thirty as at ten years before. At thirty an organ-grinder is a more or less moth-eaten man who grinds an organ—and once he was an organ-grinder! The unmistakable stigma of humanity touches all those impersonal and beautiful things that only youth ever grasps in their impersonal glory. A brilliant ball, gay with light romantic laughter, wears through its own silks and satins to show the bare framework of a man-made thing—oh, that eternal hand!—a play, most tragic and most divine, becomes merely a succession of speeches, sweated over by the eternal plagiarist in the clammy hours and acted by men subject to cramps, cowardice, and manly sentiment.

And this time with Gloria and Anthony, this first year of marriage, and the gray house caught them in that stage when the organ-grinder was slowly undergoing his inevitable metamorphosis. She was twenty-three; he was twenty-six.

The gray house was, at first, of sheerly pastoral intent. They lived impatiently in Anthony's apartment for the first fortnight after the return from California, in a stifled atmosphere of open trunks, too many callers, and the eternal laundry-bags. They discussed with their friends the stupendous problem of their future. Dick and Maury would sit with them agreeing solemnly, almost thoughtfully, as Anthony ran through his list of what they "ought" to do, and where they "ought" to live.

"I'd like to take Gloria abroad," he complained, "except for this damn war—and next to that I'd sort of like to have a place in the country, somewhere near New York, of course, where I could write—or whatever I decide to do."

Gloria laughed.

"Isn't he cute?" she required of Maury. "'Whatever he decides to do!' But what am *I* going to do if he works? Maury, will you take me around if Anthony works?"

"Anyway, I'm not going to work yet," said Anthony quickly.

It was vaguely understood between them that on some misty day he would enter a sort of glorified diplomatic service and be envied by princes and prime ministers for his beautiful wife.

"Well," said Gloria helplessly, "I'm sure I don't know. We talk and talk and never get anywhere, and we ask all our friends and they just answer the way we want 'em to. I wish somebody'd take care of us."

"Why don't you go out to—out to Greenwich or something?" suggested Richard Caramel.

"I'd like that," said Gloria, brightening. "Do you think we could get a house there?"

Dick shrugged his shoulders and Maury laughed.

"You two amuse me," he said. "Of all the unpractical people! As soon as a place is mentioned you expect us to pull great piles of photographs out of our pockets showing the different styles of architecture available in bungalows."

"That's just what I don't want," wailed Gloria, "a hot stuffy bungalow, with a lot of babies next door and their father cutting the grass in his shirt sleeves—"

"For Heaven's sake, Gloria," interrupted Maury, "nobody wants to lock you up in a bungalow. Who in God's name brought bungalows into the conversation? But you'll never get a place anywhere unless you go out and hunt for it."

"Go where? You say 'go out and hunt for it,' but where?"

With dignity Maury waved his hand paw-like about the room.

"Out anywhere. Out in the country. There're lots of places."

"Thanks."

"Look here!" Richard Caramel brought his yellow eye rakishly into play. "The trouble with you two is that you're all disorganized. Do you know anything about New York State? Shut up, Anthony, I'm talking to Gloria."

"Well," she admitted finally, "I've been to two or three house parties in Portchester and around in Connecticut—but, of course, that isn't in New York State, is it? And neither is Morristown," she finished with drowsy irrelevance.

There was a shout of laughter.

"Oh, Lord!" cried Dick, "neither is Morristown!' No, and neither is Santa Barbara, Gloria. Now listen. To begin with, unless you have a fortune there's no use considering any place like Newport or Southhampton or Tuxedo. They're out of the question."

They all agreed to this solemnly.

"And personally I hate New Jersey. Then, of course, there's upper New York, above Tuxedo."

"Too cold," said Gloria briefly. "I was there once in an automobile."

"Well, it seems to me there're a lot of towns like Rye between New York and Greenwich where you could buy a little gray house of some—"

Gloria leaped at the phrase triumphantly. For the first time since their return East she knew what she wanted.

"Oh, *yes*!" she cried. "Oh, *yes*! that's it: a little gray house with sort of white around and a whole lot of swamp maples just as brown and gold as an October picture in a gallery. Where can we find one?"

"Unfortunately, I've mislaid my list of little gray houses with swamp maples around them—but I'll try to find it. Meanwhile you take a piece of paper and write down the names of seven possible towns. And every day this week you take a trip to one of those towns."

"Oh, gosh!" protested Gloria, collapsing mentally, "why won't you do it for us? I hate trains."

"Well, hire a car, and—"

Gloria yawned.

"I'm tired of discussing it. Seems to me all we do is talk about where to live."

"My exquisite wife wearies of thought," remarked Anthony ironically. "She must have a tomato sandwich to stimulate her jaded nerves. Let's go out to tea."

As the unfortunate upshot of this conversation, they took Dick's advice literally, and two days later went out to Rye, where they wandered around with an irritated real estate agent, like bewildered babes in the wood. They were shown houses at a hundred a month which closely adjoined other houses at a hundred a month; they were shown isolated houses to which they invariably took violent dislikes, though they submitted weakly to the agent's desire that they "look at that stove—some stove!" and to a great shaking of doorposts and tapping of walls, intended evidently to show that the house would not immediately collapse, no matter how convincingly it gave that impression. They gazed through windows into interiors furnished either "commercially" with slab-like chairs and unyielding settees, or "home-like" with the melancholy bric-à-brac of other summers—crossed tennis rackets, fit-form couches, and depressing Gibson girls. With a feeling of guilt they looked at a few really nice houses, aloof, dignified, and cool—at three hundred a month. They went away from Rye thanking the real estate agent very much indeed.

On the crowded train back to New York the seat behind was occupied by a super-respirating Latin whose last few meals had obviously been composed entirely of garlic. They reached the apartment gratefully, almost hysterically, and Gloria rushed for a hot bath in the reproachless bathroom. So far as the question of a future abode was concerned both of them were incapacitated for a week.

The matter eventually worked itself out with unhoped-for romance. Anthony ran into the living room one afternoon fairly radiating "the idea."

"I've got it," he was exclaiming as though he had just caught a mouse. "We'll get a car."

"Gee whiz! Haven't we got troubles enough taking care of ourselves?"

"Give me a second to explain, can't you? just let's leave our stuff with Dick and just pile a couple of suitcases in our car, the one we're going to buy—we'll have to have one in the country anyway—and just start out in the direction of New Haven. You see, as we get out of commuting distance from New York, the rents'll get cheaper, and as soon as we find a house we want we'll just settle down."

By his frequent and soothing interpolation of the word "just" he aroused her lethargic enthusiasm. Strutting violently about the room, he simulated a dynamic and irresistible efficiency. "We'll buy a car to-morrow."

Life, limping after imagination's ten-league boots, saw them out of town a week later in a cheap but sparkling new roadster, saw them through the chaotic unintelligible Bronx, then over a wide murky district which alternated cheerless blue-green wastes with suburbs of tremendous and sordid activity. They left New York at eleven and it was well past a hot and beatific noon when they moved rakishly through Pelham.

"These aren't towns," said Gloria scornfully, "these are just city blocks plumped down coldly into waste acres. I imagine all the men here have their mustaches stained from drinking their coffee too quickly in the morning."

"And play pinochle on the commuting trains."

"What's pinochle?"

"Don't be so literal. How should I know? But it sounds as though they ought to play it."

"I like it. It sounds as if it were something where you sort of cracked your knuckles or something.... Let me drive."

Anthony looked at her suspiciously.

"You swear you're a good driver?"

"Since I was fourteen."

He stopped the car cautiously at the side of the road and they changed seats. Then with a horrible grinding noise the car was put in gear, Gloria adding an accompaniment of laughter which seemed to Anthony disquieting and in the worst possible taste.

"Here we go!" she yelled. "Whoo-oop!"

Their heads snapped back like marionettes on a single wire as the car leaped ahead and curved retchingly about a standing milk-wagon, whose driver stood up on his seat and bellowed after them. In the immemorial tradition of the road Anthony retorted with a few brief epigrams as to the grossness of the milk-delivering profession. He cut his remarks short, however, and turned to Gloria with the growing conviction that he had made a grave mistake in relinquishing control and that Gloria was a driver of many eccentricities and of infinite carelessness.

"Remember now!" he warned her nervously, "the man said we oughtn't to go over twenty miles an hour for the first five thousand miles."

She nodded briefly, but evidently intending to accomplish the prohibitive distance as quickly as possible, slightly increased her speed. A moment later he made another attempt.

"See that sign? Do you want to get us pinched?"

"Oh, for Heaven's sake," cried Gloria in exasperation, "you *always* exaggerate things so!"

"Well, I don't want to get arrested."

"Who's arresting you? You're so persistent—just like you were about my cough medicine last night."

"It was for your own good."

"Ha! I might as well be living with mama."

"What a thing to say to me!"

A standing policeman swerved into view, was hastily passed.

"See him?" demanded Anthony.

"Oh, you drive me crazy! He didn't arrest us, did he?"

"When he does it'll be too late," countered Anthony brilliantly.

Her reply was scornful, almost injured.

"Why, this old thing won't *go* over thirty-five."

"It isn't old."

"It is in spirit."

That afternoon the car joined the laundry-bags and Gloria's appetite as one of the trinity of contention. He warned her of railroad tracks; he pointed out approaching automobiles; finally he insisted on taking the wheel and a furious, insulted Gloria sat silently beside him between the towns of Larchmont and Rye.

But it was due to this furious silence of hers that the gray house materialized from its abstraction, for just beyond Rye he surrendered gloomily to it and re-relinquished the wheel. Mutely he beseeched her and Gloria, instantly cheered, vowed to be more careful. But because a discourteous street-car persisted callously in remaining upon its track Gloria ducked down a side-street—and thereafter that afternoon was never able to find her way back to the Post Road. The street they finally mistook for it lost its Post-Road aspect when it had gone five miles from Cos Cob. Its macadam became gravel, then dirt—moreover, it narrowed and developed a border of maple trees, through which filtered the weltering sun, making its endless experiments with shadow designs upon the long grass.

"We're lost now," complained Anthony.

"Read that sign!"

"Marietta—Five Miles. What's Marietta?"

"Never heard of it, but let's go on. We can't turn here and there's probably a detour back to the Post Road."

The way became scarred with deepening ruts and insidious shoulders of stone. Three farmhouses faced them momentarily, slid by. A town sprang up in a cluster of dull roofs around a white tall steeple.

Then Gloria, hesitating between two approaches, and making her choice too late, drove over a fire-hydrant and ripped the transmission violently from the car.

It was dark when the real-estate agent of Marietta showed them the gray house. They came upon it just west of the village, where it rested against a sky that was a warm blue cloak buttoned with tiny stars. The gray house had been there when women who kept cats were probably witches, when Paul Revere made false teeth in Boston preparatory to arousing the great commercial people, when our ancestors were gloriously deserting Washington in droves. Since those days the house had been bolstered up in a feeble corner, considerably repartitioned and newly plastered inside, amplified by a kitchen and added to by a side-porch—but, save for where some jovial oaf had roofed the new kitchen with red tin, Colonial it defiantly remained.

"How did you happen to come to Marietta?" demanded the real-estate agent in a tone that was first cousin to suspicion. He was showing them through four spacious and airy bedrooms.

"We broke down," explained Gloria. "I drove over a fire-hydrant and we had ourselves towed to the garage and then we saw your sign."

The man nodded, unable to follow such a sally of spontaneity. There was something subtly immoral in doing anything without several months' consideration.

They signed a lease that night and, in the agent's car, returned jubilantly to the somnolent and dilapidated Marietta Inn, which was too broken for even the chance immoralities and consequent gaieties of a country road-house. Half the night they lay awake planning the things they were to do there. Anthony was going to work at an astounding pace on his history and thus ingratiate himself with his cynical grandfather.... When the car was repaired they would explore the country and join the nearest "really nice" club, where Gloria would play golf "or something" while Anthony wrote. This, of course, was Anthony's idea—Gloria was sure she wanted but to read and dream and be fed tomato sandwiches and lemonades by some angelic servant still in a shadowy hinterland. Between paragraphs Anthony would come and kiss her as she lay indolently in the hammock.... The hammock! a host of new dreams in tune to its imagined rhythm, while the wind stirred it and waves of sun undulated over the shadows of blown wheat, or the dusty road freckled and darkened with quiet summer rain....

And guests—here they had a long argument, both of them trying to be extraordinarily mature and far-sighted. Anthony claimed that they would need people at least every other week-end "as a sort of change." This provoked an involved and extremely sentimental conversation as to whether Anthony did not consider Gloria change enough. Though he assured her that he did, she insisted upon doubting him.... Eventually the conversation assumed its eternal monotone: "What then? Oh, what'll we do then?"

"Well, we'll have a dog," suggested Anthony.

"I don't want one. I want a kitty." She went thoroughly and with great enthusiasm into the history, habits, and tastes of a cat she had once possessed. Anthony considered that it must have been a horrible character with neither personal magnetism nor a loyal heart.

Later they slept, to wake an hour before dawn with the gray house dancing in phantom glory before their dazzled eyes.

THE SOUL OF GLORIA

For that autumn the gray house welcomed them with a rush of sentiment that falsified its cynical old age. True, there were the laundry-bags, there was Gloria's appetite, there was Anthony's tendency to brood and his imaginative "nervousness," but there were intervals also of an unhoped-for serenity. Close together on the porch they would wait for the moon to stream across the silver acres of farmland, jump a thick wood and tumble waves of radiance at their feet. In such a moonlight Gloria's face was of a pervading, reminiscent white, and with a modicum of effort they would slip off the blinders of custom and each would find in the other almost the quintessential romance of the vanished June.

One night while her head lay upon his heart and their cigarettes glowed in swerving buttons of light through the dome of darkness over the bed, she spoke for the first time and fragmentarily of the men who had hung for brief moments on her beauty.

"Do you ever think of them?" he asked her.

"Only occasionally—when something happens that recalls a particular man."

"What do you remember—their kisses?"

"All sorts of things.... Men are different with women."

"Different in what way?"

"Oh, entirely—and quite inexpressibly. Men who had the most firmly rooted reputation for being this way or that would sometimes be surprisingly inconsistent with me. Brutal men were tender, negligible men were astonishingly loyal and lovable, and, often, honorable men took attitudes that were anything but honorable."

"For instance?"

"Well, there was a boy named Percy Wolcott from Cornell who was quite a hero in college, a great athlete, and saved a lot of people from a fire or something like that. But I soon found he was stupid in a rather dangerous way."

"What way?"

"It seems he had some naïve conception of a woman 'fit to be his wife,' a particular conception that I used to run into a lot and that always drove me wild. He demanded a girl who'd never been kissed and who liked to sew and sit home and pay tribute to his self-esteem. And I'll bet a hat if he's gotten an idiot to sit and be stupid with him he's tearing out on the side with some much speedier lady."

"I'd be sorry for his wife."

"I wouldn't. Think what an ass she'd be not to realize it before she married him. He's the sort whose idea of honoring and respecting a woman would be never to give her any excitement. With the best intentions, he was deep in the dark ages."

"What was his attitude toward you?"

"I'm coming to that. As I told you—or did I tell you?—he was mighty good-looking: big brown honest eyes and one of those smiles that guarantee the heart behind it is twenty-karat gold. Being young and credulous, I thought he had some discretion, so I kissed him fervently one night when we were riding around after a dance at the Homestead at Hot Springs. It had been a wonderful week, I remember—with the most luscious trees spread like green lather, sort of, all over the valley and a mist rising out of them on October mornings like bonfires lit to turn them brown—"

"How about your friend with the ideals?" interrupted Anthony.

"It seems that when he kissed me he began to think that perhaps he could get away with a little more, that I needn't be 'respected' like this Beatrice Fairfax glad-girl of his imagination."

"What'd he do?"

"Not much. I pushed him off a sixteen-foot embankment before he was well started."

"Hurt him?" inquired Anthony with a laugh.

"Broke his arm and sprained his ankle. He told the story all over Hot Springs, and when his arm healed a man named Barley who liked me fought him and broke it over again. Oh, it was all an awful mess. He threatened to sue Barley, and Barley—he was from Georgia—was seen buying a gun in town. But before that mama had dragged me North again, much against my will, so I never did find out all that happened—though I saw Barley once in the Vanderbilt lobby."

Anthony laughed long and loud.

"What a career! I suppose I ought to be furious because you've kissed so many men. I'm not, though."

At this she sat up in bed.

"It's funny, but I'm so sure that those kisses left no mark on me—no taint of promiscuity, I mean—even though a man once told me in all seriousness that he hated to think I'd been a public drinking glass."

"He had his nerve."

"I just laughed and told him to think of me rather as a loving-cup that goes from hand to hand but should be valued none the less."

"Somehow it doesn't bother me—on the other hand it would, of course, if you'd done any more than kiss them. But I believe *you're* absolutely incapable of jealousy except as hurt vanity. Why don't you care what I've done? Wouldn't you prefer it if I'd been absolutely innocent?"

"It's all in the impression it might have made on you. *My* kisses were because the man was good-looking, or because there was a slick moon, or even because I've felt vaguely sentimental and a little stirred. But that's all—it's had utterly no effect on me. But you'd remember and let memories haunt you and worry you."

"Haven't you ever kissed any one like you've kissed me?"

"No," she answered simply. "As I've told you, men have tried—oh, lots of things. Any pretty girl has that experience.... You see," she resumed, "it doesn't matter to me how many women you've stayed with in the past, so long as it was merely a physical satisfaction, but I don't believe I could endure the idea of your ever having lived with another woman for a protracted period or even having wanted to marry some possible girl. It's different somehow. There'd be all the little intimacies remembered—and they'd dull that freshness that after all is the most precious part of love."

Rapturously he pulled her down beside him on the pillow.

"Oh, my darling," he whispered, "as if I remembered anything but your dear kisses."

Then Gloria, in a very mild voice:

"Anthony, did I hear anybody say they were thirsty?"

Anthony laughed abruptly and with a sheepish and amused grin got out of bed.

"With just a *little* piece of ice in the water," she added. "Do you suppose I could have that?"

Gloria used the adjective "little" whenever she asked a favor—it made the favor sound less arduous. But Anthony laughed again—whether she wanted a cake of ice or a marble of it, he must go down-stairs to the kitchen.... Her voice followed him through the hall: "And just a *little* cracker with just a *little* marmalade on it...."

"Oh, gosh!" sighed Anthony in rapturous slang, "she's wonderful, that girl! She *has* it!"

"When we have a baby," she began one day—this, it had already been decided, was to be after three years—"I want it to look like you."

"Except its legs," he insinuated slyly.

"Oh, yes, except his legs. He's got to have my legs. But the rest of him can be you."

"My nose?"

Gloria hesitated.

"Well, perhaps my nose. But certainly your eyes—and my mouth, and I guess my shape of the face. I wonder; I think he'd be sort of cute if he had my hair."

"My dear Gloria, you've appropriated the whole baby."

"Well, I didn't mean to," she apologized cheerfully.

"Let him have my neck at least," he urged, regarding himself gravely in the glass. "You've often said you liked my neck because the Adam's apple doesn't show, and, besides, your neck's too short."

"Why, it is *not*!" she cried indignantly, turning to the mirror, "it's just right. I don't believe I've ever seen a better neck."

"It's too short," he repeated teasingly.

"Short?" Her tone expressed exasperated wonder.

"Short? You're crazy!" She elongated and contracted it to convince herself of its reptilian sinuousness. "Do you call *that* a short neck?"

"One of the shortest I've ever seen."

For the first time in weeks tears started from Gloria's eyes and the look she gave him had a quality of real pain.

"Oh, Anthony—"

"My Lord, Gloria!" He approached her in bewilderment and took her elbows in his hands. "Don't cry, *please*! Didn't you know I was only kidding? Gloria, look at me! Why, dearest, you've got the longest neck I've ever seen. Honestly."

Her tears dissolved in a twisted smile.

"Well—you shouldn't have said that, then. Let's talk about the b-baby."

Anthony paced the floor and spoke as though rehearsing for a debate.

"To put it briefly, there are two babies we could have, two distinct and logical babies, utterly differentiated. There's the baby that's the combination of the best of both of us. Your body, my eyes, my mind, your intelligence—and then there is the baby which is our worst—my body, your disposition, and my irresolution."

"I like that second baby," she said.

"What I'd really like," continued Anthony, "would be to have two sets of triplets one year apart and then experiment with the six boys—"

"Poor me," she interjected.

"—I'd educate them each in a different country and by a different system and when they were twenty-three I'd call them together and see what they were like."

"Let's have 'em all with my neck," suggested Gloria.

THE END OF A CHAPTER

The car was at length repaired and with a deliberate vengeance took up where it left off the business of causing infinite dissension. Who should drive? How fast should Gloria go? These two questions and the eternal recriminations involved ran through the days. They motored to the Post-Road towns, Rye, Portchester, and Greenwich, and called on a dozen friends, mostly Gloria's, who all seemed to be in different stages of having babies and in this respect as well as in others bored her to a point of nervous distraction. For an hour after each visit she would bite her fingers furiously and be inclined to take out her rancor on Anthony.

"I loathe women," she cried in a mild temper. "What on earth can you say to them—except talk 'lady-lady'? I've enthused over a dozen babies that I've wanted only to choke. And every one of those girls is either incipiently jealous and suspicious of her husband if he's charming or beginning to be bored with him if he isn't."

"Don't you ever intend to see any women?"

"I don't know. They never seem clean to me—never—never. Except just a few. Constance Shaw—you know, the Mrs. Merriam who came over to see us last Tuesday—is almost the only one. She's so tall and fresh-looking and stately."

"I don't like them so tall."

Though they went to several dinner dances at various country clubs, they decided that the autumn was too nearly over for them to "go out" on any scale, even had they been so inclined. He hated golf; Gloria liked it only mildly, and though she enjoyed a violent rush that some undergraduates gave her one night and was glad that Anthony should be proud of her beauty, she also perceived that their hostess for the evening, a Mrs. Granby, was somewhat disquieted by the fact that Anthony's classmate, Alec Granby, joined with enthusiasm in the rush. The Granbys never phoned again, and though Gloria laughed, it piqued her not a little.

"You see," she explained to Anthony, "if I wasn't married it wouldn't worry her—but she's been to the movies in her day and she thinks I may be a vampire. But the point is that placating such people requires an effort that I'm simply unwilling to make.... And those cute little freshmen making eyes at me and paying me idiotic compliments! I've grown up, Anthony."

Marietta itself offered little social life. Half a dozen farm-estates formed a hectagon around it, but these belonged to ancient men who displayed themselves only as inert, gray-thatched lumps in the back of limousines on their way to the station, whither they were sometimes accompanied by equally ancient and doubly massive wives. The townspeople were a particularly uninteresting type—unmarried females were predominant for the most part—with school-festival horizons and souls bleak as the forbidding white architecture of the three churches. The only native with whom they came into close contact was the broad-hipped, broad-shouldered Swedish girl who came every day to do their work. She was silent and efficient, and Gloria, after finding her weeping violently into her bowed arms upon the kitchen table, developed an uncanny fear of her and stopped complaining about the food. Because of her untold and esoteric grief the girl stayed on.

Gloria's penchant for premonitions and her bursts of vague supernaturalism were a surprise to Anthony. Either some complex, properly and scientifically inhibited in the early years with her Bilphistic mother, or some inherited hypersensitiveness, made her susceptible to any suggestion of the psychic, and, far from gullible about the motives of people, she was inclined to credit any extraordinary happening attributed to the whimsical perambulations of the buried. The desperate squeakings about the old house on windy nights that to Anthony were burglars with revolvers ready in hand represented to Gloria the auras, evil and restive, of dead generations, expiating the inexpiable upon the ancient and romantic hearth. One night, because of two swift bangs down-stairs, which Anthony fearfully but unavailingly investigated, they lay awake nearly until dawn asking each other examination-paper questions about the history of the world.

In October Muriel came out for a two weeks' visit. Gloria had called her on long-distance, and Miss Kane ended the conversation characteristically by saying "All-ll-ll righty. I'll be there with bells!" She arrived with a dozen popular songs under her arm.

"You ought to have a phonograph out here in the country," she said, "just a little Vic—they don't cost much. Then whenever you're lonesome you can have Caruso or Al Jolson right at your door."

She worried Anthony to distraction by telling him that "he was the first clever man she had ever known and she got so tired of shallow people." He wondered that people fell in love with such women. Yet he supposed that under a certain impassioned glance even she might take on a softness and promise.

But Gloria, violently showing off her love for Anthony, was diverted into a state of purring content.

Finally Richard Caramel arrived for a garrulous and to Gloria painfully literary week-end, during which he discussed himself with Anthony long after she lay in childlike sleep up-stairs.

"It's been mighty funny, this success and all," said Dick. "Just before the novel appeared I'd been trying, without success, to sell some short stories. Then, after my book came out, I polished up three and had them accepted by one of the magazines that had rejected them before. I've done a lot of them since; publishers don't pay me for my book till this winter."

"Don't let the victor belong to the spoils."

"You mean write trash?" He considered. "If you mean deliberately injecting a slushy fade-out into each one, I'm not. But I don't suppose I'm being so careful. I'm certainly writing faster and I don't seem to be thinking as much as I used to. Perhaps it's because I don't get any conversation, now that you're married and Maury's gone to Philadelphia. Haven't the old urge and ambition. Early success and all that."

"Doesn't it worry you?"

"Frantically. I get a thing I call sentence-fever that must be like buck-fever—it's a sort of intense literary self-consciousness that comes when I try to force myself. But the really awful days aren't when I think I can't write. They're when I wonder whether any writing is worth while at all—I mean whether I'm not a sort of glorified buffoon."

"I like to hear you talk that way," said Anthony with a touch of his old patronizing insolence. "I was afraid you'd gotten a bit idiotic over your work. Read the damnedest interview you gave out——"

Dick interrupted with an agonized expression.

"Good Lord! Don't mention it. Young lady wrote it—most admiring young lady. Kept telling me my work was 'strong,' and I sort of lost my head and made a lot of strange pronouncements. Some of it was good, though, don't you think?"

"Oh, yes; that part about the wise writer writing for the youth of his generation, the critic of the next, and the schoolmaster of ever afterward."

"Oh, I believe a lot of it," admitted Richard Caramel with a faint beam. "It simply was a mistake to give it out."

In November they moved into Anthony's apartment, from which they sallied triumphantly to the Yale-Harvard and Harvard-Princeton football games, to the St. Nicholas ice-skating rink, to a thorough round of the theatres and to a miscellany of entertainments—from small, staid dances to the great affairs that Gloria loved, held in those few houses where lackeys with powdered wigs scurried around in magnificent Anglomania under the direction of gigantic majordomos. Their intention was to go abroad the first of the year or, at any rate, when the war was over. Anthony had actually completed a Chestertonian essay on the twelfth century by way of introduction to his proposed book and Gloria had done some extensive research work on the question of Russian sable coats—in fact the winter was approaching quite comfortably, when the Bilphistic demiurge decided suddenly in mid-December that Mrs. Gilbert's soul had aged sufficiently in its present incarnation. In consequence Anthony took a miserable and hysterical Gloria out to Kansas City, where, in the fashion of mankind, they paid the terrible and mind-shaking deference to the dead.

Mr. Gilbert became, for the first and last time in his life, a truly pathetic figure. That woman he had broken to wait upon his body and play congregation to his mind had ironically deserted him—just when he could not much longer have supported her. Never again would he be able so satisfactorily to bore and bully a human soul.

II. SYMPOSIUM

GLORIA had lulled Anthony's mind to sleep. She, who seemed of all women the wisest and the finest, hung like a brilliant curtain across his doorways, shutting out the light of the sun. In those first years what he believed bore invariably the stamp of Gloria; he saw the sun always through the pattern of the curtain.

It was a sort of lassitude that brought them back to Marietta for another summer. Through a golden enervating spring they had loitered, restive and lazily extravagant, along the California coast, joining other parties intermittently and drifting from Pasadena to Coronado, from Coronado to Santa Barbara, with no purpose more apparent than Gloria's desire to dance by different music or catch some infinitesimal variant among the changing colors of the sea. Out of the Pacific there rose to greet them savage rocklands and equally barbaric hostelries built that at tea-time one might drowse into a languid wicker bazaar glorified by the polo costumes of Southhampton and Lake Forest and Newport and Palm Beach. And, as the waves met and splashed and glittered in the most placid of the bays, so they joined this group and that, and with them shifted stations, murmuring ever of those strange unsubstantial gaieties in wait just over the next green and fruitful valley.

A simple healthy leisure class it was—the best of the men not unpleasantly undergraduate—they seemed to be on a perpetual candidates list for some etherealized "Porcellian" or "Skull and Bones" extended out indefinitely into the world; the women, of more than average beauty, fragilely athletic, somewhat idiotic as hostesses but charming and infinitely decorative as guests. Sedately and gracefully they danced the steps of their selection in the balmy tea hours, accomplishing with a certain dignity the movements so horribly burlesqued by clerk and chorus girl the country over. It seemed ironic that in this lone and discredited offspring of the arts Americans should excel, unquestionably.

Having danced and splashed through a lavish spring, Anthony and Gloria found that they had spent too much money and for this must go into retirement for a certain period. There was Anthony's "work," they said. Almost before they knew it they were back in the gray house, more aware now that other lovers had slept there, other names had been called over the banisters, other couples had sat upon the porch steps watching the gray-green fields and the black bulk of woods beyond.

It was the same Anthony, more restless, inclined to quicken only under the stimulus of several high-balls, faintly, almost imperceptibly, apathetic toward Gloria. But Gloria—she would be twenty-four in August and was in an attractive but sincere panic about it. Six years to thirty! Had she been less in love with Anthony her sense of the flight of time would have expressed itself in a reawakened interest in other men, in a deliberate intention of extracting a transient gleam of romance from every potential lover who glanced at her with lowered brows over a shining dinner table. She said to Anthony one day:

"How I feel is that if I wanted anything I'd take it. That's what I've always thought all my life. But it happens that I want you, and so I just haven't room for any other desires."

They were bound eastward through a parched and lifeless Indiana, and she had looked up from one of her beloved moving picture magazines to find a casual conversation suddenly turned grave.

Anthony frowned out the car window. As the track crossed a country road a farmer appeared momentarily in his wagon; he was chewing on a straw and was apparently the same farmer they had passed a dozen times before, sitting in silent and malignant symbolism. As Anthony turned to Gloria his frown intensified.

"You worry me," he objected; "I can imagine *wanting* another woman under certain transitory circumstances, but I can't imagine taking her."

"But I don't feel that way, Anthony. I can't be bothered resisting things I want. My way is not to want them—to want nobody but you."

"Yet when I think that if you just happened to take a fancy to some one—"

"Oh, don't be an idiot!" she exclaimed. "There'd be nothing casual about it. And I can't even imagine the possibility."

This emphatically closed the conversation. Anthony's unfailing appreciation made her happier in his company than in any one's else. She definitely enjoyed him—she loved him. So the summer began very much as had the one before.

There was, however, one radical change in ménage. The icy-hearted Scandinavian, whose austere cooking and sardonic manner of waiting on table had so depressed Gloria, gave way to an exceedingly efficient Japanese whose name was Tanalahaka, but who confessed that he heeded any summons which included the dissyllable "Tana."

Tana was unusually small even for a Japanese, and displayed a somewhat naïve conception of himself as a man of the world. On the day of his arrival from "R. Gugimoniki, Japanese Reliable Employment Agency," he called Anthony into his room to see the treasures of his trunk. These included a large collection of Japanese post cards, which he was all for explaining to his employer at once, individually and at great length. Among them were half a dozen of pornographic intent and plainly of American origin, though the makers had modestly omitted both their names and the form for mailing. He next brought out some of his own handiwork—a pair of American pants, which he had made himself, and two suits of solid silk underwear. He informed Anthony confidentially as to the purpose for which these latter were reserved. The next exhibit was a rather good copy of an etching of Abraham Lincoln, to whose face he had given an unmistakable Japanese cast. Last came a flute; he had made it himself but it was broken: he was going to fix it soon.

After these polite formalities, which Anthony conjectured must be native to Japan, Tana delivered a long harangue in splintered English on the relation of master and servant from which Anthony gathered that he had worked on large estates but had always quarrelled with the other servants because they were not honest. They had a great time over the word "honest," and in fact became rather irritated with each other, because Anthony persisted stubbornly that Tana was trying to say "hornets," and even went to the extent of buzzing in the manner of a bee and flapping his arms to imitate wings.

After three-quarters of an hour Anthony was released with the warm assurance that they would have other nice chats in which Tana would tell "how we do in my countree."

Such was Tana's garrulous première in the gray house—and he fulfilled its promise. Though he was conscientious and honorable, he was unquestionably a terrific bore. He seemed unable to control his tongue, sometimes continuing from paragraph to paragraph with a look akin to pain in his small brown eyes.

Sunday and Monday afternoons he read the comic sections of the newspapers. One cartoon which contained a facetious Japanese butler diverted him enormously, though he claimed that the protagonist, who to Anthony appeared clearly Oriental, had really an American face. The difficulty with the funny paper was that when, aided by Anthony, he had spelled out the last three pictures and assimilated their context with a concentration surely adequate for Kant's "Critique," he had entirely forgotten what the first pictures were about.

In the middle of June Anthony and Gloria celebrated their first anniversary by having a "date." Anthony knocked at the door and she ran to let him in. Then they sat together on the couch calling over those names they had made for each other, new combinations of endearments ages old. Yet to this "date" was appended no attenuated good-night with its ecstasy of regret.

Later in June horror leered out at Gloria, struck at her and frightened her bright soul back half a generation. Then slowly it faded out, faded back into that impenetrable darkness whence it had come—taking relentlessly its modicum of youth.

With an infallible sense of the dramatic it chose a little railroad station in a wretched village near Portchester. The station platform lay all day bare as a prairie, exposed to the dusty yellow sun and to the glance of that most obnoxious type of countryman who lives near a metropolis and has attained its cheap smartness without its urbanity. A dozen of these yokels, red-eyed, cheerless as scarecrows, saw the incident. Dimly it passed across their confused and uncomprehending minds, taken at its broadest for a coarse joke, at its subtlest for a "shame." Meanwhile there upon the platform a measure of brightness faded from the world.

With Eric Merriam, Anthony had been sitting over a decanter of Scotch all the hot summer afternoon, while Gloria and Constance Merriam swam and sunned themselves at the Beach Club, the latter under a striped parasol-awning, Gloria stretched sensuously upon the soft hot sand, tanning her inevitable legs. Later they had all four played with inconsequential sandwiches; then Gloria had risen, tapping Anthony's knee with her parasol to get his attention.

"We've got to go, dear."

"Now?" He looked at her unwillingly. At that moment nothing seemed of more importance than to idle on that shady porch drinking mellowed Scotch, while his host reminisced interminably on the byplay of some forgotten political campaign.

"We've really got to go," repeated Gloria. "We can get a taxi to the station.... Come on, Anthony!" she commanded a bit more imperiously.

"Now see here—" Merriam, his yarn cut off, made conventional objections, meanwhile provocatively filling his guest's glass with a high-ball that should have been sipped through ten minutes. But at Gloria's annoyed "We really *must!*" Anthony drank it off, got to his feet and made an elaborate bow to his hostess.

"It seems we 'must,'" he said, with little grace.

In a minute he was following Gloria down a garden-walk between tall rose-bushes, her parasol brushing gently the June-blooming leaves. Most inconsiderate, he thought, as they reached the road. He felt with injured naïvete that Gloria should not have interrupted such innocent and harmless enjoyment. The whiskey had both soothed and clarified the restless things in his mind. It occurred to him that she had taken this same attitude several times before. Was he always to retreat from pleasant episodes at a touch of her parasol or a flicker of her eye? His unwillingness blurred to ill will, which rose within him like a resistless bubble. He kept silent, perversely inhibiting a desire to reproach her. They found a taxi in front of the Inn; rode silently to the little station....

Then Anthony knew what he wanted—to assert his will against this cool and impervious girl, to obtain with one magnificent effort a mastery that seemed infinitely desirable.

"Let's go over to see the Barneses," he said without looking at her. "I don't feel like going home."

—Mrs. Barnes, née Rachael Jerryl, had a summer place several miles from Redgate.

"We went there day before yesterday," she answered shortly.

"I'm sure they'd be glad to see us." He felt that that was not a strong enough note, braced himself stubbornly, and added: "I want to see the Barneses. I haven't any desire to go home."

"Well, I haven't any desire to go to the Barneses."

Suddenly they stared at each other.

"Why, Anthony," she said with annoyance, "this is Sunday night and they probably have guests for supper. Why we should go in at this hour—"

"Then why couldn't we have stayed at the Merriams'?" he burst out. "Why go home when we were having a perfectly decent time? They asked us to supper."

"They had to. Give me the money and I'll get the railroad tickets."

"I certainly will not! I'm in no humour for a ride in that damn hot train."

Gloria stamped her foot on the platform.

"Anthony, you act as if you're tight!"

"On the contrary, I'm perfectly sober."

But his voice had slipped into a husky key and she knew with certainty that this was untrue.

"If you're sober you'll give me the money for the tickets."

But it was too late to talk to him that way. In his mind was but one idea—that Gloria was being selfish, that she was always being selfish and would continue to be unless here and now he asserted himself as her master. This was the occasion of all occasions, since for a whim she had deprived him of a pleasure. His determination solidified, approached momentarily a dull and sullen hate.

"I won't go in the train," he said, his voice trembling a little with anger. "We're going to the Barneses."

"I'm not!" she cried. "If you go I'm going home alone."

"Go on, then."

Without a word she turned toward the ticket office; simultaneously he remembered that she had some money with her and that this was not the sort of victory he wanted, the sort he must have. He took a step after her and seized her arm.

"See here!" he muttered, "you're *not* going alone!"

"I certainly am—why, Anthony!" This exclamation as she tried to pull away from him and he only tightened his grasp.

He looked at her with narrowed and malicious eyes.

"Let go!" Her cry had a quality of fierceness. "If you have *any* decency you'll let go."

"Why?" He knew why. But he took a confused and not quite confident pride in holding her there.

"I'm going home, do you understand? And you're going to let me go!"

"No, I'm not."

Her eyes were burning now.

"Are you going to make a scene here?"

"I say you're not going! I'm tired of your eternal selfishness!"

"I only want to go home." Two wrathful tears started from her eyes.

"This time you're going to do what *I* say."

Slowly her body straightened: her head went back in a gesture of infinite scorn.

"I hate you!" Her low words were expelled like venom through her clenched teeth. "Oh, *let* me go! Oh, I *hate* you!" She tried to jerk herself away but he only grasped the other arm. "I hate you! I hate you!"

At Gloria's fury his uncertainty returned, but he felt that now he had gone too far to give in. It seemed that he had always given in and that in her heart she had despised him for it. Ah, she might hate him now, but afterward she would admire him for his dominance.

The approaching train gave out a premonitory siren that tumbled melodramatically toward them down the glistening blue tracks. Gloria tugged and strained to free herself, and words older than the Book of Genesis came to her lips.

"Oh, you brute!" she sobbed. "Oh, you brute! Oh, I hate you! Oh, you brute! Oh—"

On the station platform other prospective passengers were beginning to turn and stare; the drone of the train was audible, it increased to a clamor. Gloria's efforts redoubled, then ceased altogether, and she stood there trembling and hot-eyed at this helpless humiliation, as the engine roared and thundered into the station.

Low, below the flood of steam and the grinding of the brakes came her voice:

"Oh, if there was one *man* here you couldn't do this! You couldn't do this! You coward! You coward, oh, you coward!"

Anthony, silent, trembling himself, gripped her rigidly, aware that faces, dozens of them, curiously unmoved, shadows of a dream, were regarding him. Then the bells distilled metallic crashes that were like physical pain, the smoke-stacks volleyed in slow acceleration at the sky, and in a moment of noise and gray gaseous turbulence the line of faces ran by, moved off, became indistinct—until suddenly there was only the sun slanting east across the tracks and a volume of sound decreasing far off like a train made out of tin thunder. He dropped her arms. He had won.

Now, if he wished, he might laugh. The test was done and he had sustained his will with violence. Let leniency walk in the wake of victory.

"We'll hire a car here and drive back to Marietta," he said with fine reserve.

For answer Gloria seized his hand with both of hers and raising it to her mouth bit deeply into his thumb. He scarcely noticed the pain; seeing the blood spurt he absent-mindedly drew out his handkerchief and wrapped the wound. That too was part of the triumph he supposed—it was inevitable that defeat should thus be resented—and as such was beneath notice.

She was sobbing, almost without tears, profoundly and bitterly.

"I won't go! I won't go! You—can't—make—me—go! You've—you've killed any love I ever had for you, and any respect. But all that's left in me would die before I'd move from this place. Oh, if I'd thought *you'd* lay your hands on me—"

"You're going with me," he said brutally, "if I have to carry you."

He turned, beckoned to a taxicab, told the driver to go to Marietta. The man dismounted and swung the door open. Anthony faced his wife and said between his clenched teeth:

"Will you get in?—or will I *put* you in?"

With a subdued cry of infinite pain and despair she yielded herself up and got into the car.

All the long ride, through the increasing dark of twilight, she sat huddled in her side of the car, her silence broken by an occasional dry and solitary sob. Anthony stared out the window, his mind working dully on the slowly changing significance of what had occurred. Something was wrong—that last cry of Gloria's had struck a chord which echoed posthumously and with incongruous disquiet in his heart. He must be right—yet, she seemed such a pathetic little thing now, broken and dispirited, humiliated beyond the measure of her lot to bear. The sleeves of her dress were torn; her parasol was gone, forgotten on the platform. It was a new costume, he remembered, and she had been so proud of it that very morning when they had left the house.... He began wondering if any one they knew had seen the incident. And persistently there recurred to him her cry:

"All that's left in me would die—"

This gave him a confused and increasing worry. It fitted so well with the Gloria who lay in the corner—no longer a proud Gloria, nor any Gloria he had known. He asked himself if it were possible. While he did not believe she would cease to love him—this, of course, was unthinkable—it was yet problematical whether Gloria without her arrogance, her independence, her virginal confidence and courage, would be the girl of his glory, the radiant woman who was precious and charming because she was ineffably, triumphantly herself.

He was very drunk even then, so drunk as not to realize his own drunkenness. When they reached the gray house he went to his own room and, his mind still wrestling helplessly and sombrely with what he had done, fell into a deep stupor on his bed.

It was after one o'clock and the hall seemed extraordinarily quiet when Gloria, wide-eyed and sleepless, traversed it and pushed open the door of his room. He had been too befuddled to open the windows and the air was stale and thick with whiskey. She stood for a moment by his bed, a slender, exquisitely graceful figure in her boyish silk pajamas—then with abandon she flung herself upon him, half waking him in the frantic emotion of her embrace, dropping her warm tears upon his throat.

"Oh, Anthony!" she cried passionately, "oh, my darling, you don't know what you did!"

Yet in the morning, coming early into her room, he knelt down by her bed and cried like a little boy, as though it was his heart that had been broken.

"It seemed, last night," she said gravely, her fingers playing in his hair, "that all the part of me you loved, the part that was worth knowing, all the pride and fire, was gone. I knew that what was left of me would always love you, but never in quite the same way."

Nevertheless, she was aware even then that she would forget in time and that it is the manner of life seldom to strike but always to wear away. After that morning the incident was never mentioned and its deep wound healed with Anthony's hand—and if there was triumph some darker force than theirs possessed it, possessed the knowledge and the victory.

NIETZSCHEAN INCIDENT

Gloria's independence, like all sincere and profound qualities, had begun unconsciously, but, once brought to her attention by Anthony's fascinated discovery of it, it assumed more nearly the proportions of a formal code. From her conversation it might be assumed that all her energy and vitality went into a violent affirmation of the negative principle "Never give a damn."

"Not for anything or anybody," she said, "except myself and, by implication, for Anthony. That's the rule of all life and if it weren't I'd be that way anyhow. Nobody'd do anything for me if it didn't gratify them to, and I'd do as little for them."

She was on the front porch of the nicest lady in Marietta when she said this, and as she finished she gave a curious little cry and sank in a dead faint to the porch floor.

The lady brought her to and drove her home in her car. It had occurred to the estimable Gloria that she was probably with child.

She lay upon the long lounge down-stairs. Day was slipping warmly out the window, touching the late roses on the porch pillars.

"All I think of ever is that I love you," she wailed. "I value my body because you think it's beautiful. And this body of mine—of yours—to have it grow ugly and shapeless? It's simply intolerable. Oh, Anthony, I'm not afraid of the pain."

He consoled her desperately—but in vain. She continued:

"And then afterward I might have wide hips and be pale, with all my freshness gone and no radiance in my hair."

He paced the floor with his hands in his pockets, asking:

"Is it certain?"

"I don't know anything. I've always hated obstrics, or whatever you call them. I thought I'd have a child some time. But not now."

"Well, for God's sake don't lie there and go to pieces."

Her sobs lapsed. She drew down a merciful silence from the twilight which filled the room. "Turn on the lights," she pleaded. "These days seem so short—June seemed—to—have—longer days when I was a little girl."

The lights snapped on and it was as though blue drapes of softest silk had been dropped behind the windows and the door. Her pallor, her immobility, without grief now, or joy, awoke his sympathy.

"Do you want me to have it?" she asked listlessly.

"I'm indifferent. That is, I'm neutral. If you have it I'll probably be glad. If you don't—well, that's all right too."

"I wish you'd make up your mind one way or the other!"

"Suppose you make up *your* mind."

She looked at him contemptuously, scorning to answer.

"You'd think you'd been singled out of all the women in the world for this crowning indignity."

"What if I do!" she cried angrily. "It isn't an indignity for them. It's their one excuse for living. It's the one thing they're good for. It *is* an indignity for *me*.

"See here, Gloria, I'm with you whatever you do, but for God's sake be a sport about it."

"Oh, don't *fuss* at me!" she wailed.

They exchanged a mute look of no particular significance but of much stress. Then Anthony took a book from the shelf and dropped into a chair.

Half an hour later her voice came out of the intense stillness that pervaded the room and hung like incense on the air.

"I'll drive over and see Constance Merriam to-morrow."

"All right. And I'll go to Tarrytown and see Grampa."

"—You see," she added, "it isn't that I'm afraid—of this or anything else. I'm being true to me, you know."

"I know," he agreed.

THE PRACTICAL MEN

Adam Patch, in a pious rage against the Germans, subsisted on the war news. Pin maps plastered his walls; atlases were piled deep on tables convenient to his hand together with "Photographic Histories of the World War," official Explain-alls, and the "Personal Impressions" of war correspondents and of Privates X, Y, and Z. Several times during Anthony's visit his grandfather's secretary, Edward Shuttleworth, the one-time "Accomplished Gin-physician" of "Pat's Place" in Hoboken, now shod with righteous indignation, would appear with an extra. The old man attacked each paper with untiring fury, tearing out those columns which appeared to him of sufficient pregnancy for preservation and thrusting them into one of his already bulging files.

"Well, what have you been doing?" he asked Anthony blandly. "Nothing? Well, I thought so. I've been intending to drive over and see you, all summer."

"I've been writing. Don't you remember the essay I sent you—the one I sold to The Florentine last winter?"

"Essay? You never sent *me* any essay."

"Oh, yes, I did. We talked about it."

Adam Patch shook his head mildly.

"Oh, no. You never sent *me* any essay. You may have thought you sent it but it never reached me."

"Why, you read it, Grampa," insisted Anthony, somewhat exasperated, "you read it and disagreed with it."

The old man suddenly remembered, but this was made apparent only by a partial falling open of his mouth, displaying rows of gray gums. Eying Anthony with a green and ancient stare he hesitated between confessing his error and covering it up.

"So you're writing," he said quickly. "Well, why don't you go over and write about these Germans? Write something real, something about what's going on, something people can read."

"Anybody can't be a war correspondent," objected Anthony. "You have to have some newspaper willing to buy your stuff. And I can't spare the money to go over as a free-lance."

"I'll send you over," suggested his grandfather surprisingly. "I'll get you over as an authorized correspondent of any newspaper you pick out."

Anthony recoiled from the idea—almost simultaneously he bounded toward it.

"I—don't—know—"

He would have to leave Gloria, whose whole life yearned toward him and enfolded him. Gloria was in trouble. Oh, the thing wasn't feasible—yet—he saw himself in khaki, leaning, as all war correspondents lean, upon a heavy stick, portfolio at shoulder—trying to look like an Englishman. "I'd like to think it over," he, confessed. "It's certainly very kind of you. I'll think it over and I'll let you know."

Thinking it over absorbed him on the journey to New York. He had had one of those sudden flashes of illumination vouchsafed to all men who are dominated by a strong and beloved woman, which show them a world of harder men, more fiercely trained and grappling with the abstractions of thought and war. In that world the arms of Gloria would exist only as the hot embrace of a chance mistress, coolly sought and quickly forgotten....

These unfamiliar phantoms were crowding closely about him when he boarded his train for Marietta, in the Grand Central Station. The car was crowded; he secured the last vacant seat and it was only after several minutes that he gave even a casual glance to the man beside him. When he did he saw a heavy lay of jaw and nose, a curved chin and small, puffed-under eyes. In a moment he recognized Joseph Bloeckman.

Simultaneously they both half rose, were half embarrassed, and exchanged what amounted to a half handshake. Then, as though to complete the matter, they both half laughed.

"Well," remarked Anthony without inspiration, "I haven't seen you for a long time." Immediately he regretted his words and started to add: "I didn't know you lived out this way." But Bloeckman anticipated him by asking pleasantly:

"How's your wife? ..."

"She's very well. How've you been?"

"Excellent." His tone amplified the grandeur of the word.

It seemed to Anthony that during the last year Bloeckman had grown tremendously in dignity. The boiled look was gone, he seemed "done" at last. In addition he was no longer overdressed. The inappropriate facetiousness he had affected in ties had given way to a sturdy dark pattern, and his right hand, which had formerly displayed two heavy rings, was now innocent of ornament and even without the raw glow of a manicure.

This dignity appeared also in his personality. The last aura of the successful travelling-man had faded from him, that deliberate ingratiation of which the lowest form is the bawdy joke in the Pullman smoker. One imagined that, having been fawned upon financially, he had attained aloofness; having been snubbed socially, he had acquired reticence. But whatever had given him weight instead of bulk, Anthony no longer felt a correct superiority in his presence.

"D'you remember Caramel, Richard Caramel? I believe you met him one night."

"I remember. He was writing a book."

"Well, he sold it to the movies. Then they had some scenario man named Jordan work on it. Well, Dick subscribes to a clipping bureau and he's furious because about half the movie reviewers speak of the 'power and strength of William Jordan's "Demon Lover."' Didn't mention old Dick at all. You'd think this fellow Jordan had actually conceived and developed the thing."

Bloeckman nodded comprehensively.

"Most of the contracts state that the original writer's name goes into all the paid publicity. Is Caramel still writing?"

"Oh, yes. Writing hard. Short stories."

"Well, that's fine, that's fine.... You on this train often?"

"About once a week. We live in Marietta."

"Is that so? Well, well! I live near Cos Cob myself. Bought a place there only recently. We're only five miles apart."

"You'll have to come and see us." Anthony was surprised at his own courtesy. "I'm sure Gloria'd be delighted to see an old friend. Anybody'll tell you where the house is—it's our second season there."

"Thank you." Then, as though returning a complementary politeness: "How is your grandfather?"

"He's been well. I had lunch with him to-day."

"A great character," said Bloeckman severely. "A fine example of an American."

THE TRIUMPH OF LETHARGY

Anthony found his wife deep in the porch hammock voluptuously engaged with a lemonade and a tomato sandwich and carrying on an apparently cheery conversation with Tana upon one of Tana's complicated themes.

"In my countree," Anthony recognized his invariable preface, "all time—peoples—eat rice—because haven't got. Cannot eat what no have got." Had his nationality not been desperately apparent one would have thought he had acquired his knowledge of his native land from American primary-school geographies.

When the Oriental had been squelched and dismissed to the kitchen, Anthony turned questioningly to Gloria:

"It's all right," she announced, smiling broadly. "And it surprised me more than it does you."

"There's no doubt?"

"None! Couldn't be!"

They rejoiced happily, gay again with reborn irresponsibility. Then he told her of his opportunity to go abroad, and that he was almost ashamed to reject it.

"What do *you* think? Just tell me frankly."

"Why, Anthony!" Her eyes were startled. "Do you want to go? Without me?"

His face fell—yet he knew, with his wife's question, that it was too late. Her arms, sweet and strangling, were around him, for he had made all such choices back in that room in the Plaza the year before. This was an anachronism from an age of such dreams.

"Gloria," he lied, in a great burst of comprehension, "of course I don't. I was thinking you might go as a nurse or something." He wondered dully if his grandfather would consider this.

As she smiled he realized again how beautiful she was, a gorgeous girl of miraculous freshness and sheerly honorable eyes. She embraced his suggestion with luxurious intensity, holding it aloft like a sun of her own making and basking in its beams. She strung together an amazing synopsis for an extravaganza of martial adventure.

After supper, surfeited with the subject, she yawned. She wanted not to talk but only to read "Penrod," stretched upon the lounge until at midnight she fell asleep. But Anthony, after he had carried her romantically up the stairs, stayed awake to brood upon the day, vaguely angry with her, vaguely dissatisfied.

"What am I going to do?" he began at breakfast. "Here we've been married a year and we've just worried around without even being efficient people of leisure."

"Yes, you ought to do something," she admitted, being in an agreeable and loquacious humor. This was not the first of these discussions, but as they usually developed Anthony in the rôle of protagonist, she had come to avoid them.

"It's not that I have any moral compunctions about work," he continued, "but grampa may die to-morrow and he may live for ten years. Meanwhile we're living above our income and all we've got to show for it is a farmer's car and a few clothes. We keep an apartment that we've only lived in three months and a little old house way off in nowhere. We're frequently bored and yet we won't make any effort to know any one except the same crowd who drift around California all summer wearing sport clothes and waiting for their families to die."

"How you've changed!" remarked Gloria. "Once you told me you didn't see why an American couldn't loaf gracefully."

"Well, damn it, I wasn't married. And the old mind was working at top speed and now it's going round and round like a cog-wheel with nothing to catch it. As a matter of fact I think that if I hadn't met you I *would* have done something. But you make leisure so subtly attractive—"

"Oh, it's all my fault—"

"I didn't mean that, and you know I didn't. But here I'm almost twenty-seven and—"

"Oh," she interrupted in vexation, "you make me tired! Talking as though I were objecting or hindering you!"

"I was just discussing it, Gloria. Can't I discuss—"

"I should think you'd be strong enough to settle—"

"—something with you without—"

"—your own problems without coming to me. You *talk* a lot about going to work. I could use more money very easily, but *I'm* not complaining. Whether you work or not I love you." Her last words were gentle as fine snow upon hard ground. But for the moment neither was attending to the other—they were each engaged in polishing and perfecting his own attitude.

"I have worked—some." This by Anthony was an imprudent bringing up of raw reserves. Gloria laughed, torn between delight and derision; she resented his sophistry as at the same time she admired his nonchalance. She would never blame him for being the ineffectual idler so long as he did it sincerely, from the attitude that nothing much was worth doing.

"Work!" she scoffed. "Oh, you sad bird! You bluffer! Work—that means a great arranging of the desk and the lights, a great sharpening of pencils, and 'Gloria, don't sing!' and 'Please keep that damn Tana away from me,' and 'Let me read you my opening sentence,' and 'I won't be through for a long time, Gloria, so don't stay up for me,' and a tremendous consumption of tea or coffee. And that's all. In just about an hour I hear the old pencil stop scratching and look over. You've got out a book and you're 'looking up' something. Then you're reading. Then yawns—then bed and a great tossing about because you're all full of caffeine and can't sleep. Two weeks later the whole performance over again."

With much difficulty Anthony retained a scanty breech-clout of dignity.

"Now that's a *slight* exaggeration. You know *darn well* I sold an essay to The Florentine—and it attracted a lot of attention considering the circulation of The

Florentine. And what's more, Gloria, you know I sat up till five o'clock in the morning finishing it."

She lapsed into silence, giving him rope. And if he had not hanged himself he had certainly come to the end of it.

"At least," he concluded feebly, "I'm perfectly willing to be a war correspondent."

But so was Gloria. They were both willing—anxious; they assured each other of it. The evening ended on a note of tremendous sentiment, the majesty of leisure, the ill health of Adam Patch, love at any cost.

"Anthony!" she called over the banister one afternoon a week later, "there's some one at the door." Anthony, who had been lolling in the hammock on the sun-speckled south porch, strolled around to the front of the house. A foreign car, large and impressive, crouched like an immense and saturnine bug at the foot of the path. A man in a soft pongee suit, with cap to match, hailed him.

"Hello there, Patch. Ran over to call on you."

It was Bloeckman; as always, infinitesimally improved, of subtler intonation, of more convincing ease.

"I'm awfully glad you did." Anthony raised his voice to a vine-covered window: "Glor-i-*a*! We've got a visitor!"

"I'm in the tub," wailed Gloria politely.

With a smile the two men acknowledged the triumph of her alibi.

"She'll be down. Come round here on the side-porch. Like a drink? Gloria's always in the tub—good third of every day."

"Pity she doesn't live on the Sound."

"Can't afford it."

As coming from Adam Patch's grandson, Bloeckman took this as a form of pleasantry. After fifteen minutes filled with estimable brilliancies, Gloria appeared, fresh in starched yellow, bringing atmosphere and an increase of vitality.

"I want to be a successful sensation in the movies," she announced. "I hear that Mary Pickford makes a million dollars annually."

"You could, you know," said Bloeckman. "I think you'd film very well."

"Would you let me, Anthony? If I only play unsophisticated rôles?"

As the conversation continued in stilted commas, Anthony wondered that to him and Bloeckman both this girl had once been the most stimulating, the most tonic personality they had ever known—and now the three sat like overoiled machines, without conflict, without fear, without elation, heavily enamelled little figures secure beyond enjoyment in a world where death and war, dull emotion and noble savagery were covering a continent with the smoke of terror.

In a moment he would call Tana and they would pour into themselves a gay and delicate poison which would restore them momentarily to the pleasurable excitement of childhood, when every face in a crowd had carried its suggestion of splendid and significant transactions taking place somewhere to some magnificent and illimitable purpose.... Life was no more than this summer afternoon;

a faint wind stirring the lace collar of Gloria's dress; the slow baking drowsiness of the veranda.... Intolerably unmoved they all seemed, removed from any romantic imminency of action. Even Gloria's beauty needed wild emotions, needed poignancy, needed death....

"... Any day next week," Bloeckman was saying to Gloria. "Here—take this card. What they do is to give you a test of about three hundred feet of film, and they can tell pretty accurately from that."

"How about Wednesday?"

"Wednesday's fine. Just phone me and I'll go around with you—"

He was on his feet, shaking hands briskly—then his car was a wraith of dust down the road. Anthony turned to his wife in bewilderment.

"Why, Gloria!"

"You don't mind if I have a trial, Anthony. Just a trial? I've got to go to town Wednesday, *any*how."

"But it's so silly! You don't want to go into the movies—moon around a studio all day with a lot of cheap chorus people."

"Lot of mooning around Mary Pickford does!"

"Everybody isn't a Mary Pickford."

"Well, I can't see how you'd object to my *try*ing."

"I do, though. I hate actors."

"Oh, you make me tired. Do you imagine I have a very thrilling time dozing on this damn porch?"

"You wouldn't mind if you loved me."

"Of course I love you," she said impatiently, making out a quick case for herself. "It's just because I do that I hate to see you go to pieces by just lying around and saying you ought to work. Perhaps if I *did* go into this for a while it'd stir you up so you'd do something."

"It's just your craving for excitement, that's all it is."

"Maybe it is! It's a perfectly natural craving, isn't it?"

"Well, I'll tell you one thing. If you go to the movies I'm going to Europe."

"Well, go on then! *I'm* not stopping you!"

To show she was not stopping him she melted into melancholy tears. Together they marshalled the armies of sentiment—words, kisses, endearments, self-reproaches. They attained nothing. Inevitably they attained nothing. Finally, in a burst of gargantuan emotion each of them sat down and wrote a letter. Anthony's was to his grandfather; Gloria's was to Joseph Bloeckman. It was a triumph of lethargy.

One day early in July Anthony, returned from an afternoon in New York, called up-stairs to Gloria. Receiving no answer he guessed she was asleep and so went into the pantry for one of the little sandwiches that were always prepared for them. He found Tana seated at the kitchen table before a miscellaneous assortment of odds and ends—cigar-boxes, knives, pencils, the tops of cans, and some scraps of paper covered with elaborate figures and diagrams.

"What the devil you doing?" demanded Anthony curiously.

Tana politely grinned.

"I show you," he exclaimed enthusiastically. "I tell—"

"You making a dog-house?"

"No, sa." Tana grinned again. "Make typewutta."

"Typewriter?"

"Yes, sa. I think, oh all time I think, lie in bed think 'bout typewutta."

"So you thought you'd make one, eh?"

"Wait. I tell."

Anthony, munching a sandwich, leaned leisurely against the sink. Tana opened and closed his mouth several times as though testing its capacity for action. Then with a rush he began:

"I been think—typewutta—has, oh, many many many many *thing*. Oh many many many many." "Many keys. I see."

"No-o? *Yes*-key! Many many many many lettah. Like so a-b-c."

"Yes, you're right."

"Wait. I tell." He screwed his face up in a tremendous effort to express himself: "I been think—many words—end same. Like i-n-g."

"You bet. A whole raft of them."

"So—I make—typewutta—quick. Not so many lettah—"

"That's a great idea, Tana. Save time. You'll make a fortune. Press one key and there's 'ing.' Hope you work it out."

Tana laughed disparagingly. "Wait. I tell—" "Where's Mrs. Patch?"

"She out. Wait, I tell—" Again he screwed up his face for action. "*My* typewutta——"

"Where is she?"

"Here—I make." He pointed to the miscellany of junk on the table.

"I mean Mrs. Patch."

"She out." Tana reassured him. "She be back five o'clock, she say."

"Down in the village?"

"No. Went off before lunch. She go Mr. Bloeckman."

Anthony started.

"Went out with Mr. Bloeckman?"

"She be back five."

Without a word Anthony left the kitchen with Tana's disconsolate "I tell" trailing after him. So this was Gloria's idea of excitement, by God! His fists were clenched; within a moment he had worked himself up to a tremendous pitch of indignation. He went to the door and looked out; there was no car in sight and his watch stood at four minutes of five. With furious energy he dashed down to the end of the path—as far as the bend of the road a mile off he could see no car—except—but it was a farmer's flivver. Then, in an undignified pursuit of dignity, he rushed back to the shelter of the house as quickly as he had rushed out.

Pacing up and down the living room he began an angry rehearsal of the speech he would make to her when she came in—

"So this is love!" he would begin—or no, it sounded too much like the popular phrase "So this is Paris!" He must be dignified, hurt, grieved. Anyhow—"So this is what *you* do when I have to go up and trot all day around the hot city on business. No wonder I can't write! No wonder I don't dare let you out of my sight!" He was expanding now, warming to his subject. "I'll tell you," he continued, "I'll tell you—" He paused, catching a familiar ring in the words—then he realized—it was Tana's "I tell."

Yet Anthony neither laughed nor seemed absurd to himself. To his frantic imagination it was already six—seven—eight, and she was never coming! Bloeckman finding her bored and unhappy had persuaded her to go to California with him....

—There was a great to-do out in front, a joyous "Yoho, Anthony!" and he rose trembling, weakly happy to see her fluttering up the path. Bloeckman was following, cap in hand.

"Dearest!" she cried.

"We've been for the best jaunt—all over New York State."

"I'll have to be starting home," said Bloeckman, almost immediately. "Wish you'd both been here when I came."

"I'm sorry I wasn't," answered Anthony dryly. When he had departed Anthony hesitated. The fear was gone from his heart, yet he felt that some protest was ethically apropos. Gloria resolved his uncertainty.

"I knew you wouldn't mind. He came just before lunch and said he had to go to Garrison on business and wouldn't I go with him. He looked so lonesome, Anthony. And I drove his car all the way."

Listlessly Anthony dropped into a chair, his mind tired—tired with nothing, tired with everything, with the world's weight he had never chosen to bear. He was ineffectual and vaguely helpless here as he had always been. One of those personalities who, in spite of all their words, are inarticulate, he seemed to have inherited only the vast tradition of human failure—that, and the sense of death.

"I suppose I don't care," he answered.

One must be broad about these things, and Gloria being young, being beautiful, must have reasonable privileges. Yet it wearied him that he failed to understand.

WINTER

She rolled over on her back and lay still for a moment in the great bed watching the February sun suffer one last attenuated refinement in its passage through the leaded panes into the room. For a time she had no accurate sense of her whereabouts or of the events of the day before, or the day before that; then, like a suspended pendulum, memory began to beat out its story, releasing with each swing a burdened quota of time until her life was given back to her.

She could hear, now, Anthony's troubled breathing beside her; she could smell whiskey and cigarette smoke. She noticed that she lacked complete muscular control; when she moved it was not a sinuous motion with the resultant strain distributed easily over her body—it was a tremendous effort of her nervous system as though each time she were hypnotizing herself into performing an impossible action....

She was in the bathroom, brushing her teeth to get rid of that intolerable taste; then back by the bedside listening to the rattle of Bounds's key in the outer door.

"Wake up, Anthony!" she said sharply.

She climbed into bed beside him and closed her eyes. Almost the last thing she remembered was a conversation with Mr. and Mrs. Lacy. Mrs. Lacy had said, "Sure you don't want us to get you a taxi?" and Anthony had replied that he guessed they could walk over to Fifth all right. Then they had both attempted, imprudently, to bow—and collapsed absurdly into a battalion of empty milk bottles just outside the door. There must have been two dozen milk bottles standing open-mouthed in the dark. She could conceive of no plausible explanation of those milk bottles. Perhaps they had been attracted by the singing in the Lacy house and had hurried over agape with wonder to see the fun. Well, they'd had the worst of it—though it seemed that she and Anthony never would get up, the perverse things rolled so....

Still, they had found a taxi. "My meter's broken and it'll cost you a dollar and a half to get home," said the taxi driver. "Well," said Anthony, "I'm young Packy McFarland and if you'll come down here I'll beat you till you can't stand up." ...At that point the man had driven off without them. They must have found another taxi, for they were in the apartment....

"What time is it?" Anthony was sitting up in bed, staring at her with owlish precision.

This was obviously a rhetorical question. Gloria could think of no reason why she should be expected to know the time.

"Golly, I feel like the devil!" muttered Anthony dispassionately. Relaxing, he tumbled back upon his pillow. "Bring on your grim reaper!"

"Anthony, how'd we finally get home last night?"

"Taxi."

"Oh!" Then, after a pause: "Did you put me to bed?"

"I don't know. Seems to me you put *me* to bed. What day is it?"

"Tuesday."

"Tuesday? I hope so. If it's Wednesday, I've got to start work at that idiotic place. Supposed to be down at nine or some such ungodly hour."

"Ask Bounds," suggested Gloria feebly.

"Bounds!" he called.

Sprightly, sober—a voice from a world that it seemed in the past two days they had left forever, Bounds sprang in short steps down the hall and appeared in the half darkness of the door.

"What day, Bounds?"

"February the twenty-second, I think, sir."

"I mean day of the week."

"Tuesday, sir." "Thanks." After a pause: "Are you ready for breakfast, sir?"

"Yes, and Bounds, before you get it, will you make a pitcher of water, and set it here beside the bed? I'm a little thirsty."

"Yes, sir."

Bounds retreated in sober dignity down the hallway.

"Lincoln's birthday," affirmed Anthony without enthusiasm, "or St. Valentine's or somebody's. When did we start on this insane party?"

"Sunday night."

"After prayers?" he suggested sardonically.

"We raced all over town in those hansoms and Maury sat up with his driver, don't you remember? Then we came home and he tried to cook some bacon—came out of the pantry with a few blackened remains, insisting it was 'fried to the proverbial crisp.'"

Both of them laughed, spontaneously but with some difficulty, and lying there side by side reviewed the chain of events that had ended in this rusty and chaotic dawn.

They had been in New York for almost four months, since the country had grown too cool in late October. They had given up California this year, partly because of lack of funds, partly with the idea of going abroad should this interminable war, persisting now into its second year, end during the winter. Of late their income had lost elasticity; no longer did it stretch to cover gay whims and pleasant extravagances, and Anthony had spent many puzzled and unsatisfactory hours over a densely figured pad, making remarkable budgets that left huge margins for "amusements, trips, etc.," and trying to apportion, even approximately, their past expenditures.

He remembered a time when in going on a "party" with his two best friends, he and Maury had invariably paid more than their share of the expenses. They would buy the tickets for the theatre or squabble between themselves for the dinner check. It had seemed fitting; Dick, with his naïveté and his astonishing fund of information about himself, had been a diverting, almost juvenile, figure—court jester to their royalty. But this was no longer true. It was Dick who always had money; it was Anthony who entertained within limitations—always excepting occasional wild, wine-inspired, check-cashing parties—and it was Anthony who was solemn about it next morning and told the scornful and disgusted Gloria that they'd have to be "more careful next time."

In the two years since the publication of "The Demon Lover," Dick had made over twenty-five thousand dollars, most of it lately, when the reward of the author of fiction had begun to swell unprecedentedly as a result of the voracious hunger of the motion pictures for plots. He received seven hundred dollars for every story, at that time a large emolument for such a young man—he was not quite thirty—and for every one that contained enough "action" (kissing, shooting, and sacrificing) for the movies, he obtained an additional thousand. His stories varied; there was a measure of vitality and a sort of instinctive in all of them, but none attained the personality of "The Demon Lover," and there were several that Anthony considered downright cheap. These, Dick explained severely, were to widen his audience. Wasn't it true that men who had attained real permanence from Shakespeare to Mark Twain had appealed to the many as well as to the elect?

Though Anthony and Maury disagreed, Gloria told him to go ahead and make as much money as he could—that was the only thing that counted anyhow....

Maury, a little stouter, faintly mellower, and more complaisant, had gone to work in Philadelphia. He came to New York once or twice a month and on such occasions the four of them travelled the popular routes from dinner to the theatre, thence to the Frolic or, perhaps, at the urging of the ever-curious Gloria, to one of the cellars of Greenwich Village, notorious through the furious but short-lived vogue of the "new poetry movement."

In January, after many monologues directed at his reticent wife, Anthony determined to "get something to do," for the winter at any rate. He wanted to please his grandfather and even, in a measure, to see how he liked it himself. He discovered during several tentative semi-social calls that employers were not interested in a young man who was only going to "try it for a few months or so." As the grandson of Adam Patch he was received everywhere with marked courtesy, but the old man was a back number now—the heyday of his fame as first an "oppressor" and then an uplifter of the people had been during the twenty years preceding his retirement. Anthony even found several of the younger men who were under the impression that Adam Patch had been dead for some years.

Eventually Anthony went to his grandfather and asked his advice, which turned out to be that he should enter the bond business as a salesman, a tedious suggestion to Anthony, but one that in the end he determined to follow. Sheer money in deft manipulation had fascinations under all circumstances, while almost any side of manufacturing would be insufferably dull. He considered newspaper work but decided that the hours were not ordered for a married man. And he lingered over pleasant fancies of himself either as editor of a brilliant weekly of opinion, an American Mercure de France, or as scintillant producer of satiric comedy and Parisian musical revue. However, the approaches to these latter guilds seemed to be guarded by professional secrets. Men drifted into them by the devious highways of writing and acting. It was palpably impossible to get on a magazine unless you had been on one before.

So in the end he entered, by way of his grandfather's letter, that Sanctum Americanum where sat the president of Wilson, Hiemer and Hardy at his "cleared desk," and issued therefrom employed. He was to begin work on the twenty-third of February.

In tribute to the momentous occasion this two-day revel had been planned, since, he said, after he began working he'd have to get to bed early during the week. Maury Noble had arrived from Philadelphia on a trip that had to do with seeing some man in Wall Street (whom, incidentally, he failed to see), and Richard Caramel had been half persuaded, half tricked into joining them. They had condescended to a wet and fashionable wedding on Monday afternoon, and in the evening had occurred the dénouement: Gloria, going beyond her accustomed limit of four precisely timed cocktails, led them on as gay and joyous a bacchanal as they had ever known, disclosing an astonishing knowledge of ballet steps, and singing songs which she confessed had been taught her by her cook when she was innocent and seventeen. She repeated these by request at intervals throughout the evening with such frank conviviality that Anthony, far from being annoyed, was gratified at this fresh source of entertainment. The occasion was memorable in other ways—a long conversation between Maury and a defunct crab, which he was dragging around on the end of a string, as to whether the crab was fully conversant with the applications of the binomial theorem, and the aforementioned race in two hansom cabs with the sedate and impressive shadows of Fifth Avenue for audience, ending in a labyrinthine escape into the darkness of Central Park. Finally Anthony and Gloria had paid a call on some wild young married people—the Lacys—and collapsed in the empty milk bottles.

Morning now—theirs to add up the checks cashed here and there in clubs, stores, restaurants. Theirs to air the dank staleness of wine and cigarettes out of the tall blue front room, to pick up the broken glass and brush at the stained fabric of chairs and sofas; to give Bounds suits and dresses for the cleaners; finally, to take their smothery half-feverish bodies and faded depressed spirits out into the chill air of February, that life might go on and Wilson, Hiemer and Hardy obtain the services of a vigorous man at nine next morning.

"Do you remember," called Anthony from the bathroom, "when Maury got out at the corner of One Hundred and Tenth Street and acted as a traffic cop, beckoning cars forward and motioning them back? They must have thought he was a private detective."

After each reminiscence they both laughed inordinately, their overwrought nerves responding as acutely and janglingly to mirth as to depression.

Gloria at the mirror was wondering at the splendid color and freshness of her face—it seemed that she had never looked so well, though her stomach hurt her and her head was aching furiously.

The day passed slowly. Anthony, riding in a taxi to his broker's to borrow money on a bond, found that he had only two dollars in his pocket. The fare would cost all of that, but he felt that on this particular afternoon he could not have endured the subway. When the taximetre reached his limit he must get out and walk.

With this his mind drifted off into one of its characteristic day-dreams.... In this dream he discovered that the metre was going too fast—the driver had dishonestly adjusted it. Calmly he reached his destination and then nonchalantly handed the man what he justly owed him. The man showed fight, but almost before his hands were up Anthony had knocked him down with one terrific blow. And when he rose Anthony quickly sidestepped and floored him definitely with a crack in the temple.

... He was in court now. The judge had fined him five dollars and he had no money. Would the court take his check? Ah, but the court did not know him. Well, he could identify himself by having them call his apartment.

... They did so. Yes, it was Mrs. Anthony Patch speaking—but how did she know that this man was her husband? How could she know? Let the police sergeant ask her if she remembered the milk bottles ...

He leaned forward hurriedly and tapped at the glass. The taxi was only at Brooklyn Bridge, but the metre showed a dollar and eighty cents, and Anthony would never have omitted the ten per cent tip.

Later in the afternoon he returned to the apartment. Gloria had also been out—shopping—and was asleep, curled in a corner of the sofa with her purchase locked securely in her arms. Her face was as untroubled as a little girl's, and the bundle that she pressed tightly to her bosom was a child's doll, a profound and infinitely healing balm to her disturbed and childish heart.

DESTINY

It was with this party, more especially with Gloria's part in it, that a decided change began to come over their way of living. The magnificent attitude of not giving a damn altered overnight; from being a mere tenet of Gloria's it became the entire solace and justification for what they chose to do and what consequence it brought. Not to be sorry, not to loose one cry of regret, to live according to a clear code of honor toward each other, and to seek the moment's happiness as fervently and persistently as possible.

"No one cares about us but ourselves, Anthony," she said one day. "It'd be ridiculous for me to go about pretending I felt any obligations toward the world, and as for worrying what people think about me, I simply *don't*, that's all. Since I was a little girl in dancing-school I've been criticised by the mothers of all the little girls who weren't as popular as I was, and I've always looked on criticism as a sort of envious tribute."

This was because of a party in the "Boul' Mich'" one night, where Constance Merriam had seen her as one of a highly stimulated party of four. Constance

Merriam, "as an old school friend," had gone to the trouble of inviting her to lunch next day in order to inform her how terrible it was.

"I told her I couldn't see it," Gloria told Anthony. "Eric Merriam is a sort of sublimated Percy Wolcott—you remember that man in Hot Springs I told you about—his idea of respecting Constance is to leave her at home with her sewing and her baby and her book, and such innocuous amusements, whenever he's going on a party that promises to be anything but deathly dull."

"Did you tell her that?"

"I certainly did. And I told her that what she really objected to was that I was having a better time than she was."

Anthony applauded her. He was tremendously proud of Gloria, proud that she never failed to eclipse whatever other women might be in the party, proud that men were always glad to revel with her in great rowdy groups, without any attempt to do more than enjoy her beauty and the warmth of her vitality.

These "parties" gradually became their chief source of entertainment. Still in love, still enormously interested in each other, they yet found as spring drew near that staying at home in the evening palled on them; books were unreal; the old magic of being alone had long since vanished—instead they preferred to be bored by a stupid musical comedy, or to go to dinner with the most uninteresting of their acquaintances, so long as there would be enough cocktails to keep the conversation from becoming utterly intolerable. A scattering of younger married people who had been their friends in school or college, as well as a varied assortment of single men, began to think instinctively of them whenever color and excitement were needed, so there was scarcely a day without its phone call, its "Wondered what you were doing this evening." Wives, as a rule, were afraid of Gloria—her facile attainment of the centre of the stage, her innocent but nevertheless disturbing way of becoming a favorite with husbands—these things drove them instinctively into an attitude of profound distrust, heightened by the fact that Gloria was largely unresponsive to any intimacy shown her by a woman.

On the appointed Wednesday in February Anthony had gone to the imposing offices of Wilson, Hiemer and Hardy and listened to many vague instructions delivered by an energetic young man of about his own age, named Kahler, who wore a defiant yellow pompadour, and in announcing himself as an assistant secretary gave the impression that it was a tribute to exceptional ability.

"There's two kinds of men here, you'll find," he said. "There's the man who gets to be an assistant secretary or treasurer, gets his name on our folder here, before he's thirty, and there's the man who gets his name there at forty-five. The man who gets his name there at forty-five stays there the rest of his life."

"How about the man who gets it there at thirty?" inquired Anthony politely.

"Why, he gets up here, you see." He pointed to a list of assistant vice-presidents upon the folder. "Or maybe he gets to be president or secretary or treasurer."

"And what about these over here?"

"Those? Oh, those are the trustees—the men with capital."

"I see."

"Now some people," continued Kahler, "think that whether a man gets started early or late depends on whether he's got a college education. But they're wrong."

"I see."

"I had one; I was Buckleigh, class of nineteen-eleven, but when I came down to the Street I soon found that the things that would help me here weren't the fancy things I learned in college. In fact, I had to get a lot of fancy stuff out of my head."

Anthony could not help wondering what possible "fancy stuff" he had learned at Buckleigh in nineteen-eleven. An irrepressible idea that it was some sort of needlework recurred to him throughout the rest of the conversation.

"See that fellow over there?" Kahler pointed to a youngish-looking man with handsome gray hair, sitting at a desk inside a mahogany railing. "That's Mr. Ellinger, the first vice-president. Been everywhere, seen everything; got a fine education."

In vain did Anthony try to open his mind to the romance of finance; he could think of Mr. Ellinger only as one of the buyers of the handsome leather sets of Thackeray, Balzac, Hugo, and Gibbon that lined the walls of the big bookstores.

Through the damp and uninspiring month of March he was prepared for salesmanship. Lacking enthusiasm he was capable of viewing the turmoil and bustle that surrounded him only as a fruitless circumambient striving toward an incomprehensible goal, tangibly evidenced only by the rival mansions of Mr. Frick and Mr. Carnegie on Fifth Avenue. That these portentous vice-presidents and trustees should be actually the fathers of the "best men" he had known at Harvard seemed to him incongruous.

He ate in an employees' lunch-room up-stairs with an uneasy suspicion that he was being uplifted, wondering through that first week if the dozens of young clerks, some of them alert and immaculate, and just out of college, lived in flamboyant hope of crowding onto that narrow slip of cardboard before the catastrophic thirties. The conversation that interwove with the pattern of the day's work was all much of a piece. One discussed how Mr. Wilson had made his money, what method Mr. Hiemer had employed, and the means resorted to by Mr. Hardy. One related age-old but eternally breathless anecdotes of the fortunes stumbled on precipitously in the Street by a "butcher" or a "bartender," or "a darn *mess*enger boy, by golly!" and then one talked of the current gambles, and whether it was best to go out for a hundred thousand a year or be content with twenty. During the preceding year one of the assistant secretaries had invested all his savings in Bethlehem Steel. The story of his spectacular magnificence, of his haughty resignation in January, and of the triumphal palace he was now building in California, was the favorite office subject. The man's very name had acquired a magic significance, symbolizing as he did the aspirations of all good

Americans. Anecdotes were told about him—how one of the vice-presidents had advised him to sell, by golly, but he had hung on, even bought on margin, "and *now* look where he is!"

Such, obviously, was the stuff of life—a dizzy triumph dazzling the eyes of all of them, a gypsy siren to content them with meagre wage and with the arithmetical improbability of their eventual success.

To Anthony the notion became appalling. He felt that to succeed here the idea of success must grasp and limit his mind. It seemed to him that the essential element in these men at the top was their faith that their affairs were the very core of life. All other things being equal, self-assurance and opportunism won out over technical knowledge; it was obvious that the more expert work went on near the bottom—so, with appropriate efficiency, the technical experts were kept there.

His determination to stay in at night during the week did not survive, and a good half of the time he came to work with a splitting, sickish headache and the crowded horror of the morning subway ringing in his ears like an echo of hell.

Then, abruptly, he quit. He had remained in bed all one Monday, and late in the evening, overcome by one of those attacks of moody despair to which he periodically succumbed, he wrote and mailed a letter to Mr. Wilson, confessing that he considered himself ill adapted to the work. Gloria, coming in from the theatre with Richard Caramel, found him on the lounge, silently staring at the high ceiling, more depressed and discouraged than he had been at any time since their marriage.

She wanted him to whine. If he had she would have reproached him bitterly, for she was not a little annoyed, but he only lay there so utterly miserable that she felt sorry for him, and kneeling down she stroked his head, saying how little it mattered, how little anything mattered so long as they loved each other. It was like their first year, and Anthony, reacting to her cool hand, to her voice that was soft as breath itself upon his ear, became almost cheerful, and talked with her of his future plans. He even regretted, silently, before he went to bed that he had so hastily mailed his resignation.

"Even when everything seems rotten you can't trust that judgment," Gloria had said. "It's the sum of all your judgments that counts."

In mid-April came a letter from the real-estate agent in Marietta, encouraging them to take the gray house for another year at a slightly increased rental, and enclosing a lease made out for their signatures. For a week lease and letter lay carelessly neglected on Anthony's desk. They had no intention of returning to Marietta. They were weary of the place, and had been bored most of the preceding summer. Besides, their car had deteriorated to a rattling mass of hypochondriacal metal, and a new one was financially inadvisable.

But because of another wild revel, enduring through four days and participated in, at one time or another, by more than a dozen people, they did sign the lease; to their utter horror they signed it and sent it, and immediately it seemed as though they heard the gray house, drably malevolent at last, licking its white chops and waiting to devour them.

"Anthony, where's that lease?" she called in high alarm one Sunday morning, sick and sober to reality. "Where did you leave it? It was here!"

Then she knew where it was. She remembered the house party they had planned on the crest of their exuberance; she remembered a room full of men to whose less exhilarated moments she and Anthony were of no importance, and Anthony's boast of the transcendent merit and seclusion of the gray house, that it was so isolated that it didn't matter how much noise went on there. Then Dick, who had visited them, cried enthusiastically that it was the best little house imaginable, and that they were idiotic not to take it for another summer. It had been easy to work themselves up to a sense of how hot and deserted the city was getting, of how cool and ambrosial were the charms of Marietta. Anthony had picked up the lease and waved it wildly, found Gloria happily acquiescent, and with one last burst of garrulous decision during which all the men agreed with solemn handshakes that they would come out for a visit ...

"Anthony," she cried, "we've signed and sent it!"

"What?"

"The lease!"

"What the devil!"

"Oh, *An*thony!" There was utter misery in her voice. For the summer, for eternity, they had built themselves a prison. It seemed to strike at the last roots of their stability. Anthony thought they might arrange it with the real-estate agent. They could no longer afford the double rent, and going to Marietta meant giving up his apartment, his reproachless apartment with the exquisite bath and the rooms for which he had bought his furniture and hangings—it was the closest to a home that he had ever had—familiar with memories of four colorful years.

But it was not arranged with the real-estate agent, nor was it arranged at all. Dispiritedly, without even any talk of making the best of it, without even Gloria's all-sufficing "I don't care," they went back to the house that they now knew heeded neither youth nor love—only those austere and incommunicable memories that they could never share.

THE SINISTER SUMMER

There was a horror in the house that summer. It came with them and settled itself over the place like a sombre pall, pervasive through the lower rooms, gradually spreading and climbing up the narrow stairs until it oppressed their very sleep. Anthony and Gloria grew to hate being there alone. Her bedroom, which had seemed so pink and young and delicate, appropriate to her pastel-shaded lingerie tossed here and there on chair and bed, seemed now to whisper with its rustling curtains:

"Ah, my beautiful young lady, yours is not the first daintiness and delicacy that has faded here under the summer suns ... generations of unloved women have adorned themselves by that glass for rustic lovers who paid no heed.... Youth has come into this room in palest blue and left it in the gray cerements of despair, and through long nights many girls have lain awake where that bed stands pouring out waves of misery into the darkness."

Gloria finally tumbled all her clothes and unguents ingloriously out of it, declaring that she had come to live with Anthony, and making the excuse that one of her screens was rotten and admitted bugs. So her room was abandoned to insensitive guests, and they dressed and slept in her husband's chamber, which Gloria considered somehow "good," as though Anthony's presence there had acted as exterminator of any uneasy shadows of the past that might have hovered about its walls.

The distinction between "good" and "bad," ordered early and summarily out of both their lives, had been reinstated in another form. Gloria insisted that any one invited to the gray house must be "good," which, in the case of a girl, meant that she must be either simple and reproachless or, if otherwise, must possess a certain solidity and strength. Always intensely sceptical of her sex, her judgments were now concerned with the question of whether women were or were not clean. By uncleanliness she meant a variety of things, a lack of pride, a slackness in fibre and, most of all, the unmistakable aura of promiscuity.

"Women soil easily," she said, "far more easily than men. Unless a girl's very young and brave it's almost impossible for her to go down-hill without a certain hysterical animality, the cunning, dirty sort of animality. A man's different—and I suppose that's why one of the commonest characters of romance is a man going gallantly to the devil."

She was disposed to like many men, preferably those who gave her frank homage and unfailing entertainment—but often with a flash of insight she told Anthony that some one of his friends was merely using him, and consequently had best be left alone. Anthony customarily demurred, insisting that the accused was a "good one," but he found that his judgment was more fallible than hers, memorably when, as it happened on several occasions, he was left with a succession of restaurant checks for which to render a solitary account.

More from their fear of solitude than from any desire to go through the fuss and bother of entertaining, they filled the house with guests every week-end, and often on through the week. The week-end parties were much the same. When the three or four men invited had arrived, drinking was more or less in order, followed by a hilarious dinner and a ride to the Cradle Beach Country Club, which they had joined because it was inexpensive, lively if not fashionable, and almost a necessity for just such occasions as these. Moreover, it was of no great moment what one did there, and so long as the Patch party were reasonably inaudible, it mattered little whether or not the social dictators of Cradle Beach saw the gay Gloria imbibing cocktails in the supper room at frequent intervals during the evening.

Saturday ended, generally, in a glamourous confusion—it proving often necessary to assist a muddled guest to bed. Sunday brought the New York papers and a quiet morning of recuperating on the porch—and Sunday afternoon meant good-by to the one or two guests who must return to the city, and a great revival of drinking among the one or two who remained until next day, concluding in a convivial if not hilarious evening.

The faithful Tana, pedagogue by nature and man of all work by profession, had returned with them. Among their more frequent guests a tradition had sprung up about him. Maury Noble remarked one afternoon that his real name was Tannenbaum, and that he was a German agent kept in this country to disseminate Teutonic propaganda through Westchester County, and, after that, mysterious letters began to arrive from Philadelphia addressed to the bewildered Oriental as "Lt. Emile Tannenbaum," containing a few cryptic messages signed "General Staff," and adorned with an atmospheric double column of facetious Japanese. Anthony always handed them to Tana without a smile; hours afterward the recipient could be found puzzling over them in the kitchen and declaring earnestly that the perpendicular symbols were not Japanese, nor anything resembling Japanese.

Gloria had taken a strong dislike to the man ever since the day when, returning unexpectedly from the village, she had discovered him reclining on Anthony's bed, puzzling out a newspaper. It was the instinct of all servants to be fond of Anthony and to detest Gloria, and Tana was no exception to the rule. But he was thoroughly afraid of her and made plain his aversion only in his moodier moments by subtly addressing Anthony with remarks intended for her ear:

"What Miz Pats want dinner?" he would say, looking at his master. Or else he would comment about the bitter selfishness of "'Merican peoples" in such manner that there was no doubt who were the "peoples" referred to.

But they dared not dismiss him. Such a step would have been abhorrent to their inertia. They endured Tana as they endured ill weather and sickness of the body and the estimable Will of God—as they endured all things, even themselves.

IN DARKNESS

One sultry afternoon late in July Richard Caramel telephoned from New York that he and Maury were coming out, bringing a friend with them. They arrived about five, a little drunk, accompanied by a small, stocky man of thirty-five, whom they introduced as Mr. Joe Hull, one of the best fellows that Anthony and Gloria had ever met.

Joe Hull had a yellow beard continually fighting through his skin and a low voice which varied between basso profundo and a husky whisper. Anthony, carrying Maury's suitcase up-stairs, followed into the room and carefully closed the door.

"Who is this fellow?" he demanded.

Maury chuckled enthusiastically.

"Who, Hull? Oh, *he's* all right. He's a good one."

"Yes, but who is he?"

"Hull? He's just a good fellow. He's a prince." His laughter redoubled, culminating in a succession of pleasant catlike grins. Anthony hesitated between a smile and a frown.

"He looks sort of funny to me. Weird-looking clothes"—he paused—"I've got a sneaking suspicion you two picked him up somewhere last night."

"Ridiculous," declared Maury. "Why, I've known him all my life." However, as he capped this statement with another series of chuckles, Anthony was impelled to remark: "The devil you have!"

Later, just before dinner, while Maury and Dick were conversing uproariously, with Joe Hull listening in silence as he sipped his drink, Gloria drew Anthony into the dining room:

"I don't like this man Hull," she said. "I wish he'd use Tana's bathtub."

"I can't very well ask him to."

"Well, I don't want him in ours."

"He seems to be a simple soul."

"He's got on white shoes that look like gloves. I can see his toes right through them. Uh! Who is he, anyway?"

"You've got me."

"Well, I think they've got their nerve to bring him out here. This isn't a Sailor's Rescue Home!"

"They were tight when they phoned. Maury said they've been on a party since yesterday afternoon."

Gloria shook her head angrily, and saying no more returned to the porch. Anthony saw that she was trying to forget her uncertainty and devote herself to enjoying the evening.

It had been a tropical day, and even into late twilight the heat-waves emanating from the dry road were quivering faintly like undulating panes of isinglass. The sky was cloudless, but far beyond the woods in the direction of the Sound a faint and persistent rolling had commenced. When Tana announced dinner the men, at a word from Gloria, remained coatless and went inside.

Maury began a song, which they accomplished in harmony during the first course. It had two lines and was sung to a popular air called Daisy Dear. The lines were:

"The—pan-ic—has—come—over us,
So *ha-a-as*—the moral de*cline*!"

Each rendition was greeted with bursts of enthusiasm and prolonged applause.

"Cheer up, Gloria!" suggested Maury. "You seem the least bit depressed."

"I'm not," she lied.

"Here, Tannenbaum!" he called over his shoulder. "I've filled you a drink. Come on!"

Gloria tried to stay his arm.

"Please don't, Maury!"

"Why not? Maybe he'll play the flute for us after dinner. Here, Tana."

Tana, grinning, bore the glass away to the kitchen. In a few moments Maury gave him another.

"Cheer up, Gloria!" he cried. "For Heaven's sakes everybody, cheer up Gloria."

"Dearest, have another drink," counselled Anthony.

"Do, please!"

"Cheer up, Gloria," said Joe Hull easily.

Gloria winced at this uncalled-for use of her first name, and glanced around to see if any one else had noticed it. The word coming so glibly from the lips of a man to whom she had taken an inordinate dislike repelled her. A moment later she noticed that Joe Hull had given Tana another drink, and her anger increased, heightened somewhat from the effects of the alcohol.

"—and once," Maury was saying, "Peter Granby and I went into a Turkish bath in Boston, about two o'clock at night. There was no one there but the proprietor, and we jammed him into a closet and locked the door. Then a fella came in and wanted a Turkish bath. Thought we were the rubbers, by golly! Well, we just picked him up and tossed him into the pool with all his clothes on. Then we dragged him out and laid him on a slab and slapped him until he was black and blue. 'Not so rough, fellows!' he'd say in a little squeaky voice, 'please! ...'"

—Was this Maury? thought Gloria. From any one else the story would have amused her, but from Maury, the infinitely appreciative, the apotheosis of tact and consideration....

"The—pan-ic—has—come—over us,
So *ha-a-as*—"

A drum of thunder from outside drowned out the rest of the song; Gloria shivered and tried to empty her glass, but the first taste nauseated her, and she set it down. Dinner was over and they all marched into the big room, bearing several bottles and decanters. Some one had closed the porch door to keep out the wind, and in consequence circular tentacles of cigar smoke were twisting already upon the heavy air.

"Paging Lieutenant Tannenbaum!" Again it was the changeling Maury. "Bring us the flute!"

Anthony and Maury rushed into the kitchen; Richard Caramel started the phonograph and approached Gloria.

"Dance with your well-known cousin."

"I don't want to dance."

"Then I'm going to carry you around."

As though he were doing something of overpowering importance, he picked her up in his fat little arms and started trotting gravely about the room.

"Set me down, Dick! I'm dizzy!" she insisted.

He dumped her in a bouncing bundle on the couch, and rushed off to the kitchen, shouting "Tana! Tana!"

Then, without warning, she felt other arms around her, felt herself lifted from the lounge. Joe Hull had picked her up and was trying, drunkenly, to imitate Dick.

"Put me down!" she said sharply.

His maudlin laugh, and the sight of that prickly yellow jaw close to her face stirred her to intolerable disgust.

"At once!"

"The—pan-ic—" he began, but got no further, for Gloria's hand swung around swiftly and caught him in the cheek. At this he all at once let go of her, and she fell to the floor, her shoulder hitting the table a glancing blow in transit....

Then the room seemed full of men and smoke. There was Tana in his white coat reeling about supported by Maury. Into his flute he was blowing a weird blend of sound that was known, cried Anthony, as the Japanese train-song. Joe Hull had found a box of candles and was juggling them, yelling "One down!" every time he missed, and Dick was dancing by himself in a fascinated whirl around and about the room. It appeared to her that everything in the room was staggering in grotesque fourth-dimensional gyrations through intersecting planes of hazy blue.

Outside, the storm had come up amazingly—the lulls within were filled with the scrape of the tall bushes against the house and the roaring of the rain on the tin roof of the kitchen. The lightning was interminable, letting down thick drips of thunder like pig iron from the heart of a white-hot furnace. Gloria could see that the rain was spitting in at three of the windows—but she could not move to shut them....

... She was in the hall. She had said good night but no one had heard or heeded her. It seemed for an instant as though something had looked down over the head of the banister, but she could not have gone back into the living room—better madness than the madness of that clamor.... Up-stairs she fumbled for the electric switch and missed it in the darkness; a roomful of lightning showed her the button plainly on the wall. But when the impenetrable black shut down, it again eluded her fumbling fingers, so she slipped off her dress and petticoat and threw herself weakly on the dry side of the half-drenched bed.

She shut her eyes. From down-stairs arose the babel of the drinkers, punctured suddenly by a tinkling shiver of broken glass, and then another, and by a soaring fragment of unsteady, irregular song....

She lay there for something over two hours—so she calculated afterward, sheerly by piecing together the bits of time. She was conscious, even aware, after a long while that the noise down-stairs had lessened, and that the storm was moving off westward, throwing back lingering showers of sound that fell, heavy and lifeless as her soul, into the soggy fields. This was succeeded by a slow, reluctant scattering of the rain and wind, until there was nothing outside her windows but a gentle dripping and the swishing play of a cluster of wet vine against the sill. She was in a state half-way between sleeping and waking, with neither condition predominant ... and she was harassed by a desire to rid herself of a weight pressing down upon her breast. She felt that if she could cry the weight would be lifted, and forcing the lids of her eyes together she tried to raise a lump in her throat ... to no avail....

Drip! Drip! Drip! The sound was not unpleasant—like spring, like a cool rain of her childhood, that made cheerful mud in her back yard and watered the tiny garden she had dug with miniature rake and spade and hoe. Drip—dri-ip! It was like days when the rain came out of yellow skies that melted just before twilight and shot one radiant shaft of sunlight diagonally down the heavens into the damp green trees. So cool, so clear and clean—and her mother there at the centre of the world, at the centre of the rain, safe and dry and strong. She wanted her mother now, and her mother was dead, beyond sight and touch forever. And this weight was pressing on her, pressing on her—oh, it pressed on her so!

She became rigid. Some one had come to the door and was standing regarding her, very quiet except for a slight swaying motion. She could see the outline of his figure distinct against some indistinguishable light. There was no sound anywhere, only a great persuasive silence—even the dripping had ceased ... only this figure, swaying, swaying in the doorway, an indiscernible and subtly menacing terror, a personality filthy under its varnish, like smallpox spots under a layer of powder. Yet her tired heart, beating until it shook her breasts, made her sure that there was still life in her, desperately shaken, threatened....

The minute or succession of minutes prolonged itself interminably, and a swimming blur began to form before her eyes, which tried with childish persistence to pierce the gloom in the direction of the door. In another instant it seemed that some unimaginable force would shatter her out of existence ... and then the figure in the doorway—it was Hull, she saw, Hull—turned deliberately and, still slightly swaying, moved back and off, as if absorbed into that incomprehensible light that had given him dimension.

Blood rushed back into her limbs, blood and life together. With a start of energy she sat upright, shifting her body until her feet touched the floor over the side of the bed. She knew what she must do—now, now, before it was too late. She must go out into this cool damp, out, away, to feel the wet swish of the grass around her feet and the fresh moisture on her forehead. Mechanically she struggled into her clothes, groping in the dark of the closet for a hat. She must go from this house where the thing hovered that pressed upon her bosom, or else made itself into stray, swaying figures in the gloom.

In a panic she fumbled clumsily at her coat, found the sleeve just as she heard Anthony's footsteps on the lower stair. She dared not wait; he might not let her go, and even Anthony was part of this weight, part of this evil house and the sombre darkness that was growing up about it....

Through the hall then ... and down the back stairs, hearing Anthony's voice in the bedroom she had just left—

"Gloria! Gloria!"

But she had reached the kitchen now, passed out through the doorway into the night. A hundred drops, startled by a flare of wind from a dripping tree, scattered on her and she pressed them gladly to her face with hot hands.

"Gloria! Gloria!"

The voice was infinitely remote, muffed and made plaintive by the walls she had just left. She rounded the house and started down the front path toward the road, almost exultant as she turned into it, and followed the carpet of short grass alongside, moving with caution in the intense darkness.

"Gloria!"

She broke into a run, stumbled over the segment of a branch twisted off by the wind. The voice was outside the house now. Anthony, finding the bedroom deserted, had come onto the porch. But this thing was driving her forward; it was back there with Anthony, and she must go on in her flight under this dim and oppressive heaven, forcing herself through the silence ahead as though it were a tangible barrier before her.

She had gone some distance along the barely discernible road, probably half a mile, passed a single deserted barn that loomed up, black and foreboding, the only building of any sort between the gray house and Marietta; then she turned the fork, where the road entered the wood and ran between two high walls of leaves and branches that nearly touched overhead. She noticed suddenly a thin, longitudinal gleam of silver upon the road before her, like a bright sword half embedded in the mud. As she came closer she gave a little cry of satisfaction—it was a wagon-rut full of water, and glancing heavenward she saw a light rift of sky and knew that the moon was out.

"Gloria!"

She started violently. Anthony was not two hundred feet behind her.

"Gloria, wait for me!"

She shut her lips tightly to keep from screaming, and increased her gait. Before she had gone another hundred yards the woods disappeared, rolling back like a dark stocking from the leg of the road. Three minutes' walk ahead of her, suspended in the now high and limitless air, she saw a thin interlacing of attenuated gleams and glitters, centred in a regular undulation on some one invisible point. Abruptly she knew where she would go. That was the great cascade of wires that rose high over the river, like the legs of a gigantic spider whose eye was the little green light in the switch-house, and ran with the railroad bridge in the direction of the station. The station! There would be the train to take her away.

"Gloria, it's me! It's Anthony! Gloria, I won't try to stop you! For God's sake, where are you?"

She made no answer but began to run, keeping on the high side of the road and leaping the gleaming puddles—dimensionless pools of thin, unsubstantial gold. Turning sharply to the left, she followed a narrow wagon road, serving to avoid a dark body on the ground. She looked up as an owl hooted mournfully from a solitary tree. Just ahead of her she could see the trestle that led to the railroad bridge and the steps mounting up to it. The station lay across the river.

Another sounds startled her, the melancholy siren of an approaching train, and almost simultaneously, a repeated call, thin now and far away.

"Gloria! Gloria!"

Anthony must have followed the main road. She laughed with a sort of malicious cunning at having eluded him; she could spare the time to wait until the train went by.

The siren soared again, closer at hand, and then, with no anticipatory roar and clamor, a dark and sinuous body curved into view against the shadows far down the high-banked track, and with no sound but the rush of the cleft wind and the clocklike tick of the rails, moved toward the bridge—it was an electric train. Above the engine two vivid blurs of blue light formed incessantly a radiant crackling bar between them, which, like a spluttering flame in a lamp beside a corpse, lit for an instant the successive rows of trees and caused Gloria to draw back instinctively to the far side of the road. The light was tepid, the temperature of warm blood.... The clicking blended suddenly with itself in a rush of even sound, and then, elongating in sombre elasticity, the thing roared blindly by her and thundered onto the bridge, racing the lurid shaft of fire it cast into the solemn river alongside. Then it contracted swiftly, sucking in its sound until it left only a reverberant echo, which died upon the farther bank.

Silence crept down again over the wet country; the faint dripping resumed, and suddenly a great shower of drops tumbled upon Gloria stirring her out of the trance-like torpor which the passage of the train had wrought. She ran swiftly down a descending level to the bank and began climbing the iron stairway to the bridge, remembering that it was something she had always wanted to do, and that she would have the added excitement of traversing the yard-wide plank that ran beside the tracks over the river.

There! This was better. She was at the top now and could see the lands about her as successive sweeps of open country, cold under the moon, coarsely patched and seamed with thin rows and heavy clumps of trees. To her right, half a mile down the river, which trailed away behind the light like the shiny, slimy path of a snail, winked the scattered lights of Marietta. Not two hundred yards away at the end of the bridge squatted the station, marked by a sullen lantern.

The oppression was lifted now—the tree-tops below her were rocking the young starlight to a haunted doze. She stretched out her arms with a gesture of free dom. This was what she had wanted, to stand alone where it was high and cool.

"Gloria!"

Like a startled child she scurried along the plank, hopping, skipping, jumping, with an ecstatic sense of her own physical lightness. Let him come now—she no longer feared that, only she must first reach the station, because that was part of the game. She was happy. Her hat, snatched off, was clutched tightly in her hand, and her short curled hair bobbed up and down about her ears. She had thought she would never feel so young again, but this was her night, her world. Triumphantly she laughed as she left the plank, and reaching the wooden platform flung herself down happily beside an iron roof-post.

"Here I am!" she called, gay as the dawn in her elation. "Here I am, Anthony, dear—old, worried Anthony."

"Gloria!" He reached the platform, ran toward her. "Are you all right?" Coming up he knelt and took her in his arms.

"Yes."

"What was the matter? Why did you leave?" he queried anxiously.

"I had to—there was something"—she paused and a flicker of uneasiness lashed at her mind—"there was something sitting on me—here." She put her hand on her breast. "I had to go out and get away from it."

"What do you mean by 'something'?"

"I don't know—that man Hull—"

"Did he bother you?"

"He came to my door, drunk. I think I'd gotten sort of crazy by that time."

"Gloria, dearest—"

Wearily she laid her head upon his shoulder.

"Let's go back," he suggested.

She shivered.

"Uh! No, I couldn't. It'd come and sit on me again." Her voice rose to a cry that hung plaintive on the darkness. "That thing—"

"There—there," he soothed her, pulling her close to him. "We won't do anything you don't want to do. What do you want to do? Just sit here?"

"I want—I want to go away."

"Where?"

"Oh—anywhere."

"By golly, Gloria," he cried, "you're still tight!"

"No, I'm not. I haven't been, all evening. I went up-stairs about, oh, I don't know, about half an hour after dinner ...Ouch!"

He had inadvertently touched her right shoulder.

"It hurts me. I hurt it some way. I don't know—somebody picked me up and dropped me."

"Gloria, come home. It's late and damp."

"I can't," she wailed. "Oh, Anthony, don't ask me to! I will to-morrow. You go home and I'll wait here for a train. I'll go to a hotel—"

"I'll go with you."

"No, I don't want you with me. I want to be alone. I want to sleep—oh, I want to sleep. And then to-morrow, when you've got all the smell of whiskey and cigarettes out of the house, and everything straight, and Hull is gone, then I'll come home. If I went now, that thing—oh—!" She covered her eyes with her hand; Anthony saw the futility of trying to persuade her.

"I was all sober when you left," he said. "Dick was asleep on the lounge and Maury and I were having a discussion. That fellow Hull had wandered off somewhere. Then I began to realize I hadn't seen you for several hours, so I went upstairs—"

He broke off as a salutatory "Hello, there!" boomed suddenly out of the darkness. Gloria sprang to her feet and he did likewise.

"It's Maury's voice," she cried excitedly. "If it's Hull with him, keep them away, keep them away!"

"Who's there?" Anthony called.

"Just Dick and Maury," returned two voices reassuringly.

"Where's Hull?"

"He's in bed. Passed out."

Their figures appeared dimly on the platform.

"What the devil are you and Gloria doing here?" inquired Richard Caramel with sleepy bewilderment.

"What are *you* two doing here?"

Maury laughed.

"Damned if I know. We followed you, and had the deuce of a time doing it. I heard you out on the porch yelling for Gloria, so I woke up the Caramel here and got it through his head, with some difficulty, that if there was a search-party we'd better be on it. He slowed me up by sitting down in the road at intervals and asking me what it was all about. We tracked you by the pleasant scent of Canadian Club."

There was a rattle of nervous laughter under the low train-shed.

"How did you track us, really?"

"Well, we followed along down the road and then we suddenly lost you. Seems you turned off at a wagontrail. After a while somebody hailed us and asked us if we were looking for a young girl. Well, we came up and found it was a little shivering old man, sitting on a fallen tree like somebody in a fairy tale. 'She turned down here,' he said, 'and most steppud on me, goin' somewhere in an awful hustle, and then a fella in short golfin' pants come runnin' along and went after her. He throwed me this.' The old fellow had a dollar bill he was waving around—"

"Oh, the poor old man!" ejaculated Gloria, moved.

"I threw him another and we went on, though he asked us to stay and tell him what it was all about."

"Poor old man," repeated Gloria dismally.

Dick sat down sleepily on a box.

"And now what?" he inquired in the tone of stoic resignation.

"Gloria's upset," explained Anthony. "She and I are going to the city by the next train."

Maury in the darkness had pulled a time-table from his pocket.

"Strike a match."

A tiny flare leaped out of the opaque background illuminating the four faces, grotesque and unfamiliar here in the open night.

"Let's see. Two, two-thirty—no, that's evening. By gad, you won't get a train till five-thirty."

Anthony hesitated.

"Well," he muttered uncertainly, "we've decided to stay here and wait for it. You two might as well go back and sleep."

"You go, too, Anthony," urged Gloria; "I want you to have some sleep, dear. You've been as pale as a ghost all day."

"Why, you little idiot!"

Dick yawned.

"Very well. You stay, we stay."

He walked out from under the shed and surveyed the heavens.

"Rather a nice night, after all. Stars are out and everything. Exceptionally tasty assortment of them."

"Let's see." Gloria moved after him and the other two followed her. "Let's sit out here," she suggested. "I like it much better."

Anthony and Dick converted a long box into a backrest and found a board dry enough for Gloria to sit on. Anthony dropped down beside her and with some effort Dick hoisted himself onto an apple-barrel near them.

"Tana went to sleep in the porch hammock," he remarked. "We carried him in and left him next to the kitchen stove to dry. He was drenched to the skin."

"That awful little man!" sighed Gloria.

"How do you do!" The voice, sonorous and funereal, had come from above, and they looked up startled to find that in some manner Maury had climbed to the roof of the shed, where he sat dangling his feet over the edge, outlined as a shadowy and fantastic gargoyle against the now brilliant sky.

"It must be for such occasions as this," he began softly, his words having the effect of floating down from an immense height and settling softly upon his auditors, "that the righteous of the land decorate the railroads with bill-boards asserting in red and yellow that 'Jesus Christ is God,' placing them, appropriately enough, next to announcements that 'Gunter's Whiskey is Good.'"

There was gentle laughter and the three below kept their heads tilted upward.

"I think I shall tell you the story of my education," continued Maury, "under these sardonic constellations."

"Do! Please!"

"Shall I, really?"

They waited expectantly while he directed a ruminative yawn toward the white smiling moon.

"Well," he began, "as an infant I prayed. I stored up prayers against future wickedness. One year I stored up nineteen hundred 'Now I lay me's.'"

"Throw down a cigarette," murmured some one.

A small package reached the platform simultaneously with the stentorian command:

"Silence! I am about to unburden myself of many memorable remarks reserved for the darkness of such earths and the brilliance of such skies."

Below, a lighted match was passed from cigarette to cigarette. The voice resumed:

"I was adept at fooling the deity. I prayed immediately after all crimes until eventually prayer and crime became indistinguishable to me. I believed that because a man cried out 'My God!' when a safe fell on him, it proved that belief was rooted deep in the human breast. Then I went to school. For fourteen years half a hundred earnest men pointed to ancient flint-locks and cried to me: 'There's the real thing. These new rifles are only shallow, superficial imitations.' They damned the books I read and the things I thought by calling them immoral; later the fashion changed, and they damned things by calling them 'clever'.

"And so I turned, canny for my years, from the professors to the poets, listening—to the lyric tenor of Swinburne and the tenor robusto of Shelley, to Shakespeare with his first bass and his fine range, to Tennyson with his second bass and his occasional falsetto, to Milton and Marlow, bassos profundo. I gave ear to Browning chatting, Byron declaiming, and Wordsworth droning. This, at least, did me no harm. I learned a little of beauty—enough to know that it had nothing to do with truth—and I found, moreover, that there was no great literary tradition; there was only the tradition of the eventful death of every literary tradition....

"Then I grew up, and the beauty of succulent illusions fell away from me. The fibre of my mind coarsened and my eyes grew miserably keen. Life rose around my island like a sea, and presently I was swimming.

"The transition was subtle—the thing had lain in wait for me for some time. It has its insidious, seemingly innocuous trap for every one. With me? No—I didn't try to seduce the janitor's wife—nor did I run through the streets unclothed, proclaiming my virility. It is never quite passion that does the business—it is the dress that passion wears. I became bored—that was all. Boredom, which is another name and a frequent disguise for vitality, became the unconscious motive of all my acts. Beauty was behind me, do you understand?—

I was grown." He paused. "End of school and college period. Opening of Part Two."

Three quietly active points of light showed the location of his listeners. Gloria was now half sitting, half lying, in Anthony's lap. His arm was around her so tightly that she could hear the beating of his heart. Richard Caramel, perched on the apple-barrel, from time to time stirred and gave off a faint grunt.

"I grew up then, into this land of jazz, and fell immediately into a state of almost audible confusion. Life stood over me like an immoral schoolmistress, editing my ordered thoughts. But, with a mistaken faith in intelligence, I plodded on. I read Smith, who laughed at charity and insisted that the sneer was the highest form of self-expression—but Smith himself replaced charity as an obscurer of the light. I read Jones, who neatly disposed of individualism—and behold! Jones was still in my way. I did not think—I was a battle-ground for the thoughts of many men; rather was I one of those desirable but impotent countries over which the great powers surge back and forth.

"I reached maturity under the impression that I was gathering the experience to order my life for happiness. Indeed, I accomplished the not unusual feat of solving each question in my mind long before it presented itself to me in life—and of being beaten and bewildered just the same.

"But after a few tastes of this latter dish I had had enough. Here! I said, Experience is not worth the getting. It's not a thing that happens pleasantly to a passive you—it's a wall that an active you runs up against. So I wrapped myself in what I thought was my invulnerable scepticism and decided that my education was complete. But it was too late. Protect myself as I might by making no new ties with tragic and predestined humanity, I was lost with the rest. I had traded the fight against love for the fight against loneliness, the fight against life for the fight against death."

He broke off to give emphasis to his last observation—after a moment he yawned and resumed.

"I suppose that the beginning of the second phase of my education was a ghastly dissatisfaction at being used in spite of myself for some inscrutable purpose of whose ultimate goal I was unaware—if, indeed, there *was* an ultimate goal. It was a difficult choice. The schoolmistress seemed to be saying, 'We're going to play football and nothing but football. If you don't want to play football you can't play at all—'

"What was I to do—the playtime was so short!

"You see, I felt that we were even denied what consolation there might have been in being a figment of a corporate man rising from his knees. Do you think that I leaped at this pessimism, grasped it as a sweetly smug superior thing, no more depressing really than, say, a gray autumn day before a fire?—I don't think I did that. I was a great deal too warm for that, and too alive.

"For it seemed to me that there was no ultimate goal for man. Man was beginning a grotesque and bewildered fight with nature—nature, that by the divine and magnificent accident had brought us to where we could fly in her face. She had invented ways to rid the race of the inferior and thus give the remainder strength to fill her higher—or, let us say, her more amusing—though still unconscious and accidental intentions. And, actuated by the highest gifts of the enlightenment, we were seeking to circumvent her. In this republic I saw the black beginning to mingle with the white—in Europe there was taking place an economic catastrophe to save three or four diseased and wretchedly governed races from the one mastery that might organize them for material prosperity.

"We produce a Christ who can raise up the leper—and presently the breed of the leper is the salt of the earth. If any one can find any lesson in that, let him stand forth."

"There's only one lesson to be learned from life, anyway," interrupted Gloria, not in contradiction but in a sort of melancholy agreement.

"What's that?" demanded Maury sharply.

"That there's no lesson to be learned from life."

After a short silence Maury said:

"Young Gloria, the beautiful and merciless lady, first looked at the world with the fundamental sophistication I have struggled to attain, that Anthony never will attain, that Dick will never fully understand."

There was a disgusted groan from the apple-barrel. Anthony, grown accustomed to the dark, could see plainly the flash of Richard Caramel's yellow eye and the look of resentment on his face as he cried:

"You're crazy! By your own statement I should have attained some experience by trying."

"Trying what?" cried Maury fiercely. "Trying to pierce the darkness of political idealism with some wild, despairing urge toward truth? Sitting day after day supine in a rigid chair and infinitely removed from life staring at the tip of a steeple through the trees, trying to separate, definitely and for all time, the knowable from the unknowable? Trying to take a piece of actuality and give it glamour from your own soul to make for that inexpressible quality it possessed in life and lost in transit to paper or canvas? Struggling in a laboratory through weary years for one iota of relative truth in a mass of wheels or a test tube—"

"Have you?"

Maury paused, and in his answer, when it came, there was a measure of weariness, a bitter overnote that lingered for a moment in those three minds before it floated up and off like a bubble bound for the moon.

"Not I," he said softly. "I was born tired—but with the quality of mother wit, the gift of women like Gloria—to that, for all my talking and listening, my waiting in vain for the eternal generality that seems to lie just beyond every argument and every speculation, to that I have added not one jot."

In the distance a deep sound that had been audible for some moments identified itself by a plaintive mooing like that of a gigantic cow and by the pearly spot of a headlight apparent half a mile away. It was a steam-driven train this time, rumbling and groaning, and as it tumbled by with a monstrous complaint it sent a shower of sparks and cinders over the platform.

"Not one jot!" Again Maury's voice dropped down to them as from a great height. "What a feeble thing intelligence is, with its short steps, its waverings, its pacings back and forth, its disastrous retreats! Intelligence is a mere instrument of circumstances. There are people who say that intelligence must have built the universe—why, intelligence never built a steam engine! Circumstances built a steam engine. Intelligence is little more than a short foot-rule by which we measure the infinite achievements of Circumstances.

"I could quote you the philosophy of the hour—but, for all we know, fifty years may see a complete reversal of this abnegation that's absorbing the intellectuals to-day, the triumph of Christ over Anatole France—" He hesitated, and then added: "But all I know—the tremendous importance of myself to me, and the necessity of acknowledging that importance to myself—these things the wise and lovely Gloria was born knowing these things and the painful futility of trying to know anything else.

"Well, I started to tell you of my education, didn't I? But I learned nothing, you see, very little even about myself. And if I had I should die with my lips shut and the guard on my fountain pen—as the wisest men have done since—oh, since the failure of a certain matter—a strange matter, by the way. It concerned some sceptics who thought they were far-sighted, just as you and I. Let me tell you about them by way of an evening prayer before you all drop off to sleep.

"Once upon a time all the men of mind and genius in the world became of one belief—that is to say, of no belief. But it wearied them to think that within a few years after their death many cults and systems and prognostications would be ascribed to them which they had never meditated nor intended. So they said to one another:

"'Let's join together and make a great book that will last forever to mock the credulity of man. Let's persuade our more erotic poets to write about the delights of the flesh, and induce some of our robust journalists to contribute stories of famous amours. We'll include all the most preposterous old wives' tales now current. We'll choose the keenest satirist alive to compile a deity from all the deities worshipped by mankind, a deity who will be more magnificent than any of them, and yet so weakly human that he'll become a byword for laughter the world over—and we'll ascribe to him all sorts of jokes and vanities and rages, in which he'll be supposed to indulge for his own diversion, so that the people will read our book and ponder it, and there'll be no more nonsense in the world.

"'Finally, let us take care that the book possesses all the virtues of style, so that it may last forever as a witness to our profound scepticism and our universal irony.'

"So the men did, and they died.

"But the book lived always, so beautifully had it been written, and so astounding the quality of imagination with which these men of mind and genius had endowed it. They had neglected to give it a name, but after they were dead it became known as the Bible."

When he concluded there was no comment. Some damp languor sleeping on the air of night seemed to have bewitched them all.

"As I said, I started on the story of my education. But my high-balls are dead and the night's almost over, and soon there'll be an awful jabbering going on everywhere, in the trees and the houses, and the two little stores over there behind the station, and there'll be a great running up and down upon the earth for a few hours—Well," he concluded with a laugh, "thank God we four can all pass to our eternal rest knowing we've left the world a little better for having lived in it."

A breeze sprang up, blowing with it faint wisps of life which flattened against the sky.

"Your remarks grow rambling and inconclusive," said Anthony sleepily. "You expected one of those miracles of illumination by which you say your most brilliant and pregnant things in exactly the setting that should provoke the ideal symposium. Meanwhile Gloria has shown her far-sighted detachment by falling asleep—I can tell that by the fact that she has managed to concentrate her entire weight upon my broken body."

"Have I bored you?" inquired Maury, looking down with some concern.

"No, you have disappointed us. You've shot a lot of arrows but did you shoot any birds?"

"I leave the birds to Dick," said Maury hurriedly. "I speak erratically, in dissociated fragments."

"You can get no rise from me," muttered Dick. "My mind is full of any number of material things. I want a warm bath too much to worry about the importance of my work or what proportion of us are pathetic figures."

Dawn made itself felt in a gathering whiteness eastward over the river and an intermittent cheeping in the near-by trees.

"Quarter to five," sighed Dick; "almost another hour to wait. Look! Two gone." He was pointing to Anthony, whose lids had sagged over his eyes. "Sleep of the Patch family—"

But in another five minutes, despite the amplifying cheeps and chirrups, his own head had fallen forward, nodded down twice, thrice....

Only Maury Noble remained awake, seated upon the station roof, his eyes wide open and fixed with fatigued intensity upon the distant nucleus of morning. He was wondering at the unreality of ideas, at the fading radiance of existence, and at the little absorptions that were creeping avidly into his life, like rats into a ruined house. He was sorry for no one now—on Monday morning there would be his business, and later there would be a girl of another class whose whole life he was; these were the things nearest his heart. In the strangeness of the brightening day it seemed presumptuous that with this feeble, broken instrument of his mind he had ever tried to think.

There was the sun, letting down great glowing masses of heat; there was life, active and snarling, moving about them like a fly swarm—the dark pants of smoke from the engine, a crisp "all aboard!" and a bell ringing. Confusedly Maury saw eyes in the milk train staring curiously up at him, heard Gloria and Anthony in quick controversy as to whether he should go to the city with her, then another clamor and she was gone and the three men, pale as ghosts, were standing alone upon the platform while a grimy coal-heaver went down the road on top of a motor truck, carolling hoarsely at the summer morning.

III. THE BROKEN LUTE

It is seven-thirty of an August evening. The windows in the living room of the gray house are wide open, patiently exchanging the tainted inner atmosphere of liquor and smoke for the fresh drowsiness of the late hot dusk. There are dying flower scents upon the air, so thin, so fragile, as to hint already of a summer laid away in time. But August is still proclaimed relentlessly by a thousand crickets around the side-porch, and by one who has broken into the house and concealed himself confidently behind a bookcase, from time to time shrieking of his cleverness and his indomitable will.

The room itself is in messy disorder. On the table is a dish of fruit, which is real but appears artificial. Around it are grouped an ominous assortment of decanters, glasses, and heaped ash-trays, the latter still raising wavy smoke-ladders into the stale air, the effect on the whole needing but a skull to resemble that venerable chromo, once a fixture in every "den," which presents the appendages to the life of pleasure with delightful and awe-inspiring sentiment.

After a while the sprightly solo of the supercricket is interrupted rather than joined by a new sound—the melancholy wail of an erratically fingered flute. It is obvious that the musician is practising rather than performing, for from time to time the gnarled strain breaks off and, after an interval of indistinct mutterings, recommences.

Just prior to the seventh false start a third sound contributes to the subdued discord. It is a taxi outside. A minute's silence, then the taxi again, its boisterous retreat almost obliterating the scrape of footsteps on the cinder walk. The door-bell shrieks alarmingly through the house.

From the kitchen enters a small, fatigued Japanese, hastily buttoning a servant's coat of white duck. He opens the front screen-door and admits a handsome young man of thirty, clad in the sort of well-intentioned clothes peculiar to those who serve mankind. To his whole personality clings a well-intentioned air: his glance about the room is compounded of curiosity and a determined optimism; when he looks at Tana the entire burden of uplifting the godless Oriental is in his eyes. His name is FREDERICK E. PARAMORE. *He was at Harvard with* ANTHONY, *where because of the initials of their surnames they were constantly placed next to each other in classes. A fragmentary acquaintance developed—but since that time they have never met.*

Nevertheless, PARAMORE *enters the room with a certain air of arriving for the evening. Tana is answering a question.*

TANA: (*Grinning with ingratiation*) Gone to Inn for dinnah. Be back half-hour. Gone since ha' past six.

PARAMORE: (*Regarding the glasses on the table*) Have they company?

TANA: Yes. Company. Mistah Caramel, Mistah and Missays Barnes, Miss Kane, all stay here.

PARAMORE: I see. (*Kindly*) They've been having a spree, I see.

TANA: I no un'stan'.

PARAMORE: They've been having a fling.

TANA: Yes, they have drink. Oh, many, many, many drink.

PARAMORE: (*Receding delicately from the subject*) "Didn't I hear the sounds of music as I approached the house"?

TANA:(*With a spasmodic giggle*)Yes, I play.

PARAMORE: One of the Japanese instruments.

(*He is quite obviously a subscriber to the "National Geographic Magazine."*)

TANA: I play flu-u-ute, Japanese flu-u-ute.

PARAMORE: What song were you playing? One of your Japanese melodies?

TANA:(*His brow undergoing preposterous contraction*) I play train song. How you call?—railroad song. So call in my countree. Like train. It go so-o-o; that mean whistle; train start. Then go so-o-o; that mean train go. Go like that. Vera nice song in my countree. Children song.

PARAMORE: It sounded very nice.

(It is apparent at this point that only a gigantic effort at control restrains Tana from rushing up-stairs for his post cards, including the six made in America.)

TANA: I fix high-ball for gentleman?

PARAMORE: "No, thanks. I don't use it". (*He smiles.*)

(TANA *withdraws into the kitchen, leaving the intervening door slightly ajar. From the crevice there suddenly issues again the melody of the Japanese train song—this time not a practice, surely, but a performance, a lusty, spirited performance.*

The phone rings. TANA, *absorbed in his harmonics, gives no heed, so* PARAMORE *takes up the receiver.)*

PARAMORE: Hello.... Yes.... No, he's not here now, but he'll be back any moment.... Butterworth? Hello, I didn't quite catch the name.... Hello, hello, hello. Hello! ... Huh!

(The phone obstinately refuses to yield up any more sound. Paramore replaces the receiver.

At this point the taxi motif re-enters, wafting with it a second young man; he carries a suitcase and opens the front door without ringing the bell.)

MAURY: (*In the hall*) "Oh, Anthony! Yoho"! (*He comes into the large room and sees* PARAMORE) How do?

PARAMORE: (*Gazing at him with gathering intensity*) Is this—is this Maury Noble?

MAURY: "That's it". (*He advances, smiling, and holding out his hand*) How are you, old boy? Haven't seen you for years.

(He has vaguely associated the face with Harvard, but is not even positive about that. The name, if he ever knew it, he has long since forgotten. However, with a fine sensitiveness and an equally commendable charity PARAMORE *recognizes the fact and tactfully relieves the situation.)*

PARAMORE: You've forgotten Fred Paramore? We were both in old Unc Robert's history class.

MAURY: No, I haven't, Unc—I mean Fred. Fred was—I mean Unc was a great old fellow, wasn't he?

PARAMORE: *(Nodding his head humorously several times)* Great old character. Great old character.

MAURY: *(After a short pause)* Yes—he was. Where's Anthony?

PARAMORE: The Japanese servant told me he was at some inn. Having dinner, I suppose.

MAURY: *(Looking at his watch)* Gone long?

PARAMORE: I guess so. The Japanese told me they'd be back shortly.

MAURY: Suppose we have a drink.

PARAMORE: No, thanks. I don't use it. *(He smiles.)*

MAURY: Mind if I do? *(Yawning as he helps himself from a bottle)* What have you been doing since you left college?

PARAMORE: Oh, many things. I've led a very active life. Knocked about here and there. *(His tone implies anything front lion-stalking to organized crime.)*

MAURY: Oh, been over to Europe?

PARAMORE: No, I haven't—unfortunately.

MAURY: I guess we'll all go over before long.

PARAMORE: Do you really think so?

MAURY: Sure! Country's been fed on sensationalism for more than two years. Everybody getting restless. Want to have some fun.

PARAMORE: Then you don't believe any ideals are at stake?

MAURY: Nothing of much importance. People want excitement every so often.

PARAMORE: *(Intently)* It's very interesting to hear you say that. Now I was talking to a man who'd been over there——

(During the ensuing testament, left to be filled in by the reader with such phrases as "Saw with his own eyes," "Splendid spirit of France," and "Salvation of civilization," MAURY *sits with lowered eyelids, dispassionately bored.)*

MAURY: *(At the first available opportunity)* By the way, do you happen to know that there's a German agent in this very house?

PARAMORE: *(Smiling cautiously)* Are you serious?

MAURY: Absolutely. Feel it my duty to warn you.

PARAMORE: *(Convinced)* A governess?

MAURY: *(In a whisper, indicating the kitchen with his thumb) Tana!* That's not his real name. I understand he constantly gets mail addressed to Lieutenant Emile Tannenbaum.

PARAMORE: (*Laughing with hearty tolerance*) You were kidding me.

MAURY: I may be accusing him falsely. But, you haven't told me what you've been doing.

PARAMORE: For one thing—writing.

MAURY: Fiction?

PARAMORE: No. Non-fiction.

MAURY: What's that? A sort of literature that's half fiction and half fact?

PARAMORE: Oh, I've confined myself to fact. I've been doing a good deal of social-service work.

MAURY: Oh!

(*An immediate glow of suspicion leaps into his eyes. It is as though* PARAMORE *had announced himself as an amateur pickpocket.*)

PARAMORE: At present I'm doing service work in Stamford. Only last week some one told me that Anthony Patch lived so near.

(*They are interrupted by a clamor outside, unmistakable as that of two sexes in conversation and laughter. Then there enter the room in a body* ANTHONY, GLORIA, RICHARD CARAMEL, MURIEL KANE, RACHAEL BARNES *and* RODMAN BARNES, *her husband. They surge about* MAURY, *illogically replying "Fine!" to his general "Hello." ...* ANTHONY, *meanwhile, approaches his other guest.*)

ANTHONY: Well, I'll be darned. How are you? Mighty glad to see you.

PARAMORE: It's good to see you, Anthony. I'm stationed in Stamford, so I thought I'd run over. (*Roguishly*) We have to work to beat the devil most of the time, so we're entitled to a few hours' vacation.

(*In an agony of concentration* ANTHONY *tries to recall the name. After a struggle of parturition his memory gives up the fragment "Fred," around which he hastily builds the sentence "Glad you did, Fred!" Meanwhile the slight hush prefatory to an introduction has fallen upon the company.* MAURY, *who could help, prefers to look on in malicious enjoyment.*)

ANTHONY: (*In desperation*) Ladies and gentlemen, this is—this is Fred.

MURIEL: (*With obliging levity*) Hello, Fred!

(RICHARD CARAMEL *and* PARAMORE *greet each other intimately by their first names, the latter recollecting that* DICK *was one of the men in his class who had never before troubled to speak to him.* DICK *fatuously imagines that* PARAMORE *is some one he has previously met in* ANTHONY'S *house.*

The three young women go up-stairs.)

MAURY: (*In an undertone to* DICK) Haven't seen Muriel since Anthony's wedding.

DICK: She's now in her prime. Her latest is "I'll say so!"

(ANTHONY *struggles for a while with* PARAMORE *and at length attempts to make the conversation general by asking every one to have a drink.*)

MAURY: I've done pretty well on this bottle. I've gone from "Proof" down to "Distillery." (*He indicates the words on the label.*)

ANTHONY: (*To* PARAMORE) Never can tell when these two will turn up. Said good-by to them one afternoon at five and darned if they didn't appear about two in the morning. A big hired touring-car from New York drove up to the door and out they stepped, drunk as lords, of course.

(*In an ecstasy of consideration* PARAMORE *regards the cover of a book which he holds in his hand.* MAURY *and* DICK *exchange a glance.*)

DICK: (*Innocently, to* PARAMORE) You work here in town?

PARAMORE: No, I'm in the Laird Street Settlement in Stamford. (*To* ANTHONY) You have no idea of the amount of poverty in these small Connecticut towns. Italians and other immigrants. Catholics mostly, you know, so it's very hard to reach them.

ANTHONY: (*Politely*) Lot of crime?

PARAMORE: Not so much crime as ignorance and dirt.

MAURY: That's my theory: immediate electrocution of all ignorant and dirty people. I'm all for the criminals—give color to life. Trouble is if you started to punish ignorance you'd have to begin in the first families, then you could take up the moving picture people, and finally Congress and the clergy.

PARAMORE: (*Smiling uneasily*) I was speaking of the more fundamental ignorance—of even our language.

MAURY: (*Thoughtfully*) I suppose it is rather hard. Can't even keep up with the new poetry.

PARAMORE: It's only when the settlement work has gone on for months that one realizes how bad things are. As our secretary said to me, your fingernails never seem dirty until you wash your hands. Of course we're already attracting much attention.

MAURY: (*Rudely*) As your secretary might say, if you stuff paper into a grate it'll burn brightly for a moment.

(*At this point* GLORIA, *freshly tinted and lustful of admiration and entertainment, rejoins the party, followed by her two friends. For several moments the conversation becomes entirely fragmentary.* GLORIA *calls* ANTHONY *aside.*)

GLORIA: Please don't drink much, Anthony.

ANTHONY: Why?

GLORIA: Because you're so simple when you're drunk.

ANTHONY: Good Lord! What's the matter now?

GLORIA: (*After a pause during which her eyes gaze coolly into his*) Several things. In the first place, why do you insist on paying for everything? Both those men have more money than you!

ANTHONY: Why, Gloria! They're my guests!

GLORIA: That's no reason why you should pay for a bottle of champagne Rachael Barnes smashed. Dick tried to fix that second taxi bill, and you wouldn't let him.

ANTHONY: Why, Gloria—

GLORIA: When we have to keep selling bonds to even pay our bills, it's time to cut down on excess generosities. Moreover, I wouldn't be quite so attentive to Rachael Barnes. Her husband doesn't like it any more than I do!

ANTHONY: Why, Gloria—

GLORIA: (*Mimicking him sharply*) "Why, Gloria!" But that's happened a little too often this summer—with every pretty woman you meet. It's grown to be a sort of habit, and I'm *not* going to stand it! If you can play around, I can, too. (*Then, as an afterthought*) By the way, this Fred person isn't a second Joe Hull, is he?

ANTHONY: Heavens, no! He probably came up to get me to wheedle some money out of grandfather for his flock.

*(*GLORIA *turns away from a very depressed* ANTHONY *and returns to her guests.*

By nine o'clock these can be divided into two classes—those who have been drinking consistently and those who have taken little or nothing. In the second group are the BARNESES, MURIEL, *and* FREDERICK E. PARAMORE.*)*

MURIEL: I wish I could write. I get these ideas but I never seem to be able to put them in words.

DICK: As Goliath said, he understood how David felt, but he couldn't express himself. The remark was immediately adopted for a motto by the Philistines.

MURIEL: I don't get you. I must be getting stupid in my old age.

GLORIA: (*Weaving unsteadily among the company like an exhilarated angel*) If any one's hungry there's some French pastry on the dining room table.

MAURY: Can't tolerate those Victorian designs it comes in.

MURIEL: (*Violently amused*) *I'll* say you're tight, Maury.

(Her bosom is still a pavement that she offers to the hoofs of many passing stallions, hoping that their iron shoes may strike even a spark of romance in the darkness ...

Messrs. BARNES *and* PARAMORE *have been engaged in conversation upon some wholesome subject, a subject so wholesome that* MR. BARNES *has been trying for several moments to creep into the more tainted air around the central lounge. Whether* PARAMORE *is lingering in the gray house out of politeness or curiosity, or in order at some future time to make a sociological report on the decadence of American life, is problematical.)*

MAURY: Fred, I imagined you were very broad-minded.

PARAMORE: I am.

MURIEL: Me, too. I believe one religion's as good as another and everything.

PARAMORE: There's some good in all religions.

MURIEL: I'm a Catholic but, as I always say, I'm not working at it.

PARAMORE: (*With a tremendous burst of tolerance*) The Catholic religion is a very—a very powerful religion.

MAURY: Well, such a broad-minded man should consider the raised plane of sensation and the stimulated optimism contained in this cocktail.

PARAMORE: (*Taking the drink, rather defiantly*) Thanks, I'll try—one.

MAURY: One? Outrageous! Here we have a class of 'nineteen ten reunion, and you refuse to be even a little pickled. Come on!

"Here's a health to King Charles,
Here's a health to King Charles,
Bring the bowl that you boast——"

(PARAMORE *joins in with a hearty voice.*)

MAURY: Fill the cup, Frederick. You know everything's subordinated to nature's purposes with us, and her purpose with you is to make you a rip-roaring tippler.

PARAMORE: If a fellow can drink like a gentleman—

MAURY: What is a gentleman, anyway?

ANTHONY: A man who never has pins under his coat lapel.

MAURY: Nonsense! A man's social rank is determined by the amount of bread he eats in a sandwich.

DICK: He's a man who prefers the first edition of a book to the last edition of a newspaper.

RACHAEL: A man who never gives an impersonation of a dope-fiend.

MAURY: An American who can fool an English butler into thinking he's one.

MURIEL: A man who comes from a good family and went to Yale or Harvard or Princeton, and has money and dances well, and all that.

MAURY: At last—the perfect definition! Cardinal Newman's is now a back number.

PARAMORE: I think we ought to look on the question more broad-mindedly. Was it Abraham Lincoln who said that a gentleman is one who never inflicts pain?

MAURY: It's attributed, I believe, to General Ludendorff.

PARAMORE: Surely you're joking.

MAURY: Have another drink.

PARAMORE: I oughtn't to. (*Lowering his voice for* MAURY'S *ear alone*) What if I were to tell you this is the third drink I've ever taken in my life?

(DICK *starts the phonograph, which provokes* MURIEL *to rise and sway from side to side, her elbows against her ribs, her forearms perpendicular to her body and out like fins.*)

MURIEL: Oh, let's take up the rugs and dance!

(*This suggestion is received by* ANTHONY *and* GLORIA *with interior groans and sickly smiles of acquiescence.*)

MURIEL: Come on, you lazy-bones. Get up and move the furniture back.

DICK: Wait till I finish my drink.

MAURY: (*Intent on his purpose toward* PARAMORE) I'll tell you what. Let's each fill one glass, drink it off and then we'll dance.

(*A wave of protest which breaks against the rock of* MAURY'S *insistence.*)

MURIEL: My head is simply going *round* now.

RACHAEL: (*In an undertone to* ANTHONY) Did Gloria tell you to stay away from me?

ANTHONY: (*Confused*) Why, certainly not. Of course not.

(RACHAEL *smiles at him inscrutably. Two years have given her a sort of hard, well-groomed beauty.*)

MAURY: (*Holding up his glass*) Here's to the defeat of democracy and the fall of Christianity.

MURIEL: Now really!

(She flashes a mock-reproachful glance at MAURY *and then drinks.*

They all drink, with varying degrees of difficulty.)

MURIEL: Clear the floor!

(It seems inevitable that this process is to be gone through, so ANTHONY *and* GLORIA *join in the great moving of tables, piling of chairs, rolling of carpets, and breaking of lamps. When the furniture has been stacked in ugly masses at the sides, there appears a space about eight feet square.)*

MURIEL: Oh, let's have music!

MAURY: Tana will render the love song of an eye, ear, nose, and throat specialist.

(*Amid some confusion due to the fact that* TANA *has retired for the night, preparations are made for the performance. The pajamaed Japanese, flute in hand, is wrapped in a comforter and placed in a chair atop one of the tables, where he makes a ludicrous and grotesque spectacle.* PARAMORE *is perceptibly drunk and so enraptured with the notion that he increases the effect by simulating funny-paper staggers and even venturing on an occasional hiccough.*)

PARAMORE: (*To* GLORIA) Want to dance with me?

GLORIA: No, sir! Want to do the swan dance. Can you do it?

PARAMORE: Sure. Do them all.

GLORIA: All right. You start from that side of the room and I'll start from this.

MURIEL: Let's go!

(Then Bedlam creeps screaming out of the bottles: TANA *plunges into the recondite mazes of the train song, the plaintive "tootle toot-toot" blending its melancholy cadences with the "Poor Butter-fly (tink-atink), by the blossoms wait-ing" of the phonograph.* MURIEL *is too weak with laughter to do more than cling desperately to* BARNES, *who, dancing with the ominous rigidity of an army officer, tramps without humor around the small space.* ANTHONY *is trying to hear* RACHAEL'S *whisper—without attracting* GLORIA'*s attention....*

But the grotesque, the unbelievable, the histrionic incident is about to occur, one of those incidents in which life seems set upon the passionate imitation of the lowest forms of literature. PARAMORE *has been trying to emulate* GLORIA, *and as the commotion reaches its height he begins to spin round and round, more and more dizzily—he staggers, recovers, staggers again and then falls in the direction of the hall ... almost into the arms of old* ADAM PATCH, *whose approach has been rendered inaudible by the pandemonium in the room.*

ADAM PATCH *is very white. He leans upon a stick. The man with him is* EDWARD SHUTTLEWORTH, *and it is he who seizes* PARAMORE *by the shoulder and deflects the course of his fall away from the venerable philanthropist.*

The time required for quiet to descend upon the room like a monstrous pall may be estimated at two minutes, though for a short period after that the phonograph gags and the notes of the Japanese train song dribble from the end of TANA'S *flute. Of the nine people only* BARNES, PARAMORE, *and* TANA *are unaware of the late-comer's identity. Of the nine not one is aware that* ADAM PATCH *has that morning made a contribution of fifty thousand dollars to the cause of national prohibition.*

It is given to PARAMORE *to break the gathering silence; the high tide of his life's depravity is reached in his incredible remark.*)

PARAMORE: (*Crawling rapidly toward the kitchen on his hands and knees*) I'm not a guest here—I work here.

(*Again silence falls—so deep now, so weighted with intolerably contagious apprehension, that* RACHAEL *gives a nervous little giggle, and* DICK *finds himself telling over and over a line from Swinburne, grotesquely appropriate to the scene:*

"One gaunt bleak blossom of scentless breath."

... *Out of the hush the voice of* ANTHONY, *sober and strained, saying something to* ADAM PATCH; *then this, too, dies away.*)

SHUTTLEWORTH: (*Passionately*) Your grandfather thought he would motor over to see your house. I phoned from Rye and left a message.

(*A series of little gasps, emanating, apparently, from nowhere, from no one, fall into the next pause.* ANTHONY *is the color of chalk.* GLORIA'S *lips are parted and her level gaze at the old man is tense and frightened. There is not one smile in the room. Not one? Or does* CROSS PATCH'S *drawn mouth tremble slightly open, to expose the even rows of his thin teeth? He speaks—five mild and simple words.*)

ADAM PATCH: We'll go back now, Shuttleworth——

(And that is all. He turns, and assisted by his cane goes out through the hall, through the front door, and with hellish portentousness his uncertain footsteps crunch on the gravel path under the August moon.)

RETROSPECT

In this extremity they were like two goldfish in a bowl from which all the water had been drawn; they could not even swim across to each other.

Gloria would be twenty-six in May. There was nothing, she had said, that she wanted, except to be young and beautiful for a long time, to be gay and happy, and to have money and love. She wanted what most women want, but she wanted it much more fiercely and passionately. She had been married over two years. At first there had been days of serene understanding, rising to ecstasies of proprietorship and pride. Alternating with these periods had occurred sporadic hates, enduring a short hour, and forgetfulnesses lasting no longer than an afternoon. That had been for half a year.

Then the serenity, the content, had become less jubilant, had become, gray—very rarely, with the spur of jealousy or forced separation, the ancient ecstasies returned, the apparent communion of soul and soul, the emotional excitement. It was possible for her to hate Anthony for as much as a full day, to be carelessly incensed at him for as long as a week. Recrimination had displaced affection as an indulgence, almost as an entertainment, and there were nights when they would go to sleep trying to remember who was angry and who should be reserved next morning. And as the second year waned there had entered two new elements. Gloria realized that Anthony had become capable of utter indifference toward her, a temporary indifference, more than half lethargic, but one from which she could no longer stir him by a whispered word, or a certain intimate smile. There were days when her caresses affected him as a sort of suffocation. She was conscious of these things; she never entirely admitted them to herself.

It was only recently that she perceived that in spite of her adoration of him, her jealousy, her servitude, her pride, she fundamentally despised him—and her contempt blended indistinguishably with her other emotions.... All this was her love—the vital and feminine illusion that had directed itself toward him one April night, many months before.

On Anthony's part she was, in spite of these qualifications, his sole preoccupation. Had he lost her he would have been a broken man, wretchedly and sentimentally absorbed in her memory for the remainder of life. He seldom took pleasure in an entire day spent alone with her—except on occasions he preferred to have a third person with them. There were times when he felt that if he were not left absolutely alone he would go mad—there were a few times when he definitely hated her. In his cups he was capable of short attractions toward other women, the hitherto-suppressed outcroppings of an experimental temperament.

That spring, that summer, they had speculated upon future happiness—how they were to travel from summer land to summer land, returning eventually to a gorgeous estate and possible idyllic children, then entering diplomacy or politics, to accomplish, for a while, beautiful and important things, until finally as a white-haired (beautifully, silkily, white-haired) couple they were to loll about in serene glory, worshipped by the bourgeoisie of the land.... These times were to begin "when we get our money"; it was on such dreams rather than on any satisfaction with their increasingly irregular, increasingly dissipated life that their hope rested. On gray mornings when the jests of the night before had shrunk to ribaldries without wit or dignity, they could, after a fashion, bring out this batch of common hopes and count them over, then smile at each other and repeat, by way of clinching the matter, the terse yet sincere Nietzscheanism of Gloria's defiant "I don't care!"

Things had been slipping perceptibly. There was the money question, increasingly annoying, increasingly ominous; there was the realization that liquor had become a practical necessity to their amusement—not an uncommon phenomenon in the British aristocracy of a hundred years ago, but a somewhat alarming one in a civilization steadily becoming more temperate and more circumspect. Moreover, both of them seemed vaguely weaker in fibre, not so much in what they did as in their subtle reactions to the civilization about them. In Gloria had been born something that she had hitherto never needed—the skeleton, incomplete but nevertheless unmistakable, of her ancient abhorrence, a conscience. This admission to herself was coincidental with the slow decline of her physical courage.

Then, on the August morning after Adam Patch's unexpected call, they awoke, nauseated and tired, dispirited with life, capable only of one pervasive emotion—fear.

PANIC

"Well?" Anthony sat up in bed and looked down at her. The corners of his lips were drooping with depression, his voice was strained and hollow.

Her reply was to raise her hand to her mouth and begin a slow, precise nibbling at her finger.

"We've done it," he said after a pause; then, as she was still silent, he became exasperated. "Why don't you say something?"

"What on earth do you want me to say?"

"What are you thinking?"

"Nothing."

"Then stop biting your finger!"

Ensued a short confused discussion of whether or not she had been thinking. It seemed essential to Anthony that she should muse aloud upon last night's disaster. Her silence was a method of settling the responsibility on him. For her part she saw no necessity for speech—the moment required that she should gnaw at her finger like a nervous child.

"I've got to fix up this damn mess with my grandfather," he said with uneasy conviction. A faint newborn respect was indicated by his use of "my grandfather" instead of "grampa."

"You can't," she affirmed abruptly. "You can't—*ever*. He'll never forgive you as long as he lives."

"Perhaps not," agreed Anthony miserably. "Still—I might possibly square myself by some sort of reformation and all that sort of thing—"

"He looked sick," she interrupted, "pale as flour."

"He *is* sick. I told you that three months ago."

"I wish he'd died last week!" she said petulantly. "Inconsiderate old fool!"

Neither of them laughed.

"But just let me say," she added quietly, "the next time I see you acting with any woman like you did with Rachael Barnes last night, I'll leave you—*just—like—that!* I'm simply *not* going to stand it!"

Anthony quailed.

"Oh, don't be absurd," he protested. "You know there's no woman in the world for me except you—none, dearest."

His attempt at a tender note failed miserably—the more imminent danger stalked back into the foreground.

"If I went to him," suggested Anthony, "and said with appropriate biblical quotations that I'd walked too long in the way of unrighteousness and at last seen the light—" He broke off and glanced with a whimsical expression at his wife. "I wonder what he'd do?"

"I don't know."

She was speculating as to whether or not their guests would have the acumen to leave directly after breakfast.

Not for a week did Anthony muster the courage to go to Tarrytown. The prospect was revolting and left alone he would have been incapable of making the trip—but if his will had deteriorated in these past three years, so had his power to resist urging. Gloria compelled him to go. It was all very well to wait a week, she said, for that would give his grandfather's violent animosity time to cool—but to wait longer would be an error—it would give it a chance to harden.

He went, in trepidation ... and vainly. Adam Patch was not well, said Shuttleworth indignantly. Positive instructions had been given that no one was to see him. Before the ex-"gin-physician's" vindictive eye Anthony's front wilted. He walked out to his taxicab with what was almost a slink—recovering only a little of his self-respect as he boarded the train; glad to escape, boylike, to the wonder palaces of consolation that still rose and glittered in his own mind.

Gloria was scornful when he returned to Marietta. Why had he not forced his way in? That was what she would have done!

Between them they drafted a letter to the old man, and after considerable revision sent it off. It was half an apology, half a manufactured explanation. The letter was not answered.

Came a day in September, a day slashed with alternate sun and rain, sun without warmth, rain without freshness. On that day they left the gray house, which had seen the flower of their love. Four trunks and three monstrous crates were piled in the dismantled room where, two years before, they had sprawled lazily, thinking in terms of dreams, remote, languorous, content. The room echoed with emptiness. Gloria, in a new brown dress edged with fur, sat upon a trunk in silence, and Anthony walked nervously to and fro smoking, as they waited for the truck that would take their things to the city.

"What are those?" she demanded, pointing to some books piled upon one of the crates.

"That's my old stamp collection," he confessed sheepishly. "I forgot to pack it."

"Anthony, it's so silly to carry it around."

"Well, I was looking through it the day we left the apartment last spring, and I decided not to store it."

"Can't you sell it? Haven't we enough junk?"

"I'm sorry," he said humbly.

With a thunderous rattling the truck rolled up to the door. Gloria shook her fist defiantly at the four walls.

"I'm so glad to go!" she cried, "so glad. Oh, my God, how I hate this house!"

So the brilliant and beautiful lady went up with her husband to New York. On the very train that bore them away they quarrelled—her bitter words had the frequency, the regularity, the inevitability of the stations they passed.

"Don't be cross," begged Anthony piteously. "We've got nothing but each other, after all."

"We haven't even that, most of the time," cried Gloria.

"When haven't we?"

"A lot of times—beginning with one occasion on the station platform at Redgate."

"You don't mean to say that—"

"No," she interrupted coolly, "I don't brood over it. It came and went—and when it went it took something with it."

She finished abruptly. Anthony sat in silence, confused, depressed. The drab visions of train-side Mamaroneck, Larchmont, Rye, Pelham Manor, succeeded each other with intervals of bleak and shoddy wastes posing ineffectually as country. He found himself remembering how on one summer morning they two had started from New York in search of happiness. They had never expected to find it, perhaps, yet in itself that quest had been happier than anything he expected forevermore. Life, it seemed, must be a setting up of props around one—otherwise it was disaster. There was no rest, no quiet. He had been futile in longing to drift and dream; no one drifted except to maelstroms, no one dreamed, without his dreams becoming fantastic nightmares of indecision and regret.

Pelham! They had quarrelled in Pelham because Gloria must drive. And when she set her little foot on the accelerator the car had jumped off spunkily, and their two heads had jerked back like marionettes worked by a single string.

The Bronx—the houses gathering and gleaming in the sun, which was falling now through wide refulgent skies and tumbling caravans of light down into the streets. New York, he supposed, was home—the city of luxury and mystery, of preposterous hopes and exotic dreams. Here on the outskirts absurd stucco palaces reared themselves in the cool sunset, poised for an instant in cool unreality, glided off far away, succeeded by the mazed confusion of the Harlem River. The train moved in through the deepening twilight, above and past half a hundred cheerful sweating streets of the upper East Side, each one passing the car window like the space between the spokes of a gigantic wheel, each one with its vigorous colorful revelation of poor children swarming in feverish activity like vivid ants in alleys of red sand. From the tenement windows leaned rotund, moon-shaped mothers, as constellations of this sordid heaven; women like dark imperfect jewels, women like vegetables, women like great bags of abominably dirty laundry.

"I like these streets," observed Anthony aloud. "I always feel as though it's a performance being staged for me; as though the second I've passed they'll all stop leaping and laughing and, instead, grow very sad, remembering how poor they are, and retreat with bowed heads into their houses. You often get that effect abroad, but seldom in this country."

Down in a tall busy street he read a dozen Jewish names on a line of stores; in the door of each stood a dark little man watching the passers from intent eyes—eyes gleaming with suspicion, with pride, with clarity, with cupidity, with comprehension. New York—he could not dissociate it now from the slow, upward creep of this people—the little stores, growing, expanding, consolidating, moving, watched over with hawk's eyes and a bee's attention to detail—they slathered out on all sides. It was impressive—in perspective it was tremendous.

Gloria's voice broke in with strange appropriateness upon his thoughts.

"I wonder where Bloeckman's been this summer."

THE APARTMENT

After the sureties of youth there sets in a period of intense and intolerable complexity. With the soda-jerker this period is so short as to be almost negligible. Men higher in the scale hold out longer in the attempt to preserve the ultimate niceties of relationship, to retain "impractical" ideas of integrity. But by the late twenties the business has grown too intricate, and what has hitherto been imminent and confusing has become gradually remote and dim. Routine comes down like twilight on a harsh landscape, softening it until it is tolerable. The complexity is too subtle, too varied; the values are changing utterly with each lesion of vitality; it has begun to appear that we can learn nothing from the past with which to face the future—so we cease to be impulsive, convincible men, interested in what is ethically true by fine margins, we substitute rules of conduct for ideas of integrity, we value safety above romance, we become, quite unconsciously, pragmatic. It is left to the few to be persistently concerned with the nuances of relationships—and even this few only in certain hours especially set aside for the task.

Anthony Patch had ceased to be an individual of mental adventure, of curiosity, and had become an individual of bias and prejudice, with a longing to be emotionally undisturbed. This gradual change had taken place through the past several years, accelerated by a succession of anxieties preying on his mind. There was, first of all, the sense of waste, always dormant in his heart, now awakened by the circumstances of his position. In his moments of insecurity he was haunted by the suggestion that life might be, after all, significant. In his early twenties the conviction of the futility of effort, of the wisdom of abnegation, had been confirmed by the philosophies he had admired as well as by his association with Maury Noble, and later with his wife. Yet there had been occasions—just before his first meeting with Gloria, for example, and when his grandfather had suggested that he should go abroad as a war correspondent—upon which his dissatisfaction had driven him almost to a positive step.

One day just before they left Marietta for the last time, in carelessly turning over the pages of a Harvard Alumni Bulletin, he had found a column which told him what his contemporaries had been about in this six years since graduation. Most of them were in business, it was true, and several were converting the heathen of China or America to a nebulous protestantism; but a few, he found, were working constructively at jobs that were neither sinecures nor routines. There was Calvin Boyd, for instance, who, though barely out of medical school, had discovered a new treatment for typhus, had shipped abroad and was mitigating some of the civilization that the Great Powers had brought to Servia; there was Eugene Bronson, whose articles in The New Democracy were stamping him as a man with ideas transcending both vulgar timeliness and popular hysteria; there was a man named Daly who had been suspended from the faculty of a righteous university for preaching Marxian doctrines in the classroom: in art, science, politics, he saw the authentic personalities of his time emerging—there was even Severance, the quarter-back, who had given up his life rather neatly and gracefully with the Foreign Legion on the Aisne.

He laid down the magazine and thought for a while about these diverse men. In the days of his integrity he would have defended his attitude to the last—an Epicurus in Nirvana, he would have cried that to struggle was to believe, to believe was to limit. He would as soon have become a churchgoer because the prospect of immortality gratified him as he would have considered entering the leather business because the intensity of the competition would have kept him from unhappiness. But at present he had no such delicate scruples. This autumn, as his twenty-ninth year began, he was inclined to close his mind to many things, to avoid prying deeply into motive and first causes, and mostly to long passionately for security from the world and from himself. He hated to be alone, as has been said he often dreaded being alone with Gloria.

Because of the chasm which his grandfather's visit had opened before him, and the consequent revulsion from his late mode of life, it was inevitable that he should look around in this suddenly hostile city for the friends and environments that had once seemed the warmest and most secure. His first step was a desperate attempt to get back his old apartment.

In the spring of 1912 he had signed a four-year lease at seventeen hundred a year, with an option of renewal. This lease had expired the previous May. When he had first rented the rooms they had been mere potentialities, scarcely to be discerned as that, but Anthony had seen into these potentialities and arranged in the lease that he and the landlord should each spend a certain amount in improvements. Rents had gone up in the past four years, and last spring when Anthony had waived his option the landlord, a Mr. Sohenberg, had realized that he could get a much bigger price for what was now a prepossessing apartment. Accordingly, when Anthony approached him on the subject in September he was met with Sohenberg's offer of a three-year lease at twenty-five hundred a year. This, it seemed to Anthony, was outrageous. It meant that well over a third of their income would be consumed in rent. In vain he argued that his own money, his own ideas on the repartitioning, had made the rooms attractive.

In vain he offered two thousand dollars—twenty-two hundred, though they could ill afford it: Mr. Sohenberg was obdurate. It seemed that two other gentlemen were considering it; just that sort of an apartment was in demand for the moment, and it would scarcely be business to *give* it to Mr. Patch. Besides, though he had never mentioned it before, several of the other tenants had complained of noise during the previous winter—singing and dancing late at night, that sort of thing.

Internally raging Anthony hurried back to the Ritz to report his discomfiture to Gloria.

"I can just see you," she stormed, "letting him back you down!"

"What could I say?"

"You could have told him what he *was*. I wouldn't have *stood* it. No other man in the world would have stood it! You just let people order you around and cheat you and bully you and take advantage of you as if you were a silly little boy. It's absurd!"

"Oh, for Heaven's sake, don't lose your temper."

"I know, Anthony, but you *are* such an ass!"

"Well, possibly. Anyway, we can't afford that apartment. But we can afford it better than living here at the Ritz."

"You were the one who insisted on coming here."

"Yes, because I knew you'd be miserable in a cheap hotel."

"Of course I would!"

"At any rate we've got to find a place to live."

"How much can we pay?" she demanded.

"Well, we can pay even his price if we sell more bonds, but we agreed last night that until I had gotten something definite to do we-"

"Oh, I know all that. I asked you how much we can pay out of just our income."

"They say you ought not to pay more than a fourth."

"How much is a fourth?"

"One hundred and fifty a month."

"Do you mean to say we've got only six hundred dollars coming in every month?" A subdued note crept into her voice.

"Of course!" he answered angrily. "Do you think we've gone on spending more than twelve thousand a year without cutting way into our capital?"

"I knew we'd sold bonds, but—have we spent that much a year? How did we?" Her awe increased.

"Oh, I'll look in those careful account-books we kept," he remarked ironically, and then added: "Two rents a good part of the time, clothes, travel—why, each of those springs in California cost about four thousand dollars. That darn car was an expense from start to finish. And parties and amusements and—oh, one thing or another."

They were both excited now and inordinately depressed. The situation seemed worse in the actual telling Gloria than it had when he had first made the discovery himself.

"You've got to make some money," she said suddenly.

"I know it."

"And you've got to make another attempt to see your grandfather."

"I will."

"When?"

"When we get settled."

This eventuality occurred a week later. They rented a small apartment on Fifty-seventh Street at one hundred and fifty a month. It included bedroom, living-room, kitchenette, and bath, in a thin, white-stone apartment house, and though the rooms were too small to display Anthony's best furniture, they were clean, new, and, in a blonde and sanitary way, not unattractive. Bounds had gone abroad to enlist in the British army, and in his place they tolerated rather than enjoyed the services of a gaunt, big-boned Irishwoman, whom Gloria loathed because she discussed the glories of Sinn Fein as she served breakfast. But they vowed they would have no more Japanese, and English servants were for the present hard to obtain. Like Bounds, the woman prepared only breakfast. Their other meals they took at restaurants and hotels.

What finally drove Anthony post-haste up to Tarrytown was an announcement in several New York papers that Adam Patch, the multimillionaire, the philanthropist, the venerable uplifter, was seriously ill and not expected to recover.

THE KITTEN

Anthony could not see him. The doctors' instructions were that he was to talk to no one, said Mr. Shuttleworth—who offered kindly to take any message that Anthony might care to intrust with him, and deliver it to Adam Patch when his condition permitted. But by obvious innuendo he confirmed Anthony's melancholy inference that the prodigal grandson would be particularly unwelcome at the bedside. At one point in the conversation Anthony, with Gloria's positive instructions in mind, made a move as though to brush by the secretary, but Shuttleworth with a smile squared his brawny shoulders, and Anthony saw how futile such an attempt would be.

Miserably intimidated, he returned to New York, where husband and wife passed a restless week. A little incident that occurred one evening indicated to what tension their nerves were drawn.

Walking home along a cross-street after dinner, Anthony noticed a night-bound cat prowling near a railing.

"I always have an instinct to kick a cat," he said idly.

"I like them."

"I yielded to it once."

"When?"

"Oh, years ago; before I met you. One night between the acts of a show. Cold night, like this, and I was a little tight—one of the first times I was ever tight," he added. "The poor little beggar was looking for a place to sleep, I guess, and I was in a mean mood, so it took my fancy to kick it—"

"Oh, the poor kitty!" cried Gloria, sincerely moved. Inspired with the narrative instinct, Anthony enlarged on the theme.

"It was pretty bad," he admitted. "The poor little beast turned around and looked at me rather plaintively as though hoping I'd pick him up and be kind to him—he was really just a kitten—and before he knew it a big foot launched out at him and caught his little back"

"Oh!" Gloria's cry was full of anguish.

"It was such a cold night," he continued, perversely, keeping his voice upon a melancholy note. "I guess it expected kindness from somebody, and it got only pain—"

He broke off suddenly—Gloria was sobbing. They had reached home, and when they entered the apartment she threw herself upon the lounge, crying as though he had struck at her very soul.

"Oh, the poor little kitty!" she repeated piteously, "the poor little kitty. So cold—"

"Gloria"

"Don't come near me! Please, don't come near me. You killed the soft little kitty."

Touched, Anthony knelt beside her.

"Dear," he said. "Oh, Gloria, darling. It isn't true. I invented it—every word of it."

But she would not believe him. There had been something in the details he had chosen to describe that made her cry herself asleep that night, for the kitten, for Anthony for herself, for the pain and bitterness and cruelty of all the world.

THE PASSING OF AN AMERICAN MORALIST

Old Adam died on a midnight of late November with a pious compliment to his God on his thin lips. He, who had been flattered so much, faded out flattering the Omnipotent Abstraction which he fancied he might have angered in the more lascivious moments of his youth. It was announced that he had arranged some sort of an armistice with the deity, the terms of which were not made public, though they were thought to have included a large cash payment. All the newspapers printed his biography, and two of them ran short editorials on his sterling worth, and his part in the drama of industrialism, with which he had grown up. They referred guardedly to the reforms he had sponsored and financed. The memories of Comstock and Cato the Censor were resuscitated and paraded like gaunt ghosts through the columns.

Every newspaper remarked that he was survived by a single grandson, Anthony Comstock Patch, of New York.

The burial took place in the family plot at Tarrytown. Anthony and Gloria rode in the first carriage, too worried to feel grotesque, both trying desperately to glean presage of fortune from the faces of retainers who had been with him at the end.

They waited a frantic week for decency, and then, having received no notification of any kind, Anthony called up his grandfather's lawyer. Mr. Brett was not he was expected back in an hour. Anthony left his telephone number.

It was the last day of November, cool and crackling outside, with a lustreless sun peering bleakly in at the windows. While they waited for the call, ostensibly engaged in reading, the atmosphere, within and without, seemed pervaded with a deliberate rendition of the pathetic fallacy. After an interminable while, the bell jingled, and Anthony, starting violently, took up the receiver.

"Hello ..." His voice was strained and hollow. "Yes—I did leave word. Who is this, please? ... Yes.... Why, it was about the estate. Naturally I'm interested, and I've received no word about the reading of the will—I thought you might not have my address.... What? ... Yes ..."

Gloria fell on her knees. The intervals between Anthony's speeches were like tourniquets winding on her heart. She found herself helplessly twisting the large buttons from a velvet cushion. Then:

"That's—that's very, very odd—that's very odd—that's very odd. Not even any—ah—mention or any—ah—reason?"

His voice sounded faint and far away. She uttered a little sound, half gasp, half cry.

"Yes, I'll see.... All right, thanks ... thanks...."

The phone clicked. Her eyes looking along the floor saw his feet cut the pattern of a patch of sunlight on the carpet. She arose and faced him with a gray, level glance just as his arms folded about her.

"My dearest," he whispered huskily. "He did it, God damn him!"

NEXT DAY

"Who are the heirs?" asked Mr. Haight. "You see when you can tell me so little about it—"

Mr. Haight was tall and bent and beetle-browed. He had been recommended to Anthony as an astute and tenacious lawyer.

"I only know vaguely," answered Anthony. "A man named Shuttleworth, who was a sort of pet of his, has the whole thing in charge as administrator or trustee or something—all except the direct bequests to charity and the provisions for servants and for those two cousins in Idaho."

"How distant are the cousins?"

"Oh, third or fourth, anyway. I never even heard of them."

Mr. Haight nodded comprehensively.

"And you want to contest a provision of the will?"

"I guess so," admitted Anthony helplessly. "I want to do what sounds most hopeful—that's what I want you to tell me."

"You want them to refuse probate to the will?"

Anthony shook his head.

"You've got me. I haven't any idea what 'probate' is. I want a share of the estate."

"Suppose you tell me some more details. For instance, do you know why the testator disinherited you?"

"Why—yes," began Anthony. "You see he was always a sucker for moral reform, and all that—"

"I know," interjected Mr. Haight humorlessly.

"—and I don't suppose he ever thought I was much good. I didn't go into business, you see. But I feel certain that up to last summer I was one of the beneficiaries. We had a house out in Marietta, and one night grandfather got the notion he'd come over and see us. It just happened that there was a rather gay party going on and he arrived without any warning. Well, he took one look, he and this fellow Shuttleworth, and then turned around and tore right back to Tarrytown. After that he never answered my letters or even let me see him."

"He was a prohibitionist, wasn't he?"

"He was everything—regular religious maniac."

"How long before his death was the will made that disinherited you?"

"Recently—I mean since August."

"And you think that the direct reason for his not leaving you the majority of the estate was his displeasure with your recent actions?"

"Yes."

Mr. Haight considered. Upon what grounds was Anthony thinking of contesting the will?

"Why, isn't there something about evil influence?"

"Undue influence is one ground—but it's the most difficult. You would have to show that such pressure was brought to bear so that the deceased was in a condition where he disposed of his property contrary to his intentions—"

"Well, suppose this fellow Shuttleworth dragged him over to Marietta just when he thought some sort of a celebration was probably going on?"

"That wouldn't have any bearing on the case. There's a strong division between advice and influence. You'd have to prove that the secretary had a sinister intention. I'd suggest some other grounds. A will is automatically refused probate in case of insanity, drunkenness"—here Anthony smiled—"or feeble-mindedness through premature old age."

"But," objected Anthony, "his private physician, being one of the beneficiaries, would testify that he wasn't feeble-minded. And he wasn't. As a matter of fact he probably did just what he intended to with his money—it was perfectly consistent with everything he'd ever done in his life—"

"Well, you see, feeble-mindedness is a great deal like undue influence—it implies that the property wasn't disposed of as originally intended. The most common ground is duress—physical pressure."

Anthony shook his head.

"Not much chance on that, I'm afraid. Undue influence sounds best to me."

After more discussion, so technical as to be largely unintelligible to Anthony, he retained Mr. Haight as counsel. The lawyer proposed an interview with Shuttleworth, who, jointly with Wilson, Hiemer and Hardy, was executor of the will. Anthony was to come back later in the week.

It transpired that the estate consisted of approximately forty million dollars. The largest bequest to an individual was of one million, to Edward Shuttleworth, who received in addition thirty thousand a year salary as administrator of the thirty-million-dollar trust fund, left to be doled out to various charities and reform societies practically at his own discretion. The remaining nine millions were proportioned among the two cousins in Idaho and about twenty-five other beneficiaries: friends, secretaries, servants, and employees, who had, at one time or another, earned the seal of Adam Patch's approval.

At the end of another fortnight Mr. Haight, on a retainer's fee of fifteen thousand dollars, had begun preparations for contesting the will.

THE WINTER OF DISCONTENT

Before they had been two months in the little apartment on Fifty-seventh Street, it had assumed for both of them the same indefinable but almost material taint that had impregnated the gray house in Marietta. There was the odor of tobacco always—both of them smoked incessantly; it was in their clothes, their blankets, the curtains, and the ash-littered carpets. Added to this was the wretched aura of stale wine, with its inevitable suggestion of beauty gone foul and revelry remembered in disgust. About a particular set of glass goblets on the sideboard the odor was particularly noticeable, and in the main room the mahogany table was ringed with white circles where glasses had been set down upon it. There had been many parties—people broke things; people became sick in Gloria's bathroom; people spilled wine; people made unbelievable messes of the kitchenette.

These things were a regular part of their existence. Despite the resolutions of many Mondays it was tacitly understood as the week end approached that it should be observed with some sort of unholy excitement. When Saturday came they would not discuss the matter, but would call up this person or that from among their circle of sufficiently irresponsible friends, and suggest a rendezvous. Only after the friends had gathered and Anthony had set out decanters, would he murmur casually "I guess I'll have just one high-ball myself—"

Then they were off for two days—realizing on a wintry dawn that they had been the noisiest and most conspicuous members of the noisiest and most conspicuous party at the Boul' Mich', or the Club Ramée, or at other resorts much less particular about the hilarity of their clientèle. They would find that they had, somehow, squandered eighty or ninety dollars, how, they never knew; they customarily attributed it to the general penury of the "friends" who had accompanied them.

It began to be not unusual for the more sincere of their friends to remonstrate with them, in the very course of a party, and to predict a sombre end for them in the loss of Gloria's "looks" and Anthony's "constitution."

The story of the summarily interrupted revel in Marietta had, of course, leaked out in detail—"Muriel doesn't mean to tell every one she knows," said Gloria to Anthony, "but she thinks every one she tells is the only one she's going to tell"—and, diaphanously veiled, the tale had been given a conspicuous place in Town Tattle. When the terms of Adam Patch's will were made public and the newspapers printed items concerning Anthony's suit, the story was beautifully rounded out—to Anthony's infinite disparagement. They began to hear rumors about themselves from all quarters, rumors founded usually on a soupcon of truth, but overlaid with preposterous and sinister detail.

Outwardly they showed no signs of deterioration. Gloria at twenty-six was still the Gloria of twenty; her complexion a fresh damp setting for her candid eyes; her hair still a childish glory, darkening slowly from corn color to a deep russet gold; her slender body suggesting ever a nymph running and dancing through Orphic groves. Masculine eyes, dozens of them, followed her with a fascinated stare when she walked through a hotel lobby or down the aisle of a theatre. Men asked to be introduced to her, fell into prolonged states of sincere admiration, made definite love to her—for she was still a thing of exquisite and unbelievable beauty. And for his part Anthony had rather gained than lost in appearance; his face had taken on a certain intangible air of tragedy, romantically contrasted with his trim and immaculate person.

Early in the winter, when all conversation turned on the probability of America's going into the war, when Anthony was making a desperate and sincere attempt to write, Muriel Kane arrived in New York and came immediately to see them. Like Gloria, she seemed never to change. She knew the latest slang, danced the latest dances, and talked of the latest songs and plays with all the fervor of her first season as a New York drifter. Her coyness was eternally new, eternally ineffectual; her clothes were extreme; her black hair was bobbed, now, like Gloria's.

"I've come up for the midwinter prom at New Haven," she announced, imparting her delightful secret. Though she must have been older then than any of the boys in college, she managed always to secure some sort of invitation, imagining vaguely that at the next party would occur the flirtation which was to end at the romantic altar.

"Where've you been?" inquired Anthony, unfailingly amused.

"I've been at Hot Springs. It's been slick and peppy this fall—more *men!*"

"Are you in love, Muriel?"

"What do you mean 'love'?" This was the rhetorical question of the year. "I'm going to tell you something," she said, switching the subject abruptly. "I suppose it's none of my business, but I think it's time for you two to settle down."

"Why, we are settled down."

"Yes, you are!" she scoffed archly. "Everywhere I go I hear stories of your escapades. Let me tell you, I have an awful time sticking up for you."

"You needn't bother," said Gloria coldly.

"Now, Gloria," she protested, "you know I'm one of your best friends."

Gloria was silent. Muriel continued:

"It's not so much the idea of a woman drinking, but Gloria's so pretty, and so many people know her by sight all around, that it's naturally conspicuous—"

"What have you heard recently?" demanded Gloria, her dignity going down before her curiosity.

"Well, for instance, that that party in Marietta *killed* Anthony's grandfather."

Instantly husband and wife were tense with annoyance.

"Why, I think that's outrageous."

"That's what they say," persisted Muriel stubbornly.

Anthony paced the room. "It's preposterous!" he declared. "The very people we take on parties shout the story around as a great joke—and eventually it gets back to us in some such form as this."

Gloria began running her finger through a stray red-dish curl. Muriel licked her veil as she considered her next remark.

"You ought to have a baby."

Gloria looked up wearily.

"We can't afford it."

"All the people in the slums have them," said Muriel triumphantly.

Anthony and Gloria exchanged a smile. They had reached the stage of violent quarrels that were never made up, quarrels that smouldered and broke out again at intervals or died away from sheer indifference—but this visit of Muriel's drew them temporarily together. When the discomfort under which they were living was remarked upon by a third party, it gave them the impetus to face this hostile world together. It was very seldom, now, that the impulse toward reunion sprang from within.

Anthony found himself associating his own existence with that of the apartment's night elevator man, a pale, scraggly bearded person of about sixty, with an air of being somewhat above his station. It was probably because of this quality that he had secured the position; it made him a pathetic and memorable figure of failure. Anthony recollected, without humor, a hoary jest about the elevator man's career being a matter of ups and downs—it was, at any rate, an enclosed life of infinite dreariness. Each time Anthony stepped into the car he waited breathlessly for the old man's "Well, I guess we're going to have some sunshine to-day." Anthony thought how little rain or sunshine he would enjoy shut into that close little cage in the smoke-colored, windowless hall.

A darkling figure, he attained tragedy in leaving the life that had used him so shabbily. Three young gunmen came in one night, tied him up and left him on a pile of coal in the cellar while they went through the trunk room. When the janitor found him next morning he had collapsed from chill. He died of pneumonia four days later.

He was replaced by a glib Martinique negro, with an incongruous British accent and a tendency to be surly, whom Anthony detested. The passing of the old man had approximately the same effect on him that the kitten story had had on Gloria. He was reminded of the cruelty of all life and, in consequence, of the increasing bitterness of his own.

He was writing—and in earnest at last. He had gone to Dick and listened for a tense hour to an elucidation of those minutiae of procedure which hitherto he had rather scornfully looked down upon. He needed money immediately—he was selling bonds every month to pay their bills. Dick was frank and explicit:

"So far as articles on literary subjects in these obscure magazines go, you couldn't make enough to pay your rent. Of course if a man has the gift of humor, or a chance at a big biography, or some specialized knowledge, he may strike it rich. But for you, fiction's the only thing. You say you need money right away?"

"I certainly do."

"Well, it'd be a year and a half before you'd make any money out of a novel. Try some popular short stories. And, by the way, unless they're exceptionally brilliant they have to be cheerful and on the side of the heaviest artillery to make you any money."

Anthony thought of Dick's recent output, which had been appearing in a well-known monthly. It was concerned chiefly with the preposterous actions of a class of sawdust effigies who, one was assured, were New York society people, and it turned, as a rule, upon questions of the heroine's technical purity, with mock-sociological overtones about the "mad antics of the four hundred."

"But your stories—" exclaimed Anthony aloud, almost involuntarily.

"Oh, that's different," Dick asserted astoundingly. "I have a reputation, you see, so I'm expected to deal with strong themes."

Anthony gave an interior start, realizing with this remark how much Richard Caramel had fallen off. Did he actually think that these amazing latter productions were as good as his first novel?

Anthony went back to the apartment and set to work. He found that the business of optimism was no mean task. After half a dozen futile starts he went to the public library and for a week investigated the files of a popular magazine. Then, better equipped, he accomplished his first story, "The Dictaphone of Fate." It was founded upon one of his few remaining impressions of that six weeks in Wall Street the year before. It purported to be the sunny tale of an office boy who, quite by accident, hummed a wonderful melody into the dictaphone. The cylinder was discovered by the boss's brother, a well-known producer of musical comedy—and then immediately lost. The body of the story was concerned with the pursuit of the missing cylinder and the eventual marriage of the noble office boy (now a successful composer) to Miss Rooney, the virtuous stenographer, who was half Joan of Arc and half Florence Nightingale.

He had gathered that this was what the magazines wanted. He offered, in his protagonists, the customary denizens of the pink-and-blue literary world, immersing them in a saccharine plot that would offend not a single stomach in Marietta. He had it typed in double space—this last as advised by a booklet, "Success as a Writer Made Easy," by R. Meggs Widdlestien, which assured the ambitious plumber of the futility of perspiration, since after a six-lesson course he could make at least a thousand dollars a month.

After reading it to a bored Gloria and coaxing from her the immemorial remark that it was "better than a lot of stuff that gets published," he satirically affixed the nom de plume of "Gilles de Sade," enclosed the proper return envelope, and sent it off.

Following the gigantic labor of conception he decided to wait until he heard from the first story before beginning another. Dick had told him that he might get as much as two hundred dollars. If by any chance it did happen to be unsuited, the editor's letter would, no doubt, give him an idea of what changes should be made.

"It is, without question, the most abominable piece of writing in existence," said Anthony.

The editor quite conceivably agreed with him. He returned the manuscript with a rejection slip. Anthony sent it off elsewhere and began another story. The second one was called "The Little Open Doors"; it was written in three days. It concerned the occult: an estranged couple were brought together by a medium in a vaudeville show.

There were six altogether, six wretched and pitiable efforts to "write down" by a man who had never before made a consistent effort to write at all. Not one of them contained a spark of vitality, and their total yield of grace and felicity was less than that of an average newspaper column. During their circulation they collected, all told, thirty-one rejection slips, headstones for the packages that he would find lying like dead bodies at his door.

In mid-January Gloria's father died, and they went again to Kansas City—a miserable trip, for Gloria brooded interminably, not upon her father's death, but on her mother's. Russel Gilbert's affairs having been cleared up they came into possession of about three thousand dollars, and a great amount of furniture. This was in storage, for he had spent his last days in a small hotel. It was due to his death that Anthony made a new discovery concerning Gloria. On the journey East she disclosed herself, astonishingly, as a Bilphist.

"Why, Gloria," he cried, "you don't mean to tell me you believe that stuff."

"Well," she said defiantly, "why not?"

"Because it's—it's fantastic. You know that in every sense of the word you're an agnostic. You'd laugh at any orthodox form of Christianity—and then you come out with the statement that you believe in some silly rule of reincarnation."

"What if I do? I've heard you and Maury, and every one else for whose intellect I have the slightest respect, agree that life as it appears is utterly meaningless. But it's always seemed to me that if I were unconsciously learning something here it might not be so meaningless."

"You're not learning anything—you're just getting tired. And if you must have a faith to soften things, take up one that appeals to the reason of some one beside a lot of hysterical women. A person like you oughtn't to accept anything unless it's decently demonstrable."

"I don't care about truth. I want some happiness."

"Well, if you've got a decent mind the second has got to be qualified by the first. Any simple soul can delude himself with mental garbage."

"I don't care," she held out stoutly, "and, what's more, I'm not propounding any doctrine."

The argument faded off, but reoccurred to Anthony several times thereafter. It was disturbing to find this old belief, evidently assimilated from her mother, inserting itself again under its immemorial disguise as an innate idea.

They reached New York in March after an expensive and ill-advised week spent in Hot Springs, and Anthony resumed his abortive attempts at fiction. As it became plainer to both of them that escape did not lie in the way of popular literature, there was a further slipping of their mutual confidence and courage. A complicated struggle went on incessantly between them. All efforts to keep down expenses died away from sheer inertia, and by March they were again using any pretext as an excuse for a "party." With an assumption of recklessness Gloria tossed out the suggestion that they should take all their money and go on a real spree while it lasted—anything seemed better than to see it go in unsatisfactory driblets.

"Gloria, you want parties as much as I do."

"It doesn't matter about me. Everything I do is in accordance with my ideas: to use every minute of these years, when I'm young, in having the best time I possibly can."

"How about after that?"

"After that I won't care."

"Yes, you will."

"Well, I may—but I won't be able to do anything about it. And I'll have had my good time."

"You'll be the same then. After a fashion, we *have* had our good time, raised the devil, and we're in the state of paying for it."

Nevertheless, the money kept going. There would be two days of gaiety, two days of moroseness—an endless, almost invariable round. The sharp pull-ups, when they occurred, resulted usually in a spurt of work for Anthony, while Gloria, nervous and bored, remained in bed or else chewed abstractedly at her fingers. After a day or so of this, they would make an engagement, and then—Oh, what did it matter? This night, this glow, the cessation of anxiety and the sense that if living was not purposeful it was, at any rate, essentially romantic! Wine gave a sort of gallantry to their own failure.

Meanwhile the suit progressed slowly, with interminable examinations of witnesses and marshallings of evidence. The preliminary proceedings of settling the estate were finished. Mr. Haight saw no reason why the case should not come up for trial before summer.

Bloeckman appeared in New York late in March; he had been in England for nearly a year on matters concerned with "Films Par Excellence." The process of general refinement was still in progress—always he dressed a little better, his intonation was mellower, and in his manner there was perceptibly more assurance that the fine things of the world were his by a natural and inalienable right. He called at the apartment, remained only an hour, during which he talked chiefly of the war, and left telling them he was coming again. On his second visit Anthony was not at home, but an absorbed and excited Gloria greeted her husband later in the afternoon.

"Anthony," she began, "would you still object if I went in the movies?"

His whole heart hardened against the idea. As she seemed to recede from him, if only in threat, her presence became again not so much precious as desperately necessary.

"Oh, Gloria—!"

"Blockhead said he'd put me in—only if I'm ever going to do anything I'll have to start now. They only want young women. Think of the money, Anthony!"

"For you—yes. But how about me?"

"Don't you know that anything I have is yours too?"

"It's such a hell of a career!" he burst out, the moral, the infinitely circumspect Anthony, "and such a hell of a bunch. And I'm so utterly tired of that fellow Bloeckman coming here and interfering. I hate theatrical things."

"It isn't theatrical! It's utterly different."

"What am I supposed to do? Chase you all over the country? Live on your money?"

"Then make some yourself."

The conversation developed into one of the most violent quarrels they had ever had. After the ensuing reconciliation and the inevitable period of moral inertia, she realized that he had taken the life out of the project. Neither of them ever mentioned the probability that Bloeckman was by no means disinterested, but they both knew that it lay back of Anthony's objection.

In April war was declared with Germany. Wilson and his cabinet—a cabinet that in its lack of distinction was strangely reminiscent of the twelve apostles—let loose the carefully starved dogs of war, and the press began to whoop hysterically against the sinister morals, sinister philosophy, and sinister music produced by the Teutonic temperament. Those who fancied themselves particularly broad-minded made the exquisite distinction that it was only the German Government which aroused them to hysteria; the rest were worked up to a condition of retching indecency. Any song which contained the word "mother" and the word "kaiser" was assured of a tremendous success. At last every one had something to talk about—and almost every one fully enjoyed it, as though they had been cast for parts in a sombre and romantic play.

Anthony, Maury, and Dick sent in their applications for officers' training-camps and the two latter went about feeling strangely exalted and reproachless; they chattered to each other, like college boys, of war's being the one excuse for, and justification of, the aristocrat, and conjured up an impossible caste of officers, to be composed, it appeared, chiefly of the more attractive alumni of three or four Eastern colleges. It seemed to Gloria that in this huge red light streaming across the nation even Anthony took on a new glamour.

The Tenth Infantry, arriving in New York from Panama, were escorted from saloon to saloon by patriotic citizens, to their great bewilderment. West Pointers began to be noticed for the first time in years, and the general impression was that everything was glorious, but not half so glorious as it was going to be pretty soon, and that everybody was a fine fellow, and every race a great race—always excepting the Germans—and in every strata of society outcasts and scapegoats had but to appear in uniform to be forgiven, cheered, and wept over by relatives, ex-friends, and utter strangers.

Unfortunately, a small and precise doctor decided that there was something the matter with Anthony's blood-pressure. He could not conscientiously pass him for an officers' training-camp.

THE BROKEN LUTE

Their third anniversary passed, uncelebrated, unnoticed. The season warmed in thaw, melted into hotter summer, simmered and boiled away. In July the will was offered for probate, and upon the contestation was assigned by the surrogate to trial term for trial. The matter was prolonged into September—there was difficulty in empanelling an unbiassed jury because of the moral sentiments involved. To Anthony's disappointment a verdict was finally returned in favor of the testator, whereupon Mr. Haight caused a notice of appeal to be served upon Edward Shuttleworth.

As the summer waned Anthony and Gloria talked of the things they were to do when the money was theirs, and of the places they were to go to after the war, when they would "agree on things again," for both of them looked forward to a time when love, springing like the phoenix from its own ashes, should be born again in its mysterious and unfathomable haunts.

He was drafted early in the fall, and the examining doctor made no mention of low blood-pressure. It was all very purposeless and sad when Anthony told Gloria one night that he wanted, above all things, to be killed. But, as always, they were sorry for each other for the wrong things at the wrong times....

They decided that for the present she was not to go with him to the Southern camp where his contingent was ordered. She would remain in New York to "use the apartment," to save money, and to watch the progress of the case—which was pending now in the Appellate Division, of which the calendar, Mr. Haight told them, was far behind.

Almost their last conversation was a senseless quarrel about the proper division of the income—at a word either would have given it all to the other. It was typical of the muddle and confusion of their lives that on the October night when Anthony reported at the Grand Central Station for the journey to camp, she arrived only in time to catch his eye over the anxious heads of a gathered crowd. Through the dark light of the enclosed train-sheds their glances stretched across a hysterical area, foul with yellow sobbing and the smells of poor women. They must have pondered upon what they had done to one another, and each must have accused himself of drawing this sombre pattern through which they were tracing tragically and obscurely. At the last they were too far away for either to see the other's tears.

BOOK THREE

I. A MATTER OF CIVILIZATION

AT a frantic command from some invisible source, Anthony groped his way inside. He was thinking that for the first time in more than three years he was to remain longer than a night away from Gloria. The finality of it appealed to him drearily. It was his clean and lovely girl that he was leaving.

They had arrived, he thought, at the most practical financial settlement: she was to have three hundred and seventy-five dollars a month—not too much considering that over half of that would go in rent—and he was taking fifty to supplement his pay. He saw no need for more: food, clothes, and quarters would be provided—there were no social obligations for a private.

The car was crowded and already thick with breath. It was one of the type known as "tourist" cars, a sort of brummagem Pullman, with a bare floor, and straw seats that needed cleaning. Nevertheless, Anthony greeted it with relief. He had vaguely expected that the trip South would be made in a freight-car, in one end of which would stand eight horses and in the other forty men. He had heard the "hommes 40, chevaux 8" story so often that it had become confused and ominous.

As he rocked down the aisle with his barrack-bag slung at his shoulder like a monstrous blue sausage, he saw no vacant seats, but after a moment his eye fell on a single space at present occupied by the feet of a short swarthy Sicilian, who, with his hat drawn over his eyes, hunched defiantly in the corner. As Anthony stopped beside him he stared up with a scowl, evidently intended to be intimidating; he must have adopted it as a defense against this entire gigantic equation. At Anthony's sharp "That seat taken?" he very slowly lifted the feet as though they were a breakable package, and placed them with some care upon the floor. His eyes remained on Anthony, who meanwhile sat down and unbuttoned the uniform coat issued him at Camp Upton the day before. It chafed him under the arms.

Before Anthony could scrutinize the other occupants of the section a young second lieutenant blew in at the upper end of the car and wafted airily down the aisle, announcing in a voice of appalling acerbity:

"There will be no smoking in this car! No smoking! Don't smoke, men, in this car!"

As he sailed out at the other end a dozen little clouds of expostulation arose on all sides.

"Oh, cripe!"

"Jeese!"

"No smokin'?"

"Hey, come back here, fella!"

"What's 'ee idea?"

Two or three cigarettes were shot out through the open windows. Others were retained inside, though kept sketchily away from view. From here and there in accents of bravado, of mockery, of submissive humor, a few remarks were dropped that soon melted into the listless and pervasive silence.

The fourth occupant of Anthony's section spoke up suddenly.

"G'by, liberty," he said sullenly. "G'by, everything except bein' an officer's dog."

Anthony looked at him. He was a tall Irishman with an expression moulded of indifference and utter disdain. His eyes fell on Anthony, as though he expected an answer, and then upon the others. Receiving only a defiant stare from the Italian he groaned and spat noisily on the floor by way of a dignified transition back into taciturnity.

A few minutes later the door opened again and the second lieutenant was borne in upon his customary official zephyr, this time singing out a different tiding:

"All right, men, smoke if you want to! My mistake, men! It's all right, men! Go on and smoke—my mistake!"

This time Anthony had a good look at him. He was young, thin, already faded; he was like his own mustache; he was like a great piece of shiny straw. His chin receded, faintly; this was offset by a magnificent and unconvincing scowl, a scowl that Anthony was to connect with the faces of many young officers during the ensuing year.

Immediately every one smoked—whether they had previously desired to or not. Anthony's cigarette contributed to the hazy oxidation which seemed to roll back and forth in opalescent clouds with every motion of the train. The conversation, which had lapsed between the two impressive visits of the young officer, now revived tepidly; the men across the aisle began making clumsy experiments with their straw seats' capacity for comparative comfort; two card games, half-heartedly begun, soon drew several spectators to sitting positions on the arms of seats. In a few minutes Anthony became aware of a persistently obnoxious sound—the small, defiant Sicilian had fallen audibly asleep. It was wearisome to contemplate that animate protoplasm, reasonable by courtesy only, shut up in a car by an incomprehensible civilization, taken somewhere, to do a vague something without aim or significance or consequence. Anthony sighed, opened a newspaper which he had no recollection of buying, and began to read by the dim yellow light.

Ten o'clock bumped stuffily into eleven; the hours clogged and caught and slowed down. Amazingly the train halted along the dark countryside, from time to time indulging in short, deceitful movements backward or forward, and whistling harsh paeans into the high October night. Having read his newspaper through, editorials, cartoons, and war-poems, his eye fell on a half-column headed *Shakespeareville, Kansas.* It seemed that the Shakespeareville Chamber of Commerce had recently held an enthusiastic debate as to whether the American soldiers should be known as "Sammies" or "Battling Christians." The thought gagged him. He dropped the newspaper, yawned, and let his mind drift off at a tangent. He wondered why Gloria had been late. It seemed so long ago already—he had a pang of illusive loneliness. He tried to imagine from what angle she would regard her new position, what place in her considerations he would continue to hold. The thought acted as a further depressant—he opened his paper and began to read again.

The members of the Chamber of Commerce in Shakespeareville had decided upon "Liberty Lads."

For two nights and two days they rattled southward, making mysterious inexplicable stops in what were apparently arid wastes, and then rushing through large cities with a pompous air of hurry. The whimsicalities of this train foreshadowed for Anthony the whimsicalities of all army administration.

In the arid wastes they were served from the baggage-car with beans and bacon that at first he was unable to eat—he dined scantily on some milk chocolate distributed by a village canteen. But on the second day the baggage-car's output began to appear surprisingly palatable. On the third morning the rumor was passed along that within the hour they would arrive at their destination, Camp Hooker.

It had become intolerably hot in the car, and the men were all in shirt sleeves. The sun came in through the windows, a tired and ancient sun, yellow as parchment and stretched out of shape in transit. It tried to enter in triumphant squares and produced only warped splotches—but it was appallingly steady; so much so that it disturbed Anthony not to be the pivot of all the inconsequential sawmills and trees and telegraph poles that were turning around him so fast. Outside it played its heavy tremolo over olive roads and fallow cotton-fields, back of which ran a ragged line of woods broken with eminences of gray rock. The foreground was dotted sparsely with wretched, ill-patched shanties, among which there would flash by, now and then, a specimen of the languid yokelry of South Carolina, or else a strolling darky with sullen and bewildered eyes.

Then the woods moved off and they rolled into a broad space like the baked top of a gigantic cake, sugared with an infinity of tents arranged in geometric figures over its surface. The train came to an uncertain stop, and the sun and the poles and the trees faded, and his universe rocked itself slowly back to its old usualness, with Anthony Patch in the centre. As the men, weary and perspiring, crowded out of the car, he smelt that unforgetable aroma that impregnates all permanent camps—the odor of garbage.

Camp Hooker was an astonishing and spectacular growth, suggesting "A Mining Town in 1870—The Second Week." It was a thing of wooden shacks and whitish-gray tents, connected by a pattern of roads, with hard tan drill-grounds fringed with trees. Here and there stood green Y.M.C.A. houses, unpromising oases, with their muggy odor of wet flannels and closed telephone-booths—and across from each of them there was usually a canteen, swarming with life, presided over indolently by an officer who, with the aid of a side-car, usually managed to make his detail a pleasant and chatty sinecure.

Up and down the dusty roads sped the soldiers of the quartermaster corps, also in side-cars. Up and down drove the generals in their government automobiles, stopping now and then to bring unalert details to attention, to frown heavily upon captains marching at the heads of companies, to set the pompous pace in that gorgeous game of showing off which was taking place triumphantly over the entire area.

The first week after the arrival of Anthony's draft was filled with a series of interminable inoculations and physical examinations, and with the preliminary drilling. The days left him desperately tired. He had been issued the wrong size shoes by a popular, easy-going supply-sergeant, and in consequence his feet were so swollen that the last hours of the afternoon were an acute torture. For the first time in his life he could throw himself down on his cot between dinner and afternoon drill-call, and seeming to sink with each moment deeper into a bottomless bed, drop off immediately to sleep, while the noise and laughter around him faded to a pleasant drone of drowsy summer sound. In the morning he awoke stiff and aching, hollow as a ghost, and hurried forth to meet the other ghostly figures who swarmed in the wan company streets, while a harsh bugle shrieked and spluttered at the gray heavens.

He was in a skeleton infantry company of about a hundred men. After the invariable breakfast of fatty bacon, cold toast, and cereal, the entire hundred would rush for the latrines, which, however well-policed, seemed always intolerable, like the lavatories in cheap hotels. Out on the field, then, in ragged order—the lame man on his left grotesquely marring Anthony's listless efforts to keep in step, the platoon sergeants either showing off violently to impress the officers and recruits, or else quietly lurking in close to the line of march, avoiding both labor and unnecessary visibility.

When they reached the field, work began immediately—they peeled off their shirts for calisthenics. This was the only part of the day that Anthony enjoyed. Lieutenant Kretching, who presided at the antics, was sinewy and muscular, and Anthony, followed his movements faithfully, with a feeling that he was doing something of positive value to himself. The other officers and sergeants walked about among the men with the malice of schoolboys, grouping here and there around some unfortunate who lacked muscular control, giving him confused instructions and commands. When they discovered a particularly forlorn, ill-nourished specimen, they would linger the full half-hour making cutting remarks and snickering among themselves.

One little officer named Hopkins, who had been a sergeant in the regular army, was particularly annoying. He took the war as a gift of revenge from the high gods to himself, and the constant burden of his harangues was that these rookies did not appreciate the full gravity and responsibility of "the service." He considered that by a combination of foresight and dauntless efficiency he had raised himself to his current magnificence. He aped the particular tyrannies of every officer under whom he had served in times gone by. His frown was frozen on his brow—before giving a private a pass to go to town he would ponderously weigh the effect of such an absence upon the company, the army, and the welfare of the military profession the world over.

Lieutenant Kretching, blond, dull and phlegmatic, introduced Anthony ponderously to the problems of attention, right face, about face, and at ease. His principal defect was his forgetfulness. He often kept the company straining and aching at attention for five minutes while he stood out in front and explained a new movement—as a result only the men in the centre knew what it was all about—those on both flanks had been too emphatically impressed with the necessity of staring straight ahead.

The drill continued until noon. It consisted of stressing a succession of infinitely remote details, and though Anthony perceived that this was consistent with the logic of war, it none the less irritated him. That the same faulty blood-pressure which would have been indecent in an officer did not interfere with the duties of a private was a preposterous incongruity. Sometimes, after listening to a sustained invective concerned with a dull and, on the face of it, absurd subject known as military "courtesy," he suspected that the dim purpose of the war was to let the regular army officers—men with the mentality and aspirations of schoolboys—have their fling with some real slaughter. He was being grotesquely sacrificed to the twenty-year patience of a Hopkins!

Of his three tent-mates—a flat-faced, conscientious objector from Tennessee, a big, scared Pole, and the disdainful Celt whom he had sat beside on the train—the two former spent the evenings in writing eternal letters home, while the Irishman sat in the tent door whistling over and over to himself half a dozen shrill and monotonous bird-calls. It was rather to avoid an hour of their company than with any hope of diversion that, when the quarantine was lifted at the end of the week, he went into town. He caught one of the swarm of jitneys that overran the camp each evening, and in half an hour was set down in front of the Stonewall Hotel on the hot and drowsy main street.

Under the gathering twilight the town was unexpectedly attractive. The sidewalks were peopled by vividly dressed, overpainted girls, who chattered volubly in low, lazy voices, by dozens of taxi-drivers who assailed passing officers with "Take y' anywheh, *Lieu*tenant," and by an intermittent procession of ragged, shuffling, subservient negroes. Anthony, loitering along through the warm dusk, felt for the first time in years the slow, erotic breath of the South, imminent in the hot softness of the air, in the pervasive lull, of thought and time.

He had gone about a block when he was arrested suddenly by a harsh command at his elbow.

"Haven't you been taught to salute officers?"

He looked dumbly at the man who addressed him, a stout, black-haired captain, who fixed him menacingly with brown pop-eyes.

"*Come to attention!*" The words were literally thundered. A few pedestrians near by stopped and stared. A soft-eyed girl in a lilac dress tittered to her companion.

Anthony came to attention.

"What's your regiment and company?"

Anthony told him.

"After this when you pass an officer on the street you straighten up and salute!"

"All right!"

"Say 'Yes, sir!'"

"Yes, sir."

The stout officer grunted, turned sharply, and marched down the street. After a moment Anthony moved on; the town was no longer indolent and exotic; the magic was suddenly gone out of the dusk. His eyes were turned precipitately inward upon the indignity of his position. He hated that officer, every officer—life was unendurable.

After he had gone half a block he realized that the girl in the lilac dress who had giggled at his discomfiture was walking with her friend about ten paces ahead of him. Several times she had turned and stared at Anthony, with cheerful laughter in the large eyes that seemed the same color as her gown.

At the corner she and her companion visibly slackened their pace—he must make his choice between joining them and passing obliviously by. He passed, hesitated, then slowed down. In a moment the pair were abreast of him again, dissolved in laughter now—not such strident mirth as he would have expected in the North from actresses in this familiar comedy, but a soft, low rippling, like the overflow from some subtle joke, into which he had inadvertently blundered.

"How do you do?" he said.

Her eyes were soft as shadows. Were they violet, or was it their blue darkness mingling with the gray hues of dusk?

"Pleasant evening," ventured Anthony uncertainly.

"Sure is," said the second girl.

"Hasn't been a very pleasant evening for you," sighed the girl in lilac. Her voice seemed as much a part of the night as the drowsy breeze stirring the wide brim of her hat.

"He had to have a chance to show off," said Anthony with a scornful laugh.

"Reckon so," she agreed.

They turned the corner and moved lackadaisically up a side street, as if following a drifting cable to which they were attached. In this town it seemed entirely natural to turn corners like that, it seemed natural to be bound nowhere in particular, to be thinking nothing.... The side street was dark, a sudden offshoot into a district of wild rose hedges and little quiet houses set far back from the street.

"Where're you going?" he inquired politely.

"Just goin'." The answer was an apology, a question, an explanation.

"Can I stroll along with you?"

"Reckon so."

It was an advantage that her accent was different. He could not have determined the social status of a Southerner from her talk—in New York a girl of a lower class would have been raucous, unendurable—except through the rosy spectacles of intoxication.

Dark was creeping down. Talking little—Anthony in careless, casual questions, the other two with provincial economy of phrase and burden—they sauntered past another corner, and another. In the middle of a block they stopped beneath a lamp-post.

"I live near here," explained the other girl.

"I live around the block," said the girl in lilac.

"Can I see you home?"

"To the corner, if you want to."

The other girl took a few steps backward. Anthony removed his hat.

"You're supposed to salute," said the girl in lilac with a laugh. "All the soldiers salute."

"I'll learn," he responded soberly.

The other girl said, "Well—" hesitated, then added, "call me up to-morrow, Dot," and retreated from the yellow circle of the street-lamp. Then, in silence, Anthony and the girl in lilac walked the three blocks to the small rickety house which was her home. Outside the wooden gate she hesitated.

"Well—thanks."

"Must you go in so soon?"

"I ought to."

"Can't you stroll around a little longer?" She regarded him dispassionately.

"I don't even know you."

Anthony laughed.

"It's not too late."

"I reckon I better go in."

"I thought we might walk down and see a movie."

"I'd like to."

"Then I could bring you home. I'd have just enough time. I've got to be in camp by eleven."

It was so dark that he could scarcely see her now. She was a dress swayed infinitesimally by the wind, two limpid, reckless eyes ...

"Why don't you come—Dot? Don't you like movies? Better come."

She shook her head.

"I oughtn't to."

He liked her, realizing that she was temporizing for the effect on him. He came closer and took her hand.

"If we get back by ten, can't you? just to the movies?"

"Well—I reckon so—"

Hand in hand they walked back toward down-town, along a hazy, dusky street where a negro newsboy was calling an extra in the cadence of the local venders' tradition, a cadence that was as musical as song.

DOT

Anthony's affair with Dorothy Raycroft was an inevitable result of his increasing carelessness about himself. He did not go to her desiring to possess the desirable, nor did he fall before a personality more vital, more compelling than his own, as he had done with Gloria four years before. He merely slid into the matter through his inability to make definite judgments. He could say "No!" neither to man nor woman; borrower and temptress alike found him tender-minded and pliable. Indeed he seldom made decisions at all, and when he did they were but half-hysterical resolves formed in the panic of some aghast and irreparable awakening.

The particular weakness he indulged on this occasion was his need of excitement and stimulus from without. He felt that for the first time in four years he could express and interpret himself anew. The girl promised rest; the hours in her company each evening alleviated the morbid and inevitably futile poundings of his imagination. He had become a coward in earnest—completely the slave of a hundred disordered and prowling thoughts which were released by the collapse of the authentic devotion to Gloria that had been the chief jailer of his insufficiency.

On that first night, as they stood by the gate, he kissed Dorothy and made an engagement to meet her the following Saturday. Then he went out to camp, and with the light burning lawlessly in his tent, he wrote a long letter to Gloria, a glowing letter, full of the sentimental dark, full of the remembered breath of flowers, full of a true and exceeding tenderness—these things he had learned again for a moment in a kiss given and taken under a rich warm moonlight just an hour before.

When Saturday night came he found Dot waiting at the entrance of the Bijou Moving Picture Theatre. She was dressed as on the preceding Wednesday in her lilac gown of frailest organdy, but it had evidently been washed and starched since then, for it was fresh and unrumpled. Daylight confirmed the impression he had received that in a sketchy, faulty way she was lovely. She was clean, her features were small, irregular, but eloquent and appropriate to each other. She was a dark, unenduring little flower—yet he thought he detected in her some quality of spiritual reticence, of strength drawn from her passive acceptance of all things. In this he was mistaken.

Dorothy Raycroft was nineteen. Her father had kept a small, unprosperous corner store, and she had graduated from high school in the lowest fourth of her class two days before he died. At high school she had enjoyed a rather unsavory reputation. As a matter of fact her behavior at the class picnic, where the rumors started, had been merely indiscreet—she had retained her technical purity until over a year later. The boy had been a clerk in a store on Jackson Street, and on the day after the incident he departed unexpectedly to New York. He had been intending to leave for some time, but had tarried for the consummation of his amorous enterprise.

After a while she confided the adventure to a girl friend, and later, as she watched her friend disappear down the sleepy street of dusty sunshine she knew in a flash of intuition that her story was going out into the world. Yet after telling it she felt much better, and a little bitter, and made as near an approach to character as she was capable of by walking in another direction and meeting another man with the honest intention of gratifying herself again. As a rule things happened to Dot. She was not weak, because there was nothing in her to tell her she was being weak. She was not strong, because she never knew that some of the things she did were brave. She neither defied nor conformed nor compromised.

She had no sense of humor, but, to take its place, a happy disposition that made her laugh at the proper times when she was with men. She had no definite intentions—sometimes she regretted vaguely that her reputation precluded what chance she had ever had for security. There had been no open discovery: her mother was interested only in starting her off on time each morning for the jewelry store where she earned fourteen dollars a week. But some of the boys she had known in high school now looked the other way when they were walking with "nice girls," and these incidents hurt her feelings. When they occurred she went home and cried.

Besides the Jackson Street clerk there had been two other men, of whom the first was a naval officer, who passed through town during the early days of the war. He had stayed over a night to make a connection, and was leaning idly against one of the pillars of the Stonewall Hotel when she passed by. He remained in town four days. She thought she loved him—lavished on him that first hysteria of passion that would have gone to the pusillanimous clerk. The naval officer's uniform—there were few of them in those days—had made the magic. He left with vague promises on his lips, and, once on the train, rejoiced that he had not told her his real name.

Her resultant depression had thrown her into the arms of Cyrus Fielding, the son of a local clothier, who had hailed her from his roadster one day as she passed along the sidewalk. She had always known him by name. Had she been born to a higher stratum he would have known her before. She had descended a little lower—so he met her after all. After a month he had gone away to training-camp, a little afraid of the intimacy, a little relieved in perceiving that she had not cared deeply for him, and that she was not the sort who would ever make trouble. Dot romanticized this affair and conceded to her vanity that the war had taken these men away from her. She told herself that she could have married the naval officer. Nevertheless, it worried her that within eight months there had been three men in her life. She thought with more fear than wonder in her heart that she would soon be like those "bad girls" on Jackson Street at whom she and her gum-chewing, giggling friends had stared with fascinated glances three years before.

For a while she attempted to be more careful. She let men "pick her up"; she let them kiss her, and even allowed certain other liberties to be forced upon her, but she did not add to her trio. After several months the strength of her resolution—or rather the poignant expediency of her fears—was worn away. She grew restless drowsing there out of life and time while the summer months faded. The soldiers she met were either obviously below her or, less obviously, above her—in which case they desired only to use her; they were Yankees, harsh and ungracious; they swarmed in large crowds.... And then she met Anthony.

On that first evening he had been little more than a pleasantly unhappy face, a voice, the means with which to pass an hour, but when she kept her engagement with him on Saturday she regarded him with consideration. She liked him. Unknowingly she saw her own tragedies mirrored in his face.

Again they went to the movies, again they wandered along the shadowy, scented streets, hand in hand this time, speaking a little in hushed voices. They passed through the gate—up toward the little porch—

"I can stay a while, can't I?"

"Sh!" she whispered, "we've got to be very quiet. Mother sits up reading Snappy Stories." In confirmation he heard the faint crackling inside as a page was turned. The open-shutter slits emitted horizontal rods of light that fell in thin parallels across Dorothy's skirt. The street was silent save for a group on the steps of a house across the way, who, from time to time, raised their voices in a soft, bantering song.

"*—When you wa-ake*
You shall ha-ave
All the pretty little hawsiz—"

Then, as though it had been waiting on a near-by roof for their arrival, the moon came slanting suddenly through the vines and turned the girl's face to the color of white roses.

Anthony had a start of memory, so vivid that before his closed eyes there formed a picture, distinct as a flashback on a screen—a spring night of thaw set out of time in a half-forgotten winter five years before—another face, radiant, flower-like, upturned to lights as transforming as the stars—

Ah, *la belle dame sans merci* who lived in his heart, made known to him in transitory fading splendor by dark eyes in the Ritz-Carlton, by a shadowy glance from a passing carriage in the Bois de Boulogne! But those nights were only part of a song, a remembered glory—here again were the faint winds, the illusions, the eternal present with its promise of romance.

"Oh," she whispered, "do you love me? Do you love me?"

The spell was broken—the drifted fragments of the stars became only light, the singing down the street diminished to a monotone, to the whimper of locusts in the grass. With almost a sigh he kissed her fervent mouth, while her arms crept up about his shoulders.

THE MAN-AT-ARMS

As the weeks dried up and blew away, the range of Anthony's travels extended until he grew to comprehend the camp and its environment. For the first time in his life he was in constant personal contact with the waiters to whom he had given tips, the chauffeurs who had touched their hats to him, the carpenters, plumbers, barbers, and farmers who had previously been remarkable only in the subservience of their professional genuflections. During his first two months in camp he did not hold ten minutes' consecutive conversation with a single man.

On the service record his occupation stood as "student"; on the original questionnaire he had prematurely written "author"; but when men in his company asked his business he commonly gave it as bank clerk—had he told the truth, that he did no work, they would have been suspicious of him as a member of the leisure class.

His platoon sergeant, Pop Donnelly, was a scraggly "old soldier," worn thin with drink. In the past he had spent unnumbered weeks in the guard-house, but recently, thanks to the drill-master famine, he had been elevated to his present pinnacle. His complexion was full of shell-holes—it bore an unmistakable resemblance to those aerial photographs of "the battle-field at Blank." Once a week he got drunk down-town on white liquor, returned quietly to camp and collapsed upon his bunk, joining the company at reveille looking more than ever like a white mask of death.

He nursed the astounding delusion that he was astutely "slipping it over" on the government—he had spent eighteen years in its service at a minute wage, and he was soon to retire (here he usually winked) on the impressive income of fifty-five dollars a month. He looked upon it as a gorgeous joke that he had played upon the dozens who had bullied and scorned him since he was a Georgia country boy of nineteen.

At present there were but two lieutenants—Hopkins and the popular Kretching. The latter was considered a good fellow and a fine leader, until a year later, when he disappeared with a mess fund of eleven hundred dollars and, like so many leaders, proved exceedingly difficult to follow.

Eventually there was Captain Dunning, god of this brief but self-sufficing microcosm. He was a reserve officer, nervous, energetic, and enthusiastic. This latter quality, indeed, often took material form and was visible as fine froth in the corners of his mouth. Like most executives he saw his charges strictly from the front, and to his hopeful eyes his command seemed just such an excellent unit as such an excellent war deserved. For all his anxiety and absorption he was having the time of his life.

Baptiste, the little Sicilian of the train, fell foul of him the second week of drill. The captain had several times ordered the men to be clean-shaven when they fell in each morning. One day there was disclosed an alarming breech of this rule, surely a case of Teutonic connivance—during the night four men had grown hair upon their faces. The fact that three of the four understood a minimum of English made a practical object-lesson only the more necessary, so Captain Dunning resolutely sent a volunteer barber back to the company street for a razor. Whereupon for the safety of democracy a half-ounce of hair was scraped dry from the cheeks of three Italians and one Pole.

Outside the world of the company there appeared, from time to time, the colonel, a heavy man with snarling teeth, who circumnavigated the battalion drill-field upon a handsome black horse. He was a West Pointer, and, mimetically, a gentleman. He had a dowdy wife and a dowdy mind, and spent much of his time in town taking advantage of the army's lately exalted social position. Last of all was the general, who traversed the roads of the camp preceded by his flag—a figure so austere, so removed, so magnificent, as to be scarcely comprehensible.

December. Cool winds at night now, and damp, chilly mornings on the drill-grounds. As the heat faded, Anthony found himself increasingly glad to be alive. Renewed strangely through his body, he worried little and existed in the present with a sort of animal content. It was not that Gloria or the life that Gloria represented was less often in his thoughts—it was simply that she became, day by day, less real, less vivid. For a week they had corresponded passionately, almost hysterically—then by an unwritten agreement they had ceased to write more than twice, and then once, a week. She was bored, she said; if his brigade was to be there a long time she was coming down to join him. Mr. Haight was going to be able to submit a stronger brief than he had expected, but doubted that the appealed case would come up until late spring. Muriel was in the city doing Red Cross work, and they went out together rather often. What would Anthony think if *she* went into the Red Cross? Trouble was she had heard that she might have to bathe negroes in alcohol, and after that she hadn't felt so patriotic. The city was full of soldiers and she'd seen a lot of boys she hadn't laid eyes on for years....

Anthony did not want her to come South. He told himself that this was for many reasons—he needed a rest from her and she from him. She would be bored beyond measure in town, and she would be able to see Anthony for only a few hours each day. But in his heart he feared that it was because he was attracted to Dorothy. As a matter of fact he lived in terror that Gloria should learn by some chance or intention of the relation he had formed. By the end of a fortnight the entanglement began to give him moments of misery at his own faithlessness. Nevertheless, as each day ended he was unable to withstand the lure that would draw him irresistibly out of his tent and over to the telephone at the Y.M.C.A.

"Dot."

"Yes?"

"I may be able to get in to-night."

"I'm so glad."

"Do you want to listen to my splendid eloquence for a few starry hours?"

"Oh, you funny—" For an instant he had a memory of five years before—of Geraldine. Then—

"I'll arrive about eight."

At seven he would be in a jitney bound for the city, where hundreds of little Southern girls were waiting on moonlit porches for their lovers. He would be excited already for her warm retarded kisses, for the amazed quietude of the glances she gave him—glances nearer to worship than any he had ever inspired. Gloria and he had been equals, giving without thought of thanks or obligation. To this girl his very caresses were an inestimable boon. Crying quietly she had confessed to him that he was not the first man in her life; there had been one other—he gathered that the affair had no sooner commenced than it had been over.

Indeed, so far as she was concerned, she spoke the truth. She had forgotten the clerk, the naval officer, the clothier's son, forgotten her vividness of emotion, which is true forgetting. She knew that in some opaque and shadowy existence some one had taken her—it was as though it had occurred in sleep.

Almost every night Anthony came to town. It was too cool now for the porch, so her mother surrendered to them the tiny sitting room, with its dozens of cheaply framed chromos, its yard upon yard of decorative fringe, and its thick atmosphere of several decades in the proximity of the kitchen. They would build a fire—then, happily, inexhaustibly, she would go about the business of love. Each evening at ten she would walk with him to the door, her black hair in disarray, her face pale without cosmetics, paler still under the whiteness of the moon. As a rule it would be bright and silver outside; now and then there was a slow warm rain, too indolent, almost, to reach the ground.

"Say you love me," she would whisper.

"Why, of course, you sweet baby."

"Am I a baby?" This almost wistfully.

"Just a little baby."

She knew vaguely of Gloria. It gave her pain to think of it, so she imagined her to be haughty and proud and cold. She had decided that Gloria must be older than Anthony, and that there was no love between husband and wife. Sometimes she let herself dream that after the war Anthony would get a divorce and they would be married—but she never mentioned this to Anthony, she scarcely knew why. She shared his company's idea that he was a sort of bank clerk—she thought that he was respectable and poor. She would say:

"If I had some money, darlin', I'd give ev'y bit of it to you.... I'd like to have about fifty thousand dollars."

"I suppose that'd be plenty," agreed Anthony.

—In her letter that day Gloria had written: "I suppose if we *could* settle for a million it would be better to tell Mr. Haight to go ahead and settle. But it'd seem a pity...."

... "We could have an automobile," exclaimed Dot, in a final burst of triumph.

AN IMPRESSIVE OCCASION

Captain Dunning prided himself on being a great reader of character. Half an hour after meeting a man he was accustomed to place him in one of a number of astonishing categories—fine man, good man, smart fellow, theorizer, poet, and "worthless." One day early in February he caused Anthony to be summoned to his presence in the orderly tent.

"Patch," he said sententiously, "I've had my eye on you for several weeks."

Anthony stood erect and motionless.

"And I think you've got the makings of a good soldier."

He waited for the warm glow, which this would naturally arouse, to cool—and then continued:

"This is no child's play," he said, narrowing his brows.

Anthony agreed with a melancholy "No, sir."

"It's a man's game—and we need leaders." Then the climax, swift, sure, and electric: "Patch, I'm going to make you a corporal."

At this point Anthony should have staggered slightly backward, overwhelmed. He was to be one of the quarter million selected for that consummate trust. He was going to be able to shout the technical phrase, "Follow me!" to seven other frightened men.

"You seem to be a man of some education," said Captain Dunning.

"Yes, Sir."

"That's good, that's good. Education's a great thing, but don't let it go to your head. Keep on the way you're doing and you'll be a good soldier."

With these parting words lingering in his ears, Corporal Patch saluted, executed a right about face, and left the tent.

Though the conversation amused Anthony, it did generate the idea that life would be more amusing as a sergeant or, should he find a less exacting medical examiner, as an officer. He was little interested in the work, which seemed to belie the army's boasted gallantry. At the inspections one did not dress up to look well, one dressed up to keep from looking badly.

But as winter wore away—the short, snowless winter marked by damp nights and cool, rainy days—he marvelled at how quickly the system had grasped him. He was a soldier—all who were not soldiers were civilians. The world was divided primarily into those two classifications.

It occurred to him that all strongly accentuated classes, such as the military, divided men into two kinds: their own kind—and those without. To the clergyman there were clergy and laity, to the Catholic there were Catholics and non-Catholics, to the negro there were blacks and whites, to the prisoner there were the imprisoned and the free, and to the sick man there were the sick and the well.... So, without thinking of it once in his lifetime, he had been a civilian, a layman, a non-Catholic, a Gentile, white, free, and well....

As the American troops were poured into the French and British trenches he began to find the names of many Harvard men among the casualties recorded in the Army and Navy Journal. But for all the sweat and blood the situation appeared unchanged, and he saw no prospect of the war's ending in the perceptible future. In the old chronicles the right wing of one army always defeated the left wing of the other, the left wing being, meanwhile, vanquished by the enemy's right. After that the mercenaries fled. It had been so simple, in those days, almost as if prearranged....

Gloria wrote that she was reading a great deal. What a mess they had made of their affairs, she said. She had so little to do now that she spent her time imagining how differently things might have turned out. Her whole environment appeared insecure—and a few years back she had seemed to hold all the strings in her own little hand....

In June her letters grew hurried and less frequent. She suddenly ceased to write about coming South.

DEFEAT

March in the country around was rare with jasmine and jonquils and patches of violets in the warming grass. Afterward he remembered especially one afternoon of such a fresh and magic glamour that as he stood in the rifle-pit marking targets he recited "Atalanta in Calydon" to an uncomprehending Pole, his voice mingling with the rip, sing, and splatter of the bullets overhead.

"When the hounds of spring ..."

Spang!

"Are on winter's traces ..."

Whirr-r-r-r! ...

"The mother of months ..."

"Hey! Come to! Mark three-e-e! ..."

In town the streets were in a sleepy dream again, and together Anthony and Dot idled in their own tracks of the previous autumn until he began to feel a drowsy attachment for this South—a South, it seemed, more of Algiers than of Italy, with faded aspirations pointing back over innumerable generations to some warm, primitive Nirvana, without hope or care. Here there was an inflection of cordiality, of comprehension, in every voice. "Life plays the same lovely and agonizing joke on all of us," they seemed to say in their plaintive pleasant cadence, in the rising inflection terminating on an unresolved minor.

He liked his barber shop where he was "Hi, corporal!" to a pale, emaciated young man, who shaved him and pushed a cool vibrating machine endlessly over his insatiable head. He liked "Johnston's Gardens" where they danced, where a tragic negro made yearning, aching music on a saxophone until the garish hall became an enchanted jungle of barbaric rhythms and smoky laughter, where to forget the uneventful passage of time upon Dorothy's soft sighs and tender whisperings was the consummation of all aspiration, of all content.

There was an undertone of sadness in her character, a conscious evasion of all except the pleasurable minutiae of life. Her violet eyes would remain for hours apparently insensate as, thoughtless and reckless, she basked like a cat in the sun. He wondered what the tired, spiritless mother thought of them, and whether in her moments of uttermost cynicism she ever guessed at their relationship.

On Sunday afternoons they walked along the countryside, resting at intervals on the dry moss in the outskirts of a wood. Here the birds had gathered and the clusters of violets and white dogwood; here the hoar trees shone crystalline and cool, oblivious to the intoxicating heat that waited outside; here he would talk, intermittently, in a sleepy monologue, in a conversation of no significance, of no replies.

July came scorching down. Captain Dunning was ordered to detail one of his men to learn blacksmithing. The regiment was filling up to war strength, and he needed most of his veterans for drill-masters, so he selected the little Italian, Baptiste, whom he could most easily spare. Little Baptiste had never had anything to do with horses. His fear made matters worse. He reappeared in the orderly room one day and told Captain Dunning that he wanted to die if he couldn't be relieved. The horses kicked at him, he said; he was no good at the work. Finally he fell on his knees and besought Captain Dunning, in a mixture of broken English and scriptural Italian, to get him out of it. He had not slept for three days; monstrous stallions reared and cavorted through his dreams.

Captain Dunning reproved the company clerk (who had burst out laughing), and told Baptiste he would do what he could. But when he thought it over he decided that he couldn't spare a better man. Little Baptiste went from bad to worse. The horses seemed to divine his fear and take every advantage of it. Two weeks later a great black mare crushed his skull in with her hoofs while he was trying to lead her from her stall.

In mid-July came rumors, and then orders, that concerned a change of camp. The brigade was to move to an empty cantonment, a hundred miles farther south, there to be expanded into a division. At first the men thought they were departing for the trenches, and all evening little groups jabbered in the company street, shouting to each other in swaggering exclamations: "Su-u-ure we are!" When the truth leaked out, it was rejected indignantly as a blind to conceal their real destination. They revelled in their own importance. That night they told their girls in town that they were "going to get the Germans." Anthony circulated for a while among the groups—then, stopping a jitney, rode down to tell Dot that he was going away.

She was waiting on the dark veranda in a cheap white dress that accentuated the youth and softness of her face.

"Oh," she whispered, "I've wanted you so, honey. All this day."

"I have something to tell you."

She drew him down beside her on the swinging seat, not noticing his ominous tone.

"Tell me."

"We're leaving next week."

Her arms seeking his shoulders remained poised upon the dark air, her chin tipped up. When she spoke the softness was gone from her voice.

"Leaving for France?"

"No. Less luck than that. Leaving for some darn camp in Mississippi."

She shut her eyes and he could see that the lids were trembling.

"Dear little Dot, life is so damned hard."

She was crying upon his shoulder.

"So damned hard, so damned hard," he repeated aimlessly; "it just hurts people and hurts people, until finally it hurts them so that they can't be hurt ever any more. That's the last and worst thing it does."

Frantic, wild with anguish, she strained him to her breast.

"Oh, God!" she whispered brokenly, "you can't go way from me. I'd die."

He was finding it impossible to pass off his departure as a common, impersonal blow. He was too near to her to do more than repeat "Poor little Dot. Poor little Dot."

"And then what?" she demanded wearily.

"What do you mean?"

"You're my whole life, that's all. I'd die for you right now if you said so. I'd get a knife and kill myself. You can't leave me here."

Her tone frightened him.

"These things happen," he said evenly.

"Then I'm going with you." Tears were streaming down her checks. Her mouth was trembling in an ecstasy of grief and fear.

"Sweet," he muttered sentimentally, "sweet little girl. Don't you see we'd just be putting off what's bound to happen? I'll be going to France in a few months—"

She leaned away from him and clinching her fists lifted her face toward the sky.

"I want to die," she said, as if moulding each word carefully in her heart.

"Dot," he whispered uncomfortably, "you'll forget. Things are sweeter when they're lost. I know—because once I wanted something and got it. It was the only thing I ever wanted badly, Dot. And when I got it it turned to dust in my hands."

"All right."

Absorbed in himself, he continued:

"I've often thought that if I hadn't got what I wanted things might have been different with me. I might have found something in my mind and enjoyed putting it in circulation. I might have been content with the work of it, and had some sweet vanity out of the success. I suppose that at one time I could have had anything I wanted, within reason, but that was the only thing I ever wanted with any fervor. God! And that taught me you can't have *any*thing, you can't have anything at *all.* Because desire just cheats you. It's like a sunbeam skipping here and there about a room. It stops and gilds some inconsequential object, and we poor fools try to grasp it—but when we do the sunbeam moves on to something else, and you've got the inconsequential part, but the glitter that made you want it is gone—" He broke off uneasily. She had risen and was standing, dry-eyed, picking little leaves from a dark vine.

"Dot—"

"Go way," she said coldly. "What? Why?"

"I don't want just words. If that's all you have for me you'd better go."

"Why, Dot—"

"What's death to me is just a lot of words to you. You put 'em together so pretty."

"I'm sorry. I was talking about you, Dot."

"Go way from here."

He approached her with arms outstretched, but she held him away.

"You don't want me to go with you," she said evenly; "maybe you're going to meet that—that girl—" She could not bring herself to say wife. "How do I know? Well, then, I reckon you're not my fellow any more. So go way."

For a moment, while conflicting warnings and desires prompted Anthony, it seemed one of those rare times when he would take a step prompted from within. He hesitated. Then a wave of weariness broke against him. It was too late—everything was too late. For years now he had dreamed the world away, basing his decisions upon emotions unstable as water. The little girl in the white dress dominated him, as she approached beauty in the hard symmetry of her desire. The fire blazing in her dark and injured heart seemed to glow around her like a flame. With some profound and uncharted pride she had made herself remote and so achieved her purpose.

"I didn't—mean to seem so callous, Dot."

"It don't matter."

The fire rolled over Anthony. Something wrenched at his bowels, and he stood there helpless and beaten.

"Come with me, Dot—little loving Dot. Oh, come with me. I couldn't leave you now—"

With a sob she wound her arms around him and let him support her weight while the moon, at its perennial labor of covering the bad complexion of the world, showered its illicit honey over the drowsy street.

THE CATASTROPHE

Early September in Camp Boone, Mississippi. The darkness, alive with insects, beat in upon the mosquito-netting, beneath the shelter of which Anthony was trying to write a letter. An intermittent chatter over a poker game was going on in the next tent, and outside a man was strolling up the company street singing a current bit of doggerel about "K-K-K-Katy."

With an effort Anthony hoisted himself to his elbow and, pencil in hand, looked down at his blank sheet of paper. Then, omitting any heading, he began:

I can't imagine what the matter is, Gloria. I haven't had a line from you for two weeks and it's only natural to be worried—

He threw this away with a disturbed grunt and began again:

I don't know what to think, Gloria. Your last letter, short, cold, without a word of affection or even a decent account of what you've been doing, came two weeks ago. It's only natural that I should wonder. If your love for me isn't absolutely dead it seems that you'd at least keep me from worry—

Again he crumpled the page and tossed it angrily through a tear in the tent wall, realizing simultaneously that he would have to pick it up in the morning. He felt disinclined to try again. He could get no warmth into the lines—only a persistent jealousy and suspicion. Since midsummer these discrepancies in Gloria's correspondence had grown more and more noticeable. At first he had scarcely perceived them. He was so inured to the perfunctory "dearest" and "darlings" scattered through her letters that he was oblivious to their presence or absence. But in this last fortnight he had become increasingly aware that there was something amiss.

He had sent her a night-letter saying that he had passed his examinations for an officers' training-camp, and expected to leave for Georgia shortly. She had not answered. He had wired again—when he received no word he imagined that she might be out of town. But it occurred and recurred to him that she was not out of town, and a series of distraught imaginings began to plague him. Supposing Gloria, bored and restless, had found some one, even as he had. The thought terrified him with its possibility—it was chiefly because he had been so sure of her personal integrity that he had considered her so sparingly during the year. And now, as a doubt was born, the old angers, the rages of possession, swarmed back a thousandfold. What more natural than that she should be in love again?

He remembered the Gloria who promised that should she ever want anything, she would take it, insisting that since she would act entirely for her own satisfaction she could go through such an affair unsmirched—it was only the effect on a person's mind that counted, anyhow, she said, and her reaction would be the masculine one, of satiation and faint dislike.

But that had been when they were first married. Later, with the discovery that she could be jealous of Anthony, she had, outwardly at least, changed her mind. There were no other men in the world for her. This he had known only too surely. Perceiving that a certain fastidiousness would restrain her, he had grown lax in preserving the completeness of her love—which, after all, was the keystone of the entire structure.

Meanwhile all through the summer he had been maintaining Dot in a boarding-house down-town. To do this it had been necessary to write to his broker for money. Dot had covered her journey south by leaving her house a day before the brigade broke camp, informing her mother in a note that she had gone to New York. On the evening following Anthony had called as though to see her. Mrs. Raycroft was in a state of collapse and there was a policeman in the parlor. A questionnaire had ensued, from which Anthony had extricated himself with some difficulty.

In September, with his suspicions of Gloria, the company of Dot had become tedious, then almost intolerable. He was nervous and irritable from lack of sleep; his heart was sick and afraid. Three days ago he had gone to Captain Dunning and asked for a furlough, only to be met with benignant procrastination. The division was starting overseas, while Anthony was going to an officers' training-camp; what furloughs could be given must go to the men who were leaving the country.

Upon this refusal Anthony had started to the telegraph office intending to wire Gloria to come South—he reached the door and receded despairingly, seeing the utter impracticability of such a move. Then he had spent the evening quarrelling irritably with Dot, and returned to camp morose and angry with the world. There had been a disagreeable scene, in the midst of which he had precipitately departed. What was to be done with her did not seem to concern him vitally at present—he was completely absorbed in the disheartening silence of his wife....

The flap of the tent made a sudden triangle back upon itself, and a dark head appeared against the night.

"Sergeant Patch?" The accent was Italian, and Anthony saw by the belt that the man was a headquarters orderly.

"Want me?"

"Lady call up headquarters ten minutes ago. Say she have speak with you. Ver' important."

Anthony swept aside the mosquito-netting and stood up. It might be a wire from Gloria telephoned over.

"She say to get you. She call again ten o'clock."

"All right, thanks." He picked up his hat and in a moment was striding beside the orderly through the hot, almost suffocating, darkness. Over in the headquarters shack he saluted a dozing night-service officer.

"Sit down and wait," suggested the lieutenant nonchalantly. "Girl seemed awful anxious to speak to you."

Anthony's hopes fell away.

"Thank you very much, sir." And as the phone squeaked on the side-wall he knew who was calling.

"This is Dot," came an unsteady voice, "I've got to see you."

"Dot, I told you I couldn't get down for several days."

"I've got to see you to-night. It's important."

"It's too late," he said coldly; "it's ten o'clock, and I have to be in camp at eleven."

"All right." There was so much wretchedness compressed into the two words that Anthony felt a measure of compunction.

"What's the matter?"

"I want to tell you good-by.

"Oh, don't be a little idiot!" he exclaimed. But his spirits rose. What luck if she should leave town this very night! What a burden from his soul. But he said: "You can't possibly leave before to-morrow."

Out of the corner of his eye he saw the night-service officer regarding him quizzically. Then, startlingly, came Dot's next words:

"I don't mean 'leave' that way."

Anthony's hand clutched the receiver fiercely. He felt his nerves turning cold as if the heat was leaving his body.

"What?"

Then quickly in a wild broken voice he heard:

"Good-by—oh, good-by!"

Cul-*lup!* She had hung up the receiver. With a sound that was half a gasp, half a cry, Anthony hurried from the headquarters building. Outside, under the stars that dripped like silver tassels through the trees of the little grove, he stood motionless, hesitating. Had she meant to kill herself?—oh, the little fool! He was filled with bitter hate toward her. In this dénouement he found it impossible to realize that he had ever begun such an entanglement, such a mess, a sordid mélange of worry and pain.

He found himself walking slowly away, repeating over and over that it was futile to worry. He had best go back to his tent and sleep. He needed sleep. God! Would he ever sleep again? His mind was in a vast clamor and confusion; as he reached the road he turned around in a panic and began running, not toward his company but away from it. Men were returning now—he could find a taxicab. After a minute two yellow eyes appeared around a bend. Desperately he ran toward them.

"Jitney! Jitney!" ... It was an empty Ford.... "I want to go to town."

"Cost you a dollar."

"All right. If you'll just hurry—"

After an interminable time he ran up the steps of a dark ramshackle little house, and through the door, almost knocking over an immense negress who was walking, candle in hand, along the hall.

"Where's my wife?" he cried wildly.

"She gone to bed."

Up the stairs three at a time, down the creaking passage. The room was dark and silent, and with trembling fingers he struck a match. Two wide eyes looked up at him from a wretched ball of clothes on the bed.

"Ah, I knew you'd come," she murmured brokenly.

Anthony grew cold with anger.

"So it was just a plan to get me down here, get me in trouble!" he said. "God damn it, you've shouted 'wolf' once too often!"

She regarded him pitifully.

"I had to see you. I couldn't have lived. Oh, I had to see you—"

He sat down on the side of the bed and slowly shook his head.

"You're no good," he said decisively, talking unconsciously as Gloria might have talked to him. "This sort of thing isn't fair to me, you know."

"Come closer." Whatever he might say Dot was happy now. He cared for her. She had brought him to her side.

"Oh, God," said Anthony hopelessly. As weariness rolled along its inevitable wave his anger subsided, receded, vanished. He collapsed suddenly, fell sobbing beside her on the bed.

"Oh, my darling," she begged him, "don't cry! Oh, don't cry!"

She took his head upon her breast and soothed him, mingled her happy tears with the bitterness of his. Her hand played gently with his dark hair.

"I'm such a little fool," she murmured brokenly, "but I love you, and when you're cold to me it seems as if it isn't worth while to go on livin'."

After all, this was peace—the quiet room with the mingled scent of women's powder and perfume, Dot's hand soft as a warm wind upon his hair, the rise and fall of her bosom as she took breath—for a moment it was as though it were Gloria there, as though he were at rest in some sweeter and safer home than he had ever known.

An hour passed. A clock began to chime in the hall. He jumped to his feet and looked at the phosphorescent hands of his wrist watch. It was twelve o'clock.

He had trouble in finding a taxi that would take him out at that hour. As he urged the driver faster along the road he speculated on the best method of entering camp. He had been late several times recently, and he knew that were he caught again his name would probably be stricken from the list of officer candidates. He wondered if he had not better dismiss the taxi and take a chance on passing the sentry in the dark. Still, officers often rode past the sentries after midnight....

"Halt!" The monosyllable came from the yellow glare that the headlights dropped upon the changing road. The taxi-driver threw out his clutch and a sentry walked up, carrying his rifle at the port. With him, by an ill chance, was the officer of the guard.

"Out late, sergeant."

"Yes, sir. Got delayed."

"Too bad. Have to take your name."

As the officer waited, note-book and pencil in hand, something not fully intended crowded to Anthony's lips, something born of panic, of muddle, of despair.

"Sergeant R.A. Foley," he answered breathlessly.

"And the outfit?"

"Company Q, Eighty-third Infantry."

"All right. You'll have to walk from here, sergeant."

Anthony saluted, quickly paid his taxi-driver, and set off for a run toward the regiment he had named. When he was out of sight he changed his course, and with his heart beating wildly, hurried to his company, feeling that he had made a fatal error of judgment.

Two days later the officer who had been in command of the guard recognized him in a barber shop down-town. In charge of a military policeman he was taken back to the camp, where he was reduced to the ranks without trial, and confined for a month to the limits of his company street.

With this blow a spell of utter depression overtook him, and within a week he was again caught down-town, wandering around in a drunken daze, with a pint of bootleg whiskey in his hip pocket. It was because of a sort of craziness in his behavior at the trial that his sentence to the guard-house was for only three weeks.

NIGHTMARE

Early in his confinement the conviction took root in him that he was going mad. It was as though there were a quantity of dark yet vivid personalities in his mind, some of them familiar, some of them strange and terrible, held in check by a little monitor, who sat aloft somewhere and looked on. The thing that worried him was that the monitor was sick, and holding out with difficulty. Should he give up, should he falter for a moment, out would rush these intolerable things—only Anthony could know what a state of blackness there would be if the worst of him could roam his consciousness unchecked.

The heat of the day had changed, somehow, until it was a burnished darkness crushing down upon a devastated land. Over his head the blue circles of ominous uncharted suns, of unnumbered centres of fire, revolved interminably before his eyes as though he were lying constantly exposed to the hot light and in a state of feverish coma. At seven in the morning something phantasmal, something almost absurdly unreal that he knew was his mortal body, went out with seven other prisoners and two guards to work on the camp roads. One day they loaded and unloaded quantities of gravel, spread it, raked it—the next day they worked with huge barrels of red-hot tar, flooding the gravel with black, shining pools of molten heat. At night, locked up in the guard-house, he would lie without thought, without courage to compass thought, staring at the irregular beams of the ceiling overhead until about three o'clock, when he would slip into a broken, troubled sleep.

During the work hours he labored with uneasy haste, attempting, as the day bore toward the sultry Mississippi sunset, to tire himself physically so that in the evening he might sleep deeply from utter exhaustion.... Then one afternoon in the second week he had a feeling that two eyes were watching him from a place a few feet beyond one of the guards. This aroused him to a sort of terror. He turned his back on the eyes and shovelled feverishly, until it became necessary for him to face about and go for more gravel. Then they entered his vision again, and his already taut nerves tightened up to the breaking-point. The eyes were leering at him. Out of a hot silence he heard his name called in a tragic voice, and the earth tipped absurdly back and forth to a babel of shouting and confusion.

When next he became conscious he was back in the guard-house, and the other prisoners were throwing him curious glances. The eyes returned no more. It was many days before he realized that the voice must have been Dot's, that she had called out to him and made some sort of disturbance. He decided this just previous to the expiration of his sentence, when the cloud that oppressed him had lifted, leaving him in a deep, dispirited lethargy. As the conscious mediator, the monitor who kept that fearsome ménage of horror, grew stronger, Anthony became physically weaker. He was scarcely able to get through the two days of toil, and when he was released, one rainy afternoon, and returned to his company, he reached his tent only to fall into a heavy doze, from which he awoke before dawn, aching and unrefreshed. Beside his cot were two letters that had been awaiting him in the orderly tent for some time. The first was from Gloria; it was short and cool:

The case is coming to trial late in November. Can you possibly get leave?

I've tried to write you again and again but it just seems to make things worse. I want to see you about several matters, but you know that you have once prevented me from coming and I am disinclined to try again. In view of a number of things it seems necessary that we have a conference. I'm very glad about your appointment.

GLORIA.

He was too tired to try to understand—or to care. Her phrases, her intentions, were all very far away in an incomprehensible past. At the second letter he scarcely glanced; it was from Dot—an incoherent, tear-swollen scrawl, a flood of protest, endearment, and grief. After a page he let it slip from his inert hand and drowsed back into a nebulous hinterland of his own. At drill-call he awoke with a high fever and fainted when he tried to leave his tent—at noon he was sent to the base hospital with influenza.

He was aware that this sickness was providential. It saved him from a hysterical relapse—and he recovered in time to entrain on a damp November day for New York, and for the interminable massacre beyond.

When the regiment reached Camp Mills, Long Island, Anthony's single idea was to get into the city and see Gloria as soon as possible. It was now evident that an armistice would be signed within the week, but rumor had it that in any case troops would continue to be shipped to France until the last moment. Anthony was appalled at the notion of the long voyage, of a tedious debarkation at a French port, and of being kept abroad for a year, possibly, to replace the troops who had seen actual fighting.

His intention had been to obtain a two-day furlough, but Camp Mills proved to be under a strict influenza quarantine—it was impossible for even an officer to leave except on official business. For a private it was out of the question.

The camp itself was a dreary muddle, cold, wind-swept, and filthy, with the accumulated dirt incident to the passage through of many divisions. Their train came in at seven one night, and they waited in line until one while a military tangle was straightened out somewhere ahead. Officers ran up and down ceaselessly, calling orders and making a great uproar. It turned out that the trouble was due to the colonel, who was in a righteous temper because he was a West Pointer, and the war was going to stop before he could get overseas. Had the militant governments realized the number of broken hearts among the older West Pointers during that week, they would indubitably have prolonged the slaughter another month. The thing was pitiable!

Gazing out at the bleak expanse of tents extending for miles over a trodden welter of slush and snow, Anthony saw the impracticability of trudging to a telephone that night. He would call her at the first opportunity in the morning.

Aroused in the chill and bitter dawn he stood at reveille and listened to a passionate harangue from Captain Dunning:

"You men may think the war is over. Well, let me tell you, it isn't! Those fellows aren't going to sign the armistice. It's another trick, and we'd be crazy to let anything slacken up here in the company, because, let me tell you, we're going to sail from here within a week, and when we do we're going to see some real fighting." He paused that they might get the full effect of his pronouncement. And then: "If you think the war's over, just talk to any one who's been in it and see if *they* think the Germans are all in. They don't. Nobody does. I've talked to the people that *know*, and they say there'll be, anyways, a year longer of war. *They* don't think it's over. So you men better not get any foolish ideas that it is."

Doubly stressing this final admonition, he ordered the company dismissed.

At noon Anthony set off at a run for the nearest canteen telephone. As he approached what corresponded to the down-town of the camp, he noticed that many other soldiers were running also, that a man near him had suddenly leaped into the air and clicked his heels together. The tendency to run became general, and from little excited groups here and there came the sounds of cheering. He stopped and listened—over the cold country whistles were blowing and the chimes of the Garden City churches broke suddenly into reverberatory sound.

Anthony began to run again. The cries were clear and distinct now as they rose with clouds of frosted breath into the chilly air:

"Germany's surrendered! Germany's surrendered!"

THE FALSE ARMISTICE

That evening in the opaque gloom of six o'clock Anthony slipped between two freight-cars, and once over the railroad, followed the track along to Garden City, where he caught an electric train for New York. He stood some chance of apprehension—he knew that the military police were often sent through the cars to ask for passes, but he imagined that to-night the vigilance would be relaxed. But, in any event, he would have tried to slip through, for he had been unable to locate Gloria by telephone, and another day of suspense would have been intolerable.

After inexplicable stops and waits that reminded him of the night he had left New York, over a year before, they drew into the Pennsylvania Station, and he followed the familiar way to the taxi-stand, finding it grotesque and oddly stimulating to give his own address.

Broadway was a riot of light, thronged as he had never seen it with a carnival crowd which swept its glittering way through scraps of paper, piled ankle-deep on the sidewalks. Here and there, elevated upon benches and boxes, soldiers addressed the heedless mass, each face in which was clear cut and distinct under the white glare overhead. Anthony picked out half a dozen figures—a drunken sailor, tipped backward and supported by two other gobs, was waving his hat and emitting a wild series of roars; a wounded soldier, crutch in hand, was borne along in an eddy on the shoulders of some shrieking civilians; a dark-haired girl sat cross-legged and meditative on top of a parked taxicab. Here surely the victory had come in time, the climax had been scheduled with the uttermost celestial foresight. The great rich nation had made triumphant war, suffered enough for poignancy but not enough for bitterness—hence the carnival, the feasting, the triumph. Under these bright lights glittered the faces of peoples whose glory had long since passed away, whose very civilizations were dead-men whose ancestors had heard the news of victory in Babylon, in Nineveh, in Bagdad, in Tyre, a hundred generations before; men whose ancestors had seen a flower-decked, slave-adorned cortege drift with its wake of captives down the avenues of Imperial Rome....

Past the Rialto, the glittering front of the Astor, the jewelled magnificence of Times Square ... a gorgeous alley of incandescence ahead.... Then—was it years later?—he was paying the taxi-driver in front of a white building on Fifty-seventh Street. He was in the hall—ah, there was the negro boy from Martinique, lazy, indolent, unchanged.

"Is Mrs. Patch in?"

"I have just came on, sah," the man announced with his incongruous British accent.

"Take me up—"

Then the slow drone of the elevator, the three steps to the door, which swung open at the impetus of his knock.

"Gloria!" His voice was trembling. No answer. A faint string of smoke was rising from a cigarette-tray—a number of Vanity Fair sat astraddle on the table.

"Gloria!"

He ran into the bedroom, the bath. She was not there. A negligée of robin's-egg blue laid out upon the bed diffused a faint perfume, illusive and familiar. On a chair were a pair of stockings and a street dress; an open powder box yawned upon the bureau. She must just have gone out.

The telephone rang abruptly and he started—answered it with all the sensations of an impostor.

"Hello. Is Mrs. Patch there?"

"No, I'm looking for her myself. Who is this?"

"This is Mr. Crawford."

"This is Mr. Patch speaking. I've just arrived unexpectedly, and I don't know where to find her."

"Oh." Mr. Crawford sounded a bit taken aback. "Why, I imagine she's at the Armistice Ball. I know she intended going, but I didn't think she'd leave so early."

"Where's the Armistice Ball?"

"At the Astor."

"Thanks."

Anthony hung up sharply and rose. Who was Mr. Crawford? And who was it that was taking her to the ball? How long had this been going on? All these questions asked and answered themselves a dozen times, a dozen ways. His very proximity to her drove him half frantic.

In a frenzy of suspicion he rushed here and there about the apartment, hunting for some sign of masculine occupation, opening the bathroom cupboard, searching feverishly through the bureau drawers. Then he found something that made him stop suddenly and sit down on one of the twin beds, the corners of his mouth drooping as though he were about to weep. There in a corner of her drawer, tied with a frail blue ribbon, were all the letters and telegrams he had written her during the year past. He was suffused with happy and sentimental shame.

"I'm not fit to touch her," he cried aloud to the four walls. "I'm not fit to touch her little hand."

Nevertheless, he went out to look for her.

In the Astor lobby he was engulfed immediately in a crowd so thick as to make progress almost impossible. He asked the direction of the ballroom from half a dozen people before he could get a sober and intelligible answer. Eventually, after a last long wait, he checked his military overcoat in the hall.

It was only nine but the dance was in full blast. The panorama was incredible. Women, women everywhere—girls gay with wine singing shrilly above the clamor of the dazzling confetti-covered throng; girls set off by the uniforms of a dozen nations; fat females collapsing without dignity upon the floor and retaining self-respect by shouting "Hurraw for the Allies!"; three women with white hair dancing hand in hand around a sailor, who revolved in a dizzying spin upon the floor, clasping to his heart an empty bottle of champagne.

Breathlessly Anthony scanned the dancers, scanned the muddled lines trailing in single file in and out among the tables, scanned the horn-blowing, kissing, coughing, laughing, drinking parties under the great full-bosomed flags which leaned in glowing color over the pageantry and the sound.

Then he saw Gloria. She was sitting at a table for two directly across the room. Her dress was black, and above it her animated face, tinted with the most glamourous rose, made, he thought, a spot of poignant beauty on the room. His heart leaped as though to a new music. He jostled his way toward her and called her name just as the gray eyes looked up and found him. For that instant as their bodies met and melted, the world, the revel, the tumbling whimper of the music faded to an ecstatic monotone hushed as a song of bees.

"Oh, my Gloria!" he cried.

Her kiss was a cool rill flowing from her heart.

II. A MATTER OF AESTHETICS

ON the night when Anthony had left for Camp Hooker one year before, all that was left of the beautiful Gloria Gilbert—her shell, her young and lovely body—moved up the broad marble steps of the Grand Central Station with the rhythm of the engine beating in her ears like a dream, and out onto Vanderbilt Avenue, where the huge bulk of the Biltmore overhung, the street and, down at its low, gleaming entrance, sucked in the many-colored opera-cloaks of gorgeously dressed girls. For a moment she paused by the taxi-stand and watched them—wondering that but a few years before she had been of their number, ever setting out for a radiant Somewhere, always just about to have that ultimate passionate adventure for which the girls' cloaks were delicate and beautifully furred, for which their cheeks were painted and their hearts higher than the transitory dome of pleasure that would engulf them, coiffure, cloak, and all.

It was growing colder and the men passing had flipped up the collars of their overcoats. This change was kind to her. It would have been kinder still had everything changed, weather, streets, and people, and had she been whisked away, to wake in some high, fresh-scented room, alone, and statuesque within and without, as in her virginal and colorful past.

Inside the taxicab she wept impotent tears. That she had not been happy with Anthony for over a year mattered little. Recently his presence had been no more than what it would awake in her of that memorable June. The Anthony of late, irritable, weak, and poor, could do no less than make her irritable in turn—and bored with everything except the fact that in a highly imaginative and eloquent youth they had come together in an ecstatic revel of emotion. Because of this mutually vivid memory she would have done more for Anthony than for any other human—so when she got into the taxicab she wept passionately, and wanted to call his name aloud.

Miserable, lonesome as a forgotten child, she sat in the quiet apartment and wrote him a letter full of confused sentiment:

... I can almost look down the tracks and see you going but without you, dearest, dearest, I can't see or hear or feel or think. Being apart—whatever has happened or will happen to

us—is like begging for mercy from a storm, Anthony; it's like growing old. I want to kiss you so—in the back of your neck where your old black hair starts. Because I love you and whatever we do or say to each other, or have done, or have said, you've got to feel how much I do, how inanimate I am when you're gone. I can't even hate the damnable presence of PEOPLE, *those people in the station who haven't any right to live—I can't resent them even though they're dirtying up our world, because I'm engrossed in wanting you so.*

If you hated me, if you were covered with sores like a leper, if you ran away with another woman or starved me or beat me—how absurd this sounds—I'd still want you, I'd still love you. I KNOW, *my darling.*

It's late—I have all the windows open and the air outside, is just as soft as spring, yet, somehow, much more young and frail than spring. Why do they make spring a young girl, why does that illusion dance and yodel its way for three months through the world's preposterous barrenness. Spring is a lean old plough horse with its ribs showing—it's a pile of refuse in a field, parched by the sun and the rain to an ominous cleanliness.

In a few hours you'll wake up, my darling—and you'll be miserable, and disgusted with life. You'll be in Delaware or Carolina or somewhere and so unimportant. I don't believe there's any one alive who can contemplate themselves as an impermanent institution, as a luxury or an unnecessary evil. Very few of the people who accentuate the futility of life remark the futility of themselves. Perhaps they think that in proclaiming the evil of living they somehow salvage their own worth from the ruin—but they don't, even you and I....

... Still I can see you. There's blue haze about the trees where you'll be passing, too beautiful to be predominant. No, the fallow squares of earth will be most frequent—they'll be along beside the track like dirty coarse brown sheets drying in the sun, alive, mechanical, abominable. Nature, slovenly old hag, has been sleeping in them with every old farmer or negro or immigrant who happened to covet her....

So you see that now you're gone I've written a letter all full of contempt and despair. And that just means that I love you, Anthony, with all there is to love with in your

GLORIA.

When she had addressed the letter she went to her twin bed and lay down upon it, clasping Anthony's pillow in her arms as though by sheer force of emotion she could metamorphize it into his warm and living body. Two o'clock saw her dry-eyed, staring with steady persistent grief into the darkness, remembering, remembering unmercifully, blaming herself for a hundred fancied unkindnesses, making a likeness of Anthony akin to some martyred and transfigured Christ. For a time she thought of him as he, in his more sentimental moments, probably thought of himself.

At five she was still awake. A mysterious grinding noise that went on every morning across the areaway told her the hour. She heard an alarm clock ring, and saw a light make a yellow square on an illusory blank wall opposite. With the half-formed resolution of following him South immediately, her sorrow grew remote and unreal, and moved off from her as the dark moved westward. She fell asleep.

When she awoke the sight of the empty bed beside her brought a renewal of misery, dispelled shortly, however, by the inevitable callousness of the bright morning. Though she was not conscious of it, there was relief in eating breakfast without Anthony's tired and worried face opposite her. Now that she was alone she lost all desire to complain about the food. She would change her breakfasts, she thought—have a lemonade and a tomato sandwich instead of the sempiternal bacon and eggs and toast.

Nevertheless, at noon when she had called up several of her acquaintances, including the martial Muriel, and found each one engaged for lunch, she gave way to a quiet pity for herself and her loneliness. Curled on the bed with pencil and paper she wrote Anthony another letter.

Late in the afternoon arrived a special delivery, mailed from some small New Jersey town, and the familiarity of the phrasing, the almost audible undertone of worry and discontent, were so familiar that they comforted her. Who knew? Perhaps army discipline would harden Anthony and accustom him to the idea of work. She had immutable faith that the war would be over before he was called upon to fight, and meanwhile the suit would be won, and they could begin again, this time on a different basis. The first thing different would be that she would have a child. It was unbearable that she should be so utterly alone.

It was a week before she could stay in the apartment with the probability of remaining dry-eyed. There seemed little in the city that was amusing. Muriel had been shifted to a hospital in New Jersey, from which she took a metropolitan holiday only every other week, and with this defection Gloria grew to realize how few were the friends she had made in all these years of New York. The men she knew were in the army. "Men she knew"?—she had conceded vaguely to herself that all the men who had ever been in love with her were her friends. Each one of them had at a certain considerable time professed to value her favor above anything in life. But now—where were they? At least two were dead, half a dozen or more were married, the rest scattered from France to the Philippines. She wondered whether any of them thought of her, and how often, and in what respect. Most of them must still picture the little girl of seventeen or so, the adolescent siren of nine years before.

The girls, too, were gone far afield. She had never been popular in school. She had been too beautiful, too lazy, not sufficiently conscious of being a Farmover girl and a "Future Wife and Mother" in perpetual capital letters. And girls who had never been kissed hinted, with shocked expressions on their plain but not particularly wholesome faces, that Gloria had. Then these girls had gone east or west or south, married and become "people," prophesying, if they prophesied about Gloria, that she would come to a bad end—not knowing that no endings were bad, and that they, like her, were by no means the mistresses of their destinies.

Gloria told over to herself the people who had visited them in the gray house at Marietta. It had seemed at the time that they were always having company—

she had indulged in an unspoken conviction that each guest was ever afterward slightly indebted to her. They owed her a sort of moral ten dollars apiece, and should she ever be in need she might, so to speak, borrow from them this visionary currency. But they were gone, scattered like chaff, mysteriously and subtly vanished in essence or in fact.

By Christmas, Gloria's conviction that she should join Anthony had returned, no longer as a sudden emotion, but as a recurrent need. She decided to write him word of her coming, but postponed the announcement upon the advice of Mr. Haight, who expected almost weekly that the case was coming up for trial.

One day, early in January, as she was walking on Fifth Avenue, bright now with uniforms and hung with the flags of the virtuous nations, she met Rachael Barnes, whom she had not seen for nearly a year. Even Rachael, whom she had grown to dislike, was a relief from ennui, and together they went to the Ritz for tea.

After a second cocktail they became enthusiastic. They liked each other. They talked about their husbands, Rachael in that tone of public vainglory, with private reservations, in which wives are wont to speak.

"Rodman's abroad in the Quartermaster Corps. He's a captain. He was bound he would go, and he didn't think he could get into anything else."

"Anthony's in the Infantry." The words in their relation to the cocktail gave Gloria a sort of glow. With each sip she approached a warm and comforting patriotism.

"By the way," said Rachael half an hour later, as they were leaving, "can't you come up to dinner to-morrow night? I'm having two awfully sweet officers who are just going overseas. I think we ought to do all we can to make it attractive for them."

Gloria accepted gladly. She took down the address—recognizing by its number a fashionable apartment building on Park Avenue.

"It's been awfully good to have seen you, Rachael."

"It's been wonderful. I've wanted to."

With these three sentences a certain night in Marietta two summers before, when Anthony and Rachael had been unnecessarily attentive to each other, was forgiven—Gloria forgave Rachael, Rachael forgave Gloria. Also it was forgiven that Rachael had been witness to the greatest disaster in the lives of Mr. and Mrs. Anthony Patch—

Compromising with events time moves along.

THE WILES OF CAPTAIN COLLINS

The two officers were captains of the popular craft, machine gunnery. At dinner they referred to themselves with conscious boredom as members of the "Suicide Club"—in those days every recondite branch of the service referred to itself as the Suicide Club. One of the captains—Rachael's captain, Gloria observed—was a tall horsy man of thirty with a pleasant mustache and ugly teeth. The other, Captain Collins, was chubby, pink-faced, and inclined to laugh with abandon every time he caught Gloria's eye. He took an immediate fancy to her, and throughout dinner showered her with inane compliments. With her second glass of champagne Gloria decided that for the first time in months she was thoroughly enjoying herself.

After dinner it was suggested that they all go somewhere and dance. The two officers supplied themselves with bottles of liquor from Rachael's sideboard—a law forbade service to the military—and so equipped they went through innumerable fox trots in several glittering caravanseries along Broadway, faithfully alternating partners—while Gloria became more and more uproarious and more and more amusing to the pink-faced captain, who seldom bothered to remove his genial smile at all.

At eleven o'clock to her great surprise she was in the minority for staying out. The others wanted to return to Rachael's apartment—to get some more liquor, they said. Gloria argued persistently that Captain Collins's flask was half full—she had just seen it—then catching Rachael's eye she received an unmistakable wink. She deduced, confusedly, that her hostess wanted to get rid of the officers and assented to being bundled into a taxicab outside.

Captain Wolf sat on the left with Rachael on his knees. Captain Collins sat in the middle, and as he settled himself he slipped his arm about Gloria's shoulder. It rested there lifelessly for a moment and then tightened like a vise. He leaned over her.

"You're awfully pretty," he whispered.

"Thank you kindly, sir." She was neither pleased nor annoyed. Before Anthony came so many arms had done likewise that it had become little more than a gesture, sentimental but without significance.

Up in Rachael's long front room a low fire and two lamps shaded with orange silk gave all the light, so that the corners were full of deep and somnolent shadows. The hostess, moving about in a dark-figured gown of loose chiffon, seemed to accentuate the already sensuous atmosphere. For a while they were all four together, tasting the sandwiches that waited on the tea table—then Gloria found herself alone with Captain Collins on the fireside lounge; Rachael and Captain Wolf had withdrawn to the other side of the room, where they were conversing in subdued voices.

"I wish you weren't married," said Collins, his face a ludicrous travesty of "in all seriousness."

"Why?" She held out her glass to be filled with a high-ball.

"Don't drink any more," he urged her, frowning.

"Why not?"

"You'd be nicer—if you didn't."

Gloria caught suddenly the intended suggestion of the remark, the atmosphere he was attempting to create. She wanted to laugh—yet she realized that there was nothing to laugh at. She had been enjoying the evening, and she had no desire to go home—at the same time it hurt her pride to be flirted with on just that level.

"Pour me another drink," she insisted.

"Please—"

"Oh, don't be ridiculous!" she cried in exasperation.

"Very well." He yielded with ill grace.

Then his arm was about her again, and again she made no protest. But when his pink cheek came close she leaned away.

"You're awfully sweet," he said with an aimless air.

She began to sing softly, wishing now that he would take down his arm. Suddenly her eye fell on an intimate scene across the room—Rachael and Captain Wolf were engrossed in a long kiss. Gloria shivered slightly—she knew not why.... Pink face approached again.

"You shouldn't look at them," he whispered. Almost immediately his other arm was around her ... his breath was on her cheek. Again absurdity triumphed over disgust, and her laugh was a weapon that needed no edge of words.

"Oh, I thought you were a sport," he was saying.

"What's a sport?"

"Why, a person that likes to—to enjoy life."

"Is kissing you generally considered a joyful affair?"

They were interrupted as Rachael and Captain Wolf appeared suddenly before them.

"It's late, Gloria," said Rachael—she was flushed and her hair was dishevelled. "You'd better stay here all night."

For an instant Gloria thought the officers were being dismissed. Then she understood, and, understanding, got to her feet as casually as she was able.

Uncomprehendingly Rachael continued:

"You can have the room just off this one. I can lend you everything you need."

Collins's eyes implored her like a dog's; Captain Wolf's arm had settled familiarly around Rachael's waist; they were waiting.

But the lure of promiscuity, colorful, various, labyrinthine, and ever a little odorous and stale, had no call or promise for Gloria. Had she so desired she would have remained, without hesitation, without regret; as it was she could face coolly the six hostile and offended eyes that followed her out into the hall with forced politeness and hollow words.

"*He* wasn't even sport, enough to try to take me home," she thought in the taxi, and then with a quick surge of resentment: "How *utterly* common!"

GALLANTRY

In February she had an experience of quite a different sort. Tudor Baird, an ancient flame, a young man whom at one time she had fully intended to marry, came to New York by way of the Aviation Corps, and called upon her. They went several times to the theatre, and within a week, to her great enjoyment, he was as much in love with her as ever. Quite deliberately she brought it about, realizing too late that she had done a mischief. He reached the point of sitting with her in miserable silence whenever they went out together.

A Scroll and Keys man at Yale, he possessed the correct reticences of a "good egg," the correct notions of chivalry and *noblesse oblige*—and, of course but unfortunately, the correct biases and the correct lack of ideas—all those traits which Anthony had taught her to despise, but which, nevertheless, she rather admired. Unlike the majority of his type, she found that he was not a bore. He was handsome, witty in a light way, and when she was with him she felt that because of some quality he possessed—call it stupidity, loyalty, sentimentality, or something not quite as definite as any of the three—he would have done anything in his power to please her.

He told her this among other things, very correctly and with a ponderous manliness that masked a real suffering. Loving him not at all she grew sorry for him and kissed him sentimentally one night because he was so charming, a relic of a vanishing generation which lived a priggish and graceful illusion and was being replaced by less gallant fools. Afterward she was glad she had kissed him, for next day when his plane fell fifteen hundred feet at Mineola a piece of a gasolene engine smashed through his heart.

GLORIA ALONE

When Mr. Haight told her that the trial would not take place until autumn she decided that without telling Anthony she would go into the movies. When he saw her successful, both histrionically and financially, when he saw that she could have her will of Joseph Bloeckman, yielding nothing in return, he would lose his silly prejudices. She lay awake half one night planning her career and enjoying her successes in anticipation, and the next morning she called up "Films Par Excellence." Mr. Bloeckman was in Europe.

But the idea had gripped her so strongly this time that she decided to go the rounds of the moving picture employment agencies. As so often had been the case, her sense of smell worked against her good intentions. The employment agency smelt as though it had been dead a very long time. She waited five minutes inspecting her unprepossessing competitors—then she walked briskly out into the farthest recesses of Central Park and remained so long that she caught a cold. She was trying to air the employment agency out of her walking suit.

In the spring she began to gather from Anthony's letters—not from any one in particular but from their culminative effect—that he did not want her to come South. Curiously repeated excuses that seemed to haunt him by their very insufficiency occurred with Freudian regularity. He set them down in each letter as though he feared he had forgotten them the last time, as though it were desperately necessary to impress her with them. And the dilutions of his letters with affectionate diminutives began to be mechanical and unspontaneous—almost as though, having completed the letter, he had looked it over and literally stuck them in, like epigrams in an Oscar Wilde play. She jumped to the solution, rejected it, was angry and depressed by turns—finally she shut her mind to it proudly, and allowed an increasing coolness to creep into her end of the correspondence.

Of late she had found a good deal to occupy her attention. Several aviators whom she had met through Tudor Baird came into New York to see her and two other ancient beaux turned up, stationed at Camp Dix. As these men were ordered overseas they, so to speak, handed her down to their friends. But after another rather disagreeable experience with a potential Captain Collins she made it plain that when any one was introduced to her he should be under no misapprehensions as to her status and personal intentions.

When summer came she learned, like Anthony, to watch the officers' casualty list, taking a sort of melancholy pleasure in hearing of the death of some one with whom she had once danced a german and in identifying by name the younger brothers of former suitors—thinking, as the drive toward Paris progressed, that here at length went the world to inevitable and well-merited destruction.

She was twenty-seven. Her birthday fled by scarcely noticed. Years before it had frightened her when she became twenty, to some extent when she reached twenty-six—but now she looked in the glass with calm self-approval seeing the British freshness of her complexion and her figure boyish and slim as of old.

She tried not to think of Anthony. It was as though she were writing to a stranger. She told her friends that he had been made a corporal and was annoyed when they were politely unimpressed. One night she wept because she was sorry for him—had he been even slightly responsive she would have gone to him without hesitation on the first train—whatever he was doing he needed to be taken care of spiritually, and she felt that now she would be able to do even that. Recently, without his continual drain upon her moral strength she found herself wonderfully revived. Before he left she had been inclined through sheer association to brood on her wasted opportunities—now she returned to her normal state of mind, strong, disdainful, existing each day for each day's worth. She bought a doll and dressed it; one week she wept over "Ethan Frome"; the next she revelled in some novels of Galsworthy's, whom she liked for his power of recreating, by spring in darkness, that illusion of young romantic love to which women look forever forward and forever back.

In October Anthony's letters multiplied, became almost frantic—then suddenly ceased. For a worried month it needed all her powers of control to refrain from leaving immediately for Mississippi. Then a telegram told her that he had been in the hospital and that she could expect him in New York within ten days. Like a figure in a dream he came back into her life across the ballroom on that November evening—and all through long hours that held familiar gladness she took him close to her breast, nursing an illusion of happiness and security she had not thought that she would know again.

DISCOMFITURE OF THE GENERALS

After a week Anthony's regiment went back to the Mississippi camp to be discharged. The officers shut themselves up in the compartments on the Pullman cars and drank the whiskey they had bought in New York, and in the coaches the soldiers got as drunk as possible also—and pretended whenever the train stopped at a village that they were just returned from France, where they had practically put an end to the German army. As they all wore overseas caps and claimed that they had not had time to have their gold service stripes sewed on, the yokelry of the seaboard were much impressed and asked them how they liked the trenches—to which they replied "Oh, *boy!*" with great smacking of tongues and shaking of heads. Some one took a piece of chalk and scrawled on the side of the train, "We won the war—now we're going home," and the officers laughed and let it stay. They were all getting what swagger they could out of this ignominious return.

As they rumbled on toward camp, Anthony was uneasy lest he should find Dot awaiting him patiently at the station. To his relief he neither saw nor heard anything of her and thinking that were she still in town she would certainly attempt to communicate with him, he concluded that she had gone—whither he neither knew nor cared. He wanted only to return to Gloria—Gloria reborn and wonderfully alive. When eventually he was discharged he left his company on the rear of a great truck with a crowd who had given tolerant, almost sentimental, cheers for their officers, especially for Captain Dunning. The captain, on his part, had addressed them with tears in his eyes as to the pleasure, etc., and the work, etc., and time not wasted, etc., and duty, etc. It was very dull and human; having given ear to it Anthony, whose mind was freshened by his week in New York, renewed his deep loathing for the military profession and all it connoted. In their childish hearts two out of every three professional officers considered that wars were made for armies and not armies for wars. He rejoiced to see general and field-officers riding desolately about the barren camp deprived of their commands. He rejoiced to hear the men in his company laugh scornfully at the inducements tendered them to remain in the army. They were to attend "schools." He knew what these "schools" were.

Two days later he was with Gloria in New York.

ANOTHER WINTER

Late one February afternoon Anthony came into the apartment and groping through the little hall, pitch-dark in the winter dusk, found Gloria sitting by the window. She turned as he came in.

"What did Mr. Haight have to say?" she asked listlessly.

"Nothing," he answered, "usual thing. Next month, perhaps."

She looked at him closely; her ear attuned to his voice caught the slightest thickness in the dissyllable.

"You've been drinking," she remarked dispassionately.

"Couple glasses."

"Oh."

He yawned in the armchair and there was a moment's silence between them. Then she demanded suddenly:

"Did you go to Mr. Haight? Tell me the truth."

"No." He smiled weakly. "As a matter of fact I didn't have time."

"I thought you didn't go.... He sent for you."

"I don't give a damn. I'm sick of waiting around his office. You'd think he was doing *me* a favor." He glanced at Gloria as though expecting moral support, but she had turned back to her contemplation of the dubious and unprepossessing out-of-doors.

"I feel rather weary of life to-day," he offered tentatively. Still she was silent. "I met a fellow and we talked in the Biltmore bar."

The dusk had suddenly deepened but neither of them made any move to turn on the lights. Lost in heaven knew what contemplation, they sat there until a flurry of snow drew a languid sigh from Gloria.

"What've you been doing?" he asked, finding the silence oppressive.

"Reading a magazine—all full of idiotic articles by prosperous authors about how terrible it is for poor people to buy silk shirts. And while I was reading it I could think of nothing except how I wanted a gray squirrel coat—and how we can't afford one."

"Yes, we can."

"Oh, no."

"Oh, yes! If you want a fur coat you can have one."

Her voice coming through the dark held an implication of scorn.

"You mean we can sell another bond?"

"If necessary. I don't want to go without things. We have spent a lot, though, since I've been back."

"Oh, shut up!" she said in irritation.

"Why?"

"Because I'm sick and tired of hearing you talk about what we've spent or what we've done. You came back two months ago and we've been on some sort of a party practically every night since. We've both wanted to go out, and we've gone. Well, you haven't heard me complain, have you? But all you do is whine, whine, whine. I don't care any more what we do or what becomes of us and at least I'm consistent. But I will *not* tolerate your complaining and calamity-howling——"

"You're not very pleasant yourself sometimes, you know."

"I'm under no obligations to be. You're not making any attempt to make things different."

"But I am—"

"Huh! Seems to me I've heard that before. This morning you weren't going to touch another thing to drink until you'd gotten a position. And you didn't even have the spunk to go to Mr. Haight when he sent for you about the suit."

Anthony got to his feet and switched on the lights.

"See here!" he cried, blinking, "I'm getting sick of that sharp tongue of yours."

"Well, what are you going to do about it?"

"Do you think *I'm* particularly happy?" he continued, ignoring her question. "Do you think I don't know we're not living as we ought to?"

In an instant Gloria stood trembling beside him.

"I won't *stand* it!" she burst out. "I won't be lectured to. You and your suffering! You're just a pitiful weakling and you always have been!"

They faced one another idiotically, each of them unable to impress the other, each of them tremendously, achingly, bored. Then she went into the bedroom and shut the door behind her.

His return had brought into the foreground all their pre-bellum exasperations. Prices had risen alarmingly and in perverse ratio their income had shrunk to a little over half of its original size. There had been the large retainer's fee to Mr. Haight; there were stocks bought at one hundred, now down to thirty and forty and other investments that were not paying at all. During the previous spring Gloria had been given the alternative of leaving the apartment or of signing a year's lease at two hundred and twenty-five a month. She had signed it. Inevitably as the necessity for economy had increased they found themselves as a pair quite unable to save. The old policy of prevarication was resorted to. Weary of their incapabilities they chattered of what they would do—oh—to-morrow, of how they would "stop going on parties" and of how Anthony would go to work. But when dark came down Gloria, accustomed to an engagement every night, would feel the ancient restlessness creeping over her. She would stand in the doorway of the bedroom, chewing furiously at her fingers and sometimes meeting Anthony's eyes as he glanced up from his book. Then the telephone, and her nerves would relax, she would answer it with ill-concealed eagerness. Some one was coming up "for just a few minutes"—and oh, the weariness of pretense, the appearance of the wine table, the revival of their jaded spirits—and the awakening, like the mid-point of a sleepless night in which they moved.

As the winter passed with the march of the returning troops along Fifth Avenue they became more and more aware that since Anthony's return their relations had entirely changed. After that reflowering of tenderness and passion each of them had returned into some solitary dream unshared by the other and what endearments passed between them passed, it seemed, from empty heart to empty heart, echoing hollowly the departure of what they knew at last was gone.

Anthony had again made the rounds of the metropolitan newspapers and had again been refused encouragement by a motley of office boys, telephone girls, and city editors. The word was: "We're keeping any vacancies open for our own men who are still in France." Then, late in March, his eye fell on an advertisement in the morning paper and in consequence he found at last the semblance of an occupation.

YOU CAN SELL!!!

Why not earn while you learn?
Our salesmen make $50-$200 weekly.

There followed an address on Madison Avenue, and instructions to appear at one o'clock that afternoon. Gloria, glancing over his shoulder after one of their usual late breakfasts, saw him regarding it idly.

"Why don't you try it?" she suggested.

"Oh—it's one of these crazy schemes."

"It might not be. At least it'd be experience."

At her urging he went at one o'clock to the appointed address, where he found himself one of a dense miscellany of men waiting in front of the door. They ranged from a messenger-boy evidently misusing his company's time to an immemorial individual with a gnarled body and a gnarled cane. Some of the men were seedy, with sunken cheeks and puffy pink eyes—others were young; possibly still in high school. After a jostled fifteen minutes during which they all eyed one another with apathetic suspicion there appeared a smart young shepherd clad in a "waist-line" suit and wearing the manner of an assistant rector who herded them up-stairs into a large room, which resembled a school-room and contained innumerable desks. Here the prospective salesmen sat down—and again waited. After an interval a platform at the end of the hall was clouded with half a dozen sober but sprightly men who, with one exception, took seats in a semicircle facing the audience.

The exception was the man who seemed the soberest, the most sprightly and the youngest of the lot, and who advanced to the front of the platform. The audience scrutinized him hopefully. He was rather small and rather pretty, with the commercial rather than the thespian sort of prettiness. He had straight blond bushy brows and eyes that were almost preposterously honest, and as he reached the edge of his rostrum he seemed to throw these eyes out into the audience, simultaneously extending his arm with two fingers outstretched. Then while he rocked himself to a state of balance an expectant silence settled over the hall. With perfect assurance the young man had taken his listeners in hand and his words when they came were steady and confident and of the school of "straight from the shoulder."

"Men!"—he began, and paused. The word died with a prolonged echo at the end of the hall, the faces regarding him, hopefully, cynically, wearily, were alike arrested, engrossed. Six hundred eyes were turned slightly upward. With an even graceless flow that reminded Anthony of the rolling of bowling balls he launched himself into the sea of exposition.

"This bright and sunny morning you picked up your favorite newspaper and you found an advertisement which made the plain, unadorned statement that *you* could sell. That was all it said—it didn't say 'what,' it didn't say 'how,' it didn't say 'why.' It just made one single solitary assertion that *you* and *you* and *you*"—business of pointing—"could sell. Now my job isn't to make a success of you, because every man is born a success, he makes himself a failure; it's not to teach you how to talk, because each man is a natural orator and only makes himself a clam; my business is to tell you one thing in a way that will make you *know* it—it's to tell you that *you* and *you* and *you* have the heritage of money and prosperity waiting for you to come and claim it."

At this point an Irishman of saturnine appearance rose from his desk near the rear of the hall and went out.

"That man thinks he'll go look for it in the beer parlor around the corner. (Laughter.) He won't find it there. Once upon a time I looked for it there myself (laughter), but that was before I did what every one of you men no matter how young or how old, how poor or how rich (a faint ripple of satirical laughter), can do. It was before I found—*myself*!

"Now I wonder if any of you men know what a 'Heart Talk' is. A 'Heart Talk' is a little book in which I started, about five years ago, to write down what I had discovered were the principal reasons for a man's failure and the principal reasons for a man's success—from John D. Rockerfeller back to John D. Napoleon (laughter), and before that, back in the days when Abel sold his birthright for a mess of pottage. There are now one hundred of these 'Heart Talks.' Those of you who are sincere, who are interested in our proposition, above all who are dissatisfied with the way things are breaking for you at present will be handed one to take home with you as you go out yonder door this afternoon.

"Now in my own pocket I have four letters just received concerning 'Heart Talks.' These letters have names signed to them that are familiar in every household in the U.S.A. Listen to this one from Detroit:

"DEAR MR. CARLETON:

"I want to order three thousand more copies of 'Heart Talks' for distribution among my salesmen. They have done more for getting work out of the men than any bonus proposition ever considered. I read them myself constantly, and I desire to heartily congratulate you on getting at the roots of the biggest problem that faces our generation to-day—the problem of salesmanship. The rock bottom on which the country is founded is the problem of salesmanship. With many felicitations I am

"Yours very cordially,
"HENRY W. TERRAL."

He brought the name out in three long booming triumphancies—pausing for it to produce its magical effect. Then he read two more letters, one from a manufacturer of vacuum cleaners and one from the president of the Great Northern Doily Company.

"And now," he continued, "I'm going to tell you in a few words what the proposition is that's going to *make* those of you who go into it in the right spirit. Simply put, it's this: 'Heart Talks' have been incorporated as a company. We're going to put these little pamphlets into the hands of every big business organization, every salesman, and every man who *knows*—I don't say 'thinks,' I say '*knows*'—that he can sell! We are offering some of the stock of the 'Heart Talks' concern upon the market, and in order that the distribution may be as wide as possible, and in order also that we can furnish a living, concrete, flesh-and-blood example of what salesmanship is, or rather what it may be, we're going to give those of you who are the real thing a chance to sell that stock. Now, I don't care what you've tried to sell before or how you've tried to sell it. It don't matter how old you are or how young you are. I only want to know two things—first, do you *want* success, and, second, will you work for it?

"My name is Sammy Carleton. Not 'Mr.' Carleton, but just plain Sammy. I'm a regular no-nonsense man with no fancy frills about me. I want you to call me Sammy.

"Now this is all I'm going to say to you to-day. To-morrow I want those of you who have thought it over and have read the copy of 'Heart Talks' which will be given to you at the door, to come back to this same room at this same time, then we'll go into the proposition further and I'll explain to you what I've found the principles of success to be. I'm going to make you *feel* that *you* and *you* and *you* can sell!"

Mr. Carleton's voice echoed for a moment through the hall and then died away. To the stamping of many feet Anthony was pushed and jostled with the crowd out of the room.

FURTHER ADVENTURES WITH "HEART TALKS"

With an accompaniment of ironic laughter Anthony told Gloria the story of his commercial adventure. But she listened without amusement.

"You're going to give up again?" she demanded coldly.

"Why—you don't expect me to—"

"I never expected anything of you."

He hesitated.

"Well—I can't see the slightest benefit in laughing myself sick over this sort of affair. If there's anything older than the old story, it's the new twist."

It required an astonishing amount of moral energy on Gloria's part to intimidate him into returning, and when he reported next day, somewhat depressed from his perusal of the senile bromides skittishly set forth in "Heart Talks on Ambition," he found only fifty of the original three hundred awaiting the appearance of the vital and compelling Sammy Carleton. Mr. Carleton's powers of vitality and compulsion were this time exercised in elucidating that magnificent piece of speculation—how to sell. It seemed that the approved method was to state one's proposition and then to say not "And now, will you buy?"—this was not the way—oh, no!—the way was to state one's proposition and then, having reduced one's adversary to a state of exhaustion, to deliver oneself of the categorical imperative: "Now see here! You've taken up my time explaining this matter to you. You've admitted my points—all I want to ask is how many do you want?"

As Mr. Carleton piled assertion upon assertion Anthony began to feel a sort of disgusted confidence in him. The man appeared to know what he was talking about. Obviously prosperous, he had risen to the position of instructing others. It did not occur to Anthony that the type of man who attains commercial success seldom knows how or why, and, as in his grandfather's case, when he ascribes reasons, the reasons are generally inaccurate and absurd.

Anthony noted that of the numerous old men who had answered the original advertisement, only two had returned, and that among the thirty odd who assembled on the third day to get actual selling instructions from Mr. Carleton, only one gray head was in evidence. These thirty were eager converts; with their mouths they followed the working of Mr. Carleton's mouth; they swayed in their seats with enthusiasm, and in the intervals of his talk they spoke to each other in tense approving whispers. Yet of the chosen few who, in the words of Mr. Carleton, "were determined to get those deserts that rightly and truly belonged to them," less than half a dozen combined even a modicum of personal appearance with that great gift of being a "pusher." But they were told that they were all natural pushers—it was merely necessary that they should believe with a sort of savage passion in what they were selling. He even urged each one to buy some stock himself, if possible, in order to increase his own sincerity.

On the fifth day then, Anthony sallied into the street with all the sensations of a man wanted by the police. Acting according to instructions he selected a tall office building in order that he might ride to the top story and work downward, stopping in every office that had a name on the door. But at the last minute he hesitated. Perhaps it would be more practicable to acclimate himself to the chilly atmosphere which he felt was awaiting him by trying a few offices on, say, Madison Avenue. He went into an arcade that seemed only semi-prosperous, and seeing a sign which read Percy B. Weatherbee, Architect, he opened the door heroically and entered. A starchy young woman looked up questioningly.

"Can I see Mr. Weatherbee?" He wondered if his voice sounded tremulous.

She laid her hand tentatively on the telephone-receiver.

"What's the name, please?"

"He wouldn't—ah—know me. He wouldn't know my name."

"What's your business with him? You an insurance agent?"

"Oh, no, nothing like that!" denied Anthony hurriedly. "Oh, no. It's a—it's a personal matter." He wondered if he should have said this. It had all sounded so simple when Mr. Carleton had enjoined his flock:

"Don't allow yourself to be kept out! Show them you've made up your mind to talk to them, and they'll listen."

The girl succumbed to Anthony's pleasant, melancholy face, and in a moment the door to the inner room opened and admitted a tall, splay-footed man with slicked hair. He approached Anthony with ill-concealed impatience.

"You wanted to see me on a personal matter?"

Anthony quailed.

"I wanted to talk to you," he said defiantly.

"About what?"

"It'll take some time to explain."

"Well, what's it about?" Mr. Weatherbee's voice indicated rising irritation.

Then Anthony, straining at each word, each syllable, began:

"I don't know whether or not you've ever heard of a series of pamphlets called 'Heart Talks'—"

"Good grief!" cried Percy B. Weatherbee, Architect, "are you trying to touch my heart?"

"No, it's business. 'Heart Talks' have been incorporated and we're putting some shares on the market—"

His voice faded slowly off, harassed by a fixed and contemptuous stare from his unwilling prey. For another minute he struggled on, increasingly sensitive, entangled in his own words. His confidence oozed from him in great retching emanations that seemed to be sections of his own body. Almost mercifully Percy B. Weatherbee, Architect, terminated the interview:

"Good grief!" he exploded in disgust, "and you call that a *personal* matter!" He whipped about and strode into his private office, banging the door behind him. Not daring to look at the stenographer, Anthony in some shameful and mysterious way got himself from the room. Perspiring profusely he stood in the hall wondering why they didn't come and arrest him; in every hurried look he discerned infallibly a glance of scorn.

After an hour and with the help of two strong whiskies he brought himself up to another attempt. He walked into a plumber's shop, but when he mentioned his business the plumber began pulling on his coat in a great hurry, gruffly announcing that he had to go to lunch. Anthony remarked politely that it was futile to try to sell a man anything when he was hungry, and the plumber heartily agreed.

This episode encouraged Anthony; he tried to think that had the plumber not been bound for lunch he would at least have listened.

Passing by a few glittering and formidable bazaars he entered a grocery store. A talkative proprietor told him that before buying any stocks he was going to see how the armistice affected the market. To Anthony this seemed almost unfair. In Mr. Carleton's salesman's Utopia the only reason prospective buyers ever gave for not purchasing stock was that they doubted it to be a promising investment. Obviously a man in that state was almost ludicrously easy game, to be brought down merely by the judicious application of the correct selling points. But these men—why, actually they weren't considering buying anything at all.

Anthony took several more drinks before he approached his fourth man, a real-estate agent; nevertheless, he was floored with a coup as decisive as a syllogism. The real-estate agent said that he had three brothers in the investment business. Viewing himself as a breaker-up of homes Anthony apologized and went out.

After another drink he conceived the brilliant plan of selling the stock to the bartenders along Lexington Avenue. This occupied several hours, for it was necessary to take a few drinks in each place in order to get the proprietor in the proper frame of mind to talk business. But the bartenders one and all contended that if they had any money to buy bonds they would not be bartenders. It was as though they had all convened and decided upon that rejoinder. As he approached a dark and soggy five o'clock he found that they were developing a still more annoying tendency to turn him off with a jest.

At five, then, with a tremendous effort at concentration he decided that he must put more variety into his canvassing. He selected a medium-sized delicatessen store, and went in. He felt, illuminatingly, that the thing to do was to cast a spell not only over the storekeeper but over all the customers as well—and perhaps through the psychology of the herd instinct they would buy as an astounded and immediately convinced whole.

"Af'ernoon," he began in a loud thick voice. "Ga l'il prop'sition."

If he had wanted silence he obtained it. A sort of awe descended upon the half-dozen women marketing and upon the gray-haired ancient who in cap and apron was slicing chicken.

Anthony pulled a batch of papers from his flapping briefcase and waved them cheerfully.

"Buy a bon'," he suggested, "good as liberty bon'!" The phrase pleased him and he elaborated upon it. "Better'n liberty bon'. Every one these bon's worth *two* liberty bon's." His mind made a hiatus and skipped to his peroration, which he delivered with appropriate gestures, these being somewhat marred by the necessity of clinging to the counter with one or both hands.

"Now see here. You taken up my time. I don't want know *why* you won't buy. I just want you say *why*. Want you say *how many!*"

At this point they should have approached him with check-books and fountain pens in hand. Realizing that they must have missed a cue Anthony, with the instincts of an actor, went back and repeated his finale.

"Now see here! You taken up my time. You followed prop'sition. You agreed 'th reasonin'? Now, all I want from *you* is, how many lib'ty bon's?"

"See here!" broke in a new voice. A portly man whose face was adorned with symmetrical scrolls of yellow hair had come out of a glass cage in the rear of the store and was bearing down upon Anthony. "See here, you!"

"How many?" repeated the salesman sternly. "You taken up my time—"

"Hey, you!" cried the proprietor, "I'll have you taken up by the police."

"You mos' cert'nly won't!" returned Anthony with fine defiance. "All I want know is how many."

From here and there in the store went up little clouds of comment and expostulation.

"How terrible!"

"He's a raving maniac."

"He's disgracefully drunk."

The proprietor grasped Anthony's arm sharply.

"Get out, or I'll call a policeman."

Some relics of rationality moved Anthony to nod and replace his bonds clumsily in the case.

"How many?" he reiterated doubtfully.

"The whole force if necessary!" thundered his adversary, his yellow mustache trembling fiercely.

"Sell 'em all a bon'."

With this Anthony turned, bowed gravely to his late auditors, and wabbled from the store. He found a taxicab at the corner and rode home to the apartment. There he fell sound asleep on the sofa, and so Gloria found him, his breath filling the air with an unpleasant pungency, his hand still clutching his open brief case.

Except when Anthony was drinking, his range of sensation had become less than that of a healthy old man and when prohibition came in July he found that, among those who could afford it, there was more drinking than ever before. One's host now brought out a bottle upon the slightest pretext. The tendency to display liquor was a manifestation of the same instinct that led a man to deck his wife with jewels. To have liquor was a boast, almost a badge of respectability.

In the mornings Anthony awoke tired, nervous, and worried. Halcyon summer twilights and the purple chill of morning alike left him unresponsive. Only for a brief moment every day in the warmth and renewed life of a first high-ball did his mind turn to those opalescent dreams of future pleasure—the mutual heritage of the happy and the damned. But this was only for a little while. As he grew drunker the dreams faded and he became a confused spectre, moving in odd crannies of his own mind, full of unexpected devices, harshly contemptuous at best and reaching sodden and dispirited depths. One night in June he had quarrelled violently with Maury over a matter of the utmost triviality. He remembered dimly next morning that it had been about a broken pint bottle of champagne. Maury had told him to sober up and Anthony's feelings had been hurt, so with an attempted gesture of dignity he had risen from the table and seizing Gloria's arm half led, half shamed her into a taxicab outside, leaving Maury with three dinners ordered and tickets for the opera.

This sort of semi-tragic fiasco had become so usual that when they occurred he was no longer stirred into making amends. If Gloria protested—and of late she was more likely to sink into contemptuous silence—he would either engage in a bitter defense of himself or else stalk dismally from the apartment. Never since the incident on the station platform at Redgate had he laid his hands on her in anger—though he was withheld often only by some instinct that itself made him tremble with rage. Just as he still cared more for her than for any other creature, so did he more intensely and frequently hate her.

So far, the judges of the Appellate Division had failed to hand down a decision, but after another postponement they finally affirmed the decree of the lower court—two justices dissenting. A notice of appeal was served upon Edward Shuttleworth. The case was going to the court of last resort, and they were in for another interminable wait. Six months, perhaps a year. It had grown enormously unreal to them, remote and uncertain as heaven.

Throughout the previous winter one small matter had been a subtle and omnipresent irritant—the question of Gloria's gray fur coat. At that time women enveloped in long squirrel wraps could be seen every few yards along Fifth Avenue. The women were converted to the shape of tops. They seemed porcine and obscene; they resembled kept women in the concealing richness, the feminine animality of the garment. Yet—Gloria wanted a gray squirrel coat.

Discussing the matter—or, rather, arguing it, for even more than in the first year of their marriage did every discussion take the form of bitter debate full of such phrases as "most certainly," "utterly outrageous," "it's so, nevertheless," and the ultra-emphatic "regardless"—they concluded that they could not afford it. And so gradually it began to stand as a symbol of their growing financial anxiety.

To Gloria the shrinkage of their income was a remarkable phenomenon, without explanation or precedent—that it could happen at all within the space of five years seemed almost an intended cruelty, conceived and executed by a sardonic God. When they were married seventy-five hundred a year had seemed ample for a young couple, especially when augmented by the expectation of many millions. Gloria had failed to realize that it was decreasing not only in amount but in purchasing power until the payment of Mr. Haight's retaining fee of fifteen thousand dollars made the fact suddenly and startlingly obvious. When Anthony was drafted they had calculated their income at over four hundred a month, with the dollar even then decreasing in value, but on his return to New York they discovered an even more alarming condition of affairs. They were receiving only forty-five hundred a year from their investments. And though the suit over the will moved ahead of them like a persistent mirage and the financial danger-mark loomed up in the near distance they found, nevertheless, that living within their income was impossible.

So Gloria went without the squirrel coat and every day upon Fifth Avenue she was a little conscious of her well-worn, half-length leopard skin, now hopelessly old-fashioned. Every other month they sold a bond, yet when the bills were paid it left only enough to be gulped down hungrily by their current expenses. Anthony's calculations showed that their capital would last about seven years longer. So Gloria's heart was very bitter, for in one week, on a prolonged hysterical party during which Anthony whimsically divested himself of coat, vest, and shirt in a theatre and was assisted out by a posse of ushers, they spent twice what the gray squirrel coat would have cost.

It was November, Indian summer rather, and a warm, warm night—which was unnecessary, for the work of the summer was done. Babe Ruth had smashed the home-run record for the first time and Jack Dempsey had broken Jess Willard's cheek-bone out in Ohio. Over in Europe the usual number of children had swollen stomachs from starvation, and the diplomats were at their customary business of making the world safe for new wars. In New York City the proletariat were being "disciplined," and the odds on Harvard were generally quoted at five to three. Peace had come down in earnest, the beginning of new days.

Up in the bedroom of the apartment on Fifty-seventh Street Gloria lay upon her bed and tossed from side to side, sitting up at intervals to throw off a superfluous cover and once asking Anthony, who was lying awake beside her, to bring her a glass of ice-water. "Be sure and put ice in it," she said with insistence; "it isn't cold enough the way it comes from the faucet."

Looking through the frail curtains she could see the rounded moon over the roofs and beyond it on the sky the yellow glow from Times Square—and watching the two incongruous lights, her mind worked over an emotion, or rather an interwoven complex of emotions, that had occupied it through the day, and the day before that and back to the last time when she could remember having thought clearly and consecutively about anything—which must have been while Anthony was in the army.

She would be twenty-nine in February. The month assumed an ominous and inescapable significance—making her wonder, through these nebulous half-fevered hours whether after all she had not wasted her faintly tired beauty, whether there was such a thing as use for any quality bounded by a harsh and inevitable mortality.

Years before, when she was twenty-one, she had written in her diary: "Beauty is only to be admired, only to be loved—to be harvested carefully and then flung at a chosen lover like a gift of roses. It seems to me, so far as I can judge clearly at all, that my beauty should be used like that...."

And now, all this November day, all this desolate day, under a sky dirty and white, Gloria had been thinking that perhaps she had been wrong. To preserve the integrity of her first gift she had looked no more for love. When the first flame and ecstasy had grown dim, sunk down, departed, she had begun preserving—what? It puzzled her that she no longer knew just what she was preserving—a sentimental memory or some profound and fundamental concept of honor. She was doubting now whether there had been any moral issue involved in her way of life—to walk unworried and unregretful along the gayest of all possible lanes and to keep her pride by being always herself and doing what it seemed beautiful that she should do. From the first little boy in an Eton collar whose "girl" she had been, down to the latest casual man whose eyes had grown alert and appreciative as they rested upon her, there was needed only that matchless candor she could throw into a look or clothe with an inconsequent clause—for she had talked always in broken clauses—to weave about her immeasurable illusions, immeasurable distances, immeasurable light. To create souls in men, to create fine happiness and fine despair she must remain deeply proud—proud to be inviolate, proud also to be melting, to be passionate and possessed.

She knew that in her breast she had never wanted children. The reality, the earthiness, the intolerable sentiment of child-bearing, the menace to her beauty—had appalled her. She wanted to exist only as a conscious flower, prolonging and preserving itself. Her sentimentality could cling fiercely to her own illusions, but her ironic soul whispered that motherhood was also the privilege of the female baboon. So her dreams were of ghostly children only—the early, the perfect symbols of her early and perfect love for Anthony.

In the end then, her beauty was all that never failed her. She had never seen beauty like her own. What it meant ethically or aesthetically faded before the gorgeous concreteness of her pink-and-white feet, the clean perfectness of her body, and the baby mouth that was like the material symbol of a kiss.

She would be twenty-nine in February. As the long night waned she grew supremely conscious that she and beauty were going to make use of these next three months. At first she was not sure for what, but the problem resolved itself gradually into the old lure of the screen. She was in earnest now. No material want could have moved her as this fear moved her. No matter for Anthony, Anthony the poor in spirit, the weak and broken man with bloodshot eyes, for whom she still had moments of tenderness. No matter. She would be twenty-nine in February—a hundred days, so many days; she would go to Bloeckman to-morrow.

With the decision came relief. It cheered her that in some manner the illusion of beauty could be sustained, or preserved perhaps in celluloid after the reality had vanished. Well—to-morrow.

The next day she felt weak and ill. She tried to go out, and saved herself from collapse only by clinging to a mail box near the front door. The Martinique elevator boy helped her up-stairs, and she waited on the bed for Anthony's return without energy to unhook her brassiere.

For five days she was down with influenza, which, just as the month turned the corner into winter, ripened into double pneumonia. In the feverish perambulations of her mind she prowled through a house of bleak unlighted rooms hunting for her mother. All she wanted was to be a little girl, to be efficiently taken care of by some yielding yet superior power, stupider and steadier than herself. It seemed that the only lover she had ever wanted was a lover in a dream.

"ODI PROFANUM VULGUS"

One day in the midst of Gloria's illness there occurred a curious incident that puzzled Miss McGovern, the trained nurse, for some time afterward. It was noon, but the room in which the patient lay was dark and quiet. Miss McGovern was standing near the bed mixing some medicine, when Mrs. Patch, who had apparently been sound asleep, sat up and began to speak vehemently:

"Millions of people," she said, "swarming like rats, chattering like apes, smelling like all hell ... monkeys! Or lice, I suppose. For one really exquisite palace ... on Long Island, say—or even in Greenwich ... for one palace full of pictures from the Old World and exquisite things—with avenues of trees and green lawns and a view of the blue sea, and lovely people about in slick dresses ... I'd sacrifice a hundred thousand of them, a million of them." She raised her hand feebly and snapped her fingers. "I care nothing for them—understand me?"

The look she bent upon Miss McGovern at the conclusion of this speech was curiously elfin, curiously intent. Then she gave a short little laugh polished with scorn, and tumbling backward fell off again to sleep.

Miss McGovern was bewildered. She wondered what were the hundred thousand things that Mrs. Patch would sacrifice for her palace. Dollars, she supposed—yet it had not sounded exactly like dollars.

THE MOVIES

It was February, seven days before her birthday, and the great snow that had filled up the cross-streets as dirt fills the cracks in a floor had turned to slush and was being escorted to the gutters by the hoses of the street-cleaning department. The wind, none the less bitter for being casual, whipped in through the open windows of the living room bearing with it the dismal secrets of the areaway and clearing the Patch apartment of stale smoke in its cheerless circulation.

Gloria, wrapped in a warm kimona, came into the chilly room and taking up the telephone receiver called Joseph Bloeckman.

"Do you mean Mr. Joseph *Black*?" demanded the telephone girl at "Films Par Excellence."

"Bloeckman, Joseph Bloeckman. B-l-o—"

"Mr. Joseph Bloeckman has changed his name to Black. Do you want him?"

"Why—yes." She remembered nervously that she had once called him "Blockhead" to his face.

His office was reached by courtesy of two additional female voices; the last was a secretary who took her name. Only with the flow through the transmitter of his own familiar but faintly impersonal tone did she realize that it had been three years since they had met. And he had changed his name to Black.

"Can you see me?" she suggested lightly. "It's on a business matter, really. I'm going into the movies at last—if I can."

"I'm awfully glad. I've always thought you'd like it."

"Do you think you can get me a trial?" she demanded with the arrogance peculiar to all beautiful women, to all women who have ever at any time considered themselves beautiful.

He assured her that it was merely a question of when she wanted the trial. Any time? Well, he'd phone later in the day and let her know a convenient hour. The conversation closed with conventional padding on both sides. Then from three o'clock to five she sat close to the telephone—with no result.

But next morning came a note that contented and excited her:

My dear Gloria:

Just by luck a matter came to my attention that I think will be just suited to you. I would like to see you start with something that would bring you notice. At the same time if a very beautiful girl of your sort is put directly into a picture next to one of the rather shop-worn stars with which every company is afflicted, tongues would very likely wag. But there is a "flapper" part in a Percy B. Debris production that I think would be just suited to you and would bring you notice. Willa Sable plays opposite Gaston Mears in a sort of character part and your part I believe would be her younger sister.

Anyway Percy B. Debris who is directing the picture says if you'll come to the studios day after to-morrow (Thursday) he will run off a test. If ten o'clock is suited to you I will meet you there at that time.

With all good wishes

Ever Faithfully

JOSEPH BLACK.

Gloria had decided that Anthony was to know nothing of this until she had obtained a definite position, and accordingly she was dressed and out of the apartment next morning before he awoke. Her mirror had given her, she thought, much the same account as ever. She wondered if there were any lingering traces of her sickness. She was still slightly under weight, and she had fancied, a few days before, that her cheeks were a trifle thinner—but she felt that those were merely transitory conditions and that on this particular day she looked as fresh as ever. She had bought and charged a new hat, and as the day was warm she had left the leopard skin coat at home.

At the "Films Par Excellence" studios she was announced over the telephone and told that Mr. Black would be down directly. She looked around her. Two girls were being shown about by a little fat man in a slash-pocket coat, and one of them had indicated a stack of thin parcels, piled breast-high against the wall, and extending along for twenty feet.

"That's studio mail," explained the fat man. "Pictures of the stars who are with 'Films Par Excellence.'"

"Oh."

"Each one's autographed by Florence Kelley or Gaston Mears or Mack Dodge—" He winked confidentially. "At least when Minnie McGlook out in Sauk Center gets the picture she wrote for, she *thinks* it's autographed."

"Just a stamp?"

"Sure. It'd take 'em a good eight-hour day to autograph half of 'em. They say Mary Pickford's studio mail costs her fifty thousand a year."

"Say!"

"Sure. Fifty thousand. But it's the best kinda advertising there is—"

They drifted out of earshot and almost immediately Bloeckman appeared—Bloeckman, a dark suave gentleman, gracefully engaged in the middle forties, who greeted her with courteous warmth and told her she had not changed a bit in three years. He led the way into a great hall, as large as an armory and broken intermittently with busy sets and blinding rows of unfamiliar light. Each piece of scenery was marked in large white letters "Gaston Mears Company," "Mack Dodge Company," or simply "Films Par Excellence."

"Ever been in a studio before?"

"Never have."

She liked it. There was no heavy closeness of greasepaint, no scent of soiled and tawdry costumes which years before had revolted her behind the scenes of a musical comedy. This work was done in the clean mornings; the appurtenances seemed rich and gorgeous and new. On a set that was joyous with Manchu hangings a perfect Chinaman was going through a scene according to megaphone directions as the great glittering machine ground out its ancient moral tale for the edification of the national mind.

A red-headed man approached them and spoke with familiar deference to Bloeckman, who answered:

"Hello, Debris. Want you to meet Mrs. Patch.... Mrs. Patch wants to go into pictures, as I explained to you.... All right, now, where do we go?"

Mr. Debris—the great Percy B. Debris, thought Gloria—showed them to a set which represented the interior of an office. Some chairs were drawn up around the camera, which stood in front of it, and the three of them sat down.

"Ever been in a studio before?" asked Mr. Debris, giving her a glance that was surely the quintessence of keenness. "No? Well, I'll explain exactly what's going to happen. We're going to take what we call a test in order to see how your features photograph and whether you've got natural stage presence and how you respond to coaching. There's no need to be nervous over it. I'll just have the camera-man take a few hundred feet in an episode I've got marked here in the scenario. We can tell pretty much what we want to from that."

He produced a typewritten continuity and explained to her the episode she was to enact. It developed that one Barbara Wainwright had been secretly married to the junior partner of the firm whose office was there represented. Entering the deserted office one day by accident she was naturally interested in seeing where her husband worked. The telephone rang and after some hesitation she answered it. She learned that her husband had been struck by an automobile and instantly killed. She was overcome. At first she was unable to realize the truth, but finally she succeeded in comprehending it, and went into a dead faint on the floor.

"Now that's all we want," concluded Mr. Debris. "I'm going to stand here and tell you approximately what to do, and you're to act as though I wasn't here, and just go on do it your own way. You needn't be afraid we're going to judge this too severely. We simply want to get a general idea of your screen personality."

"I see."

"You'll find make-up in the room in back of the set. Go light on it. Very little red."

"I see," repeated Gloria, nodding. She touched her lips nervously with the tip of her tongue.

THE TEST

As she came into the set through the real wooden door and closed it carefully behind her, she found herself inconveniently dissatisfied with her clothes. She should have bought a "misses'" dress for the occasion—she could still wear them, and it might have been a good investment if it had accentuated her airy youth.

Her mind snapped sharply into the momentous present as Mr. Debris's voice came from the glare of the white lights in front.

"You look around for your husband.... Now—you don't see him ... you're curious about the office...."

She became conscious of the regular sound of the camera. It worried her. She glanced toward it involuntarily and wondered if she had made up her face correctly. Then, with a definite effort she forced herself to act—and she had never felt that the gestures of her body were so banal, so awkward, so bereft of grace or distinction. She strolled around the office, picking up articles here and there and looking at them inanely. Then she scrutinized the ceiling, the floor, and thoroughly inspected an inconsequential lead pencil on the desk. Finally, because she could think of nothing else to do, and less than nothing to express, she forced a smile.

"All right. Now the phone rings. Ting-a-ling-a-ling! Hesitate, and then answer it."

She hesitated—and then, too quickly, she thought, picked up the receiver.

"Hello."

Her voice was hollow and unreal. The words rang in the empty set like the ineffectualities of a ghost. The absurdities of their requirements appalled her—Did they expect that on an instant's notice she could put herself in the place of this preposterous and unexplained character?

"... No ... no.... Not yet! Now listen: 'John Sumner has just been knocked over by an automobile and instantly killed!'"

Gloria let her baby mouth drop slowly open. Then:

"Now hang up! With a bang!"

She obeyed, clung to the table with her eyes wide and staring. At length she was feeling slightly encouraged and her confidence increased.

"My God!" she cried. Her voice was good, she thought. "Oh, my God!"

"Now faint."

She collapsed forward to her knees and throwing her body outward on the ground lay without breathing.

"All right!" called Mr. Debris. "That's enough, thank you. That's plenty. Get up—that's enough."

Gloria arose, mustering her dignity and brushing off her skirt.

"Awful!" she remarked with a cool laugh, though her heart was bumping tumultuously. "Terrible, wasn't it?"

"Did you mind it?" said Mr. Debris, smiling blandly. "Did it seem hard? I can't tell anything about it until I have it run off."

"Of course not," she agreed, trying to attach some sort of meaning to his remark—and failing. It was just the sort of thing he would have said had he been trying not to encourage her.

A few moments later she left the studio. Bloeckman had promised that she should hear the result of the test within the next few days. Too proud to force any definite comment she felt a baffling uncertainty and only now when the step had at last been taken did she realize how the possibility of a successful screen career had played in the back of her mind for the past three years. That night she tried to tell over to herself the elements that might decide for or against her. Whether or not she had used enough make-up worried her, and as the part was that of a girl of twenty, she wondered if she had not been just a little too grave. About her acting she was least of all satisfied. Her entrance had been abominable—in fact not until she reached the phone had she displayed a shred of poise—and then the test had been over. If they had only realized! She wished that she could try it again. A mad plan to call up in the morning and ask for a new trial took possession of her, and as suddenly faded. It seemed neither politic nor polite to ask another favor of Bloeckman.

The third day of waiting found her in a highly nervous condition. She had bitten the insides of her mouth until they were raw and smarting, and burnt unbearably when she washed them with listerine. She had quarrelled so persistently with Anthony that he had left the apartment in a cold fury. But because he was intimidated by her exceptional frigidity, he called up an hour afterward, apologized and said he was having dinner at the Amsterdam Club, the only one in which he still retained membership.

It was after one o'clock and she had breakfasted at eleven, so, deciding to forego luncheon, she started for a walk in the Park. At three there would be a mail. She would be back by three.

It was an afternoon of premature spring. Water was drying on the walks and in the Park little girls were gravely wheeling white doll-buggies up and down under the thin trees while behind them followed bored nursery-maids in two's, discussing with each other those tremendous secrets that are peculiar to nursery-maids.

Two o'clock by her little gold watch. She should have a new watch, one made in a platinum oblong and incrusted with diamonds—but those cost even more than squirrel coats and of course they were out of her reach now, like everything else—unless perhaps the right letter was awaiting her ... in about an hour ... fifty-eight minutes exactly. Ten to get there left forty-eight ... forty-seven now ...

Little girls soberly wheeling their buggies along the damp sunny walks. The nursery-maids chattering in pairs about their inscrutable secrets. Here and there a raggedy man seated upon newspapers spread on a drying bench, related not to the radiant and delightful afternoon but to the dirty snow that slept exhausted in obscure corners, waiting for extermination....

Ages later, coming into the dim hall she saw the Martinique elevator boy standing incongruously in the light of the stained-glass window.

"Is there any mail for us?" she asked.

"Up-stays, madame."

The switchboard squawked abominably and Gloria waited while he ministered to the telephone. She sickened as the elevator groaned its way up—the floors passed like the slow lapse of centuries, each one ominous, accusing, significant. The letter, a white leprous spot, lay upon the dirty tiles of the hall....

My dear Gloria:

We had the test run off yesterday afternoon, and Mr. Debris seemed to think that for the part he had in mind he needed a younger woman. He said that the acting was not bad, and that there was a small character part supposed to be a very haughty rich widow that he thought you might——

Desolately Gloria raised her glance until it fell out across the areaway. But she found she could not see the opposite wall, for her gray eyes were full of tears. She walked into the bedroom, the letter crinkled tightly in her hand, and sank down upon her knees before the long mirror on the wardrobe floor. This was her twenty-ninth birthday, and the world was melting away before her eyes. She tried to think that it had been the make-up, but her emotions were too profound, too overwhelming for any consolation that the thought conveyed.

She strained to see until she could feel the flesh on her temples pull forward. Yes—the cheeks were ever so faintly thin, the corners of the eyes were lined with tiny wrinkles. The eyes were different. Why, they were different! ... And then suddenly she knew how tired her eyes were.

"Oh, my pretty face," she whispered, passionately grieving. "Oh, my pretty face! Oh, I don't want to live without my pretty face! Oh, what's *happened?*"

Then she slid toward the mirror and, as in the test, sprawled face downward upon the floor—and lay there sobbing. It was the first awkward movement she had ever made.

III. NO MATTER!

WITHIN another year Anthony and Gloria had become like players who had lost their costumes, lacking the pride to continue on the note of tragedy—so that when Mrs. and Miss Hulme of Kansas City cut them dead in the Plaza one evening, it was only that Mrs. and Miss Hulme, like most people, abominated mirrors of their atavistic selves.

Their new apartment, for which they paid eighty-five dollars a month, was situated on Claremont Avenue, which is two blocks from the Hudson in the dim hundreds. They had lived there a month when Muriel Kane came to see them late one afternoon.

It was a reproachless twilight on the summer side of spring. Anthony lay upon the lounge looking up One Hundred and Twenty-seventh Street toward the river, near which he could just see a single patch of vivid green trees that guaranteed the brummagem umbrageousness of Riverside Drive. Across the water were the Palisades, crowned by the ugly framework of the amusement park—yet soon it would be dusk and those same iron cobwebs would be a glory against the heavens, an enchanted palace set over the smooth radiance of a tropical canal.

The streets near the apartment, Anthony had found, were streets where children played—streets a little nicer than those he had been used to pass on his way to Marietta, but of the same general sort, with an occasional hand organ or hurdy-gurdy, and in the cool of the evening many pairs of young girls walking down to the corner drug-store for ice cream soda and dreaming unlimited dreams under the low heavens.

Dusk in the streets now, and children playing, shouting up incoherent ecstatic words that faded out close to the open window—and Muriel, who had come to find Gloria, chattering to him from an opaque gloom over across the room.

"Light the lamp, why don't we?" she suggested. "It's getting *ghostly* in here."

With a tired movement he arose and obeyed; the gray window-panes vanished. He stretched himself. He was heavier now, his stomach was a limp weight against his belt; his flesh had softened and expanded. He was thirty-two and his mind was a bleak and disordered wreck.

"Have a little drink, Muriel?"

"Not me, thanks. I don't use it anymore. What're you doing these days, Anthony?" she asked curiously.

"Well, I've been pretty busy with this lawsuit," he answered indifferently. "It's gone to the Court of Appeals—ought to be settled up one way or another by autumn. There's been some objection as to whether the Court of Appeals has jurisdiction over the matter."

Muriel made a clicking sound with her tongue and cocked her head on one side.

"Well, you tell'em! I never heard of anything taking so long."

"Oh, they all do," he replied listlessly; "all will cases. They say it's exceptional to have one settled under four or five years."

"Oh ..." Muriel daringly changed her tack, "why don't you go to work, you la-azy!"

"At what?" he demanded abruptly.

"Why, at anything, I suppose. You're still a young man."

"If that's encouragement, I'm much obliged," he answered dryly—and then with sudden weariness: "Does it bother you particularly that I don't want to work?"

"It doesn't bother me—but, it does bother a lot of people who claim—"

"Oh, God!" he said brokenly, "it seems to me that for three years I've heard nothing about myself but wild stories and virtuous admonitions. I'm tired of it. If you don't want to see us, let us alone. I don't bother my former friends. But I need no charity calls, and no criticism disguised as good advice—" Then he added apologetically: "I'm sorry—but really, Muriel, you mustn't talk like a lady slum-worker even if you are visiting the lower middle classes." He turned his bloodshot eyes on her reproachfully—eyes that had once been a deep, clear blue, that were weak now, strained, and half-ruined from reading when he was drunk.

"Why do you say such awful things?" she protested. You talk as if you and Gloria were in the middle classes."

"Why pretend we're not? I hate people who claim to be great aristocrats when they can't even keep up the appearances of it."

"Do you think a person has to have money to be aristocratic?"

Muriel ... the horrified democrat ...!

"Why, of course. Aristocracy's only an admission that certain traits which we call fine—courage and honor and beauty and all that sort of thing—can best be developed in a favorable environment, where you don't have the warpings of ignorance and necessity."

Muriel bit her lower lip and waved her head from side to side.

"Well, all *I* say is that if a person comes from a good family they're always nice people. That's the trouble with you and Gloria. You think that just because things aren't going your way right now all your old friends are trying to avoid you. You're too sensitive—"

"As a matter of fact," said Anthony, "you know nothing at all about it. With me it's simply a matter of pride, and for once Gloria's reasonable enough to agree that we oughtn't go where we're not wanted. And people don't want us. We're too much the ideal bad examples."

"Nonsense! You can't park your pessimism in my little sun parlor. I think you ought to forget all those morbid speculations and go to work."

"Here I am, thirty-two. Suppose I did start in at some idiotic business. Perhaps in two years I might rise to fifty dollars a week—with luck. That's *if* I could get a job at all; there's an awful lot of unemployment. Well, suppose I made fifty a week. Do you think I'd be any happier? Do you think that if I don't get this money of my grandfather's life will be *endurable?*"

Muriel smiled complacently.

"Well," she said, "that may be clever but it isn't common sense."

A few minutes later Gloria came in seeming to bring with her into the room some dark color, indeterminate and rare. In a taciturn way she was happy to see Muriel. She greeted Anthony with a casual "Hi!"

"I've been talking philosophy with your husband," cried the irrepressible Miss Kane.

"We took up some fundamental concepts," said Anthony, a faint smile disturbing his pale cheeks, paler still under two days' growth of beard.

Oblivious to his irony Muriel rehashed her contention. When she had done, Gloria said quietly:

"Anthony's right. It's no fun to go around when you have the sense that people are looking at you in a certain way."

He broke in plaintively:

"Don't you think that when even Maury Noble, who was my best friend, won't come to see us it's high time to stop calling people up?" Tears were standing in his eyes.

"That was your fault about Maury Noble," said Gloria coolly.

"It wasn't."

"It most certainly was."

Muriel intervened quickly:

"I met a girl who knew Maury, the other day, and she says he doesn't drink any more. He's getting pretty cagey."

"Doesn't?"

"Practically not at all. He's making *piles* of money. He's sort of changed since the war. He's going to marry a girl in Philadelphia who has millions, Ceci Larrabee—anyhow, that's what Town Tattle said."

"He's thirty-three," said Anthony, thinking aloud. But it's odd to imagine his getting married. I used to think he was so brilliant."

"He was," murmured Gloria, "in a way."

"But brilliant people don't settle down in business—or do they? Or what do they do? Or what becomes of everybody you used to know and have so much in common with?"

"You drift apart," suggested Muriel with the appropriate dreamy look.

"They change," said Gloria. "All the qualities that they don't use in their daily lives get cobwebbed up."

"The last thing he said to me," recollected Anthony, "was that he was going to work so as to forget that there was nothing worth working for."

Muriel caught at this quickly.

"That's what *you* ought to do," she exclaimed triumphantly. "Of course I shouldn't think anybody would want to work for nothing. But it'd give you something to do. What do you do with yourselves, anyway? Nobody ever sees you at Montmartre or—or anywhere. Are you economizing?"

Gloria laughed scornfully, glancing at Anthony from the corners of her eyes.

"Well," he demanded, "what are you laughing at?"

"You know what I'm laughing at," she answered coldly.

"At that case of whiskey?"

"Yes"—she turned to Muriel—"he paid seventy-five dollars for a case of whiskey yesterday."

"What if I did? It's cheaper that way than if you get it by the bottle. You needn't pretend that you won't drink any of it."

"At least I don't drink in the daytime."

"That's a fine distinction!" he cried, springing to his feet in a weak rage. "What's more, I'll be damned if you can hurl that at me every few minutes!"

"It's true."

"It is *not!* And I'm getting sick of this eternal business of criticising me before visitors!" He had worked himself up to such a state that his arms and shoulders were visibly trembling. "You'd think everything was my fault. You'd think you hadn't encouraged me to spend money—and spent a lot more on yourself than I ever did by a long shot."

Now Gloria rose to her feet.

"I *won't* let you talk to me that way!"

"All right, then; by Heaven, you don't have to!"

In a sort of rush he left the room. The two women heard his steps in the hall and then the front door banged. Gloria sank back into her chair. Her face was lovely in the lamplight, composed, inscrutable.

"Oh—!" cried Muriel in distress. "Oh, what *is* the matter?"

"Nothing particularly. He's just drunk."

"Drunk? Why, he's perfectly sober. He talked——"

Gloria shook her head.

"Oh, no, he doesn't show it any more unless he can hardly stand up, and he talks all right until he gets excited. He talks much better than he does when he's sober. But he's been sitting here all day drinking—except for the time it took him to walk to the corner for a newspaper."

"Oh, how terrible!" Muriel was sincerely moved. Her eyes filled with tears. "Has this happened much?"

"Drinking, you mean?"

"No, this—leaving you?"

"Oh, yes. Frequently. He'll come in about midnight—and weep and ask me to forgive him."

"And do you?"

"I don't know. We just go on."

The two women sat there in the lamplight and looked at each other, each in a different way helpless before this thing. Gloria was still pretty, as pretty as she would ever be again—her cheeks were flushed and she was wearing a new dress that she had bought—imprudently—for fifty dollars. She had hoped she could persuade Anthony to take her out to-night, to a restaurant or even to one of the great, gorgeous moving picture palaces where there would be a few people to look at her, at whom she could bear to look in turn. She wanted this because she knew her cheeks were flushed and because her dress was new and becomingly fragile. Only very occasionally, now, did they receive any invitations. But she did not tell these things to Muriel.

"Gloria, dear, I wish we could have dinner together, but I promised a man and it's seven-thirty already. I've got to *tear*."

"Oh, I couldn't, anyway. In the first place I've been ill all day. I couldn't eat a thing."

After she had walked with Muriel to the door, Gloria came back into the room, turned out the lamp, and leaning her elbows on the window sill looked out at Palisades Park, where the brilliant revolving circle of the Ferris wheel was like a trembling mirror catching the yellow reflection of the moon. The street was quiet now; the children had gone in—over the way she could see a family at dinner. Pointlessly, ridiculously, they rose and walked about the table; seen thus, all that they did appeared incongruous—it was as though they were being jiggled carelessly and to no purpose by invisible overhead wires.

She looked at her watch—it was eight o'clock. She had been pleased for a part of the day—the early afternoon—in walking along that Broadway of Harlem, One Hundred and Twenty-fifth Street, with her nostrils alert to many odors, and her mind excited by the extraordinary beauty of some Italian children. It affected her curiously—as Fifth Avenue had affected her once, in the days when, with the placid confidence of beauty, she had known that it was all hers, every shop and all it held, every adult toy glittering in a window, all hers for the asking. Here on One Hundred and Twenty-fifth Street there were Salvation Army bands and spectrum-shawled old ladies on door-steps and sugary, sticky candy in the grimy hands of shiny-haired children—and the late sun striking down on the sides of the tall tenements. All very rich and racy and savory, like a dish by a provident French chef that one could not help enjoying, even though one knew that the ingredients were probably left-overs....

Gloria shuddered suddenly as a river siren came moaning over the dusky roofs, and leaning back in till the ghostly curtains fell from her shoulder, she turned on the electric lamp. It was growing late. She knew there was some change in her purse, and she considered whether she would go down and have some coffee and rolls where the liberated subway made a roaring cave of Manhattan Street or eat the devilled ham and bread in the kitchen. Her purse decided for her. It contained a nickel and two pennies.

After an hour the silence of the room had grown unbearable, and she found that her eyes were wandering from her magazine to the ceiling, toward which she stared without thought. Suddenly she stood up, hesitated for a moment, biting at her finger—then she went to the pantry, took down a bottle of whiskey from the shelf and poured herself a drink. She filled up the glass with ginger ale, and returning to her chair finished an article in the magazine. It concerned the last revolutionary widow, who, when a young girl, had married an ancient veteran of the Continental Army and who had died in 1906. It seemed strange and oddly romantic to Gloria that she and this woman had been contemporaries.

She turned a page and learned that a candidate for Congress was being accused of atheism by an opponent. Gloria's surprise vanished when she found that the charges were false. The candidate had merely denied the miracle of the loaves and fishes. He admitted, under pressure, that he gave full credence to the stroll upon the water.

Finishing her first drink, Gloria got herself a second. After slipping on a negligée and making herself comfortable on the lounge, she became conscious that she was miserable and that the tears were rolling down her cheeks. She wondered if they were tears of self-pity, and tried resolutely not to cry, but this existence without hope, without happiness, oppressed her, and she kept shaking her head from side to side, her mouth drawn down tremulously in the corners, as though she were denying an assertion made by some one, somewhere. She did not know that this gesture of hers was years older than history, that, for a hundred generations of men, intolerable and persistent grief has offered that gesture, of denial, of protest, of bewilderment, to something more profound, more powerful than the God made in the image of man, and before which that God, did he exist, would be equally impotent. It is a truth set at the heart of tragedy that this force never explains, never answers—this force intangible as air, more definite than death.

RICHARD CARAMEL

Early in the summer Anthony resigned from his last club, the Amsterdam. He had come to visit it hardly twice a year, and the dues were a recurrent burden. He had joined it on his return from Italy because it had been his grandfather's club and his father's, and because it was a club that, given the opportunity, one indisputably joined—but as a matter of fact he had preferred the Harvard Club, largely because of Dick and Maury. However, with the decline of his fortunes, it had seemed an increasingly desirable bauble to cling to.... It was relinquished at the last, with some regret....

His companions numbered now a curious dozen. Several of them he had met in a place called "Sammy's," on Forty-third Street, where, if one knocked on the door and were favorably passed on from behind a grating, one could sit around a great round table drinking fairly good whiskey. It was here that he encountered a man named Parker Allison, who had been exactly the wrong sort of rounder at Harvard, and who was running through a large "yeast" fortune as rapidly as possible. Parker Allison's notion of distinction consisted in driving a noisy red-and-yellow racing-car up Broadway with two glittering, hard-eyed girls beside him. He was the sort who dined with two girls rather than with one—his imagination was almost incapable of sustaining a dialogue.

Besides Allison there was Pete Lytell, who wore a gray derby on the side of his head. He always had money and he was customarily cheerful, so Anthony held aimless, long-winded conversation with him through many afternoons of the summer and fall. Lytell, he found, not only talked but reasoned in phrases. His philosophy was a series of them, assimilated here and there through an active, thoughtless life. He had phrases about Socialism—the immemorial ones; he had phrases pertaining to the existence of a personal deity—something about one time when he had been in a railroad accident; and he had phrases about the Irish problem, the sort of woman he respected, and the futility of prohibition. The only time his conversation ever rose superior to these muddled clauses, with which he interpreted the most rococo happenings in a life that had been more than usually eventful, was when he got down to the detailed discussion of his most animal existence: he knew, to a subtlety, the foods, the liquor, and the women that he preferred.

He was at once the commonest and the most remarkable product of civilization. He was nine out of ten people that one passes on a city street—and he was a hairless ape with two dozen tricks. He was the hero of a thousand romances of life and art—and he was a virtual moron, performing staidly yet absurdly a series of complicated and infinitely astounding epics over a span of threescore years.

With such men as these two Anthony Patch drank and discussed and drank and argued. He liked them because they knew nothing about him, because they lived in the obvious and had not the faintest conception of the inevitable continuity of life. They sat not before a motion picture with consecutive reels, but at a musty old-fashioned travelogue with all values stark and hence all implications confused. Yet they themselves were not confused, because there was nothing in them to be confused—they changed phrases from month to month as they changed neckties.

Anthony, the courteous, the subtle, the perspicacious, was drunk each day—in Sammy's with these men, in the apartment over a book, some book he knew, and, very rarely, with Gloria, who, in his eyes, had begun to develop the unmistakable outlines of a quarrelsome and unreasonable woman. She was not the Gloria of old, certainly—the Gloria who, had she been sick, would have preferred to inflict misery upon every one around her, rather than confess that she needed sympathy or assistance. She was not above whining now; she was not above being sorry for herself. Each night when she prepared for bed she smeared her face with some new unguent which she hoped illogically would give back the glow and freshness to her vanishing beauty. When Anthony was drunk he taunted her about this. When he was sober he was polite to her, on occasions even tender; he seemed to show for short hours a trace of that old quality of understanding too well to blame—that quality which was the best of him and had worked swiftly and ceaselessly toward his ruin.

But he hated to be sober. It made him conscious of the people around him, of that air of struggle, of greedy ambition, of hope more sordid than despair, of incessant passage up or down, which in every metropolis is most in evidence through the unstable middle class. Unable to live with the rich he thought that his next choice would have been to live with the very poor. Anything was better than this cup of perspiration and tears.

The sense of the enormous panorama of life, never strong in Anthony, had become dim almost to extinction. At long intervals now some incident, some gesture of Gloria's, would take his fancy—but the gray veils had come down in earnest upon him. As he grew older those things faded—after that there was wine.

There was a kindliness about intoxication—there was that indescribable gloss and glamour it gave, like the memories of ephemeral and faded evenings. After a few high-balls there was magic in the tall glowing Arabian night of the Bush Terminal Building—its summit a peak of sheer grandeur, gold and dreaming against the inaccessible sky. And Wall Street, the crass, the banal—again it was the triumph of gold, a gorgeous sentient spectacle; it was where the great kings kept the money for their wars....

... The fruit of youth or of the grape, the transitory magic of the brief passage from darkness to darkness—the old illusion that truth and beauty were in some way entwined.

As he stood in front of Delmonico's lighting a cigarette one night he saw two hansoms drawn up close to the curb, waiting for a chance drunken fare. The outmoded cabs were worn and dirty—the cracked patent leather wrinkled like an old man's face, the cushions faded to a brownish lavender; the very horses were ancient and weary, and so were the white-haired men who sat aloft, cracking their whips with a grotesque affectation of gallantry. A relic of vanished gaiety!

Anthony Patch walked away in a sudden fit of depression, pondering the bitterness of such survivals. There was nothing, it seemed, that grew stale so soon as pleasure.

On Forty-second Street one afternoon he met Richard Caramel for the first time in many months, a prosperous, fattening Richard Caramel, whose face was filling out to match the Bostonian brow.

"Just got in this week from the coast. Was going to call you up, but I didn't know your new address."

"We've moved."

Richard Caramel noticed that Anthony was wearing a soiled shirt, that his cuffs were slightly but perceptibly frayed, that his eyes were set in half-moons the color of cigar smoke.

"So I gathered," he said, fixing his friend with his bright-yellow eye. "But where and how is Gloria? My God, Anthony, I've been hearing the dog-gonedest stories about you two even out in California—and when I get back to New York I find you've sunk absolutely out of sight. Why don't you pull yourself together?"

"Now, listen," chattered Anthony unsteadily, "I can't stand a long lecture. We've lost money in a dozen ways, and naturally people have talked—on account of the lawsuit, but the thing's coming to a final decision this winter, surely—"

"You're talking so fast that I can't understand you," interrupted Dick calmly.

"Well, I've said all I'm going to say," snapped Anthony. "Come and see us if you like—or don't!"

With this he turned and started to walk off in the crowd, but Dick overtook him immediately and grasped his arm.

"Say, Anthony, don't fly off the handle so easily! You know Gloria's my cousin, and you're one of my oldest friends, so it's natural for me to be interested when I hear that you're going to the dogs—and taking her with you."

"I don't want to be preached to."

"Well, then, all right—How about coming up to my apartment and having a drink? I've just got settled. I've bought three cases of Gordon gin from a revenue officer."

As they walked along he continued in a burst of exasperation:

"And how about your grandfather's money—you going to get it?"

"Well," answered Anthony resentfully, "that old fool Haight seems hopeful, especially because people are tired of reformers right now—you know it might make a slight difference, for instance, if some judge thought that Adam Patch made it harder for him to get liquor."

"You can't do without money," said Dick sententiously. "Have you tried to write any—lately?"

Anthony shook his head silently.

"That's funny," said Dick. "I always thought that you and Maury would write some day, and now he's grown to be a sort of tight-fisted aristocrat, and you're—"

"I'm the bad example."

"I wonder why?"

"You probably think you know," suggested Anthony, with an effort at concentration. "The failure and the success both believe in their hearts that they have accurately balanced points of view, the success because he's succeeded, and the failure because he's failed. The successful man tells his son to profit by his father's good fortune, and the failure tells *his* son to profit by his father's mistakes."

"I don't agree with you," said the author of "A Shave-tail in France." "I used to listen to you and Maury when we were young, and I used to be impressed because you were so consistently cynical, but now—well, after all, by God, which of us three has taken to the—to the intellectual life? I don't want to sound vainglorious, but—it's me, and I've always believed that moral values existed, and I always will."

"Well," objected Anthony, who was rather enjoying himself, "even granting that, you know that in practice life never presents problems as clear cut, does it?"

"It does to me. There's nothing I'd violate certain principles for."

"But how do you know when you're violating them? You have to guess at things just like most people do. You have to apportion the values when you look back. You finish up the portrait then—paint in the details and shadows."

Dick shook his head with a lofty stubbornness. "Same old futile cynic," he said. "It's just a mode of being sorry for yourself. You don't do anything—so nothing matters."

"Oh, I'm quite capable of self-pity," admitted Anthony, "nor am I claiming that I'm getting as much fun out of life as you are."

"You say—at least you used to—that happiness is the only thing worth while in life. Do you think you're any happier for being a pessimist?"

Anthony grunted savagely. His pleasure in the conversation began to wane. He was nervous and craving for a drink.

"My golly!" he cried, "where do you live? I can't keep walking forever."

"Your endurance is all mental, eh?" returned Dick sharply. "Well, I live right here."

He turned in at the apartment house on Forty-ninth Street, and a few minutes later they were in a large new room with an open fireplace and four walls lined with books. A colored butler served them gin rickeys, and an hour vanished politely with the mellow shortening of their drinks and the glow of a light mid-autumn fire.

"The arts are very old," said Anthony after a while. With a few glasses the tension of his nerves relaxed and he found that he could think again.

"Which art?"

"All of them. Poetry is dying first. It'll be absorbed into prose sooner or later. For instance, the beautiful word, the colored and glittering word, and the beautiful simile belong in prose now. To get attention poetry has got to strain for the unusual word, the harsh, earthy word that's never been beautiful before. Beauty, as the sum of several beautiful parts, reached its apotheosis in Swinburne. It can't go any further—except in the novel, perhaps."

Dick interrupted him impatiently:

"You know these new novels make me tired. My God! Everywhere I go some silly girl asks me if I've read 'This Side of Paradise.' Are our girls really like that? If it's true to life, which I don't believe, the next generation is going to the dogs. I'm sick of all this shoddy realism. I think there's a place for the romanticist in literature."

Anthony tried to remember what he had read lately of Richard Caramel's. There was "A Shave-tail in France," a novel called "The Land of Strong Men," and several dozen short stories, which were even worse. It had become the custom among young and clever reviewers to mention Richard Caramel with a smile of scorn. "Mr." Richard Caramel, they called him. His corpse was dragged obscenely through every literary supplement. He was accused of making a great fortune by writing trash for the movies. As the fashion in books shifted he was becoming almost a byword of contempt.

While Anthony was thinking this, Dick had got to his feet and seemed to be hesitating at an avowal.

"I've gathered quite a few books," he said suddenly.

"So I see."

"I've made an exhaustive collection of good American stuff, old and new. I don't mean the usual Longfellow-Whittier thing—in fact, most of it's modern."

He stepped to one of the walls and, seeing that it was expected of him, Anthony arose and followed.

"Look!"

Under a printed tag *Americana* he displayed six long rows of books, beautifully bound and, obviously, carefully chosen.

"And here are the contemporary novelists."

Then Anthony saw the joker. Wedged in between Mark Twain and Dreiser were eight strange and inappropriate volumes, the works of Richard Caramel—"The Demon Lover," true enough ... but also seven others that were execrably awful, without sincerity or grace.

Unwillingly Anthony glanced at Dick's face and caught a slight uncertainty there.

"I've put my own books in, of course," said Richard Caramel hastily, "though one or two of them are uneven—I'm afraid I wrote a little too fast when I had that magazine contract. But I don't believe in false modesty. Of course some of the critics haven't paid so much attention to me since I've been established—but, after all, it's not the critics that count. They're just sheep."

For the first time in so long that he could scarcely remember, Anthony felt a touch of the old pleasant contempt for his friend. Richard Caramel continued:

"My publishers, you know, have been advertising me as the Thackeray of America—because of my New York novel."

"Yes," Anthony managed to muster, "I suppose there's a good deal in what you say."

He knew that his contempt was unreasonable. He, knew that he would have changed places with Dick unhesitatingly. He himself had tried his best to write with his tongue in his cheek. Ah, well, then—can a man disparage his life-work so readily? ...

—And that night while Richard Caramel was hard at toil, with great hittings of the wrong keys and screwings up of his weary, unmatched eyes, laboring over his trash far into those cheerless hours when the fire dies down, and the head is swimming from the effect of prolonged concentration—Anthony, abominably drunk, was sprawled across the back seat of a taxi on his way to the flat on Claremont Avenue.

THE BEATING

As winter approached it seemed that a sort of madness seized upon Anthony. He awoke in the morning so nervous that Gloria could feel him trembling in the bed before he could muster enough vitality to stumble into the pantry for a drink. He was intolerable now except under the influence of liquor, and as he seemed to decay and coarsen under her eyes, Gloria's soul and body shrank away from him; when he stayed out all night, as he did several times, she not only failed to be sorry but even felt a measure of relief. Next day he would be faintly repentant, and would remark in a gruff, hang-dog fashion that he guessed he was drinking a little too much.

For hours at a time he would sit in the great armchair that had been in his apartment, lost in a sort of stupor—even his interest in reading his favorite books seemed to have departed, and though an incessant bickering went on between husband and wife, the one subject upon which they ever really conversed was the progress of the will case. What Gloria hoped in the tenebrous depths of her soul, what she expected that great gift of money to bring about, is difficult to imagine. She was being bent by her environment into a grotesque similitude of a housewife. She who until three years before had never made coffee, prepared sometimes three meals a day. She walked a great deal in the afternoons, and in the evenings she read—books, magazines, anything she found at hand. If now she wished for a child, even a child of the Anthony who sought her bed blind drunk, she neither said so nor gave any show or sign of interest in children. It is doubtful if she could have made it clear to any one what it was she wanted, or indeed what there was to want—a lonely, lovely woman, thirty now, retrenched behind some impregnable inhibition born and coexistent with her beauty.

One afternoon when the snow was dirty again along Riverside Drive, Gloria, who had been to the grocer's, entered the apartment to find Anthony pacing the floor in a state of aggravated nervousness. The feverish eyes he turned on her were traced with tiny pink lines that reminded her of rivers on a map. For a moment she received the impression that he was suddenly and definitely old.

"Have you any money?" he inquired of her precipitately.

"What? What do you mean?"

"Just what I said. Money! Money! Can't you speak English?"

She paid no attention but brushed by him and into the pantry to put the bacon and eggs in the ice-box. When his drinking had been unusually excessive he was invariably in a whining mood. This time he followed her and, standing in the pantry door, persisted in his question.

"You heard what I said. Have you any money?"

She turned about from the ice-box and faced him.

"Why, Anthony, you must be crazy! You know I haven't any money—except a dollar in change."

He executed an abrupt about-face and returned to the living room, where he renewed his pacing. It was evident that he had something portentous on his mind—he quite obviously wanted to be asked what was the matter. Joining him a moment later she sat upon the long lounge and began taking down her hair. It was no longer bobbed, and it had changed in the last year from a rich gold dusted with red to an unresplendent light brown. She had bought some shampoo soap and meant to wash it now; she had considered putting a bottle of peroxide into the rinsing water.

"—Well?" she implied silently.

"That darn bank!" he quavered. "They've had my account for over ten years—ten *years*. Well, it seems they've got some autocratic rule that you have to keep over five hundred dollars there or they won't carry you. They wrote me a letter a few months ago and told me I'd been running too low. Once I gave out two bum checks—remember? that night in Reisenweber's?—but I made them good the very next day. Well, I promised old Halloran—he's the manager, the greedy Mick—that I'd watch out. And I thought I was going all right; I kept up the stubs in my check-book pretty regular. Well, I went in there to-day to cash a check, and Halloran came up and told me they'd have to close my account. Too many bad checks, he said, and I never had more than five hundred to my credit—and that only for a day or so at a time. And by God! What do you think he said then?"

"What?"

"He said this was a good time to do it because I didn't have a damn penny in there!"

"You didn't?"

"That's what he told me. Seems I'd given these Bedros people a check for sixty for that last case of liquor—and I only had forty-five dollars in the bank. Well, the Bedros people deposited fifteen dollars to my account and drew the whole thing out."

In her ignorance Gloria conjured up a spectre of imprisonment and disgrace.

"Oh, they won't do anything," he assured her. "Bootlegging's too risky a business. They'll send me a bill for fifteen dollars and I'll pay it."

"Oh." She considered a moment. "—Well, we can sell another bond."

He laughed sarcastically.

"Oh, yes, that's always easy. When the few bonds we have that are paying any interest at all are only worth between fifty and eighty cents on the dollar. We lose about half the bond every time we sell."

"What else can we do?"

"Oh, we'll sell something—as usual. We've got paper worth eighty thousand dollars at par." Again he laughed unpleasantly. "Bring about thirty thousand on the open market."

"I distrusted those ten per cent investments."

"The deuce you did!" he said. "You pretended you did, so you could claw at me if they went to pieces, but you wanted to take a chance as much as I did."

She was silent for a moment as if considering, then:

"Anthony," she cried suddenly, "two hundred a month is worse than nothing. Let's sell all the bonds and put the thirty thousand dollars in the bank—and if we lose the case we can live in Italy for three years, and then just die." In her excitement as she talked she was aware of a faint flush of sentiment, the first she had felt in many days.

"Three years," he said nervously, "three years! You're crazy. Mr. Haight'll take more than that if we lose. Do you think he's working for charity?"

"I forgot that."

"—And here it is Saturday," he continued, "and I've only got a dollar and some change, and we've got to live till Monday, when I can get to my broker's.... And not a drink in the house," he added as a significant afterthought.

"Can't you call up Dick?"

"I did. His man says he's gone down to Princeton to address a literary club or some such thing. Won't be back till Monday."

"Well, let's see—Don't you know some friend you might go to?"

"I tried a couple of fellows. Couldn't find anybody in. I wish I'd sold that Keats letter like I started to last week."

"How about those men you play cards with in that Sammy place?"

"Do you think I'd ask *them?*" His voice rang with righteous horror. Gloria winced. He would rather contemplate her active discomfort than feel his own skin crawl at asking an inappropriate favor. "I thought of Muriel," he suggested.

"She's in California."

"Well, how about some of those men who gave you such a good time while I was in the army? You'd think they might be glad to do a little favor for you."

She looked at him contemptuously, but he took no notice.

"Or how about your old friend Rachael—or Constance Merriam?"

"Constance Merriam's been dead a year, and I wouldn't ask Rachael."

"Well, how about that gentleman who was so anxious to help you once that he could hardly restrain himself, Bloeckman?"

"Oh—!" He had hurt her at last, and he was not too obtuse or too careless to perceive it.

"Why not him?" he insisted callously.

"Because—he doesn't like me any more," she said with difficulty, and then as he did not answer but only regarded her cynically: "If you want to know why, I'll tell you. A year ago I went to Bloeckman—he's changed his name to Black—and asked him to put me into pictures."

"You went to Bloeckman?"

"Yes."

"Why didn't you tell me?" he demanded incredulously, the smile fading from his face.

"Because you were probably off drinking somewhere. He had them give me a test, and they decided that I wasn't young enough for anything except a character part."

"A character part?"

"The 'woman of thirty' sort of thing. I wasn't thirty, and I didn't think I—looked thirty."

"Why, damn him!" cried Anthony, championing her violently with a curious perverseness of emotion, "why—"

"Well, that's why I can't go to him."

"Why, the insolence!" insisted Anthony nervously, "the insolence!"

"Anthony, that doesn't matter now; the thing is we've got to live over Sunday and there's nothing in the house but a loaf of bread and a half-pound of bacon and two eggs for breakfast." She handed him the contents of her purse. "There's seventy, eighty, a dollar fifteen. With what you have that makes about two and a half altogether, doesn't it? Anthony, we can get along on that. We can buy lots of food with that—more than we can possibly eat."

Jingling the change in his hand he shook his head. "No. I've got to have a drink. I'm so darn nervous that I'm shivering." A thought struck him. "Perhaps Sammy'd cash a check. And then Monday I could rush down to the bank with the money." "But they've closed your account."

"That's right, that's right—I'd forgotten. I'll tell you what: I'll go down to Sammy's and I'll find somebody there who'll lend me something. I hate like the devil to ask them, though...." He snapped his fingers suddenly. "I know what I'll do. I'll hock my watch. I can get twenty dollars on it, and get it back Monday for sixty cents extra. It's been hocked before—when I was at Cambridge."

He had put on his overcoat, and with a brief good-by he started down the hall toward the outer door.

Gloria got to her feet. It had suddenly occurred to her where he would probably go first.

"Anthony!" she called after him, "hadn't you better leave two dollars with me? You'll only need car-fare."

The outer door slammed—he had pretended not to hear her. She stood for a moment looking after him; then she went into the bathroom among her tragic unguents and began preparations for washing her hair.

Down at Sammy's he found Parker Allison and Pete Lytell sitting alone at a table, drinking whiskey sours. It was just after six o'clock, and Sammy, or Samuele Bendiri, as he had been christened, was sweeping an accumulation of cigarette butts and broken glass into a corner.

"Hi, Tony!" called Parker Allison to Anthony. Sometimes he addressed him as Tony, at other times it was Dan. To him all Anthonys must sail under one of these diminutives.

"Sit down. What'll you have?"

On the subway Anthony had counted his money and found that he had almost four dollars. He could pay for two rounds at fifty cents a drink—which meant that he would have six drinks. Then he would go over to Sixth Avenue and get twenty dollars and a pawn ticket in exchange for his watch.

"Well, roughnecks," he said jovially, "how's the life of crime?"

"Pretty good," said Allison. He winked at Pete Lytell. "Too bad you're a married man. We've got some pretty good stuff lined up for about eleven o'clock, when the shows let out. Oh, boy! Yes, sir—too bad he's married—isn't it, Pete?"

"'Sa shame."

At half past seven, when they had completed the six rounds, Anthony found that his intentions were giving audience to his desires. He was happy and cheerful now—thoroughly enjoying himself. It seemed to him that the story which Pete had just finished telling was unusually and profoundly humorous—and he decided, as he did every day at about this point, that they were "damn good fellows, by golly!" who would do a lot more for him than any one else he knew. The pawnshops would remain open until late Saturday nights, and he felt that if he took just one more drink he would attain a gorgeous rose-colored exhilaration.

Artfully, he fished in his vest pockets, brought up his two quarters, and stared at them as though in surprise.

"Well, I'll be darned," he protested in an aggrieved tone, "here I've come out without my pocketbook."

"Need some cash?" asked Lytell easily.

"I left my money on the dresser at home. And I wanted to buy you another drink."

"Oh—knock it." Lytell waved the suggestion away disparagingly. "I guess we can blow a good fella to all the drinks he wants. What'll you have—same?"

"I tell you," suggested Parker Allison, "suppose we send Sammy across the street for some sandwiches and eat dinner here."

The other two agreed.

"Good idea."

"Hey, Sammy, wantcha do somep'm for us...."

Just after nine o'clock Anthony staggered to his feet and, bidding them a thick good night, walked unsteadily to the door, handing Sammy one of his two quarters as he passed out. Once in the street he hesitated uncertainly and then started in the direction of Sixth Avenue, where he remembered to have frequently passed several loan offices. He went by a news-stand and two drugstores—and then he realized that he was standing in front of the place which he sought, and that it was shut and barred. Unperturbed he continued; another one, half a block down, was also closed—so were two more across the street, and a fifth in the square below. Seeing a faint light in the last one, he began to knock on the glass door; he desisted only when a watchman appeared in the back of the shop and motioned him angrily to move on. With growing discouragement, with growing befuddlement, he crossed the street and walked back toward Forty-third. On the corner near Sammy's he paused undecided—if he went back to the apartment, as he felt his body required, he would lay himself open to bitter reproach; yet, now that the pawnshops were closed, he had no notion where to get the money. He decided finally that he might ask Parker Allison, after all—but he approached Sammy's only to find the door locked and the lights out. He looked at his watch; nine-thirty. He began walking.

Ten minutes later he stopped aimlessly at the corner of Forty-third Street and Madison Avenue, diagonally across from the bright but nearly deserted entrance to the Biltmore Hotel. Here he stood for a moment, and then sat down heavily on a damp board amid some debris of construction work. He rested there for almost half an hour, his mind a shifting pattern of surface thoughts, chiefest among which were that he must obtain some money and get home before he became too sodden to find his way.

Then, glancing over toward the Biltmore, he saw a man standing directly under the overhead glow of the porte-cochère lamps beside a woman in an ermine coat. As Anthony watched, the couple moved forward and signalled to a taxi. Anthony perceived by the infallible identification that lurks in the walk of a friend that it was Maury Noble.

He rose to his feet.

"Maury!" he shouted.

Maury looked in his direction, then turned back to the girl just as the taxi came up into place. With the chaotic idea of borrowing ten dollars, Anthony began to run as fast as he could across Madison Avenue and along Forty-third Street.

As he came up Maury was standing beside the yawning door of the taxicab. His companion turned and looked curiously at Anthony.

"Hello, Maury!" he said, holding out his hand. "How are you?"

"Fine, thank you."

Their hands dropped and Anthony hesitated. Maury made no move to introduce him, but only stood there regarding him with an inscrutable feline silence.

"I wanted to see you—" began Anthony uncertainly. He did not feel that he could ask for a loan with the girl not four feet away, so he broke off and made a perceptible motion of his head as if to beckon Maury to one side.

"I'm in rather a big hurry, Anthony."

"I know—but can you, can you—" Again he hesitated.

"I'll see you some other time," said Maury. "It's important."

"I'm sorry, Anthony."

Before Anthony could make up his mind to blurt out his request, Maury had turned coolly to the girl, helped her into the car and, with a polite "good evening," stepped in after her. As he nodded from the window it seemed to Anthony that his expression had not changed by a shade or a hair. Then with a fretful clatter the taxi moved off, and Anthony was left standing there alone under the lights.

Anthony went on into the Biltmore, for no reason in particular except that the entrance was at hand, and ascending the wide stair found a seat in an alcove. He was furiously aware that he had been snubbed; he was as hurt and angry as it was possible for him to be when in that condition. Nevertheless, he was stubbornly preoccupied with the necessity of obtaining some money before he went home, and once again he told over on his fingers the acquaintances he might conceivably call on in this emergency. He thought, eventually, that he might approach Mr. Howland, his broker, at his home.

After a long wait he found that Mr. Howland was out. He returned to the operator, leaning over her desk and fingering his quarter as though loath to leave unsatisfied.

"Call Mr. Bloeckman," he said suddenly. His own words surprised him. The name had come from some crossing of two suggestions in his mind.

"What's the number, please?"

Scarcely conscious of what he did, Anthony looked up Joseph Bloeckman in the telephone directory. He could find no such person, and was about to close the book when it flashed into his mind that Gloria had mentioned a change of name. It was the matter of a minute to find Joseph Black—then he waited in the booth while central called the number.

"Hello-o. Mr. Bloeckman—I mean Mr. Black in?"

"No, he's out this evening. Is there any message?" The intonation was cockney; it reminded him of the rich vocal deferences of Bounds.

"Where is he?"

"Why, ah, who is this, please, sir?"

"This Mr. Patch. Matter of vi'al importance." "Why, he's with a party at the Boul' Mich', sir."

"Thanks."

Anthony got his five cents change and started for the Boul' Mich', a popular dancing resort on Forty-fifth Street. It was nearly ten but the streets were dark and sparsely peopled until the theatres should eject their spawn an hour later. Anthony knew the Boul' Mich', for he had been there with Gloria during the year before, and he remembered the existence of a rule that patrons must be in evening dress. Well, he would not go up-stairs—he would send a boy up for Bloeckman and wait for him in the lower hall. For a moment he did not doubt that the whole project was entirely natural and graceful. To his distorted imagination Bloeckman had become simply one of his old friends.

The entrance hall of the Boul' Mich' was warm. There were high yellow lights over a thick green carpet, from the centre of which a white stairway rose to the dancing floor.

Anthony spoke to the hallboy:

"I want to see Mr. Bloeckman—Mr. Black," he said. "He's up-stairs—have him paged."

The boy shook his head.

"'Sagainsa rules to have him paged. You know what table he's at?"

"No. But I've got see him."

"Wait an' I'll getcha waiter."

After a short interval a head waiter appeared, bearing a card on which were charted the table reservations. He darted a cynical look at Anthony—which, however, failed of its target. Together they bent over the cardboard and found the table without difficulty—a party of eight, Mr. Black's own.

"Tell him Mr. Patch. Very, very important."

Again he waited, leaning against the banister and listening to the confused harmonies of "Jazz-mad" which came floating down the stairs. A check-girl near him was singing:

"Out in—the shimmee sanitarium
The jazz-mad nuts reside.
Out in—the shimmee sanitarium
I left my blushing bride.
She went and shook herself insane,
So let her shiver back again—"

Then he saw Bloeckman descending the staircase, and took a step forward to meet him and shake hands.

"You wanted to see me?" said the older man coolly.

"Yes," answered Anthony, nodding, "personal matter. Can you jus' step over here?"

Regarding him narrowly Bloeckman followed Anthony to a half bend made by the staircase where they were beyond observation or earshot of any one entering or leaving the restaurant.

"Well?" he inquired.

"Wanted talk to you."

"What about?"

Anthony only laughed—a silly laugh; he intended it to sound casual.

"What do you want to talk to me about?" repeated Bloeckman.

"Wha's hurry, old man?" He tried to lay his hand in a friendly gesture upon Bloeckman's shoulder, but the latter drew away slightly. "How've been?"

"Very well, thanks.... See here, Mr. Patch, I've got a party up-stairs. They'll think it's rude if I stay away too long. What was it you wanted to see me about?"

For the second time that evening Anthony's mind made an abrupt jump, and what he said was not at all what he had intended to say.

"Un'erstand you kep' my wife out of the movies."

"What?" Bloeckman's ruddy face darkened in parallel planes of shadows.

"You heard me."

"Look here, Mr. Patch," said Bloeckman, evenly and without changing his expression, "you're drunk. You're disgustingly and insultingly drunk."

"Not too drunk talk to you," insisted Anthony with a leer. "Firs' place, my wife wants nothin' whatever do with you. Never did. Un'erstand me?"

"Be quiet!" said the older man angrily. "I should think you'd respect your wife enough not to bring her into the conversation under these circumstances."

"Never you min' how I expect my wife. One thing—you leave her alone. You go to hell!"

"See here—I think you're a little crazy!" exclaimed Bloeckman. He took two paces forward as though to pass by, but Anthony stepped in his way.

"Not so fas', you Goddam Jew."

For a moment they stood regarding each other, Anthony swaying gently from side to side, Bloeckman almost trembling with fury.

"Be careful!" he cried in a strained voice.

Anthony might have remembered then a certain look Bloeckman had given him in the Biltmore Hotel years before. But he remembered nothing, nothing——

"I'll say it again, you God——"

Then Bloeckman struck out, with all the strength in the arm of a well-conditioned man of forty-five, struck out and caught Anthony squarely in the mouth. Anthony cracked up against the staircase, recovered himself and made a wild drunken swing at his opponent, but Bloeckman, who took exercise every day and knew something of sparring, blocked it with ease and struck him twice in the face with two swift smashing jabs. Anthony gave a little grunt and toppled over onto the green plush carpet, finding, as he fell, that his mouth was full of blood and seemed oddly loose in front. He struggled to his feet, panting and spitting, and then as he started toward Bloeckman, who stood a few feet away, his fists clenched but not up, two waiters who had appeared from nowhere seized his arms and held him, helpless. In back of them a dozen people had miraculously gathered.

"I'll kill him," cried Anthony, pitching and straining from side to side. "Let me kill——"

"Throw him out!" ordered Bloeckman excitedly, just as a small man with a pockmarked face pushed his way hurriedly through the spectators.

"Any trouble, Mr. Black?"

"This bum tried to blackmail me!" said Bloeckman, and then, his voice rising to a faintly shrill note of pride: "He got what was coming to him!"

The little man turned to a waiter.

"Call a policeman!" he commanded.

"Oh, no," said Bloeckman quickly. "I can't be bothered. Just throw him out in the street.... Ugh! What an outrage!" He turned and with conscious dignity walked toward the wash-room just as six brawny hands seized upon Anthony and dragged him toward the door. The "bum" was propelled violently to the sidewalk, where he landed on his hands and knees with a grotesque slapping sound and rolled over slowly onto his side.

The shock stunned him. He lay there for a moment in acute distributed pain. Then his discomfort became centralized in his stomach, and he regained consciousness to discover that a large foot was prodding him.

"You've got to move on, y' bum! Move on!"

It was the bulky doorman speaking. A town car had stopped at the curb and its occupants had disembarked—that is, two of the women were standing on the dashboard, waiting in offended delicacy until this obscene obstacle should be removed from their path.

"Move on! Or else I'll *throw* y'on!"

"Here—I'll get him."

This was a new voice; Anthony imagined that it was somehow more tolerant, better disposed than the first. Again arms were about him, half lifting, half dragging him into a welcome shadow four doors up the street and propping him against the stone front of a millinery shop.

"Much obliged," muttered Anthony feebly. Some one pushed his soft hat down upon his head and he winced.

"Just sit still, buddy, and you'll feel better. Those guys sure give you a bump."

"I'm going back and kill that dirty—" He tried to get to his feet but collapsed backward against the wall.

"You can't do nothin' now," came the voice. "Get 'em some other time. I'm tellin' you straight, ain't I? I'm helpin' you."

Anthony nodded.

"An' you better go home. You dropped a tooth to-night, buddy. You know that?"

Anthony explored his mouth with his tongue, verifying the statement. Then with an effort he raised his hand and located the gap.

"I'm agoin' to get you home, friend. Whereabouts do you live—"

"Oh, by God! By God!" interrupted Anthony, clenching his fists passionately. "I'll show the dirty bunch. You help me show 'em and I'll fix it with you. My grandfather's Adam Patch, of Tarrytown"—

"Who?"

"Adam Patch, by God!"

"You wanna go all the way to Tarrytown?"

"No."

"Well, you tell me where to go, friend, and I'll get a cab."

Anthony made out that his Samaritan was a short, broad-shouldered individual, somewhat the worse for wear.

"Where d'you live, hey?"

Sodden and shaken as he was, Anthony felt that his address would be poor collateral for his wild boast about his grandfather.

"Get me a cab," he commanded, feeling in his pockets.

A taxi drove up. Again Anthony essayed to rise, but his ankle swung loose, as though it were in two sections. The Samaritan must needs help him in—and climb in after him.

"See here, fella," said he, "you're soused and you're bunged up, and you won't be able to get in your house 'less somebody carries you in, so I'm going with you, and I know you'll make it all right with me. Where d'you live?"

With some reluctance Anthony gave his address. Then, as the cab moved off, he leaned his head against the man's shoulder and went into a shadowy, painful torpor. When he awoke, the man had lifted him from the cab in front of the apartment on Claremont Avenue and was trying to set him on his feet.

"Can y' walk?"

"Yes—sort of. You better not come in with me." Again he felt helplessly in his pockets. "Say," he continued, apologetically, swaying dangerously on his feet, "I'm afraid I haven't got a cent."

"Huh?"

"I'm cleaned out."

"Sa-a-ay! Didn't I hear you promise you'd fix it with me? Who's goin' to pay the taxi bill?" He turned to the driver for confirmation. "Didn't you hear him say he'd fix it? All that about his grandfather?"

"Matter of fact," muttered Anthony imprudently, "it was you did all the talking; however, if you come round, to-morrow—"

At this point the taxi-driver leaned from his cab and said ferociously:

"Ah, poke him one, the dirty cheap skate. If he wasn't a bum they wouldn'ta throwed him out."

In answer to this suggestion the fist of the Samaritan shot out like a battering-ram and sent Anthony crashing down against the stone steps of the apartment-house, where he lay without movement, while the tall buildings rocked to and fro above him....

After a long while he awoke and was conscious that it had grown much colder. He tried to move himself but his muscles refused to function. He was curiously anxious to know the time, but he reached for his watch, only to find the pocket empty. Involuntarily his lips formed an immemorial phrase:

"What a night!"

Strangely enough, he was almost sober. Without moving his head he looked up to where the moon was anchored in mid-sky, shedding light down into Claremont Avenue as into the bottom of a deep and uncharted abyss. There was no sign or sound of life save for the continuous buzzing in his own ears, but after a moment Anthony himself broke the silence with a distinct and peculiar murmur. It was the sound that he had consistently attempted to make back there in the Boul' Mich', when he had been face to face with Bloeckman—the unmistakable sound of ironic laughter. And on his torn and bleeding lips it was like a pitiful retching of the soul.

Three weeks later the trial came to an end. The seemingly endless spool of legal red tape having unrolled over a period of four and a half years, suddenly snapped off. Anthony and Gloria and, on the other side, Edward Shuttleworth and a platoon of beneficiaries testified and lied and ill-behaved generally in varying degrees of greed and desperation. Anthony awoke one morning in March realizing that the verdict was to be given at four that afternoon, and at the thought he got up out of his bed and began to dress. With his extreme nervousness there was mingled an unjustified optimism as to the outcome. He believed that the decision of the lower court would be reversed, if only because of the reaction, due to excessive prohibition, that had recently set in against reforms and reformers. He counted more on the personal attacks that they had levelled at Shuttleworth than on the more sheerly legal aspects of the proceedings.

Dressed, he poured himself a drink of whiskey and then went into Gloria's room, where he found her already wide awake. She had been in bed for a week, humoring herself, Anthony fancied, though the doctor had said that she had best not be disturbed.

"Good morning," she murmured, without smiling. Her eyes seemed unusually large and dark.

"How do you feel?" he asked grudgingly. "Better?"

"Yes."

"Much?"

"Yes."

"Do you feel well enough to go down to court with me this afternoon?"

She nodded.

"Yes. I want to. Dick said yesterday that if the weather was nice he was coming up in his car and take me for a ride in Central Park—and look, the room's all full of sunshine."

Anthony glanced mechanically out the window and then sat down upon the bed.

"God, I'm nervous!" he exclaimed.

"Please don't sit there," she said quickly.

"Why not?"

"You smell of whiskey. I can't stand it."

He got up absent-mindedly and left the room. A little later she called to him and he went out and brought her some potato salad and cold chicken from the delicatessen.

At two o'clock Richard Caramel's car arrived at the door and, when he phoned up, Anthony took Gloria down in the elevator and walked with her to the curb.

She told her cousin that it was sweet of him to take her riding. "Don't be simple," Dick replied disparagingly. "It's nothing."

But he did not mean that it was nothing and this was a curious thing. Richard Caramel had forgiven many people for many offenses. But he had never forgiven his cousin, Gloria Gilbert, for a statement she had made just prior to her wedding, seven years before. She had said that she did not intend to read his book.

Richard Caramel remembered this—he had remembered it well for seven years.

"What time will I expect you back?" asked Anthony.

"We won't come back," she answered, "we'll meet you down there at four."

"All right," he muttered, "I'll meet you."

Up-stairs he found a letter waiting for him. It was a mimeographed notice urging "the boys" in condescendingly colloquial language to pay the dues of the American Legion. He threw it impatiently into the waste-basket and sat down with his elbows on the window sill, looking down blindly into the sunny street.

Italy—if the verdict was in their favor it meant Italy. The word had become a sort of talisman to him, a land where the intolerable anxieties of life would fall away like an old garment. They would go to the watering-places first and among the bright and colorful crowds forget the gray appendages of despair. Marvellously renewed, he would walk again in the Piazza di Spanga at twilight, moving in that drifting flotsam of dark women and ragged beggars, of austere, barefooted friars. The thought of Italian women stirred him faintly—when his purse hung heavy again even romance might fly back to perch upon it—the romance of blue canals in Venice, of the golden green hills of Fiesole after rain, and of women, women who changed, dissolved, melted into other women and receded from his life, but who were always beautiful and always young.

But it seemed to him that there should be a difference in his attitude. All the distress that he had ever known, the sorrow and the pain, had been because of women. It was something that in different ways they did to him, unconsciously, almost casually—perhaps finding him tender-minded and afraid, they killed the things in him that menaced their absolute sway.

Turning about from the window he faced his reflection in the mirror, contemplating dejectedly the wan, pasty face, the eyes with their crisscross of lines like shreds of dried blood, the stooped and flabby figure whose very sag was a document in lethargy. He was thirty three—he looked forty. Well, things would be different.

The door-bell rang abruptly and he started as though he had been dealt a blow. Recovering himself, he went into the hall and opened the outer door. It was Dot.

THE ENCOUNTER

He retreated before her into the living room, comprehending only a word here and there in the slow flood of sentences that poured from her steadily, one after the other, in a persistent monotone. She was decently and shabbily dressed—a somehow pitiable little hat adorned with pink and blue flowers covered and hid her dark hair. He gathered from her words that several days before she had seen an item in the paper concerning the lawsuit, and had obtained his address from the clerk of the Appellate Division. She had called up the apartment and had been told that Anthony was out by a woman to whom she had refused to give her name.

In a living room he stood by the door regarding her with a sort of stupefied horror as she rattled on.... His predominant sensation was that all the civilization and convention around him was curiously unreal.... She was in a milliner's shop on Sixth Avenue, she said. It was a lonesome life. She had been sick for a long while after he left for Camp Mills; her mother had come down and taken her home again to Carolina.... She had come to New York with the idea of finding Anthony.

She was appallingly in earnest. Her violet eyes were red with tears; her soft intonation was ragged with little gasping sobs.

That was all. She had never changed. She wanted him now, and if she couldn't have him she must die....

"You'll have to get out," he said at length, speaking with tortuous intensity. "Haven't I enough to worry me now without you coming here? My *God*! You'll have to get *out!*"

Sobbing, she sat down in a chair.

"I love you," she cried; "I don't care what you say to me! I love you."

"I don't care!" he almost shrieked; "get out—oh, get out! Haven't you done me harm enough? Haven't—you—done—*enough*?"

"Hit me!" she implored him—wildly, stupidly. "Oh, hit me, and I'll kiss the hand you hit me with!"

His voice rose until it was pitched almost at a scream. "I'll kill you!" he cried. "If you don't get out I'll kill you, I'll kill you!"

There was madness in his eyes now, but, unintimidated, Dot rose and took a step toward him.

"Anthony! Anthony!—"

He made a little clicking sound with his teeth and drew back as though to spring at her—then, changing his purpose, he looked wildly about him on the floor and wall.

"I'll kill you!" he was muttering in short, broken gasps. "I'll *kill* you!" He seemed to bite at the word as though to force it into materialization. Alarmed at last she made no further movement forward, but meeting his frantic eyes took a step back toward the door. Anthony began to race here and there on his side of the room, still giving out his single cursing cry. Then he found what he had been seeking—a stiff oaken chair that stood beside the table. Uttering a harsh, broken shout, he seized it, swung it above his head and let it go with all his raging strength straight at the white, frightened face across the room ... then a thick, impenetrable darkness came down upon him and blotted out thought, rage, and madness together—with almost a tangible snapping sound the face of the world changed before his eyes....

Gloria and Dick came in at five and called his name. There was no answer—they went into the living room and found a chair with its back smashed lying in the doorway, and they noticed that all about the room there was a sort of disorder—the rugs had slid, the pictures and bric-à-brac were upset upon the centre table. The air was sickly sweet with cheap perfume.

They found Anthony sitting in a patch of sunshine on the floor of his bedroom. Before him, open, were spread his three big stamp-books, and when they entered he was running his hands through a great pile of stamps that he had dumped from the back of one of them. Looking up and seeing Dick and Gloria he put his head critically on one side and motioned them back.

"Anthony!" cried Gloria tensely, "we've won! They reversed the decision!"

"Don't come in," he murmured wanly, "you'll muss them. I'm sorting, and I know you'll step in them. Everything always gets mussed."

"What are you doing?" demanded Dick in astonishment. "Going back to childhood? Don't you realize you've won the suit? They've reversed the decision of the lower courts. You're worth thirty millions!"

Anthony only looked at him reproachfully.

"Shut the door when you go out." He spoke like a pert child.

With a faint horror dawning in her eyes, Gloria gazed at him—

"Anthony!" she cried, "what is it? What's the matter? Why didn't you come—why, what *is* it?"

"See here," said Anthony softly, "you two get out—now, both of you. Or else I'll tell my grandfather."

He held up a handful of stamps and let them come drifting down about him like leaves, varicolored and bright, turning and fluttering gaudily upon the sunny air: stamps of England and Ecuador, Venezuela and Spain—Italy....

TOGETHER WITH THE SPARROWS

That exquisite heavenly irony which has tabulated the demise of so many generations of sparrows doubtless records the subtlest verbal inflections of the passengers of such ships as *The Berengaria.* And doubtless it was listening when the young man in the plaid cap crossed the deck quickly and spoke to the pretty girl in yellow.

"That's him," he said, pointing to a bundled figure seated in a wheel chair near the rail. "That's Anthony Patch. First time he's been on deck."

"Oh—that's him?"

"Yes. He's been a little crazy, they say, ever since he got his money, four or five months ago. You see, the other fellow, Shuttleworth, the religious fellow, the one that didn't get the money, he locked himself up in a room in a hotel and shot himself—

"Oh, he did—"

"But I guess Anthony Patch don't care much. He got his thirty million. And he's got his private physician along in case he doesn't feel just right about it. Has *she* been on deck?" he asked.

The pretty girl in yellow looked around cautiously.

"She was here a minute ago. She had on a Russian-sable coat that must have cost a small fortune." She frowned and then added decisively: "I can't stand her, you know. She seems sort of—sort of dyed and *unclean*, if you know what I mean. Some people just have that look about them whether they are or not."

"Sure, I know," agreed the man with the plaid cap. "She's not bad-looking, though." He paused. "Wonder what he's thinking about—his money, I guess, or maybe he's got remorse about that fellow Shuttleworth."

"Probably...."

But the man in the plaid cap was quite wrong. Anthony Patch, sitting near the rail and looking out at the sea, was not thinking of his money, for he had seldom in his life been really preoccupied with material vainglory, nor of Edward Shuttleworth, for it is best to look on the sunny side of these things. No—he was concerned with a series of reminiscences, much as a general might look back upon a successful campaign and analyze his victories. He was thinking of the hardships, the insufferable tribulations he had gone through. They had tried to penalize him for the mistakes of his youth. He had been exposed to ruthless misery, his very craving for romance had been punished, his friends had deserted him—even Gloria had turned against him. He had been alone, alone—facing it all.

Only a few months before people had been urging him to give in, to submit to mediocrity, to go to work. But he had known that he was justified in his way of life—and he had stuck it out stanchly. Why, the very friends who had been most unkind had come to respect him, to know he had been right all along. Had not the Lacys and the Merediths and the Cartwright-Smiths called on Gloria and him at the Ritz-Carlton just a week before they sailed?

Great tears stood in his eyes, and his voice was tremulous as he whispered to himself.

"I showed them," he was saying. "It was a hard fight, but I didn't give up and I came through!"

THE GREAT GATSBY

ONCE AGAIN
TO
ZELDA

Then wear the gold hat, if that will move her;
If you can bounce high, bounce for her too,
Till she cry "Lover, gold-hatted, high-bouncing lover,
I must have you!"

THOMAS PARKE D'INVILLIERS

I

In my younger and more vulnerable years my father gave me some advice that I've been turning over in my mind ever since.

"Whenever you feel like criticizing anyone," he told me, "just remember that all the people in this world haven't had the advantages that you've had."

He didn't say any more, but we've always been unusually communicative in a reserved way, and I understood that he meant a great deal more than that. In consequence, I'm inclined to reserve all judgements, a habit that has opened up many curious natures to me and also made me the victim of not a few veteran bores. The abnormal mind is quick to detect and attach itself to this quality when it appears in a normal person, and so it came about that in college I was unjustly accused of being a politician, because I was privy to the secret griefs of wild, unknown men. Most of the confidences were unsought—frequently I have feigned sleep, preoccupation, or a hostile levity when I realized by some unmistakable sign that an intimate revelation was quivering on the horizon; for the intimate revelations of young men, or at least the terms in which they express them, are usually plagiaristic and marred by obvious suppressions. Reserving judgements is a matter of infinite hope. I am still a little afraid of missing something if I forget that, as my father snobbishly suggested, and I snobbishly repeat, a sense of the fundamental decencies is parcelled out unequally at birth.

And, after boasting this way of my tolerance, I come to the admission that it has a limit. Conduct may be founded on the hard rock or the wet marshes, but after a certain point I don't care what it's founded on. When I came back from the East last autumn I felt that I wanted the world to be in uniform and at a sort of moral attention forever; I wanted no more riotous excursions with privileged glimpses into the human heart. Only Gatsby, the man who gives his name to this book, was exempt from my reaction—Gatsby, who represented everything for which I have an unaffected scorn. If personality is an unbroken series of successful gestures, then there was something gorgeous about him, some heightened sensitivity to the promises of life, as if he were related to one of those intricate machines that register earthquakes ten thousand miles away. This responsiveness had nothing to do with that flabby impressionability which is dignified under the name of the "creative temperament"—it was an extraordinary gift for hope, a romantic readiness such as I have never found in any other person and which it is not likely I shall ever find again. No—Gatsby turned out all right at the end; it is what preyed on Gatsby, what foul dust floated in the wake of his dreams that temporarily closed out my interest in the abortive sorrows and short-winded elations of men.

My family have been prominent, well-to-do people in this Middle Western city for three generations. The Carraways are something of a clan, and we have a tradition that we're descended from the Dukes of Buccleuch, but the actual founder of my line was my grandfather's brother, who came here in fifty-one, sent a substitute to the Civil War, and started the wholesale hardware business that my father carries on today.

I never saw this great-uncle, but I'm supposed to look like him—with special reference to the rather hard-boiled painting that hangs in father's office. I graduated from New Haven in 1915, just a quarter of a century after my father, and a little later I participated in that delayed Teutonic migration known as the Great War. I enjoyed the counter-raid so thoroughly that I came back restless. Instead of being the warm centre of the world, the Middle West now seemed like the ragged edge of the universe—so I decided to go East and learn the bond business. Everybody I knew was in the bond business, so I supposed it could support one more single man. All my aunts and uncles talked it over as if they were choosing a prep school for me, and finally said, "Why—ye-es," with very grave, hesitant faces. Father agreed to finance me for a year, and after various delays I came East, permanently, I thought, in the spring of twenty-two.

The practical thing was to find rooms in the city, but it was a warm season, and I had just left a country of wide lawns and friendly trees, so when a young man at the office suggested that we take a house together in a commuting town, it sounded like a great idea. He found the house, a weather-beaten cardboard bungalow at eighty a month, but at the last minute the firm ordered him to Washington, and I went out to the country alone. I had a dog—at least I had him for a few days until he ran away—and an old Dodge and a Finnish woman, who made my bed and cooked breakfast and muttered Finnish wisdom to herself over the electric stove.

It was lonely for a day or so until one morning some man, more recently arrived than I, stopped me on the road.

"How do you get to West Egg village?" he asked helplessly.

I told him. And as I walked on I was lonely no longer. I was a guide, a pathfinder, an original settler. He had casually conferred on me the freedom of the neighbourhood.

And so with the sunshine and the great bursts of leaves growing on the trees, just as things grow in fast movies, I had that familiar conviction that life was beginning over again with the summer.

There was so much to read, for one thing, and so much fine health to be pulled down out of the young breath-giving air. I bought a dozen volumes on banking and credit and investment securities, and they stood on my shelf in red and gold like new money from the mint, promising to unfold the shining secrets that only Midas and Morgan and Maecenas knew. And I had the high intention of reading many other books besides. I was rather literary in college—one year I wrote a series of very solemn and obvious editorials for the Yale News—and now I was going to bring back all such things into my life and become again that most limited of all specialists, the "well-rounded man." This isn't just an epigram—life is much more successfully looked at from a single window, after all.

It was a matter of chance that I should have rented a house in one of the strangest communities in North America. It was on that slender riotous island which extends itself due east of New York—and where there are, among other natural curiosities, two unusual formations of land. Twenty miles from the city a pair of enormous eggs, identical in contour and separated only by a courtesy bay, jut out into the most domesticated body of salt water in the Western hemisphere, the great wet barnyard of Long Island Sound. They are not perfect ovals—like the egg in the Columbus story, they are both crushed flat at the contact end—but their physical resemblance must be a source of perpetual wonder to the gulls that fly overhead. To the wingless a more interesting phenomenon is their dissimilarity in every particular except shape and size.

I lived at West Egg, the—well, the less fashionable of the two, though this is a most superficial tag to express the bizarre and not a little sinister contrast between them. My house was at the very tip of the egg, only fifty yards from the Sound, and squeezed between two huge places that rented for twelve or fifteen thousand a season. The one on my right was a colossal affair by any standard—it was a factual imitation of some Hôtel de Ville in Normandy, with a tower on one side, spanking new under a thin beard of raw ivy, and a marble swimming pool, and more than forty acres of lawn and garden. It was Gatsby's mansion. Or, rather, as I didn't know Mr. Gatsby, it was a mansion inhabited by a gentleman of that name. My own house was an eyesore, but it was a small eyesore, and it had been overlooked, so I had a view of the water, a partial view of my neighbour's lawn, and the consoling proximity of millionaires—all for eighty dollars a month.

Across the courtesy bay the white palaces of fashionable East Egg glittered along the water, and the history of the summer really begins on the evening I drove over there to have dinner with the Tom Buchanans. Daisy was my second cousin once removed, and I'd known Tom in college. And just after the war I spent two days with them in Chicago.

Her husband, among various physical accomplishments, had been one of the most powerful ends that ever played football at New Haven—a national figure in a way, one of those men who reach such an acute limited excellence at twenty-one that everything afterward savours of anticlimax. His family were enormously wealthy—even in college his freedom with money was a matter for reproach—but now he'd left Chicago and come East in a fashion that rather took your breath away: for instance, he'd brought down a string of polo ponies from Lake Forest. It was hard to realize that a man in my own generation was wealthy enough to do that.

Why they came East I don't know. They had spent a year in France for no particular reason, and then drifted here and there unrestfully wherever people played polo and were rich together. This was a permanent move, said Daisy over the telephone, but I didn't believe it—I had no sight into Daisy's heart, but I felt that Tom would drift on forever seeking, a little wistfully, for the dramatic turbulence of some irrecoverable football game.

And so it happened that on a warm windy evening I drove over to East Egg to see two old friends whom I scarcely knew at all. Their house was even more elaborate than I expected, a cheerful red-and-white Georgian Colonial mansion, overlooking the bay. The lawn started at the beach and ran towards the front door for a quarter of a mile, jumping over sundials and brick walks and burning gardens—finally when it reached the house drifting up the side in bright vines as though from the momentum of its run. The front was broken by a line of French windows, glowing now with reflected gold and wide open to the warm windy afternoon, and Tom Buchanan in riding clothes was standing with his legs apart on the front porch.

He had changed since his New Haven years. Now he was a sturdy straw-haired man of thirty, with a rather hard mouth and a supercilious manner. Two shining arrogant eyes had established dominance over his face and gave him the appearance of always leaning aggressively forward. Not even the effeminate swank of his riding clothes could hide the enormous power of that body—he seemed to fill those glistening boots until he strained the top lacing, and you could see a great pack of muscle shifting when his shoulder moved under his thin coat. It was a body capable of enormous leverage—a cruel body.

His speaking voice, a gruff husky tenor, added to the impression of fractiousness he conveyed. There was a touch of paternal contempt in it, even toward people he liked—and there were men at New Haven who had hated his guts.

"Now, don't think my opinion on these matters is final," he seemed to say, "just because I'm stronger and more of a man than you are." We were in the same senior society, and while we were never intimate I always had the impression that he approved of me and wanted me to like him with some harsh, defiant wistfulness of his own.

We talked for a few minutes on the sunny porch.

"I've got a nice place here," he said, his eyes flashing about restlessly.

Turning me around by one arm, he moved a broad flat hand along the front vista, including in its sweep a sunken Italian garden, a half acre of deep, pungent roses, and a snub-nosed motorboat that bumped the tide offshore.

"It belonged to Demaine, the oil man." He turned me around again, politely and abruptly. "We'll go inside."

We walked through a high hallway into a bright rosy-coloured space, fragilely bound into the house by French windows at either end. The windows were ajar and gleaming white against the fresh grass outside that seemed to grow a little way into the house. A breeze blew through the room, blew curtains in at one end and out the other like pale flags, twisting them up toward the frosted wedding-cake of the ceiling, and then rippled over the wine-coloured rug, making a shadow on it as wind does on the sea.

The only completely stationary object in the room was an enormous couch on which two young women were buoyed up as though upon an anchored balloon. They were both in white, and their dresses were rippling and fluttering as if they had just been blown back in after a short flight around the house. I must have stood for a few moments listening to the whip and snap of the curtains and the groan of a picture on the wall. Then there was a boom as Tom Buchanan shut the rear windows and the caught wind died out about the room, and the curtains and the rugs and the two young women ballooned slowly to the floor.

The younger of the two was a stranger to me. She was extended full length at her end of the divan, completely motionless, and with her chin raised a little, as if she were balancing something on it which was quite likely to fall. If she saw me out of the corner of her eyes she gave no hint of it—indeed, I was almost surprised into murmuring an apology for having disturbed her by coming in.

The other girl, Daisy, made an attempt to rise—she leaned slightly forward with a conscientious expression—then she laughed, an absurd, charming little laugh, and I laughed too and came forward into the room.

"I'm p-paralysed with happiness."

She laughed again, as if she said something very witty, and held my hand for a moment, looking up into my face, promising that there was no one in the world she so much wanted to see. That was a way she had. She hinted in a murmur that the surname of the balancing girl was Baker. (I've heard it said that Daisy's murmur was only to make people lean toward her; an irrelevant criticism that made it no less charming.)

At any rate, Miss Baker's lips fluttered, she nodded at me almost imperceptibly, and then quickly tipped her head back again—the object she was balancing had obviously tottered a little and given her something of a fright. Again a sort of apology arose to my lips. Almost any exhibition of complete self-sufficiency draws a stunned tribute from me.

I looked back at my cousin, who began to ask me questions in her low, thrilling voice. It was the kind of voice that the ear follows up and down, as if each speech is an arrangement of notes that will never be played again. Her face was sad and lovely with bright things in it, bright eyes and a bright passionate mouth, but there was an excitement in her voice that men who had cared for her found difficult to forget: a singing compulsion, a whispered "Listen," a promise that she had done gay, exciting things just a while since and that there were gay, exciting things hovering in the next hour.

I told her how I had stopped off in Chicago for a day on my way East, and how a dozen people had sent their love through me.

"Do they miss me?" she cried ecstatically.

"The whole town is desolate. All the cars have the left rear wheel painted black as a mourning wreath, and there's a persistent wail all night along the north shore."

"How gorgeous! Let's go back, Tom. Tomorrow!" Then she added irrelevantly: "You ought to see the baby."

"I'd like to."

"She's asleep. She's three years old. Haven't you ever seen her?"

"Never."

"Well, you ought to see her. She's—"

Tom Buchanan, who had been hovering restlessly about the room, stopped and rested his hand on my shoulder.

"What you doing, Nick?"

"I'm a bond man."

"Who with?"

I told him.

"Never heard of them," he remarked decisively.

This annoyed me.

"You will," I answered shortly. "You will if you stay in the East."

"Oh, I'll stay in the East, don't you worry," he said, glancing at Daisy and then back at me, as if he were alert for something more. "I'd be a God damned fool to live anywhere else."

At this point Miss Baker said: "Absolutely!" with such suddenness that I started—it was the first word she had uttered since I came into the room. Evidently it surprised her as much as it did me, for she yawned and with a series of rapid, deft movements stood up into the room.

"I'm stiff," she complained, "I've been lying on that sofa for as long as I can remember."

"Don't look at me," Daisy retorted, "I've been trying to get you to New York all afternoon."

"No, thanks," said Miss Baker to the four cocktails just in from the pantry. "I'm absolutely in training."

Her host looked at her incredulously.

"You are!" He took down his drink as if it were a drop in the bottom of a glass. "How you ever get anything done is beyond me."

I looked at Miss Baker, wondering what it was she "got done." I enjoyed looking at her. She was a slender, small-breasted girl, with an erect carriage, which she accentuated by throwing her body backward at the shoulders like a young cadet. Her grey sun-strained eyes looked back at me with polite reciprocal curiosity out of a wan, charming, discontented face. It occurred to me now that I had seen her, or a picture of her, somewhere before.

"You live in West Egg," she remarked contemptuously. "I know somebody there."

"I don't know a single—"

"You must know Gatsby."

"Gatsby?" demanded Daisy. "What Gatsby?"

Before I could reply that he was my neighbour dinner was announced; wedging his tense arm imperatively under mine, Tom Buchanan compelled me from the room as though he were moving a checker to another square.

Slenderly, languidly, their hands set lightly on their hips, the two young women preceded us out on to a rosy-coloured porch, open toward the sunset, where four candles flickered on the table in the diminished wind.

"Why *candles*?" objected Daisy, frowning. She snapped them out with her fingers. "In two weeks it'll be the longest day in the year." She looked at us all radiantly. "Do you always watch for the longest day of the year and then miss it? I always watch for the longest day in the year and then miss it."

"We ought to plan something," yawned Miss Baker, sitting down at the table as if she were getting into bed.

"All right," said Daisy. "What'll we plan?" She turned to me helplessly: "What do people plan?"

Before I could answer her eyes fastened with an awed expression on her little finger.

"Look!" she complained; "I hurt it."

We all looked—the knuckle was black and blue.

"You did it, Tom," she said accusingly. "I know you didn't mean to, but you *did* do it. That's what I get for marrying a brute of a man, a great, big, hulking physical specimen of a—"

"I hate that word 'hulking,'" objected Tom crossly, "even in kidding."

"Hulking," insisted Daisy.

Sometimes she and Miss Baker talked at once, unobtrusively and with a bantering inconsequence that was never quite chatter, that was as cool as their white dresses and their impersonal eyes in the absence of all desire. They were here, and they accepted Tom and me, making only a polite pleasant effort to entertain or to be entertained. They knew that presently dinner would be over and a little later the evening too would be over and casually put away. It was sharply different from the West, where an evening was hurried from phase to phase towards its close, in a continually disappointed anticipation or else in sheer nervous dread of the moment itself.

"You make me feel uncivilized, Daisy," I confessed on my second glass of corky but rather impressive claret. "Can't you talk about crops or something?"

I meant nothing in particular by this remark, but it was taken up in an unexpected way.

"Civilization's going to pieces," broke out Tom violently. "I've gotten to be a terrible pessimist about things. Have you read *The Rise of the Coloured Empires* by this man Goddard?"

"Why, no," I answered, rather surprised by his tone.

"Well, it's a fine book, and everybody ought to read it. The idea is if we don't look out the white race will be—will be utterly submerged. It's all scientific stuff; it's been proved."

"Tom's getting very profound," said Daisy, with an expression of unthoughtful sadness. "He reads deep books with long words in them. What was that word we—"

"Well, these books are all scientific," insisted Tom, glancing at her impatiently. "This fellow has worked out the whole thing. It's up to us, who are the dominant race, to watch out or these other races will have control of things."

"We've got to beat them down," whispered Daisy, winking ferociously toward the fervent sun.

"You ought to live in California—" began Miss Baker, but Tom interrupted her by shifting heavily in his chair.

"This idea is that we're Nordics. I am, and you are, and you are, and—" After an infinitesimal hesitation he included Daisy with a slight nod, and she winked at me again. "—And we've produced all the things that go to make civilization—oh, science and art, and all that. Do you see?"

There was something pathetic in his concentration, as if his complacency, more acute than of old, was not enough to him any more. When, almost immediately, the telephone rang inside and the butler left the porch Daisy seized upon the momentary interruption and leaned towards me.

"I'll tell you a family secret," she whispered enthusiastically. "It's about the butler's nose. Do you want to hear about the butler's nose?"

"That's why I came over tonight."

"Well, he wasn't always a butler; he used to be the silver polisher for some people in New York that had a silver service for two hundred people. He had to polish it from morning till night, until finally it began to affect his nose—"

"Things went from bad to worse," suggested Miss Baker.

"Yes. Things went from bad to worse, until finally he had to give up his position."

For a moment the last sunshine fell with romantic affection upon her glowing face; her voice compelled me forward breathlessly as I listened—then the glow faded, each light deserting her with lingering regret, like children leaving a pleasant street at dusk.

The butler came back and murmured something close to Tom's ear, whereupon Tom frowned, pushed back his chair, and without a word went inside. As if his absence quickened something within her, Daisy leaned forward again, her voice glowing and singing.

"I love to see you at my table, Nick. You remind me of a—of a rose, an absolute rose. Doesn't he?" She turned to Miss Baker for confirmation: "An absolute rose?"

This was untrue. I am not even faintly like a rose. She was only extemporizing, but a stirring warmth flowed from her, as if her heart was trying to come out to you concealed in one of those breathless, thrilling words. Then suddenly she threw her napkin on the table and excused herself and went into the house.

Miss Baker and I exchanged a short glance consciously devoid of meaning. I was about to speak when she sat up alertly and said "*Sh!*" in a warning voice. A subdued impassioned murmur was audible in the room beyond, and Miss Baker leaned forward unashamed, trying to hear. The murmur trembled on the verge of coherence, sank down, mounted excitedly, and then ceased altogether.

"This Mr. Gatsby you spoke of is my neighbour—" I began.

"Don't talk. I want to hear what happens."

"Is something happening?" I inquired innocently.

"You mean to say you don't know?" said Miss Baker, honestly surprised. "I thought everybody knew."

"I don't."

"Why—" she said hesitantly. "Tom's got some woman in New York."

"Got some woman?" I repeated blankly.

Miss Baker nodded.

"She might have the decency not to telephone him at dinner time. Don't you think?"

Almost before I had grasped her meaning there was the flutter of a dress and the crunch of leather boots, and Tom and Daisy were back at the table.

"It couldn't be helped!" cried Daisy with tense gaiety.

She sat down, glanced searchingly at Miss Baker and then at me, and continued: "I looked outdoors for a minute, and it's very romantic outdoors. There's a bird on the lawn that I think must be a nightingale come over on the Cunard or White Star Line. He's singing away—" Her voice sang: "It's romantic, isn't it, Tom?"

"Very romantic," he said, and then miserably to me: "If it's light enough after dinner, I want to take you down to the stables."

The telephone rang inside, startlingly, and as Daisy shook her head decisively at Tom the subject of the stables, in fact all subjects, vanished into air. Among the broken fragments of the last five minutes at table I remember the candles being lit again, pointlessly, and I was conscious of wanting to look squarely at everyone, and yet to avoid all eyes. I couldn't guess what Daisy and Tom were thinking, but I doubt if even Miss Baker, who seemed to have mastered a certain hardy scepticism, was able utterly to put this fifth guest's shrill metallic urgency out of mind. To a certain temperament the situation might have seemed intriguing—my own instinct was to telephone immediately for the police.

The horses, needless to say, were not mentioned again. Tom and Miss Baker, with several feet of twilight between them, strolled back into the library, as if to a vigil beside a perfectly tangible body, while, trying to look pleasantly interested and a little deaf, I followed Daisy around a chain of connecting verandas to the porch in front. In its deep gloom we sat down side by side on a wicker settee.

Daisy took her face in her hands as if feeling its lovely shape, and her eyes moved gradually out into the velvet dusk. I saw that turbulent emotions possessed her, so I asked what I thought would be some sedative questions about her little girl.

"We don't know each other very well, Nick," she said suddenly. "Even if we are cousins. You didn't come to my wedding."

"I wasn't back from the war."

"That's true." She hesitated. "Well, I've had a very bad time, Nick, and I'm pretty cynical about everything."

Evidently she had reason to be. I waited but she didn't say any more, and after a moment I returned rather feebly to the subject of her daughter.

"I suppose she talks, and—eats, and everything."

"Oh, yes." She looked at me absently. "Listen, Nick; let me tell you what I said when she was born. Would you like to hear?"

"Very much."

"It'll show you how I've gotten to feel about—things. Well, she was less than an hour old and Tom was God knows where. I woke up out of the ether with an utterly abandoned feeling, and asked the nurse right away if it was a boy or a girl. She told me it was a girl, and so I turned my head away and wept. 'All right,' I said, 'I'm glad it's a girl. And I hope she'll be a fool—that's the best thing a girl can be in this world, a beautiful little fool.'

"You see I think everything's terrible anyhow," she went on in a convinced way. "Everybody thinks so—the most advanced people. And I *know*. I've been everywhere and seen everything and done everything." Her eyes flashed around her in a defiant way, rather like Tom's, and she laughed with thrilling scorn. "Sophisticated—God, I'm sophisticated!"

The instant her voice broke off, ceasing to compel my attention, my belief, I felt the basic insincerity of what she had said. It made me uneasy, as though the whole evening had been a trick of some sort to exact a contributory emotion from me. I waited, and sure enough, in a moment she looked at me with an absolute smirk on her lovely face, as if she had asserted her membership in a rather distinguished secret society to which she and Tom belonged.

Inside, the crimson room bloomed with light. Tom and Miss Baker sat at either end of the long couch and she read aloud to him from the *Saturday Evening Post*—the words, murmurous and uninflected, running together in a soothing tune. The lamplight, bright on his boots and dull on the autumn-leaf yellow of her hair, glinted along the paper as she turned a page with a flutter of slender muscles in her arms.

When we came in she held us silent for a moment with a lifted hand.

"To be continued," she said, tossing the magazine on the table, "in our very next issue."

Her body asserted itself with a restless movement of her knee, and she stood up.

"Ten o'clock," she remarked, apparently finding the time on the ceiling. "Time for this good girl to go to bed."

"Jordan's going to play in the tournament tomorrow," explained Daisy, "over at Westchester."

"Oh—you're *Jor*dan Baker."

I knew now why her face was familiar—its pleasing contemptuous expression had looked out at me from many rotogravure pictures of the sporting life at Asheville and Hot Springs and Palm Beach. I had heard some story of her too, a critical, unpleasant story, but what it was I had forgotten long ago.

"Good night," she said softly. "Wake me at eight, won't you."

"If you'll get up."

"I will. Good night, Mr. Carraway. See you anon."

"Of course you will," confirmed Daisy. "In fact I think I'll arrange a marriage. Come over often, Nick, and I'll sort of—oh—fling you together. You know—lock you up accidentally in linen closets and push you out to sea in a boat, and all that sort of thing—"

"Good night," called Miss Baker from the stairs. "I haven't heard a word."

"She's a nice girl," said Tom after a moment. "They oughtn't to let her run around the country this way."

"Who oughtn't to?" inquired Daisy coldly.

"Her family."

"Her family is one aunt about a thousand years old. Besides, Nick's going to look after her, aren't you, Nick? She's going to spend lots of weekends out here this summer. I think the home influence will be very good for her."

Daisy and Tom looked at each other for a moment in silence.

"Is she from New York?" I asked quickly.

"From Louisville. Our white girlhood was passed together there. Our beautiful white—"

"Did you give Nick a little heart to heart talk on the veranda?" demanded Tom suddenly.

"Did I?" She looked at me. "I can't seem to remember, but I think we talked about the Nordic race. Yes, I'm sure we did. It sort of crept up on us and first thing you know—"

"Don't believe everything you hear, Nick," he advised me.

I said lightly that I had heard nothing at all, and a few minutes later I got up to go home. They came to the door with me and stood side by side in a cheerful square of light. As I started my motor Daisy peremptorily called: "Wait!"

"I forgot to ask you something, and it's important. We heard you were engaged to a girl out West."

"That's right," corroborated Tom kindly. "We heard that you were engaged."

"It's a libel. I'm too poor."

"But we heard it," insisted Daisy, surprising me by opening up again in a flower-like way. "We heard it from three people, so it must be true."

Of course I knew what they were referring to, but I wasn't even vaguely engaged. The fact that gossip had published the banns was one of the reasons I had come East. You can't stop going with an old friend on account of rumours, and on the other hand I had no intention of being rumoured into marriage.

Their interest rather touched me and made them less remotely rich—nevertheless, I was confused and a little disgusted as I drove away. It seemed to me that the thing for Daisy to do was to rush out of the house, child in arms—but apparently there were no such intentions in her head. As for Tom, the fact that he "had some woman in New York" was really less surprising than that he had been depressed by a book. Something was making him nibble at the edge of stale ideas as if his sturdy physical egotism no longer nourished his peremptory heart.

Already it was deep summer on roadhouse roofs and in front of wayside garages, where new red petrol-pumps sat out in pools of light, and when I reached my estate at West Egg I ran the car under its shed and sat for a while on an abandoned grass roller in the yard. The wind had blown off, leaving a loud, bright night, with wings beating in the trees and a persistent organ sound as the full bellows of the earth blew the frogs full of life. The silhouette of a moving cat wavered across the moonlight, and, turning my head to watch it, I saw that I was not alone—fifty feet away a figure had emerged from the shadow of my neighbour's mansion and was standing with his hands in his pockets regarding the silver pepper of the stars. Something in his leisurely movements and the secure position of his feet upon the lawn suggested that it was Mr. Gatsby himself, come out to determine what share was his of our local heavens.

I decided to call to him. Miss Baker had mentioned him at dinner, and that would do for an introduction. But I didn't call to him, for he gave a sudden intimation that he was content to be alone—he stretched out his arms toward the dark water in a curious way, and, far as I was from him, I could have sworn he was trembling. Involuntarily I glanced seaward—and distinguished nothing except a single green light, minute and far away, that might have been the end of a dock. When I looked once more for Gatsby he had vanished, and I was alone again in the unquiet darkness.

II

About halfway between West Egg and New York the motor road hastily joins the railroad and runs beside it for a quarter of a mile, so as to shrink away from a certain desolate area of land. This is a valley of ashes—a fantastic farm where ashes grow like wheat into ridges and hills and grotesque gardens; where ashes take the forms of houses and chimneys and rising smoke and, finally, with a transcendent effort, of ash-grey men, who move dimly and already crumbling through the powdery air. Occasionally a line of grey cars crawls along an invisible track, gives out a ghastly creak, and comes to rest, and immediately the ash-grey men swarm up with leaden spades and stir up an impenetrable cloud, which screens their obscure operations from your sight.

But above the grey land and the spasms of bleak dust which drift endlessly over it, you perceive, after a moment, the eyes of Doctor T. J. Eckleburg. The eyes of Doctor T. J. Eckleburg are blue and gigantic—their retinas are one yard high. They look out of no face, but, instead, from a pair of enormous yellow spectacles which pass over a nonexistent nose. Evidently some wild wag of an oculist set them there to fatten his practice in the borough of Queens, and then sank down himself into eternal blindness, or forgot them and moved away. But his eyes, dimmed a little by many paintless days, under sun and rain, brood on over the solemn dumping ground.

The valley of ashes is bounded on one side by a small foul river, and, when the drawbridge is up to let barges through, the passengers on waiting trains can stare at the dismal scene for as long as half an hour. There is always a halt there of at least a minute, and it was because of this that I first met Tom Buchanan's mistress.

The fact that he had one was insisted upon wherever he was known. His acquaintances resented the fact that he turned up in popular cafés with her and, leaving her at a table, sauntered about, chatting with whomsoever he knew. Though I was curious to see her, I had no desire to meet her—but I did. I went up to New York with Tom on the train one afternoon, and when we stopped by the ash-heaps he jumped to his feet and, taking hold of my elbow, literally forced me from the car.

"We're getting off," he insisted. "I want you to meet my girl."

I think he'd tanked up a good deal at luncheon, and his determination to have my company bordered on violence. The supercilious assumption was that on Sunday afternoon I had nothing better to do.

I followed him over a low whitewashed railroad fence, and we walked back a hundred yards along the road under Doctor Eckleburg's persistent stare. The only building in sight was a small block of yellow brick sitting on the edge of the waste land, a sort of compact Main Street ministering to it, and contiguous to absolutely nothing. One of the three shops it contained was for rent and another was an all-night restaurant, approached by a trail of ashes; the third was a garage—*Repairs.* GEORGE B. WILSON. *Cars bought and sold.*—and I followed Tom inside.

The interior was unprosperous and bare; the only car visible was the dust-covered wreck of a Ford which crouched in a dim corner. It had occurred to me that this shadow of a garage must be a blind, and that sumptuous and romantic apartments were concealed overhead, when the proprietor himself appeared in the door of an office, wiping his hands on a piece of waste. He was a blond, spiritless man, anaemic, and faintly handsome. When he saw us a damp gleam of hope sprang into his light blue eyes.

"Hello, Wilson, old man," said Tom, slapping him jovially on the shoulder. "How's business?"

"I can't complain," answered Wilson unconvincingly. "When are you going to sell me that car?"

"Next week; I've got my man working on it now."

"Works pretty slow, don't he?"

"No, he doesn't," said Tom coldly. "And if you feel that way about it, maybe I'd better sell it somewhere else after all."

"I don't mean that," explained Wilson quickly. "I just meant—"

His voice faded off and Tom glanced impatiently around the garage. Then I heard footsteps on a stairs, and in a moment the thickish figure of a woman blocked out the light from the office door. She was in the middle thirties, and faintly stout, but she carried her flesh sensuously as some women can. Her face, above a spotted dress of dark blue crêpe-de-chine, contained no facet or gleam of beauty, but there was an immediately perceptible vitality about her as if the nerves of her body were continually smouldering. She smiled slowly and, walking through her husband as if he were a ghost, shook hands with Tom, looking him flush in the eye. Then she wet her lips, and without turning around spoke to her husband in a soft, coarse voice:

"Get some chairs, why don't you, so somebody can sit down."

"Oh, sure," agreed Wilson hurriedly, and went toward the little office, mingling immediately with the cement colour of the walls. A white ashen dust veiled his dark suit and his pale hair as it veiled everything in the vicinity—except his wife, who moved close to Tom.

"I want to see you," said Tom intently. "Get on the next train."

"All right."

"I'll meet you by the newsstand on the lower level."

She nodded and moved away from him just as George Wilson emerged with two chairs from his office door.

We waited for her down the road and out of sight. It was a few days before the Fourth of July, and a grey, scrawny Italian child was setting torpedoes in a row along the railroad track.

"Terrible place, isn't it," said Tom, exchanging a frown with Doctor Eckleburg.

"Awful."

"It does her good to get away."

"Doesn't her husband object?"

"Wilson? He thinks she goes to see her sister in New York. He's so dumb he doesn't know he's alive."

So Tom Buchanan and his girl and I went up together to New York—or not quite together, for Mrs. Wilson sat discreetly in another car. Tom deferred that much to the sensibilities of those East Eggers who might be on the train.

She had changed her dress to a brown figured muslin, which stretched tight over her rather wide hips as Tom helped her to the platform in New York. At the newsstand she bought a copy of *Town Tattle* and a moving-picture magazine, and in the station drugstore some cold cream and a small flask of perfume. Upstairs, in the solemn echoing drive she let four taxicabs drive away before she selected a new one, lavender-coloured with grey upholstery, and in this we slid out from the mass of the station into the glowing sunshine. But immediately she turned sharply from the window and, leaning forward, tapped on the front glass.

"I want to get one of those dogs," she said earnestly. "I want to get one for the apartment. They're nice to have—a dog."

We backed up to a grey old man who bore an absurd resemblance to John D. Rockefeller. In a basket swung from his neck cowered a dozen very recent puppies of an indeterminate breed.

"What kind are they?" asked Mrs. Wilson eagerly, as he came to the taxi-window.

"All kinds. What kind do you want, lady?"

"I'd like to get one of those police dogs; I don't suppose you got that kind?"

The man peered doubtfully into the basket, plunged in his hand and drew one up, wriggling, by the back of the neck.

"That's no police dog," said Tom.

"No, it's not exactly a police dog," said the man with disappointment in his voice. "It's more of an Airedale." He passed his hand over the brown washrag of a back. "Look at that coat. Some coat. That's a dog that'll never bother you with catching cold."

"I think it's cute," said Mrs. Wilson enthusiastically. "How much is it?"

"That dog?" He looked at it admiringly. "That dog will cost you ten dollars."

The Airedale—undoubtedly there was an Airedale concerned in it somewhere, though its feet were startlingly white—changed hands and settled down into Mrs. Wilson's lap, where she fondled the weatherproof coat with rapture.

"Is it a boy or a girl?" she asked delicately.

"That dog? That dog's a boy."

"It's a bitch," said Tom decisively. "Here's your money. Go and buy ten more dogs with it."

We drove over to Fifth Avenue, warm and soft, almost pastoral, on the summer Sunday afternoon. I wouldn't have been surprised to see a great flock of white sheep turn the corner.

"Hold on," I said, "I have to leave you here."

"No you don't," interposed Tom quickly. "Myrtle'll be hurt if you don't come up to the apartment. Won't you, Myrtle?"

"Come on," she urged. "I'll telephone my sister Catherine. She's said to be very beautiful by people who ought to know."

"Well, I'd like to, but—"

We went on, cutting back again over the Park toward the West Hundreds. At 158th Street the cab stopped at one slice in a long white cake of apartment-houses. Throwing a regal homecoming glance around the neighbourhood, Mrs. Wilson gathered up her dog and her other purchases, and went haughtily in.

"I'm going to have the McKees come up," she announced as we rose in the elevator. "And, of course, I got to call up my sister, too."

The apartment was on the top floor—a small living-room, a small dining-room, a small bedroom, and a bath. The living-room was crowded to the doors with a set of tapestried furniture entirely too large for it, so that to move about was to stumble continually over scenes of ladies swinging in the gardens of Versailles. The only picture was an over-enlarged photograph, apparently a hen sitting on a blurred rock. Looked at from a distance, however, the hen resolved itself into a bonnet, and the countenance of a stout old lady beamed down into the room. Several old copies of *Town Tattle* lay on the table together with a copy of *Simon Called Peter*, and some of the small scandal magazines of Broadway. Mrs. Wilson was first concerned with the dog. A reluctant elevator boy went for a box full of straw and some milk, to which he added on his own initiative a tin of large, hard dog biscuits—one of which decomposed apathetically in the saucer of milk all afternoon. Meanwhile Tom brought out a bottle of whisky from a locked bureau door.

I have been drunk just twice in my life, and the second time was that afternoon; so everything that happened has a dim, hazy cast over it, although until after eight o'clock the apartment was full of cheerful sun. Sitting on Tom's lap Mrs. Wilson called up several people on the telephone; then there were no cigarettes, and I went out to buy some at the drugstore on the corner. When I came back they had both disappeared, so I sat down discreetly in the living-room and read a chapter of *Simon Called Peter*—either it was terrible stuff or the whisky distorted things, because it didn't make any sense to me.

Just as Tom and Myrtle (after the first drink Mrs. Wilson and I called each other by our first names) reappeared, company commenced to arrive at the apartment door.

The sister, Catherine, was a slender, worldly girl of about thirty, with a solid, sticky bob of red hair, and a complexion powdered milky white. Her eyebrows had been plucked and then drawn on again at a more rakish angle, but the efforts of nature toward the restoration of the old alignment gave a blurred air to her face. When she moved about there was an incessant clicking as innumerable pottery bracelets jingled up and down upon her arms. She came in with such a proprietary haste, and looked around so possessively at the furniture that I wondered if she lived here. But when I asked her she laughed immoderately, repeated my question aloud, and told me she lived with a girl friend at a hotel.

Mr. McKee was a pale, feminine man from the flat below. He had just shaved, for there was a white spot of lather on his cheekbone, and he was most respectful in his greeting to everyone in the room. He informed me that he was in the "artistic game," and I gathered later that he was a photographer and had made the dim enlargement of Mrs. Wilson's mother which hovered like an ectoplasm on the wall. His wife was shrill, languid, handsome, and horrible. She told me with pride that her husband had photographed her a hundred and twenty-seven times since they had been married.

Mrs. Wilson had changed her costume some time before, and was now attired in an elaborate afternoon dress of cream-coloured chiffon, which gave out a continual rustle as she swept about the room. With the influence of the dress her personality had also undergone a change. The intense vitality that had been so remarkable in the garage was converted into impressive hauteur. Her laughter, her gestures, her assertions became more violently affected moment by moment, and as she expanded the room grew smaller around her, until she seemed to be revolving on a noisy, creaking pivot through the smoky air.

"My dear," she told her sister in a high, mincing shout, "most of these fellas will cheat you every time. All they think of is money. I had a woman up here last week to look at my feet, and when she gave me the bill you'd of thought she had my appendicitis out."

"What was the name of the woman?" asked Mrs. McKee.

"Mrs. Eberhardt. She goes around looking at people's feet in their own homes."

"I like your dress," remarked Mrs. McKee, "I think it's adorable."

Mrs. Wilson rejected the compliment by raising her eyebrow in disdain.

"It's just a crazy old thing," she said. "I just slip it on sometimes when I don't care what I look like."

"But it looks wonderful on you, if you know what I mean," pursued Mrs. McKee. "If Chester could only get you in that pose I think he could make something of it."

We all looked in silence at Mrs. Wilson, who removed a strand of hair from over her eyes and looked back at us with a brilliant smile. Mr. McKee regarded her intently with his head on one side, and then moved his hand back and forth slowly in front of his face.

"I should change the light," he said after a moment. "I'd like to bring out the modelling of the features. And I'd try to get hold of all the back hair."

"I wouldn't think of changing the light," cried Mrs. McKee. "I think it's—"

Her husband said "*Sh!*" and we all looked at the subject again, whereupon Tom Buchanan yawned audibly and got to his feet.

"You McKees have something to drink," he said. "Get some more ice and mineral water, Myrtle, before everybody goes to sleep."

"I told that boy about the ice." Myrtle raised her eyebrows in despair at the shiftlessness of the lower orders. "These people! You have to keep after them all the time."

She looked at me and laughed pointlessly. Then she flounced over to the dog, kissed it with ecstasy, and swept into the kitchen, implying that a dozen chefs awaited her orders there.

"I've done some nice things out on Long Island," asserted Mr. McKee.

Tom looked at him blankly.

"Two of them we have framed downstairs."

"Two what?" demanded Tom.

"Two studies. One of them I call *Montauk Point—The Gulls*, and the other I call *Montauk Point—The Sea.*"

The sister Catherine sat down beside me on the couch.

"Do you live down on Long Island, too?" she inquired.

"I live at West Egg."

"Really? I was down there at a party about a month ago. At a man named Gatsby's. Do you know him?"

"I live next door to him."

"Well, they say he's a nephew or a cousin of Kaiser Wilhelm's. That's where all his money comes from."

"Really?"

She nodded.

"I'm scared of him. I'd hate to have him get anything on me."

This absorbing information about my neighbour was interrupted by Mrs. McKee's pointing suddenly at Catherine:

"Chester, I think you could do something with *her*," she broke out, but Mr. McKee only nodded in a bored way, and turned his attention to Tom.

"I'd like to do more work on Long Island, if I could get the entry. All I ask is that they should give me a start."

"Ask Myrtle," said Tom, breaking into a short shout of laughter as Mrs. Wilson entered with a tray. "She'll give you a letter of introduction, won't you, Myrtle?"

"Do what?" she asked, startled.

"You'll give McKee a letter of introduction to your husband, so he can do some studies of him." His lips moved silently for a moment as he invented, " 'George B. Wilson at the Gasoline Pump,' or something like that."

Catherine leaned close to me and whispered in my ear:

"Neither of them can stand the person they're married to."

"Can't they?"

"Can't *stand* them." She looked at Myrtle and then at Tom. "What I say is, why go on living with them if they can't stand them? If I was them I'd get a divorce and get married to each other right away."

"Doesn't she like Wilson either?"

The answer to this was unexpected. It came from Myrtle, who had overheard the question, and it was violent and obscene.

"You see," cried Catherine triumphantly. She lowered her voice again. "It's really his wife that's keeping them apart. She's a Catholic, and they don't believe in divorce."

Daisy was not a Catholic, and I was a little shocked at the elaborateness of the lie.

"When they do get married," continued Catherine, "they're going West to live for a while until it blows over."

"It'd be more discreet to go to Europe."

"Oh, do you like Europe?" she exclaimed surprisingly. "I just got back from Monte Carlo."

"Really."

"Just last year. I went over there with another girl."

"Stay long?"

"No, we just went to Monte Carlo and back. We went by way of Marseilles. We had over twelve hundred dollars when we started, but we got gyped out of it all in two days in the private rooms. We had an awful time getting back, I can tell you. God, how I hated that town!"

The late afternoon sky bloomed in the window for a moment like the blue honey of the Mediterranean—then the shrill voice of Mrs. McKee called me back into the room.

"I almost made a mistake, too," she declared vigorously. "I almost married a little kike who'd been after me for years. I knew he was below me. Everybody kept saying to me: 'Lucille, that man's way below you!' But if I hadn't met Chester, he'd of got me sure."

"Yes, but listen," said Myrtle Wilson, nodding her head up and down, "at least you didn't marry him."

"I know I didn't."

"Well, I married him," said Myrtle, ambiguously. "And that's the difference between your case and mine."

"Why did you, Myrtle?" demanded Catherine. "Nobody forced you to."

Myrtle considered.

"I married him because I thought he was a gentleman," she said finally. "I thought he knew something about breeding, but he wasn't fit to lick my shoe."

"You were crazy about him for a while," said Catherine.

"Crazy about him!" cried Myrtle incredulously. "Who said I was crazy about him? I never was any more crazy about him than I was about that man there."

She pointed suddenly at me, and everyone looked at me accusingly. I tried to show by my expression that I expected no affection.

"The only *crazy* I was was when I married him. I knew right away I made a mistake. He borrowed somebody's best suit to get married in, and never even told me about it, and the man came after it one day when he was out: 'Oh, is that your suit?' I said. 'This is the first I ever heard about it.' But I gave it to him and then I lay down and cried to beat the band all afternoon."

"She really ought to get away from him," resumed Catherine to me. "They've been living over that garage for eleven years. And Tom's the first sweetie she ever had."

The bottle of whisky—a second one—was now in constant demand by all present, excepting Catherine, who "felt just as good on nothing at all." Tom rang for the janitor and sent him for some celebrated sandwiches, which were a complete supper in themselves. I wanted to get out and walk eastward toward the park through the soft twilight, but each time I tried to go I became entangled in some wild, strident argument which pulled me back, as if with ropes, into my chair. Yet high over the city our line of yellow windows must have contributed their share of human secrecy to the casual watcher in the darkening streets, and I saw him too, looking up and wondering. I was within and without, simultaneously enchanted and repelled by the inexhaustible variety of life.

Myrtle pulled her chair close to mine, and suddenly her warm breath poured over me the story of her first meeting with Tom.

"It was on the two little seats facing each other that are always the last ones left on the train. I was going up to New York to see my sister and spend the night. He had on a dress suit and patent leather shoes, and I couldn't keep my eyes off him, but every time he looked at me I had to pretend to be looking at the advertisement over his head. When we came into the station he was next to me, and his white shirtfront pressed against my arm, and so I told him I'd have to call a policeman, but he knew I lied. I was so excited that when I got into a taxi with him I didn't hardly know I wasn't getting into a subway train. All I kept thinking about, over and over, was 'You can't live forever; you can't live forever.'"

She turned to Mrs. McKee and the room rang full of her artificial laughter.

"My dear," she cried, "I'm going to give you this dress as soon as I'm through with it. I've got to get another one tomorrow. I'm going to make a list of all the things I've got to get. A massage and a wave, and a collar for the dog, and one of those cute little ashtrays where you touch a spring, and a wreath with a black silk bow for mother's grave that'll last all summer. I got to write down a list so I won't forget all the things I got to do."

It was nine o'clock—almost immediately afterward I looked at my watch and found it was ten. Mr. McKee was asleep on a chair with his fists clenched in his lap, like a photograph of a man of action. Taking out my handkerchief I wiped from his cheek the spot of dried lather that had worried me all the afternoon.

The little dog was sitting on the table looking with blind eyes through the smoke, and from time to time groaning faintly. People disappeared, reappeared, made plans to go somewhere, and then lost each other, searched for each other, found each other a few feet away. Some time toward midnight Tom Buchanan and Mrs. Wilson stood face to face discussing, in impassioned voices, whether Mrs. Wilson had any right to mention Daisy's name.

"Daisy! Daisy! Daisy!" shouted Mrs. Wilson. "I'll say it whenever I want to! Daisy! Dai—"

Making a short deft movement, Tom Buchanan broke her nose with his open hand.

Then there were bloody towels upon the bathroom floor, and women's voices scolding, and high over the confusion a long broken wail of pain. Mr. McKee awoke from his doze and started in a daze toward the door. When he had gone halfway he turned around and stared at the scene—his wife and Catherine scolding and consoling as they stumbled here and there among the crowded furniture with articles of aid, and the despairing figure on the couch, bleeding fluently, and trying to spread a copy of *Town Tattle* over the tapestry scenes of Versailles. Then Mr. McKee turned and continued on out the door. Taking my hat from the chandelier, I followed.

"Come to lunch some day," he suggested, as we groaned down in the elevator.

"Where?"

"Anywhere."

"Keep your hands off the lever," snapped the elevator boy.

"I beg your pardon," said Mr. McKee with dignity, "I didn't know I was touching it."

"All right," I agreed, "I'll be glad to."

... I was standing beside his bed and he was sitting up between the sheets, clad in his underwear, with a great portfolio in his hands.

"Beauty and the Beast... Loneliness... Old Grocery Horse... Brook'n Bridge..."

Then I was lying half asleep in the cold lower level of the Pennsylvania Station, staring at the morning *Tribune*, and waiting for the four o'clock train.

III

There was music from my neighbour's house through the summer nights. In his blue gardens men and girls came and went like moths among the whisperings and the champagne and the stars. At high tide in the afternoon I watched his guests diving from the tower of his raft, or taking the sun on the hot sand of his beach while his two motorboats slit the waters of the Sound, drawing aquaplanes over cataracts of foam. On weekends his Rolls-Royce became an omnibus, bearing parties to and from the city between nine in the morning and long past midnight, while his station wagon scampered like a brisk yellow bug to meet all trains. And on Mondays eight servants, including an extra gardener, toiled all day with mops and scrubbing-brushes and hammers and garden-shears, repairing the ravages of the night before.

Every Friday five crates of oranges and lemons arrived from a fruiterer in New York—every Monday these same oranges and lemons left his back door in a pyramid of pulpless halves. There was a machine in the kitchen which could extract the juice of two hundred oranges in half an hour if a little button was pressed two hundred times by a butler's thumb.

At least once a fortnight a corps of caterers came down with several hundred feet of canvas and enough coloured lights to make a Christmas tree of Gatsby's enormous garden. On buffet tables, garnished with glistening hors-d'oeuvre, spiced baked hams crowded against salads of harlequin designs and pastry pigs and turkeys bewitched to a dark gold. In the main hall a bar with a real brass rail was set up, and stocked with gins and liquors and with cordials so long forgotten that most of his female guests were too young to know one from another.

By seven o'clock the orchestra has arrived, no thin five-piece affair, but a whole pitful of oboes and trombones and saxophones and viols and cornets and piccolos, and low and high drums. The last swimmers have come in from the beach now and are dressing upstairs; the cars from New York are parked five deep in the drive, and already the halls and salons and verandas are gaudy with primary colours, and hair bobbed in strange new ways, and shawls beyond the dreams of Castile. The bar is in full swing, and floating rounds of cocktails permeate the garden outside, until the air is alive with chatter and laughter, and casual innuendo and introductions forgotten on the spot, and enthusiastic meetings between women who never knew each other's names.

The lights grow brighter as the earth lurches away from the sun, and now the orchestra is playing yellow cocktail music, and the opera of voices pitches a key higher. Laughter is easier minute by minute, spilled with prodigality, tipped out at a cheerful word. The groups change more swiftly, swell with new arrivals, dissolve and form in the same breath; already there are wanderers, confident girls who weave here and there among the stouter and more stable, become for a sharp, joyous moment the centre of a group, and then, excited with triumph, glide on through the sea-change of faces and voices and colour under the constantly changing light.

Suddenly one of these gypsies, in trembling opal, seizes a cocktail out of the air, dumps it down for courage and, moving her hands like Frisco, dances out alone on the canvas platform. A momentary hush; the orchestra leader varies his rhythm obligingly for her, and there is a burst of chatter as the erroneous news goes around that she is Gilda Gray's understudy from the Follies. The party has begun.

I believe that on the first night I went to Gatsby's house I was one of the few guests who had actually been invited. People were not invited—they went there. They got into automobiles which bore them out to Long Island, and somehow they ended up at Gatsby's door. Once there they were introduced by somebody who knew Gatsby, and after that they conducted themselves according to the rules of behaviour associated with an amusement park. Sometimes they came and went without having met Gatsby at all, came for the party with a simplicity of heart that was its own ticket of admission.

I had been actually invited. A chauffeur in a uniform of robin's-egg blue crossed my lawn early that Saturday morning with a surprisingly formal note from his employer: the honour would be entirely Gatsby's, it said, if I would attend his "little party" that night. He had seen me several times, and had intended to call on me long before, but a peculiar combination of circumstances had prevented it—signed Jay Gatsby, in a majestic hand.

Dressed up in white flannels I went over to his lawn a little after seven, and wandered around rather ill at ease among swirls and eddies of people I didn't know—though here and there was a face I had noticed on the commuting train. I was immediately struck by the number of young Englishmen dotted about; all well dressed, all looking a little hungry, and all talking in low, earnest voices to solid and prosperous Americans. I was sure that they were selling something: bonds or insurance or automobiles. They were at least agonizingly aware of the easy money in the vicinity and convinced that it was theirs for a few words in the right key.

As soon as I arrived I made an attempt to find my host, but the two or three people of whom I asked his whereabouts stared at me in such an amazed way, and denied so vehemently any knowledge of his movements, that I slunk off in the direction of the cocktail table—the only place in the garden where a single man could linger without looking purposeless and alone.

I was on my way to get roaring drunk from sheer embarrassment when Jordan Baker came out of the house and stood at the head of the marble steps, leaning a little backward and looking with contemptuous interest down into the garden.

Welcome or not, I found it necessary to attach myself to someone before I should begin to address cordial remarks to the passersby.

"Hello!" I roared, advancing toward her. My voice seemed unnaturally loud across the garden.

"I thought you might be here," she responded absently as I came up. "I remembered you lived next door to—"

She held my hand impersonally, as a promise that she'd take care of me in a minute, and gave ear to two girls in twin yellow dresses, who stopped at the foot of the steps.

"Hello!" they cried together. "Sorry you didn't win."

That was for thc golf tournament. She had lost in the finals the week before.

"You don't know who we are," said one of the girls in yellow, "but we met you here about a month ago."

"You've dyed your hair since then," remarked Jordan, and I started, but the girls had moved casually on and her remark was addressed to the premature moon, produced like the supper, no doubt, out of a caterer's basket. With Jordan's slender golden arm resting in mine, we descended the steps and sauntered about the garden. A tray of cocktails floated at us through the twilight, and we sat down at a table with the two girls in yellow and three men, each one introduced to us as Mr. Mumble.

"Do you come to these parties often?" inquired Jordan of the girl beside her.

"The last one was the one I met you at," answered the girl, in an alert confident voice. She turned to her companion: "Wasn't it for you, Lucille?"

It was for Lucille, too.

"I like to come," Lucille said. "I never care what I do, so I always have a good time. When I was here last I tore my gown on a chair, and he asked me my name and address—inside of a week I got a package from Croirier's with a new evening gown in it."

"Did you keep it?" asked Jordan.

"Sure I did. I was going to wear it tonight, but it was too big in the bust and had to be altered. It was gas blue with lavender beads. Two hundred and sixty-five dollars."

"There's something funny about a fellow that'll do a thing like that," said the other girl eagerly. "He doesn't want any trouble with *any*body."

"Who doesn't?" I inquired.

"Gatsby. Somebody told me—"

The two girls and Jordan leaned together confidentially.

"Somebody told me they thought he killed a man once."

A thrill passed over all of us. The three Mr. Mumbles bent forward and listened eagerly.

"I don't think it's so much *that*," argued Lucille sceptically; "It's more that he was a German spy during the war."

One of the men nodded in confirmation.

"I heard that from a man who knew all about him, grew up with him in Germany," he assured us positively.

"Oh, no," said the first girl, "it couldn't be that, because he was in the American army during the war." As our credulity switched back to her she leaned forward with enthusiasm. "You look at him sometimes when he thinks nobody's looking at him. I'll bet he killed a man."

She narrowed her eyes and shivered. Lucille shivered. We all turned and looked around for Gatsby. It was testimony to the romantic speculation he inspired that there were whispers about him from those who had found little that it was necessary to whisper about in this world.

The first supper—there would be another one after midnight—was now being served, and Jordan invited me to join her own party, who were spread around a table on the other side of the garden. There were three married couples and Jordan's escort, a persistent undergraduate given to violent innuendo, and obviously under the impression that sooner or later Jordan was going to yield him up her person to a greater or lesser degree. Instead of rambling, this party had preserved a dignified homogeneity, and assumed to itself the function of representing the staid nobility of the countryside—East Egg condescending to West Egg and carefully on guard against its spectroscopic gaiety.

"Let's get out," whispered Jordan, after a somehow wasteful and inappropriate half-hour; "this is much too polite for me."

We got up, and she explained that we were going to find the host: I had never met him, she said, and it was making me uneasy. The undergraduate nodded in a cynical, melancholy way.

The bar, where we glanced first, was crowded, but Gatsby was not there. She couldn't find him from the top of the steps, and he wasn't on the veranda. On a chance we tried an important-looking door, and walked into a high Gothic library, panelled with carved English oak, and probably transported complete from some ruin overseas.

A stout, middle-aged man, with enormous owl-eyed spectacles, was sitting somewhat drunk on the edge of a great table, staring with unsteady concentration at the shelves of books. As we entered he wheeled excitedly around and examined Jordan from head to foot.

"What do you think?" he demanded impetuously.

"About what?"

He waved his hand toward the bookshelves.

"About that. As a matter of fact you needn't bother to ascertain. I ascertained. They're real."

"The books?"

He nodded.

"Absolutely real—have pages and everything. I thought they'd be a nice durable cardboard. Matter of fact, they're absolutely real. Pages and—Here! Lemme show you."

Taking our scepticism for granted, he rushed to the bookcases and returned with Volume One of the *Stoddard Lectures*.

"See!" he cried triumphantly. "It's a bona-fide piece of printed matter. It fooled me. This fella's a regular Belasco. It's a triumph. What thoroughness! What realism! Knew when to stop, too—didn't cut the pages. But what do you want? What do you expect?"

He snatched the book from me and replaced it hastily on its shelf, muttering that if one brick was removed the whole library was liable to collapse.

"Who brought you?" he demanded. "Or did you just come? I was brought. Most people were brought."

Jordan looked at him alertly, cheerfully, without answering.

"I was brought by a woman named Roosevelt," he continued. "Mrs. Claud Roosevelt. Do you know her? I met her somewhere last night. I've been drunk for about a week now, and I thought it might sober me up to sit in a library."

"Has it?"

"A little bit, I think. I can't tell yet. I've only been here an hour. Did I tell you about the books? They're real. They're—"

"You told us."

We shook hands with him gravely and went back outdoors.

There was dancing now on the canvas in the garden; old men pushing young girls backward in eternal graceless circles, superior couples holding each other tortuously, fashionably, and keeping in the corners—and a great number of single girls dancing individually or relieving the orchestra for a moment of the burden of the banjo or the traps. By midnight the hilarity had increased. A celebrated tenor had sung in Italian, and a notorious contralto had sung in jazz, and between the numbers people were doing "stunts" all over the garden, while happy, vacuous bursts of laughter rose toward the summer sky. A pair of stage twins, who turned out to be the girls in yellow, did a baby act in costume, and champagne was served in glasses bigger than finger-bowls. The moon had risen higher, and floating in the Sound was a triangle of silver scales, trembling a little to the stiff, tinny drip of the banjoes on the lawn.

I was still with Jordan Baker. We were sitting at a table with a man of about my age and a rowdy little girl, who gave way upon the slightest provocation to uncontrollable laughter. I was enjoying myself now. I had taken two finger-bowls of champagne, and the scene had changed before my eyes into something significant, elemental, and profound.

At a lull in the entertainment the man looked at me and smiled.

"Your face is familiar," he said politely. "Weren't you in the First Division during the war?"

"Why yes. I was in the Twenty-eighth Infantry."

"I was in the Sixteenth until June nineteen-eighteen. I knew I'd seen you somewhere before."

We talked for a moment about some wet, grey little villages in France. Evidently he lived in this vicinity, for he told me that he had just bought a hydroplane, and was going to try it out in the morning.

"Want to go with me, old sport? Just near the shore along the Sound."

"What time?"

"Any time that suits you best."

It was on the tip of my tongue to ask his name when Jordan looked around and smiled.

"Having a gay time now?" she inquired.

"Much better." I turned again to my new acquaintance. "This is an unusual party for me. I haven't even seen the host. I live over there—" I waved my hand at the invisible hedge in the distance, "and this man Gatsby sent over his chauffeur with an invitation."

For a moment he looked at me as if he failed to understand.

"I'm Gatsby," he said suddenly.

"What!" I exclaimed. "Oh, I beg your pardon."

"I thought you knew, old sport. I'm afraid I'm not a very good host."

He smiled understandingly—much more than understandingly. It was one of those rare smiles with a quality of eternal reassurance in it, that you may come across four or five times in life. It faced—or seemed to face—the whole eternal world for an instant, and then concentrated on *you* with an irresistible prejudice in your favour. It understood you just so far as you wanted to be understood, believed in you as you would like to believe in yourself, and assured you that it had precisely the impression of you that, at your best, you hoped to convey. Precisely at that point it vanished—and I was looking at an elegant young roughneck, a year or two over thirty, whose elaborate formality of speech just missed being absurd. Some time before he introduced himself I'd got a strong impression that he was picking his words with care.

Almost at the moment when Mr. Gatsby identified himself a butler hurried toward him with the information that Chicago was calling him on the wire. He excused himself with a small bow that included each of us in turn.

"If you want anything just ask for it, old sport," he urged me. "Excuse me. I will rejoin you later."

When he was gone I turned immediately to Jordan—constrained to assure her of my surprise. I had expected that Mr. Gatsby would be a florid and corpulent person in his middle years.

"Who is he?" I demanded. "Do you know?"

"He's just a man named Gatsby."

"Where is he from, I mean? And what does he do?"

"Now *you're* started on the subject," she answered with a wan smile. "Well, he told me once he was an Oxford man."

A dim background started to take shape behind him, but at her next remark it faded away.

"However, I don't believe it."

"Why not?"

"I don't know," she insisted, "I just don't think he went there."

Something in her tone reminded me of the other girl's "I think he killed a man," and had the effect of stimulating my curiosity. I would have accepted without question the information that Gatsby sprang from the swamps of Louisiana or from the lower East Side of New York. That was comprehensible. But young men didn't—at least in my provincial inexperience I believed they didn't—drift coolly out of nowhere and buy a palace on Long Island Sound.

"Anyhow, he gives large parties," said Jordan, changing the subject with an urban distaste for the concrete. "And I like large parties. They're so intimate. At small parties there isn't any privacy."

There was the boom of a bass drum, and the voice of the orchestra leader rang out suddenly above the echolalia of the garden.

"Ladies and gentlemen," he cried. "At the request of Mr. Gatsby we are going to play for you Mr. Vladmir Tostoff's latest work, which attracted so much attention at Carnegie Hall last May. If you read the papers you know there was a big sensation." He smiled with jovial condescension, and added: "Some sensation!" Whereupon everybody laughed.

"The piece is known," he concluded lustily, "as 'Vladmir Tostoff's Jazz History of the World!'"

The nature of Mr. Tostoff's composition eluded me, because just as it began my eyes fell on Gatsby, standing alone on the marble steps and looking from one group to another with approving eyes. His tanned skin was drawn attractively tight on his face and his short hair looked as though it were trimmed every day. I could see nothing sinister about him. I wondered if the fact that he was not drinking helped to set him off from his guests, for it seemed to me that he grew more correct as the fraternal hilarity increased. When the "Jazz History of the World" was over, girls were putting their heads on men's shoulders in a puppyish, convivial way, girls were swooning backward playfully into men's arms, even into groups, knowing that someone would arrest their falls—but no one swooned backward on Gatsby, and no French bob touched Gatsby's shoulder, and no singing quartets were formed with Gatsby's head for one link.

"I beg your pardon."

Gatsby's butler was suddenly standing beside us.

"Miss Baker?" he inquired. "I beg your pardon, but Mr. Gatsby would like to speak to you alone."

"With me?" she exclaimed in surprise.

"Yes, madame."

She got up slowly, raising her eyebrows at me in astonishment, and followed the butler toward the house. I noticed that she wore her evening-dress, all her dresses, like sports clothes—there was a jauntiness about her movements as if she had first learned to walk upon golf courses on clean, crisp mornings.

I was alone and it was almost two. For some time confused and intriguing sounds had issued from a long, many-windowed room which overhung the terrace. Eluding Jordan's undergraduate, who was now engaged in an obstetrical conversation with two chorus girls, and who implored me to join him, I went inside.

The large room was full of people. One of the girls in yellow was playing the piano, and beside her stood a tall, red-haired young lady from a famous chorus, engaged in song. She had drunk a quantity of champagne, and during the course of her song she had decided, ineptly, that everything was very, very sad—she was not only singing, she was weeping too. Whenever there was a pause in the song she filled it with gasping, broken sobs, and then took up the lyric again in a quavering soprano. The tears coursed down her cheeks—not freely, however, for when they came into contact with her heavily beaded eyelashes they assumed an inky colour, and pursued the rest of their way in slow black rivulets. A humorous suggestion was made that she sing the notes on her face, whereupon she threw up her hands, sank into a chair, and went off into a deep vinous sleep.

"She had a fight with a man who says he's her husband," explained a girl at my elbow.

I looked around. Most of the remaining women were now having fights with men said to be their husbands. Even Jordan's party, the quartet from East Egg, were rent asunder by dissension. One of the men was talking with curious intensity to a young actress, and his wife, after attempting to laugh at the situation in a dignified and indifferent way, broke down entirely and resorted to flank attacks—at intervals she appeared suddenly at his side like an angry diamond, and hissed: "You promised!" into his ear.

The reluctance to go home was not confined to wayward men. The hall was at present occupied by two deplorably sober men and their highly indignant wives. The wives were sympathizing with each other in slightly raised voices.

"Whenever he sees I'm having a good time he wants to go home."

"Never heard anything so selfish in my life."

"We're always the first ones to leave."

"So are we."

"Well, we're almost the last tonight," said one of the men sheepishly. "The orchestra left half an hour ago."

In spite of the wives' agreement that such malevolence was beyond credibility, the dispute ended in a short struggle, and both wives were lifted, kicking, into the night.

As I waited for my hat in the hall the door of the library opened and Jordan Baker and Gatsby came out together. He was saying some last word to her, but the eagerness in his manner tightened abruptly into formality as several people approached him to say goodbye.

Jordan's party were calling impatiently to her from the porch, but she lingered for a moment to shake hands.

"I've just heard the most amazing thing," she whispered. "How long were we in there?"

"Why, about an hour."

"It was… simply amazing," she repeated abstractedly. "But I swore I wouldn't tell it and here I am tantalizing you." She yawned gracefully in my face. "Please come and see me… Phone book… Under the name of Mrs. Sigourney Howard… My aunt…" She was hurrying off as she talked—her brown hand waved a jaunty salute as she melted into her party at the door.

Rather ashamed that on my first appearance I had stayed so late, I joined the last of Gatsby's guests, who were clustered around him. I wanted to explain that I'd hunted for him early in the evening and to apologize for not having known him in the garden.

"Don't mention it," he enjoined me eagerly. "Don't give it another thought, old sport." The familiar expression held no more familiarity than the hand which reassuringly brushed my shoulder. "And don't forget we're going up in the hydroplane tomorrow morning, at nine o'clock."

Then the butler, behind his shoulder:

"Philadelphia wants you on the phone, sir."

"All right, in a minute. Tell them I'll be right there... Good night."

"Good night."

"Good night." He smiled—and suddenly there seemed to be a pleasant significance in having been among the last to go, as if he had desired it all the time. "Good night, old sport... Good night."

But as I walked down the steps I saw that the evening was not quite over. Fifty feet from the door a dozen headlights illuminated a bizarre and tumultuous scene. In the ditch beside the road, right side up, but violently shorn of one wheel, rested a new coupé which had left Gatsby's drive not two minutes before. The sharp jut of a wall accounted for the detachment of the wheel, which was now getting considerable attention from half a dozen curious chauffeurs. However, as they had left their cars blocking the road, a harsh, discordant din from those in the rear had been audible for some time, and added to the already violent confusion of the scene.

A man in a long duster had dismounted from the wreck and now stood in the middle of the road, looking from the car to the tyre and from the tyre to the observers in a pleasant, puzzled way.

"See!" he explained. "It went in the ditch."

The fact was infinitely astonishing to him, and I recognized first the unusual quality of wonder, and then the man—it was the late patron of Gatsby's library.

"How'd it happen?"

He shrugged his shoulders.

"I know nothing whatever about mechanics," he said decisively.

"But how did it happen? Did you run into the wall?"

"Don't ask me," said Owl Eyes, washing his hands of the whole matter. "I know very little about driving—next to nothing. It happened, and that's all I know."

"Well, if you're a poor driver you oughtn't to try driving at night."

"But I wasn't even trying," he explained indignantly, "I wasn't even trying."

An awed hush fell upon the bystanders.

"Do you want to commit suicide?"

"You're lucky it was just a wheel! A bad driver and not even *trying*!"

"You don't understand," explained the criminal. "I wasn't driving. There's another man in the car."

The shock that followed this declaration found voice in a sustained "Ah-h-h!" as the door of the coupé swung slowly open. The crowd—it was now a crowd—stepped back involuntarily, and when the door had opened wide there was a ghostly pause. Then, very gradually, part by part, a pale, dangling individual stepped out of the wreck, pawing tentatively at the ground with a large uncertain dancing shoe.

Blinded by the glare of the headlights and confused by the incessant groaning of the horns, the apparition stood swaying for a moment before he perceived the man in the duster.

"Wha's matter?" he inquired calmly. "Did we run outa gas?"

"Look!"

Half a dozen fingers pointed at the amputated wheel—he stared at it for a moment, and then looked upward as though he suspected that it had dropped from the sky.

"It came off," someone explained.

He nodded.

"At first I din' notice we'd stopped."

A pause. Then, taking a long breath and straightening his shoulders, he remarked in a determined voice:

"Wonder'ff tell me where there's a gas'line station?"

At least a dozen men, some of them a little better off than he was, explained to him that wheel and car were no longer joined by any physical bond.

"Back out," he suggested after a moment. "Put her in reverse."

"But the *wheel*'s off!"

He hesitated.

"No harm in trying," he said.

The caterwauling horns had reached a crescendo and I turned away and cut across the lawn toward home. I glanced back once. A wafer of a moon was shining over Gatsby's house, making the night fine as before, and surviving the laughter and the sound of his still glowing garden. A sudden emptiness seemed to flow now from the windows and the great doors, endowing with complete isolation the figure of the host, who stood on the porch, his hand up in a formal gesture of farewell.

Reading over what I have written so far, I see I have given the impression that the events of three nights several weeks apart were all that absorbed me. On the contrary, they were merely casual events in a crowded summer, and, until much later, they absorbed me infinitely less than my personal affairs.

Most of the time I worked. In the early morning the sun threw my shadow westward as I hurried down the white chasms of lower New York to the Probity Trust. I knew the other clerks and young bond-salesmen by their first names, and lunched with them in dark, crowded restaurants on little pig sausages and mashed potatoes and coffee. I even had a short affair with a girl who lived in Jersey City and worked in the accounting department, but her brother began throwing mean looks in my direction, so when she went on her vacation in July I let it blow quietly away.

I took dinner usually at the Yale Club—for some reason it was the gloomiest event of my day—and then I went upstairs to the library and studied investments and securities for a conscientious hour. There were generally a few rioters around, but they never came into the library, so it was a good place to work. After that, if the night was mellow, I strolled down Madison Avenue past the old Murray Hill Hotel, and over 33rd Street to the Pennsylvania Station.

I began to like New York, the racy, adventurous feel of it at night, and the satisfaction that the constant flicker of men and women and machines gives to the restless eye. I liked to walk up Fifth Avenue and pick out romantic women from the crowd and imagine that in a few minutes I was going to enter into their lives, and no one would ever know or disapprove. Sometimes, in my mind, I followed them to their apartments on the corners of hidden streets, and they turned and smiled back at me before they faded through a door into warm darkness. At the enchanted metropolitan twilight I felt a haunting loneliness sometimes, and felt it in others—poor young clerks who loitered in front of windows waiting until it was time for a solitary restaurant dinner—young clerks in the dusk, wasting the most poignant moments of night and life.

Again at eight o'clock, when the dark lanes of the Forties were lined five deep with throbbing taxicabs, bound for the theatre district, I felt a sinking in my heart. Forms leaned together in the taxis as they waited, and voices sang, and there was laughter from unheard jokes, and lighted cigarettes made unintelligible circles inside. Imagining that I, too, was hurrying towards gaiety and sharing their intimate excitement, I wished them well.

For a while I lost sight of Jordan Baker, and then in midsummer I found her again. At first I was flattered to go places with her, because she was a golf champion, and everyone knew her name. Then it was something more. I wasn't actually in love, but I felt a sort of tender curiosity. The bored haughty face that she turned to the world concealed something—most affectations conceal something eventually, even though they don't in the beginning—and one day I found what it was. When we were on a house-party together up in Warwick, she left a borrowed car out in the rain with the top down, and then lied about it—and suddenly I remembered the story about her that had eluded me that night at Daisy's. At her first big golf tournament there was a row that nearly reached the newspapers—a suggestion that she had moved her ball from a bad lie in the semifinal round. The thing approached the proportions of a scandal—then died away. A caddy retracted his statement, and the only other witness admitted that he might have been mistaken. The incident and the name had remained together in my mind.

Jordan Baker instinctively avoided clever, shrewd men, and now I saw that this was because she felt safer on a plane where any divergence from a code would be thought impossible. She was incurably dishonest. She wasn't able to endure being at a disadvantage and, given this unwillingness, I suppose she had begun dealing in subterfuges when she was very young in order to keep that cool, insolent smile turned to the world and yet satisfy the demands of her hard, jaunty body.

It made no difference to me. Dishonesty in a woman is a thing you never blame deeply—I was casually sorry, and then I forgot. It was on that same house-party that we had a curious conversation about driving a car. It started because she passed so close to some workmen that our fender flicked a button on one man's coat.

"You're a rotten driver," I protested. "Either you ought to be more careful, or you oughtn't to drive at all."

"I am careful."

"No, you're not."

"Well, other people are," she said lightly.

"What's that got to do with it?"

"They'll keep out of my way," she insisted. "It takes two to make an accident."

"Suppose you met somebody just as careless as yourself."

"I hope I never will," she answered. "I hate careless people. That's why I like you."

Her grey, sun-strained eyes stared straight ahead, but she had deliberately shifted our relations, and for a moment I thought I loved her. But I am slow-thinking and full of interior rules that act as brakes on my desires, and I knew that first I had to get myself definitely out of that tangle back home. I'd been writing letters once a week and signing them: "Love, Nick," and all I could think of was how, when that certain girl played tennis, a faint moustache of perspiration appeared on her upper lip. Nevertheless there was a vague understanding that had to be tactfully broken off before I was free.

Everyone suspects himself of at least one of the cardinal virtues, and this is mine: I am one of the few honest people that I have ever known.

IV

On Sunday morning while church bells rang in the villages alongshore, the world and its mistress returned to Gatsby's house and twinkled hilariously on his lawn.

"He's a bootlegger," said the young ladies, moving somewhere between his cocktails and his flowers. "One time he killed a man who had found out that he was nephew to Von Hindenburg and second cousin to the devil. Reach me a rose, honey, and pour me a last drop into that there crystal glass."

Once I wrote down on the empty spaces of a timetable the names of those who came to Gatsby's house that summer. It is an old timetable now, disintegrating at its folds, and headed "This schedule in effect July 5th, 1922." But I can still read the grey names, and they will give you a better impression than my generalities of those who accepted Gatsby's hospitality and paid him the subtle tribute of knowing nothing whatever about him.

From East Egg, then, came the Chester Beckers and the Leeches, and a man named Bunsen, whom I knew at Yale, and Doctor Webster Civet, who was drowned last summer up in Maine. And the Hornbeams and the Willie Voltaires, and a whole clan named Blackbuck, who always gathered in a corner and flipped up their noses like goats at whosoever came near. And the Ismays and the Chrysties (or rather Hubert Auerbach and Mr. Chrystie's wife), and Edgar Beaver, whose hair, they say, turned cotton-white one winter afternoon for no good reason at all.

Clarence Endive was from East Egg, as I remember. He came only once, in white knickerbockers, and had a fight with a bum named Etty in the garden. From farther out on the Island came the Cheadles and the O. R. P. Schraeders, and the Stonewall Jackson Abrams of Georgia, and the Fishguards and the Ripley Snells. Snell was there three days before he went to the penitentiary, so drunk out on the gravel drive that Mrs. Ulysses Swett's automobile ran over his right hand. The Dancies came, too, and S. B. Whitebait, who was well over sixty, and Maurice A. Flink, and the Hammerheads, and Beluga the tobacco importer, and Beluga's girls.

From West Egg came the Poles and the Mulreadys and Cecil Roebuck and Cecil Schoen and Gulick the State senator and Newton Orchid, who controlled Films Par Excellence, and Eckhaust and Clyde Cohen and Don S. Schwartz (the son) and Arthur McCarty, all connected with the movies in one way or another. And the Catlips and the Bembergs and G. Earl Muldoon, brother to that Muldoon who afterward strangled his wife. Da Fontano the promoter came there, and Ed Legros and James B. ("Rot-Gut") Ferret and the De Jongs and Ernest Lilly—they came to gamble, and when Ferret wandered into the garden it meant he was cleaned out and Associated Traction would have to fluctuate profitably next day.

A man named Klipspringer was there so often that he became known as "the boarder"—I doubt if he had any other home. Of theatrical people there were Gus Waize and Horace O'Donavan and Lester Myer and George Duckweed and Francis Bull. Also from New York were the Chromes and the Backhyssons and the Dennickers and Russel Betty and the Corrigans and the Kellehers and the Dewars and the Scullys and S. W. Belcher and the Smirkes and the young

Quinns, divorced now, and Henry L. Palmetto, who killed himself by jumping in front of a subway train in Times Square.

Benny McClenahan arrived always with four girls. They were never quite the same ones in physical person, but they were so identical one with another that it inevitably seemed they had been there before. I have forgotten their names—Jaqueline, I think, or else Consuela, or Gloria or Judy or June, and their last names were either the melodious names of flowers and months or the sterner ones of the great American capitalists whose cousins, if pressed, they would confess themselves to be.

In addition to all these I can remember that Faustina O'Brien came there at least once and the Baedeker girls and young Brewer, who had his nose shot off in the war, and Mr. Albrucksburger and Miss Haag, his fiancée, and Ardita Fitz-Peters and Mr. P. Jewett, once head of the American Legion, and Miss Claudia Hip, with a man reputed to be her chauffeur, and a prince of something, whom we called Duke, and whose name, if I ever knew it, I have forgotten.

All these people came to Gatsby's house in the summer.

At nine o'clock, one morning late in July, Gatsby's gorgeous car lurched up the rocky drive to my door and gave out a burst of melody from its three-noted horn.

It was the first time he had called on me, though I had gone to two of his parties, mounted in his hydroplane, and, at his urgent invitation, made frequent use of his beach.

"Good morning, old sport. You're having lunch with me today and I thought we'd ride up together."

He was balancing himself on the dashboard of his car with that resourcefulness of movement that is so peculiarly American—that comes, I suppose, with the absence of lifting work in youth and, even more, with the formless grace of our nervous, sporadic games. This quality was continually breaking through his punctilious manner in the shape of restlessness. He was never quite still; there was always a tapping foot somewhere or the impatient opening and closing of a hand.

He saw me looking with admiration at his car.

"It's pretty, isn't it, old sport?" He jumped off to give me a better view. "Haven't you ever seen it before?"

I'd seen it. Everybody had seen it. It was a rich cream colour, bright with nickel, swollen here and there in its monstrous length with triumphant hatboxes and supper-boxes and toolboxes, and terraced with a labyrinth of windshields that mirrored a dozen suns. Sitting down behind many layers of glass in a sort of green leather conservatory, we started to town.

I had talked with him perhaps half a dozen times in the past month and found, to my disappointment, that he had little to say. So my first impression, that he was a person of some undefined consequence, had gradually faded and he had become simply the proprietor of an elaborate roadhouse next door.

And then came that disconcerting ride. We hadn't reached West Egg village before Gatsby began leaving his elegant sentences unfinished and slapping himself indecisively on the knee of his caramel-coloured suit.

"Look here, old sport," he broke out surprisingly, "what's your opinion of me, anyhow?"

A little overwhelmed, I began the generalized evasions which that question deserves.

"Well, I'm going to tell you something about my life," he interrupted. "I don't want you to get a wrong idea of me from all these stories you hear."

So he was aware of the bizarre accusations that flavoured conversation in his halls.

"I'll tell you God's truth." His right hand suddenly ordered divine retribution to stand by. "I am the son of some wealthy people in the Middle West—all dead now. I was brought up in America but educated at Oxford, because all my ancestors have been educated there for many years. It is a family tradition."

He looked at me sideways—and I knew why Jordan Baker had believed he was lying. He hurried the phrase "educated at Oxford," or swallowed it, or choked on it, as though it had bothered him before. And with this doubt, his whole statement fell to pieces, and I wondered if there wasn't something a little sinister about him, after all.

"What part of the Middle West?" I inquired casually.

"San Francisco."

"I see."

"My family all died and I came into a good deal of money."

His voice was solemn, as if the memory of that sudden extinction of a clan still haunted him. For a moment I suspected that he was pulling my leg, but a glance at him convinced me otherwise.

"After that I lived like a young rajah in all the capitals of Europe—Paris, Venice, Rome—collecting jewels, chiefly rubies, hunting big game, painting a little, things for myself only, and trying to forget something very sad that had happened to me long ago."

With an effort I managed to restrain my incredulous laughter. The very phrases were worn so threadbare that they evoked no image except that of a turbaned "character" leaking sawdust at every pore as he pursued a tiger through the Bois de Boulogne.

"Then came the war, old sport. It was a great relief, and I tried very hard to die, but I seemed to bear an enchanted life. I accepted a commission as first lieutenant when it began. In the Argonne Forest I took the remains of my machine-gun battalion so far forward that there was a half mile gap on either side of us where the infantry couldn't advance. We stayed there two days and two nights, a hundred and thirty men with sixteen Lewis guns, and when the infantry came up at last they found the insignia of three German divisions among the piles of dead. I was promoted to be a major, and every Allied government gave me a decoration—even Montenegro, little Montenegro down on the Adriatic Sea!"

Little Montenegro! He lifted up the words and nodded at them—with his smile. The smile comprehended Montenegro's troubled history and sympathized with the brave struggles of the Montenegrin people. It appreciated fully the chain of national circumstances which had elicited this tribute from Montenegro's warm little heart. My incredulity was submerged in fascination now; it was like skimming hastily through a dozen magazines.

He reached in his pocket, and a piece of metal, slung on a ribbon, fell into my palm.

"That's the one from Montenegro."

To my astonishment, the thing had an authentic look. "Orderi di Danilo," ran the circular legend, "Montenegro, Nicolas Rex."

"Turn it."

"Major Jay Gatsby," I read, "For Valour Extraordinary."

"Here's another thing I always carry. A souvenir of Oxford days. It was taken in Trinity Quad—the man on my left is now the Earl of Doncaster."

It was a photograph of half a dozen young men in blazers loafing in an archway through which were visible a host of spires. There was Gatsby, looking a little, not much, younger—with a cricket bat in his hand.

Then it was all true. I saw the skins of tigers flaming in his palace on the Grand Canal; I saw him opening a chest of rubies to ease, with their crimson-lighted depths, the gnawings of his broken heart.

"I'm going to make a big request of you today," he said, pocketing his souvenirs with satisfaction, "so I thought you ought to know something about me. I didn't want you to think I was just some nobody. You see, I usually find myself among strangers because I drift here and there trying to forget the sad things that happened to me." He hesitated. "You'll hear about it this afternoon."

"At lunch?"

"No, this afternoon. I happened to find out that you're taking Miss Baker to tea."

"Do you mean you're in love with Miss Baker?"

"No, old sport, I'm not. But Miss Baker has kindly consented to speak to you about this matter."

I hadn't the faintest idea what "this matter" was, but I was more annoyed than interested. I hadn't asked Jordan to tea in order to discuss Mr. Jay Gatsby. I was sure the request would be something utterly fantastic, and for a moment I was sorry I'd ever set foot upon his overpopulated lawn.

He wouldn't say another word. His correctness grew on him as we neared the city. We passed Port Roosevelt, where there was a glimpse of red-belted oceangoing ships, and sped along a cobbled slum lined with the dark, undeserted saloons of the faded-gilt nineteen-hundreds. Then the valley of ashes opened out on both sides of us, and I had a glimpse of Mrs. Wilson straining at the garage pump with panting vitality as we went by.

With fenders spread like wings we scattered light through half Astoria—only half, for as we twisted among the pillars of the elevated I heard the familiar "jug-jug-*spat*!" of a motorcycle, and a frantic policeman rode alongside.

"All right, old sport," called Gatsby. We slowed down. Taking a white card from his wallet, he waved it before the man's eyes.

"Right you are," agreed the policeman, tipping his cap. "Know you next time, Mr. Gatsby. Excuse *me*!"

"What was that?" I inquired. "The picture of Oxford?"

"I was able to do the commissioner a favour once, and he sends me a Christmas card every year."

Over the great bridge, with the sunlight through the girders making a constant flicker upon the moving cars, with the city rising up across the river in white heaps and sugar lumps all built with a wish out of nonolfactory money. The city seen from the Queensboro Bridge is always the city seen for the first time, in its first wild promise of all the mystery and the beauty in the world.

A dead man passed us in a hearse heaped with blooms, followed by two carriages with drawn blinds, and by more cheerful carriages for friends. The friends looked out at us with the tragic eyes and short upper lips of southeastern Europe, and I was glad that the sight of Gatsby's splendid car was included in their sombre holiday. As we crossed Blackwell's Island a limousine passed us, driven by a white chauffeur, in which sat three modish negroes, two bucks and a girl. I laughed aloud as the yolks of their eyeballs rolled toward us in haughty rivalry.

"Anything can happen now that we've slid over this bridge," I thought; "anything at all…"

Even Gatsby could happen, without any particular wonder.

Roaring noon. In a well-fanned Forty-second Street cellar I met Gatsby for lunch. Blinking away the brightness of the street outside, my eyes picked him out obscurely in the anteroom, talking to another man.

"Mr. Carraway, this is my friend Mr. Wolfshiem."

A small, flat-nosed Jew raised his large head and regarded me with two fine growths of hair which luxuriated in either nostril. After a moment I discovered his tiny eyes in the half-darkness.

"—So I took one look at him," said Mr. Wolfshiem, shaking my hand earnestly, "and what do you think I did?"

"What?" I inquired politely.

But evidently he was not addressing me, for he dropped my hand and covered Gatsby with his expressive nose.

"I handed the money to Katspaugh and I said: 'All right, Katspaugh, don't pay him a penny till he shuts his mouth.' He shut it then and there."

Gatsby took an arm of each of us and moved forward into the restaurant, whereupon Mr. Wolfshiem swallowed a new sentence he was starting and lapsed into a somnambulatory abstraction.

"Highballs?" asked the head waiter.

"This is a nice restaurant here," said Mr. Wolfshiem, looking at the presbyterian nymphs on the ceiling. "But I like across the street better!"

"Yes, highballs," agreed Gatsby, and then to Mr. Wolfshiem: "It's too hot over there."

"Hot and small—yes," said Mr. Wolfshiem, "but full of memories."

"What place is that?" I asked.

"The old Metropole."

"The old Metropole," brooded Mr. Wolfshiem gloomily. "Filled with faces dead and gone. Filled with friends gone now forever. I can't forget so long as I live the night they shot Rosy Rosenthal there. It was six of us at the table, and Rosy had eat and drunk a lot all evening. When it was almost morning the waiter came up to him with a funny look and says somebody wants to speak to him outside. 'All right,' says Rosy, and begins to get up, and I pulled him down in his chair.

"'Let the bastards come in here if they want you, Rosy, but don't you, so help me, move outside this room.'

"It was four o'clock in the morning then, and if we'd of raised the blinds we'd of seen daylight."

"Did he go?" I asked innocently.

"Sure he went." Mr. Wolfshiem's nose flashed at me indignantly. "He turned around in the door and says: 'Don't let that waiter take away my coffee!' Then he went out on the sidewalk, and they shot him three times in his full belly and drove away."

"Four of them were electrocuted," I said, remembering.

"Five, with Becker." His nostrils turned to me in an interested way. "I understand you're looking for a business gonnegtion."

The juxtaposition of these two remarks was startling. Gatsby answered for me:

"Oh, no," he exclaimed, "this isn't the man."

"No?" Mr. Wolfshiem seemed disappointed.

"This is just a friend. I told you we'd talk about that some other time."

"I beg your pardon," said Mr. Wolfshiem, "I had a wrong man."

A succulent hash arrived, and Mr. Wolfshiem, forgetting the more sentimental atmosphere of the old Metropole, began to eat with ferocious delicacy.

His eyes, meanwhile, roved very slowly all around the room—he completed the arc by turning to inspect the people directly behind. I think that, except for my presence, he would have taken one short glance beneath our own table.

"Look here, old sport," said Gatsby, leaning toward me, "I'm afraid I made you a little angry this morning in the car."

There was the smile again, but this time I held out against it.

"I don't like mysteries," I answered, "and I don't understand why you won't come out frankly and tell me what you want. Why has it all got to come through Miss Baker?"

"Oh, it's nothing underhand," he assured me. "Miss Baker's a great sportswoman, you know, and she'd never do anything that wasn't all right."

Suddenly he looked at his watch, jumped up, and hurried from the room, leaving me with Mr. Wolfshiem at the table.

"He has to telephone," said Mr. Wolfshiem, following him with his eyes. "Fine fellow, isn't he? Handsome to look at and a perfect gentleman."

"Yes."

"He's an Oggsford man."

"Oh!"

"He went to Oggsford College in England. You know Oggsford College?"

"I've heard of it."

"It's one of the most famous colleges in the world."

"Have you known Gatsby for a long time?" I inquired.

"Several years," he answered in a gratified way. "I made the pleasure of his acquaintance just after the war. But I knew I had discovered a man of fine breeding after I talked with him an hour. I said to myself: 'There's the kind of man you'd like to take home and introduce to your mother and sister.'" He paused. "I see you're looking at my cuff buttons."

I hadn't been looking at them, but I did now. They were composed of oddly familiar pieces of ivory.

"Finest specimens of human molars," he informed me.

"Well!" I inspected them. "That's a very interesting idea."

"Yeah." He flipped his sleeves up under his coat. "Yeah, Gatsby's very careful about women. He would never so much as look at a friend's wife."

When the subject of this instinctive trust returned to the table and sat down Mr. Wolfshiem drank his coffee with a jerk and got to his feet.

"I have enjoyed my lunch," he said, "and I'm going to run off from you two young men before I outstay my welcome."

"Don't hurry Meyer," said Gatsby, without enthusiasm. Mr. Wolfshiem raised his hand in a sort of benediction.

"You're very polite, but I belong to another generation," he announced solemnly. "You sit here and discuss your sports and your young ladies and your—" He supplied an imaginary noun with another wave of his hand. "As for me, I am fifty years old, and I won't impose myself on you any longer."

As he shook hands and turned away his tragic nose was trembling. I wondered if I had said anything to offend him.

"He becomes very sentimental sometimes," explained Gatsby. "This is one of his sentimental days. He's quite a character around New York—a denizen of Broadway."

"Who is he, anyhow, an actor?"

"No."

"A dentist?"

"Meyer Wolfshiem? No, he's a gambler." Gatsby hesitated, then added, coolly: "He's the man who fixed the World's Series back in 1919."

"Fixed the World's Series?" I repeated.

The idea staggered me. I remembered, of course, that the World's Series had been fixed in 1919, but if I had thought of it at all I would have thought of it as a thing that merely *happened*, the end of some inevitable chain. It never occurred to me that one man could start to play with the faith of fifty million people—with the single-mindedness of a burglar blowing a safe.

"How did he happen to do that?" I asked after a minute.

"He just saw the opportunity."

"Why isn't he in jail?"

"They can't get him, old sport. He's a smart man."

I insisted on paying the check. As the waiter brought my change I caught sight of Tom Buchanan across the crowded room.

"Come along with me for a minute," I said; "I've got to say hello to someone."

When he saw us Tom jumped up and took half a dozen steps in our direction.

"Where've you been?" he demanded eagerly. "Daisy's furious because you haven't called up."

"This is Mr. Gatsby, Mr. Buchanan."

They shook hands briefly, and a strained, unfamiliar look of embarrassment came over Gatsby's face.

"How've you been, anyhow?" demanded Tom of me. "How'd you happen to come up this far to eat?"

"I've been having lunch with Mr. Gatsby."

I turned toward Mr. Gatsby, but he was no longer there.

One October day in nineteen-seventeen—

(said Jordan Baker that afternoon, sitting up very straight on a straight chair in the tea-garden at the Plaza Hotel)

—I was walking along from one place to another, half on the sidewalks and half on the lawns. I was happier on the lawns because I had on shoes from England with rubber knobs on the soles that bit into the soft ground. I had on a new plaid skirt also that blew a little in the wind, and whenever this happened the red, white, and blue banners in front of all the houses stretched out stiff and said *tut-tut-tut-tut*, in a disapproving way.

The largest of the banners and the largest of the lawns belonged to Daisy Fay's house. She was just eighteen, two years older than me, and by far the most popular of all the young girls in Louisville. She dressed in white, and had a little white roadster, and all day long the telephone rang in her house and excited young officers from Camp Taylor demanded the privilege of monopolizing her that night. "Anyways, for an hour!"

When I came opposite her house that morning her white roadster was beside the kerb, and she was sitting in it with a lieutenant I had never seen before. They were so engrossed in each other that she didn't see me until I was five feet away.

"Hello, Jordan," she called unexpectedly. "Please come here."

I was flattered that she wanted to speak to me, because of all the older girls I admired her most. She asked me if I was going to the Red Cross to make bandages. I was. Well, then, would I tell them that she couldn't come that day? The officer looked at Daisy while she was speaking, in a way that every young girl wants to be looked at sometime, and because it seemed romantic to me I have remembered the incident ever since. His name was Jay Gatsby, and I didn't lay eyes on him again for over four years—even after I'd met him on Long Island I didn't realize it was the same man.

That was nineteen-seventeen. By the next year I had a few beaux myself, and I began to play in tournaments, so I didn't see Daisy very often. She went with a slightly older crowd—when she went with anyone at all. Wild rumours were circulating about her—how her mother had found her packing her bag one winter night to go to New York and say goodbye to a soldier who was going overseas. She was effectually prevented, but she wasn't on speaking terms with her family for several weeks. After that she didn't play around with the soldiers any more, but only with a few flat-footed, shortsighted young men in town, who couldn't get into the army at all.

By the next autumn she was gay again, gay as ever. She had a début after the armistice, and in February she was presumably engaged to a man from New Orleans. In June she married Tom Buchanan of Chicago, with more pomp and circumstance than Louisville ever knew before. He came down with a hundred people in four private cars, and hired a whole floor of the Muhlbach Hotel, and the day before the wedding he gave her a string of pearls valued at three hundred and fifty thousand dollars.

I was a bridesmaid. I came into her room half an hour before the bridal dinner, and found her lying on her bed as lovely as the June night in her flowered dress—and as drunk as a monkey. She had a bottle of Sauterne in one hand and a letter in the other.

"'Gratulate me," she muttered. "Never had a drink before, but oh how I do enjoy it."

"What's the matter, Daisy?"

I was scared, I can tell you; I'd never seen a girl like that before.

"Here, dearies." She groped around in a wastebasket she had with her on the bed and pulled out the string of pearls. "Take 'em downstairs and give 'em back to whoever they belong to. Tell 'em all Daisy's change' her mine. Say: 'Daisy's change' her mine!'"

She began to cry—she cried and cried. I rushed out and found her mother's maid, and we locked the door and got her into a cold bath. She wouldn't let go of the letter. She took it into the tub with her and squeezed it up in a wet ball, and only let me leave it in the soap-dish when she saw that it was coming to pieces like snow.

But she didn't say another word. We gave her spirits of ammonia and put ice on her forehead and hooked her back into her dress, and half an hour later, when we walked out of the room, the pearls were around her neck and the incident was over. Next day at five o'clock she married Tom Buchanan without so much as a shiver, and started off on a three months' trip to the South Seas.

I saw them in Santa Barbara when they came back, and I thought I'd never seen a girl so mad about her husband. If he left the room for a minute she'd look around uneasily, and say: "Where's Tom gone?" and wear the most abstracted expression until she saw him coming in the door. She used to sit on the sand with his head in her lap by the hour, rubbing her fingers over his eyes and looking at him with unfathomable delight. It was touching to see them together—it made you laugh in a hushed, fascinated way. That was in August. A week after I left Santa Barbara Tom ran into a wagon on the Ventura road one night, and ripped a front wheel off his car. The girl who was with him got into the papers, too, because her arm was broken—she was one of the chambermaids in the Santa Barbara Hotel.

The next April Daisy had her little girl, and they went to France for a year. I saw them one spring in Cannes, and later in Deauville, and then they came back to Chicago to settle down. Daisy was popular in Chicago, as you know. They moved with a fast crowd, all of them young and rich and wild, but she came out with an absolutely perfect reputation. Perhaps because she doesn't drink. It's a great advantage not to drink among hard-drinking people. You can hold your tongue and, moreover, you can time any little irregularity of your own so that everybody else is so blind that they don't see or care. Perhaps Daisy never went in for amour at all—and yet there's something in that voice of hers...

Well, about six weeks ago, she heard the name Gatsby for the first time in years. It was when I asked you—do you remember?—if you knew Gatsby in West Egg. After you had gone home she came into my room and woke me up, and said: "What Gatsby?" and when I described him—I was half asleep—she said in the strangest voice that it must be the man she used to know. It wasn't until then that I connected this Gatsby with the officer in her white car.

When Jordan Baker had finished telling all this we had left the Plaza for half an hour and were driving in a victoria through Central Park. The sun had gone down behind the tall apartments of the movie stars in the West Fifties, and the clear voices of children, already gathered like crickets on the grass, rose through the hot twilight:

"I'm the Sheik of Araby.
Your love belongs to me.
At night when you're asleep
Into your tent I'll creep—"

"It was a strange coincidence," I said.

"But it wasn't a coincidence at all."

"Why not?"

"Gatsby bought that house so that Daisy would be just across the bay."

Then it had not been merely the stars to which he had aspired on that June night. He came alive to me, delivered suddenly from the womb of his purposeless splendour.

"He wants to know," continued Jordan, "if you'll invite Daisy to your house some afternoon and then let him come over."

The modesty of the demand shook me. He had waited five years and bought a mansion where he dispensed starlight to casual moths—so that he could "come over" some afternoon to a stranger's garden.

"Did I have to know all this before he could ask such a little thing?"

"He's afraid, he's waited so long. He thought you might be offended. You see, he's regular tough underneath it all."

Something worried me.

"Why didn't he ask you to arrange a meeting?"

"He wants her to see his house," she explained. "And your house is right next door."

"Oh!"

"I think he half expected her to wander into one of his parties, some night," went on Jordan, "but she never did. Then he began asking people casually if they knew her, and I was the first one he found. It was that night he sent for me at his dance, and you should have heard the elaborate way he worked up to it. Of course, I immediately suggested a luncheon in New York—and I thought he'd go mad:

"'I don't want to do anything out of the way!' he kept saying. 'I want to see her right next door.'

"When I said you were a particular friend of Tom's, he started to abandon the whole idea. He doesn't know very much about Tom, though he says he's read a Chicago paper for years just on the chance of catching a glimpse of Daisy's name."

It was dark now, and as we dipped under a little bridge I put my arm around Jordan's golden shoulder and drew her toward me and asked her to dinner. Suddenly I wasn't thinking of Daisy and Gatsby any more, but of this clean, hard, limited person, who dealt in universal scepticism, and who leaned back jauntily just within the circle of my arm. A phrase began to beat in my ears with a sort of heady excitement: "There are only the pursued, the pursuing, the busy, and the tired."

"And Daisy ought to have something in her life," murmured Jordan to me.

"Does she want to see Gatsby?"

"She's not to know about it. Gatsby doesn't want her to know. You're just supposed to invite her to tea."

We passed a barrier of dark trees, and then the façade of Fifty-Ninth Street, a block of delicate pale light, beamed down into the park. Unlike Gatsby and Tom Buchanan, I had no girl whose disembodied face floated along the dark cornices and blinding signs, and so I drew up the girl beside me, tightening my arms. Her wan, scornful mouth smiled, and so I drew her up again closer, this time to my face.

V

When I came home to West Egg that night I was afraid for a moment that my house was on fire. Two o'clock and the whole corner of the peninsula was blazing with light, which fell unreal on the shrubbery and made thin elongating glints upon the roadside wires. Turning a corner, I saw that it was Gatsby's house, lit from tower to cellar.

At first I thought it was another party, a wild rout that had resolved itself into "hide-and-go-seek" or "sardines-in-the-box" with all the house thrown open to the game. But there wasn't a sound. Only wind in the trees, which blew the wires and made the lights go off and on again as if the house had winked into the darkness. As my taxi groaned away I saw Gatsby walking toward me across his lawn.

"Your place looks like the World's Fair," I said.

"Does it?" He turned his eyes toward it absently. "I have been glancing into some of the rooms. Let's go to Coney Island, old sport. In my car."

"It's too late."

"Well, suppose we take a plunge in the swimming pool? I haven't made use of it all summer."

"I've got to go to bed."

"All right."

He waited, looking at me with suppressed eagerness.

"I talked with Miss Baker," I said after a moment. "I'm going to call up Daisy tomorrow and invite her over here to tea."

"Oh, that's all right," he said carelessly. "I don't want to put you to any trouble."

"What day would suit you?"

"What day would suit *you*?" he corrected me quickly. "I don't want to put you to any trouble, you see."

"How about the day after tomorrow?"

He considered for a moment. Then, with reluctance: "I want to get the grass cut," he said.

We both looked down at the grass—there was a sharp line where my ragged lawn ended and the darker, well-kept expanse of his began. I suspected that he meant my grass.

"There's another little thing," he said uncertainly, and hesitated.

"Would you rather put it off for a few days?" I asked.

"Oh, it isn't about that. At least—" He fumbled with a series of beginnings. "Why, I thought—why, look here, old sport, you don't make much money, do you?"

"Not very much."

This seemed to reassure him and he continued more confidently.

"I thought you didn't, if you'll pardon my—you see, I carry on a little business on the side, a sort of side line, you understand. And I thought that if you don't make very much—You're selling bonds, aren't you, old sport?"

"Trying to."

"Well, this would interest you. It wouldn't take up much of your time and you might pick up a nice bit of money. It happens to be a rather confidential sort of thing."

I realize now that under different circumstances that conversation might have been one of the crises of my life. But, because the offer was obviously and tactlessly for a service to be rendered, I had no choice except to cut him off there.

"I've got my hands full," I said. "I'm much obliged but I couldn't take on any more work."

"You wouldn't have to do any business with Wolfshiem." Evidently he thought that I was shying away from the "gonnegtion" mentioned at lunch, but I assured him he was wrong. He waited a moment longer, hoping I'd begin a conversation, but I was too absorbed to be responsive, so he went unwillingly home.

The evening had made me lightheaded and happy; I think I walked into a deep sleep as I entered my front door. So I don't know whether or not Gatsby went to Coney Island, or for how many hours he "glanced into rooms" while his house blazed gaudily on. I called up Daisy from the office next morning, and invited her to come to tea.

"Don't bring Tom," I warned her.

"What?"

"Don't bring Tom."

"Who is 'Tom'?" she asked innocently.

The day agreed upon was pouring rain. At eleven o'clock a man in a raincoat, dragging a lawn-mower, tapped at my front door and said that Mr. Gatsby had sent him over to cut my grass. This reminded me that I had forgotten to tell my Finn to come back, so I drove into West Egg Village to search for her among soggy whitewashed alleys and to buy some cups and lemons and flowers.

The flowers were unnecessary, for at two o'clock a greenhouse arrived from Gatsby's, with innumerable receptacles to contain it. An hour later the front door opened nervously, and Gatsby in a white flannel suit, silver shirt, and gold-coloured tie, hurried in. He was pale, and there were dark signs of sleeplessness beneath his eyes.

"Is everything all right?" he asked immediately.

"The grass looks fine, if that's what you mean."

"What grass?" he inquired blankly. "Oh, the grass in the yard." He looked out the window at it, but, judging from his expression, I don't believe he saw a thing.

"Looks very good," he remarked vaguely. "One of the papers said they thought the rain would stop about four. I think it was *The Journal*. Have you got everything you need in the shape of—of tea?"

I took him into the pantry, where he looked a little reproachfully at the Finn. Together we scrutinized the twelve lemon cakes from the delicatessen shop.

"Will they do?" I asked.

"Of course, of course! They're fine!" and he added hollowly, "... old sport."

The rain cooled about half-past three to a damp mist, through which occasional thin drops swam like dew. Gatsby looked with vacant eyes through a copy of Clay's *Economics*, starting at the Finnish tread that shook the kitchen floor, and peering towards the bleared windows from time to time as if a series of invisible but alarming happenings were taking place outside. Finally he got up and informed me, in an uncertain voice, that he was going home.

"Why's that?"

"Nobody's coming to tea. It's too late!" He looked at his watch as if there was some pressing demand on his time elsewhere. "I can't wait all day."

"Don't be silly; it's just two minutes to four."

He sat down miserably, as if I had pushed him, and simultaneously there was the sound of a motor turning into my lane. We both jumped up, and, a little harrowed myself, I went out into the yard.

Under the dripping bare lilac-trees a large open car was coming up the drive. It stopped. Daisy's face, tipped sideways beneath a three-cornered lavender hat, looked out at me with a bright ecstatic smile.

"Is this absolutely where you live, my dearest one?"

The exhilarating ripple of her voice was a wild tonic in the rain. I had to follow the sound of it for a moment, up and down, with my ear alone, before any words came through. A damp streak of hair lay like a dash of blue paint across her cheek, and her hand was wet with glistening drops as I took it to help her from the car.

"Are you in love with me," she said low in my ear, "or why did I have to come alone?"

"That's the secret of Castle Rackrent. Tell your chauffeur to go far away and spend an hour."

"Come back in an hour, Ferdie." Then in a grave murmur: "His name is Ferdie."

"Does the gasoline affect his nose?"

"I don't think so," she said innocently. "Why?"

We went in. To my overwhelming surprise the living-room was deserted.

"Well, that's funny," I exclaimed.

"What's funny?"

She turned her head as there was a light dignified knocking at the front door. I went out and opened it. Gatsby, pale as death, with his hands plunged like weights in his coat pockets, was standing in a puddle of water glaring tragically into my eyes.

With his hands still in his coat pockets he stalked by me into the hall, turned sharply as if he were on a wire, and disappeared into the living-room. It wasn't a bit funny. Aware of the loud beating of my own heart I pulled the door to against the increasing rain.

For half a minute there wasn't a sound. Then from the living-room I heard a sort of choking murmur and part of a laugh, followed by Daisy's voice on a clear artificial note:

"I certainly am awfully glad to see you again."

A pause; it endured horribly. I had nothing to do in the hall, so I went into the room.

Gatsby, his hands still in his pockets, was reclining against the mantelpiece in a strained counterfeit of perfect ease, even of boredom. His head leaned back so far that it rested against the face of a defunct mantelpiece clock, and from this position his distraught eyes stared down at Daisy, who was sitting, frightened but graceful, on the edge of a stiff chair.

"We've met before," muttered Gatsby. His eyes glanced momentarily at me, and his lips parted with an abortive attempt at a laugh. Luckily the clock took this moment to tilt dangerously at the pressure of his head, whereupon he turned and caught it with trembling fingers, and set it back in place. Then he sat down, rigidly, his elbow on the arm of the sofa and his chin in his hand.

"I'm sorry about the clock," he said.

My own face had now assumed a deep tropical burn. I couldn't muster up a single commonplace out of the thousand in my head.

"It's an old clock," I told them idiotically.

I think we all believed for a moment that it had smashed in pieces on the floor.

"We haven't met for many years," said Daisy, her voice as matter-of-fact as it could ever be.

"Five years next November."

The automatic quality of Gatsby's answer set us all back at least another minute. I had them both on their feet with the desperate suggestion that they help me make tea in the kitchen when the demoniac Finn brought it in on a tray.

Amid the welcome confusion of cups and cakes a certain physical decency established itself. Gatsby got himself into a shadow and, while Daisy and I talked, looked conscientiously from one to the other of us with tense, unhappy eyes. However, as calmness wasn't an end in itself, I made an excuse at the first possible moment, and got to my feet.

"Where are you going?" demanded Gatsby in immediate alarm.

"I'll be back."

"I've got to speak to you about something before you go."

He followed me wildly into the kitchen, closed the door, and whispered: "Oh, God!" in a miserable way.

"What's the matter?"

"This is a terrible mistake," he said, shaking his head from side to side, "a terrible, terrible mistake."

"You're just embarrassed, that's all," and luckily I added: "Daisy's embarrassed too."

"She's embarrassed?" he repeated incredulously.

"Just as much as you are."

"Don't talk so loud."

"You're acting like a little boy," I broke out impatiently. "Not only that, but you're rude. Daisy's sitting in there all alone."

He raised his hand to stop my words, looked at me with unforgettable reproach, and, opening the door cautiously, went back into the other room.

I walked out the back way—just as Gatsby had when he had made his nervous circuit of the house half an hour before—and ran for a huge black knotted tree, whose massed leaves made a fabric against the rain. Once more it was pouring, and my irregular lawn, well-shaved by Gatsby's gardener, abounded in small muddy swamps and prehistoric marshes. There was nothing to look at from under the tree except Gatsby's enormous house, so I stared at it, like Kant at his church steeple, for half an hour. A brewer had built it early in the "period" craze, a decade before, and there was a story that he'd agreed to pay five years' taxes on all the neighbouring cottages if the owners would have their roofs thatched with straw. Perhaps their refusal took the heart out of his plan to Found a Family—he went into an immediate decline. His children sold his house with the black wreath still on the door. Americans, while willing, even eager, to be serfs, have always been obstinate about being peasantry.

After half an hour, the sun shone again, and the grocer's automobile rounded Gatsby's drive with the raw material for his servants' dinner—I felt sure he wouldn't eat a spoonful. A maid began opening the upper windows of his house, appeared momentarily in each, and, leaning from the large central bay, spat meditatively into the garden. It was time I went back. While the rain continued it had seemed like the murmur of their voices, rising and swelling a little now and then with gusts of emotion. But in the new silence I felt that silence had fallen within the house too.

I went in—after making every possible noise in the kitchen, short of pushing over the stove—but I don't believe they heard a sound. They were sitting at either end of the couch, looking at each other as if some question had been asked, or was in the air, and every vestige of embarrassment was gone. Daisy's face was smeared with tears, and when I came in she jumped up and began wiping at it with her handkerchief before a mirror. But there was a change in Gatsby that was simply confounding. He literally glowed; without a word or a gesture of exultation a new well-being radiated from him and filled the little room.

"Oh, hello, old sport," he said, as if he hadn't seen me for years. I thought for a moment he was going to shake hands.

"It's stopped raining."

"Has it?" When he realized what I was talking about, that there were twinkle-bells of sunshine in the room, he smiled like a weather man, like an ecstatic patron of recurrent light, and repeated the news to Daisy. "What do you think of that? It's stopped raining."

"I'm glad, Jay." Her throat, full of aching, grieving beauty, told only of her unexpected joy.

"I want you and Daisy to come over to my house," he said, "I'd like to show her around."

"You're sure you want me to come?"

"Absolutely, old sport."

Daisy went upstairs to wash her face—too late I thought with humiliation of my towels—while Gatsby and I waited on the lawn.

"My house looks well, doesn't it?" he demanded. "See how the whole front of it catches the light."

I agreed that it was splendid.

"Yes." His eyes went over it, every arched door and square tower. "It took me just three years to earn the money that bought it."

"I thought you inherited your money."

"I did, old sport," he said automatically, "but I lost most of it in the big panic—the panic of the war."

I think he hardly knew what he was saying, for when I asked him what business he was in he answered: "That's my affair," before he realized that it wasn't an appropriate reply.

"Oh, I've been in several things," he corrected himself. "I was in the drug business and then I was in the oil business. But I'm not in either one now." He looked at me with more attention. "Do you mean you've been thinking over what I proposed the other night?"

Before I could answer, Daisy came out of the house and two rows of brass buttons on her dress gleamed in the sunlight.

"That huge place *there*?" she cried pointing.

"Do you like it?"

"I love it, but I don't see how you live there all alone."

"I keep it always full of interesting people, night and day. People who do interesting things. Celebrated people."

Instead of taking the shortcut along the Sound we went down to the road and entered by the big postern. With enchanting murmurs Daisy admired this aspect or that of the feudal silhouette against the sky, admired the gardens, the sparkling odour of jonquils and the frothy odour of hawthorn and plum blossoms and the pale gold odour of kiss-me-at-the-gate. It was strange to reach the marble steps and find no stir of bright dresses in and out the door, and hear no sound but bird voices in the trees.

And inside, as we wandered through Marie Antoinette music-rooms and Restoration Salons, I felt that there were guests concealed behind every couch and table, under orders to be breathlessly silent until we had passed through. As Gatsby closed the door of "the Merton College Library" I could have sworn I heard the owl-eyed man break into ghostly laughter.

We went upstairs, through period bedrooms swathed in rose and lavender silk and vivid with new flowers, through dressing-rooms and poolrooms, and bathrooms with sunken baths—intruding into one chamber where a dishevelled man in pyjamas was doing liver exercises on the floor. It was Mr. Klipspringer, the "boarder." I had seen him wandering hungrily about the beach that morning. Finally we came to Gatsby's own apartment, a bedroom and a bath, and an Adam's study, where we sat down and drank a glass of some Chartreuse he took from a cupboard in the wall.

He hadn't once ceased looking at Daisy, and I think he revalued everything in his house according to the measure of response it drew from her well-loved eyes. Sometimes too, he stared around at his possessions in a dazed way, as though in her actual and astounding presence none of it was any longer real. Once he nearly toppled down a flight of stairs.

His bedroom was the simplest room of all—except where the dresser was garnished with a toilet set of pure dull gold. Daisy took the brush with delight, and smoothed her hair, whereupon Gatsby sat down and shaded his eyes and began to laugh.

"It's the funniest thing, old sport," he said hilariously. "I can't—When I try to—"

He had passed visibly through two states and was entering upon a third. After his embarrassment and his unreasoning joy he was consumed with wonder at her presence. He had been full of the idea so long, dreamed it right through to the end, waited with his teeth set, so to speak, at an inconceivable pitch of intensity. Now, in the reaction, he was running down like an over-wound clock.

Recovering himself in a minute he opened for us two hulking patent cabinets which held his massed suits and dressing-gowns and ties, and his shirts, piled like bricks in stacks a dozen high.

"I've got a man in England who buys me clothes. He sends over a selection of things at the beginning of each season, spring and fall."

He took out a pile of shirts and began throwing them, one by one, before us, shirts of sheer linen and thick silk and fine flannel, which lost their folds as they fell and covered the table in many-coloured disarray. While we admired he brought more and the soft rich heap mounted higher—shirts with stripes and scrolls and plaids in coral and apple-green and lavender and faint orange, with monograms of indian blue. Suddenly, with a strained sound, Daisy bent her head into the shirts and began to cry stormily.

"They're such beautiful shirts," she sobbed, her voice muffled in the thick folds. "It makes me sad because I've never seen such—such beautiful shirts before."

After the house, we were to see the grounds and the swimming pool, and the hydroplane, and the midsummer flowers—but outside Gatsby's window it began to rain again, so we stood in a row looking at the corrugated surface of the Sound.

"If it wasn't for the mist we could see your home across the bay," said Gatsby. "You always have a green light that burns all night at the end of your dock."

Daisy put her arm through his abruptly, but he seemed absorbed in what he had just said. Possibly it had occurred to him that the colossal significance of that light had now vanished forever. Compared to the great distance that had separated him from Daisy it had seemed very near to her, almost touching her. It had seemed as close as a star to the moon. Now it was again a green light on a dock. His count of enchanted objects had diminished by one.

I began to walk about the room, examining various indefinite objects in the half darkness. A large photograph of an elderly man in yachting costume attracted me, hung on the wall over his desk.

"Who's this?"

"That? That's Mr. Dan Cody, old sport."

The name sounded faintly familiar.

"He's dead now. He used to be my best friend years ago."

There was a small picture of Gatsby, also in yachting costume, on the bureau—Gatsby with his head thrown back defiantly—taken apparently when he was about eighteen.

"I adore it," exclaimed Daisy. "The pompadour! You never told me you had a pompadour—or a yacht."

"Look at this," said Gatsby quickly. "Here's a lot of clippings—about you."

They stood side by side examining it. I was going to ask to see the rubies when the phone rang, and Gatsby took up the receiver.

"Yes... Well, I can't talk now... I can't talk now, old sport... I said a *small* town... He must know what a small town is... Well, he's no use to us if Detroit is his idea of a small town..."

He rang off.

"Come here *quick*!" cried Daisy at the window.

The rain was still falling, but the darkness had parted in the west, and there was a pink and golden billow of foamy clouds above the sea.

"Look at that," she whispered, and then after a moment: "I'd like to just get one of those pink clouds and put you in it and push you around."

I tried to go then, but they wouldn't hear of it; perhaps my presence made them feel more satisfactorily alone.

"I know what we'll do," said Gatsby, "we'll have Klipspringer play the piano."

He went out of the room calling "Ewing!" and returned in a few minutes accompanied by an embarrassed, slightly worn young man, with shell-rimmed glasses and scanty blond hair. He was now decently clothed in a "sport shirt," open at the neck, sneakers, and duck trousers of a nebulous hue.

"Did we interrupt your exercise?" inquired Daisy politely.

"I was asleep," cried Mr. Klipspringer, in a spasm of embarrassment. "That is, I'd *been* asleep. Then I got up..."

"Klipspringer plays the piano," said Gatsby, cutting him off. "Don't you, Ewing, old sport?"

"I don't play well. I don't—hardly play at all. I'm all out of prac—"

"We'll go downstairs," interrupted Gatsby. He flipped a switch. The grey windows disappeared as the house glowed full of light.

In the music-room Gatsby turned on a solitary lamp beside the piano. He lit Daisy's cigarette from a trembling match, and sat down with her on a couch far across the room, where there was no light save what the gleaming floor bounced in from the hall.

When Klipspringer had played "The Love Nest" he turned around on the bench and searched unhappily for Gatsby in the gloom.

"I'm all out of practice, you see. I told you I couldn't play. I'm all out of prac—"

"Don't talk so much, old sport," commanded Gatsby. "Play!"

"In the morning,

In the evening,
Ain't we got fun—"

Outside the wind was loud and there was a faint flow of thunder along the Sound. All the lights were going on in West Egg now; the electric trains, men-carrying, were plunging home through the rain from New York. It was the hour of a profound human change, and excitement was generating on the air.

"One thing's sure and nothing's surer
The rich get richer and the poor get—children.
In the meantime,
In between time—"

As I went over to say goodbye I saw that the expression of bewilderment had come back into Gatsby's face, as though a faint doubt had occurred to him as to the quality of his present happiness. Almost five years! There must have been moments even that afternoon when Daisy tumbled short of his dreams—not through her own fault, but because of the colossal vitality of his illusion. It had gone beyond her, beyond everything. He had thrown himself into it with a creative passion, adding to it all the time, decking it out with every bright feather that drifted his way. No amount of fire or freshness can challenge what a man can store up in his ghostly heart.

As I watched him he adjusted himself a little, visibly. His hand took hold of hers, and as she said something low in his ear he turned toward her with a rush of emotion. I think that voice held him most, with its fluctuating, feverish warmth, because it couldn't be over-dreamed—that voice was a deathless song.

They had forgotten me, but Daisy glanced up and held out her hand; Gatsby didn't know me now at all. I looked once more at them and they looked back at me, remotely, possessed by intense life. Then I went out of the room and down the marble steps into the rain, leaving them there together.

VI

About this time an ambitious young reporter from New York arrived one morning at Gatsby's door and asked him if he had anything to say.

"Anything to say about what?" inquired Gatsby politely.

"Why—any statement to give out."

It transpired after a confused five minutes that the man had heard Gatsby's name around his office in a connection which he either wouldn't reveal or didn't fully understand. This was his day off and with laudable initiative he had hurried out "to see."

It was a random shot, and yet the reporter's instinct was right. Gatsby's notoriety, spread about by the hundreds who had accepted his hospitality and so become authorities upon his past, had increased all summer until he fell just short of being news. Contemporary legends such as the "underground pipeline to Canada" attached themselves to him, and there was one persistent story that he didn't live in a house at all, but in a boat that looked like a house and was moved secretly up and down the Long Island shore. Just why these inventions were a source of satisfaction to James Gatz of North Dakota, isn't easy to say.

James Gatz—that was really, or at least legally, his name. He had changed it at the age of seventeen and at the specific moment that witnessed the beginning of his career—when he saw Dan Cody's yacht drop anchor over the most insidious flat on Lake Superior. It was James Gatz who had been loafing along the beach that afternoon in a torn green jersey and a pair of canvas pants, but it was already Jay Gatsby who borrowed a rowboat, pulled out to the *Tuolomee*, and informed Cody that a wind might catch him and break him up in half an hour.

I suppose he'd had the name ready for a long time, even then. His parents were shiftless and unsuccessful farm people—his imagination had never really accepted them as his parents at all. The truth was that Jay Gatsby of West Egg, Long Island, sprang from his Platonic conception of himself. He was a son of God—a phrase which, if it means anything, means just that—and he must be about His Father's business, the service of a vast, vulgar, and meretricious beauty. So he invented just the sort of Jay Gatsby that a seventeen-year-old boy would be likely to invent, and to this conception he was faithful to the end.

For over a year he had been beating his way along the south shore of Lake Superior as a clam-digger and a salmon-fisher or in any other capacity that brought him food and bed. His brown, hardening body lived naturally through the half-fierce, half-lazy work of the bracing days. He knew women early, and since they spoiled him he became contemptuous of them, of young virgins because they were ignorant, of the others because they were hysterical about things which in his overwhelming self-absorption he took for granted.

But his heart was in a constant, turbulent riot. The most grotesque and fantastic conceits haunted him in his bed at night. A universe of ineffable gaudiness spun itself out in his brain while the clock ticked on the washstand and the moon soaked with wet light his tangled clothes upon the floor. Each night he added to the pattern of his fancies until drowsiness closed down upon some vivid scene with an oblivious embrace. For a while these reveries provided an outlet for his imagination; they were a satisfactory hint of the unreality of reality, a promise that the rock of the world was founded securely on a fairy's wing.

An instinct toward his future glory had led him, some months before, to the small Lutheran College of St. Olaf's in southern Minnesota. He stayed there two weeks, dismayed at its ferocious indifference to the drums of his destiny, to destiny itself, and despising the janitor's work with which he was to pay his way through. Then he drifted back to Lake Superior, and he was still searching for something to do on the day that Dan Cody's yacht dropped anchor in the shallows alongshore.

Cody was fifty years old then, a product of the Nevada silver fields, of the Yukon, of every rush for metal since seventy-five. The transactions in Montana copper that made him many times a millionaire found him physically robust but on the verge of soft-mindedness, and, suspecting this, an infinite number of women tried to separate him from his money. The none too savoury ramifications by which Ella Kaye, the newspaper woman, played Madame de Maintenon to his weakness and sent him to sea in a yacht, were common property of the turgid journalism in 1902. He had been coasting along all too hospitable shores for five years when he turned up as James Gatz's destiny in Little Girl Bay.

To young Gatz, resting on his oars and looking up at the railed deck, that yacht represented all the beauty and glamour in the world. I suppose he smiled at Cody—he had probably discovered that people liked him when he smiled. At any rate Cody asked him a few questions (one of them elicited the brand new name) and found that he was quick and extravagantly ambitious. A few days later he took him to Duluth and bought him a blue coat, six pairs of white duck trousers, and a yachting cap. And when the *Tuolomee* left for the West Indies and the Barbary Coast, Gatsby left too.

He was employed in a vague personal capacity—while he remained with Cody he was in turn steward, mate, skipper, secretary, and even jailor, for Dan Cody sober knew what lavish doings Dan Cody drunk might soon be about, and he provided for such contingencies by reposing more and more trust in Gatsby. The arrangement lasted five years, during which the boat went three times around the Continent. It might have lasted indefinitely except for the fact that Ella Kaye came on board one night in Boston and a week later Dan Cody inhospitably died.

I remember the portrait of him up in Gatsby's bedroom, a grey, florid man with a hard, empty face—the pioneer debauchee, who during one phase of American life brought back to the Eastern seaboard the savage violence of the frontier brothel and saloon. It was indirectly due to Cody that Gatsby drank so little. Sometimes in the course of gay parties women used to rub champagne into his hair; for himself he formed the habit of letting liquor alone.

And it was from Cody that he inherited money—a legacy of twenty-five thousand dollars. He didn't get it. He never understood the legal device that was used against him, but what remained of the millions went intact to Ella Kaye. He was left with his singularly appropriate education; the vague contour of Jay Gatsby had filled out to the substantiality of a man.

He told me all this very much later, but I've put it down here with the idea of exploding those first wild rumours about his antecedents, which weren't even faintly true. Moreover he told it to me at a time of confusion, when I had reached the point of believing everything and nothing about him. So I take advantage of this short halt, while Gatsby, so to speak, caught his breath, to clear this set of misconceptions away.

It was a halt, too, in my association with his affairs. For several weeks I didn't see him or hear his voice on the phone—mostly I was in New York, trotting around with Jordan and trying to ingratiate myself with her senile aunt—but finally I went over to his house one Sunday afternoon. I hadn't been there two minutes when somebody brought Tom Buchanan in for a drink. I was startled, naturally, but the really surprising thing was that it hadn't happened before.

They were a party of three on horseback—Tom and a man named Sloane and a pretty woman in a brown riding-habit, who had been there previously.

"I'm delighted to see you," said Gatsby, standing on his porch. "I'm delighted that you dropped in."

As though they cared!

"Sit right down. Have a cigarette or a cigar." He walked around the room quickly, ringing bells. "I'll have something to drink for you in just a minute."

He was profoundly affected by the fact that Tom was there. But he would be uneasy anyhow until he had given them something, realizing in a vague way that that was all they came for. Mr. Sloane wanted nothing. A lemonade? No, thanks. A little champagne? Nothing at all, thanks… I'm sorry—

"Did you have a nice ride?"

"Very good roads around here."

"I suppose the automobiles—"

"Yeah."

Moved by an irresistible impulse, Gatsby turned to Tom, who had accepted the introduction as a stranger.

"I believe we've met somewhere before, Mr. Buchanan."

"Oh, yes," said Tom, gruffly polite, but obviously not remembering. "So we did. I remember very well."

"About two weeks ago."

"That's right. You were with Nick here."

"I know your wife," continued Gatsby, almost aggressively.

"That so?"

Tom turned to me.

"You live near here, Nick?"

"Next door."

"That so?"

Mr. Sloane didn't enter into the conversation, but lounged back haughtily in his chair; the woman said nothing either—until unexpectedly, after two highballs, she became cordial.

"We'll all come over to your next party, Mr. Gatsby," she suggested. "What do you say?"

"Certainly; I'd be delighted to have you."

"Be ver' nice," said Mr. Sloane, without gratitude. "Well—think ought to be starting home."

"Please don't hurry," Gatsby urged them. He had control of himself now, and he wanted to see more of Tom. "Why don't you—why don't you stay for supper? I wouldn't be surprised if some other people dropped in from New York."

"You come to supper with *me*," said the lady enthusiastically. "Both of you."

This included me. Mr. Sloane got to his feet.

"Come along," he said—but to her only.

"I mean it," she insisted. "I'd love to have you. Lots of room."

Gatsby looked at me questioningly. He wanted to go and he didn't see that Mr. Sloane had determined he shouldn't.

"I'm afraid I won't be able to," I said.

"Well, you come," she urged, concentrating on Gatsby.

Mr. Sloane murmured something close to her ear.

"We won't be late if we start now," she insisted aloud.

"I haven't got a horse," said Gatsby. "I used to ride in the army, but I've never bought a horse. I'll have to follow you in my car. Excuse me for just a minute."

The rest of us walked out on the porch, where Sloane and the lady began an impassioned conversation aside.

"My God, I believe the man's coming," said Tom. "Doesn't he know she doesn't want him?"

"She says she does want him."

"She has a big dinner party and he won't know a soul there." He frowned. "I wonder where in the devil he met Daisy. By God, I may be old-fashioned in my ideas, but women run around too much these days to suit me. They meet all kinds of crazy fish."

Suddenly Mr. Sloane and the lady walked down the steps and mounted their horses.

"Come on," said Mr. Sloane to Tom, "we're late. We've got to go." And then to me: "Tell him we couldn't wait, will you?"

Tom and I shook hands, the rest of us exchanged a cool nod, and they trotted quickly down the drive, disappearing under the August foliage just as Gatsby, with hat and light overcoat in hand, came out the front door.

Tom was evidently perturbed at Daisy's running around alone, for on the following Saturday night he came with her to Gatsby's party. Perhaps his presence gave the evening its peculiar quality of oppressiveness—it stands out in my memory from Gatsby's other parties that summer. There were the same people, or at least the same sort of people, the same profusion of champagne, the same many-coloured, many-keyed commotion, but I felt an unpleasantness in the air, a pervading harshness that hadn't been there before. Or perhaps I had merely grown used to it, grown to accept West Egg as a world complete in itself, with its own standards and its own great figures, second to nothing because it had no consciousness of being so, and now I was looking at it again, through Daisy's eyes. It is invariably saddening to look through new eyes at things upon which you have expended your own powers of adjustment.

They arrived at twilight, and, as we strolled out among the sparkling hundreds, Daisy's voice was playing murmurous tricks in her throat.

"These things excite me *so*," she whispered. "If you want to kiss me any time during the evening, Nick, just let me know and I'll be glad to arrange it for you. Just mention my name. Or present a green card. I'm giving out green—"

"Look around," suggested Gatsby.

"I'm looking around. I'm having a marvellous—"

"You must see the faces of many people you've heard about."

Tom's arrogant eyes roamed the crowd.

"We don't go around very much," he said; "in fact, I was just thinking I don't know a soul here."

"Perhaps you know that lady." Gatsby indicated a gorgeous, scarcely human orchid of a woman who sat in state under a white-plum tree. Tom and Daisy stared, with that peculiarly unreal feeling that accompanies the recognition of a hitherto ghostly celebrity of the movies.

"She's lovely," said Daisy.

"The man bending over her is her director."

He took them ceremoniously from group to group:

"Mrs. Buchanan… and Mr. Buchanan—" After an instant's hesitation he added: "the polo player."

"Oh no," objected Tom quickly, "not me."

But evidently the sound of it pleased Gatsby for Tom remained "the polo player" for the rest of the evening.

"I've never met so many celebrities," Daisy exclaimed. "I liked that man—what was his name?—with the sort of blue nose."

Gatsby identified him, adding that he was a small producer.

"Well, I liked him anyhow."

"I'd a little rather not be the polo player," said Tom pleasantly, "I'd rather look at all these famous people in—in oblivion."

Daisy and Gatsby danced. I remember being surprised by his graceful, conservative foxtrot—I had never seen him dance before. Then they sauntered over to my house and sat on the steps for half an hour, while at her request I remained watchfully in the garden. "In case there's a fire or a flood," she explained, "or any act of God."

Tom appeared from his oblivion as we were sitting down to supper together. "Do you mind if I eat with some people over here?" he said. "A fellow's getting off some funny stuff."

"Go ahead," answered Daisy genially, "and if you want to take down any addresses here's my little gold pencil."… She looked around after a moment and told me the girl was "common but pretty," and I knew that except for the half-hour she'd been alone with Gatsby she wasn't having a good time.

We were at a particularly tipsy table. That was my fault—Gatsby had been called to the phone, and I'd enjoyed these same people only two weeks before. But what had amused me then turned septic on the air now.

"How do you feel, Miss Baedeker?"

The girl addressed was trying, unsuccessfully, to slump against my shoulder. At this inquiry she sat up and opened her eyes.

"Wha'?"

A massive and lethargic woman, who had been urging Daisy to play golf with her at the local club tomorrow, spoke in Miss Baedeker's defence:

"Oh, she's all right now. When she's had five or six cocktails she always starts screaming like that. I tell her she ought to leave it alone."

"I do leave it alone," affirmed the accused hollowly.

"We heard you yelling, so I said to Doc Civet here: 'There's somebody that needs your help, Doc.'"

"She's much obliged, I'm sure," said another friend, without gratitude, "but you got her dress all wet when you stuck her head in the pool."

"Anything I hate is to get my head stuck in a pool," mumbled Miss Baedeker. "They almost drowned me once over in New Jersey."

"Then you ought to leave it alone," countered Doctor Civet.

"Speak for yourself!" cried Miss Baedeker violently. "Your hand shakes. I wouldn't let you operate on me!"

It was like that. Almost the last thing I remember was standing with Daisy and watching the moving-picture director and his Star. They were still under the white-plum tree and their faces were touching except for a pale, thin ray of moonlight between. It occurred to me that he had been very slowly bending toward her all evening to attain this proximity, and even while I watched I saw him stoop one ultimate degree and kiss at her cheek.

"I like her," said Daisy, "I think she's lovely."

But the rest offended her—and inarguably because it wasn't a gesture but an emotion. She was appalled by West Egg, this unprecedented "place" that Broadway had begotten upon a Long Island fishing village—appalled by its raw vigour that chafed under the old euphemisms and by the too obtrusive fate that herded its inhabitants along a shortcut from nothing to nothing. She saw something awful in the very simplicity she failed to understand.

I sat on the front steps with them while they waited for their car. It was dark here in front; only the bright door sent ten square feet of light volleying out into the soft black morning. Sometimes a shadow moved against a dressing-room blind above, gave way to another shadow, an indefinite procession of shadows, who rouged and powdered in an invisible glass.

"Who is this Gatsby anyhow?" demanded Tom suddenly. "Some big bootlegger?"

"Where'd you hear that?" I inquired.

"I didn't hear it. I imagined it. A lot of these newly rich people are just big bootleggers, you know."

"Not Gatsby," I said shortly.

He was silent for a moment. The pebbles of the drive crunched under his feet.

"Well, he certainly must have strained himself to get this menagerie together."

A breeze stirred the grey haze of Daisy's fur collar.

"At least they are more interesting than the people we know," she said with an effort.

"You didn't look so interested."

"Well, I was."

Tom laughed and turned to me.

"Did you notice Daisy's face when that girl asked her to put her under a cold shower?"

Daisy began to sing with the music in a husky, rhythmic whisper, bringing out a meaning in each word that it had never had before and would never have again. When the melody rose her voice broke up sweetly, following it, in a way contralto voices have, and each change tipped out a little of her warm human magic upon the air.

"Lots of people come who haven't been invited," she said suddenly. "That girl hadn't been invited. They simply force their way in and he's too polite to object."

"I'd like to know who he is and what he does," insisted Tom. "And I think I'll make a point of finding out."

"I can tell you right now," she answered. "He owned some drugstores, a lot of drugstores. He built them up himself."

The dilatory limousine came rolling up the drive.

"Good night, Nick," said Daisy.

Her glance left me and sought the lighted top of the steps, where "Three O'Clock in the Morning," a neat, sad little waltz of that year, was drifting out the open door. After all, in the very casualness of Gatsby's party there were romantic possibilities totally absent from her world. What was it up there in the song that seemed to be calling her back inside? What would happen now in the dim, incalculable hours? Perhaps some unbelievable guest would arrive, a person infinitely rare and to be marvelled at, some authentically radiant young girl who with one fresh glance at Gatsby, one moment of magical encounter, would blot out those five years of unwavering devotion.

I stayed late that night. Gatsby asked me to wait until he was free, and I lingered in the garden until the inevitable swimming party had run up, chilled and exalted, from the black beach, until the lights were extinguished in the guestrooms overhead. When he came down the steps at last the tanned skin was drawn unusually tight on his face, and his eyes were bright and tired.

"She didn't like it," he said immediately.

"Of course she did."

"She didn't like it," he insisted. "She didn't have a good time."

He was silent, and I guessed at his unutterable depression.

"I feel far away from her," he said. "It's hard to make her understand."

"You mean about the dance?"

"The dance?" He dismissed all the dances he had given with a snap of his fingers. "Old sport, the dance is unimportant."

He wanted nothing less of Daisy than that she should go to Tom and say: "I never loved you." After she had obliterated four years with that sentence they could decide upon the more practical measures to be taken. One of them was that, after she was free, they were to go back to Louisville and be married from her house—just as if it were five years ago.

"And she doesn't understand," he said. "She used to be able to understand. We'd sit for hours—"

He broke off and began to walk up and down a desolate path of fruit rinds and discarded favours and crushed flowers.

"I wouldn't ask too much of her," I ventured. "You can't repeat the past."

"Can't repeat the past?" he cried incredulously. "Why of course you can!"

He looked around him wildly, as if the past were lurking here in the shadow of his house, just out of reach of his hand.

"I'm going to fix everything just the way it was before," he said, nodding determinedly. "She'll see."

He talked a lot about the past, and I gathered that he wanted to recover something, some idea of himself perhaps, that had gone into loving Daisy. His life had been confused and disordered since then, but if he could once return to a certain starting place and go over it all slowly, he could find out what that thing was...

... One autumn night, five years before, they had been walking down the street when the leaves were falling, and they came to a place where there were no trees and the sidewalk was white with moonlight. They stopped here and turned toward each other. Now it was a cool night with that mysterious excitement in it which comes at the two changes of the year. The quiet lights in the houses were humming out into the darkness and there was a stir and bustle among the stars. Out of the corner of his eye Gatsby saw that the blocks of the sidewalks really formed a ladder and mounted to a secret place above the trees—he could climb to it, if he climbed alone, and once there he could suck on the pap of life, gulp down the incomparable milk of wonder.

His heart beat faster as Daisy's white face came up to his own. He knew that when he kissed this girl, and forever wed his unutterable visions to her perishable breath, his mind would never romp again like the mind of God. So he waited, listening for a moment longer to the tuning-fork that had been struck upon a star. Then he kissed her. At his lips' touch she blossomed for him like a flower and the incarnation was complete.

Through all he said, even through his appalling sentimentality, I was reminded of something—an elusive rhythm, a fragment of lost words, that I had heard somewhere a long time ago. For a moment a phrase tried to take shape in my mouth and my lips parted like a dumb man's, as though there was more struggling upon them than a wisp of startled air. But they made no sound, and what I had almost remembered was uncommunicable forever.

VII

It was when curiosity about Gatsby was at its highest that the lights in his house failed to go on one Saturday night—and, as obscurely as it had begun, his career as Trimalchio was over. Only gradually did I become aware that the automobiles which turned expectantly into his drive stayed for just a minute and then drove sulkily away. Wondering if he were sick I went over to find out—an unfamiliar butler with a villainous face squinted at me suspiciously from the door.

"Is Mr. Gatsby sick?"

"Nope." After a pause he added "sir" in a dilatory, grudging way.

"I hadn't seen him around, and I was rather worried. Tell him Mr. Carraway came over."

"Who?" he demanded rudely.

"Carraway."

"Carraway. All right, I'll tell him."

Abruptly he slammed the door.

My Finn informed me that Gatsby had dismissed every servant in his house a week ago and replaced them with half a dozen others, who never went into West Egg village to be bribed by the tradesmen, but ordered moderate supplies over the telephone. The grocery boy reported that the kitchen looked like a pigsty, and the general opinion in the village was that the new people weren't servants at all.

Next day Gatsby called me on the phone.

"Going away?" I inquired.

"No, old sport."

"I hear you fired all your servants."

"I wanted somebody who wouldn't gossip. Daisy comes over quite often—in the afternoons."

So the whole caravansary had fallen in like a card house at the disapproval in her eyes.

"They're some people Wolfshiem wanted to do something for. They're all brothers and sisters. They used to run a small hotel."

"I see."

He was calling up at Daisy's request—would I come to lunch at her house tomorrow? Miss Baker would be there. Half an hour later Daisy herself telephoned and seemed relieved to find that I was coming. Something was up. And yet I couldn't believe that they would choose this occasion for a scene—especially for the rather harrowing scene that Gatsby had outlined in the garden.

The next day was broiling, almost the last, certainly the warmest, of the summer. As my train emerged from the tunnel into sunlight, only the hot whistles of the National Biscuit Company broke the simmering hush at noon. The straw seats of the car hovered on the edge of combustion; the woman next to me perspired delicately for a while into her white shirtwaist, and then, as her newspaper dampened under her fingers, lapsed despairingly into deep heat with a desolate cry. Her pocketbook slapped to the floor.

"Oh, my!" she gasped.

I picked it up with a weary bend and handed it back to her, holding it at arm's length and by the extreme tip of the corners to indicate that I had no designs upon it—but everyone near by, including the woman, suspected me just the same.

"Hot!" said the conductor to familiar faces. "Some weather!... Hot!... Hot!... Hot!... Is it hot enough for you? Is it hot? Is it...?"

My commutation ticket came back to me with a dark stain from his hand. That anyone should care in this heat whose flushed lips he kissed, whose head made damp the pyjama pocket over his heart!

... Through the hall of the Buchanans' house blew a faint wind, carrying the sound of the telephone bell out to Gatsby and me as we waited at the door.

"The master's body?" roared the butler into the mouthpiece. "I'm sorry, madame, but we can't furnish it—it's far too hot to touch this noon!"

What he really said was: "Yes... Yes... I'll see."

He set down the receiver and came toward us, glistening slightly, to take our stiff straw hats.

"Madame expects you in the salon!" he cried, needlessly indicating the direction. In this heat every extra gesture was an affront to the common store of life.

The room, shadowed well with awnings, was dark and cool. Daisy and Jordan lay upon an enormous couch, like silver idols weighing down their own white dresses against the singing breeze of the fans.

"We can't move," they said together.

Jordan's fingers, powdered white over their tan, rested for a moment in mine.

"And Mr. Thomas Buchanan, the athlete?" I inquired.

Simultaneously I heard his voice, gruff, muffled, husky, at the hall telephone.

Gatsby stood in the centre of the crimson carpet and gazed around with fascinated eyes. Daisy watched him and laughed, her sweet, exciting laugh; a tiny gust of powder rose from her bosom into the air.

"The rumour is," whispered Jordan, "that that's Tom's girl on the telephone."

We were silent. The voice in the hall rose high with annoyance: "Very well, then, I won't sell you the car at all… I'm under no obligations to you at all… and as for your bothering me about it at lunch time, I won't stand that at all!"

"Holding down the receiver," said Daisy cynically.

"No, he's not," I assured her. "It's a bona-fide deal. I happen to know about it."

Tom flung open the door, blocked out its space for a moment with his thick body, and hurried into the room.

"Mr. Gatsby!" He put out his broad, flat hand with well-concealed dislike. "I'm glad to see you, sir… Nick…"

"Make us a cold drink," cried Daisy.

As he left the room again she got up and went over to Gatsby and pulled his face down, kissing him on the mouth.

"You know I love you," she murmured.

"You forget there's a lady present," said Jordan.

Daisy looked around doubtfully.

"You kiss Nick too."

"What a low, vulgar girl!"

"I don't care!" cried Daisy, and began to clog on the brick fireplace. Then she remembered the heat and sat down guiltily on the couch just as a freshly laundered nurse leading a little girl came into the room.

"Bles-sed pre-cious," she crooned, holding out her arms. "Come to your own mother that loves you."

The child, relinquished by the nurse, rushed across the room and rooted shyly into her mother's dress.

"The bles-sed pre-cious! Did mother get powder on your old yellowy hair? Stand up now, and say—How-de-do."

Gatsby and I in turn leaned down and took the small reluctant hand. Afterward he kept looking at the child with surprise. I don't think he had ever really believed in its existence before.

"I got dressed before luncheon," said the child, turning eagerly to Daisy.

"That's because your mother wanted to show you off." Her face bent into the single wrinkle of the small white neck. "You dream, you. You absolute little dream."

"Yes," admitted the child calmly. "Aunt Jordan's got on a white dress too."

"How do you like mother's friends?" Daisy turned her around so that she faced Gatsby. "Do you think they're pretty?"

"Where's Daddy?"

"She doesn't look like her father," explained Daisy. "She looks like me. She's got my hair and shape of the face."

Daisy sat back upon the couch. The nurse took a step forward and held out her hand.

"Come, Pammy."

"Goodbye, sweetheart!"

With a reluctant backward glance the well-disciplined child held to her nurse's hand and was pulled out the door, just as Tom came back, preceding four gin rickeys that clicked full of ice.

Gatsby took up his drink.

"They certainly look cool," he said, with visible tension.

We drank in long, greedy swallows.

"I read somewhere that the sun's getting hotter every year," said Tom genially. "It seems that pretty soon the earth's going to fall into the sun—or wait a minute—it's just the opposite—the sun's getting colder every year.

"Come outside," he suggested to Gatsby, "I'd like you to have a look at the place."

I went with them out to the veranda. On the green Sound, stagnant in the heat, one small sail crawled slowly toward the fresher sea. Gatsby's eyes followed it momentarily; he raised his hand and pointed across the bay.

"I'm right across from you."

"So you are."

Our eyes lifted over the rose-beds and the hot lawn and the weedy refuse of the dog-days alongshore. Slowly the white wings of the boat moved against the blue cool limit of the sky. Ahead lay the scalloped ocean and the abounding blessed isles.

"There's sport for you," said Tom, nodding. "I'd like to be out there with him for about an hour."

We had luncheon in the dining-room, darkened too against the heat, and drank down nervous gaiety with the cold ale.

"What'll we do with ourselves this afternoon?" cried Daisy, "and the day after that, and the next thirty years?"

"Don't be morbid," Jordan said. "Life starts all over again when it gets crisp in the fall."

"But it's so hot," insisted Daisy, on the verge of tears, "and everything's so confused. Let's all go to town!"

Her voice struggled on through the heat, beating against it, moulding its senselessness into forms.

"I've heard of making a garage out of a stable," Tom was saying to Gatsby, "but I'm the first man who ever made a stable out of a garage."

"Who wants to go to town?" demanded Daisy insistently. Gatsby's eyes floated toward her. "Ah," she cried, "you look so cool."

Their eyes met, and they stared together at each other, alone in space. With an effort she glanced down at the table.

"You always look so cool," she repeated.

She had told him that she loved him, and Tom Buchanan saw. He was astounded. His mouth opened a little, and he looked at Gatsby, and then back at Daisy as if he had just recognized her as someone he knew a long time ago.

"You resemble the advertisement of the man," she went on innocently. "You know the advertisement of the man—"

"All right," broke in Tom quickly, "I'm perfectly willing to go to town. Come on—we're all going to town."

He got up, his eyes still flashing between Gatsby and his wife. No one moved.

"Come on!" His temper cracked a little. "What's the matter, anyhow? If we're going to town, let's start."

His hand, trembling with his effort at self-control, bore to his lips the last of his glass of ale. Daisy's voice got us to our feet and out on to the blazing gravel drive.

"Are we just going to go?" she objected. "Like this? Aren't we going to let anyone smoke a cigarette first?"

"Everybody smoked all through lunch."

"Oh, let's have fun," she begged him. "It's too hot to fuss."

He didn't answer.

"Have it your own way," she said. "Come on, Jordan."

They went upstairs to get ready while we three men stood there shuffling the hot pebbles with our feet. A silver curve of the moon hovered already in the western sky. Gatsby started to speak, changed his mind, but not before Tom wheeled and faced him expectantly.

"Have you got your stables here?" asked Gatsby with an effort.

"About a quarter of a mile down the road."

"Oh."

A pause.

"I don't see the idea of going to town," broke out Tom savagely. "Women get these notions in their heads—"

"Shall we take anything to drink?" called Daisy from an upper window.

"I'll get some whisky," answered Tom. He went inside.

Gatsby turned to me rigidly:

"I can't say anything in his house, old sport."

"She's got an indiscreet voice," I remarked. "It's full of—" I hesitated.

"Her voice is full of money," he said suddenly.

That was it. I'd never understood before. It was full of money—that was the inexhaustible charm that rose and fell in it, the jingle of it, the cymbals' song of it... High in a white palace the king's daughter, the golden girl...

Tom came out of the house wrapping a quart bottle in a towel, followed by Daisy and Jordan wearing small tight hats of metallic cloth and carrying light capes over their arms.

"Shall we all go in my car?" suggested Gatsby. He felt the hot, green leather of the seat. "I ought to have left it in the shade."

"Is it standard shift?" demanded Tom.

"Yes."

"Well, you take my coupé and let me drive your car to town."

The suggestion was distasteful to Gatsby.

"I don't think there's much gas," he objected.

"Plenty of gas," said Tom boisterously. He looked at the gauge. "And if it runs out I can stop at a drugstore. You can buy anything at a drugstore nowadays."

A pause followed this apparently pointless remark. Daisy looked at Tom frowning, and an indefinable expression, at once definitely unfamiliar and vaguely recognizable, as if I had only heard it described in words, passed over Gatsby's face.

"Come on, Daisy" said Tom, pressing her with his hand toward Gatsby's car. "I'll take you in this circus wagon."

He opened the door, but she moved out from the circle of his arm.

"You take Nick and Jordan. We'll follow you in the coupé."

She walked close to Gatsby, touching his coat with her hand. Jordan and Tom and I got into the front seat of Gatsby's car, Tom pushed the unfamiliar gears tentatively, and we shot off into the oppressive heat, leaving them out of sight behind.

"Did you see that?" demanded Tom.

"See what?"

He looked at me keenly, realizing that Jordan and I must have known all along.

"You think I'm pretty dumb, don't you?" he suggested. "Perhaps I am, but I have a—almost a second sight, sometimes, that tells me what to do. Maybe you don't believe that, but science—"

He paused. The immediate contingency overtook him, pulled him back from the edge of theoretical abyss.

"I've made a small investigation of this fellow," he continued. "I could have gone deeper if I'd known—"

"Do you mean you've been to a medium?" inquired Jordan humorously.

"What?" Confused, he stared at us as we laughed. "A medium?"

"About Gatsby."

"About Gatsby! No, I haven't. I said I'd been making a small investigation of his past."

"And you found he was an Oxford man," said Jordan helpfully.

"An Oxford man!" He was incredulous. "Like hell he is! He wears a pink suit."

"Nevertheless he's an Oxford man."

"Oxford, New Mexico," snorted Tom contemptuously, "or something like that."

"Listen, Tom. If you're such a snob, why did you invite him to lunch?" demanded Jordan crossly.

"Daisy invited him; she knew him before we were married—God knows where!"

We were all irritable now with the fading ale, and aware of it we drove for a while in silence. Then as Doctor T. J. Eckleburg's faded eyes came into sight down the road, I remembered Gatsby's caution about gasoline.

"We've got enough to get us to town," said Tom.

"But there's a garage right here," objected Jordan. "I don't want to get stalled in this baking heat."

Tom threw on both brakes impatiently, and we slid to an abrupt dusty stop under Wilson's sign. After a moment the proprietor emerged from the interior of his establishment and gazed hollow-eyed at the car.

"Let's have some gas!" cried Tom roughly. "What do you think we stopped for—to admire the view?"

"I'm sick," said Wilson without moving. "Been sick all day."

"What's the matter?"

"I'm all run down."

"Well, shall I help myself?" Tom demanded. "You sounded well enough on the phone."

With an effort Wilson left the shade and support of the doorway and, breathing hard, unscrewed the cap of the tank. In the sunlight his face was green.

"I didn't mean to interrupt your lunch," he said. "But I need money pretty bad, and I was wondering what you were going to do with your old car."

"How do you like this one?" inquired Tom. "I bought it last week."

"It's a nice yellow one," said Wilson, as he strained at the handle.

"Like to buy it?"

"Big chance," Wilson smiled faintly. "No, but I could make some money on the other."

"What do you want money for, all of a sudden?"

"I've been here too long. I want to get away. My wife and I want to go West."

"Your wife does," exclaimed Tom, startled.

"She's been talking about it for ten years." He rested for a moment against the pump, shading his eyes. "And now she's going whether she wants to or not. I'm going to get her away."

The coupé flashed by us with a flurry of dust and the flash of a waving hand.

"What do I owe you?" demanded Tom harshly.

"I just got wised up to something funny the last two days," remarked Wilson. "That's why I want to get away. That's why I been bothering you about the car."

"What do I owe you?"

"Dollar twenty."

The relentless beating heat was beginning to confuse me and I had a bad moment there before I realized that so far his suspicions hadn't alighted on Tom. He had discovered that Myrtle had some sort of life apart from him in another world, and the shock had made him physically sick. I stared at him and then at Tom, who had made a parallel discovery less than an hour before—and it occurred to me that there was no difference between men, in intelligence or race, so profound as the difference between the sick and the well. Wilson was so sick that he looked guilty, unforgivably guilty—as if he had just got some poor girl with child.

"I'll let you have that car," said Tom. "I'll send it over tomorrow afternoon."

That locality was always vaguely disquieting, even in the broad glare of afternoon, and now I turned my head as though I had been warned of something behind. Over the ash-heaps the giant eyes of Doctor T. J. Eckleburg kept their vigil, but I perceived, after a moment, that other eyes were regarding us with peculiar intensity from less than twenty feet away.

In one of the windows over the garage the curtains had been moved aside a little, and Myrtle Wilson was peering down at the car. So engrossed was she that she had no consciousness of being observed, and one emotion after another crept into her face like objects into a slowly developing picture. Her expression was curiously familiar—it was an expression I had often seen on women's faces, but on Myrtle Wilson's face it seemed purposeless and inexplicable until I realized that her eyes, wide with jealous terror, were fixed not on Tom, but on Jordan Baker, whom she took to be his wife.

There is no confusion like the confusion of a simple mind, and as we drove away Tom was feeling the hot whips of panic. His wife and his mistress, until an hour ago secure and inviolate, were slipping precipitately from his control. Instinct made him step on the accelerator with the double purpose of overtaking Daisy and leaving Wilson behind, and we sped along toward Astoria at fifty miles an hour, until, among the spidery girders of the elevated, we came in sight of the easygoing blue coupé.

"Those big movies around Fiftieth Street are cool," suggested Jordan. "I love New York on summer afternoons when everyone's away. There's something very sensuous about it—overripe, as if all sorts of funny fruits were going to fall into your hands."

The word "sensuous" had the effect of further disquieting Tom, but before he could invent a protest the coupé came to a stop, and Daisy signalled us to draw up alongside.

"Where are we going?" she cried.

"How about the movies?"

"It's so hot," she complained. "You go. We'll ride around and meet you after." With an effort her wit rose faintly. "We'll meet you on some corner. I'll be the man smoking two cigarettes."

"We can't argue about it here," Tom said impatiently, as a truck gave out a cursing whistle behind us. "You follow me to the south side of Central Park, in front of the Plaza."

Several times he turned his head and looked back for their car, and if the traffic delayed them he slowed up until they came into sight. I think he was afraid they would dart down a side-street and out of his life forever.

But they didn't. And we all took the less explicable step of engaging the parlour of a suite in the Plaza Hotel.

The prolonged and tumultuous argument that ended by herding us into that room eludes me, though I have a sharp physical memory that, in the course of it, my underwear kept climbing like a damp snake around my legs and intermittent beads of sweat raced cool across my back. The notion originated with Daisy's suggestion that we hire five bathrooms and take cold baths, and then assumed more tangible form as "a place to have a mint julep." Each of us said over and over that it was a "crazy idea"—we all talked at once to a baffled clerk and thought, or pretended to think, that we were being very funny...

The room was large and stifling, and, though it was already four o'clock, opening the windows admitted only a gust of hot shrubbery from the Park. Daisy went to the mirror and stood with her back to us, fixing her hair.

"It's a swell suite," whispered Jordan respectfully, and everyone laughed.

"Open another window," commanded Daisy, without turning around.

"There aren't any more."

"Well, we'd better telephone for an axe—"

"The thing to do is to forget about the heat," said Tom impatiently. "You make it ten times worse by crabbing about it."

He unrolled the bottle of whisky from the towel and put it on the table.

"Why not let her alone, old sport?" remarked Gatsby. "You're the one that wanted to come to town."

There was a moment of silence. The telephone book slipped from its nail and splashed to the floor, whereupon Jordan whispered, "Excuse me"—but this time no one laughed.

"I'll pick it up," I offered.

"I've got it." Gatsby examined the parted string, muttered "Hum!" in an interested way, and tossed the book on a chair.

"That's a great expression of yours, isn't it?" said Tom sharply.

"What is?"

"All this 'old sport' business. Where'd you pick that up?"

"Now see here, Tom," said Daisy, turning around from the mirror, "if you're going to make personal remarks I won't stay here a minute. Call up and order some ice for the mint julep."

As Tom took up the receiver the compressed heat exploded into sound and we were listening to the portentous chords of Mendelssohn's Wedding March from the ballroom below.

"Imagine marrying anybody in this heat!" cried Jordan dismally.

"Still—I was married in the middle of June," Daisy remembered. "Louisville in June! Somebody fainted. Who was it fainted, Tom?"

"Biloxi," he answered shortly.

"A man named Biloxi. 'Blocks' Biloxi, and he made boxes—that's a fact—and he was from Biloxi, Tennessee."

"They carried him into my house," appended Jordan, "because we lived just two doors from the church. And he stayed three weeks, until Daddy told him he had to get out. The day after he left Daddy died." After a moment she added. "There wasn't any connection."

"I used to know a Bill Biloxi from Memphis," I remarked.

"That was his cousin. I knew his whole family history before he left. He gave me an aluminium putter that I use today."

The music had died down as the ceremony began and now a long cheer floated in at the window, followed by intermittent cries of "Yea—ea—ea!" and finally by a burst of jazz as the dancing began.

"We're getting old," said Daisy. "If we were young we'd rise and dance."

"Remember Biloxi," Jordan warned her. "Where'd you know him, Tom?"

"Biloxi?" He concentrated with an effort. "I didn't know him. He was a friend of Daisy's."

"He was not," she denied. "I'd never seen him before. He came down in the private car."

"Well, he said he knew you. He said he was raised in Louisville. Asa Bird brought him around at the last minute and asked if we had room for him."

Jordan smiled.

"He was probably bumming his way home. He told me he was president of your class at Yale."

Tom and I looked at each other blankly.

"Bil*oxi*?"

"First place, we didn't have any president—"

Gatsby's foot beat a short, restless tattoo and Tom eyed him suddenly.

"By the way, Mr. Gatsby, I understand you're an Oxford man."

"Not exactly."

"Oh, yes, I understand you went to Oxford."

"Yes—I went there."

A pause. Then Tom's voice, incredulous and insulting:

"You must have gone there about the time Biloxi went to New Haven."

Another pause. A waiter knocked and came in with crushed mint and ice but the silence was unbroken by his "thank you" and the soft closing of the door. This tremendous detail was to be cleared up at last.

"I told you I went there," said Gatsby.

"I heard you, but I'd like to know when."

"It was in nineteen-nineteen, I only stayed five months. That's why I can't really call myself an Oxford man."

Tom glanced around to see if we mirrored his unbelief. But we were all looking at Gatsby.

"It was an opportunity they gave to some of the officers after the armistice," he continued. "We could go to any of the universities in England or France."

I wanted to get up and slap him on the back. I had one of those renewals of complete faith in him that I'd experienced before.

Daisy rose, smiling faintly, and went to the table.

"Open the whisky, Tom," she ordered, "and I'll make you a mint julep. Then you won't seem so stupid to yourself… Look at the mint!"

"Wait a minute," snapped Tom, "I want to ask Mr. Gatsby one more question."

"Go on," Gatsby said politely.

"What kind of a row are you trying to cause in my house anyhow?"

They were out in the open at last and Gatsby was content.

"He isn't causing a row," Daisy looked desperately from one to the other. "You're causing a row. Please have a little self-control."

"Self-control!" repeated Tom incredulously. "I suppose the latest thing is to sit back and let Mr. Nobody from Nowhere make love to your wife. Well, if that's the idea you can count me out… Nowadays people begin by sneering at family life and family institutions, and next they'll throw everything overboard and have intermarriage between black and white."

Flushed with his impassioned gibberish, he saw himself standing alone on the last barrier of civilization.

"We're all white here," murmured Jordan.

"I know I'm not very popular. I don't give big parties. I suppose you've got to make your house into a pigsty in order to have any friends—in the modern world."

Angry as I was, as we all were, I was tempted to laugh whenever he opened his mouth. The transition from libertine to prig was so complete.

"I've got something to tell *you*, old sport—" began Gatsby. But Daisy guessed at his intention.

"Please don't!" she interrupted helplessly. "Please let's all go home. Why don't we all go home?"

"That's a good idea," I got up. "Come on, Tom. Nobody wants a drink."

"I want to know what Mr. Gatsby has to tell me."

"Your wife doesn't love you," said Gatsby. "She's never loved you. She loves me."

"You must be crazy!" exclaimed Tom automatically.

Gatsby sprang to his feet, vivid with excitement.

"She never loved you, do you hear?" he cried. "She only married you because I was poor and she was tired of waiting for me. It was a terrible mistake, but in her heart she never loved anyone except me!"

At this point Jordan and I tried to go, but Tom and Gatsby insisted with competitive firmness that we remain—as though neither of them had anything to conceal and it would be a privilege to partake vicariously of their emotions.

"Sit down, Daisy," Tom's voice groped unsuccessfully for the paternal note. "What's been going on? I want to hear all about it."

"I told you what's been going on," said Gatsby. "Going on for five years—and you didn't know."

Tom turned to Daisy sharply.

"You've been seeing this fellow for five years?"

"Not seeing," said Gatsby. "No, we couldn't meet. But both of us loved each other all that time, old sport, and you didn't know. I used to laugh sometimes"—but there was no laughter in his eyes—"to think that you didn't know."

"Oh—that's all." Tom tapped his thick fingers together like a clergyman and leaned back in his chair.

"You're crazy!" he exploded. "I can't speak about what happened five years ago, because I didn't know Daisy then—and I'll be damned if I see how you got within a mile of her unless you brought the groceries to the back door. But all the rest of that's a God damned lie. Daisy loved me when she married me and she loves me now."

"No," said Gatsby, shaking his head.

"She does, though. The trouble is that sometimes she gets foolish ideas in her head and doesn't know what she's doing." He nodded sagely. "And what's more, I love Daisy too. Once in a while I go off on a spree and make a fool of myself, but I always come back, and in my heart I love her all the time."

"You're revolting," said Daisy. She turned to me, and her voice, dropping an octave lower, filled the room with thrilling scorn: "Do you know why we left Chicago? I'm surprised that they didn't treat you to the story of that little spree."

Gatsby walked over and stood beside her.

"Daisy, that's all over now," he said earnestly. "It doesn't matter any more. Just tell him the truth—that you never loved him—and it's all wiped out forever."

She looked at him blindly. "Why—how could I love him—possibly?"

"You never loved him."

She hesitated. Her eyes fell on Jordan and me with a sort of appeal, as though she realized at last what she was doing—and as though she had never, all along, intended doing anything at all. But it was done now. It was too late.

"I never loved him," she said, with perceptible reluctance.

"Not at Kapiolani?" demanded Tom suddenly.

"No."

From the ballroom beneath, muffled and suffocating chords were drifting up on hot waves of air.

"Not that day I carried you down from the Punch Bowl to keep your shoes dry?" There was a husky tenderness in his tone… "Daisy?"

"Please don't." Her voice was cold, but the rancour was gone from it. She looked at Gatsby. "There, Jay," she said—but her hand as she tried to light a cigarette was trembling. Suddenly she threw the cigarette and the burning match on the carpet.

"Oh, you want too much!" she cried to Gatsby. "I love you now—isn't that enough? I can't help what's past." She began to sob helplessly. "I did love him once—but I loved you too."

Gatsby's eyes opened and closed.

"You loved me *too*?" he repeated.

"Even that's a lie," said Tom savagely. "She didn't know you were alive. Why—there's things between Daisy and me that you'll never know, things that neither of us can ever forget."

The words seemed to bite physically into Gatsby.

"I want to speak to Daisy alone," he insisted. "She's all excited now—"

"Even alone I can't say I never loved Tom," she admitted in a pitiful voice. "It wouldn't be true."

"Of course it wouldn't," agreed Tom.

She turned to her husband.

"As if it mattered to you," she said.

"Of course it matters. I'm going to take better care of you from now on."

"You don't understand," said Gatsby, with a touch of panic. "You're not going to take care of her any more."

"I'm not?" Tom opened his eyes wide and laughed. He could afford to control himself now. "Why's that?"

"Daisy's leaving you."

"Nonsense."

"I am, though," she said with a visible effort.

"She's not leaving me!" Tom's words suddenly leaned down over Gatsby. "Certainly not for a common swindler who'd have to steal the ring he put on her finger."

"I won't stand this!" cried Daisy. "Oh, please let's get out."

"Who are you, anyhow?" broke out Tom. "You're one of that bunch that hangs around with Meyer Wolfshiem—that much I happen to know. I've made a little investigation into your affairs—and I'll carry it further tomorrow."

"You can suit yourself about that, old sport," said Gatsby steadily.

"I found out what your 'drugstores' were." He turned to us and spoke rapidly. "He and this Wolfshiem bought up a lot of side-street drugstores here and in Chicago and sold grain alcohol over the counter. That's one of his little stunts. I picked him for a bootlegger the first time I saw him, and I wasn't far wrong."

"What about it?" said Gatsby politely. "I guess your friend Walter Chase wasn't too proud to come in on it."

"And you left him in the lurch, didn't you? You let him go to jail for a month over in New Jersey. God! You ought to hear Walter on the subject of *you*."

"He came to us dead broke. He was very glad to pick up some money, old sport."

"Don't you call me 'old sport'!" cried Tom. Gatsby said nothing. "Walter could have you up on the betting laws too, but Wolfshiem scared him into shutting his mouth."

That unfamiliar yet recognizable look was back again in Gatsby's face.

"That drugstore business was just small change," continued Tom slowly, "but you've got something on now that Walter's afraid to tell me about."

I glanced at Daisy, who was staring terrified between Gatsby and her husband, and at Jordan, who had begun to balance an invisible but absorbing object on the tip of her chin. Then I turned back to Gatsby—and was startled at his expression. He looked—and this is said in all contempt for the babbled slander of his garden—as if he had "killed a man." For a moment the set of his face could be described in just that fantastic way.

It passed, and he began to talk excitedly to Daisy, denying everything, defending his name against accusations that had not been made. But with every word she was drawing further and further into herself, so he gave that up, and only the dead dream fought on as the afternoon slipped away, trying to touch what was no longer tangible, struggling unhappily, undespairingly, toward that lost voice across the room.

The voice begged again to go.

"*Please*, Tom! I can't stand this any more."

Her frightened eyes told that whatever intentions, whatever courage she had had, were definitely gone.

"You two start on home, Daisy," said Tom. "In Mr. Gatsby's car."

She looked at Tom, alarmed now, but he insisted with magnanimous scorn.

"Go on. He won't annoy you. I think he realizes that his presumptuous little flirtation is over."

They were gone, without a word, snapped out, made accidental, isolated, like ghosts, even from our pity.

After a moment Tom got up and began wrapping the unopened bottle of whisky in the towel.

"Want any of this stuff? Jordan?... Nick?"

I didn't answer.

"Nick?" He asked again.

"What?"

"Want any?"

"No... I just remembered that today's my birthday."

I was thirty. Before me stretched the portentous, menacing road of a new decade.

It was seven o'clock when we got into the coupé with him and started for Long Island. Tom talked incessantly, exulting and laughing, but his voice was as remote from Jordan and me as the foreign clamour on the sidewalk or the tumult of the elevated overhead. Human sympathy has its limits, and we were content to let all their tragic arguments fade with the city lights behind. Thirty—the promise of a decade of loneliness, a thinning list of single men to know, a thinning briefcase of enthusiasm, thinning hair. But there was Jordan beside me, who, unlike Daisy, was too wise ever to carry well-forgotten dreams from age to age. As we passed over the dark bridge her wan face fell lazily against my coat's shoulder and the formidable stroke of thirty died away with the reassuring pressure of her hand.

So we drove on toward death through the cooling twilight.

The young Greek, Michaelis, who ran the coffee joint beside the ash-heaps was the principal witness at the inquest. He had slept through the heat until after five, when he strolled over to the garage, and found George Wilson sick in his office—really sick, pale as his own pale hair and shaking all over. Michaelis advised him to go to bed, but Wilson refused, saying that he'd miss a lot of business if he did. While his neighbour was trying to persuade him a violent racket broke out overhead.

"I've got my wife locked in up there," explained Wilson calmly. "She's going to stay there till the day after tomorrow, and then we're going to move away."

Michaelis was astonished; they had been neighbours for four years, and Wilson had never seemed faintly capable of such a statement. Generally he was one of these worn-out men: when he wasn't working, he sat on a chair in the doorway and stared at the people and the cars that passed along the road. When anyone spoke to him he invariably laughed in an agreeable, colourless way. He was his wife's man and not his own.

So naturally Michaelis tried to find out what had happened, but Wilson wouldn't say a word—instead he began to throw curious, suspicious glances at his visitor and ask him what he'd been doing at certain times on certain days. Just as the latter was getting uneasy, some workmen came past the door bound for his restaurant, and Michaelis took the opportunity to get away, intending to come back later. But he didn't. He supposed he forgot to, that's all. When he came outside again, a little after seven, he was reminded of the conversation because he heard Mrs. Wilson's voice, loud and scolding, downstairs in the garage.

"Beat me!" he heard her cry. "Throw me down and beat me, you dirty little coward!"

A moment later she rushed out into the dusk, waving her hands and shouting—before he could move from his door the business was over.

The "death car" as the newspapers called it, didn't stop; it came out of the gathering darkness, wavered tragically for a moment, and then disappeared around the next bend. Mavro Michaelis wasn't even sure of its colour—he told the first policeman that it was light green. The other car, the one going toward New York, came to rest a hundred yards beyond, and its driver hurried back to where Myrtle Wilson, her life violently extinguished, knelt in the road and mingled her thick dark blood with the dust.

Michaelis and this man reached her first, but when they had torn open her shirtwaist, still damp with perspiration, they saw that her left breast was swinging loose like a flap, and there was no need to listen for the heart beneath. The mouth was wide open and ripped a little at the corners, as though she had choked a little in giving up the tremendous vitality she had stored so long.

We saw the three or four automobiles and the crowd when we were still some distance away.

"Wreck!" said Tom. "That's good. Wilson'll have a little business at last."

He slowed down, but still without any intention of stopping, until, as we came nearer, the hushed, intent faces of the people at the garage door made him automatically put on the brakes.

"We'll take a look," he said doubtfully, "just a look."

I became aware now of a hollow, wailing sound which issued incessantly from the garage, a sound which as we got out of the coupé and walked toward the door resolved itself into the words "Oh, my God!" uttered over and over in a gasping moan.

"There's some bad trouble here," said Tom excitedly.

He reached up on tiptoes and peered over a circle of heads into the garage, which was lit only by a yellow light in a swinging metal basket overhead. Then he made a harsh sound in his throat, and with a violent thrusting movement of his powerful arms pushed his way through.

The circle closed up again with a running murmur of expostulation; it was a minute before I could see anything at all. Then new arrivals deranged the line, and Jordan and I were pushed suddenly inside.

Myrtle Wilson's body, wrapped in a blanket, and then in another blanket, as though she suffered from a chill in the hot night, lay on a worktable by the wall, and Tom, with his back to us, was bending over it, motionless. Next to him stood a motorcycle policeman taking down names with much sweat and correction in a little book. At first I couldn't find the source of the high, groaning words that echoed clamorously through the bare garage—then I saw Wilson standing on the raised threshold of his office, swaying back and forth and holding to the doorposts with both hands. Some man was talking to him in a low voice and attempting, from time to time, to lay a hand on his shoulder, but Wilson neither heard nor saw. His eyes would drop slowly from the swinging light to the laden table by the wall, and then jerk back to the light again, and he gave out incessantly his high, horrible call:

"Oh, my Ga-od! Oh, my Ga-od! Oh, Ga-od! Oh, my Ga-od!"

Presently Tom lifted his head with a jerk and, after staring around the garage with glazed eyes, addressed a mumbled incoherent remark to the policeman.

"*M-a-v—*" the policeman was saying, "*—o—*"

"No, *r—*" corrected the man, "*M-a-v-r-o—*"

"Listen to me!" muttered Tom fiercely.

"*r—*" said the policeman, "*o—*"

"*g—*"

"*g—*" He looked up as Tom's broad hand fell sharply on his shoulder. "What you want, fella?"

"What happened?—that's what I want to know."

"Auto hit her. Ins'antly killed."

"Instantly killed," repeated Tom, staring.

"She ran out ina road. Son-of-a-bitch didn't even stopus car."

"There was two cars," said Michaelis, "one comin', one goin', see?"

"Going where?" asked the policeman keenly.

"One goin' each way. Well, she"—his hand rose toward the blankets but stopped halfway and fell to his side—"she ran out there an' the one comin' from N'York knock right into her, goin' thirty or forty miles an hour."

"What's the name of this place here?" demanded the officer.

"Hasn't got any name."

A pale well-dressed negro stepped near.

"It was a yellow car," he said, "big yellow car. New."

"See the accident?" asked the policeman.

"No, but the car passed me down the road, going faster'n forty. Going fifty, sixty."

"Come here and let's have your name. Look out now. I want to get his name."

Some words of this conversation must have reached Wilson, swaying in the office door, for suddenly a new theme found voice among his grasping cries:

"You don't have to tell me what kind of car it was! I know what kind of car it was!"

Watching Tom, I saw the wad of muscle back of his shoulder tighten under his coat. He walked quickly over to Wilson and, standing in front of him, seized him firmly by the upper arms.

"You've got to pull yourself together," he said with soothing gruffness.

Wilson's eyes fell upon Tom; he started up on his tiptoes and then would have collapsed to his knees had not Tom held him upright.

"Listen," said Tom, shaking him a little. "I just got here a minute ago, from New York. I was bringing you that coupé we've been talking about. That yellow car I was driving this afternoon wasn't mine—do you hear? I haven't seen it all afternoon."

Only the negro and I were near enough to hear what he said, but the policeman caught something in the tone and looked over with truculent eyes.

"What's all that?" he demanded.

"I'm a friend of his." Tom turned his head but kept his hands firm on Wilson's body. "He says he knows the car that did it... It was a yellow car."

Some dim impulse moved the policeman to look suspiciously at Tom.

"And what colour's your car?"

"It's a blue car, a coupé."

"We've come straight from New York," I said.

Someone who had been driving a little behind us confirmed this, and the policeman turned away.

"Now, if you'll let me have that name again correct—"

Picking up Wilson like a doll, Tom carried him into the office, set him down in a chair, and came back.

"If somebody'll come here and sit with him," he snapped authoritatively. He watched while the two men standing closest glanced at each other and went unwillingly into the room. Then Tom shut the door on them and came down the single step, his eyes avoiding the table. As he passed close to me he whispered: "Let's get out."

Self-consciously, with his authoritative arms breaking the way, we pushed through the still gathering crowd, passing a hurried doctor, case in hand, who had been sent for in wild hope half an hour ago.

Tom drove slowly until we were beyond the bend—then his foot came down hard, and the coupé raced along through the night. In a little while I heard a low husky sob, and saw that the tears were overflowing down his face.

"The God damned coward!" he whimpered. "He didn't even stop his car."

The Buchanans' house floated suddenly toward us through the dark rustling trees. Tom stopped beside the porch and looked up at the second floor, where two windows bloomed with light among the vines.

"Daisy's home," he said. As we got out of the car he glanced at me and frowned slightly.

"I ought to have dropped you in West Egg, Nick. There's nothing we can do tonight."

A change had come over him, and he spoke gravely, and with decision. As we walked across the moonlight gravel to the porch he disposed of the situation in a few brisk phrases.

"I'll telephone for a taxi to take you home, and while you're waiting you and Jordan better go in the kitchen and have them get you some supper—if you want any." He opened the door. "Come in."

"No, thanks. But I'd be glad if you'd order me the taxi. I'll wait outside."

Jordan put her hand on my arm.

"Won't you come in, Nick?"

"No, thanks."

I was feeling a little sick and I wanted to be alone. But Jordan lingered for a moment more.

"It's only half-past nine," she said.

I'd be damned if I'd go in; I'd had enough of all of them for one day, and suddenly that included Jordan too. She must have seen something of this in my expression, for she turned abruptly away and ran up the porch steps into the house. I sat down for a few minutes with my head in my hands, until I heard the phone taken up inside and the butler's voice calling a taxi. Then I walked slowly down the drive away from the house, intending to wait by the gate.

I hadn't gone twenty yards when I heard my name and Gatsby stepped from between two bushes into the path. I must have felt pretty weird by that time, because I could think of nothing except the luminosity of his pink suit under the moon.

"What are you doing?" I inquired.

"Just standing here, old sport."

Somehow, that seemed a despicable occupation. For all I knew he was going to rob the house in a moment; I wouldn't have been surprised to see sinister faces, the faces of "Wolfshiem's people," behind him in the dark shrubbery.

"Did you see any trouble on the road?" he asked after a minute.

"Yes."

He hesitated.

"Was she killed?"

"Yes."

"I thought so; I told Daisy I thought so. It's better that the shock should all come at once. She stood it pretty well."

He spoke as if Daisy's reaction was the only thing that mattered.

"I got to West Egg by a side road," he went on, "and left the car in my garage. I don't think anybody saw us, but of course I can't be sure."

I disliked him so much by this time that I didn't find it necessary to tell him he was wrong.

"Who was the woman?" he inquired.

"Her name was Wilson. Her husband owns the garage. How the devil did it happen?"

"Well, I tried to swing the wheel—" He broke off, and suddenly I guessed at the truth.

"Was Daisy driving?"

"Yes," he said after a moment, "but of course I'll say I was. You see, when we left New York she was very nervous and she thought it would steady her to drive—and this woman rushed out at us just as we were passing a car coming the other way. It all happened in a minute, but it seemed to me that she wanted to speak to us, thought we were somebody she knew. Well, first Daisy turned away from the woman toward the other car, and then she lost her nerve and turned back. The second my hand reached the wheel I felt the shock—it must have killed her instantly."

"It ripped her open—"

"Don't tell me, old sport." He winced. "Anyhow—Daisy stepped on it. I tried to make her stop, but she couldn't, so I pulled on the emergency brake. Then she fell over into my lap and I drove on.

"She'll be all right tomorrow," he said presently. "I'm just going to wait here and see if he tries to bother her about that unpleasantness this afternoon. She's locked herself into her room, and if he tries any brutality she's going to turn the light out and on again."

"He won't touch her," I said. "He's not thinking about her."

"I don't trust him, old sport."

"How long are you going to wait?"

"All night, if necessary. Anyhow, till they all go to bed."

A new point of view occurred to me. Suppose Tom found out that Daisy had been driving. He might think he saw a connection in it—he might think anything. I looked at the house; there were two or three bright windows downstairs and the pink glow from Daisy's room on the ground floor.

"You wait here," I said. "I'll see if there's any sign of a commotion."

I walked back along the border of the lawn, traversed the gravel softly, and tiptoed up the veranda steps. The drawing-room curtains were open, and I saw that the room was empty. Crossing the porch where we had dined that June night three months before, I came to a small rectangle of light which I guessed was the pantry window. The blind was drawn, but I found a rift at the sill.

Daisy and Tom were sitting opposite each other at the kitchen table, with a plate of cold fried chicken between them, and two bottles of ale. He was talking intently across the table at her, and in his earnestness his hand had fallen upon and covered her own. Once in a while she looked up at him and nodded in agreement.

They weren't happy, and neither of them had touched the chicken or the ale—and yet they weren't unhappy either. There was an unmistakable air of natural intimacy about the picture, and anybody would have said that they were conspiring together.

As I tiptoed from the porch I heard my taxi feeling its way along the dark road toward the house. Gatsby was waiting where I had left him in the drive.

"Is it all quiet up there?" he asked anxiously.

"Yes, it's all quiet." I hesitated. "You'd better come home and get some sleep."

He shook his head.

"I want to wait here till Daisy goes to bed. Good night, old sport."

He put his hands in his coat pockets and turned back eagerly to his scrutiny of the house, as though my presence marred the sacredness of the vigil. So I walked away and left him standing there in the moonlight—watching over nothing.

VIII

I couldn't sleep all night; a foghorn was groaning incessantly on the Sound, and I tossed half-sick between grotesque reality and savage, frightening dreams. Toward dawn I heard a taxi go up Gatsby's drive, and immediately I jumped out of bed and began to dress—I felt that I had something to tell him, something to warn him about, and morning would be too late.

Crossing his lawn, I saw that his front door was still open and he was leaning against a table in the hall, heavy with dejection or sleep.

"Nothing happened," he said wanly. "I waited, and about four o'clock she came to the window and stood there for a minute and then turned out the light."

His house had never seemed so enormous to me as it did that night when we hunted through the great rooms for cigarettes. We pushed aside curtains that were like pavilions, and felt over innumerable feet of dark wall for electric light switches—once I tumbled with a sort of splash upon the keys of a ghostly piano. There was an inexplicable amount of dust everywhere, and the rooms were musty, as though they hadn't been aired for many days. I found the humidor on an unfamiliar table, with two stale, dry cigarettes inside. Throwing open the French windows of the drawing-room, we sat smoking out into the darkness.

"You ought to go away," I said. "It's pretty certain they'll trace your car."

"Go away *now*, old sport?"

"Go to Atlantic City for a week, or up to Montreal."

He wouldn't consider it. He couldn't possibly leave Daisy until he knew what she was going to do. He was clutching at some last hope and I couldn't bear to shake him free.

It was this night that he told me the strange story of his youth with Dan Cody—told it to me because "Jay Gatsby" had broken up like glass against Tom's hard malice, and the long secret extravaganza was played out. I think that he would have acknowledged anything now, without reserve, but he wanted to talk about Daisy.

She was the first "nice" girl he had ever known. In various unrevealed capacities he had come in contact with such people, but always with indiscernible barbed wire between. He found her excitingly desirable. He went to her house, at first with other officers from Camp Taylor, then alone. It amazed him—he had never been in such a beautiful house before. But what gave it an air of breathless intensity, was that Daisy lived there—it was as casual a thing to her as his tent out at camp was to him. There was a ripe mystery about it, a hint of bedrooms upstairs more beautiful and cool than other bedrooms, of gay and radiant activities taking place through its corridors, and of romances that were not musty and laid away already in lavender but fresh and breathing and redolent of this year's shining motorcars and of dances whose flowers were scarcely withered. It excited him, too, that many men had already loved Daisy—it increased her value in his eyes. He felt their presence all about the house, pervading the air with the shades and echoes of still vibrant emotions.

But he knew that he was in Daisy's house by a colossal accident. However glorious might be his future as Jay Gatsby, he was at present a penniless young man without a past, and at any moment the invisible cloak of his uniform might slip from his shoulders. So he made the most of his time. He took what he could get, ravenously and unscrupulously—eventually he took Daisy one still October night, took her because he had no real right to touch her hand.

He might have despised himself, for he had certainly taken her under false pretences. I don't mean that he had traded on his phantom millions, but he had deliberately given Daisy a sense of security; he let her believe that he was a person from much the same strata as herself—that he was fully able to take care of her. As a matter of fact, he had no such facilities—he had no comfortable family standing behind him, and he was liable at the whim of an impersonal government to be blown anywhere about the world.

But he didn't despise himself and it didn't turn out as he had imagined. He had intended, probably, to take what he could and go—but now he found that he had committed himself to the following of a grail. He knew that Daisy was extraordinary, but he didn't realize just how extraordinary a "nice" girl could be. She vanished into her rich house, into her rich, full life, leaving Gatsby—nothing. He felt married to her, that was all.

When they met again, two days later, it was Gatsby who was breathless, who was, somehow, betrayed. Her porch was bright with the bought luxury of starshine; the wicker of the settee squeaked fashionably as she turned toward him and he kissed her curious and lovely mouth. She had caught a cold, and it made her voice huskier and more charming than ever, and Gatsby was overwhelmingly aware of the youth and mystery that wealth imprisons and preserves, of the freshness of many clothes, and of Daisy, gleaming like silver, safe and proud above the hot struggles of the poor.

"I can't describe to you how surprised I was to find out I loved her, old sport. I even hoped for a while that she'd throw me over, but she didn't, because she was in love with me too. She thought I knew a lot because I knew different things from her... Well, there I was, way off my ambitions, getting deeper in love every minute, and all of a sudden I didn't care. What was the use of doing great things if I could have a better time telling her what I was going to do?"

On the last afternoon before he went abroad, he sat with Daisy in his arms for a long, silent time. It was a cold fall day, with fire in the room and her cheeks flushed. Now and then she moved and he changed his arm a little, and once he kissed her dark shining hair. The afternoon had made them tranquil for a while, as if to give them a deep memory for the long parting the next day promised. They had never been closer in their month of love, nor communicated more profoundly one with another, than when she brushed silent lips against his coat's shoulder or when he touched the end of her fingers, gently, as though she were asleep.

He did extraordinarily well in the war. He was a captain before he went to the front, and following the Argonne battles he got his majority and the command of the divisional machine-guns. After the armistice he tried frantically to get home, but some complication or misunderstanding sent him to Oxford instead. He was worried now—there was a quality of nervous despair in Daisy's letters. She didn't see why he couldn't come. She was feeling the pressure of the world outside, and she wanted to see him and feel his presence beside her and be reassured that she was doing the right thing after all.

For Daisy was young and her artificial world was redolent of orchids and pleasant, cheerful snobbery and orchestras which set the rhythm of the year, summing up the sadness and suggestiveness of life in new tunes. All night the saxophones wailed the hopeless comment of the "Beale Street Blues" while a hundred pairs of golden and silver slippers shuffled the shining dust. At the grey tea hour there were always rooms that throbbed incessantly with this low, sweet fever, while fresh faces drifted here and there like rose petals blown by the sad horns around the floor.

Through this twilight universe Daisy began to move again with the season; suddenly she was again keeping half a dozen dates a day with half a dozen men, and drowsing asleep at dawn with the beads and chiffon of an evening-dress tangled among dying orchids on the floor beside her bed. And all the time something within her was crying for a decision. She wanted her life shaped now, immediately—and the decision must be made by some force—of love, of money, of unquestionable practicality—that was close at hand.

That force took shape in the middle of spring with the arrival of Tom Buchanan. There was a wholesome bulkiness about his person and his position, and Daisy was flattered. Doubtless there was a certain struggle and a certain relief. The letter reached Gatsby while he was still at Oxford.

It was dawn now on Long Island and we went about opening the rest of the windows downstairs, filling the house with grey-turning, gold-turning light. The shadow of a tree fell abruptly across the dew and ghostly birds began to sing among the blue leaves. There was a slow, pleasant movement in the air, scarcely a wind, promising a cool, lovely day.

"I don't think she ever loved him." Gatsby turned around from a window and looked at me challengingly. "You must remember, old sport, she was very excited this afternoon. He told her those things in a way that frightened her—that made it look as if I was some kind of cheap sharper. And the result was she hardly knew what she was saying."

He sat down gloomily.

"Of course she might have loved him just for a minute, when they were first married—and loved me more even then, do you see?"

Suddenly he came out with a curious remark.

"In any case," he said, "it was just personal."

What could you make of that, except to suspect some intensity in his conception of the affair that couldn't be measured?

He came back from France when Tom and Daisy were still on their wedding trip, and made a miserable but irresistible journey to Louisville on the last of his army pay. He stayed there a week, walking the streets where their footsteps had clicked together through the November night and revisiting the out-of-the-way places to which they had driven in her white car. Just as Daisy's house had always seemed to him more mysterious and gay than other houses, so his idea of the city itself, even though she was gone from it, was pervaded with a melancholy beauty.

He left feeling that if he had searched harder, he might have found her—that he was leaving her behind. The day-coach—he was penniless now—was hot. He went out to the open vestibule and sat down on a folding-chair, and the station slid away and the backs of unfamiliar buildings moved by. Then out into the spring fields, where a yellow trolley raced them for a minute with people in it who might once have seen the pale magic of her face along the casual street.

The track curved and now it was going away from the sun, which, as it sank lower, seemed to spread itself in benediction over the vanishing city where she had drawn her breath. He stretched out his hand desperately as if to snatch only a wisp of air, to save a fragment of the spot that she had made lovely for him. But it was all going by too fast now for his blurred eyes and he knew that he had lost that part of it, the freshest and the best, forever.

It was nine o'clock when we finished breakfast and went out on the porch. The night had made a sharp difference in the weather and there was an autumn flavour in the air. The gardener, the last one of Gatsby's former servants, came to the foot of the steps.

"I'm going to drain the pool today, Mr. Gatsby. Leaves'll start falling pretty soon, and then there's always trouble with the pipes."

"Don't do it today," Gatsby answered. He turned to me apologetically. "You know, old sport, I've never used that pool all summer?"

I looked at my watch and stood up.

"Twelve minutes to my train."

I didn't want to go to the city. I wasn't worth a decent stroke of work, but it was more than that—I didn't want to leave Gatsby. I missed that train, and then another, before I could get myself away.

"I'll call you up," I said finally.

"Do, old sport."

"I'll call you about noon."

We walked slowly down the steps.

"I suppose Daisy'll call too." He looked at me anxiously, as if he hoped I'd corroborate this.

"I suppose so."

"Well, goodbye."

We shook hands and I started away. Just before I reached the hedge I remembered something and turned around.

"They're a rotten crowd," I shouted across the lawn. "You're worth the whole damn bunch put together."

I've always been glad I said that. It was the only compliment I ever gave him, because I disapproved of him from beginning to end. First he nodded politely, and then his face broke into that radiant and understanding smile, as if we'd been in ecstatic cahoots on that fact all the time. His gorgeous pink rag of a suit made a bright spot of colour against the white steps, and I thought of the night when I first came to his ancestral home, three months before. The lawn and drive had been crowded with the faces of those who guessed at his corruption—and he had stood on those steps, concealing his incorruptible dream, as he waved them goodbye.

I thanked him for his hospitality. We were always thanking him for that—I and the others.

"Goodbye," I called. "I enjoyed breakfast, Gatsby."

Up in the city, I tried for a while to list the quotations on an interminable amount of stock, then I fell asleep in my swivel-chair. Just before noon the phone woke me, and I started up with sweat breaking out on my forehead. It was Jordan Baker; she often called me up at this hour because the uncertainty of her own movements between hotels and clubs and private houses made her hard to find in any other way. Usually her voice came over the wire as something fresh and cool, as if a divot from a green golf-links had come sailing in at the office window, but this morning it seemed harsh and dry.

"I've left Daisy's house," she said. "I'm at Hempstead, and I'm going down to Southampton this afternoon."

Probably it had been tactful to leave Daisy's house, but the act annoyed me, and her next remark made me rigid.

"You weren't so nice to me last night."

"How could it have mattered then?"

Silence for a moment. Then:

"However—I want to see you."

"I want to see you, too."

"Suppose I don't go to Southampton, and come into town this afternoon?"

"No—I don't think this afternoon."

"Very well."

"It's impossible this afternoon. Various—"

We talked like that for a while, and then abruptly we weren't talking any longer. I don't know which of us hung up with a sharp click, but I know I didn't care. I couldn't have talked to her across a tea-table that day if I never talked to her again in this world.

I called Gatsby's house a few minutes later, but the line was busy. I tried four times; finally an exasperated central told me the wire was being kept open for long distance from Detroit. Taking out my timetable, I drew a small circle around the three-fifty train. Then I leaned back in my chair and tried to think. It was just noon.

When I passed the ash-heaps on the train that morning I had crossed deliberately to the other side of the car. I supposed there'd be a curious crowd around there all day with little boys searching for dark spots in the dust, and some garrulous man telling over and over what had happened, until it became less and less real even to him and he could tell it no longer, and Myrtle Wilson's tragic achievement was forgotten. Now I want to go back a little and tell what happened at the garage after we left there the night before.

They had difficulty in locating the sister, Catherine. She must have broken her rule against drinking that night, for when she arrived she was stupid with liquor and unable to understand that the ambulance had already gone to Flushing. When they convinced her of this, she immediately fainted, as if that was the intolerable part of the affair. Someone, kind or curious, took her in his car and drove her in the wake of her sister's body.

Until long after midnight a changing crowd lapped up against the front of the garage, while George Wilson rocked himself back and forth on the couch inside. For a while the door of the office was open, and everyone who came into the garage glanced irresistibly through it. Finally someone said it was a shame, and closed the door. Michaelis and several other men were with him; first, four or five men, later two or three men. Still later Michaelis had to ask the last stranger to wait there fifteen minutes longer, while he went back to his own place and made a pot of coffee. After that, he stayed there alone with Wilson until dawn.

About three o'clock the quality of Wilson's incoherent muttering changed—he grew quieter and began to talk about the yellow car. He announced that he had a way of finding out whom the yellow car belonged to, and then he blurted out that a couple of months ago his wife had come from the city with her face bruised and her nose swollen.

But when he heard himself say this, he flinched and began to cry "Oh, my God!" again in his groaning voice. Michaelis made a clumsy attempt to distract him.

"How long have you been married, George? Come on there, try and sit still a minute, and answer my question. How long have you been married?"

"Twelve years."

"Ever had any children? Come on, George, sit still—I asked you a question. Did you ever have any children?"

The hard brown beetles kept thudding against the dull light, and whenever Michaelis heard a car go tearing along the road outside it sounded to him like the car that hadn't stopped a few hours before. He didn't like to go into the garage, because the work bench was stained where the body had been lying, so he moved uncomfortably around the office—he knew every object in it before morning—and from time to time sat down beside Wilson trying to keep him more quiet.

"Have you got a church you go to sometimes, George? Maybe even if you haven't been there for a long time? Maybe I could call up the church and get a priest to come over and he could talk to you, see?"

"Don't belong to any."

"You ought to have a church, George, for times like this. You must have gone to church once. Didn't you get married in a church? Listen, George, listen to me. Didn't you get married in a church?"

"That was a long time ago."

The effort of answering broke the rhythm of his rocking—for a moment he was silent. Then the same half-knowing, half-bewildered look came back into his faded eyes.

"Look in the drawer there," he said, pointing at the desk.

"Which drawer?"

"That drawer—that one."

Michaelis opened the drawer nearest his hand. There was nothing in it but a small, expensive dog-leash, made of leather and braided silver. It was apparently new.

"This?" he inquired, holding it up.

Wilson stared and nodded.

"I found it yesterday afternoon. She tried to tell me about it, but I knew it was something funny."

"You mean your wife bought it?"

"She had it wrapped in tissue paper on her bureau."

Michaelis didn't see anything odd in that, and he gave Wilson a dozen reasons why his wife might have bought the dog-leash. But conceivably Wilson had heard some of these same explanations before, from Myrtle, because he began saying "Oh, my God!" again in a whisper—his comforter left several explanations in the air.

"Then he killed her," said Wilson. His mouth dropped open suddenly.

"Who did?"

"I have a way of finding out."

"You're morbid, George," said his friend. "This has been a strain to you and you don't know what you're saying. You'd better try and sit quiet till morning."

"He murdered her."

"It was an accident, George."

Wilson shook his head. His eyes narrowed and his mouth widened slightly with the ghost of a superior "Hm!"

"I know," he said definitely. "I'm one of these trusting fellas and I don't think any harm to *no*body, but when I get to know a thing I know it. It was the man in that car. She ran out to speak to him and he wouldn't stop."

Michaelis had seen this too, but it hadn't occurred to him that there was any special significance in it. He believed that Mrs. Wilson had been running away from her husband, rather than trying to stop any particular car.

"How could she of been like that?"

"She's a deep one," said Wilson, as if that answered the question. "Ah-h-h—"

He began to rock again, and Michaelis stood twisting the leash in his hand.

"Maybe you got some friend that I could telephone for, George?"

This was a forlorn hope—he was almost sure that Wilson had no friend: there was not enough of him for his wife. He was glad a little later when he noticed a change in the room, a blue quickening by the window, and realized that dawn wasn't far off. About five o'clock it was blue enough outside to snap off the light.

Wilson's glazed eyes turned out to the ash-heaps, where small grey clouds took on fantastic shapes and scurried here and there in the faint dawn wind.

"I spoke to her," he muttered, after a long silence. "I told her she might fool me but she couldn't fool God. I took her to the window"—with an effort he got up and walked to the rear window and leaned with his face pressed against it—"and I said 'God knows what you've been doing, everything you've been doing. You may fool me, but you can't fool God!'"

Standing behind him, Michaelis saw with a shock that he was looking at the eyes of Doctor T. J. Eckleburg, which had just emerged, pale and enormous, from the dissolving night.

"God sees everything," repeated Wilson.

"That's an advertisement," Michaelis assured him. Something made him turn away from the window and look back into the room. But Wilson stood there a long time, his face close to the window pane, nodding into the twilight.

By six o'clock Michaelis was worn out, and grateful for the sound of a car stopping outside. It was one of the watchers of the night before who had promised to come back, so he cooked breakfast for three, which he and the other man ate together. Wilson was quieter now, and Michaelis went home to sleep; when he awoke four hours later and hurried back to the garage, Wilson was gone.

His movements—he was on foot all the time—were afterward traced to Port Roosevelt and then to Gad's Hill, where he bought a sandwich that he didn't eat, and a cup of coffee. He must have been tired and walking slowly, for he didn't reach Gad's Hill until noon. Thus far there was no difficulty in accounting for his time—there were boys who had seen a man "acting sort of crazy," and motorists at whom he stared oddly from the side of the road. Then for three hours he disappeared from view. The police, on the strength of what he said to Michaelis, that he "had a way of finding out," supposed that he spent that time going from garage to garage thereabout, inquiring for a yellow car. On the other hand, no garage man who had seen him ever came forward, and perhaps he had an easier, surer way of finding out what he wanted to know. By half-past two he was in West Egg, where he asked someone the way to Gatsby's house. So by that time he knew Gatsby's name.

At two o'clock Gatsby put on his bathing-suit and left word with the butler that if anyone phoned word was to be brought to him at the pool. He stopped at the garage for a pneumatic mattress that had amused his guests during the summer, and the chauffeur helped him to pump it up. Then he gave instructions that the open car wasn't to be taken out under any circumstances—and this was strange, because the front right fender needed repair.

Gatsby shouldered the mattress and started for the pool. Once he stopped and shifted it a little, and the chauffeur asked him if he needed help, but he shook his head and in a moment disappeared among the yellowing trees.

No telephone message arrived, but the butler went without his sleep and waited for it until four o'clock—until long after there was anyone to give it to if it came. I have an idea that Gatsby himself didn't believe it would come, and perhaps he no longer cared. If that was true he must have felt that he had lost the old warm world, paid a high price for living too long with a single dream. He must have looked up at an unfamiliar sky through frightening leaves and shivered as he found what a grotesque thing a rose is and how raw the sunlight was upon the scarcely created grass. A new world, material without being real, where poor ghosts, breathing dreams like air, drifted fortuitously about… like that ashen, fantastic figure gliding toward him through the amorphous trees.

The chauffeur—he was one of Wolfshiem's protégés—heard the shots—afterwards he could only say that he hadn't thought anything much about them. I drove from the station directly to Gatsby's house and my rushing anxiously up the front steps was the first thing that alarmed anyone. But they knew then, I firmly believe. With scarcely a word said, four of us, the chauffeur, butler, gardener, and I hurried down to the pool.

There was a faint, barely perceptible movement of the water as the fresh flow from one end urged its way toward the drain at the other. With little ripples that were hardly the shadows of waves, the laden mattress moved irregularly down the pool. A small gust of wind that scarcely corrugated the surface was enough to disturb its accidental course with its accidental burden. The touch of a cluster of leaves revolved it slowly, tracing, like the leg of transit, a thin red circle in the water.

It was after we started with Gatsby toward the house that the gardener saw Wilson's body a little way off in the grass, and the holocaust was complete.

IX

After two years I remember the rest of that day, and that night and the next day, only as an endless drill of police and photographers and newspaper men in and out of Gatsby's front door. A rope stretched across the main gate and a policeman by it kept out the curious, but little boys soon discovered that they could enter through my yard, and there were always a few of them clustered open-mouthed about the pool. Someone with a positive manner, perhaps a detective, used the expression "madman" as he bent over Wilson's body that afternoon, and the adventitious authority of his voice set the key for the newspaper reports next morning.

Most of those reports were a nightmare—grotesque, circumstantial, eager, and untrue. When Michaelis's testimony at the inquest brought to light Wilson's suspicions of his wife I thought the whole tale would shortly be served up in racy pasquinade—but Catherine, who might have said anything, didn't say a word. She showed a surprising amount of character about it too—looked at the coroner with determined eyes under that corrected brow of hers, and swore that her sister had never seen Gatsby, that her sister was completely happy with her husband, that her sister had been into no mischief whatever. She convinced herself of it, and cried into her handkerchief, as if the very suggestion was more than she could endure. So Wilson was reduced to a man "deranged by grief" in order that the case might remain in its simplest form. And it rested there.

But all this part of it seemed remote and unessential. I found myself on Gatsby's side, and alone. From the moment I telephoned news of the catastrophe to West Egg village, every surmise about him, and every practical question, was referred to me. At first I was surprised and confused; then, as he lay in his house and didn't move or breathe or speak, hour upon hour, it grew upon me that I was responsible, because no one else was interested—interested, I mean, with that intense personal interest to which everyone has some vague right at the end.

I called up Daisy half an hour after we found him, called her instinctively and without hesitation. But she and Tom had gone away early that afternoon, and taken baggage with them.

"Left no address?"

"No."

"Say when they'd be back?"

"No."

"Any idea where they are? How I could reach them?"

"I don't know. Can't say."

I wanted to get somebody for him. I wanted to go into the room where he lay and reassure him: "I'll get somebody for you, Gatsby. Don't worry. Just trust me and I'll get somebody for you—"

Meyer Wolfshiem's name wasn't in the phone book. The butler gave me his office address on Broadway, and I called Information, but by the time I had the number it was long after five, and no one answered the phone.

"Will you ring again?"

"I've rung three times."

"It's very important."

"Sorry. I'm afraid no one's there."

I went back to the drawing-room and thought for an instant that they were chance visitors, all these official people who suddenly filled it. But, though they drew back the sheet and looked at Gatsby with shocked eyes, his protest continued in my brain:

"Look here, old sport, you've got to get somebody for me. You've got to try hard. I can't go through this alone."

Someone started to ask me questions, but I broke away and going upstairs looked hastily through the unlocked parts of his desk—he'd never told me definitely that his parents were dead. But there was nothing—only the picture of Dan Cody, a token of forgotten violence, staring down from the wall.

Next morning I sent the butler to New York with a letter to Wolfshiem, which asked for information and urged him to come out on the next train. That request seemed superfluous when I wrote it. I was sure he'd start when he saw the newspapers, just as I was sure there'd be a wire from Daisy before noon—but neither a wire nor Mr. Wolfshiem arrived; no one arrived except more police and photographers and newspaper men. When the butler brought back

Wolfshiem's answer I began to have a feeling of defiance, of scornful solidarity between Gatsby and me against them all.

> Dear Mr. Carraway. This has been one of the most terrible shocks of my life to me I hardly can believe it that it is true at all. Such a mad act as that man did should make us all think. I cannot come down now as I am tied up in some very important business and cannot get mixed up in this thing now. If there is anything I can do a little later let me know in a letter by Edgar. I hardly know where I am when I hear about a thing like this and am completely knocked down and out.
>
> Yours truly
Meyer Wolfshiem

and then hasty addenda beneath:

> Let me know about the funeral etc do not know his family at all.

When the phone rang that afternoon and Long Distance said Chicago was calling I thought this would be Daisy at last. But the connection came through as a man's voice, very thin and far away.

"This is Slagle speaking..."

"Yes?" The name was unfamiliar.

"Hell of a note, isn't it? Get my wire?"

"There haven't been any wires."

"Young Parke's in trouble," he said rapidly. "They picked him up when he handed the bonds over the counter. They got a circular from New York giving 'em the numbers just five minutes before. What d'you know about that, hey? You never can tell in these hick towns—"

"Hello!" I interrupted breathlessly. "Look here—this isn't Mr. Gatsby. Mr. Gatsby's dead."

There was a long silence on the other end of the wire, followed by an exclamation... then a quick squawk as the connection was broken.

I think it was on the third day that a telegram signed Henry C. Gatz arrived from a town in Minnesota. It said only that the sender was leaving immediately and to postpone the funeral until he came.

It was Gatsby's father, a solemn old man, very helpless and dismayed, bundled up in a long cheap ulster against the warm September day. His eyes leaked continuously with excitement, and when I took the bag and umbrella from his hands he began to pull so incessantly at his sparse grey beard that I had difficulty in getting off his coat. He was on the point of collapse, so I took him into the music-room and made him sit down while I sent for something to eat. But he wouldn't eat, and the glass of milk spilled from his trembling hand.

"I saw it in the Chicago newspaper," he said. "It was all in the Chicago newspaper. I started right away."

"I didn't know how to reach you."

His eyes, seeing nothing, moved ceaselessly about the room.

"It was a madman," he said. "He must have been mad."

"Wouldn't you like some coffee?" I urged him.

"I don't want anything. I'm all right now, Mr.—"

"Carraway."

"Well, I'm all right now. Where have they got Jimmy?"

I took him into the drawing-room, where his son lay, and left him there. Some little boys had come up on the steps and were looking into the hall; when I told them who had arrived, they went reluctantly away.

After a little while Mr. Gatz opened the door and came out, his mouth ajar, his face flushed slightly, his eyes leaking isolated and unpunctual tears. He had reached an age where death no longer has the quality of ghastly surprise, and when he looked around him now for the first time and saw the height and splendour of the hall and the great rooms opening out from it into other rooms, his grief began to be mixed with an awed pride. I helped him to a bedroom upstairs; while he took off his coat and vest I told him that all arrangements had been deferred until he came.

"I didn't know what you'd want, Mr. Gatsby—"

"Gatz is my name."

"—Mr. Gatz. I thought you might want to take the body West."

He shook his head.

"Jimmy always liked it better down East. He rose up to his position in the East. Were you a friend of my boy's, Mr.—?"

"We were close friends."

"He had a big future before him, you know. He was only a young man, but he had a lot of brain power here."

He touched his head impressively, and I nodded.

"If he'd of lived, he'd of been a great man. A man like James J. Hill. He'd of helped build up the country."

"That's true," I said, uncomfortably.

He fumbled at the embroidered coverlet, trying to take it from the bed, and lay down stiffly—was instantly asleep.

That night an obviously frightened person called up, and demanded to know who I was before he would give his name.

"This is Mr. Carraway," I said.

"Oh!" He sounded relieved. "This is Klipspringer."

I was relieved too, for that seemed to promise another friend at Gatsby's grave. I didn't want it to be in the papers and draw a sightseeing crowd, so I'd been calling up a few people myself. They were hard to find.

"The funeral's tomorrow," I said. "Three o'clock, here at the house. I wish you'd tell anybody who'd be interested."

"Oh, I will," he broke out hastily. "Of course I'm not likely to see anybody, but if I do."

His tone made me suspicious.

"Of course you'll be there yourself."

"Well, I'll certainly try. What I called up about is—"

"Wait a minute," I interrupted. "How about saying you'll come?"

"Well, the fact is—the truth of the matter is that I'm staying with some people up here in Greenwich, and they rather expect me to be with them tomorrow. In fact, there's a sort of picnic or something. Of course I'll do my best to get away."

I ejaculated an unrestrained "Huh!" and he must have heard me, for he went on nervously:

"What I called up about was a pair of shoes I left there. I wonder if it'd be too much trouble to have the butler send them on. You see, they're tennis shoes, and I'm sort of helpless without them. My address is care of B. F.—"

I didn't hear the rest of the name, because I hung up the receiver.

After that I felt a certain shame for Gatsby—one gentleman to whom I telephoned implied that he had got what he deserved. However, that was my fault, for he was one of those who used to sneer most bitterly at Gatsby on the courage of Gatsby's liquor, and I should have known better than to call him.

The morning of the funeral I went up to New York to see Meyer Wolfshiem; I couldn't seem to reach him any other way. The door that I pushed open, on the advice of an elevator boy, was marked "The Swastika Holding Company," and at first there didn't seem to be anyone inside. But when I'd shouted "hello" several times in vain, an argument broke out behind a partition, and presently a lovely Jewess appeared at an interior door and scrutinized me with black hostile eyes.

"Nobody's in," she said. "Mr. Wolfshiem's gone to Chicago."

The first part of this was obviously untrue, for someone had begun to whistle "The Rosary," tunelessly, inside.

"Please say that Mr. Carraway wants to see him."

"I can't get him back from Chicago, can I?"

At this moment a voice, unmistakably Wolfshiem's, called "Stella!" from the other side of the door.

"Leave your name on the desk," she said quickly. "I'll give it to him when he gets back."

"But I know he's there."

She took a step toward me and began to slide her hands indignantly up and down her hips.

"You young men think you can force your way in here any time," she scolded. "We're getting sickantired of it. When I say he's in Chicago, he's in Chicago."

I mentioned Gatsby.

"Oh-h!" She looked at me over again. "Will you just—What was your name?"

She vanished. In a moment Meyer Wolfshiem stood solemnly in the doorway, holding out both hands. He drew me into his office, remarking in a reverent voice that it was a sad time for all of us, and offered me a cigar.

"My memory goes back to when first I met him," he said. "A young major just out of the army and covered over with medals he got in the war. He was so hard up he had to keep on wearing his uniform because he couldn't buy some regular clothes. First time I saw him was when he came into Winebrenner's poolroom at Forty-third Street and asked for a job. He hadn't eat anything for a couple of days. 'Come on have some lunch with me,' I said. He ate more than four dollars' worth of food in half an hour."

"Did you start him in business?" I inquired.

"Start him! I made him."

"Oh."

"I raised him up out of nothing, right out of the gutter. I saw right away he was a fine-appearing, gentlemanly young man, and when he told me he was at Oggsford I knew I could use him good. I got him to join the American Legion and he used to stand high there. Right off he did some work for a client of mine up to Albany. We were so thick like that in everything"—he held up two bulbous fingers—"always together."

I wondered if this partnership had included the World's Series transaction in 1919.

"Now he's dead," I said after a moment. "You were his closest friend, so I know you'll want to come to his funeral this afternoon."

"I'd like to come."

"Well, come then."

The hair in his nostrils quivered slightly, and as he shook his head his eyes filled with tears.

"I can't do it—I can't get mixed up in it," he said.

"There's nothing to get mixed up in. It's all over now."

"When a man gets killed I never like to get mixed up in it in any way. I keep out. When I was a young man it was different—if a friend of mine died, no matter how, I stuck with them to the end. You may think that's sentimental, but I mean it—to the bitter end."

I saw that for some reason of his own he was determined not to come, so I stood up.

"Are you a college man?" he inquired suddenly.

For a moment I thought he was going to suggest a "gonnegtion," but he only nodded and shook my hand.

"Let us learn to show our friendship for a man when he is alive and not after he is dead," he suggested. "After that my own rule is to let everything alone."

When I left his office the sky had turned dark and I got back to West Egg in a drizzle. After changing my clothes I went next door and found Mr. Gatz walking up and down excitedly in the hall. His pride in his son and in his son's possessions was continually increasing and now he had something to show me.

"Jimmy sent me this picture." He took out his wallet with trembling fingers. "Look there."

It was a photograph of the house, cracked in the corners and dirty with many hands. He pointed out every detail to me eagerly. "Look there!" and then sought admiration from my eyes. He had shown it so often that I think it was more real to him now than the house itself.

"Jimmy sent it to me. I think it's a very pretty picture. It shows up well."

"Very well. Had you seen him lately?"

"He come out to see me two years ago and bought me the house I live in now. Of course we was broke up when he run off from home, but I see now there was a reason for it. He knew he had a big future in front of him. And ever since he made a success he was very generous with me."

He seemed reluctant to put away the picture, held it for another minute, lingeringly, before my eyes. Then he returned the wallet and pulled from his pocket a ragged old copy of a book called *Hopalong Cassidy*.

"Look here, this is a book he had when he was a boy. It just shows you."

He opened it at the back cover and turned it around for me to see. On the last flyleaf was printed the word SCHEDULE, and the date September 12, 1906. And underneath:

Rise from bed	6:00	a.m.
Dumbell exercise and wall-scaling	6:15–6:30	"
Study electricity, etc.	7:15–8:15	"
Work	8:30–4:30	p.m.
Baseball and sports	4:30–5:00	"
Practise elocution, poise and how to attain it	5:00–6:00	"
Study needed inventions	7:00–9:00	"

GENERAL RESOLVES

No wasting time at Shafters or [a name, indecipherable]

No more smokeing or chewing.

Bath every other day

Read one improving book or magazine per week

Save $5.00 [crossed out] $3.00 per week

Be better to parents

"I came across this book by accident," said the old man. "It just shows you, don't it?"

"It just shows you."

"Jimmy was bound to get ahead. He always had some resolves like this or something. Do you notice what he's got about improving his mind? He was always great for that. He told me I et like a hog once, and I beat him for it."

He was reluctant to close the book, reading each item aloud and then looking eagerly at me. I think he rather expected me to copy down the list for my own use.

A little before three the Lutheran minister arrived from Flushing, and I began to look involuntarily out the windows for other cars. So did Gatsby's father. And as the time passed and the servants came in and stood waiting in the hall, his eyes began to blink anxiously, and he spoke of the rain in a worried, uncertain way. The minister glanced several times at his watch, so I took him aside and asked him to wait for half an hour. But it wasn't any use. Nobody came.

About five o'clock our procession of three cars reached the cemetery and stopped in a thick drizzle beside the gate—first a motor hearse, horribly black and wet, then Mr. Gatz and the minister and me in the limousine, and a little later four or five servants and the postman from West Egg, in Gatsby's station wagon, all wet to the skin. As we started through the gate into the cemetery I heard a car stop and then the sound of someone splashing after us over the soggy ground. I looked around. It was the man with owl-eyed glasses whom I had found marvelling over Gatsby's books in the library one night three months before.

I'd never seen him since then. I don't know how he knew about the funeral, or even his name. The rain poured down his thick glasses, and he took them off and wiped them to see the protecting canvas unrolled from Gatsby's grave.

I tried to think about Gatsby then for a moment, but he was already too far away, and I could only remember, without resentment, that Daisy hadn't sent a message or a flower. Dimly I heard someone murmur "Blessed are the dead that the rain falls on," and then the owl-eyed man said "Amen to that," in a brave voice.

We straggled down quickly through the rain to the cars. Owl-eyes spoke to me by the gate.

"I couldn't get to the house," he remarked.

"Neither could anybody else."

"Go on!" He started. "Why, my God! they used to go there by the hundreds."

He took off his glasses and wiped them again, outside and in.

"The poor son-of-a-bitch," he said.

One of my most vivid memories is of coming back West from prep school and later from college at Christmas time. Those who went farther than Chicago would gather in the old dim Union Station at six o'clock of a December evening, with a few Chicago friends, already caught up into their own holiday gaieties, to bid them a hasty goodbye. I remember the fur coats of the girls returning from Miss This-or-That's and the chatter of frozen breath and the hands waving overhead as we caught sight of old acquaintances, and the matchings of invitations: "Are you going to the Ordways'? the Herseys'? the Schultzes'?" and the long green tickets clasped tight in our gloved hands. And last the murky yellow cars of the Chicago, Milwaukee and St. Paul railroad looking cheerful as Christmas itself on the tracks beside the gate.

When we pulled out into the winter night and the real snow, our snow, began to stretch out beside us and twinkle against the windows, and the dim lights of small Wisconsin stations moved by, a sharp wild brace came suddenly into the air. We drew in deep breaths of it as we walked back from dinner through the cold vestibules, unutterably aware of our identity with this country for one strange hour, before we melted indistinguishably into it again.

That's my Middle West—not the wheat or the prairies or the lost Swede towns, but the thrilling returning trains of my youth, and the street lamps and sleigh bells in the frosty dark and the shadows of holly wreaths thrown by lighted windows on the snow. I am part of that, a little solemn with the feel of those long winters, a little complacent from growing up in the Carraway house in a city where dwellings are still called through decades by a family's name. I see now that this has been a story of the West, after all—Tom and Gatsby, Daisy and Jordan and I, were all Westerners, and perhaps we possessed some deficiency in common which made us subtly unadaptable to Eastern life.

Even when the East excited me most, even when I was most keenly aware of its superiority to the bored, sprawling, swollen towns beyond the Ohio, with their interminable inquisitions which spared only the children and the very old—even then it had always for me a quality of distortion. West Egg, especially, still figures in my more fantastic dreams. I see it as a night scene by El Greco: a hundred houses, at once conventional and grotesque, crouching under a sullen, overhanging sky and a lustreless moon. In the foreground four solemn men in dress suits are walking along the sidewalk with a stretcher on which lies a drunken woman in a white evening dress. Her hand, which dangles over the side, sparkles cold with jewels. Gravely the men turn in at a house—the wrong house. But no one knows the woman's name, and no one cares.

After Gatsby's death the East was haunted for me like that, distorted beyond my eyes' power of correction. So when the blue smoke of brittle leaves was in the air and the wind blew the wet laundry stiff on the line I decided to come back home.

There was one thing to be done before I left, an awkward, unpleasant thing that perhaps had better have been let alone. But I wanted to leave things in order and not just trust that obliging and indifferent sea to sweep my refuse away. I saw Jordan Baker and talked over and around what had happened to us together, and what had happened afterward to me, and she lay perfectly still, listening, in a big chair.

She was dressed to play golf, and I remember thinking she looked like a good illustration, her chin raised a little jauntily, her hair the colour of an autumn leaf, her face the same brown tint as the fingerless glove on her knee. When I had finished she told me without comment that she was engaged to another man. I doubted that, though there were several she could have married at a nod of her head, but I pretended to be surprised. For just a minute I wondered if I wasn't making a mistake, then I thought it all over again quickly and got up to say good-bye.

"Nevertheless you did throw me over," said Jordan suddenly. "You threw me over on the telephone. I don't give a damn about you now, but it was a new experience for me, and I felt a little dizzy for a while."

We shook hands.

"Oh, and do you remember"—she added—"a conversation we had once about driving a car?"

"Why—not exactly."

"You said a bad driver was only safe until she met another bad driver? Well, I met another bad driver, didn't I? I mean it was careless of me to make such a wrong guess. I thought you were rather an honest, straightforward person. I thought it was your secret pride."

"I'm thirty," I said. "I'm five years too old to lie to myself and call it honour."

She didn't answer. Angry, and half in love with her, and tremendously sorry, I turned away.

One afternoon late in October I saw Tom Buchanan. He was walking ahead of me along Fifth Avenue in his alert, aggressive way, his hands out a little from his body as if to fight off interference, his head moving sharply here and there, adapting itself to his restless eyes. Just as I slowed up to avoid overtaking him he stopped and began frowning into the windows of a jewellery store. Suddenly he saw me and walked back, holding out his hand.

"What's the matter, Nick? Do you object to shaking hands with me?"

"Yes. You know what I think of you."

"You're crazy, Nick," he said quickly. "Crazy as hell. I don't know what's the matter with you."

"Tom," I inquired, "what did you say to Wilson that afternoon?"

He stared at me without a word, and I knew I had guessed right about those missing hours. I started to turn away, but he took a step after me and grabbed my arm.

"I told him the truth," he said. "He came to the door while we were getting ready to leave, and when I sent down word that we weren't in he tried to force his way upstairs. He was crazy enough to kill me if I hadn't told him who owned the car. His hand was on a revolver in his pocket every minute he was in the house—" He broke off defiantly. "What if I did tell him? That fellow had it coming to him. He threw dust into your eyes just like he did in Daisy's, but he was a tough one. He ran over Myrtle like you'd run over a dog and never even stopped his car."

There was nothing I could say, except the one unutterable fact that it wasn't true.

"And if you think I didn't have my share of suffering—look here, when I went to give up that flat and saw that damn box of dog biscuits sitting there on the sideboard, I sat down and cried like a baby. By God it was awful—"

I couldn't forgive him or like him, but I saw that what he had done was, to him, entirely justified. It was all very careless and confused. They were careless people, Tom and Daisy—they smashed up things and creatures and then retreated back into their money or their vast carelessness, or whatever it was that kept them together, and let other people clean up the mess they had made…

I shook hands with him; it seemed silly not to, for I felt suddenly as though I were talking to a child. Then he went into the jewellery store to buy a pearl necklace—or perhaps only a pair of cuff buttons—rid of my provincial squeamishness forever.

Gatsby's house was still empty when I left—the grass on his lawn had grown as long as mine. One of the taxi drivers in the village never took a fare past the entrance gate without stopping for a minute and pointing inside; perhaps it was he who drove Daisy and Gatsby over to East Egg the night of the accident, and perhaps he had made a story about it all his own. I didn't want to hear it and I avoided him when I got off the train.

I spent my Saturday nights in New York because those gleaming, dazzling parties of his were with me so vividly that I could still hear the music and the laughter, faint and incessant, from his garden, and the cars going up and down his drive. One night I did hear a material car there, and saw its lights stop at his front steps. But I didn't investigate. Probably it was some final guest who had been away at the ends of the earth and didn't know that the party was over.

On the last night, with my trunk packed and my car sold to the grocer, I went over and looked at that huge incoherent failure of a house once more. On the white steps an obscene word, scrawled by some boy with a piece of brick, stood out clearly in the moonlight, and I erased it, drawing my shoe raspingly along the stone. Then I wandered down to the beach and sprawled out on the sand.

Most of the big shore places were closed now and there were hardly any lights except the shadowy, moving glow of a ferryboat across the Sound. And as the moon rose higher the inessential houses began to melt away until gradually I became aware of the old island here that flowered once for Dutch sailors' eyes—a fresh, green breast of the new world. Its vanished trees, the trees that had made way for Gatsby's house, had once pandered in whispers to the last and greatest of all human dreams; for a transitory enchanted moment man must have held his breath in the presence of this continent, compelled into an aesthetic contemplation he neither understood nor desired, face to face for the last time in history with something commensurate to his capacity for wonder.

And as I sat there brooding on the old, unknown world, I thought of Gatsby's wonder when he first picked out the green light at the end of Daisy's dock. He had come a long way to this blue lawn, and his dream must have seemed so close that he could hardly fail to grasp it. He did not know that it was already behind him, somewhere back in that vast obscurity beyond the city, where the dark fields of the republic rolled on under the night.

Gatsby believed in the green light, the orgastic future that year by year recedes before us. It eluded us then, but that's no matter—tomorrow we will run faster, stretch out our arms further… And one fine morning—

So we beat on, boats against the current, borne back ceaselessly into the past.

TENDER IS THE NIGHT

Already with thee! tender is the night. . .
. . . But here there is no light,
Save what from heaven is with the breezes blown
Through verdurous glooms and winding mossy ways.

--Ode to a Nightingale

TO

GERALD and SARA

MANY FÊTES

BOOK ONE

I

On the pleasant shore of the French Riviera, about half way between Marseilles and the Italian border, stands a large, proud, rose-colored hotel. Deferential palms cool its flushed façade, and before it stretches a short dazzling beach. Lately it has become a summer resort of notable and fashionable people; a decade ago it was almost deserted after its English clientele went north in April. Now, many bungalows cluster near it, but when this story begins only the cupolas of a dozen old villas rotted like water lilies among the massed pines between Gausse's Hôtel des Étrangers and Cannes, five miles away.

The hotel and its bright tan prayer rug of a beach were one. In the early morning the distant image of Cannes, the pink and cream of old fortifications, the purple Alp that bounded Italy, were cast across the water and lay quavering in the ripples and rings sent up by sea-plants through the clear shallows. Before eight a man came down to the beach in a blue bathrobe and with much preliminary application to his person of the chilly water, and much grunting and loud breathing, floundered a minute in the sea. When he had gone, beach and bay were quiet for an hour. Merchantmen crawled westward on the horizon; bus boys shouted in the hotel court; the dew dried upon the pines. In another hour the horns of motors began to blow down from the winding road along the low range of the Maures, which separates the littoral from true Provençal France.

A mile from the sea, where pines give way to dusty poplars, is an isolated railroad stop, whence one June morning in 1925 a victoria brought a woman and her daughter down to Gausse's Hotel. The mother's face was of a fading prettiness that would soon be patted with broken veins; her expression was both tranquil and aware in a pleasant way. However, one's eye moved on quickly to her daughter, who had magic in her pink palms and her cheeks lit to a lovely flame, like the thrilling flush of children after their cold baths in the evening. Her fine forehead sloped gently up to where her hair, bordering it like an armorial shield, burst into lovelocks and waves and curlicues of ash blonde and gold. Her eyes were bright, big, clear, wet, and shining, the color of her cheeks was real, breaking close to the surface from the strong young pump of her heart. Her body hovered delicately on the last edge of childhood--she was almost eighteen, nearly complete, but the dew was still on her.

As sea and sky appeared below them in a thin, hot line the mother said:

"Something tells me we're not going to like this place."

"I want to go home anyhow," the girl answered.

They both spoke cheerfully but were obviously without direction and bored by the fact--moreover, just any direction would not do. They wanted high excitement, not from the necessity of stimulating jaded nerves but with the avidity of prize-winning schoolchildren who deserved their vacations.

"We'll stay three days and then go home. I'll wire right away for steamer tickets."

At the hotel the girl made the reservation in idiomatic but rather flat French, like something remembered. When they were installed on the ground floor she walked into the glare of the French windows and out a few steps onto the stone veranda that ran the length of the hotel. When she walked she carried herself like a ballet-dancer, not slumped down on her hips but held up in the small of her back. Out there the hot light clipped close her shadow and she retreated--it was too bright to see. Fifty yards away the Mediterranean yielded up its pigments, moment by moment, to the brutal sunshine; below the balustrade a faded Buick cooked on the hotel drive.

Indeed, of all the region only the beach stirred with activity. Three British nannies sat knitting the slow pattern of Victorian England, the pattern of the forties, the sixties, and the eighties, into sweaters and socks, to the tune of gossip as formalized as incantation; closer to the sea a dozen persons kept house under striped umbrellas, while their dozen children pursued unintimidated fish through the shallows or lay naked and glistening with cocoanut oil out in the sun.

As Rosemary came onto the beach a boy of twelve ran past her and dashed into the sea with exultant cries. Feeling the impactive scrutiny of strange faces, she took off her bathrobe and followed. She floated face down for a few yards and finding it shallow staggered to her feet and plodded forward, dragging slim legs like weights against the resistance of the water. When it was about breast high, she glanced back toward shore: a bald man in a monocle and a pair of tights, his tufted chest thrown out, his brash navel sucked in, was regarding her attentively. As Rosemary returned the gaze the man dislodged the monocle, which went into hiding amid the facetious whiskers of his chest, and poured himself a glass of something from a bottle in his hand.

Rosemary laid her face on the water and swam a choppy little four-beat crawl out to the raft. The water reached up for her, pulled her down tenderly out of the heat, seeped in her hair and ran into the corners of her body. She turned round and round in it, embracing it, wallowing in it. Reaching the raft she was out of breath, but a tanned woman with very white teeth looked down at her, and Rosemary, suddenly conscious of the raw whiteness of her own body, turned on her back and drifted toward shore. The hairy man holding the bottle spoke to her as she came out.

"I say--they have sharks out behind the raft." He was of indeterminate nationality, but spoke English with a slow Oxford drawl. "Yesterday they devoured two British sailors from the flotte at Golfe Juan."

"Heavens!" exclaimed Rosemary.

"They come in for the refuse from the flotte."

Glazing his eyes to indicate that he had only spoken in order to warn her, he minced off two steps and poured himself another drink.

Not unpleasantly self-conscious, since there had been a slight sway of attention toward her during this conversation, Rosemary looked for a place to sit. Obviously each family possessed the strip of sand immediately in front of its umbrella; besides there was much visiting and talking back and forth--the atmosphere of a community upon which it would be presumptuous to intrude. Farther up, where the beach was strewn with pebbles and dead sea-weed, sat a group with flesh as white as her own. They lay under small hand-parasols instead of beach umbrellas and were obviously less indigenous to the place. Between the dark people and the light, Rosemary found room and spread out her peignoir on the sand.

Lying so, she first heard their voices and felt their feet skirt her body and their shapes pass between the sun and herself. The breath of an inquisitive dog blew warm and nervous on her neck; she could feel her skin broiling a little in the heat and hear the small exhausted wa-*waa* of the expiring waves. Presently her ear distinguished individual voices and she became aware that some one referred to scornfully as "that North guy" had kidnapped a waiter from a café in Cannes last night in order to saw him in two. The sponsor of the story was a white-haired woman in full evening dress, obviously a relic of the previous evening, for a tiara still clung to her head and a discouraged orchid expired from her shoulder. Rosemary, forming a vague antipathy to her and her companions, turned away.

Nearest her, on the other side, a young woman lay under a roof of umbrellas making out a list of things from a book open on the sand. Her bathing suit was pulled off her shoulders and her back, a ruddy, orange brown, set off by a string of creamy pearls, shone in the sun. Her face was hard and lovely and pitiful. Her eyes met Rosemary's but did not see her. Beyond her was a fine man in a jockey cap and red-striped tights; then the woman Rosemary had seen on the raft, and who looked back at her, seeing her; then a man with a long face and a golden, leonine head, with blue tights and no hat, talking very seriously to an unmistakably Latin young man in black tights, both of them picking at little pieces of seaweed in the sand. She thought they were mostly Americans, but something made them unlike the Americans she had known of late.

After a while she realized that the man in the jockey cap was giving a quiet little performance for this group; he moved gravely about with a rake, ostensibly removing gravel and meanwhile developing some esoteric burlesque held in suspension by his grave face. Its faintest ramification had become hilarious, until whatever he said released a burst of laughter. Even those who, like herself, were too far away to hear, sent out antennæ of attention until the only person on the beach not caught up in it was the young woman with the string of pearls. Perhaps from modesty of possession she responded to each salvo of amusement by bending closer over her list.

The man of the monocle and bottle spoke suddenly out of the sky above Rosemary.

"You are a ripping swimmer."

She demurred.

"Jolly good. My name is Campion. Here is a lady who says she saw you in Sorrento last week and knows who you are and would so like to meet you."

Glancing around with concealed annoyance Rosemary saw the untanned people were waiting. Reluctantly she got up and went over to them.

"Mrs. Abrams--Mrs. McKisco--Mr. McKisco--Mr. Dumphry--

"We know who you are," spoke up the woman in evening dress. "You're Rosemary Hoyt and I recognized you in Sorrento and asked the hotel clerk and we all think you're perfectly marvellous and we want to know why you're not back in America making another marvellous moving picture."

They made a superfluous gesture of moving over for her. The woman who had recognized her was not a Jewess, despite her name. She was one of those elderly "good sports" preserved by an imperviousness to experience and a good digestion into another generation.

"We wanted to warn you about getting burned the first day," she continued cheerily, "because *your* skin is important, but there seems to be so darn much formality on this beach that we didn't know whether you'd mind."

II

"We thought maybe you were in the plot," said Mrs. McKisco. She was a shabby-eyed, pretty young woman with a disheartening intensity. "We don't know who's in the plot and who isn't. One man my husband had been particularly nice to turned out to be a chief character--practically the assistant hero."

"The plot?" inquired Rosemary, half understanding. "Is there a plot?"

"My dear, we don't *know,"* said Mrs. Abrams, with a convulsive, stout woman's chuckle. "We're not in it. We're the gallery."

Mr. Dumphry, a tow-headed effeminate young man, remarked: "Mama Abrams is a plot in herself," and Campion shook his monocle at him, saying: "Now, Royal, don't be too ghastly for words." Rosemary looked at them all uncomfortably, wishing her mother had come down here with her. She did not like these people, especially in her immediate comparison of them with those who had interested her at the other end of the beach. Her mother's modest but compact social gift got them out of unwelcome situations swiftly and firmly. But Rosemary had been a celebrity for only six months, and sometimes the French manners of her early adolescence and the democratic manners of America, these latter superimposed, made a certain confusion and let her in for just such things.

Mr. McKisco, a scrawny, freckle-and-red man of thirty, did not find the topic of the "plot" amusing. He had been staring at the sea--now after a swift glance at his wife he turned to Rosemary and demanded aggressively:

"Been here long?"

"Only a day."

"Oh."

Evidently feeling that the subject had been thoroughly changed, he looked in turn at the others.

"Going to stay all summer?" asked Mrs. McKisco, innocently. "If you do you can watch the plot unfold."

"For God's sake, Violet, drop the subject!" exploded her husband. "Get a new joke, for God's sake!"

Mrs. McKisco swayed toward Mrs. Abrams and breathed audibly:

"He's nervous."

"I'm not nervous," disagreed McKisco. "It just happens I'm not nervous at all."

He was burning visibly--a grayish flush had spread over his face, dissolving all his expressions into a vast ineffectuality. Suddenly remotely conscious of his condition he got up to go in the water, followed by his wife, and seizing the opportunity Rosemary followed.

Mr. McKisco drew a long breath, flung himself into the shallows and began a stiff-armed batting of the Mediterranean, obviously intended to suggest a crawl--his breath exhausted he arose and looked around with an expression of surprise that he was still in sight of shore.

"I haven't learned to breathe yet. I never quite understood how they breathed." He looked at Rosemary inquiringly.

"I think you breathe out under water," she explained. "And every fourth beat you roll your head over for air."

"The breathing's the hardest part for me. Shall we go to the raft?"

The man with the leonine head lay stretched out upon the raft, which tipped back and forth with the motion of the water. As Mrs. McKisco reached for it a sudden tilt struck her arm up roughly, whereupon the man started up and pulled her on board.

"I was afraid it hit you." His voice was slow and shy; he had one of the saddest faces Rosemary had ever seen, the high cheekbones of an Indian, a long upper lip, and enormous deep-set dark golden eyes. He had spoken out of the side of his mouth, as if he hoped his words would reach Mrs. McKisco by a circuitous and unobtrusive route; in a minute he had shoved off into the water and his long body lay motionless toward shore.

Rosemary and Mrs. McKisco watched him. When he had exhausted his momentum he abruptly bent double, his thin thighs rose above the surface, and he disappeared totally, leaving scarcely a fleck of foam behind.

"He's a good swimmer," Rosemary said.

Mrs. McKisco's answer came with surprising violence.

"Well, he's a rotten musician." She turned to her husband, who after two unsuccessful attempts had managed to climb on the raft, and having attained his balance was trying to make some kind of compensatory flourish, achieving only an extra stagger. "I was just saying that Abe North may be a good swimmer but he's a rotten musician."

"Yes," agreed McKisco, grudgingly. Obviously he had created his wife's world, and allowed her few liberties in it.

"Antheil's my man." Mrs. McKisco turned challengingly to Rosemary, "Anthiel and Joyce. I don't suppose you ever hear much about those sort of people in Hollywood, but my husband wrote the first criticism of Ulysses that ever appeared in America."

"I wish I had a cigarette," said McKisco calmly. "That's more important to me just now."

"He's got insides--don't you think so, Albert?"

Her voice faded off suddenly. The woman of the pearls had joined her two children in the water, and now Abe North came up under one of them like a volcanic island, raising him on his shoulders. The child yelled with fear and delight and the woman watched with a lovely peace, without a smile.

"Is that his wife?" Rosemary asked.

"No, that's Mrs. Diver. They're not at the hotel." Her eyes, photographic, did not move from the woman's face. After a moment she turned vehemently to Rosemary.

"Have you been abroad before?"

"Yes--I went to school in Paris."

"Oh! Well then you probably know that if you want to enjoy yourself here the thing is to get to know some real French families. What do these people get out of it?" She pointed her left shoulder toward shore. "They just stick around with each other in little cliques. Of course, we had letters of introduction and met all the best French artists and writers in Paris. That made it very nice."

"I should think so."

"My husband is finishing his first novel, you see."

Rosemary said: "Oh, he is?" She was not thinking anything special, except wondering whether her mother had got to sleep in this heat.

"It's on the idea of Ulysses," continued Mrs. McKisco. "Only instead of taking twenty-four hours my husband takes a hundred years. He takes a decayed old French aristocrat and puts him in contrast with the mechanical age--"

"Oh, for God's sake, Violet, don't go telling everybody the idea," protested McKisco. "I don't want it to get all around before the book's published."

Rosemary swam back to the shore, where she threw her peignoir over her already sore shoulders and lay down again in the sun. The man with the jockey cap was now going from umbrella to umbrella carrying a bottle and little glasses in his hands; presently he and his friends grew livelier and closer together and now they were all under a single assemblage of umbrellas--she gathered that some one was leaving and that this was a last drink on the beach. Even the children knew that excitement was generating under that umbrella and turned toward it--and it seemed to Rosemary that it all came from the man in the jockey cap.

Noon dominated sea and sky--even the white line of Cannes, five miles off, had faded to a mirage of what was fresh and cool; a robin-breasted sailing boat pulled in behind it a strand from the outer, darker sea. It seemed that there was no life anywhere in all this expanse of coast except under the filtered sunlight of those umbrellas, where something went on amid the color and the murmur.

Campion walked near her, stood a few feet away and Rosemary closed her eyes, pretending to be asleep; then she half-opened them and watched two dim, blurred pillars that were legs. The man tried to edge his way into a sand-colored cloud, but the cloud floated off into the vast hot sky. Rosemary fell really asleep.

She awoke drenched with sweat to find the beach deserted save for the man in the jockey cap, who was folding a last umbrella. As Rosemary lay blinking, he walked nearer and said:

"I was going to wake you before I left. It's not good to get too burned right away."

"Thank you." Rosemary looked down at her crimson legs.

"Heavens!"

She laughed cheerfully, inviting him to talk, but Dick Diver was already carrying a tent and a beach umbrella up to a waiting car, so she went into the water to wash off the sweat. He came back and gathering up a rake, a shovel, and a sieve, stowed them in a crevice of a rock. He glanced up and down the beach to see if he had left anything.

"Do you know what time it is?" Rosemary asked.

"It's about half-past one."

They faced the seascape together momentarily.

"It's not a bad time," said Dick Diver. "It's not one of worst times of the day."

He looked at her and for a moment she lived in the bright blue worlds of his eyes, eagerly and confidently. Then he shouldered his last piece of junk and went up to his car, and Rosemary came out of the water, shook out her peignoir and walked up to the hotel.

III

It was almost two when they went into the dining-room. Back and forth over the deserted tables a heavy pattern of beams and shadows swayed with the motion of the pines outside. Two waiters, piling plates and talking loud Italian, fell silent when they came in and brought them a tired version of the table d'hôte luncheon.

"I fell in love on the beach," said Rosemary.

"Who with?"

"First with a whole lot of people who looked nice. Then with one man."

"Did you talk to him?"

"Just a little. Very handsome. With reddish hair." She was eating, ravenously. "He's married though--it's usually the way."

Her mother was her best friend and had put every last possibility into the guiding of her, not so rare a thing in the theatrical profession, but rather special in that Mrs. Elsie Speers was not recompensing herself for a defeat of her own. She had no personal bitterness or resentments about life--twice satisfactorily married and twice widowed, her cheerful stoicism had each time deepened. One of her husbands had been a cavalry officer and one an army doctor, and they both left something to her that she tried to present intact to Rosemary. By not sparing Rosemary she had made her hard--by not sparing her own labor and devotion she had cultivated an idealism in Rosemary, which at present was directed toward herself and saw the world through her eyes. So that while Rosemary was a "simple" child she was protected by a double sheath of her mother's armor and her own--she had a mature distrust of the trivial, the facile and the vulgar. However, with Rosemary's sudden success in pictures Mrs. Speers felt that it was time she were spiritually weaned; it would please rather than pain her if this somewhat bouncing, breathless and exigent idealism would focus on something except herself.

"Then you like it here?" she asked.

"It might be fun if we knew those people. There were some other people, but they weren't nice. They recognized me--no matter where we go everybody's seen 'Daddy's Girl.'"

Mrs. Speers waited for the glow of egotism to subside; then she said in a matter-of-fact way: "That reminds me, when are you going to see Earl Brady?"

"I thought we might go this afternoon--if you're rested."

"You go--I'm not going."

"We'll wait till to-morrow then."

"I want you to go alone. It's only a short way--it isn't as if you didn't speak French."

"Mother--aren't there some things I don't have to do?"

"Oh, well then go later--but some day before we leave."

"All right, Mother."

After lunch they were both overwhelmed by the sudden flatness that comes over American travellers in quiet foreign places. No stimuli worked upon them, no voices called them from without, no fragments of their own thoughts came suddenly from the minds of others, and missing the clamor of Empire they felt that life was not continuing here.

"Let's only stay three days, Mother," Rosemary said when they were back in their rooms. Outside a light wind blew the heat around, straining it through the trees and sending little hot gusts through the shutters.

"How about the man you fell in love with on the beach?"

"I don't love anybody but you, Mother, darling."

Rosemary stopped in the lobby and spoke to Gausse père about trains. The concierge, lounging in light-brown khaki by the desk, stared at her rigidly, then suddenly remembered the manners of his métier. She took the bus and rode with a pair of obsequious waiters to the station, embarrassed by their deferential silence, wanting to urge them: "Go on, talk, enjoy yourselves. It doesn't bother me."

The first-class compartment was stifling; the vivid advertising cards of the railroad companies--The Pont du Gard at Arles, the Amphitheatre at Orange, winter sports at Chamonix--were fresher than the long motionless sea outside. Unlike American trains that were absorbed in an intense destiny of their own, and scornful of people on another world less swift and breathless, this train was part of the country through which it passed. Its breath stirred the dust from the palm leaves, the cinders mingled with the dry dung in the gardens. Rosemary was sure she could lean from the window and pull flowers with her hand.

A dozen cabbies slept in their hacks outside the Cannes station. Over on the promenade the Casino, the smart shops, and the great hotels turned blank iron masks to the summer sea. It was unbelievable that there could ever have been a "season," and Rosemary, half in the grip of fashion, became a little self-conscious, as though she were displaying an unhealthy taste for the moribund; as though people were wondering why she was here in the lull between the gaiety of last winter and next winter, while up north the true world thundered by.

As she came out of a drug store with a bottle of cocoanut oil, a woman, whom she recognized as Mrs. Diver, crossed her path with arms full of sofa cushions, and went to a car parked down the street. A long, low black dog barked at her, a dozing chauffeur woke with a start. She sat in the car, her lovely face set, controlled, her eyes brave and watchful, looking straight ahead toward nothing. Her dress was bright red and her brown legs were bare. She had thick, dark, gold hair like a chow's.

With half an hour to wait for her train Rosemary sat down in the Café des Alliés on the Croisette, where the trees made a green twilight over the tables and an orchestra wooed an imaginary public of cosmopolites with the Nice Carnival

Song and last year's American tune. She had bought *Le Temps* and *The Saturday Evening Post* for her mother, and as she drank her citronade she opened the latter at the memoirs of a Russian princess, finding the dim conventions of the nineties realer and nearer than the headlines of the French paper. It was the same feeling that had oppressed her at the hotel--accustomed to seeing the starkest grotesqueries of a continent heavily underlined as comedy or tragedy, untrained to the task of separating out the essential for herself, she now began to feel that French life was empty and stale. This feeling was surcharged by listening to the sad tunes of the orchestra, reminiscent of the melancholy music played for acrobats in vaudeville. She was glad to go back to Gausse's Hotel.

Her shoulders were too burned to swim with the next day, so she and her mother hired a car--after much haggling, for Rosemary had formed her valuations of money in France--and drove along the Riviera, the delta of many rivers. The chauffeur, a Russian Czar of the period of Ivan the Terrible, was a self-appointed guide, and the resplendent names--Cannes, Nice, Monte Carlo--began to glow through their torpid camouflage, whispering of old kings come here to dine or die, of rajahs tossing Buddha's eyes to English ballerinas, of Russian princes turning the weeks into Baltic twilights in the lost caviare days. Most of all, there was the scent of the Russians along the coast--their closed book shops and grocery stores. Ten years ago, when the season ended in April, the doors of the Orthodox Church were locked, and the sweet champagnes they favored were put away until their return. "We'll be back next season," they said, but this was premature, for they were never coming back any more.

It was pleasant to drive back to the hotel in the late afternoon, above a sea as mysteriously colored as the agates and cornelians of childhood, green as green milk, blue as laundry water, wine dark. It was pleasant to pass people eating outside their doors, and to hear the fierce mechanical pianos behind the vines of country estaminets. When they turned off the Corniche d'Or and down to Gausse's Hotel through the darkening banks of trees, set one behind another in many greens, the moon already hovered over the ruins of the aqueducts. . . .

Somewhere in the hills behind the hotel there was a dance, and Rosemary listened to the music through the ghostly moonshine of her mosquito net, realizing that there was gaiety too somewhere about, and she thought of the nice people on the beach. She thought she might meet them in the morning, but they obviously formed a self-sufficient little group, and once their umbrellas, bamboo rugs, dogs, and children were set out in place the part of the plage was literally fenced in. She resolved in any case not to spend her last two mornings with the other ones.

IV

The matter was solved for her. The McKiscos were not yet there and she had scarcely spread her peignoir when two men--the man with the jockey cap and the tall blonde man, given to sawing waiters in two--left the group and came down toward her.

"Good morning," said Dick Diver. He broke down. "Look--sunburn or no sunburn, why did you stay away yesterday? We worried about you."

She sat up and her happy little laugh welcomed their intrusion.

"We wondered," Dick Diver said, "if you wouldn't come over this morning. We go in, we take food and drink, so it's a substantial invitation."

He seemed kind and charming--his voice promised that he would take care of her, and that a little later he would open up whole new worlds for her, unroll an endless succession of magnificent possibilities. He managed the introduction so that her name wasn't mentioned and then let her know easily that everyone knew who she was but were respecting the completeness of her private life--a courtesy that Rosemary had not met with save from professional people since her success.

Nicole Diver, her brown back hanging from her pearls, was looking through a recipe book for chicken Maryland. She was about twenty-four, Rosemary guessed--her face could have been described in terms of conventional prettiness, but the effect was that it had been made first on the heroic scale with strong structure and marking, as if the features and vividness of brow and coloring, everything we associate with temperament and character had been molded with a Rodinesque intention, and then chiseled away in the direction of prettiness to a point where a single slip would have irreparably diminished its force and quality. With the mouth the sculptor had taken desperate chances--it was the cupid's bow of a magazine cover, yet it shared the distinction of the rest.

"Are you here for a long time?" Nicole asked. Her voice was low, almost harsh.

Suddenly Rosemary let the possibility enter her mind that they might stay another week.

"Not very long," she answered vaguely. "We've been abroad a long time--we landed in Sicily in March and we've been slowly working our way north. I got pneumonia making a picture last January and I've been recuperating."

"Mercy! How did that happen?"

"Well, it was from swimming," Rosemary was rather reluctant at embarking upon personal revelations. "One day I happened to have the grippe and didn't know it, and they were taking a scene where I dove into a canal in Venice. It was a very expensive set, so I had to dive and dive and dive all morning. Mother had a doctor right there, but it was no use--I got pneumonia." She changed the subject determinedly before they could speak. "Do you like it here--this place?"

"They have to like it," said Abe North slowly. "They invented it." He turned his noble head slowly so that his eyes rested with tenderness and affection on the two Divers.

"Oh, did you?"

"This is only the second season that the hotel's been open in summer," Nicole explained. "We persuaded Gausse to keep on a cook and a garçon and a chasseur--it paid its way and this year it's doing even better."

"But you're not in the hotel."

"We built a house, up at Tarmes."

"The theory is," said Dick, arranging an umbrella to clip a square of sunlight off Rosemary's shoulder, "that all the northern places, like Deauville, were picked out by Russians and English who don't mind the cold, while half of us Americans come from tropical climates--that's why we're beginning to come here."

The young man of Latin aspect had been turning the pages of *The New York Herald.*

"Well, what nationality are these people?" he demanded, suddenly, and read with a slight French intonation, "'Registered at the Hotel Palace at Vevey are Mr. Pandely Vlasco, Mme. Bonneasse'--I don't exaggerate--'Corinna Medonca, Mme. Pasche, Seraphim Tullio, Maria Amalia Roto Mais, Moises Teubel, Mme. Paragoris, Apostle Alexandre, Yolanda Yosfuglu and Geneveva de Momus!' She attracts me most--Geneveva de Momus. Almost worth running up to Vevey to take a look at Geneveva de Momus."

He stood up with sudden restlessness, stretching himself with one sharp movement. He was a few years younger than Diver or North. He was tall and his body was hard but overspare save for the bunched force gathered in his shoulders and upper arms. At first glance he seemed conventionally handsome--but there was a faint disgust always in his face which marred the full fierce lustre of his brown eyes. Yet one remembered them afterward, when one had forgotten the inability of the mouth to endure boredom and the young forehead with its furrows of fretful and unprofitable pain.

"We found some fine ones in the news of Americans last week," said Nicole. "Mrs. Evelyn Oyster and--what were the others?"

"There was Mr. S. Flesh," said Diver, getting up also. He took his rake and began to work seriously at getting small stones out of the sand.

"Oh, yes--S. Flesh--doesn't he give you the creeps?"

It was quiet alone with Nicole--Rosemary found it even quieter than with her mother. Abe North and Barban, the Frenchman, were talking about Morocco, and Nicole having copied her recipe picked up a piece of sewing. Rosemary examined their appurtenances--four large parasols that made a canopy of shade, a portable bath house for dressing, a pneumatic rubber horse, new things that Rosemary had never seen, from the first burst of luxury manufacturing after the War, and probably in the hands of the first of purchasers. She had gathered that they were fashionable people, but though her mother had brought her up to beware such people as drones, she did not feel that way here. Even in their absolute immobility, complete as that of the morning, she felt a purpose, a working over something, a direction, an act of creation different from any she had known. Her immature mind made no speculations upon the nature of their relation to each other, she was only concerned with their attitude toward herself--but she perceived the web of some pleasant interrelation, which she expressed with the thought that they seemed to have a very good time.

She looked in turn at the three men, temporarily expropriating them. All three were personable in different ways; all were of a special gentleness that she felt was part of their lives, past and future, not circumstanced by events, not at all like the company manners of actors, and she detected also a far-reaching delicacy that was different from the rough and ready good fellowship of directors, who represented the intellectuals in her life. Actors and directors--those were the only men she had ever known, those and the heterogeneous, indistinguishable mass of college boys, interested only in love at first sight, whom she had met at the Yale prom last fall.

These three were different. Barban was less civilized, more skeptical and scoffing, his manners were formal, even perfunctory. Abe North had, under his shyness, a desperate humor that amused but puzzled her. Her serious nature distrusted its ability to make a supreme impression on him.

But Dick Diver--he was all complete there. Silently she admired him. His complexion was reddish and weather-burned, so was his short hair--a light growth of it rolled down his arms and hands. His eyes were of a bright, hard blue. His nose was somewhat pointed and there was never any doubt at whom he was looking or talking--and this is a flattering attention, for who looks at us?--glances fall upon us, curious or disinterested, nothing more. His voice, with some faint Irish melody running through it, wooed the world, yet she felt the layer of hardness in him, of self-control and of self-discipline, her own virtues. Oh, she chose him, and Nicole, lifting her head saw her choose him, heard the little sigh at the fact that he was already possessed.

Toward noon the McKiscos, Mrs. Abrams, Mr. Dumphry, and Signor Campion came on the beach. They had brought a new umbrella that they set up with side glances toward the Divers, and crept under with satisfied expressions--all save Mr. McKisco, who remained derisively without. In his raking Dick had passed near them and now he returned to the umbrellas.

"The two young men are reading the Book of Etiquette together," he said in a low voice.

"Planning to mix wit de quality," said Abe.

Mary North, the very tanned young woman whom Rosemary had encountered the first day on the raft, came in from swimming and said with a smile that was a rakish gleam:

"So Mr. and Mrs. Neverquiver have arrived."

"They're this man's friends," Nicole reminded her, indicating Abe. "Why doesn't he go and speak to them? Don't you think they're attractive?"

"I think they're very attractive," Abe agreed. "I just don't think they're attractive, that's all."

"Well, I *have* felt there were too many people on the beach this summer," Nicole admitted. *"Our* beach that Dick made out of a pebble pile." She considered, and then lowering her voice out of the range of the trio of nannies who sat back under another umbrella. "Still, they're preferable to those British last summer who kept shouting about: 'Isn't the sea blue? Isn't the sky white? Isn't little Nellie's nose red?'"

Rosemary thought she would not like to have Nicole for an enemy.

"But you didn't see the fight," Nicole continued. "The day before you came, the married man, the one with the name that sounds like a substitute for gasoline or butter--"

"McKisco?"

"Yes--well they were having words and she tossed some sand in his face. So naturally he sat on top of her and rubbed her face in the sand. We were--electrified. I wanted Dick to interfere."

"I think," said Dick Diver, staring down abstractedly at the straw mat, "that I'll go over and invite them to dinner."

"No, you won't," Nicole told him quickly.

"I think it would be a very good thing. They're here--let's adjust ourselves."

"We're very well adjusted," she insisted, laughing. "I'm not going to have *my* nose rubbed in the sand. I'm a mean, hard woman," she explained to Rosemary, and then raising her voice, "Children, put on your bathing suits!"

Rosemary felt that this swim would become the typical one of her life, the one that would always pop up in her memory at the mention of swimming. Simultaneously the whole party moved toward the water, super-ready from the long, forced inaction, passing from the heat to the cool with the gourmandise of a tingling curry eaten with chilled white wine. The Divers' day was spaced like the day of the older civilizations to yield the utmost from the materials at hand, and to give all the transitions their full value, and she did not know that there would be another transition presently from the utter absorption of the swim to the garrulity of the Provençal lunch hour. But again she had the sense that Dick was taking care of her, and she delighted in responding to the eventual movement as if it had been an order.

Nicole handed her husband the curious garment on which she had been working. He went into the dressing tent and inspired a commotion by appearing in a moment clad in transparent black lace drawers. Close inspection revealed that actually they were lined with flesh-colored cloth.

"Well, if that isn't a pansys trick!" exclaimed Mr. McKisco contemptuously--then turning quickly to Mr. Dumphry and Mr. Campion, he added, "Oh, I beg your pardon."

Rosemary bubbled with delight at the trunks. Her naïveté responded wholeheartedly to the expensive simplicity of the Divers, unaware of its complexity and its lack of innocence, unaware that it was all a selection of quality rather than quantity from the run of the world's bazaar; and that the simplicity of behavior also, the nursery-like peace and good will, the emphasis on the simpler virtues, was part of a desperate bargain with the gods and had been attained through struggles she could not have guessed at. At that moment the Divers represented externally the exact furthermost evolution of a class, so that most people seemed awkward beside them--in reality a qualitative change had already set in that was not at all apparent to Rosemary.

She stood with them as they took sherry and ate crackers. Dick Diver looked at her with cold blue eyes; his kind, strong mouth said thoughtfully and deliberately:

"You're the only girl I've seen for a long time that actually did look like something blooming."

In her mother's lap afterward Rosemary cried and cried.

"I love him, Mother. I'm desperately in love with him--I never knew I could feel that way about anybody. And he's married and I like her too--it's just hopeless. Oh, I love him so!"

"I'm curious to meet him."

"She invited us to dinner Friday."

"If you're in love it ought to make you happy. You ought to laugh."

Rosemary looked up and gave a beautiful little shiver of her face and laughed. Her mother always had a great influence on her.

V

Rosemary went to Monte Carlo nearly as sulkily as it was possible for her to be. She rode up the rugged hill to La Turbie, to an old Gaumont lot in process of reconstruction, and as she stood by the grilled entrance waiting for an answer to the message on her card, she might have been looking into Hollywood. The bizarre débris of some recent picture, a decayed street scene in India, a great cardboard whale, a monstrous tree bearing cherries large as basketballs, bloomed there by exotic dispensation, autochthonous as the pale amaranth, mimosa, cork oak or dwarfed pine. There were a quick-lunch shack and two barnlike stages and everywhere about the lot, groups of waiting, hopeful, painted faces.

After ten minutes a young man with hair the color of canary feathers hurried down to the gate.

"Come in, Miss Hoyt. Mr. Brady's on the set, but he's very anxious to see you. I'm sorry you were kept waiting, but you know some of these French dames are worse about pushing themselves in--"

The studio manager opened a small door in the blank wall of stage building and with sudden glad familiarity Rosemary followed him into half darkness. Here and there figures spotted the twilight, turning up ashen faces to her like souls in purgatory watching the passage of a mortal through. There were whispers and soft voices and, apparently from afar, the gentle tremolo of a small organ. Turning the corner made by some flats, they came upon the white crackling glow of a stage, where a French actor--his shirt front, collar, and cuffs tinted a brilliant pink--and an American actress stood motionless face to face. They stared at each other with dogged eyes, as though they had been in the same position for hours; and still for a long time nothing happened, no one moved. A bank of lights went off with a savage hiss, went on again; the plaintive tap of a hammer begged admission to nowhere in the distance; a blue face appeared among the blinding lights above, called something unintelligible into the upper blackness. Then the silence was broken by a voice in front of Rosemary.

"Baby, you don't take off the stockings, you can spoil ten more pairs. That dress is fifteen pounds."

Stepping backward the speaker ran against Rosemary, whereupon the studio manager said, "Hey, Earl--Miss Hoyt."

They were meeting for the first time. Brady was quick and strenuous. As he took her hand she saw him look her over from head to foot, a gesture she recognized and that made her feel at home, but gave her always a faint feeling of superiority to whoever made it. If her person was property she could exercise whatever advantage was inherent in its ownership.

"I thought you'd be along any day now," Brady said, in a voice that was just a little too compelling for private life, and that trailed with it a faintly defiant cockney accent. "Have a good trip?"

"Yes, but we're glad to be going home."

"No-o-o!" he protested. "Stay awhile--I want to talk to you. Let me tell you that was some picture of yours--that 'Daddy's Girl.' I saw it in Paris. I wired the coast right away to see if you were signed."

"I just had--I'm sorry."

"God, what a picture!"

Not wanting to smile in silly agreement Rosemary frowned.

"Nobody wants to be thought of forever for just one picture," she said.

"Sure--that's right. What're your plans?"

"Mother thought I needed a rest. When I get back we'll probably either sign up with First National or keep on with Famous."

"Who's we?"

"My mother. She decides business matters. I couldn't do without her."

Again he looked her over completely, and, as he did, something in Rosemary went out to him. It was not liking, not at all the spontaneous admiration she had felt for the man on the beach this morning. It was a click. He desired her and, so far as her virginal emotions went, she contemplated a surrender with equanimity. Yet she knew she would forget him half an hour after she left him--like an actor kissed in a picture.

"Where are you staying?" Brady asked. "Oh, yes, at Gausse's. Well, my plans are made for this year, too, but that letter I wrote you still stands. Rather make a picture with you than any girl since Connie Talmadge was a kid."

"I feel the same way. Why don't you come back to Hollywood?"

"I can't stand the damn place. I'm fine here. Wait till after this shot and I'll show you around."

Walking onto the set he began to talk to the French actor in a low, quiet voice.

Five minutes passed--Brady talked on, while from time to time the Frenchman shifted his feet and nodded. Abruptly, Brady broke off, calling something to the lights that startled them into a humming glare. Los Angeles was loud about Rosemary now. Unappalled she moved once more through the city of thin partitions, wanting to be back there. But she did not want to see Brady in the mood she sensed he would be in after he had finished and she left the lot with a spell still upon her. The Mediterranean world was less silent now that she knew the studio was there. She liked the people on the streets and bought herself a pair of espadrilles on the way to the train.

Her mother was pleased that she had done so accurately what she was told to do, but she still wanted to launch her out and away. Mrs. Speers was fresh in appearance but she was tired; death beds make people tired indeed and she had watched beside a couple.

VI

Feeling good from the rosy wine at lunch, Nicole Diver folded her arms high enough for the artificial camellia on her shoulder to touch her cheek, and went out into her lovely grassless garden. The garden was bounded on one side by the house, from which it flowed and into which it ran, on two sides by the old village, and on the last by the cliff falling by ledges to the sea.

Along the walls on the village side all was dusty, the wriggling vines, the lemon and eucalyptus trees, the casual wheel-barrow, left only a moment since, but already grown into the path, atrophied and faintly rotten. Nicole was invariably somewhat surprised that by turning in the other direction past a bed of peonies she walked into an area so green and cool that the leaves and petals were curled with tender damp.

Knotted at her throat she wore a lilac scarf that even in the achromatic sunshine cast its color up to her face and down around her moving feet in a lilac shadow. Her face was hard, almost stern, save for the soft gleam of piteous doubt that looked from her green eyes. Her once fair hair had darkened, but she was lovelier now at twenty-four than she had been at eighteen, when her hair was brighter than she.

Following a walk marked by an intangible mist of bloom that followed the white border stones she came to a space overlooking the sea where there were lanterns asleep in the fig trees and a big table and wicker chairs and a great market umbrella from Sienna, all gathered about an enormous pine, the biggest tree in the garden. She paused there a moment, looking absently at a growth of nasturtiums and iris tangled at its foot, as though sprung from a careless handful of seeds, listening to the plaints and accusations of some nursery squabble in the house. When this died away on the summer air, she walked on, between kaleidoscopic peonies massed in pink clouds, black and brown tulips and fragile mauve-stemmed roses, transparent like sugar flowers in a confectioner's window--until, as if the scherzo of color could reach no further intensity, it broke off suddenly in mid-air, and moist steps went down to a level five feet below.

Here there was a well with the boarding around it dank and slippery even on the brightest days. She went up the stairs on the other side and into the vegetable garden; she walked rather quickly; she liked to be active, though at times she gave an impression of repose that was at once static and evocative. This was because she knew few words and believed in none, and in the world she was rather silent, contributing just her share of urbane humor with a precision that approached meagreness. But at the moment when strangers tended to grow uncomfortable in the presence of this economy she would seize the topic and rush off with it, feverishly surprised with herself--then bring it back and relinquish it abruptly, almost timidly, like an obedient retriever, having been adequate and something more.

As she stood in the fuzzy green light of the vegetable garden, Dick crossed the path ahead of her going to his work house. Nicole waited silently till he had passed; then she went on through lines of prospective salads to a little menagerie where pigeons and rabbits and a parrot made a medley of insolent noises at her. Descending to another ledge she reached a low, curved wall and looked down seven hundred feet to the Mediterranean Sea.

She stood in the ancient hill village of Tarmes. The villa and its grounds were made out of a row of peasant dwellings that abutted on the cliff--five small houses had been combined to make the house and four destroyed to make the garden. The exterior walls were untouched so that from the road far below it was indistinguishable from the violet gray mass of the town.

For a moment Nicole stood looking down at the Mediterranean but there was nothing to do with that, even with her tireless hands. Presently Dick came out of his one-room house carrying a telescope and looked east toward Cannes. In a moment Nicole swam into his field of vision, whereupon he disappeared into his house and came out with a megaphone. He had many light mechanical devices.

"Nicole," he shouted, "I forgot to tell you that as a final apostolic gesture I invited Mrs. Abrams, the woman with the white hair."

"I suspected it. It's an outrage."

The ease with which her reply reached him seemed to belittle his megaphone, so she raised her voice and called, "Can you hear me?"

"Yes." He lowered the megaphone and then raised it stubbornly. "I'm going to invite some more people too. I'm going to invite the two young men."

"All right," she agreed placidly.

"I want to give a really *bad* party. I mean it. I want to give a party where there's a brawl and seductions and people going home with their feelings hurt and women passed out in the cabinet de toilette. You wait and see."

He went back into his house and Nicole saw that one of his most characteristic moods was upon him, the excitement that swept everyone up into it and was inevitably followed by his own form of melancholy, which he never displayed but at which she guessed. This excitement about things reached an intensity out of proportion to their importance, generating a really extraordinary virtuosity with people. Save among a few of the tough-minded and perennially suspicious, he had the power of arousing a fascinated and uncritical love. The reaction came when he realized the waste and extravagance involved. He sometimes looked back with awe at the carnivals of affection he had given, as a general might gaze upon a massacre he had ordered to satisfy an impersonal blood lust.

But to be included in Dick Diver's world for a while was a remarkable experience: people believed he made special reservations about them, recognizing the proud uniqueness of their destinies, buried under the compromises of how many years. He won everyone quickly with an exquisite consideration and a politeness that moved so fast and intuitively that it could be examined only in its effect. Then, without caution, lest the first bloom of the relation wither, he opened the gate to his amusing world. So long as they subscribed to it completely, their happiness was his preoccupation, but at the first flicker of doubt as to its all-inclusiveness he evaporated before their eyes, leaving little communicable memory of what he had said or done.

At eight-thirty that evening he came out to meet his first guests, his coat carried rather ceremoniously, rather promisingly, in his hand, like a toreador's cape. It was characteristic that after greeting Rosemary and her mother he waited for them to speak first, as if to allow them the reassurance of their own voices in new surroundings.

To resume Rosemary's point of view it should be said that, under the spell of the climb to Tarmes and the fresher air, she and her mother looked about appreciatively. Just as the personal qualities of extraordinary people can make themselves plain in an unaccustomed change of expression, so the intensely calculated perfection of Villa Diana transpired all at once through such minute failures as the chance apparition of a maid in the background or the perversity of a cork. While the first guests arrived bringing with them the excitement of the night, the domestic activity of the day receded past them gently, symbolized by the Diver children and their governess still at supper on the terrace.

"What a beautiful garden!" Mrs. Speers exclaimed.

"Nicole's garden," said Dick. "She won't let it alone--she nags it all the time, worries about its diseases. Any day now I expect to have her come down with *Powdery Mildew or Fly Speck, or Late Blight." He pointed his forefinger decisively at Rosemary, saying with a lightness seeming to conceal a paternal interest, "I'm going to save your reason--I'm going to give you a hat to wear on the beach."

He turned them from the garden to the terrace, where he poured a cocktail. Earl Brady arrived, discovering Rosemary with surprise. His manner was softer than at the studio, as if his differentness had been put on at the gate, and Rosemary, comparing him instantly with Dick Diver, swung sharply toward the latter. In comparison Earl Brady seemed faintly gross, faintly ill-bred; once more, though, she felt an electric response to his person.

He spoke familiarly to the children who were getting up from their outdoor supper.

"Hello, Lanier, how about a song? Will you and Topsy sing me a song?"

"What shall we sing?" agreed the little boy, with the odd chanting accent of American children brought up in France.

"That song about 'Mon Ami Pierrot.'"

Brother and sister stood side by side without self-consciousness and their voices soared sweet and shrill upon the evening air.

"Au clair de la lune
Mon Ami Pierrot
Prête-moi ta plume
Pour écrire un mot
Ma chandelle est morte
Je n'ai plus de feu
Ouvre-moi ta porte
Pour l'amour de Dieu."

The singing ceased and the children, their faces aglow with the late sunshine, stood smiling calmly at their success. Rosemary was thinking that the Villa Diana was the centre of the world. On such a stage some memorable thing was sure to happen. She lighted up higher as the gate tinkled open and the rest of the guests arrived in a body--the McKiscos, Mrs. Abrams, Mr. Dumphry, and Mr. Campion came up to the terrace.

Rosemary had a sharp feeling of disappointment--she looked quickly at Dick, as though to ask an explanation of this incongruous mingling. But there was nothing unusual in his expression. He greeted his new guests with a proud bearing and an obvious deference to their infinite and unknown possibilities. She believed in him so much that presently she accepted the rightness of the McKiscos' presence as if she had expected to meet them all along.

"I've met you in Paris," McKisco said to Abe North, who with his wife had arrived on their heels, "in fact I've met you twice."

"Yes, I remember," Abe said.

"Then where was it?" demanded McKisco, not content to let well enough alone.

"Why, I think--" Abe got tired of the game, "I can't remember."

The interchange filled a pause and Rosemary's instinct was that something tactful should be said by somebody, but Dick made no attempt to break up the grouping formed by these late arrivals, not even to disarm Mrs. McKisco of her air of supercilious amusement. He did not solve this social problem because he knew it was not of importance at the moment and would solve itself. He was saving his newness for a larger effort, waiting a more significant moment for his guests to be conscious of a good time.

Rosemary stood beside Tommy Barban--he was in a particularly scornful mood and there seemed to be some special stimulus working upon him. He was leaving in the morning.

"Going home?"

"Home? I have no home. I am going to a war."

"What war?"

"What war? Any war. I haven't seen a paper lately but I suppose there's a war--there always is."

"Don't you care what you fight for?"

"Not at all--so long as I'm well treated. When I'm in a rut I come to see the Divers, because then I know that in a few weeks I'll want to go to war."

Rosemary stiffened.

"You like the Divers," she reminded him.

"Of course--especially her--but they make me want to go to war."

She considered this, to no avail. The Divers made her want to stay near them forever.

"You're half American," she said, as if that should solve the problem.

"Also I'm half French, and I was educated in England and since I was eighteen I've worn the uniforms of eight countries. But I hope I did not give you the impression that I am not fond of the Divers--I am, especially of Nicole."

"How could any one help it?" she said simply.

She felt far from him. The undertone of his words repelled her and she withdrew her adoration for the Divers from the profanity of his bitterness. She was glad he was not next to her at dinner and she was still thinking of his words "especially her" as they moved toward the table in the garden.

For a moment now she was beside Dick Diver on the path. Alongside his hard, neat brightness everything faded into the surety that he knew everything. For a year, which was forever, she had had money and a certain celebrity and contact with the celebrated, and these latter had presented themselves merely as powerful enlargements of the people with whom the doctor's widow and her daughter had associated in a hôtel-pension in Paris. Rosemary was a romantic and her career had not provided many satisfactory opportunities on that score. Her mother, with the idea of a career for Rosemary, would not tolerate any such spurious substitutes as the excitations available on all sides, and indeed Rosemary was already beyond that--she was In the movies but not at all At them. So when she had seen approval of Dick Diver in her mother's face it meant that he was "the real thing"; it meant permission to go as far as she could.

"I was watching you," he said, and she knew he meant it. "We've grown very fond of you."

"I fell in love with you the first time I saw you," she said quietly. He pretended not to have heard, as if the compliment were purely formal.

"New friends," he said, as if it were an important point, "can often have a better time together than old friends."

With that remark, which she did not understand precisely, she found herself at the table, picked out by slowly emerging lights against the dark dusk. A chord of delight struck inside her when she saw that Dick had taken her mother on his right hand; for herself she was between Luis Campion and Brady.

Surcharged with her emotion she turned to Brady with the intention of confiding in him, but at her first mention of Dick a hard-boiled sparkle in his eyes gave her to understand that he refused the fatherly office. In turn she was equally firm when he tried to monopolize her hand, so they talked shop or rather she listened while he talked shop, her polite eyes never leaving his face, but her mind was so definitely elsewhere that she felt he must guess the fact. Intermittently she caught the gist of his sentences and supplied the rest from her subconscious, as one picks up the striking of a clock in the middle with only the rhythm of the first uncounted strokes lingering in the mind.

VII

In a pause Rosemary looked away and up the table where Nicole sat between Tommy Barban and Abe North, her chow's hair foaming and frothing in the candlelight. Rosemary listened, caught sharply by the rich clipped voice in infrequent speech:

"The poor man," Nicole exclaimed. "Why did you want to saw him in two?"

"Naturally I wanted to see what was inside a waiter. Wouldn't you like to know what was inside a waiter?"

"Old menus," suggested Nicole with a short laugh. "Pieces of broken china and tips and pencil stubs."

"Exactly--but the thing was to prove it scientifically. And of course doing it with that musical saw would have eliminated any sordidness."

"Did you intend to play the saw while you performed the operation?" Tommy inquired.

"We didn't get quite that far. We were alarmed by the screams. We thought he might rupture something."

"All sounds very peculiar to me," said Nicole. "Any musician that'll use another musician's saw to--"

They had been at table half an hour and a perceptible change had set in--person by person had given up something, a preoccupation, an anxiety, a suspicion, and now they were only their best selves and the Divers' guests. Not to have been friendly and interested would have seemed to reflect on the Divers, so now they were all trying, and seeing this, Rosemary liked everyone--except McKisco, who had contrived to be the unassimilated member of the party. This was less from ill will than from his determination to sustain with wine the good spirits he had enjoyed on his arrival. Lying back in his place between Earl Brady, to whom he had addressed several withering remarks about the movies, and Mrs. Abrams, to whom he said nothing, he stared at Dick Diver with an expression of devastating irony, the effect being occasionally interrupted by his attempts to engage Dick in a cater-cornered conversation across the table.

"Aren't you a friend of Van Buren Denby?" he would say.

"I don't believe I know him."

"I thought you were a friend of his," he persisted irritably.

When the subject of Mr. Denby fell of its own weight, he essayed other equally irrelative themes, but each time the very deference of Dick's attention seemed to paralyze him, and after a moment's stark pause the conversation that he had interrupted would go on without him. He tried breaking into other dialogues, but it was like continually shaking hands with a glove from which the hand had been withdrawn--so finally, with a resigned air of being among children, he devoted his attention entirely to the champagne.

Rosemary's glance moved at intervals around the table, eager for the others' enjoyment, as if they were her future stepchildren. A gracious table light, emanating from a bowl of spicy pinks, fell upon Mrs. Abrams' face, cooked to a turn in Veuve Cliquot, full of vigor, tolerance, adolescent good will; next to her sat Mr. Royal Dumphry, his girl's comeliness less startling in the pleasure world of evening. Then Violet McKisco, whose prettiness had been piped to the surface of her, so that she ceased her struggle to make tangible to herself her shadowy position as the wife of an arriviste who had not arrived.

Then came Dick, with his arms full of the slack he had taken up from others, deeply merged in his own party.

Then her mother, forever perfect.

Then Barban talking to her mother with an urbane fluency that made Rosemary like him again. Then Nicole. Rosemary saw her suddenly in a new way and found her one of the most beautiful people she had ever known. Her face, the face of a saint, a viking Madonna, shone through the faint motes that snowed across the candlelight, drew down its flush from the wine-colored lanterns in the pine. She was still as still.

Abe North was talking to her about his moral code: "Of course I've got one," he insisted, "--a man can't live without a moral code. Mine is that I'm against the burning of witches. Whenever they burn a witch I get all hot under the collar." Rosemary knew from Brady that he was a musician who after a brilliant and precocious start had composed nothing for seven years.

Next was Campion, managing somehow to restrain his most blatant effeminacy, and even to visit upon those near him a certain disinterested motherliness. Then Mary North with a face so merry that it was impossible not to smile back into the white mirrors of her teeth--the whole area around her parted lips was a lovely little circle of delight.

Finally Brady, whose heartiness became, moment by moment, a social thing instead of a crude assertion and reassertion of his own mental health, and his preservation of it by a detachment from the frailties of others.

Rosemary, as dewy with belief as a child from one of Mrs. Burnett's vicious tracts, had a conviction of homecoming, of a return from the derisive and salacious improvisations of the frontier. There were fireflies riding on the dark air and a dog baying on some low and far-away ledge of the cliff. The table seemed to have risen a little toward the sky like a mechanical dancing platform, giving the people around it a sense of being alone with each other in the dark universe, nourished by its only food, warmed by its only lights. And, as if a curious hushed laugh from Mrs. McKisco were a signal that such a detachment from the world had been attained, the two Divers began suddenly to warm and glow and expand, as if to make up to their guests, already so subtly assured of their importance, so flattered with politeness, for anything they might still miss from that country well left behind. Just for a moment they seemed to speak to every one at the table, singly and together, assuring them of their friendliness, their affection. And for a moment the faces turned up toward them were like the faces of poor children at a Christmas tree. Then abruptly the table broke up--the moment when the guests had been daringly lifted above conviviality into the rarer atmosphere of sentiment, was over before it could be irreverently breathed, before they had half realized it was there.

But the diffused magic of the hot sweet South had withdrawn into them--the soft-pawed night and the ghostly wash of the Mediterranean far below--the magic left these things and melted into the two Divers and became part of them.

Rosemary watched Nicole pressing upon her mother a yellow evening bag she had admired, saying, "I think things ought to belong to the people that like them"--and then sweeping into it all the yellow articles she could find, a pencil, a lipstick, a little note book, "because they all go together."

Nicole disappeared and presently Rosemary noticed that Dick was no longer there; the guests distributed themselves in the garden or drifted in toward the terrace.

"Do you want," Violet McKisco asked Rosemary, "to go to the bathroom?"

Not at that precise moment.

"I want," insisted Mrs. McKisco, "to go to the bathroom." As a frank outspoken woman she walked toward the house, dragging her secret after her, while Rosemary looked after with reprobation. Earl Brady proposed that they walk down to the sea wall but she felt that this was her time to have a share of Dick Diver when he reappeared, so she stalled, listening to McKisco quarrel with Barban.

"Why do you want to fight the Soviets?" McKisco said. "The greatest experiment ever made by humanity? And the Riff? It seems to me it would be more heroic to fight on the just side."

"How do you find out which it is?" asked Barban dryly.

"Why--usually everybody intelligent knows."

"Are you a Communist?"

"I'm a Socialist," said McKisco, "I sympathize with Russia."

"Well, I'm a soldier," Barban answered pleasantly. "My business is to kill people. I fought against the Riff because I am a European, and I have fought the Communists because they want to take my property from me."

"Of all the narrow-minded excuses," McKisco looked around to establish a derisive liaison with some one else, but without success. He had no idea what he was up against in Barban, neither of the simplicity of the other man's bag of ideas nor of the complexity of his training. McKisco knew what ideas were, and as his mind grew he was able to recognize and sort an increasing number of them--but faced by a man whom he considered "dumb," one in whom he found no ideas he could recognize as such, and yet to whom he could not feel personally superior, he jumped at the conclusion that Barban was the end product of an archaic world, and as such, worthless. McKisco's contacts with the princely classes in America had impressed upon him their uncertain and fumbling snobbery, their delight in ignorance and their deliberate rudeness, all lifted from the English with no regard paid to factors that make English philistinism and rudeness purposeful, and applied in a land where a little knowledge and civility buy more than they do anywhere else--an attitude which reached its apogee in the "Harvard manner" of about 1900. He thought that this Barban was of that type, and being drunk rashly forgot that he was in awe of him--this led up to the trouble in which he presently found himself.

Feeling vaguely ashamed for McKisco, Rosemary waited, placid but inwardly on fire, for Dick Diver's return. From her chair at the deserted table with Barban, McKisco, and Abe she looked up along the path edged with shadowy myrtle and fern to the stone terrace, and falling in love with her mother's profile against a lighted door, was about to go there when Mrs. McKisco came hurrying down from the house.

She exuded excitement. In the very silence with which she pulled out a chair and sat down, her eyes staring, her mouth working a little, they all recognized a person crop-full of news, and her husband's "What's the matter, Vi?" came naturally, as all eyes turned toward her.

"My dear--" she said at large, and then addressed Rosemary, "my dear--it's nothing. I really can't say a word."

"You're among friends," said Abe.

"Well, upstairs I came upon a scene, my dears--"

Shaking her head cryptically she broke off just in time, for Tommy arose and addressed her politely but sharply:

"It's inadvisable to comment on what goes on in this house."

VIII

Violet breathed loud and hard once and with an effort brought another expression into her face.

Dick came finally and with a sure instinct he separated Barban and the McKiscos and became excessively ignorant and inquisitive about literature with McKisco--thus giving the latter the moment of superiority which he required. The others helped him carry lamps up--who would not be pleased at carrying lamps helpfully through the darkness? Rosemary helped, meanwhile responding patiently to Royal Dumphry's inexhaustible curiosity about Hollywood.

Now--she was thinking--I've earned a time alone with him. He must know that because his laws are like the laws Mother taught me.

Rosemary was right--presently he detached her from the company on the terrace, and they were alone together, borne away from the house toward the seaside wall with what were less steps than irregularly spaced intervals through some of which she was pulled, through others blown.

They looked out over the Mediterranean. Far below, the last excursion boat from the Isles des Lerins floated across the bay like a Fourth-of-July balloon foot-loose in the heavens. Between the black isles it floated, softly parting the dark tide.

"I understand why you speak as you do of your mother," he said. "Her attitude toward you is very fine, I think. She has a sort of wisdom that's rare in America."

"Mother is perfect," she prayed.

"I was talking to her about a plan I have--she told me that how long you both stayed in France depended on you."

On *you,* Rosemary all but said aloud.

"So since things are over down here--"

"Over?" she inquired.

"Well, this is over--this part of the summer is over. Last week Nicole's sister left, to-morrow Tommy Barban leaves, Monday Abe and Mary North are leaving. Maybe we'll have more fun this summer but this particular fun is over. I want it to die violently instead of fading out sentimentally--that's why I gave this party. What I'm coming to is--Nicole and I are going up to Paris to see Abe North off for America--I wonder if you'd like to go with us."

"What did Mother say?"

"She seemed to think it would be fine. She doesn't want to go herself. She wants you to go alone."

"I haven't seen Paris since I've been grown," said Rosemary. "I'd love to see it with you."

"That's nice of you." Did she imagine that his voice was suddenly metallic? "Of course we've been excited about you from the moment you came on the beach. That vitality, we were sure it was professional--especially Nicole was. It'd never use itself up on any one person or group."

Her instinct cried out to her that he was passing her along slowly toward Nicole and she put her own brakes on, saying with an equal harness:

"I wanted to know all of you too--especially you. I told you I fell in love with you the first time I saw you."

She was right going at it that way. But the space between heaven and earth had cooled his mind, destroyed the impulsiveness that had led him to bring her here, and made him aware of the too obvious appeal, the struggle with an unrehearsed scene and unfamiliar words.

He tried now to make her want to go back to the house and it was difficult, and he did not quite want to lose her. She felt only the draft blowing as he joked with her good-humoredly.

"You don't know what you want. You go and ask your mother what you want."

She was stricken. She touched him, feeling the smooth cloth of his dark coat like a chasuble. She seemed about to fall to her knees--from that position she delivered her last shot.

"I think you're the most wonderful person I ever met--except my mother."

"You have romantic eyes."

His laughter swept them on up toward the terrace where he delivered her to Nicole. . . .

Too soon it had become time to go and the Divers helped them all to go quickly. In the Divers' big Isotta there would be Tommy Barban and his baggage--he was spending the night at the hotel to catch an early train--with Mrs.

Abrams, the McKiscos and Campion. Earl Brady was going to drop Rosemary and her mother on his way to Monte Carlo, and Royal Dumphry rode with them because the Divers' car was crowded. Down in the garden lanterns still glowed over the table where they had dined, as the Divers stood side by side in the gate, Nicole blooming away and filling the night with graciousness, and Dick bidding good-by to everyone by name. To Rosemary it seemed very poignant to drive away and leave them in their house. Again she wondered what Mrs. McKisco had seen in the bathroom.

IX

It was a limpid black night, hung as in a basket from a single dull star. The horn of the car ahead was muffled by the resistance of the thick air. Brady's chauffeur drove slowly; the tail-light of the other car appeared from time to time at turnings--then not at all. But after ten minutes it came into sight again, drawn up at the side of the road. Brady's chauffeur slowed up behind but immediately it began to roll forward slowly and they passed it. In the instant they passed it they heard a blur of voices from behind the reticence of the limousine and saw that the Divers' chauffeur was grinning. Then they went on, going fast through the alternating banks of darkness and thin night, descending at last in a series of roller-coaster swoops, to the great bulk of Gausse's hotel.

Rosemary dozed for three hours and then lay awake, suspended in the moonshine. Cloaked by the erotic darkness she exhausted the future quickly, with all the eventualities that might lead up to a kiss, but with the kiss itself as blurred as a kiss in pictures. She changed position in bed deliberately, the first sign of insomnia she had ever had, and tried to think with her mother's mind about the question. In this process she was often acute beyond her experience, with remembered things from old conversations that had gone into her half-heard.

Rosemary had been brought up with the idea of work. Mrs. Speers had spent the slim leavings of the men who had widowed her on her daughter's education, and when she blossomed out at sixteen with that extraordinary hair, rushed her to Aix-les-Bains and marched her unannounced into the suite of an American producer who was recuperating there. When the producer went to New York they went too. Thus Rosemary had passed her entrance examinations. With the ensuing success and the promise of comparative stability that followed, Mrs. Speers had felt free to tacitly imply tonight:

"You were brought up to work--not especially to marry. Now you've found your first nut to crack and it's a good nut--go ahead and put whatever happens down to experience. Wound yourself or him--whatever happens it can't spoil you because economically you're a boy, not a girl."

Rosemary had never done much thinking, save about the illimitability of her mother's perfections, so this final severance of the umbilical cord disturbed her sleep. A false dawn sent the sky pressing through the tall French windows, and getting up she walked out on the terrace, warm to her bare feet. There were secret noises in the air, an insistent bird achieved an ill-natured triumph with regularity in the trees above the tennis court; footfalls followed a round drive in the rear of the hotel, taking their tone in turn from the dust road, the crushed-stone walk, the cement steps, and then reversing the process in going away. Beyond the inky sea and far up that high, black shadow of a hill lived the Divers. She thought of them both together, heard them still singing faintly a song like rising smoke, like a hymn, very remote in time and far away. Their children slept, their gate was shut for the night.

She went inside and dressing in a light gown and espadrilles went out her window again and along the continuous terrace toward the front door, going fast since she found that other private rooms, exuding sleep, gave upon it. She stopped at the sight of a figure seated on the wide white stairway of the formal entrance--then she saw that it was Luis Campion and that he was weeping.

He was weeping hard and quietly and shaking in the same parts as a weeping woman. A scene in a role she had played last year swept over her irresistibly and advancing she touched him on the shoulder. He gave a little yelp before he recognized her.

"What is it?" Her eyes were level and kind and not slanted into him with hard curiosity. "Can I help you?"

"Nobody can help me. I knew it. I have only myself to blame. It's always the same."

"What is it--do you want to tell me?"

He looked at her to see.

"No," he decided. "When you're older you'll know what people who love suffer. The agony. It's better to be cold and young than to love. It's happened to me before but never like this--so accidental--just when everything was going well."

His face was repulsive in the quickening light. Not by a flicker of her personality, a movement of the smallest muscle, did she betray her sudden disgust with whatever it was. But Campion's sensitivity realized it and he changed the subject rather suddenly.

"Abe North is around here somewhere."

"Why, he's staying at the Divers'!"

"Yes, but he's up--don't you know what happened?"

A shutter opened suddenly in a room two stories above and an English voice spat distinctly:

"Will you kaindlay stup tucking!"

Rosemary and Luis Campion went humbly down the steps and to a bench beside the road to the beach.

"Then you have no idea what's happened? My dear, the most extraordinary thing--" He was warming up now, hanging on to his revelation. "I've never seen a thing come so suddenly--I have always avoided violent people--they upset me so I sometimes have to go to bed for days."

He looked at her triumphantly. She had no idea what he was talking about.

"My dear," he burst forth, leaning toward her with his whole body as he touched her on the upper leg, to show it was no mere irresponsible venture of his hand--he was so sure of himself. "There's going to be a duel."

"Wh-at?"

"A duel with--we don't know what yet."

"Who's going to duel?"

"I'll tell you from the beginning." He drew a long breath and then said, as if it were rather to her discredit but he wouldn't hold it against her. "Of course, you were in the other automobile. Well, in a way you were lucky--I lost at least two years of my life, it came so suddenly."

"What came?" she demanded.

"I don't know what began it. First she began to talk--"

"Who?"

"Violet McKisco." He lowered his voice as if there were people under the bench. "But don't mention the Divers because he made threats against anybody who mentioned it."

"Who did?"

"Tommy Barban, so don't you say I so much as mentioned them. None of us ever found out anyhow what it was Violet had to say because he kept interrupting her, and then her husband got into it and now, my dear, we have the duel. This morning--at five o'clock--in an hour." He sighed suddenly thinking of his own griefs. "I almost wish it were I. I might as well be killed now I have nothing to live for." He broke off and rocked to and fro with sorrow.

Again the iron shutter parted above and the same British voice said:

"Rilly, this must stup immejetely."

Simultaneously Abe North, looking somewhat distracted, came out of the hotel, perceived them against the sky, white over the sea. Rosemary shook her head warningly before he could speak and they moved another bench further down the road. Rosemary saw that Abe was a little tight.

"What are *you* doing up?" he demanded.

"I just got up." She started to laugh, but remembering the voice above, she restrained herself.

"Plagued by the nightingale," Abe suggested, and repeated, "probably plagued by the nightingale. Has this sewing-circle member told you what happened?"

Campion said with dignity:

"I only know what I heard with my own ears."

He got up and walked swiftly away; Abe sat down beside Rosemary.

"Why did you treat him so badly?"

"Did I?" he asked surprised. "He's been weeping around here all morning."

"Well, maybe he's sad about something."

"Maybe he is."

"What about a duel? Who's going to duel? I thought there was something strange in that car. Is it true?"

"It certainly is coo-coo but it seems to be true."

X

The trouble began at the time Earl Brady's car passed the Divers' car stopped on the road--Abe's account melted impersonally into the thronged night--Violet McKisco was telling Mrs. Abrams something she had found out about the Divers--she had gone upstairs in their house and she had come upon something there which had made a great impression on her. But Tommy is a watch-dog about the Divers. As a matter of fact she is inspiring and formidable--but it's a mutual thing, and the fact of The Divers together is more important to their friends than many of them realize. Of course it's done at a certain sacrifice--sometimes they seem just rather charming figures in a ballet, and worth just the attention you give a ballet, but it's more than that--you'd have to know the story. Anyhow Tommy is one of those men that Dick's passed along to Nicole and when Mrs. McKisco kept hinting at her story, he called them on it. He said:

"Mrs. McKisco, please don't talk further about Mrs. Diver."

"I wasn't talking to you," she objected.

"I think it's better to leave them out."

"Are they so sacred?"

"Leave them out. Talk about something else."

He was sitting on one of the two little seats beside Campion. Campion told me the story.

"Well, you're pretty high-handed," Violet came back.

You know how conversations are in cars late at night, some people murmuring and some not caring, giving up after the party, or bored or asleep. Well, none of them knew just what happened until the car stopped and Barban cried in a voice that shook everybody, a voice for cavalry.

"Do you want to step out here--we're only a mile from the hotel and you can walk it or I'll drag you there. *You've got to shut up and shut your wife up!*"

"You're a bully," said McKisco. "You know you're stronger muscularly than I am. But I'm not afraid of you--what they ought to have is the code duello--"

There's where he made his mistake because Tommy, being French, leaned over and clapped him one, and then the chauffeur drove on. That was where you passed them. Then the women began. That was still the state of things when the car got to the hotel.

Tommy telephoned some man in Cannes to act as second and McKisco said he wasn't going to be seconded by Campion, who wasn't crazy for the job anyhow, so he telephoned me not to say anything but to come right down. Violet McKisco collapsed and Mrs. Abrams took her to her room and gave her a bromide whereupon she fell comfortably asleep on the bed. When I got there I tried to argue with Tommy but the latter wouldn't accept anything short of an apology and McKisco rather spunkily wouldn't give it.

When Abe had finished Rosemary asked thoughtfully:

"Do the Divers know it was about them?"

"No--and they're not ever going to know they had anything to do with it. That damn Campion had no business talking to you about it, but since he did--I told the chauffeur I'd get out the old musical saw if he opened his mouth about it. This fight's between two men--what Tommy needs is a good war."

"I hope the Divers don't find out," Rosemary said.

Abe peered at his watch.

"I've got to go up and see McKisco--do you want to come?--he feels sort of friendless--I bet he hasn't slept."

Rosemary had a vision of the desperate vigil that high-strung, badly organized man had probably kept. After a moment balanced between pity and repugnance she agreed, and full of morning energy, bounced upstairs beside Abe.

McKisco was sitting on his bed with his alcoholic combativeness vanished, in spite of the glass of champagne in his hand. He seemed very puny and cross and white. Evidently he had been writing and drinking all night. He stared confusedly at Abe and Rosemary and asked:

"Is it time?"

"No, not for half an hour."

The table was covered with papers which he assembled with some difficulty into a long letter; the writing on the last pages was very large and illegible. In the delicate light of electric lamps fading, he scrawled his name at the bottom, crammed it into an envelope and handed it to Abe. "For my wife."

"You better souse your head in cold water," Abe suggested.

"You think I'd better?" inquired McKisco doubtfully. "I don't want to get too sober."

"Well, you look terrible now."

Obediently McKisco went into the bathroom.

"I'm leaving everything in an awful mess," he called. "I don't know how Violet will get back to America. I don't carry any insurance. I never got around to it."

"Don't talk nonsense, you'll be right here eating breakfast in an hour."

"Sure, I know." He came back with his hair wet and looked at Rosemary as if he saw her for the first time. Suddenly tears stood in his eyes. "I never have finished my novel. That's what makes me so sore. You don't like me," he said to Rosemary, "but that can't be helped. I'm primarily a literary man." He made a vague discouraged sound and shook his head helplessly. "I've made lots of mistakes in my life--many of them. But I've been one of the most prominent--in some ways--"

He gave this up and puffed at a dead cigarette.

"I do like you," said Rosemary, "but I don't think you ought to fight a duel."

"Yeah, I should have tried to beat him up, but it's done now. I've let myself be drawn into something that I had no right to be. I have a very violent temper--" He looked closely at Abe as if he expected the statement to be challenged. Then with an aghast laugh he raised the cold cigarette butt toward his mouth. His breathing quickened.

"The trouble was I suggested the duel--if Violet had only kept her mouth shut I could have fixed it. Of course even now I can just leave, or sit back and laugh at the whole thing--but I don't think Violet would ever respect me again."

"Yes, she would," said Rosemary. "She'd respect you more."

"No--you don't know Violet. She's very hard when she gets an advantage over you. We've been married twelve years, we had a little girl seven years old and she died and after that you know how it is. We both played around on the side a little, nothing serious but drifting apart--she called me a coward out there tonight."

Troubled, Rosemary didn't answer.

"Well, we'll see there's as little damage done as possible," said Abe. He opened the leather case. "These are Barban's duelling pistols--I borrowed them so you could get familiar with them. He carries them in his suitcase." He weighed one of the archaic weapons in his hand. Rosemary gave an exclamation of uneasiness and McKisco looked at the pistols anxiously.

"Well--it isn't as if we were going to stand up and pot each other with forty-fives," he said.

"I don't know," said Abe cruelly; "the idea is you can sight better along a long barrel."

"How about distance?" asked McKisco.

"I've inquired about that. If one or the other parties has to be definitely eliminated they make it eight paces, if they're just good and sore it's twenty paces, and if it's only to vindicate their honor it's forty paces. His second agreed with me to make it forty."

"That's good."

"There's a wonderful duel in a novel of Pushkin's," recollected Abe. "Each man stood on the edge of a precipice, so if he was hit at all he was done for."

This seemed very remote and academic to McKisco, who stared at him and said, "What?"

"Do you want to take a quick dip and freshen up?"

"No--no, I couldn t swim." He sighed. "I don't see what it's all about," he said helplessly. "I don't see why I'm doing it."

It was the first thing he had ever done in his life. Actually he was one of those for whom the sensual world does not exist, and faced with a concrete fact he brought to it a vast surprise.

"We might as well be going," said Abe, seeing him fail a little.

"All right." He drank off a stiff drink of brandy, put the flask in his pocket, and said with almost a savage air: "What'll happen if I kill him--will they throw me in jail?"

"I'll run you over the Italian border."

He glanced at Rosemary--and then said apologetically to Abe:

"Before we start there's one thing I'd like to see you about alone."

"I hope neither of you gets hurt," Rosemary said. "I think it's very foolish and you ought to try to stop it."

XI

She found Campion downstairs in the deserted lobby.

"I saw you go upstairs," he said excitedly. "Is he all right? When is the duel going to be?"

"I don't know." She resented his speaking of it as a circus, with McKisco as the tragic clown.

"Will you go with me?" he demanded, with the air of having seats. "I've hired the hotel car."

"I don't want to go."

"Why not? I imagine it'll take years off my life but I wouldn't miss it for worlds. We could watch it from quite far away."

"Why don't you get Mr. Dumphry to go with you?"

His monocle fell out, with no whiskers to hide in--he drew himself up.

"I never want to see him again."

"Well, I'm afraid I can't go. Mother wouldn't like it."

As Rosemary entered her room Mrs. Speers stirred sleepily and called to her:

"Where've you been?"

"I just couldn't sleep. You go back to sleep, Mother."

"Come in my room." Hearing her sit up in bed, Rosemary went in and told her what had happened.

"Why don't you go and see it?" Mrs. Speers suggested. "You needn't go up close and you might be able to help afterwards."

Rosemary did not like the picture of herself looking on and she demurred, but Mrs. Speer's consciousness was still clogged with sleep and she was reminded of night calls to death and calamity when she was the wife of a doctor. "I like you to go places and do things on your own initiative without me--you did much harder things for Rainy's publicity stunts."

Still Rosemary did not see why she should go, but she obeyed the sure, clear voice that had sent her into the stage entrance of the Odeon in Paris when she was twelve and greeted her when she came out again.

She thought she was reprieved when from the steps she saw Abe and McKisco drive away--but after a moment the hotel car came around the corner. Squealing delightedly Luis Campion pulled her in beside him.

"I hid there because they might not let us come. I've got my movie camera, you see."

She laughed helplessly. He was so terrible that he was no longer terrible, only dehumanized.

"I wonder why Mrs. McKisco didn't like the Divers?" she said. "They were very nice to her."

"Oh, it wasn't that. It was something she saw. We never did find exactly what it was because of Barban."

"Then that wasn't what made you so sad."

"Oh, no," he said, his voice breaking, "that was something else that happened when we got back to the hotel. But now I don't care--I wash my hands of it completely."

They followed the other car east along the shore past Juan les Pins, where the skeleton of the new Casino was rising. It was past four and under a blue-gray sky the first fishing boats were creaking out into a glaucous sea. Then they turned off the main road and into the back country.

"It's the golf course," cried Campion, "I'm sure that's where it's going to be."

He was right. When Abe's car pulled up ahead of them the east was crayoned red and yellow, promising a sultry day. Ordering the hotel car into a grove of pines Rosemary and Campion kept in the shadow of a wood and skirted the bleached fairway where Abe and McKisco were walking up and down, the latter raising his head at intervals like a rabbit scenting. Presently there were moving figures over by a farther tee and the watchers made out Barban and his French second--the latter carried the box of pistols under his arm.

Somewhat appalled, McKisco slipped behind Abe and took a long swallow of brandy. He walked on choking and would have marched directly up into the other party, but Abe stopped him and went forward to talk to the Frenchman. The sun was over the horizon.

Campion grabbed Rosemary's arm.

"I can't stand it," he squeaked, almost voiceless. "It's too much. This will cost me--"

"Let go," Rosemary said peremptorily. She breathed a frantic prayer in French.

The principals faced each other, Barban with the sleeve rolled up from his arm. His eyes gleamed restlessly in the sun, but his motion was deliberate as he wiped his palm on the seam of his trousers. McKisco, reckless with brandy, pursed his lips in a whistle and pointed his long nose about nonchalantly, until

Abe stepped forward with a handkerchief in his hand. The French second stood with his face turned away. Rosemary caught her breath in terrible pity and gritted her teeth with hatred for Barban; then:

"One--two--three!" Abe counted in a strained voice.

They fired at the same moment. McKisco swayed but recovered himself. Both shots had missed.

"Now, that's enough!" cried Abe.

The duellists walked in, and everyone looked at Barban inquiringly.

"I declare myself unsatisfied."

"What? Sure you're satisfied," said Abe impatiently. "You just don't know it."

"Your man refuses another shot?"

"You're damn right, Tommy. You insisted on this and my client went through with it."

Tommy laughed scornfully.

"The distance was ridiculous," he said. "I'm not accustomed to such farces--your man must remember he's not now in America."

"No use cracking at America," said Abe rather sharply. And then, in a more conciliatory tone, "This has gone far enough, Tommy." They parleyed briskly for a moment--then Barban nodded and bowed coldly to his late antagonist.

"No shake hand?" suggested the French doctor.

"They already know each other," said Abe.

He turned to McKisco.

"Come on, let's get out."

As they strode off, McKisco, in exultation, gripped his arm.

"Wait a minute!" Abe said. "Tommy wants his pistol back. He might need it again."

McKisco handed it over.

"To hell with him," he said in a tough voice. "Tell him he can--"

"Shall I tell him you want another shot?"

"Well, I did it," cried McKisco, as they went along. "And I did it pretty well, didn't I? I wasn't yellow."

"You were pretty drunk," said Abe bluntly.

"No, I wasn't."

"All right, then, you weren't."

"Why would it make any difference if I had a drink or so?"

As his confidence mounted he looked resentfully at Abe.

"What difference does that make?" he repeated.

"If you can't see it, there's no use going into it."

"Don't you know everybody was drunk all the time during the war?"

"Well, let's forget it."

But the episode was not quite over. There were urgent footsteps in the heather behind them and the doctor drew up alongside.

"Pardon, Messieurs," he panted. "Voulez-vous regler mes honorairies? Naturellement c'est pour soins médicaux seulement. M. Barban n'a qu'un billet de mille et ne peut pas les régler et l'autre a laissé son porte-monnaie chez lui."

"Trust a Frenchman to think of that," said Abe, and then to the doctor. "Combien?"

"Let me pay this," said McKisco.

"No, I've got it. We were all in about the same danger."

Abe paid the doctor while McKisco suddenly turned into the bushes and was sick there. Then paler than before he strutted on with Abe toward the car through the now rosy morning.

Campion lay gasping on his back in the shrubbery, the only casualty of the duel, while Rosemary suddenly hysterical with laughter kept kicking at him with her espadrille. She did this persistently until she roused him--the only matter of importance to her now was that in a few hours she would see the person whom she still referred to in her mind as "the Divers" on the beach.

XII

They were at Voisins waiting for Nicole, six of them, Rosemary, the Norths, Dick Diver and two young French musicians. They were looking over the other patrons of the restaurant to see if they had repose--Dick said no American men had any repose, except himself, and they were seeking an example to confront him with. Things looked black for them--not a man had come into the restaurant for ten minutes without raising his hand to his face.

"We ought never to have given up waxed mustaches," said Abe. "Nevertheless Dick isn't the *only* man with repose--"

"Oh, yes, I am."

"--but he may be the only sober man with repose."

A well-dressed American had come in with two women who swooped and fluttered unselfconsciously around a table. Suddenly, he perceived that he was being watched--whereupon his hand rose spasmodically and arranged a phantom bulge in his necktie. In another unseated party a man endlessly patted his shaven cheek with his palm, and his companion mechanically raised and lowered the stub of a cold cigar. The luckier ones fingered eyeglasses and facial hair, the unequipped stroked blank mouths, or even pulled desperately at the lobes of their ears.

A well-known general came in, and Abe, counting on the man's first year at West Point--that year during which no cadet can resign and from which none ever recovers--made a bet with Dick of five dollars.

His hands hanging naturally at his sides, the general waited to be seated. Once his arms swung suddenly backward like a jumper's and Dick said, "Ah!"

supposing he had lost control, but the general recovered and they breathed again--the agony was nearly over, the garçon was pulling out his chair . . .

With a touch of fury the conqueror shot up his hand and scratched his gray immaculate head.

"You see," said Dick smugly, "I'm the only one."

Rosemary was quite sure of it and Dick, realizing that he never had a better audience, made the group into so bright a unit that Rosemary felt an impatient disregard for all who were not at their table. They had been two days in Paris but actually they were still under the beach umbrella. When, as at the ball of the Corps des Pages the night before, the surroundings seemed formidable to Rosemary, who had yet to attend a Mayfair party in Hollywood, Dick would bring the scene within range by greeting a few people, a sort of selection--the Divers seemed to have a large acquaintance, but it was always as if the person had not seen them for a long, long time, and was utterly bowled over, "Why, where do you *keep* yourselves?"--and then re-create the unity of his own party by destroying the outsiders softly but permanently with an ironic coup de grâce. Presently Rosemary seemed to have known those people herself in some deplorable past, and then got on to them, rejected them, discarded them.

Their own party was overwhelmingly American and sometimes scarcely American at all. It was themselves he gave back to them, blurred by the compromises of how many years.

Into the dark, smoky restaurant, smelling of the rich raw foods on the buffet, slid Nicole's sky-blue suit like a stray segment of the weather outside. Seeing from their eyes how beautiful she was, she thanked them with a smile of radiant appreciation. They were all very nice people for a while, very courteous and all that. Then they grew tired of it and they were funny and bitter, and finally they made a lot of plans. They laughed at things that they would not remember clearly afterward--laughed a lot and the men drank three bottles of wine. The trio of women at the table were representative of the enormous flux of American life. Nicole was the granddaughter of a self-made American capitalist and the granddaughter of a Count of the House of Lippe Weissenfeld. Mary North was the daughter of a journeyman paper-hanger and a descendant of President Tyler. Rosemary was from the middle of the middle class, catapulted by her mother onto the uncharted heights of Hollywood. Their point of resemblance to each other and their difference from so many American women, lay in the fact that they were all happy to exist in a man's world--they preserved their individuality through men and not by opposition to them. They would all three have made alternatively good courtesans or good wives not by the accident of birth but through the greater accident of finding their man or not finding him.

So Rosemary found it a pleasant party, that luncheon, nicer in that there were only seven people, about the limit of a good party. Perhaps, too, the fact that she was new to their world acted as a sort of catalytic agent to precipitate out all their old reservations about one another. After the table broke up, a waiter directed Rosemary back into the dark hinterland of all French restaurants, where she looked up a phone number by a dim orange bulb, and called Franco-American Films. Sure, they had a print of "Daddy's Girl"--it was out for the moment, but they would run it off later in the week for her at 341 Rue des Saintes Anges--ask for Mr. Crowder.

The semi-booth gave on the vestiaire and as Rosemary hung up the receiver she heard two low voices not five feet from her on the other side of a row of coats.

"--So you love me?"

"Oh, *do* I!"

It Was Nicole--Rosemary hesitated in the door of the booth--then she heard Dick say:

"I want you terribly--let's go to the hotel now." Nicole gave a little gasping sigh. For a moment the words conveyed nothing at all to Rosemary--but the tone did. The vast secretiveness of it vibrated to herself.

"I want you."

"I'll be at the hotel at four."

Rosemary stood breathless as the voices moved away. She was at first even astonished--she had seen them in their relation to each other as people without personal exigencies--as something cooler. Now a strong current of emotion flowed through her, profound and unidentified. She did not know whether she was attracted or repelled, but only that she was deeply moved. It made her feel very alone as she went back into the restaurant, but it was touching to look in upon, and the passionate gratitude of Nicole's "Oh, *do* I!" echoed in her mind. The particular mood of the passage she had witnessed lay ahead of her; but however far she was from it her stomach told her it was all right--she had none of the aversion she had felt in the playing of certain love scenes in pictures.

Being far away from it she nevertheless irrevocably participated in it now, and shopping with Nicole she was much more conscious of the assignation than Nicole herself. She looked at Nicole in a new way, estimating her attractions. Certainly she was the most attractive woman Rosemary had ever met--with her hardness, her devotions and loyalties, and a certain elusiveness, which Rosemary, thinking now through her mother's middle-class mind, associated with her attitude about money. Rosemary spent money she had earned--she was here in Europe due to the fact that she had gone in the pool six times that January day with her temperature roving from 99° in the early morning to 103°, when her mother stopped it.

With Nicole's help Rosemary bought two dresses and two hats and four pairs of shoes with her money. Nicole bought from a great list that ran two pages, and bought the things in the windows besides. Everything she liked that she couldn't possibly use herself, she bought as a present for a friend. She bought colored beads, folding beach cushions, artificial flowers, honey, a guest bed, bags, scarfs, love birds, miniatures for a doll's house and three yards of some new cloth the color of prawns. She bought a dozen bathing suits, a rubber alligator, a travelling chess set of gold and ivory, big linen handkerchiefs for Abe, two chamois leather jackets of kingfisher blue and burning bush from Hermes--bought all these things not a bit like a high-class courtesan buying underwear and jewels, which were after all professional equipment and insurance--but with an entirely different point of view. Nicole was the product of much ingenuity and toil. For her sake trains began their run at Chicago and traversed the round belly of the continent to California; chicle factories fumed and link belts grew link by link in factories; men mixed toothpaste in vats and drew mouthwash out of copper hogsheads; girls canned tomatoes quickly in August or worked rudely at the Five-and-Tens on Christmas Eve; half-breed Indians toiled on Brazilian coffee plantations and dreamers were muscled out of patent rights in new tractors--these were some of the people who gave a tithe to Nicole, and as the whole system swayed and thundered onward it lent a feverish bloom to such processes of hers as wholesale buying, like the flush of a fireman's face holding his post before a spreading blaze. She illustrated very simple principles, containing in herself her own doom, but illustrated them so accurately that there was grace in the procedure, and presently Rosemary would try to imitate it.

It was almost four. Nicole stood in a shop with a love bird on her shoulder, and had one of her infrequent outbursts of speech.

"Well, what if you hadn't gone in that pool that day--I sometimes wonder about such things. Just before the war we were in Berlin--I was thirteen, it was just before Mother died. My sister was going to a court ball and she had three of the royal princes on her dance card, all arranged by a chamberlain and everything. Half an hour before she was going to start she had a side ache and a high fever. The doctor said it was appendicitis and she ought to be operated on. But Mother had her plans made, so Baby went to the ball and danced till two with an ice pack strapped on under her evening dress. She was operated on at seven o'clock next morning."

It was good to be hard, then; all nice people were hard on themselves. But it was four o'clock and Rosemary kept thinking of Dick waiting for Nicole now at the hotel. She must go there, she must not make him wait for her. She kept thinking, "Why don't you go?" and then suddenly, "Or let me go if you don't want to." But Nicole went to one more place to buy corsages for them both and sent one to Mary North. Only then she seemed to remember and with sudden abstraction she signalled for a taxi.

"Good-by," said Nicole. "We had fun, didn't we?"

"Loads of fun," said Rosemary. It was more difficult than she thought and her whole self protested as Nicole drove away.

XIII

Dick turned the corner of the traverse and continued along the trench walking on the duckboard. He came to a periscope, looked through it a moment; then he got up on the step and peered over the parapet. In front of him beneath a dingy sky was Beaumont Hamel; to his left the tragic hill of Thiepval. Dick stared at them through his field glasses, his throat straining with sadness.

He went on along the trench, and found the others waiting for him in the next traverse. He was full of excitement and he wanted to communicate it to them, to make them understand about this, though actually Abe North had seen battle service and he had not.

"This land here cost twenty lives a foot that summer," he said to Rosemary. She looked out obediently at the rather bare green plain with its low trees of six years' growth. If Dick had added that they were now being shelled she would have believed him that afternoon. Her love had reached a point where now at last she was beginning to be unhappy, to be desperate. She didn't know what to do--she wanted to talk to her mother.

"There are lots of people dead since and we'll all be dead soon," said Abe consolingly.

Rosemary waited tensely for Dick to continue.

"See that little stream--we could walk to it in two minutes. It took the British a month to walk to it--a whole empire walking very slowly, dying in front and pushing forward behind. And another empire walked very slowly backward a few inches a day, leaving the dead like a million bloody rugs. No Europeans will ever do that again in this generation."

"Why, they've only just quit over in Turkey," said Abe. "And in Morocco--"

"That's different. This western-front business couldn't be done again, not for a long time. The young men think they could do it but they couldn't. They could fight the first Marne again but not this. This took religion and years of plenty and tremendous sureties and the exact relation that existed between the classes. The Russians and Italians weren't any good on this front. You had to have a whole-souled sentimental equipment going back further than you could remember. You had to remember Christmas, and postcards of the Crown Prince and his fiancée, and little cafés in Valence and beer gardens in Unter den Linden and weddings at the mairie, and going to the Derby, and your grandfather's whiskers."

"General Grant invented this kind of battle at Petersburg in sixty-five."

"No, he didn't--he just invented mass butchery. This kind of battle was invented by Lewis Carroll and Jules Verne and whoever wrote Undine, and country deacons bowling and marraines in Marseilles and girls seduced in the back lanes of Wurtemburg and Westphalia. Why, this was a love battle--there was a century of middle-class love spent here. This was the last love battle."

"You want to hand over this battle to D. H. Lawrence," said Abe.

"All my beautiful lovely safe world blew itself up here with a great gust of high explosive love," Dick mourned persistently. "Isn't that true, Rosemary?"

"I don't know," she answered with a grave face. "You know everything."

They dropped behind the others. Suddenly a shower of earth gobs and pebbles came down on them and Abe yelled from the next traverse:

"The war spirit's getting into me again. I have a hundred years of Ohio love behind me and I'm going to bomb out this trench." His head popped up over the embankment. "You're dead--don't you know the rules? That was a grenade."

Rosemary laughed and Dick picked up a retaliatory handful of stones and then put them down.

"I couldn't kid here," he said rather apologetically. "The silver cord is cut and the golden bowl is broken and all that, but an old romantic like me can't do anything about it."

"I'm romantic too."

They came out of the neat restored trench, and faced a memorial to the Newfoundland dead. Reading the inscription Rosemary burst into sudden tears. Like most women she liked to be told how she should feel, and she liked Dick's telling her which things were ludicrous and which things were sad. But most of all she wanted him to know how she loved him, now that the fact was upsetting everything, now that she was walking over the battlefield in a thrilling dream.

After that they got in their car and started back toward Amiens. A thin warm rain was falling on the new scrubby woods and underbrush and they passed great funeral pyres of sorted duds, shells, bombs, grenades, and equipment, helmets, bayonets, gun stocks and rotten leather, abandoned six years in the ground. And suddenly around a bend the white caps of a great sea of graves. Dick asked the chauffeur to stop.

"There's that girl--and she still has her wreath."

They watched as he got out and went over to the girl, who stood uncertainly by the gate with a wreath in her hand. Her taxi waited. She was a red-haired girl from Tennessee whom they had met on the train this morning, come from Knoxville to lay a memorial on her brother's grave. There were tears of vexation on her face.

"The War Department must have given me the wrong number," she whimpered. "It had another name on it. I been lookin' for it since two o'clock, and there's so many graves."

"Then if I were you I'd just lay it on any grave without looking at the name," Dick advised her.

"You reckon that's what I ought to do?"

"I think that's what he'd have wanted you to do."

It was growing dark and the rain was coming down harder.

She left the wreath on the first grave inside the gate, and accepted Dick's suggestion that she dismiss her taxi-cab and ride back to Amiens with them.

Rosemary shed tears again when she heard of the mishap--altogether it had been a watery day, but she felt that she had learned something, though exactly what it was she did not know. Later she remembered all the hours of the afternoon as happy--one of those uneventful times that seem at the moment only a link between past and future pleasure but turn out to have been the pleasure itself.

Amiens was an echoing purple town, still sad with the war, as some railroad stations were:--the Gare du Nord and Waterloo station in London. In the daytime one is deflated by such towns, with their little trolley cars of twenty years ago crossing the great gray cobble-stoned squares in front of the cathedral, and the very weather seems to have a quality of the past, faded weather like that of old photographs. But after dark all that is most satisfactory in French life swims back into the picture--the sprightly tarts, the men arguing with a hundred Voilàs in the cafés, the couples drifting, head to head, toward the satisfactory inexpensiveness of nowhere. Waiting for the train they sat in a big arcade, tall enough to release the smoke and chatter and music upward and obligingly the orchestra launched into "Yes, We Have No Bananas,"--they clapped, because the leader looked so pleased with himself. The Tennessee girl forgot her sorrow and enjoyed herself, even began flirtations of tropical eye-rollings and pawings, with Dick and Abe. They teased her gently.

Then, leaving infinitesimal sections of Wurtemburgers, Prussian Guards, Chasseurs Alpins, Manchester mill hands and old Etonians to pursue their eternal dissolution under the warm rain, they took the train for Paris. They ate sandwiches of mortadel sausage and bel paese cheese made up in the station restaurant, and drank Beaujolais. Nicole was abstracted, biting her lip restlessly and reading over the guide-books to the battle-field that Dick had brought along--indeed, he had made a quick study of the whole affair, simplifying it always until it bore a faint resemblance to one of his own parties.

XIV

When they reached Paris Nicole was too tired to go on to the grand illumination at the Decorative Art Exposition as they had planned. They left her at the Hotel Roi George, and as she disappeared between the intersecting planes made by lobby lights of the glass doors, Rosemary's oppression lifted. Nicole was a force--not necessarily well disposed or predictable like her mother--an incalculable force. Rosemary was somewhat afraid of her.

At eleven she sat with Dick and the Norths at a houseboat café just opened on the Seine. The river shimmered with lights from the bridges and cradled many cold moons. On Sundays sometimes when Rosemary and her mother had lived in Paris they had taken the little steamer up to Suresnes and talked about plans for the future. They had little money but Mrs. Speers was so sure of Rosemary's beauty and had implanted in her so much ambition, that she was willing to gamble the money on "advantages"; Rosemary in turn was to repay her mother when she got her start. . . .

Since reaching Paris Abe North had had a thin vinous fur over him; his eyes were bloodshot from sun and wine. Rosemary realized for the first time that he was always stopping in places to get a drink, and she wondered how Mary North liked it. Mary was quiet, so quiet save for her frequent laughter that Rosemary had learned little about her. She liked the straight dark hair brushed back until it met some sort of natural cascade that took care of it--from time to time it eased with a jaunty slant over the corner of her temple, until it was almost in her eye when she tossed her head and caused it to fall sleek into place once more.

"We'll turn in early to-night, Abe, after this drink." Mary's voice was light but it held a little flicker of anxiety. "You don't want to be poured on the boat."

"It's pretty late now," Dick said. "We'd all better go."

The noble dignity of Abe's face took on a certain stubbornness, and he remarked with determination:

"Oh, no." He paused gravely. "Oh, no, not yet. We'll have another bottle of champagne."

"No more for me," said Dick.

"It's Rosemary I'm thinking of. She's a natural alcoholic--keeps a bottle of gin in the bathroom and all that--her mother told me."

He emptied what was left of the first bottle into Rosemary's glass. She had made herself quite sick the first day in Paris with quarts of lemonade; after that she had taken nothing with them but now she raised the champagne and drank at it.

"But what's this?" exclaimed Dick. "You told me you didn't drink."

"I didn't say I was never going to."

"What about your mother?"

"I'm just going to drink this one glass." She felt some necessity for it. Dick drank, not too much, but he drank, and perhaps it would bring her closer to him, be a part of the equipment for what she had to do. She drank it quickly, choked and then said, "Besides, yesterday was my birthday--I was eighteen."

"Why didn't you tell us?" they said indignantly.

"I knew you'd make a fuss over it and go to a lot of trouble." She finished the champagne. "So this is the celebration."

"It most certainly is not," Dick assured her. "The dinner tomorrow night is your birthday party and don't forget it. Eighteen--why that's a terribly important age."

"I used to think until you're eighteen nothing matters," said Mary.

"That's right," Abe agreed. "And afterward it's the same way."

"Abe feels that nothing matters till he gets on the boat," said Mary. "This time he really has got everything planned out when he gets to New York." She spoke as though she were tired of saying things that no longer had a meaning for her, as if in reality the course that she and her husband followed, or failed to follow, had become merely an intention.

"He'll be writing music in America and I'll be working at singing in Munich, so when we get together again there'll be nothing we can't do."

"That's wonderful," agreed Rosemary, feeling the champagne.

"Meanwhile, another touch of champagne for Rosemary. Then she'll be more able to rationalize the acts of her lymphatic glands. They only begin to function at eighteen."

Dick laughed indulgently at Abe, whom he loved, and in whom he had long lost hope: "That's medically incorrect and we're going." Catching the faint patronage Abe said lightly:

"Something tells me I'll have a new score on Broadway long before you've finished your scientific treatise."

"I hope so," said Dick evenly. "I hope so. I may even abandon what you call my 'scientific treatise.'"

"Oh, Dick!" Mary's voice was startled, was shocked. Rosemary had never before seen Dick's face utterly expressionless; she felt that this announcement was something momentous and she was inclined to exclaim with Mary "Oh, Dick!"

But suddenly Dick laughed again, added to his remark "--abandon it for another one," and got up from the table.

"But Dick, sit down. I want to know--"

"I'll tell you some time. Good night, Abe. Good night, Mary."

"Good night, dear Dick." Mary smiled as if she were going to be perfectly happy sitting there on the almost deserted boat. She was a brave, hopeful woman and she was following her husband somewhere, changing herself to this kind of person or that, without being able to lead him a step out of his path, and sometimes realizing with discouragement how deep in him the guarded secret of her direction lay. And yet an air of luck clung about her, as if she were a sort of token. . . .

XV

"What is it you are giving up?" demanded Rosemary, facing Dick earnestly in the taxi.

"Nothing of importance."

"Are you a scientist?"

"I'm a doctor of medicine."

"Oh-h!" she smiled delightedly. "My father was a doctor too. Then why don't you--" she stopped.

"There's no mystery. I didn't disgrace myself at the height of my career, and hide away on the Riviera. I'm just not practising. You can't tell, I'll probably practise again some day."

Rosemary put up her face quietly to be kissed. He looked at her for a moment as if he didn't understand. Then holding her in the hollow of his arm he rubbed his cheek against her cheek's softness, and then looked down at her for another long moment.

"Such a lovely child," he said gravely.

She smiled up at him; her hands playing conventionally with the lapels of his coat. "I'm in love with you and Nicole. Actually that's my secret--I can't even talk about you to anybody because I don't want any more people to know how wonderful you are. Honestly--I love you and Nicole--I do."

--So many times he had heard this--even the formula was the same.

Suddenly she came toward him, her youth vanishing as she passed inside the focus of his eyes and he had kissed her breathlessly as if she were any age at all. Then she lay back against his arm and sighed.

"I've decided to give you up," she said.

Dick started--had he said anything to imply that she possessed any part of him?

"But that's very mean," he managed to say lightly, "just when I was getting interested."

"I've loved you so--" As if it had been for years. She was weeping a little now. "I've loved you so-o-o."

Then he should have laughed, but he heard himself saying, "Not only are you beautiful but you are somehow on the grand scale. Everything you do, like pretending to be in love or pretending to be shy gets across."

In the dark cave of the taxi, fragrant with the perfume Rosemary had bought with Nicole, she came close again, clinging to him. He kissed her without enjoying it. He knew that there was passion there, but there was no shadow of it in her eyes or on her mouth; there was a faint spray of champagne on her breath. She clung nearer desperately and once more he kissed her and was chilled by the innocence of her kiss, by the glance that at the moment of contact looked beyond him out into the darkness of the night, the darkness of the world. She did not know yet that splendor is something in the heart; at the moment when she realized that and melted into the passion of the universe he could take her without question or regret.

Her room in the hotel was diagonally across from theirs and nearer the elevator. When they reached the door she said suddenly:

"I know you don't love me--I don't expect it. But you said I should have told you about my birthday. Well, I did, and now for my birthday present I want you to come into my room a minute while I tell you something. Just one minute."

They went in and he closed the door, and Rosemary stood close to him, not touching him. The night had drawn the color from her face--she was pale as pale now, she was a white carnation left after a dance.

"When you smile--" He had recovered his paternal attitude, perhaps because of Nicole's silent proximity, "I always think I'll see a gap where you've lost some baby teeth."

But he was too late--she came close up against him with a forlorn whisper.

"Take me."

"Take you where?"

Astonishment froze him rigid.

"Go on," she whispered. "Oh, please go on, whatever they do. I don't care if I don't like it--I never expected to--I've always hated to think about it but now I don't. I want you to."

She was astonished at herself--she had never imagined she could talk like that. She was calling on things she had read, seen, dreamed through a decade of convent hours. Suddenly she knew too that it was one of her greatest rôles and she flung herself into it more passionately.

"This is not as it should be," Dick deliberated. "Isn't it just the champagne? Let's more or less forget it."

"Oh, no, *now*. I want you to do it now, take me, show me, I'm absolutely yours and I want to be."

"For one thing, have you thought how much it would hurt Nicole?"

"She won't know--this won't have anything to do with her."

He continued kindly.

"Then there's the fact that I love Nicole."

"But you can love more than just one person, can't you? Like I love Mother and I love you--more. I love you more now."

"--the fourth place you're not in love with me but you might be afterwards, and that would begin your life with a terrible mess."

"No, I promise I'll never see you again. I'll get Mother and go to America right away."

He dismissed this. He was remembering too vividly the youth and freshness of her lips. He took another tone.

"You're just in that mood."

"Oh, please, I don't care even if I had a baby. I could go into Mexico like a girl at the studio. Oh, this is so different from anything I ever thought--I used to hate it when they kissed me seriously." He saw she was still under the impression that it must happen. "Some of them had great big teeth, but you're all different and beautiful. I want you to do it."

"I believe you think people just kiss some way and you want me to kiss you."

"Oh, don't tease me--I'm not a baby. I know you're not in love with me." She was suddenly humble and quiet. "I didn't expect that much. I know I must seem just nothing to you."

"Nonsense. But you seem young to me." His thoughts added, "--there'd be so much to teach you."

Rosemary waited, breathing eagerly till Dick said: "And lastly things aren't arranged so that this could be as you want."

Her face drooped with dismay and disappointment and Dick said automatically, "We'll have to simply--" He stopped himself, followed her to the bed, sat down beside her while she wept. He was suddenly confused, not about the ethics of the matter, for the impossibility of it was sheerly indicated from all angles but simply confused, and for a moment his usual grace, the tensile strength of his balance, was absent.

"I knew you wouldn't," she sobbed. "It was just a forlorn hope."

He stood up.

"Good night, child. This is a damn shame. Let's drop it out of the picture." He gave her two lines of hospital patter to go to sleep on. "So many people are going to love you and it might be nice to meet your first love all intact, emotionally too. That's an old-fashioned idea, isn't it?" She looked up at him as he took a step toward the door; she looked at him without the slightest idea as to what was in his head, she saw him take another step in slow motion, turn and look at her again, and she wanted for a moment to hold him and devour him, wanted his mouth, his ears, his coat collar, wanted to surround him and engulf him; she saw his hand fall on the doorknob. Then she gave up and sank back on the bed. When the door closed she got up and went to the mirror, where she began brushing her hair, sniffling a little. One hundred and fifty strokes Rosemary gave it, as usual, then a hundred and fifty more. She brushed it until her arm ached, then she changed arms and went on brushing. . . .

XVI

She woke up cooled and shamed. The sight of her beauty in the mirror did not reassure her but only awakened the ache of yesterday and a letter, forwarded by her mother, from the boy who had taken her to the Yale prom last fall, which announced his presence in Paris was no help--all that seemed far away. She emerged from her room for the ordeal of meeting the Divers weighted with a double trouble. But it was hidden by a sheath as impermeable as Nicole's when they met and went together to a series of fittings. It was consoling, though, when Nicole remarked, apropos of a distraught saleswoman: "Most people think everybody feels about them much more violently than they actually do--they think other people's opinions of them swing through great arcs of approval or disapproval." Yesterday in her expansiveness Rosemary would have resented that remark--to-day in her desire to minimize what had happened she welcomed it eagerly. She admired Nicole for her beauty and her wisdom, and also for the first time in her life she was jealous. Just before leaving Gausse's hotel her mother had said in that casual tone, which Rosemary knew concealed her most significant opinions, that Nicole was a great beauty, with the frank implication that Rosemary was not. This did not bother Rosemary, who had only recently been allowed to learn that she was even personable; so that her prettiness never seemed exactly her own but rather an acquirement, like her French. Nevertheless, in the taxi she looked at Nicole, matching herself against her. There were all the potentialities for romantic love in that lovely body and in the delicate mouth, sometimes tight, sometimes expectantly half open to the world. Nicole had been a beauty as a young girl and she would be a beauty later when her skin stretched tight over her high cheekbones--the essential structure was there. She had been white-Saxon-blonde but she was more beautiful now that her hair had darkened than when it had been like a cloud and more beautiful than she.

"We lived there," Rosemary suddenly pointed to a building in the Rue des Saints-Péres.

"That's strange. Because when I was twelve Mother and Baby and I once spent a winter there," and she pointed to a hotel directly across the street. The two dingy fronts stared at them, gray echoes of girlhood.

"We'd just built our Lake Forest house and we were economizing," Nicole continued. "At least Baby and I and the governess economized and Mother travelled."

"We were economizing too," said Rosemary, realizing that the word meant different things to them.

"Mother always spoke of it very carefully as a small hotel--" Nicole gave her quick magnetic little laugh, "--I mean instead of saying a 'cheap' hotel. If any swanky friends asked us our address we'd never say, 'We're in a dingy little hole over in the apache quarter where we're glad of running water,'--we'd say 'We're in a small hotel.' As if all the big ones were too noisy and vulgar for us. Of course the friends always saw through us and told everyone about it, but Mother always said it showed we knew our way around Europe. She did, of course: she was born a German citizen. But her mother was American, and she was brought up in Chicago, and she was more American than European."

They were meeting the others in two minutes, and Rosemary reconstructed herself once more as they got out of the taxi in the Rue Guynemer, across from the Luxembourg Gardens. They were lunching in the Norths' already dismantled apartment high above the green mass of leaves. The day seemed different to Rosemary from the day before--When she saw him face to face their eyes met and brushed like birds' wings. After that everything was all right, everything was wonderful, she knew that he was beginning to fall in love with her. She felt wildly happy, felt the warm sap of emotion being pumped through her body. A cool, clear confidence deepened and sang in her. She scarcely looked at Dick but she knew everything was all right.

After luncheon the Divers and the Norths and Rosemary went to the Franco-American Films, to be joined by Collis Clay, her young man from New Haven, to whom she had telephoned. He was a Georgian, with the peculiarly regular, even stencilled ideas of Southerners who are educated in the North. Last winter she had thought him attractive--once they held hands in an automobile going from New Haven to New York; now he no longer existed for her.

In the projection room she sat between Collis Clay and Dick while the mechanic mounted the reels of *Daddy's Girl* and a French executive fluttered about her trying to talk American slang. "Yes, boy," he said when there was trouble with the projector, "I have not any benenas." Then the lights went out, there was the sudden click and a flickering noise and she was alone with Dick at last. They looked at each other in the half darkness.

"Dear Rosemary," he murmured. Their shoulders touched. Nicole stirred restlessly at the end of the row and Abe coughed convulsively and blew his nose; then they all settled down and the picture ran.

There she was--the school girl of a year ago, hair down her back and rippling out stiffly like the solid hair of a tanagra figure; there she was--*so* young and innocent--the product of her mother's loving care; there she was--embodying all the immaturity of the race, cutting a new cardboard paper doll to pass before its empty harlot's mind. She remembered how she had felt in that dress, especially fresh and new under the fresh young silk.

Daddy's girl. Was it a 'itty-bitty bravekins and did it suffer? Ooo-ooo-tweet, de tweetest thing, wasn't she dest too tweet? Before her tiny fist the forces of lust and corruption rolled away; nay, the very march of destiny stopped; inevitable became evitable, syllogism, dialectic, all rationality fell away. Women would forget the dirty dishes at home and weep, even within the picture one woman wept so long that she almost stole the film away from Rosemary. She wept all over a set that cost a fortune, in a Duncan Phyfe dining-room, in an aviation port, and during a yacht-race that was only used in two flashes, in a subway and finally in a bathroom. But Rosemary triumphed. Her fineness of character, her courage and steadfastness intruded upon by the vulgarity of the world, and Rosemary showing what it took with a face that had not yet become mask-like--yet it was actually so moving that the emotions of the whole row of people went out to her at intervals during the picture. There was a break once and the light went on and after the chatter of applause Dick said to her sincerely: "I'm simply astounded. You're going to be one of the best actresses on the stage."

Then back to *Daddy's Girl:* happier days now, and a lovely shot of Rosemary and her parent united at the last in a father complex so apparent that Dick winced for all psychologists at the vicious sentimentality. The screen vanished, the lights went on, the moment had come.

"I've arranged one other thing," announced Rosemary to the company at large, "I've arranged a test for Dick."

"A what?"

"A screen test, they'll take one now."

There was an awful silence--then an irrepressible chortle from the Norths. Rosemary watched Dick comprehend what she meant, his face moving first in an Irish way; simultaneously she realized that she had made some mistake in the playing of her trump and still she did not suspect that the card was at fault.

"I don't want a test," said Dick firmly; then, seeing the situation as a whole, he continued lightly, "Rosemary, I'm disappointed. The pictures make a fine career for a woman--but my God, they can't photograph me. I'm an old scientist all wrapped up in his private life."

Nicole and Mary urged him ironically to seize the opportunity; they teased him, both faintly annoyed at not having been asked for a sitting. But Dick closed the subject with a somewhat tart discussion of actors: "The strongest guard is placed at the gateway to nothing," he said. "Maybe because the condition of emptiness is too shameful to be divulged."

In the taxi with Dick and Collis Clay--they were dropping Collis, and Dick was taking Rosemary to a tea from which Nicole and the Norths had resigned in order to do the things Abe had left undone till the last--in the taxi Rosemary reproached him.

"I thought if the test turned out to be good I could take it to California with me. And then maybe if they liked it you'd come out and be my leading man in a picture."

He was overwhelmed. "It was a darn sweet thought, but I'd rather look at *you*. You were about the nicest sight I ever looked at."

"That's a great picture," said Collis. "I've seen it four times. I know one boy at New Haven who's seen it a dozen times--he went all the way to Hartford to see it one time. And when I brought Rosemary up to New Haven he was so shy he wouldn't meet her. Can you beat that? This little girl knocks them cold."

Dick and Rosemary looked at each other, wanting to be alone, but Collis failed to understand.

"I'll drop you where you're going," he suggested. "I'm staying at the Lutetia."

"We'll drop you," said Dick.

"It'll be easier for me to drop you. No trouble at all."

"I think it will be better if we drop you."

"But--" began Collis; he grasped the situation at last and began discussing with Rosemary when he would see her again.

Finally, he was gone, with the shadowy unimportance but the offensive bulk of the third party. The car stopped unexpectedly, unsatisfactorily, at the address Dick had given. He drew a long breath.

"Shall we go in?"

"I don't care," Rosemary said. "I'll do anything you want."

He considered.

"I almost have to go in--she wants to buy some pictures from a friend of mine who needs the money."

Rosemary smoothed the brief expressive disarray of her hair.

"We'll stay just five minutes," he decided. "You're not going to like these people."

She assumed that they were dull and stereotyped people, or gross and drunken people, or tiresome, insistent people, or any of the sorts of people that the Divers avoided. She was entirely unprepared for the impression that the scene made on her.

XVII

It was a house hewn from the frame of Cardinal de Retz's palace in the Rue Monsieur, but once inside the door there was nothing of the past, nor of any present that Rosemary knew. The outer shell, the masonry, seemed rather to enclose the future so that it was an electric-like shock, a definite nervous experience, perverted as a breakfast of oatmeal and hashish, to cross that threshold, if it could be so called, into the long hall of blue steel, silver-gilt, and the myriad facets of many oddly bevelled mirrors. The effect was unlike that of any part of the Decorative Arts Exhibition--for there were people *in* it, not in front of it. Rosemary had the detached false-and-exalted feeling of being on a set and she guessed that every one else present had that feeling too.

There were about thirty people, mostly women, and all fashioned by Louisa M. Alcott or Madame de Ségur; and they functioned on this set as cautiously, as precisely, as does a human hand picking up jagged broken glass. Neither individually nor as a crowd could they be said to dominate the environment, as one comes to dominate a work of art he may possess, no matter how esoteric, no one knew what this room meant because it was evolving into something else, becoming everything a room was not; to exist in it was as difficult as walking on a highly polished moving stairway, and no one could succeed at all save with the aforementioned qualities of a hand moving among broken glass--which qualities limited and defined the majority of those present.

These were of two sorts. There were the Americans and English who had been dissipating all spring and summer, so that now everything they did had a purely nervous inspiration. They were very quiet and lethargic at certain hours and then they exploded into sudden quarrels and breakdowns and seductions. The other class, who might be called the exploiters, was formed by the sponges, who were sober, serious people by comparison, with a purpose in life and no time for fooling. These kept their balance best in that environment, and what tone there was, beyond the apartment's novel organization of light values, came from them.

The Frankenstein took down Dick and Rosemary at a gulp--it separated them immediately and Rosemary suddenly discovered herself to be an insincere little person, living all in the upper registers of her throat and wishing the director would come. There was however such a wild beating of wings in the room that she did not feel her position was more incongruous than any one else's. In addition, her training told and after a series of semi-military turns, shifts, and marches she found herself presumably talking to a neat, slick girl with a lovely boy's face, but actually absorbed by a conversation taking place on a sort of gun-metal ladder diagonally opposite her and four feet away.

There was a trio of young women sitting on the bench. They were all tall and slender with small heads groomed like manikins' heads, and as they talked the heads waved gracefully about above their dark tailored suits, rather like long-stemmed flowers and rather like cobras' hoods.

"Oh, they give a good show," said one of them, in a deep rich voice. "Practically the best show in Paris--I'd be the last one to deny that. But after all--" She sighed. "Those phrases he uses over and over--'Oldest inhabitant gnawed by rodents.' You laugh once."

"I prefer people whose lives have more corrugated surfaces," said the second, "and I don't like her."

"I've never really been able to get very excited about them, or their entourage either. Why, for example, the entirely liquid Mr. North?"

"He's out," said the first girl. "But you must admit that the party in question can be one of the most charming human beings you have ever met."

It was the first hint Rosemary had had that they were talking about the Divers, and her body grew tense with indignation. But the girl talking to her, in the starched blue shirt with the bright blue eyes and the red cheeks and the very gray suit, a poster of a girl, had begun to play up. Desperately she kept sweeping things from between them, afraid that Rosemary couldn't see her, sweeping them away until presently there was not so much as a veil of brittle humor hiding the girl, and with distaste Rosemary saw her plain.

"Couldn't you have lunch, or maybe dinner, or lunch the day after?" begged the girl. Rosemary looked about for Dick, finding him with the hostess, to whom he had been talking since they came in. Their eyes met and he nodded slightly, and simultaneously the three cobra women noticed her; their long necks darted toward her and they fixed finely critical glances upon her. She looked back at them defiantly, acknowledging that she had heard what they said. Then she threw off her exigent vis-à-vis with a polite but clipped parting that she had just learned from Dick, and went over to join him. The hostess--she was another tall rich American girl, promenading insouciantly upon the national prosperity--was asking Dick innumerable questions about Gausse's Hôtel, whither she evidently wanted to come, and battering persistently against his reluctance. Rosemary's presence reminded her that she had been recalcitrant as a hostess and glancing about she said: "Have you met any one amusing, have you met Mr.--" Her eyes groped for a male who might interest Rosemary, but Dick said they must go. They left immediately, moving over the brief threshold of the future to the sudden past of the stone façade without.

"Wasn't it terrible?" he said.

"Terrible," she echoed obediently.

"Rosemary?"

She murmured, "What?" in an awed voice.

"I feel terribly about this."

She was shaken with audibly painful sobs. "Have you got a handkerchief?" she faltered. But there was little time to cry, and lovers now they fell ravenously on the quick seconds while outside the taxi windows the green and cream twilight faded, and the fire-red, gas-blue, ghost-green signs began to shine smokily through the tranquil rain. It was nearly six, the streets were in movement, the bistros gleamed, the Place de la Concorde moved by in pink majesty as the cab turned north.

They looked at each other at last, murmuring names that were a spell. Softly the two names lingered on the air, died away more slowly than other words, other names, slower than music in the mind.

"I don't know what came over me last night," Rosemary said. "That glass of champagne? I've never done anything like that before."

"You simply said you loved me."

"I do love you--I can't change that." It was time for Rosemary to cry, so she cried a little in her handkerchief.

"I'm afraid I'm in love with you," said Dick, "and that's not the best thing that could happen."

Again the names--then they lurched together as if the taxi had swung them. Her breasts crushed flat against him, her mouth was all new and warm, owned in common. They stopped thinking with an almost painful relief, stopped seeing; they only breathed and sought each other. They were both in the gray gentle world of a mild hangover of fatigue when the nerves relax in bunches like piano strings, and crackle suddenly like wicker chairs. Nerves so raw and tender must surely join other nerves, lips to lips, breast to breast. . . .

They were still in the happier stage of love. They were full of brave illusions about each other, tremendous illusions, so that the communion of self with self seemed to be on a plane where no other human relations mattered. They both seemed to have arrived there with an extraordinary innocence as though a series of pure accidents had driven them together, so many accidents that at last they were forced to conclude that they were for each other. They had arrived with clean hands, or so it seemed, after no traffic with the merely curious and clandestine.

But for Dick that portion of the road was short; the turning came before they reached the hotel.

"There's nothing to do about it," he said, with a feeling of panic. "I'm in love with you but it doesn't change what I said last night."

"That doesn't matter now. I just wanted to make you love me--if you love me everything's all right."

"Unfortunately I do. But Nicole mustn't know--she mustn't suspect even faintly. Nicole and I have got to go on together. In a way that's more important than just wanting to go on."

"Kiss me once more."

He kissed her, but momentarily he had left her.

"Nicole mustn't suffer--she loves me and I love her--you understand that."

She did understand--it was the sort of thing she understood well, not hurting people. She knew the Divers loved each other because it had been her primary assumption. She had thought however that it was a rather cooled relation, and actually rather like the love of herself and her mother. When people have so much for outsiders didn't it indicate a lack of inner intensity?

"And I mean love," he said, guessing her thoughts. "Active love--it's more complicated than I can tell you. It was responsible for that crazy duel."

"How did you know about the duel? I thought we were to keep it from you."

"Do you think Abe can keep a secret?" He spoke with incisive irony. "Tell a secret over the radio, publish it in a tabloid, but never tell it to a man who drinks more than three or four a day."

She laughed in agreement, staying close to him.

"So you understand my relations with Nicole are complicated. She's not very strong--she looks strong but she isn't. And this makes rather a mess."

"Oh, say that later! But kiss me now--love me now. I'll love you and never let Nicole see."

"You darling."

They reached the hotel and Rosemary walked a little behind him, to admire him, to adore him. His step was alert as if he had just come from some great doings and was hurrying on toward others. Organizer of private gaiety, curator of a richly incrusted happiness. His hat was a perfect hat and he carried a heavy stick and yellow gloves. She thought what a good time they would all have being with him to-night.

They walked upstairs--five flights. At the first landing they stopped and kissed; she was careful on the next landing, on the third more careful still. On the next--there were two more--she stopped half way and kissed him fleetingly good-by. At his urgency she walked down with him to the one below for a minute--and then up and up. Finally it was good-by with their hands stretching to touch along the diagonal of the banister and then the fingers slipping apart. Dick went back downstairs to make some arrangements for the evening--Rosemary ran to her room and wrote a letter to her mother; she was conscience-stricken because she did not miss her mother at all.

XVIII

Although the Divers were honestly apathetic to organized fashion, they were nevertheless too acute to abandon its contemporaneous rhythm and beat--Dick's parties were all concerned with excitement, and a chance breath of fresh night air was the more precious for being experienced in the intervals of the excitement.

The party that night moved with the speed of a slapstick comedy. They were twelve, they were sixteen, they were quartets in separate motors bound on a quick Odyssey over Paris. Everything had been foreseen. People joined them as if by magic, accompanied them as specialists, almost guides, through a phase of the evening, dropped out and were succeeded by other people, so that it appeared as if the freshness of each one had been husbanded for them all day. Rosemary appreciated how different it was from any party in Hollywood, no matter how splendid in scale. There was, among many diversions, the car of the Shah of Persia. Where Dick had commandeered this vehicle, what bribery was employed, these were facts of irrelevance. Rosemary accepted it as merely a new facet of the fabulous, which for two years had filled her life. The car had been built on a special chassis in America. Its wheels were of silver, so was the radiator. The inside of the body was inlaid with innumerable brilliants which would be replaced with true gems by the court jeweller when the car arrived in Teheran the following week. There was only one real seat in back, because the Shah must ride alone, so they took turns riding in it and sitting on the marten fur that covered the floor.

But always there was Dick. Rosemary assured the image of her mother, ever carried with her, that never, never had she known any one so nice, so thoroughly nice as Dick was that night. She compared him with the two Englishmen, whom Abe addressed conscientiously as "Major Hengest and Mr. Horsa," and with the heir to a Scandinavian throne and the novelist just back from Russia, and with Abe, who was desperate and witty, and with Collis Clay, who joined them somewhere and stayed along--and felt there was no comparison. The enthusiasm, the selflessness behind the whole performance ravished her, the technic of moving many varied types, each as immobile, as dependent on supplies of attention as an infantry battalion is dependent on rations, appeared so effortless that he still had pieces of his own most personal self for everyone.

--Afterward she remembered the times when she had felt the happiest. The first time was when she and Dick danced together and she felt her beauty sparkling bright against his tall, strong form as they floated, hovering like people in an amusing dream--he turned her here and there with such a delicacy of suggestion that she was like a bright bouquet, a piece of precious cloth being displayed before fifty eyes. There was a moment when they were not dancing at all, simply clinging together. Some time in the early morning they were alone, and her damp powdery young body came up close to him in a crush of tired cloth, and stayed there, crushed against a background of other people's hats and wraps. . . .

The time she laughed most was later, when six of them, the best of them, noblest relics of the evening, stood in the dusky front lobby of the Ritz telling the night concierge that General Pershing was outside and wanted caviare and champagne. "He brooks no delay. Every man, every gun is at his service." Frantic waiters emerged from nowhere, a table was set in the lobby, and Abe came in representing General Pershing while they stood up and mumbled remembered fragments of war songs at him. In the waiters' injured reaction to this anti-climax they found themselves neglected, so they built a waiter trap--a huge and fantastic device constructed of all the furniture in the lobby and functioning like one of the bizarre machines of a Goldberg cartoon. Abe shook his head doubtfully at it.

"Perhaps it would be better to steal a musical saw and--"

"That's enough," Mary interrupted. "When Abe begins bringing up that it's time to go home." Anxiously she confided to Rosemary:

"I've got to get Abe home. His boat train leaves at eleven. It's so important--I feel the whole future depends on his catching it, but whenever I argue with him he does the exact opposite."

"I'll try and persuade him," offered Rosemary.

"Would you?" Mary said doubtfully. "Maybe you could."

Then Dick came up to Rosemary:

"Nicole and I are going home and we thought you'd want to go with us."

Her face was pale with fatigue in the false dawn. Two wan dark spots in her cheek marked where the color was by day.

"I can't," she said. "I promised Mary North to stay along with them--or Abe'll never go to bed. Maybe you could do something."

"Don't you know you can't do anything about people?" he advised her. "If Abe was my room-mate in college, tight for the first time, it'd be different. Now there's nothing to do."

"Well, I've got to stay. He says he'll go to bed if we only come to the Halles with him," she said, almost defiantly.

He kissed the inside of her elbow quickly.

"Don't let Rosemary go home alone," Nicole called to Mary as they left. "We feel responsible to her mother."

--Later Rosemary and the Norths and a manufacturer of dolls' voices from Newark and ubiquitous Collis and a big splendidly dressed oil Indian named George T. Horseprotection were riding along on top of thousands of carrots in a market wagon. The earth in the carrot beards was fragrant and sweet in the darkness, and Rosemary was so high up in the load that she could hardly see the others in the long shadow between infrequent street lamps. Their voices came from far off, as if they were having experiences different from hers, different and far away, for she was with Dick in her heart, sorry she had come with the

Norths, wishing she was at the hotel and him asleep across the hall, or that he was here beside her with the warm darkness streaming down.

"Don't come up," she called to Collis, "the carrots will all roll." She threw one at Abe who was sitting beside the driver, stiffly like an old man. . . .

Later she was homeward bound at last in broad daylight, with the pigeons already breaking over Saint-Sulpice. All of them began to laugh spontaneously because they knew it was still last night while the people in the streets had the delusion that it was bright hot morning.

"At last I've been on a wild party," thought Rosemary, "but it's no fun when Dick isn't there."

She felt a little betrayed and sad, but presently a moving object came into sight. It was a huge horse-chestnut tree in full bloom bound for the Champs Élysées, strapped now into a long truck and simply shaking with laughter--like a lovely person in an undignified position yet confident none the less of being lovely. Looking at it with fascination Rosemary identified herself with it, and laughed cheerfully with it, and everything all at once seemed gorgeous.

XIX

Abe left from the Gare Saint Lazare at eleven--he stood alone under the fouled glass dome, relic of the seventies, era of the Crystal Palace; his hands, of that vague gray color that only twenty-four hours can produce, were in his coat pockets to conceal the trembling fingers. With his hat removed it was plain that only the top layer of his hair was brushed back--the lower levels were pointed resolutely sidewise. He was scarcely recognizable as the man who had swum upon Gausse's Beach a fortnight ago.

He was early; he looked from left to right with his eyes only; it would have taken nervous forces out of his control to use any other part of his body. New-looking baggage went past him; presently prospective passengers, with dark little bodies, were calling: "Jew-uls-*Hoo-oo!*" in dark piercing voices.

At the minute when he wondered whether or not he had time for a drink at the buffet, and began clutching at the soggy wad of thousand-franc notes in his pocket, one end of his pendulous glance came to rest upon the apparition of Nicole at the stairhead. He watched her--she was self-revelatory in her little expressions as people seem to some one waiting for them, who as yet is himself unobserved. She was frowning, thinking of her children, less gloating over them than merely animally counting them--a cat checking her cubs with a paw.

When she saw Abe, the mood passed out of her face; the glow of the morning skylight was sad, and Abe made a gloomy figure with dark circles that showed through the crimson tan under his eyes. They sat down on a bench.

"I came because you asked me," said Nicole defensively. Abe seemed to have forgotten why he asked her and Nicole was quite content to look at the travellers passing by.

"That's going to be the belle of your boat--that one with all the men to say good-by--you see why she bought that dress?" Nicole talked faster and faster. "You see why nobody else would buy it except the belle of the world cruise? See? No? Wake up! That's a story dress--that extra material tells a story and somebody on world cruise would be lonesome enough to want to hear it."

She bit close her last words; she had talked too much for her; and Abe found it difficult to gather from her serious set face that she had spoken at all. With an effort he drew himself up to a posture that looked as if he were standing up while he was sitting down.

"The afternoon you took me to that funny ball--you know, St. Genevieve's--" he began.

"I remember. It was fun, wasn't it?"

"No fun for me. I haven't had fun seeing you this time. I'm tired of you both, but it doesn't show because you're even more tired of me--you know what I mean. If I had any enthusiasm, I'd go on to new people."

There was a rough nap on Nicole's velvet gloves as she slapped him back:

"Seems rather foolish to be unpleasant, Abe. Anyhow you don't mean that. I can't see why you've given up about everything."

Abe considered, trying hard not to cough or blow his nose.

"I suppose I got bored; and then it was such a long way to go back in order to get anywhere."

Often a man can play the helpless child in front of a woman, but he can almost never bring it off when he feels most like a helpless child.

"No excuse for it," Nicole said crisply.

Abe was feeling worse every minute--he could think of nothing but disagreeable and sheerly nervous remarks. Nicole thought that the correct attitude for her was to sit staring straight ahead, hands in her lap. For a while there was no communication between them--each was racing away from the other, breathing only insofar as there was blue space ahead, a sky not seen by the other. Unlike lovers they possessed no past; unlike man and wife, they possessed no future; yet up to this morning Nicole had liked Abe better than any one except Dick--and he had been heavy, belly-frightened, with love for her for years.

"Tired of women's worlds," he spoke up suddenly.

"Then why don't you make a world of your own?"

"Tired of friends. The thing is to have sycophants."

Nicole tried to force the minute hand around on the station clock, but, "You agree?" he demanded.

"I am a woman and my business is to hold things together."

"My business is to tear them apart."

"When you get drunk you don't tear anything apart except yourself," she said, cold now, and frightened and unconfident. The station was filling but no one she knew came. After a moment her eyes fell gratefully on a tall girl with straw hair like a helmet, who was dropping letters in the mail slot.

"A girl I have to speak to, Abe. Abe, wake up! You fool!"

Patiently Abe followed her with his eyes. The woman turned in a startled way to greet Nicole, and Abe recognized her as some one he had seen around Paris. He took advantage of Nicole's absence to cough hard and retchingly into his handkerchief, and to blow his nose loud. The morning was warmer and his underwear was soaked with sweat. His fingers trembled so violently that it took four matches to light a cigarette; it seemed absolutely necessary to make his way into the buffet for a drink, but immediately Nicole returned.

"That was a mistake," she said with frosty humor. "After begging me to come and see her, she gave me a good snubbing. She looked at me as if I were rotted." Excited, she did a little laugh, as with two fingers high in the scales. "Let people come to you."

Abe recovered from a cigarette cough and remarked:

"Trouble is when you're sober you don't want to see anybody, and when you're tight nobody wants to see you."

"Who, me?" Nicole laughed again; for some reason the late encounter had cheered her.

"No--me."

"Speak for yourself. I like people, a lot of people--I like--"

Rosemary and Mary North came in sight, walking slowly and searching for Abe, and Nicole burst forth grossly with "Hey! Hi! Hey!" and laughed and waved the package of handkerchiefs she had bought for Abe.

They stood in an uncomfortable little group weighted down by Abe's gigantic presence: he lay athwart them like the wreck of a galleon, dominating with his presence his own weakness and self-indulgence, his narrowness and bitterness. All of them were conscious of the solemn dignity that flowed from him, of his achievement, fragmentary, suggestive and surpassed. But they were frightened at his survivant will, once a will to live, now become a will to die.

Dick Diver came and brought with him a fine glowing surface on which the three women sprang like monkeys with cries of relief, perching on his shoulders, on the beautiful crown of his hat or the gold head of his cane. Now, for a moment, they could disregard the spectacle of Abe's gigantic obscenity. Dick saw the situation quickly and grasped it quietly. He pulled them out of themselves into the station, making plain its wonders. Nearby, some Americans were saying good-by in voices that mimicked the cadence of water running into a large old bathtub. Standing in the station, with Paris in back of them, it seemed as if they were vicariously leaning a little over the ocean, already undergoing a sea-change, a shifting about of atoms to form the essential molecule of a new people.

So the well-to-do Americans poured through the station onto the platforms with frank new faces, intelligent, considerate, thoughtless, thought-for. An occasional English face among them seemed sharp and emergent. When there were enough Americans on the platform the first impression of their immaculacy and their money began to fade into a vague racial dusk that hindered and blinded both them and their observers.

Nicole seized Dick's arm crying, "Look!" Dick turned in time to see what took place in half a minute. At a Pullman entrance two cars off, a vivid scene detached itself from the tenor of many farewells. The young woman with the helmet-like hair to whom Nicole had spoken made an odd dodging little run away from the man to whom she was talking and plunged a frantic hand into her purse; then the sound of two revolver shots cracked the narrow air of the platform. Simultaneously the engine whistled sharply and the train began to move, momentarily dwarfing the shots in significance. Abe waved again from his window, oblivious to what had happened. But before the crowd closed in, the others had seen the shots take effect, seen the target sit down upon the platform.

Only after a hundred years did the train stop; Nicole, Mary, and Rosemary waited on the outskirts while Dick fought his way through. It was five minutes before he found them again--by this time the crowd had split into two sections, following, respectively, the man on a stretcher and the girl walking pale and firm between distraught gendarmes.

"It was Maria Wallis," Dick said hurriedly. "The man she shot was an Englishman--they had an awful time finding out who, because she shot him through his identification card." They were walking quickly from the train, swayed along with the crowd. "I found out what poste de police they're taking her to so I'll go there--"

"But her sister lives in Paris," Nicole objected. "Why not phone her? Seems very peculiar nobody thought of that. She's married to a Frenchman, and he can do more than we can."

Dick hesitated, shook his head and started off.

"Wait!" Nicole cried after him. "That's foolish--how can you do any good--with your French?"

"At least I'll see they don't do anything outrageous to her."

"They're certainly going to hold on to her," Nicole assured him briskly. "She *did* shoot the man. The best thing is to phone right away to Laura--she can do more than we can."

Dick was unconvinced--also he was showing off for Rosemary.

"You wait," said Nicole firmly, and hurried off to a telephone booth.

"When Nicole takes things into her hands," he said with affectionate irony, "there is nothing more to be done."

He saw Rosemary for the first time that morning. They exchanged glances, trying to recognize the emotions of the day before. For a moment each seemed unreal to the other--then the slow warm hum of love began again.

"You like to help everybody, don't you?" Rosemary said.

"I only pretend to."

"Mother likes to help everybody--of course she can't help as many people as you do." She sighed. "Sometimes I think I'm the most selfish person in the world."

For the first time the mention of her mother annoyed rather than amused Dick. He wanted to sweep away her mother, remove the whole affair from the nursery footing upon which Rosemary persistently established it. But he realized that this impulse was a loss of control--what would become of Rosemary's urge toward him if, for even a moment, he relaxed. He saw, not without panic, that the affair was sliding to rest; it could not stand still, it must go on or go back; for the first time it occurred to him that Rosemary had her hand on the lever more authoritatively than he.

Before he had thought out a course of procedure, Nicole returned.

"I found Laura. It was the first news she had and her voice kept fading away and then getting loud again--as if she was fainting and then pulling herself together. She said she knew something was going to happen this morning."

"Maria ought to be with Diaghileff," said Dick in a gentle tone, in order to bring them back to quietude. "She has a nice sense of decor--not to say rhythm. Will any of us ever see a train pulling out without hearing a few shots?"

They bumped down the wide steel steps. "I'm sorry for the poor man," Nicole said. "Course that's why she talked so strange to me--she was getting ready to open fire."

She laughed, Rosemary laughed too, but they were both horrified, and both of them deeply wanted Dick to make a moral comment on the matter and not leave it to them. This wish was not entirely conscious, especially on the part of Rosemary, who was accustomed to having shell fragments of such events shriek past her head. But a totality of shock had piled up in her too. For the moment, Dick was too shaken by the impetus of his newly recognized emotion to resolve things into the pattern of the holiday, so the women, missing something, lapsed into a vague unhappiness.

Then, as if nothing had happened, the lives of the Divers and their friends flowed out into the street.

However, everything had happened--Abe's departure and Mary's impending departure for Salzburg this afternoon had ended the time in Paris. Or perhaps the shots, the concussions that had finished God knew what dark matter, had terminated it. The shots had entered into all their lives: echoes of violence followed them out onto the pavement where two porters held a post-mortem beside them as they waited for a taxi.

"Tu as vu le revolver? Il était très petit, vraie perle--un jouet."

"Mais, assez puissant!" said the other porter sagely. "Tu as vu sa chemise? Assez de sang pour se croire à la guerre."

XX

In the square, as they came out, a suspended mass of gasoline exhaust cooked slowly in the July sun. It was a terrible thing--unlike pure heat it held no promise of rural escape but suggested only roads choked with the same foul asthma. During their luncheon, outdoors, across from the Luxembourg Gardens, Rosemary had cramps and felt fretful and full of impatient lassitude--it was the foretaste of this that had inspired her self-accusation of selfishness in the station.

Dick had no suspicion of the sharpness of the change; he was profoundly unhappy and the subsequent increase of egotism tended momentarily to blind him to what was going on round about him, and deprive him of the long groundswell of imagination that he counted on for his judgments.

After Mary North left them, accompanied by the Italian singing teacher who had joined them for coffee and was taking her to her train, Rosemary, too, stood up, bound for an engagement at her studio: "meet some officials."

"And oh--" she proposed "--if Collis Clay, that Southern boy--if he comes while you are still sitting here, just tell him I couldn't wait; tell him to call me tomorrow."

Too insouciant, in reaction from the late disturbance, she had assumed the privileges of a child--the result being to remind the Divers of their exclusive love for their own children; Rosemary was sharply rebuked in a short passage between the women: "You'd better leave the message with a waiter," Nicole's voice was stern and unmodulated, "we're leaving immediately."

Rosemary got it, took it without resentment.

"I'll let it go then. Good-by, you darlings."

Dick asked for the check; the Divers relaxed, chewing tentatively on toothpicks.

"Well--" they said together.

He saw a flash of unhappiness on her mouth, so brief that only he would have noticed, and he could pretend not to have seen. What did Nicole think? Rosemary was one of a dozen people he had "worked over" in the past years: these had included a French circus clown, Abe and Mary North, a pair of dancers, a writer, a painter, a comedienne from the Grand Guignol, a half-crazy pederast from the Russian Ballet, a promising tenor they had staked to a year in Milan. Nicole well knew how seriously these people interpreted his interest and enthusiasm; but she realized also that, except while their children were being born, Dick had not spent a night apart from her since their marriage. On the other hand, there was a pleasingness about him that simply had to be used--those who possessed that pleasingness had to keep their hands in, and go along attaching people that they had no use to make of.

Now Dick hardened himself and let minutes pass without making any gesture of confidence, any representation of constantly renewed surprise that they were one together.

Collis Clay out of the South edged a passage between the closely packed tables and greeted the Divers cavalierly. Such salutations always astonished Dick--acquaintances saying "Hi!" to them, or speaking only to one of them. He felt so intensely about people that in moments of apathy he preferred to remain concealed; that one could parade a casualness into his presence was a challenge to the key on which he lived.

Collis, unaware that he was without a wedding garment, heralded his arrival with: "I reckon I'm late--the beyed has flown." Dick had to wrench something out of himself before he could forgive him for not having first complimented Nicole.

She left almost immediately and he sat with Collis, finishing the last of his wine. He rather liked Collis--he was "post-war"; less difficult than most of the Southerners he had known at New Haven a decade previously. Dick listened with amusement to the conversation that accompanied the slow, profound stuffing of a pipe. In the early afternoon children and nurses were trekking into the Luxembourg Gardens; it was the first time in months that Dick had let this part of the day out of his hands.

Suddenly his blood ran cold as he realized the content of Collis's confidential monologue.

"--she's not so cold as you'd probably think. I admit I thought she was cold for a long time. But she got into a jam with a friend of mine going from New York to Chicago at Easter--a boy named Hillis she thought was pretty nutsey at New Haven--she had a compartment with a cousin of mine but she and Hillis wanted to be alone, so in the afternoon my cousin came and played cards in our compartment. Well, after about two hours we went back and there was Rosemary and Bill Hillis standing in the vestibule arguing with the conductor--Rosemary white as a sheet. Seems they locked the door and pulled down the blinds and I guess there was some heavy stuff going on when the conductor came for the tickets and knocked on the door. They thought it was us kidding them and wouldn't let him in at first, and when they did, he was plenty sore. He asked Hillis if that was his compartment and whether he and Rosemary were married that they locked the door, and Hillis lost his temper trying to explain there was nothing wrong. He said the conductor had insulted Rosemary and he wanted him to fight, but that conductor could have made trouble--and believe me I had an awful time smoothing it over."

With every detail imagined, with even envy for the pair's community of misfortune in the vestibule, Dick felt a change taking place within him. Only the image of a third person, even a vanished one, entering into his relation with Rosemary was needed to throw him off his balance and send through him waves of pain, misery, desire, desperation. The vividly pictured hand on Rosemary's cheek, the quicker breath, the white excitement of the event viewed from outside, the inviolable secret warmth within.

--Do you mind if I pull down the curtain?

--Please do. It's too light in here.

Collis Clay was now speaking about fraternity politics at New Haven, in the same tone, with the same emphasis. Dick had gathered that he was in love with Rosemary in some curious way Dick could not have understood. The affair with Hillis seemed to have made no emotional impression on Collis save to give him the joyful conviction that Rosemary was "human."

"Bones got a wonderful crowd," he said. "We all did, as a matter of fact. New Haven's so big now the sad thing is the men we have to leave out."

--Do you mind if I pull down the curtain?

--Please do. It's too light in here.

. . . Dick went over Paris to his bank--writing a check, he looked along the row of men at the desks deciding to which one he would present it for an O.K. As he wrote he engrossed himself in the material act, examining meticulously the pen, writing laboriously upon the high glass-topped desk. Once he raised glazed eyes to look toward the mail department, then glazed his spirit again by concentration upon the objects he dealt with.

Still he failed to decide to whom the check should be presented, which man in the line would guess least of the unhappy predicament in which he found himself and, also, which one would be least likely to talk. There was Perrin, the suave New Yorker, who had asked him to luncheons at the American Club, there was Casasus, the Spaniard, with whom he usually discussed a mutual friend in spite of the fact that the friend had passed out of his life a dozen years before; there was Muchhause, who always asked him whether he wanted to draw upon his wife's money or his own.

As he entered the amount on the stub, and drew two lines under it, he decided to go to Pierce, who was young and for whom he would have to put on only a small show. It was often easier to give a show than to watch one.

He went to the mail desk first--as the woman who served him pushed up with her bosom a piece of paper that had nearly escaped the desk, he thought how differently women use their bodies from men. He took his letters aside to open: There was a bill for seventeen psychiatric books from a German concern, a bill from Brentano's, a letter from Buffalo from his father, in a handwriting that year by year became more indecipherable; there was a card from Tommy Barban postmarked Fez and bearing a facetious communication; there were letters from doctors in Zurich, both in German; a disputed bill from a plasterer in Cannes; a bill from a furniture maker; a letter from the publisher of a medical journal in Baltimore, miscellaneous announcements and an invitation to a showing of pictures by an incipient artist; also there were three letters for Nicole, and a letter for Rosemary sent in his care.

--Do you mind if I pull down the curtain?

He went toward Pierce but he was engaged with a woman, and Dick saw with his heels that he would have to present his check to Casasus at the next desk, who was free.

"How are you, Diver?" Casasus was genial. He stood up, his mustache spreading with his smile. "We were talking about Featherstone the other day and I thought of you--he's out in California now."

Dick widened his eyes and bent forward a little.

"In Cali*for*nia?"

"That's what I heard."

Dick held the check poised; to focus the attention of Casasus upon it he looked toward Pierce's desk, holding the latter for a moment in a friendly eye-play conditioned by an old joke of three years before when Pierce had been involved with a Lithuanian countess. Pierce played up with a grin until Casasus had authorized the check and had no further recourse to detain Dick, whom he liked, than to stand up holding his pince-nez and repeat, "Yes, he's in California."

Meanwhile Dick had seen that Perrin, at the head of the line of desks, was in conversation with the heavyweight champion of the world; from a sidesweep of Perrin's eye Dick saw that he was considering calling him over and introducing him, but that he finally decided against it.

Cutting across the social mood of Casasus with the intensity he had accumulated at the glass desk--which is to say he looked hard at the check, studying it, and then fixed his eyes on grave problems beyond the first marble pillar to the right of the banker's head and made a business of shifting the cane, hat, and letters he carried--he said good-by and went out. He had long ago purchased the doorman; his taxi sprang to the curb.

"I want to go to the Films Par Excellence Studio--it's on a little street in Passy. Go to the Muette. I'll direct you from there."

He was rendered so uncertain by the events of the last forty-eight hours that he was not even sure of what he wanted to do; he paid off the taxi at the Muette and walked in the direction of the studio, crossing to the opposite side of the street before he came to the building. Dignified in his fine clothes, with their fine accessories, he was yet swayed and driven as an animal. Dignity could come only with an overthrowing of his past, of the effort of the last six years. He went briskly around the block with the fatuousness of one of Tarkington's adolescents, hurrying at the blind places lest he miss Rosemary's coming out of the studio. It was a melancholy neighborhood. Next door to the place he saw a sign: "1000 chemises." The shirts filled the window, piled, cravated, stuffed, or draped with shoddy grace on the showcase floor: "1000 chemises"--count them! On either side he read: "Papeterie," "Pâtisserie," "Solde," "Réclame"--and Constance Talmadge in "Déjeuner de Soleil," and farther away there were more sombre announcements: "Vêtements Ecclésiastiques," "Déclaration de Décès" and "Pompes Funèbres." Life and death.

He knew that what he was now doing marked a turning point in his life--it was out of line with everything that had preceded it--even out of line with what effect he might hope to produce upon Rosemary. Rosemary saw him always as a model of correctness--his presence walking around this block was an intrusion.

But Dick's necessity of behaving as he did was a projection of some submerged reality: he was compelled to walk there, or stand there, his shirt-sleeve fitting his wrist and his coat sleeve encasing his shirt-sleeve like a sleeve valve, his collar molded plastically to his neck, his red hair cut exactly, his hand holding his small briefcase like a dandy--just as another man once found it necessary to stand in front of a church in Ferrara, in sackcloth and ashes. Dick was paying some tribute to things unforgotten, unshriven, unexpurgated.

XXI

After three-quarters of an hour of standing around, he became suddenly involved in a human contact. It was just the sort of thing that was likely to happen to him when he was in the mood of not wanting to see any one. So rigidly did he sometimes guard his exposed self-consciousness that frequently he defeated his own purposes; as an actor who underplays a part sets up a craning forward, a stimulated emotional attention in an audience, and seems to create in others an ability to bridge the gap he has left open. Similarly we are seldom sorry for those who need and crave our pity--we reserve this for those who, by other means, make us exercise the abstract function of pity.

So Dick might, himself, have analyzed the incident that ensued. As he paced the Rue des Saintes-Anges he was spoken to by a thin-faced American, perhaps thirty, with an air of being scarred and a slight but sinister smile. As Dick gave him the light he requested, he placed him as one of a type of which he had been conscious since early youth--a type that loafed about tobacco stores with one elbow on the counter and watched, through heaven knew what small chink of the mind, the people who came in and out. Intimate to garages, where he had vague business conducted in undertones, to barber shops, to the lobbies of theatres--in such places, at any rate, Dick placed him. Sometimes the face bobbed up in one of Tad's more savage cartoons--in boyhood Dick had often thrown an uneasy glance at the dim borderland of crime on which he stood.

"How do you like Paris, Buddy?"

Not waiting for an answer the man tried to fit in his footsteps with Dick's: "Where you from?" he asked encouragingly.

"From Buffalo."

"I'm from San Antone--but I been over here since the war."

"You in the army?"

"*I'll* say I was. Eighty-fourth Division--ever heard of that outfit?"

The man walked a little ahead of him and fixed him with eyes that were practically menacing.

"Staying in Paris awhile, Buddy? Or just passing through."

"Passing through."

"What hotel you staying at?"

Dick had begun laughing to himself--the party had the intention of rifling his room that night. His thoughts were read apparently without self-consciousness.

"With a build like yours you oughtn't to be afraid of me, Buddy. There's a lot of bums around just laying for American tourists, but you needn't be afraid of me."

Becoming bored, Dick stopped walking: "I just wonder why you've got so much time to waste."

"I'm in business here in Paris."

"In what line?"

"Selling papers."

The contrast between the formidable manner and the mild profession was absurd--but the man amended it with:

"Don't worry; I made plenty money last year--ten or twenty francs for a Sunny Times that cost six."

He produced a newspaper clipping from a rusty wallet and passed it over to one who had become a fellow stroller--the cartoon showed a stream of Americans pouring from the gangplank of a liner freighted with gold.

"Two hundred thousand--spending ten million a summer."

"What you doing out here in Passy?"

His companion looked around cautiously. "Movies," he said darkly. "They got an American studio over there. And they need guys can speak English. I'm waiting for a break."

Dick shook him off quickly and firmly.

It had become apparent that Rosemary either had escaped on one of his early circuits of the block or else had left before he came into the neighborhood; he went into the bistro on the corner, bought a lead disk and, squeezed in an alcove between the kitchen and the foul toilet, he called the Roi George. He recognized Cheyne-Stokes tendencies in his respiration--but like everything the symptom served only to turn him in toward his emotion. He gave the number of the hotel; then stood holding the phone and staring into the café; after a long while a strange little voice said hello.

"This is Dick--I had to call you."

A pause from her--then bravely, and in key with his emotion: "I'm glad you did."

"I came to meet you at your studio--I'm out in Passy across the way from it. I thought maybe we'd ride around through the Bois."

"Oh, I only stayed there a minute! I'm so sorry." A silence.

"Rosemary."

"Yes, Dick."

"Look, I'm in an extraordinary condition about you. When a child can disturb a middle-aged gent--things get difficult."

"You're not middle-aged, Dick--you're the youngest person in the world."

"Rosemary?" Silence while he stared at a shelf that held the humbler poisons of France--bottles of Otard, Rhum St. James, Marie Brizzard, Punch Orangeade, André Fernet Blanco, Cherry Rochet, and Armagnac.

"Are you alone?"

--Do you mind if I pull down the curtain?

"Who do you think I'd be with?"

"That's the state I'm in. I'd like to be with you now."

Silence, then a sigh and an answer. "I wish you were with me now."

There was the hotel room where she lay behind a telephone number, and little gusts of music wailed around her--

"And two--for tea.
And me for you,
And you for me
Alow-own."

There was the remembered dust of powder over her tan--when he kissed her face it was damp around the corners of her hair; there was the flash of a white face under his own, the arc of a shoulder.

"It's impossible," he said to himself. In a minute he was out in the street marching along toward the Muette, or away from it, his small brief-case still in his hand, his gold-headed stick held at a sword-like angle.

Rosemary returned to her desk and finished a letter to her mother.

"--I only saw him for a little while but I thought he was wonderful looking. I fell in love with him (Of course I Do Love Dick Best but you know what I mean). He really is going to direct the picture and is leaving immediately for Hollywood, and I think we ought to leave, too. Collis Clay has been here. I like him all right but have not seen much of him because of the Divers, who really are divine, about the Nicest People I ever Knew. I am feeling not very well today and am taking the Medicine, though see No need for it. I'm not even Going to Try to tell you All that's Happened until I see *You!!!* So when you get this letter *wire, wire, wire!* Are you coming north or shall I come south with the Divers?"

At six Dick called Nicole.

"Have you any special plans?" he asked. "Would you like to do something quiet--dinner at the hotel and then a play?"

"Would you? I'll do whatever you want. I phoned Rosemary a while ago and she's having dinner in her room. I think this upset all of us, don't you?"

"It didn't upset me," he objected. "Darling, unless you're physically tired let's do something. Otherwise we'll get south and spend a week wondering why we didn't see Boucher. It's better than brooding--"

This was a blunder and Nicole took him up sharply.

"Brooding about what?"

"About Maria Wallis."

She agreed to go to a play. It was a tradition between them that they should never be too tired for anything, and they found it made the days better on the whole and put the evenings more in order. When, inevitably, their spirits flagged they shifted the blame to the weariness and fatigue of others. Before they went out, as fine-looking a couple as could be found in Paris, they knocked softly at Rosemary's door. There was no answer; judging that she was asleep they walked into a warm strident Paris night, snatching a vermouth and bitters in the shadow by Fouquet's bar.

XXII

Nicole awoke late, murmuring something back into her dream before she parted her long lashes tangled with sleep. Dick's bed was empty--only after a minute did she realize that she had been awakened by a knock at their salon door.

"Entrez!" she called, but there was no answer, and after a moment she slipped on a dressing-gown and went to open it. A sergent-de-ville confronted her courteously and stepped inside the door.

"Mr. Afghan North--he is here?"

"What? No--he's gone to America."

"When did he leave, Madame?"

"Yesterday morning."

He shook his head and waved his forefinger at her in a quicker rhythm.

"He was in Paris last night. He is registered here but his room is not occupied. They told me I had better ask at this room."

"Sounds very peculiar to me--we saw him off yesterday morning on the boat train."

"Be that as it may, he has been seen here this morning. Even his carte d'identité has been seen. And there you are."

"We know nothing about it," she proclaimed in amazement.

He considered. He was an ill-smelling, handsome man.

"You were not with him at all last night?"

"But no."

"We have arrested a Negro. We are convinced we have at last arrested the correct Negro."

"I assure you that I haven't an idea what you're talking about. If it's the Mr. Abraham North, the one we know, well, if he was in Paris last night we weren't aware of it."

The man nodded, sucked his upper lip, convinced but disappointed.

"What happened?" Nicole demanded.

He showed his palms, puffing out his closed mouth. He had begun to find her attractive and his eyes flickered at her.

"What do you wish, Madame? A summer affair. Mr. Afghan North was robbed and he made a complaint. We have arrested the miscreant. Mr. Afghan should come to identify him and make the proper charges."

Nicole pulled her dressing-gown closer around her and dismissed him briskly. Mystified she took a bath and dressed. By this time it was after ten and she called Rosemary but got no answer--then she phoned the hotel office and found that Abe had indeed registered, at six-thirty this morning. His room, however, was still unoccupied. Hoping for a word from Dick she waited in the parlor of the suite; just as she had given up and decided to go out, the office called and announced:

"Meestaire Crawshow, un nègre."

"On what business?" she demanded.

"He says he knows you and the doctaire. He says there is a Meestaire Freeman into prison that is a friend of all the world. He says there is injustice and he wishes to see Meestaire North before he himself is arrested."

"We know nothing about it." Nicole disclaimed the whole business with a vehement clap of the receiver. Abe's bizarre reappearance made it plain to her how fatigued she was with his dissipation. Dismissing him from her mind she went out, ran into Rosemary at the dressmaker's, and shopped with her for artificial flowers and all-colored strings of colored beads on the Rue de Rivoli. She helped Rosemary choose a diamond for her mother, and some scarfs and novel cigarette cases to take home to business associates in California. For her son she bought Greek and Roman soldiers, a whole army of them, costing over a thousand francs. Once again they spent their money in different ways and again Rosemary admired Nicole's method of spending. Nicole was sure that the money she spent was hers--Rosemary still thought her money was miraculously lent to her and she must consequently be very careful of it.

It was fun spending money in the sunlight of the foreign city with healthy bodies under them that sent streams of color up to their faces; with arms and hands, legs and ankles that they stretched out confidently, reaching or stepping with the confidence of women lovely to men.

When they got back to the hotel and found Dick, all bright and new in the morning, both of them had a moment of complete childish joy.

He had just received a garbled telephone call from Abe who, so it appeared, had spent the forenoon in hiding.

"It was one of the most extraordinary telephone conversations I've ever held."

Dick had talked not only to Abe but to a dozen others. On the phone these supernumeraries had been typically introduced as: "--man wants to talk to you is in the teput dome, well he says he was in it--what is it?

"Hey, somebody, shut-up--anyhow, he was in some shandel-scandal and he kaa *possibly* go home. My own *personal* is that--my personal is he's had a--" Gulps sounded and thereafter what the party had, rested with the unknown.

The phone yielded up a supplementary offer:

"I thought it would appeal to you anyhow as a psychologist." The vague personality who corresponded to this statement was eventually hung on to the phone; in the sequence he failed to appeal to Dick, as a psychologist, or indeed as anything else. Abe's conversation flowed on as follows:

"Hello."

"Well?"

"Well, hello."

"Who are you?"

"Well." There were interpolated snorts of laughter.

"Well, I'll put somebody else on the line."

Sometimes Dick could hear Abe's voice, accompanied by scufflings, droppings of the receiver, far-away fragments such as, "No, I don't, Mr. North. . . ." Then a pert decided voice had said: "If you are a friend of Mr. North you will come down and take him away."

Abe cut in, solemn and ponderous, beating it all down with an overtone of earth-bound determination.

"Dick, I've launched a race riot in Montmartre. I'm going over and get Freeman out of jail. If a Negro from Copenhagen that makes shoe polish--hello, can you hear me--well, look, if anybody comes there--" Once again the receiver was a chorus of innumerable melodies.

"Why you back in Paris?" Dick demanded.

"I got as far as Evreux, and I decided to take a plane back so I could compare it with St. Sulpice. I mean I don't intend to bring St. Sulpice back to Paris. I don't even mean Baroque! I meant St. Germain. For God's sake, wait a minute and I'll put the chasseur on the wire."

"For God's sake, don't."

"Listen--did Mary get off all right?"

"Yes."

"Dick, I want you to talk with a man I met here this morning, the son of a naval officer that's been to every doctor in Europe. Let me tell you about him--"

Dick had rung off at this point--perhaps that was a piece of ingratitude for he needed grist for the grinding activity of his mind.

"Abe used to be so nice," Nicole told Rosemary. "So nice. Long ago--when Dick and I were first married. If you had known him then. He'd come to stay with us for weeks and weeks and we scarcely knew he was in the house. Sometimes he'd play--sometimes he'd be in the library with a muted piano, making love to it by the hour--Dick, do you remember that maid? She thought he was a ghost and sometimes Abe used to meet her in the hall and moo at her, and it cost us a whole tea service once--but we didn't care."

So much fun--so long ago. Rosemary envied them their fun, imagining a life of leisure unlike her own. She knew little of leisure but she had the respect for it of those who have never had it. She thought of it as a resting, without realizing that the Divers were as far from relaxing as she was herself.

"What did this to him?" she asked. "Why does he have to drink?"

Nicole shook her head right and left, disclaiming responsibility for the matter: "So many smart men go to pieces nowadays."

"And when haven't they?" Dick asked. "Smart men play close to the line because they have to--some of them can't stand it, so they quit."

"It must lie deeper than that." Nicole clung to her conversation; also she was irritated that Dick should contradict her before Rosemary. "Artists like--well, like Fernand don't seem to have to wallow in alcohol. Why is it just Americans who dissipate?"

There were so many answers to this question that Dick decided to leave it in the air, to buzz victoriously in Nicole's ears. He had become intensely critical of her. Though he thought she was the most attractive human creature he had ever seen, though he got from her everything he needed, he scented battle from afar, and subconsciously he had been hardening and arming himself, hour by hour. He was not given to self-indulgence and he felt comparatively graceless at this moment of indulging himself, blinding his eyes with the hope that Nicole guessed at only an emotional excitement about Rosemary. He was not sure--last night at the theatre she had referred pointedly to Rosemary as a child.

The trio lunched downstairs in an atmosphere of carpets and padded waiters, who did not march at the stomping quick-step of those men who brought good food to the tables whereon they had recently dined. Here there were families of Americans staring around at families of Americans, and trying to make conversation with one another.

There was a party at the next table that they could not account for. It consisted of an expansive, somewhat secretarial, would-you-mind-repeating young man, and a score of women. The women were neither young nor old nor of any particular social class; yet the party gave the impression of a unit, held more closely together for example than a group of wives stalling through a professional congress of their husbands. Certainly it was more of a unit than any conceivable tourist party.

An instinct made Dick suck back the grave derision that formed on his tongue; he asked the waiter to find out who they were.

"Those are the gold-star muzzers," explained the waiter.

Aloud and in low voices they exclaimed. Rosemary's eyes filled with tears.

"Probably the young ones are the wives," said Nicole.

Over his wine Dick looked at them again; in their happy faces, the dignity that surrounded and pervaded the party, he perceived all the maturity of an older

America. For a while the sobered women who had come to mourn for their dead, for something they could not repair, made the room beautiful. Momentarily, he sat again on his father's knee, riding with Moseby while the old loyalties and devotions fought on around him. Almost with an effort he turned back to his two women at the table and faced the whole new world in which he believed.

--Do you mind if I pull down the curtain?

XXIII

Abe North was still in the Ritz bar, where he had been since nine in the morning. When he arrived seeking sanctuary the windows were open and great beams were busy at pulling up the dust from smoky carpets and cushions. Chasseurs tore through the corridors, liberated and disembodied, moving for the moment in pure space. The sit-down bar for women, across from the bar proper, seemed very small--it was hard to imagine what throngs it could accommodate in the afternoon.

The famous Paul, the concessionaire, had not arrived, but Claude, who was checking stock, broke off his work with no improper surprise to make Abe a pick-me-up. Abe sat on a bench against a wall. After two drinks he began to feel better--so much better that he mounted to the barber's shop and was shaved. When he returned to the bar Paul had arrived--in his custom-built motor, from which he had disembarked correctly at the Boulevard des Capucines. Paul liked Abe and came over to talk.

"I was supposed to ship home this morning," Abe said. "I mean yesterday morning, or whatever this is."

"Why din you?" asked Paul.

Abe considered, and happened finally to a reason: "I was reading a serial in Liberty and the next installment was due here in Paris--so if I'd sailed I'd have missed it--then I never would have read it."

"It must be a very good story."

"It's a terr-r-rible story."

Paul arose chuckling and paused, leaning on the back of a chair:

"If you really want to get off, Mr. North, there are friends of yours going tomorrow on the France--Mister what is this name--and Slim Pearson. Mister--I'll think of it--tall with a new beard."

"Yardly," Abe supplied.

"Mr. Yardly. They're both going on the France."

He was on his way to his duties but Abe tried to detain him: "If I didn't have to go by way of Cherbourg. The baggage went that way."

"Get your baggage in New York," said Paul, receding.

The logic of the suggestion fitted gradually into Abe's pitch--he grew rather enthusiastic about being cared for, or rather of prolonging his state of irresponsibility.

Other clients had meanwhile drifted in to the bar: first came a huge Dane whom Abe had somewhere encountered. The Dane took a seat across the room, and Abe guessed he would be there all the day, drinking, lunching, talking or reading newspapers. He felt a desire to out-stay him. At eleven the college boys began to step in, stepping gingerly lest they tear one another bag from bag. It was about then he had the chasseur telephone to the Divers; by the time he was in touch with them he was in touch also with other friends--and his hunch was to put them all on different phones at once--the result was somewhat general. From time to time his mind reverted to the fact that he ought to go over and get Freeman out of jail, but he shook off all facts as parts of the nightmare.

By one o'clock the bar was jammed; amidst the consequent mixture of voices the staff of waiters functioned, pinning down their clients to the facts of drink and money.

"That makes two stingers . . . and one more . . . two martinis and one . . . nothing for you, Mr. Quarterly . . . that makes three rounds. That makes seventy-five francs, Mr. Quarterly. Mr. Schaeffer said he had this--you had the last . . . I can only do what you say . . . thanks vera-much."

In the confusion Abe had lost his seat; now he stood gently swaying and talking to some of the people with whom he had involved himself. A terrier ran a leash around his legs but Abe managed to extricate himself without upsetting and became the recipient of profuse apologies. Presently he was invited to lunch, but declined. It was almost Briglith, he explained, and there was something he had to do at Briglith. A little later, with the exquisite manners of the alcoholic that are like the manners of a prisoner or a family servant, he said good-by to an acquaintance, and turning around discovered that the bar's great moment was over as precipitately as it had begun.

Across from him the Dane and his companions had ordered luncheon. Abe did likewise but scarcely touched it. Afterwards, he just sat, happy to live in the past. The drink made past happy things contemporary with the present, as if they were still going on, contemporary even with the future as if they were about to happen again.

At four the chasseur approached him:

"You wish to see a colored fellow of the name Jules Peterson?"

"God! How did he find me?"

"I didn't tell him you were present."

"Who did?" Abe fell over his glasses but recovered himself.

"Says he's already been around to all the American bars and hotels."

"Tell him I'm not here--" As the chasseur turned away Abe asked: "Can he come in here?"

"I'll find out."

Receiving the question Paul glanced over his shoulder; he shook his head, then seeing Abe he came over.

"I'm sorry; I can't allow it."

Abe got himself up with an effort and went out to the Rue Cambon.

XXIV

With his miniature leather brief-case in his hand Richard Diver walked from the seventh arrondisement--where he left a note for Maria Wallis signed "Dicole," the word with which he and Nicole had signed communications in the first days of love--to his shirt-makers where the clerks made a fuss over him out of proportion to the money he spent. Ashamed at promising so much to these poor Englishmen, with his fine manners, his air of having the key to security, ashamed of making a tailor shift an inch of silk on his arm. Afterward he went to the bar of the Crillon and drank a small coffee and two fingers of gin.

As he entered the hotel the halls had seemed unnaturally bright; when he left he realized that it was because it had already turned dark outside. It was a windy four-o'clock night with the leaves on the Champs Élysées singing and failing, thin and wild. Dick turned down the Rue de Rivoli, walking two squares under the arcades to his bank where there was mail. Then he took a taxi and started up the Champs Élysées through the first patter of rain, sitting alone with his love.

Back at two o'clock in the Roi George corridor the beauty of Nicole had been to the beauty of Rosemary as the beauty of Leonardo's girl was to that of the girl of an illustrator. Dick moved on through the rain, demoniac and frightened, the passions of many men inside him and nothing simple that he could see.

Rosemary opened her door full of emotions no one else knew of. She was now what is sometimes called a "little wild thing"--by twenty-four full hours she was not yet unified and she was absorbed in playing around with chaos; as if her destiny were a picture puzzle--counting benefits, counting hopes, telling off Dick, Nicole, her mother, the director she met yesterday, like stops on a string of beads.

When Dick knocked she had just dressed and been watching the rain, thinking of some poem, and of full gutters in Beverly Hills. When she opened the door she saw him as something fixed and Godlike as he had always been, as older people are to younger, rigid and unmalleable. Dick saw her with an inevitable sense of disappointment. It took him a moment to respond to the unguarded sweetness of her smile, her body calculated to a millimeter to suggest a bud yet guarantee a flower. He was conscious of the print of her wet foot on a rug through the bathroom door.

"Miss Television," he said with a lightness he did not feel. He put his gloves, his brief-case on the dressing-table, his stick against the wall. His chin dominated the lines of pain around his mouth, forcing them up into his forehead and the corner of his eyes, like fear that cannot be shown in public.

"Come and sit on my lap close to me," he said softly, "and let me see about your lovely mouth."

She came over and sat there and while the dripping slowed down outside--drip--dri-i-ip, she laid her lips to the beautiful cold image she had created.

Presently she kissed him several times in the mouth, her face getting big as it came up to him; he had never seen anything so dazzling as the quality of her skin, and since sometimes beauty gives back the images of one's best thoughts he thought of his responsibility about Nicole, and of the responsibility of her being two doors down across the corridor.

"The rain's over," he said. "Do you see the sun on the slate?"

Rosemary stood up and leaned down and said her most sincere thing to him: "Oh, we're such *actors*--you and I."

She went to her dresser and the moment that she laid her comb flat against her hair there was a slow persistent knocking at the door.

They were shocked motionless; the knock was repeated insistently, and in the sudden realization that the door was not locked Rosemary finished her hair with one stroke, nodded at Dick who had quickly jerked the wrinkles out of the bed where they had been sitting, and started for the door. Dick said in quite a natural voice, not too loud:

"--so if you don't feel up to going out, I'll tell Nicole and we'll have a very quiet last evening."

The precautions were needless for the situation of the parties outside the door was so harassed as to preclude any but the most fleeting judgments on matters not pertinent to themselves. Standing there was Abe, aged by several months in the last twenty-four hours, and a very frightened, concerned colored man whom Abe introduced as Mr. Peterson of Stockholm.

"He's in a terrible situation and it's my fault," said Abe. "We need some good advice."

"Come in our rooms," said Dick.

Abe insisted that Rosemary come too and they crossed the hall to the Divers' suite. Jules Peterson, a small, respectable Negro, on the suave model that heels the Republican party in the border States, followed.

It appeared that the latter had been a legal witness to the early morning dispute in Montparnasse; he had accompanied Abe to the police station and supported his assertion that a thousand franc note had been seized out of his hand by a Negro, whose identification was one of the points of the case. Abe and Jules Peterson, accompanied by an agent of police, returned to the bistro and too hastily identified as the criminal a Negro, who, so it was established after an hour, had only entered the place after Abe left. The police had further complicated the situation by arresting the prominent Negro restaurateur, Freeman, who had only drifted through the alcoholic fog at a very early stage and then vanished. The true culprit, whose case, as reported by his friends, was that he had merely commandeered a fifty-franc note to pay for drinks that Abe had ordered, had only recently and in a somewhat sinister rôle, reappeared upon the scene.

In brief, Abe had succeeded in the space of an hour in entangling himself with the personal lives, consciences, and emotions of one Afro-European and three Afro-Americans inhabiting the French Latin quarter. The disentanglement was not even faintly in sight and the day had passed in an atmosphere of unfamiliar Negro faces bobbing up in unexpected places and around unexpected corners, and insistent Negro voices on the phone.

In person, Abe had succeeded in evading all of them, save Jules Peterson. Peterson was rather in the position of the friendly Indian who had helped a white. The Negroes who suffered from the betrayal were not so much after Abe as after Peterson, and Peterson was very much after what protection he might get from Abe.

Up in Stockholm Peterson had failed as a small manufacturer of shoe polish and now possessed only his formula and sufficient trade tools to fill a small box; however, his new protector had promised in the early hours to set him up in business in Versailles. Abe's former chauffeur was a shoemaker there and Abe had handed Peterson two hundred francs on account.

Rosemary listened with distaste to this rigmarole; to appreciate its grotesquerie required a more robust sense of humor than hers. The little man with his portable manufactory, his insincere eyes that, from time to time, rolled white semicircles of panic into view; the figure of Abe, his face as blurred as the gaunt fine lines of it would permit--all this was as remote from her as sickness.

"I ask only a chance in life," said Peterson with the sort of precise yet distorted intonation peculiar to colonial countries. "My methods are simple, my formula is so good that I was drove away from Stockholm, ruined, because I did not care to dispose of it."

Dick regarded him politely--interest formed, dissolved, he turned to Abe:

"You go to some hotel and go to bed. After you're all straight Mr. Peterson will come and see you."

"But don't you appreciate the mess that Peterson's in?" Abe protested.

"I shall wait in the hall," said Mr. Peterson with delicacy. "It is perhaps hard to discuss my problems in front of me."

He withdrew after a short travesty of a French bow; Abe pulled himself to his feet with the deliberation of a locomotive.

"I don't seem highly popular to-day."

"Popular but not probable," Dick advised him. "My advice is to leave this hotel--by way of the bar, if you want. Go to the Chambord, or if you'll need a lot of service, go over to the Majestic."

"Could I annoy you for a drink?"

"There's not a thing up here," Dick lied.

Resignedly Abe shook hands with Rosemary; he composed his face slowly, holding her hand a long time and forming sentences that did not emerge.

"You are the most--one of the most--"

She was sorry, and rather revolted at his dirty hands, but she laughed in a well-bred way, as though it were nothing unusual to her to watch a man walking in a slow dream. Often people display a curious respect for a man drunk, rather like the respect of simple races for the insane. Respect rather than fear. There is something awe-inspiring in one who has lost all inhibitions, who will do anything. Of course we make him pay afterward for his moment of superiority, his moment of impressiveness. Abe turned to Dick with a last appeal.

"If I go to a hotel and get all steamed and curry-combed, and sleep awhile, and fight off these Senegalese--could I come and spend the evening by the fireside?"

Dick nodded at him, less in agreement than in mockery and said: "You have a high opinion of your current capacities."

"I bet if Nicole was here she'd let me come back."

"All right." Dick went to a trunk tray and brought a box to the central table; inside were innumerable cardboard letters.

"You can come if you want to play anagrams."

Abe eyed the contents of the box with physical revulsion, as though he had been asked to eat them like oats.

"What are anagrams? Haven't I had enough strange--"

"It's a quiet game. You spell words with them--any word except alcohol."

"I bet you can spell alcohol," Abe plunged his hand among the counters. "Can I come back if I can spell alcohol?"

"You can come back if you want to play anagrams."

Abe shook his head resignedly.

"If you're in that frame of mind there's no use--I'd just be in the way." He waved his finger reproachfully at Dick. "But remember what George the third said, that if Grant was drunk he wished he would bite the other generals."

With a last desperate glance at Rosemary from the golden corners of his eyes, he went out. To his relief Peterson was no longer in the corridor. Feeling lost and homeless he went back to ask Paul the name of that boat.

XXV

When he had tottered out, Dick and Rosemary embraced fleetingly. There was a dust of Paris over both of them through which they scented each other: the rubber guard on Dick's fountain pen, the faintest odor of warmth from

Rosemary's neck and shoulders. For another half-minute Dick clung to the situation; Rosemary was first to return to reality.

"I must go, youngster," she said.

They blinked at each other across a widening space, and Rosemary made an exit that she had learned young, and on which no director had ever tried to improve.

She opened the door of her room and went directly to her desk where she had suddenly remembered leaving her wristwatch. It was there; slipping it on she glanced down at the daily letter to her mother, finishing the last sentence in her mind. Then, rather gradually, she realized without turning about that she was not alone in the room.

In an inhabited room there are refracting objects only half noticed: varnished wood, more or less polished brass, silver and ivory, and beyond these a thousand conveyers of light and shadow so mild that one scarcely thinks of them as that, the tops of picture-frames, the edges of pencils or ash-trays, of crystal or china ornaments; the totality of this refraction--appealing to equally subtle reflexes of the vision as well as to those associational fragments in the subconscious that we seem to hang on to, as a glass-fitter keeps the irregularly shaped pieces that may do some time--this fact might account for what Rosemary afterward mystically described as "realizing" that there was some one in the room, before she could determine it. But when she did realize it she turned swift in a sort of ballet step and saw that a dead Negro was stretched upon her bed.

As she cried "aaouu!" and her still unfastened wristwatch banged against the desk she had the preposterous idea that it was Abe North. Then she dashed for the door and across the hall.

Dick was straightening up; he had examined the gloves worn that day and thrown them into a pile of soiled gloves in a corner of a trunk. He had hung up coat and vest and spread his shirt on another hanger--a trick of his own. "You'll wear a shirt that's a little dirty where you won't wear a mussed shirt." Nicole had come in and was dumping one of Abe's extraordinary ash-trays into the waste-basket when Rosemary tore into the room.

"*Dick! Dick!* Come and see!"

Dick jogged across the hall into her room. He knelt to Peterson's heart, and felt the pulse--the body was warm, the face, harassed and indirect in life, was gross and bitter in death; the box of materials was held under one arm but the shoe that dangled over the bedside was bare of polish and its sole was worn through. By French law Dick had no right to touch the body but he moved the arm a little to see something--there was a stain on the green coverlet, there would be faint blood on the blanket beneath.

Dick closed the door and stood thinking; he heard cautious steps in the corridor and then Nicole calling him by name. Opening the door he whispered: "Bring the couverture and top blanket from one of our beds--don't let any one see you." Then, noticing the strained look on her face, he added quickly, "Look here, you mustn't get upset over this--it's only some nigger scrap."

"I want it to be over."

The body, as Dick lifted it, was light and ill-nourished. He held it so that further hemorrhages from the wound would flow into the man's clothes. Laying it beside the bed he stripped off the coverlet and top blanket and then opening the door an inch, listened--there was a clank of dishes down the hall followed by a loud patronizing "Mer*ci*, Madame," but the waiter went in the other direction, toward the service stairway. Quickly Dick and Nicole exchanged bundles across the corridor; after spreading this covering on Rosemary's bed, Dick stood sweating in the warm twilight, considering. Certain points had become apparent to him in the moment following his examination of the body; first, that Abe's first hostile Indian had tracked the friendly Indian and discovered him in the corridor, and when the latter had taken desperate refuge in Rosemary's room, had hunted down and slain him; second, that if the situation were allowed to develop naturally, no power on earth could keep the smear off Rosemary--the paint was scarcely dry on the Arbuckle case. Her contract was contingent upon an obligation to continue rigidly and unexceptionally as "Daddy's Girl."

Automatically Dick made the old motion of turning up his sleeves though he wore a sleeveless undershirt, and bent over the body. Getting a purchase on the shoulders of the coat he kicked open the door with his heel, and dragged the body quickly into a plausible position in the corridor. He came back into Rosemary's room and smoothed back the grain of the plush floor rug. Then he went to the phone in his suite and called the manager-owner of the hotel.

"McBeth?--it's Doctor Diver speaking--something very important. Are we on a more or less private line?"

It was good that he had made the extra effort which had firmly entrenched him with Mr. McBeth. Here was one use for all the pleasingness that Dick had expended over a large area he would never retrace. . . .

"Going out of the suite we came on a dead Negro . . . in the hall . . . no, no, he's a civilian. Wait a minute now--I knew you didn't want any guests to blunder on the body so I'm phoning you. Of course I must ask you to keep my name out of it. I don't want any French red tape just because I discovered the man."

What exquisite consideration for the hotel! Only because Mr. McBeth, with his own eyes, had seen these traits in Doctor Diver two nights before, could he credit the story without question.

In a minute Mr. McBeth arrived and in another minute he was joined by a gendarme. In the interval he found time to whisper to Dick, "You can be sure the name of any guest will be protected. I'm only too grateful to you for your pains."

Mr. McBeth took an immediate step that may only be imagined, but that influenced the gendarme so as to make him pull his mustaches in a frenzy of uneasiness and greed. He made perfunctory notes and sent a telephone call to his post. Meanwhile with a celerity that Jules Peterson, as a business man, would have quite understood, the remains were carried into another apartment of one of the most fashionable hotels in the world.

Dick went back to his salon.

"What *hap*pened?" cried Rosemary. "Do all the Americans in Paris just shoot at each other all the time?"

"This seems to be the open season," he answered. "Where's Nicole?"

"I think she's in the bathroom."

She adored him for saving her--disasters that could have attended upon the event had passed in prophecy through her mind; and she had listened in wild worship to his strong, sure, polite voice making it all right. But before she reached him in a sway of soul and body his attention focussed on something else: he went into the bedroom and toward the bathroom. And now Rosemary, too, could hear, louder and louder, a verbal inhumanity that penetrated the key-holes and the cracks in the doors, swept into the suite and in the shape of horror took form again.

With the idea that Nicole had fallen in the bathroom and hurt herself, Rose-mary followed Dick. That was not the condition of affairs at which she stared before Dick shouldered her back and brusquely blocked her view.

Nicole knelt beside the tub swaying sidewise and sidewise. "It's you!" she cried, "--it's you come to intrude on the only privacy I have in the world--with your spread with red blood on it. I'll wear it for you--I'm not ashamed, though it was such a pity. On All Fools Day we had a party on the Zurichsee, and all the fools were there, and I wanted to come dressed in a spread but they wouldn't let me--"

"Control yourself!"

"--so I sat in the bathroom and they brought me a domino and said wear that. I did. What else could I do?"

"Control yourself, Nicole!"

"I never expected you to love me--it was too late--only don't come in the bathroom, the only place I can go for privacy, dragging spreads with red blood on them and asking me to fix them."

"Control yourself. Get up--"

Rosemary, back in the salon, heard the bathroom door bang, and stood trem-bling: now she knew what Violet McKisco had seen in the bathroom at Villa Diana. She answered the ringing phone and almost cried with relief when she found it was Collis Clay, who had traced her to the Divers' apartment. She asked him to come up while she got her hat, because she was afraid to go into her room alone.

BOOK TWO

I

In the spring of 1917, when Doctor Richard Diver first arrived in Zurich, he was twenty-six years old, a fine age for a man, indeed the very acme of bachelorhood. Even in war-time days, it was a fine age for Dick, who was already too valuable, too much of a capital investment to be shot off in a gun. Years later it seemed to him that even in this sanctuary he did not escape lightly, but about that he never fully made up his mind--in 1917 he laughed at the idea, saying apologetically that the war didn't touch him at all. Instructions from his local board were that he was to complete his studies in Zurich and take a degree as he had planned.

Switzerland was an island, washed on one side by the waves of thunder around Gorizia and on another by the cataracts along the Somme and the Aisne. For once there seemed more intriguing strangers than sick ones in the cantons, but that had to be guessed at--the men who whispered in the little cafés of Berne and Geneva were as likely to be diamond salesmen or commercial travellers. However, no one had missed the long trains of blinded or one-legged men, or dying trunks, that crossed each other between the bright lakes of Constance and Neuchâtel. In the beer-halls and shop-windows were bright posters presenting the Swiss defending their frontiers in 1914--with inspiring ferocity young men and old men glared down from the mountains at phantom French and Germans; the purpose was to assure the Swiss heart that it had shared the contagious glory of those days. As the massacre continued the posters withered away, and no country was more surprised than its sister republic when the United States bungled its way into the war.

Doctor Diver had seen around the edges of the war by that time: he was an Oxford Rhodes Scholar from Connecticut in 1914. He returned home for a final year at Johns Hopkins, and took his degree. In 1916 he managed to get to Vienna under the impression that, if he did not make haste, the great Freud would eventually succumb to an aeroplane bomb. Even then Vienna was old with death but Dick managed to get enough coal and oil to sit in his room in the Damenstiff

Strasse and write the pamphlets that he later destroyed, but that, rewritten, were the backbone of the book he published in Zurich in 1920.

Most of us have a favorite, a heroic period, in our lives and that was Dick Diver's. For one thing he had no idea that he was charming, that the affection he gave and inspired was anything unusual among healthy people. In his last year at New Haven some one referred to him as "lucky Dick"--the name lingered in his head.

"Lucky Dick, you big stiff," he would whisper to himself, walking around the last sticks of flame in his room. "You hit it, my boy. Nobody knew it was there before you came along."

At the beginning of 1917, when it was becoming difficult to find coal, Dick burned for fuel almost a hundred textbooks that he had accumulated; but only, as he laid each one on the fire, with an assurance chuckling inside him that he was himself a digest of what was within the book, that he could brief it five years from now, if it deserved to be briefed. This went on at any odd hour, if necessary, with a floor rug over his shoulders, with the fine quiet of the scholar which is nearest of all things to heavenly peace--but which, as will presently be told, had to end.

For its temporary continuance he thanked his body that had done the flying rings at New Haven, and now swam in the winter Danube. With Elkins, second secretary at the Embassy, he shared an apartment, and there were two nice girl visitors--which was that and not too much of it, nor too much of the Embassy either. His contact with Ed Elkins aroused in him a first faint doubt as to the quality of his mental processes; he could not feel that they were profoundly different from the thinking of Elkins--Elkins, who would name you all the quarterbacks in New Haven for thirty years.

"--And Lucky Dick can't be one of these clever men; he must be less intact, even faintly destroyed. If life won't do it for him it's not a substitute to get a disease, or a broken heart, or an inferiority complex, though it'd be nice to build out some broken side till it was better than the original structure."

He mocked at his reasoning, calling it specious and "American"--his criteria of uncerebral phrase-making was that it was American. He knew, though, that the price of his intactness was incompleteness.

"The best I can wish you, my child," so said the Fairy Blackstick in Thackeray's The Rose and the Ring, "is a little misfortune."

In some moods he griped at his own reasoning: Could I help it that Pete Livingstone sat in the locker-room Tap Day when everybody looked all over hell for him? And I got an election when otherwise I wouldn't have got Elihu, knowing so few men. He was good and right and I ought to have sat in the locker-room instead. Maybe I would, if I'd thought I had a chance at an election. But Mercer kept coming to my room all those weeks. I guess I knew I had a chance all right, all right. But it would have served me right if I'd swallowed my pin in the shower and set up a conflict.

After the lectures at the university he used to argue this point with a young Rumanian intellectual who reassured him: "There's no evidence that Goethe ever had a 'conflict' in the modern sense, or a man like Jung, for instance. You're not a romantic philosopher--you're a scientist. Memory, force, character--especially good sense. That's going to be your trouble--judgment about yourself--once I knew a man who worked two years on the brain of an armadillo, with the idea that he would sooner or later know more about the brain of an armadillo than any one. I kept arguing with him that he was not really pushing out the extension of the human range--it was too arbitrary. And sure enough, when he sent his work to the medical journal they refused it--they had just accepted a thesis by another man on the same subject."

Dick got up to Zurich on less Achilles' heels than would be required to equip a centipede, but with plenty--the illusions of eternal strength and health, and of the essential goodness of people; illusions of a nation, the lies of generations of frontier mothers who had to croon falsely, that there were no wolves outside the cabin door. After he took his degree, he received his orders to join a neurological unit forming in Bar-sur-Aube.

In France, to his disgust, the work was executive rather than practical. In compensation he found time to complete the short textbook and assemble the material for his next venture. He returned to Zurich in the spring of 1919 discharged.

The foregoing has the ring of a biography, without the satisfaction of knowing that the hero, like Grant, lolling in his general store in Galena, is ready to be called to an intricate destiny. Moreover it is confusing to come across a youthful photograph of some one known in a rounded maturity and gaze with a shock upon a fiery, wiry, eagle-eyed stranger. Best to be reassuring--Dick Diver's moment now began.

II

It was a damp April day, with long diagonal clouds over the Albishorn and water inert in the low places. Zurich is not unlike an American city. Missing something ever since his arrival two days before, Dick perceived that it was the sense he had had in finite French lanes that there was nothing more. In Zurich there was a lot besides Zurich--the roofs upled the eyes to tinkling cow pastures, which in turn modified hilltops further up--so life was a perpendicular starting off to a postcard heaven. The Alpine lands, home of the toy and the funicular, the merry-go-round and the thin chime, were not a being *here,* as in France with French vines growing over one's feet on the ground.

In Salzburg once Dick had felt the superimposed quality of a bought and borrowed century of music; once in the laboratories of the university in Zurich, delicately poking at the cervical of a brain, he had felt like a toy-maker rather than like the tornado who had hurried through the old red buildings of Hopkins, two years before, unstayed by the irony of the gigantic Christ in the entrance hall.

Yet he had decided to remain another two years in Zurich, for he did not underestimate the value of toy-making, in infinite precision, of infinite patience.

To-day he went out to see Franz Gregorovius at Dohmler's clinic on the Zurichsee. Franz, resident pathologist at the clinic, a Vaudois by birth, a few years older than Dick, met him at the tram stop. He had a dark and magnificent aspect of Cagliostro about him, contrasted with holy eyes; he was the third of the Gregoroviuses--his grandfather had instructed Krapaelin when psychiatry was just emerging from the darkness of all time. In personality he was proud, fiery, and sheeplike--he fancied himself as a hypnotist. If the original genius of the family had grown a little tired, Franz would without doubt become a fine clinician.

On the way to the clinic he said: "Tell me of your experiences in the war. Are you changed like the rest? You have the same stupid and unaging American face, except I know you're not stupid, Dick."

"I didn't see any of the war--you must have gathered that from my letters, Franz."

"That doesn't matter--we have some shell-shocks who merely heard an air raid from a distance. We have a few who merely read newspapers."

"It sounds like nonsense to me."

"Maybe it is, Dick. But, we're a rich person's clinic--we don't use the word nonsense. Frankly, did you come down to see me or to see that girl?"

They looked sideways at each other; Franz smiled enigmatically.

"Naturally I saw all the first letters," he said in his official basso. "When the change began, delicacy prevented me from opening any more. Really it had become your case."

"Then she's well?" Dick demanded.

"Perfectly well, I have charge of her, in fact I have charge of the majority of the English and American patients. They call me Doctor Gregory."

"Let me explain about that girl," Dick said. "I only saw her one time, that's a fact. When I came out to say good-by to you just before I went over to France. It was the first time I put on my uniform and I felt very bogus in it--went around saluting private soldiers and all that."

"Why didn't you wear it to-day?"

"Hey! I've been discharged three weeks. Here's the way I happened to see that girl. When I left you I walked down toward that building of yours on the lake to get my bicycle."

"--toward the 'Cedars'?"

"--a wonderful night, you know--moon over that mountain--"

"The Krenzegg."

"--I caught up with a nurse and a young girl. I didn't think the girl was a patient; I asked the nurse about tram times and we walked along. The girl was about the prettiest thing I ever saw."

"She still is."

"She'd never seen an American uniform and we talked, and I didn't think anything about it." He broke off, recognizing a familiar perspective, and then resumed: "--except, Franz, I'm not as hard-boiled as you are yet; when I see a beautiful shell like that I can't help feeling a regret about what's inside it. That was absolutely all--till the letters began to come."

"It was the best thing that could have happened to her," said Franz dramatically, "a transference of the most fortuitous kind. That's why I came down to meet you on a very busy day. I want you to come into my office and talk a long time before you see her. In fact, I sent her into Zurich to do errands." His voice was tense with enthusiasm. "In fact, I sent her without a nurse, with a less stable patient. I'm intensely proud of this case, which I handled, with your accidental assistance."

The car had followed the shore of the Zurichsee into a fertile region of pasture farms and low hills, steepled with châlets. The sun swam out into a blue sea of sky and suddenly it was a Swiss valley at its best--pleasant sounds and murmurs and a good fresh smell of health and cheer.

Professor Dohmler's plant consisted of three old buildings and a pair of new ones, between a slight eminence and the shore of the lake. At its founding, ten years before, it had been the first modern clinic for mental illness; at a casual glance no layman would recognize it as a refuge for the broken, the incomplete, the menacing, of this world, though two buildings were surrounded with vine-softened walls of a deceptive height. Some men raked straw in the sunshine; here and there, as they rode into the grounds, the car passed the white flag of a nurse waving beside a patient on a path.

After conducting Dick to his office, Franz excused himself for half an hour. Left alone Dick wandered about the room and tried to reconstruct Franz from the litter of his desk, from his books and the books of and by his father and grandfather; from the Swiss piety of a huge claret-colored photo of the former on the wall. There was smoke in the room; pushing open a French window, Dick let in a cone of sunshine. Suddenly his thoughts swung to the patient, the girl.

He had received about fifty letters from her written over a period of eight months. The first one was apologetic, explaining that she had heard from America how girls wrote to soldiers whom they did not know. She had obtained the name and address from Doctor Gregory and she hoped he would not mind if she sometimes sent word to wish him well, etc., etc.

So far it was easy to recognize the tone--from "Daddy-Long-Legs" and "Molly-Make-Believe," sprightly and sentimental epistolary collections enjoying a vogue in the States. But there the resemblance ended.

The letters were divided into two classes, of which the first class, up to about the time of the armistice, was of marked pathological turn, and of which the second class, running from thence up to the present, was entirely normal, and displayed a richly maturing nature. For these latter letters Dick had come to wait eagerly in the last dull months at Bar-sur-Aube--yet even from the first letters he had pieced together more than Franz would have guessed of the story.

MON CAPITAINE:

I thought when I saw you in your uniform you were so handsome. Then I thought Je m'en fiche French too and German. You thought I was pretty too but I've had that before and a long time I've stood it. If you come here again with that attitude base and criminal and not even faintly what I had been taught to associate with the role of gentleman then heaven help you. However you seem quieter than the others,

(2)

all soft like a big cat. I have only gotten to like boys who are rather sissies. Are you a sissy? There were some somewhere.

Excuse all this, it is the third letter I have written you and will send immediately or will never send. I've thought a lot about moonlight too, and there are many witnesses I could find if I could only be out of here.

(3)

They said you were a doctor, but so long as you are a cat it is different. My head aches so, so excuse this walking there like an ordinary with a white cat will explain, I think. I can speak three languages, four with English, and am sure I could be useful interpreting if you arrange such thing in France I'm sure I could control everything with the belts all bound around everybody like it was Wednesday. It is now Saturday and

(4)

you are far away, perhaps killed.

Come back to me some day, for I will be here always on this green hill. Unless they will let me write my father, whom I loved dearly. Excuse this. I am not myself today. I will write when I feel better.

Cherio

NICOLE WARREN.

Excuse all this.

CAPTAIN DIVER:

I know introspection is not good for a highly nervous state like mine, but I would like you to know where I stand. Last year or whenever it was in Chicago when I got so I couldn't speak to servants or walk in the street I kept waiting for some one to tell me. It was the duty of some one who understood. The blind must be led. Only no one would tell me everything--they would just tell me half and I was already too muddled to put two and two together. One man was nice--he was a French officer and he understood. He gave me a flower and said it was "plus petite et

(2)

moins entendue." We were friends. Then he took it away. I grew sicker and there was no one to explain to me. They had a song about Joan of Arc that they used to sing at me but that was just mean--it would just make me cry, for there was nothing the matter with my head then. They kept making reference to sports, too, but I didn't care by that time. So there was that day I went walking on Michigan Boulevard on and on for miles and finally they followed me in an automobile, but I wouldn't get

(3)

in. Finally they pulled me in and there were nurses. After that time I began to realize it all, because I could feel what was happening in others. So you see how I stand. And what good can it be for me to stay here with the doctors harping constantly in the things I was here to get over. So today I have written my father to come and take me away. I am glad

(4)

you are so interested in examining people and sending them back. It must be so much fun.

And again, from another letter:

You might pass up your next examination and write me a letter. They just sent me some phonograph records in case I should forget my lesson and I broke them all so the nurse won't speak to me. They were in English, so that the nurses would not understand. One doctor in Chicago said I was bluffing, but what he really meant was that I was a twin six and he had never seen one before. But I was very busy being mad then, so I didn't care what he said, when I am very busy being mad I don't usually care what they say, not if I were a million girls.

You told me that night you'd teach me to play. Well, I think love is all

(2)

there is or should be. Anyhow I am glad your interest in examinations keeps you busy.

Tout à vous,

NICOLE WARREN.

There were other letters among whose helpless cæsuras lurked darker rhythms.

DEAR CAPTAIN DIVER:

I write to you because there is no one else to whom I can turn and it seems to me if this farcicle situation is apparent to one as sick as me it should be apparent to you. The mental trouble is all over and besides that I am completely broken and humiliated, if that was what they wanted. My family have shamefully neglected me, there's no use asking them for help or pity. I have had enough and it is simply ruining my health and wasting my time pretending that what is the matter with my

(2)

head is curable.

Here I am in what appears to be a semi-insane-asylum, all because nobody saw fit to tell me the truth about anything. If I had only known what was going on like I know now I could have stood it I guess for I am pretty strong, but those who should have, did not see fit to enlighten me.

(3)

And now, when I know and have paid such a price for knowing, they sit there with their dogs lives and say I should believe what I did believe. Especially one does but I know now.

I am lonesome all the time far away from friends and family across the Atlantic I roam all over the place in a half daze. If you could get me a position as interpreter (I know French and German like a native, fair

(4)

Italian and a little Spanish) or in the Red Cross Ambulance or as a trained nurse, though I would have to train you would prove a great blessing.

And again:

Since you will not accept my explanation of what is the matter you could at least explain to me what you think, because you have a kind cat's face, and not that funny look that seems to be so fashionable here. Dr. Gregory gave me a snapshot of you, not as handsome as you are in your uniform, but younger looking.

MON CAPITAINE:

It was fine to have your postcard. I am so glad you take such interest in disqualifying nurses--oh, I understood your note very well indeed. Only I thought from the moment I met you that you were different.

DEAR CAPITAINE:

I think one thing today and another tomorrow. That is really all that's the matter with me, except a crazy defiance and a lack of proportion. I would gladly welcome any alienist you might suggest. Here they lie in their bath tubs and sing Play in Your Own Backyard as if I had my

(2)

backyard to play in or any hope which I can find by looking either backward or forward. They tried it again in the candy store again and I almost hit the man with the weight, but they held me.

I am not going to write you any more. I am too unstable.

And then a month with no letters. And then suddenly the change.

--I am slowly coming back to life . . .

--Today the flowers and the clouds . . .

--The war is over and I scarcely knew there was a war . . .

--How kind you have been! You must be very wise behind your face like a white cat, except you don't look like that in the picture Dr. Gregory gave me . . .

--Today I went to Zurich, how strange a feeling to see a city again.

--Today we went to Berne, it was so nice with the clocks.

--Today we climbed high enough to find asphodel and edelweiss . . .

After that the letters were fewer, but he answered them all. There was one:

I wish someone were in love with me like boys were ages ago before I was sick. I suppose it will be years, though, before I could think of anything like that.

But when Dick's answer was delayed for any reason, there was a fluttering burst of worry--like a worry of a lover: "Perhaps I have bored you," and: "Afraid I have presumed," and: "I keep thinking at night you have been sick."

In actuality Dick was sick with the flu. When he recovered, all except the formal part of his correspondence was sacrificed to the consequent fatigue, and shortly afterward the memory of her became overlaid by the vivid presence of a Wisconsin telephone girl at headquarters in Bar-sur-Aube. She was red-lipped like a poster, and known obscenely in the messes as "The Switchboard."

Franz came back into his office feeling self-important. Dick thought he would probably be a fine clinician, for the sonorous or staccato cadences by which he disciplined nurse or patient came not from his nervous system but from a tremendous and harmless vanity. His true emotions were more ordered and kept to himself.

"Now about the girl, Dick," he said. "Of course, I want to find out about you and tell you about myself, but first about the girl, because I have been waiting to tell you about it so long."

He searched for and found a sheaf of papers in a filing cabinet but after shuffling through them he found they were in his way and put them on his desk. Instead he told Dick the story.

III

About a year and a half before, Doctor Dohmler had some vague correspondence with an American gentleman living in Lausanne, a Mr. Devereux Warren, of the Warren family of Chicago. A meeting was arranged and one day Mr. Warren arrived at the clinic with his daughter Nicole, a girl of sixteen. She was obviously not well and the nurse who was with her took her to walk about the grounds while Mr. Warren had his consultation.

Warren was a strikingly handsome man looking less than forty. He was a fine American type in every way, tall, broad, well-made--"un homme très chic," as Doctor Dohmler described him to Franz. His large gray eyes were sun-veined from rowing on Lake Geneva, and he had that special air about him of having known the best of this world. The conversation was in German, for it developed that he had been educated at Göttingen. He was nervous and obviously very moved by his errand.

"Doctor Dohmler, my daughter isn't right in the head. I've had lots of specialists and nurses for her and she's taken a couple of rest cures but the thing has grown too big for me and I've been strongly recommended to come to you."

"Very well," said Doctor Dohmler. "Suppose you start at the beginning and tell me everything."

"There isn't any beginning, at least there isn't any insanity in the family that I know of, on either side. Nicole's mother died when she was eleven and I've sort of been father and mother both to her, with the help of governesses--father and mother both to her."

He was very moved as he said this. Doctor Dohmler saw that there were tears in the corners of his eyes and noticed for the first time that there was whiskey on his breath.

"As a child she was a darling thing--everybody was crazy about her, everybody that came in contact with her. She was smart as a whip and happy as the day is long. She liked to read or draw or dance or play the piano--anything. I used to hear my wife say she was the only one of our children who never cried at night. I've got an older girl, too, and there was a boy that died, but Nicole was--Nicole was--Nicole--"

He broke off and Doctor Dohmler helped him.

"She was a perfectly normal, bright, happy child."

"Perfectly."

Doctor Dohmler waited. Mr. Warren shook his head, blew a long sigh, glanced quickly at Doctor Dohmler and then at the floor again.

"About eight months ago, or maybe it was six months ago or maybe ten--I try to figure but I can't remember exactly where we were when she began to do funny things--crazy things. Her sister was the first one to say anything to me about it--because Nicole was always the same to me," he added rather hastily, as if some one had accused him of being to blame, "--the same loving little girl. The first thing was about a valet."

"Oh, yes," said Doctor Dohmler, nodding his venerable head, as if, like Sherlock Holmes, he had expected a valet and only a valet to be introduced at this point.

"I had a valet--been with me for years--Swiss, by the way." He looked up for Doctor Dohmler's patriotic approval. "And she got some crazy idea about him. She thought he was making up to her--of course, at the time I believed her and I let him go, but I know now it was all nonsense."

"What did she claim he had done?"

"That was the first thing--the doctors couldn't pin her down. She just looked at them as if they ought to know what he'd done. But she certainly meant he'd made some kind of indecent advances to her--she didn't leave us in any doubt of that."

"I see."

"Of course, I've read about women getting lonesome and thinking there's a man under the bed and all that, but why should Nicole get such an idea? She could have all the young men she wanted. We were in Lake Forest--that's a summer place near Chicago where we have a place--and she was out all day playing golf or tennis with boys. And some of them pretty gone on her at that."

All the time Warren was talking to the dried old package of Doctor Dohmler, one section of the latter's mind kept thinking intermittently of Chicago. Once in his youth he could have gone to Chicago as fellow and docent at the university, and perhaps become rich there and owned his own clinic instead of being only a minor shareholder in a clinic. But when he had thought of what he considered his own thin knowledge spread over that whole area, over all those wheat fields, those endless prairies, he had decided against it. But he had read about Chicago in those days, about the great feudal families of Armour, Palmer, Field, Crane, Warren, Swift, and McCormick and many others, and since that time not a few patients had come to him from that stratum of Chicago and New York.

"She got worse," continued Warren. "She had a fit or something--the things she said got crazier and crazier. Her sister wrote some of them down--" He handed a much-folded piece of paper to the doctor. "Almost always about men going to attack her, men she knew or men on the street--anybody--"

He told of their alarm and distress, of the horrors families go through under such circumstances, of the ineffectual efforts they had made in America, finally of the faith in a change of scene that had made him run the submarine blockade and bring his daughter to Switzerland.

"--on a United States cruiser," he specified with a touch of hauteur. "It was possible for me to arrange that, by a stroke of luck. And, may I add," he smiled apologetically, "that as they say: money is no object."

"Certainly not," agreed Dohmler dryly.

He was wondering why and about what the man was lying to him. Or, if he was wrong about that, what was the falsity that pervaded the whole room, the handsome figure in tweeds sprawling in his chair with a sportsman's ease? That was a tragedy out there, in the February day, the young bird with wings crushed somehow, and inside here it was all too thin, thin and wrong.

"I would like--to talk to her--a few minutes now," said Doctor Dohmler, going into English as if it would bring him closer to Warren.

Afterward when Warren had left his daughter and returned to Lausanne, and several days had passed, the doctor and Franz entered upon Nicole's card:

> Diagnostic: Schizophrénie. Phase aiguë en décroissance. La peur des hommes est un symptôme de la maladie, et n'est point constitutionnelle. . . . Le pronostic doit rester réservé.*

> * Diagnosis: Divided Personality. Acute and down-hill phase of the illness. The fear of men is a symptom of the illness and is not at all constitutional. . . . The prognosis must be reserved.

And then they waited with increasing interest as the days passed for Mr. Warren's promised second visit.

It was slow in coming. After a fortnight Doctor Dohmler wrote. Confronted with further silence he committed what was for those days "une folie," and telephoned to the Grand Hotel at Vevey. He learned from Mr. Warren's valet that he was at the moment packing to sail for America. But reminded that the forty francs Swiss for the call would show up on the clinic books, the blood of the Tuileries Guard rose to Doctor Dohmler's aid and Mr. Warren was got to the phone.

"It is--absolutely necessary--that you come. Your daughter's health--all depends. I can take no responsibility."

"But look here, Doctor, that's just what you're for. I have a hurry call to go home!"

Doctor Dohmler had never yet spoken to any one so far away but he dispatched his ultimatum so firmly into the phone that the agonized American at the other end yielded. Half an hour after this second arrival on the Zurichsee, Warren had broken down, his fine shoulders shaking with awful sobs inside his easy fitting coat, his eyes redder than the very sun on Lake Geneva, and they had the awful story.

"It just happened," he said hoarsely. "I don't know--I don't know.

"After her mother died when she was little she used to come into my bed every morning, sometimes she'd sleep in my bed. I was sorry for the little thing. Oh, after that, whenever we went places in an automobile or a train we used to hold hands. She used to sing to me. We used to say, 'Now let's not pay any attention to anybody else this afternoon--let's just have each other--for this morning you're mine.'" A broken sarcasm came into his voice. "People used to say what a wonderful father and daughter we were--they used to wipe their eyes. We were just like lovers--and then all at once we were lovers--and ten minutes after it happened I could have shot myself--except I guess I'm such a God-damned degenerate I didn't have the nerve to do it."

"Then what?" said Doctor Dohmler, thinking again of Chicago and of a mild pale gentleman with a pince-nez who had looked him over in Zurich thirty years before. "Did this thing go on?"

"Oh, no! She almost--she seemed to freeze up right away. She'd just say, 'Never mind, never mind, Daddy. It doesn't matter. Never mind.'"

"There were no consequences?"

"No." He gave one short convulsive sob and blew his nose several times. "Except now there're plenty of consequences."

As the story concluded Dohmler sat back in the focal armchair of the middle class and said to himself sharply, "Peasant!"--it was one of the few absolute worldly judgments that he had permitted himself for twenty years. Then he said:

"I would like for you to go to a hotel in Zurich and spend the night and come see me in the morning."

"And then what?"

Doctor Dohmler spread his hands wide enough to carry a young pig.

"Chicago," he suggested.

IV

"Then we knew where we stood," said Franz. "Dohmler told Warren we would take the case if he would agree to keep away from his daughter indefinitely, with an absolute minimum of five years. After Warren's first collapse, he seemed chiefly concerned as to whether the story would ever leak back to America."

"We mapped out a routine for her and waited. The prognosis was bad--as you know, the percentage of cures, even so-called social cures, is very low at that age."

"Those first letters looked bad," agreed Dick.

"Very bad--very typical. I hesitated about letting the first one get out of the clinic. Then I thought it will be good for Dick to know we're carrying on here. It was generous of you to answer them."

Dick sighed. "She was such a pretty thing--she enclosed a lot of snapshots of herself. And for a month there I didn't have anything to do. All I said in my letters was 'Be a good girl and mind the doctors.'"

"That was enough--it gave her somebody to think of outside. For a while she didn't have anybody--only one sister that she doesn't seem very close to. Besides, reading her letters helped us here--they were a measure of her condition."

"I'm glad."

"You see now what happened? She felt complicity--that's neither here nor there, except as we want to revalue her ultimate stability and strength of character. First came this shock. Then she went off to a boarding-school and heard the girls talking--so from sheer self-protection she developed the idea that she had had no complicity--and from there it was easy to slide into a phantom world where all men, the more you liked them and trusted them, the more evil--"

"Did she ever go into the--horror directly?"

"No, and as a matter of fact when she began to seem normal, about October, we were in a predicament. If she had been thirty years old we would have let her make her own adjustment, but she was so young we were afraid she might harden with it all twisted inside her. So Doctor Dohmler said to her frankly, 'Your duty now is to yourself. This doesn't by any account mean the end of anything for you--your life is just at its beginning,' and so forth and so forth. She really has an excellent mind, so he gave her a little Freud to read, not too much, and she was very interested. In fact, we've made rather a pet of her around here. But she is reticent," he added; he hesitated: "We have wondered if in her recent letters to you which she mailed herself from Zurich, she has said anything that would be illuminating about her state of mind and her plans for the future."

Dick considered.

"Yes and no--I'll bring the letters out here if you want. She seems hopeful and normally hungry for life--even rather romantic. Sometimes she speaks of 'the past' as people speak who have been in prison. But you never know whether they refer to the crime or the imprisonment or the whole experience. After all I'm only a sort of stuffed figure in her life."

"Of course, I understand your position exactly, and I express our gratitude once again. That was why I wanted to see you before you see her."

Dick laughed.

"You think she's going to make a flying leap at my person?"

"No, not that. But I want to ask you to go very gently. You are attractive to women, Dick."

"Then God help me! Well, I'll be gentle and repulsive--I'll chew garlic whenever I'm going to see her and wear a stubble beard. I'll drive her to cover."

"Not garlic!" said Franz, taking him seriously. "You don't want to compromise your career. But you're partly joking."

"--and I can limp a little. And there's no real bathtub where I'm living, anyhow."

"You're entirely joking," Franz relaxed--or rather assumed the posture of one relaxed. "Now tell me about yourself and your plans?"

"I've only got one, Franz, and that's to be a good psychologist--maybe to be the greatest one that ever lived."

Franz laughed pleasantly, but he saw that this time Dick wasn't joking.

"That's very good--and very American," he said. "It's more difficult for us." He got up and went to the French window. "I stand here and I see Zurich--there is the steeple of the Gross-Münster. In its vault my grandfather is buried. Across the bridge from it lies my ancestor Lavater, who would not be buried in any church. Nearby is the statue of another ancestor, Heinrich Pestalozzi, and one of Doctor Alfred Escher. And over everything there is always Zwingli--I am continually confronted with a pantheon of heroes."

"Yes, I see." Dick got up. "I was only talking big. Everything's just starting over. Most of the Americans in France are frantic to get home, but not me--I draw military pay all the rest of the year if I only attend lectures at the university. How's that for a government on the grand scale that knows its future great men? Then I'm going home for a month and see my father. Then I'm coming back--I've been offered a job."

"Where?"

"Your rivals--Gisler's Clinic on Interlacken."

"Don't touch it," Franz advised him. "They've had a dozen young men there in a year. Gisler's a manic-depressive himself, his wife and her lover run the clinic--of course, you understand that's confidential."

"How about your old scheme for America?" asked Dick lightly. "We were going to New York and start an up-to-date establishment for billionaires."

"That was students' talk."

Dick dined with Franz and his bride and a small dog with a smell of burning rubber, in their cottage on the edge of the grounds, He felt vaguely oppressed, not by the atmosphere of modest retrenchment, nor by Frau Gregorovius, who might have been prophesied, but by the sudden contracting of horizons to which Franz seemed so reconciled. For him the boundaries of asceticism were differently marked--he could see it as a means to an end, even as a carrying on with a glory it would itself supply, but it was hard to think of deliberately cutting life down to the scale of an inherited suit. The domestic gestures of Franz and his wife as they turned in a cramped space lacked grace and adventure. The post-war months in France, and the lavish liquidations taking place under the ægis of American splendor, had affected Dick's outlook. Also, men and women had made much of him, and perhaps what had brought him back to the centre of the great Swiss watch, was an intuition that this was not too good for a serious man.

He made Kaethe Gregorovius feel charming, meanwhile becoming increasingly restless at the all-pervading cauliflower--simultaneously hating himself too for this incipience of he knew not what superficiality.

"God, am I like the rest after all?"--So he used to think starting awake at night--"Am I like the rest?"

This was poor material for a socialist but good material for those who do much of the world's rarest work. The truth was that for some months he had been going through that partitioning of the things of youth wherein it is decided whether or not to die for what one no longer believes. In the dead white hours in Zurich staring into a stranger's pantry across the upshine of a street-lamp, he used to think that he wanted to be good, he wanted to be kind, he wanted to be brave and wise, but it was all pretty difficult. He wanted to be loved, too, if he could fit it in.

V

The veranda of the central building was illuminated from open French windows, save where the black shadows of stripling walls and the fantastic shadows of iron chairs slithered down into a gladiola bed. From the figures that shuffled between the rooms Miss Warren emerged first in glimpses and then sharply when she saw him; as she crossed the threshold her face caught the room's last light and brought it outside with her. She walked to a rhythm--all that week there had been singing in her ears, summer songs of ardent skies and wild shade, and with his arrival the singing had become so loud she could have joined in with it.

"How do you do, Captain," she said, unfastening her eyes from his with difficulty, as though they had become entangled. "Shall we sit out here?" She stood still, her glance moving about for a moment. "It's summer practically."

A woman had followed her out, a dumpy woman in a shawl, and Nicole presented Dick: "Señora--"

Franz excused himself and Dick grouped three chairs together.

"The lovely night," the Señora said.

"Muy bella," agreed Nicole; then to Dick, "Are you here for a long time?"

"I'm in Zurich for a long time, if that's what you mean."

"This is really the first night of real spring," the Señora suggested.

"To stay?"

"At least till July."

"I'm leaving in June."

"June is a lovely month here," the Señora commented. "You should stay for June and then leave in July when it gets really too hot."

"You're going where?" Dick asked Nicole.

"Somewhere with my sister--somewhere exciting, I hope, because I've lost so much time. But perhaps they'll think I ought to go to a quiet place at first--perhaps Como. Why don't you come to Como?"

"Ah, Como--" began the Señora.

Within the building a trio broke into Suppe's "Light Cavalry." Nicole took advantage of this to stand up and the impression of her youth and beauty grew on Dick until it welled up inside him in a compact paroxysm of emotion. She smiled, a moving childish smile that was like all the lost youth in the world.

"The music's too loud to talk against--suppose we walk around. Buenas noches, Señora."

"G't night--g't night."

They went down two steps to the path--where in a moment a shadow cut across it. She took his arm.

"I have some phonograph records my sister sent me from America," she said. "Next time you come here I'll play them for you--I know a place to put the phonograph where no one can hear."

"That'll be nice."

"Do you know 'Hindustan'?" she asked wistfully. "I'd never heard it before, but I like it. And I've got 'Why Do They Call Them Babies?' and 'I'm Glad I Can Make You Cry.' I suppose you've danced to all those tunes in Paris?"

"I haven't been to Paris."

Her cream-colored dress, alternately blue or gray as they walked, and her very blonde hair, dazzled Dick--whenever he turned toward her she was smiling a little, her face lighting up like an angel's when they came into the range of a roadside arc. She thanked him for everything, rather as if he had taken her to some party, and as Dick became less and less certain of his relation to her, her confidence increased--there was that excitement about her that seemed to reflect all the excitement of the world.

"I'm not under any restraint at all," she said. "I'll play you two good tunes called 'Wait Till the Cows Come Home' and 'Good-by, Alexander.'"

He was late the next time, a week later, and Nicole was waiting for him at a point in the path which he would pass walking from Franz's house. Her hair drawn back of her ears brushed her shoulders in such a way that the face seemed to have just emerged from it, as if this were the exact moment when she was coming from a wood into clear moonlight. The unknown yielded her up; Dick wished she had no background, that she was just a girl lost with no address save the night from which she had come. They went to the cache where she had left the phonograph, turned a corner by the workshop, climbed a rock, and sat down behind a low wall, facing miles and miles of rolling night.

They were in America now, even Franz with his conception of Dick as an irresistible Lothario would never have guessed that they had gone so far away. They were so sorry, dear; they went down to meet each other in a taxi, honey; they had preferences in smiles and had met in Hindustan, and shortly afterward they must have quarrelled, for nobody knew and nobody seemed to care--yet finally one of them had gone and left the other crying, only to feel blue, to feel sad.

The thin tunes, holding lost times and future hopes in liaison, twisted upon the Valais night. In the lulls of the phonograph a cricket held the scene together with a single note. By and by Nicole stopped playing the machine and sang to him.

"Lay a silver dollar
On the ground
And watch it roll
Because it's round--"

On the pure parting of her lips no breath hovered. Dick stood up suddenly.

"What's the matter, you don't like it?"

"Of course I do."

"Our cook at home taught it to me:

"A woman never knows
What a good man she's got
Till after she turns him down . . ."

"You like it?"

She smiled at him, making sure that the smile gathered up everything inside her and directed it toward him, making him a profound promise of herself for so little, for the beat of a response, the assurance of a complimentary vibration in him. Minute by minute the sweetness drained down into her out of the willow trees, out of the dark world.

She stood up too, and stumbling over the phonograph, was momentarily against him, leaning into the hollow of his rounded shoulder.

"I've got one more record," she said. "--Have you heard 'So Long, Letty'? I suppose you have."

"Honestly, you don't understand--I haven't heard a thing."

Nor known, nor smelt, nor tasted, he might have added; only hot-cheeked girls in hot secret rooms. The young maidens he had known at New Haven in 1914 kissed men, saying "There!", hands at the man's chest to push him away. Now there was this scarcely saved waif of disaster bringing him the essence of a continent. . . .

VI

It was May when he next found her. The luncheon in Zurich was a council of caution; obviously the logic of his life tended away from the girl; yet when a stranger stared at her from a nearby table, eyes burning disturbingly like an uncharted light, he turned to the man with an urbane version of intimidation and broke the regard.

"He was just a peeper," he explained cheerfully. "He was just looking at your clothes. Why do you have so many different clothes?"

"Sister says we're very rich," she offered humbly. "Since Grandmother is dead."

"I forgive you."

He was enough older than Nicole to take pleasure in her youthful vanities and delights, the way she paused fractionally in front of the hall mirror on leaving the restaurant, so that the incorruptible quicksilver could give her back to herself. He delighted in her stretching out her hands to new octaves now that she found herself beautiful and rich. He tried honestly to divorce her from any obsession that he had stitched her together--glad to see her build up happiness and confidence apart from him; the difficulty was that, eventually, Nicole brought everything to his feet, gifts of sacrificial ambrosia, of worshipping myrtle.

The first week of summer found Dick re-established in Zurich. He had arranged his pamphlets and what work he had done in the Service into a pattern from which he intended to make his revise of "A Psychology for Psychiatrists." He thought he had a publisher; he had established contact with a poor student who would iron out his errors in German. Franz considered it a rash business, but Dick pointed out the disarming modesty of the theme.

"This is stuff I'll never know so well again," he insisted. "I have a hunch it's a thing that only fails to be basic because it's never had material recognition. The weakness of this profession is its attraction for the man a little crippled and broken. Within the walls of the profession he compensates by tending toward the clinical, the 'practical'--he has won his battle without a struggle.

"On the contrary, you are a good man, Franz, because fate selected you for your profession before you were born. You better thank God you had no 'bent'--I got to be a psychiatrist because there was a girl at St. Hilda's in Oxford that went to the same lectures. Maybe I'm getting trite but I don't want to let my current ideas slide away with a few dozen glasses of beer."

"All right," Franz answered. "You are an American. You can do this without professional harm. I do not like these generalities. Soon you will be writing little books called 'Deep Thoughts for the Layman,' so simplified that they are positively guaranteed not to cause thinking. If my father were alive he would look at you and grunt, Dick. He would take his napkin and fold it so, and hold his napkin ring, this very one--" he held it up, a boar's head was carved in the brown wood--"and he would say, 'Well my impression is--' then he would look at you and think suddenly 'What is the use?' then he would stop and grunt again; then we would be at the end of dinner."

"I am alone to-day," said Dick testily. "But I may not be alone to-morrow. After that I'll fold up my napkin like your father and grunt."

Franz waited a moment.

"How about our patient?" he asked.

"I don't know."

"Well, you should know about her by now."

"I like her. She's attractive. What do you want me to do--take her up in the edelweiss?"

"No, I thought since you go in for scientific books you might have an idea."

"--devote my life to her?"

Franz called his wife in the kitchen: "Du lieber Gott! Bitte, bringe Dick noch ein Glas-Bier."

"I don't want any more if I've got to see Dohmler."

"We think it's best to have a program. Four weeks have passed away--apparently the girl is in love with you. That's not our business if we were in the world, but here in the clinic we have a stake in the matter."

"I'll do whatever Doctor Dohmler says," Dick agreed.

But he had little faith that Dohmler would throw much light on the matter; he himself was the incalculable element involved. By no conscious volition of his own, the thing had drifted into his hands. It reminded him of a scene in his childhood when everyone in the house was looking for the lost key to the silver closet, Dick knowing he had hid it under the handkerchiefs in his mother's top drawer; at that time he had experienced a philosophical detachment, and this was repeated now when he and Franz went together to Professor Dohmler's office.

The professor, his face beautiful under straight whiskers, like a vine-overgrown veranda of some fine old house, disarmed him. Dick knew some individuals with more talent, but no person of a class qualitatively superior to Dohmler.

--Six months later he thought the same way when he saw Dohmler dead, the light out on the veranda, the vines of his whiskers tickling his stiff white collar, the many battles that had swayed before the chink-like eyes stilled forever under the frail delicate lids--

". . . Good morning, sir." He stood formally, thrown back to the army.

Professor Dohmler interlaced his tranquil fingers. Franz spoke in terms half of liaison officer, half of secretary, till his senior cut through him in mid-sentence.

"We have gone a certain way," he said mildly. "It's you, Doctor Diver, who can best help us now."

Routed out, Dick confessed: "I'm not so straight on it myself."

"I have nothing to do with your personal reactions," said Dohmler. "But I have much to do with the fact that this so-called 'transference,'" he darted a short ironic look at Franz which the latter returned in kind, "must be terminated. Miss Nicole does well indeed, but she is in no condition to survive what she might interpret as a tragedy."

Again Franz began to speak, but Doctor Dohmler motioned him silent.

"I realize that your position has been difficult."

"Yes, it has."

Now the professor sat back and laughed, saying on the last syllable of his laughter, with his sharp little gray eyes shining through: "Perhaps you have got sentimentally involved yourself."

Aware that he was being drawn on, Dick, too, laughed.

"She's a pretty girl--anybody responds to that to a certain extent. I have no intention--"

Again Franz tried to speak--again Dohmler stopped him with a question directed pointedly at Dick. "Have you thought of going away?"

"I can't go away."

Doctor Dohmler turned to Franz: "Then we can send Miss Warren away."

"As you think best, Professor Dohmler," Dick conceded. "It's certainly a situation."

Professor Dohmler raised himself like a legless man mounting a pair of crutches.

"But it is a professional situation," he cried quietly.

He sighed himself back into his chair, waiting for the reverberating thunder to die out about the room. Dick saw that Dohmler had reached his climax, and he was not sure that he himself had survived it. When the thunder had diminished Franz managed to get his word in.

"Doctor Diver is a man of fine character," he said. "I feel he only has to appreciate the situation in order to deal correctly with it. In my opinion Dick can co-operate right here, without any one going away."

"How do you feel about that?" Professor Dohmler asked Dick.

Dick felt churlish in the face of the situation; at the same time he realized in the silence after Dohmler's pronouncement that the state of inanimation could not be indefinitely prolonged; suddenly he spilled everything.

"I'm half in love with her--the question of marrying her has passed through my mind."

"Tch! Tch!" uttered Franz.

"Wait." Dohmler warned him. Franz refused to wait: "What! And devote half your life to being doctor and nurse and all--never! I know what these cases are. One time in twenty it's finished in the first push--better never see her again!"

"What do you think?" Dohmler asked Dick.

"Of course Franz is right."

VII

It was late afternoon when they wound up the discussion as to what Dick should do, he must be most kind and yet eliminate himself. When the doctors stood up at last, Dick's eyes fell outside the window to where a light rain was falling--Nicole was waiting, expectant, somewhere in that rain. When, presently, he went out buttoning his oil-skin at the throat, pulling down the brim of his hat, he came upon her immediately under the roof of the main entrance.

"I know a new place we can go," she said. "When I was ill I didn't mind sitting inside with the others in the evening--what they said seemed like everything else. Naturally now I see them as ill and it's--it's--"

"You'll be leaving soon."

"Oh, soon. My sister, Beth, but she's always been called Baby, she's coming in a few weeks to take me somewhere; after that I'll be back here for a last month."

"The older sister?"

"Oh, quite a bit older. She's twenty-four--she's very English. She lives in London with my father's sister. She was engaged to an Englishman but he was killed--I never saw him."

Her face, ivory gold against the blurred sunset that strove through the rain, had a promise Dick had never seen before: the high cheek-bones, the faintly wan quality, cool rather than feverish, was reminiscent of the frame of a promising colt--a creature whose life did not promise to be only a projection of youth upon a grayer screen, but instead, a true growing; the face would be handsome in middle life; it would be handsome in old age: the essential structure and the economy were there.

"What are you looking at?"

"I was just thinking that you're going to be rather happy."

Nicole was frightened: "Am I? All right--things couldn't be worse than they have been."

In the covered woodshed to which she had led him, she sat cross-legged upon her golf shoes, her burberry wound about her and her cheeks stung alive by the damp air. Gravely she returned his gaze, taking in his somewhat proud carriage that never quite yielded to the wooden post against which he leaned; she looked into his face that always tried to discipline itself into molds of attentive seriousness, after excursions into joys and mockeries of its own. That part of him which seemed to fit his reddish Irish coloring she knew least; she was afraid of it, yet more anxious to explore--this was his more masculine side: the other part, the trained part, the consideration in the polite eyes, she expropriated without question, as most women did.

"At least this institution has been good for languages," said Nicole. "I've spoken French with two doctors, and German with the nurses, and Italian, or something like it, with a couple of scrub-women and one of the patients, and I've picked up a lot of Spanish from another."

"That's fine."

He tried to arrange an attitude but no logic seemed forthcoming.

"--Music too. Hope you didn't think I was only interested in ragtime. I practise every day--the last few months I've been taking a course in Zurich on the history of music. In fact it was all that kept me going at times--music and the drawing." She leaned suddenly and twisted a loose strip from the sole of her shoe and then looked up. "I'd like to draw you just the way you are now."

It made him sad when she brought out her accomplishments for his approval.

"I envy you. At present I don't seem to be interested in anything except my work."

"Oh, I think that's fine for a man," she said quickly. "But for a girl I think she ought to have lots of minor accomplishments and pass them on to her children."

"I suppose so," said Dick with deliberated indifference.

Nicole sat quiet. Dick wished she would speak so that he could play the easy rôle of wet blanket, but now she sat quiet.

"You're all well," he said. "Try to forget the past; don't overdo things for a year or so. Go back to America and be a débutante and fall in love--and be happy."

"I couldn't fall in love." Her injured shoe scraped a cocoon of dust from the log on which she sat.

"Sure you can," Dick insisted. "Not for a year maybe, but sooner or later." Then he added brutally: "You can have a perfectly normal life with a houseful of beautiful descendants. The very fact that you could make a complete comeback at your age proves that the precipitating factors were pretty near everything. Young woman, you'll be pulling your weight long after your friends are carried off screaming."

--But there was a look of pain in her eyes as she took the rough dose, the harsh reminder.

"I know I wouldn't be fit to marry any one for a long time," she said humbly.

Dick was too upset to say any more. He looked out into the grain field trying to recover his hard brassy attitude.

"You'll be all right--everybody here believes in you. Why, Doctor Gregory is so proud of you that he'll probably--"

"I hate Doctor Gregory."

"Well, you shouldn't."

Nicole's world had fallen to pieces, but it was only a flimsy and scarcely created world; beneath it her emotions and instincts fought on. Was it an hour ago she had waited by the entrance, wearing her hope like a corsage at her belt?

. . . Dress stay crisp for him, button stay put, bloom narcissus--air stay still and sweet.

"It will be nice to have fun again," she fumbled on. For a moment she entertained a desperate idea of telling him how rich she was, what big houses she lived in, that really she was a valuable property--for a moment she made herself into her grandfather, Sid Warren, the horse-trader. But she survived the temptation to confuse all values and shut these matters into their Victorian side-chambers--even though there was no home left to her, save emptiness and pain.

"I have to go back to the clinic. It's not raining now."

Dick walked beside her, feeling her unhappiness, and wanting to drink the rain that touched her cheek.

"I have some new records," she said. "I can hardly wait to play them. Do you know--"

After supper that evening, Dick thought, he would finish the break; also he wanted to kick Franz's bottom for having partially introduced him to such a sordid business. He waited in the hall. His eyes followed a beret, not wet with waiting like Nicole's beret, but covering a skull recently operated on. Beneath it human eyes peered, found him and came over:

"Bonjour, Docteur."

"Bonjour, Monsieur."

"Il fait beau temps."

"Oui, merveilleux."

"Vous êtes ici maintenant?"

"Non, pour la journée seulement."

"Ah, bon. Alors--au revoir, Monsieur."

Glad at having survived another contact, the wretch in the beret moved away. Dick waited. Presently a nurse came downstairs and delivered him a message.

"Miss Warren asks to be excused, Doctor. She wants to lie down. She wants to have dinner upstairs to-night."

The nurse hung on his response, half expecting him to imply that Miss Warren's attitude was pathological.

"Oh, I see. Well--" He rearranged the flow of his own saliva, the pulse of his heart. "I hope she feels better. Thanks."

He was puzzled and discontent. At any rate it freed him.

Leaving a note for Franz begging off from supper, he walked through the countryside to the tram station. As he reached the platform, with spring twilight gilding the rails and the glass in the slot machines, he began to feel that the station, the hospital, was hovering between being centripetal and centrifugal. He felt frightened. He was glad when the substantial cobble-stones of Zurich clicked once more under his shoes.

He expected to hear from Nicole next day but there was no word. Wondering if she was ill, he called the clinic and talked to Franz.

"She came downstairs to luncheon yesterday and to-day," said Franz. "She seemed a little abstracted and in the clouds. How did it go off?"

Dick tried to plunge over the Alpine crevasse between the sexes.

"We didn't get to it--at least I didn't think we did. I tried to be distant, but I didn't think enough happened to change her attitude if it ever went deep."

Perhaps his vanity had been hurt that there was no coup de grâce to administer.

"From some things she said to her nurse I'm inclined to think she understood."

"All right."

"It was the best thing that could have happened. She doesn't seem over-agitated--only a little in the clouds."

"All right, then."

"Dick, come soon and see me."

VIII

During the next weeks Dick experienced a vast dissatisfaction. The pathological origin and mechanistic defeat of the affair left a flat and metallic taste. Nicole's emotions had been used unfairly--what if they turned out to have been his own? Necessarily he must absent himself from felicity a while--in dreams he saw her walking on the clinic path swinging her wide straw hat. . . .

One time he saw her in person; as he walked past the Palace Hotel, a magnificent Rolls curved into the half-moon entrance. Small within its gigantic proportions, and buoyed up by the power of a hundred superfluous horses, sat Nicole and a young woman whom he assumed was her sister. Nicole saw him and momentarily her lips parted in an expression of fright. Dick shifted his hat and passed, yet for a moment the air around him was loud with the circlings of all the goblins on the Gross-Münster. He tried to write the matter out of his mind in a memorandum that went into detail as to the solemn régime before her; the possibilities of another "push" of the malady under the stresses which the world would inevitably supply--in all a memorandum that would have been convincing to any one save to him who had written it.

The total value of this effort was to make him realize once more how far his emotions were involved; thenceforth he resolutely provided antidotes. One was the telephone girl from Bar-sur-Aube, now touring Europe from Nice to Coblenz, in a desperate roundup of the men she had known in her never-to-beequalled holiday; another was the making of arrangements to get home on a government transport in August; a third was a consequent intensification of work on his proofs for the book that this autumn was to be presented to the German-speaking world of psychiatry.

Dick had outgrown the book; he wanted now to do more spade work; if he got an exchange fellowship he could count on plenty of routine.

Meanwhile he had projected a new work: *An Attempt at a Uniform and Pragmatic Classification of the Neuroses and Psychoses, Based on an Examination of Fifteen Hundred Pre-Krapælin and Post-Krapælin Cases as they would be Diagnosed in the Terminology of the Different Contemporary Schools*--and another sonorous paragraph--*Together with a Chronology of Such Subdivisions of Opinion as Have Arisen Independently.*

This title would look monumental in German.*

*Ein Versuch die Neurosen und Psychosen gleichmässig und pragmatisch zu klassifizieren auf Grund der Untersuchung von fünfzehn hundert pre-Krapaelin und post-Krapaelin Fällen wie siz diagnostiziert sein würden in der Terminologie von den verschiedenen Schulen der Gegenwart--and another sonorous paragraph--Zusammen mit einer Chronologic solcher Subdivisionen der Meinung welche unabhängig entstanden sind.

Going into Montreux Dick pedalled slowly, gaping at the Jugenhorn whenever possible, and blinded by glimpses of the lake through the alleys of the shore hotels. He was conscious of the groups of English, emergent after four years and walking with detective-story suspicion in their eyes, as though they were about to be assaulted in this questionable country by German trained-bands. There were building and awakening everywhere on this mound of débris formed by a mountain torrent. At Berne and at Lausanne on the way south, Dick had been eagerly asked if there would be Americans this year. "By August, if not in June?"

He wore leather shorts, an army shirt, mountain shoes. In his knapsack were a cotton suit and a change of underwear. At the Glion funicular he checked his bicycle and took a small beer on the terrace of the station buffet, meanwhile watching the little bug crawl down the eighty-degree slope of the hill. His ear was full of dried blood from La Tour de Pelz, where he had sprinted under the impression that he was a spoiled athlete. He asked for alcohol and cleared up the exterior while the funicular slid down port. He saw his bicycle embarked, slung his knapsack into the lower compartment of the car, and followed it in.

Mountain-climbing cars are built on a slant similar to the angle of a hat-brim of a man who doesn't want to be recognized. As water gushed from the chamber under the car, Dick was impressed with the ingenuity of the whole idea--a complimentary car was now taking on mountain water at the top and would pull the lightened car up by gravity, as soon as the brakes were released. It must have been a great inspiration. In the seat across, a couple of British were discussing the cable itself.

"The ones made in England always last five or six years. Two years ago the Germans underbid us, and how long do you think their cable lasted?"

"How long?"

"A year and ten months. Then the Swiss sold it to the Italians. They don't have rigid inspections of cables."

"I can see it would be a terrible thing for Switzerland if a cable broke."

The conductor shut a door; he telephoned his confrere among the undulati, and with a jerk the car was pulled upward, heading for a pinpoint on an emerald hill above. After it cleared the low roofs, the skies of Vaud, Valais, Swiss Savoy, and Geneva spread around the passengers in cyclorama. On the centre of the lake, cooled by the piercing current of the Rhône, lay the true centre of the Western World. Upon it floated swans like boats and boats like swans, both lost in the nothingness of the heartless beauty. It was a bright day, with sun glittering on the grass beach below and the white courts of the Kursal. The figures on the courts threw no shadows.

When Chillon and the island palace of Salagnon came into view Dick turned his eyes inward. The funicular was above the highest houses of the shore; on both sides a tangle of foliage and flowers culminated at intervals in masses of color. It was a rail-side garden, and in the car was a sign: *Défense de cueillir les fleurs.*

Though one must not pick flowers on the way up, the blossoms trailed in as they passed--Dorothy Perkins roses dragged patiently through each compartment slowly waggling with the motion of the funicular, letting go at the last to swing back to their rosy cluster. Again and again these branches went through the car.

In the compartment above and in front of Dick's, a group of English were standing up and exclaiming upon the backdrop of sky, when suddenly there was a confusion among them--they parted to give passage to a couple of young people who made apologies and scrambled over into the rear compartment of the funicular--Dick's compartment. The young man was a Latin with the eyes of a stuffed deer; the girl was Nicole.

The two climbers gasped momentarily from their efforts; as they settled into seats, laughing and crowding the English to the corners, Nicole said, "Hel*lo.*" She was lovely to look at; immediately Dick saw that something was different; in a second he realized it was her fine-spun hair, bobbed like Irene Castle's and fluffed into curls. She wore a sweater of powder blue and a white tennis skirt--she was the first morning in May and every taint of the clinic was departed.

"Plunk!" she gasped. "Whoo-oo that guard. They'll arrest us at the next stop. Doctor Diver, the Conte de Marmora."

"Gee-imminy!" She felt her new hair, panting. "Sister bought first-class tickets--it's a matter of principle with her." She and Marmora exchanged glances and shouted: "Then we found that first-class is the hearse part behind the chauffeur--shut in with curtains for a rainy day, so you can't see anything. But Sister's very dignified--" Again Nicole and Marmora laughed with young intimacy.

"Where you bound?" asked Dick.

"Caux. You too?" Nicole looked at his costume. "That your bicycle they got up in front?"

"Yes. I'm going to coast down Monday."

"With me on your handle-bars? I mean, really--will you? I can't think of more fun."

"But I will carry you down in my arms," Marmora protested intensely. "I will roller-skate you--or I will throw you and you will fall slowly like a feather."

The delight in Nicole's face--to be a feather again instead of a plummet, to float and not to drag. She was a carnival to watch--at times primly coy, posing, grimacing and gesturing--sometimes the shadow fell and the dignity of old suffering flowed down into her finger tips. Dick wished himself away from her, fearing that he was a reminder of a world well left behind. He resolved to go to the other hotel.

When the funicular came to rest those new to it stirred in suspension between the blues of two heavens. It was merely for a mysterious exchange between the conductor of the car going up and the conductor of the car coming down. Then up and up over a forest path and a gorge--then again up a hill that became solid with narcissus, from passengers to sky. The people in Montreux playing tennis in the lakeside courts were pinpoints now. Something new was in the air; freshness--freshness embodying itself in music as the car slid into Glion and they heard the orchestra in the hotel garden.

When they changed to the mountain train the music was drowned by the rushing water released from the hydraulic chamber. Almost overhead was Caux, where the thousand windows of a hotel burned in the late sun.

But the approach was different--a leather-lunged engine pushed the passengers round and round in a corkscrew, mounting, rising; they chugged through low-level clouds and for a moment Dick lost Nicole's face in the spray of the slanting donkey engine; they skirted a lost streak of wind with the hotel growing in size at each spiral, until with a vast surprise they were there, on top of the sunshine.

In the confusion of arrival, as Dick slung his knapsack and started forward on the platform to get his bicycle, Nicole was beside him.

"Aren't you at our hotel?" she asked.

"I'm economizing."

"Will you come down and have dinner?" Some confusion with baggage ensued. "This is my sister--Doctor Diver from Zurich."

Dick bowed to a young woman of twenty-five, tall and confident. She was both formidable and vulnerable, he decided, remembering other women with flower-like mouths grooved for bits.

"I'll drop in after dinner," Dick promised. "First I must get acclimated."

He wheeled off his bicycle, feeling Nicole's eyes following him, feeling her helpless first love, feeling it twist around inside him. He went three hundred yards up the slope to the other hotel, he engaged a room and found himself washing without a memory of the intervening ten minutes, only a sort of drunken flush pierced with voices, unimportant voices that did not know how much he was loved.

IX

They were waiting for him and incomplete without him. He was still the incalculable element; Miss Warren and the young Italian wore their anticipation as obviously as Nicole. The salon of the hotel, a room of fabled acoustics, was stripped for dancing but there was a small gallery of Englishwomen of a certain age, with neckbands, dyed hair and faces powdered pinkish gray; and of American women of a certain age, with snowy-white transformations, black dresses and lips of cherry red. Miss Warren and Marmora were at a corner table--Nicole was diagonally across from them forty yards away, and as Dick arrived he heard her voice:

"Can you hear me? I'm speaking naturally."

"Perfectly,"

"Hello, Doctor Diver."

"What's this?"

"You realize the people in the centre of the floor can't hear what I say, but you can?"

"A waiter told us about it," said Miss Warren. "Corner to corner--it's like wireless."

It was exciting up on the mountain, like a ship at sea. Presently Marmora's parents joined them. They treated the Warrens with respect--Dick gathered that their fortunes had something to do with a bank in Milan that had something to do with the Warren fortunes. But Baby Warren wanted to talk to Dick, wanted to talk to him with the impetus that sent her out vagrantly toward all new men, as though she were on an inelastic tether and considered that she might as well get to the end of it as soon as possible. She crossed and recrossed her knees frequently in the manner of tall restless virgins.

"--Nicole told me that you took part care of her, and had a lot to do with her getting well. What I can't understand is what *we're* supposed to do--they were so indefinite at the sanitarium; they only told me she ought to be natural and gay. I knew the Marmoras were up here so I asked Tino to meet us at the funicular. And you see what happens--the very first thing Nicole has him crawling over the sides of the car as if they were both insane--"

"That was absolutely normal," Dick laughed. "I'd call it a good sign. They were showing off for each other."

"But how can *I* tell? Before I knew it, almost in front of my eyes, she had her hair cut off, in Zurich, because of a picture in 'Vanity Fair.'"

"That's all right. She's a schizoid--a permanent eccentric. You can't change that."

"What is it?"

"Just what I said--an eccentric."

"Well, how can any one tell what's eccentric and what's crazy?"

"Nothing is going to be crazy--Nicole is all fresh and happy, you needn't be afraid."

Baby shifted her knees about--she was a compendium of all the discontented women who had loved Byron a hundred years before, yet, in spite of the tragic affair with the guards' officer there was something wooden and onanistic about her.

"I don't mind the responsibility," she declared, "but I'm in the air. We've never had anything like this in the family before--we know Nicole had some shock and my opinion is it was about a boy, but we don't really know. Father says he would have shot him if he could have found out."

The orchestra was playing "Poor Butterfly"; young Marmora was dancing with his mother. It was a tune new enough to them all. Listening, and watching Nicole's shoulders as she chattered to the elder Marmora, whose hair was dashed with white like a piano keyboard, Dick thought of the shoulders of a violin, and then he thought of the dishonor, the secret. Oh, butterfly--the moments pass into hours--

"Actually *I* have a plan," Baby continued with apologetic hardness. "It may seem absolutely impractical to you but they say Nicole will need to be looked after for a few years. I don't know whether you know Chicago or not--"

"I don't."

"Well, there's a North Side and a South Side and they're very much separated. The North Side is chic and all that, and we've always lived over there, at least for many years, but lots of old families, old Chicago families, if you know what I mean, still live on the South Side. The University is there. I mean it's stuffy to some people, but anyhow it's different from the North Side. I don't know whether you understand."

He nodded. With some concentration he had been able to follow her.

"Now of course we have lots of connections there--Father controls certain chairs and fellowships and so forth at the University, and I thought if we took Nicole home and threw her with that crowd--you see she's quite musical and speaks all these languages--what could be better in her condition than if she fell in love with some good doctor--"

A burst of hilarity surged up in Dick, the Warrens were going to buy Nicole a doctor--You got a nice doctor you can let us use? There was no use worrying about Nicole when they were in the position of being able to buy her a nice young doctor, the paint scarcely dry on him.

"But how about the doctor?" he said automatically.

"There must be many who'd jump at the chance."

The dancers were back, but Baby whispered quickly:

"This is the sort of thing I mean. Now where is Nicole--she's gone off somewhere. Is she upstairs in her room? What am *I* supposed to do? I never know whether it's something innocent or whether I ought to go find her."

"Perhaps she just wants to be by herself--people living alone get used to loneliness." Seeing that Miss Warren was not listening he stopped. "I'll take a look around."

For a moment all the outdoors shut in with mist was like spring with the curtains drawn. Life was gathered near the hotel. Dick passed some cellar windows where bus boys sat on bunks and played cards over a litre of Spanish wine. As he approached the promenade, the stars began to come through the white crests of the high Alps. On the horseshoe walk overlooking the lake Nicole was the figure motionless between two lamp stands, and he approached silently across the grass. She turned to him with an expression of: "Here *you* are," and for a moment he was sorry he had come.

"Your sister wondered."

"Oh!" She was accustomed to being watched. With an effort she explained herself: "Sometimes I get a little--it gets a little too much. I've lived so quietly. To-night that music was too much. It made me want to cry--"

"I understand."

"This has been an awfully exciting day."

"I know."

"I don't want to do anything anti-social--I've caused everybody enough trouble. But to-night I wanted to get away."

It occurred to Dick suddenly, as it might occur to a dying man that he had forgotten to tell where his will was, that Nicole had been "re-educated" by Dohmler and the ghostly generations behind him; it occurred to him also that there would be so much she would have to be told. But having recorded this wisdom within himself, he yielded to the insistent face-value of the situation and said:

"You're a nice person--just keep using your own judgment about yourself."

"You like me?"

"Of course."

"Would you--" They were strolling along toward the dim end of the horseshoe, two hundred yards ahead. "If I hadn't been sick would you--I mean, would I have been the sort of girl you might have--oh, slush, you know what I mean."

He was in for it now, possessed by a vast irrationality. She was so near that he felt his breathing change but again his training came to his aid in a boy's laugh and a trite remark.

"You're teasing yourself, my dear. Once I knew a man who fell in love with his nurse--" The anecdote rambled on, punctuated by their footsteps. Suddenly Nicole interrupted in succinct Chicagoese: "Bull!"

"That's a very vulgar expression."

"What about it?" she flared up. "You don't think I've got any common sense--before I was sick I didn't have any, but I have now. And if I don't know you're the most attractive man I ever met you must think I'm still crazy. It's my hard luck, all right--but don't pretend I don't *know*--I know everything about you and me."

Dick was at an additional disadvantage. He remembered the statement of the elder Miss Warren as to the young doctors that could be purchased in the intellectual stockyards of the South Side of Chicago, and he hardened for a moment. "You're a fetching kid, but I couldn't fall in love."

"You won't give me a chance."

"What!"

The impertinence, the right to invade implied, astounded him. Short of anarchy he could not think of any chance that Nicole Warren deserved.

"Give me a chance now."

The voice fell low, sank into her breast and stretched the tight bodice over her heart as she came up close. He felt the young lips, her body sighing in relief against the arm growing stronger to hold her. There were now no more plans than if Dick had arbitrarily made some indissoluble mixture, with atoms joined and inseparable; you could throw it all out but never again could they fit back into atomic scale. As he held her and tasted her, and as she curved in further and further toward him, with her own lips, new to herself, drowned and engulfed in love, yet solaced and triumphant, he was thankful to have an existence at all, if only as a reflection in her wet eyes.

"My God," he gasped, "you're fun to kiss."

That was talk, but Nicole had a better hold on him now and she held it; she turned coquette and walked away, leaving him as suspended as in the funicular of the afternoon. She felt: There, that'll show him, how conceited; how he could do with me; oh, wasn't it wonderful! I've got him, he's mine. Now in the sequence came flight, but it was all so sweet and new that she dawdled, wanting to draw all of it in.

She shivered suddenly. Two thousand feet below she saw the necklace and bracelet of lights that were Montreux and Vevey, beyond them a dim pendant of Lausanne. From down there somewhere ascended a faint sound of dance music. Nicole was up in her head now, cool as cool, trying to collate the sentimentalities of her childhood, as deliberate as a man getting drunk after battle. But she was still afraid of Dick, who stood near her, leaning, characteristically, against the iron fence that rimmed the horseshoe; and this prompted her to say: "I can remember how I stood waiting for you in the garden--holding all my self in my arms like a basket of flowers. It was that to me anyhow--I thought I was sweet--waiting to hand that basket to you."

He breathed over her shoulder and turned her insistently about; she kissed him several times, her face getting big every time she came close, her hands holding him by the shoulders.

"It's raining hard."

Suddenly there was a booming from the wine slopes across the lake; cannons were shooting at hail-bearing clouds in order to break them. The lights of the promenade went off, went on again. Then the storm came swiftly, first falling from the heavens, then doubly falling in torrents from the mountains and washing loud down the roads and stone ditches; with it came a dark, frightening sky and savage filaments of lightning and world-splitting thunder, while ragged, destroying clouds fled along past the hotel. Mountains and lake disappeared--the hotel crouched amid tumult, chaos and darkness.

By this time Dick and Nicole had reached the vestibule, where Baby Warren and the three Marmoras were anxiously awaiting them. It was exciting coming out of the wet fog--with the doors banging, to stand and laugh and quiver with emotion, wind in their ears and rain on their clothes. Now in the ballroom the orchestra was playing a Strauss waltz, high and confusing.

. . . For Doctor Diver to marry a mental patient? How did it happen? Where did it begin?

"Won't you come back after you've changed?" Baby Warren asked after a close scrutiny.

"I haven't got any change, except some shorts."

As he trudged up to his hotel in a borrowed raincoat he kept laughing derisively in his throat.

"Big chance--oh, yes. My God!--they decided to buy a doctor? Well, they better stick to whoever they've got in Chicago." Revolted by his harshness he made amends to Nicole, remembering that nothing had ever felt so young as her lips, remembering rain like tears shed for him that lay upon her softly shining porcelain cheeks . . . the silence of the storm ceasing woke him about three o'clock and he went to the window. Her beauty climbed the rolling slope, it came into the room, rustling ghostlike through the curtains. . . .

. . . He climbed two thousand meters to Rochers de Naye the following morning, amused by the fact that his conductor of the day before was using his day off to climb also.

Then Dick descended all the way to Montreux for a swim, got back to his hotel in time for dinner. Two notes awaited him.

> "I'm not ashamed about last night--it was the nicest thing that ever happened to me and even if I never saw you again, Mon Capitaine, I would be glad it happened."

That was disarming enough--the heavy shade of Dohmler retreated as Dick opened the second envelope:

DEAR DOCTOR DIVER: I phoned but you were out. I wonder if I may ask you a great big favor. Unforeseen circumstances call me back to Paris, and I find I can make better time by way of Lausanne. Can you let Nicole ride as far as Zurich with you, since you are going back Monday? and drop her at the sanitarium? Is this too much to ask?

Sincerely,

BETH EVAN WARREN.

Dick was furious--Miss Warren had known he had a bicycle with him; yet she had so phrased her note that it was impossible to refuse. Throw us together! Sweet propinquity and the Warren money!

He was wrong; Baby Warren had no such intentions. She had looked Dick over with worldly eyes, she had measured him with the warped rule of an Anglophile and found him wanting--in spite of the fact that she found him toothsome. But for her he was too "intellectual" and she pigeonholed him with a shabby-snobby crowd she had once known in London--he put himself out too much to be really of the correct stuff. She could not see how he could be made into her idea of an aristocrat.

In addition to that he was stubborn--she had seen him leave her conversation and get down behind his eyes in that odd way that people did, half a dozen times. She had not liked Nicole's free and easy manner as a child and now she was sensibly habituated to thinking of her as a "gone coon"; and anyhow Doctor Diver was not the sort of medical man she could envisage in the family.

She only wanted to use him innocently as a convenience.

But her request had the effect that Dick assumed she desired. A ride in a train can be a terrible, heavy-hearted or comic thing; it can be a trial flight; it can be a prefiguration of another journey just as a given day with a friend can be long, from the taste of hurry in the morning up to the realization of both being hungry and taking food together. Then comes the afternoon with the journey fading and dying, but quickening again at the end. Dick was sad to see Nicole's meagre joy; yet it was a relief for her, going back to the only home she knew. They made no love that day, but when he left her outside the sad door on the Zurichsee and she turned and looked at him he knew her problem was one they had together for good now.

X

In Zurich in September Doctor Diver had tea with Baby Warren.

"I think it's ill advised," she said, "I'm not sure I truly understand your motives."

"Don't let's be unpleasant."

"After all I'm Nicole's sister."

"That doesn't give you the right to be unpleasant." It irritated Dick that he knew so much that he could not tell her. "Nicole's rich, but that doesn't make me an adventurer."

"That's just it," complained Baby stubbornly. "Nicole's rich."

"Just how much money has she got?" he asked.

She started; and with a silent laugh he continued, "You see how silly this is? I'd rather talk to some man in your family--"

"Everything's been left to me," she persisted. "It isn't we think you're an adventurer. We don't know who you are."

"I'm a doctor of medicine," he said. "My father is a clergyman, now retired. We lived in Buffalo and my past is open to investigation. I went to New Haven; afterward I was a Rhodes scholar. My great-grandfather was Governor of North Carolina and I'm a direct descendant of Mad Anthony Wayne."

"Who was Mad Anthony Wayne?" Baby asked suspiciously.

"Mad Anthony Wayne?"

"I think there's enough madness in this affair."

He shook his head hopelessly, just as Nicole came out on the hotel terrace and looked around for them.

"He was too mad to leave as much money as Marshall Field," he said.

"That's all very well--"

Baby was right and she knew it. Face to face, her father would have it on almost any clergyman. They were an American ducal family without a title--the very name written in a hotel register, signed to an introduction, used in a difficult situation, caused a psychological metamorphosis in people, and in return this change had crystallized her own sense of position. She knew these facts from the English, who had known them for over two hundred years. But she did not know that twice Dick had come close to flinging the marriage in her face. All that saved it this time was Nicole finding their table and glowing away, white and fresh and new in the September afternoon.

How do you do, lawyer. We're going to Como tomorrow for a week and then back to Zurich. That's why I wanted you and sister to settle this, because it doesn't matter to us how much I'm allowed. We're going to live very quietly in Zurich for two years and Dick has enough to take care of us. No, Baby, I'm more practical than you think--It's only for clothes and things I'll need it. . . . Why, that's more than--can the estate really afford to give me all that? I know I'll never manage to spend it. Do you have that much? Why do you have more--is it because I'm supposed to be incompetent? All right, let my share pile up then. . . . No, Dick refuses to have anything whatever to do with it. I'll have to feel bloated for us both. . . . Baby, you have no more idea of what Dick is like than, than--Now where do I sign? Oh, I'm sorry.

. . . Isn't it funny and lonely being together, Dick. No place to go except close. Shall we just love and love? Ah, but I love the most, and I can tell when you're away from me, even a little. I think it's wonderful to be just like everybody else, to reach out and find you all warm beside me in the bed.

. . . If you will kindly call my husband at the hospital. Yes, the little book is selling everywhere--they want it published in six languages. I was to do the French translation but I'm tired these days--I'm afraid of falling, I'm so heavy and clumsy--like a broken roly-poly that can't stand up straight. The cold stethoscope against my heart and my strongest feeling "Je m'en fiche de tout."--Oh, that poor woman in the hospital with the blue baby, much better dead. Isn't it fine there are three of us now?

. . . That seems unreasonable, Dick--we have every reason for taking the bigger apartment. Why should we penalize ourselves just because there's more Warren money than Diver money. Oh, thank you, cameriere, but we've changed our minds. This English clergyman tells us that your wine here in Orvieto is excellent. It doesn't travel? That must be why we have never heard of it, because we love wine.

The lakes are sunk in the brown clay and the slopes have all the creases of a belly. The photographer gave us the picture of me, my hair limp over the rail on the boat to Capri. "Good-by, Blue Grotte," sang the boatman, "come again soooon." And afterward tracing down the hot sinister shin of the Italian boot with the wind soughing around those eerie castles, the dead watching from up on those hills.

. . . This ship is nice, with our heels hitting the deck together. This is the blowy corner and each time we turn it I slant forward against the wind and pull my coat together without losing step with Dick. We are chanting nonsense:

"Oh--oh--oh--oh
Other flamingoes than me,
Oh--oh--oh--oh
Other flamingoes than me--"

Life is fun with Dick--the people in deck chairs look at us, and a woman is trying to hear what we are singing. Dick is tired of singing it, so go on alone, Dick. You will walk differently alone, dear, through a thicker atmosphere, forcing your way through the shadows of chairs, through the dripping smoke of the funnels. You will feel your own reflection sliding along the eyes of those who look at you. You are no longer insulated; but I suppose you must touch life in order to spring from it.

Sitting on the stanchion of this life-boat I look seaward and let my hair blow and shine. I am motionless against the sky and the boat is made to carry my form onward into the blue obscurity of the future, I am Pallas Athene carved reverently on the front of a galley. The waters are lapping in the public toilets and the agate green foliage of spray changes and complains about the stern.

. . . We travelled a lot that year--from Woolloomooloo Bay to Biskra. On the edge of the Sahara we ran into a plague of locusts and the chauffeur explained kindly that they were bumble-bees. The sky was low at night, full of the presence of a strange and watchful God. Oh, the poor little naked Ouled Naïl; the night was noisy with drums from Senegal and flutes and whining camels, and the natives pattering about in shoes made of old automobile tires.

But I was gone again by that time--trains and beaches they were all one. That was why he took me travelling but after my second child, my little girl, Topsy, was born everything got dark again.

. . . If I could get word to my husband who has seen fit to desert me here, to leave me in the hands of incompetents. You tell me my baby is black--that's farcical, that's very cheap. We went to Africa merely to see Timgad, since my principal interest in life is archeology. I am tired of knowing nothing and being reminded of it all the time.

. . . When I get well I want to be a fine person like you, Dick--I would study medicine except it's too late. We must spend my money and have a house--I'm tired of apartments and waiting for you. You're bored with Zurich and you can't find time for writing here and you say that it's a confession of weakness for a scientist not to write. And I'll look over the whole field of knowledge and pick out something and really know about it, so I'll have it to hang on to if I go to pieces again. You'll help me, Dick, so I won't feel so guilty. We'll live near a warm beach where we can be brown and young together.

. . . This is going to be Dick's work house. Oh, the idea came to us both at the same moment. We had passed Tarmes a dozen times and we rode up here and found the houses empty, except two stables. When we bought we acted through a Frenchman but the navy sent spies up here in no time when they found that Americans had bought part of a hill village. They looked for cannons all through the building material, and finally Baby had to twitch wires for us at the *Affaires Etrangères* in Paris.

No one comes to the Riviera in summer, so we expect to have a few guests and to work. There are some French people here--Mistinguet last week, surprised to find the hotel open, and Picasso and the man who wrote *Pas sur la Bouche.*

. . . Dick, why did you register Mr. and Mrs. Diver instead of Doctor and Mrs. Diver? I just wondered--it just floated through my mind.--You've taught me that work is everything and I believe you. You used to say a man knows things and when he stops knowing things he's like anybody else, and the thing is to get power before he stops knowing things. If you want to turn things topsy-turvy, all right, but must your Nicole follow you walking on her hands, darling?

. . . Tommy says I am silent. Since I was well the first time I talked a lot to Dick late at night, both of us sitting up in bed and lighting cigarettes, then diving down afterward out of the blue dawn and into the pillows, to keep the light from our eyes. Sometimes I sing, and play with the animals, and I have a few friends too--Mary, for instance. When Mary and I talk neither of us listens to the other. Talk is men. When I talk I say to myself that I am probably Dick. Already I have even been my son, remembering how wise and slow he is. Sometimes I am Doctor Dohmler and one time I may even be an aspect of you, Tommy Barban. Tommy is in love with me, I think, but gently, reassuringly. Enough, though, so that he and Dick have begun to disapprove of each other. All in all, everything has never gone better. I am among friends who like me. I am here on this tranquil beach with my husband and two children. Everything is all right--if I can finish translating this damn recipe for chicken a la Maryland into French. My toes feel warm in the sand.

"Yes, I'll look. More new people--oh, that girl--yes. Who did you say she looked like. . . . No, I haven't, we don't get much chance to see the new American pictures over here. Rosemary who? Well, we're getting very fashionable for July--seems very peculiar to me. Yes, she's lovely, but there can be too many people."

XI

Doctor Richard Diver and Mrs. Elsie Speers sat in the Café des Alliées in August, under cool and dusty trees. The sparkle of the mica was dulled by the baked ground, and a few gusts of mistral from down the coast seeped through the Esterel and rocked the fishing boats in the harbor, pointing the masts here and there at a featureless sky.

"I had a letter this morning," said Mrs. Speers. "What a terrible time you all must have had with those Negroes! But Rosemary said you were perfectly wonderful to her."

"Rosemary ought to have a service stripe. It was pretty harrowing--the only person it didn't disturb was Abe North--he flew off to Havre--he probably doesn't know about it yet."

"I'm sorry Mrs. Diver was upset," she said carefully.

Rosemary had written:

> Nicole seemed Out of her Mind. I didn't want to come South with them because I felt Dick had enough on his hands.

"She's all right now." He spoke almost impatiently. "So you're leaving tomorrow. When will you sail?"

"Right away."

"My God, it's awful to have you go."

"We're glad we came here. We've had a good time, thanks to you. You're the first man Rosemary ever cared for."

Another gust of wind strained around the porphyry hills of la Napoule. There was a hint in the air that the earth was hurrying on toward other weather; the lush midsummer moment outside of time was already over.

"Rosemary's had crushes but sooner or later she always turned the man over to me--" Mrs. Speers laughed, "--for dissection."

"So I was spared."

"There was nothing I could have done. She was in love with you before I ever saw you. I told her to go ahead."

He saw that no provision had been made for him, or for Nicole, in Mrs. Speers' plans--and he saw that her amorality sprang from the conditions of her own withdrawal. It was her right, the pension on which her own emotions had retired. Women are necessarily capable of almost anything in their struggle for survival and can scarcely be convicted of such man-made crimes as "cruelty." So long as the shuffle of love and pain went on within proper walls Mrs. Speers could view it with as much detachment and humor as a eunuch. She had not even allowed for the possibility of Rosemary's being damaged--or was she certain that she couldn't be?

"If what you say is true I don't think it did her any harm." He was keeping up to the end the pretense that he could still think objectively about Rosemary. "She's over it already. Still--so many of the important times in life begin by seeming incidental."

"This wasn't incidental," Mrs. Speers insisted. "You were the first man--you're an ideal to her. In every letter she says that."

"She's so polite."

"You and Rosemary are the politest people I've ever known, but she means this."

"My politeness is a trick of the heart."

This was partly true. From his father Dick had learned the somewhat conscious good manners of the young Southerner coming north after the Civil War. Often he used them and just as often he despised them because they were not a protest against how unpleasant selfishness was but against how unpleasant it looked.

"I'm in love with Rosemary," he told her suddenly. "It's a kind of self-indulgence saying that to you."

It seemed very strange and official to him, as if the very tables and chairs in the Café des Alliées would remember it forever. Already he felt her absence from these skies: on the beach he could only remember the sun-torn flesh of her shoulder; at Tarmes he crushed out her footprints as he crossed the garden; and now the orchestra launching into the Nice Carnival Song, an echo of last year's vanished gaieties, started the little dance that went on all about her. In a hundred hours she had come to possess all the world's dark magic; the blinding belladonna, the caffein converting physical into nervous energy, the mandragora that imposes harmony.

With an effort he once more accepted the fiction that he shared Mrs. Speers' detachment.

"You and Rosemary aren't really alike," he said. "The wisdom she got from you is all molded up into her persona, into the mask she faces the world with. She doesn't think; her real depths are Irish and romantic and illogical."

Mrs. Speers knew too that Rosemary, for all her delicate surface, was a young mustang, perceptibly by Captain Doctor Hoyt, U.S.A. Cross-sectioned, Rosemary would have displayed an enormous heart, liver and soul, all crammed close together under the lovely shell.

Saying good-by, Dick was aware of Elsie Speers' full charm, aware that she meant rather more to him than merely a last unwillingly relinquished fragment of Rosemary. He could possibly have made up Rosemary--he could never have made up her mother. If the cloak, spurs and brilliants in which Rosemary had walked off were things with which he had endowed her, it was nice in contrast to watch her mother's grace knowing it was surely something he had not evoked. She had an air of seeming to wait, as if for a man to get through with something more important than herself, a battle or an operation, during which he must not be hurried or interfered with. When the man had finished she would be waiting, without fret or impatience, somewhere on a highstool, turning the pages of a newspaper.

"Good-by--and I want you both to remember always how fond of you Nicole and I have grown."

Back at the Villa Diana, he went to his work-room, and opened the shutters, closed against the mid-day glare. On his two long tables, in ordered confusion, lay the materials of his book. Volume I, concerned with Classification, had achieved some success in a small subsidized edition. He was negotiating for its reissue. Volume II was to be a great amplification of his first little book, *A Psychology for Psychiatrists*. Like so many men he had found that he had only one or two ideas--that his little collection of pamphlets now in its fiftieth German edition contained the germ of all he would ever think or know.

But he was currently uneasy about the whole thing. He resented the wasted years at New Haven, but mostly he felt a discrepancy between the growing luxury in which the Divers lived, and the need for display which apparently went along with it. Remembering his Rumanian friend's story, about the man who had worked for years on the brain of an armadillo, he suspected that patient Germans were sitting close to the libraries of Berlin and Vienna callously anticipating him. He had about decided to brief the work in its present condition and publish it in an undocumented volume of a hundred thousand words as an introduction to more scholarly volumes to follow.

He confirmed this decision walking around the rays of late afternoon in his work-room. With the new plan he could be through by spring. It seemed to him that when a man with his energy was pursued for a year by increasing doubts, it indicated some fault in the plan.

He laid the bars of gilded metal that he used as paperweights along the sheaves of notes. He swept up, for no servant was allowed in here, treated his washroom sketchily with Bon Ami, repaired a screen and sent off an order to a publishing house in Zurich. Then he drank an ounce of gin with twice as much water.

He saw Nicole in the garden. Presently he must encounter her and the prospect gave him a leaden feeling. Before her he must keep up a perfect front, now and to-morrow, next week and next year. All night in Paris he had held her in his arms while she slept light under the luminol; in the early morning he broke in upon her confusion before it could form, with words of tenderness and protection, and she slept again with his face against the warm scent of her hair. Before she woke he had arranged everything at the phone in the next room. Rosemary was to move to another hotel. She was to be "Daddy's Girl" and even to give up saying good-by to them. The proprietor of the hotel, Mr. McBeth, was to be the three Chinese monkeys. Packing amid the piled boxes and tissue paper of many purchases, Dick and Nicole left for the Riviera at noon.

Then there was a reaction. As they settled down in the wagon-lit Dick saw that Nicole was waiting for it, and it came quickly and desperately, before the train was out of the ceinture--his only instinct was to step off while the train was still going slow, rush back and see where Rosemary was, what she was doing. He opened a book and bent his pince-nez upon it, aware that Nicole was watching him from her pillow across the compartment. Unable to read, he pretended to be tired and shut his eyes but she was still watching him, and though still she was half asleep from the hangover of the drug, she was relieved and almost happy that he was hers again.

It was worse with his eyes shut for it gave a rhythm of finding and losing, finding and losing; but so as not to appear restless he lay like that until noon. At luncheon things were better--it was always a fine meal; a thousand lunches in inns and restaurants, wagon-lits, buffets, and aeroplanes were a mighty collation to have taken together. The familiar hurry of the train waiters, the little bottles of wine and mineral water, the excellent food of the Paris-Lyons-Méditerranee gave them the illusion that everything was the same as before, but it was almost the first trip he had ever taken with Nicole that was a going away rather than a going toward. He drank a whole bottle of wine save for Nicole's single glass; they talked about the house and the children. But once back in the compartment a silence fell over them like the silence in the restaurant across from the Luxembourg. Receding from a grief, it seems necessary to retrace the same steps that brought us there. An unfamiliar impatience settled on Dick; suddenly Nicole said:

"It seemed too bad to leave Rosemary like that--do you suppose she'll be all right?"

"Of course. She could take care of herself anywhere--" Lest this belittle Nicole's ability to do likewise, he added, "After all, she's an actress, and even though her mother's in the background she *has* to look out for herself."

"She's very attractive."

"She's an infant."

"She's attractive though."

They talked aimlessly back and forth, each speaking for the other.

"She's not as intelligent as I thought," Dick offered.

"She's quite smart."

"Not very, though--there's a persistent aroma of the nursery."

"She's very--very pretty," Nicole said in a detached, emphatic way, "and I thought she was very good in the picture."

"She was well directed. Thinking it over, it wasn't very individual."

"I thought it was. I can see how she'd be very attractive to men."

His heart twisted. To what men? How many men?

--Do you mind if I pull down the curtain?

--Please do, it's too light in here.

Where now? And with whom?

"In a few years she'll look ten years older than you."

"On the contrary. I sketched her one night on a theatre program, I think she'll last."

They were both restless in the night. In a day or two Dick would try to banish the ghost of Rosemary before it became walled up with them, but for the moment he had no force to do it. Sometimes it is harder to deprive oneself of a pain than of a pleasure and the memory so possessed him that for the moment there was nothing to do but to pretend. This was more difficult because he was currently annoyed with Nicole, who, after all these years, should recognize symptoms of strain in herself and guard against them. Twice within a fortnight she had broken up: there had been the night of the dinner at Tarmes when he had found her in her bedroom dissolved in crazy laughter telling Mrs. McKisco she could not go in the bathroom because the key was thrown down the well. Mrs. McKisco was astonished and resentful, baffled and yet in a way comprehending. Dick had not been particularly alarmed then, for afterward Nicole was repentant. She called at Gausse's Hotel but the McKiscos were gone.

The collapse in Paris was another matter, adding significance to the first one. It prophesied possibly a new cycle, a new pousse of the malady. Having gone through unprofessional agonies during her long relapse following Topsy's birth, he had, perforce, hardened himself about her, making a cleavage between Nicole sick and Nicole well. This made it difficult now to distinguish between his self-protective professional detachment and some new coldness in his heart. As an indifference cherished, or left to atrophy, becomes an emptiness, to this extent he had learned to become empty of Nicole, serving her against his will with negations and emotional neglect. One writes of scars healed, a loose parallel to the pathology of the skin, but there is no such thing in the life of an individual. There are open wounds, shrunk sometimes to the size of a pin-prick but wounds still. The marks of suffering are more comparable to the loss of a finger, or of the sight of an eye. We may not miss them, either, for one minute in a year, but if we should there is nothing to be done about it.

XII

He found Nicole in the garden with her arms folded high on her shoulders. She looked at him with straight gray eyes, with a child's searching wonder.

"I went to Cannes," he said. "I ran into Mrs. Speers. She's leaving to-morrow. She wanted to come up and say good-by to you, but I slew the idea."

"I'm sorry. I'd like to have seen her. I like her."

"Who else do you think I saw--Bartholomew Tailor."

"You didn't."

"I couldn't have missed that face of his, the old experienced weasel. He was looking over the ground for Ciro's Menagerie--they'll all be down next year. I suspected Mrs. Abrams was a sort of outpost."

"And Baby was outraged the first summer we came here."

"They don't really give a damn where they are, so I don't see why they don't stay and freeze in Deauville."

"Can't we start rumors about cholera or something?"

"I told Bartholomew that some categories died off like flies here--I told him the life of a suck was as short as the life of a machine-gunner in the war."

"You didn't."

"No, I didn't," he admitted. "He was very pleasant. It was a beautiful sight, he and I shaking hands there on the boulevard. The meeting of Sigmund Freud and Ward McAllister."

Dick didn't want to talk--he wanted to be alone so that his thoughts about work and the future would overpower his thoughts of love and to-day. Nicole knew about it but only darkly and tragically, hating him a little in an animal way, yet wanting to rub against his shoulder.

"The darling," Dick said lightly.

He went into the house, forgetting something he wanted to do there, and then remembering it was the piano. He sat down whistling and played by ear:

"Just picture you upon my knee
With tea for two and two for tea
And me for you and you for me--"

Through the melody flowed a sudden realization that Nicole, hearing it, would guess quickly at a nostalgia for the past fortnight. He broke off with a casual chord and left the piano.

It was hard to know where to go. He glanced about the house that Nicole had made, that Nicole's grandfather had paid for. He owned only his work house and the ground on which it stood. Out of three thousand a year and what dribbled in from his publications he paid for his clothes and personal expenses, for cellar charges, and for Lanier's education, so far confined to a nurse's wage. Never had a move been contemplated without Dick's figuring his share. Living rather ascetically, travelling third-class when he was alone, with the cheapest wine, and good care of his clothes, and penalizing himself for any extravagances, he maintained a qualified financial independence. After a certain point, though, it was difficult--again and again it was necessary to decide together as to the uses to which Nicole's money should be put. Naturally Nicole, wanting to own him, wanting him to stand still forever, encouraged any slackness on his part, and in multiplying ways he was constantly inundated by a trickling of goods and money. The inception of the idea of the cliff villa which they had elaborated as a fantasy one day was a typical example of the forces divorcing them from the first simple arrangements in Zurich.

"Wouldn't it be fun if--" it had been; and then, "Won't it be fun when--"

It was not so much fun. His work became confused with Nicole's problems; in addition, her income had increased so fast of late that it seemed to belittle his work. Also, for the purpose of her cure, he had for many years pretended to a rigid domesticity from which he was drifting away, and this pretense became more arduous in this effortless immobility, in which he was inevitably subjected to microscopic examination. When Dick could no longer play what he wanted to play on the piano, it was an indication that life was being refined down to a point. He stayed in the big room a long time listening to the buzz of the electric clock, listening to time.

In November the waves grew black and dashed over the sea wall onto the shore road--such summer life as had survived disappeared and the beaches were melancholy and desolate under the mistral and rain. Gausse's Hotel was closed for repairs and enlargement and the scaffolding of the summer Casino at Juan les Pins grew larger and more formidable. Going into Cannes or Nice, Dick and Nicole met new people--members of orchestras, restaurateurs, horticultural enthusiasts, shipbuilders--for Dick had bought an old dinghy--and members of the Syndicat d'Initiative. They knew their servants well and gave thought to the children's education. In December, Nicole seemed well-knit again; when a month had passed without tension, without the tight mouth, the unmotivated smile, the unfathomable remark, they went to the Swiss Alps for the Christmas holidays.

XIII

With his cap, Dick slapped the snow from his dark blue ski-suit before going inside. The great hall, its floor pockmarked by two decades of hobnails, was cleared for the tea dance, and four-score young Americans, domiciled in schools near Gstaad, bounced about to the frolic of "Don't Bring Lulu," or exploded violently with the first percussions of the Charleston. It was a colony of the young, simple, and expensive--the *Sturmtruppen* of the rich were at St. Moritz. Baby Warren felt that she had made a gesture of renunciation in joining the Divers here.

Dick picked out the two sisters easily across the delicately haunted, soft-swaying room--they were poster-like, formidable in their snow costumes, Nicole's of cerulean blue, Baby's of brick red. The young Englishman was talking to them; but they were paying no attention, lulled to the staring point by the adolescent dance.

Nicole's snow-warm face lighted up further as she saw Dick. "Where is he?"

"He missed the train--I'm meeting him later." Dick sat down, swinging a heavy boot over his knee. "You two look very striking together. Every once in a while I forget we're in the same party and get a big shock at seeing you."

Baby was a tall, fine-looking woman, deeply engaged in being almost thirty. Symptomatically she had pulled two men with her from London, one scarcely down from Cambridge, one old and hard with Victorian lecheries. Baby had certain spinsters' characteristics--she was alien from touch, she started if she was touched suddenly, and such lingering touches as kisses and embraces slipped directly through the flesh into the forefront of her consciousness. She made few gestures with her trunk, her body proper--instead, she stamped her foot and tossed her head in almost an old-fashioned way. She relished the foretaste of death, prefigured by the catastrophes of friends--persistently she clung to the idea of Nicole's tragic destiny.

Baby's younger Englishman had been chaperoning the women down appropriate inclines and harrowing them on the bob-run. Dick, having turned an ankle in a too ambitious telemark, loafed gratefully about the "nursery slope" with the children or drank kvass with a Russian doctor at the hotel.

"Please be happy, Dick," Nicole urged him. "Why don't you meet some of these ickle durls and dance with them in the afternoon?"

"What would I say to them?"

Her low almost harsh voice rose a few notes, simulating a plaintive coquetry: "Say: 'Ickle durl, oo is de pwettiest sing.' What do you think you say?"

"I don't like ickle durls. They smell of castile soap and peppermint. When I dance with them, I feel as if I'm pushing a baby carriage."

It was a dangerous subject--he was careful, to the point of self-consciousness, to stare far over the heads of young maidens.

"There's a lot of business," said Baby. "First place, there's news from home--the property we used to call the station property. The railroads only bought the centre of it at first. Now they've bought the rest, and it belonged to Mother. It's a question of investing the money."

Pretending to be repelled by this gross turn in the conversation, the Englishman made for a girl on the floor. Following him for an instant with the uncertain eyes of an American girl in the grip of a life-long Anglophilia, Baby continued defiantly:

"It's a lot of money. It's three hundred thousand apiece. I keep an eye on my own investments but Nicole doesn't know anything about securities, and I don't suppose you do either."

"I've got to meet the train," Dick said evasively.

Outside he inhaled damp snowflakes that he could no longer see against the darkening sky. Three children sledding past shouted a warning in some strange language; he heard them yell at the next bend and a little farther on he heard sleigh-bells coming up the hill in the dark. The holiday station glittered with expectancy, boys and girls waiting for new boys and girls, and by the time the train arrived, Dick had caught the rhythm, and pretended to Franz Gregorovius that he was clipping off a half-hour from an endless roll of pleasures. But Franz had some intensity of purpose at the moment that fought through any superimposition of mood on Dick's part. "I may get up to Zurich for a day," Dick had written, "or you can manage to come to Lausanne." Franz had managed to come all the way to Gstaad.

He was forty. Upon his healthy maturity reposed a set of pleasant official manners, but he was most at home in a somewhat stuffy safety from which he could despise the broken rich whom he re-educated. His scientific heredity might have bequeathed him a wider world but he seemed to have deliberately chosen the standpoint of an humbler class, a choice typified by his selection of a wife. At the hotel Baby Warren made a quick examination of him, and failing to find any of the hall-marks she respected, the subtler virtues or courtesies by which the privileged classes recognized one another, treated him thereafter with her second manner. Nicole was always a little afraid of him. Dick liked him, as he liked his friends, without reservations.

For the evening they were sliding down the hill into the village, on those little sleds which serve the same purpose as gondolas do in Venice. Their destination was a hotel with an old-fashioned Swiss tap-room, wooden and resounding, a room of clocks, kegs, steins, and antlers. Many parties at long tables blurred into one great party and ate fondue--a peculiarly indigestible form of Welsh rarebit, mitigated by hot spiced wine.

It was jolly in the big room; the younger Englishman remarked it and Dick conceded that there was no other word. With the pert heady wine he relaxed and pretended that the world was all put together again by the gray-haired men of the golden nineties who shouted old glees at the piano, by the young voices and the bright costumes toned into the room by the swirling smoke. For a moment he felt that they were in a ship with landfall just ahead; in the faces of all the girls was the same innocent expectation of the possibilities inherent in the situation and the night. He looked to see if that special girl was there and got an impression that she was at the table behind them--then he forgot her and invented a rigmarole and tried to make his party have a good time.

"I must talk to you," said Franz in English. "I have only twenty-four hours to spend here."

"I suspected you had something on your mind."

"I have a plan that is--so marvellous." His hand fell upon Dick's knee. "I have a plan that will be the making of us two."

"Well?"

"Dick--there is a clinic we could have together--the old clinic of Braun on the Zugersee. The plant is all modern except for a few points. He is sick--he wants to go up in Austria, to die probably. It is a chance that is just insuperable. You and me--what a pair! Now don't say anything yet until I finish."

From the yellow glint in Baby's eyes, Dick saw she was listening.

"We must undertake it together. It would not bind you too tight--it would give you a base, a laboratory, a centre. You could stay in residence say no more than half the year, when the weather is fine. In winter you could go to France or America and write your texts fresh from clinical experience." He lowered his voice. "And for the convalescence in your family, there are the atmosphere and regularity of the clinic at hand." Dick's expression did not encourage this note so Franz dropped it with the punctuation of his tongue leaving his lip quickly. "We could be partners. I the executive manager, you the theoretician, the brilliant consultant and all that. I know myself--I know I have no genius and you have. But, in my way, I am thought very capable; I am utterly competent at the most modern clinical methods. Sometimes for months I have served as the practical head of the old clinic. The professor says this plan is excellent, he advises me to go ahead. He says he is going to live forever, and work up to the last minute."

Dick formed imaginary pictures of the prospect as a preliminary to any exercise of judgment.

"What's the financial angle?" he asked.

Franz threw up his chin, his eyebrows, the transient wrinkles of his forehead, his hands, his elbows, his shoulders; he strained up the muscles of his legs, so that the cloth of his trousers bulged, pushed up his heart into his throat and his voice into the roof of his mouth.

"There we have it! Money!" he bewailed. "I have little money. The price in American money is two hundred thousand dollars. The innovation--ary--" he tasted the coinage doubtfully, "--steps, that you will agree are necessary, will cost twenty thousand dollars American. But the clinic is a gold mine--I tell you, I haven't seen the books. For an investment of two hundred and twenty thousand dollars we have an assured income of--"

Baby's curiosity was such that Dick brought her into the conversation.

"In your experience, Baby," he demanded, "have you found that when a European wants to see an American *very* pressingly it is invariably something concerned with money?"

"What is it?" she said innocently.

"This young Privat-dozent thinks that he and I ought to launch into big business and try to attract nervous breakdowns from America."

Worried, Franz stared at Baby as Dick continued:

"But who are we, Franz? You bear a big name and I've written two textbooks. Is that enough to attract anybody? And I haven't got that much money--I haven't got a tenth of it." Franz smiled cynically. "Honestly I haven't. Nicole and Baby are rich as Croesus but I haven't managed to get my hands on any of it yet."

They were all listening now--Dick wondered if the girl at the table behind was listening too. The idea attracted him. He decided to let Baby speak for him, as one often lets women raise their voices over issues that are not in their hands. Baby became suddenly her grandfather, cool and experimental.

"I think it's a suggestion you ought to consider, Dick. I don't know what Doctor Gregory was saying--but it seems to me--"

Behind him the girl had leaned forward into a smoke ring and was picking up something from the floor. Nicole's face, fitted into his own across the table--her beauty, tentatively nesting and posing, flowed into his love, ever braced to protect it.

"Consider it, Dick," Franz urged excitedly. "When one writes on psychiatry, one should have actual clinical contacts. Jung writes, Bleuler writes, Freud writes, Forel writes, Adler writes--also they are in constant contact with mental disorder."

"Dick has me," laughed Nicole. "I should think that'd be enough mental disorder for one man."

"That's different," said Franz cautiously.

Baby was thinking that if Nicole lived beside a clinic she would always feel quite safe about her.

"We must think it over carefully," she said.

Though amused at her insolence, Dick did not encourage it.

"The decision concerns me, Baby," he said gently. "It's nice of you to want to buy me a clinic."

Realizing she had meddled, Baby withdrew hurriedly:

"Of course, it's entirely your affair."

"A thing as important as this will take weeks to decide. I wonder how I like the picture of Nicole and me anchored to Zurich--" He turned to Franz, anticipating: "--I know. Zurich has a gashouse and running water and electric light--I lived there three years."

"I will leave you to think it over," said Franz. "I am confident--"

One hundred pair of five-pound boots had begun to clump toward the door, and they joined the press. Outside in the crisp moonlight, Dick saw the girl tying her sled to one of the sleighs ahead. They piled into their own sleigh and at the crisp-cracking whips the horses strained, breasting the dark air. Past them figures ran and scrambled, the younger ones shoving each other from sleds and runners, landing in the soft snow, then panting after the horses to drop exhausted on a sled or wail that they were abandoned. On either side the fields were beneficently tranquil; the space through which the cavalcade moved was high and limitless. In the country there was less noise as though they were all listening atavistically for wolves in the wide snow.

In Saanen, they poured into the municipal dance, crowded with cow herders, hotel servants, shop-keepers, ski teachers, guides, tourists, peasants. To come into the warm enclosed place after the pantheistic animal feeling without, was to reassume some absurd and impressive knightly name, as thunderous as spurred boots in war, as football cleats on the cement of a locker-room floor. There was conventional yodelling, and the familiar rhythm of it separated Dick from what he had first found romantic in the scene. At first he thought it was because he had hounded the girl out of his consciousness; then it came to him under the form of what Baby had said: "We must think it over carefully--" and the unsaid lines back of that: "We own you, and you'll admit it sooner or later. It is absurd to keep up the pretense of independence."

It had been years since Dick had bottled up malice against a creature--since freshman year at New Haven when he had come upon a popular essay about "mental hygiene." Now he lost his temper at Baby and simultaneously tried to coop it up within him, resenting her cold rich insolence. It would be hundreds of years before any emergent Amazons would ever grasp the fact that a man is vulnerable only in his pride, but delicate as Humpty-Dumpty once that is meddled with--though some of them paid the fact a cautious lip-service. Doctor Diver's profession of sorting the broken shells of another sort of egg had given him a dread of breakage. But:

"There's too much good manners," he said on the way back to Gstaad in the smooth sleigh.

"Well, I think that's nice," said Baby.

"No, it isn't," he insisted to the anonymous bundle of fur. "Good manners are an admission that everybody is so tender that they have to be handled with gloves. Now, human respect--you don't call a man a coward or a liar lightly, but if you spend your life sparing people's feelings and feeding their vanity, you get so you can't distinguish what *should* be respected in them."

"I think Americans take their manners rather seriously," said the elder Englishman.

"I guess so," said Dick. "My father had the kind of manners he inherited from the days when you shot first and apologized afterward. Men armed--why, you Europeans haven't carried arms in civil life since the beginning of the eighteenth century--"

"Not actually, perhaps--"

"Not *act*ually. Not really."

"Dick, you've always had such beautiful manners," said Baby conciliatingly.

The women were regarding him across the zoo of robes with some alarm. The younger Englishman did not understand--he was one of the kind who were always jumping around cornices and balconies, as if they thought they were in the rigging of a ship--and filled the ride to the hotel with a preposterous story about a boxing match with his best friend in which they loved and bruised each other for an hour, always with great reserve. Dick became facetious.

"So every time he hit you you considered him an even better friend?"

"I respected him more."

"It's the premise I don't understand. You and your best friend scrap about a trivial matter--"

"If you don't understand, I can't explain it to you," said the young Englishman coldly.

--This is what I'll get if I begin saying what I think, Dick said to himself.

He was ashamed at baiting the man, realizing that the absurdity of the story rested in the immaturity of the attitude combined with the sophisticated method of its narration.

The carnival spirit was strong and they went with the crowd into the grill, where a Tunisian barman manipulated the illumination in a counterpoint, whose other melody was the moon off the ice rink staring in the big windows. In that light, Dick found the girl devitalized, and uninteresting--he turned from her to enjoy the darkness, the cigarette points going green and silver when the lights shone red, the band of white that fell across the dancers as the door to the bar was opened and closed.

"Now tell me, Franz," he demanded, "do you think after sitting up all night drinking beer, you can go back and convince your patients that you have any character? Don't you think they'll see you're a gastropath?"

"I'm going to bed," Nicole announced. Dick accompanied her to the door of the elevator.

"I'd come with you but I must show Franz that I'm not intended for a clinician."

Nicole walked into the elevator.

"Baby has lots of common sense," she said meditatively.

"Baby is one of--"

The door slashed shut--facing a mechanical hum, Dick finished the sentence in his mind, "--Baby is a trivial, selfish woman."

But two days later, sleighing to the station with Franz, Dick admitted that he thought favorably upon the matter.

"We're beginning to turn in a circle," he admitted. "Living on this scale, there's an unavoidable series of strains, and Nicole doesn't survive them. The pastoral quality down on the summer Riviera is all changing anyhow--next year they'll have a Season."

They passed the crisp green rinks where Wiener waltzes blared and the colors of many mountain schools flashed against the pale-blue skies.

"--I hope we'll be able to do it, Franz. There's nobody I'd rather try it with than you--"

Good-by, Gstaad! Good-by, fresh faces, cold sweet flowers, flakes in the darkness. Good-by, Gstaad, good-by!

XIV

Dick awoke at five after a long dream of war, walked to the window and stared out it at the Zugersee. His dream had begun in sombre majesty; navy blue uniforms crossed a dark plaza behind bands playing the second movement of Prokofieff's "Love of Three Oranges." Presently there were fire engines, symbols of disaster, and a ghastly uprising of the mutilated in a dressing station. He turned on his bed-lamp light and made a thorough note of it ending with the half-ironic phrase: "Non-combatant's shell-shock."

As he sat on the side of his bed, he felt the room, the house and the night as empty. In the next room Nicole muttered something desolate and he felt sorry for whatever loneliness she was feeling in her sleep. For him time stood still and then every few years accelerated in a rush, like the quick re-wind of a film, but for Nicole the years slipped away by clock and calendar and birthday, with the added poignance of her perishable beauty.

Even this past year and a half on the Zugersee seemed wasted time for her, the seasons marked only by the workmen on the road turning pink in May, brown in July, black in September, white again in Spring. She had come out of her first illness alive with new hopes, expecting so much, yet deprived of any subsistence except Dick, bringing up children she could only pretend gently to love, guided orphans. The people she liked, rebels mostly, disturbed her and were bad for her--she sought in them the vitality that had made them independent or creative or rugged, sought in vain--for their secrets were buried deep in childhood struggles they had forgotten. They were more interested in Nicole's exterior harmony and charm, the other face of her illness. She led a lonely life owning Dick who did not want to be owned.

Many times he had tried unsuccessfully to let go his hold on her. They had many fine times together, fine talks between the loves of the white nights, but always when he turned away from her into himself he left her holding Nothing in her hands and staring at it, calling it many names, but knowing it was only the hope that he would come back soon.

He scrunched his pillow hard, lay down, and put the back of his neck against it as a Japanese does to slow the circulation, and slept again for a time. Later, while he shaved, Nicole awoke and marched around, giving abrupt, succinct orders to children and servants. Lanier came in to watch his father shave--living beside a psychiatric clinic he had developed an extraordinary confidence in and admiration for his father, together with an exaggerated indifference toward most other adults; the patients appeared to him either in their odd aspects, or else as devitalized, over-correct creatures without personality. He was a handsome, promising boy and Dick devoted much time to him, in the relationship of a sympathetic but exacting officer and respectful enlisted man.

"Why," Lanier asked, "do you always leave a little lather on the top of your hair when you shave?"

Cautiously Dick parted soapy lips: "I have never been able to find out. I've often wondered. I think it's because I get the first finger soapy when I make the line of my side-burn, but how it gets up on top of my head I don't know."

"I'm going to watch it all to-morrow."

"That's your only question before breakfast?"

"I don't really call it a question."

"That's one on you."

Half an hour later Dick started up to the administration building. He was thirty-eight--still declining a beard he yet had a more medical aura about him than he had worn upon the Riviera. For eighteen months now he had lived at the clinic--certainly one of the best-appointed in Europe. Like Dohmler's it was of the modern type--no longer a single dark and sinister building but a small, scattered, yet deceitfully integrated village--Dick and Nicole had added much in the domain of taste, so that the plant was a thing of beauty, visited by every psychologist passing through Zurich. With the addition of a caddy house it might very well have been a country club. The Eglantine and the Beeches, houses for those sunk into eternal darkness, were screened by little copses from the main building, camouflaged strong-points. Behind was a large truck farm, worked partly by the patients. The workshops for ergo-therapy were three, placed under a single roof and there Doctor Diver began his morning's inspection. The carpentry shop, full of sunlight, exuded the sweetness of sawdust, of a lost age of wood; always half a dozen men were there, hammering, planing, buzzing--silent men, who lifted solemn eyes from their work as he passed through. Himself a good carpenter, he discussed with them the efficiency of some tools for a moment in a quiet, personal, interested voice. Adjoining was the book-bindery, adapted to the most mobile of patients who were not always, however, those who had the greatest chance for recovery. The last chamber was devoted to beadwork, weaving and work in brass. The faces of the patients here wore the expression of one who had just sighed profoundly, dismissing something insoluble--but their sighs only marked the beginning of another ceaseless round of ratiocination, not in a line as with normal people but in the same circle. Round, round, and round. Around forever. But the bright colors of the stuffs they worked with gave strangers a momentary illusion that all was well, as in a kindergarten. These patients brightened as Doctor Diver came in. Most of them liked him better than they liked Doctor Gregorovius. Those who had once lived in the great world invariably liked him better. There were a few who thought he neglected them, or that he was not simple, or that he posed. Their responses were not dissimilar to those that Dick evoked in non-professional life, but here they were warped and distorted.

One Englishwoman spoke to him always about a subject which she considered her own.

"Have we got music to-night?"

"I don't know," he answered. "I haven't seen Doctor Ladislau. How did you enjoy the music that Mrs. Sachs and Mr. Longstreet gave us last night?"

"It was so-so."

"I thought it was fine--especially the Chopin."

"I thought it was so-so."

"When are you going to play for us yourself?"

She shrugged her shoulders, as pleased at this question as she had been for several years.

"Some time. But I only play so-so."

They knew that she did not play at all--she had had two sisters who were brilliant musicians, but she had never been able to learn the notes when they had been young together.

From the workshop Dick went to visit the Eglantine and the Beeches. Exteriorly these houses were as cheerful as the others; Nicole had designed the decoration and the furniture on a necessary base of concealed grills and bars and immovable furniture. She had worked with so much imagination--the inventive quality, which she lacked, being supplied by the problem itself--that no instructed visitor would have dreamed that the light, graceful filagree work at a window was a strong, unyielding end of a tether, that the pieces reflecting modern tubular tendencies were stancher than the massive creations of the Edwardians--even the flowers lay in iron fingers and every casual ornament and fixture was as necessary as a girder in a skyscraper. Her tireless eyes had made each room yield up its greatest usefulness. Complimented, she referred to herself brusquely as a master plumber.

For those whose compasses were not depolarized there seemed many odd things in these houses. Doctor Diver was often amused in the Eglantine, the men's building--here there was a strange little exhibitionist who thought that if he could walk unclothed and unmolested from the Êtoile to the Place de la Concorde he would solve many things--and, perhaps, Dick thought, he was quite right.

His most interesting case was in the main building. The patient was a woman of thirty who had been in the clinic six months; she was an American painter who had lived long in Paris. They had no very satisfactory history of her. A cousin had happened upon her all mad and gone and after an unsatisfactory interlude at one of the whoopee cures that fringed the city, dedicated largely to tourist victims of drug and drink, he had managed to get her to Switzerland. On her admittance she had been exceptionally pretty--now she was a living agonizing sore. All blood tests had failed to give a positive reaction and the trouble was unsatisfactorily catalogued as nervous eczema. For two months she had lain under it, as imprisoned as in the Iron Maiden. She was coherent, even brilliant, within the limits of her special hallucinations.

She was particularly his patient. During spells of overexcitement he was the only doctor who could "do anything with her." Several weeks ago, on one of many nights that she had passed in sleepless torture Franz had succeeded in hypnotizing her into a few hours of needed rest, but he had never again succeeded. Hypnosis was a tool that Dick had distrusted and seldom used, for he knew that he could not always summon up the mood in himself--he had once tried it on Nicole and she had scornfully laughed at him.

The woman in room twenty could not see him when he came in--the area about her eyes was too tightly swollen. She spoke in a strong, rich, deep, thrilling voice.

"How long will this last? Is it going to be forever?"

"It's not going to be very long now. Doctor Ladislau tells me there are whole areas cleared up."

"If I knew what I had done to deserve this I could accept it with equanimity."

"It isn't wise to be mystical about it--we recognize it as a nervous phenomenon. It's related to the blush--when you were a girl, did you blush easily?"

She lay with her face turned to the ceiling.

"I have found nothing to blush for since I cut my wisdom teeth."

"Haven't you committed your share of petty sins and mistakes?"

"I have nothing to reproach myself with."

"You're very fortunate."

The woman thought a moment; her voice came up through her bandaged face afflicted with subterranean melodies:

"I'm sharing the fate of the women of my time who challenged men to battle."

"To your vast surprise it was just like all battles," he answered, adopting her formal diction.

"Just like all battles." She thought this over. "You pick a set-up, or else win a Pyrrhic victory, or you're wrecked and ruined--you're a ghostly echo from a broken wall."

"You are neither wrecked nor ruined," he told her. "Are you quite sure you've been in a real battle?"

"Look at me!" she cried furiously.

"You've suffered, but many women suffered before they mistook themselves for men." It was becoming an argument and he retreated. "In any case you mustn't confuse a single failure with a final defeat."

She sneered. "Beautiful words," and the phrase transpiring up through the crust of pain humbled him.

"We would like to go into the true reasons that brought you here--" he began but she interrupted.

"I am here as a symbol of something. I thought perhaps you would know what it was."

"You are sick," he said mechanically.

"Then what was it I had almost found?"

"A greater sickness."

"That's all?"

"That's all." With disgust he heard himself lying, but here and now the vastness of the subject could only be compressed into a lie. "Outside of that there's only confusion and chaos. I won't lecture to you--we have too acute a realization of your physical suffering. But it's only by meeting the problems of every day, no matter how trifling and boring they seem, that you can make things drop back into place again. After that--perhaps you'll be able again to examine--"

He had slowed up to avoid the inevitable end of his thought: "--the frontiers of consciousness." The frontiers that artists must explore were not for her, ever. She was fine-spun, inbred--eventually she might find rest in some quiet mysticism. Exploration was for those with a measure of peasant blood, those with big thighs and thick ankles who could take punishment as they took bread and salt, on every inch of flesh and spirit.

--Not for you, he almost said. It's too tough a game for you.

Yet in the awful majesty of her pain he went out to her unreservedly, almost sexually. He wanted to gather her up in his arms, as he so often had Nicole, and cherish even her mistakes, so deeply were they part of her. The orange light through the drawn blind, the sarcophagus of her figure on the bed, the spot of face, the voice searching the vacuity of her illness and finding only remote abstractions.

As he arose the tears fled lava-like into her bandages.

"That is for something," she whispered. "Something must come out of it."

He stooped and kissed her forehead.

"We must all try to be good," he said.

Leaving her room he sent the nurse in to her. There were other patients to see: an American girl of fifteen who had been brought up on the basis that childhood was intended to be all fun--his visit was provoked by the fact that she had just hacked off all her hair with a nail scissors. There was nothing much to be done for her--a family history of neurosis and nothing stable in her past to build on. The father, normal and conscientious himself, had tried to protect a nervous brood from life's troubles and had succeeded merely in preventing them from developing powers of adjustment to life's inevitable surprises. There was little that Dick could say: "Helen, when you're in doubt you must ask a nurse, you must learn to take advice. Promise me you will."

What was a promise with the head sick? He looked in upon a frail exile from the Caucasus buckled securely in a sort of hammock which in turn was submerged in a warm medical bath, and upon the three daughters of a Portuguese general who slid almost imperceptibly toward paresis. He went into the room next to them and told a collapsed psychiatrist that he was better, always better, and the man tried to read his face for conviction, since he hung on the real world only through such reassurance as he could find in the resonance, or lack of it, in Doctor Diver's voice. After that Dick discharged a shiftless orderly and by then it was the lunch hour.

XV

Meals with the patients were a chore he approached with apathy. The gathering, which of course did not include residents at the Eglantine or the Beeches, was conventional enough at first sight, but over it brooded always a heavy melancholy. Such doctors as were present kept up a conversation but most of the patients, as if exhausted by their morning's endeavor, or depressed by the company, spoke little, and ate looking into their plates.

Luncheon over, Dick returned to his villa. Nicole was in the salon wearing a strange expression.

"Read that," she said.

He opened the letter. It was from a woman recently discharged, though with skepticism on the part of the faculty. It accused him in no uncertain terms of having seduced her daughter, who had been at her mother's side during the crucial stage of the illness. It presumed that Mrs. Diver would be glad to have this information and learn what her husband was "really like."

Dick read the letter again. Couched in clear and concise English he yet recognized it as the letter of a maniac. Upon a single occasion he had let the girl, a flirtatious little brunette, ride into Zurich with him, upon her request, and in the evening had brought her back to the clinic. In an idle, almost indulgent way, he kissed her. Later, she tried to carry the affair further, but he was not interested and subsequently, probably consequently, the girl had come to dislike him, and taken her mother away.

"This letter is deranged," he said. "I had no relations of any kind with that girl. I didn't even like her."

"Yes, I've tried thinking that," said Nicole.

"Surely you don't believe it?"

"I've been sitting here."

He sank his voice to a reproachful note and sat beside her.

"This is absurd. This is a letter from a mental patient."

"I was a mental patient."

He stood up and spoke more authoritatively.

"Suppose we don't have any nonsense, Nicole. Go and round up the children and we'll start."

In the car, with Dick driving, they followed the little promontories of the lake, catching the burn of light and water in the windshield, tunnelling through cascades of evergreen. It was Dick's car, a Renault so dwarfish that they all stuck out of it except the children, between whom Mademoiselle towered mastlike in the rear seat. They knew every kilometer of the road--where they would smell the pine needles and the black stove smoke. A high sun with a face traced on it beat fierce on the straw hats of the children.

Nicole was silent; Dick was uneasy at her straight hard gaze. Often he felt lonely with her, and frequently she tired him with the short floods of personal revelations that she reserved exclusively for him, "I'm like this--I'm more like that," but this afternoon he would have been glad had she rattled on in staccato for a while and given him glimpses of her thoughts. The situation was always most threatening when she backed up into herself and closed the doors behind her.

At Zug Mademoiselle got out and left them. The Divers approached the Agiri Fair through a menagerie of mammoth steamrollers that made way for them. Dick parked the car, and as Nicole looked at him without moving, he said: "Come on, darl." Her lips drew apart into a sudden awful smile, and his belly quailed, but as if he hadn't seen it he repeated: "Come on. So the children can get out."

"Oh, I'll come all right," she answered, tearing the words from some story spinning itself out inside her, too fast for him to grasp. "Don't worry about that. I'll come--"

"Then come."

She turned from him as he walked beside her but the smile still flickered across her face, derisive and remote. Only when Lanier spoke to her several times did she manage to fix her attention upon an object, a Punch-and-Judy show, and to orient herself by anchoring to it.

Dick tried to think what to do. The dualism in his views of her--that of the husband, that of the psychiatrist--was increasingly paralyzing his faculties. In these six years she had several times carried him over the line with her, disarming him by exciting emotional pity or by a flow of wit, fantastic and disassociated, so that only after the episode did he realize with the consciousness of his own relaxation from tension, that she had succeeded in getting a point against his better judgment.

A discussion with Topsy about the guignol--as to whether the Punch was the same Punch they had seen last year in Cannes--having been settled, the family walked along again between the booths under the open sky. The women's bonnets, perching over velvet vests, the bright, spreading skirts of many cantons, seemed demure against the blue and orange paint of the wagons and displays. There was the sound of a whining, tinkling hootchy-kootchy show.

Nicole began to run very suddenly, so suddenly that for a moment Dick did not miss her. Far ahead he saw her yellow dress twisting through the crowd, an ochre stitch along the edge of reality and unreality, and started after her. Secretly she ran and secretly he followed. As the hot afternoon went shrill and terrible with her flight he had forgotten the children; then he wheeled and ran back to them, drawing them this way and that by their arms, his eyes jumping from booth to booth.

"Madame," he cried to a young woman behind a white lottery wheel, "Est-ce que je peux laisser ces petits avec vous deux minutes? C'est très urgent--je vous donnerai dix francs."

"Mais oui."

He headed the children into the booth. "Alors--restez avec cette gentille dame."

"Oui, Dick."

He darted off again but he had lost her; he circled the merry-go-round keeping up with it till he realized he was running beside it, staring always at the same horse. He elbowed through the crowd in the buvette; then remembering a predilection of Nicole's he snatched up an edge of a fortuneteller's tent and peered within. A droning voice greeted him: "La septième fille d'une septième fille née sur les rives du Nil--entrez, Monsieur--"

Dropping the flap he ran along toward where the plaisance terminated at the lake and a small ferris wheel revolved slowly against the sky. There he found her.

She was alone in what was momentarily the top boat of the wheel, and as it descended he saw that she was laughing hilariously; he slunk back in the crowd, a crowd which, at the wheel's next revolution, spotted the intensity of Nicole's hysteria.

"Regardez-moi ça!"

"Regarde donc cette Anglaise!"

Down she dropped again--this time the wheel and its music were slowing and a dozen people were around her car, all of them impelled by the quality of her laughter to smile in sympathetic idiocy. But when Nicole saw Dick her laughter died--she made a gesture of slipping by and away from him but he caught her arm and held it as they walked away.

"Why did you lose control of yourself like that?"

"You know very well why."

"No, I don't."

"That's just preposterous--let me loose--that's an insult to my intelligence. Don't you think I saw that girl look at you--that little dark girl. Oh, this is farcical--a child, not more than fifteen. Don't you think I saw?"

"Stop here a minute and quiet down."

They sat at a table, her eyes in a profundity of suspicion, her hand moving across her line of sight as if it were obstructed. "I want a drink--I want a brandy."

"You can't have brandy--you can have a bock if you want it."

"Why can't I have a brandy?"

"We won't go into that. Listen to me--this business about a girl is a delusion, do you understand that word?"

"It's always a delusion when I see what you don't want me to see."

He had a sense of guilt as in one of those nightmares where we are accused of a crime which we recognize as something undeniably experienced, but which upon waking we realize we have not committed. His eyes wavered from hers.

"I left the children with a gypsy woman in a booth. We ought to get them."

"Who do you think you are?" she demanded. "Svengali?"

Fifteen minutes ago they had been a family. Now as she was crushed into a corner by his unwilling shoulder, he saw them all, child and man, as a perilous accident.

"We're going home."

"Home!" she roared in a voice so abandoned that its louder tones wavered and cracked. "And sit and think that we're all rotting and the children's ashes are rotting in every box I open? That filth!"

Almost with relief he saw that her words sterilized her, and Nicole, sensitized down to the corium of the skin, saw the withdrawal in his face. Her own face softened and she begged, "Help me, help me, Dick!"

A wave of agony went over him. It was awful that such a fine tower should not be erected, only suspended, suspended from him. Up to a point that was right: men were for that, beam and idea, girder and logarithm; but somehow Dick and Nicole had become one and equal, not opposite and complementary; she was Dick too, the drought in the marrow of his bones. He could not watch her disintegrations without participating in them. His intuition rilled out of him as tenderness and compassion--he could only take the characteristically modern course, to interpose--he would get a nurse from Zurich, to take her over to-night.

"You *can* help me."

Her sweet bullying pulled him forward off his feet. "You've helped me be-fore--you can help me now."

"I can only help you the same old way."

"Some one can help me."

"Maybe so. You can help yourself most. Let's find the children."

There were numerous lottery booths with white wheels--Dick was startled when he inquired at the first and encountered blank disavowals. Evil-eyed, Nicole stood apart, denying the children, resenting them as part of a downright world she sought to make amorphous. Presently Dick found them, surrounded by women who were examining them with delight like fine goods, and by peasant children staring.

"Merci, Monsieur, ah Monsieur est trop généreux. C'était un plaisir, M'sieur, Madame. Au revoir, mes petits."

They started back with a hot sorrow streaming down upon them; the car was weighted with their mutual apprehension and anguish, and the children's mouths were grave with disappointment. Grief presented itself in its terrible, dark unfamiliar color. Somewhere around Zug, Nicole, with a convulsive effort, reiterated a remark she had made before about a misty yellow house set back from the road that looked like a painting not yet dry, but it was just an attempt to catch at a rope that was playing out too swiftly.

Dick tried to rest--the struggle would come presently at home and he might have to sit a long time, restating the universe for her. A "schizophrêne" is well named as a split personality--Nicole was alternately a person to whom nothing need be explained and one to whom nothing *could* be explained. It was necessary to treat her with active and affirmative insistence, keeping the road to reality always open, making the road to escape harder going. But the brilliance, the versatility of madness is akin to the resourcefulness of water seeping through, over and around a dike. It requires the united front of many people to work against it. He felt it necessary that this time Nicole cure herself; he wanted to wait until she remembered the other times, and revolted from them. In a tired way, he planned that they would again resume the régime relaxed a year before.

He had turned up a hill that made a short cut to the clinic, and now as he stepped on the accelerator for a short straightaway run parallel to the hillside the car swerved violently left, swerved right, tipped on two wheels and, as Dick, with Nicole's voice screaming in his ear, crushed down the mad hand clutching the steering wheel, righted itself, swerved once more and shot off the road; it tore through low underbrush, tipped again and settled slowly at an angle of ninety degrees against a tree.

The children were screaming and Nicole was screaming and cursing and trying to tear at Dick's face. Thinking first of the list of the car and unable to estimate it Dick bent away Nicole's arm, climbed over the top side and lifted out the children; then he saw the car was in a stable position. Before doing anything else he stood there shaking and panting.

"You--!" he cried.

She was laughing hilariously, unashamed, unafraid, unconcerned. No one coming on the scene would have imagined that she had caused it; she laughed as after some mild escape of childhood.

"You were scared, weren't you?" she accused him. "You wanted to live!"

She spoke with such force that in his shocked state Dick wondered if he had been frightened for himself--but the strained faces of the children, looking from parent to parent, made him want to grind her grinning mask into jelly.

Directly above them, half a kilometer by the winding road but only a hundred yards climbing, was an inn; one of its wings showed through the wooded hill.

"Take Topsy's hand," he said to Lanier, "like that, tight, and climb up that hill--see the little path? When you get to the inn tell them 'La voiture Divare est cassée.' Some one must come right down."

Lanier, not sure what had happened, but suspecting the dark and unprecedented, asked:

"What will you do, Dick?"

"We'll stay here with the car."

Neither of them looked at their mother as they started off. "Be careful crossing the road up there! Look both ways!" Dick shouted after them.

He and Nicole looked at each other directly, their eyes like blazing windows across a court of the same house. Then she took out a compact, looked in its mirror, and smoothed back the temple hair. Dick watched the children climbing for a moment until they disappeared among the pines half way up; then he walked around the car to see the damage and plan how to get it back on the road. In the dirt he could trace the rocking course they had pursued for over a hundred feet; he was filled with a violent disgust that was not like anger.

In a few minutes the proprietor of the inn came running down.

"My God!" he exclaimed. "How did it happen, were you going fast? What luck! Except for that tree you'd have rolled down hill!"

Taking advantage of Emile's reality, the wide black apron, the sweat upon the rolls of his face, Dick signalled to Nicole in a matter-of-fact way to let him help her from the car; whereupon she jumped over the lower side, lost her balance on the slope, fell to her knees and got up again. As she watched the men trying to move the car her expression became defiant. Welcoming even that mood Dick said:

"Go and wait with the children, Nicole."

Only after she had gone did he remember that she had wanted cognac, and that there was cognac available up there--he told Emile never mind about the car; they would wait for the chauffeur and the big car to pull it up onto the road. Together they hurried up to the inn.

XVI

"I want to go away," he told Franz. "For a month or so, for as long as I can."

"Why not, Dick? That was our original arrangement--it was you who insisted on staying. If you and Nicole--"

"I don't want to go away with Nicole. I want to go away alone. This last thing knocked me sideways--if I get two hours' sleep in twenty-four, it's one of Zwingli's miracles."

"You wish a real leave of abstinence."

"The word is 'absence.' Look here: if I go to Berlin to the Psychiatric Congress could you manage to keep the peace? For three months she's been all right and she likes her nurse. My God, you're the only human being in this world I can ask this of."

Franz grunted, considering whether or not he could be trusted to think always of his partner's interest.

In Zurich the next week Dick drove to the airport and took the big plane for Munich. Soaring and roaring into the blue he felt numb, realizing how tired he was. A vast persuasive quiet stole over him, and he abandoned sickness to the sick, sound to the motors, direction to the pilot. He had no intention of attending so much as a single session of the congress--he could imagine it well enough, new pamphlets by Bleuler and the elder Forel that he could much better digest at home, the paper by the American who cured dementia præcox by pulling out his patient's teeth or cauterizing their tonsils, the half-derisive respect with which this idea would be greeted, for no more reason than that America was such a rich and powerful country. The other delegates from America--red-headed Schwartz with his saint's face and his infinite patience in straddling two worlds, as well as dozens of commercial alienists with hang-dog faces, who would be present partly to increase their standing, and hence their reach for the big plums of the criminal practice, partly to master novel sophistries that they could weave into their stock in trade, to the infinite confusion of all values. There would be cynical Latins, and some man of Freud's from Vienna. Articulate among them would be the great Jung, bland, super-vigorous, on his rounds between the forests of anthropology and the neuroses of school-boys. At first there would be an American cast to the congress, almost Rotarian in its forms and ceremonies, then the closer-knit European vitality would fight through, and finally the Americans would play their trump card, the announcement of colossal gifts and endowments, of great new plants and training schools, and in the presence of the figures the Europeans would blanch and walk timidly. But he would not be there to see.

They skirted the Vorarlberg Alps, and Dick felt a pastoral delight in watching the villages. There were always four or five in sight, each one gathered around a church. It was simple looking at the earth from far off, simple as playing grim games with dolls and soldiers. This was the way statesmen and commanders and all retired people looked at things. Anyhow, it was a good draft of relief.

An Englishman spoke to him from across the aisle but he found something antipathetic in the English lately. England was like a rich man after a disastrous orgy who makes up to the household by chatting with them individually, when it is obvious to them that he is only trying to get back his self-respect in order to usurp his former power.

Dick had with him what magazines were available on the station quays: The Century, The Motion Picture, L'Illustration, and the Fliegende Blätter, but it was more fun to descend in his imagination into the villages and shake hands with the rural characters. He sat in the churches as he sat in his father's church in Buffalo, amid the starchy must of Sunday clothes. He listened to the wisdom of the Near East, was Crucified, Died, and was Buried in the cheerful church, and once more worried between five or ten cents for the collection plate, because of the girl who sat in the pew behind.

The Englishman suddenly borrowed his magazines with a little small change of conversation, and Dick, glad to see them go, thought of the voyage ahead of him. Wolf-like under his sheep's clothing of long-staple Australian wool, he considered the world of pleasure--the incorruptible Mediterranean with sweet old dirt caked in the olive trees, the peasant girl near Savona with a face as green and rose as the color of an illuminated missal. He would take her in his hands and snatch her across the border . . .

. . . but there he deserted her--he must press on toward the Isles of Greece, the cloudy waters of unfamiliar ports, the lost girl on shore, the moon of popular songs. A part of Dick's mind was made up of the tawdry souvenirs of his boyhood. Yet in that somewhat littered Five-and-Ten, he had managed to keep alive the low painful fire of intelligence.

XVII

Tommy Barban was a ruler, Tommy was a hero--Dick happened upon him in the Marienplatz in Munich, in one of those cafés, where small gamblers diced on "tapestry" mats. The air was full of politics, and the slap of cards.

Tommy was at a table laughing his martial laugh: "Um-buh--ha-ha! Um-buh--ha-ha!" As a rule, he drank little; courage was his game and his companions were always a little afraid of him. Recently an eighth of the area of his skull had been removed by a Warsaw surgeon and was knitting under his hair, and the weakest person in the café could have killed him with a flip of a knotted napkin.

"--this is Prince Chillicheff--" A battered, powder-gray Russian of fifty, "--and Mr. McKibben--and Mr. Hannan--" the latter was a lively ball of black eyes and hair, a clown; and he said immediately to Dick:

"The first thing before we shake hands--what do you mean by fooling around with my aunt?"

"Why, I--"

"You heard me. What are you doing here in Munich anyhow?"

"Um-bah--ha-ha!" laughed Tommy.

"Haven't you got aunts of your own? Why don't you fool with them?"

Dick laughed, whereupon the man shifted his attack:

"Now let's not have any more talk about aunts. How do I know you didn't make up the whole thing? Here you are a complete stranger with an acquaintance of less than half an hour, and you come up to me with a cock-and-bull story about your aunts. How do I know what you have concealed about you?"

Tommy laughed again, then he said good-naturedly, but firmly, "That's enough, Carly. Sit down, Dick--how're you? How's Nicole?"

He did not like any man very much nor feel their presence with much intensity--he was all relaxed for combat; as a fine athlete playing secondary defense in any sport is really resting much of the time, while a lesser man only pretends to rest and is at a continual and self-destroying nervous tension.

Hannan, not entirely suppressed, moved to an adjoining piano, and with recurring resentment on his face whenever he looked at Dick, played chords, from time to time muttering, "Your aunts," and, in a dying cadence, "I didn't say aunts anyhow. I said pants."

"Well, how're you?" repeated Tommy. "You don't look so--" he fought for a word, "--so jaunty as you used to, so spruce, you know what I mean."

The remark sounded too much like one of those irritating accusations of waning vitality and Dick was about to retort by commenting on the extraordinary suits worn by Tommy and Prince Chillicheff, suits of a cut and pattern fantastic enough to have sauntered down Beale Street on a Sunday--when an explanation was forthcoming.

"I see you are regarding our clothes," said the Prince. "We have just come out of Russia."

"These were made in Poland by the court tailor," said Tommy. "That's a fact--Pilsudski's own tailor."

"You've been touring?" Dick asked.

They laughed, the Prince inordinately meanwhile clapping Tommy on the back.

"Yes, we have been touring. That's it, touring. We have made the grand Tour of all the Russias. In state."

Dick waited for an explanation. It came from Mr. McKibben in two words.

"They escaped."

"Have you been prisoners in Russia?"

"It was I," explained Prince Chillicheff, his dead yellow eyes staring at Dick. "Not a prisoner but in hiding."

"Did you have much trouble getting out?"

"Some trouble. We left three Red Guards dead at the border. Tommy left two--" He held up two fingers like a Frenchman--"I left one."

"That's the part I don't understand," said Mr. McKibben. "Why they should have objected to your leaving."

Hannan turned from the piano and said, winking at the others: "Mac thinks a Marxian is somebody who went to St. Mark's school."

It was an escape story in the best tradition--an aristocrat hiding nine years with a former servant and working in a government bakery; the eighteen-year-old daughter in Paris who knew Tommy Barban. . . . During the narrative Dick decided that this parched papier mâché relic of the past was scarcely worth the lives of three young men. The question arose as to whether Tommy and Chillicheff had been frightened.

"When I was cold," Tommy said. "I always get scared when I'm cold. During the war I was always frightened when I was cold."

McKibben stood up.

"I must leave. To-morrow morning I'm going to Innsbruck by car with my wife and children--and the governess."

"I'm going there to-morrow, too," said Dick.

"Oh, are you?" exclaimed McKibben. "Why not come with us? It's a big Packard and there's only my wife and my children and myself--and the governess--"

"I can't possibly--"

"Of course she's not really a governess," McKibben concluded, looking rather pathetically at Dick. "As a matter of fact my wife knows your sister-in-law, Baby Warren."

But Dick was not to be drawn in a blind contract.

"I've promised to travel with two men."

"Oh," McKibben's face fell. "Well, I'll say good-by." He unscrewed two blooded wire-hairs from a nearby table and departed; Dick pictured the jammed Packard pounding toward Innsbruck with the McKibbens and their children and their baggage and yapping dogs--and the governess.

"The paper says they know the man who killed him," said Tommy. "But his cousins did not want it in the papers, because it happened in a speakeasy. What do you think of that?"

"It's what's known as family pride."

Hannan played a loud chord on the piano to attract attention to himself.

"I don't believe his first stuff holds up," he said. "Even barring the Europeans there are a dozen Americans can do what North did."

It was the first indication Dick had had that they were talking about Abe North.

"The only difference is that Abe did it first," said Tommy.

"I don't agree," persisted Hannan. "He got the reputation for being a good musician because he drank so much that his friends had to explain him away somehow--"

"What's this about Abe North? What about him? Is he in a jam?"

"Didn't you read The Herald this morning?"

"No."

"He's dead. He was beaten to death in a speakeasy in New York. He just managed to crawl home to the Racquet Club to die--"

"Abe North?"

"Yes, sure, they--"

"Abe North?" Dick stood up. "Are you sure he's dead?"

Hannan turned around to McKibben: "It wasn't the Racquet Club he crawled to--it was the Harvard Club. I'm sure he didn't belong to the Racquet."

"The paper said so," McKibben insisted.

"It must have been a mistake. I'm quite sure."

"Beaten to death in a speakeasy."

"But I happen to know most of the members of the Racquet Club," said Hannan. "It *must* have been the Harvard Club."

Dick got up, Tommy too. Prince Chillicheff started out of a wan study of nothing, perhaps of his chances of ever getting out of Russia, a study that had occupied him so long that it was doubtful if he could give it up immediately, and joined them in leaving.

"Abe North beaten to death."

On the way to the hotel, a journey of which Dick was scarcely aware, Tommy said:

"We're waiting for a tailor to finish some suits so we can get to Paris. I'm going into stock-broking and they wouldn't take me if I showed up like this. Everybody in your country is making millions. Are you really leaving to-morrow? We can't even have dinner with you. It seems the Prince had an old girl in Munich. He called her up but she'd been dead five years and we're having dinner with the two daughters."

The Prince nodded.

"Perhaps I could have arranged for Doctor Diver."

"No, no," said Dick hastily.

He slept deep and awoke to a slow mournful march passing his window. It was a long column of men in uniform, wearing the familiar helmet of 1914, thick men in frock coats and silk hats, burghers, aristocrats, plain men. It was a society of veterans going to lay wreaths on the tombs of the dead. The column marched slowly with a sort of swagger for a lost magnificence, a past effort, a forgotten sorrow. The faces were only formally sad but Dick's lungs burst for a moment with regret for Abe's death, and his own youth of ten years ago.

XVIII

He reached Innsbruck at dusk, sent his bags up to a hotel and walked into town. In the sunset the Emperor Maximilian knelt in prayer above his bronze mourners; a quartet of Jesuit novices paced and read in the university garden. The marble souvenirs of old sieges, marriages, anniversaries, faded quickly when the sun was down, and he had erbsen-suppe with würstchen cut up in it, drank four helles of Pilsener and refused a formidable dessert known as "kaiser-schmarren."

Despite the overhanging mountains Switzerland was far away, Nicole was far away. Walking in the garden later when it was quite dark he thought about her with detachment, loving her for her best self. He remembered once when the grass was damp and she came to him on hurried feet, her thin slippers drenched with dew. She stood upon his shoes nestling close and held up her face, showing it as a book open at a page.

"Think how you love me," she whispered. "I don't ask you to love me always like this, but I ask you to remember. Somewhere inside me there'll always be the person I am to-night."

But Dick had come away for his soul's sake, and he began thinking about that. He had lost himself--he could not tell the hour when, or the day or the week, the month or the year. Once he had cut through things, solving the most complicated equations as the simplest problems of his simplest patients. Between the time he found Nicole flowering under a stone on the Zurichsee and the moment of his meeting with Rosemary the spear had been blunted.

Watching his father's struggles in poor parishes had wedded a desire for money to an essentially unacquisitive nature. It was not a healthy necessity for security--he had never felt more sure of himself, more thoroughly his own man, than at the time of his marriage to Nicole. Yet he had been swallowed up like a gigolo, and somehow permitted his arsenal to be locked up in the Warren safety-deposit vaults.

"There should have been a settlement in the Continental style; but it isn't over yet. I've wasted eight years teaching the rich the ABC's of human decency, but I'm not done. I've got too many unplayed trumps in my hand."

He loitered among the fallow rose bushes and the beds of damp sweet indistinguishable fern. It was warm for October but cool enough to wear a heavy tweed coat buttoned by a little elastic tape at the neck. A figure detached itself from the black shape of a tree and he knew it was the woman whom he had passed in the lobby coming out. He was in love with every pretty woman he saw now, their forms at a distance, their shadows on a wall.

Her back was toward him as she faced the lights of the town. He scratched a match that she must have heard, but she remained motionless.

--Was it an invitation? Or an indication of obliviousness? He had long been outside of the world of simple desires and their fulfillments, and he was inept and uncertain. For all he knew there might be some code among the wanderers of obscure spas by which they found each other quickly.

--Perhaps the next gesture was his. Strange children should smile at each other and say, "Let's play."

He moved closer, the shadow moved sideways. Possibly he would be snubbed like the scapegrace drummers he had heard of in youth. His heart beat loud in contact with the unprobed, undissected, unanalyzed, unaccounted for. Suddenly he turned away, and, as he did, the girl, too, broke the black frieze she made with the foliage, rounded a bench at a moderate but determined pace and took the path back to the hotel.

With a guide and two other men, Dick started up the Birkkarspitze next morning. It was a fine feeling once they were above the cowbells of the highest pastures--Dick looked forward to the night in the shack, enjoying his own fatigue, enjoying the captaincy of the guide, feeling a delight in his own anonymity. But at mid-day the weather changed to black sleet and hail and mountain thunder. Dick and one of the other climbers wanted to go on but the guide refused. Regretfully they struggled back to Innsbruck to start again to-morrow.

After dinner and a bottle of heavy local wine in the deserted dining-room, he felt excited, without knowing why, until he began thinking of the garden. He had passed the girl in the lobby before supper and this time she had looked at him and approved of him, but it kept worrying him: Why? When I could have had a good share of the pretty women of my time for the asking, why start that now? With a wraith, with a fragment of my desire? Why?

His imagination pushed ahead--the old asceticism, the actual unfamiliarity, triumphed: God, I might as well go back to the Riviera and sleep with Janice Caricamento or the Wilburhazy girl. To belittle all these years with something cheap and easy?

He was still excited, though, and he turned from the veranda and went up to his room to think. Being alone in body and spirit begets loneliness, and loneliness begets more loneliness.

Upstairs he walked around thinking of the matter and laying out his climbing clothes advantageously on the faint heater; he again encountered Nicole's telegram, still unopened, with which diurnally she accompanied his itinerary. He had delayed opening it before supper--perhaps because of the garden. It was a cablegram from Buffalo, forwarded through Zurich.

"Your father died peacefully tonight. HOLMES."

He felt a sharp wince at the shock, a gathering of the forces of resistance; then it rolled up through his loins and stomach and throat.

He read the message again. He sat down on the bed, breathing and staring; thinking first the old selfish child's thought that comes with the death of a parent, how will it affect me now that this earliest and strongest of protections is gone?

The atavism passed and he walked the room still, stopping from time to time to look at the telegram. Holmes was formally his father's curate but actually, and for a decade, rector of the church. How did he die? Of old age--he was seventy-five. He had lived a long time.

Dick felt sad that he had died alone--he had survived his wife, and his brothers and sisters; there were cousins in Virginia but they were poor and not able to come North, and Holmes had had to sign the telegram. Dick loved his father--again and again he referred judgments to what his father would probably have thought or done. Dick was born several months after the death of two young sisters and his father, guessing what would be the effect on Dick's mother, had saved him from a spoiling by becoming his moral guide. He was of tired stock yet he raised himself to that effort.

In the summer father and son walked downtown together to have their shoes shined--Dick in his starched duck sailor suit, his father always in beautifully cut clerical clothes--and the father was very proud of his handsome little boy. He told Dick all he knew about life, not much but most of it true, simple things, matters of behavior that came within his clergyman's range. "Once in a strange town when I was first ordained, I went into a crowded room and was confused as to who was my hostess. Several people I knew came toward me, but I disregarded them because I had seen a gray-haired woman sitting by a window far across the room. I went over to her and introduced myself. After that I made many friends in that town."

His father had done that from a good heart--his father had been sure of what he was, with a deep pride of the two proud widows who had raised him to believe that nothing could be superior to "good instincts," honor, courtesy, and courage.

The father always considered that his wife's small fortune belonged to his son, and in college and in medical school sent him a check for all of it four times a year. He was one of those about whom it was said with smug finality in the gilded age: "very much the gentleman, but not much get-up-and-go about him."

. . . Dick sent down for a newspaper. Still pacing to and from the telegram open on his bureau, he chose a ship to go to America. Then he put in a call for Nicole in Zurich, remembering so many things as he waited, and wishing he had always been as good as he had intended to be.

XIX

For an hour, tied up with his profound reaction to his father's death, the magnificent façade of the homeland, the harbor of New York, seemed all sad and glorious to Dick, but once ashore the feeling vanished, nor did he find it again in the streets or the hotels or the trains that bore him first to Buffalo, and then south to Virginia with his father's body. Only as the local train shambled into the low-forested clayland of Westmoreland County, did he feel once more identified with his surroundings; at the station he saw a star he knew, and a cold moon bright over Chesapeake Bay; he heard the rasping wheels of buckboards turning, the lovely fatuous voices, the sound of sluggish primeval rivers flowing softly under soft Indian names.

Next day at the churchyard his father was laid among a hundred Divers, Dorseys, and Hunters. It was very friendly leaving him there with all his relations around him. Flowers were scattered on the brown unsettled earth. Dick had no more ties here now and did not believe he would come back. He knelt on the hard soil. These dead, he knew them all, their weather-beaten faces with blue flashing eyes, the spare violent bodies, the souls made of new earth in the forest-heavy darkness of the seventeenth century.

"Good-by, my father--good-by, all my fathers."

On the long-roofed steamship piers one is in a country that is no longer here and not yet there. The hazy yellow vault is full of echoing shouts. There are the rumble of trucks and the clump of trunks, the strident chatter of cranes, the first salt smell of the sea. One hurries through, even though there's time; the past, the continent, is behind; the future is the glowing mouth in the side of the ship; the dim, turbulent alley is too confusedly the present.

Up the gangplank and the vision of the world adjusts itself, narrows. One is a citizen of a commonwealth smaller than Andorra, no longer sure of anything. The men at the purser's desk are as oddly shaped as the cabins; disdainful are the eyes of voyagers and their friends. Next the loud mournful whistles, the portentous vibration and the boat, the human idea--is in motion. The pier and its faces slide by and for a moment the boat is a piece accidentally split off from them; the faces become remote, voiceless, the pier is one of many blurs along the water front. The harbor flows swiftly toward the sea.

With it flowed Albert McKisco, labelled by the newspapers as its most precious cargo. McKisco was having a vogue. His novels were pastiches of the work of the best people of his time, a feat not to be disparaged, and in addition he possessed a gift for softening and debasing what he borrowed, so that many readers were charmed by the ease with which they could follow him. Success had improved him and humbled him. He was no fool about his capacities--he realized that he possessed more vitality than many men of superior talent, and he was resolved to enjoy the success he had earned. "I've done nothing yet," he would say. "I don't think I've got any real genius. But if I keep trying I may write a good book." Fine dives have been made from flimsier spring-boards. The innumerable snubs of the past were forgotten. Indeed, his success was founded psychologically upon his duel with Tommy Barban, upon the basis of which, as it withered in his memory, he had created, afresh, a new self-respect.

Spotting Dick Diver the second day out, he eyed him tentatively, then introduced himself in a friendly way and sat down. Dick laid aside his reading and, after the few minutes that it took to realize the change in McKisco, the disappearance of the man's annoying sense of inferiority, found himself pleased to talk to him. McKisco was "well-informed" on a range of subjects wider than Goethe's--it was interesting to listen to the innumerable facile combinations that he referred to as his opinions. They struck up an acquaintance, and Dick had several meals with them. The McKiscos had been invited to sit at the captain's table but with nascent snobbery they told Dick that they "couldn't stand that bunch."

Violet was very grand now, decked out by the grand couturières, charmed about the little discoveries that well-bred girls make in their teens. She could, indeed, have learned them from her mother in Boise but her soul was born dismally in the small movie houses of Idaho, and she had had no time for her mother. Now she "belonged"--together with several million other people--and she was happy, though her husband still shushed her when she grew violently naïve.

The McKiscos got off at Gibraltar. Next evening in Naples Dick picked up a lost and miserable family of two girls and their mother in the bus from the hotel to the station. He had seen them on the ship. An overwhelming desire to help, or to be admired, came over him: he showed them fragments of gaiety; tentatively he bought them wine, with pleasure saw them begin to regain their proper egotism. He pretended they were this and that, and falling in with his own plot, and drinking too much to sustain the illusion, and all this time the women, thought only that this was a windfall from heaven. He withdrew from them as the night waned and the train rocked and snorted at Cassino and Frosinone. After weird American partings in the station at Rome, Dick went to the Hotel Quirinal, somewhat exhausted.

At the desk he suddenly stared and upped his head. As if a drink were acting on him, warming the lining of his stomach, throwing a flush up into his brain, he saw the person he had come to see, the person for whom he had made the Mediterranean crossing.

Simultaneously Rosemary saw him, acknowledging him before placing him; she looked back startled, and, leaving the girl she was with, she hurried over. Holding himself erect, holding his breath, Dick turned to her. As she came across the lobby, her beauty all groomed, like a young horse dosed with Blackseed oil, and hoops varnished, shocked him awake; but it all came too quick for him to do anything except conceal his fatigue as best he could. To meet her starry-eyed confidence he mustered an insincere pantomime implying, "You *would* turn up here--of all the people in the world."

Her gloved hands closed over his on the desk; "Dick--we're making *The Grandeur that was Rome*--at least we think we are; we may quit any day."

He looked at her hard, trying to make her a little self-conscious, so that she would observe less closely his unshaven face, his crumpled and slept-in collar. Fortunately, she was in a hurry.

"We begin early because the mists rise at eleven--phone me at two."

In his room Dick collected his faculties. He left a call for noon, stripped off his clothes and dove literally into a heavy sleep.

He slept over the phone call but awoke at two, refreshed. Unpacking his bag, he sent out suits and laundry. He shaved, lay for half an hour in a warm bath and had breakfast. The sun had dipped into the Via Nazionale and he let it through the portières with a jingling of old brass rings. Waiting for a suit to be pressed, he discovered from the Corriere della Sera that "una novella di Sinclair Lewis 'Wall Street' nella quale autore analizza la vita sociale di una piccola citta Americana." Then he tried to think about Rosemary.

At first he thought nothing. She was young and magnetic, but so was Topsy. He guessed that she had had lovers and had loved them in the last four years. Well, you never knew exactly how much space you occupied in people's lives. Yet from this fog his affection emerged--the best contacts are when one knows the obstacles and still wants to preserve a relation. The past drifted back and he wanted to hold her eloquent giving-of-herself in its precious shell, till he enclosed it, till it no longer existed outside him. He tried to collect all that might attract her--it was less than it had been four years ago. Eighteen might look at thirty-four through a rising mist of adolescence; but twenty-two would see thirty-eight with discerning clarity. Moreover, Dick had been at an emotional peak at the time of the previous encounter; since then there had been a lesion of enthusiasm.

When the valet returned he put on a white shirt and collar and a black tie with a pearl; the cords of his reading-glasses passed through another pearl of the same size that swung a casual inch below. After sleep, his face had resumed the ruddy brown of many Riviera summers, and to limber himself up he stood on his hands on a chair until his fountain pen and coins fell out. At three he called Rosemary and was bidden to come up. Momentarily dizzy from his acrobatics, he stopped in the bar for a gin-and-tonic.

"Hi, Doctor Diver!"

Only because of Rosemary's presence in the hotel did Dick place the man immediately as Collis Clay. He had his old confidence and an air of prosperity and big sudden jowls.

"Do you know Rosemary's here?" Collis asked.

"I ran into her."

"I was in Florence and I heard she was here so I came down last week. You'd never know Mama's little girl." He modified the remark, "I mean she was so carefully brought up and now she's a woman of the world--if you know what I mean. Believe me, has she got some of these Roman boys tied up in bags! And how!"

"You studying in Florence?"

"Me? Sure, I'm studying architecture there. I go back Sunday--I'm staying for the races."

With difficulty Dick restrained him from adding the drink to the account he carried in the bar, like a stock-market report.

XX

When Dick got out of the elevator he followed a tortuous corridor and turned at length toward a distant voice outside a lighted door. Rosemary was in black pajamas; a luncheon table was still in the room; she was having coffee.

"You're still beautiful," he said. "A little more beautiful than ever."

"Do you want coffee, youngster?"

"I'm sorry I was so unpresentable this morning."

"You didn't look well--you all right now? Want coffee?"

"No, thanks."

"You're fine again, I was scared this morning. Mother's coming over next month, if the company stays. She always asks me if I've seen you over here, as if she thought we were living next door. Mother always liked you--she always felt you were some one I ought to know."

"Well, I'm glad she still thinks of me."

"Oh, she does," Rosemary reassured him. "A very great deal."

"I've seen you here and there in pictures," said Dick. "Once I had *Daddy's Girl* run off just for myself!"

"I have a good part in this one if it isn't cut."

She crossed behind him, touching his shoulder as she passed. She phoned for the table to be taken away and settled in a big chair.

"I was just a little girl when I met you, Dick. Now I'm a woman."

"I want to hear everything about you."

"How is Nicole--and Lanier and Topsy?"

"They're fine. They often speak of you--"

The phone rang. While she answered it Dick examined two novels--one by Edna Ferber, one by Albert McKisco. The waiter came for the table; bereft of its presence Rosemary seemed more alone in her black pajamas.

". . . I have a caller. . . . No, not very well. I've got to go to the costumer's for a long fitting. . . . No, not now . . ."

As though with the disappearance of the table she felt released, Rosemary smiled at Dick--that smile as if they two together had managed to get rid of all the trouble in the world and were now at peace in their own heaven . . .

"That's done," she said. "Do you realize I've spent the last hour getting ready for you?"

But again the phone called her. Dick got up to change his hat from the bed to the luggage stand, and in alarm Rosemary put her hand over the mouthpiece of the phone. "You're not going!"

"No."

When the communication was over he tried to drag the afternoon together saying: "I expect some nourishment from people now."

"Me too," Rosemary agreed. "The man that just phoned me once knew a second cousin of mine. Imagine calling anybody up for a reason like that!"

Now she lowered the lights for love. Why else should she want to shut off his view of her? He sent his words to her like letters, as though they left him some time before they reached her.

"Hard to sit here and be close to you, and not kiss you." Then they kissed passionately in the centre of the floor. She pressed against him, and went back to her chair.

It could not go on being merely pleasant in the room. Forward or backward; when the phone rang once more he strolled into the bedchamber and lay down on her bed, opening Albert McKisco's novel. Presently Rosemary came in and sat beside him.

"You have the longest eyelashes," she remarked.

"We are now back at the Junior Prom. Among those present are Miss Rosemary Hoyt, the eyelash fancier--"

She kissed him and he pulled her down so that they lay side by side, and then they kissed till they were both breathless. Her breathing was young and eager and exciting. Her lips were faintly chapped but soft in the corners.

When they were still limbs and feet and clothes, struggles of his arms and back, and her throat and breasts, she whispered, "No, not now--those things are rhythmic."

Disciplined he crushed his passion into a corner of his mind, but bearing up her fragility on his arms until she was poised half a foot above him, he said lightly:

"Darling--that doesn't matter."

Her face had changed with his looking up at it; there was the eternal moonlight in it.

"That would be poetic justice if it should be you," she said. She twisted away from him, walked to the mirror, and boxed her disarranged hair with her hands. Presently she drew a chair close to the bed and stroked his cheek.

"Tell me the truth about you," he demanded.

"I always have."

"In a way--but nothing hangs together."

They both laughed but he pursued.

"Are you actually a virgin?"

"No-o-o!" she sang. "I've slept with six hundred and forty men--if that's the answer you want."

"It's none of my business."

"Do you want me for a case in psychology?"

"Looking at you as a perfectly normal girl of twenty-two, living in the year nineteen twenty-eight, I guess you've taken a few shots at love."

"It's all been--abortive," she said.

Dick couldn't believe her. He could not decide whether she was deliberately building a barrier between them or whether this was intended to make an eventual surrender more significant.

"Let's go walk in the Pincio," he suggested.

He shook himself straight in his clothes and smoothed his hair. A moment had come and somehow passed. For three years Dick had been the ideal by which Rosemary measured other men and inevitably his stature had increased to heroic size. She did not want him to be like other men, yet here were the same exigent demands, as if he wanted to take some of herself away, carry it off in his pocket.

Walking on the greensward between cherubs and philosophers, fauns and falling water, she took his arm snugly, settling into it with a series of little readjustments, as if she wanted it to be right because it was going to be there forever. She plucked a twig and broke it, but she found no spring in it. Suddenly seeing what she wanted in Dick's face she took his gloved hand and kissed it. Then she cavorted childishly for him until he smiled and she laughed and they began having a good time.

"I can't go out with you to-night, darling, because I promised some people a long time ago. But if you'll get up early I'll take you out to the set to-morrow."

He dined alone at the hotel, went to bed early, and met Rosemary in the lobby at half-past six. Beside him in the car she glowed away fresh and new in the morning sunshine. They went out through the Porta San Sebastiano and along the Appian Way until they came to the huge set of the forum, larger than the forum itself. Rosemary turned him over to a man who led him about the great props; the arches and tiers of seats and the sanded arena. She was working on a stage which represented a guard-room for Christian prisoners, and presently they went there and watched Nicotera, one of many hopeful Valentinos, strut and pose before a dozen female "captives," their eyes melancholy and startling with mascara.

Rosemary appeared in a knee-length tunic.

"Watch this," she whispered to Dick. "I want your opinion. Everybody that's seen the rushes says--"

"What are the rushes?"

"When they run off what they took the day before. They say it's the first thing I've had sex appeal in."

"I don't notice it."

"You wouldn't! But I have."

Nicotera in his leopard skin talked attentively to Rosemary while the electrician discussed something with the director, meanwhile leaning on him. Finally the director pushed his hand off roughly and wiped a sweating forehead, and Dick's guide remarked: "He's on the hop again, and how!"

"Who?" asked Dick, but before the man could answer the director walked swiftly over to them.

"Who's on the hop--you're on the hop yourself." He spoke vehemently to Dick, as if to a jury. "When he's on the hop he always thinks everybody else is, and how!" He glared at the guide a moment longer, then he clapped his hands: "All right--everybody on the set."

It was like visiting a great turbulent family. An actress approached Dick and talked to him for five minutes under the impression that he was an actor recently arrived from London. Discovering her mistake she scuttled away in panic. The majority of the company felt either sharply superior or sharply inferior to the world outside, but the former feeling prevailed. They were people of bravery and industry; they were risen to a position of prominence in a nation that for a decade had wanted only to be entertained.

The session ended as the light grew misty--a fine light for painters, but, for the camera, not to be compared with the clear California air. Nicotera followed Rosemary to the car and whispered something to her--she looked at him without smiling as she said good-by.

Dick and Rosemary had luncheon at the Castelli dei Cæsari, a splendid restaurant in a high-terraced villa overlooking the ruined forum of an undetermined period of the decadence. Rosemary took a cocktail and a little wine, and Dick took enough so that his feeling of dissatisfaction left him. Afterward they drove back to the hotel, all flushed and happy, in a sort of exalted quiet. She wanted to be taken and she was, and what had begun with a childish infatuation on a beach was accomplished at last.

XXI

Rosemary had another dinner date, a birthday party for a member of the company. Dick ran into Collis Clay in the lobby, but he wanted to dine alone, and pretended an engagement at the Excelsior. He drank a cocktail with Collis and his vague dissatisfaction crystallized as impatience--he no longer had an excuse for playing truant to the clinic. This was less an infatuation than a romantic memory. Nicole was his girl--too often he was sick at heart about her, yet she was his girl. Time with Rosemary was self-indulgence--time with Collis was nothing plus nothing.

In the doorway of the Excelsior he ran into Baby Warren. Her large beautiful eyes, looking precisely like marbles, stared at him with surprise and curiosity. "I thought you were in America, Dick! Is Nicole with you?"

"I came back by way of Naples."

The black band on his arm reminded her to say: "I'm so sorry to hear of your trouble."

Inevitably they dined together.

"Tell me about everything," she demanded.

Dick gave her a version of the facts, and Baby frowned. She found it necessary to blame some one for the catastrophe in her sister's life.

"Do you think Doctor Dohmler took the right course with her from the first?"

"There's not much variety in treatment any more--of course you try to find the right personality to handle a particular case."

"Dick, I don't pretend to advise you or to know much about it but don't you think a change might be good for her--to get out of that atmosphere of sickness and live in the world like other people?"

"But you were keen for the clinic," he reminded her. "You told me you'd never feel really safe about her--"

"That was when you were leading that hermit's life on the Riviera, up on a hill way off from anybody. I didn't mean to go back to that life. I meant, for instance, London. The English are the best-balanced race in the world."

"They are not," he disagreed.

"They are. I know them, you see. I meant it might be nice for you to take a house in London for the spring season--I know a dove of a house in Talbot Square you could get, furnished. I mean, living with sane, well-balanced English people."

She would have gone on to tell him all the old propaganda stories of 1914 if he had not laughed and said:

"I've been reading a book by Michael Arlen and if that's--"

She ruined Michael Arlen with a wave of her salad spoon.

"He only writes about degenerates. I mean the worthwhile English."

As she thus dismissed her friends they were replaced in Dick's mind only by a picture of the alien, unresponsive faces that peopled the small hotels of Europe.

"Of course it's none of my business," Baby repeated, as a preliminary to a further plunge, "but to leave her alone in an atmosphere like that--"

"I went to America because my father died."

"I understand that, I told you how sorry I was." She fiddled with the glass grapes on her necklace. "But there's so *much* money now. Plenty for everything, and it ought to be used to get Nicole well."

"For one thing I can't see myself in London."

"Why not? I should think you could work there as well as anywhere else."

He sat back and looked at her. If she had ever suspected the rotted old truth, the real reason for Nicole's illness, she had certainly determined to deny it to herself, shoving it back in a dusty closet like one of the paintings she bought by mistake.

They continued the conversation in the Ulpia, where Collis Clay came over to their table and sat down, and a gifted guitar player thrummed and rumbled "Suona Fanfara Mia" in the cellar piled with wine casks.

"It's possible that I was the wrong person for Nicole," Dick said. "Still she would probably have married some one of my type, some one she thought she could rely on--indefinitely."

"You think she'd be happier with somebody else?" Baby thought aloud suddenly. "Of course it could be arranged."

Only as she saw Dick bend forward with helpless laughter did she realize the preposterousness of her remark.

"Oh, you understand," she assured him. "Don't think for a moment that we're not grateful for all you've done. And we know you've had a hard time--"

"For God's sake," he protested. "If I didn't love Nicole it might be different."

"But you do love Nicole?" she demanded in alarm.

Collis was catching up with the conversation now and Dick switched it quickly: "Suppose we talk about something else--about you, for instance. Why don't you get married? We heard you were engaged to Lord Paley, the cousin of the--"

"Oh, no." She became coy and elusive. "That was last year."

"Why don't you marry?" Dick insisted stubbornly.

"I don't know. One of the men I loved was killed in the war, and the other one threw me over."

"Tell me about it. Tell me about your private life, Baby, and your opinions. You never do--we always talk about Nicole."

"Both of them were Englishmen. I don't think there's any higher type in the world than a first-rate Englishman, do you? If there is I haven't met him. This man--oh, it's a long story. I hate long stories, don't you?"

"And how!" said Collis.

"Why, no--I like them if they're good."

"That's something you do so well, Dick. You can keep a party moving by just a little sentence or a saying here and there. I think that's a wonderful talent."

"It's a trick," he said gently. That made three of her opinions he disagreed with.

"Of course I like formality--I like things to be just so, and on the grand scale. I know you probably don't but you must admit it's a sign of solidity in me."

Dick did not even bother to dissent from this.

"Of course I know people say, Baby Warren is racing around over Europe, chasing one novelty after another, and missing the best things in life, but I think on the contrary that I'm one of the few people who really go after the best things. I've known the most interesting people of my time." Her voice blurred with the tinny drumming of another guitar number, but she called over it, "I've made very few big mistakes--"

"--Only the very big ones, Baby."

She had caught something facetious in his eye and she changed the subject. It seemed impossible for them to hold anything in common. But he admired something in her, and he deposited her at the Excelsior with a series of compliments that left her shimmering.

Rosemary insisted on treating Dick to lunch next day. They went to a little *trattoria* kept by an Italian who had worked in America, and ate ham and eggs and waffles. Afterward, they went to the hotel. Dick's discovery that he was not in love with her, nor she with him, had added to rather than diminished his passion for her. Now that he knew he would not enter further into her life, she became the strange woman for him. He supposed many men meant no more than that when they said they were in love--not a wild submergence of soul, a dipping of all colors into an obscuring dye, such as his love for Nicole had been. Certain thoughts about Nicole, that she should die, sink into mental darkness, love another man, made him physically sick.

Nicotera was in Rosemary's sitting-room, chattering about a professional matter. When Rosemary gave him his cue to go, he left with humorous protests and a rather insolent wink at Dick. As usual the phone clamored and Rosemary was engaged at it for ten minutes, to Dick's increasing impatience.

"Let's go up to my room," he suggested, and she agreed.

She lay across his knees on a big sofa; he ran his fingers through the lovely forelocks of her hair.

"Let me be curious about you again?" he asked.

"What do you want to know?"

"About men. I'm curious, not to say prurient."

"You mean how long after I met you?"

"Or before."

"Oh, no." She was shocked. "There was nothing before. You were the first man I cared about. You're still the only man I really care about." She considered. "It was about a year, I think."

"Who was it?"

"Oh, a man."

He closed in on her evasion.

"I'll bet I can tell you about it: the first affair was unsatisfactory and after that there was a long gap. The second was better, but you hadn't been in love with the man in the first place. The third was all right--"

Torturing himself he ran on. "Then you had one real affair that fell of its own weight, and by that time you were getting afraid that you wouldn't have anything to give to the man you finally loved." He felt increasingly Victorian. "Afterwards there were half a dozen just episodic affairs, right up to the present. Is that close?"

She laughed between amusement and tears.

"It's about as wrong as it could be," she said, to Dick's relief. "But some day I'm going to find somebody and love him and love him and never let him go."

Now his phone rang and Dick recognized Nicotera's voice, asking for Rosemary. He put his palm over the transmitter.

"Do you want to talk to him?"

She went to the phone and jabbered in a rapid Italian Dick could not understand.

"This telephoning takes time," he said. "It's after four and I have an engagement at five. You better go play with Signor Nicotera."

"Don't be silly."

"Then I think that while I'm here you ought to count him out."

"It's difficult." She was suddenly crying. "Dick, I do love you, never anybody like you. But what have you got for me?"

"What has Nicotera got for anybody?"

"That's different."

--Because youth called to youth.

"He's a spic!" he said. He was frantic with jealousy, he didn't want to be hurt again.

"He's only a baby," she said, sniffling. "You know I'm yours first."

In reaction he put his arms about her but she relaxed wearily backward; he held her like that for a moment as in the end of an adagio, her eyes closed, her hair falling straight back like that of a girl drowned.

"Dick, let me go. I never felt so mixed up in my life."

He was a gruff red bird and instinctively she drew away from him as his unjustified jealousy began to snow over the qualities of consideration and understanding with which she felt at home.

"I want to know the truth," he said.

"Yes, then. We're a lot together, he wants to marry me, but I don't want to. What of it? What do you expect me to do? You never asked me to marry you. Do you want me to play around forever with half-wits like Collis Clay?"

"You were with Nicotera last night?"

"That's none of your business," she sobbed. "Excuse me, Dick, it is your business. You and Mother are the only two people in the world I care about."

"How about Nicotera?"

"How do I know?"

She had achieved the elusiveness that gives hidden significance to the least significant remarks.

"Is it like you felt toward me in Paris?"

"I feel comfortable and happy when I'm with you. In Paris it was different. But you never know how you once felt. Do you?"

He got up and began collecting his evening clothes--if he had to bring all the bitterness and hatred of the world into his heart, he was not going to be in love with her again.

"I don't care about Nicotera!" she declared. "But I've got to go to Livorno with the company to-morrow. Oh, why did this have to happen?" There was a new flood of tears. "It's such a shame. Why did you come here? Why couldn't we just have the memory anyhow? I feel as if I'd quarrelled with Mother."

As he began to dress, she got up and went to the door.

"I won't go to the party to-night." It was her last effort. "I'll stay with you. I don't want to go anyhow."

The tide began to flow again, but he retreated from it.

"I'll be in my room," she said. "Good-by, Dick."

"Good-by."

"Oh, such a shame, such a shame. Oh, such a shame. What's it all about anyhow?"

"I've wondered for a long time."

"But why bring it to me?"

"I guess I'm the Black Death," he said slowly. "I don't seem to bring people happiness any more."

XXII

There were five people in the Quirinal bar after dinner, a high-class Italian frail who sat on a stool making persistent conversation against the bartender's bored: "Si . . . Si . . . Si," a light, snobbish Egyptian who was lonely but chary of the woman, and the two Americans.

Dick was always vividly conscious of his surroundings, while Collis Clay lived vaguely, the sharpest impressions dissolving upon a recording apparatus that had early atrophied, so the former talked and the latter listened, like a man sitting in a breeze.

Dick, worn away by the events of the afternoon, was taking it out on the inhabitants of Italy. He looked around the bar as if he hoped an Italian had heard him and would resent his words.

"This afternoon I had tea with my sister-in-law at the Excelsior. We got the last table and two men came up and looked around for a table and couldn't find one. So one of them came up to us and said, 'Isn't this table reserved for the Princess Orsini?' and I said: 'There was no sign on it,' and he said: 'But I think it's reserved for the Princess Orsini.' I couldn't even answer him."

"What'd he do?"

"He retired." Dick switched around in his chair. "I don't like these people. The other day I left Rosemary for two minutes in front of a store and an officer started walking up and down in front of her, tipping his hat."

"I don't know," said Collis after a moment. "I'd rather be here than up in Paris with somebody picking your pocket every minute."

He had been enjoying himself, and he held out against anything that threatened to dull his pleasure.

"I don't know," he persisted. "I don't mind it here."

Dick evoked the picture that the few days had imprinted on his mind, and stared at it. The walk toward the American Express past the odorous confectioneries of the Via Nationale, through the foul tunnel up to the Spanish Steps, where his spirit soared before the flower stalls and the house where Keats had died. He cared only about people; he was scarcely conscious of places except for their weather, until they had been invested with color by tangible events. Rome was the end of his dream of Rosemary.

A bell-boy came in and gave him a note.

"I did not go to the party," it said. *"I am in my room. We leave for Livorno early in the morning."*

Dick handed the note and a tip to the boy.

"Tell Miss Hoyt you couldn't find me." Turning to Collis he suggested the Bonbonieri.

They inspected the tart at the bar, granting her the minimum of interest exacted by her profession, and she stared back with bright boldness; they went through the deserted lobby oppressed by draperies holding Victorian dust in stuffy folds, and they nodded at the night concierge who returned the gesture with the bitter servility peculiar to night servants. Then in a taxi they rode along cheerless streets through a dank November night. There were no women in the streets, only pale men with dark coats buttoned to the neck, who stood in groups beside shoulders of cold stone.

"My God!" Dick sighed.

"What's a matter?"

"I was thinking of that man this afternoon: 'This table is reserved for the Princess Orsini.' Do you know what these old Roman families are? They're bandits, they're the ones who got possession of the temples and palaces after Rome went to pieces and preyed on the people."

"I like Rome," insisted Collis. "Why won't you try the races?"

"I don't like races."

"But all the women turn out--"

"I know I wouldn't like anything here. I like France, where everybody thinks he's Napoleon--down here everybody thinks he's Christ."

At the Bonbonieri they descended to a panelled cabaret, hopelessly impermanent amid the cold stone. A listless band played a tango and a dozen couples covered the wide floor with those elaborate and dainty steps so offensive to the American eye. A surplus of waiters precluded the stir and bustle that even a few busy men can create; over the scene as its form of animation brooded an air of waiting for something, for the dance, the night, the balance of forces which kept it stable, to cease. It assured the impressionable guest that whatever he was seeking he would not find it here.

This was plain as plain to Dick. He looked around, hoping his eye would catch on something, so that spirit instead of imagination could carry on for an hour. But there was nothing and after a moment he turned back to Collis. He had told Collis some of his current notions, and he was bored with his audience's short memory and lack of response. After half an hour of Collis he felt a distinct lesion of his own vitality.

They drank a bottle of Italian mousseaux, and Dick became pale and somewhat noisy. He called the orchestra leader over to their table; this was a Bahama Negro, conceited and unpleasant, and in a few minutes there was a row.

"You asked me to sit down."

"All right. And I gave you fifty lire, didn't I?"

"All right. All right. All right."

"All right, I gave you fifty lire, didn't I? Then you come up and asked me to put some more in the horn!"

"You asked me to sit down, didn't you? Didn't you?"

"I asked you to sit down but I gave you fifty lire, didn't I?"

"All right. All right."

The Negro got up sourly and went away, leaving Dick in a still more evil humor. But he saw a girl smiling at him from across the room and immediately the pale Roman shapes around him receded into decent, humble perspective. She was a young English girl, with blonde hair and a healthy, pretty English face and she smiled at him again with an invitation he understood, that denied the flesh even in the act of tendering it.

"There's a quick trick or else I don't know bridge," said Collis.

Dick got up and walked to her across the room.

"Won't you dance?"

The middle-aged Englishman with whom she was sitting said, almost apologetically: "I'm going out soon."

Sobered by excitement Dick danced. He found in the girl a suggestion of all the pleasant English things; the story of safe gardens ringed around by the sea was implicit in her bright voice and as he leaned back to look at her, he meant what he said to her so sincerely that his voice trembled. When her current escort should leave, she promised to come and sit with them. The Englishman accepted her return with repeated apologies and smiles.

Back at his table Dick ordered another bottle of spumante.

"She looks like somebody in the movies," he said. "I can't think who." He glanced impatiently over his shoulder. "Wonder what's keeping her?"

"I'd like to get in the movies," said Collis thoughtfully. "I'm supposed to go into my father's business but it doesn't appeal to me much. Sit in an office in Birmingham for twenty years--"

His voice resisted the pressure of materialistic civilization.

"Too good for it?" suggested Dick.

"No, I don't mean that."

"Yes, you do."

"How do you know what I mean? Why don't you practise as a doctor, if you like to work so much?"

Dick had made them both wretched by this time, but simultaneously they had become vague with drink and in a moment they forgot; Collis left, and they shook hands warmly.

"Think it over," said Dick sagely.

"Think what over?"

"You know." It had been something about Collis going into his father's business--good sound advice.

Clay walked off into space. Dick finished his bottle and then danced with the English girl again, conquering his unwilling body with bold revolutions and stern determined marches down the floor. The most remarkable thing suddenly happened. He was dancing with the girl, the music stopped--and she had disappeared.

"Have you seen her?"

"Seen who?"

"The girl I was dancing with. Su'nly disappeared. Must be in the building."

"No! No! That's the ladies' room."

He stood up by the bar. There were two other men there, but he could think of no way of starting a conversation. He could have told them all about Rome and the violent origins of the Colonna and Gaetani families but he realized that as a beginning that would be somewhat abrupt. A row of Yenci dolls on the cigar counter fell suddenly to the floor; there was a subsequent confusion and he had a sense of having been the cause of it, so he went back to the cabaret and drank a cup of black coffee. Collis was gone and the English girl was gone and there seemed nothing to do but go back to the hotel and lie down with his black heart. He paid his check and got his hat and coat.

There was dirty water in the gutters and between the rough cobblestones; a marshy vapor from the Campagna, a sweat of exhausted cultures tainted the morning air. A quartet of taxi-drivers, their little eyes bobbing in dark pouches, surrounded him. One who leaned insistently in his face he pushed harshly away.

"Quanto a Hotel Quirinal?"

"Cento lire."

Six dollars. He shook his head and offered thirty lire which was twice the day-time fare, but they shrugged their shoulders as one pair, and moved off.

"Trente-cinque lire e mancie," he said firmly.

"Cento lire."

He broke into English.

"To go half a mile? You'll take me for forty lire."

"Oh, no."

He was very tired. He pulled open the door of a cab and got in.

"Hotel Quirinal!" he said to the driver who stood obstinately outside the window. "Wipe that sneer off your face and take me to the Quirinal."

"Ah, no."

Dick got out. By the door of the Bonbonieri some one was arguing with the taxi-drivers, some one who now tried to explain their attitude to Dick; again one of the men pressed close, insisting and gesticulating and Dick shoved him away.

"I want to go to the Quirinal Hotel."

"He says wan huner lire," explained the interpreter.

"I understand. I'll give him fif'y lire. Go on away." This last to the insistent man who had edged up once more. The man looked at him and spat contemptuously.

The passionate impatience of the week leaped up in Dick and clothed itself like a flash in violence, the honorable, the traditional resource of his land; he stepped forward and slapped the man's face.

They surged about him, threatening, waving their arms, trying ineffectually to close in on him--with his back against the wall Dick hit out clumsily, laughing a little and for a few minutes the mock fight, an affair of foiled rushes and padded, glancing blows, swayed back and forth in front of the door. Then Dick tripped and fell; he was hurt somewhere but he struggled up again wrestling in arms that suddenly broke apart. There was a new voice and a new argument but he leaned against the wall, panting and furious at the indignity of his position. He saw there was no sympathy for him but he was unable to believe that he was wrong.

They were going to the police station and settle it there. His hat was retrieved and handed to him, and with some one holding his arm lightly he strode around the corner with the taxi-men and entered a bare barrack where carabinieri lounged under a single dim light.

At a desk sat a captain, to whom the officious individual who had stopped the battle spoke at length in Italian, at times pointing at Dick, and letting himself be interrupted by the taxi-men who delivered short bursts of invective and denunciation. The captain began to nod impatiently. He held up his hand and the hydra-headed address, with a few parting exclamations, died away. Then he turned to Dick.

"Spick Italiano?" he asked.

"No."

"Spick Français?"

"Oui," said Dick, glowering.

"Alors. Écoute. Va au Quirinal. Espèce d'endormi. Écoute: vous êtes saoûl. Payez ce que le chauffeur demande. Comprenez-vous?"

Diver shook his head.

"Non, je ne veux pas."

"Come?"

"Je paierai quarante lires. C'est bien assez."

The captain stood up.

"Écoute!" he cried portentously. "Vous êtes saoûl. Vous avez battu le chauffeur. Comme ci, comme ça." He struck the air excitedly with right hand and left,

"C'est bon que je vous donne la liberté. Payez ce qu'il a dit--cento lire. Va au Quirinal."

Raging with humiliation, Dick stared back at him.

"All right." He turned blindly to the door--before him, leering and nodding, was the man who had brought him to the police station. "I'll go home," he shouted, "but first I'll fix this baby."

He walked past the staring carabinieri and up to the grinning face, hit it with a smashing left beside the jaw. The man dropped to the floor.

For a moment he stood over him in savage triumph--but even as a first pang of doubt shot through him the world reeled; he was clubbed down, and fists and boots beat on him in a savage tattoo. He felt his nose break like a shingle and his eyes jerk as if they had snapped back on a rubber band into his head. A rib splintered under a stamping heel. Momentarily he lost consciousness, regained it as he was raised to a sitting position and his wrists jerked together with handcuffs. He struggled automatically. The plainclothes lieutenant whom he had knocked down, stood dabbing his jaw with a handkerchief and looking into it for blood; he came over to Dick, poised himself, drew back his arm and smashed him to the floor.

When Doctor Diver lay quite still a pail of water was sloshed over him. One of his eyes opened dimly as he was being dragged along by the wrists through a bloody haze and he made out the human and ghastly face of one of the taxi-drivers.

"Go to the Excelsior hotel," he cried faintly. "Tell Miss Warren. Two hundred lire! Miss Warren. Due centi lire! Oh, you dirty--you God--"

Still he was dragged along through the bloody haze, choking and sobbing, over vague irregular surfaces into some small place where he was dropped upon a stone floor. The men went out, a door clanged, he was alone.

XXIII

Until one o'clock Baby Warren lay in bed, reading one of Marion Crawford's curiously inanimate Roman stories; then she went to a window and looked down into the street. Across from the hotel two carabinieri, grotesque in swaddling capes and harlequin hats, swung voluminously from this side and that, like mains'ls coming about, and watching them she thought of the guards' officer who had stared at her so intensely at lunch. He had possessed the arrogance of a tall member of a short race, with no obligation save to be tall. Had he come up to her and said: "Let's go along, you and I," she would have answered: "Why not?"--at least it seemed so now, for she was still disembodied by an unfamiliar background.

Her thoughts drifted back slowly through the guardsman to the two carabinieri, to Dick--she got into bed and turned out the light.

A little before four she was awakened by a brusque knocking.

"Yes--what is it?"

"It's the concierge, Madame."

She pulled on her kimono and faced him sleepily.

"Your friend name Deever he's in trouble. He had trouble with the police, and they have him in the jail. He sent a taxi up to tell, the driver says that he promised him two hundred lire." He paused cautiously for this to be approved. "The driver says Mr. Deever in the bad trouble. He had a fight with the police and is terribly bad hurt."

"I'll be right down."

She dressed to an accompaniment of anxious heartbeats and ten minutes later stepped out of the elevator into the dark lobby. The chauffeur who brought the message was gone; the concierge hailed another one and told him the location of the jail. As they rode, the darkness lifted and thinned outside and Baby's nerves, scarcely awake, cringed faintly at the unstable balance between night and day. She began to race against the day; sometimes on the broad avenues she gained but whenever the thing that was pushing up paused for a moment, gusts of wind blew here and there impatiently and the slow creep of light began once more. The cab went past a loud fountain splashing in a voluminous shadow, turned into an alley so curved that the buildings were warped and strained following it, bumped and rattled over cobblestones, and stopped with a jerk where two sentry boxes were bright against a wall of green damp. Suddenly from the violet darkness of an archway came Dick's voice, shouting and screaming.

"Are there any English? Are there any Americans? Are there any English? Are there any--oh, my God! You dirty Wops!"

His voice died away and she heard a dull sound of beating on the door. Then the voice began again.

"Are there any Americans? Are there any English?"

Following the voice she ran through the arch into a court, whirled about in momentary confusion and located the small guard-room whence the cries came. Two carabinieri started to their feet, but Baby brushed past them to the door of the cell.

"Dick!" she called. "What's the trouble?"

"They've put out my eye," he cried. "They handcuffed me and then they beat me, the goddamn--the--"

Flashing around Baby took a step toward the two carabinieri.

"What have you done to him?" she whispered so fiercely that they flinched before her gathering fury.

"Non capisco inglese."

In French she execrated them; her wild, confident rage filled the room, enveloped them until they shrank and wriggled from the garments of blame with which she invested them. "Do something! Do something!"

"We can do nothing until we are ordered."

"Bene. *Bay-nay! Bene!*"

Once more Baby let her passion scorch around them until they sweated out apologies for their impotence, looking at each other with the sense that something had after all gone terribly wrong. Baby went to the cell door, leaned against it, almost caressing it, as if that could make Dick feel her presence and power, and cried: "I'm going to the Embassy, I'll be back." Throwing a last glance of infinite menace at the carabinieri she ran out.

She drove to the American Embassy where she paid off the taxi-driver upon his insistence. It was still dark when she ran up the steps and pressed the bell. She had pressed it three times before a sleepy English porter opened the door to her.

"I want to see some one," she said. "Any one--but right away."

"No one's awake, Madame. We don't open until nine o'clock."

Impatiently she waved the hour away.

"This is important. A man--an American has been terribly beaten. He's in an Italian jail."

"No one's awake now. At nine o'clock--"

"I can't wait. They've put out a man's eye--my brother-in-law, and they won't let him out of jail. I must talk to some one--can't you see? Are you crazy? Are you an idiot, you stand there with that look in your face?"

"Hime unable to do anything, Madame."

"You've got to wake some one up!" She seized him by the shoulders and jerked him violently. "It's a matter of life and death. If you won't wake some one a terrible thing will happen to you--"

"Kindly don't lay hands on me, Madame."

From above and behind the porter floated down a weary Groton voice.

"What is it there?"

The porter answered with relief.

"It's a lady, sir, and she has shook me." He had stepped back to speak and Baby pushed forward into the hall. On an upper landing, just aroused from sleep and wrapped in a white embroidered Persian robe, stood a singular young man. His face was of a monstrous and unnatural pink, vivid yet dead, and over his mouth was fastened what appeared to be a gag. When he saw Baby he moved his head back into a shadow.

"What is it?" he repeated.

Baby told him, in her agitation edging forward to the stairs. In the course of her story she realized that the gag was in reality a mustache bandage and that the man's face was covered with pink cold cream, but the fact fitted quietly into the nightmare. The thing to do, she cried passionately, was for him to come to the jail with her at once and get Dick out.

"It's a bad business," he said.

"Yes," she agreed conciliatingly. "Yes?"

"This trying to fight the police." A note of personal affront crept into his voice, "I'm afraid there's nothing to be done until nine o'clock."

"Till nine o'clock," she repeated aghast. "But you can do something, certainly! You can come to the jail with me and see that they don't hurt him any more."

"We aren't permitted to do anything like that. The Consulate handles these things. The Consulate will be open at nine."

His face, constrained to impassivity by the binding strap, infuriated Baby.

"I can't wait until nine. My brother-in-law says they've put his eye out--he's seriously hurt! I have to get to him. I have to find a doctor." She let herself go and began to cry angrily as she talked, for she knew that he would respond to her agitation rather than her words. "You've got to do something about this. It's your business to protect American citizens in trouble."

But he was of the Eastern seaboard and too hard for her. Shaking his head patiently at her failure to understand his position he drew the Persian robe closer about him and came down a few steps.

"Write down the address of the Consulate for this lady," he said to the porter, "and look up Doctor Colazzo's address and telephone number and write that down too." He turned to Baby, with the expression of an exasperated Christ. "My dear lady, the diplomatic corps represents the Government of the United States to the Government of Italy. It has nothing to do with the protection of citizens, except under specific instructions from the State Department. Your brother-in-law has broken the laws of this country and been put in jail, just as an Italian might be put in jail in New York. The only people who can let him go are the Italian courts and if your brother-in-law has a case you can get aid and advice from the Consulate, which protects the rights of American citizens. The consulate does not open until nine o'clock. Even if it were my brother I couldn't do anything--"

"Can you phone the Consulate?" she broke in.

"We can't interfere with the Consulate. When the Consul gets there at nine--"

"Can you give me his home address?"

After a fractional pause the man shook his head. He took the memorandum from the porter and gave it to her.

"Now I'll ask you to excuse me."

He had manoeuvred her to the door: for an instant the violet dawn fell shrilly upon his pink mask and upon the linen sack that supported his mustache; then Baby was standing on the front steps alone. She had been in the embassy ten minutes.

The piazza whereon it faced was empty save for an old man gathering cigarette butts with a spiked stick. Baby caught a taxi presently and went to the Consulate but there was no one there save a trio of wretched women scrubbing the stairs. She could not make them understand that she wanted the Consul's home address--in a sudden resurgence of anxiety she rushed out and told the chauffeur to take her to the jail. He did not know where it was, but by the use of the words *semper dritte, dextra* and *sinestra* she manoeuvred him to its approximate locality, where she dismounted and explored a labyrinth of familiar alleys. But the buildings and the alleys all looked alike. Emerging from one trail into the Piazzo d'Espagna she saw the American Express Company and her heart lifted at the word "American" on the sign. There was a light in the window and hurrying across the square she tried the door, but it was locked, and inside the clock stood at seven. Then she thought of Collis Clay.

She remembered the name of his hotel, a stuffy villa sealed in red plush across from the Excelsior. The woman on duty at the office was not disposed to help her--she had no authority to disturb Mr. Clay, and refused to let Miss Warren go up to his room alone; convinced finally that this was not an affair of passion she accompanied her.

Collis lay naked upon his bed. He had come in tight and, awakening, it took him some moments to realize his nudity. He atoned for it by an excess of modesty. Taking his clothes into the bathroom he dressed in haste, muttering to himself "Gosh. She certainly musta got a good look at me." After some telephoning, he and Baby found the jail and went to it.

The cell door was open and Dick was slumped on a chair in the guard-room. The carabinieri had washed some of the blood from his face, brushed him and set his hat concealingly upon his head.

Baby stood in the doorway trembling.

"Mr. Clay will stay with you," she said. "I want to get the Consul and a doctor."

"All right."

"Just stay quiet."

"All right."

"I'll be back."

She drove to the Consulate; it was after eight now, and she was permitted to sit in the ante-room. Toward nine the Consul came in and Baby, hysterical with impotence and exhaustion, repeated her story. The Consul was disturbed. He warned her against getting into brawls in strange cities, but he was chiefly concerned that she should wait outside--with despair she read in his elderly eye that he wanted to be mixed up as little as possible in this catastrophe. Waiting on his action, she passed the minutes by phoning a doctor to go to Dick. There were other people in the ante-room and several were admitted to the Consul's office. After half an hour she chose the moment of some one's coming out and pushed past the secretary into the room.

"This is outrageous! An American has been beaten half to death and thrown into prison and you make no move to help."

"Just a minute, Mrs--"

"I've waited long enough. You come right down to the jail and get him out!"

"Mrs--"

"We're people of considerable standing in America--" Her mouth hardened as she continued. "If it wasn't for the scandal we can--I shall see that your indifference to this matter is reported in the proper quarter. If my brother-in-law were a British citizen he'd have been free hours ago, but you're more concerned with what the police will think than about what you're here for."

"Mrs.--"

"You put on your hat and come with me right away."

The mention of his hat alarmed the Consul who began to clean his spectacles hurriedly and to ruffle his papers. This proved of no avail: the American Woman, aroused, stood over him; the clean-sweeping irrational temper that had broken the moral back of a race and made a nursery out of a continent, was too much for him. He rang for the vice-consul--Baby had won.

Dick sat in the sunshine that fell profusely through the guard-room window. Collis was with him and two carabinieri, and they were waiting for something to happen. With the narrowed vision of his one eye Dick could see the carabinieri; they were Tuscan peasants with short upper lips and he found it difficult to associate them with the brutality of last night. He sent one of them to fetch him a glass of beer.

The beer made him light-headed and the episode was momentarily illumined by a ray of sardonic humor. Collis was under the impression that the English girl had something to do with the catastrophe, but Dick was sure she had disappeared long before it happened. Collis was still absorbed by the fact that Miss Warren had found him naked on his bed.

Dick's rage had retreated into him a little and he felt a vast criminal irresponsibility. What had happened to him was so awful that nothing could make any difference unless he could choke it to death, and, as this was unlikely, he was hopeless. He would be a different person henceforward, and in his raw state he had bizarre feelings of what the new self would be. The matter had about it the impersonal quality of an act of God. No mature Aryan is able to profit by a humiliation; when he forgives it has become part of his life, he has identified himself with the thing which has humiliated him--an upshot that in this case was impossible.

When Collis spoke of retribution, Dick shook his head and was silent. A lieutenant of carabinieri, pressed, burnished, vital, came into the room like three men and the guards jumped to attention. He seized the empty beer bottle and directed a stream of scolding at his men. The new spirit was in him, and the first thing was to get the beer bottle out of the guard-room. Dick looked at Collis and laughed.

The vice-consul, an over-worked young man named Swanson, arrived, and they started to the court; Collis and Swanson on either side of Dick and the two carabinieri close behind. It was a yellow, hazy morning; the squares and arcades were crowded and Dick, pulling his hat low over his head, walked fast, setting the pace, until one of the short-legged carabinieri ran alongside and protested. Swanson arranged matters.

"I've disgraced you, haven't I?" said Dick jovially.

"You're liable to get killed fighting Italians," replied Swanson sheepishly. "They'll probably let you go this time but if you were an Italian you'd get a couple of months in prison. And how!"

"Have you ever been in prison?"

Swanson laughed.

"I like him," announced Dick to Clay. "He's a very likeable young man and he gives people excellent advice, but I'll bet he's been to jail himself. Probably spent weeks at a time in jail."

Swanson laughed.

"I mean you want to be careful. You don't know how these people are."

"Oh, I know how they are," broke out Dick, irritably. "They're god damn stinkers." He turned around to the carabinieri: "Did you get that?"

"I'm leaving you here," Swanson said quickly. "I told your sister-in-law I would--our lawyer will meet you upstairs in the courtroom. You want to be careful."

"Good-by." Dick shook hands politely. "Thank you very much. I feel you have a future--"

With another smile Swanson hurried away, resuming his official expression of disapproval.

Now they came into a courtyard on all four sides of which outer stairways mounted to the chambers above. As they crossed the flags a groaning, hissing, booing sound went up from the loiterers in the courtyard, voices full of fury and scorn. Dick stared about.

"What's that?" he demanded, aghast.

One of the carabinieri spoke to a group of men and the sound died away.

They came into the court-room. A shabby Italian lawyer from the Consulate spoke at length to the judge while Dick and Collis waited aside. Some one who knew English turned from the window that gave on the yard and explained the sound that had accompanied their passage through. A native of Frascati had raped and slain a five-year-old child and was to be brought in that morning--the crowd had assumed it was Dick.

In a few minutes the lawyer told Dick that he was freed--the court considered him punished enough.

"Enough!" Dick cried. "Punished for what?"

"Come along," said Collis. "You can't do anything now."

"But what did I do, except get into a fight with some taxi-men?"

"They claim you went up to a detective as if you were going to shake hands with him and hit him--"

"That's not true! I told him I was going to hit him--I didn't know he was a detective."

"You better go along," urged the lawyer.

"Come along." Collis took his arm and they descended the steps.

"I want to make a speech," Dick cried. "I want to explain to these people how I raped a five-year-old girl. Maybe I did--"

"Come along."

Baby was waiting with a doctor in a taxi-cab. Dick did not want to look at her and he disliked the doctor, whose stern manner revealed him as one of that least palpable of European types, the Latin moralist. Dick summed up his conception of the disaster, but no one had much to say. In his room in the Quirinal the doctor washed off the rest of the blood and the oily sweat, set his nose, his fractured ribs and fingers, disinfected the smaller wounds and put a hopeful dressing on the eye. Dick asked for a quarter of a grain of morphine, for he was still wide awake and full of nervous energy. With the morphine he fell asleep; the doctor and Collis left and Baby waited with him until a woman could arrive from the English nursing home. It had been a hard night but she had the satisfaction of feeling that, whatever Dick's previous record was, they now possessed a moral superiority over him for as long as he proved of any use.

BOOK THREE

I

Frau Kaethe Gregorovius overtook her husband on the path of their villa.

"How was Nicole?" she asked mildly; but she spoke out of breath, giving away the fact that she had held the question in her mind during her run.

Franz looked at her in surprise.

"Nicole's not sick. What makes you ask, dearest one?"

"You see her so much--I thought she must be sick."

"We will talk of this in the house."

Kaethe agreed meekly. His study was over in the administration building and the children were with their tutor in the living-room; they went up to the bedroom.

"Excuse me, Franz," said Kaethe before he could speak. "Excuse me, dear, I had no right to say that. I know my obligations and I am proud of them. But there is a bad feeling between Nicole and me."

"Birds in their little nests agree," Franz thundered. Finding the tone inappropriate to the sentiment he repeated his command in the spaced and considered rhythm with which his old master, Doctor Dohmler, could cast significance on the tritest platitude. "Birds--in--their--nests--*agree!*"

"I realize that. You haven't seen me fail in courtesy toward Nicole."

"I see you failing in common sense. Nicole is half a patient--she will possibly remain something of a patient all her life. In the absence of Dick I am responsible." He hesitated; sometimes as a quiet joke he tried to keep news from Kaethe. "There was a cable from Rome this morning. Dick has had grippe and is starting home to-morrow."

Relieved, Kaethe pursued her course in a less personal tone:

"I think Nicole is less sick than any one thinks--she only cherishes her illness as an instrument of power. She ought to be in the cinema, like your Norma Talmadge--that's where all American women would be happy."

"Are you jealous of Norma Talmadge, on a film?"

"I don't like Americans. They're selfish, *self*ish!"

"You like Dick?"

"I like him," she admitted. "He's different, he thinks of others."

--And so does Norma Talmadge, Franz said to himself. Norma Talmadge must be a fine, noble woman beyond her loveliness. They must compel her to play foolish rôles; Norma Talmadge must be a woman whom it would be a great privilege to know.

Kaethe had forgotten about Norma Talmadge, a vivid shadow that she had fretted bitterly upon one night as they were driving home from the movies in Zurich.

"--Dick married Nicole for her money," she said. "That was his weakness--you hinted as much yourself one night."

"You're being malicious."

"I shouldn't have said that," she retracted. "We must all live together like birds, as you say. But it's difficult when Nicole acts as--when Nicole pulls herself back a little, as if she were holding her breath--as if I *smelt* bad!"

Kaethe had touched a material truth. She did most of her work herself, and, frugal, she bought few clothes. An American shopgirl, laundering two changes of underwear every night, would have noticed a hint of yesterday's reawakened sweat about Kaethe's person, less a smell than an ammoniacal reminder of the eternity of toil and decay. To Franz this was as natural as the thick dark scent of Kaethe's hair, and he would have missed it equally; but to Nicole, born hating the smell of a nurse's fingers dressing her, it was an offense only to be endured.

"And the children," Kaethe continued. "She doesn't like them to play with our children--" but Franz had heard enough:

"Hold your tongue--that kind of talk can hurt me professionally, since we owe this clinic to Nicole's money. Let us have lunch."

Kaethe realized that her outburst had been ill-advised, but Franz's last remark reminded her that other Americans had money, and a week later she put her dislike of Nicole into new words.

The occasion was the dinner they tendered the Divers upon Dick's return. Hardly had their footfalls ceased on the path when she shut the door and said to Franz:

"Did you see around his eyes? He's been on a debauch!"

"Go gently," Franz requested. "Dick told me about that as soon as he came home. He was boxing on the trans-Atlantic ship. The American passengers box a lot on these trans-Atlantic ships."

"I believe that?" she scoffed. "It hurts him to move one of his arms and he has an unhealed scar on his temple--you can see where the hair's been cut away."

Franz had not noticed these details.

"But what?" Kaethe demanded. "Do you think that sort of thing does the Clinic any good? The liquor I smelt on him tonight, and several other times since he's been back."

She slowed her voice to fit the gravity of what she was about to say: "Dick is no longer a serious man."

Franz rocked his shoulders up the stairs, shaking off her persistence. In their bedroom he turned on her.

"He is most certainly a serious man and a brilliant man. Of all the men who have recently taken their degrees in neuropathology in Zurich, Dick has been regarded as the most brilliant--more brilliant than I could ever be."

"For shame!"

"It's the truth--the shame would be not to admit it. I turn to Dick when cases are highly involved. His publications are still standard in their line--go into any medical library and ask. Most students think he's an Englishman--they don't believe that such thoroughness could come out of America." He groaned domestically, taking his pajamas from under the pillow, "I can't understand why you talk this way, Kaethe--I thought you liked him."

"For shame!" Kaethe said. "You're the solid one, you do the work. It's a case of hare and tortoise--and in my opinion the hare's race is almost done."

"Tch! Tch!"

"Very well, then. It's true."

With his open hand he pushed down air briskly.

"Stop!"

The upshot was that they had exchanged viewpoints like debaters. Kaethe admitted to herself that she had been too hard on Dick, whom she admired and of whom she stood in awe, who had been so appreciative and understanding of herself. As for Franz, once Kaethe's idea had had time to sink in, he never after believed that Dick was a serious person. And as time went on he convinced himself that he had never thought so.

II

Dick told Nicole an expurgated version of the catastrophe in Rome--in his version he had gone philanthropically to the rescue of a drunken friend. He could trust Baby Warren to hold her tongue, since he had painted the disastrous effect of the truth upon Nicole. All this, however, was a low hurdle compared to the lingering effect of the episode upon him.

In reaction he took himself for an intensified beating in his work, so that Franz, trying to break with him, could find no basis on which to begin a disagreement. No friendship worth the name was ever destroyed in an hour without some painful flesh being torn--so Franz let himself believe with ever-increasing conviction that Dick travelled intellectually and emotionally at such a rate of speed that the vibrations jarred him--this was a contrast that had previously been considered a virtue in their relation. So, for the shoddiness of needs, are shoes made out of last year's hide.

Yet it was May before Franz found an opportunity to insert the first wedge. Dick came into his office white and tired one noon and sat down, saying:

"Well, she's gone."

"She's dead?"

"The heart quit."

Dick sat exhausted in the chair nearest the door. During three nights he had remained with the scabbed anonymous woman-artist he had come to love, formally to portion out the adrenaline, but really to throw as much wan light as he could into the darkness ahead.

Half appreciating his feeling, Franz travelled quickly over an opinion:

"It was neuro-syphilis. All the Wassermans we took won't tell me differently. The spinal fluid--"

"Never mind," said Dick. "Oh, God, never mind! If she cared enough about her secret to take it away with her, let it go at that."

"You better lay off for a day."

"Don't worry, I'm going to."

Franz had his wedge; looking up from the telegram that he was writing to the woman's brother he inquired: "Or do you want to take a little trip?"

"Not now."

"I don't mean a vacation. There's a case in Lausanne. I've been on the phone with a Chilian all morning--"

"She was so damn brave," said Dick. "And it took her so long." Franz shook his head sympathetically and Dick got himself together. "Excuse me for interrupting you."

"This is just a change--the situation is a father's problem with his son--the father can't get the son up here. He wants somebody to come down there."

"What is it? Alcoholism? Homosexuality? When you say Lausanne--"

"A little of everything."

"I'll go down. Is there any money in it?"

"Quite a lot, I'd say. Count on staying two or three days, and get the boy up here if he needs to be watched. In any case take your time, take your ease; combine business with pleasure."

After two hours' train sleep Dick felt renewed, and he approached the interview with Señor Pardo y Cuidad Real in good spirits.

These interviews were much of a type. Often the sheer hysteria of the family representative was as interesting psychologically as the condition of the patient. This one was no exception: Señor Pardo y Cuidad Real, a handsome iron-gray Spaniard, noble of carriage, with all the appurtenances of wealth and power, raged up and down his suite in the Hôtel de Trois Mondes and told the story of his son with no more self-control than a drunken woman.

"I am at the end of my invention. My son is corrupt. He was corrupt at Harrow, he was corrupt at King's College, Cambridge. He's incorrigibly corrupt. Now that there is this drinking it is more and more obvious how he is, and there is continual scandal. I have tried everything--I worked out a plan with a doctor friend of mine, sent them together for a tour of Spain. Every evening Francisco had an injection of cantharides and then the two went together to a reputable bordello--for a week or so it seemed to work but the result was nothing. Finally last week in this very room, rather in that bathroom--" he pointed at it, "--I made Francisco strip to the waist and lashed him with a whip--"

Exhausted with his emotion he sat down and Dick spoke:

"That was foolish--the trip to Spain was futile also--" He struggled against an upsurging hilarity--that any reputable medical man should have lent himself to such an amateurish experiment! "--Señor, I must tell you that in these cases we can promise nothing. In the case of the drinking we can often accomplish something--with proper co-operation. The first thing is to see the boy and get enough of his confidence to find whether he has any insight into the matter."

--The boy, with whom he sat on the terrace, was about twenty, handsome and alert.

"I'd like to know your attitude," Dick said. "Do you feel that the situation is getting worse? And do you want to do anything about it?"

"I suppose I do," said Francisco, "I am very unhappy."

"Do you think it's from the drinking or from the abnormality?"

"I think the drinking is caused by the other." He was serious for a while--suddenly an irrepressible facetiousness broke through and he laughed, saying, "It's hopeless. At King's I was known as the Queen of Chili. That trip to Spain--all it did was to make me nauseated by the sight of a woman."

Dick caught him up sharply.

"If you're happy in this mess, then I can't help you and I'm wasting my time."

"No, let's talk--I despise most of the others so." There was some manliness in the boy, perverted now into an active resistance to his father. But he had that typically roguish look in his eyes that homosexuals assume in discussing the subject.

"It's a hole-and-corner business at best," Dick told him. "You'll spend your life on it, and its consequences, and you won't have time or energy for any other decent or social act. If you want to face the world you'll have to begin by controlling your sensuality--and, first of all, the drinking that provokes it--"

He talked automatically, having abandoned the case ten minutes before. They talked pleasantly through another hour about the boy's home in Chili and about his ambitions. It was as close as Dick had ever come to comprehending such a character from any but the pathological angle--he gathered that this very charm made it possible for Francisco to perpetrate his outrages, and, for Dick, charm always had an independent existence, whether it was the mad gallantry of the wretch who had died in the clinic this morning, or the courageous grace which this lost young man brought to a drab old story. Dick tried to dissect it into pieces small enough to store away--realizing that the totality of a life may be different in quality from its segments, and also that life during the forties seemed capable of being observed only in segments. His love for Nicole and Rosemary, his friendship with Abe North, with Tommy Barban in the broken universe of the war's ending--in such contacts the personalities had seemed to press up so close to him that he became the personality itself--there seemed some necessity of taking all or nothing; it was as if for the remainder of his life he was condemned to carry with him the egos of certain people, early met and early loved, and to be only as complete as they were complete themselves. There was some element of loneliness involved--so easy to be loved--so hard to love.

As he sat on the veranda with young Francisco, a ghost of the past swam into his ken. A tall, singularly swaying male detached himself from the shrubbery and approached Dick and Francisco with feeble resolution. For a moment he formed such an apologetic part of the vibrant landscape that Dick scarcely remarked him--then Dick was on his feet, shaking hands with an abstracted air, thinking, "My God, I've stirred up a nest!" and trying to collect the man's name.

"This is Doctor Diver, isn't it?"

"Well, well--Mr. Dumphry, isn't it?"

"Royal Dumphry. I had the pleasure of having dinner one night in that lovely garden of yours."

"Of course." Trying to dampen Mr. Dumphry's enthusiasm, Dick went into impersonal chronology. "It was in nineteen--twenty-four--or twenty-five--"

He had remained standing, but Royal Dumphry, shy as he had seemed at first, was no laggard with his pick and spade; he spoke to Francisco in a flip, intimate manner, but the latter, ashamed of him, joined Dick in trying to freeze him away.

"Doctor Diver--one thing I want to say before you go. I've never forgotten that evening in your garden--how nice you and your wife were. To me it's one of the finest memories in my life, one of the happiest ones. I've always thought of it as the most civilized gathering of people that I have ever known."

Dick continued a crab-like retreat toward the nearest door of the hotel.

"I'm glad you remembered it so pleasantly. Now I've got to see--"

"I understand," Royal Dumphry pursued sympathetically. "I hear he's dying."

"Who's dying?"

"Perhaps I shouldn't have said that--but we have the same physician."

Dick paused, regarding him in astonishment. "Who're you talking about?"

"Why, your wife's father--perhaps I--"

"My *what*?"

"I suppose--you mean I'm the first person--"

"You mean my wife's father is here, in Lausanne?"

"Why, I thought you knew--I thought that was why you were here."

"What doctor is taking care of him?"

Dick scrawled the name in a notebook, excused himself, and hurried to a telephone booth.

It was convenient for Doctor Dangeu to see Doctor Diver at his house immediately.

Doctor Dangeu was a young Génevois; for a moment he was afraid that he was going to lose a profitable patient, but, when Dick reassured him, he divulged the fact that Mr. Warren was indeed dying.

"He is only fifty but the liver has stopped restoring itself; the precipitating factor is alcoholism."

"Doesn't respond?"

"The man can take nothing except liquids--I give him three days, or at most, a week."

"Does his elder daughter, Miss Warren, know his condition?"

"By his own wish no one knows except the man-servant. It was only this morning I felt I had to tell him--he took it excitedly, although he has been in a very religious and resigned mood from the beginning of his illness."

Dick considered: "Well--" he decided slowly, "in any case I'll take care of the family angle. But I imagine they would want a consultation."

"As you like."

"I know I speak for them when I ask you to call in one of the best-known medicine men around the lake--Herbrugge, from Geneva."

"I was thinking of Herbrugge."

"Meanwhile I'm here for a day at least and I'll keep in touch with you."

That evening Dick went to Señor Pardo y Cuidad Real and they talked.

"We have large estates in Chili--" said the old man. "My son could well be taking care of them. Or I can get him in any one of a dozen enterprises in Paris--" He shook his head and paced across the windows against a spring rain so cheerful that it didn't even drive the swans to cover, "My only son! Can't you take him with you?"

The Spaniard knelt suddenly at Dick's feet.

"Can't you cure my only son? I believe in you--you can take him with you, cure him."

"It's impossible to commit a person on such grounds. I wouldn't if I could."

The Spaniard got up from his knees.

"I have been hasty--I have been driven--"

Descending to the lobby Dick met Doctor Dangeu in the elevator.

"I was about to call your room," the latter said. "Can we speak out on the terrace?"

"Is Mr. Warren dead?" Dick demanded.

"He is the same--the consultation is in the morning. Meanwhile he wants to see his daughter--your wife--with the greatest fervor. It seems there was some quarrel--"

"I know all about that."

The doctors looked at each other, thinking.

"Why don't you talk to him before you make up your mind?" Dangeu suggested. "His death will be graceful--merely a weakening and sinking."

With an effort Dick consented.

"All right."

The suite in which Devereux Warren was gracefully weakening and sinking was of the same size as that of the Señor Pardo y Cuidad Real--throughout this hotel there were many chambers wherein rich ruins, fugitives from justice, claimants to the thrones of mediatized principalities, lived on the derivatives of opium or barbitol listening eternally as to an inescapable radio, to the coarse melodies of old sins. This corner of Europe does not so much draw people as accept them without inconvenient questions. Routes cross here--people bound for private sanitariums or tuberculosis resorts in the mountains, people who are no longer *persona gratis* in France or Italy.

The suite was darkened. A nun with a holy face was nursing the man whose emaciated fingers stirred a rosary on the white sheet. He was still handsome and his voice summoned up a thick burr of individuality as he spoke to Dick, after Dangeu had left them together.

"We get a lot of understanding at the end of life. Only now, Doctor Diver, do I realize what it was all about."

Dick waited.

"I've been a bad man. You must know how little right I have to see Nicole again, yet a Bigger Man than either of us says to forgive and to pity." The rosary slipped from his weak hands and slid off the smooth bed covers. Dick picked it up for him. "If I could see Nicole for ten minutes I would go happy out of the world."

"It's not a decision I can make for myself," said Dick. "Nicole is not strong." He made his decision but pretended to hesitate. "I can put it up to my professional associate."

"What your associate says goes with me--very well, Doctor. Let me tell you my debt to you is so large--"

Dick stood up quickly.

"I'll let you know the result through Doctor Dangeu."

In his room he called the clinic on the Zugersee. After a long time Kaethe answered from her own house.

"I want to get in touch with Franz."

"Franz is up on the mountain. I'm going up myself--is it something I can tell him, Dick?"

"It's about Nicole--her father is dying here in Lausanne. Tell Franz that, to show him it's important; and ask him to phone me from up there."

"I will."

"Tell him I'll be in my room here at the hotel from three to five, and again from seven to eight, and after that to page me in the dining-room."

In plotting these hours he forgot to add that Nicole was not to be told; when he remembered it he was talking into a dead telephone. Certainly Kaethe should realize.

. . . Kaethe had no exact intention of telling Nicole about the call when she rode up the deserted hill of mountain wild-flowers and secret winds, where the patients were taken to ski in winter and to climb in spring. Getting off the train she saw Nicole shepherding the children through some organized romp. Approaching, she drew her arm gently along Nicole's shoulder, saying: "You are clever with children--you must teach them more about swimming in the summer."

In the play they had grown hot, and Nicole's reflex in drawing away from Kaethe's arm was automatic to the point of rudeness. Kaethe's hand fell awkwardly into space, and then she too reacted, verbally, and deplorably.

"Did you think I was going to embrace you?" she demanded sharply. "It was only about Dick, I talked on the phone to him and I was sorry--"

"Is anything the matter with Dick?"

Kaethe suddenly realized her error, but she had taken a tactless course and there was no choice but to answer as Nicole pursued her with reiterated questions: ". . . then why were you sorry?"

"Nothing about Dick. I must talk to Franz."

"It is about Dick."

There was terror in her face and collaborating alarm in the faces of the Diver children, near at hand. Kaethe collapsed with: "Your father is ill in Lausanne--Dick wants to talk to Franz about it."

"Is he very sick?" Nicole demanded--just as Franz came up with his hearty hospital manner. Gratefully Kaethe passed the remnant of the buck to him--but the damage was done.

"I'm going to Lausanne," announced Nicole.

"One minute," said Franz. "I'm not sure it's advisable. I must first talk on the phone to Dick."

"Then I'll miss the train down," Nicole protested, "and then I'll miss the three o'clock from Zurich! If my father is dying I must--" She left this in the air, afraid to formulate it. "I *must* go. I'll have to run for the train." She was running even as she spoke toward the sequence of flat cars that crowned the bare hill with bursting steam and sound. Over her shoulder she called back, "If you phone Dick tell him I'm coming, Franz!" . . .

. . . Dick was in his own room in the hotel reading The New York Herald when the swallow-like nun rushed in--simultaneously the phone rang.

"Is he dead?" Dick demanded of the nun, hopefully.

"Monsieur, il est parti--he has gone away."

"Com*ment*?"

"Il est parti--his man and his baggage have gone away too!"

It was incredible. A man in that condition to arise and depart.

Dick answered the phone-call from Franz. "You shouldn't have told Nicole," he protested.

"Kaethe told her, very unwisely."

"I suppose it was my fault. Never tell a thing to a woman till it's done. However, I'll meet Nicole . . . say, Franz, the craziest thing has happened down here--the old boy took up his bed and walked. . . ."

"At what? What did you say?"

"I say he walked, old Warren--he walked!"

"But why not?"

"He was supposed to be dying of general collapse . . . he got up and walked away, back to Chicago, I guess. . . . I don't know, the nurse is here now. . . . I don't know, Franz--I've just heard about it. . . . Call me later."

He spent the better part of two hours tracing Warren's movements. The patient had found an opportunity between the change of day and night nurses to resort to the bar where he had gulped down four whiskeys; he paid his hotel bill with a thousand dollar note, instructing the desk that the change should be sent after him, and departed, presumably for America. A last minute dash by Dick and Dangeu to overtake him at the station resulted only in Dick's failing to meet Nicole; when they did meet in the lobby of the hotel she seemed suddenly tired, and there was a tight purse to her lips that disquieted him.

"How's father?" she demanded.

"He's much better. He seemed to have a good deal of reserve energy after all." He hesitated, breaking it to her easy. "In fact he got up and went away."

Wanting a drink, for the chase had occupied the dinner hour, he led her, puzzled, toward the grill, and continued as they occupied two leather easy-chairs and ordered a high-ball and a glass of beer: "The man who was taking care of him made a wrong prognosis or something--wait a minute, I've hardly had time to think the thing out myself."

"He's *gone?"*

"He got the evening train for Paris."

They sat silent. From Nicole flowed a vast tragic apathy.

"It was instinct," Dick said, finally. "He was really dying, but he tried to get a resumption of rhythm--he's not the first person that ever walked off his death-bed--like an old clock--you know, you shake it and somehow from sheer habit it gets going again. Now your father--"

"Oh, don't tell me," she said.

"His principal fuel was fear," he continued. "He got afraid, and off he went. He'll probably live till ninety--"

"Please don't tell me any more," she said. "Please don't--I couldn't stand any more."

"All right. The little devil I came down to see is hopeless. We may as well go back to-morrow."

"I don't see why you have to--come in contact with all this," she burst forth.

"Oh, don't you? Sometimes I don't either."

She put her hand on his.

"Oh, I'm sorry I said that, Dick."

Some one had brought a phonograph into the bar and they sat listening to The Wedding of the Painted Doll.

III

One morning a week later, stopping at the desk for his mail, Dick became aware of some extra commotion outside: Patient Von Cohn Morris was going away. His parents, Australians, were putting his baggage vehemently into a large limousine, and beside them stood Doctor Ladislau protesting with ineffectual attitudes against the violent gesturings of Morris, senior. The young man was regarding his embarkation with aloof cynicism as Doctor Diver approached.

"Isn't this a little sudden, Mr. Morris?"

Mr. Morris started as he saw Dick--his florid face and the large checks on his suit seemed to turn off and on like electric lights. He approached Dick as though to strike him.

"High time we left, we and those who have come with us," he began, and paused for breath. "It is high time, Doctor Diver. High time."

"Will you come in my office?" Dick suggested.

"Not I! I'll talk to you, but I'm washing my hands of you and your place."

He shook his finger at Dick. "I was just telling this doctor here. We've wasted our time and our money."

Doctor Ladislau stirred in a feeble negative, signalling up a vague Slavic evasiveness. Dick had never liked Ladislau. He managed to walk the excited Australian along the path in the direction of his office, trying to persuade him to enter; but the man shook his head.

"It's you, Doctor Diver, *you,* the very man. I went to Doctor Ladislau because you were not to be found, Doctor Diver, and because Doctor Gregorovius is not expected until the nightfall, and I would not wait. No, sir! I would not wait a minute after my son told me the truth."

He came up menacingly to Dick, who kept his hands loose enough to drop him if it seemed necessary. "My son is here for alcoholism, and he told us he smelt liquor on your breath. Yes, sir!" He made a quick, apparently unsuccessful sniff. "Not once, but twice Von Cohn says he has smelt liquor on your breath. I and my lady have never touched a drop of it in our lives. We hand Von Cohn to you to be cured, and within a month he twice smells liquor on your breath! What kind of cure is that there?"

Dick hesitated; Mr. Morris was quite capable of making a scene on the clinic drive.

"After all, Mr. Morris, some people are not going to give up what they regard as food because of your son--"

"But you're a doctor, man!" cried Morris furiously. "When the workmen drink their beer that's bad 'cess to them--but you're here supposing to cure--"

"This has gone too far. Your son came to us because of kleptomania."

"What was behind it?" The man was almost shrieking. "Drink--black drink. Do you know what color black is? It's black! My own uncle was hung by the neck because of it, you hear? My son comes to a sanitarium, and a doctor reeks of it!"

"I must ask you to leave."

"You *ask* me! We *are* leaving!"

"If you could be a little temperate we could tell you the results of the treatment to date. Naturally, since you feel as you do, we would not want your son as a patient--"

"You dare to use the word temperate to me?"

Dick called to Doctor Ladislau and as he approached, said: "Will you represent us in saying good-by to the patient and to his family?"

He bowed slightly to Morris and went into his office, and stood rigid for a moment just inside the door. He watched until they drove away, the gross parents, the bland, degenerate offspring: it was easy to prophesy the family's swing around Europe, bullying their betters with hard ignorance and hard money. But what absorbed Dick after the disappearance of the caravan was the question as to what extent he had provoked this. He drank claret with each meal, took a nightcap, generally in the form of hot rum, and sometimes he tippled with gin in the afternoons--gin was the most difficult to detect on the breath. He was averaging a half-pint of alcohol a day, too much for his system to burn up.

Dismissing a tendency to justify himself, he sat down at his desk and wrote out, like a prescription, a régime that would cut his liquor in half. Doctors, chauffeurs, and Protestant clergymen could never smell of liquor, as could painters, brokers, cavalry leaders; Dick blamed himself only for indiscretion. But the matter was by no means clarified half an hour later when Franz, revivified by an Alpine fortnight, rolled up the drive, so eager to resume work that he was plunged in it before he reached his office. Dick met him there.

"How was Mount Everest?"

"We could very well have done Mount Everest the rate we were doing. We thought of it. How goes it all? How is my Kaethe, how is your Nicole?"

"All goes smooth domestically. But my God, Franz, we had a rotten scene this morning."

"How? What was it?"

Dick walked around the room while Franz got in touch with his villa by telephone. After the family exchange was over, Dick said: "The Morris boy was taken away--there was a row."

Franz's buoyant face fell.

"I knew he'd left. I met Ladislau on the veranda."

"What did Ladislau say?"

"Just that young Morris had gone--that you'd tell me about it. What about it?"

"The usual incoherent reasons."

"He was a devil, that boy."

"He was a case for anesthesia," Dick agreed. "Anyhow, the father had beaten Ladislau into a colonial subject by the time I came along. What about Ladislau? Do we keep him? I say no--he's not much of a man, he can't seem to cope with anything." Dick hesitated on the verge of the truth, swung away to give himself space within which to recapitulate. Franz perched on the edge of a desk, still in his linen duster and travelling gloves. Dick said:

"One of the remarks the boy made to his father was that your distinguished collaborator was a drunkard. The man is a fanatic, and the descendant seems to have caught traces of vin-du-pays on me."

Franz sat down, musing on his lower lip. "You can tell me at length," he said finally.

"Why not now?" Dick suggested. "You must know I'm the last man to abuse liquor." His eyes and Franz's glinted on each other, pair on pair. "Ladislau let the man get so worked up that I was on the defensive. It might have happened in front of patients, and you can imagine how hard it could be to defend yourself in a situation like that!"

Franz took off his gloves and coat. He went to the door and told the secretary, "Don't disturb us." Coming back into the room he flung himself at the long table and fooled with his mail, reasoning as little as is characteristic of people in such postures, rather summoning up a suitable mask for what he had to say.

"Dick, I know well that you are a temperate, well-balanced man, even though we do not entirely agree on the subject of alcohol. But a time has come--Dick, I must say frankly that I have been aware several times that you have had a drink when it was not the moment to have one. There is some reason. Why not try another leave of abstinence?"

"Absence," Dick corrected him automatically. "It's no solution for me to go away."

They were both chafed, Franz at having his return marred and blurred.

"Sometimes you don't use your common sense, Dick."

"I never understood what common sense meant applied to complicated problems--unless it means that a general practitioner can perform a better operation than a specialist."

He was seized by an overwhelming disgust for the situation. To explain, to patch--these were not natural functions at their age--better to continue with the cracked echo of an old truth in the ears.

"This is no go," he said suddenly.

"Well, that's occurred to me," Franz admitted. "Your heart isn't in this project any more, Dick."

"I know. I want to leave--we could strike some arrangement about taking Nicole's money out gradually."

"I have thought about that too, Dick--I have seen this coming. I am able to arrange other backing, and it will be possible to take all your money out by the end of the year."

Dick had not intended to come to a decision so quickly, nor was he prepared for Franz's so ready acquiescence in the break, yet he was relieved. Not without desperation he had long felt the ethics of his profession dissolving into a lifeless mass.

IV

The Divers would return to the Riviera, which was home. The Villa Diana had been rented again for the summer, so they divided the intervening time between German spas and French cathedral towns where they were always happy for a few days. Dick wrote a little with no particular method; it was one of those parts of life that is an awaiting; not upon Nicole's health, which seemed to thrive on travel, nor upon work, but simply an awaiting. The factor that gave purposefulness to the period was the children.

Dick's interest in them increased with their ages, now eleven and nine. He managed to reach them over the heads of employees on the principle that both the forcing of children and the fear of forcing them were inadequate substitutes for the long, careful watchfulness, the checking and balancing and reckoning of accounts, to the end that there should be no slip below a certain level of duty. He came to know them much better than Nicole did, and in expansive moods over the wines of several countries he talked and played with them at length. They had that wistful charm, almost sadness, peculiar to children who have learned early not to cry or laugh with abandon; they were apparently moved to no extremes of emotion, but content with a simple regimentation and the simple pleasures allowed them. They lived on the even tenor found advisable in the experience of old families of the Western world, brought up rather than brought out. Dick thought, for example, that nothing was more conducive to the development of observation than compulsory silence.

Lanier was an unpredictable boy with an inhuman curiosity. "Well, how many Pomeranians would it take to lick a lion, father?" was typical of the questions with which he harassed Dick. Topsy was easier. She was nine and very fair and exquisitely made like Nicole, and in the past Dick had worried about that. Lately she had become as robust as any American child. He was satisfied with them both, but conveyed the fact to them only in a tacit way. They were not let off breaches of good conduct--"Either one learns politeness at home," Dick said, "or the world teaches it to you with a whip and you may get hurt in the process. What do I care whether Topsy 'adores' me or not? I'm not bringing her up to be my wife."

Another element that distinguished this summer and autumn for the Divers was a plenitude of money. Due to the sale of their interest in the clinic, and to developments in America, there was now so much that the mere spending of it, the care of goods, was an absorption in itself. The style in which they travelled seemed fabulous.

Regard them, for example, as the train slows up at Boyen where they are to spend a fortnight visiting. The shifting from the wagon-lit has begun at the Italian frontier. The governess's maid and Madame Diver's maid have come up from second class to help with the baggage and the dogs. Mlle. Bellois will superintend the hand-luggage, leaving the Sealyhams to one maid and the pair of Pekinese to the other. It is not necessarily poverty of spirit that makes a woman surround herself with life--it can be a superabundance of interest, and, except during her flashes of illness, Nicole was capable of being curator of it all. For example with the great quantity of heavy baggage--presently from the van would be unloaded four wardrobe trunks, a shoe trunk, three hat trunks, and two hat boxes, a chest of servants' trunks, a portable filing-cabinet, a medicine case, a spirit lamp container, a picnic set, four tennis rackets in presses and cases, a phonograph, a typewriter. Distributed among the spaces reserved for family and entourage were two dozen supplementary grips, satchels and packages, each one numbered, down to the tag on the cane case. Thus all of it could be checked up in two minutes on any station platform, some for storage, some for accompaniment from the "light trip list" or the "heavy trip list," constantly revised, and carried on metal-edged plaques in Nicole's purse. She had devised the system as a child when travelling with her failing mother. It was equivalent to the system of a regimental supply officer who must think of the bellies and equipment of three thousand men.

The Divers flocked from the train into the early gathered twilight of the valley. The village people watched the debarkation with an awe akin to that which followed the Italian pilgrimages of Lord Byron a century before. Their hostess was the Contessa di Minghetti, lately Mary North. The journey that had begun in a room over the shop of a paperhanger in Newark had ended in an extraordinary marriage.

"Conte di Minghetti" was merely a papal title--the wealth of Mary's husband flowed from his being ruler-owner of manganese deposits in southwestern Asia. He was not quite light enough to travel in a pullman south of Mason-Dixon; he was of the Kyble-Berber-Sabaean-Hindu strain that belts across north Africa and Asia, more sympathetic to the European than the mongrel faces of the ports.

When these princely households, one of the East, one of the West, faced each other on the station platform, the splendor of the Divers seemed pioneer simplicity by comparison. Their hosts were accompanied by an Italian major-domo carrying a staff, by a quartet of turbaned retainers on motorcycles, and by two half-veiled females who stood respectfully a little behind Mary and salaamed at Nicole, making her jump with the gesture.

To Mary as well as to the Divers the greeting was faintly comic; Mary gave an apologetic, belittling giggle; yet her voice, as she introduced her husband by his Asiatic title, flew proud and high.

In their rooms as they dressed for dinner, Dick and Nicole grimaced at each other in an awed way: such rich as want to be thought democratic pretend in private to be swept off their feet by swank.

"Little Mary North knows what she wants," Dick muttered through his shaving cream. "Abe educated her, and now she's married to a Buddha. If Europe ever goes Bolshevik she'll turn up as the bride of Stalin."

Nicole looked around from her dressing-case. "Watch your tongue, Dick, will you?" But she laughed. "They're very swell. The warships all fire at them or salute them or something. Mary rides in the royal bus in London."

"All right," he agreed. As he heard Nicole at the door asking for pins, he called, "I wonder if I could have some whiskey; I feel the mountain air!"

"She'll see to it," presently Nicole called through the bathroom door. "It was one of those women who were at the station. She has her veil off."

"What did Mary tell you about life?" he asked.

"She didn't say so much--she was interested in high life--she asked me a lot of questions about my genealogy and all that sort of thing, as if I knew anything about it. But it seems the bridegroom has two very tan children by another marriage--one of them ill with some Asiatic thing they can't diagnose. I've got to warn the children. Sounds very peculiar to me. Mary will see how we'd feel about it." She stood worrying a minute.

"She'll understand," Dick reassured her. "Probably the child's in bed."

At dinner Dick talked to Hosain, who had been at an English public school. Hosain wanted to know about stocks and about Hollywood and Dick, whipping up his imagination with champagne, told him preposterous tales.

"Billions?" Hosain demanded.

"Trillions," Dick assured him.

"I didn't truly realize--"

"Well, perhaps millions," Dick conceded. "Every hotel guest is assigned a harem--or what amounts to a harem."

"Other than the actors and directors?"

"Every hotel guest--even travelling salesmen. Why, they tried to send me up a dozen candidates, but Nicole wouldn't stand for it."

Nicole reproved him when they were in their room alone. "Why so many highballs? Why did you use your word spic in front of him?"

"Excuse me, I meant smoke. The tongue slipped."

"Dick, this isn't faintly like you."

"Excuse me again. I'm not much like myself any more."

That night Dick opened a bathroom window, giving on a narrow and tubular court of the château, gray as rats but echoing at the moment to plaintive and peculiar music, sad as a flute. Two men were chanting in an Eastern language or dialect full of k's and l's--he leaned out but he could not see them; there was obviously a religious significance in the sounds, and tired and emotionless he let them pray for him too, but what for, save that he should not lose himself in his increasing melancholy, he did not know.

Next day, over a thinly wooded hillside they shot scrawny birds, distant poor relations to the partridge. It was done in a vague imitation of the English manner, with a corps of inexperienced beaters whom Dick managed to miss by firing only directly overhead.

On their return Lanier was waiting in their suite.

"Father, you said tell you immediately if we were near the sick boy."

Nicole whirled about, immediately on guard.

"--so, Mother," Lanier continued, turning to her, "the boy takes a bath every evening and to-night he took his bath just before mine and I had to take mine in his water, and it was dirty."

"What? Now what?"

"I saw them take Tony out of it, and then they called me into it and the water was dirty."

"But--did you take it?"

"Yes, Mother."

"Heavens!" she exclaimed to Dick.

He demanded: "Why didn't Lucienne draw your bath?"

"Lucienne can't. It's a funny heater--it reached out of itself and burned her arm last night and she's afraid of it, so one of those two women--"

"You go in this bathroom and take a bath now."

"Don't say *I* told you," said Lanier from the doorway.

Dick went in and sprinkled the tub with sulphur; closing the door he said to Nicole:

"Either we speak to Mary or we'd better get out."

She agreed and he continued: "People think their children are constitutionally cleaner than other people's, and their diseases are less contagious."

Dick came in and helped himself from the decanter, chewing a biscuit savagely in the rhythm of the pouring water in the bathroom.

"Tell Lucienne that she's got to learn about the heater--" he suggested. At that moment the Asiatic woman came in person to the door.

"El Contessa--"

Dick beckoned her inside and closed the door.

"Is the little sick boy better?" he inquired pleasantly.

"Better, yes, but he still has the eruptions frequently."

"That's too bad--I'm very sorry. But you see our children mustn't be bathed in his water. That's out of the question--I'm sure your mistress would be furious if she had known you had done a thing like that."

"I?" She seemed thunderstruck. "Why, I merely saw your maid had difficulty with the heater--I told her about it and started the water."

"But with a sick person you must empty the bathwater entirely out, and clean the tub."

"I?"

Chokingly the woman drew a long breath, uttered a convulsed sob and rushed from the room.

"She mustn't get up on western civilization at our expense," he said grimly.

At dinner that night he decided that it must inevitably be a truncated visit: about his own country Hosain seemed to have observed only that there were many mountains and some goats and herders of goats. He was a reserved young man--to draw him out would have required the sincere effort that Dick now reserved for his family. Soon after dinner Hosain left Mary and the Divers to themselves, but the old unity was split--between them lay the restless social fields that Mary was about to conquer. Dick was relieved when, at nine-thirty, Mary received and read a note and got up.

"You'll have to excuse me. My husband is leaving on a short trip--and I must be with him."

Next morning, hard on the heels of the servant bringing coffee, Mary entered their room. She was dressed and they were not dressed, and she had the air of having been up for some time. Her face was toughened with quiet jerky fury.

"What is this story about Lanier having been bathed in a dirty bath?"

Dick began to protest, but she cut through:

"What is this story that you commanded my husband's sister to clean Lanier's tub?"

She remained on her feet staring at them, as they sat impotent as idols in their beds, weighted by their trays. Together they exclaimed: "His *sister!*"

"That you ordered one of his sisters to clean out a tub!"

"We didn't--" their voices rang together saying the same thing, "--I spoke to the native servant--"

"You spoke to Hosain's sister."

Dick could only say: "I supposed they were two maids."

"You were told they were Himadoun."

"What?" Dick got out of bed and into a robe.

"I explained it to you at the piano night before last. Don't tell me you were too merry to understand."

"Was that what you said? I didn't hear the beginning. I didn't connect the--we didn't make any connection, Mary. Well, all we can do is see her and apologize."

"See her and apologize! I explained to you that when the oldest member of the family--when the oldest one marries, well, the two oldest sisters consecrate themselves to being Himadoun, to being his wife's ladies-in-waiting."

"Was that why Hosain left the house last night?"

Mary hesitated; then nodded.

"He had to--they all left. His honor makes it necessary."

Now both the Divers were up and dressing; Mary went on:

"And what's all that about the bathwater. As if a thing like that could happen in this house! We'll ask Lanier about it."

Dick sat on the bedside indicating in a private gesture to Nicole that she should take over. Meanwhile Mary went to the door and spoke to an attendant in Italian.

"Wait a minute," Nicole said. "I won't have that."

"You accused us," answered Mary, in a tone she had never used to Nicole before. "Now I have a right to see."

"I won't have the child brought in." Nicole threw on her clothes as though they were chain mail.

"That's all right," said Dick. "Bring Lanier in. We'll settle this bathtub matter--fact or myth."

Lanier, half clothed mentally and physically, gazed at the angered faces of the adults.

"Listen, Lanier," Mary demanded, "how did you come to think you were bathed in water that had been used before?"

"Speak up," Dick added.

"It was just dirty, that was all."

"Couldn't you hear the new water running, from your room, next door?"

Lanier admitted the possibility but reiterated his point--the water was dirty. He was a little awed; he tried to see ahead:

"It couldn't have been running, because--"

They pinned him down.

"Why not?"

He stood in his little kimono arousing the sympathy of his parents and further arousing Mary's impatience--then he said:

"The water was dirty, it was full of soap-suds."

"When you're not sure what you're saying--" Mary began, but Nicole interrupted.

"Stop it, Mary. If there were dirty suds in the water it was logical to think it was dirty. His father told him to come--"

"There couldn't have been dirty suds in the water."

Lanier looked reproachfully at his father, who had betrayed him. Nicole turned him about by the shoulders and sent him out of the room; Dick broke the tensity with a laugh.

Then, as if the sound recalled the past, the old friendship, Mary guessed how far away from them she had gone and said in a mollifying tone: "It's always like that with children."

Her uneasiness grew as she remembered the past. "You'd be silly to go--Hosain wanted to make this trip anyhow. After all, you're my guests and you just blundered into the thing." But Dick, made more angry by this obliqueness and the use of the word blunder, turned away and began arranging his effects, saying:

"It's too bad about the young women. I'd like to apologize to the one who came in here."

"If you'd only listened on the piano seat!"

"But you've gotten so damned dull, Mary. I listened as long as I could."

"Be quiet!" Nicole advised him.

"I return his compliment," said Mary bitterly. "Good-by, Nicole." She went out.

After all that there was no question of her coming to see them off; the major-domo arranged the departure. Dick left formal notes for Hosain and the sisters. There was nothing to do except to go, but all of them, especially Lanier, felt bad about it.

"I insist," insisted Lanier on the train, "that it was dirty bathwater."

"That'll do," his father said. "You better forget it--unless you want me to divorce you. Did you know there was a new law in France that you can divorce a child?"

Lanier roared with delight and the Divers were unified again--Dick wondered how many more times it could be done.

V

Nicole went to the window and bent over the sill to take a look at the rising altercation on the terrace; the April sun shone pink on the saintly face of Augustine, the cook, and blue on the butcher's knife she waved in her drunken hand. She had been with them since their return to Villa Diana in February.

Because of an obstruction of an awning she could see only Dick's head and his hand holding one of his heavy canes with a bronze knob on it. The knife and the cane, menacing each other, were like tripos and short sword in a gladiatorial combat. Dick's words reached her first:

"--care how much kitchen wine you drink but when I find you digging into a bottle of Chablis Moutonne--"

"You talk about drinking!" Augustine cried, flourishing her sabre. "You drink--all the time!"

Nicole called over the awning: "What's the matter, Dick?" and he answered in English:

"The old girl has been polishing off the vintage wines. I'm firing her--at least I'm trying to."

"Heavens! Well, don't let her reach you with that knife."

Augustine shook her knife up at Nicole. Her old mouth was made of two small intersecting cherries.

"I would like to say, Madame, if you knew that your husband drinks over at his Bastide comparatively as a day-laborer--"

"Shut up and get out!" interrupted Nicole. "We'll get the gendarmes."

"You'll get the gendarmes! With my brother in the corps! You--a disgusting American?"

In English Dick called up to Nicole:

"Get the children away from the house till I settle this."

"--disgusting Americans who come here and drink up our finest wines," screamed Augustine with the voice of the commune.

Dick mastered a firmer tone.

"You must leave now! I'll pay you what we owe you."

"Very sure you'll pay me! And let me tell you--" she came close and waved the knife so furiously that Dick raised his stick, whereupon she rushed into the kitchen and returned with the carving knife reinforced by a hatchet.

The situation was not prepossessing--Augustine was a strong woman and could be disarmed only at the risk of serious results to herself--and severe legal complications which were the lot of one who molested a French citizen. Trying a bluff Dick called up to Nicole:

"Phone the poste de police." Then to Augustine, indicating her armament, "This means arrest for you."

"Ha-*ha!"* she laughed demoniacally; nevertheless she came no nearer. Nicole phoned the police but was answered with what was almost an echo of Augustine's laugh. She heard mumbles and passings of the word around--the connection was suddenly broken.

Returning to the window she called down to Dick: "Give her something extra!"

"If I could get to that phone!" As this seemed impracticable, Dick capitulated. For fifty francs, increased to a hundred as he succumbed to the idea of getting her out hastily, Augustine yielded her fortress, covering the retreat with stormy grenades of "Salaud!" She would leave only when her nephew could come for her baggage. Waiting cautiously in the neighborhood of the kitchen Dick heard a cork pop, but he yielded the point. There was no further trouble--when the nephew arrived, all apologetic, Augustine bade Dick a cheerful, convivial good-by and called up "All revoir, Madame! Bonne chance!" to Nicole's window.

The Divers went to Nice and dined on a bouillabaisse, which is a stew of rock fish and small lobsters, highly seasoned with saffron, and a bottle of cold Chablis. He expressed pity for Augustine.

"I'm not sorry a bit," said Nicole.

"I'm sorry--and yet I wish I'd shoved her over the cliff."

There was little they dared talk about in these days; seldom did they find the right word when it counted, it arrived always a moment too late when one could not reach the other any more. To-night Augustine's outburst had shaken them from their separate reveries; with the burn and chill of the spiced broth and the parching wine they talked.

"We can't go on like this," Nicole suggested. "Or can we?--what do you think?" Startled that for the moment Dick did not deny it, she continued, "Some of the time I think it's my fault--I've ruined you."

"So I'm ruined, am I?" he inquired pleasantly.

"I didn't mean that. But you used to want to create things--now you seem to want to smash them up."

She trembled at criticizing him in these broad terms--but his enlarging silence frightened her even more. She guessed that something was developing behind the silence, behind the hard, blue eyes, the almost unnatural interest in the children. Uncharacteristic bursts of temper surprised her--he would suddenly unroll a long scroll of contempt for some person, race, class, way of life, way of thinking. It was as though an incalculable story was telling itself inside him, about which she could only guess at in the moments when it broke through the surface.

"After all, what do you get out of this?" she demanded.

"Knowing you're stronger every day. Knowing that your illness follows the law of diminishing returns."

His voice came to her from far off, as though he were speaking of something remote and academic; her alarm made her exclaim, "Dick!" and she thrust her hand forward to his across the table. A reflex pulled Dick's hand back and he added: "There's the whole situation to think of, isn't there? There's not just you." He covered her hand with his and said in the old pleasant voice of a conspirator for pleasure, mischief, profit, and delight:

"See that boat out there?"

It was the motor yacht of T. F. Golding lying placid among the little swells of the Nicean Bay, constantly bound upon a romantic voyage that was not dependent upon actual motion. "We'll go out there now and ask the people on board what's the matter with them. We'll find out if they're happy."

"We hardly know him," Nicole objected.

"He urged us. Besides, Baby knows him--she practically married him, doesn't she--didn't she?"

When they put out from the port in a hired launch it was already summer dusk and lights were breaking out in spasms along the rigging of the *Margin.* As they drew up alongside, Nicole's doubts reasserted themselves.

"He's having a party--"

"It's only a radio," he guessed.

They were hailed--a huge white-haired man in a white suit looked down at them, calling:

"Do I recognize the Divers?"

"Boat ahoy, *Margin*!"

Their boat moved under the companionway; as they mounted Golding doubled his huge frame to give Nicole a hand.

"Just in time for dinner."

A small orchestra was playing astern.

"I'm yours for the asking--but till then you can't ask me to behave--"

And as Golding's cyclonic arms blew them aft without touching them, Nicole was sorrier they had come, and more impatient at Dick. Having taken up an attitude of aloofness from the gay people here, at the time when Dick's work and her health were incompatible with going about, they had a reputation as refusers. Riviera replacements during the ensuing years interpreted this as a vague unpopularity. Nevertheless, having taken such a stand, Nicole felt it should not be cheaply compromised for a momentary self-indulgence.

As they passed through the principal salon they saw ahead of them figures that seemed to dance in the half light of the circular stern. This was an illusion made by the enchantment of the music, the unfamiliar lighting, and the surrounding presence of water. Actually, save for some busy stewards, the guests loafed on a wide divan that followed the curve of the deck. There were a white, a red, a blurred dress, the laundered chests of several men, of whom one, detaching and identifying himself, brought from Nicole a rare little cry of delight.

"Tommy!"

Brushing aside the Gallicism of his formal dip at her hand, Nicole pressed her face against his. They sat, or rather lay down together on the Antoninian bench. His handsome face was so dark as to have lost the pleasantness of deep tan, without attaining the blue beauty of Negroes--it was just worn leather. The foreignness of his depigmentation by unknown suns, his nourishment by strange soils, his tongue awkward with the curl of many dialects, his reactions attuned to odd alarms--these things fascinated and rested Nicole--in the moment of meeting she lay on his bosom, spiritually, going out and out. . . . Then self-preservation reasserted itself and retiring to her own world she spoke lightly.

"You look just like all the adventurers in the movies--but why do you have to stay away so long?"

Tommy Barban looked at her, uncomprehending but alert; the pupils of his eyes flashed.

"Five years," she continued, in throaty mimicry of nothing. "*Much* too long. Couldn't you only slaughter a certain number of creatures and then come back, and breathe our air for a while?"

In her cherished presence Tommy Europeanized himself quickly.

"Mais pour nous héros," he said, "il nous faut du temps, Nicole. Nous ne pouvons pas faire de petits exercises d'héroisme--il faut faire les grandes compositions."

"Talk English to me, Tommy."

"Parlez français avec moi, Nicole."

"But the meanings are different--in French you can be heroic and gallant with dignity, and you know it. But in English you can't be heroic and gallant without being a little absurd, and you know that too. That gives me an advantage."

"But after all--" He chuckled suddenly. "Even in English I'm brave, heroic and all that."

She pretended to be groggy with wonderment but he was not abashed.

"I only know what I see in the cinema," he said.

"Is it all like the movies?"

"The movies aren't so bad--now this Ronald Colman--have you seen his pictures about the Corps d'Afrique du Nord? They're not bad at all."

"Very well, whenever I go to the movies I'll know you're going through just that sort of thing at that moment."

As she spoke, Nicole was aware of a small, pale, pretty young woman with lovely metallic hair, almost green in the deck lights, who had been sitting on the other side of Tommy and might have been part either of their conversation or of the one next to them. She had obviously had a monopoly of Tommy, for now she abandoned hope of his attention with what was once called ill grace, and petulantly crossed the crescent of the deck.

"After all, I am a hero," Tommy said calmly, only half joking. "I have ferocious courage, *us*ually, something like a lion, something like a drunken man."

Nicole waited until the echo of his boast had died away in his mind--she knew he had probably never made such a statement before. Then she looked among the strangers, and found as usual, the fierce neurotics, pretending calm, liking the country only in horror of the city, of the sound of their own voices which had set the tone and pitch. . . . She asked:

"Who is the woman in white?"

"The one who was beside me? Lady Caroline Sibly-Biers."--They listened for a moment to her voice across the way:

"The man's a scoundrel, but he's a cat of the stripe. We sat up all night playing two-handed chemin-de-fer, and he owes me a mille Swiss."

Tommy laughed and said: "She is now the wickedest woman in London--whenever I come back to Europe there is a new crop of the wickedest women from London. She's the very latest--though I believe there is now one other who's considered almost as wicked."

Nicole glanced again at the woman across the deck--she was fragile, tubercular--it was incredible that such narrow shoulders, such puny arms could bear aloft the pennon of decadence, last ensign of the fading empire. Her resemblance was rather to one of John Held's flat-chested flappers than to the hierarchy of tall languid blondes who had posed for painters and novelists since before the war.

Golding approached, fighting down the resonance of his huge bulk, which transmitted his will as through a gargantuan amplifier, and Nicole, still reluctant, yielded to his reiterated points: that the *Margin* was starting for Cannes immediately after dinner; that they could always pack in some caviare and champagne, even though they had dined; that in any case Dick was now on the phone, telling their chauffeur in Nice to drive their car back to Cannes and leave it in front of the Café des Alliées where the Divers could retrieve it.

They moved into the dining salon and Dick was placed next to Lady Sibly-Biers. Nicole saw that his usually ruddy face was drained of blood; he talked in a dogmatic voice, of which only snatches reached Nicole:

". . . It's all right for you English, you're doing a dance of death. . . . Sepoys in the ruined fort, I mean Sepoys at the gate and gaiety in the fort and all that. The green hat, the crushed hat, no future."

Lady Caroline answered him in short sentences spotted with the terminal "What?" the double-edged "Quite!" the depressing "Cheerio!" that always had a connotation of imminent peril, but Dick appeared oblivious to the warning signals. Suddenly he made a particularly vehement pronouncement, the purport of which eluded Nicole, but she saw the young woman turn dark and sinewy, and heard her answer sharply:

"After all a chep's a chep and a chum's a chum."

Again he had offended some one--couldn't he hold his tongue a little longer? How long? To death then.

At the piano, a fair-haired young Scotsman from the orchestra (entitled by its drum "The Ragtime College Jazzes of Edinboro") had begun singing in a Danny Deever monotone, accompanying himself with low chords on the piano. He pronounced his words with great precision, as though they impressed him almost intolerably.

"There was a young lady from hell,
Who jumped at the sound of a bell,
Because she was bad--bad--bad,
She jumped at the sound of a bell,
From hell (BOOMBOOM)
From hell (TOOTTOOT)
There was a young lady from hell--"

"What is all this?" whispered Tommy to Nicole.

The girl on the other side of him supplied the answer:

"Caroline Sibly-Biers wrote the words. He wrote the music."

"Quelle enfanterie!" Tommy murmured as the next verse began, hinting at the jumpy lady's further predilections. "On dirait qu'il récite Racine!"

On the surface at least, Lady Caroline was paying no attention to the performance of her work. Glancing at her again Nicole found herself impressed, neither with the character nor the personality, but with the sheer strength derived from an attitude; Nicole thought that she was formidable, and she was confirmed in this point of view as the party rose from table. Dick remained in his seat wearing an odd expression; then he crashed into words with a harsh ineptness.

"I don't like innuendo in these deafening English whispers."

Already half-way out of the room Lady Caroline turned and walked back to him; she spoke in a low clipped voice purposely audible to the whole company.

"You came to me asking for it--disparaging my countrymen, disparaging my friend, Mary Minghetti. I simply said you were observed associating with a questionable crowd in Lausanne. Is that a deafening whisper? Or does it simply deafen *you?"*

"It's still not loud enough," said Dick, a little too late. "So I am actually a notorious--"

Golding crushed out the phrase with his voice saying:

"What! What!" and moved his guests on out, with the threat of his powerful body. Turning the corner of the door Nicole saw that Dick was still sitting at the table. She was furious at the woman for her preposterous statement, equally furious at Dick for having brought them here, for having become fuddled, for having untipped the capped barbs of his irony, for having come off humiliated--she was a little more annoyed because she knew that her taking possession of Tommy Barban on their arrival had first irritated the Englishwoman.

A moment later she saw Dick standing in the gangway, apparently in complete control of himself as he talked with Golding; then for half an hour she did not see him anywhere about the deck and she broke out of an intricate Malay game, played with string and coffee beans, and said to Tommy:

"I've got to find Dick."

Since dinner the yacht had been in motion westward. The fine night streamed away on either side, the Diesel engines pounded softly, there was a spring wind that blew Nicole's hair abruptly when she reached the bow, and she had a sharp lesion of anxiety at seeing Dick standing in the angle by the flagstaff. His voice was serene as he recognized her.

"It's a nice night."

"I was worried."

"Oh, you were worried?"

"Oh, don't talk that way. It would give me so much pleasure to think of a little something I could do for you, Dick."

He turned away from her, toward the veil of starlight over Africa.

"I believe that's true, Nicole. And sometimes I believe that the littler it was, the more pleasure it would give you."

"Don't talk like that--don't say such things."

His face, wan in the light that the white spray caught and tossed back to the brilliant sky had none of the lines of annoyance she had expected. It was even detached; his eyes focussed upon her gradually as upon a chessman to be moved; in the same slow manner he caught her wrist and drew her near.

"You ruined me, did you?" he inquired blandly. "Then we're both ruined. So--"

Cold with terror she put her other wrist into his grip. All right, she would go with him--again she felt the beauty of the night vividly in one moment of complete response and abnegation--all right, then--

--but now she was unexpectedly free and Dick turned his back sighing. "Tch! tch!"

Tears streamed down Nicole's face--in a moment she heard some one approaching; it was Tommy.

"You found him! Nicole thought maybe you jumped overboard, Dick," he said, "because that little English poule slanged you."

"It'd be a good setting to jump overboard," said Dick mildly.

"Wouldn't it?" agreed Nicole hastily. "Let's borrow life-preservers and jump over. I think we should do something spectacular. I feel that all our lives have been too restrained."

Tommy sniffed from one to the other trying to breathe in the situation with the night. "We'll go ask the Lady Beer-and-Ale what to do--she should know the latest things. And we should memorize her song 'There was a young lady from l'enfer.' I shall translate it, and make a fortune from its success at the Casino."

"Are you rich, Tommy?" Dick asked him, as they retraced the length of the boat.

"Not as things go now. I got tired of the brokerage business and went away. But I have good stocks in the hands of friends who are holding it for me. All goes well."

"Dick's getting rich," Nicole said. In reaction her voice had begun to tremble.

On the after deck Golding had fanned three pairs of dancers into action with his colossal paws. Nicole and Tommy joined them and Tommy remarked: "Dick seems to be drinking."

"Only moderately," she said loyally.

"There are those who can drink and those who can't. Obviously Dick can't. You ought to tell him not to."

"I!" she exclaimed in amazement. "*I* tell Dick what he should do or shouldn't do!"

But in a reticent way Dick was still vague and sleepy when they reached the pier at Cannes. Golding buoyed him down into the launch of the *Margin* whereupon Lady Caroline shifted her place conspicuously. On the dock he bowed good-by with exaggerated formality, and for a moment he seemed about to speed her with a salty epigram, but the bone of Tommy's arm went into the soft part of his and they walked to the attendant car.

"I'll drive you home," Tommy suggested.

"Don't bother--we can get a cab."

"I'd like to, if you can put me up."

On the back seat of the car Dick remained quiescent until the yellow monolith of Golfe Juan was passed, and then the constant carnival at Juan les Pins where the night was musical and strident in many languages. When the car turned up the hill toward Tarmes, he sat up suddenly, prompted by the tilt of the vehicle and delivered a peroration:

"A charming representative of the--" he stumbled momentarily, "--a firm of--bring me Brains addled a l'Anglaise." Then he went into an appeased sleep, belching now and then contentedly into the soft warm darkness.

VI

Next morning Dick came early into Nicole's room. "I waited till I heard you up. Needless to say I feel badly about the evening--but how about no postmortems?"

"I'm agreed," she answered coolly, carrying her face to the mirror.

"Tommy drove us home? Or did I dream it?"

"You know he did."

"Seems probable," he admitted, "since I just heard him coughing. I think I'll call on him."

She was glad when he left her, for almost the first time in her life--his awful faculty of being right seemed to have deserted him at last.

Tommy was stirring in his bed, waking for café au lait.

"Feel all right?" Dick asked.

When Tommy complained of a sore throat he seized at a professional attitude.

"Better have a gargle or something."

"You have one?"

"Oddly enough I haven't--probably Nicole has."

"Don't disturb her."

"She's up."

"How is she?"

Dick turned around slowly. "Did you expect her to be dead because I was tight?" His tone was pleasant. "Nicole is now made of--of Georgia pine, which is the hardest wood known, except lignum vitæ from New Zealand--"

Nicole, going downstairs, heard the end of the conversation. She knew, as she had always known, that Tommy loved her; she knew he had come to dislike Dick, and that Dick had realized it before he did, and would react in some positive way to the man's lonely passion. This thought was succeeded by a moment of sheerly feminine satisfaction. She leaned over her children's breakfast table and told off instructions to the governess, while upstairs two men were concerned about her.

Later in the garden she was happy; she did not want anything to happen, but only for the situation to remain in suspension as the two men tossed her from one mind to another; she had not existed for a long time, even as a ball.

"Nice, Rabbits, isn't it--Or is it? Hey, Rabbit--hey you! Is it nice?--hey? Or does it sound very peculiar to you?"

The rabbit, after an experience of practically nothing else and cabbage leaves, agreed after a few tentative shiftings of the nose.

Nicole went on through her garden routine. She left the flowers she cut in designated spots to be brought to the house later by the gardener. Reaching the sea wall she fell into a communicative mood and no one to communicate with; so she stopped and deliberated. She was somewhat shocked at the idea of being interested in another man--but other women have lovers--why not me? In the fine spring morning the inhibitions of the male world disappeared and she reasoned as gaily as a flower, while the wind blew her hair until her head moved with it. Other women have had lovers--the same forces that last night had made her yield to Dick up to the point of death, now kept her head nodding to the wind, content and happy with the logic of, Why shouldn't I?

She sat upon the low wall and looked down upon the sea. But from another sea, the wide swell of fantasy, she had fished out something tangible to lay beside the rest of her loot. If she need not, in her spirit, be forever one with Dick as he had appeared last night, she must be something in addition, not just an image on his mind, condemned to endless parades around the circumference of a medal.

Nicole had chosen this part of the wall on which to sit, because the cliff shaded to a slanting meadow with a cultivated vegetable garden. Through a cluster of boughs she saw two men carrying rakes and spades and talking in a counterpoint of Niçoise and Provençal. Attracted by their words and gestures she caught the sense:

"I laid her down here."

"I took her behind the vines there."

"She doesn't care--neither does he. It was that sacred dog. Well, I laid her down here--"

"You got the rake?"

"You got it yourself, you clown."

"Well, I don't care where you laid her down. Until that night I never even felt a woman's breast against my chest since I married--twelve years ago. And now you tell me--"

"But listen about the dog--"

Nicole watched them through the boughs; it seemed all right what they were saying--one thing was good for one person, another for another. Yet it was a man's world she had overheard; going back to the house she became doubtful again.

Dick and Tommy were on the terrace. She walked through them and into the house, brought out a sketch pad and began a head of Tommy.

"Hands never idle--distaff flying," Dick said lightly. How could he talk so trivially with the blood still drained down from his cheeks so that the auburn lather of beard showed red as his eyes? She turned to Tommy saying:

"I can always do something. I used to have a nice active little Polynesian ape and juggle him around for hours till people began to make the most dismal rough jokes--"

She kept her eyes resolutely away from Dick. Presently he excused himself and went inside--she saw him pour himself two glasses of water, and she hardened further.

"Nicole--" Tommy began but interrupted himself to clear the harshness from his throat.

"I'm going to get you some special camphor rub," she suggested. "It's American--Dick believes in it. I'll be just a minute."

"I must go really."

Dick came out and sat down. "Believes in what?" When she returned with the jar neither of the men had moved, though she gathered they had had some sort of excited conversation about nothing.

The chauffeur was at the door, with a bag containing Tommy's clothes of the night before. The sight of Tommy in clothes borrowed from Dick moved her sadly, falsely, as though Tommy were not able to afford such clothes.

"When you get to the hotel rub this into your throat and chest and then inhale it," she said.

"Say, there," Dick murmured as Tommy went down the steps, "don't give Tommy the whole jar--it has to be ordered from Paris--it's out of stock down here."

Tommy came back within hearing and the three of them stood in the sunshine, Tommy squarely before the car so that it seemed by leaning forward he would tip it upon his back.

Nicole stepped down to the path.

"Now catch it," she advised him. "It's extremely rare."

She heard Dick grow silent at her side; she took a step off from him and waved as the car drove off with Tommy and the special camphor rub. Then she turned to take her own medicine.

"There was no necessity for that gesture," Dick said. "There are four of us here--and for years whenever there's a cough--"

They looked at each other.

"We can always get another jar--" then she lost her nerve and presently followed him upstairs where he lay down on his own bed and said nothing.

"Do you want lunch to be brought up to you?" she asked.

He nodded and continued to lie quiescent, staring at the ceiling. Doubtfully she went to give the order. Upstairs again she looked into his room--the blue eyes, like searchlights, played on a dark sky. She stood a minute in the doorway, aware of the sin she had committed against him, half afraid to come in. . . . She put out her hand as if to rub his head, but he turned away like a suspicious animal. Nicole could stand the situation no longer; in a kitchen-maid's panic she ran downstairs, afraid of what the stricken man above would feed on while she must still continue her dry suckling at his lean chest.

In a week Nicole forgot her flash about Tommy--she had not much memory for people and forgot them easily. But in the first hot blast of June she heard he was in Nice. He wrote a little note to them both--and she opened it under the parasol, together with other mail they had brought from the house. After reading it she tossed it over to Dick, and in exchange he threw a telegram into the lap of her beach pajamas:

> Dears will be at Gausses to-morrow unfortunately without mother am counting on seeing you.

"I'll be glad to see her," said Nicole, grimly.

VII

But she went to the beach with Dick next morning with a renewal of her apprehension that Dick was contriving at some desperate solution. Since the evening on Golding's yacht she had sensed what was going on. So delicately balanced was she between an old foothold that had always guaranteed her security, and the imminence of a leap from which she must alight changed in the very chemistry of blood and muscle, that she did not dare bring the matter into the true forefront of consciousness. The figures of Dick and herself, mutating, undefined, appeared as spooks caught up into a fantastic dance. For months every word had seemed to have an overtone of some other meaning, soon to be resolved under circumstances that Dick would determine. Though this state of mind was perhaps more hopeful,--the long years of sheer being had had an enlivening effect on the parts of her nature that early illness had killed, that Dick had not reached--through no fault of his but simply because no one nature can extend entirely inside another--it was still disquieting. The most unhappy aspect of their relations was Dick's growing indifference, at present personified by too much drink; Nicole did not know whether she was to be crushed or spared--Dick's voice, throbbing with insincerity, confused the issue; she couldn't guess how he was going to behave next upon the tortuously slow unrolling of the carpet, nor what would happen at the end, at the moment of the leap.

For what might occur thereafter she had no anxiety--she suspected that that would be the lifting of a burden, an unblinding of eyes. Nicole had been designed for change, for flight, with money as fins and wings. The new state of things would be no more than if a racing chassis, concealed for years under the body of a family limousine, should be stripped to its original self. Nicole could feel the fresh breeze already--the wrench it was she feared, and the dark manner of its coming.

The Divers went out on the beach with her white suit and his white trunks very white against the color of their bodies. Nicole saw Dick peer about for the children among the confused shapes and shadows of many umbrellas, and as his mind temporarily left her, ceasing to grip her, she looked at him with detachment, and decided that he was seeking his children, not protectively but for protection. Probably it was the beach he feared, like a deposed ruler secretly visiting an old court. She had come to hate his world with its delicate jokes and politenesses, forgetting that for many years it was the only world open to her. Let him look at it--his beach, perverted now to the tastes of the tasteless; he could search it for a day and find no stone of the Chinese Wall he had once erected around it, no footprint of an old friend.

For a moment Nicole was sorry it was so; remembering the glass he had raked out of the old trash heap, remembering the sailor trunks and sweaters they had bought in a Nice back street--garments that afterward ran through a vogue in silk among the Paris couturiers, remembering the simple little French girls climbing on the breakwaters crying "Dites donc! Dites donc!" like birds, and the ritual of the morning time, the quiet restful extraversion toward sea and sun--many inventions of his, buried deeper than the sand under the span of so few years. . . .

Now the swimming place was a "club," though, like the international society it represented, it would be hard to say who was not admitted.

Nicole hardened again as Dick knelt on the straw mat and looked about for Rosemary. Her eyes followed his, searching among the new paraphernalia, the trapezes over the water, the swinging rings, the portable bathhouses, the floating towers, the searchlights from last night's fêtes, the modernistic buffet, white with a hackneyed motif of endless handlebars.

The water was almost the last place he looked for Rosemary, because few people swam any more in that blue paradise, children and one exhibitionistic valet who punctuated the morning with spectacular dives from a fifty-foot rock--most of Gausse's guests stripped the concealing pajamas from their flabbiness only for a short hangover dip at one o'clock.

"There she is," Nicole remarked.

She watched Dick's eyes following Rosemary's track from raft to raft; but the sigh that rocked out of her bosom was something left over from five years ago.

"Let's swim out and speak to Rosemary," he suggested.

"You go."

"We'll both go." She struggled a moment against his pronouncement, but eventually they swam out together, tracing Rosemary by the school of little fish who followed her, taking their dazzle from her, the shining spoon of a trout hook.

Nicole stayed in the water while Dick hoisted himself up beside Rosemary, and the two sat dripping and talking, exactly as if they had never loved or touched each other. Rosemary was beautiful--her youth was a shock to Nicole, who rejoiced, however, that the young girl was less slender by a hairline than herself. Nicole swam around in little rings, listening to Rosemary who was acting amusement, joy, and expectation--more confident than she had been five years ago.

"I miss Mother so, but she's meeting me in Paris, Monday."

"Five years ago you came here," said Dick. "And what a funny little thing you were, in one of those hotel peignoirs!"

"How you remember things! You always did--and always the nice things."

Nicole saw the old game of flattery beginning again and she dove under water, coming up again to hear:

"I'm going to pretend it's five years ago and I'm a girl of eighteen again. You could always make me feel some you know, kind of, you know, kind of happy way--you and Nicole. I feel as if you're still on the beach there, under one of those umbrellas--the nicest people I'd ever known, maybe ever will."

Swimming away, Nicole saw that the cloud of Dick's heart-sickness had lifted a little as he began to play with Rosemary, bringing out his old expertness with people, a tarnished object of art; she guessed that with a drink or so he would have done his stunts on the swinging rings for her, fumbling through stunts he had once done with ease. She noticed that this summer, for the first time, he avoided high diving.

Later, as she dodged her way from raft to raft, Dick overtook her.

"Some of Rosemary's friends have a speed boat, the one out there. Do you want to aquaplane? I think it would be amusing."

Remembering that once he could stand on his hands on a chair at the end of a board, she indulged him as she might have indulged Lanier. Last summer on the Zugersee they had played at that pleasant water game, and Dick had lifted a two-hundred-pound man from the board onto his shoulders and stood up. But women marry all their husbands' talents and naturally, afterwards, are not so impressed with them as they may keep up the pretense of being. Nicole had not even pretended to be impressed, though she had said "Yes" to him, and "Yes, I thought so too."

She knew, though, that he was somewhat tired, that it was only the closeness of Rosemary's exciting youth that prompted the impending effort--she had seen him draw the same inspiration from the new bodies of her children and she wondered coldly if he would make a spectacle of himself. The Divers were older than the others in the boat--the young people were polite, deferential, but Nicole felt an undercurrent of "Who are these Numbers anyhow?" and she missed Dick's easy talent of taking control of situations and making them all right--he had concentrated on what he was going to try to do.

The motor throttled down two hundred yards from shore and one of the young men dove flat over the edge. He swam at the aimless twisting board, steadied it, climbed slowly to his knees on it--then got on his feet as the boat accelerated. Leaning back he swung his light vehicle ponderously from side to side in slow, breathless arcs that rode the trailing side-swell at the end of each swing. In the direct wake of the boat he let go his rope, balanced for a moment, then back-flipped into the water, disappearing like a statue of glory, and reappearing as an insignificant head while the boat made the circle back to him.

Nicole refused her turn; then Rosemary rode the board neatly and conservatively, with facetious cheers from her admirers. Three of them scrambled egotistically for the honor of pulling her into the boat, managing, among them, to bruise her knee and hip against the side.

"Now you. Doctor," said the Mexican at the wheel.

Dick and the last young man dove over the side and swam to the board. Dick was going to try his lifting trick and Nicole began to watch with smiling scorn. This physical showing-off for Rosemary irritated her most of all.

When the men had ridden long enough to find their balance, Dick knelt, and putting the back of his neck in the other man's crotch, found the rope through his legs, and slowly began to rise.

The people in the boat, watching closely, saw that he was having difficulties. He was on one knee; the trick was to straighten all the way up in the same motion with which he left his kneeling position. He rested for a moment, then his face contracted as he put his heart into the strain, and lifted.

The board was narrow, the man, though weighing less than a hundred and fifty, was awkward with his weight and grabbed clumsily at Dick's head. When, with a last wrenching effort of his back, Dick stood upright, the board slid sidewise and the pair toppled into the sea.

In the boat Rosemary exclaimed: "Wonderful! They almost had it."

But as they came back to the swimmers Nicole watched for a sight of Dick's face. It was full of annoyance as she expected, because he had done the thing with ease only two years ago.

The second time he was more careful. He rose a little testing the balance of his burden, settled down again on his knee; then, grunting "Alley oop!" began to rise--but before he could really straighten out, his legs suddenly buckled and he shoved the board away with his feet to avoid being struck as they fell off.

This time when the Baby Gar came back it was apparent to all the passengers that he was angry.

"Do you mind if I try that once more?" he called, treading water. "We almost had it then."

"Sure. Go ahead."

To Nicole he looked white-around-the-gills, and she cautioned him:

"Don't you think that's enough for now?"

He didn't answer. The first partner had had plenty and was hauled over the side, the Mexican driving the motor boat obligingly took his place.

He was heavier than the first man. As the boat gathered motion, Dick rested for a moment, belly-down on the board. Then he got beneath the man and took the rope, and his muscles flexed as he tried to rise.

He could not rise. Nicole saw him shift his position and strain upward again but at the instant when the weight of his partner was full upon his shoulders he became immovable. He tried again--lifting an inch, two inches--Nicole felt the sweat glands of her forehead open as she strained with him--then he was simply holding his ground, then he collapsed back down on his knees with a smack, and they went over, Dick's head barely missing a kick of the board.

"Hurry back!" Nicole called to the driver; even as she spoke she saw him slide under water and she gave a little cry; but he came up again and turned on his back, and "Château" swam near to help. It seemed forever till the boat reached them but when they came alongside at last and Nicole saw Dick floating exhausted and expressionless, alone with the water and the sky, her panic changed suddenly to contempt.

"We'll help you up, Doctor. . . . Get his foot . . . all right . . . now altogether. . . ."

Dick sat panting and looking at nothing.

"I knew you shouldn't have tried it," Nicole could not help saying.

"He'd tired himself the first two times," said the Mexican.

"It was a foolish thing," Nicole insisted. Rosemary tactfully said nothing.

After a minute Dick got his breath, panting, "I couldn't have lifted a paper doll that time."

An explosive little laugh relieved the tension caused by his failure. They were all attentive to Dick as he disembarked at the dock. But Nicole was annoyed--everything he did annoyed her now.

She sat with Rosemary under an umbrella while Dick went to the buffet for a drink--he returned presently with some sherry for them.

"The first drink I ever had was with you," Rosemary said, and with a spurt of enthusiasm she added, "Oh, I'm so glad to see you and *know* you're all right. I was worried--" Her sentence broke as she changed direction "that maybe you wouldn't be."

"Did you hear I'd gone into a process of deterioration?"

"Oh, no. I simply--just heard you'd changed. And I'm glad to see with my own eyes it isn't true."

"It is true," Dick answered, sitting down with them. "The change came a long way back--but at first it didn't show. The manner remains intact for some time after the morale cracks."

"Do you practise on the Riviera?" Rosemary demanded hastily.

"It'd be a good ground to find likely specimens." He nodded here and there at the people milling about in the golden sand. "Great candidates. Notice our old friend, Mrs. Abrams, playing duchess to Mary North's queen? Don't get jealous about it--think of Mrs. Abram's long climb up the back stairs of the Ritz on her hands and knees and all the carpet dust she had to inhale."

Rosemary interrupted him. "But is that really Mary North?" She was regarding a woman sauntering in their direction followed by a small group who behaved as if they were accustomed to being looked at. When they were ten feet away, Mary's glance flickered fractionally over the Divers, one of those unfortunate glances that indicate to the glanced-upon that they have been observed but are to be overlooked, the sort of glance that neither the Divers nor Rosemary Hoyt had ever permitted themselves to throw at any one in their lives. Dick was amused when Mary perceived Rosemary, changed her plans and came over. She spoke to Nicole with pleasant heartiness, nodded unsmilingly to Dick as if he were somewhat contagious--whereupon he bowed in ironic respect--as she greeted Rosemary.

"I heard you were here. For how long?"

"Until to-morrow," Rosemary answered.

She, too, saw how Mary had walked through the Divers to talk to her, and a sense of obligation kept her unenthusiastic. No, she could not dine to-night.

Mary turned to Nicole, her manner indicating affection blended with pity.

"How are the children?" she asked.

They came up at the moment, and Nicole gave ear to a request that she overrule the governess on a swimming point.

"No," Dick answered for her. "What Mademoiselle says must go."

Agreeing that one must support delegated authority, Nicole refused their request, whereupon Mary--who in the manner of an Anita Loos' heroine had dealings only with Faits Accomplis, who indeed could not have house-broken a French poodle puppy--regarded Dick as though he were guilty of a most flagrant bullying. Dick, chafed by the tiresome performance, inquired with mock solicitude:

"How are your children--and their aunts?"

Mary did not answer; she left them, first draping a sympathetic hand over Lanier's reluctant head. After she had gone Dick said: "When I think of the time I spent working over her."

"I like her," said Nicole.

Dick's bitterness had surprised Rosemary, who had thought of him as all-forgiving, all-comprehending. Suddenly she recalled what it was she had heard about him. In conversation with some State Department people on the boat,--Europeanized Americans who had reached a position where they could scarcely have been said to belong to any nation at all, at least not to any great power though perhaps to a Balkan-like state composed of similar citizens--the name of the ubiquitously renowned Baby Warren had occurred and it was remarked that Baby's younger sister had thrown herself away on a dissipated doctor. "He's not received anywhere any more," the woman said.

The phrase disturbed Rosemary, though she could not place the Divers as living in any relation to society where such a fact, if fact it was, could have any meaning, yet the hint of a hostile and organized public opinion rang in her ears. "He's not received anywhere any more." She pictured Dick climbing the steps of a mansion, presenting cards and being told by a butler: "We're not receiving you any more"; then proceeding down an avenue only to be told the same thing by the countless other butlers of countless Ambassadors, Ministers, Chargés d'Affaires. . . .

Nicole wondered how she could get away. She guessed that Dick, stung into alertness, would grow charming and would make Rosemary respond to him. Sure enough, in a moment his voice managed to qualify everything unpleasant he had said:

"Mary's all right--she's done very well. But it's hard to go on liking people who don't like you."

Rosemary, falling into line, swayed toward Dick and crooned:

"Oh, you're so nice. I can't imagine anybody not forgiving you anything, no matter what you did to them." Then feeling that her exuberance had transgressed on Nicole's rights, she looked at the sand exactly between them: "I wanted to ask you both what you thought of my latest pictures--if you saw them."

Nicole said nothing, having seen one of them and thought little about it.

"It'll take a few minutes to tell you," Dick said. "Let's suppose that Nicole says to you that Lanier is ill. What do you do in life? What does anyone do? They *act*--face, voice, words--the face shows sorrow, the voice shows shock, the words show sympathy."

"Yes--I understand."

"But in the theatre, No. In the theatre all the best comediennes have built up their reputations by burlesquing the correct emotional responses--fear and love and sympathy."

"I see." Yet she did not quite see.

Losing the thread of it, Nicole's impatience increased as Dick continued:

"The danger to an actress is in responding. Again, let's suppose that somebody told you, 'Your lover is dead.' In life you'd probably go to pieces. But on the stage you're trying to entertain--the audience can do the 'responding' for themselves. First the actress has lines to follow, then she has to get the audience's attention back on herself, away from the murdered Chinese or whatever the thing is. So she must do something unexpected. If the audience thinks the character is hard she goes soft on them--if they think she's soft she goes hard. You go all *out* of character--you understand?"

"I don't quite," admitted Rosemary. "How do you mean out of character?"

"You do the unexpected thing until you've manoeuvred the audience back from the objective fact to yourself. *Then* you slide into character again."

Nicole could stand no more. She stood up sharply, making no attempt to conceal her impatience. Rosemary, who had been for a few minutes half-conscious of this, turned in a conciliatory way to Topsy.

"Would you like to be an actress when you grow up? I think you'd make a fine actress."

Nicole stared at her deliberately and in her grandfather's voice said, slow and distinct:

"It's absolutely *out* to put such ideas in the heads of other people's children. Remember, we may have quite different plans for them." She turned sharply to Dick. "I'm going to take the car home. I'll send Michelle for you and the children."

"You haven't driven for months," he protested.

"I haven't forgotten how."

Without a glance at Rosemary whose face was "responding" violently, Nicole left the umbrella.

In the bathhouse, she changed to pajamas, her expression still hard as a plaque. But as she turned into the road of arched pines and the atmosphere changed,--with a squirrel's flight on a branch, a wind nudging at the leaves, a cock splitting distant air, with a creep of sunlight transpiring through the immobility, then the voices of the beach receded--Nicole relaxed and felt new and happy; her thoughts were clear as good bells--she had a sense of being cured and in a new way. Her ego began blooming like a great rich rose as she scrambled back along the labyrinths in which she had wandered for years. She hated the beach, resented the places where she had played planet to Dick's sun.

"Why, I'm almost complete," she thought. "I'm practically standing alone, without him." And like a happy child, wanting the completion as soon as possible, and knowing vaguely that Dick had planned for her to have it, she lay on her bed as soon as she got home and wrote Tommy Barban in Nice a short provocative letter.

But that was for the daytime--toward evening with the inevitable diminution of nervous energy, her spirits flagged, and the arrows flew a little in the twilight. She was afraid of what was in Dick's mind; again she felt that a plan underlay his current actions and she was afraid of his plans--they worked well and they had an all-inclusive logic about them which Nicole was not able to command. She had somehow given over the thinking to him, and in his absences her every action seemed automatically governed by what he would like, so that now she felt inadequate to match her intentions against his. Yet think she must; she knew at last the number on the dreadful door of fantasy, the threshold to the escape that was no escape; she knew that for her the greatest sin now and in the future was to delude herself. It had been a long lesson but she had learned it. Either you think--or else others have to think for you and take power from you, pervert and discipline your natural tastes, civilize and sterilize you.

They had a tranquil supper with Dick drinking much beer and being cheerful with the children in the dusky room. Afterward he played some Schubert songs and some new jazz from America that Nicole hummed in her harsh, sweet contralto over his shoulder.

"Thank y' father-r
Thank y' mother-r
Thanks for meetingup with one another--"

"I don't like that one," Dick said, starting to turn the page.

"Oh, play it!" she exclaimed. "Am I going through the rest of life flinching at the word 'father'?"

"--Thank the horse that pulled the buggy that night!
Thank you both for being justabit tight--"

Later they sat with the children on the Moorish roof and watched the fireworks of two casinos, far apart, far down on the shore. It was lonely and sad to be so empty-hearted toward each other.

Next morning, back from shopping in Cannes, Nicole found a note saying that Dick had taken the small car and gone up into Provence for a few days by himself. Even as she read it the phone rang--it was Tommy Barban from Monte Carlo, saying that he had received her letter and was driving over. She felt her lips' warmth in the receiver as she welcomed his coming.

VIII

She bathed and anointed herself and covered her body with a layer of powder, while her toes crunched another pile on a bath towel. She looked microscopically at the lines of her flanks, wondering how soon the fine, slim edifice would begin to sink squat and earthward. In about six years, but now I'll do--in fact I'll do as well as any one I know.

She was not exaggerating. The only physical disparity between Nicole at present and the Nicole of five years before was simply that she was no longer a young girl. But she was enough ridden by the current youth worship, the moving pictures with their myriad faces of girl-children, blandly represented as carrying on the work and wisdom of the world, to feel a jealousy of youth.

She put on the first ankle-length day dress that she had owned for many years, and crossed herself reverently with Chanel Sixteen. When Tommy drove up at one o'clock she had made her person into the trimmest of gardens.

How good to have things like this, to be worshipped again, to pretend to have a mystery! She had lost two of the great arrogant years in the life of a pretty girl--now she felt like making up for them; she greeted Tommy as if he were one of many men at her feet, walking ahead of him instead of beside him as they crossed the garden toward the market umbrella. Attractive women of nineteen and of twenty-nine are alike in their breezy confidence; on the contrary, the exigent womb of the twenties does not pull the outside world centripetally around itself. The former are ages of insolence, comparable the one to a young cadet, the other to a fighter strutting after combat.

But whereas a girl of nineteen draws her confidence from a surfeit of attention, a woman of twenty-nine is nourished on subtler stuff. Desirous, she chooses her apéritifs wisely, or, content, she enjoys the caviare of potential power. Happily she does not seem, in either case, to anticipate the subsequent years when her insight will often be blurred by panic, by the fear of stopping or the fear of going on. But on the landings of nineteen or twenty-nine she is pretty sure that there are no bears in the hall.

Nicole did not want any vague spiritual romance--she wanted an "affair"; she wanted a change. She realized, thinking with Dick's thoughts, that from a superficial view it was a vulgar business to enter, without emotion, into an indulgence that menaced all of them. On the other hand, she blamed Dick for the immediate situation, and honestly thought that such an experiment might have a therapeutic value. All summer she had been stimulated by watching people do exactly what they were tempted to do and pay no penalty for it--moreover, in spite of her intention of no longer lying to herself, she preferred to consider that she was merely feeling her way and that at any moment she could withdraw. . . .

In the light shade Tommy caught her up in his white-duck arms and pulled her around to him, looking at her eyes.

"Don't move," he said. "I'm going to look at you a great deal from now on."

There was some scent on his hair, a faint aura of soap from his white clothes. Her lips were tight, not smiling and they both simply looked for a moment.

"Do you like what you see?" she murmured.

"Parle français."

"Very well," and she asked again in French. "Do you like what you see?"

He pulled her closer.

"I like whatever I see about you." He hesitated. "I thought I knew your face but it seems there are some things I didn't know about it. When did you begin to have white crook's eyes?"

She broke away, shocked and indignant, and cried in English:

"Is that why you wanted to talk French?" Her voice quieted as the butler came with sherry. "So you could be offensive more accurately?"

She parked her small seat violently on the cloth-of-silver chair cushion.

"I have no mirror here," she said, again in French, but decisively, "but if my eyes have changed it's because I'm well again. And being well perhaps I've gone back to my true self--I suppose my grandfather was a crook and I'm a crook by heritage, so there we are. Does that satisfy your logical mind?"

He scarcely seemed to know what she was talking about.

"Where's Dick--is he lunching with us?"

Seeing that his remark had meant comparatively little to him she suddenly laughed away its effect.

"Dick's on a tour," she said. "Rosemary Hoyt turned up, and either they're together or she upset him so much that he wants to go away and dream about her."

"You know, you're a little complicated after all."

"Oh no," she assured him hastily. "No, I'm not really--I'm just a--I'm just a whole lot of different simple people."

Marius brought out melon and an ice pail, and Nicole, thinking irresistibly about her crook's eyes did not answer; he gave one an entire nut to crack, this man, instead of giving it in fragments to pick at for meat.

"Why didn't they leave you in your natural state?" Tommy demanded presently. "You are the most dramatic person I have known."

She had no answer.

"All this taming of women!" he scoffed.

"In any society there are certain--" She felt Dick's ghost prompting at her elbow but she subsided at Tommy's overtone:

"I've brutalized many men into shape but I wouldn't take a chance on half the number of women. Especially this 'kind' bullying--what good does it do anybody?--you or him or anybody?"

Her heart leaped and then sank faintly with a sense of what she owed Dick.

"I suppose I've got--"

"You've got too much money," he said impatiently. "That's the crux of the matter. Dick can't beat that."

She considered while the melons were removed.

"What do you think I ought to do?"

For the first time in ten years she was under the sway of a personality other than her husband's. Everything Tommy said to her became part of her forever.

They drank the bottle of wine while a faint wind rocked the pine needles and the sensuous heat of early afternoon made blinding freckles on the checkered luncheon cloth. Tommy came over behind her and laid his arms along hers, clasping her hands. Their cheeks touched and then their lips and she gasped half with passion for him, half with the sudden surprise of its force. . . .

"Can't you send the governess and the children away for the afternoon?"

"They have a piano lesson. Anyhow I don't want to stay here."

"Kiss me again."

A little later, riding toward Nice, she thought: So I have white crook's eyes, have I? Very well then, better a sane crook than a mad puritan.

His assertion seemed to absolve her from all blame or responsibility and she had a thrill of delight in thinking of herself in a new way. New vistas appeared ahead, peopled with the faces of many men, none of whom she need obey or even love. She drew in her breath, hunched her shoulders with a wriggle and turned to Tommy.

"Have we *got* to go all the way to your hotel at Monte Carlo?"

He brought the car to a stop with a squeak of tires.

"No!" he answered. "And, my God, I have never been so happy as I am this minute."

They had passed through Nice following the blue coast and begun to mount to the middling-high Corniche. Now Tommy turned sharply down to the shore, ran out a blunt peninsula, and stopped in the rear of a small shore hotel.

Its tangibility frightened Nicole for a moment. At the desk an American was arguing interminably with the clerk about the rate of exchange. She hovered, outwardly tranquil but inwardly miserable, as Tommy filled out the police blanks--his real, hers false. Their room was a Mediterranean room, almost ascetic, almost clean, darkened to the glare of the sea. Simplest of pleasures--simplest of places. Tommy ordered two cognacs, and when the door closed behind the waiter, he sat in the only chair, dark, scarred and handsome, his eyebrows arched and upcurling, a fighting Puck, an earnest Satan.

Before they had finished the brandy they suddenly moved together and met standing up; then they were sitting on the bed and he kissed her hardy knees. Struggling a little still, like a decapitated animal she forgot about Dick and her new white eyes, forgot Tommy himself and sank deeper and deeper into the minutes and the moment.

. . . When he got up to open a shutter and find out what caused the increasing clamor below their windows, his figure was darker and stronger than Dick's, with high lights along the rope-twists of muscle. Momentarily he had forgotten her too--almost in the second of his flesh breaking from hers she had a foretaste that things were going to be different than she had expected. She felt the nameless fear which precedes all emotions, joyous or sorrowful, inevitable as a hum of thunder precedes a storm.

Tommy peered cautiously from the balcony and reported.

"All I can see is two women on the balcony below this. They're talking about weather and tipping back and forth in American rocking-chairs."

"Making all that noise?"

"The noise is coming from somewhere below them. Listen."

> "Oh, way down South in the land of cotton
> Hotels bum and business rotten
> Look away--"

"It's Americans."

Nicole flung her arms wide on the bed and stared at the ceiling; the powder had dampened on her to make a milky surface. She liked the bareness of the room, the sound of the single fly navigating overhead. Tommy brought the chair over to the bed and swept the clothes off it to sit down; she liked the economy of the weightless dress and espadrilles that mingled with his ducks upon the floor.

He inspected the oblong white torso joined abruptly to the brown limbs and head, and said, laughing gravely:

"You are all new like a baby."

"With white eyes."

"I'll take care of that."

"It's very hard taking care of white eyes--especially the ones made in Chicago."

"I know all the old Languedoc peasant remedies."

"Kiss me, on the lips, Tommy."

"That's so American," he said, kissing her nevertheless. "When I was in America last there were girls who would tear you apart with their lips, tear themselves too, until their faces were scarlet with the blood around the lips all brought out in a patch--but nothing further."

Nicole leaned up on one elbow.

"I like this room," she said.

"I find it somewhat meagre. Darling, I'm glad you wouldn't wait until we got to Monte Carlo."

"Why only meagre? Why, this is a wonderful room, Tommy--like the bare tables in so many Cézannes and Picassos."

"I don't know." He did not try to understand her. "There's that noise again. My God, has there been a murder?"

He went to the window and reported once more:

"It seems to be two American sailors fighting and a lot more cheering them on. They are from your battleship off shore." He wrapped a towel around himself and went farther out on the balcony. "They have poules with them. I have heard about this now--the women follow them from place to place wherever the ship goes. But what women! One would think with their pay they could find better women! Why the women who followed Korniloff! Why we never looked at anything less than a ballerina!"

Nicole was glad he had known so many women, so that the word itself meant nothing to him; she would be able to hold him so long as the person in her transcended the universals of her body.

"Hit him where it hurts!"

"Yah-h-h-h!"

"Hey, what I tell you get inside that right!"

"Come on, Dulschmit, you son!"

"Yaa-Yaa!"

"YA-YEH-YAH!"

Tommy turned away.

"This place seems to have outlived its usefulness, you agree?"

She agreed, but they clung together for a moment before dressing, and then for a while longer it seemed as good enough a palace as any. . . .

Dressing at last Tommy exclaimed:

"My God, those two women in the rocking-chairs on the balcony below us haven't moved. They're trying to talk this matter out of existence. They're here on an economical holiday, and all the American navy and all the whores in Europe couldn't spoil it."

He came over gently and surrounded her, pulling the shoulder strap of her slip into place with his teeth; then a sound split the air outside: Cr-ACK--BOOM-M-m-*m*! It was the battleship sounding a recall.

Now, down below their window, it was pandemonium indeed--for the boat was moving to shores as yet unannounced. Waiters called accounts and demanded settlements in impassioned voices, there were oaths and denials; the tossing of bills too large and change too small; passouts were assisted to the boats, and the voices of the naval police chopped with quick commands through all voices. There were cries, tears, shrieks, promises as the first launch shoved off and the women crowded forward on the wharf, screaming and waving.

Tommy saw a girl rush out upon the balcony below waving a napkin, and before he could see whether or not the rocking Englishwomen gave in at last and acknowledged her presence, there was a knock at their own door. Outside, excited female voices made them agree to unlock it, disclosing two girls, young, thin and barbaric, unfound rather than lost, in the hall. One of them wept chokingly.

"Kwee wave off your porch?" implored the other in passionate American. "Kwee please? Wave at the boy friends? Kwee, please. The other rooms is all locked."

"With pleasure," Tommy said.

The girls rushed out on the balcony and presently their voices struck a loud treble over the din.

"'By, Charlie! Charlie, look *up!"*

"Send a wire gen'al alivery Nice!"

"Charlie! He don't see me."

One of the girls hoisted her skirt suddenly, pulled and ripped at her pink step-ins and tore them to a sizable flag; then, screaming "Ben! Ben!" she waved it wildly. As Tommy and Nicole left the room it still fluttered against the blue sky. Oh, say can you see the tender color of remembered flesh?--while at the stern of the battleship arose in rivalry the Star-Spangled Banner.

They dined at the new Beach Casino at Monte Carlo . . . much later they swam in Beaulieu in a roofless cavern of white moonlight formed by a circlet of pale boulders about a cup of phosphorescent water, facing Monaco and the blur of Mentone. She liked his bringing her there to the eastward vision and the novel tricks of wind and water; it was all as new as they were to each other. Symbolically she lay across his saddle-bow as surely as if he had wolfed her away from Damascus and they had come out upon the Mongolian plain. Moment by moment all that Dick had taught her fell away and she was ever nearer to what she had been in the beginning, prototype of that obscure yielding up of swords that was going on in the world about her. Tangled with love in the moonlight she welcomed the anarchy of her lover.

They awoke together finding the moon gone down and the air cool. She struggled up demanding the time and Tommy called it roughly at three.

"I've got to go home then."

"I thought we'd sleep in Monte Carlo."

"No. There's a governess and the children. I've got to roll in before daylight."

"As you like."

They dipped for a second, and when he saw her shivering he rubbed her briskly with a towel. As they got into the car with their heads still damp, their skins fresh and glowing, they were loath to start back. It was very bright where they were and as Tommy kissed her she felt him losing himself in the whiteness of her cheeks and her white teeth and her cool brow and the hand that touched his face. Still attuned to Dick, she waited for interpretation or qualification; but none was forthcoming. Reassured sleepily and happily that none would be, she sank low in the seat and drowsed until the sound of the motor changed and she felt them climbing toward Villa Diana. At the gate she kissed him an almost automatic good-by. The sound of her feet on the walk was changed, the night noises of the garden were suddenly in the past but she was glad, none the less, to be back. The day had progressed at a staccato rate, and in spite of its satisfactions she was not habituated to such strain.

IX

At four o'clock next afternoon a station taxi stopped at the gate and Dick got out. Suddenly off balance, Nicole ran from the terrace to meet him, breathless with her effort at self-control.

"Where's the car?" she asked.

"I left it in Arles. I didn't feel like driving any more."

"I thought from your note that you'd be several days."

"I ran into a mistral and some rain."

"Did you have fun?"

"Just as much fun as anybody has running away from things. I drove Rosemary as far as Avignon and put her on her train there." They walked toward the terrace together, where he deposited his bag. "I didn't tell you in the note because I thought you'd imagine a lot of things."

"That was very considerate of you." Nicole felt surer of herself now.

"I wanted to find out if she had anything to offer--the only way was to see her alone."

"Did she have--anything to offer?"

"Rosemary didn't grow up," he answered. "It's probably better that way. What have you been doing?"

She felt her face quiver like a rabbit's.

"I went dancing last night--with Tommy Barban. We went--"

He winced, interrupting her.

"Don't tell me about it. It doesn't matter what you do, only I don't want to know anything definitely."

"There isn't anything to know."

"All right, all right." Then as if he had been away a week: "How are the children?"

The phone rang in the house.

"If it's for me I'm not home," said Dick turning away quickly. "I've got some things to do over in the work-room."

Nicole waited till he was out of sight behind the well; then she went into the house and took up the phone.

"Nicole, comment vas-tu?"

"Dick's home."

He groaned.

"Meet me here in Cannes," he suggested. "I've got to talk to you."

"I can't."

"Tell me you love me." Without speaking she nodded at the receiver; he repeated, "Tell me you love me."

"Oh, I do," she assured him. "But there's nothing to be done right now."

"Of course there is," he said impatiently. "Dick sees it's over between you two--it's obvious he has quit. What does he expect you to do?"

"I don't know. I'll have to--" She stopped herself from saying "--to wait until I can ask Dick," and instead finished with: "I'll write and I'll phone you to-morrow."

She wandered about the house rather contentedly, resting on her achievement. She was a mischief, and that was a satisfaction; no longer was she a huntress of corralled game. Yesterday came back to her now in innumerable detail--detail that began to overlay her memory of similar moments when her love for Dick was fresh and intact. She began to slight that love, so that it seemed to have been tinged with sentimental habit from the first. With the opportunistic memory of women she scarcely recalled how she had felt when she and Dick had possessed each other in secret places around the corners of the world, during the month before they were married. Just so had she lied to Tommy last night, swearing to him that never before had she so entirely, so completely, so utterly. . . .

. . . then remorse for this moment of betrayal, which so cavalierly belittled a decade of her life, turned her walk toward Dick's sanctuary.

Approaching noiselessly she saw him behind his cottage, sitting in a steamer chair by the cliff wall, and for a moment she regarded him silently. He was thinking, he was living a world completely his own and in the small motions of his face, the brow raised or lowered, the eyes narrowed or widened, the lips set and reset, the play of his hands, she saw him progress from phase to phase of his own story spinning out inside him, his own, not hers. Once he clenched his fists and leaned forward, once it brought into his face an expression of torment and despair--when this passed its stamp lingered in his eyes. For almost the first time in her life she was sorry for him--it is hard for those who have once been mentally afflicted to be sorry for those who are well, and though Nicole often paid lip service to the fact that he had led her back to the world she had forfeited, she had thought of him really as an inexhaustible energy, incapable of fatigue--she forgot the troubles she caused him at the moment when she forgot the troubles of her own that had prompted her. That he no longer controlled her--did he know that? Had he willed it all?--she felt as sorry for him as she had sometimes felt for Abe North and his ignoble destiny, sorry as for the helplessness of infants and the old.

She went up putting her arm around his shoulder and touching their heads together said:

"Don't be sad."

He looked at her coldly.

"Don't touch me!" he said.

Confused she moved a few feet away.

"Excuse me," he continued abstractedly. "I was just thinking what I thought of you--"

"Why not add the new classification to your book?"

"I have thought of it--'Furthermore and beyond the psychoses and the neuroses--'"

"I didn't come over here to be disagreeable."

"Then why *did* you come, Nicole? I can't do anything for you any more. I'm trying to save myself."

"From my contamination?"

"Profession throws me in contact with questionable company sometimes."

She wept with anger at the abuse.

"You're a coward! You've made a failure of your life, and you want to blame it on me."

While he did not answer she began to feel the old hypnotism of his intelligence, sometimes exercised without power but always with substrata of truth under truth which she could not break or even crack. Again she struggled with it, fighting him with her small, fine eyes, with the plush arrogance of a top dog, with her nascent transference to another man, with the accumulated resentment of years; she fought him with her money and her faith that her sister disliked him and was behind her now; with the thought of the new enemies he was making with his bitterness, with her quick guile against his wine-ing and dine-ing slowness, her health and beauty against his physical deterioration, her unscrupulousness against his moralities--for this inner battle she used even her weaknesses--fighting bravely and courageously with the old cans and crockery and bottles, empty receptacles of her expiated sins, outrages, mistakes. And suddenly, in the space of two minutes she achieved her victory and justified herself to herself without lie or subterfuge, cut the cord forever. Then she walked, weak in the legs, and sobbing coolly, toward the household that was hers at last.

Dick waited until she was out of sight. Then he leaned his head forward on the parapet. The case was finished. Doctor Diver was at liberty.

X

At two o'clock that night the phone woke Nicole and she heard Dick answer it from what they called the restless bed, in the next room.

"Oui, oui . . . mais à qui est-ce-que je parle? . . . Oui . . ." His voice woke up with surprise. "But can I speak to one of the ladies, Sir the Officer? They are both ladies of the very highest prominence, ladies of connections that might cause political complications of the most serious. . . . It is a fact, I swear to you. . . . Very well, you will see."

He got up and, as he absorbed the situation, his self-knowledge assured him that he would undertake to deal with it--the old fatal pleasingness, the old forceful charm, swept back with its cry of "Use me!" He would have to go fix this thing that he didn't care a damn about, because it had early become a habit to be loved, perhaps from the moment when he had realized that he was the last hope of a decaying clan. On an almost parallel occasion, back in Dohmler's clinic on the Zürichsee, realizing this power, he had made his choice, chosen Ophelia, chosen the sweet poison and drunk it. Wanting above all to be brave and kind, he had wanted, even more than that, to be loved. So it had been. So it would ever be, he saw, simultaneously with the slow archaic tinkle from the phone box as he rang off.

There was a long pause. Nicole called, "What is it? Who is it?"

Dick had begun to dress even as he hung up the phone.

"It's the poste de police in Antibes--they're holding Mary North and that Sibley-Biers. It's something serious--the agent wouldn't tell me; he kept saying 'pas de mortes--pas d'automobiles' but he implied it was just about everything else."

"Why on earth did they call on *you?* It sounds very peculiar to me."

"They've got to get out on bail to save their faces; and only some property owner in the Alpes Maritimes can give bail."

"They had their nerve."

"I don't mind. However I'll pick up Gausse at the hotel--"

Nicole stayed awake after he had departed wondering what offense they could have committed; then she slept. A little after three when Dick came in she sat up stark awake saying, "What?" as if to a character in her dream.

"It was an extraordinary story--" Dick said. He sat on the foot of her bed, telling her how he had roused old Gausse from an Alsatian coma, told him to clean out his cash drawer, and driven with him to the police station.

"I don't like to do something for that Anglaise," Gausse grumbled.

Mary North and Lady Caroline, dressed in the costume of French sailors, lounged on a bench outside the two dingy cells. The latter had the outraged air of a Briton who momentarily expected the Mediterranean fleet to steam up to her assistance. Mary Minghetti was in a condition of panic and collapse--she literally flung herself at Dick's stomach as though that were the point of greatest association, imploring him to do something. Meanwhile the chief of police explained the matter to Gausse who listened to each word with reluctance, divided between being properly appreciative of the officer's narrative gift and showing that, as the perfect servant, the story had no shocking effect on him. "It was merely a lark," said Lady Caroline with scorn. "We were pretending to be sailors on leave, and we picked up two silly girls. They got the wind up and made a rotten scene in a lodging house."

Dick nodded gravely, looking at the stone floor, like a priest in the confessional--he was torn between a tendency to ironic laughter and another tendency to order fifty stripes of the cat and a fortnight of bread and water. The lack, in Lady Caroline's face, of any sense of evil, except the evil wrought by cowardly Provençal girls and stupid police, confounded him; yet he had long concluded that certain classes of English people lived upon a concentrated essence of the anti-social that, in comparison, reduced the gorgings of New York to something like a child contracting indigestion from ice cream.

"I've got to get out before Hosain hears about this," Mary pleaded. "Dick, you can always arrange things--you always could. Tell 'em we'll go right home, tell 'em we'll pay anything."

"I shall not," said Lady Caroline disdainfully. "Not a shilling. But I shall jolly well find out what the Consulate in Cannes has to say about this."

"No, no!" insisted Mary. "We've got to get out to-night."

"I'll see what I can do," said Dick, and added, "but money will certainly have to change hands." Looking at them as though they were the innocents that he knew they were not, he shook his head: "Of all the crazy stunts!"

Lady Caroline smiled complacently.

"You're an insanity doctor, aren't you? You ought to be able to help us--and Gausse has *got* to!"

At this point Dick went aside with Gausse and talked over the old man's findings. The affair was more serious than had been indicated--one of the girls whom they had picked up was of a respectable family. The family were furious, or pretended to be; a settlement would have to be made with them. The other one, a girl of the port, could be more easily dealt with. There were French statutes that would make conviction punishable by imprisonment or, at the very least, public expulsion from the country. In addition to the difficulties, there was a growing difference in tolerance between such townspeople as benefited by the foreign colony and the ones who were annoyed by the consequent rise of prices. Gausse, having summarized the situation, turned it over to Dick. Dick called the chief of police into conference.

"Now you know that the French government wants to encourage American touring--so much so that in Paris this summer there's an order that Americans can't be arrested except for the most serious offenses."

"This is serious enough, my God."

"But look now--you have their Cartes d'Identité?"

"They had none. They had nothing--two hundred francs and some rings. Not even shoe-laces that they could have hung themselves with!"

Relieved that there had been no Cartes d'Identité Dick continued.

"The Italian Countess is still an American citizen. She is the grand-daughter--" he told a string of lies slowly and portentously, "of John D. Rockefeller Mellon. You have heard of him?"

"Yes, oh heavens, yes. You mistake me for a nobody?"

"In addition she is the niece of Lord Henry Ford and so connected with the Renault and Citroën companies--" He thought he had better stop here. However the sincerity of his voice had begun to affect the officer, so he continued: "To arrest her is just as if you arrested a great royalty of England. It might mean--War!"

"But how about the Englishwoman?"

"I'm coming to that. She is affianced to the brother of the Prince of Wales--the Duke of Buckingham."

"She will be an exquisite bride for him."

"Now we are prepared to give--" Dick calculated quickly, "one thousand francs to each of the girls--and an additional thousand to the father of the 'serious' one. Also two thousand in addition, for you to distribute as you think best--" he shrugged his shoulders, "--among the men who made the arrest, the lodging-house keeper and so forth. I shall hand you the five thousand and expect you to do the negotiating immediately. Then they can be released on bail on some charge like disturbing the peace, and whatever fine there is will be paid before the magistrate tomorrow--by messenger."

Before the officer spoke Dick saw by his expression that it would be all right. The man said hesitantly, "I have made no entry because they have no Cartes d'Identité. I must see--give me the money."

An hour later Dick and M. Gausse dropped the women by the Majestic Hotel, where Lady Caroline's chauffeur slept in her landaulet.

"Remember," said Dick, "you owe Monsieur Gausse a hundred dollars a piece."

"All right," Mary agreed, "I'll give him a check to-morrow--and something more."

"Not I!" Startled, they all turned to Lady Caroline, who, now entirely recovered, was swollen with righteousness. "The whole thing was an outrage. By no means did I authorize you to give a hundred dollars to those people."

Little Gausse stood beside the car, his eyes blazing suddenly.

"You won't pay me?"

"Of course she will," said Dick.

Suddenly the abuse that Gausse had once endured as a bus boy in London flamed up and he walked through the moonlight up to Lady Caroline.

He whipped a string of condemnatory words about her, and as she turned away with a frozen laugh, he took a step after her and swiftly planted his little foot in the most celebrated of targets. Lady Caroline, taken by surprise, flung up her hands like a person shot as her sailor-clad form sprawled forward on the sidewalk.

Dick's voice cut across her raging: "Mary, you quiet her down! or you'll both be in leg-irons in ten minutes!"

On the way back to the hotel old Gausse said not a word, until they passed the Juan-les-Pins Casino, still sobbing and coughing with jazz; then he sighed forth:

"I have never seen women like this sort of women. I have known many of the great courtesans of the world, and for them I have much respect often, but women like these women I have never seen before."

XI

Dick and Nicole were accustomed to go together to the barber, and have haircuts and shampoos in adjoining rooms. From Dick's side Nicole could hear the snip of shears, the count of changes, the Voilàs and Pardons. The day after his return they went down to be shorn and washed in the perfumed breeze of the fans.

In front of the Carleton Hotel, its windows as stubbornly blank to the summer as so many cellar doors, a car passed them and Tommy Barban was in it. Nicole's momentary glimpse of his expression, taciturn and thoughtful and, in the second of seeing her, wide-eyed and alert, disturbed her. She wanted to be going where he was going. The hour with the hair-dresser seemed one of the wasteful intervals that composed her life, another little prison. The coiffeuse in her white uniform, faintly sweating lip-rouge and cologne reminded her of many nurses.

In the next room Dick dozed under an apron and a lather of soap. The mirror in front of Nicole reflected the passage between the men's side and the women's, and Nicole started up at the sight of Tommy entering and wheeling sharply into the men's shop. She knew with a flush of joy that there was going to be some sort of showdown.

She heard fragments of its beginning.

"Hello, I want to see you."

". . . serious."

". . . serious."

". . . perfectly agreeable."

In a minute Dick came into Nicole's booth, his expression emerging annoyed from behind the towel of his hastily rinsed face.

"Your friend has worked himself up into a state. He wants to see us together, so I agreed to have it over with. Come along!"

"But my hair--it's half cut."

"Nevermind--come along!"

Resentfully she had the staring coiffeuse remove the towels.

Feeling messy and unadorned she followed Dick from the hotel. Outside Tommy bent over her hand.

"We'll go to the Café des Alliées," said Dick.

"Wherever we can be alone," Tommy agreed.

Under the arching trees, central in summer, Dick asked: "Will you take anything, Nicole?"

"A citron pressé."

"For me a demi," said Tommy.

"The Blackenwite with siphon," said Dick.

"Il n'y a plus de Blackenwite. Nous n'avons que le Johnny Walkair."

"Ca va."

> "She's--not--wired for sound
> but on the quiet
> you ought to try it--"

"Your wife does not love you," said Tommy suddenly. "She loves me."

The two men regarded each other with a curious impotence of expression. There can be little communication between men in that position, for their relation is indirect, and consists of how much each of them has possessed or will possess of the woman in question, so that their emotions pass through her divided self as through a bad telephone connection.

"Wait a minute," Dick said. "Donnez moi du gin et du siphon."

"Bien, Monsieur."

"All right, go on, Tommy."

"It's very plain to me that your marriage to Nicole has run its course. She is through. I've waited five years for that to be so."

"What does Nicole say?"

They both looked at her.

"I've gotten very fond of Tommy, Dick."

He nodded.

"You don't care for me any more," she continued. "It's all just habit. Things were never the same after Rosemary."

Unattracted to this angle, Tommy broke in sharply with:

"You don't understand Nicole. You treat her always like a patient because she was once sick."

They were suddenly interrupted by an insistent American, of sinister aspect, vending copies of *The Herald* and of *The Times* fresh from New York.

"Got everything here, Buddies," he announced. "Been here long?"

"Cessez cela! Allez Ouste!" Tommy cried and then to Dick, "Now no woman would stand such--"

"Buddies," interrupted the American again. "You think I'm wasting my time--but lots of others don't." He brought a gray clipping from his purse--and Dick recognized it as he saw it. It cartooned millions of Americans pouring from liners with bags of gold. "You think I'm not going to get part of that? Well, I am. I'm just over from Nice for the Tour de France."

As Tommy got him off with a fierce "allez-vous-en," Dick identified him as the man who had once hailed him in the Rue de Saints Anges, five years before.

"When does the Tour de France get here?" he called after him.

"Any minute now, Buddy."

He departed at last with a cheery wave and Tommy returned to Dick.

"Elle doit avoir plus avec moi qu'avec vous."

"Speak English! What do you mean 'doit avoir'?"

"'Doit avoir?' Would have more happiness with me."

"You'd be new to each other. But Nicole and I have had much happiness together, Tommy."

"L'amour de famille," Tommy said, scoffing.

"If you and Nicole married won't that be 'l'amour de famille'?" The increasing commotion made him break off; presently it came to a serpentine head on the promenade and a group, presently a crowd, of people sprung from hidden siestas, lined the curbstone.

Boys sprinted past on bicycles, automobiles jammed with elaborate betasselled sportsmen slid up the street, high horns tooted to announce the approach of the race, and unsuspected cooks in undershirts appeared at restaurant doors as around a bend a procession came into sight. First was a lone cyclist in a red jersey, toiling intent and confident out of the westering sun, passing to the melody of a high chattering cheer. Then three together in a harlequinade of faded color, legs caked yellow with dust and sweat, faces expressionless, eyes heavy and endlessly tired.

Tommy faced Dick, saying: "I think Nicole wants a divorce--I suppose you'll make no obstacles?"

A troupe of fifty more swarmed after the first bicycle racers, strung out over two hundred yards; a few were smiling and self-conscious, a few obviously exhausted, most of them indifferent and weary. A retinue of small boys passed, a few defiant stragglers, a light truck carried the dupes of accident and defeat. They were back at the table. Nicole wanted Dick to take the initiative, but he seemed content to sit with his face half-shaved matching her hair half-washed.

"Isn't it true you're not happy with me any more?" Nicole continued. "Without me you could get to your work again--you could work better if you didn't worry about me."

Tommy moved impatiently.

"That is so useless. Nicole and I love each other, that's all there is to it."

"Well, then," said the Doctor, "since it's all settled, suppose we go back to the barber shop."

Tommy wanted a row: "There are several points--"

"Nicole and I will talk things over," said Dick equitably. "Don't worry--I agree in principal, and Nicole and I understand each other. There's less chance of unpleasantness if we avoid a three-cornered discussion."

Unwillingly acknowledging Dick's logic, Tommy was moved by an irresistible racial tendency to chisel for an advantage.

"Let it be understood that from this moment," he said, "I stand in the position of Nicole's protector until details can be arranged. And I shall hold you strictly accountable for any abuse of the fact that you continue to inhabit the same house."

"I never did go in for making love to dry loins," said Dick.

He nodded, and walked off toward the hotel with Nicole's whitest eyes following him.

"He was fair enough," Tommy conceded. "Darling, will we be together tonight?"

"I suppose so."

So it had happened--and with a minimum of drama; Nicole felt outguessed, realizing that from the episode of the camphor-rub, Dick had anticipated everything. But also she felt happy and excited, and the odd little wish that she could tell Dick all about it faded quickly. But her eyes followed his figure until it became a dot and mingled with the other dots in the summer crowd.

XII

The day before Doctor Diver left the Riviera he spent all his time with his children. He was not young any more with a lot of nice thoughts and dreams to have about himself, so he wanted to remember them well. The children had been told that this winter they would be with their aunt in London and that soon they were going to come and see him in America. Fräulein was not to be discharged without his consent.

He was glad he had given so much to the little girl--about the boy he was more uncertain--always he had been uneasy about what he had to give to the ever-climbing, ever-clinging, breast-searching young. But, when he said good-by to them, he wanted to lift their beautiful heads off their necks and hold them close for hours.

He embraced the old gardener who had made the first garden at Villa Diana six years ago; he kissed the Provençal girl who helped with the children. She had been with them for almost a decade and she fell on her knees and cried until Dick jerked her to her feet and gave her three hundred francs. Nicole was sleeping late, as had been agreed upon--he left a note for her, and one for Baby Warren who was just back from Sardinia and staying at the house. Dick took a big drink from a bottle of brandy three feet high, holding ten quarts, that some one had presented them with.

Then he decided to leave his bags by the station in Cannes and take a last look at Gausse's Beach.

The beach was peopled with only an advance guard of children when Nicole and her sister arrived that morning. A white sun, chivied of outline by a white sky, boomed over a windless day. Waiters were putting extra ice into the bar; an American photographer from the A. and P. worked with his equipment in a precarious shade and looked up quickly at every footfall descending the stone steps. At the hotel his prospective subjects slept late in darkened rooms upon their recent opiate of dawn.

When Nicole started out on the beach she saw Dick, not dressed for swimming, sitting on a rock above. She shrank back in the shadow of her dressing-tent. In a minute Baby joined her, saying:

"Dick's still there."

"I saw him."

"I think he might have the delicacy to go."

"This is his place--in a way, he discovered it. Old Gausse always says he owes everything to Dick."

Baby looked calmly at her sister.

"We should have let him confine himself to his bicycle excursions," she remarked. "When people are taken out of their depths they lose their heads, no matter how charming a bluff they put up."

"Dick was a good husband to me for six years," Nicole said. "All that time I never suffered a minute's pain because of him, and he always did his best never to let anything hurt me."

Baby's lower jaw projected slightly as she said:

"That's what he was educated for."

The sisters sat in silence; Nicole wondering in a tired way about things; Baby considering whether or not to marry the latest candidate for her hand and money, an authenticated Hapsburg. She was not quite *thinking* about it. Her affairs had long shared such a sameness, that, as she dried out, they were more important for their conversational value than for themselves. Her emotions had their truest existence in the telling of them.

"Is he gone?" Nicole asked after a while. "I think his train leaves at noon."

Baby looked.

"No. He's moved up higher on the terrace and he's talking to some women. Anyhow there are so many people now that he doesn't *have* to see us."

He had seen them though, as they left their pavilion, and he followed them with his eyes until they disappeared again. He sat with Mary Minghetti, drinking anisette.

"You were like you used to be the night you helped us," she was saying, "except at the end, when you were horrid about Caroline. Why aren't you nice like that always? You can be."

It seemed fantastic to Dick to be in a position where Mary North could tell him about things.

"Your friends still like you, Dick. But you say awful things to people when you've been drinking. I've spent most of my time defending you this summer."

"That remark is one of Doctor Eliot's classics."

"It's true. Nobody cares whether you drink or not--" She hesitated, "even when Abe drank hardest, he never offended people like you do."

"You're all so dull," he said.

"But we're all there is!" cried Mary. "If you don't like nice people, try the ones who aren't nice, and see how you like that! All people want is to have a good time and if you make them unhappy you cut yourself off from nourishment."

"Have I been nourished?" he asked.

Mary was having a good time, though she did not know it, as she had sat down with him only out of fear. Again she refused a drink and said: "Self-indulgence is back of it. Of course, after Abe you can imagine how I feel about it--since I watched the progress of a good man toward alcoholism--"

Down the steps tripped Lady Caroline Sibly-Biers with blithe theatricality.

Dick felt fine--he was already well in advance of the day; arrived at where a man should be at the end of a good dinner, yet he showed only a fine, considered, restrained interest in Mary. His eyes, for the moment clear as a child's, asked her sympathy and stealing over him he felt the old necessity of convincing her that he was the last man in the world and she was the last woman.

. . . Then he would not have to look at those two other figures, a man and a woman, black and white and metallic against the sky. . . .

"You once liked me, didn't you?" he asked.

"Liked you--I *loved* you. Everybody loved you. You could've had anybody you wanted for the asking--"

"There has always been something between you and me."

She bit eagerly. "Has there, Dick?"

"Always--I knew your troubles and how brave you were about them." But the old interior laughter had begun inside him and he knew he couldn't keep it up much longer.

"I always thought you knew a lot," Mary said enthusiastically. "More about me than any one has ever known. Perhaps that's why I was so afraid of you when we didn't get along so well."

His glance fell soft and kind upon hers, suggesting an emotion underneath; their glances married suddenly, bedded, strained together. Then, as the laughter inside of him became so loud that it seemed as if Mary must hear it, Dick switched off the light and they were back in the Riviera sun.

"I must go," he said. As he stood up he swayed a little; he did not feel well any more--his blood raced slow. He raised his right hand and with a papal cross he blessed the beach from the high terrace. Faces turned upward from several umbrellas.

"I'm going to him." Nicole got to her knees.

"No, you're not," said Tommy, pulling her down firmly. "Let well enough alone."

XIII

Nicole kept in touch with Dick after her new marriage; there were letters on business matters, and about the children. When she said, as she often did, "I loved Dick and I'll never forget him," Tommy answered, "Of course not--why should you?"

Dick opened an office in Buffalo, but evidently without success. Nicole did not find what the trouble was, but she heard a few months later that he was in a little town named Batavia, N.Y., practising general medicine, and later that he was in Lockport, doing the same thing. By accident she heard more about his life there than anywhere: that he bicycled a lot, was much admired by the ladies, and always had a big stack of papers on his desk that were known to be an important treatise on some medical subject, almost in process of completion. He was considered to have fine manners and once made a good speech at a public health meeting on the subject of drugs; but he became entangled with a girl who worked in a grocery store, and he was also involved in a lawsuit about some medical question; so he left Lockport.

After that he didn't ask for the children to be sent to America and didn't answer when Nicole wrote asking him if he needed money. In the last letter she had from him he told her that he was practising in Geneva, New York, and she got the impression that he had settled down with some one to keep house for him. She looked up Geneva in an atlas and found it was in the heart of the Finger Lakes Section and considered a pleasant place. Perhaps, so she liked to think, his career was biding its time, again like Grant's in Galena; his latest note was post-marked from Hornell, New York, which is some distance from Geneva and a very small town; in any case he is almost certainly in that section of the country, in one town or another.

Also from Benediction Books …

Wandering Between Two Worlds: Essays on Faith and Art
Anita Mathias
Benediction Books, 2007
152 pages
ISBN: 0955373700

In these wide-ranging lyrical essays, Anita Mathias writes, in lush, lovely prose, of her naughty Catholic childhood in Jamshedpur, India; her large, eccentric family in Mangalore, a sea-coast town converted by the Portuguese in the sixteenth century; her rebellion and atheism as a teenager in her Himalayan boarding school, run by German missionary nuns, St. Mary's Convent, Nainital; and her abrupt religious conversion after which she entered Mother Teresa's convent in Calcutta as a novice. Later rich, elegant essays explore the dualities of her life as a writer, mother, and Christian in the United States-- Domesticity and Art, Writing and Prayer, and the experience of being "an alien and stranger" as an immigrant in America, sensing the need for roots.

The Story of Dirk Willems: The Man who Died to Save his Enemy
Anita Mathias
Benediction Classics, 2019
18 pages, Full colour.
ISBN: 9781789430448

The religious wars of the Reformation had heroes and villains. There were giants like Luther and Calvin, and quieter unsung heroes. Five hundred years later, one of these stands out: the Dutch Anabaptist, Dirk Willems, who sacrificed his life to save his enemy.

The Meek Shall Inherit the Earth
Anita Mathias
Benediction Books, 2013
38 pages
ISBN: 9781781393956

"Blessed are the meek, for they shall inherit the earth," Jesus says in his most puzzling Beatitude. Puzzling, because, if we are honest, it does not feel true to our experience. So do the meek inherit the earth? Is this true? Or isn't it? In The Meek Shall Inherit the Earth, an extended meditation on the power of gentleness, Anita Mathias grapples with this mystifying Beatitude.

Francesco, Artist of Florence: The Man Who Gave Too Much
Anita Mathias
Benediction Books, 2014
52 pages (full colour)
ISBN: 978-1781394175

In this lavishly illustrated book by Anita Mathias, Francesco, artist of Florence, creates magic in pietre dure, inlaying precious stones in marble in life-like "paintings." While he works, placing lapis lazuli birds on clocks, and jade dragonflies on vases, he is purely happy. However, he must sell his art to support his family. Francesco, who is incorrigibly soft-hearted, cannot stand up to his haggling customers. He ends up almost giving away an exquisite jewellery box to Signora Farnese's bambina, who stands, captivated, gazing at a jade parrot nibbling a cherry. Signora Stallardi uses her daughter's wedding to cajole him into discounting his rainbowed marriage chest. His old friend Girolamo bullies him into letting him have the opulent table he hoped to sell to the Medici almost at cost. Carrara is raising the price of marble; the price of gems keeps rising. His wife is in despair. Francesco fears ruin.

* * *

Sitting in the church of Santa Maria Novella at Mass, very worried, Francesco hears the words of Christ. The lilies of the field and the birds of the air do not worry, yet their Heavenly Father looks after them. As He will look after us. He resolves not to worry. And as he repeats the prayer the Saviour taught us, Francesco resolves to forgive the friends and neighbours who repeatedly put their own interests above his. But can he forgive himself for his own weakness, as he waits for the eternal city of gold whose walls are made of jasper, whose gates are made of pearls, and whose foundations are sapphire, emerald, ruby and amethyst? There time and money shall be no more, the lion shall live with the lamb, and we shall dwell trustfully together. Francesco leaves Santa Maria Novella, resolving to trust the One who told him to live like the lilies and the birds, deciding to forgive those who haggled him into bad bargains--while making a little resolution for the future.

About the Author
Anita Mathias is the author of *Wandering Between Two Worlds: Essays on Faith and Art.* She has a B.A. and M.A. in English from Somerville College, Oxford University, and an M.A. in Creative Writing from the Ohio State University, USA. Anita won a National Endowment of the Arts fellowship in Creative Nonfiction in 1997. She lives in Oxford, England with her husband, Roy, and her daughters, Zoe and Irene.
Visit Anita at http://www.anitamathias.com.

www.ingramcontent.com/pod-product-compliance
Lightning Source LLC
Chambersburg PA
CBHW060820310726
48980CB00002B/351

* 9 7 8 1 7 8 9 4 3 3 3 6 4 *